BEFORE THE GOLDEN AGE

Science fiction anthologies
edited by Isaac Asimov

THE HUGO WINNERS, *Volume One*
FIFTY SHORT SCIENCE FICTION TALES (*with Groff Conklin*)
TOMORROW'S CHILDREN
WHERE DO WE GO FROM HERE?
THE HUGO WINNERS, *Volume Two*
BEFORE THE GOLDEN AGE

BEFORE THE GOLDEN AGE

A SCIENCE FICTION ANTHOLOGY

OF THE 1930S

EDITED BY

Isaac Asimov

DOUBLEDAY & COMPANY, INC.
GARDEN CITY, NEW YORK

"The Man Who Evolved," by Edmond Hamilton, copyright © 1931 by Gernsback Publications, Inc.; reprinted by permission of the author and the agents for the author, Scott Meredith Literary Agency, Inc.

"The Jameson Satellite," by Neil R. Jones, copyright © 1931 by Radio-Science Publications, Inc.; reprinted by permission of the author.

"Submicroscopic," by Capt. S. P. Meek, copyright ©1931 by Radio-Science Publications, Inc.

"Awlo of Ulm," by Capt. S. P. Meek, copyright © 1931 by Teck Publishing Corporation.

"Tetrahedra of Space," by P. Schuyler Miller, copyright © 1931 by Gernsback Publications, Inc.; reprinted by permission of the author.

"The World of the Red Sun," by Clifford D. Simak, copyright © 1931 by Gernsback Publications, Inc.; reprinted by permission of the author.

"Tumithak of the Corridors," by Charles R. Tanner, copyright © 1931 by Teck Publishing Corporation; reprinted by permission of the author.

"The Moon Era," by Jack Williamson, copyright © 1931 by Gernsback Publications, Inc.; reprinted by permission of the author.

"The Man Who Awoke," by Laurence Manning, copyright © 1933 by Gernsback Publications, Inc.; reprinted by permission of Edith B. Manning.

TO SAM MOSKOWITZ, AND MYSELF,
AND ALL THE OTHER MEMBERS OF FIRST FANDOM
(THOSE DINOSAURS OF SCIENCE FICTION),
FOR WHOM SOME OF THE GLITTER WENT
OUT OF THE WORLD IN 1938.

Contents

INTRODUCTION

TO MANY science fiction readers who are now in their middle years, there was a Golden Age of Science Fiction—in capital letters.

That Golden Age began in 1938, when John Campbell became editor of *Astounding Stories* and remolded it, and the whole field, into something closer to his heart's desire. During the Golden Age, he and the magazine he edited so dominated science fiction that to read *Astounding* was to know the field entire.

In that sense, the Golden Age endured till 1950, when other magazines, such as *Galaxy* and *The Magazine of Fantasy and Science Fiction,* entered the field. The editorial personalities of H. L. Gold and Anthony Boucher were as strong in their ways as Campbell's, so the field grew wider and more diverse. In many ways, it improved still further as it spilled out of the magazines and into the books, the paperbacks, and the electronic media.

But then the individual could no longer comprehend the field entire. It grew too large for one to do more than sample, and the Golden Age, when all of science fiction could belong to the reader, was over.

I lived through the Golden Age in the best possible way, for I was among the first of the new writers Campbell discovered, and I am sure there was no other in whom he took so personal and paternal an interest. My book *The Early Asimov* (Doubleday, 1972) is both my memorial to those years and my tribute to John.

But let us forget the capital-letter Golden Age, and let us be more personal. To anyone who has lived a life that has not been utterly disastrous, there is an iridescent aura permeating its second decade. Memories of the first decade, extending back to before the age of ten, are dim, uncertain, and incomplete. Beginning with the third decade, after twenty, life becomes filled with adult responsibility and turns to lead. But that second decade, from ten to twenty, is gold; it is in those years that we remember bliss.

It is the second decade that is the golden age for each individual; it is the memory of life as it was then, that we consider to be life as it ought to be. For any science fiction reader, the gold of the second decade of his life permeates the stories he read at that time, so I frequently hear enthusiasts of thirty speak of "the golden age of the 1950s." If I live out my normal lifetime, I fully expect to hear some rotten kid talk to me of "the golden age of the 1970s." (I will rise from my wheel chair and hit him with my cane.)

Well, then, what about me? My own golden age (small letters) lay in the 1930s. It came in the decade just before the Golden Age (capital letters), and it had a glory for me—and a glory for everyone, for it was in *my* golden age that the personalities that molded the Golden Age, including Campbell himself, were themselves molded.

The science fiction stories I read in the 1930s were in magazines I could not keep. I took each magazine, as it arrived, from my father's newsstand and then, having read it as quickly as I could, I returned it to my father's newsstand so that it might be sold. I cultivated a light hand, which left the magazine in its pristine crispness even though I had read, rabidly, every word on every page. (I *had* to, for if the magazine suffered, my father would have issued a ukase forbidding me to touch any of them, and I don't know about you, but *my* father expected, and got, instant obedience.)

So I never reread those science fiction stories of my personal golden age after that first reading. Oh, a very few of them, yes, when they were reprinted. However, very few stories published before the Golden Age have been reprinted. The Coming of Campbell wiped out all that went before.

The science fiction of the thirties seems, to anyone who has experienced the Campbell Revolution, to be clumsy, primitive, and naïve. The stories are old-fashioned and unsophisticated.

All right, grant that they are all those things. Nevertheless, there was a rough-hewn vigor about them that sophistication has, to some extent, lost us.

Besides, I remember them. Some of them, although I read them only once at a very early age, I remember over a space of forty years. Through all that has happened and all that I have read and, for that matter, written, I remember them—and love them still.

Those stories were dear to me because they roused my enthusiasm, gave me the joy of life at a time and in a place and under conditions when not terribly many joys existed. They helped shape me and even educate me, and I am filled with gratitude to those stories and to the men who wrote them.

And aside from my personal involvement, the stories form an essential part of the history of science fiction, a part that has been unfairly neglected and is in danger of being forgotten altogether, since virtually no important anthologies have dealt with pre-1938 science fiction.

You would have thought that a person of my incredible ingenuity would have conceived *years ago* the notion of repairing this omission and editing an anthology of the great stories of the 1930s. Oddly enough, that is not so. Never once, in my conscious moments, did so obvious a project occur to me.

Fortunately, I am not always conscious.

On the morning of April 3, 1973, I woke and said to my good lady, "Hey, I remember a dream I had." (I virtually never remember my dreams, so this came under the heading of a stop-the-presses bulletin.)

My good lady is professionally interested in dreams, so she said, "What was it?"

"I dreamed," I said, "I had prepared an anthology of all those good old stories I read when I was a kid and I was getting a chance to read them again. There was 'Tumithak of the Corridors' and 'Awlo of Ulm' and 'The World of the—'"

I think that's about as far as I got. I had been chuckling as I talked about the dream, because it seemed like such a ridiculous thing to do. But was it ridiculous?

Simply talking about it filled me, quite suddenly, with a burning urge to do it. I've had those burning urges before, and I know it means I will have to do it at once regardless of any commitments I may have. But who would publish such a thing? —A ridiculous question. After all, in a quarter century of association, the good people at Doubleday & Company, Inc., had never once said "No" to me.

It was at 7 A.M. that I told my dream, and I had to wait for the opening of the business day to do something about it. At 9:05 A.M. (I gave them five minutes' grace) I was on the phone, talking rapidly and earnestly to Lawrence P. Ashmead and to Michele Tempesta, two splendid editorial representatives of that estimable publishing house. They did not say "No" to me.

I then thought about it some more. As I told you, I did not have those old magazines, and it is most difficult to get copies these days. Difficult, but not impossible.

There was always my old friend Sam Moskowitz, who shared my golden age but bought and kept every magazine that was published, memorized them all, and can quote them all word by word at any time of day or night.

He has put his knowledge and expertise to good use by becoming a historian of science fiction, perhaps the only true specialist in this unusual section of human knowledge in the whole world. He has written two volumes of biographies of great science fiction writers, *Explorers of the Infinite* and *Seekers of Tomorrow*. (One of these biographies dealt with none other than your un-humble servant, Isaac Asimov. Sam, never one to skimp on hyperbole, called that one *Genius in a Candy Store.*)

He also produced *Science Fiction by Gaslight,* a history and anthology of science fiction in the popular magazines of the period from 1891 to 1911, and *Under the Moons of Mars,* a history and anthology of science fiction in the Munsey magazines from 1912 to 1929.

Doubleday published his *The Crystal Man,* dealing with nineteenth-century American science fiction. Sam even wrote an account of the tremendous and earth-shaking feuds among the handful of science fiction fans in the American Northeast, which he very dashingly entitled *The Immortal Storm.*

It was to Sam Moskowitz that I therefore turned. Swearing him to secrecy, I asked him if he had ever himself done an anthology of this sort and if he was in the process of doing so. He answered, no, he hadn't and he wasn't. He would like to if he could find a publisher.

"Well, I can," I said, "and I would make it an autobiographical anthology. Would you object if I moved in on your territory?"

He sighed a little and said that he didn't.

Then I reached the crucial point. "Would you get me the stories, Sam?" I asked.

And goodhearted Sam said, "Oh, sure!" and in three weeks he had them, every one, with word counts and copyright information and comments on each. (I was only too glad to pay him for the time and trouble he took.)

So now here I am, all set to do the anthology, and, if you don't mind, I intend to make it more than a mere anthology. I am not going to include the stories bareboned.

With your permission (or without, if necessary), I intend to do as I did in *The Early Asimov* and place the stories within the context of my life. As I told Larry, Michele, and Sam, I intend the book to be autobiographical.

I am doing this partly because one pronounced facet of my personality is a kind of cheerful self-appreciation ("a monster of vanity and arrogance" is what my good friends call me) but also, believe it or not, as a matter of self-protection and as almost a kind of public service.

My numerous readers (bless them, one and all) never tire of writing letters in which they ask eagerly after all the most intimate statistics of my early life, and it has long since passed the point where I can possibly satisfy them, one by one, and still find time to do anything else. *The Early Asimov* has already performed miracles in that respect, since I can send back post cards saying, "Please read *The Early Asimov* for the information you request."

And now I will be able to add, "Also read *Before the Golden Age.*"

Part One

1920 TO 1930

I HAVE always wanted to start a book in the fashion of a nineteenth-century novelist. You know: "I was born in the little town of P———— in the year 19——." Here's my chance:

I was born in the little town of Petrovichi (accent on the second syllable, I believe), in the U.S.S.R. I say the U.S.S.R. and not Russia, because I was born two years after the Russian Revolution.

More than once, I have been asked where Petrovichi is relative to some place that might be considered reasonably familiar. It is thirty-five miles due west of Roslavl and fifty-five miles due south of Smolensk (where a great battle was fought during Napoleon's invasion of 1812, and another during Hitler's invasion of 1941), but that doesn't seem to help any. I had better say, then, that Petrovichi is 240 miles southwest of Moscow and fifteen miles east of the White Russian S.S.R., so I was born on the soil of Holy Russia itself, for what that's worth.

The date of my birth is January 2, 1920. For those of you who are interested in casting horoscopes, forget it! I am not only unaware of the exact hour and minute of my birth but even, actually, of the exact day. January 2 is the official day and that's what I celebrate, but at the time of my birth the Soviet Union was on the Julian calendar, which was thirteen days behind our Gregorian, and my parents in those days didn't even pay much attention to the Julian. They dated things according to the holy days of the Jewish calendar.

Under the Tsars, Russia had never indulged in careful statistical accounting of its less important subjects, and during World War I and the hectic years immediately following, things were more slovenly than ever. So when a birth certificate finally had to be drawn up for me, my parents had to rely on memory, and that worked out to January 2.

And that's good enough. Anyway, it's official.

I remained in the Soviet Union for less than three years and remember nothing of those days except for a few vague impressions, some of which my mother claims she can date back to the time I was two years old.

About the only event of personal note worth mentioning from those years is the fact that sometime in 1921 I fell ill of double pneumonia at a time when antibiotics were non-existent and such medical care as did exist was extremely primitive. My mother tells me (though I never know how much to allow for her innate sense of the dramatic) that seventeen children came down with it in our village at that time and that sixteen died. Apparently, I was the sole survivor.

In 1922, after my sister, Marcia, was born, my father decided to emigrate to the United States. My mother had a half brother living in New York who was willing to guarantee that we would not become a charge on the country; that, plus permission from the Soviet Government, was all we needed.

I am sometimes asked to give the details of how we left the Soviet Union, and I get the distinct feeling that the questioners will be satisfied with nothing less than having my mother jumping from ice floe to ice floe across the Dnieper River with myself in her arms and the entire Red Army hot on our heels.

Sorry! Nothing like that at all! My father applied for an exit visa, or whatever it's called, got it, and off we went by commercial transportation. While we were getting the visa, the family had to go to Moscow, so in the year 1922 I was actually there. My mother says the temperature was forty below and she had to keep me inside her coat lest I freeze solid, but she may be exaggerating.

Needless to say, I am not sorry we left. I dare say that if my family had remained in the Soviet Union, I would have received an education similar to the one I actually did get, that I might well have become a chemist and might even have become a science fiction writer. On the other hand, there is a very good chance that I would then have been killed in the course of the German invasion of the Soviet Union in 1941 to 1945, and while I hope I would have done my bit first, I am glad I didn't have to. I am prejudiced in favor of life.

The four of us—my father Judah, my mother Anna, my sister Marcia, and myself—traveled by way of Danzig, Liverpool, and the good ship *Baltic*, and arrived at Ellis Island in February 1923. It was the last year in which immigration was relatively open and in which Ellis Island was working full steam. In 1924, the quota system was established and the United States began to welcome only sharply limited amounts of the tired, the poor, and the wretched refuse of Europe's teeming shores.

One more year, then, and we wouldn't have made it. Even if we could have come in at some later time, it wouldn't have been the same. Arriving at the age of three, I was, of course, already speaking (Yiddish), but I was still young enough to learn English as a native language and not as an acquired one (which is never the same).

My parents, both of whom spoke Russian fluently, made no effort to teach me Russian, but insisted on my learning English as rapidly and as well as possible. They even set about learning English themselves, with reasonable, but limited, success.

In a way, I am sorry. It would have been good to know the language of Pushkin, Tolstoy, and Dostoevski. On the other hand, I would not have been willing to let anything get in the way of the complete mastery of English. Allow me my prejudice: surely there is no language more majestic than that of Shakespeare, Milton, and the King James Bible, and if I am to have one language that I know as only a native can know it, I consider myself unbelievably fortunate that it is English.

Now my memory starts. I remember, quite distinctly, the first place we lived in after having arrived in the United States. I even remember the address. It was 425 Van Siclen Avenue, in the East New York section of Brooklyn.* I lived in Brooklyn for nineteen years after my arrival in the United States, and my Brooklyn accent is with me to this day.

The Van Siclen Avenue abode was nothing lavish. There was no electricity; we used gas jets. There was no central heating; we had a cast-iron stove, which my mother started with paper and kindling.

Fortunately, I didn't know that this represented slum living. It was home to me, and I was happy. I was particularly fascinated by the stove, and I was always on hand to watch the fire start and my mother knead dough and make noodles. In 1925, when we moved to more advanced quarters, at 434 Miller Avenue, one block away, I cried bitterly.

In February 1925, shortly after my fifth birthday, I began school: kindergarten. If you want further statistics, the school was P.S. 182.

In the ordinary course of events, I would have entered first grade a year later, shortly after my sixth birthday. My mother, however, could not wait.

You see, I had already taught myself to read by hounding the older boys to write out the alphabet for me (which I had learned from a rope-skipping game) and identify each letter and tell me what it "sounds like." I then practiced on street signs and newspaper headlines, sounding the letters till words made sense. To this day, I remember the sudden surge of triumph when I realized there must be such things as silent letters

* I feel a little silly giving statistics of this sort. I mean, who could possibly care what the exact address is? However, these are among the questions I am sometimes asked: "Exactly where did you live when you first came to the United States?" I hope that no one is thinking of making a pilgrimage to the site. It was a slum when I lived there and it has gone downhill steadily ever since.

and that the word I was trying to pronounce, ISland, which meant nothing to me, was really EYEland. That made "Coney Island" luminously clear all of a sudden. On the other hand, I remember being completely defeated by "ought." I could not pronounce it, nor could any of the other boys tell me what it meant when *they* pronounced it.

My parents, of course, couldn't read English and so couldn't help me, and the fact that I learned to read without their help seemed to impress them the more. (My sister was much luckier. When she was five years old, I was seven and a past master at the art. Considerably against her will, I taught her to read quite efficiently, so that when it came time for her to enter school, they put her into the second grade directly.)

In September 1925, I remember, my mother took me to school. My mother's half brother came along, too, as interpreter. (He was my "Uncle Joe.") At the time, I did not know what they were doing, but in later years it dawned on me that they must have been altering my birth date. My mother, backed by Uncle Joe, assured the school authorities that I was born on September 7, 1919. (Considering the uncertainty of my birth date, it was less of a lie than it looked, but it was a little of a lie, because, allowing for all uncertainties, I could not possibly have been born earlier than October at the outside.)

With a September 7, 1919 birthday, that made me six years old the day before the fall term started in 1925, and I was allowed to enter the first grade.

The reason I know that this is what must have happened is that when I was in the third grade, the teacher (for some reason) had the children recite their birth dates. In all innocence, I said January 2, 1920, and she frowned and told me it was September 7, 1919.

Well! I have always been quite certain of knowing what I *know*, and I became very emphatic about having been born on January 2, 1920. So energetic did I become in the matter, in fact, that the school records were changed accordingly. If that had not been done, my official birthday would have been September 7, 1919, to this day.

Oddly enough, that turned out to have an important influence on my life. During World War II, I was working at the U. S. Navy Yard in Philadelphia as a chemist and was periodically deferred from the draft because of the war-related importance of my labors. After V-E day, May 8, 1945, the upper age for those liable to the draft was lowered to twenty-six, and those who were still under that age and had thus far escaped being drafted were scrutinized with special care.

On September 7, 1945, I received my notice of induction, and, two months later, was taken into the warm bosom of the Army of the United States as a private. It was no great tragedy, as it turned out, since by that time the war was over, and I remained in the Army only nine months.

However, had I kept my little third-grade yap shut, my birthday would have stayed September 7, 1919, and that notice of induction would have arrived on my twenty-sixth birthday and I would have been ineligible for the draft.

My stay in grade school was hectic. On two different occasions, my despairing teachers got rid of me by shoving me ahead a semester. This had its elements of trauma, for on each occasion I lost the friends I had made in the old class and was forced to associate with the strangers of the new one.

Besides that, there was always that panic-laden moment when I realized the class had learned things I didn't yet know and that it would take me days of frightened activity to catch up and move ahead again. On the first occasion on which I was "skipped," I found myself in a class that was solving problems in multiplication, something I had never heard of.

I went home crying. My mother, unable to tell what it was that I did not know, called in a neighboring girl, aged twelve. (I found out in later years that she had been aged twelve; at the time, I thought she was a grownup.) The girl began drilling me in 2×1=2, 2×2=4, 2×3=6, and so on.

After a while it began to seem very familiar. I asked her to wait a moment and got my five-cent copybook. On the back were reference tables telling me that there were 12 inches to a foot, 16 ounces to a pound, and so on. There was also a large square array of mysterious numbers.

"What is this?" I asked.

"That," she said, "is the multiplication table."

"In that case," I said, "I know how to multiply," and I sent her home. Having nothing better to do, I had memorized the numbers long before, and from what she told me, I saw how the multiplication table worked.

The other time when I was pushed ahead, I found the class was studying geography, something of which I was utterly innocent. I remember the teacher had asked me where Yucatan was, and I drew a complete blank and the class laughed. (The less advanced a student was, the louder he laughed at someone else's ignorance.)

Quite humiliated, I asked the teacher after class if we had a book on the subject, and she pointed out the largest of the new books I had been given and said it was the geography book. That night, I went over every map in the book, and you can bet I was never caught again.

It turned out quite early, you see, that I was a child prodigy. My parents apparently knew it, but never told me so, because they didn't believe in giving children swelled heads. I wish they had, though, since then I wouldn't have thought it so unreasonable that every time I came back with less than 100 in any test I took, it would be interpreted as an unsatisfactory performance deserving of punishment. (And my mother, who knew nothing about modern child psychology, always punished by means of a physical assault.)

But then I didn't really need the information from them, since I gathered it by myself when I made the astonishing discovery that other people didn't understand something till it was explained and then didn't remember it after it was explained.

I don't know how it is with other prodigies, for I have never gone into the subject. Perhaps many of them have had a sense of unhappiness, of isolation, of drudgery, and may have wanted to be like other people.

Not so in my case, however. I enjoyed every minute of my prodigiousness, because, nasty little devil that I was, I enjoyed knowing more than the other kids and being far quicker on the uptake.

Of course, it had its difficulties. By the time I entered the fourth grade, I was a year and a half younger than anyone else in the class, and small for my age at that. And since I was still the smartest kid in the class and very self-appreciative about it, there were many of my schoolmates who lusted for my life. I found, however, that if I picked out the biggest and dumbest kid in the class and did his homework for him, he constituted himself my protector.

Another point that may have helped save my life was that I was never a teacher's pet. Never! I was a loudmouthed extrovert then, as I am now, and I could never resist the chance of upsetting the class with a funny remark. I was forever being disciplined, and when that was insufficient I was sent to the principal's office. (Believe it or not, I was evicted from class as a disruptive influence even as late as my college days.) So, of course, the other kids decided that anyone as badly behaved as I couldn't be all bad, and they resisted the impulse to eradicate me.

During our first years in the United States, my father worked in a knitting factory for a while, and then tried his hand at being a door-to-door salesman. Finally, in 1926, in a search for some sort of security, he put what money he had been able to accumulate into a candy store that existed on Sutter Avenue (good Heavens, I've forgotten the street number), right around the corner from our apartment.

A candy store is a good thing in some ways. You work for yourself and the work is steady. The profits are small but they're there, and we went through the entire period of the Great Depression without missing a meal and without ever having to spend one moment's anxiety that my father might lose his job and that we might all be on the bread lines. To those of you who know nothing of the Great Depression firsthand, let me assure you as earnestly as I can that we were very lucky.

On the other hand, a candy store is a rotten thing in some ways. Back before World War II, candy stores stayed open from 6 A.M. to I A.M. seven days a week, with no holidays. It meant that from the age of six I never had any but an occasional, fugitive hour of leisure with either parent. Furthermore, a candy store can be operated only by an entire family, which meant that I had to pitch in. Each year, I did a larger share of the chores.

The work wasn't hard, but it kept me behind the counter for much of my spare time, dishing out candy and cigarettes, making change, delivering papers, running a block and a half to call someone to the telephone, and so on. It kept me from the gay social life of my peers, eliminating punchball and ring-a-levio and many other things of the sort.

Not entirely, of course. In those days (and maybe in ours, too, for all I know) there were "seasons." One day, everyone was playing complicated games with marbles. The next day, all the marbles had disappeared and everyone was out with tops, or checkers (with which to play a marvelous game called "skelly"). I could play all the games with moderate ability, but I was considerably hampered by the fact that I was under strict instructions not to play "for keeps," because my father disapproved of gambling and it was difficult to get other kids to play me "for fun." ("There's no fun in playing for fun," they would say.)

Life was not all work, of course. There was a movie immediately across the street from the candy store. Every Saturday afternoon, my mother gave me a dime and supervised my crossing of the street. For that dime I saw two (silent) movies, a comedy, a cartoon, and, best of all, "an episode," which is what we called the movie serials of those days.

Then, too, I read a good deal. We had no books in the house (they were one of the very many luxuries we could not afford), but my father wangled a library card for me before I was seven. My very first taste of independence was that of going to the library *alone* by bus in order to pick out books.

I could go to the library only at certain times, however, and I could take out only two books at a time when I did go, and I generally finished them both before it was time to go to the library again, no matter how slowly I tried to make myself read. As a result, I constantly felt myself gravitating toward the magazine rack in my father's candy store. It was filled with apparently fascinating reading material.

Along a string stretched across the window, there were draped a dozen paper-backed novels featuring Frank Merriwell and Nick Carter, which I yearned for. There were other paper-backed objects with pictures on the cover, which I learned were called magazines, and some were particularly fascinating; there were pictures of people shooting other people with guns, and that looked great. There were even magazines with names like

Paris Nights, whose purpose I didn't quite understand but with color illustrations that roused the most intense curiosity in me.

But, standing in the way of all this was my father. He simply would not let me read any of the magazines he sold, for he considered every one of them cheap and sensational trash that would only blunt and ruin my razor-sharp mind. I disagreed, of course, but my father was a remarkably stubborn man and he still had the European notion that Papa was boss.

My fate, however, all unknown to me, was approaching.

In the spring of 1926, the first magazine ever to be devoted to science fiction exclusively was placed on the newsstands for sale. It was entitled *Amazing Stories,* the first issue was dated April, and the publisher was Hugo Gernsback.

To fill the magazine, Gernsback was at first compelled to make heavy use of reprints of the works of European writers. It wasn't till the August 1928 issue that a new world really opened. In that issue there appeared the first installment of a three-part serial entitled *The Skylark of Space,* by Edward E. Smith and Lee Hawkins Garby.

As literature, it was a total flop (may the shade of good old Doc Smith forgive me!), but it had something more than good writing, much more. It had adventure of an unprecedented kind. There was the first introduction of interstellar travel. There were mind-boggling distances and encounters; a kind of never-slowing action centered about indestructible heroes.

The readers whom *Amazing Stories* had been attracting went wild. It became the first great "classic" of American magazine science fiction, and it was the forerunner of native American science fiction, which ever since has dominated world literature in that field.

But, alas, *The Skylark of Space* came and went and I knew nothing of it. I don't even recall seeing *Amazing Stories* on my father's newsstand during the years 1926 to 1928. I must have, but no trace of it is left in my memory.

Yet 1928, the year of *The Skylark of Space,* was notable for me in a number of ways.

For one thing, I briefly made the acquaintance of a remarkable youngster, who influenced me far more strongly than I could possibly have realized at the time.

He was roughly my age, rather smaller than I was, and rather darker in complexion. Somehow I discovered he had the ability to tell stories that held me enthralled, and he discovered simultaneously that I was an audience most willing to be enthralled.

For some months, we sought each other out so that we could play the roles of storyteller and audience. He would rattle on eagerly while we walked to the library and back, or when we just sat on someone's front steps.

The importance of it was just this: for the first time, I realized stories could be "made up." Until then, I had naturally assumed that stories existed only in books and had probably been there unchanged, from the beginning of time, without human creators.

Of the tales my friend told me, I have only the dimmest of recollections. I seem to remember that they involved the adventures of a group of men who were forever facing and overcoming dangerous villains. The leader of the group, an expert in the use of all conceivable weapons, was named Dodo "Weapons" Windrows, and his lieutenant was one Jack Winslow.

Whether my friend actually made up the stories or retold me material he had read, with adaptations, I don't know. At the time, I had no doubt whatever that he was inventing it as he went along. And looking back on it now, his enthusiasm seems to me to have been that of creation and not of adaptation.

Both of us were careful never to let anyone overhear us in our enjoyment of the process. My friend once explained that the other kids would "laugh at us." I suppose he felt his stories weren't first class and that while I seemed to appreciate them, others might not. Like any true artist, he did not care to expose himself needlessly to the possibility of adverse criticism.

As for myself, my chief fear was that my father would become aware of this. Instinctively, I was certain that my friend's tales would come under the heading of "cheap literature" and that I would be forcibly rescued from their baneful influence. This I most earnestly did not want to happen, and, in so far as I recognized that my friend's stories were akin in spirit to the tales to be found in sensational magazines, my hunger for those magazines sharpened.

Ah, well, it didn't last long. The storytelling spree could not have gone on for more than a few months when my friend's family moved away from the neighborhood and, of course, took my friend with them. He never returned; he never visited; he never wrote. I never knew where they had moved, and shortly my family moved, too. Contact was broken forever.

It seems to me now that my storytelling friend could not possibly have gotten the pleasure he clearly got out of telling stories that he (to all appearances) made up as he went along, without having tried to be a writer as he grew older. I know something about that particular compulsion, and I am certain he would have tried. And if he tried, it would seem to me that he must have succeeded.

And yet I remember his name and I am certain that there is no writer by that name. Can he have used a pseudonym? Is he dead? I don't know; I wish I did.

On a less personal note, and for the sake of statistics, 1928 was also the year of our citizenship. My parents had completed their five-year residency requirement, and in September received their papers. As minor children, my sister and I were mentioned on my father's citizenship papers and automatically became American citizens in consequence. (After I married and left home, I got citizenship papers of my own, dated 1943, so that I need not be forced to send my father to his safe-deposit box every time I needed proof of citizenship. To any future biographer who may find documentation of the 1943 citizenship, however, this is to inform him that I have been a citizen since 1928.)

The year ended with another change of residence. My father, having increased his savings, thanks to the candy store, felt it was time to sell it and buy another. Partly, I suppose, he felt he would welcome a change, and partly there was always the hope that another candy store would be more profitable.

In December 1928, therefore, we moved to 651 Essex Street, on the corner of New Lots Avenue. There the second candy store was located. I had to transfer from P.S. 182 to P.S. 202, something that involved another traumatic readjustment of friendships.

Then came the crucial summer of 1929, in which everything seemed to conspire to change the direction of my life. (It was the last summer of the Roaring Twenties, the last merry spark before the stock-market crash and the beginning of the Great Depression, but no one knew that, of course.)

For one thing, it was a time of crisis for *Amazing Stories*. Though it had been doing well, there were business machinations of a kind that go beyond the capacity for understanding of my essentially simple mind (Sam Moskowitz knows the story in detail), and Gernsback was forced out of ownership of the magazine.

The last issue of what we can call the "Gernsback *Amazing*" was the June 1929 issue, I believe. (I may be wrong by one or two months here.) It had gone thirty-nine issues. The magazine was taken over by Teck Publications, so with the July 1929 issue we can speak of the "Teck *Amazing*."

Gernsback, a man of considerable resource, had no intention of leaving the magazine field or, for that matter, of abandoning science fiction. Without missing a step, he founded another science fiction magazine, which was thereafter to compete with *Amazing Stories* and was to double the supply of reading matter for the science fiction public. Gernsback's new magazine was called *Science Wonder Stories*, and its first issue was dated June 1929.

Gernsback went further indeed and started a companion magazine called *Air Wonder Stories,* which began with the July 1929 issue. The supply of science fiction was thus tripled, and the existence of these new magazines was to prove of crucial importance to me.

The June in which those two new magazines were both on the stands for the first time, I was completing my stay in the fifth grade. The teacher of the course had offered to take a selected group in the class on a post-term trip to the Statue of Liberty. I did not qualify, since my marks in "Deportment" did not meet the minimum standards. I looked so stricken, however, that the teacher (presumably recalling that I was the brightest student in the class) asked the class permission to include me. The nice kids gave it and I went.

The trip was on July 2, 1929. I remember because I was nine and a half years old that day. It was exciting in itself, but the most remarkable thing about it was that for the first time in my life I had gone a considerable distance without my parents. The fact that the teacher was along didn't count. She did not have parental authority. It gave me an extraordinary feeling of having reached manhood.

The third event of the period was the fact that my mother had entered a third pregnancy (this one, I have reason to believe, unplanned) and, in July, was nearing term. It meant she couldn't help much in the store, and my poor father with only a nine-year-old assistant was terribly harried.

Now observe the concatenation of events.

Not long after my trip to the Statue of Liberty, I noted the new magazine *Science Wonder Stories* on the newsstand. It was the August 1929 issue, the third of its existence. I noticed it, first, because it had a cover by Frank R. Paul, the artist Gernsback always used, a man who painted in primary colors exclusively, I think, and who specialized in complex, futuristic machines.

But I also noticed it because it was a new magazine and my eye hadn't grown dulled to it. Finally, I noticed it because of the word "Science" in the title. That made all the difference. I knew about science; I had already read books about science. I was perfectly aware that science was considered a mentally nourishing and spiritually wholesome study. What's more, I knew that my father thought so from our occasional talks about my schoolwork.

Well, then, the loss of my storytelling friend had left a gnawing vacancy within me; my trip to the Statue of Liberty filled me with a desire to assert my independence and argue with my father; and the word "science" gave me the necessary leverage.

I picked up the magazine and, not without considerable qualms, approached my formidable parent. (It is hard for me to believe that at the time he was only thirty-two years old. I took it for granted he was infinitely old—at least as old as Moses.)

I spoke rapidly, pointed out the word "science," pointed to paintings of futuristic machines inside as an indication of how advanced it was, and (I believe) made it plain that if he said "No" I had every intention of throwing a fit. And that's where the final item in the concatenation of events came in: my father, driven to distraction by the new baby that was on its way, was in no mood to concern himself with trivia. He granted me permission.

I then scanned the newsstand for any other magazine of the same type, planning to maintain with all the strength at my disposal the legal position that permission for one such magazine implied permission for all the others, even when the word "science" was not in the title.

Promptly I found the August 1929 issue of *Amazing Stories* and, of course, the August 1929 issue of *Air Wonder Stories*. I girded myself for the battle. It never came. My mother went to the hospital and my father conceded everything. On July 25, my brother, Stanley, was born.

I wish I could remember the stories in the very first science fiction magazines I ever read, but I can't. The nearest I can come to it is the fact that I remember the cover story in the August 1929 *Amazing Stories* to be "Barton's Island" by Harl Vincent, but I don't remember the plot.

One of the factors that surely must have helped induce my father to let me read the science fiction magazines was their respectable appearance.

At that time, there were two types of magazines on the stands. There were the smaller magazines, 7 by 10 inches in size, which were printed on cheap paper made of wood pulp, unglazed and with ragged edges. These "pulps" featured action stories in different categories, one magazine being devoted to Westerns, another to mysteries, still another to jungle stories, another to sports stories, yet another to air-war stories, and so on.

My father read some of the pulps himself (to improve his English, he said), but nothing could have induced him to let *me* read them. We quarreled over *The Shadow* and *Doc Savage* for years, and eventually, in my mid-teens, I began to read them defiantly without his permission. He would look at me sorrowfully whenever he caught me reading one of them, too; but though those looks stabbed me to the soul, I kept on reading them.

There were, however, also large-size magazines, 8½ by 11 inches or larger, published on glazed paper of good quality with smooth edges. These were the "slicks." I doubt that very many of them were any higher in literary quality than the pulps, but they looked better.

Well, *Amazing Stories, Science Wonder Stories,* and *Air Wonder Stories,* though printed on pulp paper and sometimes featuring authors who wrote regularly for the pulp magazines, were large-size and had smooth edges. They were kept with the slicks on the newsstands, not with the pulps (oh, what a kiss of death that would have been), and they therefore were to be found in respectable company.

What's more, where the pulp magazines usually charged ten cents an issue, the three science fiction magazines charged a lordly twenty-five cents, and, as always, high charge was equated with high quality.

In 1927, Gernsback had been faced with an overflow of stories and had put out a special issue of *Amazing Stories,* which he then still owned, made it thicker than an ordinary one, and called it *Amazing Stories Annual.* It was a success, and from then on he put out such issues at quarter-year intervals. This *Amazing Stories Quarterly* continued under the Teck regime, too, and Gernsback, when he started his new magazines, also began *Science Wonder Quarterly.*

The quarterlies were magnificent. Whereas the ordinary issues of the science fiction magazines contained 96 pages and about 100,000 words of fiction, the quarterlies contained 144 pages and about 150,000 words. The ordinary issues ran novels as serials (usually in three parts), but the quarterlies could run novels entire. Of course, the quarterlies cost fifty cents, an enormous price for those days, and my father didn't always receive them from the distributing companies, so I missed some copies. When I saw them, though, what an enormous feast they were!

(It occurs to me that if my father had not had a newsstand, there would not have been the slightest possibility of my ever reading science fiction magazines at that time except for such issues as I might—a very unlikely supposition—have borrowed. There was no way on Earth that I could have afforded quarters and half dollars for something as unessential as reading matter. . . . Pardon me while I overcome my trembling fit at the thought, and then I will continue.)

Toward the end of 1929, still another science fiction magazine hit the newsstands, with its first issue dated January 1930. It was called *Astounding Stories of Super-Science.* The final phrase was soon dropped and it became *Astounding Stories.* It was published by Clayton Publications and is now referred to as the "Clayton *Astounding*" to differentiate it from later incarnations.

The Clayton *Astounding* was clearly a poor relation. For one thing, it was the size and quality of the pulp magazines and was placed with them on the newsstands. I was taken aback, and almost hesitated to try to read it, thinking that I would surely be stopped. However, my father said nothing. Having retreated, he was not prepared to renew the battle.

Astounding Stories published tales that were heavy on adventure and that seemed, to my boyish mind, to be less sophisticated than those in

Amazing Stories. In fact, though I read every issue of the Clayton *Astounding,* all thirty-four, there was not one story in any of those issues that has remained with me to this day, and none are included in this anthology.

The very early stories that I still remember almost all appeared in *Amazing Stories,* which called itself "The Aristocrat of Science Fiction." And so it was, in my opinion. During the first four years of my science fiction reading, it was *Amazing Stories* all the way with me.

And it was the novels that were most impressive. The plots were most intricate, the adventures most detailed, and, most of all, there was the cliff-hanger with which each installment ended. You then had to wait the length of an arid month for the next installment. Some readers, I later discovered, saved their issues so that they could read the serials all at once, but I couldn't do that, of course. I had to return each issue to the newsstand.

The earliest serial I remember reading and slavering joyously over was *Cities in the Air,* by Edmond Hamilton, which ran in two parts in *Air Wonder Stories,* in the November and December 1929 issues.* I still remember the dramatic Paul cover illustration for that serial, with skyscraper cities shown on huge circular slabs in mid-air.

The next serial I remember is *The Universe Wreckers,* a three-parter in *Amazing Stories,* in the May, June, and July 1930 issues. This one was also by Edmond Hamilton. Considering that, and the fact that Ed is the best-represented in this anthology (three stories) of any of the authors included, I can only deduce that Ed was my favorite author in those very early days.

I have met Ed and his charming wife, Leigh Brackett—also a writer —on many occasions in my grown-up days, and I've never thought to tell him this. I guess I didn't really realize it myself till I began sorting out my memories for this book.

Then, too, there was *The Drums of Tapajos,* by Capt. S. P. Meek, another three-parter in *Amazing Stories,* the November and December 1930 and January 1931 issues. Also *The Black Star Passes,* by John W.

* I have a marvelous memory, but it is not so marvelous that I can remember exact issues for all the stories that I quote, or the exact date for the various items of historical interest I refer to in connection with early magazine science fiction. Actually, I am making liberal use of Donald B. Day's *Index to the Science-Fiction Magazines,* *1926–1950* (Perri Press, Portland, Ore., 1952), which I bought twenty years ago and which has paid me back a hundredfold in its constant usefulness as a reference book to the early history of magazine science fiction. There have been a number of supplements put out for the period since 1950 by computers at M.I.T., but they lack the taste and flavor of the Day *Index.*

Campbell, Jr., published complete in the fall 1930 *Amazing Stories Quarterly*.

These stories, which are full-length novels, can't be included, alas, in this anthology, which is restricted to stories of fewer than forty thousand words.

In my first couple of years as a science fiction reader, I was given an unexpected bonus of time in which to read. When my brother was an infant, I was freed of some of my candy-store chores because I was put in charge of his welfare.

Watching Stanley was much better than standing behind the counter, because virtually no work was required. Aside from giving him his bottle if he cried (or shaking the carriage) and making sure that he didn't fall out or that no eagle swooped down to carry him off, I had only to sit there. I remember the warm summer days of 1930 when I was counting the hours till the Monday after Labor Day, when I could start the adventure of junior high school. I would be sitting next to the carriage, my chair tipped back against the brick wall of the house, and reading a science fiction magazine, dead to all the world except for my automatic response to any wail from the carriage.

Sometimes, to avoid being cramped, I would wheel the carriage sixty or seventy times around the block with the science fiction magazine propped against the handlebar.

Of course the nation as a whole was not going through my own idyllic experience that summer. The stock market had crashed in October 1929, and the economic situation had grown steadily worse ever since. The Great Depression was on. My father's customers had less money, so less money was spent in the candy store. Things grew tighter, and the second candy store, after half a year of moderate promise, showed clearly that it was to be no more a highway to riches than the first.

The science fiction magazines suffered along with everyone else. *Amazing Stories* and *Science Wonder Stories*, which never paid their authors very much, paid them more and more slowly. (The grim joke was that they paid a quarter cent a word on lawsuit.) *Astounding Stories*, for all its lower quality, paid higher rates more quickly, and it began to draw the authors its way, which made things harder than ever for the large-size magazines.

Amazing Stories withstood the strain stolidly and continued without apparent alteration. The Gernsback magazines, however, underwent ominous changes.

Air Wonder Stories was simply too specialized. Its stories dealt with futurized air travel in one way or another, and that did not allow for sufficient variety. I presume its circulation suffered, and the May 1930 issue, its eleventh, was also its last. With the next issue, that of June 1930, it was combined with *Science Wonder Stories* and the combined magazine was given the logical name of *Wonder Stories*.

After five issues, however, the combined magazine found that matters were still too tight for it and it attempted to improve its competitive stance by more closely imitating *Astounding Stories*. With the November 1930 issue, *Wonder Stories* went pulp size and left *Amazing Stories* as the only large-size science fiction magazine.

Part Two

1931

IN 1931, I finished my first year at Junior High School 149. It gave a three-year course: seventh, eighth, and ninth grades. For the better students, it offered, however, a "rapid advance" course in which both seventh and eighth grades were completed in the first year. That was the course I took.

On promotion day in June 1931, therefore, I received my final report card and was told that I would enter ninth grade in September. This was the equivalent of first year high school. I had expected this, of course, and had arranged with my mother that I would not go directly home. I ran to the library instead and came up against the librarian's desk with a bang.

"I want an adult library card, please," I panted, handing her my children's card.

I was still a week short of being eleven and a half, and very skinny, so the librarian said to me, kindly, "You can't have an adult card till you're in high school, little boy."

"I *am* in high school," I snarled, and slammed down my report card. She consulted another official, and I got my card.

This meant I could roam at will among the mysterious stacks containing adult books. The card was stamped "H.S.," however, which still restricted me to two books at a time.

Science fiction helped fill the gaps, and, as it happened, that spring, three months before my exciting promotion to an adult library card, I had read the first science fiction short story (as opposed to novel) that impressed me so much it stayed in my mind permanently.

I never read it again after that first reading, *never*, until I got a copy of old, fading, and brittle tear sheets of the story from Sam Moskowitz for the preparation of this anthology. And then, when I read it again, after forty-two years, I found I remembered it all in complete detail.

This cannot merely be a quirk of my excellent memory, for there are hundreds of science fiction stories I read both before and after this one that I have completely forgotten, including one or two that I read last month.

No, it's the story, "The Man Who Evolved," by (no surprise!) Edmond Hamilton. It appeared in the April 1931 *Wonder Stories*.

THE MAN WHO EVOLVED

by Edmond Hamilton

There were three of us in Pollard's house on that night that I try vainly to forget. Dr. John Pollard himself, Hugh Dutton and I, Arthur Wright—we were the three. Pollard met that night a fate whose horror none could dream; Dutton has since that night inhabited a state institution reserved for the insane, and I alone am left to tell what happened.

It was on Pollard's invitation that Dutton and I went up to his isolated cottage. We three had been friends and room-mates at the New York Technical University. Our friendship was perhaps a little unusual, for Pollard was a number of years older than Dutton and myself and was different in temperament, being rather quieter by nature. He had followed an intensive course of biological studies, too, instead of the ordinary engineering courses Dutton and I had taken.

As Dutton and I drove northward along the Hudson on that afternoon, we found ourselves reviewing what we knew of Pollard's career. We had known of his taking his master's and doctor's degrees, and had heard of his work under Braun, the Vienna biologist whose theories had stirred up such turmoil. We had heard casually, too, that afterwards he had come back to plunge himself in private research at the country-house beside the Hudson he had inherited. But since then we had had no word from him and had been somewhat surprised to receive his telegrams inviting us to spend the week-end with him.

It was drawing into early-summer twilight when Dutton and I reached a small riverside village and were directed to Pollard's place, a mile or so beyond. We found it easily enough, a splendid old pegged-frame house that for a hundred-odd years had squatted on a low hill above the river. Its outbuildings were clustered around the big house like the chicks about some protecting hen.

Pollard himself came out to greet us. "Why, you boys have grown up!"

was his first exclamation. "Here I've remembered you as Hughie and Art,
the campus trouble-raisers, and you look as though you belong to business
clubs and talk everlastingly about sales-resistance!"

"That's the sobering effect of commercial life," Dutton explained, grinning. "It hasn't touched you, you old oyster—you look the same as you
did five years ago."

He did, too, his lanky figure and slow smile and curiously thoughtful
eyes having changed not a jot. Yet Pollard's bearing seemed to show some
rather more than usual excitement and I commented on it.

"If I seem a little excited it's because this is a great day for me," he
answered.

"Well, you *are* in luck to get two fine fellows like Dutton and me to
trail up to this hermitage of yours," I began, but he shook his head
smilingly.

"I don't refer to that, Art, though I'm mighty glad you've come. As
for my hermitage, as you call it, don't say a word against it. I've been
able to do work here I could never have done amid the distractions of
a city laboratory."

His eyes were alight. "If you two knew what—but there, you'll hear
it soon enough. Let's get inside—I suppose you're hungry?"

"Hungry—not I," I assured him. "I might devour half a steer or some
trifle like that, but I have really no appetite for anything else today."

"Same here," Dutton said. "I just pick at my food lately. Give me a
few dozen sandwiches and a bucket of coffee and I consider it a full meal."

"Well, we'll see what we can do to tempt your delicate appetites," said
Pollard, as we went inside.

We found his big house comfortable enough, with long, low-ceilinged
rooms and broad windows looking riverward. After putting our bags in
a bedroom, and while his housekeeper and cook prepared dinner, Pollard
escorted us on a tour of inspection of the place. We were most interested
in his laboratory.

It was a small wing he had added to the house, of frame construction
outside to harmonize with the rest of the building, but inside offering
a gleaming vista of white-tiled walls and polished instruments. A big cube-
like structure of transparent metal surmounted by a huge metal cylinder
resembling a monster vacuum tube, took up the room's center, and he
showed us in an adjoining stone-floored room the dynamos and motors
of his private power-plant.

Night had fallen by the time we finished dinner, the meal having been
prolonged by our reminiscences. The housekeeper and cook had gone, Pollard explaining that the servants did not sleep in the place. We sat smoking
for a while in his living-room, Dutton looking appreciatively around at
our comfortable surroundings.

"Your hermitage doesn't seem half-bad, Pollard," he commented. "I wouldn't mind this easy life for a while myself."

"Easy life?" repeated Pollard. "That's all you know about it, Hugh. The fact is that I've never worked so hard in my life as I've done up here in the last two years."

"What in the world have you been working at?" I asked. "Something so unholy you've had to keep it hidden here?"

A Mad Scheme

Pollard chuckled. "That's what they think down in the village. They know I'm a biologist and have a laboratory here, so it's a foregone conclusion with them that I'm doing vivisection of a specially dreadful nature. That's why the servants won't stay here at night.

"As a matter of fact," he added, "if they knew down in the village what I've really been working on they'd be ten times as fearful as they are now."

"Are you trying to play the mysterious great scientist for our benefit?" Dutton demanded. "If you are you're wasting time—I know you, stranger, so take off that mask."

"That's right," I told him. "If you're trying to get our curiosity worked up you'll find we can scram you as neatly as we could five years ago."

"Which scramming generally ended in black eyes for both of you," he retorted. "But I've no intention of working up your curiosity—as a matter of fact I asked you up here to see what I've been doing and help me finish it."

"Help you?" echoed Dutton. "What can we help you do—dissect worms? Some week-end, I can see right now!"

"There's more to this than dissecting worms," Pollard said. He leaned back and smoked for a little time in silence before he spoke again.

"Do you two have any knowledge at all of evolution?" he asked.

"I know that it's a fighting word in some states," I answered, "and that when you say it you've got to smile, damn you."

He smiled, himself. "I suppose you're aware of the fact, however, that all life on this earth began as simple uni-cellular protoplasm, and by successive evolutionary mutations or changes developed into its present forms and is still slowly developing?"

"We know that much—just because we're not biologists you needn't think we're totally ignorant of biology," Dutton said.

"Shut up, Dutton," I warned. "What's evolution got to do with your work up here, Pollard?"

"It *is* my work up here," Pollard answered.

He bent forward. "I'll try to make this clear to you from the start. You know, or say you know, the main steps of evolutionary development. Life began on this earth as simple protoplasm, a jelly-like mass from which developed small protoplasmic organisms. From these developed in turn sea-creatures, land-lizards, mammals, by successive mutations. This infinitely slow evolutionary process has reached its highest point so far in the mammal man, and is still going on with the same slowness.

"This much is certain biological knowledge, but two great questions concerning this process of evolution have remained hitherto unanswered. First, what is the cause of evolutionary change, the cause of these slow, steady mutations into higher forms? Second, what is the future course of man's evolution going to be, what will the forms into which in the future man will evolve, and where will his evolution stop? Those two questions biology has so far been unable to answer."

Pollard was silent a moment and then said quietly, "I have found the answer to one of those questions, and am going to find the answer to the other tonight."

We stared at him. "Are you trying to spoof us?" I asked finally.

"I'm absolutely serious, Arthur. I have actually solved the first of those problems, have found the cause of evolution."

"What is it, then?" burst out of Dutton.

"What it has been thought by some biologists for years to be," Pollard answered. "The cosmic rays."

"The cosmic rays?" I echoed. "The vibrations from space that Millikan discovered?"

"Yes, the cosmic rays, the shortest wavelength and most highly penetrating of all vibratory forces. It has been known that they beat unceasingly upon the earth from outer space, cast forth by the huge generators of the stars, and it has also been known that they must have some great effect in one way or another upon the life of the earth."

"I have proved that they do have such an effect, and that that effect is what we call evolution! For it is the cosmic rays, beating upon every living organism on earth, that cause the profound changes in the structure of those organisms which we call mutations. Those changes are slow indeed, but it is due to them that through the ages life has been raised from the first protoplasm to man, and is still being raised higher."

"Good Lord, you can't be serious on this, Pollard!" Dutton protested.

"I am so serious that I am going to stake my life on my discovery tonight," Pollard answered, quietly.

We were startled. "What do you mean?"

"I mean that I have found in the cosmic rays the cause of evolution, the answer to the first question, and that tonight by means of them

I am going to answer the second question and find out what the future
evolutionary development of man will be!"

"But how could you possibly—"

Pollard interrupted. "Easily enough. I have been able in the last months
to do something no physicist has been able to do, to concentrate the cosmic rays and yet remove from them their harmful properties. You saw
the cylinder over the metal cube in my laboratory? That cylinder literally
gathers in for an immense distance the cosmic rays that strike this part
of earth, and reflects them down inside the cube.

"Now suppose those concentrated cosmic rays, millions of times stronger
than the ordinary cosmic rays that strike one spot on earth, fall upon a
man standing inside the cube. What will be the result? It is the cosmic
rays that cause evolutionary change, and you heard me say that they are
still changing all life on earth, still changing man, but so slowly as to
be unnoticeable. But what about the man under those terrifically intensi-
fied rays? He will be changed millions of times faster than ordinarily, will
go forward in hours or minutes through the evolutionary mutations that
all mankind will go forward through in eons to come!"

"And you propose to try that experiment?" I cried.

"I propose to try it on myself," said Pollard gravely, "and to find out
for myself the evolutionary changes that await humankind."

"Why, it's insane!" Dutton exclaimed.

Pollard smiled. "The old cry," he commented. "Never an attempt has
been made yet to tamper with nature's laws, but that cry has been raised."

"But Dutton's right!" I cried. "Pollard, you've worked here alone too
long—you've let your mind become warped—"

"You are trying to tell me that I have become a little mad," he said.
"No, I am sane—perhaps wonderfully sane, in trying this."

His expression changed, his eyes brooding. "Can't you two see what
this may mean to humanity? As we are to the apes, so must the men
of the future be to us. If we could use this method of mine to take all
mankind forward through millions of years of evolutionary development
at one stride, wouldn't it be sane to do so?"

My mind was whirling. "Good heavens, the whole thing is so crazy,"
I protested. "To accelerate the evolution of the human race? It seems somehow a thing forbidden."

"It's a thing glorious if it can be done," he returned, "and I know that
it can be done. But first one must go ahead, must travel on through stage
after stage of man's future development to find out to which stage it would
be most desirable for all mankind to be transferred. I know there is such
an age."

"And you asked us up here to take part in that?"

"Just that. I mean to enter the cube and let the concentrated rays whirl me forward along the paths of evolution, but I must have someone to turn the rays on and off at the right moments."

"It's all incredible!" Dutton exclaimed. "Pollard, if this is a joke it's gone far enough for me."

For answer Pollard rose. "We will go to the laboratory now," he said simply. "I am eager to get started."

I cannot remember following Pollard and Dutton to the laboratory, my thoughts were spinning so at the time. It was not until we stood before the great cube from which the huge metal cylinder towered that I was aware of the reality of it all.

Pollard had gone into the dynamo-room and as Dutton and I stared wordlessly at the great cube and cylinder, at the retorts and flasks of acids and strange equipment about us, we heard the hum of motor-generators. Pollard came back to the switchboard supported in a steel frame beside the cube, and as he closed a switch there came a crackling and the cylinder glowed with white light.

Pollard pointed to it and the big quartz-like disk in the cubical chamber's ceiling, from which the white force-shafts shot downward.

"The cylinder is now gathering cosmic rays from an immense area of space," he said, "and those concentrated rays are falling through that disk into the cube's interior. To cut off the rays it is necessary only to open this switch." He reached to open the switch, the light died.

The Man Who Evolved

Quickly, while we stared, he removed his clothing, donning in place of it a loose white running suit.

"I will want to observe the changes of my own body as much as possible," he explained. "Now, I will stand inside the cube and you will turn on the rays and let them play upon me for fifteen minutes. Roughly, that should represent a period of some fifty million years of future evolutionary change. At the end of fifteen minutes you will turn the rays off and we will be able to observe what changes they have caused. We will then resume the process, going forward by fifteen-minute or rather fifty million year periods."

"But where will it stop—where will we quit the process?" Dutton asked.

Pollard shrugged. "We'll stop where evolution stops, that is, where the rays no longer affect me. You know, biologists have often wondered what the last change or final development of man will be, the last mutation. Well, we are going to see tonight what it will be."

He stepped toward the cube and then paused, went to a desk and brought from it a sealed envelope he handed to me.

"This is just in case something happens to me of a fatal nature," he said. "It contains an attestation signed by myself that you two are in no way responsible for what I am undertaking."

"Pollard, give up this unholy business!" I cried, clutching his arm. "It's not too late, and this whole thing seems ghastly to me!"

"I'm afraid it is too late," he smiled. "If I backed out now I'd be ashamed to look in a mirror hereafter. And no explorer was ever more eager than I am to start down the path of man's future evolution!"

He stepped up into the cube, standing directly beneath the disk in its ceiling. He motioned imperatively, and like an automaton I closed the door and then threw the switch.

The cylinder broke again into glowing white light, and as the shafts of glowing white force shot down from the disk in the cube's ceiling upon Pollard, we glimpsed his whole body writhing as though beneath a terrifically concentrated electrical force. The shaft of glowing emanations almost hid him from our view. I knew that the cosmic rays in themselves were invisible but guessed that the light of the cylinder and shaft was in some way a transformation of part of the rays into visible light.

Dutton and I stared with beating hearts into the cubical chamber, having but fleeting glimpses of Pollard's form. My watch was in one hand, the other hand on the switch. The fifteen minutes that followed seemed to me to pass with the slowness of fifteen eternities. Neither of us spoke and the only sounds were the hum of the generators and the crackling of the cylinder that from the far spaces was gathering and concentrating the rays of evolution.

At last the watch's hand marked the quarter-hour and I snapped off the switch, the light of the cylinder and inside the cube dying. Exclamations burst from us both.

Pollard stood inside the cube, staggering as though still dazed by the impact of the experience, but he was not the Pollard who had entered the chamber! He was transfigured, godlike! His body had literally expanded into a great figure of such physical power and beauty as we had not imagined could exist! He was many inches taller and broader, his skin a clear pink, every limb and muscle molded as though by some master sculptor.

The greatest change, though, was in his face. Pollard's homely, good-humored features were gone, replaced by a face whose perfectly-cut features held the stamp of immense intellectual power that shone almost overpoweringly from the clear dark eyes. It was not Pollard who stood before us, I told myself, but a being as far above us as the most advanced man of today is above the troglodyte!

He was stepping out of the cube and his voice reached our ears, clear and bell-like, triumphant.

"You see? It worked as I knew it would work! I'm fifty million years ahead of the rest of humanity in evolutionary development!"

"Pollard!" My lips moved with difficulty. "Pollard, this is terrible—this change—"

His radiant eyes flashed. "Terrible? It's wonderful! Do you two realize what I now am, can you realize it? This body of mine is the kind of body all men will have in fifty million years, and the brain inside it is a brain fifty million years ahead of yours in development!"

He swept his hand about. "Why, all this laboratory and former work of mine seems infinitely petty, childish, to me! The problems that I worked on for years I could solve now in minutes. I could do more for mankind now than all the men now living could do together!"

"Then you're going to stop at this stage?" Dutton cried eagerly. "You're not going further with this?"

"Of course I am! If fifty million years development makes this much change in man, what will a hundred million years, two hundred million make? I'm going to find that out."

I grasped his hand. "Pollard, listen to me! Your experiment has succeeded, has fulfilled your wildest dreams. Stop it now! Think what you can accomplish, man! I know your ambition has always been to be one of humanity's great benefactors—by stopping here you can be the greatest! You can be a living proof to mankind of what your process can make it, and with that proof before it all humanity will be eager to become the same as you!"

He freed himself from my grasp. "No, Arthur—I have gone part of the way into humanity's future and I'm going on."

He stepped back into the chamber, while Dutton and I stared helplessly. It seemed half a dream, the laboratory, the cubical chamber, the godlike figure inside that was and still was not Pollard.

"Turn on the rays, and let them play for fifteen minutes more," he was directing. "It will project me ahead another fifty million years."

His eyes and voice were imperative, and I glanced at my watch, and snicked over the switch. Again the cylinder broke into light, again the shaft of force shot down into the cube to hide Pollard's splendid figure.

Dutton and I waited with feverish intensity in the next minutes. Pollard was standing still beneath the broad shaft of force, and so was hidden in it from our eyes. What would its lifting disclose? Would he have changed still more, into some giant form, or would he be the same, having already reached humanity's highest possible development?

When I shut off the mechanism at the end of the appointed period, Dutton and I received a shock. For again Pollard had changed!

He was no longer the radiant, physically perfect figure of the first metamorphosis. His body instead seemed to have grown thin and shrivelled, the outlines of bones visible through its flesh. His body, indeed, seemed to have lost half its bulk and many inches of stature and breadth, but these were compensated for by the change in his head.

For the head supported by this weak body was an immense, bulging balloon that measured fully eighteen inches from brow to back! It was almost entirely hairless, its great mass balanced precariously upon his slender shoulders and neck. And his face too was changed greatly, the eyes larger and the mouth smaller, the ears seeming smaller also. The great bulging forehead dominated the face.

Could this be Pollard? His voice sounded thin and weak to our ears.

"You are surprised to see me this time? Well, you see a man a hundred million years ahead of you in development. And I must confess that you appear to me as two brutish, hairy cave-men would appear to you."

"But Pollard, this is awful!" Dutton cried. "This change is more terrible than the first . . . if you had only stopped at the first . . ."

The eyes of the shrivelled, huge-headed figure in the cube fired with anger. "Stop at that first stage? I'm glad now that I didn't! The man I was fifteen minutes ago . . . fifty million years ago in development . . . seems now to me to have been half-animal! What was his big animal-like body beside my immense brain?"

"You say that because in this change you're getting away from all human emotions and sentiments!" I burst. "Pollard, do you realize what you're doing? You're changing out of human semblance!"

"I realize it perfectly," he snapped, "and I see nothing to be deplored in the fact. It means that in a hundred million years man will be developing in brain-capacity and will care nothing for the development of body. To you two crude beings, of what is to me the past, this seems terrible; but to me it is desirable and natural. Turn on the rays again!"

"Don't do it, Art!" cried Dutton. "This madness has gone far enough!"

Pollard's great eyes surveyed us with cold menace. "You will turn on the rays," his thin voice ordered deliberately. "If you do not, it will be but the work of a moment for me to annihilate both of you and go on with this alone."

"You'd kill us?" I said dumfoundedly. "We two, two of your best friends?"

His narrow mouth seemed to sneer. "Friends? I am millions of years past such irrational emotions as friendship. The only emotion you awaken in me is a contempt for your crudity. Turn on the rays!"

The Brain Monster

His eyes blazed as he snapped the last order, and as though propelled by a force outside myself, I closed the switch. The shaft of glowing force again hid him from our view.

Of our thoughts during the following quarter-hour I can say nothing, for both Dutton and I were so rigid with awe and horror as to make our minds chaotic. I shall never forget, though, that first moment after the time had passed and I had again switched off the mechanism.

The change had continued, and Pollard—I could not call him that in my own mind—stood in the cube-chamber as a shape the sight of which stunned our minds.

He had become simply a great head! A huge hairless head fully a yard in diameter, supported on tiny legs, the arms having dwindled to mere hands that projected just below the head! The eyes were enormous, saucer-like, but the ears were mere pin-holes at either side of the head, the nose and mouth being similar holes below the eyes!

He was stepping out of the chamber on his ridiculously little limbs, and as Dutton and I reeled back in unreasoning horror, his voice came to us as an almost inaudible piping. And it held pride!

"You tried to keep me from going on, and you see what I have become? To such as you, no doubt, I seem terrible, yet you two and all like you seem as low to me as the worms that crawl!"

"Good God, Pollard, you've made yourself a monster!" The words burst from me without thought.

His enormous eyes turned on me. "You call me Pollard, yet I am no more the Pollard you knew, and who entered that chamber first, than you are the ape of millions of years ago from whom you sprang! And all mankind is like you two! Well, they will all learn the powers of one who is a hundred and fifty million years in advance of them!"

"What do you mean?" Dutton exclaimed.

"I mean that with the colossal brain I have I will master without a struggle this man-swarming planet, and make it a huge laboratory in which to pursue the experiments that please me."

"But Pollard—remember why you started this!" I cried. "To go ahead and chart the path of future evolution for humanity—to benefit humanity and not to rule it!"

The great head's enormous eyes did not change. "I remember that the creature Pollard that I was until tonight had such foolish ambitions, yes. It would stir mirth now, if I could feel such an emotion. To benefit humanity? Do you men dream of benefitting the animals you rule over? I would no sooner think of working for the benefit of you humans!

"Do you two yet realize that I am so far ahead of you in brain power now as you are ahead of the beasts that perish? Look at this . . ."

He had climbed onto a chair beside one of the laboratory tables, was reaching among the retorts and apparatus there. Swiftly he poured several compounds into a lead mortar, added others, poured upon the mixed contents another mixture made as swiftly.

There was a puff of intense green smoke from the mortar instantly, and then the great head—I can only call him that—turned the mortar upside down. A lump of shining mottled metal fell out and we gasped as we recognized the yellow sheen of pure gold, made in a moment, apparently, by a mixture of common compounds!

"You see?" the grotesque figure was asking. "What is the transformation of elements to a mind like mine? You two cannot even realize the scope of my intelligence!

"I can destroy all life on this earth from this room, if I desire. I can construct a telescope that will allow me to look on the planets of the farthest galaxies! I can send my mind forth to make contact with other minds without the slightest material connection. And you think it terrible that I should rule your race! I will not rule them, I will *own* them and this planet as you might own a farm and animals!"

"You couldn't!" I cried. "Pollard, if there is anything of Pollard left in you, give up that thought! We'll kill you ourselves before we'll let you start a monstrous rule of men!"

"We will—by God, we will!" Dutton cried, his face twitching.

We had started desperately forward toward the great head but stopped suddenly in our tracks as his great eyes met ours. I found myself walking backward to where I had stood, walking back and Dutton with me, like two automatons.

"So you two would try to kill me?" queried the head that had been Pollard. "Why, I could direct you without a word to kill yourselves and you'd do so in an instant! What chance has your puny will and brain against mine? And what chance will all the force of men have against me when a glance from me will make them puppets of my will?"

A desperate inspiration flashed through my brain. "Pollard, wait!" I exclaimed. "You were going on with the process, with the rays! If you stop here you'll not know what changes lie beyond your present form!"

He seemed to consider. "That is true," he admitted, "and though it seems impossible to me that by going on I can attain to greater intelligence than I now have, I want to find out for certain."

"Then you'll go under the rays for another fifteen minutes?" I asked quickly.

"I will," he answered, "but lest you harbor any foolish ideas, you may know that even inside the chamber I will be able to read your thoughts and can kill both of you before you can make a move to harm me."

He stepped up into the chamber again, and as I reached for the switch, Dutton trembling beside me, we glimpsed for a moment the huge head before the down-smiting white force hid it from our sight.

The minutes of this period seemed dragging even more slowly than before. It seemed hours before I reached at last to snap off the rays. We gazed into the chamber, shaking.

At first glance the great head inside seemed unchanged, but then we saw that it had changed, and greatly. Instead of being a skin-covered head with at least rudimentary arms and legs, it was now a great gray head-like shape of even greater size, supported by two gray muscular tentacles. The surface of this gray head-thing was wrinkled and folded and its only features were two eyes as small as our own.

"Oh, my God!" quaked Dutton. "He's changing from a head into a brain—he's losing all human appearance!"

Into our minds came a thought from the gray head-thing before us, a thought as clear as though spoken. "You have guessed it, for even my former head-body is disappearing, all atrophying except the brain. I am become a walking, seeing brain. As I am so all of your race will be in two hundred million years, gradually losing more and more of their atrophied bodies and developing more and more their great brains."

His eyes seemed to read us. "You need not fear now the things I threatened in my last stage of development. My mind, grown infinitely greater, would no more now want to rule you men and your little planet than you would want to rule an anthill and its inhabitants! My mind, gone fifty million years further ahead in development, can soar out now to vistas of power and knowledge unimagined by me in that last stage, and unimaginable to you."

"Great God, Pollard!" I cried. "What have you become?"

"Pollard?" Dutton was laughing hysterically. "You call that thing Pollard? Why, we had dinner with Pollard three hours ago—he was a human being, and not a thing like this!"

"I have become what all men will become in time," the thing's thought answered me, "I have gone this far along the road of man's future evolution, and am going on to the end of that road, am going to attain the development that the last mutation possible will give me!

"Turn on the rays," his thought continued. "I think that I must be approaching now the last possible mutation."

I snapped over the switch again and the white shaft of the concentrated rays veiled from us the great gray shape. I felt my own mind giving beneath the strain of horror of the last hour, and Dutton was still half-hysterical.

The humming and crackling of the great apparatus seemed thunderous to my ears as the minutes passed. With every nerve keyed to highest tension, I threw open the switch at last. The rays ceased, and the figure in the chamber was again revealed.

Dutton began to laugh shrilly, and then abruptly was sobbing. I do not know whether I was doing the same, though I have a dim memory of mouthing incoherent things as my eyes took in the shape in the chamber.

It was a great brain! A gray limp mass four feet across, it lay in the chamber, its surface ridged and wrinkled by innumerable fine convolutions. It had no features or limbs of any kind in its gray mass. It was simply a huge brain whose only visible sign of life was its slow, twitching movement.

From it thoughts beat strongly into our own horror-weighted brains.

"You see me now, a great brain only, just as all men will be far in the future. Yes, you might have known, I might have known, when I was like you, that this would be the course of human evolution, that the brain that alone gives man dominance would develop and the body that hampers that brain would atrophy until he would have developed into pure brain as I now am!

"I have no features, no senses that I could describe to you, yet I can realize the universe infinitely better than you can with your elementary senses. I am aware of planes of existence you cannot imagine. I can feed myself with pure energy without the need of a cumbersome body, to transform it, and I can move and act, despite my lack of limbs, by means and with a speed and power utterly beyond your comprehension.

"If you still have fear of the threats I made two stages back against your world and race, banish them! I am pure intelligence now and as such, though I can no more feel the emotions of love or friendship, neither can I feel those of ambition or pride. The only emotion, if such it is, that remains to me still is intellectual curiosity, and this desire for truth that has burned in man since his apehood will thus be the last of all desires to leave him!"

The Last Mutation

"A brain—a great brain!" Dutton was saying dazedly. "Here in Pollard's laboratory—but where's Pollard? He was here, too . . ."

"Then all men will some day be as you are now?" I cried.

"Yes," came the answering thought, "in two hundred and fifty million years man as you know him and as you are will be no more, and after passing all the stages through which I have passed through tonight, the human race will have developed into great brains inhabiting not only your solar system, no doubt, but the systems of other stars!"

"And that's the end of man's evolutionary road? That is the highest point that he will reach?"

"No, I think he will change from this great brain into still a higher form," the brain answered—the brain that three hours before had been Pollard!—"and I am going to find out now what that higher form will be. For I think this will be the last mutation of all and that with it I will reach the end of man's evolutionary path, the last and highest form into which he can develop!

"You will turn on the rays now," the brain's order continued, "and in fifteen minutes we will know what that last and highest form is."

My hand was on the switch but Dutton had staggered to me, was clutching my arm. "Don't, Arthur!" he was exclaiming thickly. "We've seen horrors enough—let's not see the last—get out of here . . ."

"I can't!" I cried. "Oh God, I want to stop but I can't now—I want to see the end myself—I've got to see . . ."

"Turn on the rays!" came the brain's thought-order again.

"The end of the road—the last mutation," I panted. "We've got to see—to see—" I drove the switch home.

The rays flashed down again to hide the great gray brain in the cube. Dutton's eyes were staring fixedly, he was clinging to me.

The minutes passed! Each tick of the watch in my hand was the mighty note of a great tolling bell in my ears.

An inability to move seemed gripping me. The hand of my watch was approaching the minute for which I waited, yet I could not raise my hand toward the switch!

Then as the hand reached the appointed minute I broke from my immobility and in a sheer frenzy of sudden strength pulled open the switch, rushed forward with Dutton to the cube's very edge!

The great gray brain that had been inside it was gone. There lay on the cube's floor instead of it a quite shapeless mass of clear, jelly-like matter. It was quite motionless save for a slight quivering. My shaking hand went forth to touch it, and then it was that I screamed, such a scream as all the tortures of hell's cruelest fiends could not have wrung from a human throat.

The mass inside the cube was a mass of simple *protoplasm!* This then was the end of man's evolution-road, the highest form to which time would bring him, the last mutation of all! The road of man's evolution was a circular one, returning to its beginning!

From the earth's bosom had risen the first crude organisms. Then sea-creature and land-creature and mammal and ape to man; and from man it would rise in the future through all the forms we had seen that night. There would be super-men, bodiless heads, pure brains; only to be changed by the last mutation of all into the protoplasm from which first it had sprung!

I do not know now exactly what followed. I know that I rushed upon that quivering, quiescent mass, calling Pollard's name madly and shouting things I am glad I cannot remember. I know that Dutton was shouting too, with insane laughter, and that as he struck with lunatic howls and fury about the laboratory the crash of breaking glass and the hiss of escaping gases was in my ears. And then from those mingling acids bright flames were leaping and spreading, sudden fires that alone, I think now, saved my own sanity.

For I can remember dragging the insanely laughing Dutton from the room, from the house, into the cool darkness of the night. I remember the chill of dew-wet grass against my hands and face as the flames from Pollard's house soared higher. And I remember that as I saw Dutton's crazy laughter by that crimson light, I knew that he would laugh thus until he died.

So ends my narrative of the end that came to Pollard and Pollard's house. It is, as I said in beginning, a narrative that I only can tell now, for Dutton has never spoken a sane word since. In the institution where he now is, they think his condition the result of shock from the fire, just as Pollard was believed to have perished in that fire. I have never until now told the truth.

But I am telling it now, hoping that it will in some way lessen the horror it has left with me. For there could be no horror greater than that we saw in Pollard's house that night. I have brooded upon it. With my mind's eye I have followed that tremendous cycle of change, that purposeless, eon-long climb of life up from simple protoplasm through myriads of forms and lives of ceaseless pain and struggle, only to end in simple protoplasm again.

Will that cycle of evolutionary change be repeated over and over again upon this and other worlds, ceaselessly, purposelessly, until there is no more universe for it to go on in? Is this colossal cycle of life's changes as inevitable and necessary as the cycle that in space makes of the nebulæ myriad suns, and of the suns dark-stars, and of the dark-stars colliding with one another nebula again?

Or is this evolutionary cycle we saw a cycle in appearance only, is there some change that we cannot understand, above and beyond it? I do not know which of these possibilities is truth, but I do know that the first of them haunts me. It would haunt the world if the world believed my story. Perhaps I should be thankful as I write to know that I will not be believed.

As I reread "The Man Who Evolved," I tried to remember when I had first learned about cosmic rays and evolution. I failed. It is as though I always knew about both phenomena, even though I was clearly not born with the knowledge.

I honestly believe that I learned about both from science fiction stories to begin with. I might even have come across them first in this story.

There are some pieces of knowledge that I remember clearly having learned from science fiction stories.

For instance, in Hamilton's *The Universe Wreckers*, much of the action took place on the planet Neptune, which was treated in the story as the most distant of the planets. (Pluto had not yet been discovered, and when I heard news of the discovery, in 1931, my first thought was that it messed up Hamilton's novel.) It was in that novel that, for the first time, I learned Neptune had a satellite named Triton. I remember that piece of learning quite clearly.

It was from *The Drums of Tapajos* that I first learned there was a Mato Grosso area in the Amazon basin. It was from *The Black Star Passes* and other stories by John W. Campbell, Jr., that I first heard of relativity.

The pleasure of reading about such things in the dramatic and fascinating form of science fiction gave me a push toward science that was irresistible. It was science fiction that made me want to be a scientist strongly enough to eventually make me one.

This is not to say that science fiction stories can be completely trusted as a source of specific knowledge. In the case of "The Man Who Evolved," Hamilton was on solid ground when he maintained cosmic rays to be a motive force behind evolution. They are, but only in so far as they help create random mutations. It is natural selection that supplies the direction of evolutionary change, and this works, very painfully and slowly, upon large populations, not upon individuals.

The notion that a concentration of cosmic rays would cause an individual human being to evolve, personally, in the direction inevitably to be taken by the entire species is, of course, quite wrong. Concentrated radiation would merely kill.

However, the misguidings of science fiction can be unlearned. Sometimes the unlearning process is not easy, but it is a low price to pay for the gift of fascination over science.

It was the mark of the early and rather unsophisticated science fiction stories of the 1930s, by the way, that they often opened with one scientist lecturing others on subjects those others could not fail to know in real life (but of which the readers had to be informed).

I remember that the very first story I ever wrote for publication (but which was never published), "Cosmic Corkscrew," began that way, with the scientist-hero lecturing a friend on cosmic rays and neutrinos. No doubt, that opening helped Campbell decide on an immediate rejection (see *The Early Asimov*).

In the very month in which I completed the eighth grade, I read another story that stayed with me: "The Jameson Satellite," by Neil R. Jones, in the July 1931 *Amazing Stories*.

THE JAMESON SATELLITE

by Neil R. Jones

PROLOGUE

The Rocket Satellite

In the depths of space, some twenty thousand miles from the earth, the body of Professor Jameson within its rocket container cruised upon an endless journey, circling the gigantic sphere. The rocket was a satellite of the huge, revolving world around which it held to its orbit. In the year 1958, Professor Jameson had sought for a plan whereby he might preserve his body indefinitely after his death. He had worked long and hard upon the subject.

Since the time of the Pharaohs, the human race had looked for a means by which the dead might be preserved against the ravages of time. Great had been the art of the Egyptians in the embalming of their deceased, a practice which was later lost to humanity of the ensuing mechanical age, never to be rediscovered. But even the embalming of the Egyptians—so Professor Jameson had argued—would be futile in the face of millions of years, the dissolution of the corpses being just as eventual as immediate cremation following death.

The professor had looked for a means by which the body could be preserved perfectly forever. But eventually he had come to the conclusion that nothing on earth is unchangeable beyond a certain limit of time. Just as long as he sought an earthly means of preservation, he was doomed to disappointment. All earthly elements are composed of atoms which are forever breaking down and building up, but never destroying themselves. A match may be burned, but the atoms are still unchanged, having resolved themselves into smoke, carbon dioxide, ashes, and certain basic elements. It was clear to the professor that he could never accomplish his purpose if he were to employ one system of atomic structure, such as embalming fluid or other concoction, to preserve another system of atomic structure, such as the human body, when all atomic structure is subject to universal change, no matter how slow.

He had then soliloquized upon the possibility of preserving the human body in its state of death until the end of all earthly time—to that day when the earth would return to the sun from which it had sprung. Quite suddenly one day he had conceived the answer to the puzzling problem which obsessed his mind, leaving him awed with its wild, uncanny potentialities.

He would have his body shot into space enclosed in a rocket to become a satellite of the earth as long as the earth continued to exist. He reasoned logically. Any material substance, whether of organic or inorganic origin, cast into the depths of space would exist indefinitely. He had visualized his dead body enclosed in a rocket flying off into the illimitable maw of space. He would remain in perfect preservation, while on earth millions of generations of mankind would live and die, their bodies to molder into the dust of the forgotten past. He would exist in this unchanged manner until that day when mankind, beneath a cooling sun, should fade out forever in the chill, thin atmosphere of a dying world. And still his body would remain intact and as perfect in its rocket container as on that day of the far-gone past when it had left the earth to be hurled out on its career. What a magnificent idea!

At first he had been assailed with doubts. Suppose his funeral rocket landed upon some other planet or, drawn by the pull of the great sun, were thrown into the flaming folds of the incandescent sphere? Then the rocket might continue on out of the solar system, plunging through the endless seas of space for millions of years, to finally enter the solar system of some far-off star, as meteors often enter ours. Suppose his rocket crashed upon a planet, or the star itself, or became a captive satellite of some celestial body?

It had been at this juncture that the idea of his rocket becoming the satellite of the earth had presented itself, and he had immediately incorporated it into his scheme. The professor had figured out the amount of radium necessary to carry the rocket far enough away from the earth so that it would not turn around and crash, and still be not so far away but what the earth's gravitational attraction would keep it from leaving the vicinity of the earth and the solar system. Like the moon, it would forever revolve around the earth.

He had chosen an orbit sixty-five thousand miles from the earth for his rocket to follow. The only fears he had entertained concerned the huge meteors which careened through space at tremendous rates of speed. He had overcome this obstacle, however, and had eliminated the possibilities of a collision with these stellar juggernauts. In the rocket were installed radium repulsion rays which swerved all approaching meteors from the path of the rocket as they entered the vicinity of the space wanderer.

The aged professor had prepared for every contingency, and had set

down to rest from his labors, reveling in the stupendous, unparalleled results he would obtain. Never would his body undergo decay; and never
would his bones bleach to return to the dust of the earth from which all
men originally came and to which they must return. His body would remain millions of years in a perfectly preserved state, untouched by the
hoary palm of such time as only geologists and astronomers can conceive.

His efforts would surpass even the wildest dreams of H. Rider Haggard,
who depicted the wondrous, embalming practices of the ancient nation of
Kor in his immortal novel, "She," wherein Holly, under the escort of the
incomparable Ayesha, looked upon the magnificent, lifelike masterpieces
of embalming by the long-gone peoples of Kor.

With the able assistance of a nephew, who carried out his instructions
and wishes following his death, Professor Jameson was sent upon his pilgrimage into space within the rocket he himself had built. The nephew
and heir kept the secret forever locked in his heart.

Generation after generation had passed upon its way. Gradually humanity had come to die out, finally disappearing from the earth altogether.
Mankind was later replaced by various other forms of life which dominated the globe for their allotted spaces of time before they too became
extinct. The years piled up on one another, running into millions, and
still the Jameson Satellite kept its lonely vigil around the earth, gradually
closing the distance between satellite and planet, yielding reluctantly to
the latter's powerful attraction.

Forty million years later, its orbit ranged some twenty thousand miles
from the earth while the dead world edged ever nearer the cooling sun
whose dull, red ball covered a large expanse of the sky. Surrounding the
flaming sphere, many of the stars could be perceived through the earth's
thin, rarefied atmosphere. As the earth cut in slowly and gradually toward
the solar luminary, so was the moon revolving ever nearer the earth, appearing like a great gem glowing in the twilight sky.

The rocket containing the remains of Professor Jameson continued its
endless travel around the great ball of the earth whose rotation had now
ceased entirely—one side forever facing the dying sun. There it pursued
its lonely way, a cosmic coffin, accompanied by its funeral cortege of
scintillating stars amid the deep silence of the eternal space which enshrouded it. Solitary it remained, except for the occasional passing of a
meteor flitting by at a remarkable speed on its aimless journey through the
vacuum between the far-flung worlds.

Would the satellite follow its orbit to the world's end, or would its supply of radium soon exhaust itself after so many eons of time, converting
the rocket into the prey of the first large meteor which chanced that way?
Would it some day return to the earth as its nearer approach portended,

and increase its acceleration in a long arc to crash upon the surface of the dead planet? And when the rocket terminated its career, would the body of Professor Jameson be found perfectly preserved or merely a crumbled mound of dust?

CHAPTER I

40,000,000 Years After

Entering within the boundaries of the solar system, a long, dark, pointed craft sped across the realms of space towards the tiny point of light which marked the dull red ball of the dying sun which would some day lie cold and dark forever. Like a huge meteor it flashed into the solar system from another chain of planets far out in the illimitable Universe of stars and worlds, heading towards the great red sun at an inconceivable speed.

Within the interior of the space traveler, queer creatures of metal labored at the controls of the space flyer which juggernauted on its way towards the far-off solar luminary. Rapidly it crossed the orbits of Neptune and Uranus and headed sunward. The bodies of these queer creatures were square blocks of a metal closely resembling steel, while for appendages, the metal cube was upheld by four jointed legs capable of movement. A set of six tentacles, all metal, like the rest of the body, curved outward from the upper half of the cubic body. Surmounting it was a queer-shaped head rising to a peak in the center and equipped with a circle of eyes all the way around the head. The creatures, with their mechanical eyes equipped with metal shutters, could see in all directions. A single eye pointed directly upward, being situated in the space of the peaked head, resting in a slight depression of the cranium.

These were the Zoromes of the planet Zor which rotated on its way around a star millions of light years distant from our solar system. The Zoromes, several hundred thousand years before, had reached a stage in science, where they searched for immortality and eternal relief from bodily ills and various deficiencies of flesh and blood anatomy. They had sought freedom from death, and had found it, but at the same time they had destroyed the propensities for birth. And for several hundred thousand years there had been no births and few deaths in the history of the Zoromes.

This strange race of people had built their own mechanical bodies, and by operation upon one another had removed their brains to the metal heads from which they directed the functions and movements of their inorganic anatomies. There had been no deaths due to worn-out bodies. When one part of the mechanical men wore out, it was replaced by a new part, and so the Zoromes continued living their immortal lives which saw few casualties. It was true that, since the innovation of the machines, there had been a few accidents which had seen the destruction of the metal heads with their brains. These were irreparable. Such cases had been few, however, and the population of Zor had decreased but little. The machine men of Zor had no use for atmosphere, and had it not been for the terrible coldness of space, could have just as well existed in the ether void as upon some planet. Their metal bodies, especially their metal-encased brains, did require a certain amount of heat even though they were able to exist comfortably in temperatures which would instantly have frozen to death a flesh-and-blood creature.

The most popular pastime among the machine men of Zor was the exploration of the Universe. This afforded them a never ending source of interest in the discovery of the variegated inhabitants and conditions of the various planets on which they came to rest. Hundreds of space ships were sent out in all directions, many of them being upon their expeditions for hundreds of years before they returned once more to the home planet of far-off Zor.

This particular space craft of the Zoromes had entered the solar system whose planets were gradually circling in closer to the dull red ball of the declining sun. Several of the machine men of the space craft's crew, which numbered some fifty individuals, were examining the various planets of this particular planetary system carefully through telescopes possessing immense power.

These machine men had no names and were indexed according to letters and numbers. They conversed by means of thought impulses, and were neither capable of making a sound vocally nor of hearing one uttered.

"Where shall we go?" queried one of the men at the controls questioning another who stood by his side examining a chart on the wall.

"They all appear to be dead worlds, 4R-3579," replied the one addressed, "but the second planet from the sun appears to have an atmosphere which might sustain a few living creatures, and the third planet may also prove interesting for it has a satellite. We shall examine the inner planets first of all, and explore the outer ones later if we decide it is worth the time."

"Too much trouble for nothing," ventured 9G-721. "This system of planets offers us little but what we have seen many times before in our travels. The sun is so cooled that it cannot sustain the more common life on its planets, the type of life forms we usually find in our travels. We should have visited a planetary system with a brighter sun."

"You speak of common life," remarked 25X-987. "What of the uncommon life? Have we not found life existent on cold, dead planets with no sunlight and atmosphere at all?"

"Yes, we have," admitted 9G-721, "but such occasions are exceedingly rare."

"The possibility exists, however, even in this case," reminded 4R-3579, "and what if we do spend a bit of unprofitable time in this one planetary system—haven't we all an endless lifetime before us? Eternity is ours."

"We shall visit the second planet first of all," directed 25X-987, who was in charge of this particular expedition of the Zoromes, "and on the way there we shall cruise along near the third planet to see what we can of the surface. We may be able to tell whether or not it holds anything of interest to us. If it does, after visiting the second planet, we shall then return to the third. The first world is not worth bothering with."

The space ship from Zor raced on in a direction which would take it several thousand miles above the earth and then on to the planet which we know as Venus. As the space ship rapidly neared the earth, it slackened its speed, so that the Zoromes might examine it closely with their glasses as the ship passed the third planet.

Suddenly, one of the machine men ran excitedly into the room where 25X-987 stood watching the topography of the world beneath him.

"We have found something!" he exclaimed.

"What?"

"Another space ship!"

"Where?"

"But a short distance ahead of us on our course. Come into the foreport of the ship and you can pick it up with the glass."

"Which is the way it's going?" asked 25X-987.

"It is behaving queerly," replied the machine man of Zor. "It appears to be in the act of encircling the planet."

"Do you suppose that there really is life on that dead world—intelligent beings like ourselves, and that this is one of their space craft?"

"Perhaps it is another exploration craft like our own from some other world," was the suggestion.

"But not of ours," said 25X-987.

Together, the two Zoromes now hastened into the observation room of the space ship where more of the machine men were excitedly examining the mysterious space craft, their thought impulses flying thick and fast like bodiless bullets.

"It is very small!"

"Its speed is slow!"

"The craft can hold but few men," observed one.

"We do not yet know of what size the creatures are," reminded another. "Perhaps there are thousands of them in that space craft out there. They may be of such a small size that it will be necessary to look twice before finding one of them. Such beings are not unknown."

"We shall soon overtake it and see."

"I wonder if they have seen us?"

"Where do you suppose it came from?"
"From the world beneath us," was the suggestion.
"Perhaps."

CHAPTER II

The Mysterious Space Craft

The machine men made way for their leader, 25X-987, who regarded the space craft ahead of them critically.

"Have you tried communicating with it yet?" he asked.

"There is no reply to any of our signals," came the answer.

"Come alongside of it then," ordered their commander. "It is small enough to be brought inside our carrying compartment, and we can see with our penetration rays just what manner of creatures it holds. They are intelligent, that is certain, for their space ship does imply as much."

The space flyer of the Zoromes slowed up as it approached the mysterious wanderer of the cosmic void which hovered in the vicinity of the dying world.

"What a queer shape it has," remarked 25X-987. "It is even smaller than I had previously calculated."

A rare occurrence had taken place among the machine men of Zor. They were overcome by a great curiosity which they could not allow to remain unsatiated. Accustomed as they were to witnessing strange sights and still stranger creatures, meeting up with weird adventures in various corners of the Universe, they had now become hardened to the usual run of experiences which they were in the habit of encountering. It took a great deal to arouse their unperturbed attitudes. Something new, however, about this queer space craft had gripped their imaginations, and perhaps a subconscious influence asserted to their minds that here they have come across an adventure radically unusual.

"Come alongside it," repeated 25X-987 to the operator as he returned to the control room and gazed through the side of the space ship in the direction of the smaller cosmic wanderer.

"I'm trying to," replied the machine man, "but it seems to jump away a bit every time I get within a certain distance of it. Our ship seems to jump backward a bit too."

"Are they trying to elude us?"

"I don't know. They should pick up more speed if that is their object."

"Perhaps they are now progressing at their maximum speed and cannot increase their acceleration any more."

"Look!" exclaimed the operator. "Did you just see that? The thing has jumped away from us again!"

"Our ship moved also," said 25X-987. "I saw a flash of light shoot from the side of the other craft as it jumped."

Another machine man now entered and spoke to the commander of the Zorome expedition.

"They are using radium repellent rays to keep us from approaching," he informed.

"Counteract it," instructed 25X-987.

The man left, and now the machine man at the controls of the craft tried again to close with the mysterious wanderer of the space between planets. The effort was successful, and this time there was no glow of repulsion rays from the side of the long metal cylinder.

They now entered the compartment where various objects were transferred from out of the depths of space to the interplanetary craft. Then patiently they waited for the rest of the machine men to open the side of their space ship and bring in the queer, elongated cylinder.

"Put it under the penetration ray!" ordered 25X-987. "Then we shall see what it contains!"

The entire group of Zoromes were assembled about the long cylinder, whose low nickel-plated sides shone brilliantly. With interest they regarded the fifteen-foot object which tapered a bit towards its base. The nose was pointed like a bullet. Eight cylindrical protuberances were affixed to the base while the four sides were equipped with fins such as are seen on aerial bombs to guide them in a direct, unswerving line through the atmosphere. At the base of the strange craft there projected a lever, while in one side was a door which apparently opened outward. One of the machine men reached forward to open it but was halted by the admonition of the commander.

"Do not open it up yet!" he warned. "We are not aware of what it contains!"

Guided by the hand of one of the machine men, a series of lights shone down upon the cylinder. It became enveloped in a haze of light which rendered the metal sides of the mysterious space craft dim and indistinct while the interior of the cylinder was as clearly revealed as if there had been no covering. The machine men, expecting to see at least several, perhaps many, strange creatures moving about within the metal cylinder, stared aghast at the sight they beheld. There was but one creature, and he was lying perfectly still, either in a state of suspended animation or else of death. He was about twice the height of the mechanical men of Zor. For a long time they gazed at him in a silence of thought, and then their leader instructed them.

"Take him out of the container."

The penetration rays were turned off, and two of the machine men stepped eagerly forward and opened the door. One of them peered within at the recumbent body of the weird-looking individual with the four appendages. The creature lay up against a luxuriously upholstered interior, a strap affixed to his chin while four more straps held both the upper and lower appendages securely to the insides of the cylinder. The machine man released these, and with the help of his comrade removed the body of the creature from the cosmic coffin in which they had found it.

"He is dead!" pronounced one of the machine men after a long and careful examination of the corpse. "He has been like this for a long time."

"There are strange thought impressions left upon his mind," remarked another.

One of the machine men, whose metal body was a different shade than that of his companions, stepped forward, his cubic body bent over that of the strange, cold creature who was garbed in fantastic accoutrements. He examined the dead organism a moment, and then he turned to his companions.

"Would you like to hear his story?" he asked.

"Yes!" came the concerted reply.

"You shall, then," was the ultimatum. "Bring him into my laboratory. I shall remove his brain and stimulate the cells into activity once more. We shall give him life again, transplanting his brain into the head of one of our machines."

With these words he directed two of the Zoromes to carry the corpse into the laboratory.

As the space ship cruised about in the vicinity of this third planet which 25X-987 had decided to visit on finding the metal cylinder with its queer inhabitant, 8B-52, the experimenter, worked unceasingly in his laboratory to revive the long-dead brain cells to action once more. Finally, after consummating his desires and having his efforts crowned with success, he placed the brain within the head of a machine. The brain was brought to consciousness. The creature's body was discarded after the all-important brain had been removed.

CHAPTER III

Recalled to Life

As Professor Jameson came to, he became aware of a strange feeling. He was sick. The doctors had not expected him to live; they had frankly told him so—but he had cared little in view of the long, happy years stretched out behind him. Perhaps he was not to die yet. He wondered how long he had slept. How strange he felt—as if he had no body. Why couldn't he open his eyes? He tried very hard. A mist swam before him. His eyes had been open all the time but he had not seen before. That was queer, he ruminated. All was silent about his bedside. Had all the doctors and nurses left him to sleep—or to die?

Devil take that mist which now swam before him, obscuring everything in line of vision. He would call his nephew. Vainly he attempted to shout the word "Douglas," but to no avail. Where was his mouth? It seemed as if he had none. Was it all delirium? The strange silence—perhaps he had lost his sense of hearing along with his ability to speak—and he could see nothing distinctly. The mist had transferred itself into a confused jumble of indistinct objects, some of which moved about before him.

He was now conscious of some impulse in his mind which kept questioning him as to how he felt. He was conscious of other strange ideas which seemed to be impressed upon his brain, but this one thought concerning his indisposition clamored insistently over the lesser ideas. It even seemed just as if someone was addressing him, and impulsively he attempted to utter a sound and tell them how queer he felt. It seemed as if speech had been taken from him. He could not talk, no matter how hard he tried. It was no use. Strange to say, however, the impulse within his mind appeared to be satisfied with the effort, and it now put another question to him. Where was he from? What a strange question—when he was at home. He told them as much. Had he always lived there? Why, yes, of course.

The aged professor was now becoming more astute as to his condition. At first it was only a mild, passive wonderment at his helplessness and the strange thoughts which raced through his mind. Now he attempted to arouse himself from the lethargy.

Quite suddenly his sight cleared, and what a surprise! He could see all the way around him without moving his head! And he could look at the ceiling of his room! His room? Was it his room? No— It just couldn't be. Where was he? What were those queer machines before him? They moved on four legs. Six tentacles curled outward from their cubical bodies. One of the machines stood close before him. A tentacle shot out from the object and rubbed his head. How strange it felt upon his brow. Instinctively he obeyed the impulse to shove the contraption of metal from him with his hands.

His arms did not rise, instead six tentacles projected upward to force back the machine. Professor Jameson gasped mentally in surprise as he gazed at the result of his urge to push the strange, unearthly looking machine-caricature from him. With trepidation he looked down at his own body to see where the tentacles had come from, and his surprise turned to sheer fright and amazement. His body was like the moving machine which stood before him! Where was he? What ever had happened to him so suddenly? Only a few moments ago he had been in his bed, with the doctors and his nephew bending over him, expecting him to die. The last words he had remembered hearing was the cryptic announcement of one of the doctors.

"He is going now."

But he hadn't died after all, apparently. A horrible thought struck him! Was this the life after death? Or was it an illusion of the mind? He became aware that the machine in front of him was attempting to communicate something to him. How could it, thought the professor, when he had no mouth. The desire to communicate an idea to him became more insistent. The suggestion of the machine man's question was in his mind. Telepathy, thought he.

The creature was asking about the place whence he had come. He didn't know; his mind was in such a turmoil of thoughts and conflicting ideas. He allowed himself to be led to a window where the machine with waving tentacle pointed towards an object outside. It was a queer sensation to be walking on the four metal legs. He looked from the window and he saw that which caused him to nearly drop over, so astounded was he.

The professor found himself gazing out from the boundless depths of space across the cosmic void to where a huge planet lay quiet. Now he was sure it was an illusion which made his mind and sight behave so queerly. He was troubled by a very strange dream. Carefully he examined the topography of the gigantic globe which rested off in the distance. At the same time he could see back of him the concourse of mechanical creatures crowding up behind him, and he was aware of a telepathic conversation which was being carried on behind him—or just before him. Which was it now? Eyes extended all the way around his head, while there existed no difference on any of the four sides of his cubed body. His mechanical legs were capable of moving in any of four given directions with perfect ease, he discovered.

The planet was not the earth—of that he was sure. None of the familiar continents lay before his eyes. And then he saw the great dull red ball of the dying sun. That was not the sun of his earth. It had been a great deal more brilliant.

"Did you come from that planet?" came the thought impulse from the mechanism by his side.

"No," he returned.

He then allowed the machine men—for he assumed that they were machine men, and he reasoned that, somehow or other they had by some marvelous transformation made him over just as they were—to lead him through the craft of which he now took notice for the first time. It was an interplanetary flyer, or space ship, he firmly believed.

25X-987 now took him to the compartment which they had removed him to from the strange container they had found wandering in the vicinity of the nearby world. There they showed him the long cylinder.

"It's my rocket satellite!" exclaimed Professor Jameson to himself, though in reality every one of the machine men received his thoughts plainly. "What is it doing here?"

"We found your dead body within it," answered 25X-987. "Your brain was removed to the machine after having been stimulated into activity once more. Your carcass was thrown away."

Professor Jameson just stood dumfounded by the words of the machine man.

"So I did die!" exclaimed the professor. "And my body was placed within the rocket to remain in everlasting preservation until the end of all earthly time! Success! I have now attained unrivaled success!"

He then turned to the machine man.

"How long have I been that way?" he asked excitedly.

"How should we know?" replied the Zorome. "We picked up your rocket only a short time ago, which, according to your computation, would be less than a day. This is our first visit to your planetary system and we chanced upon your rocket. So it is a satellite? We didn't watch it long enough to discover whether or not it was a satellite. At first we thought it to be another traveling space craft, but when it refused to answer our signals we investigated."

"And so that was the earth at which I looked," mused the professor. "No wonder I didn't recognize it. The topography has changed so much. How different the sun appears—it must have been over a million years ago when I died!"

"Many millions," corrected 25X-987. "Suns of such size as this one do not cool in so short a time as you suggest."

Professor Jameson, in spite of all his amazing computations before his death, was staggered by the reality.

"Who are you?" he suddenly asked.

"We are the Zoromes from Zor, a planet of a sun far across the Universe."

25X-987 then went on to tell Professor Jameson something about how the Zoromes had attained their high stage of development and had instantly put a stop to all birth, evolution and death of their people, by becoming machine men.

CHAPTER IV

The Dying World

"And now tell us of yourself," said 25X-987, "and about your world."

Professor Jameson, noted in college as a lecturer of no mean ability and perfectly capable of relating intelligently to them the story of the earth's history, evolution and march of events following the birth of civilization up until the time when he died, began his story. The mental speech hampered him for a time, but he soon became accustomed to it so as to use it easily, and he found it preferable to vocal speech after a while. The Zoromes listened interestedly to the long account until Professor Jameson had finished.

"My nephew," concluded the professor, "evidently obeyed my instructions and placed my body in the rocket I had built, shooting it out into space where I became the satellite of the earth for these many millions of years."

"Do you really want to know how long you were dead before we found you?" asked 25X-987. "It would be interesting to find out."

"Yes, I should like very much to know," replied the professor.

"Our greatest mathematician, 459C-79, will tell it to you." The mathematician stepped forward. Upon one side of his cube were many buttons arranged in long columns and squares.

"What is your unit of measuring?" he asked.

"A mile."

"How many times more is a mile than is the length of your rocket satellite?"

"My rocket is fifteen feet long. A mile is five thousand two hundred and eighty feet."

The mathematician depressed a few buttons.

"How far, or how many miles from the sun was your planet at that time?"

"Ninety-three million miles," was the reply.

"And your world's satellite—which you call moon from your planet—earth?"

"Two hundred and forty thousand miles."

"And your rocket?"

"I figured it to go about sixty-five thousand miles from the earth."

"It was only twenty thousand miles from the earth when we picked it up," said the mathematician, depressing a few more buttons. "The moon and sun are also much nearer your planet now."

Professor Jameson gave way to a mental ejaculation of amazement.

"Do you know how long you have cruised around the planet in your own satellite?" said the mathematician. "Since you began that journey, the planet which you call the earth has revolved around the sun over forty million times."

"Forty—million—years!" exclaimed Professor Jameson haltingly. "Humanity must then have all perished from the earth long ago! I'm the last man on earth!"

"It is a dead world now," interjected 25X-987.

"Of course," elucidated the mathematician, "those last few million years are much shorter than the ones in which you lived. The earth's orbit is of less diameter and its speed of revolution is greatly increased, due to its proximity to the cooling sun. I shou'd say that your year was some four times as long as the time in which it now takes your old planet to circumnavigate the sun.

"How many days were there in your year?"

"Three hundred and sixty-five."

"The planet has now ceased rotating entirely."

"Seems queer that your rocket satellite should avoid the meteors so long," observed 459C-79, the mathematician.

"Automatic radium repu'sion rays," explained the professor.

"The very rays which kept us from approaching your rocket," stated 25X-987, "until we neutralized them."

"You died and were shot out into space long before any life occurred on Zor," soliloquized one of the machine men. "Our people had not yet even been born when yours had probably disappeared entirely from the face of the earth."

"Hearken to 72N-4783," said 25X-987, "he is our philosopher, and he just loves to dwell on the past life of Zor when we were flesh and blood creatures with the threat of death hanging always over our heads. At that time, like the life you knew, we were born, we lived and died, all within a very short time, comparatively."

"Of course, time has come to mean nothing to us, especially when we are out in space," observed 72N-4783. "We never keep track of it on our expeditions, though back in Zor such accounts are accurately kept. By the way, do you know how long we stood here while you recounted to us the history of your planet? Our machine bodies never get tired, you know."

"Well," ruminated Professor Jameson, giving a generous allowance of time. "I should say about a half a day, although it seemed scarcely as long as that."

"We listened to you for four days," replied 72N-4783.

Professor Jameson was really aghast.

"Really, I hadn't meant to be such a bore," he apologized.

"That is nothing," replied the other. "Your story was interesting, and if it had been twice as long, it would not have mattered, nor would it have seemed any longer. Time is merely relative, and in space actual time does not exist at all, any more than your forty million years' cessation of life seemed more than a few moments to you. We saw that it was so when your first thought impressions reached us following your revival."

"Let us continue on to your planet earth," then said 25X-987. "Perhaps we shall find more startling disclosures there."

As the space ship of the Zoromes approached the sphere from which Professor Jameson had been hurled in his rocket forty million years before, the professor was wondering how the earth would appear, and what radical changes he would find. Already he knew that the geographical conditions of the various continents were changed. He had seen as much from the space ship.

A short time later the earth was reached. The space travelers from Zor, as well as Professor Jameson, emerged from the cosmic flyer to walk upon the surface of the planet. The earth had ceased rotating, leaving one-half its surface always toward the sun. This side of the earth was heated to a considerable degree, while its antipodes, turned always away from the solar luminary, was a cold, frigid, desolate waste. The space travelers from Zor did not dare to advance very far into either hemisphere, but landed on the narrow, thousand-mile strip of territory separating the earth's frozen half from its sun-baked antipodes.

As Professor Jameson emerged from the space ship with 25X-987, he stared in awe at the great transformation four hundred thousand centuries had wrought. The earth's surface, its sky and the sun were all so changed and unearthly appearing. Off to the east the blood red ball of the slowly cooling sun rested upon the horizon, lighting up the eternal day. The earth's rotation had ceased entirely, and it hung motionless in the sky as it revolved around its solar parent, its orbit slowly but surely cutting in toward the great body of the sun. The two inner planets, Mercury and Venus, were now very close to the blood red orb whose scintillating, dazzling brilliance had been lost in its cooling process. Soon, the two nearer planets would succumb to the great pull of the solar luminary and return to the flaming folds, from which they had been hurled out as gaseous bodies in the dim, age-old past, when their careers had just begun.

The atmosphere was nearly gone, so rarefied had it become, and through it Professor Jameson could view with amazing clarity without discomfort to his eyes the bloated body of the dying sun. It appeared many times the size he had seen it at the time of his death, on account of its relative nearness. The earth had advanced a great deal closer to the great star around which it swung.

The sky towards the west was pitch black except for the iridescent twinkle of the fiery stars which studded that section of the heavens. As he watched, a faint glow suffused the western sky, gradually growing brighter, the full moon majestically lifted itself above the horizon, casting its pale, ethereal radiance upon the dying world beneath. It was increased to many times the size Professor Jameson had ever seen it during his natural lifetime. The earth's greater attraction was drawing upon the moon just as the sun was pulling the earth ever nearer itself.

This cheerless landscape confronting the professor represented the state of existence to which the earth had come. It was a magnificent spread of loneliness which bore no witness to the fact that it had seen the teeming of life in better ages long ago. The weird, yet beautiful scene, spread in a melancholy panorama before his eyes, drove his thoughts into gloomy abstraction with its dismal, depressing influence. Its funereal, oppressive aspect smote him suddenly with the chill of a terrible loneliness.

25X-987 aroused Professor Jameson from his lethargic reverie. "Let us walk around and see what we can find. I can understand how you feel in regard to the past. It is quite a shock—but it must happen to all worlds sooner or later—even to Zor. When that time comes, the Zoromes will find a new planet on which to live. If you travel with us, you will become accustomed to the sight of seeing dead, lifeless worlds as well as new and beautiful ones pulsating with life and energy. Of course, this world being your own, holds a peculiar sentimental value to you, but it is really one planet among billions."

Professor Jameson was silent.

"I wonder whether or not there are any ruins here to be found?" queried 25X-987.

"I don't believe so," replied the professor. "I remember hearing an eminent scientist of my day state that, given fifty thousand years, every structure and other creation of man would be obliterated entirely from off the earth's surface."

"And he was right," endorsed the machine man of Zor. "Time is a great effacer."

For a long time the machine men wandered over the dreary surface of the earth, and then 25X-987 suggested a change of territory to explore. In the space ship, they moved around the earth to the other side, still keeping to the belt of shadowland which completely encircled the globe like some gigantic ring. Where they now landed arose a series of cones with hollow peaks.

"Volcanoes!" exclaimed the professor.

"Extinct ones," added the machine man.

Leaving the space ship, the fifty or more machine men, including also Professor Jameson, were soon exploring the curiously shaped peaks. The professor, in his wanderings had strayed away from the rest, and now advanced into one of the cup-like depressions of the peak, out of sight of his companions, the Zoromes.

CHAPTER V

Eternity or Death

He was well in the center of the cavity when the soft ground beneath him gave way suddenly and he catapulted below into the darkness. Through the Stygian gloom he fell in what seemed to be an endless drop. He finally crashed upon something hard. The thin crust of the volcano's mouth had broken through, precipitating him into the deep, hollow interior.

It must have been a long ways to fall—or so it had seemed. Why was he not knocked senseless or killed? Then he felt himself over with three tentacles. His metal legs were four broken, twisted masses of metal, while the lower half of his cubic body was jammed out of shape and split. He could not move, and half of his six tentacles were paralyzed.

How would he ever get out of there? he wondered. The machine men of Zor might never find him. What would happen to him, then? He would remain in this deathless, monotonous state forever in the black hole of the volcano's interior unable to move. What a horrible thought! He could not starve to death; eating was unknown among the Zoromes, the machines requiring no food. He could not even commit suicide. The only way for him to die would be to smash the strong metal head, and in his present immovable condition, this was impossible.

It suddenly occurred to him to radiate thoughts for help. Would the Zoromes receive his messages? He wondered how far the telepathic messages would carry. He concentrated the powers of his mind upon the call for help, and repeatedly stated his position and plight. He then left his mind clear to receive the thought answers of the Zoromes. He received none. Again he tried. Still he received no welcoming answer. Professor Jameson became dejected.

It was hopeless. The telepathic messages had not reached the machine men of Zor. They were too far away, just as one person may be out of earshot of another's voice. He was doomed to a terrible fate of existence! It were better that his rocket had never been found. He wished that the Zoromes had destroyed him instead of bringing him back to life—back to this!

His thoughts were suddenly broken in upon.

"We're coming!"

"Don't give up hope!"

If the professor's machine body had been equipped with a heart, it would have sung for joy at these welcome thought impressions. A short time later there appeared in the ragged break of the volcano's mouth, where he had fallen through, the metal head of one of the machine men.

"We shall have you out of there soon," he said.

The professor never knew how they managed it for he lost consciousness under some strange ray of light they projected down upon him in his prison. When he came to consciousness once more, it was to find himself inside the space ship.

"If you had fallen and had smashed your head, it would have been all over with you," were the first thought impulses which greeted him. "As it is, however, we can fix you up first rate."

"Why didn't you answer the first time I called to you?" asked the professor. "Didn't you hear me?"

"We heard you, and we answered, but you didn't hear us. You see, your brain is different than ours, and though you can send thought waves as far as we can you cannot receive them from such a great distance."

"I'm wrecked," said the professor, gazing at his twisted limbs, paralyzed tentacles and jammed body.

"We shall repair you," came the reply. "It is your good fortune that your head was not crushed."

"What are you going to do with me?" queried the professor. "Will you remove my brains to another machine?"

"No, it isn't necessary. We shall merely remove your head and place it upon another machine body."

The Zoromes immediately set to work upon the task, and soon had Professor Jameson's metal head removed from the machine which he had wrecked in his fall down the crater. All during the painless operation, the professor kept up a series of thought exchanges in conversation with the Zoromes, and it seemed but a short time before his head surmounted a new machine and he was ready for further exploration. In the course of his operation, the space ship had moved to a new position, and now as they emerged 25X-987 kept company with Professor Jameson.

"I must keep an eye on you," he said. "You will be getting into more trouble before you get accustomed to the metal bodies."

But Professor Jameson was doing a great deal of thinking. Doubtlessly, these strange machine men who had picked up his rocket in the depths of space and had brought him back to life, were expecting him to travel with them and become adopted into the ranks of the Zoromes. Did he

want to go with them? He couldn't decide. He had forgotten that the
machine men could read his innermost thoughts.

"You wish to remain here alone upon the earth?" asked 25X-987. "It
is your privilege if you really want it so."

"I don't know," replied Professor Jameson truthfully.

He gazed at the dust around his feet. It had probably been the composition of men, and had changed from time to time into various other
atomic structures—of other queer forms of life which had succeeded mankind. It was the law of the atom which never died. And now he had
within his power perpetual existence. He could be immortal if he wished!
It would be an immortality of never-ending adventures in the vast, endless
Universe among the galaxy of stars and planets.

A great loneliness seized him. Would he be happy among these machine
men of another far-off world—among these Zoromes? They were kindly
and solicitous of his welfare. What better fate could he expect? Still,
a longing for his own kind arose in him—the call of humanity. It was
irresistible. What could he do? Was it not in vain? Humanity had long
since disappeared from the earth—millions of years ago. He wondered what
lay beyond the pales of death—the real death, where the body decomposed
and wasted away to return to the dust of the earth and assume new atomic
structures.

He had begun to wonder whether or not he had been dead all these
forty millions of years—suppose he had been merely in a state of suspended
animation. He had remembered a scientist of his day, who had claimed
that the body does not die at the point of official death. According to
the claims of this man, the cells of the body did not die at the moment
at which respiration, heart beats and the blood circulation ceased, but it
existed in the semblance of life for several days afterward, especially in
the cells of the bones, which died last of all.

Perhaps when he had been sent out into space in his rocket right after
his death, the action of the cosmic void was to halt his slow death of
the cells in his body, and hold him in suspended animation during the
ensuing millions of years. Suppose he should really die—destroying his
own brain? What lay beyond real death? Would it be a better plane of
existence than the Zoromes could offer him? Would he rediscover humanity, or had they long since arisen to higher planes of existence or reincarna-
tion? Did time exist beyond the mysterious portals of death? If not, then
it was possible for him to join the souls of the human race. Had he really
been dead all this time? If so, he knew what to expect in case he really
destroyed his own brain. Oblivion!

Again the intense feeling of loneliness surged over him and held him
within its melancholy grasp. Desperately, he decided to find the nearest

cliff and jump from it—head-first! Humanity called; no man lived to companion him. His four metal limbs carried him swiftly to the summit of a nearby precipice. Why not gamble on the hereafter? 25X-987, understanding his trend of thought, did not attempt to restrain him. Instead, the machine man of Zor waited patiently.

As Professor Jameson stood there meditating upon the jump which would hurl him now into a new plane of existence—or into oblivion, the thought transference of 25X-987 reached him. It was laden with the wisdom born of many planets and thousands of centuries' experience.

"Why jump?" asked the machine man. "The dying world holds your imagination within a morbid clutch. It is all a matter of mental condition. Free your mind of this fascinating influence and come with us to visit other worlds, many of them are both beautiful and new. You will then feel a great difference."

"Will you come?"

The professor considered for a moment as he resisted the impulse to dive off the declivity to the enticing rocks far below. An inspiration seized him. Backing away from the edge of the cliff, he joined 25X-987 once more.

"I shall come," he stated.

He would become an immortal after all and join the Zoromes in their never-ending adventures from world to world. They hastened to the space ship to escape the depressing, dreary influence of the dying world, which had nearly driven Professor Jameson to take the fatal leap to oblivion.

"The Jameson Satellite" is a notable example of the faults of pre-Campbell science fiction. The scientific background is not blended with the story but is presented in indigestible blocks that halt the action. The science, moreover, is inaccurate even by the standards of its own time.

In 1931, for instance, radium still had glamour as the richest practical source of radioactivity, so it is natural to have it used vaguely as propulsive power for a satellite (launched in 1958, by the way, almost on the nose). There was no indication, however, in 1931 (or since) that radium possesses "repulsion rays."

Then, too, Jones, at this early stage in his career (he had been publishing for only a year and a half, and this was his fourth science fiction story) was clearly in imperfect command of the English language. He used the words "soliloquized upon" when he should rather have used "considered," "inspiration" rather than the more accurate "impulse," and so on. On the whole, "The Jameson Satellite" is probably the least skillfully written story in this anthology.

None of the flaws in language and construction were obvious to my eleven-and-a-half-year self, however. What I responded to was the tantalizing glimpse of possible immortality and the vision of the world's sad death, to say nothing of the contracting spirals of the planetary orbits forty million years hence (not long enough, by the way; forty billion would have been better if that were the way the Solar System were to end, which it isn't).

More important still were Jones's Zoromes, who were robots really. Their organic brains were just a detail. Jones treated them as mechanical men, making them objective without being unfeeling, benevolent without being busybodies. They made no effort to use force to keep Professor Jameson from committing suicide if he really wanted to, but they did use dignified persuasion.

One of the marks of reader enthusiasm for a story is the demand for more, and an author often wrote a sequel to a popular story. The readers (not just myself) were so taken by "The Jameson Satellite" that Jones wrote about a dozen "Professor Jameson stories" over the next seven years, carrying his Zoromes to a new and startling world in each. Although the Zoromes remained without individual personality, I could easily recite the number-letter combinations of those who appeared most often.

It is from the Zoromes, beginning with their first appearance in "The Jameson Satellite," that I got my own feeling for benevolent robots who could serve man with decency, as these had served Professor Jameson. It was the Zoromes, then, who were the spiritual ancestors of my own "positronic robots," all of them, from Robbie to R. Daneel.

Something else that was very prevalent in the science fiction of the 1930s was the adventure story fitted out with just enough scientific trappings to enable it to pass muster. And in the science fiction magazines of the early part of the decade, no one was better at it than Captain S. P. Meek.

He published some thirty stories in the magazines between 1930 and 1932—his heyday—and of them all, the best was The Drums of Tapajos, a lost-civilization-in-the-Amazon story I have already mentioned twice.

Equally typical, and short enough to include here, are his "Submicroscopic" and its sequel, "Awlo of Ulm," which ran in successive issues of Amazing Stories (August and September 1931), and which won my heart with their boy-and-girl romance. It was at a level that just suited my time in life.

SUBMICROSCOPIC

by Capt. S. P. Meek

After many weary months of toil my task has been completed. As the sun sank to rest today, I soldered up the last connection on my Electronic Vibration Adjuster and in the fading twilight I tested it. It functions perfectly and as soon as the sun rises tomorrow I will leave this plane, I hope forever. I had originally intended to disappear without trace, as I did once before, but as I sit here waiting for the dawn, such a course seems hardly fair. This plane has treated me pretty well on the whole and I really ought to leave behind me some record of my discoveries and of my adventures, possibly the strangest adventures through which a man of this plane has ever passed. Besides, it will help to pass the time which must elapse before I can start on my journey.

My name is Courtney Edwards. I was born thirty-four years ago in the city of Honolulu, the only child of the richest sugar planter in the Islands. When I arrived at high school age I was sent to the mainland to be educated and here I have stayed. The death of my parents left me wealthy and rather disinclined to return to the home of my youth.

I did my bit in the Air Corps during the war and when it was over I shed my olive drab and went back to the University of Minneconsin to finish my education. My interest in science started when I attended a lecture on the composition of matter. It was a popular lecture intended for non-science students, and so it wasn't over my head. Dr. Harvey, one of our most popular professors, was the speaker and to this day I can visualize him standing there and can even recall some of his words.

"To give you some idea of the size of an atom," he said, "I will take for an example a cubic millimeter of hydrogen gas at a temperature of o degrees Centigrade and at sea-level pressure. It contains roughly ninety quadrillions of atoms, an almost inconceivable number. Consider this enormous number of particles packed into a cube with an edge less than one-twentieth of an inch long; yet so small are the individual atoms compared with the space between them that the solar system is crowded in comparison.

"In order to get at the ultimate composition of matter, however, we are forced to consider even smaller units. An atom is not a solid particle of matter, but instead consists of smaller particles called protons and electrons. The protons are particles of positive electricity which exist at the center or the nucleus of the atoms and the electrons are particles of negative electricity some of which revolve about the central portion and in most elements some are in the nucleus. Each of these particles is as small compared to the space between them as is the case with the atoms in the molecule."

I left the lecture hall with my head in a whirl. My imagination had been captured by the idea of counting and measuring such infinitesimal particles and I went to Dr. Harvey's office the next day and sought an interview.

"I wish to ask some questions relative to your talk last night, Doctor," I said when I faced him.

His kindly grey eyes twinkled and he invited me to be seated.

"As I understood you, Doctor," I began, "the space between the atoms and between the electrons and protons in each atom is so vast compared to their bulk that if you were to jam the protons and electrons of a cubic mile of gas together until they touched, you couldn't see the result with a microscope."

"Your idea is crudely expressed, but in the main accurate," he answered.

"Then what in the name of common sense holds them apart?" I demanded.

"Each of the atoms," he replied, "is in a state of violent motion, rushing through space with a high velocity and continually colliding with other atoms and rebounding until it strikes another atom and rebounds again. The electrons are also in a state of violent motion, revolving around the protons and this combination of centrifugal force and electrical attraction holds the atom in a state of dynamic equilibrium."

"One more question, Doctor, and I'll quit. Are these things you have told me cold sober fact susceptible of proof, or are they merely the results of an overactive imagination?"

He smiled and then leaned over his desk and answered gravely.

"Some of them are solid facts which I can prove to you in the laboratory," he said. "For instance, you, yourself, with proper training could count the number of atoms in a given volume. Other things I have said are merely theories or shrewd guesses which best explain the facts which we know. There is in physical chemistry a tremendous field of work open for men who have the ability and the patience to investigate. No one knows what the future may bring forth."

The Doctor's evident enthusiasm communicated itself to me.

"I'll be one of the ones to do this work if you'll have me as a student!" I exclaimed.

"I'll be very glad to have you, Edwards," he replied. "I believe you have the ability and the will. Time alone will tell whether you have the patience."

I resigned from my course the next day and enrolled as a special student under Dr. Harvey. After a period of intensive study of methods, I was ready to plunge into the unknown. The work of Bohr and Langmuir especially attracted me, and I bent my energies to investigating the supposed motion of the electrons about the nuclear protons. This line of investigation led me to the suspicion that the motion was not circular and steady, but was periodic and simple harmonic except as the harmonic periods were interfered with by the frequent collisions.

I devised an experiment which proved this to my satisfaction and took my results to Dr. Harvey for checking. He took my data home with him that night intending to read it in bed as was his usual custom, but from that bed he never rose. Death robbed me of my preceptor and Dr. Julius became the head of the Chemistry Department. I took my results to him only to meet with scorn and laughter. Dr. Julius was an able analyst, but he lacked vision and could never see the woods for the trees. The result of my interview with him was that I promptly left Minneconsin, and resolved to carry on my work at another school.

The problem on which I wished to work was the reduction of the period of vibration of the atoms and of their constituent parts. If my theory of their motion were correct, it should be possible to damp their vibrations and thus collapse matter together and make it occupy a smaller volume in space. I soon found that men like Dr. Harvey were scarce. Not a man at the head of a university department could I find who had the vision to see the possibilities of my work and in a rage I determined to conduct my experiments alone and hidden from the world until I had proved the truth of my theories.

I was still flying for amusement and one day while flying from Salt Lake City to San Francisco, I passed over a verdant fertile valley hidden in the almost inaccessible crags of the Timpahute range in southern Nevada. I abandoned my trip temporarily and landed at Beatty to make inquiries. Not a person could I find who had ever heard of my hidden valley. Even the old desert rats professed ignorance of its location and laughed at me when I told them that I had seen flowing water and deciduous trees in the barren stretches of the Timpahutes.

I had taken the bearings of my valley and I flew on to San Francisco and made my arrangements. I flew back to Beatty and picked up a pack outfit and landed at the foot of the crags sheltering the valley and started on foot to seek an entrance. It took me a month of careful searching to find it, but find it I did. With a little blasting, the way could be made practicable for pack burros. The stuff I had ordered at San Francisco had been delivered to Beatty and I hired packers to take it out to the Timpahutes for me. I established a dump about a mile from my valley entrance and had the stuff unloaded there. When the packers had left I took my own burros and packed it in to the valley. I didn't care to have anyone find out where I was locating and so far as I know no one ever did.

When I had everything packed in, I started to work.

A few days enabled me to rig an undershot waterwheel in the stream and get enough power to turn an electric generator and thereafter I had the strength of twenty men at my call. I built a small wooden building for a laboratory with a room in it for my cooking and sleeping.

I was fortunate enough not to meet with a single major setback in my work, and in about fourteen months I had my first piece of apparatus completed. I don't intend to tell how I did it, for I do not believe that the world is ready for it yet, but I will give some idea of how it looked and how it was operated. The adjuster has a circular base of silvery metal (it is a palladium alloy) from which rise six supports which hold up the top. The top, which is made of the same alloy as the base, is parabolic in shape and concave downward. In the parabola is set an induction coil with a sparkgap surmounting it, so set that the gap is at the focus of the reflector, which is what the top really is. The coil and gap are connected with other coils and condensers which are actuated by large storage batteries set around the edge of the base. To each of the six uprights is fastened a small parabolic reflector with a small coil and gap at the focus. These small reflectors are so arranged that they bathe the top with the generated ray while the large gap in the top bathes the rest of the apparatus.

When the gaps and coils are actuated by the current, they throw out a ray of such a wavelength that it has the same period as the electronic and atomic vibrations but is half a wavelength out of phase. The ray is effective only when it can flow freely, and the base and top serve not only as conductors, but also as insulators, for they absorb and transform the vibrations falling on them so that nothing outside of the apparatus itself and anything lying between the base and the top is affected.

When I had it completed, I naturally tested it. The whole thing was controlled by a master switch and I reached in with a small steel rod and closed the switch. Immediately the whole apparatus began to shrink. I gave a loud cheer and patted myself on the back. I got down on my knees and watched it as it rapidly diminished in size until I suddenly realized that it would soon get too small to see unless I opened my switch. I tried to reach the switch with my rod but I had waited too long. The rod would not go through the interval between the side columns. I had the mortification of seeing a year's work grow smaller and smaller until it finally vanished.

The loss of my adjuster was a blow, but at least I had proved my theory and as soon as I had rested for a few days I started in to build a duplicate. The way had already been blazed and it took me less than a year to complete my second piece of apparatus. When I tested this one I stopped the shrinking process when the adjuster was about half its original size and reversed the polarity of my coils. To my delight the adjuster began to expand until it had resumed its original proportions. Then I shut it off and began to experiment to find out its limitations.

When I had determined to my satisfaction that inanimate objects placed on the base would be expanded or contracted, I tried it on living organisms. A jack rabbit was my first subject and I found that I could increase this rabbit to the size of a Shetland pony or reduce it to the size of a mouse without visible ill effects. When I had completed this experiment, I tried the adjuster on myself.

My first experiment was to increase my size. I stepped on the base plate and turned on the current, but I could feel no effects. I looked at the landscape and found to my amazement that something had gone wrong. I was remaining the same size but the house and the surrounding country had come under the influence of my device and was shrinking rapidly. In alarm I shut off my current and got out. The house had shrunk to one-half its normal size and I could not get in the door, even on hands and knees. An idea struck me and I reached in and hauled out a pair of scales and weighed myself. *I weighed a trifle over twelve hundred pounds.* I suddenly realized that I had succeeded beyond my wildest dreams and I reentered the adjuster and shrunk myself down to four inches tall, again with no ill effects and merely the impression that the house and landscape were growing. I returned myself to my normal size and while I was weak from excitement, otherwise I felt perfectly normal.

My first thought was to return and confound the men who had scoffed at me but the more I considered the matter, the more I realized the importance of my invention and the need of caution in introducing it. I felt that I needed a rest anyway, so I remained in my valley to perfect my plans before announcing my discovery.

Time soon lagged on my hands. I have always been fond of big game hunting and I had an excellent rifle and plenty of ammunition, but game does not abound in the Timpahutes. There were quite a few ants in the valley and it struck me that, were I to reduce myself and my rifle to the proper dimensions, I would have some good sport. The novelty of the idea fascinated me as much as the thought of the hunting and I promptly belted on a pistol and a full belt of ammunition and entered the adjuster.

I closed the switch and the house and landscape began to grow to Brobdingnagian proportions, but I kept my power on until the grains of sand began to look like huge boulders and then I tried to open the switch. *It was stuck.* Thoroughly alarmed, I tried to wrench it open and as a result broke the handle—the device kept on functioning and I grew smaller and smaller. The grains of sand grew to be huge mountains and presently I felt myself falling. I realized that my adjuster had been balanced on a grain of sand and that it had slipped and was falling into the chasm between two grains. Soon it became wedged in a gloomy chasm, but it was still functioning and presently I was falling again.

A glance at the dial of my relative size indicator showed me that the needle had almost reached the point which I had indicated as infinity. Desperately I battered at the switch with my rifle butt, but it was solidly made. At last I broke it loose and the whine of my coil became audible and ran down the scale until it was silent. I had stopped shrinking but I was already far smaller than any microscope could detect and an examination of the switch soon convinced me that it was completely wrecked and that it would take me hours to repair it.

When I had finished my examination, I looked around for the first time. I could hardly believe my eyes. My adjuster was standing in a beautiful sunlit glade, which was carpeted with grass and dotted with varicolored flowers. Now I will have to explain one thing. As I said, I felt no change when my size was increased and reduced; it only seemed that the familiar landscape was undergoing a change. As a result, I could never realize while I was in Ulm, that everything was really submicroscopic, but persisted in referring everything to my normal six feet of height. In actual fact, the glade in which the adjuster stood was only a minute fraction of an inch across, but to me it looked like about half a mile and it took me ten minutes to walk it. Even now I have no idea of how small I actually was, so I will not try to describe the *absolute* size of everything, but will speak of things as they appeared to me; in other words, their *relative* size to me.

I looked over that landscape and rubbed my eyes, trying to convince myself that I was dreaming, but the scene didn't change and I realized that I had stumbled on something heretofore unsuspected—namely that our world is a very complex affair and supports many kinds of life unknown to us. Everything within the range of my vision looked normal, grass, trees and even mosquitos were buzzing around and one lit on my wrist and bit me. Imagine, if you can, what the actual measurements of that mosquito must have been!

Convinced that I was not dreaming, I stepped out of the adjuster to the grass. Before I repaired that switch I meant to have a look around and see what this miniature world was like. I had gone only a few steps from the adjuster when a lordly buck rose from the grass and bounded away. Instinctively I threw up my rifle and fired and the buck went down kicking. Assured that my weapons were functioning properly, I set off at a brisk pace across the glade. I took careful bearings with my pocket compass and expected to have no trouble in finding my way back. During the ten minutes it took me to cross the glade, I had several more chances to shoot at deer, but I passed them up. I didn't wish to waste ammunition or to call attention to myself until I knew what was ahead of me.

It was hot and sultry in the glade and I glanced up at the sun, expecting it to appear enormous, but it appeared no larger than usual, a matter which I could not explain at the time and cannot even yet. Before I reached the woods which fringed the glade I noticed that the horizon was walled in on all sides with enormous mountains, higher than any I had ever seen and it gave me a shock to realize that these mighty and imposing masses of rock were in reality only grains of sand, or perhaps even smaller; they might be particles of the impalpable dust which lies between the sand grains.

It took me perhaps ten minutes to reach the edge of the jungle, for such it proved to be. Most of the trees were of species unknown to me, although I recognized several trees of peculiarly tropical habit, among them the baobab or one of its relatives and the *lignum vitae*. The scene reminded me more of the Brazilian jungles than anything else. The ground underfoot was deep with rotting vegetation and the creepers made the going hard. I plunged into the tangle and in ten minutes I was as thoroughly lost as I have ever been in my life. The gloom under the trees prevented me from using the sun as a guide and I had not read my compass when I entered the tangle.

I set a compass course and floundered forward as best I could but half an hour of steady going convinced me that I had taken the wrong direction. The jungle was too dense to back trail, so I laid a new course by compass and plunged ahead. I kept on for perhaps ten minutes on my new course when I heard a sound that brought me up standing, hardly able to believe my ears. From ahead of me came a shout, a shout given in a human voice. I strained my ears and soon I heard it again from the same direction and somewhat closer. Some one was coming toward me and I looked for a hiding place. A tangle of baobab roots concealed me pretty well and I crouched, my rifle ready, waiting for what might appear.

In a few moments I heard a sound of running footsteps and I peered out from my cover. Imagine my surprise when a girl, a white girl, came into view, running at top speed. Not fifty yards behind her came a group of men, or beasts, for I couldn't tell at first glance which they were. They were as black as pitch, with thick heavy lips, flat noses and almost no foreheads. They were or rather seemed to be about seven feet tall on the average, with enormously powerful chests and arms that hung below their knees. At times they dropped forward so that their knuckles rested on the ground and came ahead on all fours at a more rapid rate than their relatively short bandy legs could carry them when they were in an upright position. They were covered on the head, chest and arms with coarse black hair, although their legs, abdomens and backs were almost free from it. Their mouths were wide with the lower jaw protruding somewhat with yellow fangs showing between their lips, giving them a horribly bestial expression. They had two eyes, but they were not placed as is usual with animals of the monkey or human species. One eye was set in the middle of the forehead and the other in the back of the head. They were naked except for a G string and a belt from which hung a short heavy sword, and in their hands they carried spears about ten feet long. The average weight of a full grown male in our world would have been about four hundred pounds. Of course I didn't see all of this at first glance, but later I saw enough of the Mena, as they were called, to get pretty familiar with their appearance.

A glance was enough to show me that the girl was tired and that these brutes were gaining on her. She was human and the sight of these savages made my next action purely instinctive. With a shout I stepped from my hiding place and threw my rifle to my shoulder. The girl saw me and altered her direction to come toward me. The blacks saw me, too, and they turned in my direction, brandishing their spears.

I am a pretty good shot and they were close and an easy target. I had four shells in my rifle and four of the blacks went down as fast as I could work my bolt. The rest paused for a moment and gave me time to ram a fresh clip of cartridges into my rifle. As I reloaded, I picked out one of them who seemed to be a leader and I dropped him on the next shot. This made them pause again but another black devil sprang forward to take the lead and I presented him with a bit of lead in the face. He went down like a thunderbolt and as none of the rest seemed to aspire to leadership, I distributed the other three bullets where I thought they would do the most good. As I lowered my rifle to reload, another one of the blacks jumped forward and charged me, and the rest followed. I had no time to load, so I jerked out my Colt .45 and when he was about twenty-five yards away I let him have a pill in the chest and then started a little miscellaneous slaughter. By the time the Colt was empty, there were fourteen of the blacks down and the rest were retreating at full speed. I first reloaded my rifle and slipped a clip into my pistol and then looked for the girl.

I didn't see her for a moment and then I spied a lock of golden hair in the tangle at my feet. She had burrowed into the vegetation and had got pretty well covered in the few moments I was shooting. I reached down and touched her, but as soon as she found that her hiding place was discovered, she bounded up and took to her heels like a scared rabbit. I called to her and she threw a glance back over her shoulder and when she saw that I was alone she checked her speed and stood her ground. She hesitated for a moment and then came back and dropped to her knees at my feet. I lifted her up and patted her on the shoulder.

"'There, little girl, don't cry,'" I quoted inanely, partly because I didn't know what else to say and partly because I was completely bowled over by her appearance. She was absolutely the most beautiful girl I have ever seen in my life—tall and lithe, all curves and grace, with eyes as blue as the sea around Oahu and hair where sunbeams had been imprisoned and where they struggled continuously for liberty, throwing their glints out through the meshes of their prison. Bound around her head was a golden filet with a huge square cut stone of beautiful sparkle and radiance set in it. Around her waist and confining her garments of flowing green gauze was another golden band with a gold-encrusted, gem-set pouch depending from it. On the buckle of her girdle was another of the square cut gems such as adorned her head band.

I have always been pretty much at ease in the presence of girls, principally because I never cared much for them, but to this dirty little savage, as beautiful as dawn, I didn't know what to say. I could just gulp and stammer.

"Er, do you think these rapscallions will come back for more?" I blurted out at last.

She cast a sideways glance at me that made my head whirl, and my heart do all sorts of funny flip-flops, and then she spoke. Her speech was beautifully liquid and hauntingly familiar. I couldn't understand her, but I was sure that I had heard that language before. Presently I caught a word and like a flash I knew. She was speaking some dialect of Hawaiian. Desperately I strove to recall the speech of Leilani, my old nurse, but the only phrase I could remember was *"E nac iki ne puu wai."* It didn't seem quite appropriate to say "Be true to me, fair one" to a girl I had just met, but it was for the moment the only phrase I could remember so I blurted it out.

She understood it all right and she flew into a royal rage. She shot out a stream of fluent speech so fast that I couldn't understand a word of it. I thought rapidly and then brought forth another gem of speech, *"Hawaiian pau."* I had to repeat it twice before she understood and then she didn't get the word Hawaiian, but she understood *pau,* finished, all right and she presently realized that my first speech was the only bit of her language which I knew. When she understood my predicament, she forgot her anger and laughed. I was glad to see her cheerful again, but I was still worried about whether those blacks would return.

For lack of language I was forced to fall back on pantomime in order to make myself understood. She readily understood me and looked worried for a moment until her eye fell on my rifle. She touched it questioningly and then spurned the body of the nearest black with her foot and laughed.

Evidently she thought that my weapon made me invincible, but I knew better. I had only two more clips of pistol cartridges and eighty-five rounds for my rifle, not enough to repel a real attack. I tapped my rifle, shook my head sadly and said *"pau."*

The worried look again came into her face and she started talking very slowly and distinctly, repeating the word *"Ulm"* several times. Gradually my Hawaiian was coming back and while her speech was not the language I had learned in my youth, for she made use of the consonants "s" and "t," both of which are unknown in Hawaiian, presently I made out her meaning. She was asking me to go with her to Ulm. I had no idea of where Ulm was but I had given up hopes of finding my adjuster and besides, since I had met this girl, I wasn't so very anxious to find it at once. It seemed to me that it might be a good idea to go to Ulm for a while, and then make a fresh start for the glade with a competent guide. I therefore gave her to understand that her program suited me. She nodded brightly and stepped in front of me and set off toward the northeast.

For perhaps three hours we made our way through the jungle, keeping a pretty straight line as I could tell by my compass. I found later that the people of Ulm have an uncanny sense of direction and can find their way from place to place in their miniature world without the aid of any other guide. The girl kept up a steady talk in her language and as I recalled more of my early Hawaiian, I found that I could understand the sense of most of what she said if she talked very slowly and I was even able to answer her after a fashion.

"What is your name?" I asked her.

"Awlo Sibi Tam," she replied, raising her head proudly as she did so.

"My name is Courtney," I told her.

She tried to repeat it, but she had a little trouble with the "r" sound which was evidently strange to her. She repeated it several times as we went along and at last managed to get a very fair rendition. Anyhow, I thought that I had never heard it pronounced so beautifully before.

Suddenly Awlo paused in her talk and listened intently. She turned a terror-stricken face toward me and said, "They are coming."

"Who?" I asked.

"The Mena," she replied.

I listened but I could hear nothing.

"Are there many of them?" I asked.

"Many," she replied, "hundred, I believe. They are following our trail. Can't you hear them?"

I laid my ear close to the ground and could detect a faint murmur but I would never have recognized what it was.

"What shall we do?" I asked. "This," I held up my rifle, "will kill about a hundred but no more."

"Run," she said, "run as fast as we can. It will be of little use, because the Mena can catch us. You are slow and I am tired, but if we are lucky, we may win to the plains of Ulm and there we are safe."

Her advice sounded good and I started after her as swiftly as I could. I am a fair average runner, but I could not keep up with Awlo, who fled over the ground like an antelope. I was handicapped by the weight of my rifle but I hung to it like grim death. It was not long before I could plainly hear the shouts of the pursuing Mena.

"Have we far to go?" I gasped.

"No," she replied over her shoulder. "Hurry!"

I panted along in her wake. The jungle thinned before us and we debouched onto a huge open plain. Awlo stopped and uttered a cry of dismay.

"What is it?" I demanded.

She did not answer but pointed ahead. Our way was barred by a wide, gently flowing river. Over it had been thrown a bridge but a glance showed me that the center span had been removed and a gap twenty feet wide yawned in the middle of the structure.

"Can you swim?" I asked.

She looked at me interrogatively. Evidently the word was a new one.

"Swim, run through the water," I explained.

An expression of absolute terror passed over her face.

"It is *tabu*," she replied. "It is death to enter."

"It is death to stay on this side," I told her.

"It is better to die at the hands of the Mena than at the hands of the Gods," she answered.

She meant it too. She would rather face certain death at the hands of those hideous savages than to enter the stream. There was only one thing to do and that was to look for a place where I could sell my life dearly. With this in mind, I started along the river bank looking for a depression which would shelter us from the spears of the Mena. We made our way through a clump of trees in front of us and it was my turn to cry out, only the cry was one of joy and not of apprehension. There, between the trees and the river bank, stood a familiar looking object—an Electronic Vibration Adjuster.

"We are saved, Awlo," I cried joyously as I raced for the machine. A glance showed me that it was my first model which I had sent, as I thought, to infinite smallness nearly a year before. I was puzzled for a moment at the fact that it had not shrunk to nothing, but I had no time for philosophical reasoning. The shouts of the Mena were already perilously close.

"Run off a few yards, Awlo," I commanded, "and don't be frightened. I can save you easily."

She obeyed me and I entered the adjuster. A momentary fear came over me that the batteries might be exhausted but I seized the switch and threw it on in the direction of increasing size. The landscape began to diminish its size, although as before, I could feel nothing. I kept my eye on the river until it had shrunk to a point where I knew that I could easily leap it and then I opened my switch and stepped out.

For a moment I could not see Awlo, but I detected her lying face downward on the ground. I bent over her and then I saw something else. The Mena, hundreds of them, had emerged from the jungle and were coming along our trail. I hesitated no longer. As gently as I could, I picked up Awlo and leaped over the river with her. I waited to see whether the Mena were going to make any attempt to follow, but they had evidently caught a glimpse of my gargantuan proportions and they were in full retreat. I found out later that the river was as much taboo to them as it was to Awlo and they would under no circumstances have crossed the stream except by means of a bridge or in boats.

I raised Awlo to the level of my eyes to talk to her but she had fainted. I leaped back to the other side of the river, reentered my adjuster and closed the reducing switch. Since I had the machine under control, I determined not to stop it until I found what had made it cease functioning when it did. My size rapidly grew smaller until I was correctly scaled to my surroundings and then the machine abruptly ceased working. I could not make it reduce either itself or me any further. The only explanation which has ever occurred to me is that the land of Ulm must be at the limit of smallness, that is, the period of vibration of the atoms and their component parts must be at the lower limit of motion and any further reduction would result in contact and consequent nothingness.

My intention had been to swim the river while Awlo was unconscious but it occurred to me that the adjuster might be useful on the other side of the river so I again increased my size until I could step over it. Knowing that the machine would only get so small, I reached in with a piece of wood and closed the reducing switch and watched it grow to toy size. With it in my hand, I again leaped the river and used my pocket knife blade to close the increasing switch. When it had grown to the right size, I stopped it, reentered it and soon had both the adjuster and myself down to the minimum to which it would go.

Awlo was still unconscious and I bent over her and chafed her hands. She soon recovered and sat up. Her gaze wandered and it fell on the adjuster, she shuddered and turned to me with fear in her eyes.

"What happened, Courtney Siba?" she asked with a quaver in her voice. "I thought that you had changed into a *kahuma*, a wizard of the old days. Was I dreaming?"

I thought rapidly. Evidently a *kahuma* was something to be revered but also something not quite human. The advantage and disadvantages of being one flashed before me but a glance at Awlo's scared face decided me.

"I am no *kahuma*, Awlo," I replied. "What I did, I did with the aid of that. It made me appear to the Mena to be larger than I am and they ran. While they were gone, I carried you and the machine over the river. We are perfectly safe now and unless the Mena find some way of crossing, they won't bother us again."

Awlo seemed satisfied with my explanation. I suggested that she rest for a while to recover from her scare but she laughed at the idea.

"Ulm is near at hand," she told me, "and we must hurry on. I would not that my father be unduly worried by my absence."

"That reminds me of something I have been meaning to ask you, Awlo," I said as we resumed our onward way. "How did you happen to be in the jungle with the Mena after you when I found you?"

"I was visiting my uncle, Hama, at his city of Ame," she replied. "My visit was at an end and I started homeward yesterday. It has been three years since the Mena have ventured to attack us and the guard was small, only about three hundred soldiers. We were about half way between the two cities and were going peaceably through the jungle when, without warning, the Mena attacked. The soldiers fought desperately but the Mena were too many and too powerful for them and they were all killed. I and two of my maidens were captured. The Mena took us to one of their cities in the jungle and prepared for a feast."

"For a feast?" I inquired.

"We are food for the Mena," she replied simply.

I shuddered at the thought and gritted my teeth as I thought of those flying monsters who were at my mercy a few minutes before. Had I known what brutes they were, I could have taken glorious vengeance on them.

"Last night," went on Awlo, "they took first one and then the other of my maidens out from the cave where we were confined, and killed them and dragged them away to the pot. My turn was next and two of them seized me and dragged me out. They released me and one of them raised

a spear to end my life. I dropped to the ground and the spear passed over
my head and then I fled. I tried to run toward Ulm, but they suspected
the course I would pursue and a party went to head me off while others
followed my trail. As long as it was dark I was able to baffle them and go
faster than they could trail me, but with the coming of light they found
my trail and soon I heard them after me. I ran as fast as I could, but they
gained rapidly and I thought that I was lost when I heard your shout.
Awlo Sibu Tam will never forget how you saved her and neither will Ulm.
My father, Kalu, will honor you highly, Courtney Siba."

"If these Mena are such brutes, why don't your soldiers wage war on
them until there are none left?" I asked.

"They have waged war for ages," she replied, "but the Mena are too
many and we cannot hunt them all down. In ages past, there were
no Mena and then Ulm and Ame fought together. Sometimes one would
be victorious and sometimes the other, but always they ceased warring before either was destroyed. Then came the Mena through the passes from
the wilderness to the north. They came in thousands and they attacked
Ame. The men of Ulm forgot their hatred of their old rival and our
armies marched to the assistance of the threatened city. For a time our
armies drove the invaders back but more and more came from the north
and carried the battle to the gates of Ame itself. There our armies stopped
them for they could not climb the walls nor could they break in.

"When they saw that they could not win the city, they attacked Ulm.
Our army hurried back to defend the city and the men of Ame came with
them, leaving only enough to man the walls. Again the Mena fought their
way to the city walls and again they were stopped. When they found they
could not take either city, they drew back into the jungle and established
cities of huts. Such is the condition today. The Mena fight among themselves and when they are weakened in numbers, the armies of Ulm and
Ame march out to attack them. They have always defeated them and tried
to hunt them down and sometimes for a generation the Mena are not
seen, but eventually they return stronger than ever and attack one of the
cities. It has been many years now since war was waged on them and it
may be that they are planning to attack again."

"Do Ulm and Ame ever fight now?" I asked.

"No, there is peace between them. Brothers of one blood sit on the two
thrones and the old enmity is forgotten. But see, there lies Ulm!"

We had topped a little rise and had come to the cultivated fields. Before
us lay row after row of cultivated plots, most of them planted with *keili*
bushes, the nut of which is the staple food of the poorer classes of Ulm.
Two miles or so across the plain rose a massive walled city. Dotted about
on the plain were small stone structures, which reminded me of the old

blockhouses which used to be erected on our own plains to guard against Indian raids. That, in fact, was the exact function of these structures.

As we approached the nearest of them a figure appeared on the wall and scrutinized us closely. He called out a musical greeting and Awlo raised her face.

"Awlo Sibi Tam commands your presence," she cried imperiously.

The sentry rubbed his eyes and looked and then came down from that wall in a hurry. The massive gates swung open and an officer appeared and prostrated himself and kissed the ground before Awlo.

"Rise!" she commanded.

He rose and half drew his sword from its sheath and presented the hilt to Awlo. She touched it and he returned it to its scabbard with a sharp motion and stood upright.

"I would go to Ulm," she said. "Send couriers to warn my father of my approach and bid my guard come hither to escort me."

He bowed deeply and Awlo took me by the hand and led me into the building. It was a typical guardroom such as are found in all nations and at all times. We seated ourselves and I heard the sound of hoof-beats rapidly dying away in the direction of the city.

"Who are you, Awlo?" I asked. "Are you a Chief's daughter or what?"

"I am Sibi Tam," she replied.

"I don't know that rank," I answered. "How important is it?"

She looked at me in surprise and then laughed.

"You will find out in time, Courtney Siba," she said with a laugh.

I tried to press the question but she refused to answer and turned the talk to other matters. Half an hour passed and then I was aware of a confused murmur approaching from the city. Awlo rose.

"It is doubtless our escort," she said. "Let us greet them."

I followed her out into the courtyard and up on the thick wall which surrounded the building. Coming down the road was the most gorgeous cavalcade I had ever seen. First came a band of cavalry mounted on superb horses and carrying long lances. They wore golden helmets with nodding crimson horsehair plumes rising from them, a cuirass of gold and golden shin guards. Their thighs were bare. Besides the armor they wore a short crimson garment like a skirt, which fell half way to the knee, and a flowing crimson cape trimmed with brown fur. Heavy swords on the left side of their belts and a dagger on the right, together with their twelve-foot lances made up their offensive weapons.

Following the cavalry came a number of gorgeously decorated chariots, occupied by men gorgeously dressed in every imaginable hue. Another troop of cavalry, similar to the first except that their plumes and clothing were blue, brought up the rear.

As the leading troop came opposite the gate, Awlo stepped to the edge of the wall. Her appearance was greeted by a roar of applause and salutation and the red cavalry reined in their horses and pointed their lances toward her, butt foremost. She answered the salute with a wave of her hand and the troop charged forward at a word of command past the tower and then whirled to form a line facing her. The chariots came up and an elderly man dismounted from the first one and passed in through the gate. He came up the steps to the wall and dropped on one knee before Awlo, half drawing his sword and thrusting the hilt toward her as he did so.

She touched the sword and he returned it and rose to his feet.

"Greeting, Moka," she said. "Come with me for I desire a word with you."

Submissively he followed her a short distance along the wall and I could see that she was speaking rapidly. I could tell from the direction of Moka's glances that I was the topic of conversation, and his actions when Awlo had finished amply proved it. Moka came forward and drew his sword and cast it at my feet. I drew my pistol and placed it beside his weapon. Moka laid his left hand against my breast and I did the same.

"My brother and my lord," he said as he rose.

Awlo interrupted before I could say anything.

"I would go to Ulm," she said.

Moka bowed deeply and we each picked up our weapons. I followed Awlo toward the chariots. The largest and most ornate was empty and into it she sprang lightly, motioning to me to go with Moka in his chariot. I entered it and the whole cortège turned about and proceeded toward the city.

We drove in through a huge gate which was opened before us and down a wide thoroughfare which led directly into the center of the city. This avenue ended in a park in the center of which stood the largest and most beautiful building in the city. We left our chariots and made our way on foot across the park and entered the palace between rows of guards who, as Awlo passed, presented their spears, butt foremost.

At the end of the hall, Awlo paused.

"Courtney Siba," she said, "you are doubtless weary as I am. Go then with Moka, who will supply you with clothing fitting to your rank and with proper refreshment. My father will meet you when you have rested and reward you as you merit."

I had learned a little about the customs of Ulm and I dropped on one knee and presented her my pistol, butt first. She smilingly touched it and I rose and followed Moka. He led me up a flight of steps and into an apartment fit for a Prince of the Blood. Here he summoned servants and surrendered me to their tender mercies.

I did not realize how tired I was until a hot bath revealed the true extent of my fatigue. One of my servants approached and by motions indicated that I was to lie down on a couch. I did so and he massaged me thoroughly with a sweet-smelling oil, which banished my fatigue marvelously. When he had finished, other servants approached with garments which they evidently desired me to put on. I strove to talk to them but they merely shook their heads. Small wonder, for I later found that they were dumb.

The clothing which they brought me consisted of such a skirt, as I had seen on the soldiers, except that it was pure white. In addition they brought me a white cloak which hung well below the waist and which was fastened at the throat with a diamond the size of a walnut. On my feet they placed leather sandals which were thickly encrusted with gold and diamonds and around my calves they wound leather straps also heavily gemmed. About my head they bound a golden filet with a square cut diamond set in the center and around my waist they fastened a belt with a diamond buckle with a long straight sword hanging from the left and a heavily jeweled dagger from the right. As a final touch they set on my head a golden helmet somewhat like those I have seen on ancient Grecian coins, with a white horsehair plume. When they had finished they stood me in front of a mirror to see if I was suited.

I was, in every respect except one. I dug into my old clothes and got my Colt and hung the holster on my belt instead of the silly dagger. It may not have been as handsome, but if I was going to need weapons where I was going, I knew which would be of the most value to me. When I signified that I was suited, my servants withdrew with many bows and left me alone.

I hardly knew what to expect next but I threw myself on the couch to rest a little. For close to an hour I waited before the door swung open to admit Moka.

"My lord," he said with a bow, "Kalu Sabama awaits your presence."

"I am ready," I replied as I rose.

As we passed through the doorway, a detachment of guard met us. As we appeared, they grounded their spears with a ringing clash and closed around us. We passed down a corridor and down a flight of stairs to the main entrance hall and across it to a great closed double door, where we were halted by another detachment of guards and challenged. Moka answered the challenge and the great doors swung open and there was a peal of trumpets. When they had ceased a sonorous voice called out some words which I did not understand, although I was pretty sure that I caught the words "Awlo" and "Courtney." It was evidently an introduction, for, when the voice ceased, Moka motioned me to go forward. I stepped out with my head held high. The guards went with me for a few paces and

then opened out and formed a line, leaving me to advance alone down
the hall.

It was an immense and spacious hall and while the center was open,
the sides were crowded with gaily dressed people. Guards were on all sides
and at the far end was a dais or platform raised seven steps above the floor.
On the topmost level were four thrones. Before the throne, on the various
levels, were a number of men and women, dressed in every color imaginable except the green which was worn by the occupants of the thrones.
On the step next to the top level stood a lone figure, who also wore green.

Down the hall I marched until I stood at the foot of the dais. I heard
a murmur run down the hall as I passed, but whether of approval or disapproval I could not tell, so I went straight ahead until I came to the foot
of the dais and then I bowed deeply. I looked up and looked the occupants
of the thrones straight in the eye.

The two center seats were occupied by an elderly couple of great grace
and dignity of manner, the throne on the right was vacant and in the one
on the left sat Awlo. I had known by the respect accorded her that she
must be a rather important personage, but it startled me to realize that she
was one of the biggest of them all. She threw me a momentary smile and
then looked at me gravely and impersonally as the other two were doing.

The man who occupied one of the center thrones rose and spoke to me.

"Courtney Siba," he said gravely in a sonorous and ringing voice, "my
daughter has told before me, where all could hear, the mighty deeds which
you have wrought against the Mena. And you who have saved her, in
whom the hopes of the dynasty of Kalu are bound up, merit and will receive the gratitude of a nation. The gratitude of a father for the life of his
only child I freely give you.

"There is no reward within my power to grant that is great enough for
your merits, but if you will name your wishes, they shall be yours if Ulm
can supply them. Your rank of Siba I hereby confirm in Ulm and Ame
and give orders that your rank is above all others in the empire save only
the royal blood. Is there any reward you desire?"

"I thank you, oh King," I replied, "and I will bear your gracious words
in mind. Already you have honored me above my poor deserts but the time
may come when I will remind you of your words."

"My words are engraven on my memory, Courtney Siba," said the King
with a gracious smile, "and time will not erase them. Your rank entitles
you to a place on the second level of my throne, below only my beloved
nephew, Lamu Siba."

He motioned toward the man who stood on the next to the topmost level
and who I noticed was attired in green as was Kalu. I glanced at him and
found that he was watching me with a face like a thundercloud. I returned
the scowl with interest and took stock of him. He was about two inches

shorter than I was and ruggedly built and showed evidence of a great deal of strength. His black hair, which like the hair of all the men of Ulm, was worn long enough to reach his shoulders, matched the swarthy complexion. The thing that set me against him was a crafty expression in his close-set eyes, which were grey instead of the honest black or brown which should have gone with his complexion.

At a gesture from the King (or Sabama as his title really was), I mounted the dais and took my stand on the step below Lamu and directly in front of Awlo. When I had taken my place, the Sabama turned to the court and began again in his sonorous voice what was evidently a regularly recited formula.

"The house of Kalu," he said, "is as a withered tree with but one green branch. Should this branch be cut, the tree would die without trace of life remaining. Already the branch has been almost cut. It is the hope of all Ulm that this branch will make that new life may be given to the tree, yet the immemorable laws of Ulm decree that the Sibi Tam shall be free to choose her own husband when and how she will, nor may even the Sabama force her choice. Awlo, my daughter, the green branch of the tree of the house of Kalu, are you yet ready to declare your choice?"

Awlo rose and stepped forward.

"I am," she declared in ringing tone.

The reply made a sensation. The audience had been listening politely to the words of the Sabama but they evidently expected Awlo to say that she had not yet made up her mind and her reply electrified them. A hastily suppressed murmur ran through the hall and the Sabama started. I noticed that Lamu bit his lip and closed his hand on his dagger hilt.

"Whom, my daughter, have you chosen to be your prince?" asked Kalu.

Awlo stepped down two steps and stood beside me.

"When the branch was about to be cut, one arose who stayed the hand of the Mena and who saved the tree from being a desolate dying trunk today. Who but that one should be chosen to the highest honor in Ulm and as her future ruler. My father, for my husband, I choose Courtney Siba."

As she ended, she took my right hand and raised it high above my head. There was a moment of silence and then cheer after cheer rent the hall. Evidently Awlo's choice was popular. The Sabama stepped forward and held up his hand for silence. The uproar instantly hushed and he started to speak. He was interrupted in a dramatic manner.

Sword in hand, Lamu faced him.

"Grant you permission to the Sibi Tam to make such a choice?" he demanded.

"The Sibi Tam chooses whom she pleases," said Kalu sharply. "Sheath your weapon. You are in the presence of the Sabama."

"My weapon remains drawn until the honor of Ame is revenged," cried Lamu hoarsely. "Have you lost your senses, my uncle, that you give your only child, the pride and hope of Ulm, to a nameless adventurer who comes from no one knows where? Who knows that he is not a *kahuma* who will destroy the land? Awlo says that he slew the Mena by witchcraft."

"Awlo has chosen," said Kalu quietly but with an ominous ring in his voice. "By what right do you assume to question her choice?"

"For years I have sought her, seeking to consolidate the rule of Ulm and Ame," replied Lamu, "and until this stranger came into Ulm, I had reason to think that my suit was favored. Are you seeking, my uncle, to raise a barrier of blood between Ulm and Ame that the Mena may destroy both?"

"What mean you?" thundered Kalu.

"I demand that the stranger be tested before the Court of Lords to prove that he is not a *kahuma*."

"And Lamu presides over the Court of Lords," broke in Awlo with biting sarcasm. "Do you expect me to let my chosen go before your creatures for judgment?"

The shot struck home and Lamu bit his lips.

"Do you approve Awlo's choice?" he demanded of the Sabama.

"I do," was the reply.

"Then I call upon the ancient laws of Ulm for redress. It is the right of every Siba of royal blood to challenge and fight to the death with the choice of the Sibi Tam. You, Courtney, who claim the rank of Siba, I challenge you to fight to the death."

"Courtney Siba," said Kalu gravely, "do you accept this challenge? Either you must give up your rank or fight for it."

I hesitated but Awlo touched me on the arm. I looked at her and she glanced meaningly at my pistol. An idea came to me.

"I will gladly fight him," I cried, "but not to his death. If he overcomes me, he may do as he wishes, but I fight with my own weapons and if I overcome him, I spare his life."

"Then draw your weapon, Courtney Siba and defend yourself," cried Lamu as he rushed forward.

He aimed a vicious thrust at me before I had time to draw my own weapon and I avoided it only by leaping nimbly back. He came on again and I side-stepped and whipped out my Colt. As he rushed me the third time, I raised my weapon and fired. As I have said, I am a good shot and the range was close, so I didn't shoot to kill. Instead I fired at his sword hand and was lucky enough to hit the hilt of his weapon. The heavy forty-five bullet tore his sword from his grasp and sent it flying through the air.

I instantly sheathed my pistol and waited for his next move. It came quickly enough.

He rubbed his right hand for a moment; it must have stung damnably, and then he whipped out his dagger and came at me with it in his left hand. I was a little taller than he was and had the reach on him so I met him half way. He made a sweep at me with his knife which I avoided and then I took his measure and landed my right full on the point of his chin and he went down like a poled ox. A tremendous murmur went around the room and then came a volley of cheers. I judged that Lamu was not popular. When the noise subsided, the Sabama spoke.

"Does any one else wish to challenge the choice of the Sibi Tam?" he asked sardonically.

There was no reply and he nodded to Awlo. She stepped forward and took my right hand in hers and turning it over, she kissed me on the palm and then set my hand on top of her head. When she had finished the ceremony, she looked expectantly at me. I wasn't exactly sure what to do so I took her hand and kissed it and then placed it on top of my head as she had done. In a moment her arms were around me and the assembly room rang with cheers.

Presently Awlo drew back and the Sabama stepped down from his throne. Some officers came forward and removed my white cloak and replaced it with a green one and the Sabama himself bound about my brow a golden filet with a square cut stone in it, similar to the ones which he and Awlo wore, and took me by the hand and led me up the dais and seated me on the vacant throne. There came another blare of trumpets and then the Sabama formally addressed me as "Courtney Siba Tam." Thus it was that I, Courtney Edwards, a citizen of the United States of America, in the year of our Lord one thousand, nine hundred and twenty-two became a Prince of the House of Kalu, the Crown Prince of the Empire of Ulm and the husband of the reigning monarch's only child.

I quickly became settled in my position of Siba Tam. My first official task was to pronounce judgment on Lamu. When I learned the circumstances, I hardly blamed him for his outburst. He was the only son of the ruler of Ame and he had been Awlo's suitor for years. By virtue of his rank he was Commander-in-Chief of the combined armies of Ulm and Ame and when he saw me, a stranger, come in and oust him from his proud position and take his sweetheart as my wife into the bargain, he lost his head. The Sabama wished to reduce him to the grade of commoner and confine him, but Awlo and I interceded and he was eventually pardoned and I appointed him as my second in command of the army. Whatever his faults, he was a good soldier and quite popular with the military. He acted rather formally to me for a couple of years, but he got over it and became one of my closest friends.

One of my first acts was to send a detail of troops out to bring my adjuster into Ulm. There I drained the batteries and went over it thoroughly and stored it in the palace vault. I was perfectly happy and had no idea at all of ever leaving Ulm, but I was guarding against accidents. At any time some prospector might find my valley and wash out a pan of dirt and dump the rubbish on Ulm. If that happened, I meant to take Awlo and increase our size and break up through it.

For five years everything was quiet and peaceful in Ulm and Awlo and I were the happiest pair in the whole empire. She was the idol of the city and my rescue of her had given me a good start. I soon grew quite popular and when Lamu grew to be my friend, the army joined the populace in their affection for me.

In the fall of 1927 we first began to get rumors of a great gathering of the Mena. At first both Lamu and I were disposed to scout the idea, but the rumors came with more definiteness and at last we had to face the fact that the Mena were gathering for an attack in real force. We made what preparations we could for the siege and waited for them to attack. One of the peculiar things which had struck me about Ulm was that the art of projecting weapons was unknown to them. Even the crudest bow and arrow had not been developed. I thought that I saw my way clear to thrash the Mena handsomely and I made up a bow and arrow and showed it to Kalu, proposing that our army be so equipped. He smiled enigmatically and advised me to lay it before the council.

I did so and to my surprise Lamu and the council would not listen to the suggestion. When they explained their reasons, I saw that they were sound ones. The Mena, while they have no inventive ability, are adept at copying the ideas of others and the council were afraid that, while we might smash the first attack by fire superiority, on the next attack we would find the Mena armed with bows, and in such a case we would suffer heavily, even if we finally beat off the attack. The principle of the bow and arrow were well known to them, but they had never used it for this reason.

About a year ago the Mena attacked. There were millions of them, it seemed to me, and they were utterly reckless and willing to put up with huge losses to gain a small point. Man for man they were our superiors, so we did not meet them outside the walls, but contented ourselves with defending the city. They brought ladders and tried to climb the walls and they brought rams and tried to batter down the gates and we stood on the walls and dropped rocks on them and poured hot oil on them and when they got a ladder hoisted we hurled it back and killed with sword and spear those who had gained a footing on the walls. I had read of such defenses in history, and I was able to introduce a few new wrinkles which gave the

Mena some rather unpleasant surprises. After three months of fighting, the situation hadn't changed a bit. I learned that a siege of ten or even twenty years was nothing unusual. We had enough *keili* nuts stored in the city to last for fifty years and we had an abundant supply of water. We weren't strong enough to take the offensive, so all we could do was to defend ourselves and wait until the Mena got tired and quit or got to fighting among themselves; the latter always happened when the siege drew out to too great a length.

The continual fighting kept me away from Awlo a great deal and I was naturally anxious to end it as soon as possible. As I passed the arsenal one day, I saw my adjuster standing there and a great idea struck me. I was confident that if I could use propelled projectiles, I could break the back of the Mena attack in no time. The council wouldn't let me use bows and arrows for fear our enemies would copy them and use them against us, but I defied any artisan of the Mena, or any artisan of Ulm for that matter, to copy a modern rifle and its ammunition. Why couldn't I use the adjuster to increase my size to the plane where such things were to be had, load it with guns and ammunition and shrink the whole business to usable size. I hastened to lay my idea before Kalu and the council.

I doubt whether any of the council had ever believed the story I told of my origin, although they had never said so. It is never safe to dispute t] word of those in high authority. When I soberly offered to increase my size and get them guns and ammunition, they shook their heads and began to wonder. I took them up on the wall and showed them what a rifle would do to the Mena and any opposition to my going vanished. Highly elated, I refilled my batteries with the electrolyte I had drawn years before and got ready for the trip. I soon found that I had reckoned without Awlo. My Princess flatly refused to be separated from me.

For a while I was baffled but Awlo herself suggested a solution of the problem she had raised.

"Why can't I go with you, Courtney?" she asked. "If we come back safely, the trip will be an interesting one and if we do not return, at least we will be together."

The idea had merit and I presented it to Kalu. He didn't like Awlo to leave him, but he gave consent at last on my solemn promise to come back with her. I knew that some of the work up here would be rather heavy and I asked for a volunteer to accompany me. To my surprise, Lamu asked to go. I was glad of his company but I didn't want both the head of the army and the second in command to leave at once. He insisted and pointed out that the danger of the trip should be shared by the two highest ranking men in the army and I gave way and consented.

The adjuster was carried to the palace roof and I made a few adjustments to increase the speed of its action so that it wouldn't crush the whole city beneath its weight before the base expanded enough to get a wider support. At last everything was ready and the three of us crowded in and with final farewells to all I closed the switch.

I had set the machine to work faster than I realized and before I could open the switch we were twelve feet tall. I threw it back into slow speed and reduced our size until the indicator showed that I was my normal six feet and we stepped out into a new world to Awlo and Lamu and almost a new one to me.

We went into my shack and looked it over. Nothing had been disturbed and no one had been there, so there was no reason why Awlo couldn't stay there safely while Lamu and I trekked into Beatty and I got in touch with my bankers and arranged to buy the munitions that I wanted. We talked it over and Awlo wanted to come. There was no real reason why she couldn't come and indeed make a trip to New York with me if she wished, so I agreed to her coming. Lamu suggested that it might be a good idea for me to teach him how to operate the adjuster so that, in case we found it advisable to send the stuff down in several loads, he could take it down and return and thus avoid separating Awlo and me. The thought was a good one so I set the machine on slow speed and soon taught him the simple manipulation. He caught on readily and manipulated it several times to quite a small size and then professed himself satisfied with his ability. I wish that I could have seen what was in the black villain's heart!

The next morning I was in the cabin making up packs for us to carry on our hike to Beatty when I was alarmed by Awlo outside. I dropped everything and rushed out at top speed. For a moment I didn't see either her or Lamu and then I heard a low faint wail in her voice. I looked in the direction from which it came and saw the adjuster. It was less than one-tenth the size it should have been and I realized that it was shrinking. I sprinted toward it hoping to reach the switch and reverse the action, but I was too late. On my hands and knees I dropped and stared into it. Lamu had my Princess captive and his hand was on the switch. He stopped the action for a minute but the thing was already so small that I could not get my finger between the side bars had I tried and I was afraid of wrecking it. Stooping closer, I heard their tiny voices.

"Courtney Siba Tam," cried Lamu with triumph in his voice, "he laughs best who laughs last as I have heard you say. You robbed me of my kingdom once but when we return and tell them how you planned to desert Ulm in her hour of need and to steal away her Princess, I shall win back all I have lost. For years I have planned to thwart you in your ambition and for that reason I throttled my impulses and seemed your friend. Say farewell to Awlo for this is your last glimpse of her."

"Awlo," I cried in a whisper, "can't you free yourself?"

"No, Courtney," came back her tiny voice, "he is too strong for me and

I dare not struggle. Come after me, Courtney! Rescue me from this dog who is worse than the Mena from whom you saved me once. I will watch for you, Courtney!" Thus I heard her voice for the last time and responded.

"I'll be after you as soon as I can, my darling," I cried. "As for you, Lamu Siba, the game is not played out yet. When I return, your heart's blood will pay for this!"

"Ah, yes, Courtney Siba Tam," came his mocking voice, "*when* you return."

He turned again to the switch and the adjuster carrying with it all that is dear in life to me disappeared.

I don't remember much about the next few days. Somehow, I made my way to Beatty and established my identity. I made the wires hum to San Francisco, ordering the materials I needed to construct a duplicate of my adjuster. Nor did I forget my people. I ordered the guns and ammunition which I wanted shipped in with the rest of my stuff. It seemed to take forever to get to my valley, but at last it came and I have worked almost day and night since. This afternoon I finished my apparatus and moved it over to the spot where the other had stood and in the morning I will leave this plane and try to take my guns and ammunition to Ulm.

I hope to land in Ulm but I am not at all sure that I will do so. I marked the place where my former machine stood but I may have easily missed placing my new model over the old one. If I have missed setting the center point where it should be by even a fraction of an inch I may come down in Ulm miles from the city. I may even come down into a strange world far from my empire and with no knowledge of which way to go. I have done my best and time alone will tell how well I have done. One thing I know. No matter what Lamu may have done or said, Awlo is still waiting for me and she is still true to me. I have my rifle and plenty of ammunition and even though the whole Mena race block my path, some way I will fight my way through them and once more hold my Princess in my arms.

AWLO OF ULM

by Capt. S. P. Meek

When I allowed my manuscript, "Submicroscopic," to be published, I had no intention of telling to the world the balance of my adventures. Frankly, I did not expect to be believed. The events of which I told were so fantastic, so contrary to the ordinary experiences and preconceived notions of men of this plane of existence, that I expected the story to be passed off as an idle tale, told only to amuse. The editor of AMAZING STORIES was kind enough to forward to me a number of comments received. When I read them over I found, to my astonishment, that there were a small number of discerning thinkers who realized that my story was one of actual facts. Most of them expressed regret that the end of the story was, so they thought, a sealed book to them. It is to this select group, who I feel are my friends, that this story is addressed. The interest they have shown in my welfare and in that of my beloved princess is so heartfelt that I feel that I can do no less than publish for their benefit the extraordinary events which followed that seemingly endless night in my hidden Nevada valley before I started in pursuit of Awlo and her abductor.

Impatiently I watched the sun rise over the Timpahutes. The sunrise is a little later in Ulm than in this plane because of the height of the mountain (grains of sand!) which surround the empire. I judged it best to wait for broad daylight before I plunged into what might easily be the unknown. I had set my electronic vibration adjuster as nearly as possible over the spot where Lamu and my princess had disappeared but I know that a distance which could not be detected under the microscope in this plane might be miles in Ulm and I had little hope of landing in the beleaguered city.

At last I felt that the time had come. I entered my newly completed adjuster, closed the switch and was on my way. Rapidly the scenery grew to Brobdingnagian proportions and then disappeared as it grew too large for my eyes to see or my mind to comprehend. I watched the indicator dial as the needle crept toward infinity. Presently its motion ceased and the high whine of my generators became audible. The note ran down the scale of audibility and subsided into silence. I looked out from my adjuster and my heart sank. The landscape resembled not in the least the scenery around Ulm. There was no doubt that I had missed my goal by many miles.

My first inclination was to increase my size and move the adjuster but a sober second thought made me realize the futility of such an action. I had set the machine as nearly as I could over the spot where Ulm lay and any change I made would be just as likely to be away from the city as toward it. The only thing to do was to set out on my travels in the hope that I would meet some one, even were it one of the hostile Mena, who could give me some idea of the direction in which to travel. I slung a couple of extra bandoliers of ammunition over my shoulders, picked up my rifle and stepped out of the adjuster. A second thought made me pause. I retraced my steps and opened an arm locker. From it I took two small-caliber .32, automatic pistols, which I placed in shoulder holsters under my shirt. The little guns held six rounds each and while they were small, they carried hollow point bullets which would have a deadly effect at short range. With my armament thus reenforced, I was ready to start my travels.

The country in which I found myself was wild beyond description. In place of the dense semi-tropical vegetation which I had been accustomed to associate with my submicroscopic empire, there was nothing but rock, bare rugged rock. Huge masses of stone, hundreds and even thousands of feet high, lay piled one on another as though a race of giants had tossed them about in sport, recking little of where they fell. There was none of the solidity and symmetry which marks the mountains of the larger plane. Many of the stones seemed to be precariously balanced and even where they were wedged together, the effect was one of insecurity. I shuddered and caught myself afraid to stir lest even my tiny weight would start one of the masses of rock into motion and engulf me and all my possessions in cataclysmic ruin. I walked in a gingerly fashion over to one of the unstable appearing masses of rock and rested my hand against it. It was solid to the touch and I pressed, gently at first, and then with all my strength, trying in vain to budge the mass which must have weighed thousands of tons, if my own negligible weight be taken as being its normal one hundred and eighty pounds. Satisfied that it was beyond my strength to move it, I felt safer, and began to consider in which direction I should start my travels.

I racked my brain for a clue. Somewhere in memory's vaults there was an elusive something that this jumbled phantasmagoria of rock reminded me of. Suddenly I remembered it.

In the days when I had been hailed as the Crown Prince of Ulm, the husband of its ruler's only child, I had been much interested in the ancient legends which told the history of the empire. Ulm had no written language and no records to which I could refer other than the traditions and legends which had been handed down from father to son. These legends were preserved in metrical form. The learning and reciting of them on occasion was the principal duty of the class of persons known as *tamaaini*,* generally elderly men who were not of the noble class, but who, because of their profession, had an *entrée* to the court and many of the privileges of nobility. Some of them had marvelous memories and could repeat without faltering thousands after thousands of lines of the old legends. It was from them that I learned that the Mena had originally come down from the north through the barren passes in the mighty mountains which border Ulm on all sides. I had never been able to gather much information as to derivation of the people of Ulm themselves. It seemed that so far as the *tamaaini* knew, they had always lived in their present location. There were, however, here and there in the legends dim and little understood references to other places and it was one of these passages that I strove to recall. Suddenly, like a flash, the long forgotten tale came to my mind.

It told of the flight of the natural son of a ruler of Ulm who had tried to wrest the throne from his legitimate half-brother, after his father's death, and it described his own defeat and death. The victor pursued him with a handful of guards and caught him in a place where "giants played as children, tossing mountains hand to hand." There they encountered a race of *kahumas* or wizards who flew through the air like birds and who shot fire from their many hands. They could "kill from afar with fire" and they allowed no one who entered their land to return. Evidently, at least one of the party returned to Ulm with the record of the attempted usurper's death, which the legend goes on to detail at great length. The passage had always interested me, for it seemed to hint at a higher civilization than was possessed by the brave and chivalrous warriors of Ulm.

I looked about me and I did not blame the fancy of the ancient bard who had laid the condition of the landscape to the gambols of giants or to the evil machinations of wizards. Certainly his description was an apt one. The forbidden land lay, according to the legend, "toward the setting sun." *If* the tale were true and *if* I were looking on the scene of that ancient tragedy, Ulm should lie to the east and not more than a few days' journey away. It was a pretty slender clue but it was the only one I had. Without it I had no idea of which direction to take, so I decided to trust to the ac-

---

* Compare the Hawaiian word, *"kamaaini,"* an old inhabitant.

curacy and authenticity of a legend of unknown antiquity and make my way eastward.

My first step was to fix the landscape in my mind and to take bearings with my marching compass on the most prominent points of the scenery. If I found my way back to Ulm my entire labor and travail would be lost unless I were able to return to the adjuster and its precious load of weapons. Three huge peaks dominated the scene to the north and they stood so that the farther one lay exactly in the middle of the interval between the two nearer ones. The bearing of the farther peak was a quarter point west of magnetic north. Exactly south east was another peak with a peculiar cleft near its summit. A short study enabled me to fix the location of the adjuster so firmly in my mind that I was certain that I could find the place again. With a final look around, I shouldered my rifle, set my face to the east and set out.

Despite the ruggedness of the country I was able, by the aid of my marching compass, to keep going in the general direction of east pretty well although I had to make several lengthy detours around masses of rock. For several hours I pushed on and found the country gradually getting a little less rugged. There were no signs of animal life but once in a while I came across a tuft of vegetation resembling the bunch grass so common in some parts of the West.

As the sun got higher it grew intolerably hot and I began to regret that I had loaded myself so heavily with food and especially ammunition and had brought only two quarts of water. It was too late to retrace my steps, so I husbanded my water as carefully as possible and kept going. Before noon the heat got so bad that I began to look for a place where I could find a little shelter.

Ahead of me I spied what looked like a cave in the rock and I pressed forward to investigate it. It was not a true cave but it was a fair imitation of one made by two huge masses of rock leaning against one another. I had no idea how far into the rock the cavity extended but it was cool in the shade and I discarded my pack with a sigh of relief. I also unslung the heavy bandoliers of ammunition which I carried and leaned my rifle against the wall of the cavern. According to my pedometer, I had covered about ten miles. I secured a pencil and notebook from my pack and stepped to the mouth of the cavern to sight the directions of the peaks by which I had marked my landing.

I located them without any trouble and was engaged in trying to locate myself by a process of triangulation on a crude map which I had made of my morning's journey when an unfamiliar sound brought me up with a start. I listened intently and the sound faded for a moment only to increase in volume. I puzzled my brains as to what was causing it. It was a

dull humming sound and the only thing it reminded me of was the whirling of an airplane propeller, a patent impossibility in Ulm.

The sound came nearer and I started back to the cave and took up my
rifle when the cause of the noise came in sight. My flyer's ears had not
misled me. Flying along at a moderate speed about a thousand feet above
my level was an airplane. It was not of the conventional pattern with
which I was familiar although it bore certain resemblance to the planes
I had flown. The main difference was in the size and shape of the wings.
Instead of the usual rectangular wing spread on each side of the fuselage, this machine had a single heart-shaped wing mounted above the fuselage with the point of the heart to the rear. Above the wing was a
crisscross network of wires which reminded me of an aerial.

The passenger car was long and cigar-shaped although it did not extend backward much beyond the point of the heart. The sides were
pierced with windows which were glazed with glass or some other transparent material through which I fancied I could see figures moving, although the distance was too great for me to be sure.

The machine had three propellers, one mounted directly in front of the
car and about on a level with the wing while the other two, which were
smaller, were set lower and about midway from the center line of the craft
to the extremities of the wing. Not only the small wing spread and other
unconventional features of the design attracted my attention but also the
complete absence of all motor noise although the three propellers were
whirling rapidly.

Stupidly I watched the craft until it was almost overhead and then I
had sense enough to start something. Even though the occupants of the
ship were not handicapped by the roar of motors, I had no hope of making
them hear at that elevation so I hastily took off my hat and waved it frantically. The airship moved serenely on without anyone seeing, or at any
rate, heeding my signals of distress. Desperately I ransacked my brains
for a means of attracting their attention and inspiration visited me. An
old friend of mine had been experimenting with some illuminating bullets
and he had given me a handful of cartridges loaded with them. I suddenly
remembered that my pistol was loaded with them for I had intended to try
them out but had forgotten to do so. Here was an excellent chance to test
their value. I pulled my pistol from its holster and fired up into the air.

From the muzzle of the gun a bell of fire rose into the air. Up past the
airship it went and still up. It must have traveled fully eight hundred yards
before the flame died. I fired again and then turned my attention to the
airplane. My signal had evidently been seen, for the ship was swinging
around on a wide arc. Again I waved my coat. There was no question that
my signal was seen for the ship glided on a long slant toward the ground.
I looked at the small open space before me and knew that it would be im-

possible to land an ordinary plane in it without a crash, but I had not yet learned the possibilities of that stubby ship with its diminutive wing spread. The plane curved down and came to a stop not over a hundred feet from where it first touched ground. The center propeller ceased turning but the two side propellers kept up a steady hum until after the ship had come to a complete stop.

A door opened in the side of the ship and four figures climbed out and came toward me. I hastened to meet them but I stopped short in my stride before I had gone far. They had the general conformation of men but they suddenly gave me an uncanny feeling as though I were looking at huge spiders. I could not understand the feeling for a moment until I concentrated my attention on the one who was leading the advance. From his shoulders projected not one pair of arms but three. The rest of him appeared to be normal as well as I could tell through the bulky shapeless garment which he wore and the helmet which concealed his features.

The four figures spread out as they advanced and I did not interpret the action as a friendly one. I thought momentarily of retreating to the cave where I had left my rifle but I had no idea of how fast these newcomers could travel and they were as close to the cavern mouth as I was. I backed against a nearby boulder and drew my pistol. They might mean no harm but I preferred to be ready for all eventualities.

The four drew near until they were within twenty feet of me. I raised my pistol but hesitated about commencing hostilities until I was sure that they were not friendly. At my action they all stopped and stared and one of them raised an arm and pointed it at me. At this close distance I could see their features through the glass windows which formed the front of their helmets and I realized that they were like no men I had seen before. Their faces were a bright saffron yellow and their eyes were set obliquely in their heads. I raised my left hand in the universal gesture of peace and spoke.

"*Pehea oc, malahini?*" I said.

The leader looked doubtfully at me for a moment before he replied. He spoke in a strange guttural voice and while his language was not that of Ulm, I was able to understand it.

"Whence came you and what seek you here?" he demanded.

"I come from Ulm," I replied. "I came from the capital which is beleaguered by the race of the Mena and I am seeking to bring assistance to Kalu Sibama, my sovereign lord. I am lost and am trying to find my way thither. Can you direct me?"

"Ulm?" he said slowly and then burst into a harsh laugh. "You lie," he went on. "Ulm is no more than a memory. Kalu Sibama has rested, well I hope, in the stomachs of the Mena for many moons."

"Is Ulm fallen?" I gasped, hardly able to believe my ears.

"Ulm is fallen," he said, evidently amused at my horror. "As fleas desert a dying dog, so her leaders deserted her. The Mena stormed the walls and but a remnant fought their way out. That remnant are slaves of my lord, Kapioma Sibama of the Empire of Kau. He will be pleased when I bring him two slaves in place of the one I was sent to seek."

His words answered my question as to his intentions. I thought grimly that he had not captured his slave yet as I carefully covered his chest with my pistol. The illuminating bullet struck him fair in the center of his chest and exploded in a flash of red light. He staggered back under the shock of impact but did not fall. I raised my pistol for a second shot but I never fired it. A flash of blinding green light came from one of his arms and my pistol clattered to the ground. My right arm hung numb and paralyzed from the shoulder. A second flash came and my left arm was in the same condition. I turned to run but I was too late. A dozen hands gripped me and held me helpless.

At a word from their leader, the three subordinates jerked me rudely along the ground toward the strange craft and pulled me inside. I gave a rapid glance around as I entered the craft for I desired to see what type of motors they had which operated so silently. There were none in sight. In the front of the long cabin were a set of dual flying controls of the type with which I was familiar. In the forward end were three tiny motors of an unfamiliar type but there were no batteries, no generators and above all no prime movers, unless such a term could be applied to a large panel board set with switches and dials which was between the two sets of controls. One man stood at this board. There were no other occupants of the ship evident at first glance.

My captors dragged me to the rear end of the cabin and forced me to a sitting position. Two more green flashes filled the interior of the cabin momentarily and my legs from the knee down were as useless as my arms were. The three retreated to the upper end of the cabin and divested themselves of their flying suits. They were men of middle height with rather slight physique but with high foreheads and an air of great intelligence. The leader turned his slanting eyes toward me. There was power in them and intelligence but there was also the very quintessence of cruelty in them. So obsessed was I with his face, that for a moment I failed to notice that four of his six arms had disappeared.

An explanation flashed through my mind and I looked at the rest of the crew. Each of them had only the normal two arms which I had expected. On the wall was a rack and hung there were five flying suits, from the shoulders of each of which projected three sets of arms. As I examined them more closely, I saw that only two arms on each suit ended in gloves. The other arms ended in hollow tubes from which the paralyzing rays had evidently come. The sight of these garments did as much as the coldly merciless faces to impress on my mind the fact that I was dealing, not with the brave chivalrous savages of Ulm, but with a race who had developed their mental powers highly and who were well acquainted with scientific laws.

The leader gave an order and two of the crew stepped to the flying controls. The man at the switchboard manipulated some dials. The ship started upward with a rocketing motion, climbing at what was, to my judgment an entirely unsafe angle. However, the ship made it without any difficulty and leveled off at an elevation of about a thousand feet and continued on her way east. I took a rapid glance at the compass set on the roof and mentally resolved to keep track of our course.

Two of the crew stepped forward and tossed to one side a piece of cloth which had covered some long object lying on the floor. They picked it up and I suppressed an exclamation with difficulty. The object was a man and it needed only a glance to tell me that he was of a different race from the crew of the ship. Long curling yellow locks fell from his head in place of the short black hair of the Kauans and his skin was as white as mine instead of the disgusting saffron yellow which marked our captors.

His arms and legs hung limp and useless as they picked him up and bore him aft. They dumped him unceremoniously on the floor beside me and returned to the forward part of the cabin. I looked at my fellow captive with interest, an interest which he quite evidently felt as well.

"Where from?" he asked me in an undertone. His voice had none of the guttural quality which marked the speech of the crew. It was as soft and liquid as the speech of any man of Ulm.

"Ulm," I replied, also in an undertone.

"But Ulm fell months ago," he said wonderingly. "Surely you did not survive the sack of the city. If you did, how have you survived since then?"

"I was not at the fall of the city," I replied. "I was away seeking aid for Ulm when it fell. I have just returned."

He looked at me curiously.

"What was your rank?" he demanded.

"I was Siba Tam," I replied proudly.

An expression of joy crossed his face.

"My hilt to your hand, Siba Tam," he said, "had I a sword to offer. I have long hoped for a sight of the son of my ruler."

"I was not the son of Kalu," I answered, "I was the husband of his only child."

"Still my hilt to your hand," he replied. "I have not seen my native land since I was a child but no more loyal subject of her Sibama lives. Do you wish to continue on to Kau?"

"I hardly wish to go anywhere as a slave," I said briefly.

"Then we can escape," he replied. "I had planned to try to win my freedom before we reached the city, although I had little hope of success. Two of us should be more than a match for five men of Kau."

"But my legs and arms are paralyzed," I objected.

"That is of no moment. Can you keep them quiet and simulate paralysis if I remove the effects of the ray?"

"I think so."

"Then be careful and do not move them while I work."

He rolled over and fell against me. The Kauans glanced around at him for a moment but paid no further attention. In a moment I felt a sharp pain in my back and then another in my shoulder.

"Now remain perfectly quiet," said my new friend. A dull whir sounded behind me for a moment and an excruciating pain racked my limbs. I bit my lip to keep from crying out. The pain passed and to my joy I found that both feeling and motion had been restored.

"What are your orders?" asked my fellow captive softly.

"I have no plans made. You know what to do much better than I do. Issue your orders and I will obey."

"Then when I give the word, leap to your feet and rush them," he said. "Get between them and their fighting suits and keep them away from them. If they get to their weapons, we are dead or worse. Without them they have nothing but their strength to rely on."

"Wait a moment," I said cautiously, "I think I have a weapon here. I have one that will kill ordinary men but it failed against these men. However, they had their fighting suits on when I tried it. Tell me, are they vulnerable to a sword thrust?"

"Without their fighting suits, yes; with them, no."

"Fine. Lie still and let me try my hand on them. Can you fly the ship after we capture it?"

"Certainly."

"All right, I'll see what I can do. If my weapon fails, we can still rush them with bare hands."

I braced myself for an effort. The distance was short and I felt sure that the little thirty-two automatic pistols which I had providentially armed myself with would be accurate enough for my purpose. Both rested in holsters—one under each arm.

With a sudden swift movement, I sprang to my feet, a pistol in each hand. I raised the right one and fired at the leader. I watched breathlessly for a moment. He swayed back and forth and then fell headlong. The gun was effective.

The other members of the crew stared stupidly at their fallen leader. Again the little gun spoke and the odds were reduced to three to two. The remaining members of the crew made a rush for their fighting suits but they never reached them. Three times the little automatic spat forth a message of death and each time my aim was good. My companion had risen to his feet and he now raced for the controls. He got them just in time, for the pilotless ship was careening badly. In a moment he had it flying once more on a level keel.

I made the rounds of the prostrate crew. At short range the mushroom bullets with which my gun was loaded had done their work. Only one of our enemies lived and it was evident that his wound was fatal. Assured of their helplessness to harm us, I moved up to the control board.

"Which way, Siba Tam?"

I reflected before answering. There was no use in returning to fallen Ulm. The ship would be an excellent aid to me in pursuing my search for my lost princess and I had gained a loyal follower. The first step was to arm him.

"Go back to the place where I was captured and then straight west for a few miles. In the meantime, teach me how to fly this ship. What is your motive power? I see no signs of any source of energy."

"Our power is drawn from the central power house in Kaulani."

"Radio transmission of power!" I gasped.

"I do not understand your words," he said (I had unconsciously spoken in English). "The power to turn our propellers and to actuate the fighting suits is generated in Kaulani and is sent out in the form of waves which are received by wires on the top of the ship."

"I noticed them," I replied, "but did not suspect their use. I thought they were used to receive and probably transmit messages."

"Could messages be sent or received through them?"

"Certainly. Isn't that done?"

"No, Siba Tam."

"In that case we have one bit of knowledge that the Kauans don't have," I said cheerfully. "I will show you how it is done later. Now show me how to control the ship."

He motioned me to take the dual set of controls and started his explanations. It was ridiculously simple for one already well versed in flying and in five minutes I was maneuvering the ship like a veteran. The secret of the small wing spread and the short take-off and landing distance lay in the setting and position of the side propellers. They were so inclined that their blast struck the wings and gave a lifting effect to aid the take-off. Reversing them made them act as a brake and brought the craft to a standstill in a few feet. The central propeller did practically all the work of moving the ship forward.

In a short time we were over the place where I had been captured and we landed and secured my rifle and pack. We took off again and in ten minutes landed safely by the side of my adjuster.

"Now I will repay you for teaching me to fly our ship," I said with a smile, "by teaching you to manipulate a machine which I doubt if even the leader of that crew of brigands who captured us could understand. However, before I do so, tell me about yourself. Who are you and how did you get here? I have lived for years in Ulm and do not know your face and my face was not familiar to you."

"I was taken from Ulm as a child and reared in Kau."

"How did that happen?"

"My name is Olua; Olua Alii by right, for I was born the son of Muana Alii, one of the Council of Lords. When I was a child, I accompanied my father on a trip to Ame. On the way home, the Mena attacked us. My father was killed but I was saved alive and taken as a present to their chief. I was destined for his larder but he never saw me. On the way to his resting place, an airship like this one swooped down on us. The Mena fled in all directions. Men of Kau in fighting suits came from the ship and one of them, a great Alii, picked me up. His only son had died a few days before and for that reason he spared me, although the men of Kau are entirely without mercy in their dealings with those of other races. He took me to Kau and raised and educated me as his own child. There are few of the scientific secrets of Kau that I do not know."

"How did you come to be a prisoner?"

"Through loyalty to the land of my birth. Although raised in Kau, I never forgot that I was by birth an Alii of Ulm, one of the Council of Lords. I read all I could of Ulm and the more I learned of their bravery and chivalry, the more glad I became that I was one of them and not a treacherous Kauan. My loyalty was always to Kalu Sibama of Ulm and not Kapioma Sibama of Kau, although I did not speak openly of it.

"When Ulm fell to the Mena, a handful of the warriors of Ulm won their way through to the mountains between Kau and Ulm, where they were captured and brought as slaves to Kaulani. My heart leapt when I saw them come in. They were such men as I had always dreamed of, men who fought their enemies with steel and not with weapons of stealth and treachery. The dream of my life was to rescue them and flee with them to Ame, which had not fallen to the Mena. I laid my plans carefully. I was going to capture one of the largest warships, and fly with them.

"The day before I was to act, I was betrayed. A faithful slave warned me that the Sibama's guards were on their way to arrest me. I did not delay, but raced for the roof of the power house, where I know that the Sibama's private flyers, the fastest craft in Kau, were kept. I selected a fast one-man flyer and fled in the night to the west. My flight was foredoomed to be a failure.

"The power sent out by the power house in Kaulani is sent in five wavelengths. One of them is used for all machines of peace, for lighting the house, preparing the food and similar uses. A second actuates the fighting suits and other weapons of war. The other three are assigned to the ships; one to commercial ships, one to war vessels and one to the Sibama's private flyers. All they had to do was to shut down the wavelength on which I was flying and my ship crashed to the ground, a wreck.

"By their meters at Kaulani they can tell where every ship is and warships were dispatched after me. They could not locate me. Before leaving, I had rigged the flyer with a device I had perfected, which made the meters give false readings and I was many miles from the place where they sought me. I hid the wreckage of my ship under rocks and eked out a precarious living in the hope that some day I would be able to capture a small flyer and make my way to Ame alone. I knew that they would use the paralyzing ray on me when I was found and I labored to make a pocket device which would remove the effects of the ray. After seven months of toil, I perfected it. The search for me had never ended, for the Kauans knew that I could not be beyond the limits of their empire. Many times I had seen the patrol vessels pass over me and each time I had hidden myself. This morning one passed and I deliberately showed myself. Everything went as I had planned. They paralyzed my arms and legs but my pocket neutralizer destroyed the effects. I simulated paralysis and was carried on the ship a prisoner. I bided my time and was about to attack, when they saw your signal and stopped to capture you. You know the rest."

"One question, Olua Alii; you said that the survivors of Ulm were taken to Kaulani. Were there any women among them?"

"There were not, Siba Tam. They were all warriors."

Evidently Awlo and Lamu had not made their way to Ulm. Well, that was about what I had expected.

"Perhaps you had better teach me to use one of these fighting suits," I suggested.

"Certainly, Siba Tam, whatever you desire. As you can see, each suit has six arms. Two of these are control arms, the other four are weapons. Each of the weapons is different. The green ray is a paralyzing ray with whose effects you are familiar. It can be used as a crippling weapon or as a killing weapon. If the heart is paralyzed, death ensues instantly.

"In the second arm is an orange ray which neutralizes the effect of the green ray. It is used as a defensive weapon against an enemy equipped with the green paralyzing ray. It will also restore the functioning of any part of the body which has been paralyzed. The third arm contains a red or heat ray. I will show you the effect of it."

He donned a suit and directed the middle arm on the left side toward a boulder. A ray of intolerable brightness shot from the arm. The granite boulder glowed bright for a moment and a stream of molten rock ran down its face. Olua shut off the ray.

"The fourth ray is a blue one which has the effect of neutralizing the red ray of an opponent," he went on. "You see, each suit is equipped with two offensive and two defensive weapons. These are all that the common soldiers carry. The Alii have suits with more arms and more deadly weapons, both offensive and defensive. It is said that Kapioma Sibama has made a suit with forty arms but it is so heavy that he cannot walk with it on. It operates, not on the usual wavelength, but on the private wavelength on which his flyers operate.

"That, however, is not the most effective suit in Kaulani. The most deadly suit is one which I manufactured in secret and which is hidden there. I had no opportunity to bring it with me or all the forces of Kau could not have harmed me. I will tell you, Siba Tam, where it is concealed. The knowledge may never benefit you but it will do you no harm. In the power house is a laboratory where fighting suits are made and tested. One entire end of the laboratory is taken up by a screen against which all rays are helpless. Unknown to everyone, I have tampered with that screen. If you ever wish to get the suit, go to the laboratory and turn the ordinary red ray, the heat ray of the common suits, against the upper corner of the screen, fourteen inches from the top and eleven inches from the left end. Leave the ray on full force for eight seconds and then apply the orange ray for twelve seconds. A portion of the screen will open and the suit is behind it. It operates on the same wave as Kapioma's."

"Thank you, Olua," I said, after I had practised with one of the suits until I could manipulate it rapidly, "you have told me what I wished to know very frankly and fully. I will reward your confidence by being equally frank with you. Although I am Siba Tam of Ulm, I was not born in that empire. I was born in a much larger world. Do you understand the composition of matter?"

I soon found that the education of an Alii of Kau left little to be desired from a scientific standpoint. Olua was perfectly familiar with the division of matter into molecules and atoms and of the atoms into protons and electrons. One of his statements surprised me a great deal until I had time to reflect on it. He said that the atoms were static instead of in motion and that the same was true of the electrons. I started to correct him, when a sudden thought made me pause. A moment of reflection told me that he was right. In his plane, both atoms and electrons were static.

When I had first started my electronic vibration adjuster, which reduced the amplitude of vibration of the electrons, my switch had jammed and I had broken it in trying to open it. Despite this fact, the adjuster had reduced me to the size of the men of Ulm and had then ceased operation.

On each subsequent trip, the same phenomenon had occurred. The reason, on reflection, was obvious. I had reduced the amplitude of vibration to zero and in this minute plane, the electrons did not vibrate.

Once I had that idea in my head, it was a simple matter to explain to Olua the theory of the vibrating atoms of the larger planes. He did not question my theory of simple harmonic vibration of the electrons, which theory had brought so much ridicule on me at one time. He realized at once how the size of a body could be increased under such circumstances but when I told him of the world from which I had first come to Ulm, his eyes opened. He had no more idea of the existence of such a world than we of the larger plane had of the existence of Ulm before my first trip there. His first thought was to flee to the larger plane from the pursuing Kauans.

"There we will be safe," he said. "They will be after us in a few hours with ships of greater speed equipped with fighting suits against which we have no defence."

"You may go if you wish, Olua," I said, "but I have returned to Ulm for a purpose and that purpose has not been accomplished. I will stay and continue my search."

"Where the Siba Tam of Ulm stays, there stays Olua Alii of Ulm," he said quietly. "What are your plans?"

"The only place where I can obtain the information I seek is at Kaulani, where the survivors of Ulm are," I replied. "Let me tell you why I am here and what I seek."

In a few words I told him of Lamu's treachery and of my search for my lost princess.

"You will not find her in Kaulani," he said thoughtfully, "for there were no women brought there. However, some of the prisoners can tell you whether they returned to Ulm before it fell. Since that is your desire, we will wait here until the Kauans come and capture us."

"No, we won't," I replied. "If they come here, they will capture not only us but also my adjuster and the weapons I brought from the larger plane. How long will it be before they are after us?"

"At least four hours."

"Good. In that length of time, I can teach you how to manipulate a rifle and a pistol as well as the adjuster. There is one other thing you want to learn to use. Here is a wireless transmission set. It will enable you to send messages through the air, which a similar instrument will receive, and also to receive messages sent to you. If I can, I will construct one in Kaulani so that we can get into communication. You are not going back to Kaulani with me."

"I will stay with my lord."

"You will obey my orders. If you go there, it will not aid me at all and will result in your death. If you hide out here, it is possible that you may aid me. In the event that I am killed, it is my order that you take up the search for Awlo of Ulm and never abandon it while you live until you have rescued her from Lamu or have looked on her dead body. Do you understand?"

"I do, sire. It will be as you order."

"Good. Now I want to teach you all I can before we have to pull out of here."

Olua was an apt pupil and in two hours he was able to manipulate a rifle and a pistol as well as I could and even to shoot fairly well at short ranges. The weapons would be useless against men equipped with fighting suits, the simplest of which threw about the wearer a repulsive screen which no bullet could penetrate, but I felt that no knowledge was useless, since my ability with a pistol had saved us once. The radio set was elementary to him, his only wonder being that no Kauan had ever thought of so simple a device.

When he was fully instructed we entered the adjuster and increased our size slowly until we were perhaps a hundred yards tall, compared to Ulm standards. We stepped out and I used a rifle to start the adjuster and let it reduce its size to Ulmite standards. When this was done, I could pick it and its entire load up and carry it without difficulty. Olua picked up the Kauan ship and together we set out across the hills for the point where I was captured. I resolved to make that cavern our base of operations.

We found it with no trouble and reduced ourselves to our former dimensions. It was quite a task for us to move the adjuster and its load into the cavern but we did so. When the task was completed, I bade a temporary farewell to Olua and entered the Kauan ship. I drove it about thirty miles due east and then landed. I set the controls of the ship for a maximum climb and pulled the power lever to full speed forward. The ship sprang up into the air and I leaped out just in time. Upward it went for several miles before it fell out of contro When it did, it gave a sickening lurch or two and then dove at full speed toward the ground. I sat down and waited for the next Kauan ship to appear.

I did not have long to wait. In less than an hour a speck appeared in the blue to the east. The new ship was a larger one than the first and it seemed to me to be traveling at a higher speed. I was fearful lest the occupants would see the remains of the ship which had crashed but the Gods of Fate were kind to me and it escaped their notice. It probably dove into some deep dark ravine, for none of the scouts which went out from Kau in search of it ever located it. Hunting for so small an object as a five-man cruiser in the wastes of the Kau mountains was a great deal like the proverbial search for a needle in a haystack.

When the ship came in sight, I walked slowly out into the open and stood quietly awaiting its approach. I thought, and as it turned out I thought rightly, that the figure of a man would hardly escape the attention of an airship sent out to seek for one. The ship swung down on a long slant and came to a standstill less than fifty feet from where I stood. A door opened in the side of the cabin and a half a dozen figures wearing eight-armed fighting suits emerged. I advanced toward them confidently.

"Greetings, men of Kau," I said when I had approached to within twenty feet of them. They paused and their leader stepped a pace in front.

"Greetings, man of Ulm," he replied in his guttural voice. "What seek you in the mountains of Kau?"

"I seek audience with Kapioma Sibama of Kau," I said. "The way to Kaulani is long and weary and I ask your aid in traveling there."

"What manner of man are you?" he demanded. "Your color and speech mark you as a man of Ulm, yet what man of Ulm knows of Kau and Kaulani?"

"I know many things," I said haughtily, "things which I have come to Kau to impart to your Sibama."

"What is your name and rank?"

"I am Courtney Siba Tam, Crown Prince of Ulm."

A peculiar expression flickered for a moment over his face and he bowed low to me.

"Neimeha of Kau is honored to be of service to such a one," he said smoothly. "My poor ship is at your Highness' disposal to carry him to the court of Kapioma Sibama. There you may meet some of your compatriots."

"I believe that a few of my subjects did escape into the Kau mountains when Ulm fell," I said carelessly, "and I would like to see them again. I will mention your courtesy to Kapioma Sibama."

He bowed again at my words and motioned to me to precede him into the flyer. I did so, expecting every moment to feel a paralyzing ray strike me, but evidently my bluff had worked. Neimeha followed me in and he and his followers divested themselves of their fighting suits.

"It is fortunate for me that you took this path," I said cheerfully. "I had little hope of meeting a ship so soon."

"We seek one who has fled from Kau," he replied. "As long as the light holds we will continue our search. Such were my orders."

"It is unfortunate that you men of Kau do not understand some of the laws of nature with which I am familiar," I said. "If you were, it would be a simple matter to communicate with your sovereign and ask for a modification of your orders. The waves which come from your power house could easily carry a message to you."

"How would such a thing be possible?" demanded Neimeha in amazement.

I smiled enigmatically.

"It is but one of the things which I can teach you," I replied. "I could instruct one of your learning in a short time, but I do not choose to do so. Perhaps your Sibama will desire to confine this new knowledge to his Alii. How long will it take us to fly to Kaulani?"

He turned to a map hanging on the wall and I walked over and studied it. It was the first map of the submicroscopic country I had ever seen, for Ulm had not progressed to the stage of map making and probably never would have. The Ulmites were possessed of an uncanny sense of direction which enabled them to find their way readily about their domain without other aid.

I had been captured in what was apparently a "no man's land" between the empires of Ulm and Kau. Ulm lay, as nearly as I could scale distances by the eye, about ninety miles *due west* of where we were. The old legend had lied after all. Kaulani was roughly two hundred miles to the east, a hundred and fifty of which were over barren mountains.

"We can fly to Kaulani in an hour and a half," said Neimeha. "In view of your presence, I am going to alter my instructions on my own initiative and take you directly to the city."

"I thank you," I said. "I am fairly familiar with this type of ship. With your permission, I will take the dual set of controls and guide the ship a part of the way."

He nodded and for the rest of the trip I devoted my attention to improving my technique. There was really nothing to it and long before we reached Kaulani, I was as confident of my ability to fly any ship in the country as I was of my ability to fly a Bach or a Douglas.

It was nearly dark when we landed in Kaulani. The plan of the city resembled the plan of Ulm, but the architecture was of a much lighter and more graceful type. Not that Ulm had not been a beautiful city but its beauty was the beauty of grandeur and massiveness with utter simplicity marking its architectural lines. Kaulani, as well as I could tell in the gathering dusk, was made up of buildings of a much more graceful style. I could not place the type of architecture, although in the daylight it had a strong note of the best Grecian style in it.

We landed in the huge grounds surrounding the royal palace. Neimeha and two of his guards escorted me into the palace to a floor below the level of the ground.

"I am placing you in the slave's quarters," he explained, "not that your status as a guest has changed, but that it is necessary that you be kept under surveillance, until it is learned whether Kapioma Sibama will receive you. The slave's quarters are the only place where this can be done. Besides, I thought that you might like to see some of your old subjects," he added with a touch of malice in his voice.

The room into which I stepped was the central recreation room of a large suite of rooms. It was well lighted and ventilated and was fitted with a number of comfortable looking chairs and divans. At the far end of the room a half dozen men clothed in coarse white garments were grouped together talking. They turned as I entered and surveyed me from head to foot. As I approached them, one stepped in front of the rest and looked at me keenly. I suddenly became aware that I was dressed in corduroy breeches and a flannel shirt and not in the gorgeous robes of the Crown Prince of Ulm with the diadem indicative of my royal rank blazing on my brow. These garments were not suitable for rough work and I had left them at my adjuster in the care of Olua. With as much of an air of dignity as I could command, I stepped forward to face the group. Suddenly I recognized the man who had stepped forward.

"Moka!" I shouted with joy. It was indeed Moka Alii, Lord Chamberlain of Kalu's court.

The old nobleman stared at me in unbelief for a moment and then a red flush stole over his haughty face. Pointedly he turned his back on me.

"Moka!" I cried again. "Don't you remember me? I am Courtney Siba Tam, your prince; Courtney Sibama, if Olua spoke the truth when he said that Kalu Sibama was no more."

Moka turned and faced me coldly, entirely ignoring my outstretched hand.

"I recognize you, Courtney," he said in a biting tone, carefully avoiding giving me any title, "to my regret, but my lips will never touch the hand of a traitor, though I be boiled in oil for my refusal!"

"Moka!" I cried in real anguish, for the coldness of the first friend I had made in Ulm cut me to the heart. "It is not true. I am no traitor to Ulm. I was delayed in my task and was on my way to Ulm with aid when I learned that it had fallen. I surrendered to the Kauans and hastened here to bring what aid and comfort I could to those of my subjects who still lived. Never have I deserted Ulm and never has the thought of her welfare been absent from my thoughts."

"Traitor! Doubly dyed traitor!" said Moka slowly and bitingly, "and now, it seems, liar to boot! Well, I know the plan with which you left Ulm. You planned to aid her enemies and to depose Kalu Sibama, your lord, and reign in his stead. Thankful I am that Kalu, who foolishly loved you, died before he knew of your treachery."

"I am no traitor, Moka," I cried, "and who says I am, lies in his throat! Hold up, old friend," I exclaimed as he sprang at me, "I am not hitting at you but at the one who told you this pack of lies. Where did you learn what you thought were my plans?"

"Your smooth tongue, which deluded Kalu Sibama, will not avail you, Courtney," he said coldly. "Cover your face in confusion and learn that your treachery was told by Lamu Siba, whom you tried to corrupt and failed."

"Lamu!" I gasped—"Did Lamu return to Ulm?"

"He is here and he has told of the plans which you broached to him to destroy Kalu and of how he fled from you when he learned of your baseness. Your treachery is proven indeed, Courtney."

"So he got back to Ulm safely," I said. Somehow I had always had an idea that he must have missed the city as I did and thought that he and Awlo were wandering somewhere in the submicroscopic world. The news that he had reached Ulm and had managed to turn my friends against me was a bitter blow for it could mean only one thing, that Awlo was dead. Had she been alive, he could never have told that tale and been believed. With a sinking heart I put my next question.

"What of Awlo?" I asked.

I reeled back as Moka struck me a blow on the mouth.

"Dog!" he cried. "The name of a Sibimi of Ulm must not be uttered by the lips of a perjured traitor! To complete your confusion, I will tell you that the Sibimi of Ulm is in Kaulani."

"Said she that I was a traitor?" I demanded bitterly. Moka paused.

"No," he admitted slowly, "she did not, but it is unnecessary. Lamu Siba has told enough. We men of Ulm need no word from her to damn you further."

My heart leaped with joy at the thought that Awlo was alive and in the same city with me, and while her silence was inexplicable, I knew that she must have some good reason for it. Awlo knew that I was no traitor to Ulm and I would have staked my life on her love and loyalty.

"Listen, old friend," I said to Moka, "it was never your way to condemn a man unheard in his own defense on the testimony of his enemies. You have known me as your lord and as your friend for years; have you ever known me to speak an untruth?"

"No," he admitted.

"Then listen, old friend, while I tell you the truth. Lamu Siba is the traitor, not I."

Rapidly, but in great detail, I told him all that had happened since the fatal day when I left Ulm in my adjuster with Awlo and Lamu to bring back the guns and ammunition with which I hoped to rout, if not destroy the besieging Mena. I told how Lamu had learned to operate the adjuster, how he had stolen my princess and had fled with her, leaving me desolate. I told of my struggle to get material and of the months of feverish work while I had constructed a duplicate of my machine and gone in pursuit. Last, I told of how I had landed with my guns and ammunition and had met Olua and how I had surrendered to the Kauans in order to be brought to Kaulani.

Moka's face grew graver as my story progressed. My sincerity almost convinced him, but for months he had thought me a traitor. The struggle was evident in his face. He wanted to believe and yet could not. When I had ended my tale and again held out my hand to him, he hesitated, but another of the auditors, a young officer named Hiko, who had at one time been my personal aide, had no doubts.

"My sword to your hand, Courtney Sibama!" he cried, as he dropped on one knee and pressed my hand against his forehead and then to his lips. "My life is yours to command!"

His enthusiasm carried the day and in a moment, not only Moka, but the rest of the group were on their knees professing their loyalty to me.

"Forgive me for doubting you, Courtney Sibama," cried Moka with tears in his voice, "but the words of a Siba carry weight."

"Where is my Sibimi?" I demanded.

"Alas, my lord," said Moka, "she is a prisoner in the palace of Kapioma Sibama, Lord of Kau. I have seen her twice but none of us has ever spoken to her."

"Did you not speak to her in Ulm?" I asked.

"No, my lord. She or Lamu never returned to Ulm. Four months after you left us, Ulm fell to a night assault of the Mena. Had you been there, it would never have happened, but discipline was relaxed after you left and they kept watch poorly. Besides, the Mena had never before attacked at night.

"The city was given over to slaughter, but a remnant of the royal guard gathered about the palace of the Sibama and we held them at bay for eight days. At the end of that time they fired the palace and we fought our way out hardly. Both Kalu and the Sibimi were killed and most of the guards, but a few of us held together and fought our way toward the waste places where we hoped the kahumas, who were said to rule, would either defend us or kill us with honor.

"The Mena ringed us about and mile by mile our numbers lessened. There were but a hundred and twenty left and many of them sore wounded when the pressure of the Mena suddenly ceased and we saw them flying like leaves before a gale. We heard a strange noise overhead and looked up and saw a multitude of strange birds flying over us. Some of these birds lit near us and disgorged men with many arms who took us prisoners and dragged us into the interior of the birds. We thought they were kahumas. When they were in the birds they divested themselves of all their arms but two and we prepared for death. They did not kill us but saved us alive and brought us here to Kaulani.

"We had been here about a month when we learned that an Alii of Kau had planned to rescue us. We rejoiced but his plot failed and he had to flee for his life. Two months later Lamu Siba was brought to use as a slave. He told us a tale of treachery on your part and of how he and Awlo Sibimi had fled from you but had been captured in the waste places of Kau. Him we foolishly believed, the more because Awlo Sibimi was a prisoner in the palace of Kapioma and none of us could speak with her.

"Aside from the fact that we are slaves and not free men, we have no complaint. The kahumas have treated us well and mercifully, although we are forced to labor, and dire is the punishment of one who shirks. We hope that our condition will be improved, for Kapioma means to make Awlo his Sibimi as soon as the present one is killed."

"Is killed?" I echoed.

"Yes. The kahumas have a barbarous custom in Kau. A Sibimi is chosen and in one year, unless she is with child, she is slain and a new one is chosen. The present Sibimi dies in a month. Thinking you dead, Kapioma meant to make Awlo Sibimi of Kau. Hark! Here come the others from work. Hide behind us for a moment, Courtney Sibama, until I tell them of your presence."

I knew the love of the men of Ulm for dramatic scenes and I stepped behind the ranks of my followers. The door opened and in trooped a hundred men, all attired alike, in the coarse white garb which is the Kauan mark of a slave. Moka stepped forward and held up his hand for silence.

"We harbor in our midst a traitor!" he cried dramatically. "One who is a traitor to his Sibama, a worse traitor to his Sibimi and a traitor to Ulm. What is the punishment for such a one?"

"Death!" came a cry from the men of Ulm. Lamu stepped forward and confronted Moka.

"Death is his punishment and it shall be meted out when he is known," he said. "Name this traitor."

This was the answer that Moka had hoped for. He drew himself up to his full height and pointed his finger dramatically at the prince.

"Thou art the man!" he thundered. "On your knees and beg for mercy from Courtney, Sibama of Ulm!"

Taking my cue from his words I stepped forward into full view. Lamu started and turned pale as he saw me, but an ominous growl rose from the rest.

"What means this, Moka?" demanded one of them. I recognized the man as Hama Alii, a noble of Ulm and one of the Council of Lords. He was, if my memory did not play me false, a distant cousin of Lamu's. "Courtney is a traitor, as we all well know. To him shall the sentence of death be meted out."

A murmur of assent came from the ranks of the Ulmites behind him and my handful of followers closed up behind me.

"Slay him!" cried Lamu pointing at me. The crowd surged forward.

"Hold!" I cried and they paused for a moment. "Every man is entitled to a hearing. Let me tell my tale and then let the Council of Lords judge my tale. One of royal blood may be tried only by that tribunal."

My point was well taken and it appealed to the justice of the men and a cry of assent went up. Briefly, and as eloquently as I could, I retold my story. It made an impression but there was no loyal aide to turn the tables in my favor this time and at the end of my speech there was silence for a moment.

"It is a lie!" cried Lamu suddenly. "Kill the traitor and make an end of it."

There was a murmur, half of assent and half of dissent and I played the same card again.

"How many of the Council of Lords of Ulm are here?" I asked.

"Hama Alii and I," replied Moka.

"A matter touching the royal family of Ulm can be decided only by the Council of Lords," I insisted. "Neither Lamu Siba nor I can be tried by any lesser tribunal. Let Hama and Moka decide."

There was a roar of assent to my proposition and the two nobles retired into a corner to talk the matter over. For half an hour they argued the matter back and forth. Knowing Hama's relation to Lamu, I had rather expected a deadlock and that was what eventually happened. The two came forward and Moka, as the elder, announced their decision.

"When the Council of Lords is evenly divided, the decision rests with the Sibama," he said, "but here the Sibama is an interested party and it would not be fair to let him decide the matter, for traitor or not, Courtney is Sibama of Ulm until the Council of Lords declare the throne vacant. Both Courtney Sibama and Lamu Siba have spoken and the voice of each sounds as that of a true man in our ears. It is our decision that Courtney Sibama and Lamu Siba be each given the honors of their rank and both held blameless, until the matter can be laid before the Sibimi for decision. In the meantime, the disputants shall swear friendship to one another for the time being, and we will all live in harmony as becomes brothers in misfortune."

Lamu and I looked speculatively at one another. After all, there was nothing that we could do except agree with the decision, which was manifestly a just one. I knew that once Awlo spoke, the question would be settled and he doubtless hoped that she would get no chance to speak or else he had another idea in the back of his head. At any rate, he spoke first.

"The Prince of Ame defers to the Council," he said. "As Moka Alii has spoken, so shall it be."

"So shall it be," I echoed.

As Lamu and I approached one another for the ceremony of swearing temporary friendship, there came an interruption. The door opened and there stood Neimeha with a detachment of guards.

"Courtney Sibama," he said, "Kapioma Sibama requires your presence in his throne room."

With a shrug of my shoulders I followed him out of the slaves' quarters and to the ground floor of the palace. The building was a beautiful one, much more ornate than Kalu's palace in Ulm, but what it gained in beauty, to my mind at least, it lost in grandeur. At the door of the throne room we were challenged, but a word from Neimeha opened a way for us.

The scene was very similar to one of the dozens of Kalu's audiences I had taken part in. On all sides blazed the colors of the nobles and ladies, their flashing gems set off by the sombre black worn by the guards. The throne room was long and impressive, with a dais at the head bearing four thrones, the central two of which were occupied. Kapioma Sibama of Kau was a tall, slender man of about my age. He had a splendid breadth of forehead but his slanting eyes, like those of all the Kauans, were mercilessly cold and cruel. The first thing, however, that attracted my attention was the sadness of the face of the Sibimi who sat beside him. She was a slim young girl and despite her yellow skin, was beautiful, but the sadness of the ages was in her tragic eyes. Suddenly I remembered what Moka had told me of the customs of Kau and I realized that she saw death before her in a few short weeks. I squared my shoulders and advanced to the foot of the dais. Slave or prisoner, condemned to death, I might come from that interview, but as Sibama of Ulm I would go to it. I looked Kapioma squarely in the eye and he returned my gaze with an expressionless face.

"Courtney of Ulm," he said in a guttural voice, "Neimeha tells me that the wonders we have heard of you are true and that your subjects in Ulm looked on you as a powerful kahuma because you knew more of nature and her laws than they dreamed of. You are no barbarian of Ulm, fit only to be a slave, but a man of intelligence and learning. He tells me that you are able to navigate a flyer."

I bowed without speaking.

"I am duly sensible of the misfortunes which have thrown you from your high position, where you might with propriety have sat by my side, and it is not my desire to add to the burdens or sorrows of a man of royal rank. Since you are able to take your part in this community as an equal with my nobles, it is in my mind to create you an Alii of Kau and attach you to my court."

Again I bowed deeply in silence.

"Neimeha tells me further that you know ways of sending messages through the air from the power house to a ship many miles away."

"I do, sire, it is a relatively simple matter."

"I am glad to hear it, for I believe that the art will be of much use. To the rank of Alii of Kau I will raise you, but in return I will ask of you one small favor."

"I will be glad to put my knowledge at your service," I replied.

He frowned slightly at my answer.

"It is not that; that I took for granted. The favor I ask of you is of a different nature. You were married in Ulm to Awlo, daughter of Kalu Sibama. Since his death she is now Sibimi of Ulm. In a month or so," here he paused and shot a glance at the Sibimi, who quailed under it as though under a lash, "there will be no Sibimi in Kau and it is my intention to elevate the daughter of Kalu to that exalted rank in lieu of the throne she has lost. The favor I ask of you is that you divorce her."

"Divorce Awlo? Never!" I cried.

"You had better consider well before you decide so," he said with a frown. "As the wife of an Alii, I could not marry her without first getting rid of you. Were I to order your execution, I would be no better off, for the widow of an executed criminal could not be elevated to the rank of Sibimi. However, under the laws of Kau, a slave may not legally have a wife. Unless you consent, I will degrade you to the position of a slave, which will effectually dissolve the tie which binds her and leave her free to mount the throne by my side. It is immaterial to me, but it means much to you. You may have a day in which to decide. Either you become an Alii of Kau and divorce her, or you become a slave of Kau and I will marry her in either event."

"It doesn't take a day or a minute to decide that, Kapioma Sibama," I replied, "I will never divorce her."

He shrugged his shoulders.

"At any rate, I tried to be kind to you," he replied. "Neimeha, this man is a slave of Kau. Clothe him as such and take him to the slaves' quarters. He will work in the laboratory of the power house and show us a method of sending messages to our ships, which he boasts is so simple. If he refuses, or fails, flay him alive."

The guards seized me and half dragged and half led me from the throne room. Once outside the room, my clothing was stripped from me and the white garb of a slave thrown over my shoulders. Thus dressed, I was led back to the slaves' quarters which I had left a short time before. Moka and my other friends hastened to greet me and to express their indignation at the tale I had to tell. They applauded my action vociferously, although Lamu suggested that it might have been a good plan for me to have fallen in with Kapioma's plan and won the rank of Alii, which might have enabled me to aid all of them to escape. A withering glance from Moka stopped his mouth. After a short talk we dispersed to our beds in the dormitories attached to the central room.

I lay awake for some time making my plans. So far everything had fallen out better than I had dared to hope. Awlo was alive and well and in no immediate peril. I had a hundred loyal friends at my back and best of all, I was assigned to work in the laboratory to construct a wireless set, the very thing I needed to communicate with Olua. I dropped to sleep with a feeling that fortune was favoring me.

When the slaves were turned out for work the next morning, a guard was waiting for me. He took me to the power plant, which was located in the grounds of the royal palace. I was taken to the laboratory and told shortly to show how I proposed to send messages over power waves. I protested that I was unfamiliar with their methods of power transmission and that I would have to familiarize myself with their methods and equipment before I could be expected to show them anything new. After a consultation, my stand was decided to be a reasonable one and I was handed over to one of the laboratory men with orders that I be taught all that could be taught about power transmission.

My guide and instructor was a young man, about my own age. Despite his slant eyes and yellow skin, he proved to me quite a likeable fellow as well as an erudite scientist. He was a son of one of the higher Alii of Kau. During the period I worked with him, we became in a measure friends and he confided to me one day that one of his great-grandmothers had been a slave brought from Ame, the second city of the empire of Ulm. This probably accounted for the fact that he showed less interest in science and more in human beings than most of his compatriots. Altogether, I found him the most human and likeable person I met among the Kauans. Only the fact that he was passionately loyal to Kapioma prevented me from approaching Waimua, which was his name, on the subject of joining forces with us. His tragic death later was a source of lasting sorrow to me.

I had little trouble following Waimua's explanations. The power for the entire empire of Kau was generated in the one building in Kaulani and was sent out broadcast for general use. There were five distinct and separate installations, each sending out one of the five wavelengths earlier described to me by Olua. I was appalled at first by the enormous waste of energy involved in general broadcasting until I found out that only a low-power pilot wave was so sent out. The generators were so built that when a demand was received by the pilot wave, a directional wave of the proper power was automatically sent out to fill the demand. Meters registered the direction and distance from the power house of the consumption and, as a result, the location of any ship flying over the empire could be plotted to within a dozen miles on a map hung near the flying broadcasters. The smallest installation of the five was naturally the one on which the Sibama's private flyers and his fighting suits were operated.

The day passed before we were half through with the power installation but I took the time to give Waimua a rough outline of the methods of radio telegraphy. He understood the principle at once and promised to assemble everything we needed for our experiments and start the best instrument makers in the empire making tubes according to my specifications. As soon as the needed equipment could be got together, we would be in a position to start our experiments. I readily located the screen in the laboratory, behind which Olua had hid his fighting suit, but naturally I made no attempt to get possession of it and did not mention its existence to Waimua.

While I was going over the power plant, a germ of an idea came to me, which seemed to make our escape not altogether impossible. While I had no intention to strike before I had established communication with Olua and given him orders as to the part he was to play in it, nevertheless, I broached the idea to Moka in strict confidence. He promptly promised to see that our men gathered as promptly as possible certain information which I needed. He proposed to speak at first only to the most discreet and trustworthy of our men and avoid giving out information until the time came for action. As we were not interrupted that night, the remnant of the Council of Lords decided that the moment was propitious and Lamu and I swore a temporary oath of friendship.

The next day I finished my course of instruction and on the third day the instrument makers presented for my approval a dozen radio tubes which they had manufactured. Considering the fact that they had never seen a small tube for the sending of messages, they had done a very creditable job and I had little doubt of the success of my efforts. Waimua and I at once started assembling a transmitter and two receivers. One of the receivers was constructed to work only on one definite wavelength, but the other was made adjustable, so that I could not only receive from my own transmitter but also from Olua, if I finally established communication with him. A week passed before I was ready to make a test.

The receivers worked all right while they were in the room with the transmitter and on the pretext of testing them at a longer distance, I sent

Waimua fifty miles away in a military flyer. As soon as he was out of the way, I set my transmitter to the wavelength of the receiver on the adjuster and called frantically. It seemed hours before an answer came. Olua had diligently studied the international code since I had left him and he had no difficulty in receiving my messages and answering them. I quickly acquainted him with the state of affairs in Kau and told him of our plans. He was able to make some excellent suggestions, based on his knowledge of Kaulani, suggestions which I gladly fitted into my plans. On the off-chance that they might be useful, I directed him to make a trip to the larger plane in the adjuster and bring back certain supplies. I had left quite a sum in gold in my hidden Nevada valley and I told him where to find it. He promised faithful performance of his duties and I turned to the wavelength on which the receiver, which Waimua was carrying, was set.

I sent out a garbled message, varying my power from time to time so that the signals would come in strong and then fade out. I was fairly sure that Waimua would be able to get only a few words of the message, yet he would feel much encouraged. By means of a proposed modification, I intended to prolong the work for a few more days until we were ready to strike for freedom. My plan worked perfectly and Waimua came back wildly enthusiastic about the partial success we had achieved on our first attempt. We tore down both the receivers and the transmitters and proposed rebuilding them with slight modifications, which I assured him would make them entirely successful.

That night Moka reported that Hiko had brought in the last bit of information we had needed and there was no need to delay longer. Everyone, even Lamu, had by this time been informed of the plan and of the part assigned to him in carrying it out.

Briefly, our plan was this. At a given time, we were to divide into two bands. One band, under my personal leadership, was to attack the power house and shut off all power. As soon as this was done, the remainder, under the command of Moka, was to enter the palace and secure Awlo. The rest of us would sally out and meet them and we would all take refuge in the power house. We expected to capture several of the Kauan scientists in the power plant and we would force them to modify a hundred-man military flyer, which was always kept in a hangar on the roof of the power house, to fly on the Sibama's private wavelength. We would disable all generating units except the small one which sent out this power. All but a picked detail were then to leave on this modified ship and the devoted band who remained would try to hold the power plant until we were well away from Kau.

The plan was a risky one but it was the best we could think of and

I resolutely refused to allow any discussion of what would happen after those staying behind had been overpowered and our ship brought to the ground. I had another plan, which I did not divulge, even to Moka. I meant to head for my adjuster and arm my band. Kau had no firearms so far as any of us had seen and before a hundred well-armed and resolute men, the entire army of Kau would be helpless, once their fighting suits were put out of business by the shutting off of the power which actuated them. What we would do after our escape would depend on Awlo's wishes. We might wipe out the Mena and refound the empire of Ulm (Ame had not yet fallen to the Mena so far as we knew), or we might found a new empire in some remote part of our tiny world some place where neither the Mena nor the Kauans would find us.

The weakest part of our plan was the fact that we were forced to strike in broad daylight, for we were locked in at night. This could not be helped, however, and we set high noon for our attempt. We trusted to the surprise and to the fact that many of the palace attendants would be at lunch. When we left our quarters in the morning, I could not help wondering how many of my brave subjects would be alive that night.

About ten o'clock, as Waimua and I were working away at the radio transmitter, two guards appeared in the laboratory and ordered me to follow them. They refused to answer any questions, merely stating that I was wanted at once in the throne room. With a few words of instruction to Waimua, I took my place between them and walked out. As we emerged from the power house, I saw that something had gone wrong with our plans. Between rows of guards wearing fighting suits, the Ulmites were being herded to the slaves' quarters. I was taken to the door of the throne room, where I found Lamu, Moka, and Hama all waiting under guard. The door opened and I was ordered to enter the presence of the Sibama. Shaking off the hands of my guards, I walked with my head up, to the foot of the dais and stared defiantly at Kapioma. He stared back at me with an expressionless face.

"I have been informed, Courtney," he said in his guttural voice, "that there is a plot on foot among the slaves from Ulm to capture the power plant and then to escape in a military flyer, with you at the controls. What have you to say?"

"Nothing, sire," I replied briefly.

"All of the details of the plot are in my hands," he went on, "and any denial would be useless. As the ringleader, your fate is naturally death. What form it will take, I have not yet decided, nor has my Council of Lords yet debated the fate of your followers."

"Of course, I realized long ago that you had decided on my death, Kapioma Sibama," I said coldly, "since only thus can you free Awlo from her bonds to me. The laws of Kau may say what they please about a slave but we were wed by the laws of Ulm when I was free and a Prince. My enslaving does not dissolve the tie which may be set aside only by the Sibama of Ulm with the consent of his Council of Lords. I would like to know how you learned of our plan."

"One of your members, whom you basely planned to leave behind through jealousy, overheard the plan and found out the details and told them," he replied.

"None were to be left," I exclaimed in surprise.

"Did you not plan to leave Lamu here?"

"We did not. He was the leader of the band who were to seize and protect the power installation by means of which we hoped to escape."

"Then Lamu lied," said Kapioma slowly. "This is not the first lie in which he has been detected. Courtney, it seems that even a Prince of Ulm may be a traitor. Bring in the slave, Lamu!"

The trembling Lamu was dragged by guards to the foot of the dais. He prostrated himself at the foot of the throne and looked abjectly upward. His subserviency disgusted me and I kicked him sharply.

"Get up and take your medicine like a man!" I said.

Kapioma smiled coldly as Lamu struggled to his feet with a black look at me.

"Lamu," he said, "you have lied once too often. The penalty for lying to the Sibama of Kau is death and that fate you have merited. The reward for treachery to your ruler in all countries is death and you have betrayed him who is your lawful Sibama, slave though he may be in Kau. Twice do you merit death and so slowly shall you die that it will seem to you that twice have you passed through the agonies of dissolution. You were planning to escape despite what you told me."

"I was not," cried Lamu. "I first learned of the plot last night through overhearing Moka and Courtney talk. I told my guards at the first opportunity."

"Bring in Moka and Hama," directed Kapioma.

The two Alii were brought in and it pleased me to see that each of them bowed with just the right amount of deference due to a throned monarch and not a speck more.

"Was the slave, Lamu, included in the plot to escape and did he know of it before last night?" demanded the Sibama.

The two nobles glanced at me for orders.

"Speak the truth!" I said.

"He was included in the plot to escape and he was told of it four nights ago, Kapioma Sibama," said Hama. Moka nodded assent.

"By the voices of your countrymen are you condemned, Lamu," said Kapioma. "His death shall be a thing to bring the sweat of terror to the brows of condemned criminals for a generation. Courtney, the laws of Kau are not inexorable. You have been the victim of one you trusted and your suffering to learn that one of your Princes is a traitor is already a heavy punishment. It may be that you may not have to die. If you will divorce Awlo as I have requested, I will submit the question to my Council of Lords with a recommendation for clemency. No, do not answer me now; I know what your answer will be before you have had time to think the matter over. Reflect on this matter. If you die, with you will die every one of your followers who were concerned in the plot. As criminals shall they die by torture. For you, I decree a soldier's death."

"Not through any regard for me, Kapioma Sibama, but because you cannot elevate the widow of one who has died as a criminal to the rank of Sibimi," I replied hotly.

"Exactly, Courtney. Your refusal to accede to my terms will accomplish nothing. You may have two days in which to make your decision. In the meanwhile, it is my pleasure that any reasonable wish of yours be granted. Have you a desire?"

"Yes," I replied with my blood boiling, "let me be the one to execute your decree of death on that rat who has been the source of all my trouble."

Kapioma smiled slightly, while Lamu shuddered.

"Gladly," said the Sibama. "It will be an amusing spectacle. I will even let you choose the manner of his death."

"I wish to kill him in fair fight."

Kapioma studied the two of us for a moment.

"So be it," he said. "Should he kill you, the question of Awlo would be settled pleasantly. If he is the victor, his life will be spared and he shall serve as a slave in Kau for the rest of his days. If you kill him, both you and your subjects will be free. You will be taken to the Kau mountains and liberated with two weeks' supply of food and water and with arms. If any of you return to Kau, you will be put to death with torture. If you win through the mountains, the Mena will kill you. What say you?"

"And Awlo?" I asked.

"In any event, Awlo remains here and becomes my Sibimi," he said sharply.

"Then I will——" I paused in thought. I had been about to declare my preference for death in Kau rather than for a separation from Awlo, but a plan occurred to me. My death in Kau would rob Awlo of her only protector and the Kau mountains were where my precious firearms were stored.

"I accept your terms, Kapioma Sibama," I said.

"Bring fighting suits!" commanded the Sibama.

A guard hastened up with two fighting suits, each equipped with eight arms.

"A scientist such as you are, Courtney, needs no instruction to use such a simple appliance," said Kapioma in a cold voice. "Since Lamu has not your knowledge, I will personally instruct him so that the fight may be more even."

I saw at once that it was his plan that Lamu should kill me and I thought regretfully of the thirty-armed suit which Olua had told me was concealed in the laboratory. However, there was no use in crying for the moon and I devoted my attention to studying the six controls with which my suit was equipped. I soon had them located.

Kapioma put in some time instructing Lamu. When he was satisfied that my adversary understood his weapons, he gave orders for us to don the suits. We did so and the guards brought in a huge dome of some transparent crystalline material which they sat down over us. I have no idea what it was made of. It looked like glass, but since it was thirty feet in diameter and ten feet high and four men carried it with ease, it must have been made of some exceedingly light material. I could hear Kapioma's voice as plainly as though the dome were not over us.

"Let no one interfere," said the Sibama. "I will count to five. When I have given the final number you may fight, but not before. Are you ready? One! Two!"

A blinding green flash came from one of the arms of Lamu's suit. My left arm fell useless, paralyzed by the deadly ray. Lamu threw back his head and raised an arm to shield his eyes from the brilliance. The ray passed from me with no further damage. I waited for the further counting of Kapioma. I was sure that he had instructed Lamu to start the battle before the final count, but I was equally sure that I would be punished if I did the same.

"Three!" came his voice after a pause. "Four!"

Lamu had recovered from the shock and with a crafty expression he was slowly bringing his green ray, which had been blazing harmlessly against the crystalline dome covering us, to bear on me. Nearer and nearer it came and still Kapioma did not give the final word. The ray touched my paralyzed arm and traveled down toward my leg.

"Five!" came Kapioma's voice at last.

My orange ray blazed forth and Lamu's green ray disappeared. I wasted a moment by turning my orange ray against my paralyzed arm and restoring it to usefulness. With it again normal, I could use two of my weapons at once.

I turned the orange ray again on Lamu and then turned on in rapid succession my red and my green. This was a fighting trick which Olua had taught me. There was a blinding flash from Lamu's suit and his green ray disappeared. One of his most powerful weapons was out of commission.

A scared look came on his face and his red ray blazed out. I was resolved to act only on the defensive until his weapons were destroyed and I turned off my orange, green and red rays and let my blue one blaze forth. Vainly Lamu strove to pierce the shield of blue light with which I covered myself. He reached toward his suit again and a white ray began to play beside the red. Olua had told me of this terrible ray, which extracted the water from any substance on which it struck and I hurriedly turned on my yellow ray to combat it. Round and round one another we circled, his rays trying vainly to find a hole in my armor of light. I strove to remember other tricks which Olua had told me of and one came to my mind. I suddenly turned off both my rays. Lamu swung the two blazing arms of his fighting suit toward my heart. I waited until the two rays overlapped one another and then turned on my green and yellow. With only one ray to guard against, it was a simple matter to keep him at bay.

I could remember no method of putting his white ray out of operation and to avoid prolonging the battle indefinitely, I turned on my green ray suddenly and directed it against his legs. Before he could switch on his orange ray to combat it, the paralyzing ray had got in its deadly effect and he fell in a heap. I hastened forward and stood over him. Olua had told me that almost any ray was deadly against the force which generated it. I seized the arm from which the white ray was blazing and slowly twisted it around. Lamu strove to fight, but a touch of my paralyzing ray made his arms as useless as were his legs. Slowly I twisted his arm until the white ray bore back against the arm from which it came. In another moment the ray ceased to glow and Lamu was shorn of his weapons.

A touch of either of my three offensive rays would have finished him, but I was not minded to kill him in that way. I bent over him and stripped his wrecked fighting suit from him. I tossed it to one side and stepped back. My orange ray glowed for an instant and Lamu rose as well and strong as he had been at the start of the battle.

"This fight is between you and me, Lamu Siba," I said slowly and menacingly. "Prepare to die at my hands."

Quickly I ripped my fighting suit from me. Lamu watched me like a cat. Once my arms were engaged in getting out of the suit he straightened up and rushed. I stepped back and to one side and gave him an opening. His right foot flew out and caught me a violent blow in the groin. With a cry of anguish I doubled up in pain and Lamu threw himself on me, a dagger gleaming in his hand.

I had sense enough left to twist to one side and Lamu's dagger merely scored my back. The pain of his foul blow was terrible and I was unarmed, but as he closed again I wriggled out of my suit and launched myself at his throat. His dagger flashed before my eyes but I disregarded it and closed with him. I grasped him by the throat and hurled myself to the ground, dragging him with me. I felt a burning pain in my shoulder and another in my side before my knee found his chest and I could wrench the dagger from his grasp and hurl it away. My hands closed again on his throat and I began to squeeze. His face grew purple and he looked at me appealingly. I released the pressure for a moment and put my head down.

"Mercy, Courtney Sibama," came in a coarse whisper from his lips.

"When did you show mercy?" I demanded. "Where is Awlo? Where is Kalu Sibama? Where is ravaged Ulm? Your life is trebly forfeit for your treachery and there is no mercy in my heart."

Slowly I tightened my grip on his throat. His breath came in gasps and then in a rattling wheeze. His head sank back, his eyes starting from their sockets and staring horribly. I can see those eyes yet. Still kneeling on his chest, I released my grip on his throat and seized his head and twisted it slowly around. Further and further it went until the vertebrae gave with a snap and his head fell limp. So died Lamu Siba, Prince of Ame of the Empire of Ulm at the hands of his ruler, whom he had betrayed.

I staggered to my feet and faced Kapioma.

"Your decree has been executed, oh Sibama," I cried between gasps. "When may I and my subjects depart?"

"As soon as you are recovered from your wounds and can travel, Courtney," he said gravely. "I am disappointed at the showing that dog made, but the word of the Sibama once pledged, may not be recalled. You are only changing the quick and honorable death of a soldier for a lingering death of thirst and starvation in the mountains. You have made your choice. Remember, however, that my offer of your life is still open. Divorce Awlo and I give it to you freely."

I straightened up to hurl a defiance into his teeth, but I could do no more. I had lost more blood than I realized and I swayed a moment and then everything went black. I seemed to be falling through an endless distance and then I could remember nothing more.

It was four days before I recovered consciousness, but when I did, I was ready to travel. The physicians of Kau had treated me with healing rays which had healed my wounds and restored my strength. I really felt little the worse for the terrible battle I had been through. Moka wished me to rest for a few more days, but I did not dare. The date of the death of the Sibimi of Kau was only fourteen days away and unless we could return to Kau before that time, I shuddered to think of the fate of Awlo. Accordingly, I sent word to Kapioma that I held him to his promise and desired to depart at once.

Somewhere in his heart there must have been a speck of chivalry which had not been bred out, for he came to the power house in person to see our departure.

"Farewell, Courtney Sibama," he said, "for once I have released you from slavery, your royal rank returns. I am sorry that you would not accede to the very lenient terms I offered you, for I believe you would be a useful member of my court. However, I have pledged my word and you may depart. I am merely changing the form of your death. You cannot return to Kau. If you stay in the mountains, you starve, and if you go to Ulm the Mena will kill you. In any event, you will be removed from my path in a few weeks."

I humbled myself to ask one favor before I left.

"Since I am going to death, Kapioma Sibama," I said, "I ask of your mercy one thing. I wish to see Awlo before I go."

His brow darkened.

"That is impossible," he said coldly. "Awlo does not know of your presence here and thinks you are dead. You soon will be and I have no wish to refresh her memory and reawaken her sorrows. It would turn her against me."

I did not trust myself to speak further but entered the waiting transport. My men followed me and in a few moments we rose rapidly into the air and headed away to the west.

"Where shall we land you, Courtney Sibama?" asked Neimeha, who was in command.

"Land us at the spot where you found me," I replied.

He shrugged his shoulders and spoke to the pilot. Two hours after leaving Kaulani, the transport dropped to a landing and we debarked. The ship hovered over us for a few minutes and then turned back toward the capital of Kau. Moka approached me as the Kauan ship disappeared.

"What are your plans, Courtney Sibama?" he asked.

"We will return to Kau and rescue our Sibimi. Thereafter we will do as circumstances direct."

"We are but a hundred and two," said Moka doubtfully, "and the army of Kau numbers thousands. Can we hope to win through to victory?"

"A hundred men properly armed can do wonders, Moka," I replied. "Have you forgotten the weapons which I went from Ulm to bring? They are hidden in these mountains. We will go to where they are and then make our plans. With them we will find an Alii of Ulm who has lived in Kau for years and knows their weapons. Do you think that the Kauan ship will return to watch our movements?"

"Since we are forbidden to return, I think it will."

"I hope so. If they do, I have an idea that may enable us to reach Kaulani without a fight. The first thing to do is to get proper arms."

My marching compass was one of the things which the Kauans had returned to me before they left us. My automatic pistols they had kept, although they were not familiar with their use. I laid off a course with the compass and, laden down with food and water, we started our journey toward the adjuster.

Moka had been right when he said that the Kauans would keep track of us. Late that afternoon, while our cavalcade was struggling wearily over the bare rocks, the transport which had brought us to the mountains sailed over us at a low elevation. The sight of our progress evidently satisfied them, for, after a careful survey of our column, they returned toward Kaulani. Night fell before we had covered more than half the distance which I calculated separated us from the adjuster, but I was confident that we were going in the right direction.

The night was bitterly cold and as we had nothing resembling blankets, all we could do was to huddle together and pass the night as best we could. The men of Ulm were unaccustomed to cold weather and they suffered horribly but none of them complained. The next morning we took up our march.

By noon I was confident that we had come far enough, yet none of the landscape was familiar. I halted the column and sent parties of scouts off in various directions. They were all ordered to reassemble at the central point before sundown.

It was a hard task to find one's way about the rugged country, even with a compass. I nearly got lost and the sun was setting when my party returned to camp. Two of the parties were still unaccounted for. We had no material with which to make fires and all we could do was to send up occasional shouts to guide the stragglers. One party came in about eight o'clock but morning dawned without trace of the other one. I was surprised at this, for I knew of the wonderful sense of direction and location which is the gift of all Ulmites. I made some tests and soon found that this sense was not operative in the mountains. Why, I can't explain. It just wasn't.

I held a consultation with Hama and Moka the next morning. I was sure that we were close to the adjuster and the ammunition and yet we had combed the country the day before and found nothing. I had a feeling that we were too far south and favored moving the camp, but the problem of the lost party remained to be solved. We finally decided to leave ten men under Hama at our first camp and move the rest some five miles north, keeping in touch by means of messengers. At the new camp I would send out fresh search parties. This programme we carried out, but another two days of combing the hills failed to locate the adjuster and I began to fear that the Kauans had found it and moved it. The fourth and fifth days passed in similar fashion and even my staunchest supporter, Moka, began to look dubious.

The morning of the sixth day we were about to start fresh parties out on their interminable search when a faint shout was heard from the south and we saw one of Hama's party approaching at top speed. As he came nearer, it was evident that he was laboring under great excitement.

"We have found the place, Sibama!" he gasped as he came within hearing. "Hiko's party found it the first day but the messenger they sent fell and broke a leg. It was not until today that he crawled into our camp, nearly dead from pain and thirst. He says that Hiko and two men stayed there, but he does not know where it is."

The fact that the adjuster had been found near our camp was a heartening thing and we swiftly broke camp and retraced our steps to join Hama's party. We found that Hama had sent off all his men in the direction in which Hiko had left the camp and all we could do was to wait until they found the place. We had not waited more than three hours when a man arrived and told us that he had located it. He said that they had found the cave and the boxes in it, but that there were no signs of Olua or the adjuster. I started at once with a party with food and water for Hiko's men, leaving most of the men in camp until all of Hama's men returned. They were to move camp and join me the next morning.

The report of the scout was correct. In the cave were the arm chests and the boxes of ammunition, but there was no trace of either Olua or the adjuster. I racked my brains as to what could have happened. The only explanation which seemed logical was that when he had returned to the larger plane at my orders, his adjuster got moved. In such a case he might easily have come down miles away and was earnestly seeking us. The loss of the adjuster was a blow, but we still had our arms and ammunition and everything was not lost.

It was a short task to break open the rifle chests and the ammunition boxes and I felt better when I saw my tiny force armed with modern rifles and pistols, even though none of them had the slightest idea of their use and I had grave doubts of their value against the fighting suits of the Kauans. The fact that they did not know how to use the weapons did not worry me especially, for I knew that I had eight days before the Sibimi of Kau was doomed to die and I had a plan which, if successful, would enable us to travel over the two hundred miles which separated us from Kaulani in a short time. The Kauan transport had flown over us each afternoon, evidently checking our movements and my plan was a no less daring one than attempting its capture. I blessed the fact that I had not completed my radiotelegraphic apparatus before I left the city.

My first task was to teach my men the use of the pistols and rifles. I had loaded a hundred rifles and thirty thousand rounds of ammunition on the adjuster together with a hundred pistols and ten thousand rounds of pistol ammunition. I felt that I could safely expend one hundred rounds of rifle ammunition per man and half that amount of pistol ammunition on target practise. We improvised a range and posted guards to warn us of the approach of Kauan ships. The Ulmites took to the guns as ducks take to water. In five days I felt my fire discipline was adequate and I anxiously awaited the arrival of the ship I had planned to capture.

To my horror, the ship did not appear on that day, nor the next day, nor yet on the next. Our food and water were about exhausted, for we had been allowed only a fourteen-day supply. Apparently the Kauans knew that we could not return to their country and had decided that we were afraid to face the Mena and thought it useless to keep further track of us. As the sun went down on the fourteenth day after we had left Kaulani, I was in black despair. That was the day set for the execution of the Sibimi of Kau and the thought of my princess at the mercy of Kapioma nearly drove me insane.

We could not possibly cover the two hundred miles separating us from Kaulani in less than five days of forced marching, even were we adequately supplied with food and water and unopposed. I had based all my plans on the capture of a Kauan ship. The morning of the fifteenth day found us with no water and almost no food and despair settled over the camp. We felt the urge to be moving but there was no place where we could go and nothing that we could do. We went through some rifle drill in the morning in a perfunctory manner and with the feeling that it was merely a waste of time.

In an endeavor to keep my men from brooding, I took them out on the improvised range again in the afternoon, but there was no enthusiasm. We were all suffering badly from thirst. I was about to order them back to camp when a shout from one of the lookouts whom we had posted as a routine matter, brought us to our feet. The lookout was shouting and pointing to the east. In the sudden silence which fell, I could feel rather than hear, the distant hum of propellers. Our plans had been made long ago and my men rapidly took the ambush formation I had laid out, while others, as the Kauans appeared, started a dropping fire at the distant targets.

I had counted on the curiosity of the Kauans to bring them to the ground to see what we were doing, nor was I disappointed. The ship hovered over our range for fifteen agonizing minutes before it swooped to a landing, a hundred yards from our firing point. A detachment of Kauans, wearing six-armed fighting suits, debarked and approached the firing line. I was hidden behind a rock perhaps fifty yards from the ship. The angle at which the ship landed was such that I could not see the control board through the open door, a vital necessity, if we were to capture the ship. I waited until the Kauans had passed me and blew my whistle.

A burst of fire came from the line and the Kauans staggered back under the impact of the heavy bullets at short range. The fighting suits held and none of them were injured. Green and red rays shot out from the arms of the fighting suits. Half a dozen of my men dropped helpless and the Kauans advanced slowly in a line. This was the moment for which I had been waiting. Holding my fire at ready, I raced across the ground behind the fighters. The angle at which I ran brought the control panel into view through the open door. I dropped prone and cuddled my rifle to my cheek. I had been nervous, but when the moment came to fire, I was as steady as a rock. I picked out the switch which controlled the current which fed the fighting suits. The switch sat for a moment on top of my front sight as I slowly squeezed my trigger. With a crash the rifle went off. In an instant the rays died out in midair, and with a cheer my men leaped to their feet. A volley rang out and the ground was sprinkled with dead and dying Kauans. I had effectually disabled every fighting suit in the ship.

The pilot of the ship was not napping. My men raced toward the ship, but when the nearest was still fifty yards away, the central propeller began to whir and the ship moved forward. Hiko was the nearest and he almost reached it when a blinding white flash came from its side and he dropped in his tracks. The ship moved forward with rapidly gathering momentum.

My men raced after it, but I knew the use of a rifle better than they did. I rammed a fresh shell into my piece and took careful aim. As my shot rang out, the central propeller slowed down for a moment and I hastily reloaded my gun. My second shot went wild, but the third scored a bull's-eye and the propeller slowed visibly and ran out of true. A fourth shot, the last in my magazine, stopped it entirely and the ship, with only the two wing propellers turning, sank toward the ground.

"After it!" I shouted, and my men toiled valiantly toward the dropping ship. I did not dare to risk a shot at a wing propeller lest the ship crash so badly that we would be unable to repair it. The ship touched the ground and came to a standstill. My men rushed forward with a shout of triumph. They had almost reached it when another blinding crash came from the side and two of the Ulmites crumpled in their tracks.

It was apparent that the Kauans possessed other means of offense than their fighting suits, but they seemed to be effective only at short range. I called my men back and a volley from our rifles riddled the transport. A second and third volley were poured into the cabin for safety's sake before we cautiously approached. No flash greeted us and we opened the doors to find the interior of the cabin a shambles.

The soldiers removed the dead bodies while I inspected the ship. Aside from my first shot, not a one had struck the control panel, but the central propeller was wrecked. A cursory inspection showed me that the switch which controlled the fighting suits was hopelessly wrecked, but as my men did not know how to use those terrible weapons, it was a matter of small moment. I knew that every Kauan ship carried a set of spare propellers and I soon located them and set some of my men at work removing the damaged one. The Ulmites were about as clumsy with tools as it is possible to imagine and in the end I had to do most of the work myself. The result was that the sun had nearly set before I tested the new propeller with the control panel and found that it had been properly installed. Our party embarked and I took my place at the controls. A hundred-man transport was not built for one man to fly and I had my troubles. How I cursed the luck which had made Olua miss the place when he returned to Kau in the adjuster. I would have given a great deal to have had him at my side. However, what must be done can be done and I got the ship into the air and headed for Kaulani.

For half an hour we made our way east without incident. A shout from the forward lookout apprised us of danger and Moka hastened to his side. He glanced through the telescope and informed me that three Kauan warships were approaching at high speed. I dared not leave the controls for an instant, so I hastily gave him directions for the fight which I felt was approaching and I drove forward.

The leading Kauan ship approached to within fifty yards and a string of illuminated signals broke out above her wings. I had no idea what they meant. The ship passed by, swung around in a circle and flew parallel to us about a hundred yards away with the strange signals flying. I gave the word to Moka.

A burst of rifle fire came from our ports and I had the satisfaction of seeing the Kauan ship reel wildly for a moment and then plunge headlong toward the ground. The other ships had not been fired on and they approached rapidly, one on either side. As the first one swept past us there was a blinding flash of purple light from her side. I was conscious of a feeling as though I had been struck a heavy blow, but they had miscalculated the range. While our ship reeled in the air, she righted herself and went on. The fire of our riflemen was deadly and the second ship plunged to the ground after the first.

The third ship had learned caution. It swung past us at a much greater range. When it was opposite us, a tiny spot of intense light shone for an instant and every switch on our power panel flew open. Our ship reeled and started to fall, but I dropped the flying controls and rushed to the panel. With both hands I closed the switches and then grasped the controls again and tried to right the ship. I had barely succeeded when the spot of light shone again and I had to repeat the task.

"Fire at them, Moka!" I cried. "Never mind the range!"

At my words, the burst of fire came from our ship but again the light glowed, this time before I had the ship under control. We turned nose down and fell rapidly. Apparently satisfied that they had put us out of commission, the Kauan ship turned her tail to us and sped away in the gathering darkness. I closed the switches and with all three propellers whirling at top speed, I strove desperately to right the ship. Nearer and nearer we came to the ground, but I wrenched at the controls with all my strength. Just before we struck I felt the craft respond to my efforts and slowly start to gain altitude. A dropping fire had been kept up at the flying Kauan and just as we started to climb, a shout of joy from Moka, who was at the telescope, told us that it was in trouble. At our best speed we drove it and soon it was again visible, flying slowly and in evident distress. A few well-directed shots ended the fight. We left it in ruins and resumed our course for Kaulani. Again I thanked my lucky stars that Kau did not have wireless communication.

Darkness came on rapidly, but I held my course by compass and in less than an hour the lights of Kaulani loomed before us. With all my lights blazing I headed boldly for the power house and landed on the roof. A detachment of the guard came to meet us and we opened the door and emerged. Ten of my men had donned the useless fighting suits of the dead Kauans and they led the way with me in their midst and the rest of the Ulmites trooped along after as though they were prisoners.

"What means this, Homena?" demanded the officer who had approached us.

These were the last words he spoke, for Moka had him by the throat before he could utter another. Before the menace of the lifted arms of the fighting suits, the unarmed Kauan guards surrendered and were taken into the flyer and bound and gagged. The ten men equipped with fighting suits, with me again an apparent prisoner in their midst, trooped down the stairs to the laboratory. We paused outside and I heard the buzz of a wireless transmitter. Waimua was apparently at work.

I motioned my men aside and softly opened the door. Waimua was alone in the laboratory and he looked up with a smile when I entered.

"Ah, Courtney," he said, "you are just in time. I have been hearing some signals on my receiver—"

He broke off as I covered him with my pistol.

"I want to save your life, Waimua," I said, "for you were kind to me, but to do so you must surrender to me. I am in control of the power house and my men are outside. If you make a sound, I will kill you where you stand."

"What do you mean?" he asked in amazement.

"Exactly what I say. We have returned from the Kau mountains to rescue our Sibimi and we will brook no interference. Raise your hands in token of surrender or I'll shoot."

Slowly he raised his hands as I had ordered. I turned to call my men, and he sprang. Not at me, but toward a button which was on his laboratory table. I liked Waimua, but it was his life or mine and with mine, Awlo's. My pistol spat out a message of death and the luckless scientist fell in a heap. At the sound of my weapon, my men burst in. We barred the door and waited breathlessly. Not a sound came from outside. Apparently the Kauans were enough accustomed to strange sounds from the laboratory to remain unalarmed at my shot.

Satisfied that we would not be interrupted, I took an ordinary six-armed fighting suit from the wall and donned it. I measured a distance of fourteen inches from the top of the huge testing screen, which covered one entire end of the laboratory and eleven inches from the left edge. I marked the place and stepped back. I pointed my red ray at the intersection of the two lines I had drawn and left it on full force for eight seconds. I shut it off and supplied the orange ray for twelve seconds. As I shut the orange ray off, a section of the screen opened slowly forward and there, in a recess cut behind the screen, lay the fighting suit of which Olua had told me. I drew it out and examined it.

The suit weighed less than twenty pounds, despite its thirty arms. I took off the six-armed suit which I was wearing and donned the new garment. It fit me like a glove and was not much more uncomfortable than an ordinary suit of clothes.

Olua had explained the suit to me and I found detailed instructions with it. I stepped back and spent several minutes in practising the use of the various controls against the protective screen. I did not have time to try all of them and no time to learn which control actuated which weapons, but I did locate the master control, which threw on all of the protective rays at once. Satisfied that I had learned enough, I led the way out of the laboratory.

For some unknown reason, we passed through the building and into the grounds without a challenge, although the sight of a detachment of eleven men in fighting suits in the Sibama's palace ground was enough to attract attention. We stole quietly toward the royal palace until we were under the south wing, where we knew Awlo to be confined. Moka pointed out her window to me and I gave my rifle to him and grasped a creeper which clothed the wall. It was a hard climb and I was tempted several times to return to the ground and take off the cumbersome fighting suit which I wore, but better judgment prevailed and I struggled on. At last I climbed to a point where I could look into her room. It was apparently empty and I inserted the point of my dagger and pried the window open and stepped into the room.

I found myself in a luxuriously furnished apartment, but a hasty search through the rooms proved them to be as empty as the grave. My heart fell, for I feared that Awlo had already been dragged to Kapioma's chambers. I tried the doors leading from the rooms and one of them opened at my touch. I found myself in a deserted corridor and I stole softly along it. I had almost reached an intersecting way when a slight noise behind me made me swing around. A hidden panel in the wall I had just passed was slowly opening and I stepped beside it. A Kauan Alii made his appearance and turned toward me. As he saw me, he opened his mouth to shout, but my green ray blazed forth for an instant and he stopped petrified. He had done me no harm and with my orange ray I removed the paralysis from his brain. His tongue I left helpless and before I left him I treated both his legs with a dose from my paralyzing ray. I left him helpless and went on.

I found myself in a secret passage, dimly lighted, and I stole along it for a few yards and found it ended in a stairway. I debated for a moment as to what course to pursue and then stole back to the panel. It was closed and I could not find the spring or lever which operated it. It would have been an easy matter to have burnt my way through with my heat ray, but I did not care to start a possible fire in the palace. I thought of restoring to speech the Alii who lay helpless before me, but knowing the Kauans as I did, I felt certain that his first action would be to give the alarm. Despite their cruelty and treachery, they were intensely loyal to their Sibama.

There was only one alternative. With a prayer in my heart, I returned to the stairway and proceeded down it. I went down a long flight and paused on a landing place where I could hear a murmur of voices. I touched the wall before me and found that it was no wall but a hanging. Cautiously I cut a slit with my dagger and peered through.

I was looking into the throne room from a point behind and slightly to one side of the two central thrones. The room was empty save for a small group which stood before the throne. I didn't stop to count them, for my eyes were focused on one of them and my heart gave a bound which threatened to burst my ribs. The central figure was my adored princess, Awlo of Ulm. I could hear a voice speaking from the throne which was concealed from my gaze and I recognized it as Kapioma's.

"The Sibimi's throne of Kau is empty," he said in a voice which sounded as though he were repeating an argument for the hundredth time, "and I offer you the honor of filling it. I could take you without this formality, but such is not my wish. Your blood is royal and your children would be worthy of the throne of Kau, which they would occupy some day. Will you bid me lay aside the panoply of war and don the robes of peace that I may wed you honorably?"

Awlo threw back her proud head.

"Never!" she cried. "My lord, Courtney Sibama, lives and will rescue me. I could not be your Sibimi if I wished and would not if I could."

"I tell you that Courtney is dead," protested Kapioma.

"Not until I see his corpse will I believe that and when I do, my life will end as well," she said haughtily. "Beware what you do, Kapioma Sibama, the arm of my lord is long and he knows how to avenge any indignity to which I am subjected."

"Enough of this!" cried Kapioma angrily. "I am offering you no indignity but honorable marriage and the rank of Sibimi of the greatest empire in the world. If you will not wed me willingly, you will by force. Wedlock is essential that your children may be lawfully called to the throne of Kau. Where is the Mayor of the Palace?"

A gorgeously dressed functionary stepped forward.

"You shall wed us, Wiki," said Kapioma, "and as I have won her by conquest, I will be wed in the panoply of war."

He stepped down from the dais into the range of my vision. Had it not been for his voice, I would not have known him, for he wore a fighting suit from which fully forty arms protruded. The weight must have been great for he moved slowly and as if with an effort. As he approached, the Mayor of the Palace stepped forward toward Awlo, but recoiled as though she had been a deadly snake. In her hand gleamed a jeweled dagger.

"One step nearer and I will sheath this weapon in my heart!" she cried.

The Mayor stopped but Awlo could not fight alone the weapons of Kau. A green flash came momentarily from Kapioma's suit and the dagger dropped from her paralyzed arm. She turned to run but another flash, this time of a paler green, filled the room for an instant and she stopped in her tracks. Kapioma's guttural laugh rang out as he advanced to where she stood motionless. He took her hand in his and kissed it and then placed it for a moment on top of his head. He held out his hand and the Mayor of the Palace took it respectfully and raised it toward Awlo's lips. A sharp report rang out and the Mayor staggered and fell headlong. Unfamiliar as I was with Olua's fighting suit, I preferred to use the weapon I knew. I have mentioned before that I am a good shot, especially at short range.

A sweep of my dagger opened a way for me through the tapestry and I stepped out into view. The time for ordinary weapons had passed and I dropped both pistol and dagger and placed my hands on the control buttons of my fighting suit. I swung the deadly offensive arms toward Kapioma and prepared to launch my deadly assortment of rays at him. The guards, armed with spears, were approaching from all sides.

"One step nearer and your Sibama dies!" I shouted.

The Sibama stared at me for a moment and a look of wonder came into his eyes.

"Courtney Sibama!" he cried.

I bowed my head in acknowledgement but I did not take my eyes off him. It was well that I did not. Slowly his hands sought the control buttons of his massive fighting suit.

"Stop that!" I warned sharply. "If you try to use a weapon you are a dead man."

He dropped his hand and stared fixedly at me. The situation was a stalemate. Kapioma did not dare to move and I could not pick the helpless Awlo up and leave with her. I thought of trying a blast of one of my rays at Kapioma but I was not sure just which ones his fighting suit would stop instantly. Besides, if I opened hostilities, Awlo might be killed in the blasts of rays which would fill the throne room. For a full minute we stared at one another and then Kapioma spoke.

"Courtney Sibama," he said slowly, "one of us will never leave this room alive. You are wearing a fighting suit of a type I do not recognize. I wear the most powerful suit in Kau. Which of the two will win in a conflict, neither of us knows. If we fight in the open, no one can prophesy what the result to all in this room will be."

He paused and I nodded assent to his word but did not relax my vigilance.

"We both desire the same thing—the life and person of Awlo of Ulm," he went on, "and one of us will win it. Let her be won in fair fight and to the victor she shall belong."

"What do you mean?" I asked.

"Let a fighting dome be brought and placed over us. When the signal is given, we will prove which of our fighting suits is the most powerful. To the survivor shall belong the princess."

"If I win, have I the promise that Awlo and I can leave Kau with our subjects without hindrance?" I demanded.

"You may, without hindrance from me. Further than that I cannot promise. The word of a dead Sibama does not bind his successor. However, if you win, you should be able to fight your way out of the kingdom with fighting suits."

I hesitated for a minute. If I fought him and lost, my princess was doomed. If I won, all I could hope for was the chance to battle my way out with her in my arms. If, on the other hand, I refused his terms, she might easily be sacrificed during the battle in the open, which would ensue. I quickly made up my mind.

"Bring your fighting dome," I cried.

Guards hastened out to get it. Still keeping my hands on the control buttons of my suit, I walked down the steps of the dais and took my place facing Kapioma. The dome was brought in and placed over us.

"Take your hands from your controls, Courtney Sibama," said Kapioma, "in order that we may start equally."

I dropped my hands to my side. The Sibama turned to the ring of spectators.

"Noma," he said to an Alii who stood there, "take a spear from a guard and drop it. When that spear strikes the ground, the battle will commence."

The Alii took a spear and poised it. He stood in such a position that each of us could see him equally well. He poised the spear above his head for an instant and then let it fall.

The fractions of a second that passed before that spear reached the floor seemed like days and weeks. It seemed to move with infinitesimal slowness. I stole a glance around and the scene burned itself on my brain. Kapioma stood a few feet from me with a confident smile on his yellow face, his slant black eyes gleaming fiercely. All about us stood the Alii and guards of Kau, their yellow faces alight with excitement. Like a white flower stood out the form of my beloved princess, rigid in the grasp of the rays which Kapioma had poured out on her. I looked back and saw that the spear had almost reached the floor. Another glance at Kapioma showed that he had not moved but stood with muscles tense, waiting for the signal. At least, he was a fair fighter.

The spear struck the floor and my hands flew to the control buttons of my suit. I tugged the master button of the defensive weapons in the nick of time for the red and green rays flashed out from half a dozen of the arms of Kapioma's suit. They were absorbed harmlessly in the refulgence with which I was bathed. He stepped back a moment and shifted his hands. His first attack with his simpler weapons had failed and he was prepared to use weapons which were individual to his suit.

I remembered what Olua had told me and shut off my general protective ray. I hastily tugged at my fifth, sixteenth and seventeenth buttons. A dazzling kaleidoscope of colors surrounded me and I heard a report from Kapioma's suit. His simple paralyzing and heat rays had been rendered useless.

His hand found the buttons he wished and a fresh menace threatened me. From him came a cloud of purple gas which rolled rapidly toward me. I knew the weapon to use against that and I tugged at my eleventh button. The cloud of gas was drawn rapidly into one of the arms of my suit. I pressed my twelfth button and a cloud of yellow vapor rolled toward him. As his hands sought his defensive weapons, I tugged my ninth button and the gas dissolved into a blinding flash which rushed toward him. It struck him full on the chest and drove him back with the violence of the shock. I followed up my advantage with my violet ray, but he had recovered from the momentary effects of the surprise he had received and shot out a furry spiral of red flame, which twisted in and out before him and rendered the purple ray helpless.

From another arm came alternate flashes of red and white. I pulled on a defensive weapon but it had no effect. Through my protective screens the deadly ray was eating its way. I felt as though my veins were filled with liquid fire. Frantically I tugged at button after button. Clouds of deadly gases and vivid rays of various sorts leaped from the arms of my suit but Kapioma met each attack with a weapon of his own and rendered my efforts futile. And still that deadly red and white ate into my screen. It was a matter of seconds only before the end would come.

In desperation I used my final weapon. Olua had cautioned me not to use it, except as a last resort. With a sob I tugged at my thirtieth button. As I did so, a blinding flash came from one of the arms of my suit. It struck Kapioma and coiled itself around him. Fighting against the strange power at every step, he was dragged relentlessly toward me. The red and white still glowed and my body seemed parched and dried up but I could not think of that. In another moment he would be within reach.

Despite his struggles, he was drawn closer until I could reach him with my hands. I understood why Olua had warned me against this weapon for my strength was rapidly oozing away. It took a tremendous toll of the user. Kapioma reached for other buttons but he was unable to use them. This thirtieth weapon of Olua's was nothing less than an electrical harnessing of the will of the user and while Kapioma was in its grasp, his will was a slave to mine. As I realized the nature of the strange force I was wielding, I concentrated on what I wished him to do. Slowly and reluctantly his hand sought his controls. He tugged at one and the deadly red and white which was eating into my very brain died out. I was temporarily safe.

I threw all the force of my will into the struggle and the force I exerted was magnified a thousand times by the instrument which Olua's genius had evolved. Kapioma tugged button after button, until not a ray gleamed from his suit and not a single deadly gas even oozed from it. With almost my last effort I pulled my second button and bathed him for an instant in the common green paralyzing ray carried by even the simplest fighting suits. He wavered a moment and then dropped in a heap. I shut off the terrible weapon with which I had conquered and swayed in weakness for a moment.

I thought I was going to fall, but I didn't. My eyes caught a glimpse of Awlo and it acted like a dash of cold water in my face. I braced myself up and faced the spectators.

"Remove the fighting dome!" I cried, "and make way for Courtney, Sibama of Ulm!"

The dome was hastily lifted from me. As I approached Awlo, there was a disturbance at the door. I looked up and a more welcome sight never met my eyes. In the doorway stood Moka with a half dozen Ulmites with rifles in their hands ranged behind him. Four figures in six-armed fighting suits stood beside him.

"Way!" I cried imperiously, "Way for the men of Ulm! Way ere I blast a path through your living bodies!"

There was a general scurry at my words and the space between Moka and me opened. Down the path came my loyal Ulmites. At my orders two of them handed their rifles to comrades and tenderly picked up the form of my beloved princess. Down through the ranks of the scowling Kauans we passed until the door of the palace opened before us. Guards stepped forward to bar our way, long black tubes in their hands. I hesitated only a moment. The poor fellows wore no fighting suits and it was almost murder but I did not dare to hesitate. I tugged my fourteenth button and a flash of violet flame leaped in front of me. The guards went down like tenpins, their black tubes exploding with brilliant flashes of light. As we emerged from the doorway, a distant crackle of rifle fire told us that Hama's party had left the roof and were fighting their way down through the power house. In a compact group we raced across the lawn toward the building.

We had covered about half the distance before we were opposed. I heard a shout behind us and turned and looked. Emerging from the trees at one side were a group of figures in fighting suits. We were a little closer to the power house than they were, but we were handicapped by our rifles and we had to carry Awlo. It looked as though we would arrive at the door at about the same moment. My decision was made in an instant. Warning Moka to hold straight for the door, I turned at an angle and raced to meet them.

As I approached, the newcomers stopped and rays began to flash from the arms of their fighting suits. None of the suits carried more than ten arms, so I pulled on my general protective rays and charged them. They strove to run but they were too late. Again my fourteenth button came into play and they toppled in heaps. I glanced over my shoulder and saw that Moka's party had gained the doorway.

I bounded through the door and Hama slammed it shut behind me. I was positive that there were protective rays of some sort that could be brought into action but I did not dare to look for them. Hama told me that the power house was clear of Kauans except for one room in which a few were barricaded. I knew that they would soon emerge wearing fighting suits and that more men from the palace would be using more potent weapons against us in a few minutes. With Hama and Moka at my back, I ran for the central control room. I reached it just in time.

My hand was on the switch controlling the fighting suit power when a door opened and a dozen figures wearing many-armed suits entered. I let them approach a few feet and pulled the switch just as their hands were seeking the control buttons. When I pulled that switch every fighting suit and every weapon of war in the empire of Kau became useless. It took me only a few seconds to pull the other four controlling switches and everything which depended on power in the empire was useless. The science of our enemies was at an end and the battle, if battle there was, would be fought out hand to hand in the same manner as the old battles with the Mena. The only power left in the land was a tiny auxiliary generator which fed the lights in the power house itself. As we saw in the morning, my action in pulling the switches came none too soon. Two huge Kauan warships had crashed in ruins not a hundred yards from the building. Had I been a little slower, they would have landed on the roof and we would have been caught between two fires.

I left Awlo in the laboratory and hastened out to look after our defense. Although crippled by the loss of power, the Kauans were not altogether helpless. They were present in tremendous numbers and they still had a quantity of the black tubes which I had noticed in the hands of the guards at the palace gates. These tubes were not dependent on power for their discharge, although once fired, they could not be reloaded while the generators were shut down. They carried a large charge of static electricity and at short range they were very deadly.

Armed with the tubes and with spears, the Kauans made a determined assault on our fortress. The attack was doomed to failure from the first. The flash tubes were not dangerous at ranges of over fifty yards and we mowed down the attackers with our deadly rifle fire. The attack waned after a few minutes and I returned to the laboratory.

Awlo lay on a table, cold and rigid. There was a complete absence of respiration and I could not detect the slightest flicker of a pulse. I would have unhesitatingly pronounced her dead, had I not seen what had happened to her. I knew that Kapioma would never have fought for the possession of a dead body and I was confident that there was some method of reviving her, could I only find it. I ordered Moka to turn on the switch which controlled the fighting suit I had worn. He did so and I bathed her in a refulgence of the orange anti-paralysis ray. It had not the slightest effect. For an hour I experimented with various rays and combinations of them without result. I did not dare to use most of the weapons in Olua's fighting suit for I was not aware of all of their properties and I might easily do more harm than good.

As I studied her prostrate figure, I was alarmed by a crash at the main door of the house. I started down to investigate, but a messenger from Hama met me before I got there.

"A Kauan!" the man gasped, "a Kauan in a fighting suit has broken in the door and has killed a dozen of our men!"

The explanation rushed to my mind. When I had connected up the generator which had actuated my fighting suit, I had also supplied power to Kapioma's, which worked on the same wavelength. I hurried to the control room and pulled off the switch. A crackle of rifle fire from below told me that my men were engaged. I rushed down the steps to take charge, but I was no longer needed. When the fighting suit was rendered helpless, our rifles came into their own and they made short work of the Kauans, who had followed their leader in through the wrecked door.

In an hour the door was repaired and we were again in a position to bid defiance to the armies of Kau, but I learned with regret that the fleeing Kauans had carried off the body of their leader and so, of course, his fighting suit. If we had it, two of us could have walked unopposed throughout Kaulani. As it was, I did not dare to again turn on any of the generators which would arm our enemies. Since I had no idea of what to do for Awlo, even had I had plenty of power, it did not seem to matter much.

In point of fact, our situation had many elements devoid of cheer in it. To be sure we were comparatively safe in the power house, but we had no way of getting out. We had a hundred-man flyer at our service, but if we turned on power to run it, we mobilized every warship in Kau. We had plenty of powerful fighting suits, but there were more powerful ones in the hands of some of the Alii of Kau and arming our suits meant arming theirs. As far as I could figure out, in capturing the power house, I had put myself in the classic position of the man who had caught the bear by the tail; I needed a lot of help to hang on and a darned sight more help to let go.

I went back to the laboratory and studied the rigid figure of Awlo, but no new suggestion came to me and I lay down for a few minutes of rest, hoping that time would solve the problem. In any event, I felt sure that we could hold the power house indefinitely. In thinking this, however, I had underestimated the power and resourcefulness of the Alii of Kau, as the morning showed.

All night we heard the sounds of men working and saw faint lights flickering back and forth across the lawn. We tried them with a shot occasionally but we had no ammunition to waste and I ordered the men to hold their fire. When day broke, we saw on the lawn between the palace and the power house, an enormous machine made of metal. As we watched, it moved slowly forward toward the power house. I had forgotten that the Alii and even the soldiers and commoners of Kau were familiar with electricity in all of its forms. The obvious thing had occurred to them. Since their regular source of power had been shut off, they had collected or constructed batteries and were driving this tank, for that is what it looked like, toward us with direct current. From the moving mass of metal, heavy cables trailed back toward the palace.

I took a rifle and fired at that cable, directing my best shots to do the same. Despite the fire we poured in, the machine continued to advance until it was only a few yards from the building. From its side a bolt of what looked like lightning came and the power house door was again splintered and driven from its hinges. The machine moved forward for a few feet and stopped. No fresh bolts came from it and it was apparently helpless. At last a lucky shot had severed their connection with the source of power. We were temporarily saved.

As no fresh attack seemed imminent, I left Moka in charge of the defense and returned to the laboratory. It had occurred to me that direct current might have some effect on Awlo.

As I entered the laboratory, a familiar sound struck my ear. I paused and looked around but I could not locate the source. It was an intermittent buzzing and crackling and as I listened, it began to form itself into letters and words in my mind. "$-.-. $ $ --- $ $ ...- $ $.-. $ $ --. . -.--,$" I heard and then "$-.-. $ $ --- $ $ ...- .-. -.. . . -.-- .. -... .---.-$" "COURTNEY, COURTNEY SIBAMA." There was only one person in the world who would be calling me by wireless and calling me by that title. I jumped for the radio set which had stood unheeded on the laboratory table since Waimua's death. As I clamped the headphones on my ear, the message came through plainly and distinctly. It was a matter of seconds only until I had the transmitter hooked up and ready to send. Luckily both sender and receiver drew their power from the auxiliary generator which normally supplied only the lights in the power house. I pounded my key rapidly.

"Olua," I called. "Olua, can you hear me?"

"Yes, Courtney Sibama," came the reply.

"Where are you?" I tapped out.

"At the cave, where we parted. The arms are gone. Did you return for them or did the Kauans get them?"

"I have the arms here."

"Where is here?"

"At the power house in Kaulani. I'll tell you the situation."

"All right, but send a little slower."

As briefly as possible I told him the events which had happened and the situation in which we were. I told him of the deadlock and that we were afraid to turn on any power. Last I told him of the attack launched by battery driven appliances that morning.

"How long can you hold out?" he asked.

As the message came in, a crash from below, followed by a burst of rifle fire, told me that a fresh attack had been launched. I told Olua of this fact.

"Battery apparatus won't do much harm," he answered. "If you can hold out for a few hours, I'll be with you and help you."

"How can you get here?" I asked, "there is no power being broadcast."

"I'll get there," he replied. "Look for me in three hours or less."

"Wait," I demanded. "I want one bit of information."

In a few words I described the condition of Awlo.

"Was it a light green ray with yellow flecks?" he asked.

"Yes."

"Use button twenty-eight on my suit for two seconds. Goodbye. I'll be with you soon."

Without regard to the risk I was running, I dashed to the control room and threw on the switch which actuated Olua's fighting suit. Back in the laboratory, I donned the garment and with trembling hands pulled button twenty-eight. Nothing happened for two seconds and then Awlo sat up. With a shout of joy I released the button and started for her. She gave a cry of terror and strove to run. I stopped aghast at her reception of me, until I remembered the fighting suit which I wore. She took me for a Kauan.

"Awlo!" I cried as I threw back my helmet. "It is Courtney, your Courtney! Don't you know me?"

She looked at me in wonder and then with a sob of utter thankfulness threw herself into my arms. As I clasped her, there came an interruption. Moka dashed into the room.

"Sibama!" he cried. "Come quickly or we are lost. The Kauans are winning their way in."

So excited was he that he failed to notice Awlo. As I released her, his jaw dropped and he fell on one knee.

"Sibimi!" he cried and the worship in his voice made me realize anew the depth of affection which these tiny men had for their rulers. I gave him no further time.

"Come, Moka," I cried, as I pulled my helmet back into place, "we must go to the rescue."

I led the way down the stairs to the doorway. A number of Kauans equipped with fighting suits from which long leads trailed back to the palace, had crossed the lawn and forced their way through the shattered door. Bullets had no effect on them and my men went down like tenpins before the deadly rays which poured from them. Their feeble fighting suits, however, were no match for the one I wore and in three minutes after I arrived, not a live Kauan remained in the power house. My violet ray disposed of them. As the last one fell, a figure wearing Kapioma's forty-armed suit came from the palace and lumbered slowly across the lawn. Before he was close enough to do any damage I had the power shut off and he fell before a well aimed bullet from Hama's rifle. The danger was again temporarily averted and I turned my attention to my men. The improvised suits did not have enough power to kill, or else it was not a killing ray that was used, for they were merely stunned and a few minutes of care brought them to, as well as ever.

Leaving Moka in command, I hurried back to the laboratory. Awlo threw herself into my arms again as I entered. I embraced her fervently and then turned to the key of my wireless. Not an answering signal could I get. I gave up at last and devoted my attention to Awlo. Her story was soon told.

The adjuster must have been moved slightly without our knowledge when Lamu had stolen it and fled with her, for they landed in Kau, not far from Kaulani. Lamu had attempted to force his attentions on her and had threatened her with death if she did not substantiate his story of my treachery. When I heard this, I gritted my teeth and wished that I had killed Lamu more slowly and painfully.

They attempted to make their way to Ulm but they were seen and taken prisoners. They were taken to Halekala, one of the cities of Kau, several hundred miles from the capital. There they were held as prisoners for several months. Word of their presence was finally brought to Kaulani and Kapioma had ordered them sent to him. He had at once made Lamu a prisoner and confined him with the survivors of Ulm who had been meanwhile captured and brought to the city. Awlo he treated at first as an honored guest, but during the last few months he had tried unavailingly to win her consent to their union. The final scene of his attempt was the one which I had interrupted in the throne room.

She had consistently refused to give him any cause for hope, for she assured me that she never would believe that I was dead but always expected me to rescue her. Until I entered the throne room she had no idea that I had been in Kaulani.

An hour later the Kauans attacked in earnest. Wearing their improvised direct current fighting suits they came in force and repaired the broken cable which led to their machine. I went down in my fighting suit to rout them, but I did not dare to turn the power on. One of them was wearing Kapioma's suit and any attempt to render mine active would have activated his. He kept behind a screen of men and was effectually protected from our rifles.

Slowly the huge tank-like machine moved forward. We poured a storm of rifle and pistol bullets into it but they had no effect. Like the heroes they were, the loyal Ulmites threw themselves before it and strove to stop it with their bodies, only to fall before the deadly rays which it poured out. Half of my men were down and the tank was slowly but inexorably approaching the open doorway. At intervals blinding flashes of white light came from it and whatever stood in their path, be it man, wood or stone, was shattered to fragments. On it came despite all our efforts. I was about to order the power turned on and make a last desperate attempt to stop it with Olua's fighting suit, despite the one I would have opposing me, when an unfamiliar sound stopped the fighting for a moment. There was a silence and I heard a sound I had never expected to hear again, the drone of an airplane motor. The Kauans looked up and gave vent to cries of surprise. Half of them raced back toward the hangars where their war machines were kept.

Louder and louder became the sound and over the palace grounds swooped the familiar form of a tri-motored Fokker. I gave a shout of joy when I saw it and another one of exultation when I realized who the pilot must be. I suspected what Olua was up to and I called my men under shelter.

The Fokker swooped down low over the palace grounds and then up. A second time it swooped, and as it passed, a few hundred feet above our heads, something was thrown from the cockpit. It was a long black object and it fell slowly toward the ground. Square on the Kauan machine it landed. There was a deafening crash and a burst of smoke. Fragments of the machine flew in all directions. The Kauans who remained on their feet fled with cries of alarm.

Again the Fokker swept up and back over the palace. Another black cylinder fell and a huge hole was torn in one corner of Kapioma's stately residence. Apparently satisfied with the damage he had done, the pilot swung down with idling motor. I raced to the roof to meet him. The Fokker came down and made a perfect landing, although it would have rolled off the roof had not several of my men been there to check it. Removing his flying goggles, Olua climbed out and knelt at my feet.

"You came just in time, Olua Alii," I said as I raised him to his feet. "I feared that your adjuster had been moved and that you could not find your way back."

"I had no trouble, Courtney Sibama," he replied. "I exceeded your orders somewhat but I felt certain that you would approve what I did. I got to the larger plane all right and learned to fly your ship with no trouble but it took me a long time to get the explosives you wanted. I could make myself understood only with difficulty and when they understood, they would not give me what I wanted, although I offered them the metal you told me to use. At last I found one who knew you in the place they call Beatty and he got them for me. Then I returned as quickly as I could."

"And just in time," I repeated, "and you are more than welcome. I was about at the end of my resources, but with your knowledge of Kauan fighting methods, the battle will be on a more even footing now."

Olua inquired as to the details of the fight and expressed himself as surprised at the stubborn resistance we had made. As a member of the Council of Lords, he requested a private interview with Moka and Hama, a favor which I promptly granted. In an hour the three of them entered the laboratory where I was talking to Awlo and requested permission to speak.

"Speak on," I said, puzzled at their grave faces.

"It is the law of Ulm," said Moka gravely, "that when dire peril threatens the persons of the Sibama or the Sibimi, the word of the Council of Lords shall rule, if it will promise safety. Is that not so, my lord?"

"It is," I replied.

"Grave danger now threatens you and Awlo Sibimi, my lord. It is the word of the Council of Lords that you take the flying ship in which Olua Alii arrived and take the Sibimi to a place of safety."

"I'll do nothing of the sort," I said shortly.

"You must, Courtney Sibama," said Moka earnestly. "All of us have risked our lives and Olua Alii has returned from a place of safety to one of peril to assure the safety of our rulers. Unless you avail yourself of this chance, the sacrifice of those who have already died for you will be in vain. For countless generations my fathers have served the royal family of Ulm and it is just and fitting that the last member of my family should die that the royal family of Ulm should live on. Besides, the ammunition is running short."

This last was serious news. I inquired and found that we had less than sixty rounds of rifle cartridges per man left and another serious attack would settle matters. Olua gave another argument.

"You do not know the power of Kau," he said. "They have tried to conquer you quickly so far but now I think they will settle down to do it slowly. It is only a matter of time until they will construct a new power house or at least a power unit sufficient to power their fighting suits and when they do, the battle is over. I can make suits for our men but they would be outnumbered by a thousand to one. No, Courtney Sibama, what Moka says is true. You and our Sibimi must fly to safety. For this reason, I brought you your ship."

Thus reenforced, Moka returned to the attack.

"Ame has not yet fallen to the Mena," he said, "and there you and the Sibimi will find refuge and can build up again the empire of Ulm. We here are few and worthless, but the hopes of a mighty people are bound up in you. It may even be that when the Mena are defeated that you can lead a rescue party here for us."

"Wait a minute," I cried. His voice gave me an idea. I had forgotten the possibilities of my electronic vibration adjuster. Could I win my way to that, I could make my Fokker large enough to carry the entire population of Ulm, Ame and Kaulani. As the possibilities of the plan became clear, I gave a shout of joy.

"We will go," I exclaimed. "We will go, but we will return and carry you all to Ame."

In a few words I outlined my plan and Moka, Hama and Olua enthusiastically agreed to it. I don't think that any of the three expected me to succeed but the fact that Awlo and I would be safe was the thing that was uppermost in their loyal minds. In a few minutes we were on the roof and I was examining the Fokker prior to taking off. Satisfied with my inspection, Awlo and I went the rounds of our subjects to say farewell. Our plan had been told to them and man after man, the brave fellows thrust forward their gun butts for me to touch and knelt at Awlo's feet. To each of them we gave a hearty hand clasp and then, with only the three Alii in attendance, we ascended to the roof to take our departure. At the last moment I suggested that Olua accompany me to help me with the adjuster but he objected on the grounds that his knowledge would be needed to ward off the next attack. Moka dropped on one knee with the tears suspiciously near overflowing in his blue eyes.

"Farewell, my lord; farewell, my lady," he said. "It is the best end to die bravely for those we love."

"Die, nothing!" I exclaimed. "I'll be back here in five hours at the outside to take you all to Ame and safety."

"If it be so written," he replied, "but if not, remember ever, my friends, that Ulm was loyal to the last."

Awlo was sobbing openly and the tears were coming into my own eyes, so I brusquely put my princess into the plane and took the controls. Olua spun the propeller and the little craft soared into the air and at her best speed flew to the west toward the Kau mountains.

In two hours we were over the mountains and I was searching for my adjuster. At last I saw it and on a long slope we glided down toward it. We were within a hundred yards of the ground when the sun suddenly darkened and a terrific gust of wind turned the ship completely over. I strove to right it, but we were too close to the ground and in the semi-darkness, we crashed. I staggered to my feet and found that neither of us had been more than badly shaken by the fall.

As we climbed free from the wreck, the wind nearly carried us from the ground while crashes which shook the earth came from all around us. The sun was still partially obscured and I looked up and saw a marvel. Through the air were flying rocks the size of mountains, some of them apparently miles in diameter. They were flying toward the east and I realized that some of them must be falling on or near Kaulani.

"The kahumas! The giants!" cried Awlo.

"Kahumas, nothing!" I replied. "I don't know what it is, but it is no witchcraft."

As I spoke, another blast of wind came and again the sun was darkened.

When it cleared, more of the huge masses of rock were flying through the air. One boulder, which must have weighed a million tons, fell not over two miles from us.

"Quick, Awlo!" I gasped. "Come with me!"

I grasped her hand and we raced for the adjuster. The only defence against such masses of rock was to increase our size until they were small in comparison to our bulk. We entered the machine and I turned the speed control to maximum, at the same time setting an automatic stop I had put on my new model, which would halt our increase when I arrived at my normal six feet. My hand reached for the increasing switch when a fresh cloud of rock masses came hurtling through the air, this time falling to the west of us. One of them struck the mountain above us and started a slide. I looked up and saw thousands of tons of rock rushing madly toward us. Awlo gave a cry of despair and fear but before they reached us, my hand closed on the switch and I pulled downward with all my strength.

I stepped from the adjuster and faced with clenched fists a grizzled old prospector, who lay on the ground where he had been thrown by the adjuster, as it had grown almost instantaneously to its original size.

"What do you mean by digging here and killing my friends?" I demanded hotly. "This is private property."

"Taint so on the map," he retorted as he rose. "It's a public domain and I reckon a man can prospect where he pleases. Where in hell did you come from?"

Without bothering to answer him, I hastily pulled the adjuster to one side. Under where it stood was piled dirt that that wretched fool had thrown and the weight of the adjuster had packed it smooth. Ulm, Ame, Kau; all were gone; buried under what was to them miles on miles of rock.

"Where did you come from?" demanded the prospector again as he dusted off his knees. "You weren't here a minute ago!"

"I came from a better land than you'll ever see," I replied grimly. "Hand me your shovel for a moment."

I took his tool and reached in and changed the speed of the adjuster to slow and closed the reducing switch. Sadly I watched it as it shrunk down to nothing and vanished from our sight. When it disappeared, I turned to Awlo, ignoring for the moment the ancient prospector who had watched the proceedings with dropping jaw and eyes as big as saucers.

"Farewell, Awlo, Sibimi of Ulm," I said solemnly. "My dear, you have lost forever your royal title but you have gained another fully as honorable, if it is slightly less exclusive."

"What do you mean, Courtney?" she asked.

"I mean that through the action of God and this ignorant agent of his, the Empire of Ulm had ceased to exist. You have ceased to be Awlo, Sibimi of Ulm, and will henceforth have to content yourself with being Mrs. Courtney Edwards, citizen of the United States of America."

When I reread "Submicroscopic" and "Awlo of Ulm," I was made very uneasy by the touches of racism it contained. The thought crossed my mind that I ought to try to edit them out, but, you know, I can't do that. Once I started tampering with stories, where would I stop?

The trouble is that racial stereotypes, unfavorable to everyone but white men of northwest European extraction, were completely accepted and, indeed, scarcely noted in those days of only forty years ago (except perhaps by members of the groups victimized thereby).

I'm sure the readers of that day were not particularly disturbed by the fact that the brave and chivalrous people of Ulm were blond, white people; and that so was the Earthman hero. (That hero is rich, athletic, and the kind of square-shooter who longs to kill ants for sport, and who does kill an inoffensive deer the instant he sees it, even though he is not hungry at the time and has no intention of eating it.) The one member of the Ulm group who is villainous is, of course, swarthy in complexion.

The chief villains in "Submicroscopic," however, are the Mena, who are black, brutal, disgusting, and cannibalistic. In "Awlo of Ulm" the villains are the men of Kau, who are intelligent and scientifically advanced, but who are yellow in color and very, very cruel. This picture of the savage Black (given in almost every adventure story dealing with the far corners of the world, from *Robinson Crusoe* on) and the cruel Oriental (remember Fu Manchu and Ming the Merciless) was drummed into young heads until it became second nature.

Indeed, when my storytelling friend of 1928 told his tales of derring-do, the band of heroes he invented included both a Black and an Oriental, each with a full and insulting list of stereotypical characteristics. Neither he nor I knew there was anything wrong in that.

That we have come as far as we have in forty years is hopeful, though I believe it is more through the fact that Hitler's excesses made racism poisonous to any humane individual than through our own virtue. That we have much farther to go even now is incontestable.

The stories also include naïvetés of drama characteristic of the adventure stories of the day. There is the love at first sight, the princess who accepts a strange adventurer as her husband, and who threatens, "One step nearer and I will sheath this weapon in my heart!" (I had to read that line twice to make sure it was there.)

There are also the naïvetés of science that assume that slowing atomic and subatomic movement reduces size (it actually cools an object) or that mass automatically increases and decreases with size, or that the living creatures of the submicroscopic world would be of the same species as ourselves and would speak a kind of Hawaiian (which the hero fortunately understands).

But never mind. The action is rapid and violent; the hero is utterly heroic, the heroine utterly beautiful, the various villains utterly despicable. Everything breathed a kind of knightly chivalry, and at the time I asked no more.

"Submicroscopic" and "Awlo of Ulm" did not directly affect my own writing. I have never been able to throw myself into the kind of tale in which virtue just happens to have stronger muscles, readier fists, and better weapons.

Two things lingered, though. One was the seductive vision of a world in a grain of dust (something handled with much superior force in "He Who Shrank," which will appear later in the book). The notion is an old one, but it seemed to gain scientific backing in 1910, when the atom was briefly pictured as an ultramicroscopic Solar System.

Science quickly abandoned the picture as impossibly simplistic, but it caught on with science fiction writers. I never used it, because by the time I became a writer I had too good a grounding in the physical sciences to make me comfortable with the notion.

However, in 1965, when I was asked to do a novelization of a motion picture that had already been made, I found myself brought face to face with a similar notion. The picture was *Fantastic Voyage*, and it dealt with the miniaturization of human beings to the size of bacteria and with their adventures in a human blood stream. It was not the type of situation I would have chosen to use of my own accord, but since it was handed me, the dim memory of "Submicroscopic" helped persuade me to accept the task.

The other aspect of the stories that particularly impressed me was the duel with the rays in "Awlo of Ulm." The ray gun was a staple of science fiction (and came true, after a fashion, with the laser). That and the disintegrator gun were the two great hand weapons of the future. No one, however, had gone as all out as had Meek in "Awlo of Ulm."

I don't think I ever actually used ray guns myself in my stories, but the "neuronic whip" in my book *Pebble in the Sky* is a definite reminiscence of the weapons of "Awlo of Ulm."

It was not long after "Awlo of Ulm" that I read "Tetrahedra of Space," in the November 1931 issue of *Wonder Stories*, and was nearly as impressed. That was an important issue to me anyway, for after twelve months of experiment with pulp size, *Wonder Stories* went back to the large size with that issue, to my great relief.

TETRAHEDRA OF SPACE

by P. Schuyler Miller

A moon of mottled silver swam in the star-flecked sky, pouring its flood of pale light over the sea of blue-green vegetation that swelled up and up in a mighty, slow wave to break in the foaming crest of the Andes. The shadow of the plane raced far below, dipping into the troughs, breasting the summits of that vast, unbroken sea of emerald stretching on and on beyond reach of vision.

And the stars—blinking Mira nearly overhead, a great Fomalhaut blazing over the far off mountains, and to the south a host of exotic strangers, burning with a fire that we of the north seldom know—clustered like great, glowing fireflies around the invisible Pole. But I paid little heed to moon and stars and silvered jungle, for night had caught me unawares, and it is no simple matter to lay down supplies in a little clearing, marked only by a flickering camp-fire, lost somewhere among the jungles of Brazil.

Or was it Brazil? Here three great states mingled in an upland of forest and mountain and grassy valley—Peru, Bolivia, Brazil. Here ancient races had made their home, raised their massive temples in the little valleys, wrested a fortune from the mountains, given their lives to the jungles—a people more ancient by far than those others beyond the ranges whom the Incas conquered. Here none had come before to study, yet now, somewhere in the gloom beneath me, was a little oval valley hung midway between crag and forest, and there would be the tents and fires of scientists, men of my own world.

I must swoop and circle and loose my load, then soar off into the silver night like some great moth spurning the flame, out into the world of the moon and the jungles, back to the government that had sent me, to plunge once more into the hum-drum routine of government flight, the moon and the silvered jungle forgotten and forever gone.

But there came no glimmer of flame in the darkness, no flicker of white tents in the moonlight. Along the outflung cross of the plane swam the unbroken sea of green, dark and boding against its wan beauty. It takes little error of judgment to miss a tiny clearing in the dark. So, as the western ranges crept out of their alignment, I swooped and soared, and was roaring back, higher now, over the silent moon-lit forests.

But one gap had I seen in the jungle—a harsh, black scar seared by some great fire from the bowels of the planet, ugly and grim in the soft beauty of the night. Again it slipped beneath, and as the shadow of the plane vanished against its harsh blackness it seemed to me that there came a scurry of furtive motion, an instant's flicker of shadow against its deeper gloom. I half checked the course of the plane, to wheel and search it closer, then of a sudden the air about me blazed with a dull crimson fire that burned into my body with a numbing fury of unleashed energy, the drone of the engines gasped and died, and we were spinning headlong toward the silver sea beneath!

As it had come, the tingling paralysis passed, and I flattened out the mad dive of the crippled plane, cut the ignition, and dived over the side. As in a dream I felt the jerk of the parachute, saw the deserted plane, like a huge, wounded bat of the jungles, swoop and check and swoop again in a long flat dive that broke and pancaked into the upper reaches of the forest. Then the heavy pendulum of my body alone beat out the dull seconds as I swung and twisted beneath the silken hemisphere of the 'chute. And then the leafy boughs, no longer silver but like hungry, clutching talons of black horror, swept up and seized me. I crashed through a tangle of vine and brittle bough into a hot, sweet-scented darkness where little hidden things scurried away into the night and the silence.

The rain-forest is like a mighty roof stretched over the valleys of tropical America. Interlacing branches blot out the sun from a world of damp and rotting dark, where great mottled serpents writhe among tangled branches and greater vines strangle the life out of giants of the forest in the endless battle for light. And there are little, venomous things of the dark ways—savage two-inch ants with fire in their bite, tiny snakelets whose particolored beauty masks grim death—creatures of the upper reaches and of the glorious world above the tree-tops. With the sunrise, a blaze of life and flaming color breaks over the roof of the jungle—flame of orchid and of macaw, and of the great, gaudy butterflies of this upper world. Beneath, there comes but a brightening of the green gloom to a wan half-light in which dim horrors seem to lurk and creep and watch, and giant lianas twist and climb up and ever up to the living light. And lowest of all is death and damp decay—the dull, sodden carpet of mold and rotting vegetation where fat white grubs burrow in blind fear and huge centipedes scurry underfoot.

The sun was an hour gone when I fell, but it was not until its second

coming when I managed to writhe and slip through the tangle as if I too
were of the jungle, moving toward the spot where my memory placed that
blasted clearing, and the light. And with the deepening of the gloom in
the upper branches, I came upon it, quite by accident, from above.

It was a little valley, perhaps a mile long and two thirds as wide, lying
in an oval of glittering jet against the side of the mountain. Here the
Andes were beginning their swift climb up from the jungles to the snows,
and beneath me fifty-foot cliffs of sheer, black rock dropped to the valley
floor.

I have spoken of it as blasted, seared into the living heart of the jungle.
It was all of that, and more! There was a gentleness in its rocky slopes
that spoke of centuries of hungry plant-life, prying and tearing at jagged
ledges, crumbling giant boulders, dying, and laying down a soft, rich
blanket of humus over the harsh under-rock, forming a little garden-
spot of life and light in the dark heart of the forest.

Then came fire—an awful, scourging blast of fierce heat that even
Man's Hell cannot equal! It blasted that little valley, seared its verdant
beauty horribly, crumbling blossoms and long grasses into dead white ash,
stripping the rich soil of past ages from its sleeping rocks, fusing those
rocks into a harsh, glittering slag of seared, burnt black, cold and dead
and damned! The sheer cliffs of its sides, once draped with a delicate trac-
ery of flowered tendrils, had cloven away under the terrible heat, split off
in huge slabs of the living rock that had toppled into the holocaust beneath
and died with the valley.

The few thin shrubs that screened me at their summit showed blackened, blistered leaves and twigs, though here the heat had been least. As
no other spot on Earth that little upland valley was awfully, terribly dead,
yet at its center something moved!

Eagerly, fearfully, I peered through the gathering dusk. Full and
golden, the moon was rising over the forest, throwing new shadows across
the valley floor, brightening new corners, revealing new motion. And as
its smoky orange cleared to white gold and waned to limpid silver, that
glorious light seemed to soften the harsh jet of the valley. It wakened a
lustrous opalescence in the two great spheres that nestled like mighty
twin pearls against the dark rock, to create beings of the rock and of the
shadow, gliding wraithlike among the shattered boulders!

Painfully I crept through the dense growth of the brink, nearer to those
great spheres and their dreadful cargo. Within me my brain whirled and
throbbed, my throat froze against the cry of shocked incredulity that
rushed to my lips, cold, clammy sweat oozed from gaping pores! It was
beyond all reason—all possibility! And yet—it *was!* Now I could see them
clearly, rank on rank of them in orderly file, some hundred of them,

strewn in great concentric rings about the softly glowing spheres—harsh as the black rock itself, hard, and glittering, and angular—a man's height and more from summit to base—great, glittering tetrahedra—*tetrahedra of terror!*

They were tetrahedra, and they were alive—living even as you and I! They stirred restlessly in their great circles, uneasy in the dim light. Here and there little groups formed, and sometimes they clicked together in still other monstrous geometric shapes, yet always they moved with an uncanny stillness, darting with utter sureness among the scattered rocks. And now from the nearer of the twin spheres came another of their kind, yet twice their size, the pearly walls opening and closing as by thought-magic for his passing! He swept forward a little, into the full light of the moon, and the rings followed him, centered about him, until the spheres lay beyond the outermost and the giant tetrahedron faced alone the hosts of his lesser fellows!

Then came their speech—of all things the most mind-wracking! I felt it deep within my brain, before I sensed it externally, a dull, heavy rhythm of insistent throbbing, beating at my temples and throwing up a dull red haze before my staring eyes!

And then I knew it was no fancy—that the great things of the blasted valley were indeed speaking, chanting, in low, vibrant monotone that beat physically upon me in long, slow waves of the air! You have heard those deepest notes of a great organ, when the windows tremble, even the walls, the building itself vibrate in resonance, beat and beat and beat to its rhythm until you feel it throbbing against your skull, pulsing in your mind in a vast, relentless sea of thundrous sound!

Such was the speech of the tetrahedra, only deeper still beneath the threshold of sound—so deep that each tiny nerve of the skin sensed its monotonous pressure and shouted it to a reeling brain—so deep that it seemed like a great surf of more-than-sound thundering dismally against desolate, rocky shores!

For it was without inflection—only the dull, dead beat and beat and beat, mounting throb on throb in my pulsing brain, and bringing madness in its wake! I think now that it was a sort of chant, the concerted cry of all the scores of tetrahedra, dinning savagely, angrily at their giant leader in a dismal plaint of discontent and unease! I think they were restless, aware of unfulfilled promises and purposes, anxious to make sure their mission, or to be gone. I think that the seed of tetrahedral mutiny was sown among them, and that as angry convicts will drum at their prison bars and scream in monotone, even so these things of another world, another life-stuff, drummed their grievances at their mighty leader!

For soon I sensed a deeper, stronger voice beating against the din, drowning it out, thundering command and reproof, shouting down the mob until its lesser drumming sank to a mutter and ceased. But the voice of the giant tetrahedron rang on, inflected now as our own voices, rising and falling in angry speech and command, pouring out burning sarcasm, perhaps, cowing them with its great insistence!

Like all great leaders, his followers were as children to him, and the hard, harsh beat of sound swept off into a soothing, cajoling murmur of whispering ripples, tapping ever so lightly against the packed sand of some distant tropic beach, almost sibilant, if such a sound can be so, yet none the less dominant and definite in its message. And it sank to a far, hinting rumble and vanished.

For a long instant they lay quiet, like graven things of the stone itself, then through the circles, like a spreading wave, rose a thrill of slow motion, quickening, livening, until all were astir! The ranks parted, the giant tetrahedron swept swiftly over the valley floor to the two great spheres, his angular hordes flowing in swift, soft motion in his wake! Again, with that speed and silent mystery of thought, the spheres gaped open and the ranks of the tetrahedra were swallowed up within! Alone, the twin pearls of fire-flecked opalescence nestled among the black rocks—great orbs of soft light, glowing with the magic of the full moon.

For a long moment I lay there under the bushes at the cliff's edge, staring out over the valley, stunned by the weird unreality of the thing I had seen. Then, out of the dark behind me, came a hand, gripping my shoulder in a vise of iron! Mad with sudden terror I twisted free, struck blindly at the thing that had seized me, a thing that fastened with the grip of a Hercules upon my flailing arms, pinioned them to my sides—a thing that spoke, its words a hoarse mutter that barely penetrated the gloom!

"For God's sake, man, be still! Do you want *them* to hear?"

It was a man—a human like myself. My frozen tongue stammered reply.

"Who are you? What are those things out there? What Hell of Earth did they spring from?"

"None of Earth, you may rest sure!" came the grim answer. "But we will tell you all that later. We must get clear of this place! I am Marston of the Museum expedition—the biologist. I suppose you are the aviator—Valdez saw them burn you down last night. Follow me."

"Yes, I'm Hawkins. The plane is somewhere over there, if it didn't burn, with all your supplies in it. I was held up crossing the mountains. But tell me, first—those things, there—are they *alive?*"

"You've wondered that? I suppose anyone would. The Indians make them gods of a kind—realize they're beyond all experience and tradition. But I'm a biologist. I have had some experience in strange forms of life. They are as much alive as we—perhaps even more than we. After all, if life is energy, why should it not rest where it will? Need we—soft, puny things of carbon and water and a few unstable elements—be the only things to harbor life? But this is no place to moralize—come on!"

He vanished into the dark, and I followed, plunging blindly after the sound of his crashing progress, away from the seared valley and the tetrahedra, to safety of a sort in the sombre depths of the rain-forest.

They crouched beside a tiny fire of bark and twigs, like men of old Cro-Magnon, fifty thousand years ago—two gaunt skeletons hung and swathed with soiled rags, brooding over their pitiful little flame. With the crackle of our approach they sprang at bay—two hunted things of the jungle—then relaxed as we came into the firelight.

I will always remember them as I saw them then—Hornby, the Museum archaeologist, tall, grey-haired, his haggard face seamed with deep wrinkles of sleeplessness and fear and puzzled wonderment. Valdez, his colleague of the government that had sent me, short, dark, his Portuguese blood blended with that of the squat tribes of the interior, teeth gleaming in a snarl like that of some great jungle cat, cornered, crazed, and dangerous! He seemed plumper than the others, and I felt that he could and would care for himself very well if need be.

Now, too, I saw my guide for the first time as something more than a black hulk in blackness. Marston, the biologist, looked like an old-time blacksmith, a massive man of bone and muscle, with keen grey eyes under heavy brows and the beginnings of a mighty beard. A Hercules, I have said—more like an Atlas, upholding the burden of this little wilderness world from the shoulders of one who could not and one who would not share it! Muscles that had had scant padding of reserve flesh now lacked it utterly, jutting like knotted tree-roots from his rugged frame, making him seem a being rudely hewn from some twisted cypress stump by the master hand of a forest god, and given life.

"We're all there are, Hawkins," he rumbled, his unhushed voice bearing much of the quality of the speech of the tetrahedra. "We've got to find that plane soon, if it's still whole. Did you see flames, Valdez?"

"Flames, Senor Marston? No—as I have so often said, I saw merely the falling of the plane, like a great wounded bird seeking the shelter of the jungle, and Senor—Hawkins, is it—with his parachute. I am not certain that I can find it, now that a day and a night have passed, but I will try. With the guides gone, it is not easy to feed even three mouths—eh, Senor Marston?"

"Four is no worse than three, Valdez. I'm glad Hawkins is here. He's new blood, a new brain, and with his help we may lick the damn' things yet!"

Then Hornby's voice—dry and withered as his shrunken body—weary as his tired old eyes.

"You have seen the tetrahedra, Lieutenant Hawkins? You realize that they are living, intelligent beings? You can comprehend the menace of their presence here on our Earth?"

"Yes, Professor," I answered slowly, "I have seen them and heard them.

I can see that they're not like anything I know of, on Earth or off, and that there is some sort of purpose behind them. But I saw them only in the half-light, for a few moments at best. They had a great leader, twice the size of any of them, and the rest seemed to be dissatisfied with the way he was running things."

"You hear that, Marston?" cried the Professor, almost savagely. "You hear—they are impatient—they will act, soon, as soon as they have fed again! We dare not wait longer! We must do something, Marston—we must act—now!"

"Yes, I saw them too," said Marston slowly. "They're on the brink, all right. But I don't know what we can do—four men with three rifles and a couple of machetes against a hundred of them and what they can do. I don't know that we can even puncture one—they look almighty hard to me!"

"Marston," I put in eagerly, "if it's guns you want, there are two machine-guns and plenty of ammunition in the plane—it was a government ship, fresh from the uprising in the North. If we can find that, there'll be guns as well as food. I think I could find it, from the valley, in daylight."

"Valdez—you hear that? Can you help him search? You are the one who saw him fall, and you have been out with the Indians more than once. How about it?"

"Very well, Senor Marston, I will do what I can. But do not hope for too much—remember, there has been a day and a night, and I had only a glimpse. And the guns—what can they do against those devils from the spheres? We are fools to stay here, I tell you—we would do better to flee, now that there is food, and warn the world of what has come upon it!"

"I've heard that stuff preached before, Valdez. Stow it! If it comes to announcing them to the world, those things will do it for themselves faster than we could! It would be our own hides we'd be saving, and that not for long! Besides, you know the reputation these Indians have, once they're roused! Looks like you're the fool of the lot, Valdez. You'll hunt with Hawkins in the morning!"

Professor Hornby had said little—he merely crouched against a tree, staring blankly at the flames. Now, at Marston's words, he roused again.

"Marston," his voice came petulantly, "have you seen the Indians in the forest, as I have? Have you seen them, felt them staring at your back, fingering their little darts in the dark? Marston, they take those tetrahedra for gods, or devils—things to worship and propitiate with sacrifice! The forest is full of them—I feel it—I can tell! Marston, *what are they doing?*"

CHAPTER II

The Coming of the Tetrahedra

Marston's bluff rumble drowned out that final wail. "Sure, Prof, they're here, all right—all about us, out there in the jungle with the beasts. I can feel them too—watching us from the dark. But they're harmless—just inquisitive, that's all. It's the things yonder that draw them—gods, maybe, or devils, like you said, but something out of old times and old tales, when the Old People had their forts and palaces here under the shadow of the hills. It's a legend come true, for them, and until they find out different, I reckon they link us with the things that have appeared in the place where we used to be—we, with our white magic and our questions of the Old People. They're not apt to hurt us for a while yet, but it won't hurt to slip a mite closer to the valley, where we can watch the things and keep the association fresh for the Indians."

Then Valdez slipped in his acid wedge of dissent, smoothly and blandly as ever, yet deadly sharp beneath the flashing smile.

"You remember, of course, Senor Marston, that these poor Indios retain the superstitions of their ancient masters, and that in time of peril it was the way of the Old People to make blood sacrifice to their gods—the blood of their most holy priests! Old customs linger long among savages, Senor! You have a proverb, I think—'Out of sight, out of mind', is it not? There is truth in such old maxims, Senor Marston."

"Meaning we can skip out and let them forget us? We're not playing that game, as I think I've said before, Valdez. None of us—get that! We're staying, and we're fighting, just as soon as you and Hawkins locate those guns, which is tomorrow. Your memory will improve with a little sleep, I think. And, Prof—I reckon Hawkins here would like to hear about those things yonder. Tell him what there is to tell—you have it clearest of any of us, I guess."

And so, huddled there by the tiny, flickering fire, I listened as the thin, dry voice of the old Professor marched through the awful story of the coming of the tetrahedra. It was graven deep in his mind, and with every telling the tale grew more vivid to him. Even now the sweat oozed from his face as he spoke, staring in fascination at the dying flames. The eyes of Marston and Valdez watched us across the embers and those other, unseen eyes in the darkness that hung its velvet shroud beyond the waning flicker of the fire-light, peered furtively out of the night.

They had come to the little valley in the hills, three white men and a half-dozen Indian guides from the more civilized tribes to the north. Here in its oval bowl they had made their camp among flowers and waving grasses, with the dark rampart of the jungle standing about them like the walls of a prison. And from those walls, in the end, came the Indians of the forest—poor, savage creatures hag-ridden by superstition and ignorance, wracked by famine and disease—a feeble remnant of those who had been servants to the Old People in days long gone.

For they treasured weird legends and aborted ceremonies where understanding of other things had passed. Perhaps they had never known the reality of the great deeds with which they had served the Masters—cunningly fitting huge boulders into smooth-cut walls and terraces, hacking long roads into jungle and mountain, eking out a livelihood for the decadent ruling race.

But true it was that they bore memories of things that even the savage mind can ponder, memories of magic and ritual, and the adoration of fierce and powerful gods. As the newer magic of this younger, paler race gripped their childish minds, they told of the things that their fathers before them had learned of grandfathers through the centuries, tales not only of custom and life in those long-gone days, but of cities swallowed up in the rain-forest, cities of massive stone and untarnishing metal—"the metal of the Sun," that sleeps in long, fat serpents in the white rock of the mountains. In Hornby's old eyes gleamed a new, young frenzy of hope and joy, and in the little eyes of Valdez another, older lust-light wakened at the tale of the golden serpents. Marston saw it, but Marston had known that it would come, and he went about his study of the plants of valley and forest as if it had not been there—worked, and watched.

Then, one day—and Professor Hornby's hoarse voice sank almost to a whisper as he told of it—there came the little group of savages who were to lead the way to the buried ruins of a great city of the Old Ones, four little brown men with blow-guns and deadly darts, waiting patiently for the great White Ones to take up their magic and follow. Hornby had stepped to the door of his tent to call their chieftain to conference, and as he went he gazed up at the towering Andes, whence the Old Ones had sprung. There, drifting like wind-tossed bubbles just above the tree-tops, floated the spheres of the tetrahedra!

Gently they sank to rest at the other end of the little valley—lay there in the thick grass like the eggs of some huge moth out of fable. The Indians had fled in terror, but as Hardy and Marston raced down the slope toward the twin globes they sensed that furtive eyes would be peering from the undergrowth, half-fearful, half-wondering, waiting with timeless patience for new magic—new masters.

The three came to the spheres as they lay there in the lush grass— Hornby, Marston, Valdez—and in each heart must have been something of the wonder that I in my turn had felt. For the spheres were unbroken by any opening, were as twin orbs hewn from mother-of-pearl, iridescent, with delicate hues of blue and rose tinting their snowy white, and yet there came a force from them, a tingling of excess energy that thrilled in every nerve and set their minds on edge with unwonted keenness!

It grew in strength, slowly, and it was Marston who first sensed its lurking hostility, who turned his gaze from the enigmatic spheres to see the long grasses about their bases wither and shrivel to soft grey ash under the blasting radiation! It was he who cried the alarm, and in sudden panic they fled a little way up the valley, to stand like startled sheep, then flee anew as the surge of energy poured forth in ever-quickening pulses from the opal spheres.

It swept all life before it into sudden, luxuriant growth that as suddenly dropped into blighted destruction! Beside their tents, nearly in the shadow of the brooding forest, they stood at last and watched the slow torrent sweep the life of their little valley home into the sullen ash of death. And then its invisible van drifted up the slope to their feet, and again its subtle venom thrilled evilly in their veins, and they ran crazily, headlong, into the jungle!

But they could not long shun the brain-troubling enigma that had engulfed their little home. Marston, Hornby, Valdez—they struggled back and stared from the damp dark of the forest at the thing that was happening there in the sunlit oval on the mountainside. Then it was that Marston broke the spell of fear that had been laid upon him—seized rifles, blankets, food from the deserted tents in the ebbing of the invisible waves, and fled again as the second billow of devastation poured from the silent spheres! The grasses and delicate blossoms of the valley had passed under the first blight, but here and there grew hardier blooms and bushes, akin to the life of the forest, and higher forms of life—insects, rodents, birds. Again the wave of death surged, and again, and now they could see a faint flush of crimson burning angrily where it passed, a glow more of the atmosphere than of the blighted, seared life of the valley! Then, for a time, there came a lull—a peace almost of the days and hours when this little spot of light in the green dark was the home of happy, busy men—almost, yet not quite!

For there was a boding in it, an ominous sense of oppression, a tension of the very ether, a stress that spread to mind and brain and sucked hungrily at the dazed consciousness! Now they saw that the spheres were alight with a cold green radiance that glowed vividly even above the glare of the sun upon the bleaching ash! Almost an incandescence they might have called it, yet there was no feeling of heat, only a great, overpowering energy that was being hurled from those unearthly spheres upon the little valley and its walling forests. And they were not wrong, for of a sudden,

with an awful violence that shook even the stolid Marston, the storm burst
in its full fury over the valley!

It did not touch the forests—indeed, it seemed to shun their cool, damp
dark—and so the three could watch its awful progress and live. In an instant's time the tension burst into a seething, chaotic turmoil of blue-green
flame, electric fire akin to lightning, yet far surpassing any lightning of
Earth in its fury!

In a great beating sea of horrid flame it lashed the oval valley, driving
into the soil, into the very rock, waking them into an angry answer of leaping, burning crimson fires. The fires swept the thin black soil from the
underlying rock and scored the naked face of the rock itself with an awful
furnace of consuming fury. Filling all the bowl of the valley and beating
high against its bounding walls, licking away their flowery curtain of lacing vines, rending from them huge flakes of rock that burst like monster
bombs as they toppled into the fiery sea below, it rushed in a mighty pillar
of roaring fires hundreds of feet into the shuddering air!

And through the curtain where fire of heavens and fire of Earth met
in that terrible holocaust, those three saw the curving flames of the twin
spheres gape wide, saw huge angular shapes file from the darkness within
—shapes never yet associated in the Mind of Man with the meaning of
life! Careless of the flame that seethed about them, they glided out over
the fusing rock of the valley floor, score on score of them, showing in the
fierce glare as mighty, eight-foot tetrahedra of dark, glistening crystal.
They were of a purple that seemed to be of the essence of the things themselves, rather than a pigmentation of their surface; and near one apex each
had two green-yellow unstaring, unseeing eyes!

Within them one glimpsed a spherical body—purple too—from which
ran hundreds of curious filaments to the smooth surfaces. Tetrahedra they
were—living tetrahedra of chilling terror that feared neither flame nor
lightning and spread destruction on every side!

Sick at heart the three men watched, while the flames died and the
winds came and stripped the blanket of dust and ash from the blasted
rock. The tetrahedra meanwhile glided about their endless affairs, forming and reforming in geometric pattern. Or they clicked swiftly into many-
faceted forms that in turn mounted into monolithic, crystalline monstrosities, then melted with startling suddenness into their original components.
These were idle, pointless maneuverings from the human viewpoint, yet
fraught with some hidden meaning and purpose as alien to Earth as the
things themselves. They suggested the terrible energies that were under
their control—energies such as our little science has never hinted at.

"I cannot tell you of the feeling that came to me," the weary, dried-out
voice of the Professor droned despairingly on. "Here was a power absolutely at odds to all the great, painfully evolved civilization of mankind,

a power that could and would crush us as a fly, if we came into conflict with the motives of the tetrahedral race! Here were beings endowed by nature with powers beyond our science—alien to our ideas of evolution, well-nigh to our imagination and reason. I felt the latent doom of mankind and of the very life-forms of all Earth, squatting here in our little, blasted valley with an ominous, cruel indifference that struck chill fear into my heart! And I knew that if Man must die, I would die too—die fighting for *my* race and *my* civilization! I think we all felt it, knew it in our hearts, and swore our oath of undying feud upon the violated rock of our valley home!"

His voice trailed off into silence as his deadened eyes saw once more the vision of that awful day. I thought he had done, but again his voice broke the quiet.

"Perhaps we can flee, even now—hide away in some corner where they can have no motive for searching—exist for a few dreadful months or years while our planet sinks under their unearthly tyranny. Perhaps, for a little, we can save our lives, and yet—I wonder if it is not better to die foolishly, futilely, but to die with the knowledge that we have been closer than any man to the unfathomable, to the reality that underlies all life."

From the dark beyond the glowing embers came Marston's quiet rumble:

"We can't do less, Prof, and we won't. We will fight, as men fight, and if our way is greater and better than their way, you know, down in your heart, that we will win as Man has always won—and that science will have another doubtful bone to quarrel over. In the morning we must lay our plans. They are getting restless—they may strike any minute, and we must be ready and waiting. We're going to die, I guess, but we'll die as men should!" That was all.

The events of the past few hours had crowded in upon me with such staggering force and complexity that I found my mind in a whirl. I could get no clear-cut impression—no broad meaning—only a blurred, fantastic cyclorama of unearthly event and taut emotion, piling thought on thought in an orgy of color and sound and feeling that completely swamped me. Even now, with it all past and much of it clarified by time, I feel that same vagueness, that groping for concepts, that I felt then. With the morning all this changed—changed swiftly and utterly as event after event rushed upon us, broke like a tidal wave upon our outraged consciousness, and vanished before the tumultuous onslaught of another, greater clash of mind and matter.

We were up with the dawn, and after a scant breakfast of dried fruits, salvaged from the tents before the destruction of the valley, Valdez and I set out to find the plane. I wanted to return to the valley to get my bearings, but Valdez protested—claimed it was uselessly dangerous, that he could make better time from where we were. We struck into the tangle of dank underwood, Valdez leading, and within seconds of our leaving camp I was utterly lost. My companion seemed sure of his way, slipping through the maze of fine growth like a beast of the jungle, almost as if he were following an invisible trail.

For nearly an hour we plunged ahead, then of a sudden came a gap in the forest roof as the level of the ground fell in a narrow ravine, and I woke to angry realization of what was happening! The sun, on our right when we started, lay behind us! *We were traveling dead away from the valley, the camp, and the plane!*

Angrily I sprang forward, seized Valdez by the shoulder! He spun like a striking snake, fury in his half-closed eyes, fury and crazed fear! In his hand was a gun!

"So—you have awakened at last, Senor Hawkins," he sneered. "You feel that things are not quite as they seemed—is it not so? You fool—did you for one moment think I would cast my lot with those idiots back there? Do I seem mad, that I should offer my life for fools like them? You—you were not invited to our little party, but you came—you are here, and on my hands—and you will do as I say or wish you had! Am I clear?"

"You're too damn' clear!" I shouted. "You're not fit to live, Valdez, and it's high time someone told you so to your sneaking face! So you're going to sneak off and leave your comrades to the tender mercies of those tetrahedra—you want to make sure of your precious hide! Why, damn you, it's *you* that's a bigger fool than any of us! How can you expect to get clear of this filthy jungle, with the guides gone? Where are you going to find food when your shells run out? What do you think these damn' stinking savages will do to you when they catch you out here alone, running away from their new gods? You haven't the least chance in the world —you're crazy, that's it! You're stark, staring mad—a damned, yellow, mad dog!"

"You say unfortunate things, Senor Hawkins," he replied coldly, the ugly sneer still on his thin, red lips. "I think that I can dispense with your company. It might interest you to know that Valdez is the name of my father by adoption, Senor. My people are those whom you have so kindly classified as 'damned stinking savages'—my home is these very forests that you seem to find so unpleasant! And, Senor Hawkins, have I not said that I can always find your plane?"

"What do you mean by that?"

"I mean, Senor, that it has always been I who could find the plane, and I who *did* find it, not very many minutes after it crashed. You would be disappointed, Senor Hawkins, were you to see it now. The food, the guns and ammunition of which you boasted—they can never have existed save in a mind disordered by jungle fevers. Or can it be that the Indios—the 'stinking savages' that even now are all about us, there behind you in the shadows, have stolen them? It would be most interesting to know the truth of the matter, would it not?"

I stared up through the matted branches at the blandly shining sun, red hate clouding my vision! I raised both hands, fists clenched, as if to crash them down upon the evilly smiling face! But the little snub-nosed gun that bored into my belly spoke eloquent warning, and of a sudden came clear thought and cool, calculated words:

"So even in this you must lie, Valdez! It is bred in the blood, I think! I do not question that you stole the food and weapons that meant life to your comrades—it is much too characteristic an act to doubt—but, Senor Valdez, no Indian would so steal another's food. *Was it, perhaps, your mother who was white?*"

Blind fury glazed his little, bloodshot eyes and drew back his thin lips in an ugly snarl of rage! I saw murder staring at me from those eyes, and in the instant when he stood frozen with his hate I leaped—swung with all my weight on the great liana that was looped over the branch above me! Even as the gun spat flame, the tautening vine caught him full at the base of the skull and toppled him forward into the black mold of the forest floor, out, and out for good!

CHAPTER III

The Tetrahedra's Power

It was his life or mine, but I had not contemplated killing him. The vine was heavy and swung loose on the limb, and it whipped taut with the force of a snapping hawser, catching him squarely at the base of his maddened brain! It was an awful blow, every bit as heavy as the swing of a sledge hammer, and it broke his spine free from his skull as I would snap an apple from its stem! I turned him over, his features purple and contorted, and as I lifted him his head flopped forward like that of a rag dummy! With a shudder I dropped him and turned away.

Yet part of him was white, and all of him was human, and so I scooped a shallow trench in the soft mold and buried him, first searching his body for weapons and food. In his breast pocket was a rough sketch-map, showing the valley, the camp, and a small cross where the plane had fallen. Across its penciled contours ran a fine dotted line, due north from the camp nearly to the place where the plane lay, then bearing off to the west, toward the mountains, and toward a little upland river that ran down from the snows.

There was the gulley where I stood, a dried-out stream-bed leading up into the lower end of the valley, and just beyond a second little cross, to the south of the trail. I knew what it meant—the food and guns from the looted plane! I could see now that the way was cunningly marked by untangled vines and diverted branches—a path of least resistance, more than a trail—and within five minutes I had uncovered Valdez' cache, under the cover of an outcropping ledge of quartz, and loaded one of the packs we had brought along.

How to return to camp with my news was another question entirely. I knew it was hopelessly futile for me to try to follow the back trail, or to run by the rude map for either plane or camp. There remained the valley—straight south along the ravine—and I felt certain that once there I could regain my lost sense of direction or wait until one of the others found me. The valley—and the tetrahedra! Driven by instinct or intuition, I shouldered one of the very light machine-guns and wrapped three belts of ammunition about my waist, under my shirt.

The going was easier along the rim of the little ravine than at its bottom, where extra moisture made the tangle thicker. Indeed, it seemed almost like the trail Valdez had followed—a path of least resistance, carved invisibly into the underbrush by unknown hands. To right and left the thicket held like a tightly woven fabric, but ahead, parallel to the gulley, the branches slipped silently apart under a slight pressure of the hand and closed us quietly behind. It was obvious that either Valdez or the Indians had made this way to the valley, and it was not on Valdez' map.

The trail finally swung away from the stream-bed, toward the east, and suddenly emerged on a sort of peninsula jutting into the valley just above the point where the twin spheres lay. I saw the glare of sunlight through the trees, for there was a sort of clearing overlooking the parade-ground of the tetrahedra. Here were gathered the forest Indians, clustered behind the thin screen of vegetation, gazing in dumb adoration at the things below. So rapt were they that my approach went unnoticed, and I was able to retreat and bear to the west, creeping up to the edge of the valley midway between clearing and ravine.

It was nearly noon, and the fury of the blazing sun made the valley a black cauldron of flickering air-currents. They boiled up from the naked rock in vast, shimmering waves of heat that made the distant jungle and the rocky valley floor seem to engage in a weird witches' caper with the unearthly things that basked at the valley's heart.

Now, in the full light of day, I could see that it was as Professor Hornby had said. The tetrahedra were formed from some hard, crystalline mineral, black almost to invisibility, with a faint wash of rich purple running through it. As they moved, the sun sent up glittering flashes of brilliance from their polished flanks, dancing like little searchlight rays along the shadowed face of the forest. For the tetrahedra were restless, were weaving aimlessly in and out among the boulders in weird arabesques as of some unearthly dance of the crystal folk, were condensing in little groups of half a dozen or less that formed and broke again even as do restless humans, waiting impatiently for some anticipated event.

Apart from the rest, motionless in a sort of circular clearing among the rocks, squatted the giant leader of the tetrahedra. In him the deep violet of the crystal became a rich, plum-like hue, purple flushed with warm red, and the underlying black seemed less harsh. It was warmer and more like the calm velvet of the tropic night. But these are impressions, qualitative terms with which to distinguish him in some way other than by mere size from his fellows. To an observer, the distinction was apparent, but it is not easy to express in everyday terms. It must suffice that he was indefinably different from the others, that he seemed to have character and personality, where the rest were but pyramidal crystals, albeit terribly alive.

And now the giant leader was dinning out his mighty call in long, slow billows of beating sound that seemed to thrust me back, press me into the dark of the forest, away from the alien monsters of the valley! In response came thirty of the lesser tetrahedra, chosen seemingly at random from the scattered ranks, to range themselves at equal intervals about their master, forming a single great circle a dozen yards in diameter.

Again the throbbing call shattered against the cliffs about me, and now all the hordes of the tetrahedra broke into flowing motion, converging in a torrent of glittering purple crystal upon the natural amphitheater, clustering in threes at the spots that their fellows had marked—all but ten, who glided into place before every third group, forming a giant toothed wheel with hub and rim and spokes of living, sentient crystal—*crystal with a purpose!*

There under that blazing sun they lay, gleaming like giant purple gems against the jetty rock. I thought of the great stone wheel of Stonehenge, and of the other monolithic circles that men have found in England and on the Continent. Strange resemblance, between the pattern of living monsters of another world and the ancient temples of a prehistoric race! And yet, is it too far-fetched to suggest that the superstitious savages should pattern their greatest temples after the unearthly gods of their worship— gods of purple crystal that came and smote and vanished again into the skies, leaving the memory of their inevitable circling, and the thunder of their language in the great drums of worship? May it not be that they have come before, and found Earth unfitted for their usage, and passed on to other worlds? And if they have so come, and found us wanting, what lies beyond that has prevented them from bearing back the tale of their findings, marking Earth as useless for their tetrahedral purposes? Why have they had to come again and again?

I could see that the groups of three that formed the toothed rim of the giant crystal wheel were tipping inward, bringing their peaks together in a narrow focus, and more, that the ten that were the spokes, the binding members of the wheel, were of the same rich hue as their master. The shadows of the myriad tetrahedra squatted short and black about their shining bases, against the shining rock.

As the sun soared higher, pouring its blazing rays straight down upon the sweltering world, I sensed the beginning of a vague roseate glow at the foci of the circling trios, a glow as of energy, light, focussed by the tetrahedra themselves, yet not *of* themselves, but sucked from the flood of light that poured upon them from above. For the light that was reflected from their sides gleamed ever bluer, ever colder, as they drank in the warm red rays and spewed them forth again into the seething globes of leashed energy that were forming just beyond their pointing tips!

The rose-glow had deepened to angry vermillion, seemingly caged within the spheres defined by the tips of the tilted tetrahedra. Thirty glowing coals against the black, ninety great angular forms gleaming ghastly blue in the pillaged sunlight, forms that were slowly closing in upon the center, upon their mighty master, bearing him food, energy of the sun for his feasting!

Now the scarlet flame of the prisoned light was mounting swiftly in an awful pinnacle of outrageous color—pure fire torn from the warm rays of the sun—raw energy for the glutting of these tetrahedral demons of another world! It seemed to me that it must needs burst its bounding spheres and fuse all that crystal horde with its unleashed fury of living flame, must win free of the unimaginable forces that held it there between the eager, glittering facets, must burst its unnatural bonds and sweep the valley with a tempest of awful fire that would consign the furnace of the tetrahedra to pitiful insignificance! It did none of these, for the power that had reft it from the golden sunbeams could mould it to the use and will of the tetrahedra, as clay before the potter!

Slowly the great ring contracted, slowly the tetrahedra tipped toward their common center, bearing at their foci the globes of angry flame. Now they stopped, hung for a long moment in preparation. Then in an instant they loosed the cradled energy of the spheres in one mighty blaze of blinding crimson that swept out in a single huge sheet of flame, blanketing all the giant wheel with its glory, then rushing into the blazing vortex of its center. Here, all the freed energy of the flame was flowing into the body of the mighty ruler of the tetrahedra, bathing him in a fury of crimson light that sank into his glowing facets as water into parched sand of the desert, bringing a fresh, new glow of renewed life to his giant frame!

And now, as in recoil, there spouted from his towering peak a fine, thin fountain of pale blue fire, soundless, like the blaze of man-made lightning between two mightily energized electrodes—the blue of electric fire— the seepage of the giant's feast! Like slaves snatching at the crumbs from their master's board, the ten lesser tetrahedra crowded close. As their fierce hunger voiced itself in awful, yearning force, the fountain of blue flame split into ten thin tongues, barely visible against the black rock, that bent down into the pinnacles of the ten and poured through them into the crowding rim of the giant wheel, a rim where again the spheres of crimson fire were mounting to their climactic burst!

Again the crimson orbs shattered and swept over the horde in a titanic canopy of flame, and again the giant master drank in its fiery glory! Now the fountain of seepage had become a mighty geyser of sparkling sapphire light that hurtled a hundred feet into the shimmering atmosphere, and, bent by the fierce hungering of the lesser creatures, curved in a glorious parabola above the crystal wheel, down over them and into them, renewing their substance and their life!

For as I watched, each tetrahedron began to swell, visibly, creeping in horrid slow growth to a magnitude very little less than that of their giant leader. And as they mounted in size, the torrent of blue fire paled and died, leaving them glutted and expectant of the final stage!

It came, with startling suddenness! In an instant each of the hundred clustering monsters budded, burst, shattered into four of half its size that cleaved from each corner of the parent tetrahedron. They left an octohedral shape of transparent crystal, colorless and fragile, whence every evidence of life had been withdrawn into the new-born things—a shell that crumpled and fell in fine, sparkling crystal dust to the valley floor. Only the giant ruler lay unchanged beneath the downward slanting rays of the sun. The hundred had become four hundred! The tetrahedra had spawned!

Four hundred of the monstrous things where a hundred had lain the moment before! Drinking in the light of the noonday sun, sucking up its energy to give them substance, these tetrahedral beings from an alien world held it in their power to smother out the slightest opposition by sheer force of ever-mounting numbers! Against a hundred, or four hundred, the armies and the science of mankind might have waged war with some possibility of success, but when each creature of these invulnerable hosts might become four, with the passing of each noon's sun, surely hope lay dead! Man was doomed!

On the jutting point to my left I sensed new activity. The Indians were chanting, in weird low tones, to the rhythm of a great, deep-throated drum. It was some monotonous hymn or supplication to their ancient gods—gods now personified in the things below. Through the screen of shrubbery between us, I glimpsed their chieftain, taller by a head than the rest, his arms up-raised, leading the exhortation. Their voices rose, broke in an angry clamor as a dozen of their kind burst from the forest dragging the bound form of a white man—*of Marston!*

I must be closer. Here, separated from them by a hundred feet of space and a double screen of matted vines, I dared not fire for fear of slaying friend with foe! Headlong I dived into the tangle, shoving the machine-gun ahead of me! Had they not been utterly engrossed in their savage ritual, the Indians must surely have heard my blundering approach, ripping blindly through the undergrowth with caution flung to the winds! By chance or fortune the tangle was less matted than elsewhere, and I burst into the cleared space barely in the nick of time.

For all of his traitorous hypocrisy, Valdez had spoken truly of old customs and old sacrifices! Marston's huge, straining frame was bent back over a rounded slab of polished rock in the center of the clearing, the dwarfed forest-men fairly swarming over him to hold him in place! Arms raised in supplication, their chieftain stood over him, his features distorted by something more than fear of his gods, and frenzy of sacrifice! Hate and terrible rage had seized upon his bronzed visage, making of it a veritable devil-mask! And in his clenched fist he grasped a glittering knife of steel, a knife that half an hour ago I had seen buried in the black soil of the forest floor—*Valdez' knife!*

Again he was raising his chant of dedication and sacrifice, screeched to the thunderous rhythm of the drum in the manner of those Old Ones before the Incas! Again it mounted to its climactic crescendo of frenzied adoration and black hate—rose to a maddened scream, and broke as his arm swept down against that bearded throat! With a merry cackle of savage laughter, my gun woke the echoes, sweeping leaden death across the clearing, mowing its swath of lives in sacrifice more terrible than any savage mind could plan!

Through a bloody haze I saw the brown, broken bodies twisted and flung bodily from their feet by thudding missiles that tore their unresisting flesh from their broken bones and bathed the altar and the gaunt form stretched over it with spouting, smoking blood! Blood lust was in me as I raked their bewildered ranks with the laughing death, then the belt of cartridges was gone, and as I fumbled for a second the few cowering survivors fled screaming into the sheltering jungle!

Sanity came, and horror at the slaughter I had done, and with them an awful fear that in my unreasoning rage I had murdered friend as well as foe! Stumbling over the torn and bleeding windrows of slain humanity, I raced across the bloody clearing to where he lay, the gun forgotten! And as I reached the rude altar where he lay, Marston heaved his blood-soaked frame free of the bodies that covered it, sat up, and growled whimsically:

"Are you quite sure you've killed enough for the day? Or didn't you know it was loaded?"

"Marston, man!" I shouted frantically. "Are you all right? Did I hit you?"

"Oh, not at all. I'm quite all right. You're a rotten shot if I do say it—bring in a blasted flail, and then you can't hit me! Though I'll not say you didn't try hard enough. You did well by the innocent bystanders, and of course the public must come first in the mind of every good citizen."

As a matter of fact, I had nicked a chunk out of his arm—a nice, clean hit—and the blood on him was not all Indian. Still, his sarcastic joshing served its purpose and brought me out of my near-hysteria, where I was doing nobody the slightest good, into a sort of sanity in which I could at least talk without dithering like a crazy fool. Not until we were well clear of the shambles around the altar did he speak of Valdez.

"What happened?" he asked. "Did Valdez bolt?"

"He tried to," I replied glumly. "He had the stuff from the plane cached on the trail out, and—well, I wouldn't listen to reason, he pulled a gun, and we had it out. I broke his neck—killed him."

"I'm not blaming you for it. I saw it coming, and I reckon it was you or he. But it's stirred up merry hell among the Indians. Did you know he was a breed? He claimed to be pure Indian, son of a jungle chieftain and a princess of some remnants of the Old People, but he was a breed, and crossed the wrong way! The least hint that anyone had guessed the truth made a beast of him. I've seen him deliberately bash a man's head to jelly because the fellow, a Portuguese muleteer, claimed relationship— on his mother's side! He was one of their priests, a heritage from his father, and I guess they found his body. Hornby doesn't know, though, and if I were you I'd lay the blame to the Indians—the dead ones. Right?"

"I suppose so. It happened as you guessed. I slugged him in the neck with a heavy liana, too hard. But how did they get you?"

"I told you I was suspicious of Valdez. I tried to follow you, and they jumped me, south of here, near the ravine. It must have been shortly after they found Valdez, for they were all crazy mad. I think the Doc is safe, though. Do you realize that this spawning means that they're ready to go ahead and burn their way right through everything—make this whole planet a safer and better place for tetrahedra? Doc has figured they're from Mercury—overcrowded, probably, by this wholesale system of reproduction in job-lots, and hunting for new stamping-grounds. I don't know what our chances are of bucking them—about a quarter of what they were an hour ago—but they're mighty slim, armed as we are. You've got the other machine-gun?"

"It's at the cache, with most of the food, if the Indians didn't find it when they found Valdez. I have a map here, that he was using."

"Good. Let's have it. You keep an eye on the Professor tomorrow, now that the Indians are out for blood, and I'll get the stuff back to camp. Now I know they're hostile, I'll keep my weather eye open for trouble and I'll guarantee I won't be caught napping again. Come on—let's hunt him up now, while they're still scared."

"Wait, Marston," I replied. "You get the stuff now. I have a hunch we'll need it, and that soon. I can find Professor Hornby well enough, and I don't think the Indians will want any more for some time to come."

"Right you are!" he exclaimed. "So long then." And he swung off along my back-track.

CHAPTER IV

At Bay!

I had no trouble in finding the Professor. In truth, he found me. He was all but boiling over with excitement, for he had seen something we had not.

"Hawkins," he exclaimed, grabbing my shoulder fiercely, "did you see them spawn? It is remarkable—absolutely unequalled! The speed of it all—and, Hawkins, they do not have to grow before cleaving. I saw two that divided and redivided into three-inch tetrahedra—over a thousand of them! Think of it—Hawkins, they can overrun our little planet in a few days, once they start! We're done for!"

"I guess you're right, Professor," I replied. "But tell me—have you seen anything of the Indians?"

"The Indians? Yes—there seems to be something wrong with them now, Hawkins. They seem to have lost their reverence for the tetrahedra. These tribes do not paint much, but those I have seen were decorated for battle, and one old man was cursing the things from the edge of the forest, working himself up into a regular frenzy of invective. They may resist, now, if the tetrahedra try to start anything."

"Marston will be glad to hear that! Right now, I think we had better strike for the high ground across the ravine, where their flame is less likely to reach us. I'll leave you there and then look for Marston and the guns. We're going to need them before long."

"Very well, Hawkins. Your plan sounds good, and I'm glad you found the plane. But where is Valdez? Isn't he with Marston?"

"No. He's dead."

"Dead! You mean—the Indians?"

"Um. They nearly got Marston too, but I had one of the guns. Come on, we'll pick it up, and my pack of food, and find a place where we can see what happens and still be fairly safe. Follow me."

We found an ideal fortress, high on the west side of the ravine, where a little spur ran down from the highlands to the valley of the tetrahedra. Indeed, it had been used as a lookout by the ancient inhabitants of the region, ages ago, when great cities of cut stone lay in the valleys now choked by vegetation. Enough of the ancient walls remained to provide a decent bulwark against attack, and I left Professor Hornby with the gun to hold the fort until I could find Marston.

I had little difficulty in locating him, and between us we transferred the supplies from cache to lookout, while the Professor kept a perfunctory guard over them. As a matter of fact, he was more interested in digging around in the ancient floor of potsherds and tools of the former inhabitants. He explained that the ancient Pleistocene wave of immigration from Asia, via Alaska and North America, had split at Panama to pass down both sides of the Andes. On the west, along the coast, arose the ancient American civilizations, culminating in the Incas. On the east were the forest Indians, poor savage creatures of the thick jungles, such as we had seen. And here, on the boundary between these two regions, he sought a link between the two. Perhaps he had found it. We were never to know.

It was two days before the hostilities began. Meanwhile we had found the wreck of the plane, very nearly intact but quite useless in this dense jungle. We drained the tanks of what gasoline they contained, storing it in great glazed jars of painted earthenware that Professor Hornby had found intact in a niche below our present floor-level. His idea was to fight fire with fire, incidentally clearing a space about the spur on which our little fort was perched, so that we could see what we were about in case of trouble.

Marston and I cleared out the brush as best we could, and cut deep slots in the larger trees on the down-hill side. A back-fire is ticklish work in the forest, but we worked it, piling the quickly drying underbrush at the far side of our little swath, saturating it with gasoline, then digging in to one of the Professor's excavations while the fireworks went off. In a drier climate we would not have lived to tell the tale. As it was, we more or less leveled the thick forest for about two hundred feet on all sides, before the fire petered out, leaving a tangled mess of blackened wreckage that effectively kept us in and others out, as well as clearing the field of view.

Our fire may have served to set off the onslaught of the tetrahedra. Certainly, with the next morning, there was renewed activity in their rocky pocket. They cleared out a sizeable ring of forest before sun-set. The next noon they had another sunfeast, and now the blackened valley was fairly teeming with their angular forms, large and small, for many seemed to have split without growing, as the Professor had seen one do before.

Now, their army of destruction assembled, the tetrahedra began their conquest of Earth! In vast waves of horrid destruction with rays of angry yellow flame darting from apexes their flaming floods of energy swept over the jungle, and now not even its damp dark could resist. Mighty forest-giants toppled headlong, by the cleaving yellow flame, to melt into powdery ash before they touched the ground. Giant lianas writhed like tortured serpents as their juices were vaporized by the awful heat, then dropped away in death to lie in long grey coils along the stripped rock of the forest floor—rock that was fast taking on the glassy glare of the little valley, rock fused by heat such as Earth had never known.

By evening, our spur of rock was a lone peninsula, an oasis in a desert of harsh black, a height which the tetrahedra, for some unknown reason, had not attempted.

Now we could watch their plan of campaign, and our hearts sank in fear for our race, for while half of the tetrahedral army engaged in its holocaust of destruction, the remaining half fed and spawned in the full blaze of the sun. With every day dozens of square miles were added to their hellish domain and thousands of tetrahedra to their unnatural army. For now we could see that more and more of them were taking the second course, were splitting into hosts of tiny, three-inch creatures which, within a few days' time, had swelled to full size and on the following day could spawn anew! It was dreadful, but now we were hopelessly isolated—an island in a sea of black rock, untouched as yet by the blasting fires, but utterly unable to save ourselves or our world.

Aside from the vegetation which they were so methodically blasting, the Mercutian tetrahedra—for such Professor Hornby swore they were and such we later found them to be—had not yet come into real contact with the life of our planet, much less its master, Man. The worship of the Indians had been carried on from afar, and we ourselves were careful not to tempt our visitors from space. Now all that was changed in some-thing of a double-barreled fashion. It began with the Indians. It ended with us.

Now that we were shut off from the jungle, we no longer sensed the unease and stealthy activity of the forest people. Their gods had betrayed them—perhaps they thought them devils now—their sacrifice had been in-terrupted and their chief men slaughtered unmercifully by the slayers of their half-white brother. Their whole life and legend had gone wrong. The tetrahedra were to blame, and the tetrahedra must pay!

The invaders did not start their daily program of devastation until the sun was high. Of late, the people of the forest had become creatures of the night, and so it was that Marston roused us about midnight to watch the fun, as he put it. As a matter of fact, we all realized that what the Indians did would probably be of vital importance to our own situation.

The spheres were too small to hold all the tetrahedral hosts, now, and they lay crowded in great confocal ovals about them, sleeping, if such things can be said to sleep. The first indication of the attack was a tiny fire of leaves and twigs on the rocks above the ravine, now choked with slabs of rock scaled from its walls by the terrific heat. It was barely visible —merely a smudge in size, kindled for some magical purpose. Then there came a low, wailing chant, rising swiftly in vehemence and bitter hatred— a curse designed to blast the unearthly invaders where they lay. Professor Hornby was fairly gasping at the enormously ancient background of legend and superstition which it revealed, when it suddenly broke in a shrill, senile yammer of sheer madness! The strain was more than the old priest could stand.

As in answer, other, greater fires sprang up all along the walls of the valley, and by their light we could see the Indians closing in from the edge of the forest—thousands of them, drawn to worship over untold leagues of jungle paths, and now racing into battle with all the mad fanaticism of an outraged religion! It was like a tidal wave of screeching humanity, pouring down over the black rock to break over the sleeping tetrahedra! Yet, as the last Indian burst from shelter of the jungle, the attacking force was revealed as pitifully small, compared to the ranks of those whom they attacked. Like a great city of black, tetrahedral tents the Mercutians lay, dim-lit by the failing moon, as if unaware of the savage swarm, led by its gibbering priest, that raced upon them. But they were far from unaware!

It was I who first noticed the faint, rosy glow that hung over the silent ranks—a glow like that which had brought down my plane. I whispered to Marston, and he told me that it had not been there before—that the tetrahedra must be awake, and waiting!

He was right. The red glow was spreading swiftly, out over the valley floor, and there must have been another, invisible emanation that preceded it, for I saw the old priest falter, beat with clawed fists at an unseen wall, then topple with a choking scream and lie still. Now, all round the valley, the first ranks of the savages were meeting this slowly advancing wall of unseen death—meeting it, and falling before it! In long windrows they lay, body after body piling up before the momentum of the unleashed rush of the red-skinned hordes! Stones, arrows, spears flew through the thickening red mist to clatter harmlessly upon the quiescent tetrahedra! But not as harmlessly as it seemed, for here and there among them showed a little spurt of pale blue flame as one of the smaller things was crushed by a hurtling stone! They were hard, but their skins of crystal were thin, and a well-flung stone might break them! *They were not invulnerable!*

The Indians sensed this, too, for they had deserted spears and darts in favor of a hail of stones, large and small, that clattered among the tetrahedra in a veritable downpour, dealing really telling destruction among those who had not attained a fair size.

The savages were yelling in triumph, now, thrilled with success, and their blind onslaught was checked, but still the invisible barrier crept on, dealing death all along their evilly grimacing front, and still the rose-red haze followed after, dissolving the crumpled bodies in fine white ash that in turn vanished in the deepening red. The yelling circle was thinning fast, yet they had not realized the futility of their attack when suddenly the tetrahedra deserted quiet defense for active combat!

The cause was evident. Five Indians on the upslope had shoved over the cliff a huge rounded boulder that bounded like a live thing among the rocks and crashed full into the side of a great eight-foot tetrahedron, splintering its flinty flank and freeing the pent-up energy in a blinding torrent of blue flame that cascaded over the nearby ledges, fusing them into a white-hot, smoking pool of molten lava that glowed evilly in the ill-lit gloom! It was the last straw! The mad attack had become a thing of real menace to the tetrahedra, and they sprang into swift retribution. From their apexes they flashed out the flaming yellow streaks of destruction.

Now at last the Indians broke and fled before the advancing hordes, but flight came too late, for the tetrahedra were aroused and they gave no quarter! Long tongues of yellow reached out, beating down like awful flails on the fleeing savages and searing them with swift agony, dropping them in their tracks, driving them down in shapeless horror against the smoking rock, where the scarlet sea swept over them and dissolved them in drifting, fusing ash! The doomed Indians seemed to float in a yellow sea and what the sea touched was gone in an instant! Before that awful barrage nothing living could stand!

Of a sudden the tragedy was borne forcibly to our own quarter, as a handful of Indians sought the refuge of our rocky spur! Like brown apes they scrambled up its precipitous side toward our fortress and burrowed through the tangled debris of our back-fire. They were men like ourselves, men in awful danger of their lives, and Marston and Hornby sprang to the parapet, shouting at them in their native tongue. But the frightened savage knows no friend, and their reply was a volley of long arrows that toppled the Professor into my arms and sent Marston cursing for the guns! Lips set grimly, he sprayed the rocky slope with whining leaden death, mowing down the frenzied savages as I had done in the place of sacrifice!

At sight of us, their madness burst forth anew and they broke their flight to rush our pinnacle, voices raised in wild vituperation!

Laying Professor Hornby under the shelter of the wall, I dragged out the other gun and kicked open a case of ammunition, joining Marston in the defense of the fort. That other time I had had surprise and superstition to aid me in my single-handed victory, but now we two were leagued against outraged fanaticism, and the odds were great. Like locusts they came on, from every side, eyes red with blood-lust, teeth bared in hate—beasts of the jungle, ravening for the kill! It was the debris of our back-fire, piled in a matted belt around the spur, that saved us, for here the mad charge must halt and here our guns took their toll. Nor were we two alone, for now I heard the crack of a rifle and knew that Professor Hornby was covering the ledge of rock that ran back at our rear to join us to the hills.

Even so, I think our defense must have failed but for the tetrahedra. They had not been slow to recognize the changed nature of the Indians' fight, and they turned that realization to their own advantage, curving around the spur to cut off a second retreat, then laying down their fiery yellow barrage upon the rear of the clamoring savage host, licking them up as a bear licks ants. It was a matter of minutes before the last Indian lay in grey ash on the rocky slope of the crag.

For a moment matters were at a deadlock. We paused and took stock—three men with their guns against thousands of tetrahedra, armed with lightnings. Hornby had slumped back against the low wall, his eyes closed, his spare frame racked with coughs that brought back blood to his twisted lips. An arrow had pierced his lungs. Marston dropped the machine-gun, now smoking-hot, and grabbed up a rifle. I followed suit. So for perhaps two minutes the rival forces held silent, waiting.

The Mercutians took the initiative. Their yellow tongues of flame crept slowly up the hillside, scouring it clean—up, up toward our little refuge on the peak. Now they began to glide forward, on every side, beginning the ascent. In answer our rifles rang out, and now there was no doubt as to their vulnerability, for wherever the steel-jacketed lead hit, there the thin crystal splintered and the night was lit by the glare of freed energy, the life-blood of the tetrahedra! We could not save ourselves, but we would do no puny damage!

Now came a dull thunder from the rear, and by the dim light of the red mist I could see the giant leader of the Mercutians, standing at the summit of the cliff above the valley, commanding the attack. In reply, the yellow barrage began to beat upward along the rock, toward us, and with the same signal a faint, blurred scheme leapt into my fuddled brain! I raised my rifle, fired—not at the advancing front but farther back, into the body of the horde, slowly driving my fire back toward the giant commander, picking off monster after angular monster, nearer and nearer to where he squatted!

Then he was flinching, gliding back before the sea of flame that burst around him as his crystal warriors fell, and in reply I brought down one after another of those toward whom he was retreating, hemming him in with death, threatening—but not striking! I cannot tell why we did not destroy him, for Marston had followed suit, neglecting the threat of the flame, which waned and died as the tetrahedra woke to the meaning of our fire. Somehow we felt that it was wiser to spare him, and our intuition was good. For a moment he hesitated, then thundered his drumming command, and the ranks of the tetrahedra drew slowly back, leaving us in peace and safety.

So we remained, virtually prisoners, for eight days. On the third, Professor Hornby died—a blessing, for he suffered greatly. He was the only one who really understood these tetrahedra, and we shall never know how he deduced that they were from Mercury, a fact which Marston later proved. The archaeological data collected by the expedition are lost, too, since both he and Valdez are dead and we could bring out no specimens. The tetrahedra left us alone, barring us from flight with their haze of red energy, which extended up the slope to a level above that of the saddle connecting us with the forested mountain-slopes. Meanwhile they continued their barrage of the jungle, laying it waste on every side, mile after mile, day after day.

Through the binoculars we had watched them slowly advance, and noted their very human surprise as they burned the covering jungle from the great ruined city which the expedition had sought. It was their first real experience with the works of Man, and it caused a great commotion among them. Led by the purple giant, they swarmed over and through its ruined labyrinth, studying its every niche and angle, learning it. Here was their proof that Earth harbored a civilization—that they might expect real opposition. I do not think they ever realized that our puny defense was a fair example of what that civilization could do.

Later in the same day they found the wreck of the plane, and this time consternation indeed reigned. Here was a machine of some sort, evidently the product of that civilization that they feared. Moreover, it was recent where the city was ancient. Could it mean that they were watched—that the unseen creatures of this unknown ruling race were lurking in the dark of the jungle, with their engines of war and destruction—*waiting?* Now, as never before in their descent on Earth, the tetrahedra were faced by the stark blankness of the utterly unknown, and I think that they began to be afraid.

The little valley was still the center of their activity, and every day we watched their spawning as the sun rode high, saw the piling up of the hordes that would overwhelm our race and planet, and make of it a dead, black thing like that little pocket on the east slope of the Andes. There was always a double ring of the tetrahedra about us now, and their crimson sea of energy beat high about our prison. The giant who led them came often to observe us, to sit and stare with invisible eyes at our fortress and ourselves. Their drumming speech had grown familiar, too, and I felt that it would not be hard to understand, given the key to its meaning.

Marston seemed fascinated with the things and their ways. There was a spring, just above the limit of the red haze, where we got our water, and he would sit there by the hour, as close to the things as he could get, watching and listening. I could see him sway to the rhythm of their thunderous speech, see his lips move in low response, and I wondered if he were going mad.

Ever since Marston had first mentioned Professor Hornby's theory that the things were Mercutians, I had been trying to find some way of verifying it. Now that we were in semi-intimate terms with the tetrahedra, I wondered if I might not get them, somehow, to supply this evidence. I thought of stories I had read of interplanetary communication—of telepathy, of word-association, of sign-language. They had all seemed far-fetched to me, impossible of attainment, but I resolved to try my hand at the last.

There was some rather soft rock in the structure of the watch-tower, and as Valdez had rescued my tool kit from the plane, I had a hammer and chisel. With these, and a faulty memory, I set out to make a rough scale diagram of the inner planets, leaning a bit on the Professor's theory. I cut circular grooves for the orbits of the four minor planets—Mercury, Venus, Earth, Mars—and dug a deep central pit. In this I set a large nugget of gold, found in the ruins of the fortress, for the Sun, and in the grooves a tiny black pebble for Mercury, a large white one for Venus, and a jade bead from the ruins for Earth. Earth had a very small white moon, in its own deep-cut spiral orbit. Mars was a small chunk of rusty iron with two grains of sand for moons. I had a fair-sized scale, and there was no room for more.

Now I was prepared to attempt communication with the tetrahedra, but I wanted more than one diagram to work with. Consequently I attempted a map of Earth, with hollowed oceans and low mountain-ridges. All this took plenty of time and trouble, but Marston was not at all in evidence, and I was not sorry, for my scheme seemed rather pointless, and I did not relish his ridicule.

CHAPTER V

Face to Face

So things stood when the tropical storm broke over us. Its cause is not hard to explain. Remember, when those scathing fires blasted the jungle, all the superabundant moisture of the region was vaporized. Even our little spring, as it ran down into the crimson haze, vanished in plumes of steam as it passed the scarce visible boundary between life and death. To add to this, during all the long summer, the sun had been literally boiling the moisture out of the rain-forests all over the Amazon Basin. The air was nearly saturated with water-vapor, though the rainy season was normally a month off. The electrical disturbances set up by the continual barrage of fire added to the general effect. Things were ripe for a storm, and it came!

A cloud-burst, it would be called in the United States. The heavens opened in the night, and water fell in torrents, streaming from every angle of the rock, standing in pools wherever a hollow offered itself, drenching us and the world through and through. Day came, but there was no sun for the tetrahedra to feed on. Nor were they thinking of feeding, for very definite peril threatened them. *To the tetrahedra, water was death!*

As I have said, their fires had flaked huge slabs of rock from the walls of the ravine leading from the high-walled valley where they slept, choking its narrow throat with shattered stone. And now that the mountain slopes, shorn of soil and vegetation, were pouring water into its bed, the stream that had carved that ravine found its course dammed—rose against it, poured over it, but not until the valley had become a lake, a lake where only the two pearly spheres floated against the rocky wall, the thousands of tetrahedra gone forever—*dissolved!*

Water was death to them—dissolution! Only in the shelter of the spheres was there safety, and they were long since crowded. The hordes of the tetrahedral monsters perished miserably in the night, before they could summon the forces that might have spun them a fiery canopy of arching lightnings that would drive the water back in vapor and keep them safely dry beneath. A hundred had come in the twin spheres. A hundred thousand had been born. A bare hundred remained. Our way of escape was clear!

But escape had been possible before, and we stayed then as now. Flight was delay—nothing more. A miracle might save us, and I think we believed in miracles. So we vainly sought shelter from the deluge in the ruins of the tower, and stared through the falling rain at the two spheres, now clear of the water and perched on the ravine's edge, above the dam.

Our "local shower" lasted for three days. Then came the sun, and the mountains began to drain. Only the new-born lake remained to remind us of the rains, a lake stained deep violet with the slowly dissolving bodies of the crystal tetrahedra. Those in the two spheres waited for a day, then came forth to survey the ruins of their campaign—the giant leader and a scant hundred of his richly purple subordinates. And now, too, came proof of the method in Marston's madness.

The tetrahedra had resumed their guard about the base of our crag, although the crimson barrage did not beat so high nor so vividly. Their master squatted outside the ring, brooding, watching us—perhaps pondering our connection with the tempest that had wrecked his hopes. And now Marston took under his arm the great Indian drum that I had brought away from the place of sacrifice, a drum of ancient ritual, headed with well-tanned human skin, and stalked down the slope to confront the tetrahedra. I stuck by the guns and waited.

I can see them yet, giant leaders of two utterly different races, born on two planets sixty millions of miles apart at their nearest, inherently opposite and inherently enemies, squatting there on the black rock, watching each other! A rumble of speech from the great leader and the rose-hue of the barrage deepened, climbed higher about the crag. A bluff, it was. Marston did not move.

And then he took up the great drum. He had cared for it as for a child during the long rain, sheltering it as best he could, testing the tautness of its grisly membrane, drying it carefully with sun and fire during all the previous day. Now I learned the reason.

Slowly, softly, using the heel of his palm and his fingers in quick succession, he began to drum. This was not the rhythmic throb of native dances, not the choppy voice of signal drums. Faster, ever faster the great drum of sacrifice boomed forth its message, until the beats melted into a low, continuous thunder of bottomless sound, mounting in volume to a steady, rolling roar, rising and swelling in delicate inflection. His wrist must have been wonderfully strong and flexible to so control the sound! On and on in great throbbing billows rolled the drumming, and but for its thunder all the world lay still—Marston and I on the slope of the spur, the tetrahedra about its base, the purple giant beyond, on the shore of the lake. On and on, thundering through my brain in dull, insistent beatings of dead surf on the beaches of a dead world, possessing me, filling me, speaking to me in the voice of the storm—speaking—that was it! *Marston was speaking to the tetrahedra with the voice of his giant drum!*

During those long, empty days on the crag-side he had been listening, learning, drilling into his scientist's brain the meaning of every voiced command that the great master of the Mercutian tetrahedra thundered to his crystal hosts, learning their inflections, storing them in his mind! He had memorized a simple vocabulary—sounds that signified the great commander, the horde, the tetrahedra as a class; simple verbs for coming and going, for altering the barrage; words for human beings, for their planet and our own—a host of nouns and verbs that even yet seem beyond the power of any man to glean from the muttering of an alien race, coupled with the actions that fitted the words. But Marston *had* learned, and with the sullen voice of the giant drum he was replying, in rough, broken, ill-chosen words, falteringly expressed, words that the tetrahedron understood!

For the crimson mist faded, vanished. The crystal ranks split, and through the lane between them glided the giant ruler, coming to where Marston sat with his drum. He stopped, spoke in words very like those that Marston had used—simple words, such as our own babies learn, roughly connected.

"What—you?"

And the drum: "We—tetrahedra—Earth." I translate rudely, as they spoke. His words were not so literal as I must make them, to suit our limited tongue—were ideas, rather than words. And yet, they got their message across!

The giant was startled. How could we, misshapen, flabby monstrosities, be rulers of a planet, equal to themselves? He was incredulous:

"You—tetrahedra?"

The drum muttered approval, as for a fulfilled command. The idea had been transferred, but the purple giant did not seem to think much of it.

"You—weak! (Easily vulnerable, like vegetation, was the sense of the term used.) You—dead—easy. (Here he used a term with which he had designated the tetrahedra shattered in the battle with the Indians.) *We*—tetrahedra—our planet—and Earth!"

There wasn't much answer to that one. They could rule both planets with ease. And yet—Marston called to me.

"Hawkins, bring down those stones you've been chipping, and a flask of water. Wait—bring two flasks, and a gun."

So he had seen me at work and guessed my plan. Well, his own beat it hollow, but if he had an idea, I wasn't going to hinder him. I lugged the slabs down and went back for the stoppered canteens of water and the gun. At his directions I set one flask against the rock of the hillside, above him. He took the other. And all the while his drum was murmuring reassurance to the giant and his horde.

"You work the slabs, Hawkins," he said, "while I talk. I'll translate, and you act accordingly." The drum spoke:

"Sun—Sun—Sun." He pointed. "Your Sun—our Sun."

The tetrahedron approved. He came from our own Solar System.

Now he was pointing to my diagram, to the Sun, the Earth and its orbit. "Sun. Sun. Earth. Earth." I rolled the jade bead slowly along its groove, the white moon-pebble following in its spiral course. I rolled the other planets, showed him their colors and relative sizes. Marston was drumming again, as I touched planet after planet, questioning.

"Your planet—your planet? Your planet—what? This?"

The giant disapproved. It was not Mars.

"This?" It was anything but Venus! Venus must have been pretty wet for the completest comfort.

Eagerly—"This?" Assent! The Professor was right! They came from Mercury! But Marston wanted to be sure. He found a white speck of quartz in the black stone that was Mercury, and now he turned it to the golden Sun—held it there as Mercury revolved slowly in its orbit. There was emphatic approval. Mercury it was—the planet with one side always to the Sun. So far, so good. Marston took my other plaque—the relief map of Earth.

"Earth—Earth."

Yes, the Mercutian recognized it. He had seen it thus from space.

With a crystal of quartz, Marston gouged our particular section of South America, pointed to the ground, to the lake, the forests. "This—this," he said.

More approval. They knew where they were, all right.

Now he reopened a closed subject. He started up the monotone of reassurance, then superimposed on it a few deft words.

"You—tetrahedra—Mercury." They sure were!

"We—tetrahedra—Earth!" Not so good! He repeated: "You—Mercury. We—Earth. We—tetrahedra!" There were evident signs of dissent! Marston swelled the reassurance-tone, then added a sharp call to attention, raised his gun, fired twice, threw the weapon down, and redoubled his assurance of well-meaning and safety.

His aim had been good. The flask was pierced at top and bottom, and a thin stream of water was jetting forth, trickling over the glassy rock toward us. It made a little pool at his feet, lipped over, and the double rank of tetrahedra drew back to let it pass. It formed another little pool, close to the base of their giant leader. He wasn't taking bluffs! A flash of blinding energy and the pool was steam and the rock white-hot! Marston learned another word.

"Water—dead! We—tetrahedra—Mercury and Earth!"

Not so good! Marston tried another.

"You—tetrahedra—Mercury. Water—tetrahedron—Earth!"

An alarming idea that! Water the lord of Earth!

"Water—no—dead!" Decided negation in the drum. He pointed. True enough, the steam was condensing and running down the smooth rock in little droplets. Water could not be killed! It always came back!

"We—tetrahedra—water!"

Phew! That *was* a statement! He proved it. He dabbled his fingers in the pool at his feet, took some up in his hand and slicked back his hair. I gave a thunderous grunt by way of attracting attention, uncapped the other canteen, and poured a long and very visible stream of water down my throat. Marston took the canteen and did the same, then sent me for more water, a pailful.

"Water—tetrahedron—Earth!" he reiterated. He illustrated his point, dipped water from the pail with much splashing and poured it over my relief of the Earth, filling the hollows of the seas. He emphasized it, with a gloomy note in his drumming. "*Water*—tetrahedron—Earth. Water. *Water!*"

He had another hunch, rolled Venus around its orbit. "What?" asked the drum. He was answered, glumly. He dipped Venus in the water. Venus was pumice and floated.

"Water—tetrahedron—Venus?" Oh, decidedly. The purple giant was sure of that. Marston tried Mercury. Mercury sank. Time after time it sank. Water didn't like Mercury.

"*You*—tetrahedra—Mercury. Water—*no*—tetrahedron—Mercury." A pause. Then slowly, ominously—"*Water—tetrahedron—you!*"

And he was right. Water had them licked. I had a bright idea, and Marston moved camp to the brink of the lake, striding like a conqueror between the double file of tetrahedra. Arrived beside the water, with the giant fairly close and the army very much in the background, I stripped and dove in—"brought up bottom"—brought up a chunk of half-dissolved purple crystal! Marston rubbed it in, gleefully.

"Water—tetrahedron—*you!*" They had to admit it. Now he tried to coin a word—pointed to the sky and shuffled syllables on the drum. "Up—up. Water—up." The giant caught on and supplied the correct term. Marston coined a real one—a genial, murmurous "Thank-you"—on his drum. I tried my hand again, dipped up a bucket of water and doused Marston, then stepped toward the great tetrahedron with another. He retreated. I wallowed in it myself instead—childish, but convincing. By now the idea was definitely set that water was rank poison to the tetrahedra and a second home to us. Now for the real information!

Marston drummed attention and reassurance, and the great leader glided back, carefully avoiding puddles. I could see that he floated about three inches clear of the ground. Perhaps, with the lesser gravitation of Mercury, he flew.

I started demonstrating my little Solar System again, while Marston announced again that Earth was largely water—no fit place for tetrahedra —water that could be killed, but that came down again in rain. He drilled in the idea of rain, until he was sure he had made his point, securing various Mercutian expressions of disgust and dislike. He found a word for "rain"—really coined one, for it did not seem to exist in Mercutian. It was a combination of "water" and "up," so as to be quite clear, with a double-ruffle of emphasis to characterize it. The etymology of the word was quite clear to all concerned. They knew what rain was, now.

I had poked a hole through the soft, thin rock of Mercury's orbit and put clay plugs in Earth's orbit at diametrically opposite points. Now Marston demonstrated. He poured water on Mercury. It vanished.

"Mercury—no—rain. No!" The entire host had crowded in, and there was a general murmur of assent.

Venus, on the other hand, being a deep groove, held plenty of water. "Venus—rain. Water—tetrahedron—Venus."

They got that, too. Weather of Venus is ideal for ducks and frogs—*not* for tetrahedra.

He moved out one planet, and I could feel a tensing. They knew what he was driving at! He was going to describe weather-conditions of Earth. Half Earth's orbit held water to the brim. The other half was rather damp. He slowly moved Earth around her circles, showing that six months were wet and six not so wet. He took to the drum for emphasis.

"*Water*—tetrahedron—Earth. *We*—tetrahedron—water. Water—tetrahedron—*you*." A delicate inference. Then, slowly, emphatically, "Water—Venus. Water—Earth." And now his final card.

He set Mercury in its orbit, placed Venus almost opposite, paused. The giant assented. That was where the planets were at present. He skipped Earth and went to Mars, rolled it along its orbit, stopped it. Assent. All true, so far. And now I saw his point, for when he dropped Earth in place, very nearly in line between Mars and Mercury, *it fell in the middle of the dry half of the orbit!*

A hundred tetrahedra slid back a yard or so in recoil. This rain which had drowned out practically all of their army of thousands, was an example of our *dry* season! By inference, our real wet weather must have been sheer Mercutian hell to every tetrahedron of them!

But Marston was too good a diplomat to give them a hands off without suggesting an alternative. He slowly poured water on Mars. Mars apparently, and actually, had a hole in its bottom, for it drained bone dry. Mars, now, was very nice. But Earth was nasty and wet, as bad as Venus or worse. And it was inhabited by a race of super-intelligent fish, to judge from the impression he gave the tetrahedra. He picked up the drum for a last word.

"Earth—*rain*. Mars—*no*—rain. *We*—Earth. You—*no*—Earth. You—Mars?" He dwelt on the question. "Mars? Mars???" He rolled out an endless question-mark, then suddenly quit, took a long, flashing drink of water from the flask, and dove into the lake, clothes and all. I followed him, and together we splashed to the other shore, making our mastery of the water very evident, then climbed out, waiting. If things worked out, all well and good. If they didn't—well, we had the lake between us.

And it did work! For a moment they stood motionless, the mighty sixteen-foot tetrahedron of royal purple and his eight-foot purple retinue, silent, considering. Then came a sudden command, and the hundred flowed in orderly motion to the spheres, entered. Their mighty master was alone. For an instant he hesitated, then swept forward to the very edge of the lake. From this towering peak beat the white lightnings, lashing the purple waters into great billowing clouds of steam that threw up a dense wall of mist between us! Through the hiss of the steam came his thunderous voice, in last comment upon the invasion of his tetrahedral race! Marston translated, softly:

"Water—tetrahedron—Earth. *You*—tetrahedron—water. *We—kill—water!* You—Earth. We—Mars. Mars!" And a long, rolling assent, an infinitely underlined "*YES!*"

Water and Earth seemed to be synonymous, and we were perfectly at ease in that dangerous element. For all that, they, the tetrahedra of Mercury, could "kill" it, which, by inference, we could not. They weren't going to admit defeat, by Man or water, but this was a big Solar System. We could have our soggy Earth! They were going to Mars!

Up from behind the wall of "killed" water rose two great, glorious pearls, marvelously opalescent in the rays of the setting sun—up and up, smaller and smaller, until they vanished into the deepening blue above the Andes. Ironically, it began to rain.

———————

As you see, "Tetrahedra of Space" belongs in the same tradition as the stories of Meek. The setting is South America, and it is the Indians this time who are superstitious savages and clearly subhuman. When the half-breed, Valdez, is killed, the hero buries him saying, ". . . all of him was human," but also says, ". . . part of him was white."

P. Schuyler Miller has been the book reviewer for *Astounding* now for almost as many years as I have been writing, and I know him to be a liberal and humane person, one of the gentlest and most generous souls I have ever met. It is a measure of how far the unthinking stereotypes can penetrate and of how taken-for-granted they were in this type of adventure fiction, that even Miller could fall victim to them.

What fascinated me in this story and what caused it to live on in my memory was the picture of extraterrestrials who were utterly non-human. This wasn't often done in those days, or, for that matter, in the more primitive forms of science fiction even today. In so many cases, intelligent creatures are assumed to be quite human if they are virtuous, and distortedly human if they are villainous, as in "Submicroscopic."

There was, further, the picture of the tetrahedra spawning and of the final communication of the two intelligences, which was handled rather subtly, I thought then—and thought again recently, when I reread it.

One other thing that occurs to me in connection with the story is the mere word "tetrahedra." Miller doesn't define the word anywhere in the story, but the illustrations by Frank R. Paul (one of them on the cover of the magazine) made it clear to me that they were solids with four, triangular faces.

It was the first time I had ever heard the word, and, of course, I never forgot it. Any form of reading will improve one's vocabulary, but science fiction automatically improves one's scientific vocabulary.

"Tetrahedra of Space," incidentally, contains another common characteristic of early magazine science fiction: elephantiasis of the adjectives. Especially in the first portion of the story, every sentence carries a load of them that breaks it in two. Combine that with inverted word order and unnecessary italics, and you find yourself breathing heavily and losing track of the sense.

To me in my younger days, and to others in theirs, and to some, I fear, in all their days, this thick layer of fatty adjectival froth seems to be a mark of good writing. And, indeed, adjectivitis was most common in the fantasy of the time and in such admired writers as A. Merritt, H. P. Lovecraft, and Clark Ashton Smith (whom, however, I am afraid I never admired, even when I was young and might have been excused the error).

Clark Ashton Smith, in particular, had a second interesting literary aberration. He used long and unfamiliar words as another way of impressing the naïve with the quality of his writing. In the same issue with "Tetrahedra of Space," for instance, there is Smith's "Beyond the Singing Flame," and since Sam Moskowitz had sent me the complete issue in this particular case, I looked at the Smith story for old time's sake.

In the very second paragraph, I found him using "veridical" when he meant "true," and I read no further. Yes, "veridical" does mean "true," but I cannot imagine any occasion (outside a certain specialized use among psychologists) when "true" is not very greatly to be preferred.

In my early days, I tried to imitate these adjectival examples of writing. My style was most ornate in the days before I had published anything. Some of the fat had been steamed out by the time I was publishing, and my writing has grown progressively leaner with the years. I am not sorry.

During 1931, I reached the stage where my pleasure in science fiction had bubbled over and could not be confined. I began to retell the stories I had read. I did this, I remember, in distinct imitation of my storytelling friend of three years earlier. Now it was *I* who had the audience.

Of course, the stories weren't my own, but I made no pretense that they were. I carefully explained that I had read them in science fiction magazines. My classmates couldn't afford to buy the magazines any more than I could and were glad to listen.

As for myself, I discovered, for the first time in my life, that I loved to have an audience and that I could speak before a group, even when some of them were strangers to me, without embarrassment. (It was a useful piece of knowledge, for twenty years later I was to become a professional after-dinner speaker at what turned out to be, eventually, very respectable fees. The childhood experience and training helped, I am sure.)

I well remember sitting at the curb in front of the junior high school with anywhere from two to ten youngsters listening attentively while I repeated what I had read, with such personal embellishments as I could manage.

And the specific story that I most vividly recall telling was "The World of the Red Sun," by Clifford D. Simak, which appeared in the December 1931 issue of *Wonder Stories*.

THE WORLD OF THE RED SUN

by Clifford D. Simak

"Ready, Bill?" asked Harl Swanson. Bill Kressman nodded.

"Then kiss 1935 good-bye!" cried the giant Swede, and swung over the lever.

The machine quivered violently, then hung motionless in pitch blackness. In the snap of a finger the bright sunlight was blotted out and a total darkness, a darkness painted with the devil's brush, rushed in upon the two men.

Electric lights glowed above the instrument boards, but their illumination was feeble against the utter blackness which crowded in upon the quartz windows of the machine.

The sudden change astounded Bill. He had been prepared for something, for some sort of change, but nothing like this. He half started out of his seat, then settled back.

Harl observed him and grinned.

"Scared," he jested.

"Hell, no," said Bill.

"You're traveling in time, my lad," said Harl. "You aren't in space any more. You are in a time stream. Space is curved about you. Can't travel in time when you're still in space, for space binds time to a measured pace, only so fast, no faster. Curve space about you, though, and you can travel in time. And when you're out of space there's absolutely no light, therefore, utter darkness. Likewise no gravity, nor any of the universal phenomena."

Bill nodded. They had worked it all out before, many, many times. Double wall construction of a strength to withstand the vacuum into which the flier would be plunged at the move of the lever which would snatch it out of space into the time stream. An insulation to guard against the absolute zero that would rule where there could be no heat. Gravity grids at their feet so that they would still be able to orient themselves when flung into that space where there was no gravity. An elaborate heating system to keep the motors warm, to prevent the freezing of gasoline, oil and water. Powerful atmosphere generators to supply air to the passengers and the motors.

It had represented years of work, ten years of it, and a wealth that mounted into seven figures. Time after time they had blundered, again and again they had failed. The discoveries they had made would have rocked the world, would have revolutionized industry, but they had breathed no word of it. They had thought of only one thing, time travel.

To travel into the future, to delve into the past, to conquer time, to this the two young scientists had dedicated all their labors, and at last success lay beneath their hands.

It was in 1933 they had at last achieved their goal. The intervening months were spent in experiments and the building of the combination flier-time machine.

Miniature fliers were launched, with the miniature time machines set automatically. They had buzzed about the laboratory, to suddenly disappear. Perhaps at this very instant they were whirling madly through unguessed ages.

They managed to construct a small time machine, set to travel a month into the future. In a month's time, almost to the second, it had materialized on the laboratory floor where it had dropped at the end of its flight through time. That settled it! The feasibility of time travel was proved beyond all doubt.

Now Harl Swanson and Bill Kressman were out in the time stream. There had been a gasp of amazement from the crowd, on the street, which had seen the giant tri-motored plane suddenly disappear into thin air.

Harl crouched over the instrument board. His straining ears could distinguish the wheezy mutterings of the three motors as, despite the elaborate precautions taken to safeguard them, the inexorable fingers of absolute zero clutched at their throbbing metal.

This was a dangerous way, but the only safe way. Had they remained on the surface to plunge into the time stream they might have halted to find themselves and their machine buried by shifting earth; they might have found a great building over them, they might have found a canal covering them. Here in the air they were safe from all that might occur beneath them in the passing centuries through which they sped at an almost unbelievable pace. They were being fairly hurled through time.

Furthermore, the great machine would serve as a means of travel in that future day when they would roll out of the time stream back into space again. Perhaps it might serve as a means of escape, for there was no foreknowledge to tell them what they might expect a few thousand years in the future.

The motors wheezed more and more. They were operating on a closed throttle. At full speed they might dash the propellers to bits.

However, they must be warmed up. Otherwise they would simply die. It would be stark tragedy to roll out into space with three dead engines. It would mean a crash which neither of them could hope to survive.

"Give her the gun, Bill," said Harl in a tense voice.

Bill pushed the accelerator slowly. The motors protested, sputtered, and then burst into a roar. Here, in the machine, because of the artificial air, sound could be heard. Out in the time stream there could be no sound.

Harl listened anxiously, hoping fiercely that the propellers would stand.

Bill cut the acceleration and the motors, once more barely turning over, ran more smoothly.

Harl glanced at his wrist watch. Despite the fact they were in time, where actual time could not be measured by clocks, the little watch still ticked off the time-space seconds and minutes.

They had been out eight minutes. Seven minutes more and they must roll out of time into space.

Fifteen minutes was all that the tortured motors could stand of this intense cold and vacuum.

He glanced at the time dial. It read 2816. They had traveled 2816 years into the future. They should be well over 5000 when the fifteen minutes were at an end.

Bill touched his arm.

"You're sure we're still over Denver?"

Harl chuckled.

"If we aren't, we may find ourselves billions of miles out in space. It's a chance we have to take. According to all our experiments we should be in exactly the same position we were when we snapped into the time stream. We are occupying a hole in space. It should remain the same."

Their lungs began to ache. Either the atmosphere generators were failing or the air leakage out into the vacuum was greater than they had expected. Undeniably the air was becoming thinner. The motors still ran steadily, however. It must be a leakage from the cabin of the ship.

"How long?" bellowed Bill.

Harl glanced at his watch.

"Twelve minutes," he reported.

The time dial read 4224.

"Three minutes," replied Bill, "I guess we can stand it. The motors are running all right. It's getting colder, though, and the air's pretty thin."

"Leakage," said Harl gruffly.

The minutes dragged.

Bill tried to think. Here they hung, hypothetically, over the city of Denver. Less than a quarter of an hour ago, they were in the year 1935, now they were passing over years at a lightning-like speed—a speed of over 350 years in each space-minute. They must now be in about the year 6450.

He glanced at his hands. They were blue. It was intensely cold in the cabin. Their heat was leaking—leaking swiftly. It was hard to breathe. The air was rare—too rare for safety. Suppose they became unconscious. Then they would freeze—would drive endlessly through time. Frozen corpses, riding through the aeons. The earth beneath them would dissolve in space. New worlds might form, new galaxies be born as they whirled on in the time stream. The time needle would reach the pin, bend back upon itself and slip past the pin, to slam against the side of the dial, where it would still struggle to record the flight of the years.

He chafed his hands and glanced at the time dial. It read 5516.

"A quarter of a minute," snapped Harl, his teeth chattering, his right hand on the lever, his wrist watch held in front of him.

Bill placed his hands on the wheel.

"All right!" shouted Harl.

He jerked the lever.

They hung in the sky.

Harl uttered a cry of astonishment.

It was twilight. Beneath them were the ruins of a vast city. To the east lapped a sea, stretching to a murky horizon. The sea coast was a desert of heaped sand.

The motors, warming to their task, bellowed a mighty challenge.

"Where are we?" cried Harl.

Bill shook his head.

"It's not Denver," said Harl.

"Doesn't look much like it," agreed Bill, his teeth still chattering.

He circled, warming the motors.

There was no sign of humanity below them.

The motors blasted a throaty defiance to the desert sands and under Bill's hand, the machine came down in a long swoop, headed for a level stretch of sand near one of the largest of the white stone ruins.

It hit the ground, bounced high in a cloud of sand, struck and bounced again, then rolled to a stop.

Bill cut the motors.

"We're here," he said.

Harl stretched his legs wearily.

Bill glanced at the time dial. It read 5626.

"This is the year 7561," he said slowly, thoughtfully.

"Got your gun?" asked Harl.

Bill's hand went to his side, felt the reassuring touch of the .45 in its holster.

"I have it," he said.

"All right, let's get out."

Harl opened the door and they stepped out. The sand glittered under their boots.

Harl turned the key in the door lock and locked the ring to his belt.

"Wouldn't do to lose the keys," he said.

A chill wind was blowing over the desert, moaning among the ruins, carrying with it a freight of fine, hard granules. Even in their heavy clothing, the time explorers shivered.

Harl grasped Bill by the arm, pointing to the east.

There hung a huge dull red ball.

Bill's jaw fell.

"The sun," he said.

"Yes, the sun," said Harl.

They stared at one another in the half-light.

"Then this isn't the year 7561," stammered Bill.

"No, more likely the year 750,000, perhaps even more than that."

"The time dial was wrong then."

"It was wrong. Badly wrong. We were traveling through time a thousand times faster than we thought."

They were silent, studying the landscape about them. They saw only ruins which towered hundreds of feet above the sands. They were ruins of noble proportions, many of them still bearing the hint of a marvelous architecture of which the twentieth century would have been incapable. The stone was pure white, gleaming beautifully in the twilight which the feeble rays of the great brick-red sun could not expel.

"The time dial," said Bill, thoughtfully, "was registering thousands of years instead of years."

Harl nodded cheerlessly.

"Maybe," he said. "For all we know it may have been registering tens of thousands of years."

A creature, somewhat like a dog, dull gray in color, with tail hanging low, was silhouetted for a moment on a sand dune and then disappeared.

"These are the ruins of Denver," said Harl. "That sea we saw must cover the whole of eastern North America. Probably only the Rocky Mountains remain unsubmerged and they are a desert. Yes, we must have covered at least 750,000 years, perhaps seven million."

"What about the human race? Do you think there are any people left?" asked Bill.

"Possibly. Man is a hardy animal. It takes a lot to kill him and he could adapt himself to almost any kind of environment. This change, you must remember, came slowly."

Bill turned about and his cry rang in Harl's ear. Harl whirled.

Running toward them, leaping over the sands, came a motley horde of men. They were dressed in furs and they carried no weapons, but they charged down upon the two as if to attack.

Harl yanked his .45 from its holster. His great hand closed around the weapon and his finger found the trigger. It gave him a sense of power, this burly six-shooter.

The men, their furs flying behind them, were only a hundred yards away. Now they yelled, blood-curdling, vicious whoops which left no doubt that they were enemies.

No weapons. Harl grinned. They'd give 'em hell and plenty of it. There were about fifty in the mob. Big odds, but not too great.

"We might as well let them have it," he said to Bill. The two guns roared. There was disorder in the running ranks, but the mob still forged ahead, leaving two of its members prone on the ground. Again the .45's barked, spurting a stream of fire.

Men staggered, screaming, to collapse. The rest hurdled them, raced on. It seemed nothing could stop them. They were less than fifty feet away.

The guns were empty. Swiftly the two plucked cartridges from their belts and reloaded.

Before they could fire the mob was on top of them. Bill thrust his gun into the face of a running foeman and fired. He had to sidestep quickly to prevent the fellow tumbling on top of him. A knotted fist connected with his head and he slipped to his knees. From that position he drilled two more of the milling enemies before they piled on top of him.

Through the turmoil he heard the roar of Harl's gun.

He felt the grip of many hands, felt bodies pressing close about him. He fought blindly and desperately.

He fought with hands, with feet, with suddenly bared teeth. He felt bodies wilt under his blows, felt blood upon his hands. The sand, kicked up by many feet, got into his nostrils and eyes, half strangling, half blinding him.

Only a few feet away Harl fought, fought in the same manner as his companion. With their weapons knocked from their hands they resorted to the tactics of their ancient forebears.

It seemed minutes that they battled with their attackers, but it could not have been more than seconds before the sheer weight of numbers subdued them, wound thongs tightly about their hands and feet and left them, trussed like two fowls ready for the grid.

"Hurt, Bill?" called Harl.

"No," replied Bill. "Just mussed up a bit."

"Me, too," said Harl.

They lay on their backs and stared up at the sky. Their captors moved away and massed about the plane.

A loud banging came to the ears of the two. Evidently the others were trying to force an entrance into the machine.

"Let them bang," said Harl. "They can't break anything."

"Except a propeller," replied Bill.

After more banging, the men returned and untying the bonds on the feet of the captives, hoisted them up.

For the first time they had an opportunity to study their captors. They were tall men, well proportioned, clean of limb, with the stamp of well-being about them. Aside from their figures, however, they held a distinctly barbarous appearance. Their hair was roughly trimmed, as were their beards. They walked with a slouch and their feet shuffled in the sand with the gait of one who holds a purposeless existence. They were dressed in well-tanned furs, none too clean. They bore no arms and their eyes were the eyes of furtive beings, shifty, restless, as are the eyes of hunted beasts, always on the lookout for danger.

"March," said one of them, a large fellow with a protruding front tooth. The single word was English, with the pronunciation slightly different than it would have been in the twentieth century, but good, pure English.

They marched, flanked on either side by their captors. The march led back over the same route as the future-men had come. They passed the dead, but no attention was paid them, their comrades passing the sprawled figures with merely a glance. Life apparently was cheap in this place.

CHAPTER II

Orders of Golan-Kirt

They passed between monstrous ruins. The men talked among themselves, but, although the tongue was English, it was so intermixed with unfamiliar words and spoken with such an accent that the two could understand very little of it.

They reached what appeared to be a street. It led between rows of ruins and now other humans appeared, among them women and children. All stared at the captives and jabbered excitedly.

"Where are you taking us?" Bill asked a man who walked by his side.

The man ran his fingers through his beard and spat in the sand.

"To the arena," he said slowly that the twentieth century man might understand the words.

"What for?" Bill also spoke slowly and concisely.

"The games," said the man, shortly, as if displeased at being questioned.

"What are the games?" asked Harl.

"You'll find out soon enough. They are held at high sun today," growled the other. The reply brought a burst of brutal laughter from the rest.

"They will find out when they face the minions of Golan-Kirt," chortled a voice.

"The minions of Golan-Kirt!" exclaimed Harl.

"Hold your tongue," snarled the man with the protruding tooth, "or we will tear it from your mouth."

The two time-travelers asked no more questions.

They plodded on. Although the sand beneath their feet was packed, it was heavy going and their legs ached. Fortunately the future-men did not hustle their pace, seeming to be content to take their time.

A good-sized crowd of children had gathered and accompanied the procession, staring at the twentieth century men, shrieking shrill gibberish at them. A few of them, crowding too close or yelling too loudly, gained the displeasure of the guards and were slapped to one side.

For fifteen minutes they toiled up a sandy slope. Now they gained the top and in a depression below them they saw the arena. It was a great building, open to the air, which had apparently escaped the general destruction visited upon the rest of the city. Here and there repairs had been made, evident by the decidedly inferior type of workmanship.

The building was circular in shape, and about a half-mile in diameter. It was built of a pure white stone, like the rest of the ruined city.

The two twentieth century men gasped at its size.

They had little time, however, to gaze upon the building, for their captors urged them on. They walked slowly down the slope and, directed by the future-men, made their way through one of the great arching gateways and into the arena proper.

On all sides rose tier upon tier of seats, designed to hold thousands of spectators. On the opposite side of the arena was a series of steel cages, set under the seats.

The future-men urged them forward.

"They're going to lock us up, evidently," said Bill.

He of the protruding tooth laughed, as if enjoying a huge joke.

"It will not be for long," he said.

As they approached the cages, they saw that a number of them were occupied. Men clung to the bars, peering out at the group crossing the sandy arena. Others sat listlessly, regarding their approach with little or no interest. Many of them, the twentieth century men noticed, bore the marks of prolonged incarceration.

They halted before one of the cells. One of the future-men stepped to the door of the cage and unlocked it with a large key. As the door grated back on rusty hinges, the others seized the two, unbound their hands and roughly hurled them inside the prison. The door clanged to with a hollow, ringing sound and the key grated in the lock.

They struggled up out of the dirt and refuse which covered the floor of the cell and squatted on their heels to watch the future-men make their way across the arena and through the archway by which they had come.

"I guess we're in for it," said Bill.

Harl produced a pack of cigarettes.

"Light up," he said gruffly.

They lit up. Smoke from tobacco grown in 1935 floated out of their cell over the ruins of the city of Denver, upon which shone a dying sun.

They smoked their cigarettes, crushed them in the sand. Harl rose and began a minute examination of their prison. Bill joined him. They went over it inch by inch, but it was impregnable. Except for the iron gate, it was constructed of heavy masonry. An examination of the iron gate gave no hope. Again they squatted on their heels.

Harl glanced at his wrist watch.

"Six hours since we landed," he said, "and from the appearance of the shadows, it's still morning. The sun was well up in the sky, too, when we arrived."

"The days are longer than those back in 1935," explained Bill. "The earth turns slower. The days here may be twenty-four hours or longer."

"Listen," hissed Harl.

To their ears came the sound of voices. They listened intently. Mingled with the voices was the harsh grating of steel. The voices seemed to come from their right. They grew in volume.

"If we only had our guns," moaned Harl.

The clamor of voices was close and seemed to be almost beside them.

"It's the other prisoners," gasped Bill. "They must be feeding them or something."

His surmise was correct.

Before their cell appeared an old man. He was stooped and a long white beard hung over his skinny chest. His long hair curled majestically over his shoulders. In one hand he carried a jug of about a gallon capacity and a huge loaf of bread.

But it was neither the bread nor the jug which caught the attention of Harl and Bill. In his loincloth, beside a massive ring of keys, were thrust their two .45's.

He set down the jug and the loaf and fumbled with the keys. Selecting one he unlocked and slid back a panel near the bottom of the great door. Carefully he set the jug and the loaf inside the cell.

The two men inside exchanged a glance. The same thought had occurred to each. When the old man came near the door, it would be a simple matter to grasp him. With the guns there was a chance of blazing a way to the ship.

The oldster, however, was pulling the weapons from his loincloth.

Their breath held in wonder, the time-travelers saw him lay them beside the jug and the loaf.

"The command of Golan-Kirt," he muttered in explanation. "He has arrived to witness the games. He commanded that the weapons be returned. They will make the games more interesting."

"More interesting," chuckled Harl, rocking slowly on the balls of his feet.

These future-men, who seemed to possess absolutely no weapons, apparently did not appreciate the deadliness of the .45's.

"Golan-Kirt?" questioned Bill, speaking softly.

The old man seemed to see them for the first time.

"Yes," he said. "Know you not of Golan-Kirt? He-Who-Came-Out-of-the-Cosmos?"

"No," said Bill.

"Then truly can I believe what has come to my ears of you?" said the old man.

"What have you heard?"

"That you came out of time," replied the oldster, "in a great machine."

"That is true," said Harl. "We came out of the twentieth century."

The old man slowly shook his head.

"I know naught of the twentieth century."

"How could you?" asked Harl. "It must have ended close to a million years ago."

The other shook his head again.

"Years?" he asked. "What are years?"

Harl drew in his breath sharply.

"A year," he explained, "is a measurement of time."

"Time cannot be measured," replied the old man dogmatically.

"Back in the twentieth century we measured it," said Harl.

"Any man who thinks he can measure time is a fool," the future-man was uncompromising.

Harl held out his hand, palm down, and pointed to his wrist watch.

"That measures time," he asserted.

The old man scarcely glanced at it.

"That," he said, "is a foolish mechanism and has nothing to do with time."

Bill laid a warning hand on his friend's arm.

"A year," he explained slowly, "is our term for one revolution of the earth about the sun."

"So that is what it means," said the old man. "Why didn't you say so at first? The movement of the earth, however, has no association with time. Time is purely relative."

"We came from a time when the world was much different," said Bill. "Can you give us any idea of the number of revolutions the earth has made since then?"

"How can I?" asked the old man, "when we speak in terms that neither understands? I can only tell you that since Golan-Kirt came out of the Cosmos the earth has circled the sun over five million times."

Five million times! Five million years! Five million years since some event had happened, an event which may not have occurred for many other millions of years after the twentieth century. At least five million years in the future; there was no telling how much more!

Their instrument had been wrong. How wrong they could not remotely have guessed until this moment!

The twentieth century. It had a remote sound, an unreal significance. In this age, with the sun a brick red ball and the city of Denver a mass of ruins, the twentieth century was a forgotten second in the great march of time, it was as remote as the age when man emerged from the beast.

"Has the sun always been as it is?" asked Harl.

The old man shook his head.

"Our wise ones tell us that one time the sun was so hot it hurt one's eyes. They also tell us it is cooling, that in the future it will give no light or heat at all."

The oldster shrugged his shoulders.

"Of course, before that happens, all men will be dead."

The old man pulled the little panel shut and locked it. He turned to go.

"Wait," cried Harl.

The old one faced them.

"What do you want?" he asked, mumbling half-angrily in his beard.

"Sit down, friend," said Harl. "We would like to talk further."

The other hesitated, half wheeling to go, then turned back.

"We came from a time when the sun hurt one's eyes. We have seen Denver as a great and proud city. We have seen this land when the grass grew upon it and rain fell and there were broad plains where the sea now lies," said Harl.

The oldster sank to the sand in front of their cage. His eyes were lighted with a wild enthusiasm and his two skinny hands clutched the iron bars.

"You have looked upon the world when it was young," he cried. "You have seen green grass and felt rain. It seldom rains here."

"We have seen all you mention," Harl assured him. "But we would ask why we have been treated as foes. We came as friends, hoping to meet friends, but ready for war."

"Aye, ready for war," said the old man in trembling tones, his eyes on the guns. "Those are noble weapons. They tell me you strewed the sands with the dead ere you were taken."

"But why were we not treated as friends?" insisted Harl.

"There are no friends here," cackled the old man. "Not since Golan-Kirt came. All are at one another's throats."

"Who is this Golan-Kirt?"

"Golan-Kirt came out of the Cosmos to rule over the world," said the old man, as if intoning a chant. "He is neither Man nor Beast. There is no good in him. He hates and hates. He is pure Evil. For after all, there is no friendliness or goodness in the universe. We have no proof that the Cosmos is benevolent. Long ago our ancestors believed in love. This was a fallacy. Evil is greater than good."

"Tell me," asked Bill, moving closer to the bars, "have you ever seen Golan-Kirt?"

"Aye, I have."

"Tell us of him," urged Bill.

"I cannot," there was stark terror in the old man's eyes. "I cannot!"

He huddled closer to the cage and his voice dropped to an uncanny whisper.

"Men out of time, I will tell you something. He is hated, because he teaches hate. We obey him because we must. He holds our minds in the hollow of his hand. He rules by suggestion only. He is not immortal. He fears death—he is afraid—there is a way, if only one with the courage might be found—."

The old man's face blanched and a look of horror crept into his eyes. His muscles tensed and his clawlike hands clutched madly at the bars. He slumped against the gate and gasped for breath.

Faintly his whisper came, low and halting.

"Golan-Kirt—your weapons—believe nothing—close your mind to all suggestion—."

He stopped, gasping for breath.

"I have fought—" he continued, haltingly, with an effort. "I have won—. I have told you—. He has—killed me—he will not kill you—now that you—know—."

The old man was on the verge of death. Wide-eyed, the two saw him ward it off, gain a precious second.

"Your weapons—will kill him—he's easy to kill—by one who does not —believe in him—he is a—."

The whisper pinched out and the old man slid slowly to the sands in front of the cage.

The two stared at the crumpled form of humanity.

"Killed by suggestion," gasped Harl.

Bill nodded.

"He was a brave man," he said.

Harl regarded the corpse intently. His eyes lighted on the key ring and kneeling, he reached out and drew the body of the future-man close. His fingers closed on the ring and ripped it from the loincloth.

"We're going home," he said.

"And on the way out we'll bump off the big shot," added Bill.

He lifted the guns from the floor and clicked fresh cartridges into the chambers. Harl rattled the keys. He tried several before he found the correct one. The lock screeched and the gate swung open protestingly.

With quick steps they passed out of the cell. For a moment they halted in silent tribute before the body of the old man. With helmets doffed the twentieth century men stood beside the shriveled form of a man who was a hero, a man who had flung his hatred in the face of some terrible entity that taught hate to the people of the world. Scanty as was the information which he had given, it set the two on their guard, gave them an inkling of what to expect.

As they turned about they involuntarily started. Filing into the amphitheater, rapidly filling the seats, were crowds of future-men. A subdued roar, the voice of the assembling people, came to their ears.

The populace was assembling for the games.

"This may complicate matters," said Bill.

"I don't think so," replied Harl. "It's Golan-Kirt we must deal with. We would have had to in any case. These men do not count. As I understand it he exercises an absolute control over them. The removal of that control may change the habits and psychology of the future-men."

"The only thing we can do is fight Golan-Kirt and then act accordingly," said Bill.

"The man who captured us spoke of his minions," Harl said thoughtfully.

"He may be able to produce hallucinations," Bill hazarded. "He may be able to make one believe something exists when it really doesn't. In that case, the people would naturally believe them to be creatures which came at his beck and call."

"But the old man knew," objected Harl. "He knew that it was all mere suggestion. If all the people knew this the rule of Golan-Kirt would end abruptly. They would no longer believe in his omnipotence. Without this belief, suggestion, by which he rules, would be impossible."

"The old man," asserted Bill, "gained his knowledge in some mysterious manner and paid for its divulgence with his life. Still the old fellow didn't know all of it. He believed this entity came out of the Cosmos."

Harl shook his head, thoughtfully.

"It may have come out of the Cosmos. Remember, we are at least five million years in the future. I expect to find some great intelligence. It is physical, for the old man claimed to have seen it, and that should make our job easier."

"The old man said he was not immortal," commented Bill. "Therefore, he is vulnerable and our guns may do the work. Another thing—we are not to believe a single thing we feel, hear, or see. He seems to rule wholly by suggestion. He will try to kill us by suggestion, just as he killed the old fellow."

Harl nodded.

"It's a matter of will power," he said. "A matter of brain and bluff. Apparently the will power of these people has degenerated and Golan-Kirt finds it easy to control their minds. They are born, live, and die under his influence. It has almost become hereditary to accept his power. We have the advantage of coming out of an age when men were obliged to use their brains. Perhaps the human mind degenerated because, as science increased the ease of life, there was little need to use it. Some fine minds may still remain, but apparently they are few. We are doubters, schemers, bluffers. Golan-Kirt will find us tougher than these future-men."

CHAPTER III

The Struggle of the Ages

Bill produced cigarettes and the two lighted up. Slowly they walked across the vast arena, guns hanging in their right hands. People were filing into the place and the tiers were filling.

A roar came out of the tiers of seats before them. They recognized it. It was the cry of the gathering crowd, the cry for blood, the expression of a desire to see battle.

Harl grinned.

"Regular football crowd," he commented.

More and more poured into the arena, but it was apparent that the inhabitants of the ruined city could fill only a very small section of the thousands upon thousands of seats.

The two seemed lost in the mighty space. Above them, almost at the zenith, hung the vast red sun. They seemed to move in a twilight-filled desert rimmed in by enormous white cliffs.

"Denver must have been a large city at the time this place was built," commented Bill. "Think of the number of people it would hold. Wonder what it was used for?"

"Probably we'll never know," said Harl.

They had gained the approximate center of the arena.

Harl halted.

"Do you know," he said, "I've been thinking. It seems to me we must have a fairly good chance against Golan-Kirt. For the last fifteen minutes every thought of ours has been in open defiance of him, but he has not attempted our annihilation. Although it is possible he may only be biding his time. I am beginning to believe he can't read our minds as he could the mind of the old man. He killed him the moment he uttered a word of treason."

Bill nodded.

As if in answer to what Harl had said, a great weight seemed to press in upon them. Bill felt a deadly illness creeping over him. His knees sagged and his brain whirled. Spots danced before his eyes and a horrible pain gripped his stomach.

He took a step forward and stumbled. A hand clutched his shoulder and fiercely shook him. The shake momentarily cleared his brain. Through the clearing mist which seemed to hang before his eyes, he saw the face of his friend, a face white and lined.

The lips in the face moved.

"Buck up, old man. There's nothing wrong with you. You're feeling fine."

Something seemed to snap inside his head. This was suggestion—the suggestion of Golan-Kirt. He had to fight it. That was it—fight it.

He planted his feet firmly in the sand, straightened his shoulders with an effort, and smiled.

"Hell, no," he said, "there's nothing wrong with me. I'm feeling fine."

Harl slapped him on the back.

"That's the spirit," he roared. "It almost floored me for a minute. We've got to fight it, boy. We've got to fight it."

Bill laughed, harshly. His head was clear now and he could feel the strength flowing back into his body. They had won the first round!

"But where is this Golan-Kirt?" he burst out.

"Invisible," snarled Harl, "but I have a theory that he can't put in his best licks in such a state. We'll force him to show himself and then we'll give him the works."

The frenzied roar of the crowd came to their ears. Those on the bleachers had seen and appreciated the little drama out in the middle of the arena. They were crying for more.

Suddenly a spiteful rattle broke out behind the two.

They started. That sound was familiar. It was the rat-a-tat of a machine gun. With no ceremony they fell flat, pressing their bodies close against the ground, seeking to burrow into the sand.

Little puffs of sand spurted up all about them. Bill felt a searing pain in his arm. One of the bullets had found him. This was the end. There was no obstruction to shield them in this vast level expanse from the gun that chuckled and chattered at their rear. Another searing pain caught him in the leg. Another hit.

Then he laughed—a wild laugh. There was no machine gun, no bullets. It was all suggestion. A trick to make them believe they were being killed —a trick, which, if carried far enough, would kill them.

He struggled to his knees, hauling Harl up beside him. His leg and arm still pained, but he paid them no attention. There was nothing wrong with them, he told himself fiercely, absolutely nothing wrong.

"It's suggestion again," he shouted at Harl. "There isn't any machine gun."

Harl nodded. They regained their feet and turned. There, only a couple of hundred yards away, a khaki-clad figure crouched behind a gun that chattered wickedly, a red flame licking the muzzle.

"That isn't a machine gun," said Bill, speaking slowly.

"Of course, it's not a machine gun," Harl spoke as if by rote.

They walked slowly toward the flaming gun. Although bullets apparently whistled all about them, none struck them. The pain in Bill's arm and leg no longer existed.

Suddenly the gun disappeared, and with it the khaki-clad figure. One moment they were there, the next they were not.

"I thought it would do just that," said Bill.

"The old boy is still going strong, though," replied Harl. "Here is some more of his suggestion."

Harl pointed to one of the arching gateways. Through it marched file upon file of soldiers, clad in khaki, metal helmets on their heads, guns across their shoulders. An officer uttered a sharp command and the troops began to deploy over the field.

A shrill blast of a bugle drew the attention of the two time-travelers from the soldiers and through another gateway they beheld the advance of what appeared to be a cohort of Roman legionnaires. Shields flashed dully in the sun and the rattle of arms could be distinctly heard.

"Do you know what I believe?" asked Harl.

"What is it?"

"Golan-Kirt cannot suggest anything new to us. The machine guns and the soldiers and legionnaires are all things of which we have former knowledge."

"How is it," asked Bill, "that we see these things when we know they do not exist?"

"I do not know," replied Harl, "there are a lot of funny things about this business that I can't understand."

"Anyhow, he is giving the crowd a good show," observed Bill.

The bleachers were in an uproar. To the ears of the two came the shrill screaming of women, the loud roars of the men. The populace was thoroughly enjoying itself.

A lion, large and ferocious, growling fiercely, leaped past the two men. A thunder of hoof-beats announced the arrival of more of the brain creatures.

"It's about time for us to do something," said Harl.

He lifted his .45 high in the air and fired. A hush fell.

"Golan-Kirt, attention!" roared Harl, in a voice that could be heard in every part of the arena. "We challenge you to personal combat. We have no fear of your creatures. They cannot harm us. You are the one we wish to fight."

An awed silence fell over the crowd. It was the first time their god had ever been openly challenged. They waited for the two lone figures out in the arena to be stricken in a heap.

They were not stricken, however.

Again Harl's voice rang out.

"Come out of hiding, you fat-bellied toad!" he thundered. "Come and fight if you have the guts, you dirty, yellow coward!"

The crowd may not have gathered the exact meaning of the words, but the full insult of them was plain. A threatening murmur rolled out from the bleachers, and there was a sudden surging of the crowd. Men leaped over the low wall in front of the seats and raced across the arena.

Then a sonorous voice, deep and strong, rolled out.

"Stop," it said. "I, Golan-Kirt, will deal with these men."

Harl noticed that the soldiers and the lion had disappeared. The arena was empty except for him and his comrade and the score of futuremen who had halted in their tracks at the voice which had come out of nothingness.

They waited, tensed. Harl wriggled his feet into a firmer position. He slipped a cartridge in the gun to take the place of the one which had been fired. Bill mopped his brow with the sleeve of his coat.

"It's going to be brains now," Harl told his friend.

Bill grinned.

"Two mediocre intelligences against a great one," he joked.

"Look, Bill!" shouted Harl.

Directly in front and slightly above the level of their heads a field of light had formed, a small ball of brightness in the murky atmosphere. Slowly it grew. Vibrations set in.

The two watched, fascinated. The vibrations quickened until the whole field was quivering. As the vibrations increased the light faded and a monstrosity began to take form. Only vaguely could it be seen at first. Then it became clearer and clearer, began to take definite form.

Hanging in the air, suspended without visible means of support, was a gigantic brain, approximately two feet in diameter. A naked brain, with the convolutions exposed. It was a ghastly thing.

The horror of it was heightened by the two tiny, pig-like, lidless, close-set eyes and a curving beak which hung directly below the frontal portion of the brain, resting in what was apparently an atrophied face.

The two were aghast, but with a tremendous effort they kept close hold on their self-control.

"Greetings, Golan-Kirt," drawled Harl, sarcasm putting an edge to the words.

As he spoke, his arm swung up and under the pressure of his finger, the hammer of the gun slowly moved backward. But before the muzzle could be brought in line with the great brain, the arm stopped and Harl stood like a frozen man, held rigid by the frightful power which poured forth from Golan-Kirt.

Bill's arm flashed up and his .45 broke the silence with a sullen roar. However, even as he fired, his arm was flung aside as if by a mighty blow and the speeding bullet missed the huge brain by the mere fraction of an inch.

"Presumptuous fools," roared a voice, which, however, seemed not a voice, for there was no sound, merely the sense of hearing. The two, standing rigidly, as if at attention, realized that it was telepathy: that the brain before them was sending out powerful emanations.

"Presumptuous fools, you would fight me, Golan-Kirt? I, who have a hundred-fold the mental power of your combined brains? I, who hold the knowledge of all time?"

"We would fight you," snarled Harl. "We are going to fight you. We know you for what you are. You are not out of the Cosmos. You are a laboratory specimen. Unknown ages ago you were developed under artificial conditions. You are not immortal. You fear our weapons. A bullet in that dirty brain of yours will finish you."

"Who are you to judge," came the thought-wave, "you, with your tiny, twentieth century brain? You have come unbidden into my time, you have defied me. I shall destroy you. I, who came out of the Cosmos aeons ago to rule over the portion of the Universe I chose as my own, do not fear you or your ridiculous weapons."

"Yet you foiled us when we would have used our weapons on you. If I could reach you I would not need my weapon. I could tear you apart, destroy you with the strength of my two hands."

"Say on," rumbled the thought-waves. "Say what you believe me to be, and when you are done I shall obliterate you. You shall be dust floating in the air, ashes on the sands."

There was an unveiled tone of mockery in the brain emanations.

Harl raised his voice, almost shouting. It was a deliberate act, done in hopes the future-men would hear, that they might realize not too late the true nature of the tyrant Golan-Kirt. They did hear and their mouths gaped as they listened.

"You once were a man," Harl roared, "a great scientist. You studied the brain, specialized in it. At last you discovered a great secret, which gave you the power of developing the brain to an unheard-of degree. Sure of your technique, and realizing the power you might enjoy, you transformed yourself into a brain creature. You are a fraud and an impostor. You have mis-ruled these people for millions of years. You are not out of the Cosmos,—you are a man, or what once was a man. You are an atrocity, an abomination—"

The thought emanations which flowed from out the brain trembled, as if with rage.

"You lie. I am out of the Cosmos. I am immortal. I shall kill you— kill you."

Suddenly Bill laughed, a resounding guffaw. It was an escape from the terrible tension, but as he laughed a ludicrous angle presented itself—the twentieth century travelers millions of years ahead of their time wrangling with a cheat pawning himself off as a god on a people who would not be born until long after he was dead.

He felt the horrible power of Golan-Kirt centering upon him. Perspiration streamed down his face and his body trembled. He felt his strength leaving him.

He stopped laughing. As he did so, he seemed to be struck, as if by a blow. He staggered. Then sudden realization flashed through him. Laughter! Laughter, that was it. Laughter and ridicule! That would turn the trick.

"Laugh, you fool, laugh," he screamed at Harl.

Uncomprehendingly, Harl obeyed.

The two rocked with laughter. They whooped and roared.

Hardly knowing what he did, almost involuntarily, Bill screeched horrible things at the great brain, reviled it, taunted it, called it almost unspeakable names.

Harl began to understand. It was all a great game that Bill was playing. A supreme egoism such as was lodged in the brain pitted against them could not bear ridicule, would lose its grip before a storm of jeers. For uncounted centuries, through some miraculous power, it had lived and in all that time it had been accorded only the highest honor. Derision was something with which it was unacquainted, a terrible weapon suddenly loosed upon it.

Harl joined with Bill and hurled gibes at Golan-Kirt. It was a high carnival of mockery. They were not conscious of their words. Their brains responded to the emergency and their tongues formed sentences of unguessed taunts.

Between sentences they laughed, howling with satanic glee.

Through all their laughter they felt the power of the brain. They felt its anger mount at their taunting. Their bodies were racked with pain, they wanted to fall on the sands and writhe in agony, but they continued to laugh, to shout taunts.

It seemed an eternity that they fought with Golan-Kirt, all the time shrieking with laughter, while they suffered fine-edged torture from the tops of their heads to the soles of their feet. Still they dare not stop their laughter, dare not cease their hideous derision, poking fun at the huge intelligence which opposed them. That was their one weapon. Without it the engulfing waves of suggestion which poured with relentless fury upon them would have snapped asunder every nerve in their bodies.

They sensed the raging of the great brain. It was literally crazed with anger. They were "getting its goat!" They were ridiculing the very life out of it.

Unconsciously they allowed the pitch of their laughter to lower. From sheer exhaustion they lapsed into silence.

Suddenly they felt the terrible force of the brain renewed, as it drew upon some mysterious reserve strength. It struck them like a blow, doubling them over, clouding their eyes, dulling their minds, racking every nerve and joint.

Hot irons seemed to sear them, hundreds of needles seemed thrust in their flesh, sharp knives seemed to slash their bodies. They reeled blindly, gropingly, mouthing curses, crying out in pain.

Through the red haze of torture came a whisper, a soft, enchanting whisper, a whisper beckoning to them, showing them a way of escape.

"Turn your weapons on yourselves. End all of this torture. Death is painless."

The whisper fluttered through their brains. That was the way out! Why endure this seemingly endless torture? Death was painless. The muzzle against one's head, a pressure on the trigger, oblivion.

Bill placed his gun against his temple. His finger contracted against the trigger. He laughed. This was a joke. A rare joke. Robbing Golan-Kirt by his own hand.

Another voice burst through his laughter. It was Harl.

"You fool! It's Golan-Kirt! It's Golan-Kirt, you fool!"

He saw his friend staggering toward him, saw his face pinched with pain, saw the moving of the livid lips as they shouted the warning.

Bill's hand dropped to his side. Even as he continued that insane laughter, he felt chagrin steal over him. The hideous brain had played its trump card and had failed, but it had almost finished him. Had it not been for Harl he would have been stretched on the sand, a suicide, his head blown to bits.

Then suddenly they felt the power of the brain slipping, felt its strength falter and ebb. They had beaten it!

They sensed the gigantic struggle going on in that great brain, the struggle to regain the grip it had lost.

For years on end it had lived without struggle, without question that it was the ruler of the earth. They sensed the futile anger and the devastating fear which revolved in the convolutions of Golan-Kirt.

But he was beaten, beaten at last by men from out of a forgotten age. He had met defeat at the hands of ridicule, something he had never known, a thing he had not suspected.

His strength ebbed steadily. The twentieth century men felt his dread power lift from them, sensed the despair which surged through him.

They stopped their laughter, their sides sore, their throats hoarse. Then they heard. The arena resounded with laughter. The crowd was laughing. The horrible uproar beat like a tumult upon them. The future-men were roaring, bent over, stamping their feet, throwing back their heads, screaming to the murky skies. They were laughing at Golan-Kirt, screaming insults at him, hooting him. It was the end of his rule.

For generations the future-men had hated him with the very hate he had taught them. They had hated and feared. Now they feared no longer and hate rode unchained.

From a god he had fallen to the estate of a ridiculous fraud. He was a thing of pity, an uncloaked clown, simply a naked, defenseless brain that had bluffed its way through centuries of kingship.

Through bleared eyes the twentieth century men saw the great brain, writhing now under the scorn of its erstwhile subjects, being laughed powerless. No longer did it hold control over these creatures of a dying world. Its close-set eyes glowed fiercely, its beak clicked angrily. It was tired, too tired to regain its rule. It was the end of Golan-Kirt!

The revolvers of the time-travelers came up almost simultaneously. This time the sights lined on the brain. There was no power to ward off the danger.

The guns roared rapidly, spitting hateful fire. At the impact of the bullets the brain turned over in the air, blood spurted from it, great gashes appeared in it. With a thump it struck the ground, quivered and lay still.

The time-travelers, their eyes closing from sheer weariness, their knees suddenly weak, slumped to the sand, the .45's still smoking.

Over the arena floated the full-toned roar of the future-men.

"Hail to the Deliverers! Golan-Kirt is dead! His rule is ended! Hail to the saviors of the race!"

Epilogue

"It is impossible to reverse time. You cannot travel back to your own age. I have no idea of what will occur if you attempt it, but I do know it is impossible. We of this age knew travel into the future was possible, but we lacked the technique to build a machine to try it. Under the rule of Golan-Kirt there was no material progress, only a steady degeneration. We know that it is impossible to reverse time. We, as a people, beg you not to attempt it."

Old Agnar Nohl, his white beard streaming in the wind, his hair flying, spoke seriously. There was a troubled frown on his face.

"We love you," he went on, "you freed us of the tyranny of the brain which ruled over us for uncounted time. We need you. Stay with us, help us rebuild this land, help us construct machines, give us some of the marvelous knowledge which we, as a race, have lost. We can give you much in return, for we have not forgotten all the science we knew before the coming of Golan-Kirt."

Harl shook his head.

"We must at least try to go back," he said.

The two twentieth century men stood beside the plane. Before them was a solid mass of humanity, a silent humanity in the shadow of the silent ruins of the city of Denver, the future-men who had come to bid the time-travelers a regretful farewell.

A chill wind howled over the desert, carrying its freight of sand. The furs of the future-men fluttered in the gale as it played a solemn dirge between the ruined walls of humbled buildings.

"If there was a chance of your success, we would speed you on your way," said old Agnar, "but we are reluctant to let you go to what may be your death. We are selfish enough to wish to hold you for ourselves, but we love you enough to let you go. You taught us hate was wrong, you removed the hate that ruled us. We wish only the best for you.

"It is impossible to go back in time. Why not remain? We need you badly. Our land grows less and less food every year. We must discover how to make synthetic food or we shall starve. This is only one of our problems. There are many others. You cannot go back. Stay and help us!"

Again Harl shook his head.

"No, we must try it. We may fail, but we must try it at least. If we succeed we shall return and bring with us books of knowledge and tools to work with."

Agnar combed his beard with skinny fingers.

"You'll fail," he said.

"But if we don't we will return," said Bill.

"Yes, if you don't," replied the old man.

"We are going now," said Bill. "We thank you for your thoughtfulness. We must at least try. We are sorry to leave you. Please believe that."

"I do believe it," cried the old man and he seized their hands in a fare-well clasp.

Harl opened the door of the plane and Bill clambered in.

At the door Harl stood with upraised hand.

"Good-bye," he said. "Some day we will return."

The crowd burst into a roar of farewell. Harl climbed into the plane and closed the door.

The motors bellowed, droning out the shouting of the future-men and the great machine charged down the sand. With a rush it took the air. Three times Bill circled the ruined city in a last mute good-bye to the men who watched silently and sorrowfully below.

Then Harl threw the lever. Again the utter darkness, the feeling of hanging in nothingness.

The motors, barely turning, muttered at the change. A minute passed, two minutes.

"Who says we can't travel back in time!" Harl shouted triumphantly. He pointed to the needle. It was slowly creeping back across the face of the dial.

"Maybe the old man was wrong after—"

Bill never finished the sentence.

"Roll her out," he screamed at Harl, "roll her out. One of our engines is going dead!"

Harl snatched at the lever, jerked frantically at it. The faulty motor choked and coughed, sputtered, then broke into a steady drone.

The two men in the cabin regarded one another with blanched faces. They knew they had escaped a possible crash—and death—by bare seconds.

Again they hung in the air. Again they saw the brick-red sun, the desert, and the sea. Below them loomed the ruins of Denver.

"We couldn't have gone far back in time," said Harl. "It looks the same as ever."

They circled the ruins.

"We had better land out in the desert to fix up the engine," suggested Harl. "Remember we have traveled back in time and Golan-Kirt still rules over the land. We don't want to have to kill him a second time. We might not be able to do it."

The plane was flying low and he nosed it up. Again the faulty engine sputtered and missed.

"She's going dead this time for certain," yelled Bill. "We'll have to chance it, Harl. We have to land and chance getting away again."

Harl nodded grimly.

Before them lay the broad expanse of the arena. It was either that or crash.

As Bill nosed the plane down the missing motor sputtered for the last time, went dead.

They flashed over the white walls of the amphitheater and down into the arena. The plane struck the sand, raced across it, slowed to a stop.

Harl opened the door.

"Our only chance is to fix it up in a hurry and get out of here," he shouted at Bill. "We don't want to meet that damn brain again."

He stopped short.

"Bill," he spoke scarcely above a whisper, "am I seeing things?"

Before him, set on the sands of the arena, only a few yards from the plane, was a statue of heroic size, a statue of himself and Bill.

Even from where he stood he could read the inscription, carved in the white stone base of the statue in characters which closely resembled written English.

Slowly, haltingly, he read it aloud, stumbling over an occasional queer character.

"Two men, Harl Swanson, and Bill Kressman, came out of time to kill Golan-Kirt and to free the race."

Below it he saw other characters.

"They may return."

"Bill," he sobbed, "we haven't traveled back in time. We have traveled further into the future. Look at that stone—eroded, ready to crumble to pieces. That statue has stood there for thousands of years!"

Bill slumped back into his seat, his face ashen, his eyes staring.

"The old man was right," he screamed. "He was right. We'll never see the twentieth century again."

He leaned over toward the time machine.

His face twitched.

"Those instruments," he shrieked, "those damned instruments! They were wrong. They lied, they lied!"

With his bare fists he beat at them, smashing them, unaware that the glass cut deep gashes and his hands were smeared with blood.

Silence weighed down over the plain. There was absolutely no sound.

Bill broke the silence.

"The future-men," he cried, "where are the future-men?"

He answered his own question.

"They are all dead," he screamed, "all dead. They are starved—starved because they couldn't manufacture synthetic food. We are alone! Alone at the end of the world!"

Harl stood in the door of the plane.

Over the rim of the amphitheater the huge red sun hung in a sky devoid of clouds. A slight wind stirred the sand at the base of the crumbling statue.

Cliff Simak is a particularly prominent figure in the science fiction world. "The World of the Red Sun" was his first published story, and it was simply and straightforwardly told. It had a sad ending, too, and I remember that impressed me at the time. I could not help but recognize the force of a dramatic and ironic ending. ("The Man Who Evolved" had possessed one, too.)

Simak was unusual among the early authors in that he survived the Coming of Campbell. Most early authors did not. (It was rather like the coming of talking pictures, which proved the ruin of so many actors who had learned their job in the world of the silents.)

Meek, for instance, hardly wrote anything after 1932, and Miller wrote infrequently. Jones and Hamilton continued to write frequently but hardly ever appeared in Campbell's *Astounding*, which was all that counted through the 1940s.

Simak was quite different. He published four more stories in 1932 and then nothing more until the Campbell era began, in 1938. He then began to write prolifically for the various magazines, including *Astounding*, and was soon numbered among the recognized members of Campbell's "stable" —that is, those authors whom he had discovered or developed (or both).

Indeed, Simak went on to grow even larger in stature as the field expanded in the 1950s and 1960s, when Campbell no longer held the monopoly. Simak was Guest of Honor at the World Science Fiction Convention held in Boston in 1971, and just the other day I received the hardback edition of his most recent novel, *Cemetery World*.

In the gap between 1932 and 1938, I had forgotten Clifford Simak, though not "The World of the Red Sun." I rediscovered him when he wrote "Rule 18," which appeared in the July 1938 issue of *Astounding Science Fiction*. What followed from that and how we grew to be close friends I mentioned in *The Early Asimov*.

It was not till a number of years after I had become friends with Cliff that I discovered, quite by accident, that it was he who had written the story I had once told with such pleasure and success to my junior high school classmates. What a happy discovery that was!

Simak was the first to teach me, by example, of the value of an un-adorned style. I explained that in *The Early Asimov*, and I want to mention that here, too.

In the fall of 1931 (inspired, perhaps, by my success in interesting my friends in the science fiction tales I retold), I began to try my hand at making up stories of my own.

I didn't write science fiction, however. I had a most exalted notion of the intense skills and vast scientific knowledge required of authors in the field, and I dared not aspire to such things. Instead, I began to write a tale of ordinary planetbound adventure called "The Greenville Chums at College."

I worked with a pencil and a five-cent notebook and eventually wrote eight chapters before fading out. I remember trying to tell the story of the Greenville Chums to one of those friends who had listened steadily to my retelling of science fiction. With a certain precocious caution, I had chosen the one who seemed most consistently enthusiastic. After I had told him what I had written that day, he asked eagerly if he could borrow the book when I was done.

I had either neglected to make it clear to him, or he had failed to understand, that I was *writing* the book. He thought it was another already printed story I was retelling. The implied compliment staggered me, and from that day on, I secretly took myself seriously as a writer.

Part Three

1932

IN THE SPRING of 1932, I completed my stay at Junior High School 149. The class held the graduation ceremonies at a fancy auditorium somewhere in Brooklyn. My father gave me a fountain pen as a graduation present (the traditional gift, of course, but very appropriate in my case—though neither my father nor I realized that at the time).

More important, he and my mother actually managed to shake off the candy-store duties (I don't remember whether they closed the store or hired a temporary store sitter) in order to attend the graduation. They took it *very* seriously.

I remember only two things. First, the glee club sang "Gaudeamus Igitur," which included the line "Glorious youth is with us." I was at once overwhelmed with a sharp and sorrowful pang at the thought that I was graduating and that youth was slipping fast away.

Yet I was only twelve years old at the time, and here it is over forty years later and youth *still* hasn't slipped away. (Well, it hasn't, you rotten kids.)

The second thing I remember was that two awards were given out, one for excellence in biology and the other for excellence in mathematics. Both winners marched forward and onto the stage and were covered with glory in the sight of their proud parents. And I knew that somewhere in the audience my father's face was setting into lines of grim disapproval, since neither winner was I.

Sure enough, when we were all home, my father, in awful, patriarchal tones, demanded to know why it was that I had won neither prize.

"Papa," I said (for I had had time to think out the best way of putting it), "the kid who won the mathematics prize is lousy in biology. The kid who won the biology prize can't add two and two. And as for me, I was second in line for *both* prizes."

That was quite true and it took me neatly off the hook. Not another word was said.

The last months at the junior high school were enlivened for me by "Tumithak of the Corridors," by Charles R. Tanner, which appeared in the January 1932 *Amazing Stories*.

TUMITHAK OF THE CORRIDORS

by *Charles R. Tanner*

FOREWORD

It is only within the last few years that archeological science has reached a point where we may begin to appreciate the astonishing advances in science that our ancestors had achieved before the Great Invasion. Excavations in the ruins of London and New York have been especially prolific in yielding knowledge of the life that those ancestors led. That they possessed the secret of flying, and a knowledge of chemistry and electricity far beyond ours is now certain; and there is even some evidence that they surpassed us in medicine and some of the arts. Taking their civilization as a whole, it is quite doubtful if we have even yet surpassed them in general knowledge.

Until the time of the Invasion, their discoveries of the secrets of Nature seem to have been made steadily in regular geometric progression, and we have good cause to believe that it was the people of earth who first solved the secret of interplanetary flight. The many romances that have been written by novelists dealing with this time, testify to the interest which we of today take in the history of what we call the Golden Age.

But the present story deals neither with the days of the Invasion, nor with life as it was in the Golden Age before it. It tells, instead, of the life of that semi-mythical, semi-historical character, Tumithak of Loor, who, legend tells us, was the first man to rebel against the savage shelks. Although innumerable facts are still lacking, recent investigations in the Pits and Corridors have thrown much light on what was obscure in this hero's life. That he really lived and fought is now certain to be true; that he accomplished the miracles accredited to him by legend is just as certain to be untrue.

We can feel sure, for instance, that he never lived for the two hundred and fifty years that are ascribed to him; that his wonderful strength and imperviousness to the rays of the shelks are mythical, as are doubtless the stories of his destruction of the six cities.

But our knowledge of his life increases as our credibility in the legends decreases, and the time has come when we can grasp dimly, but with a more rational viewpoint, the truth about his deeds. So, in this tale, the author makes an attempt to rationalize, to place properly in its historical setting, the early life of a great hero who dared to strike boldly for Mankind, in the days when the Beasts of Venus held all the earth in thrall . . .

CHAPTER I

The Boy and the Book

As far as eye could see the long somber corridor extended. Fifteen feet high and as many wide it ran on and on, its brown, glassy walls presenting an unvarying sameness. At intervals along the center line of the ceiling large glowing lights appeared, flat plates of cool white luminescence that had shone without attention for centuries. At intervals equally frequent, were deep-cut doors, draped with a rough burlap-like cloth, their sills worn down by the passing generations of feet. Nowhere was the monotony of the scene broken unless it were in some places, where the corridor was crossed by another of equal simplicity.

The passage was by no means deserted. Here and there, throughout its length, scattered figures appeared—men, for the most part blue-eyed and red-haired and dressed in rough burlap tunics that were gathered at the waist by wide, pocketed belts with enormous buckles. A few women were also in evidence, differing from the men in the length of their hair and tunics. All moved with a furtive slinking air, for though it was many years since the Terror had been seen, the habits of a hundred generations were not easily thrown off. And so the hall, its frequenters, their clothes and even their habits combined to complete the somber monotone.

From somewhere far below this corridor came the steady beat and throb of some gigantic machine; a beat that continued unceasingly and was so much a part of the life of these people that it was only with difficulty that they could be brought to notice it at all. Yes its beat bore down on them, penetrated their minds, and, with its steady rhythm, affected all that they did.

One part of the hall seemed to be more populous than any other. The lights here glowed brighter, the cloths that covered the doorways were cleaner and newer, and many more people appeared. Sneaking in and out of the doorways they went, for all the world like rabbits engaged in some big business enterprise.

Out of one of the side doorways, a boy and girl appeared. About fourteen years of age, they were exceptionally tall for children, apparently having already reached their full growth, though their immaturity was evident. They, too, like their elders, were blue-eyed and red-haired; a complexion due to the eternal lack of sunshine and lifelong exposure to the rays of the corridor lights. There was a certain boldness and quickness about them that caused many of the folk of the corridor to frown disapprovingly as they passed. One could see that these older ones felt that the younger generation was fast riding to destruction. Certainly, sooner or later, this boldness and loudness would bring down the Terror from the Surface.

But sublimely indifferent to the disapproval that was so in evidence around them, the two youngsters continued upon their way. They turned from the main corridor into one less brilliantly lighted, and after traversing it for nearly a mile, turned into another. The hall in which they now found themselves was narrow and inclined upward at a decided angle. It was entirely deserted and the thick dust and neglected condition of the lights showed that it was long since men had lived here. The many doorways were without the draped curtains that concealed the interior of the inhabited apartments in the larger corridors; but many of the doorways were almost entirely covered with draperies of cobwebs covered with dust. The girl drew closer to the boy as they continued up the passage; but aside from this she showed no sign of fear. After some time the passageway grew steeper, and at last ended in a cul-de-sac. The two seated themselves in the rubble that littered the floor and presently began to talk in a low tone.

"It must have been years since men have come here," said the girl, softly. "Perhaps we will find something of great value which was left here when men deserted this corridor."

"I think Tumithak is too hopeful, when he tells us of possible treasures in these halls," answered the boy. "Surely there have been men in these halls, searching as we are, since they were abandoned."

"Tumithak should be here by now," the girl said, after a while. "Do you think he will come?" Her eyes strove vainly to pierce the gloom down the hallway.

"Why, of course, he will come, Thupra," said her companion. "Has Tumithak ever failed to meet us as he promised?"

"But to come here, alone!" protested Thupra. "I should die of fright, Nikadur, if you weren't here."

"There isn't really any danger here," he said. "The men of Yakra could never enter these halls without passing through the main corridor. And many, many years have passed since Loor has seen a shelk."

"Grandfather Koniak once saw a shelk," reminded Thupra.

"Yes, but not here in Loor. He saw it in Yakra, years ago, when he fought the Yakrans as a young man. Remember, the Loorians were successful in their campaign against the Yakrans and drove them out of their city and into the corridors beyond. And then suddenly there was flame and terror, and a band of shelks appeared. Grandfather Koniak saw but one, and that one almost caught him before he escaped." Nikadur smiled. "It is a wonderful tale, but I think we have only Grandfather Koniak's word for it."

"But really, Nikadur—" the girl was beginning, when she was interrupted by a rustling noise from one of the web-hung doorways. Like a flash, boy and girl both leapt to their feet and sped in panic down the passage without so much as a single glance backward, totally unaware of the youth who had stepped from the doorway and who was now leaning against the wall, watching their flight with a cynical smile on his face.

At a glance, this youth seemed not unlike the others who lived in the corridors. The same red hair and clear translucent skin, the same rough tunic and enormous belt characterized this lad as it did all the others of Loor. But the discerning eye would have noticed in the immense brow, the narrow, hooked nose and the keen eyes, a promise of the greatness that was to some day be his.

The boy watched his fleeing friends for a moment and then gave a low bird-like whistle. Thupra stopped suddenly and turned around, and then, seeing the newcomer, called to Nikadur. The boy stopped his flight, too, and together they returned, rather shamefaced, to the end of the passage.

"You frightened us, Tumithak," said the girl, reproachfully. "What in the world were you doing in that room? Weren't you afraid to go in there alone?"

"Nothing is in there to hurt me," answered Tumithak, loftily. "Often and often I have browsed around through these corridors and apartments and never yet have I seen any living thing, save the spiders and the bats. I was seeking for forgotten things," he went on, and his eyes grew suddenly brighter. "And look! I have found a book!" And, reaching into the bosom of his tunic, he drew forth his prize and exhibited it proudly to the others.

"This is an *old* book," he said. "See?"

It certainly was an old book. The cover was gone, more than half the leaves were missing, and the thin metal sheets of which the leaves were composed were even beginning to oxidize on the edges. Certainly, this book had been lying forgotten for centuries.

Nikadur and Thupra looked at it in awe, the awe that an illiterate person naturally holds for all the mysteries of the magic black marks that transmit thoughts. But Tumithak could read. He was the son of Tumlook, one of the food men, the men who held the secret of preparing the synthetic food that these people lived on, and these food men, as well as the doctors and the light and power men, retained many of the secrets of the wisdom of their ancestors. Foremost among these secrets was the very necessary art of reading; and as Tumithak was intended to follow in his father's footsteps, Tumlook had early trained him in this wonderful art.

So, after the two had looked at the book and held it in their hands, and wondered, they beseeched Tumithak to read it to them. Often, they had listened in wide-eyed wonder as he read to them from some of the rare works the food men owned, and they never wasted a chance to watch the apparently mystifying process of changing the queer marks on the metal sheets into sounds and sentences.

Tumithak smiled at their importuning, and then, because secretly he was as anxious as they to know what the long-forgotten script contained, he motioned them to be seated on the floor beside him, and opening the book, began to read:

"The manuscript of Davon Starros; written at Pitmouth, Sol 22nd, in the year of the Invasion, 161, or in the old style—A.D. 3218."

Tumithak paused.

"That *is* an old book," whispered Nikadur in an awed voice, and Tumithak nodded.

"Nearly two thousand years!" he answered, "I wonder what the figures A.D. 3218 stand for?"

He puzzled over the book for a moment and then resumed his reading.

"I am an old man, in these latter days, and to one who can remember the day when men still dared to fight, now and then, for liberty, it is indeed a bitter thing to see how the race has fallen.

"There is growing up among men in these days a hopeless superstition to the effect that man can never conquer, and must never attempt to even battle with the shelks, and it is to combat this superstition that the author here writes the story of the conquest of earth, in the hope that at some future time, a man will arise who will have the courage to face the conquerors of Man and again do battle. In the hope that this man will appear and that he may know the creatures against whom he fights, this story is written.

"The scientists who tell of the days before the Invasion, inform us that man was once little more than a beast. Through thousands of years he gradually worked his way upward to civilization, learning the arts of living, until he conquered all the world for his own.

"He learned the secret of producing food from the very elements themselves, he learned the secret of imitating the life-giving light of the sun, his great airships sped through the atmosphere as easily as his waterships

sped through the sea. Wonderful, disintegrating rays dissolved the hill
that stood in his way, and as a result, long canals brought water from the
ocean to inaccessible deserts, making them blossom like earth's most fertile
regions. From pole to pole, man's mighty cities grew, and from pole to
pole man was supreme.

"For thousands of years, men quarreled among themselves, and great
wars tore the earth, until at last their civilization reached a point where
these wars ceased. A great era of peace settled down upon the earth, sea
and land alike were conquered by man, and he began to look out to the
other worlds that swung about the sun, wondering if these, too, might
not be conquered.

"It was many centuries before they learned enough to attempt a journey
into the depths of space. A way had to be found to avoid the countless meteors that filled the paths between the planets. A way had to be
found to insulate against the deadly cosmic rays. It seemed that no sooner
was one difficulty overcome than another arose to take its place. But one
after another the difficulties in the way of interplanetary flight disappeared
and at last the day came when a mighty vessel, hundreds of feet long, lay
ready to leap into space to explore the other worlds."

Tumithak again paused in his reading.

"It must be a wonderful secret," he said. "I seem to be reading words,
but I do not know what they mean. Some one is going somewhere, but
that's about all I can make of it. Shall I go on?"

"Yes! Yes!" they cried; so he continued:

"It was under the command of a man named Henric Sudiven; and, of
all the great company that manned it, only he returned to the world of
men to tell of the terrible adventures that they met with on the planet
Venus, the world to which they traveled.

"The trip to Venus was a highly successful one, and quite uneventful.
Week after week passed, while the evening star, as men called it, grew
ever brighter and larger. The ship worked perfectly, and though the journey was a long one to those who were used to crossing an ocean in a single
night, the time did not hang heavy on their hands. The day came when
they sailed over the low rolling plains and broad valleys of Venus, under
the thick mantle of clouds that forever hides the surface of that planet
from the sun, and marveled at the great cities and works of civilization
that were in evidence everywhere.

"After hovering over a great city for some time, they landed and were
welcomed by the strange, intelligent creatures that ruled over Venus; the
same creatures that we know today by the name of shelks. The shelks
thought them demi-gods and would have worshipped them; but Sudiven
and his companions, true products of earth's noblest culture, scorned to

dissemble; and when they had learned the language of the shelks, told them quite truthfully just who they were and from whence they came.

"The astonishment of the shelks knew no bounds. They were skilled far more than men in mechanical science; their knowledge of electricity and chemistry was quite as great; but astronomy and its kindred sciences were totally unknown to them. Imprisoned as they were under the eternal canopy of clouds that hides forever the sight of outer space, they had never dreamed of other worlds than the one they knew; and it was only with difficulty that they were at last persuaded that Sudiven's story was true.

"But, once convinced, the attitude of the shelks underwent a decided change. No longer were they deferential and friendly. They suspected that man had come only to conquer them and they determined to beat him at his own game. There was a certain lack of the more humane feelings in the make-up of the shelks, and they were quite unable to conceive of a friendly visit from strangers of another world.

"The Tellurians soon found themselves locked up in a great metal tower many miles from their space flier. In a moment of carelessness, one of Sudiven's companions had let drop the remark that this flier was the only one yet built upon the earth, and the shelks decided to take advantage of this fact, to begin at once the conquest of earth.

"They took possession at once of the Tellurians' vessel, and with that unity of purpose that is so characteristic of the shelks and so lacking in man, began at once the construction of a vast number of similar machines. All over the planet, the great machine-shops hummed and clattered with the noise of the work; and while the earth awaited the triumphal return of her explorers, the day of her doom drew nearer and nearer.

"But Sudiven and the other Tellurians, locked up in their tower, had not given up to despair. Time after time, they attempted to escape, and there is no doubt but that the shelks would have slain them to a man, had they not hoped to extract further knowledge from them before they killed them. For once the shelks were in error; they should have slain the Tellurians, every one; for about a week before the date set for the departure of the shelks' great fleet of machines, Sudiven and about a dozen of his companions managed to escape.

"At terrific risk they made their way across the country to the place where their space car lay. An idea can be had of the dangers of the journey when one realizes that on Venus, that is, on the inhabited side, it is always day. There was no concealing night to enable the Tellurians to travel without hope of discovery. But at last they came upon their car, guarded only by a few unarmed shelks. The battle that ensued is one that should go down in man's history, to inspire him in all the ages to come. When it was over the shelks were all dead and only seven men were left to man the space-flier on its journey back to earth.

"For weeks, the great bullet-shaped flier sped across the vast emptiness of space and at last landed upon the earth. Sudiven alone remained alive when it landed; the others had succumbed to some strange disease, a disease that had been given to them by the shelks.

"But Sudiven was alive and remained alive long enough to warn the world. Faced with this sudden terror, the world had little time for any but defensive measures. The construction of vast underground pits and caverns was begun at once, the intention being to construct great underground cities, in which man could hide himself and from which he could emerge to conquer his enemies at his leisure. But before they were well started, the shelks arrived and the war was on!

"Never, in the days when man warred with man, had anyone dreamed of a war like this. The shelks had arrived by the millions; it was estimated that fully two hundred thousand space cars took part in the invasion. For days man's defensive measures kept the shelks from gaining a landing space on the earth; they were forced to fly far above the surface, dropping their deadly gases and explosives where they could. From his subterranean halls, man sent up vast quantities of gases as deadly as those of the shelks, and their disintegrating rays sent hundreds of the space-cars into nothingness, killing off the shelks like flies. And from their fliers, the shelks dropped vast quantities of flaming chemicals into the pits that men had dug, chemicals that burned with terrific violence and exhausted the oxygen of the caverns, causing men to perish by the thousand.

"Ever, as men found themselves defeated by the shelks, they drove deeper and deeper into the earth, their wonderful disintegrations dissolving the rock almost as fast as man could walk through the corridor it dug. Men were forced from the Surface at last, and a million intricate warrens of corridors and passages honeycombed the earth for miles beneath the surface. It was impossible for the shelks to ever thread the mazes of the innumerable labyrinths, and so man reached a position of comparative safety.

"And thus came the deadlock.

"The Surface had become the property of the savage shelks, while far below them in the pits and corridors, man labored to hold on to the dregs of civilization that were left him. An unequal game it was, for man was sadly handicapped—the supplies of elements that produced the disintegrating rays gradually diminished, and there was no way of renewing them; they were unable to secure wood, or the thousand and one varieties of vegetation on which their industries were based; the men of one set of corridors had no way of communicating with the men of another; and always came hordes of shelks, down into the corridors, hunting men for sport!

"The only thing that enabled them to live at all was the wonderful ability to create synthetic foods out of the very rock itself.

"So it was that man's civilization, fought for and won after centuries of struggle, collapsed in a dozen years; and over it was imposed the Terror. Men, like rabbits, lived a life of fear and trembling in their underground holes, daring less each year, as time went by, and spending all their time and energy in devising means to sink their pits deeper and deeper into the ground. Today it seems that man's subjugation is complete. For over a hundred years, no man has dared to think of revolt against the shelks, any more than a rat would think of revolt against man. Unable to form a unified government, unable even to communicate with his brethren in the neighboring corridors, man has come to accept, far too willingly, his place as merely the highest of the lower animals. The spider-like Beasts of Venus are the supreme Masters of our planet, and—"

The manuscript had come to an end. Although the book had originally been much longer, although, indeed, what was left of it was probably little more than an introduction to some work on the life and customs of the shelks, the remainder was missing and the droning sing-song voice of Tumithak ceased as he read the concluding unfinished sentence. For several moments there was silence and then—

"How hard it was to understand," said Thupra. "I only know that men were fighting with shelks, just as though they were Yakrans."

"Who could have conceived such a story?" murmured Nikadur. "Men fighting with shelks: Of all the impossible tales!"

Tumithak did not answer. For quite a while he sat in silence and stared at the book as one who suddenly beheld some dazzling vision.

At last he spoke.

"Nikadur, that is history!" he exclaimed. "That is no strange impossible tale of fancy. Something tells me that those men really lived; that that war was really fought: How else can we explain the life that we live. Have we not wondered often—have not our fathers wondered before us—how our wise ancestors ever gained the wisdom to build the great pits and corridors? We know that our ancestors had great knowledge; how did they come to lose it?

"Oh, I know that no legend of ours even suggests such a thing as men ruling this world," he went on, as he saw the incredulous look in the eyes of his companions. "But there is something—something in that book that tells me it is surely true. Just think, Nikadur! That book was written only a hundred and sixty years after the savage shelks invaded the earth! How much more that writer must have known than we who live two thousand years later. Nikadur, once men fought with shelks!" He arose, his eyes gleaming with the first glow of the fanatical light that, in after years, was to make him a man apart from his fellows, "*Once men fought with shelks:* and with the help of the High One, they shall do so again! Nikadur! Thupra! Some day *I* shall fight a shelk," he flung his arms wide, "some day I shall *slay* a shelk!

"And to that I dedicate my life!"

He stood for a moment with his arms outstretched, and then, as if oblivious of their presence, he dashed down the hallway and in a moment was lost in the gloom. For a moment the two stared after him in amazement, and then, clasping hands, they walked slowly, soberly after him. They knew that something had suddenly inspired their friend, but whether it was genius or madness they could not tell. And they were not to know with certainty for many years.

CHAPTER II

The Three Strange Gifts

Tumlook contemplated his son proudly. The years that had passed since he had discovered the strange manuscript and acquired his strange obsession may have ruined his mind, as some said, but they had certainly been kind to him, physically. Six feet tall, Tumithak stood (an exceptional height for these dwellers in the corridors), and every inch seemed to be of iron muscle. Today, on his twentieth birthday, there was not a man that would not have hailed him as one of the leaders of the city, had it not been for his preposterous mania. For Tumithak was resolved to kill a shelk!

For years—in fact, since he had found the manuscript, at the age of fourteen—he had directed all his studies to this end. He had pored over maps of the corridors, ancient maps that had not been used for centuries— maps that showed the way to the Surface—and he was known to be an authority on all the secret passages in the pit. He had little idea of what the Surface was really like; there was little in the stories of his people to tell him of it. But of one thing he was certain, and that was, that on the Surface he would find the shelks.

He had studied the various weapons that man could still rely on—the sling, the sword, and the bow; and had made himself proficient in the use of all three. Indeed, in every way possible, he had prepared himself for the great work to which he had decided to devote his life. Of course, he had met with the opposition of his father, of the whole tribe, for that matter, but with the singleness of purpose that only a fanatic can attain, he persisted in his idea, resolved that when he was of age he would bid his people adieu, and set out for the Surface. He had given little thought to the details of what he would do when he arrived there. That would all depend on what he found. One thing he was sure of—that he would kill a shelk and bring its body back to show his people that men could still triumph over those who thought they were man's masters.

And today he became of age; today he was twenty and Tumlook could not resist being secretly proud of this astounding son of his, even though he had done everything in his power to turn him from the impossible dream that he had conceived. Now that the day had come when Tumithak was to start on his absurd quest, Tumlook had to admit that in his heart, he had long been one with Tumithak, and that now he was eager to see the boy started on his way. He spoke:

"Tumithak," he said. "For years, I have sought to turn you from the impossible task that you have set yourself. For years, you have opposed me and persisted in believing in the actual possibility of achieving your dream. And now the day has come when you are to actually set out to achieve it. Do not think that it was anything other than a father's love that led me to oppose your ambition, and to try and keep you in Loor. But now that the day has come when you are free to do as you please, and as you are still determined to make your incredible attempt, you must at least allow your father to help you all he can."

He paused and lifted to the table a box about a foot square. He opened it and drew from it three strange-looking objects.

"Here," he said, impressively, "are three of the most precious treasures of the food-men; implements devised by our wise ancestors of old. This one," and he picked up a cylindrical tube about an inch in diameter and a foot long, "is a torch, a wonderful torch that will give you light in the dark corridors, by merely pressing this button. Take care not to waste its power, it is not made of the eternal light that our ancestors set in the ceilings. It is based on a different principle and after a certain time its power is exhausted."

Tumlook picked up the next object gingerly.

"This, too, is something that will surely help you, though it is neither so rare nor so wonderful as the other two. It is a charge of high explosive, such as we use occasionally for closing a corridor, or in mining the elements from which our food is made. There is no telling when it may come in handy, on your way to the Surface.

"And here," he picked up the last article, which looked like a small pipe with a handle set on one end, at right angles. "Here is the most wonderful article of all. It shoots a small pellet of lead, and it shoots it with such force that it will pierce even a sheet of metal! Each time this small trigger on the side is pressed, a pellet is ejected from the mouth of the pipe, with terrific force. It kills, Tumithak, kills even quicker than an arrow, and much surer. Use it carefully for there are but ten pellets, and when they are gone, the instrument is useless."

He laid the three articles on the table before him, and pushed them across to Tumithak. The younger man took them and stowed them carefully in the pockets of his wide belt.

"Father," he said, slowly, "you know it is not anything in my heart that commands me to leave you and go on this quest. There is something, higher than either of you or I, that has spoken to me and that I must obey. Since mother's death, you have been both mother and father to me, and so I probably love you more than the average man loves his father. But I have had a Vision! I dream of a time when Man will once again rule on the Surface and not a shelk will exist to oppose him. But that time can never come as long as men believe the shelks to be invincible, and so I am going to prove that they can really be slain—and by men!"

He paused and before he could continue, the door opened and Nikadur and Thupra entered. The former was a man now, the responsibility of a householder having fallen upon him at his father's death, two years before. And the latter had grown into a beautiful woman, a woman that Nikadur was soon to marry. They both greeted Tumithak with deference and when Thupra spoke, it was in an awed voice, as one who addressed a demi-god; and Nikadur, too, had obviously come to look upon Tumithak as something more than mortal. These two, with the possible exception of Tumlook, were the only ones who took Tumithak seriously, and so they were the only ones that he would call his friends.

"Do you leave us today, Tumithak?" asked Thupra.

Tumithak nodded. "Yes," he answered. "This very day. I start for the Surface. Before a month has gone by, I will lie dead in some distant corridor, or you shall look on the head of a shelk!"

Thupra shuddered. Either of these alternatives seemed terrible enough to her. But Nikadur was thinking of the more immediate dangers of the journey.

"You will have no trouble on the road to Nonone," he said, thoughtfully. "But mustn't you pass through the town of Yakra on the way to the Surface?"

"Yes," answered Tumithak. "There is no road to the Surface, except through Yakra. And beyond Yakra are the Dark Corridors, where men have not ventured for hundreds of years."

Nikadur considered. The city of Yakra had for over a century been the enemy of the people of Loor. Situated as it was, more than twenty miles nearer the Surface than Loor, it was inevitable that it should be much more conscious of the Terror. And it was just as inevitable that the people of Yakra should envy the Loorians their comparative safety, and continually make attempts to seize the city for their own. The small town of Nonone, located between the two larger cities, found itself sometimes fighting with the Yakrans, sometimes against them, as suited the convenience of the chiefs of the more powerful cities. Just as present, and indeed for the past twenty years, it was allied to Loor, and so Tumithak expected no trouble on his journey until he attempted to pass through Yakra.

"And the Dark Corridors?" questioned Nikadur.

"Beyond Yakra, there are no lights," replied Tumithak. "Men have avoided these passages for centuries. They are entirely too near the Surface for safety. Yakrans have at times attempted to explore them, but the parties that went out never returned. At least, so the men of Nonone have told me."

Thupra was about to make some remark, but Tumithak turned and busied himself with the pack of foodstuff that he intended to take with him on his journey. He slung it over his back and turned toward the door.

"The time has come for me to begin my journey," he said impressively. "This is the moment that I have awaited for years. Farewell, father! Farewell, Thupra! Nikadur, take good care of my little friend, and—if I do not return, name your first-born after me."

With a dramatic gesture that was characteristic of him, he thrust the door curtain aside and strode out into the corridor. The three followed him, calling and waving as he walked on up the hallway, but without so much as a backward glance, he strode along until he disappeared in the distant gloom.

They stood then, for a while, and then, with a dry sob, Tumlook turned and re-entered the apartment.

"He'll never return," he muttered to Nikadur. "He'll never return, of course."

Nikadur and Thupra answered nothing, only standing in uncomfortable silence. There was nothing consoling that they might say. Tumlook was right and it would have been foolish to attempt words of condolence that would have obviously been false.

The road that led from Loor to Nonone inclined very gradually upward. It was not an entirely strange road to Tumithak, for long ago he had been to that small town with his father, but the memory of the road was faint and now he found much to interest him as he left the lights of the populous portion of the town behind him. The entrances of other corridors continually appeared, corridors that were constructed to add to the labyrinthine maze, that made it impossible for the creatures from the upper Surface to find their way into the great pits. The way did not lead along the broad main corridor for long. Often Tumithak would take his own way down what appeared to be quite an insignificant hallway, only to have it suddenly branch into another larger one, farther on.

It must not be supposed that Tumithak had so quickly forgotten his home in his anxiety to be on his quest. Often, as he passed some familiar sight, a lump would come into his throat and he would almost be tempted to give up his journey and return. Twice Tumithak passed foodrooms, rooms where the familiar mystic machines throbbed eternally, building up out of the very rocks their own fuel and the tasteless biscuits of food that these people lived on. It was then that his homesickness was the greatest, for many times he had watched his father operating such machines as these, and the memory made him realize poignantly all that he was leaving behind. But like all the inspired genuises of humanity, at times such as this, it almost seemed as if something outside of himself took charge of him and forced him on.

Tumithak turned from the last large corridor to a single winding hall not more than a half dozen feet in width. There were no doorways along this hall and it was much steeper than any he had yet climbed. It ran on for several miles and then entered a larger passage through a door that was seemingly but one of a hundred similar ones that lined this new passage. These doors were apparently those of apartments, but the apartments seemed to be unused, for there were no signs of inhabitants in this district. Probably this corridor had been abandoned for some reason many years ago.

There was nothing strange in this to Tumithak, however. He knew quite well that these doorways were only to add extra confusion to the ones who sought to thread the maze of corridors, and he continued on his way, without paying the slightest attention to the many branching hallways, until he came to the room he sought.

It was an ordinary apartment, to all appearances, but when Tumithak found himself inside, he hastened to the rear and began to feel carefully over the walls. In a corner, he found what he was searching for—a ladder of metal bars, leading upwards. Confidently, he began the ascent, mounting steadily upward in the dark; and as minute followed minute, the faint glow of light that shone in from the corridor below grew smaller and smaller.

At last he reached the top of the ladder, and found himself standing at the mouth of the pit, in a room similar to the one he had left below. He strode out of the room into another of the familiar door-lined corridors and turning in the direction that led upward, continued his journey. He was on the level of Nonone now, and if he hurried, he knew that he might reach that town before the time of sleep.

He hastened along, and presently he perceived a party of men in the distance, who gradually approached him. He drew into an apartment from which he peered out cautiously, until he assured himself that they were Nononese. The red color of their tunics, their narrow belts and the peculiar way they had of dressing their hair convinced him that these were friends and so Tumithak showed himself and waited for the party to approach him. When they saw him, the foremost man, who was evidently the leader, hailed him.

"Is not this Tumithak of Loor?" he asked, and as Tumithak replied in the affirmative, he continued, "I am Nennapuss, chief of the people of Nonone. Your father has acquainted us with the facts of your journey and asked us to be looking for you about this time. We trust that you will spend the next sleep with us; and if there is anything that we can do to add to your comfort or safety on your journey, you have but to command us."

Tumithak almost smiled at the rather pompous speech which the chief had evidently prepared beforehand, but he answered gravely that he would indeed be indebted if Nennapuss could provide him with sleeping quarters. The chief assured him that the best in the town would be provided, and, turning, led Tumithak off in the direction from which he and his party had come.

They traversed several miles of deserted passages before they finally came to the inhabited halls of Nonone, but once here, the hospitality of Nennapuss knew no bounds. The people of Nonone were assembled in the "Great Square," as the juncture of the two main corridors was called, and in a florid, flowing speech that was characteristic of him, Nennapuss told them of Tumithak and his quest; and presented him, as it were, with the keys of the city.

After an answering speech by Tumithak, in which the Loorian worked himself up into a fine fury of eloquence on his favorite subject—his journey—a banquet was prepared; and even though the food was only the tasteless biscuits that constituted the sole diet of these people, they gorged themselves to repletion. When Tumithak at last fell asleep, it was with the feeling that here, at least, a tentative slayer of shelks might find appreciation. Had not the proverb been buried in centuries of ignorance and forgetfulness, he might have mused that a prophet is, verily, not without honor save in his own country.

Tumithak arose about ten hours later and prepared to bid good-by to the people of Nonone. Nennapuss insisted that the Loorian have breakfast with his family and Tumithak willingly complied. The sons of Nennapuss, two lads in their early teens, were enthusiastic during the meal, with the wonderful idea that Tumithak had conceived. Though the idea of any other man facing a shelk was incredible to them, they seemed to think that Tumithak was something more than the average mortal, and plied him with a hundred questions as to his plans. But, beyond having studied the long route to the Surface, Tumithak's plans were decidedly vague, and he was unable to tell them how he would slay his shelk.

After the meal, he again shouldered his pack and started up the corridor. The chief and his retinue followed him for several miles and as they went Tumithak questioned Nennapuss closely as to the condition of the passages to Yakra and beyond.

"The road on this level is quite safe," said Nennapuss, in answer to his questions. "It is patrolled by men of my city and no Yakran ever enters it without our being aware of it. But the pit that leads to the level of Yakra is always guarded at the top by the Yakrans, and I do not doubt but that you will have trouble when you try to get out of that pit."

Tumithak promised to use an extra amount of caution when he reached this spot, and a short time later, Nennapuss and his companions said good-by to him and he trudged on alone.

He moved more warily, now, for though the Nononese patrolled these corridors, he knew quite well that it was possible for enemies to evade the guards and raid the corridors as had often been done in the past. He kept well in the middle of the corridor, away from the many doorways, any one of which may have concealed a secret road to Yakra, and he seldom passed one of the branching ways without peering carefully up and down it, before venturing to cross it.

But Tumithak was fortunate in meeting no one in the corridors, and after half a day he came at last to another apartment in which was located a shaft almost exactly similar to the one that had brought him to Nonone.

He mounted this ladder much more stealthily than he had the first one, for he was quite confident that a Yakran guard was at the top and he had no desire to be toppled backward into the pit when he reached there. As he drew near the end of the ladder, he drew his sword, but again luck favored him, for the guard had apparently left the room at the top of the well, and Tumithak drew himself up into the room and prepared to enter the corridor.

But he had moved only a scant half dozen feet when his luck deserted him. He bumped violently into a table that he had failed to notice in the gloom, and the resulting noise brought a bull-like bellow from the corridor without. The next moment, sword in hand, a veritable giant of a man dashed through the door and made for Tumithak.

CHAPTER III

The Passing of Yakra

That the man was a Yakran, Tumithak would have known, had he met him in the depths of Loor. Though the Loorian knew of the Yakrans only through the stories of the older men, who remembered the wars with that city, he saw at once that this was just the kind of barbarian that had figured in the stories. He was fully four inches taller than Tumithak, and far broader and heavier, and his chin was covered with a tremendous, bristly growth of beard—sufficient evidence that the owner was of Yakra. His tunic was covered with bits of bone and metal sewn into the cloth, the former stained in various colors and sewn in a crude pattern. Around his neck was a necklace made of dozens of fingerbones threaded on a thin strip of skin.

Tumithak saw in an instant that he would have little chance with this huge Yakran if he were to stand fairly up to him, and so, even as he drew his sword and prepared to defend himself, he was casting about in his mind for some method to overcome him by strategy. The most probable plan, he decided at once, would be to drive him somehow into the pit; but to drive this colossus was almost as impossible as to defeat him by face to face fighting methods. And before Tumithak could devise any more subtle method of overcoming his adversary, he found his entire mind taken up with methods of defending himself.

The Yakran rushed at him, still shouting his rumbling war-cry, and it was but the merest lurch that enabled Tumithak to avoid the first terrific blow aimed at him. Tumithak dropped to one knee, but in a moment was up again and only just in time to avoid another sweep of that lightning sword. On his feet again, however, his defense was perfect, and the Yakran found it necessary to retire a step or two, in order to prepare another of his lunging rushes.

Again and again the Yakran rushed at Tumithak, and it was only the Loorian's uncanny skill at fencing, learned through many years in the hope of facing a shelk, that saved him. Around and around the table, now close to the pit and now farther away, they fought; until even Tumithak's steel-like muscles began to tire.

But as his body tired, his brain quickened, and at last a plan came to him to defeat the Yakran. He allowed himself to be gradually forced to the edge of the pit and then, as he parried a particularly powerful lunge, he suddenly threw one hand high in the air and screamed. The Yakran, believing that he had struck him, smiled a vicious smile and stepped back for a final rush. Sword pointing at Tumithak's breast, he dashed forward, and as he did so, Tumithak threw himself at his opponent's feet.

There was a wild howl from the giant as he stumbled over the recumbent form, but before he could recover himself, he dropped heavily at the very edge of the pit. Tumithak kicked wildly, and the great Yakran, grasping frantically at the air, dropped into the well! There was a hoarse cry from the darkness below, a heavy thud and then silence.

For several minutes, Tumithak lay panting at the edge of the pit. This was the first battle he had ever had with a man, and though he was the victor, it was only by a miracle, it seemed, that he had not been defeated. What would the people of Loor and Nonone say, he wondered if they knew that their self-appointed slayer of shelks had been so nearly defeated by the first enemy that had attacked him—and that enemy not a shelk, but a man, and a man of despised Yakra, at that? For several minutes, the Loorian lay, filled with self-reproach, and then, reflecting that if all his enemies were conquered with a margin even so small as this, his victory was certain, he arose, pulled himself together and left the room.

He was in Yakra now, and it was necessary for him to find some means of passing safely through the city in order to reach the dark corridors beyond. For only through these dark corridors might he win his way to the upper Surface. He continued cautiously on his way, turning over in his brain plan after plan that would enable him to deceive the Yakrans; but he was almost within sight of the inhabited walls of Yakra before he conceived an idea that seemed to him to be feasible. There was but one thing that all men in these pits feared, with a fear that was quite unreasoning. And it was upon this unreasoning fear that Tumithak decided to play.

He began to run. He ran slowly at first, a mere trot, but as he drew nearer the corridors where men lived, he increased his pace, running faster and faster until he was fleeing along like one who had all the demons of hell at his back. Which was precisely the effect that he wished to produce.

In the distance he saw a group of Yakrans approaching. They beheld him at the same time that he spied them, and in a moment more were charging down on him; quite aware, as he knew, that he was not a Yakran. Instead of trying to avoid them, he charged straight into their midst, screaming at the top of his lungs.

"Shelks!" he shouted, as though in the last stages of terror, "Shelks!"

The bellicose attitude of the men changed at once to one of extreme fright. Without a word to Tumithak or even so much as a backward glance, they turned, and as he dashed past them, they sped panic-stricken after him. Had they been men of Loor, they might have paused long enough to investigate, or at least, have held Tumithak and questioned him. But not these Yakrans. This town was many miles nearer the Surface than Loor, and many of the older men could still remember the last time that the shelks had raided these halls on one of their rare hunting expeditions, leaving a trail of death and destruction that would never be forgotten while those that witnessed it lived. So the terror was far more of a living thing to Yakra than it was to Loor, to whom it was little more than a terrible legend of the past.

And so, without a word of question, the Yakrans fled down the long corridor after Tumithak, through branching hallways and through doorways that seemed mere entrances to apartments, but were actually roads to the main corridor. Several times they passed other men or groups of men, but at the fearful cry of "Shelks" these always dropped whatever they were doing and followed the frightened throng. A good many dashed down branching corridors, in which, they imagined, lay greater safety; but the majority continued on their way to the heart of the city, the direction in which Tumithak was going.

The Loorian was no longer in the lead now, several of the fleeter Yakrans had passed him, terror lending wings to their feet. And so the size of the mob grew and was augmented by greater and greater numbers as they came closer to the town center, until at last the corridor was filled with a screaming, terrified multitude in which Tumithak was completely lost.

They neared the wide main corridor, and here they found a great mass of people that had surged in from every one of the branching corridors. How the news had traveled so quickly, Tumithak was unable to guess, but apparently the entire city was already aware of the supposed danger. And like sheep, or rather, like the humans they were, all had been seized with the same idea—the desire to reach the center of the city, where they supposed, the greatest safety lay in the presence of the greatest numbers.

But now this frenzied confusion bade fair to defeat the plan that Tumithak had devised to cross the city safely under cover of the excitement he caused. To be sure, he had almost won to the center of the city without discovery, and the inhabitants were so wrought up that there would be little chance of anyone noticing that he was a stranger, but so thickly packed was the crowd that it became more and more certain that the Loorian was not going to be able to work his way through, in order to reach the corridors beyond. Yet in spite of the apparent hopelessness, Tumithak struggled along with the frantic mob, hoping against hope that he might gain a comparatively clear corridor beyond the city's center before the fright of the people died down to the point where they would begin the inevitable search for the one who had started the panic.

The crowd, its fright enhanced by that strange sense of telepathy that is evident in any large assembly of people, was becoming dangerous. Men were using their fists freely to better their way, they passed their weaker brothers, and here and there voices could be heard, high pitched with anger. Tumithak saw a man stumble and fall, and a moment later, heard a scream as the unfortunate one was trampled on by the ones behind him. Hardly had the scream died away when there was another cry from the opposite side of the passage, where another man had fallen and found himself unable to regain his feet.

The Loorian seemed little more than a leaf borne along on the stream of shouting, gesticulating, Yakrans by the time he reached the center of the city. Time after time, he had almost been swept from his feet, only to regain his balance by what seemed a miracle. He had nearly gained the huge square that marked the crossing of the two main corridors when he stumbled over a fallen Yakran and almost went down. He attempted to pass on, and then stopped. The form beneath his feet was that of a woman with a baby in her arms!

Her face was tear-stained and bleeding, her clothes were torn in a dozen places, yet she was attempting bravely to prevent the injury of her child beneath the feet of the multitude. Tumithak instantly stooped over to raise her to her feet, but even before he could do so, the crowd had pushed him almost beyond the reach of her. Sudden anger swept over him, and plunging out wrathfully, he dealt blow after blow into the faces of the onrushing multitude of creatures, who would have crushed one of their own people in their anxiety for personal safety. The Yakrans yielded before his blows, poured on either side of him for a moment, and in that moment, Tumithak stopped and raised the woman to her feet.

She was still conscious, as the wan smile that she bestowed upon him showed, and though he knew she was an enemy of his people, Tumithak felt a momentary pity that his ruse to frighten the Yakrans had been so successful. She was trying to tell him something, but so great were the confused shouts that it was impossible for him to understand her. He bent down his head to hers to hear what she had to say.

"The doorway across the hall," she screamed in his ear. "Try to get through the crowd to the third doorway across the hall! There is safety there!"

Tumithak placed her in front of him and drove savagely into the crowd, his fists flashing out around her and protecting her as they moved. It was hard to keep from being hustled, against his will, into the central square, but at last he gained the doorway and thrust the woman through it. He followed her inside, and gave a great gasp of relief as he found himself free from the struggles of the crowd. He stood for a moment in the doorway, to assure himself that nobody intended to follow them, and then turned back to the woman with the child.

She had torn a small piece of cloth from the sleeve of her tattered garment and as he faced her, she paused from wiping the blood and tears from her face long enough to flash him a frightened, little smile. Tumithak could not but wonder at the apparent gentleness and refinement of this woman of savage Yakra. He had been taught to believe, since childhood, that the Yakrans were a strange race, not unlike our concept of goblins and witches, and yet, this woman might have been a daughter of one of the best families of Loor. Tumithak had to learn that in no matter what nation or age one finds oneself, he will find gentleness, if he looks, as well as savagery.

All this while the child, who had evidently been too frightened to cry, had been as silent as though dead, but now it set up a lusty screaming.

The mother, after attempting for several moments to silence it with croonings and whispers, at last applied nature's first silencer, and as the child quieted down and began nursing, she arose and motioning Tumithak to follow, led the way to the doorway across the room and entered the rear of the apartment. She was gone a moment, and then she called to the Loorian, and with a realization of what she meant dawning in his mind, he followed her. In the next room, sure enough, the woman pointed to the ceiling and showed him the circular hole of a shaft leading straight upward.

"Here is the entrance to an old corridor that is not known to more than twenty people in all Yakra," she said. "It leads across the square to the upper end of the city. We can hide up there for days and the shelks will probably never know that we exist. Here is safety."

Tumithak nodded and began the ascent of the ladder, pausing only long enough to assure himself that the woman was following him. The ladder extended not more than thirty feet upward and then they found themselves in the dark in a corridor that must have been unused for many centuries. So dark was it that as soon as they moved away from the pit shaft, it was impossible to distinguish the faintest glow of light. Certainly the woman was right in calling this an unknown corridor. Even Tumithak's maps had never told him of this passage.

The woman seemed to be quite at home in the passage, however, for with a whispered word to Tumithak, she began to feel her way along the wall, only stopping now and then to whisper softly to her baby. Tumithak followed her, keeping one hand on her shoulder and so they felt their way along until they came at last to a spot where a single light glowed dimly, and here the woman sat down to rest. Tumithak did likewise, and the woman, reaching into her pocket, drew out a crude needle and thread and began to stitch the tears in her garment. Presently she spoke.

"Isn't it terrible," she whispered, her voice hushed as though she feared that even here the shelks might be listening. "What has started them to hunting again, I wonder?"

Tumithak made no reply and in a moment, she continued:

"My grandfather was killed in a shelk raid. That must have been nearly forty years ago. And now they have come upon us again! My poor husband! I separated from him almost as soon as we left our apartment. Oh! I do hope he reaches safety. He doesn't know about this corridor." She looked to him for comfort. "Do you think he will be safe?"

Tumithak smiled.

"Will you believe me if I tell you that he is surely safe from the shelks?" he asked. "Truly I can assure you that he will not be slain by the shelks in this raid."

"I only hope you are right," the woman began, and then, as if she had noticed him for the first time, she continued, suddenly. "You are not of Yakra!"

And then quite positively and harshly, "You are a man of Loor!"

Tumithak realized that the woman had at last noticed the Loorian clothes that he wore, and so made no attempt to lie.

"Yes," he answered, "I am of Loor."

The woman arose in consternation, clasping her baby tighter to her breast, as though to protect it from this ogre from the lower corridors.

"What are you doing in these halls?" she asked, fearfully, "Is it you that have brought this raid down upon us? I could well believe that the men of Loor would ally themselves with the shelks, if such a thing were possible. And surely, this is the first time in history that the shelks ever came upon us from the lower end of the city."

Tumithak considered for a moment. He saw no reason why he should not tell this woman the truth. It could do her no harm, and might at least put her mind at rest, regarding the safety of her husband.

"It will probably be the last time that the shelks ever come upon you from the lower end of the city, too," he said, and in a few brief words, he explained to her his ruse and its rather appalling success.

"But why should you desire to pass through Yakra?" she asked, incredulously. "Are you going into the dark corridors? What man in his senses would desire to explore them?"

"I am not seeking to explore the dark corridors," the Loorian answered. "My goal lies even beyond them!"

"Beyond the dark corridors?"

"Yes," said Tumithak, and rose to his feet. As always when he spoke of his "mission," he was, for the moment a dreamer, a fanatic.

"I am Tumithak," he said. "I am the slayer of the shelk. You wish to know why I seek to go beyond the dark corridors? It is because I am on my way to the Surface. For on the Surface is a shelk that, all unknowing, awaits his doom! I am going to slay a shelk!"

The woman gazed at him in consternation. She was quite certain, now, that she was alone with a madman. No other could even conceive such an incredible thought. She clasped her child tighter to her and drew away from him.

Tumithak was quick to notice her attitude. He had, many times before, seen people draw away from him in just the same manner, when he spoke of his mission. And so, quite unoffended by her unflattering opinion of him, he began to explain to her why he believed it possible for men to once more engage in battle with the masters of the Surface.

The woman listened for a while, and as he waxed more and more eloquent on his subject, Tumithak saw that she was beginning to believe. He told her of the book he had found, and how it had decided for him what his mission in life should be. He told her of the three strange gifts of his father, and how he hoped they would help him to be successful in his quest. And at last, he saw the look come into her eyes that he had often seen in Thupra's and knew that she believed.

The woman's thoughts, however, had been quite different from what Tumithak believed. She had listened to be sure, but as she listened, she was thinking of the fury with which Tumithak had attacked the terror stricken mob that had nearly crushed her. She was studying the erect, handsome form of him, the smooth-shaven face and keen eyes; and comparing him with the men of Yakra. And at last she believed, not because of Tumithak's eloquence, but because of the age-old appeal of sex.

"It is well that you saved me," she said at last, when the Loorian paused in his story. "It would have hardly been possible for you to force your way through the lower corridors. Up here, you may cross Yakra at your leisure, and leave it whenever you will. I will show you the way to the upper end of the city, now, if you wish."

She arose.

"Come, I will guide you. You are a Loorian and an enemy, but you saved my life, and one who would slay a shelk is surely the true friend of all mankind."

She took him by the hand (though that was hardly necessary), and led him on into the darkness. Minute after minute passed in silence and then, at last, she paused and whispered, "The corridor ends here."

She stepped into the doorway, and following her, Tumithak discerned a faint light coming up through a shaft from the corridor below.

He dropped down the ladder that he could see dimly in the gloom, and in a moment was in the lower corridor. The woman followed him, and when she reached the ground she pointed up the corridor.

"If you are really going to the Surface, your road lies that way," she said, "and we must part here. My road lies back into the town. I wish I might know you better, O Loorian," she paused and then, as she strode off, she turned to exclaim, "Go on to the Surface, strange one, and if you succeed in your quest, do not fear to pass through Yakra on your return. All the city would worship you then, and do you reverence."

As if afraid to say more, she hurried down the passage. Tumithak watched her for a moment and then, with a shrug, turned and walked away in the opposite direction.

He had expected to reach the dark corridors soon after leaving Yakra; but although his maps told him much concerning the route he must take, they were silent concerning the conditions of the various corridors; and it soon became evident to Tumithak that he was not to reach the dark corridors that day. Fatigue overcame him at last, and entering one of the many deserted apartments that lined the passage, he threw himself upon the floor and in a moment was sound asleep.

CHAPTER IV

The Dark Corridors

Hours after, the Loorian awakened with a start. He looked about him vaguely for a moment, and then started into full wakefulness. In the corridor without he had heard a soft rustling. Scarcely breathing, he arose and, tiptoeing to the doorway, peered cautiously out. The corridor was empty, yet Tumithak was certain that he had heard soft footsteps.

He stepped back into the room, picked up his pack, which he had removed before falling asleep, and adjusted it on his back. Then, once more carefully scanning the empty corridor, he stepped out and prepared to resume his journey.

Before going on, though, he drew his sword and looked thoroughly through all the neighboring apartments. It puzzled him to find them all deserted. He was quite sure that he had heard a noise, was quite sure, he felt, that someone, from somewhere, was watching him. But at last, he was forced to admit that unless he was mistaken in their existence, the watchers were more clever than he; and so, keeping well to the center of the corridor, he took up his journey again.

For hours, he kept up a continuous, monotonous pace. The route was steadily upward, the corridor was broad, and to Tumithak's surprise the lights continued undimmed. He had almost forgotten the cause of his sudden awakening, when, after traveling some eight or nine miles, he was suddenly aware of another soft, rustling sound, quite similar to the former one. It came from one of the apartments on his left, and he had scarcely heard it, when he sprang like lightning to the door from which it came, his sword flashing from its sheath. He dashed into the apartment, through the front room and into the rear one, and then stood foolishly, looking around him at the bare brown walls. Like the apartment which he had examined in the morning, this one was quite empty. There were no ladders up which the mysterious one might have escaped, indeed, there seemed to be no way in which anyone might have escaped discovery and, at last, Tumithak was forced to continue on his way.

But he moved more warily, now. He was as cautious as he had been before entering Yakra; in fact, even more so, for then he had known what to expect, and was facing the unknown.

As the hours passed, Tumithak became increasingly certain of the fact that he was being followed—was being watched. Time after time, he would hear the slight rustling noise, sometimes from the dark recesses of an apartment, sometimes from down the path of some dimly lighted branching corridor. Once he was certain that he heard the sound far ahead of him, in the hall that he was traversing. But never was he able to catch so much as a glimpse of the beings that caused the sound.

At last he came to a section of the corridors where the lights began to dim. At first only a few were affected, their light coming from the plates with a peculiar bluish glow, but before long the bluish tint was the rule rather than the exception, and many of the lights were out entirely. Tumithak traveled on in an increasing gloom, and realized that he was, at last, really approaching the legendary dark corridors.

Now, Tumithak was the product of a hundred generations of men who had fled from the slightest suspicious sound. For hundreds of years after the Invasion, an unusual sound had meant a man-hunting shelk, and a shelk had meant death, sudden, sure and unmistakable. So man had become a skulking, fleeing race of creatures that fled panic-stricken from the least suspicion of danger.

In deep-cut Loor, however, men had made a warren so intricate and lengthy that years had passed since a shelk had been seen. And so it came about that the men grew more courageous in Loor, until there arose, at last, a visionary who dared to dream of slaying a shelk.

But although Tumithak was bolder by far than any other man of his generation, it must not be supposed that he had overcome, entirely, the heritage that was man's. Even now as he trudged so firmly up the apparently endless hallway, his heart was beating wildly, and it would have taken little to send him back on the way he had come, his heart almost smothering him in his fright.

But apparently those who followed him knew well not to agitate his fears too greatly. As the corridors grew darker, the noises lessened, and at last, Tumithak decided that he was quite alone. Whatever had been following him, he felt, had turned back or continued down one of the branching halls. For over an hour, he strained his ears in an attempt to hear again the soft noises, but only silence was his reward; so his vigilance gradually lessened and he trod more and more carelessly up the hall.

He passed from a corridor of eternal gloom to one of eternal darkness. Here the lights, if there had ever been any, had long since ceased to glow, and for some time Tumithak felt his way along the passage, depending only on his sense of touch.

And in the corridor below, a number of dark, gaunt figures moved from the gloom to the darkness and hurried silently toward him.

As they went, they would have presented a strange appearance, could anyone have seen them. Gaunt almost to the point of emaciation, with strange, slate-colored skins, perhaps the most surprising thing about their appearance was their heads, which were wrapped with layer after layer of strips of cloth which completely covered their eyes, making it impossible for the slightest ray of light to reach them.

For these were the savages of the dark corridors—men born and raised in the halls of eternal night—and so sensitive were their eyes that the least light was an intolerable pain. All day long they had been shadowing Tumithak, and all day long their eyes had been veiled with the bandages, leaving the savages to move by their astounding senses of hearing and feeling alone. But now that they were again in the halls that were their home, they hastened to remove the cumbering cloths. And when this was accomplished they gradually closed in upon their intended victim.

The first intimation of their presence that Tumithak had after entering the darkness was when he heard a sudden rush behind him. He turned quickly, drew his sword and lashed out savagely. His sword cut through the air, he heard a sardonic laugh and then silence. Furiously he lunged again, and again his sword met only empty air, and then he heard new rustling in the hall behind him.

He turned, realizing that they had surrounded him. Sword flashing furiously, he backed to the wall prepared to sell his life as dearly as possible. He felt his blade strike something that yielded, heard a cry of pain and then suddenly quiet descended on the corridor. The Loorian was not to be deceived, however, he kept up the vicious beating about him with his sword, and presently had the satisfaction of hearing another groan of pain as he struck one of the savages who had attempted to creep under his guard.

But, though Tumithak continued to defend himself to the best of his ability, and lashed about with the courage born of desperation, he had little doubt as to the outcome of the struggle. He was alone, with his back to the wall; while his enemies, already numbering he knew not how many, were constantly having their numbers added to, by the arrival of others. Tumithak prepared to die fighting; his only regret was that he must die in this stygian darkness, unable even to see the opponents who conquered him—and then suddenly he remembered the torch, the first of his father's strange gifts.

With his left hand, he fumbled in his belt and drew out the cylinder. At least he would have the satisfaction of knowing what sort of creatures these were that had attacked him. In a moment he had found the switch and filled the hall with light.

He was totally unprepared for the effect that the brilliant beam of light had upon his enemies. Cries of pain and dismay burst from them, and Tumithak's first sight of the savages was that of a dozen or more scrawny, dark-colored figures that buried their heads in their arms and turned to flee in terror down the passage. Panic-stricken, bawling strange, harsh words to their companions, they fled from the light, as if Tumithak had suddenly been reinforced by all the men of Loor.

For a moment Tumithak stood dazed. He was, of course, unable to account for the sudden flight of his attackers. The idea occurred to him that they fled from some danger that he was unable to see and he flashed his light about the corridor fearfully, but at last, as their cries diminished in the distance, the truth gradually dawned on him. These creatures were so much at home in the dark that it must really be, thought Tumithak, that they feared the light; and though he could not understand why this should be, he determined to keep the torch burning as long as his route remained in the dark.

So flashing its rays this way and that, up branching corridors and into open doorways, the Loorian continued on his way. He knew that any thought of sleeping in these dark halls was out of the question, but this bothered him little. Shut up in the pits and corridors for centuries, man had forgotten the regular hours that he had once kept, and although he usually slept eight or ten hours out of thirty, it was entirely possible for a man to go forty or fifty hours before he felt the necessity of sleep. Tumithak had often worked steadily, under his father, for as many hours as this, and so now he felt confident that he would be out of the dark corridors long before he gave way to fatigue.

He munched, now and then, on the biscuits of synthetic food that he had brought with him; but for the most part, his entire time was spent in carefully scanning the corridors before and behind him. And so the hours passed. He had almost reached the point where his fears were allayed sufficiently to allow him to enter one of the apartments and seek slumber, when he heard, far behind him in the corridor, a strange inhuman snarl. Fear seized him instantly. He felt a sudden crawling sensation at the back of his neck, and, darting instantly into the nearest doorway, he extinguished his torch and lay trembling in an excess of fear.

It must not be supposed that Tumithak had suddenly become a coward. Remember the courage with which he had faced the Yakran and the dark savages. But it was the inhumanity of the sound that terrified him. In the lower passages, with the exception of rats, bats and a few other small creatures, no animals had ever been known. Except the shelks. They alone had followed man into his pits, and so it was natural that to them alone could Tumithak attribute the sound that had certainly come from some large creature other than man. He was yet to learn that there were other animals from the Surface that had been driven into these upper corridors.

So now he cowered in the apartment, vainly attempting to lash his courage to the point where he could go out and face his enemy. Suppose it were a shelk, he argued. Had he not come all these dangerous miles for the sole purpose of facing a shelk? Was he not Tumithak, the hero whom the high one had called to deliver Man from the heritage of fear that was his? And so, with arguments such as this, his indomitable spirit lashed his body into a semblance of courage, until at last he arose and again entered the corridor.

As he might have known, it appeared empty. His flashlight lit up the passage fully five hundred feet away, but the corridor was apparently quite deserted. He continued on his way; but as he went, he now paid more attention to the lower corridor than he did to the corridor above. And so, presently, he noticed, at the very limit of the light, a number of strange, slinking figures that followed him at a safe distance. His sharp eyes told him that these creatures were neither shelks nor men; but what they were, he was at a loss to guess. It was many generations since the men of the lower corridors had even heard of man's one-time friend the dog.

He paused uncertainly and watched these strange creatures. They slunk out of reach of the torch's rays at once, and after a moment Tumithak turned and continued his journey, half convinced that, in spite of their size, they were merely some large species of rat, as cowardly as their smaller brethren.

In this he was soon to find himself mistaken. He had continued for but a short distance, when he heard a snarl in the corridor ahead of him; and as though this were a signal, the beasts behind him began to draw steadily closer. Tumithak increased his pace, broke into a trot, and finally into a run; but fast as he went, the beasts behind him were faster, and gradually closed in on him.

It was when they were but a little less than a hundred feet behind him that he noticed their masters. The savages that he had vanquished a few hours before had returned, their faces buried in the swathings that they had worn when they stalked him in the corridors beyond Yakra. And with whispered urgings, they drove the dogs on until Tumithak again found it necessary to draw forth his sword and prepare to defend himself.

The beasts from the upper end of the corridor had appeared by this time and the Loorian soon found himself surrounded by a snarling, snapping pack of creatures against whose numbers it was utterly useless to attempt to defend himself. He slew one, another fell snapping at a great gash across its mangy back; but before he could do more, his light was knocked out of his hand and he felt a half dozen hairy forms leap upon him. He fell heavily to the ground with the dogs on top of him, his sword flying from his hand and disappearing in the darkness.

Tumithak expected to die then and there. He felt the hot breath of the monsters on various parts of his body, and that strange feeling of resignation came over him that almost every one feels in the presence of almost certain death, and then—the dogs were pulled away, and he felt hands on him and heard soft, muttering words as the savages felt over his body. He was pinioned to the ground by a half dozen wiry hands, and a moment later a band was tightened around him, fastening his arms firmly to his sides. He was picked up and carried away.

They carried him on up the corridor for some distance, turned after a while into one of the branching halls and continued for a long time before they at last halted and threw him upon the ground. Around him he heard many soft sounds, whispered conversation and the rustling of moving bodies, and he decided that he had been taken to the central halls of these creatures. After lying for some time, he was rolled over and a pair of thin hands felt him all over, and then a voice spoke firmly and with authority. Again he was picked up, and carried for a short distance and then he was unceremoniously dumped down upon the floor of what he suspected was the floor of an apartment. Something metallic clanged on the floor beside him and he heard the departing footsteps of his captors in the corridor beyond the door.

For a while Tumithak lay still, gathering his thoughts. He wondered vaguely why he had not been killed, little dreaming that the savages knew well enough not to kill their meat until they were ready for the feast. For these savages had no knowledge of the preparation of the machine-made food, and lived by preying on Yakra and other smaller towns that existed far down the branching corridors. Reduced to such desperate straits, anything that would provide sustenance became their food and for many generations they had been cannibals.

After a while, Tumithak arose. He had little trouble in working loose the bonds of cloth that he was tied with; the knowledge of knots that the savages possessed was elementary, and so it took less than an hour for the Loorian to free himself. He began feeling carefully over the walls of the apartment, in an attempt to acquaint himself with the features of his prison. The room was little more than ten feet square, and the walls were broken by but a single door, the entrance. Tumithak attempted to pass through this door, but was halted immediately by a growl and a snarl, and a rough hairy body pushed against his legs, driving him back into the apartment. The savages had left the dogs to guard the entrance to his prison.

Tumithak stepped back into the room and as he did so, his foot struck an object that rolled across the floor. He remembered the metallic object that had been thrown into the apartment with him and wondered curiously what it was. Groping around, he finally located it, and to his joy realized that it was his flashlight. He was quite unable to understand why the savages had brought it here, but he decided that to their superstitious minds, it was something to fear, and that they thought it best to keep these two dangerous enemies imprisoned together. At any rate, here it was, and for that Tumithak was grateful.

He turned it on and looked around as its rays filled the apartment with light. Yes, he had been right about its size and simplicity. There was little chance, none at all, in fact, of his escaping unless he passed through the beast-guarded doorway. And in the light, Tumithak saw that the savages had left him but little chance to escape that way. The entire pack of over twenty stood just without the doorway, their eyes dazzled and blinking in the sudden light.

From within the doorway, Tumithak could look far up the corridor, and he could see no one at all in all that stretch of hallway, as far as his light reached. He flashed it down the hallway; it, too, was empty. He decided that it was probably the time of sleep for these savages, and realized that if he was to escape, no better time would offer itself than the present. He sat down on the floor of the apartment and gave himself up to thought. Somewhere in the back of his mind an idea was glimmering, a faint conviction that he possessed the means to escape those animals. He arose and looked at the pack, huddled together in the corridor as if to protect themselves from the unwelcome rays of the torch. He turned to study the room, but apparently found little there to favor his half-formed plan. Suddenly, though, he reached a decision, and feeling in the pocket of his belt, and pulling a pin from it, hurled it out among the pack and threw himself flat on his face!

It was the bomb, the second of his father's strange gifts. It struck the floor of the corridor without, and burst with a roar that was nothing short of deafening. In the confined space of the passage, the expanding gases acted with terrific force. Flat on the floor though he was, Tumithak was lifted and hurled violently against the opposite wall of the apartment. As for the beasts in the corridor without, they were practically annihilated. Torn bodies were flung in every direction, and when Tumithak, bruised and shaken, entered the corridor a few minutes later, he found it deserted of every living thing. But the scene resembled a shambles, with blood and torn bodies strewn all over the corridor.

Sick with the unaccustomed sight of blood and death, Tumithak hastened to put as much distance as possible between himself and the gruesome scene. He hurried on up the corridor, through the still smoke-laden air, until at last the air cleared and the horrors of the scene could be forgotten. He saw no signs of the savages, although twice he heard a whimpering from the doorway of some apartment and knew that a dark form probably cowered, terror-stricken, in the darkness. It would be many, many sleeps before the savages of the dark corridors forgot the enemy who had caused such destruction among them.

Tumithak emerged again into the corridor that led to the Surface. For the first time since he set out on that route, he retraced his steps, but it was with a definite object in view. He arrived at the place where he had battled with the dogs, and retrieved his sword, finding it without difficulty and noting with satisfaction that it was entirely unharmed. Then he once again took up his journey to the Surface, continuing for long without meeting with anything that could give him cause for alarm. At last he decided that he was past the dangerous parts of these halls, and entering one of the apartments he prepared himself for a long-needed rest . . .

He slept long and dreamlessly, awaking at last after more than fourteen hours of sleep. He immediately took up his journey again, partaking of his food as he went and wondering what this new march would mean for him.

But he was not to wonder for long. He was quite aware, from his maps, that he was now more than half through with his journey, and so he was not surprised when the walls of the corridors, which, ever since leaving Loor had continued as smooth and glossy as those of his own home, now began to assume a rough, irregular appearance, almost like that of a natural cavern. He was, he knew, approaching that section of the corridors which man had carved out in the days of his first panic-stricken flight into the earth. There had been little time, in those first days, to smooth down the walls of the corridors or to give them the regular rectangular appearance that they were to have in the lower corridors.

But though he was not surprised at this appearance of the passages, he was totally unprepared for their next change. He had travelled perhaps three or four miles through the winding, narrow caverns, when he came upon a well-concealed pit-mouth that led far up into the darkness. He could see that there was a light at the top and gave a sigh of gratitude, for his light had begun to show the first signs of failing. He climbed the ladder slowly, with his usual caution, and at last, emerging warily from the mouth of the shaft, he stepped into the strangest corridor he had ever beheld.

CHAPTER V

The Hall of the Esthetts

The hall in which Tumithak found himself was more brilliantly lighted than any he had ever seen. The lights were not all of the usual clear white, here and there blues and greens vied with reds and golden yellows to add beauty to a scene that was already beautiful beyond anything that Tumithak had ever imagined. For a moment, he was at a loss to understand just where the luminescence was coming from, for there were no shining plates in the center of the ceiling, such as he had always been familiar with. But after a while, an explanation of the system of lighting dawned on him, and he saw that all the plates were cleverly concealed in the walls, so that the light reflected from them produced an effect of soft, creamy mellowness.

And the walls—the walls were no longer of the familiar glossy brown stone; they were of stone of the purest milky white! And though this in itself was a wonder that must have excited the Loorian's astonishment, it was not the color of the walls that held his attention rivited to them. It was the fact that the walls were covered with designs and pictures, intaglios and bas-reliefs, to such an extent that not a clear space was visible on walls or ceiling, at any place along the corridor. And even the floor bore an intricate design of varicolored inlaid stone.

Now, Tumithak had never dreamed of the possibility of such a thing as this. There was no art in the lower corridors, there never had been. That had been lost to man long before the first passage had been blasted down to Loor. And so Tumithak stood lost in wonder at the marvel that confronted him.

Although most of the wall was covered with design, there were many pictures, too. They showed in detail many wonderful things, things that Tumithak could scarcely believe existed. Yet here they were before him, and to his simple mind the fact that they were here in pictures were proof that somewhere they existed in reality.

Here, for instance, was a group of men and women dancing. They were in a circle and they danced around something in the center, something that could only partly be seen. But as he looked at it, Tumithak again felt the hair on the back of his neck begin to rise—the creature had long and spidery legs, and from somewhere in his subconscious mind a voice whispered, "Shelk."

Turning with a puzzled feeling of disgust from that picture, he came upon another one—it depicted a long corridor, and in it a cylindrical object that must have been eighteen or twenty feet long. It was mounted on wheels and around it were gathered a group of eager, waiting humans, with happy, excited looks on their faces. Tumithak puzzled over the pictures for many moments, unable to understand them. They didn't make sense. These people did not seem to fear the shelks! He came upon a picture that proved it. It showed again the long cylindrical object, and at its side were three beings that could be nothing but shelks. And grouped around them, talking and gesticulating, were another group of humans.

There was one thing that particularly impressed Tumithak in these pictures. The people were all fat. Not a one of them but was florid and grossly overweight. But it was probably natural, thought the Loorian, of people who lived near the Surface and were apparently without any fear of the terrible shelk. Such a people would naturally have little to do but live and grow fat.

And so, musing and looking at the pictures, he continued along his way, until he saw in the distance, up the corridor a ponderous human form and realized that he was reaching the inhabited part of these corridors. The form disappeared down a branching corridor, almost as soon as he glimpsed it, but it was enough to make Tumithak realize that he must go much more carefully. So, for a long while, he slipped cautiously along the side of the passage, using every opportunity that was offered for concealment. He found a thousand things to excite his wonder; indeed, ere long he found himself in a constant state of astonishment. Great tapestries were hung along the wall at one spot; at another, his heart leapt into his mouth as he came suddenly upon a group of statues. It was hard for him to realize that these carven stones were not really men.

There had been no doorways on the sides of the corridors at first; but now the corridor widened until it must have been full forty feet broad, and apartment entrances began to appear. High and wide, these doorways were, and the "curtains" that covered them were of metal! It was Tumithak's first contact with true doors, for in Loor the cloth curtains were all that ever separated apartments from the corridor without.

Minute after minute passed, as Tumithak continued on his way. The pictures on the walls grew more elaborate, the corridor grew higher and even wider; and then, in the distance, Tumithak saw a number of human forms approaching him. He knew that he must not be seen, debated for a moment the advisability of turning about and retreating, and then he noticed an open door close to him. Before him was discovery and danger, behind him lay an unthinkable retreat. Tumithak had little choice in the matter; in a moment he had made his decision, had pushed the door wide open and stepped inside.

For a moment he stood, his eyes, used to the brilliant light without, failing him in the gloom of the apartment. Then he realized that he was not alone, for the room was occupied by a man who, to all appearances, was so frightened at Tumithak's sudden appearance as to be quite speechless. Tumithak took advantage of the other's evident fright to observe him carefully and to look about the room for some means of escape or concealment.

The room was lighted much more dimly than the hall, the light coming from two plates concealed in the wall near the ceiling. The walls were of a uniform dull blue and in the rear a tapestried door led to the back room. A table, a huge, padded chair, a bed, and a shelf that was filled with books, made up the furniture of the room. And in the midst of this bed lay this huge man.

The man was a veritable mountain of flesh. Tumithak estimated that he certainly must have weighed four hundred pounds. He was well over six feet tall and the bed on which he lay, and which would easily have held three of Tumithak's fellow citizens, was completely filled with his bulk. He was a florid, full-blooded type of man; and his pale blond hair and beard only served to accentuate the redness of his face and neck.

But the coarseness of the man's features was offset by the refinement of his surroundings. Never had such luxuries been dreamed of by the man of Loor. The clothes that the man wore were of the finest texture imaginable, sheer gauzes that were dyed in the most delicate shades of nacreous pinks, and greens, and blues. They flowed down over his form, softening and dignifying the immense obesity of him. The bed-clothes were as fine and sheer as the man's garments, but of a deep shade of green and brown. The bed itself was a revelation, a glorious triumph in inlaid metals that might have been wrought by some wonderful artisan of the Golden Age. And flung across the floor was a rug—And the pictures on the wall!—

The man suddenly regained control of himself. He set up a scream, a high-pitched womanly scream that seemed strangely absurd coming from one of his bulk. Tumithak was at his side in an instant, with his sword at the fat one's throat.

"Stop that!" he ordered peremptorily. "Stop it at once, or I'll kill you!"

The other subsided, his screams at once becoming a series of involuntary agonized groans. Tumithak stood listening, fearful that the first scream might have been effective, but the silence from without was unbroken. After fully a minute, the man spoke.

"You are a wild man," he said, and his voice was full of terror. "You are a wild man of the lower corridors! What are you doing here among the Chosen Ones?"

Tumithak ignored the question.

"Make another sound, fat one," he whispered, fiercely, "and there will be one less mouth to feed in these halls." He looked toward the door anxiously. "Is any one likely to enter here?" he asked.

The other attempted to answer, but apparently his fear had by now rendered him speechless. Tumithak laughed scornfully, a strange elation possessing him. It was indeed pleasant to the Loorian to find some one that feared him so terribly. Man had not felt this strange sense of power often in the preceding centuries and Tumithak was half tempted to increase the other's fears, but in the end this emotion was overcome by his curiosity. Seeing that the fat man's terror of the sword was a very real one, he lowered it and returned it to its sheath.

The fat man breathed easier then, but it was some moments before speech returned. Then when he did speak, it was only to repeat the question he had asked before.

"What are you doing here in the halls of the Esthetts?" he gulped fearfully.

Tumithak considered his answer carefully. These people, he knew, did not fear the shelk; clearly, then, they were friendly with them. The Loorian doubted the advisability of confiding in the obese craven, but at the same time it seemed absurd to fear him or any others like him. And the natural conceit that is a part of every great genius made Tumithak long to boast of his mission so that at last he decided to answer the question.

"I am on my way to the Surface," he said. "I come from the lowest pit of all, so far down that we have never even heard of the halls of the Esthetts, as you call them. Are you one of the Esthetts?"

"On your way to the Surface," said the other, who was now fast losing his fear. "But you have not been called! You will be killed at once. Think you that the Holy Shelks will permit any one to attain the Surface uncalled for?" His nose twitched scornfully. "And a wild man of the lower corridors at that!"

Tumithak was stung by the scorn in the other's voice.

"Listen, fat one," he said, "I do not ask the permission of any one to visit the Surface. As for the shelks, my whole object in reaching the Surface is that I might kill one of them."

The other looked at him with a look that Tumithak was at a loss to interpret.

"You will soon die," said the Esthett, calmly. "There is no need of my fearing you any longer. Surely any one who speaks such unthinkable blasphemy is doomed even as he says it." He settled himself more comfortably in his bed as he spoke, and looked at Tumithak curiously.

"From where, oh, Wild One, did such an impossible idea come to you?" he asked.

The Loorian might have had a feeling of anger at the other's attitude, had not this question shown him a loophole for expounding his favorite subject. He began to tell the Esthett, in elaborate detail, all the story of his mission. The latter listened attentively, so interested, apparently, that Tumithak grew more and more interested in the telling.

He spoke of his early life, of the finding of the book, and the inspiration it had given him; he told of the many years of preparation for his journey, and of the many adventures he had had since he left Loor.

The fat one was strangely interested, but to Tumithak, wrapped up in the story of his mission, it never once occurred that the Esthett was sparring for time. And so, when he was finished with his story at last, he was quite willing to listen to the Chosen One's story of his own life in the marble halls.

"We who live in these halls," began the Esthett, "are those chosen ones of the race of mankind who possess the one thing that the Holy Shelks lack—the power of creating beauty. Mighty as the Masters are, they have no artistic ability, but in spite of this they are quite capable of appreciating our art, and so they have come to rely upon us for the beauties of life, and they have given it to us to produce all the great works of art that decorate their wonderful palaces on the Surface! All the great art works that you see on the walls of these corridors have been executed by me and my fellow-citizens. All the rich paintings and statuary that you will see later, in our great square, all these are the rejected specimens that the Holy Shelks have no need of. Can you imagine the beauties of the accepted pieces that have found their way up to the Surface?

"And in return for our beauty, the shelks feed us and give us every luxury imaginable. Of all mankind, we alone have been chosen as worthy of being the friends and companions of the world's masters."

He paused for a moment, breathless with what was apparently an exceptionally long speech, for him. After resting a while, he went on:

"Here in these marble corridors, we of the Esthetts are born and educated. We work only at our art: we work only when it suits us, and our work is carefully examined by the shelks, and the choicest is preserved. The artists who produce this work—listen carefully wild man—the artists who produce this work are called from their homes to join the great guild of Chosen Ones who live on the Surface and spend the rest of their lives decorating the glorious palaces and gardens of the Holy Shelks! They are the happiest of men, for they know that their work is praised by the very Lords of Creation themselves."

He was panting with the effort caused by his story, but he struggled bravely on:

"Can you wonder that we feel ourselves superior to the men who have allowed themselves to become little better than animals, little more than rabbits skulking in their warrens, miles below the ground? Can you wonder that—"

His speech was suddenly cut off by a sound from the corridor without. It was the sound of a siren, whose tones grew shriller and shriller, higher and higher until it seemed to pass entirely beyond the range of sound heard by human ears. The Esthett was suddenly beside himself with eagerness. He began to struggle out of his bed, managed after several failures to get to his feet, waddled to the door and then turned.

"The Masters!" he cried. "The Holy Shelks! They have come to take another group of artists to the Surface. I knew they would be here soon, wild man, and it was not for nothing that I listened to your long, tiresome story. Try to escape if you can, but you know as well as I that none can escape from the Masters. And now I go to tell them of your presence!"

He slammed the door suddenly in Tumithak's face and was gone.

For several minutes, Tumithak remained motionless in the apartment. That shelks were so near to him seemed incredible. Yet he expected every minute to see the door open and to have the horrible spider-like creatures rush in and slay him. At last, it seemed, he was in a trap from which there was no escape. He shivered with fear, and then, as always, the very intensity of his fear shamed him and caused him to take a new grip upon himself; and though he trembled violently at what he was about to do, he moved to the door and examined it carefully. He had decided that the chances of escape would be greater in the corridor than if he waited here for the shelks to capture him. It was several minutes before he discovered the secret of the latch, but then he swung the door open and stepped into the corridor.

The corridor in Tumithak's vicinity was fortunately empty, but far up the hallway, the obese Esthett could still be seen, bustling ponderously on his way. He had been joined by others, many as fat as he; and all were hastening, as fast as their weight would let them up the corridor, in the direction in which the square of the city evidently lay. Tumithak followed them at a discreet distance, and after a while, saw them turn into another corridor. He approached the corridor cautiously, the determination forming in his mind to slay the fat one that intended to betray him at the first opportunity. It was well that he used care in his approach, for when he peered around the corner he saw that he was not a hundred feet from the town's great square.

He had never seen such a great square. It was a huge hall over a hundred yards in diameter, its tesselated marble floor and carved walls presenting an appearance that made Tumithak gasp in wonder. Here and there statues stood on vari-colored pedestals, and all the doorways were hung with beautiful tapestries. The entire square was almost filled with Esthetts, over five hundred being present.

Not the hall, its furnishings nor its inhabitants had much effect on Tumithak. His eyes were occupied in observing the great cylinder of metal that lay in the center of the hall. It was just such a cylinder as the one he had seen on the carving when he first entered the city—eighteen or twenty feet long, mounted on four thickly tired wheels and having, he now perceived a round opening in the top.

While he looked, a number of objects shot out of the opening and dropped lightly before the crowd. One after another, just as jacks from a box, they leapt from the opening, and as they nimbly struck the ground the Esthetts raised a cheer. Tumithak drew hastily back, and then, his curiosity overcoming his caution, dared to peep again into the hall. For the first time in over a hundred years, a man of Loor gazed upon a shelk!

Standing about four feet high, they were indeed spider-like, just as tradition said. But close look showed that this was only a superficial resemblance. For these creatures were hairless, and possessed ten legs, rather than the eight that belong to a true spider. The legs were long and triple jointed and on the tip of each was a short rudimentary claw much like a finger nail. There were two bunches of these legs, five on each side, and they joined the creature at a point midway between the head and the body. The body was shaped much like the abdomen of a wasp, and was about the same size as the head, which was certainly the strangest part of the entire creature.

For the head was the head of a man: The same eyes, the same broad brow, a mouth with tight, thin lips, and a chin—all these gave the head of the creature a startling resemblance to that of a man. The nose and hair alone were missing, to make the face perfectly human.

As Tumithak looked, they entered at once upon the business that had brought them down into the corridor. One of them took a paper from a pouch strapped to his body, grasping it nimbly between two of his limbs, and began to speak. His voice had a queer, metallic clack about it, but it was not a bit hard for Tumithak to distinguish every word he said.

"Brothers of the Pits," he cried, "the time has come for another group of you to make your homes on the Surface! The friends who left you last week are eagerly awaiting your arrival there, and it only remains for us to call the names of the ones to whom the great honor has fallen. Listen carefully, and let each one enter the cylinder as his name is called."

He paused, allowing his words to sink in, and then in a silence that was impressive, he began to call the names.

"Korystalis! Vintiamia! Lathrumidor!" he called, and one after another, great, bull-bodied men strutted forward and climbed up a small ladder that was lowered from the cylinder. The third man called, Tumithak noticed, was the one who had conversed with him in the apartment. The look on his face, as well as on the faces of the others, was one of surprise and joy, as if some incredible piece of good luck had befallen him.

Now, Tumithak had been so absorbed in observing the shelks and their vehicle that he had forgotten momentarily the threat that the Esthett had made, but when he saw him approaching the shelks, the Loorian's terror returned. He stood, rooted in his tracks with fear. But his fear was unnecessary, for apparently this unexpected piece of good fortune had driven everything else from the simple mind of the Chosen One, for he climbed into the cylinder without so much as a word to the shelks standing about. And Tumithak gave a great sigh of relief as he disappeared into the hole.

There were six shelks, and six Esthetts' names were called; and as fast as they were called, their owners stepped forward and clambered, puffing and grunting, into the car. At last, the sixth had struggled down into the round opening and the shelks turned and followed. A lid covered the hole from below, and silence reigned in the hall. After a moment, the Esthetts began to drift away, and as several moved toward the corridor in which Tumithak was concealed, he was forced to dart back through the passage some distance and slip into an apartment to avoid discovery.

He half expected some Esthett to enter the apartment and discover him, but this time luck was with him and after a few moments, he peered cautiously through the door to find the corridor empty. He emerged and quickly made his way to the main hall. It was deserted of Esthetts, now, but for some reason the cylinder still remained in the same spot; and Tumithak was suddenly seized with an idea that made him tremble with its magnitude.

These shelks had obviously come from the Surface in this car! And now they were going back to the Surface in it. Had not the Esthett, whom the shelks named Lathrumidor, told him that occasionally artists were called to live upon the Surface among the shelks? Yes, this car was certainly going to return to the Surface. And, with a sudden rush of inspired determination, Tumithak knew that he was going with it.

He hastened forward and in a moment was clinging to the rear of the machine, clambering for a foothold on the few projections he could find. He was not a moment too soon, for hardly had he gotten a firm grip on the machine than it leaped silently forward and sped at a vertiginous speed up the corridor!

CHAPTER VI

The Slaying of the Shelk

Tumithak's memory of that ride was a wild kaleidoscopic jumble of incidents. So fast did the car speed, that it was only occasionally, as they slowed to turn a corner or passed through an exceptionally narrow hall, that he could lift his eyes and look about him.

They passed through halls more brilliantly lighted than any he had yet seen. He saw halls of metal, polished and gleaming, and corridors of unpolished rock where the vibration of passing over rough rock threatened to hurl him at any moment from his precarious position.

Once they passed slowly through a marble passageway where Esthetts were lined on either side, chanting a solemn and sonorous hymn as the car of the shelks passed through. Tumithak was certain that he would be discovered, but if any of the singers saw him they paid little heed, evidently believing him to be a captive of the shelks. There were no longer any pits or branching hallways now, the entire road to the surface was one broad main corridor and along this corridor the car sped, carrying Tumithak ever nearer to his goal.

Although the car's speed was not great as measured by the speed of the cars we use today, it must be remembered that the fastest speed the Loorian had ever conceived was a fast run. So it seemed to him now that he rode upon the very wings of the wind, and his thankfulness knew no bounds when the car at last slowed to a speed that enabled him to drop to the ground in a section of the corridor that had apparently been uninhabited for many years. All thought of continuing the ride was abandoned now, his only desire was to end the devil's ride that he had so foolhardily undertaken.

For a moment, Tumithak was inclined to lie where he had fallen, at least long enough to regain control of his dazed faculties, but the sudden realization that the car of the shelks had stopped, not a hundred yards away, brought him instantly to his feet, and he flung himself hurriedly through the nearest open door. The apartment in which he found himself was dustladen and bare of furniture; it was obvious that it had been long unused, and so, convinced that no danger awaited him there, Tumithak returned to the door and looked out at the car.

He saw at once that the queer door or hatchway in the top of the car was open, but it was several moments before the occupants began to emerge. Then the fat head of one of the Esthetts appeared and its owner laboriously dragged himself up and over the side of the car. He was followed by a shelk, who leaped nimbly to the ground, after which the car slowly emptied until all twelve of its occupants were in the corridor. They all turned, then, and entered an apartment, the only one visible that bore a curtain over the door.

For a while, Tumithak remained in his hiding place debating his next move. His instinctive timidity urged him to remain in hiding, to wait— for days, if necessary—until the shelks had re-entered the car and departed. His curiosity demanded that he attempt to discover what the strangely allied party was doing beyond that great tapestry-covered door. And his wisdom told him that if he intended to continue on his quest, the best course was to keep on at once up the corridor, while the shelks were still within the apartment—for he knew that he was but a few short miles from the surface, toward which he had been traveling for so long.

His better judgment conquered at last and he chose the latter course, determined to forget the party, and so emerged from the room and began to run lightly and silently on his way; but as he passed the great doorway and saw how easily one might conceal himself in them, he determined to have one last look at the shelks and their strange friends before continuing. So, suiting the action to the thought, he stepped to the opening and, drawing the curtains around him, parted them slightly and looked into the room.

The first thing to strike his attention was the immense size of the room.

It must have been eighty feet long and half as many wide, truly an enormous room to the Loorian; and its ceiling was lost in gloom. So high was it that the lights, which were arranged around the room at the level of the shoulder, were not bright enough to show any of its detail. Tumithak had a queer idea that there was no ceiling, that perhaps the walls rose higher and higher until at last they reached the Surface. He had little time to speculate on this possibility, however, for he had hardly noticed it when his eyes fell upon the table. A great low table, it was, a long table covered with a cloth of snowy whiteness and piled high with strange articles that Tumithak saw were intended to be foods. But the Loorian looked at them in wonder, for they were foods such as he had never before heard of, such as his ancestors had not known for many a generation, the thousand and one succulent viands of the Surface. And around the table were a dozen low divans, and on some of these divans the Esthetts were even now reclining, greedily partaking of the varied foods.

The shelks, strangely enough were not joining them in the feast. Behind each of the ponderous artists, a shelk had taken his place, and to Tumithak's notion, there was something ominous in the way they stood, silently watching every move the Esthetts made. But the self-styled Chosen Ones were quite at ease, gobbling their food and grunting appreciative interjections to each other, until Tumithak turned from looking at them in disgust.

And then, suddenly, there came a sharp command from the shelk at the head of the table. The Esthetts looked up in consternation, dismay and a pitiable incredulity in their faces. Ere they could move, however, ere they could even cry out, on each a shelk had leaped, his thin-lipped mouth seeking, finding unerringly, the jugular vein beneath the folds of flesh in the fat one's heavy throat.

Vainly the artists struggled, their slow, helpless movements were unavailing, the nimble shelks easily avoiding their groping arms while all the time their teeth sank deeper into the flesh. Tumithak gasped in horror. As one in a trance, he watched the movements of the Esthetts become feebler until at last all motion ceased. The Loorian's brain was in a daze. What—what on Venus could be the meaning of this? What connection could this grisly scene have with the lengthy explanation of the lives of these people that Lathrumidor had given him in the marble halls below? He gazed at the scene in horror, unable to move his eyes.

The Esthetts were quiet now, and the shelks had raised themselves from them and were busy with some new occupation. From beneath the table they had drawn several large, transparent jars and half a dozen small machines with long hoses attached. These hoses were fastened to the wounds in the necks of the Esthetts and as Tumithak looked on he saw the blood swiftly pumped from the bodies and ejected into the jars.

As the jars filled with the liquid, the bodies of the Esthetts collapsed like punctured balloons, and in a few moments they lay, pallid and wrinkled, on the floor about the table. The shelks showed no excitement in their work; apparently it was merely a routine duty with them, and their calm business-like methods served only to add to Tumithak's terror, but at last he overcame the paralytic fear that held him, and he turned and sped frantically away. Up the corridor he ran faster and faster, farther and farther, and at last, spent and breathless, unable to run another step, he darted into an open door and flung himself gasping and panting on the floor of the apartment it led into.

Slowly he regained control of himself, his breath returned, and with it some small measure of confidence. He berated himself harshly for his cowardice in so losing control of himself, yet, even as he did so, he trembled at the thought of the terrible sight that he had witnessed. As he grew calmer, he began to wonder at the meaning of the events that he had seen. Lathrumidor, the Esthett, had led him to believe that the shelks were the kindly masters of the immense artists. He had spoken of the journey to the Surface as being the culminating honor of an Esthett's life. The shelk who had spoken in the great hall, too, had intimated as much. Yet for some strange reason, at the first opportunity after leaving the city, the shelks had slain their worshiping servants, and slain them in a way that seemed quite usual and commonplace to them. Strive as he might, Tumithak could not account for this apparent anomaly. And so, cowering in the rear room of the apartment, puzzling over the unnaturalness of the day's adventures, the Loorian fell into a troubled sleep.

It is not to be wondered that Tumithak was puzzled at the strange events of the day. He knew of no relationship between animals, such as existed between the Esthetts and the shelks. There were no domestic animals in the pits and man had not known of them for centuries. Other centuries were to go by before they were to know of them again, so there was nothing in Tumithak's life analogous to the status in which the shelks held the Esthetts.

Today we know that they were—cattle! Lulled into a sense of false security by hypocritical lies, bred for centuries for the full-blooded, bovine stupidity that was characteristic of them, allowed no means of intellectual expression except the artistic impulse which the shelks scorned, they had become, after many generations, the willing creatures of the Beasts of Venus.

And by a strange combination of the lies of the shelks and their own immense conceit, they had come to look forward, from earliest childhood, to that happy day when they would be taken to the Surface—to become, unknowing, the food of their masters. Such were the Esthetts, strangest, perhaps, of all the various races of men evolved by the breeding of the shelks.

All this, however, was far beyond the comprehension of Tumithak—or of any man of his generation. And so it was that even after he awoke and resumed his journey, he was still unable to account for the strange relationship. But the puzzles which a semi-savage mind cannot solve, it soon forgets, and so it was that before long Tumithak was strolling along on his way, his mind entirely at ease.

Since passing the hall of the singing Esthetts, during his wild ride, Tumithak had seen no signs of habitation. Apparently the corridors were entirely too near the surface to be inhabited by man. So Tumithak saw no one in the corridors and traveled for several miles undisturbed. At last he came to an abrupt end of the passage, and here found a ladder of metal set into the wall that rose higher and higher in the gloom. Filled with a suppressed excitement, his heart beating noticeably again, Tumithak began the ascent of what he knew to be the last pit before he reached the Surface. He emerged from it in a hall of strange black stone, and removing from his pouch the last of his father's gifts, he started along the upward slope, the weapon held gingerly in his hand. The corridor was narrower than any Tumithak had ever seen, and as he walked along, the walls drew still closer together, until it was not more than two feet wide. The grade became steeper and steeper and at last became a flight of stairs. Up these Tumithak strode, every moment his heart beating wilder, and at last he saw what he knew to be his goal. Far ahead, a light shone down in the corridor from above, a light far brighter and harsher than any of the lights of the corridors, and of a strange reddish tint. Tumithak knew, as he looked on it in awe, that the light was the light of the Surface.

He hurried forward; the ceiling became lower and lower and for the last few yards he was forced to stoop, and then, finally, he reached the top of the steps and found himself standing in a shallow pit, not more than five feet deep. He raised his head and a low gasp of absolute unbelief escaped from him.

For Tumithak had looked upon the Surface . . .

The vastness of the scene was enough to unnerve the Loorian. It seemed that he had emerged into a mighty room or hall, so tremendous that he could not even comprehend its immensity. The ceiling and walls of this room merged into each other to form a stupendous vault like an inverted bowl, which touched the floor of the vault at a distance so far away that it seemed utterly incredible. And this ceiling and these walls in places were of a beautiful blue, the color of a woman's eyes. This blue glowed like a jewel, and was mottled with great billowy areas of white and rose, and as Tumithak looked he had a vague feeling that those enormous billowy spots were slowly moving and changing in shape.

Unable to take his eyes from the sky above him, Tumithak's wonder and awe began to turn into a great fear. The more he looked, the further away the great dome seemed to be, and yet, curiously and terribly, it seemed to be closing in on him, too. He was sure, after a moment, that the great billowy spots were moving, and he had a dreadful feeling that they were about to fall and crush him. Sick and terrified at the enormity of the scene before him, he darted back into the passageway and cowered against the wall, trembling with a strange, unreasoning fear. For, raised as he had been in the close confines of the corridor walls, living his whole life under the ground, Tumithak, when he first looked upon the Surface, became a victim of agoraphobia, that strange fear of open spaces, that in some people, even today, amounts to a disease.

It was nearly an hour before his reason was able to gain control over this strange fear. Had he come thus far, he argued with himself, only to return because of the appearance of the Surface? Surely, if that mighty blue and cloudy vault was to fall, it would not have waited all these years just to fall on him. He took a deep breath, and reason prevailing at last, he again looked out upon the Surface.

But this time his eyes avoided the sky, and he directed his attention to the floor of the "room." In the vicinity of the pit this floor consisted of a thick brown dust, but not far away this dust was covered with a strange carpet consisting of thousands of long green hairs thickly matted together, completely hiding the dusty floor beneath. In the middle distance were a number of tall, irregular pillars whose tops were covered with a great huge bunch of green stuff, of the same color and appearance as the hairs of the carpet.

And then, as Tumithak looked beyond the grass and the trees, he beheld a wonder that surpassed the other wonders that he had seen, for hanging low in the dome above the trees was the light of the Surface, a brilliant, blinding orb that lit up, redly, all that vast space of the Surface.

Speechless with awe, Tumithak looked upon the sunset. Again came the dizzy, sickening rush of agoraphobia, but with it came a sense of beauty that made him forget his fear, and gradually calmed him. After a while he turned his eyes and looked in the opposite direction; and there, towering high above him, were the homes of the shelks!

Fully a dozen of the high towers were visible; obelisk-like they stood there, their metal walls gleaming redly in the light of the sinking sun. Very few of them stood perfectly erect, the strange unearthly artistic sense of the shelks causing them to be built at various angles from the perpendicular, some as much as thirty degrees. They were of varying heights, some fifty, some as much as two hundred feet high, and from their tops long cables hung, linking all the towers together. Windowless they were, and the only mode of ingress was a small round door at the bottom. Not one of all these towers was more than fifteen feet in circumference, so that they gave an appearance not unlike a bundle of huge needles.

For how long the Loorian gazed at these amazing scenes, he could not tell. Of all the wondrous sights, the strangest, to him, was the sunset, the gradual sinking of the great red light into what seemed to be the floor of the vast chamber. Even after the sun had disappeared, he remained gazing absorbedly at the walls, which still glowed redly where it had been . . . And then—

Tumithak had not heard a sound. Lost in wonder though he was, his ears had remained instinctively on the alert, and yet he had heard nothing. Until suddenly there was a scratching, rustling noise behind him and a clattering, metallic voice barked staccato words of command.

"Get—back—in—that—hole!" it spat, and Tumithak's blood turned to water as he realized that a shelk had stolen up behind him!

The next second seemed a year to the Loorian. He turned to face the beast, and in that turning a thousand thoughts raced through his mind. He thought of Nikadur and Thupra, and of the many years that he had known them; he thought of his father and even of his little remembered mother, he thought, strangely enough of the huge Yakran that he had tumbled into the pit and of how he had bellowed as he fell. All these thoughts rushed through his mind as he turned and then his arm flew up to protect himself. Utterly instinctive, the action was; it seemed that he was not in control of his body at all. Something outside of him— greater than himself—caused him to flex his fingers, and as he did, the revolver, the last of his father's three strange gifts spat flame and thunder. As in a dream, he heard its spitting bark, once, twice, thrice—seven times; and into the shallow pit tumbled the dead body of the shelk!

For a moment, the hero stared at it dumbly. Then, as the realization that he had accomplished his mission came over him, a great feeling of exultation seized him. Quickly drawing his sword, he began to slash at the ten long finger-like legs of the shelk, humming, as he did so, the song that the Loorians sang when they marched against the Yakrans; and though there were strange, questioning clacks and clatters from the direction of the homes of the shelks, he methodically continued hacking until the head was free from the body.

Then, realizing that the voices of the shelks were much nearer, he stuffed the bleeding head into the bosom of his tunic, and sped like the wind down the steps of the corridor.

CHAPTER VII

The Power and the Glory

Tumlook of Loor, the father of Tumithak, sat in the doorway of his apartment, gazing out into the corridor. It was a lonely life that he had led for the past few weeks, for although his friends had tried to cheer him with the customary optimistic chatter, he could see that they all believed that his son would never return. And indeed, it would have been a bold man that would argue that Tumithak had even so much as passed the city of Yakra.

Tumlook knew the opinions of his friends and he was beginning to believe as they did, in spite of the fact that they did their best to make him think that they expected wondrous things of his son. Why, he wondered, had he ever let the youth depart on such a hopeless quest? Why had he not been more stern with him, and driven the idea out of his head while he was still young? So he sat and berated himself, in this hour just before the time of sleep, as the life of Loor passed by him in an irregular, intermittent stream.

After a while his face brightened a little. Coming down the hall toward him were the two lovers whose long friendship with Tumithak had made a bond that Tumlook felt that he had somehow inherited. Nikadur hailed him, and as they drew near, Thupra ran up and kissed him impulsively on the cheek.

"Have you heard aught of Tumithak?" she cried, the question that had been almost a form of greeting between them.

Tumlook shook his head.

"Is it likely?" he asked. "Surely after all these weeks, we must look upon him as dead."

But Thupra was not to be discouraged. Indeed, of all Loor, it is probable that she alone still maintained the confidence that amounted to a certainty that Tumithak was safe and would return in triumph.

"I think he will return," she said now. "You know, we are sure that he reached Yakra. And has not Nennapuss told us of the huge giant that was found dead at the foot of the Yakran shaft? If Tumithak could conquer such a man as that, who could overcome him?"

"Thupra may be right," said Nikadur, gravely. "There are rumors in Nonone of a great panic in Yakra, during which a man of these corridors is supposed to have passed through the town. The rumors are vague and may be only gossip, but perhaps Tumithak did reach the dark corridors."

"Tumithak will return, I know," Thupra repeated. "He is mighty, and—" she paused. Far up the corridor, her ears caught a sound and she listened questioningly. Then Nikadur heard it, too, and last of all it reached the ears of Tumlook.

A shouting, a distant shouting that grew louder even as they listened. Several passing pedestrians heard it, too, and paused; and then two men turned and hastened off in its direction. The trio strained their ears in an endeavor to distinguish the meaning of the cries. Several more men came speeding up the corridor, running in the direction of the noise.

"Come," cried Nikadur suddenly, consternation written on his face. "If this be a raid of the Yakrans—" In spite of the cries of Thupra, he sped off, and Tumlook hesitated only long enough to dart back into his apartment and arm himself before he followed.

Thupra, however, was not to be left behind. She caught up with Nikadur in a moment, and in spite of his protestations, persisted in going with him. And so the three, joined soon by many others, rushed on in the direction of the excitement.

A man passed them, running the other way. "What is it?" came a chorus of a dozen voices, but the man's only answer was an unintelligible gabble of words as he ran on. The crowd's ignorance was not to continue for long, though, for at the very next turn of the corridor, they beheld the cause of the tumult.

Down the corridor came marching an incredible procession. A group of Loorians led the parade, dancing and cheering like mad, while behind them came marching a well-known figure—Nennapuss, chief of the Nononese, with his retinue of officers. Nennapuss was followed by what must have been almost the entire population of Nonone, all gabbling and shouting madly to the Loorians whom they passed. It was not at the Nononese that the Loorians stared, however, but at the ones who followed them. Behind Nennapuss' men came a crowd of Yakrans, each carrying aloft a white cloth on a stick that still, after so many hundreds of years, denoted a truce. Datta was there, the burly chief of the Yakrans, and his huge nephew, Thorpf, and many others of whom the Loorians had heard from the Nononese, and there, high on the shoulders of two of the mightiest Yakrans, was riding—Tumithak!

But when the eyes of the Loorians looked upon Tumithak, they looked no further. For the sight they beheld was so incredible that it seemed impossible to believe that they were not dreaming.

He was dressed in garments that, to their eyes, were beautiful beyond telling. They were of the finest texture imaginable, sheer gauzes that were dyed in the most delicate shades of nacreous pinks and greens and blues. They flowed down over his form, clinging to his body and giving him all the appearance of a god. Around his head was a metal band not unlike a crown, such a band as legend said the king shelks were wont to wear.

And, most unbelievable of all, he held his arm aloft, and in his hand was the wrinkled head of a shelk!

Tumlook, Nikadur and Thupra never knew when they joined the crowd. One moment they were rushing down the corridor toward the incredible procession, the next, it had absorbed them and they, too, were a part of the howling, enthusiastic mob that fought and laughed its way toward the great square of Loor.

They reached the crossing of the two main corridors and formed an immense crowd with Tumithak and the Yakrans in its center. The crowd continued its chattering and cheering for some moments and then Tumithak, mounting the stone pedestal that had long been used for speakers, held up his hand for silence. Quiet reigned almost instantly, and in the lull, the voice of Nennapuss, that instinctive master of ceremonies, could be heard.

"Friends of Loor," he cried. "Today is the day that will live forever in the archives of the three cities of the lower corridors. It has been unnumbered years since the three cities have all met on a friendly footing, and to bring that about it has taken an event so incredible that it is well-nigh impossible to believe. For at last a man has slain a shelk—"

He was interrupted by the booming voice of Datto, the much-decorated chief of the Yakrans.

"Enough of this talk," he shouted. "We are here to do honor to Tumithak, the Loorian, who has slain a shelk. Let us shout and sing songs in his praise. Let us bow to him, Nennapuss, we who are chiefs, let us call upon the chiefs of Loor to bow to him also, for who could slay a shelk if he were not far greater than we."

Nennapuss looked a little nettled at having been interrupted at his favorite pastime, but before he could answer, Tumithak began to speak. And at his word, Yakran and Nononese alike listened with respect.

"Fellow Loorians," he began. "Brothers of Nonone and Yakra, it was not for honor that I journeyed to the Surface and slew the beast whose head I hold in my hand. Since I was a boy I have felt that men could fight with shelks. It has been the ambition of my life to prove that fact to everyone. Surely no citizen of Loor was less of a fighter than I. Many, indeed, have scorned me for a mere dreamer of dreams. And I assure you that I was little more. Can you not see that man is not the weak, insignificant creature that you seem to think? You Yakrans have never cowered in fear when the men of Loor came against you! Loorians, have you ever trembled in your apartments when the Yakrans raided your halls?

"Yet the cry of 'Shelk!' will send you all fleeing panic-stricken to your homes! Can you not see that these shelks, although mighty, are only mortal creatures like yourselves? Listen to the story of my deeds, now, and see if I have done aught that you could not have done."

He took up the recital of his adventures. He told of the passing of Yakra, and though the Loorians cheered a bit there was silence among the people of Yakra, and then he told of the dark corridors, and the Yakrans, too, cheered as he recited his story of the slaying of the dogs. He told of the halls of the Esthetts, and in glowing colors described to them the beauties there, hoping that he might arouse in them the desire to possess these beauties.

And then he tried to tell them of the Surface, but here words failed him; it was hardly possible, in the limited vocabulary of the corridors, to tell of the slaying of the shelk, and at last the story of his return.

"For some reason the shelks did not follow me," he said, "and I reached the first halls of the Esthetts in safety. And here I was discovered, and had to fight a battle with a half dozen of the fat ones before I could go farther. I slew them all," Tumithak, in that sublime unconscious conceit of his, failed to say how easy it had been to slaughter his huge opponents, "and taking from them these garments, continued on my way.

"I came again to the dark corridors, but even here no one opposed me. Perhaps the terrible smell of shelk was so great that the savages feared to come near me. So at last I came to Yakra, and found that the woman whom I had met on my upward journey had told her story to Datto, the chief, who was ready and eager to do me honor on my return home. And so I came to Nonone, and after a time to Loor."

He ceased his story, and again the crowd broke into cheers. The cheers increased, echoed back against the walls until the great hall rang like a bell. "Great is Tumithak of the Loorians!" They cried, "Great is Tumithak, slayer of shelks!" And Tumithak folded his arms and drank in the praise, forgetful for the moment that his entire mission had been to prove that it did not take a great man to kill a shelk.

After a while, the tumult began to die and the voice of Datto was heard again.

"Loorians," he shouted. "For many, many years, the men of Yakra have fought unending war with the men of Loor. Today that war ceases. Today we have found a Loorian who is greater than all Yakrans, and so we fight with Loor no more. And to prove that I speak truth, Datto bows in allegiance to Tumithak!"

Again the cheers, and at last Nennapuss arose.

"It is a good thing that you have done, O Datto," he said, "and truly Tumithak is a chief of chiefs if there ever was one. Now there has been little enmity between Loor and Nonone in the past, and so our cases are different. For it is said that in the olden days, the people of Loor and Nonone were one. Thus, we hear of the days of the great chief, Ampithat, who ruled—" here Datto whispered something fiercely into his ear, and the Nononese flushed and went on, "But enough of that. Suffice it that

Nennapuss, too, bows to Tumithak, chief of chiefs and chief of Nonone."

Again there was a great demonstration and after a while, Datto began to speak again. Would it not be a seemly thing, he asked frowning fiercely, for the Loorians to recognize Tumithak as their chief also, thus making him king of all the lower corridors? The Loorians raised a cheer, and then Tagivos, the eldest of the doctors, arose to speak.

"The people of Loor have a government somewhat different from that of Nonone and Yakra," he said. "We have not had a chief for many years. However, it might be a good thing for the three towns to be united and so I will call a meeting of the council to decide on it."

The council was soon grouped together, Tagivos, Tumlook and old Sidango leading them, and after a while they announced that they were agreed to recognize Tumithak as their chief also. And so, amid wild cheering, that made it utterly impossible to distinguish a word that was said, Tumithak became chief of all the lower corridors.

Datto and his huge nephew, Thorpf, the foremost of the Yakrans, were the first to swear allegiance to him; then he accepted the fealty of Sidango, Tagivos and the other Loorians. It gave Tumithak a queer feeling to touch the sword of his father and to hear his oath, but he maintained his dignified bearing, and treated Tumlook in just the same fashion as the others, until the ceremony was over. Then he called for attention.

"Friends of the lower corridors," he said. "A new day dawns for man today. It has been over thirty years since war has visited these corridors and in all those years men have almost forgotten the arts of war. We have lived in a spirit of slothful peace, while above us the enemies of all mankind have grown stronger and stronger. But in making me your chief, you have ended that era of peace and brought upon yourselves new lives of action. I will not be a peaceful ruler, for I, who have seen so much of the world, will not be content to skulk idly in the deepest corridor. Already I plan to lead you against the savages of the dark corridors, to claim those halls as our own, and to fill them with the lights that still gleam in the deserted corridors that we no longer use.

"And if we conquer those savages, I shall take you against the huge Esthetts to show you what beauty can do for the life of man. And the time will surely come, if the High One be willing, when I shall lead you against the shelks themselves, for what I have done, every one of you can do, and shall do.

"And if anyone feels that the task I call upon you to do is too great, let him speak now for I will not rule over man against his will."

Again the cheers broke out, and gathered volume, and rang from wall to wall of the great square. In the excitement and enthusiasm of the moment, there was not a man in all the crowd that did not feel that he, too, might become a slayer of shelks.

And while they cheered and sang, and worked themselves into a frenzy, Tumithak stepped down from the stone and strode off in the direction of his home.

"Tumithak of the Corridors" was far and away the best and most exciting story I had ever read up to that time.

I must admit that when I reread these ancient stories, I don't, in my early fifties, get nearly the same charge I got when in my preteens. I am far more aware now than I was then of the structural and stylistic flaws. And what was new and astonishing then is not new and astonishing now.

Yet let it be said that the gap proved surprisingly small when I read "Tumithak of the Corridors." Even now, though my hair is graying, I found myself stirred very much as I had been once in junior high school.

I found the characters human and the hero all the more admirable because he could feel fear. I found the plot exciting and found a deep humanity in the sentence "Tumithak had to learn that in no matter what nation or age one finds oneself, he will find gentleness, if he looks, as well as savagery." This was an amazing viewpoint at a time when popular literature accepted racial stereotypes as a matter of course.

Most of all, though, there was (and is) something fascinating to me in the thought of endless corridors burrowing underground.

I'm a claustrophile. I enjoy the feeling of being closed in. I like tunnels and corridors and never mind the absence of windows. The office I work in I chose because it faces a court. I keep the shades pulled down and I work under perpetual artificial light.

I've always been that way. I remember that, in my younger days, when I took the subway to school I was always fascinated by the small newsstands there used to be on the stations. Late at night I would see them closed, and inside, I knew, were all those lovely pulps I never got a chance to read. And I would fantasize being shut into one of those things, with the lights on, of course, and, safely enclosed and with the sound of subway trains rushing past periodically, reading and reading and reading.

But don't get me wrong. I am not psychotic about it. The apartment I live in is on the twenty-third floor with wide windows overlooking Central Park, and the sunlight comes in steadily.

Well, I'm off the point. The corridors pleased me, and I never forgot them. When I wrote The Caves of Steel, in 1953, and lovingly described the underground city of the future, I did not forget "Tumithak of the Corridors."

One thing I noted, in rereading the story, that I had forgotten. It is told in the form of history. The narrator is in the far future looking back on events that took place in what was, to him, the legendary past. Apparently, that didn't impress me, for I did not remember.

Yet does one ever really forget? Eventually, when I wrote my Foundation Trilogy in the form of historical novels of the future, was there a dim unconscious memory of the manner of telling of "Tumithak of the Corridors?"

In my last months at junior high school, I decided to apply for entrance into Boys High School of Brooklyn. In the ordinary course of events I should have gone to Thomas Jefferson High School, which was closest to where I lived. The graduating body of J.H.S. 149 usually transferred to Jefferson *en masse* and did so this time too. I think I was one of only three boys who opted for Boys High.

You see, by this time I had ambitions of vague higher things, and Boys High School had a reputation for scholastic excellence. My parents, who wanted me to go to medical school eventually, thought this was a good move.

I have often pondered the consequences of that decision. Jefferson High was coeducational. Had I spent my early teens there, I would undoubtedly have discovered girls. Automatically, I would have had a strong motivation to broaden my interests, learn to dance, for instance, learn to handle myself easily and well with the opposite sex. On the other hand, my schoolwork might have suffered disastrously.

At Boys High, with its purely masculine student body, I was plunged into a monastic existence in which there was little to distract me from schoolwork or to encourage me to broaden out.

In consequence, throughout my teens and very early twenties I remained ill at ease in the presence of girls. I got over it, to be sure, married at the age of twenty-two, and have, for many years, been noted for my suavity with the ladies. (I have even written a book called *The Sensuous Dirty Old Man,* and no one has ever cast doubt on my qualifications for undertaking that task.)

Nevertheless, what would have happened if I had gone to Jefferson High instead of Boys High?

But what's the use of dwelling upon it? Things might have turned out much worse. After all, the girls in my class would have been, for the most part, two and a half years older than I. Not only would I have seemed ludicrously young in their eyes, but I would also have been found to be lacking in the social graces and in worldly knowledge. I would undoubtedly have suffered rejection of all sorts, and who can tell how badly that might have affected me.

Nor was the monasticism of my early teens disturbed (or relieved, if you prefer) by the science fiction I was reading. In the 1930s, science fiction was almost entirely masculine. The readership was almost entirely masculine, after all, and so were the writers.

Of course, there were women in the stories, but they were there only to be caught and then rescued, only to be fought over by hero and villain (as in "Awlo of Ulm"). They had no life of their own and left no impression.

Once, in those early years, however, I recall being really moved by the relationship between a man and a woman as pictured in a science fiction story. It is perhaps inevitable that the woman involved wasn't really a woman.

The story in question was Jack Williamson's "The Moon Era," published in the February 1932 *Wonder Stories*, and I fell in love with the Moon woman whom Williamson called the "Mother."

THE MOON ERA

by Jack Williamson

CHAPTER I

We were seated at dinner in the long dining room of my uncle's Long Island mansion. There was glistening silver plate, and the meal had been served with a formality to which I was unaccustomed. I was ill at ease, though my uncle and I sat alone at the table. The business of eating, without committing an egregious blunder before the several servants, took all my attention.

It was the first time I had ever seen my uncle, Enfield Conway. A tall man, stiffly erect, dressed severely in black. His face, though lean, was not emaciated as is usual at his age of seventy years. His hair, though almost perfectly white, was abundant, parted on the side. His eyes were blue, and strong; he wore no glasses.

A uniformed chauffeur had met me at the station, in the afternoon. The butler had sent an entirely unnecessary valet to my luxurious room. I had not met my uncle until he came down to the dining room.

"I suppose, Stephen, you are wondering why I sent for you," he said in his precise manner, when the servants had carried away the last course, leaving cigars, and a bottle of mineral water for him.

I nodded. I had been instructor of history in a small high school in Texas, where his telegram had reached me. There had been no explanation; merely a summons to Long Island.

"You are aware that some of my patents have been quite profitable." Again I nodded. "The evidence surrounds me."

"Stephen, my fortune amounts to upwards of three and a half million. How should you like to be my heir?"

"Why, sir—I should not refuse. I'd like very much to be."

"You can, if you wish, earn that fortune. And fifty thousand a year while I live."

I pushed back the chair and rose to my feet in excitement. Such riches were beyond my dreams! I felt myself trembling.

"Anything—" I stammered. "I'll do anything you say, to earn that! It means—"

"Wait," he said, looking at me calmly. "You don't know yet what I require. Don't commit yourself too soon."

"What is it?" I asked, in a quivering voice.

"Stephen, I have been working in my private laboratory here for eleven years. I have been building a machine. The best of my brains have gone into that machine. Hundreds of thousands of dollars. The efforts of able engineers and skilled mechanics.

"Now the machine is finished. It is to be tested. The engineers who worked with me refused to try the machine. They insist that it is very dangerous.

"And I am too old to make the trial. It will take a young man, with strength, endurance, and courage.

"You are young, Stephen. You look vigorous enough. I suppose your health is good? A sound heart? That's the main thing."

"I think so," I told him. "I've been coaching the Midland football team. And it isn't many years since I was playing college football, myself."

"And you have no dependents?"

"None.—But what is this machine?"

"I will show you. Come."

He rose, agilely enough for one of his seventy years, and led the way from the long room. Through several magnificent rooms of the big house. Out into the wide, landscaped grounds, beautiful and still in the moonlight.

I followed silently. My brain was confusion. A whirl of mad thought. All this wealth whose evidence surrounded me might be my own! I cared nothing for luxury, for money itself. But the fortune would mean freedom from the thankless toil of pedagogy. Books. Travel. Why I could see with my own eyes the scenes of history's dramatic moments! Finance research expeditions of my own! Delve with my own hands for the secrets of Egypt's sands, uncover the age-old enigmas of ruined mounds that once were proud cities of the East!

We approached a rough building,—resembling an airplane hangar,—of galvanized iron, which glistened like silver in the rays of the full moon.

Without speaking, Uncle Enfield produced a key from his pocket, unlocked the heavy padlock on the door. He entered the building, switching on electric lights inside it.

"Come in," he said. "Here it is. I'll explain it as well as I can."

I walked through the narrow doorway and uttered an involuntary exclamation of surprise at sight of the huge machine that rested upon the clean concrete floor.

Two huge disks of copper, with a cylinder of bright, chromium-plated metal between them. Its shape vaguely suggested that of an ordinary spool of adhesive plaster, from which a little has been used—the polished cylinder, which was of smaller diameter than the disks, took the place of the roll of plaster.

The lower of the massive disks rested on the concrete floor. Its diameter was about twenty feet. The cylinder above it was about sixteen feet in diameter, and eight feet high. The copper disk above was the same size as the lower one.

Small round windows stared from the riveted metal plates forming the cylinder. The whole was like a building, it burst on me. A circular room with bright metal walls. Copper floor and copper roof projecting beyond those walls.

My uncle walked to the other side of this astounding mechanism. He turned a projecting knob. An oval door, four feet high, swung inward in the curving wall. Four inches thick. Of plated steel. Fitting very tightly against cushions of rubber.

My uncle climbed through the door, into the dark interior. I followed with a growing sense of wonder and excitement. I groped toward him through the darkness. Then I heard the click of a switch, and lights flashed on within the round chamber.

I gazed about me in astonishment.

Walls, floor, and ceiling were covered with soft, white fiber. The little room was crowded with apparatus. Clamped against one white wall was a row of the tall steel flasks in which commercial oxygen is compressed. Across the room was a bank of storage batteries. The walls were hung with numerous instruments, all clamped neatly in place. Sextants. Compasses. Pressure gauges. Numerous dials whose functions were not apparent. Cooking utensils. An automatic pistol. Cameras. Telescopes. Binoculars.

In the center of the room stood a table or cabinet, with switches, dials, and levers upon its top. A heavy cable, apparently of aluminum, ran from it to the ceiling.

I was gazing about in bewilderment. "I don't understand all this—" I began.

"Naturally," said my uncle. "It is quite a novel invention. Even the engineers who built it did not understand it. I confess that the theory of it is yet beyond me. But what happens is quite simple.

"Eleven years ago, Stephen, I discovered a new phenomenon. I had happened to charge two parallel copper plates, whose distances apart had a certain very definite relation to their combined masses, with a high tension current at a certain frequency.

"The plates, Stephen, were in some way—how, I do not pretend to understand—cut out of the earth's gravitational field. Insulated from gravity. The effect extended to any object placed between them. By a slight variation of the current's strength, I was able to increase the repulsion, until the plates pulled upward with a force approximately equal to their own weight.

"My efforts to discover the reason for this phenomenon—it is referred to in my notes as the Conway Effect—have not been successful. But I have built this machine to make a practical application of it. Now that it is finished, the four engineers who helped design it have deserted. They refused to assist with any trials."

"Why?" I asked.

"Muller, who had the construction in charge, somehow came to the conclusion that the suspension or reversal of gravity was due to motion in a fourth dimension. He claimed that he had experimental proof of his theory, by building models of the device, setting the dials, and causing them to vanish. I would have none of it. But the other men seemed to accept his ideas. At any rate, they refused with him to have any part in the tests. They thought they would vanish, like Muller says his models did, and not come back."

"The thing is supposed to rise above the ground?" I asked.

"Quite so." My uncle smiled. "When the force of gravitation is merely suspended, it should fly off the earth at a tangent, due to the diurnal rotation. This initial velocity, which in these latitudes, amounts to considerably less than one thousand miles per hour, can be built up at will, by reversing gravitation, and falling away from the earth."

"*Falling away from the earth!*" I was staggered. "And where is one to fall."

"This machine was designed for a trip to the moon. At the beginning of the voyage, gravitation will be merely cut out, allowing the machine to fly off on a tangent, toward the point of intersection with the moon's orbit. Safely beyond the atmosphere, repulsion can be used to build up the acceleration. Within the gravitational sphere of the moon, positive gravitation can be utilized further to increase the speed. And reversed gravitation to retard the velocity, to make possible a safe landing. The return will be made in the same manner."

I was staring at him blankly. A trip to the moon seemed insane, beyond reason. Especially for a professor of history, with only a modicum of scientific knowledge. And it must be dangerous, if those engineers—. But three million—what dangers would I not face for such a fortune?

"Everything has been done," he went on, "to insure the comfort and safety of the passenger. The walls are insulated with a fiber composition especially worked out to afford protection from the cold of space, and from the unshielded radiation of the sun. The steel armor is strong enough not only to hold the necessary air pressure, but to stop any ordinary meteoric particles.

"You notice the oxygen cylinders, for maintaining that essential element in the air. There is automatic apparatus for purifying it. It is pumped through caustic soda to absorb the carbon dioxide, and through refrigerator tubes to condense the excess moisture.

"The batteries, besides energizing the plates, are amply powerful to supply lights and heat for cooking.

"That, I believe, fairly outlines the machine and the projected voyage. Now it is up to you. Take time to consider it fully. Ask me any questions you wish."

He sat down deliberately in the large, cushioned chair, beside the central table, which was evidently intended for the operator. He stared at me alertly, with calm blue eyes.

I was extremely agitated. My knees had a weak feeling, so that I desired to sit down also; though I was so nervous that I kept striding back and forth across the resilient white fiber of the floor.

Three millions! It would mean so much! Books, magazines, maps—I should have to economize no longer. Years—all my life, if I wished—abroad. The tombs of Egypt. The sand-covered cities of the Gobi. My theory that mankind originated in South Africa. All those puzzles that I had longed to be able to study. Stonehenge! Angkor! Easter Island!

But the adventure seemed madness. A voyage to the moon! In a craft condemned by the very engineers that had built it. To be hurled away from the earth at speeds no man had attained before. To face unknown perils of space. Dangers beyond guessing. Hurtling meteors. The all-penetrating cosmic ray. The burning heat of the sun. The absolute zero. What, beyond speculation and theory, did men know of space? I was no astronomer; how was I to cope with the emergencies that might rise?

"How long will it take?" I demanded suddenly.

My uncle smiled a little. "Glad you are taking it seriously," he said. "The duration of the voyage depends on the speed you make, of course. A week each way is a conservative estimate. And perhaps two or three days on the moon. To take notes. Photograph it. Move around a little, if possible; land in several different places. There is oxygen and concentrated food to last six months. But a fortnight should see you nearly back. I'll go over the charts and calculations with you."

"Can I leave the machine on the moon?"

"No. No atmosphere. And it would be too hot in the day, too cold at night. Of course an insulated suit and oxygen mask might be devised. Something like diving armor. But I haven't worked at that. You will be expected just to take a few pictures, be prepared to describe what you have seen."

I continued to pace the floor, pausing sometimes to examine some piece of apparatus. How would it feel, I wondered, to be shut up in here? Drifting in space. Far from the world of my birth. Alone. In silence. Entombed. Would it not drive me mad?

My uncle rose suddenly from the chair.

"Sleep on it, Stephen," he advised. "See how you feel in the morning. Or take longer if you wish."

He switched off the light in the machine. Led the way out into the shed. And from it into the brilliant moonlight that flooded the wide, magnificent grounds about the great house that would be one of the prizes of this mad adventure.

As he was locking the shed, I gazed up at the moon.

Broad, bright disk. Silvery, mottled. Extinguishing the stars with argent splendor. And all at once it came over me—the desire to penetrate the enigmatic mystery of this companion world, that men have watched since the race began.

What an adventure! To be the first human to tread this silver planet. To be the first to solve its age-old riddles. Why think of Angkor, or Stonehenge, of Luxor and Karnak, when I might win the secrets of the moon?

Even if death came, what did it matter against the call of this adventure? Many men would trade their lives eagerly for such a chance.

Suddenly I was strong. All weakness had left me. All fear and doubt. A few moments before I had been tired, wishing to sit down. Now vast energy filled me. I was conscious of an extraordinary elation. Swiftly I turned to my uncle.

"Let's go back," I said. "Show me as much about it as you can tonight. I am going."

He gripped my hand tightly, without a word, before he turned back to the lock.

CHAPTER II

Toward the Moon

It was in the second week, after that sudden decision came to me, that I started. At the end my uncle became a little alarmed, and tried to persuade me to stay longer, to make more elaborate preparations. I believe that he was secretly becoming fond of me, despite his brisk precise manner. I think he took the opinion of his engineers seriously enough to consider my return very uncertain.

But I could see no reason for longer delay. The operation of the machine was simple; he had explained it quite fully.

There was a switch to close, to send current from the batteries through the coils that raised it to the potential necessary to energize the copper disks. And a large rheostat that controlled the force, from a slight decrease in gravity, to a complete reversal.

The auxiliary apparatus, for control of temperature and atmosphere, was largely automatic. And not beyond my limited mechanical comprehension. I was certain that I should be able to make any necessary repairs or adjustments.

Now I was filled with the greatest haste to undertake the adventure. No doubt or hesitation had troubled me since the moment of the decision. I felt only a longing to be sweeping away from the earth. To view scenes that the ages had kept hidden from human eyes; to tread the world that has always been the symbol of the unattainable.

My uncle recalled one of the engineers, a sallow young fellow named Gorton. On the second morning, to supplement my uncle's instruction he went over the machine again, showing me the function of every part. Before he left, he warned me.

"If you are idiot enough to get in that darned contraption, and turn on the power," he told me, "you'll never come back. Muller said so. And he proved it. So long as the batteries and coil are outside the field of force between the plates, the plates act according to schedule, and rise up in the air.

"But Muller made self-contained models. With the battery and all inside. And they didn't rise up. They went out! Vanished. Just like that!" He snapped his fingers. "Muller said the things moved along another dimension, right out of our world. And he ought to know. String of degrees a mile long. Into another dimension. No telling what sort of hell you'll blunder into."

I thanked the man. But his warnings only increased my eagerness. I was about to tear aside the veil of the unknown. What if I did blunder into new worlds? Might they not yield rewards of knowledge richer than those of the barren moon? I might be a new Columbus, a greater Balboa.

I slept a few hours in the afternoon, after Gorton had gone. I felt no conscious need of slumber, but my uncle insisted upon it. And to my surprise, I fell soundly asleep, almost as soon as I lay down.

At sunset, we went down again to the shed in which the machine was housed. My uncle started a motor, which opened the roof like a pair of enormous doors, by means of pulleys and cables. The red light of the evening sky streamed down upon the machine.

We made a final inspection of all the apparatus. My uncle explained again the charts and instruments that I was to use in navigating space. Finally he questioned me for an hour, making me explain the various parts of the machine, correcting any error.

I was not to start until nearly midnight.

We returned to the house, where an elaborate dinner was waiting. I ate almost absently, hardly noticing the servants of whom I had been so conscious upon my arrival. My uncle was full of conversation. Talking of his own life, and asking me many questions about my own, and about my father, whom he had seen last when they were boys. My mind was upon the adventure before me; I could answer him only disjointedly. But I was aware that he had taken a real liking for me; I was not surprised at his request that I postpone the departure.

At last we went back down to the machine. The white moon was high; its soft radiance bathed the gleaming machine, through the opened roof. I stared up at its bright disk. Was it possible that in a short week I should be there, looking back upon the earth? It seemed madness! But the madness of glorious adventure!

Without hesitation, I clambered through the oval door. A last time my uncle wrung my hand. He had tears in his eyes. And his voice was a little husky.

"I want you to come back, Stephen."

I swung the door into its cushioned seat, upon massive hinges, tightened the screws that were to hold it. A final glance about the white-walled interior of the machine. All was in order. The chronometer by the wall, ticking steadily, told me that the moment had come.

My uncle's anxious face was pressed against one of the ports. I smiled at him. Waved. His hand moved across the port. He left the shed.

I dropped into the big chair beside the table, reached for the switch. With my fingers upon the button, I hesitated the merest second. Was there anything else? Anything neglected? Anything I had yet to do on earth? Was I ready to die, if so I must?

The deep, vibrant hum of the coils, beneath the table, answered the pressure of my finger. I took the handle of the rheostat, swung it to the zero mark, where gravitation was to be cut off completely.

My sensation was exactly as if the chair, the floor, had fallen from under me. The same sensation that one feels when an elevator drops very abruptly. Almost I floated out of the chair. I had to grasp at the arm of it to stay within it.

For a few moments I experienced nauseating vertigo. The white crowded room seemed to spin about me. To drop away endlessly beneath me. Sick, helpless, miserable, I clung weakly to the great chair. Falling . . . falling . . . falling. Would I never strike bottom?

Then I realized, with relief, that the sensation was due merely to the absence of gravity's familiar pull. The machine had worked! My last, lingering doubt was killed. Strange elation filled me.

I was flying away from the earth. Flying.

The thought seemed to work a miracle of change in my feelings. The dreadful, dizzy nausea gave way to a feeling of exhilaration. Of lightness. I was filled with a sense of power and well-being, such as I had never before experienced.

I left the great chair, floated rather than walked to one of the windows.

Already I was high in the air. So high that the moonlit earth was a dim and misty plain before me. I could see many lights; the westward sky was aglow, above New York. But already I was unable to pick out the lights at my uncle's mansion.

The machine had risen through the open roof of the shed. It was driving out into space, as it had been planned to do! The adventure was succeeding.

As I watched, the earth sank visibly. Became a great concave bowl of misty silver. Expanded slowly, as the minutes went by. And became suddenly convex. A huge dark sphere, washed with pale gray light.

Presently, after an hour, when the dials showed that I was beyond the faintest trace of atmosphere, I returned to the table and increased the power, moving the rheostat to the last contact. I looked at charts and chronometer. According to my uncle's calculations, four hours at this acceleration were required, before the controls were set again.

I returned to the window and stared in amazement at the earth, that I had left vast and silver gray and motionless.

It was spinning madly, backward!

The continents seemed to race beneath me—I was now high enough to see a vast section of the globe. Asia. North America. Europe. Asia again. In seconds.

It was madness! The earth spinning in a few moments, instead of the usual twenty-four hours. And turning backward! But I could not doubt my eyes. Even as I watched, the planet seemed to spin faster. Ever faster! The continental outlines merged into dim indistinctness.

I looked away from the mad earth, in bewilderment. The firmament was very black. And the very stars were creeping about it, with visible motions!

Then the sun came into view, plunging across the sky like a flaming comet. It swung supernally across my field of vision, vanished. Appeared again. And again. Its motion became ever swifter.

What was the meaning of such an apparent revolution of the sun about the sky? It meant, I knew, that earth and moon had swung about the star.

That a year had passed! But were years going by as fast as my chronometer ticked off the seconds?

Another strange thing. I could recognize the constellations of the Zodiac, through which the sun was plunging. And it was going backward! As the earth was spinning backward!

I moved to another window, searched for the moon, my goal. It hung still among spinning stars. But in its light there was a flicker, far more rapid than the flashing of the sun across the wild heavens. I wondered, then knew that I saw the waxing and waning of the moon. Months, passing so swiftly that soon the flicker became a gray blur.

The flashing past of the sun became more frequent. Until it was a strange belt of flame about the strange heavens, in which the stars crept and moved like living things.

A universe gone mad! Suns and planets spinning helpless in the might of a cosmic storm! The machine from which I watched the only sane thing in a runaway cosmos!

Then reason came to my rescue.

Earth, moon, sun, and stars could not all be mad. The trouble was with *myself!* My perceptions had changed. The machine—

Slowly it came to me, until I knew I had grasped the truth.

Time, true time, is measured by the movements of the heavenly bodies. Our day is the time of earth's rotation on its axis. Our year the period of its revolution about the sun.

Those intervals had become crowded so thick in my perception that they were indistinguishable. Then countless years were spinning past, while I hung still in space!

Incredible! But the conclusion was inevitable.

And the apparent motion of earth and sun had been backward.

That meant—and the thought was staggering—that the ages were reeling backward. That I was plunging at an incalculable rate into the past.

Vaguely I recalled magazine articles that I had read, upon the nature of space and time. A lecture. The subject had fascinated me, though I had only a layman's knowledge of it.

The lecturer had defined our universe in terms of space-time. A four-dimensional "continuum." Time was a fourth dimension, he had said. An extension as real as the three of what we call space, and not completely distinguishable from them. A direction in which motion would carry one into the past, or into the future.

All memory, he had said, is a groping back along this dimension, at right angles to each of the three of space. Dreams, vivid memories, he insisted, carry one's consciousness in reality back along this dimension, until the body, swept relentlessly along the stream of time, drags it forward again.

Then I recalled what my uncle had told me of the refusal of his engineers to try the machine. Recalled Gorton's warning. Muller, they both had told me, had declared that the machine would move along a fourth dimension, out of our world. He had made models of the machine, and they had vanished when the power was turned on.

Now I knew that Muller was right. His models had vanished because they had been carried into the past. Had not continued to exist in the present time.

And now I was moving along that fourth dimension. The dimension of time. And very swiftly, for the years went past too fast for counting.

The reversal of gravitation, it came to me, must be some effect of this change of direction in time. But I am not a scientist; I can explain the "Conway Effect" no better than my uncle, for all the wonders that it has brought into my life.

At first it was horribly strange and terrifying.

After I had thought out my explanation of the mad antics of the earth and sun and moon, and of the hurrying stars, I was, however, no longer frightened. I gazed out through my small round ports at the melting firmament with some degree of equanimity.

I continued to watch the charts my uncle had prepared, and to make adjustments of the rheostat when they were indicated by the chronometer.

And presently, feeling hungry, I toasted biscuits on the electric stove, cut off a generous slice of a cheese that I found in the supplies, opened a vacuum bottle of steaming chocolate, and made a hearty and very satisfactory meal.

When I had finished, the aspect of the space about me was unchanged. Crawling stars, already forming themselves into constellations the most of which were unfamiliar. The sun a broad belt of burning gold, counting off the years too swiftly for the eye to follow. A living flame that girdled the firmament. The earth was a huge gray sphere, spinning so swiftly behind me that no detail was visible.

And even the moon, hanging in space ahead, was turning slowly. No longer was the same familiar face toward me, and toward the earth. Already I had reached a point in past time at which the moon was turning on its axis more rapidly than it revolved about the earth. The tidal drag had not yet completely stopped the moon's apparent rotation.

And if already the moon was turning, what would it be when I reached it? Hurtling into the past as I was, would I see oceans cover its dry sea-floors? Would I see an atmosphere soften the harsh outlines of its rugged mountains? Would I see life, vegetation, spread over its plains? Was I to witness the rejuvenation of an aged world?

It seemed fantastic. But it was taking place. The speed of rotation slowly increased as I watched.

The hours slipped past.

I became heavy with sleep. The two days before the departure had not been easy. I had worked day and night to familiarize myself with the machine's operation. The nervous strain had been exhausting. The amazing incidents of the voyage had kept me tense, sapped my strength.

The chart told me that no change was to be made in the controls for many hours. I inspected the gauges which showed the condition of the atmosphere in the chamber. Oxygen content, humidity, temperature, were correct. The air smelled sweet and clean. I completed the rounds, found everything in order.

I adjusted the big chair to a reclining position, and threw myself upon it. For hours I slept, waking at intervals to make a tour of inspection.

Sometimes, in the following days, I wondered if I should be able to go back. Muller's models had carried no operator, of course to start them on the flight back through time to the starting point. Would I be able to reverse the time-flight? If I followed the directions on the operating chart, on the flight back, would I be flung forward through the ages, back to my own era?

I wondered. But the speculation brought forth no conclusion. A strange, unique experience was mine. Glorious adventure. Death was not too high a price to pay.

It did not even occur to me to attempt to turn back earthward, when I found that I was slipping through time. And I did not have sufficient control of the machine to have done so, had I wished. Dependent upon the chart for navigating instructions, I could not have plotted a return path from the midway point. And I knew no way to stop my flight, except by using the repulsion of the moon's reversed gravitation.

My flight lasted six days, by the chronometer.

Long before the end, the moon was spinning very swiftly. And the edges of its outline had become hazy, so that I knew it had an atmosphere.

I followed the charted directions, until I was in the upper layers of that atmosphere. The moon's surface was sliding very rapidly beneath me, and the atmosphere with it, due to the swift rotation of the satellite. Consequently, fierce winds screamed about the machine.

I hung in the atmosphere, merely using enough power to balance the moon's comparatively feeble gravitational pull, until the pressure of that rushing wind swept me with it. The mistily indistinct surface slowed, became motionless beneath me.

With power decreased still further, I settled slowly, watching alertly through the ports.

A towering, crimson mountain loomed above the mists below. I dropped toward it, increasing the power a little. At last I hovered motionless above a narrow, irregular plateau, near the peak, that seemed covered with soft scarlet moss.

Slowly I cut down the power. With hardly a shock, the machine settled in the moss.

I was on the moon! The first of my race to set foot upon an alien planet! What adventures might await me?

CHAPTER III

When the Moon Was Young

With the power cut off entirely, I ran to the ports. There had been no time to scan my surroundings during the uncertainties of the landing. Now I peered out eagerly.

The moonscape was as strange a sight as man had ever seen.

The machine had come down in thick green moss, that looked soft as a Persian rug. A foot deep it was. Dark green fibers closely intertwined. In an unbroken carpet it covered the sloping plateau upon which I had landed, and extended almost to the top of the rugged peak to northward.

To the south and west lay a great valley, almost level, miles across. Beyond it rose a dim range of green hills, rugged summits bare and black. A broad river, glinting white in the distance, flowed down the valley, from northwest, into the south. Then there must be an ocean in that direction.

Strange jungle covered that valley, below the green moss of the mountains. Masses of green. Walls of yellow lining the wide smooth river. Dense forests of gigantic plants, weirdly and grotesquely strange. They grew more luxuriant, taller, than similar plants could upon the earth, because a much feebler gravitation opposed their growth.

Equally strange was the sky.

Darker than on earth, perhaps because the atmosphere was thinner. A deep, pure, living blue. A blue that was almost violet. No cloud marred its liquid azure splendor.

The sun hung in the glorious eastward sky. Larger than I had known it. Whiter. A supernal sphere of pure white flame.

Low in the west was an amazing disk. A huge ball of white, a globe of milky light. Many times the diameter of the sun. I wondered at it. And realized that it was—the earth! The earth young as Venus had been in my time. And like Venus, shrouded in white clouds never broken. Were the rocks still glowing beneath those clouds. I wondered? Or had the life begun—the life of my farthest progenitors?

Would I ever see my native land again, upon that resplendent, cloud-hidden planet? Would the machine carry me back into the future, when I attempted return? Or would it hurl me farther into the past, to plunge flaming into the new-born and incandescent world?

That question I put resolutely from my mind. A new world was before me. A globe strange and unexplored. Why worry about return to the old?

My eyes went back to the broad valley below me, along the banks of the broad river, beneath the majestic range of green mountains. Clumps of gold, resembling distant groves of yellow trees. Patches of green that looked like meadows of grass. Queer, puzzling uprights of black.

I saw things moving. Little bright objects, that rose and fell slightly as they flew. Birds? Gigantic insects? Or creatures stranger than either?

Then I saw the balloons. Captive balloons, floating above the jungles of the valley. At first I saw only two, hanging side by side, swaying a little. Then three more, beyond. Then I distinguished dozens, scores of them, scattered all over the valley.

I strained my eyes at them. Were there intelligent beings here, who had invented the balloons? But what would be the object of hanging them about above the jungles, by the hundred?

I remembered the powerful prism binoculars hanging on the wall beside me. I seized them, focused them hurriedly. The weird jungle leaped toward me in the lenses.

The things were doubtless balloons. Huge spheres of purple, very bright in the sunlight. Anchored with long red cables. Some of them, I estimated, were thirty feet in diameter. Some, much smaller. I could make out no baskets. But there seemed to be small dark masses upon their lower sides, to which the red ropes were attached.

I left them and surveyed the jungle again.

A mass of the yellow vegetation filled the lenses. A dense tangle of slender yellow stems, armed with terrible rows of long, bayonet-like thorns. A thick tangle of sharp yellow thorns, it seemed, with no more stalk than was necessary to support them against the moon's feeble pull. A wall of cruel spikes, impenetrable.

I found a patch of green. A mass of soft, feathery foliage. A sort of creeper, it seemed, covering rocks, and other vegetation—though it did not mingle with the yellow scrub. Enormous, brilliantly white, bell-shaped blooms were open upon it here and there.

A flying thing darted across my vision. It looked like a gigantic moth, frail wings dusted with silver.

Then I made out a little cluster of curious plants. Black, smooth, upright stalks, devoid of leaf or branch. The tallest looked a foot in diameter, a score in height. It was crowned with a gorgeous red bloom. I noticed that no other vegetation grew near any of them. About each was a little cleared circle. Had they been cultivated?

Hours went by as I stared out through the ports, at this fascinating and bewildering moonscape.

Finally I recalled the pictures that my uncle had requested me to make. For two or three hours I was busy with the cameras. I made exposures in all directions, with ordinary and telescopic lenses. I photographed the scene with color filters. And finally I made motion pictures, swinging the camera to take a panoramic view.

It was almost sunset when I had done. It seemed strange that the day was passing so swiftly, until I looked at the chronometer, found that it was not keeping pace with the sun, and decided that the period of rotation must be rather less than twenty-four hours. I later found it to be about eighteen hours, divided into days and nights of very nearly equal length.

Darkness came very swiftly after sunset, due to the comparatively small size and quick rotation of the moon. The stars burst out splendidly through the clean air, burning in constellations utterly strange.

A heavy dew was soon obscuring the ports. As I later discovered, clouds almost never formed in this light atmosphere. Nearly the entire precipitation was in the form of dew, which, however, was amazingly abundant. The tiny droplets on the glass were soon running in streams.

After a few hours, a huge and glorious snow-white sphere rose in the east. The earth. Wondrous in size and brilliance. The weird jungle was visible in its silvery radiance almost as in daylight.

Suddenly I realized that I was tired, and very sleepy. The anxiety and prolonged nervous strain of the landing had been exhausting. I threw myself down upon the reclining chair, and fell into immediate oblivion.

The white sun was high when I woke. I found myself refreshed. Keenly hungry. And conscious of a great need for physical exercise. Accustomed to an active life, I had been shut up in that little round room for seven days. I felt that I must move, breathe fresh air.

Could I leave the machine?

My uncle had told me that it would be impossible, because of lack of atmosphere. But there was plainly air about me, on this young moon. Would it be breathable?

I pondered the question. The moon, I knew, was formed of materials thrown off the cooling earth. Then should its atmosphere not contain the same elements as that of earth?

I decided to try it. Open the door slightly, and sniff experimentally. Close it immediately if there seemed anything wrong.

I loosened the screws that held the heavy door, tried to pull it open. It seemed fastened immovably. In vain I tugged at it, looked to see if I had left a screw, or if something was amiss with the hinges. It refused to budge.

For minutes I was baffled. The explanation came to me suddenly. The pressure of the atmosphere outside was much less than that within the machine. Since the door opened inward, it was the unbalanced pressure upon it that held it.

I found the valve which was to be opened to free the chamber of any dangerous excess of oxygen that might escape, and spun it open. The air hissed out noisily.

I sat down in the chair to wait. At first I felt no symptoms of the lessening pressure. Then I was conscious of a sensation of lightness, of exhilaration. I noticed that I was breathing faster. My temples throbbed. For a few minutes I felt a dull ache in my lungs.

But the sensations did not become unduly alarming, and I left the valve open. The hissing sound gradually decreased, and finally died away completely.

I rose and went to the door, feeling a painful shortness of the breath as I moved. The heavy door came open quite easily now. I sniffed the air outside. It bore a strange, heavy, unfamiliar fragrance which must have been carried from the jungle in the valley. And I found it oddly stimulating—it must have been richer in oxygen than the air in the machine.

With the door flung wide, I breathed deeply of it.

At first I had thought merely of strolling up and down for a while, in the moss outside the machine. But now I decided, quite suddenly, to hike to the lower edge of the green-carpeted plateau, perhaps a mile away, and look at the edge of the jungle.

I looked about for equipment that I should take, got together a few items. A light camera, in case I should see something worth taking. The binoculars. A vacuum bottle full of water, and a little food, so that I should not have to hasten back to eat.

And finally I took down the automatic pistol on the wall, a .45 Colt. It must have been included with the machine's equipment merely as a way of merciful escape, in case some failure made life in the little round compartment unendurable. There was only one box of ammunition. Fifty cartridges. I loaded the weapon, and slipped the remainder into my pocket.

Gathering up the other articles, I scrambled through the oval door, and stood upon the rim of the lower copper disk, drawing the door to behind me, and fastening it.

And stepped off, upon the moon.

The thick, fibrous moss yielded under my foot, surprisingly. I stumbled, fell into its soft green pile. And in scrambling to my feet, I forgot the lesser gravity of the moon, threw myself into the air, tumbling once more into the yielding moss.

In a few minutes I had mastered the art of walking under the new conditions, so that I could stride along with some confidence, going clear of the ground at every step, as if I had worn seven league boots. Once I essayed a leap. It carried me twenty feet into the air, and twice as far forward. It seemed that I hung in the air an unconscionable time, and floated down very slowly. But I was helpless, aloft, sprawling about, unable to get my feet beneath me. I came down on my shoulder, and must have been painfully bruised had it not been for the thick moss.

I realized that my strength upon the moon was quite out of proportion to my weight. I had muscles developed to handle a mass of 180 pounds. Here my weight was only 30 pounds. It would be some time, I supposed, before I could learn the exact force required to produce the result desired. Actually, I found myself adapted to these new conditions in a surprisingly short space of time.

For a time I was conscious of shortness of the breath, especially after violent exertion. But soon I was accustomed to the lighter air as well as the lesser gravitation.

In half an hour I had arrived at the edge of the red plateau. A steep slope fell before me to the edge of the jungle, perhaps two-thirds of a mile farther below. A slope carpeted with the thick fiber of the green moss.

A weird scene. Clear cerulean sky, darkly, richly blue. Huge white globe of the hot earth setting beyond the farther range of green mountains. The wide valley, with the broad silvery stream, winding among golden forests, and patches of green. The purple balloons floating here and yon, huge spheres swaying on the red cables that anchored them above the jungle.

I seated myself on the moss, where I could overlook that valley of eldritch wonder. I remained there for some time, staring out across it, while I ate most of the food that I had brought, and half-emptied the bottle of water.

Then I decided to descend to the edge of the jungle.

The sun was just at the meridian—the whole of the short afternoon, four hours and a half, was yet before me. I had ample time, I thought, to go down the slope to the edge of the jungle and return before the sudden nightfall.

I had no fear of getting lost. The glittering armor of the machine was visible over the whole plateau. And the jagged, triple peak to the northward of it was a landmark which should be visible over the whole region. There should be no difficulty about return.

Nor, while I realized that the jungle might hide hostile life, did I fear attack. I intended to be cautious, and not to penetrate beyond the edge of the jungle. I had the automatic, which, I was sure, gave me greater power of destruction than any other animal on the planet. Finally in case of difficulty, I could rely upon the superior strength of my muscles, which must be far stronger, in proportion to my weight, than those of native creatures.

I found progress easy on the long, mossy incline. My skill at traveling under lunar conditions of gravity was increasing with practice: I found a way of moving by deliberate, measured leaps, each carrying me twenty feet or more.

In a few minutes I found myself approaching the edge of the jungle. But that was not so sharp a line as it had appeared from above. The first vegetation other than the moss was scattered clumps of a plant resembling the cactus of my native Southwest.

Thick, fleshy disks growing one upon another, edge to edge. They were not green, however, but of a curious pink, flesh-like color. They bore no thorns, but were studded with little black protuberances or knobs, of doubtful function. The plants I first approached were small and appeared stunted. The lower clumps seemed larger, and more thickly spaced.

I paused to examine one. Walked around it curiously. Photographed it from several angles. Then I ventured to touch it with my foot. Several of the little black knobs broke—they proved to be thin-walled vesicles, containing a black liquid. An overpowering and extremely unpleasant odor assailed me, and I retreated hastily.

A hundred yards farther on, I came upon the green creepers. Thick stems coiled like endless serpents over the ground, with innumerable fronds rising from them, terminating in feathery sprays of green. Here and there were huge white blooms, nearly six feet across, resembling great bells of burnished silver. From them, evidently, came the heavy perfume that I had noticed upon opening the door of the machine.

The creepers formed an unbroken mass of green, several feet deep. It would have been impossible to penetrate it without crushing the delicate foliage. I decided to go no farther in that direction. The creeper might have such means of protection as the malodorous sacs of the fleshy plants above. Or dangerous creatures, counterparts of terrene snakes, might lie concealed beneath the dense foliage.

For some distance I followed along the edge of the mass of creepers, pausing at intervals to make photographs. I was approaching a thicket or forest of the yellow scrub. A wall of inch-thick stems, each armed at intervals of a few inches with dagger-like thorns, all interwoven. A hundred feet high, I estimated. Interlaced so closely that a rat would have had difficulty in moving through it, without impaling himself upon a needle-sharp spike.

Then I paused to watch one of the purple balloons, which seemed swaying toward me, increasing the length of the red anchor-cable which held it to the jungle behind. A strange thing, that huge purple sphere, tugging at the thin scarlet cable that held it. Tugging almost like a thing alive, I thought.

Several times I photographed it, but its distance was so great that I feared none of the images would be satisfactory. It seemed to be moving toward me, perhaps carried by some breeze that did not reach the ground. Perhaps, I thought, it would soon be near enough for a good picture.

CHAPTER IV

The Balloon Menace

I studied it closely, trying to see if it had an intelligent pilot or occupant. But I was unable to settle the point. There was certainly no basket. But black arms or levers seemed to project in a cluster, from its lowest part, to manipulate the cables.

Nearly an hour, I waited, watching it. It moved much closer during that time; until, in fact, it was almost directly overhead, and only a few hundred feet high. The red cable slanted from it back into the jungle. It seemed to be loose, dragging.

At last I got a picture that satisfied me. I decided to go on and examine the tangle of yellow thorn-brush or scrub at closer range.

I had taken my eyes from the purple balloon, and turned to walk away, when it struck.

A red rope whipped about me.

The first I knew, it was already about my shoulders. Its end seemed to be weighted, for it whirled about my body several times, wrapping me in sticky coils.

The cable was about half an inch in diameter and made of many smaller crimson strands, fastened together with the adhesive stuff that covered it. I recall its appearance very vividly, even the odd, pungent, disagreeable odor of it.

Half a dozen coils of the red cable had whipped about me before I realized that anything was amiss. Then it tightened suddenly, dragging me across the red moss upon which I had been standing. Toward the edge of the jungle.

Looking up in horror, I saw that the rope had been thrown from the purple balloon I had been watching. Now the black arms that I had seen were working swiftly, coiling it up again—with me caught neatly on the end.

The great sphere was drawn down a little, as my weight came upon it. It seemed to swell. Then, having been dragged along until I was directly beneath it, I was lifted clear of the ground.

I was filled with unutterable terror. I was panting, my heart was beating swiftly. And I felt endowed with terrific strength. Furiously I writhed in my gluey bonds, struggled with the strength of desperation to break the red strands.

But the web had been spun to hold just such frightened, struggling animals as myself. It did not break.

Back and forth I swung over the jungle, like a pendulum. With a constantly quickening arc! For the cable was being drawn up. Once more I looked upward, and saw a sight to freeze me in dreadful stupefaction of horror.

The whole balloon was a living thing!

I saw its two black and terrible eyes, aflame with hot evil, staring at me from many bright facets. The black limbs I had seen were its legs, growing in a cluster at the bottom of its body—now furiously busy coiling up the cable that it had spun, spider-like, to catch me. I saw long jaws waiting, black and hideously fanged, drooling foul saliva. And a rapier-thin pointed snout, that must be meant for piercing, sucking body juices.

The huge purple sphere was a thin-walled, muscular sac, which must have been filled with some light gas, probably hydrogen, generated in the body of the creature. The amazing being floated above the jungle, out of harm's way, riding free on the wind, or anchored with its red web, lassoing its prey and hauling it up to feast hideously in the air.

For a moment I was petrified, dazed and helpless with the new horror of that thin snout, with black-fanged jaws behind it.

Then fear bred superhuman strength in me. I got my arms free, dragging them from beneath the sticky coils. I reached above my head, seized the red cable in both hands, tried to break it between them.

It refused to part, despite my fiercest efforts.

Only then did I recall the pistol in my pocket. If I could reach it in time, I might be able to kill the monster. And the gas should escape through the riddled sac, letting me back to the surface. I was already so high that the fall would have been dangerous, had I succeeded in my desperate effort to break the web.

The viscid stuff on the cable clung to my hands. It took all my strength to tear them loose. But at last they were free, and I fumbled desperately for the gun.

A red strand was across the pocket in which I had the weapon. I tore at it. It required every ounce of my strength to slip it upward. And it adhered to my fingers again. I wrenched them loose, snatched out the automatic. It touched the gluey rope, stuck fast. I dragged it free, moved the safety catch with sticky fingers, raised it above my head.

Though it had been seconds only since I was snatched up, already I had been lifted midway to the dreadful living balloon. I glanced downward. The distance was appalling. I noticed that the balloon was still drifting, so that I hung over a thicket of the yellow scrub.

Then I began shooting at the monster. It was difficult to aim, because of the regular jerks as the ugly black limbs hauled on the cable. I held the gun with both hands and fired deliberately, very carefully.

The first shot seemed to have no effect.

At the second, I heard a shrill, deafening scream. And I saw that one of the black limbs was hanging limp.

I shot at the black, many-faceted eyes. Though I had no knowledge of the creature's anatomy, I supposed that its highest nervous centers should be near them.

The third shot hit one of them. A great blob of transparent jelly burst through the faceted surface, hung pendulous. The thing screamed horribly again. The black arms worked furiously, hauling me up.

I felt a violent upward jerk, stronger than the regular pulls that had been raising me. In a moment I saw the reason. The creature had released the long anchor cable, which had held it to the jungle. We were plunging upward. The moon was spinning away below.

The next shot seemed to take no effect. But at the fifth, the black limbs twitched convulsively. I am sure that the creature died almost at once. The limbs ceased to haul upon the cable, hung still. But I fired the two cartridges remaining in the gun.

That was the beginning of a mad aerial voyage.

The balloon shot upward, when the anchor cable was dropped. And after it was dead, the muscular sac seemed to relax, expand, so that it rose still faster.

Within a few minutes I must have been two miles above the surface. A vast area was visible beneath me; the convexity of the moon's surface, which, of course, is much greater than that of the earth's, was quite apparent.

The great valley lay below, between the green mountain ranges. Splotched with blue and yellow. The white river twisting along it, wide and silvery. I could see into other misty valleys beyond the green ranges, and on the curving horizon were more hills, dim and black in the distance.

The plateau upon which I had landed was like a green-covered table, many thousands of feet below. I could distinguish upon it a tiny bright disk, which I knew was the machine that I had left so unwisely.

Though there had been little wind at the surface, it seemed that I rose into a stratum of air, which was moving quite rapidly into the northwest. I was carried swiftly along; the floor of the great valley glided back beneath me. In a few minutes the machine was lost to view.

I was, of course, rendered desperate at being swept away from the machine. I kept myself oriented, and tried to watch the landmarks that passed beneath me. It was fortunate, I thought, that the wind was driving me up the valley, instead of across the red ranges. I might be able to return to the machine by following down the great river, until the triple peak, near which I had left the machine, came into view. Despair came over me, however, at the realization that I was not likely to be able to traverse so vast a stretch of the unknown jungles of this world, without my ignorance of its perils leading me into some fatal blunder.

I thought of climbing the web to that monstrous body, and trying to make a great rent in the purple sac, so that I should fall more swiftly. But I could only have succeeded in entangling myself more thoroughly in the adhesive coils. And I dismissed the scheme when I realized that if I fell too rapidly, I might be killed upon striking the surface.

After the first few minutes of the flight, I could see that the balloon was sinking slowly, as the gas escaped through the bullet-holes in the muscular sac. I could only wait, and fix in my mind the route that I must follow back to the machine.

The wind bore me so swiftly along that within an hour the triple peak that I watched had dropped below the curved horizon. But still I was above the great valley, so that I should be able to find my way back by following the river. I wondered if I could build a raft, and float down it, with the current.

The balloon was carried along less rapidly as it approached the surface. But, as I neared the jungle, it was evident that it still drifted at considerable speed.

Hanging helpless in the end of the red web, I anxiously scanned the jungle into which I was descending. Like that which I had first seen, it was of dense tangles of the thorny yellow scrub, broken with areas covered largely with the luxuriant green creeper.

Never would I be able to extricate myself alive, I knew, if I had the misfortune to fall in the thorn-brush. And another danger occurred to me. Even if I first touched ground in an open space, the balloon, if the wind continued to blow, would drag me into the spiky scrub before I could tear myself free of the web.

Could I cut myself free, within a safe distance of the ground, and let the balloon go on without me? It seemed that only thus could I escape being dragged to death. I knew that I could survive a fall from a considerable height, since the moon's acceleration of gravity is only about two feet per second,—if only I could land on open ground.

But how could I cut the web? I was without a knife. I thought madly of attempting to bite it in two, realized that that would be as hopeless as attempting to bite through a manila rope.

But I still had the pistol. If I should place the muzzle against the cable and fire, the bullet should cut it.

I reached into my pocket again, past the adhesive coil, and found two cartridges. Though they clung to my sticky fingers, I got them at last into the magazine, and worked the action to throw one into the chamber.

By the time I had finished loading, I was low over an apparently endless jungle of the yellow thorns. Swaying on the end of the web, I was swept along over the spiky scrub, dropping swiftly. At last I could see the edge, and a green patch of the great creepers. For a time I hoped that I would be carried clear of the thorns.

Then they seemed suddenly to leap at me. I threw up my arms, to shelter my face, still clinging fiercely to the pistol.

In an instant, I was being dragged through the cruel yellow spikes. There was a sharp, dry, crackling sound, as they broke beneath my weight. A thousand sharp, poisoned bayonets scratched at me, stabbed, cut.

Intolerable agony racked me. I screamed. The razor-sharp spikes were tipped with poison, so that the slightest scratch burned like liquid flame. And many of the stabbing points went deep.

It seems that I struck near the edge of the thicket. For a moment I hung there in the thorns. Then, as a harder puff of wind struck it, the balloon leaped into the air, dragging me free. I swung up like a pendulum. And down again, beyond the thorny scrub—over a strip of bare sand beside the thicket.

Bleeding rapidly from my cuts, and suffering unendurable pain from the poison in my wounds, I realized that I could not long remain conscious.

Moving in a haze of agony, I seized the red cable with one hand, put the muzzle of the automatic against it, pulled the trigger. The report was crashing, stunning. My right hand, holding the gun, was flung back by the recoil—I should have lost the weapon had it not been glued to my fingers. The cable was jerked with terrific force, almost breaking my left hand, with which I held it.

And it parted! I plunged downward, sprawled on the sand.

For a few minutes I remained conscious as I lay there on the hard, cold sand—the first soil, I recall thinking vaguely in my agony, that I had seen not covered with vegetation.

The clothing had been half stripped from my tortured body by the thorns. I was bleeding freely from several deeper cuts—I remember how dark the blood was, sinking into the white sand.

All my body throbbed with insufferable pain, from the poison in my wounds. As if I had been plunged into a sea of flame. Only my face had been spared.

Weakly, dizzy with pain, I tried to stagger to my feet. But a coil of the red web still clung about my legs. It tripped me, and I fell forward again, upon the white sand.

Fell into bitter despair. Into blind, hopeless rage at my inane lack of caution in leaving the machine. At my foolhardiness in venturing into the edge of the jungle. Fell into gentle oblivion. . . .

A curious sound drew me back into wakefulness. A thin, high-pitched piping, pleasantly melodious. The musical notes beat insistently upon my brain, evidently originating quite near me.

On first awakening, I was aware of no bodily sensation. My mind was peculiarly dull and slow. I was unable to recall where I was. My first impression was that I was lying in bed in my old rooming place at Midland and that my alarm clock was ringing. But soon I realized that the liquid piping notes that had disturbed me came from no alarm.

I forced open heavy eyes. What startling nightmare was this? A tangle of green creepers, incredibly profuse. A wall of yellow thorns. A scarlet mountain beyond. And purple balloons floating in a rich blue sky.

I tried to sit up. My body burst into screaming agony when I moved. And I sank back. My skin was stiff with dry blood. The deeper wounds were aching. And the poison from the thorns seemed to have stiffened my muscles, so that the slightest motion brought exquisite pain.

The melodious pipings had been abruptly silenced at my movement. But now they rose again. Behind me. I tried to turn my head.

Recollection was returning swiftly. My uncle's telegram. The flight through space and time. My expedition to the jungle's edge, and its horrible sequel. I still lay where I had fallen, on the bare sand below the spiky scrub.

I groaned despite myself, with the pain of my stiff body. The thin musical notes stopped again. And the thing that had voiced them glided around before me, so that I could see it.

A strange and marvelous being.

Its body was slender, flexible as an eel. Perhaps five feet long, it was little thicker than my upper arm. Soft, short golden down or fur covered it. Part of it was coiled on the sand; its head was lifted two or three feet.

A small head, not much larger than my fist. A tiny mouth, with curved lips full and red as a woman's. And large eyes, dark and intelligent. They were deeply violet, almost luminous. Somehow they looked human, perhaps only because they mirrored the human qualities of curiosity and pity.

Aside from red mouth and dark eyes, the head had no human features. Golden down covered it. On the crown was a plume or crest of brilliant blue. But strange as it was, it possessed a certain beauty. A beauty of exquisite proportion, of smooth curves.

Curious wing-like appendages or mantles grew from the sides of the sleek, golden body, just below the head. Now they were stiffened, extended as if for flight. They were very white, of thin soft membrane. Their snowy surfaces were finely veined with scarlet.

Other than these white, membranous mantles, the creature had no limbs. Slim, long, pliant body, covered with golden fur. Small, delicate head, with red mouth and warm dark eyes, crested with blue. And delicate wings thrust out from its sides.

I stared at it.

Even at first sight, I did not fear it, though I was helpless. It seemed to have a magnetic power that filled me with quiet confidence, assured me that it meant only good.

The lips pursed themselves. And the thin, musical piping sound came from them again. Was the thing speaking to me? I uttered the first phrases that entered my mind, "Hello. Who are we, anyhow?"

CHAPTER V

The Mother

The thing glided toward me swiftly, its smooth round golden body leaving a little twisting track in the white sand. It lowered its head a little. And it laid one of the white mantles across my forehead.

The strange red-veined membrane was soft, yet there was an odd firmness in its pressure against my skin. A vital warmth seemed to come from it—it was vibrant with energy, with life.

The pipings came again. And they seemed to stir vague response in my mind, to call dim thoughts into being. As the same sounds were repeated again and again, definite questions formed in my mind.

"What are you? How did you come here?"

Through some strange telepathy induced by the pressure of the mantle upon my head, I was grasping the thought in the piping words.

It was a little time before I was sufficiently recovered from my astonishment to speak. Then I replied slowly, phrasing my expressions carefully, and uttering them as distinctly as I could.

"I am a native of Earth. Of the great white globe you can see in the sky. I came here in a machine which moves through space and time. I left it, and was caught and jerked up into the air by one of those purple, floating things. I broke the web, and fell here. My body was so torn by the thorns that I cannot move."

The thing piped again. A single quavering note. It was repeated until its meaning formed in my mind.

"I understand."

"Who are you?" I ventured.

I got the meaning of the reply, as it was being piped for the third time.

"I am the Mother. The Eternal Ones, who destroyed my people, pursue me. To escape them, I am going to the sea."

And the thin, musical tones came again. This time I understood them more easily.

"Your body seems slow to heal its hurts. Your mental force is feeble. May I aid you?"

"Of course," I said. "Anything you can do—"

"Lie still. Trust me. Do not resist. You must sleep." When the meaning of the notes came to me, I relaxed upon the sand, closed my eyes.

I could feel the warm, vibrant pressure of the mantle on my forehead. Vital, throbbing force seemed pulsing into me through it. I felt no fear, despite the strangeness of my situation. A living wave of confidence came over me. Serene trust in the power of this being. I felt a command to sleep. I did not resist it; a strong tide of vital energy swept me into oblivion.

It seemed but an instant later, though it must have been many hours, when an insistent voice called me back from sleep.

Vitality filled me. Even before I opened my eyes, I was conscious of a new and abounding physical vigor, of perfect health; I was bubbling with energy and high spirits. And I knew, by the complete absence of bodily pain, that my wounds were completely healed.

I opened my lids, saw the amazing creature that had called itself the Mother. Its smooth golden body coiled beside me on the sand. Its large, clear eyes watching me intently, with kind sympathy.

Abruptly I sat up. My limbs were stiff no longer. My body was still dried with blood, clothed in my tattered garments; the sticky scarlet coils of the web were still around me. But my ragged wounds were closed. Only white scars showed where they had been.

"Why, I'm well!" I told the Mother, thankfully. "How'd you do it?"

The strange being piped melodiously, and I grasped the meaning almost at once. "My vital force is stronger than your own. I merely lent you energy."

I began tearing at the coils of the crimson web about me. Their viscid covering seemed to have dried a little; otherwise I might never have got them off. After a moment the Mother glided forward and helped.

It used the white, membranous appendages like hands. Though they appeared quite frail, they seemed able to grasp the red cable powerfully when they were folded about it.

In a few minutes I was on my feet.

Again the Mother piped at me. I failed to understand, though vague images were summoned to my mind. I knelt down again on the sand, and the being glided toward me, pressed the white, red-veined mantle once more against my forehead. An amazing organ, that mantle, so delicately beautiful. So strong of grasp when used as a hand. And useful, as I was to learn, as an organ of some strange sense.

The meaning of the pipings came to me clearly now, with the warm, vibrant mantle touching my head.

"Adventurer, tell me more of your world, and how you came here. My people are old, and I have vital powers beyond your own. But we have never been able to go beyond the atmosphere of our planet. Even the Eternal Ones, with all their machines, have never been able to bridge the gulf of space. And it has been thought that the primary planet from which you say you came is yet too hot for the development of life."

For many hours we talked, I in my natural voice, the Mother in those weirdly melodious pipings. At first the transference of thought by the telepathy which the wonderful mantle made possible was slow and awkward. I, especially, had trouble in receiving, and had many times to ask the Mother to repeat a complex thought. But facility increased with practice, and I at last was able to understand, quite readily, even when the white membrane did not touch me.

The sun had been low when I woke. It set, and the dew fell upon us. We talked on in the darkness. And the earth rose, illuminating the jungle with argent glory. Still we talked, until it was day again. For a time the air was quite cold. Wet with the abundant dew, I felt chilled, and shivered.

But the Mother touched me again with the white membrane. Quick, throbbing warmth seemed to flow from it into my body, and I felt cold no longer.

I told much of the world that I had left, and of my own insignificant life upon it. Told of the machine. Of the voyage across space, and back through æons of time, to this young moon.

And the Mother told me of her life, and of her lost people.

She had been the leader of a community of beings that had lived on the highlands, near the source of the great river that I had seen. A community in some respects resembling those of ants or bees upon the earth. It had contained thousands of neuter beings, imperfectly developed females, workers. And herself, the only member capable of reproduction. She was now the sole survivor of that community.

It seemed that her race was very old, and had developed a high civilization. The Mother admitted that her people had had no machines or buildings of any kind. She declared that such things were marks of barbarism, and that her own culture was superior to mine.

"Once we had machines," she told me. "My ancient mothers lived in shells of metal and wood, such as you describe. And constructed machines to aid and protect their weak and inefficient bodies.

"But the machines tended to weaken their poor bodies still further. Their limbs atrophied, perished from lack of use. Even their brains were injured, for they lived an easy life, depending upon machines for existence, facing no new problems.

"Some of my people awoke to the danger. They left the cities, and returned to the forest and the sea, to live sternly, to depend upon their own minds and their own bodies, to remain living things, and not grow into cold machines.

"The mothers divided. And my people were those that returned to the forest."

"And what," I asked, "of those that remained in the city, that kept the machines?"

"They became the Eternal Ones—my enemies.

"Generation upon generation their bodies wasted away. Until they were no longer natural animals. They became mere brains, with eyes and feeble tentacles. In place of bodies, they use machines. Living brains, with bodies of metal.

"Too weak, they became, to reproduce their kind. So they sought immortality, with their mechanical science. And still some of them live on, in their ugly city of metal—though for ages no young have been born among them. The Eternal Ones.

"But at last they die, because that is the way of life. Even with all their knowledge they cannot live forever. One by one, they fall. Their strange machines are still, with rotting brains in their cases.

"And the few thousands that live attacked my people. They planned to take the Mothers. To change their offspring with their hideous arts, and make of them new brains for the machines.

"The Mothers were many, when the war began. And my people a thousand times more. Now only I remain. But it was no easy victory for the Eternal Ones. My people fought bravely. Many an ancient brain they killed. But the Eternal Ones had great engines of war, that we could not escape, nor destroy with our vital energy.

"All the Mothers save myself were taken. And all destroyed themselves, rather than have their children made into living machines.

"I alone escaped. Because my people sacrificed their lives for me. In my body are the seeds of a new race. I seek a home for my children. I have left our old land on the shores of the lake, and I am going down to the sea. There we shall be far from the Eternal Land. And perhaps our enemies will never find us.

"But the Eternal Ones know I have escaped. They are hunting me. Hunting me with their strange machines."

When day came, I felt very hungry. What was I to do for food in this weird jungle? Even if I could find fruits or nuts, how could I tell whether they were poisonous? I mentioned my hunger.

"Come," the Mother piped.

She glided away across the white sand, with easy, sinuous grace. Very beautiful, she was. Slim body, smooth, rounded. Compactly trim. The golden down was bright in the sunlight; sapphire rays played over the blue plume upon her head. The wondrous, red-veined mantles at her sides shone brilliantly.

Regarding her strange beauty, I stood still for a moment, and then moved after her slowly, absently.

She turned back suddenly, with something like humor flashing in her great dark violet eyes.

"Is your great body so slow you cannot keep up with me?" she piped, almost derisively. "Shall I carry you?" Her eyes were mocking.

For answer I crouched, leaped into the air. My wild spring carried me a score of feet above her, and beyond. I had the misfortune to come down head first upon the sand, though I received no injury.

I saw laughter in her eyes, as she glided swiftly to me, and grasped my arm with one of the white mantles to assist me to my feet.

"You could travel splendidly if there were two of you, one to help the other out of the thorns," she said quaintly.

A little embarrassed by her mockery, I followed meekly.

We reached a mass of the green creeper. Without hesitation, she pushed on through the feathery foliage. I broke through behind her. She led the way to one of the huge white flowers, bent it toward her, and crept into it like a golden bee.

In a moment she emerged with mantles cupped up to hold a good quantity of white, crystalline powder which she had scraped from the inside of the huge calyx.

She made me hold my hands, and dropped part of the powder into them. She lifted what she had left, upon the other mantle, and began delicately licking at it with her lips.

I tasted it. It was sweet, with a peculiar, though not at all unpleasant, acid flavor. It formed a sort of gum as it was wetted in my mouth, and this softened and dissolved as I continued to chew. I took a larger bite, and soon finished all the Mother had given me. We visited another bloom. This time I reached in, and scraped out the powder with my own hand. (The crystals must have been formed for the same purpose as the nectar in terrene flowers—to attract raiders, which carry the pollen.)

I divided my booty with the Mother. She accepted but little, and I found enough of the sweetish powder in the calyx to satisfy my own hunger.

"Now I must go on down to the sea," she piped. "Too long already have I delayed with you. For I carry the seed of my race; I must not neglect the great work that has fallen upon me.

"But I was glad to know of your strange planet. And it is good to be with an intelligent being again, when I had been so long alone. I wish I could stay longer with you. But my wishes are not my master."

Thoughts of parting from her were oddly disturbing. My feeling for her was partly gratitude for saving my life and partly something else. A sense of comradeship. We were companion adventurers in this weird and lonely jungle. Solitude and my human desire for society of any sort drew me toward her.

Then came an idea. She was going down the valley to the sea. And my way led in the same direction, until I could see the triple peak that marked the location of the machine.

"May I travel with you," I asked her, "until we reach the mountain where I left the machine in which I came to your world?"

The Mother looked at me with fine dark eyes. And glided suddenly nearer. A white membranous mantle folded about my hand, with warm pressure.

"I am glad you wish to go with me," she piped. "But you must think of the danger. Remember that I am hunted by the Eternal Ones. They will doubtless destroy you if they find us together."

"I have a weapon," I said. "I'll put up a scrap for you, if we get in a tight place. And besides, I'd very likely be killed, in one way or another, if I tried to travel alone."

"Let us go, Adventurer."

Thus it was decided.

I had dropped the camera, the binoculars, and the vacuum bottle when the balloon-creature jerked me into the air. They were lost in the jungle. But I still had the automatic. It had remained in my hand—stuck to it, in fact—when I fell upon the sand. I carried it with me.

The Mother objected to the weapon. Because it was a machine, and machines weakened all that used them. But I insisted that we should have to fight machines, if the Eternal Ones caught us, and that fire could be best fought with fire. She yielded gracefully.

"But my vital force will prove stronger than your rude slaying machine, Adventurer," she maintained.

We set out almost immediately. She glided off along the strip of bare sand beside the wall of thorny yellow scrub. And began my instruction in the ways of life upon the moon, by informing me that there was always such a clear zone about a thicket of the thorn-brush, because its roots generated a poison in the soil which prevented the growth of other vegetation near them.

When we had traveled two or three miles, we came to a crystal pool, where the abundant dew had collected at the bottom of a bare, rocky slope. We drank there. Then the Mother plunged into it joyously. With white mantles folded tight against her sides, she flashed through the water like a golden eel. I was glad to remove my own garments, and wash the grime and dried blood from my body.

I was donning my tattered clothing again, and the Mother was lying beside me, at the edge of the pool, with eyes closed, drying her golden fur in the sunshine, when I saw the ghostly bars.

Seven thin upright pillars of light, ringed about us. Straight bars of pale white radiance. They stood like phantom columns about us, enclosing a space ten yards across. They were not above two inches in diameter. And they were quite transparent, so I could see the green jungle and the yellow wall of thorn-brush quite plainly through them.

I was not particularly alarmed. In fact, I thought the ghostly pillars only some trick of my vision. I rubbed my eyes, and said rather carelessly to the Mother:

"Are the spirits building a fence around us? Or is it just my eyes?"

She lifted her golden, blue-crested head quickly. Her violet eyes went wide. I saw alarm in them. Terror. And she moved with astonishing speed. Drew her slender length into a coil. Leaped. And seized my shoulder as she leaped, with one of her mantles.

She jerked me between two of those strange columns of motionless light, out of the area they enclosed.

I fell on the sand, got quickly to my feet.

"What—" I began.

"The Eternal Ones," her sweet, whistling tones came swiftly. "They have found me. Even here, they reach me with their evil power. We must go on, quickly."

She glided swiftly away. Still buttoning my clothing, I followed, keeping pace with her easily, with my regular leaps of half a dozen yards. Followed, wondering vainly what danger there might have been in the pillars of ghostly light.

CHAPTER VI

Pursuit!

We skirted a continuous wall of the spiky yellow scrub.

The strip of clear ground we followed was usually fifty to one hundred yards wide. The mass of yellow thorn-brush, the poison from whose roots had killed the vegetation here, rose dense and impenetrable to our right.

To the left of our open way limitless stretches covered with the green creeper. Undulating seas of feathery emerald foliage. Scattered with huge white blooms. Broken, here and there, with strange plants of various kinds. Beyond were other clumps of the yellow scrub. A red mountain wall rose in the distance. Huge purple balloons swayed here and there upon this weird, sunlit moonscape, anchored with their red cables.

I suppose we followed that open strip for ten miles. I was beginning to breathe heavily, as violent exercise always made me do in the moon's light atmosphere. The Mother showed no fatigue.

Abruptly she paused ahead of me, and glided into a sort of tunnel through the forest of thorns. A passage five feet wide and six feet high, with the yellow spokes arching over it. The floor was worn smooth, hard-packed as if by constant use. It seemed almost perfectly straight, for I could see down it for a considerable distance. Twilight filled it, filtering down through the unbroken mass of cruel bayonets above.

"I am not eager to use this path," the Mother told me. "For they who made it are hostile things. And though not very intelligent, they are able to resist my vital force, so that I cannot control them. We shall be help-less if they discover us.

"But there is no other way. We must cross this forest of thorns. And I am glad to be out of sight in this tunnel. Perhaps the Eternal Ones will lose us again. We must hasten, and hope that we encounter no right-ful user of the path. If one appears, we must hide."

I was placed immediately at a disadvantage upon entering the tunnel, for I could no longer take the long leaps by which I had been traveling. My pace became a sort of trot. I had to hold my head down, to save it from the poisoned thorns above.

The Mother glided easily before me, to my relief not in such haste as before. Slender and strong and trimly beautiful—for all her strangeness. I was glad she had let me come with her. Even if peril threatened.

I found breath for speech.

"Those ghostly bars," I panted. "What were they?"

"The Eternal Ones possess strange powers of science," came the thin, whistling notes of her reply. "Something like the television you told me of. But more highly developed. They were able to see us, back by the pool.

"And the shining bars were projected through space by their rays of force. They meant some harm to us. Just what, I do not know. It is ap-parently a new weapon, which they did not use in the war."

We must have gone many miles through the tunnel. It had been almost perfectly straight. There had been no branches or cross-passages. We had come through no open space. Roof and walls of yellow thorns had been unbroken. I was wondering what sort of creature it might be, that had made a path through the thorns so long and straight.

The Mother stopped suddenly, turned back to face me.

"One of the makers of the trail is approaching," she piped. "I feel it coming. Wait for me a bit."

She sank in golden coils upon the trail. Her head was raised a little. The mantles were extended stiffly. Always before they had been white, except for their fine veining of red. But now soft, rosy colors flushed them. Her full red lips were parted a little, and her eyes had become strange, wide, staring. They seemed to look past me, to gaze upon scenes far-off, invisible to ordinary sight.

For long seconds she remained motionless, violet eyes distant, staring.

Then she stirred abruptly. Rose upon tawny, golden coils. Alarm was in her great eyes, in her thin, melodious tones.

"The creature comes behind us. Upon this trail. We have scant time to reach the open. We must go swiftly."

She waited for me to begin my stumbling run, glided easily beside me. I moved awkwardly. With only the moon's slight gravitational pull to hold me to the trail, I was in constant danger from the thorns.

For tortured hours, it seemed to me, we raced down the straight passage, through the unbroken forest of yellow thorns. My heart was laboring painfully; my breath came in short gasps of agony. My body was not equipped for such prolonged exertions in the light air.

The Mother, just ahead of me, glided along with effortless ease. I knew that she could easily have left me, had she wished.

At last I stumbled, fell headlong, and did not have energy to get at once to my feet. My lungs burned, my heart was a great ache. Sweat was pouring from me; my temples throbbed; and a red mist obscured my sight.

"Go—on," I gasped, between panting breaths. "I'll try—to stop—it."

I fumbled weakly for my gun.

The Mother stopped, came back to me. Her piping notes were quick, insistent. "Come. We are near the open now. And the thing is close. You must come!"

With a soft, flexible mantle she seized my arm. It seemed to me that a wave of new strength and energy came into me from it. At any rate, I staggered to my feet, lurched forward again. As I rose, I cast a glance backward.

A dark, indistinguishable shape was in view. So large that it filled almost the whole width of the tunnel. A dim circle of the pale light of the thorn forest showed around it.

I ran on . . . on . . . on.

My legs rose and fell, rose and fell, like the insensate levers of an automaton. I felt no sensation from them. Even my lungs had ceased to burn, since the Mother touched me. And my heart ached no longer. It seemed that I floated beside my body, and watched it run, run, run with the monotonously repeated movements of a machine.

My eyes were upon the Mother before me.

Gliding so swiftly through the twilight of the tunnel. Trim, round golden body. White mantles extended stiffly, wing-like, as if to help carry her. Delicate head raised, the blue plume upon it flashing.

I watched that blue plume as I ran. It danced mockingly before me, always retreating. Always just beyond my grasp. I followed it through the blinding mists of fatigue, when all the rest of the world melted into a gray blue, streaked with bloody crimson.

I was astonished when we came out into the sunlight. A strip of sand below the yellow wall of thorns. Cool green foliage beyond, a sea of green. Sinister purple balloons above it, straining on crimson cables. Far-off, a scarlet line of mountains, steep and rugged.

The Mother turned to the left.

I followed, automatically, mechanically. I was beyond feeling. I could see the bright moonscape, but it was strange no longer. Even the threat of the purple balloons was remote, without consequence.

I do not know how far we ran, beside the forest of thorns, before the Mother turned again and led the way into a mass of creepers.

"Lie still," she piped. "The creature may not find us."

Gratefully, I flung myself down in the delicate fronds. I lay flat, with my eyes closed, my breath coming in great, painful, sobbing gasps. The Mother folded my hand in her soft mantle again, and immediately, it seemed, I felt relief, though I still breathed heavily.

"Your reserve of vital energy is very low," she commented.

I took the automatic from my pocket, examined it to see that it was ready for action. I had cleaned and loaded it before we started. I saw the Mother raising her blue-crested head cautiously. I got to my knees, peered back along the bare strip of sand, down which we had come.

I saw the thing advancing swiftly along the sand.

A sphere of bright crimson. Nearly five feet in diameter. It rolled along, following the way we had come.

"It has found us!" the Mother piped, very softly. "And my vital power cannot reach through its armor. It will suck the fluids from our bodies."

I looked down at her. She had drawn her slender body into a golden coil. Her head rose in the center, and the mantles were outspread, pure white, veined with fine lines of scarlet, and frail as the petals of a lily. Her great dark eyes were grave and calm; there was no trace of panic in them.

I raised the automatic, determined to show no more fear than she, and to give my best to save her.

Now the scarlet globe was no more than fifty yards away. I could distinguish the individual scales of its armor, looking like plates of horn covered with ruby lacquer. No limbs or external appendages were visible then. But I saw dark ovals upon the shell, appearing at the top and seeming to drop down, as the thing rolled.

I began shooting.

At such a distance there was no possibility of missing. I knelt in the leaves of the green creeper, and emptied the magazine into the globe.

It continued to roll on toward us, without change of speed. But a deep, angry drumming sound came from within it. A reverberating roar of astonishing volume. After a few moments, I heard it repeated from several points about us. Low and distant rumblings, almost like thunder.

In desperate haste, I was filling the clip with fresh cartridges. Before I could snap it back into the gun, the creature was upon us.

Until it stopped, it had presented a sphere of unbroken surface. But suddenly six long, glistening black tentacles reached out of it, one from each of the black ovals I had seen evenly spaced about the red shell. They were a dozen feet long, slender, covered with thin black skin corrugated with innumerable wrinkles, and glistening with tiny drops of moisture. At the base of each was a single, staring, black-lidded eye.

One of those black tentacles was thrust toward me. It reeked with an overpowering, fetid odor. At its extremity was a sharp, hooked claw, beside a black opening. I think the creature sucked its food through those hideous, retractable tentacles.

I got the loaded clip into the gun, hastily snapped a cartridge into the chamber. Shrinking back from the writhing tentacular arm, I fired seven shots, as rapidly as I could press the trigger, into the black-lidded eye.

The deep drumming notes came from within the red shell again. The black tentacles writhed, thrashed about, and became suddenly stiff and rigid. The sound of it died to a curious rattle, and then ceased.

"You have killed it," the Mother whistled musically. "You use your machine well, and it is more powerful than I thought. Perhaps, after all, we may yet live."

As if in ominous answer, a reverberating roll of distant drumming came from the tangle of yellow thorns. She listened, and the white mantles were stiffened in her alarm.

"But it has called to its kind. Soon many will be here. We must hasten away."

Though I was still so tired that movement was torture, I rose and followed the Mother, as she glided on along the sand.

Only a moment did I pause to examine the very interesting creature I had killed. It seemed unique, both in shape and in means of locomotion. It must have developed the spherical shell of red armor through ages of life in the spiky scrub. By drawing its limbs inside, it was able to crash through the thorns without suffering any hurt. I supposed it contrived to roll along by some rhythmic muscular contraction, inside the shell—such movement being much easier on the moon than it would be on earth, because of the lesser gravity. Where it could not roll, it dragged or lifted itself with the long, muscular appendages that I have called tentacles.

Since we were in the open air again, I was able to resume my progression by deliberate, measured leaps, which carried me forward as fast as the Mother could move, and with much less effort than I had spent in running. I had a few moments of rest as I glided through the air between leaps, which compensated for the fiercer effort of each spring.

From time to time I looked back, nervously. At first I could see only the scarlet shell of the dead creature, there by the green vines where we had killed it. Always smaller, until it was hardly visible.

Then I saw other spheres. Emerging from the tangle of yellow thornbrush. Rolling along the strip of bare soil, to congregate about the dead being. Finally I saw that they had started in our direction, rolling along rather faster than we could move.

"They are coming," I told the Mother. "And more of them than I can kill."

"They are implacable," came her piping reply. "When one of them sets out upon the trail of some luckless creature, it never stops until it has sucked the body fluids from it—or until it is dead."

"Anything we can do?" I questioned.

"There is a rock ahead of us, beyond that thicket. A small hill, whose sides are so steep they will not be able to climb it. If we can reach it in time, we may be able to scramble to the top.

"It will be only temporary escape, since the creatures will never leave so long as we are alive upon it. But we shall delay our fate, at least—if we can reach it in time."

Again I looked back. Our pursuers were rolling along like a group of red marbles, at the edge of the yellow forest. Gaining upon us—swiftly.

The Mother glided along more rapidly. The white mantles were stiffly extended from her golden sides, and aglow with rosy colors. The muscles beneath her furry skin rippled evenly, gracefully.

I increased the force of my own leaps.

We rounded an arm of the tangle of scrub, came in sight of the rock. A jutting mass of black granite. Its sides leaped up steep and bare from a mass of green creepers. Green moss crowned it. Thirty feet high it was. Perhaps a hundred in length.

Our pursuers were no longer merely marbles when we saw the rock. They had grown to the size of baseballs. Rolling swiftly after us.

The Mother glided on, a tireless strength in her graceful tawny body. And I leaped desperately, straining to drive myself as fast as possible.

We turned. Broke through the thick masses of verdure to the rock. Stood beneath its sheer wall, grim and black.

The red spheres were no more than a hundred yards behind. A sudden rumble of drums came from them, when we halted by the rock. I could see the dark ovals on their glistening red armor, that marked their eyes and the ends of their concealed tentacles.

"I can never climb that," the Mother was piping.

"I can leap up!" I cried. "Earth muscles. I'll carry you up."

"Better that one should live than both of us die," she said. "I can delay them, until you reach the top."

She started gliding back, toward the swiftly rolling spheres.

I bent, snatched her up.

It was the first time that I had felt her body. The golden fur was short, and very soft. The rounded body beneath it was firm, muscular, warm and vibrant. It throbbed with life. I felt that a strange sudden surge of energy was coming into me from contact with it.

I threw her quickly over my shoulder, ran forward a few steps, leaped desperately up at that sheer wall of black granite.

My own weight, on the moon, was only thirty pounds. The Mother, compact and strong though she was, weighed no more than a third as much. Combined, our weight was then some forty pounds. But, as she had realized, it was an apparently hopeless undertaking to attempt to hurl that mass to the top of the cliff before us.

At first I thought I should make it, as we soared swiftly up and up, toward the crown of red moss. Then I realized that we should strike the face of the cliff before we reached the top.

The face of the black rock was sheer. But my searching eyes caught a little projecting ledge. As we fell against the vertical cliff, my fingers caught that ledge. A moment of dreadful uncertainty, for the ledge was mossy, slippery.

CHAPTER VII

The Eternal Ones Follow!

My left hand slipped suddenly off. But the right held. I drew myself upward. The Mother slipped from my shoulder to the top of the rock. Grasped my left hand with one of the white mantles, drew me to safety.

Trembling from the strain of it, I got to my feet upon the soft scarlet moss, and surveyed our fortress. The moss-covered surface was almost level, a score of feet wide at the middle, where we stood, and a hundred in length. On all sides the walls were steep, though not everywhere so steep as where I had leaped up.

"Thank you, Adventurer," the Mother whistled musically. "You have saved my life, and the lives of all my people to come."

"I was merely repaying a debt," I told her.

We watched the red globes. Very soon they reached the foot of the cliff. The rumble of drums floated up from the group of them. And they scattered, surrounding the butte.

Presently we discovered that they were attempting to climb up. They were not strong enough to make the leap as I had done. But they were finding fissures and ledges upon which their long tentacles could find a grasp, drawing themselves up.

We patrolled the sides of the rock regularly, and I shot those which seemed to be making the best progress. I was able to aim carefully at an eye or the base of a tentacle. And usually a single shot was enough to send the climber rolling back down to the green jungle.

The view from our stronghold was magnificent. On one side was an endless wall of yellow scrub, with crimson mountains towering above it in the distance. On the other, the green tangle of the luxuriant creepers swept down to the wide silver river. Yellow and green mottled the slope that stretched up to scarlet hills beyond.

We held out for an entire day.

The sun sank beyond the red mountains when we had been upon the butte only an hour or two. A dark night would have terminated our adventures on the spot. But fortunately the huge white disk of the earth rose almost immediately after sunset, and gave sufficient light throughout the night to enable us to see the spheres that persisted in attempting to climb the walls of our fort.

It was late on the following afternoon that I used my last shot. I turned to the Mother with the news that I could no longer keep the red spheres from the walls, that they would soon be overwhelming us.

"It does not matter," she piped. "The Eternal Ones have found us again."

Looking nervously about, I saw the bars of ghostly light once more. Seven thin upright pillars of silvery radiance, standing in a ring about us. They had exactly the same appearance as those from which we had fled at the pool.

"I have felt them watching for some time," she said. "Before, we escaped by running away. Now that is impossible."

Calmly she coiled her tawny length. The white mantles were folded against her golden fur. Her small head sank upon her coils, blue crest erect above it. Her violet eyes were grave, calm, alert. They reflected neither fear nor despair.

The seven pillars of light about us became continually brighter.

One of the red spheres, with black tentacles extended, dragged itself upon the top of the butte, with us. The Mother saw it, but paid it no heed. It was outside the ring formed by the seven pillars. I stood still, within that ring, beside the Mother, watching—waiting.

The seven columns of light grew brighter.

Then it seemed that they were no longer merely light, but solid metal.

At the same instant, I was blinded with a flash of light, intolerably bright. A splintering crash of sound smote my ears, sharp as the crack of a rifle, infinitely louder. A wave of pain flashed over my body, as if I had received a severe electric shock. I had a sense of abrupt movement, as if the rock beneath my feet had been jarred by a moonquake.

Then we were no longer upon the rock.

I was standing upon a broad, smooth metal plate. About its edge rose seven metal rods, shining with a white light, their positions corresponding exactly to the seven ghostly pillars. The Mother was coiled on the metal plate beside me, her violet eyes still cool and quiet, revealing no surprise.

But I was dazed with astonishment.

For we were no longer in the jungle. The metal plate upon which I stood was part of a complex mechanism, of bars and coils of shining wire, and huge tubes of transparent crystal, which stood in the center of a broad open court, paved with bright, worn metal.

About the court towered buildings. Lofty, rectangular edifices of metal and transparent crystal. They were not beautiful structures. Nor were they in good repair. The metal was covered with ugly red oxide. Many of the crystal panels were shattered.

Along the metal-paved streets, and on the wide courtyard about us, things were moving. Not human beings. Not evidently, living things at all. But grotesque things of metal. Machines. They had no common standard of form; few seemed to resemble any others. They had apparently been designed with a variety of shapes, to fill a variety of purposes. But many had a semblance to living things that was horrible mockery.

"This is the land of the Eternal Ones," the Mother piped to me softly. "These are the beings that destroyed my people, seeking new brains for their worn-out machines."

"But how did we get here?" I demanded.

"Evidently they have developed means of transmitting matter through space. A mere technical question. Resolving matter into energy, transmitting the energy without loss on a light beam, condensing it again into the original atoms.

"It is not remarkable that the Eternal Ones can do such things. When they gave up all that is life, for such power. When they sacrificed their bodies for machines. Should they not have some reward?"

"It seems impossible—"

"It must, to you. The science of your world is young. If you have television after a few hundred years, what will you not have developed after a hundred thousand?

"Even to the Eternal Ones, it is new. It is only in the time of my own life that they have been able to transmit objects between two stations, without destroying their identity. And they have never before used this apparatus, with carrier rays that could reach out to disintegrate our bodies upon the rock, and create a reflecting zone of interference that would focus the beam here—"

Her piping notes broke off sharply. Three grotesque machines were advancing upon us, about the platform. Queer bright cases, with levels and wheels projecting from them. Jointed metal limbs. Upon the top of each was a transparent crystal dome, containing a strange, shapeless gray mass. A soft helpless gray thing, with huge black staring eyes. The brain in the machine! The Eternal One.

Horrible travesties of life, were those metal things. At first they appeared almost alive, with their quick, sure movements. But mechanical sounds came from them, little clatterings and hummings. They were stark and ugly.

And their eyes roughened my skin with dread. Huge, black, and cold. There was nothing warm in them, nothing human, nothing kind. They were as emotionless as polished lenses. And filled with menace.

"They shall not take me alive!" the Mother piped, lifting herself beside me on tawny coils.

Then, as if something had snapped like a taut wire in my mind, I ran at the nearest of the Eternal Ones, my eyes searching swiftly for a weapon.

It was one of the upright metal rods that I seized. Its lower end was set in an oddly shaped mass of white crystal, which I took to be an insulator of some kind. It shattered when I threw my weight on the rod. And the rod came free in my hands, the white glow vanishing from it, so I saw it was copper.

Thus I was provided with a massive metal club, as heavy as I could readily swing. On earth, it would have weighed far more than I could lift.

Raising it over my head, I sprang in front of the foremost of the advancing machines—a case of bright metal, moving stiffly upon metal limbs, with a dome-shaped shell of crystal upon it, which housed the helpless gray brain, with its black, unpleasant eyes. I saw little tentacles—feeble translucent fingers—reaching from the brain to touch controlling levers.

The machine paused before me. An angry, insistent buzzing came from it. A great, hooked, many-jointed metal lever reached out from it suddenly, as if to seize me.

And I struck, bringing the copper bar down upon the transparent dome with all my strength. The crystal was tough. But the inertia of the copper bar was as great as it would have been upon the earth; its hundreds of pounds came down with a force indeed terrific.

The dome was shattered. And the gray brain smashed into red pulp.

The Eternal Ones would certainly have been able to seize the Mother, without suffering any harm. And probably any other creature of the moon, that might have been brought with her on the matter-transmitting beam. But they were not equipped for dealing with a being whose muscles were the stronger ones of earth.

The two fellows of the Eternal One I had destroyed fell upon me. Though the copper bar was not very heavy, it was oddly hard to swing, because of its great inertia. The metal limbs of the third machine closed about my body, even as I crushed the brain in the second with another smashing blow.

I squirmed desperately, but I was unable to twist about to get in a position to strike.

Then the Mother was gliding toward me. Blue crest erect upon her golden head, eager light of battle flashing in her violet eyes. From her smooth, tawny sides the mantles were stiffly outstretched. And they were almost scarlet with the flashing lights that played through them. My momentary despair vanished; I felt that she was invincible.

She almost reached me. And then rose upon her glossy coils, and gazed at the brain in the transparent dome of the machine that held me, her membranes still alight.

Abruptly the machine released me; its metal limbs were relaxed, motionless.

My encrimsoned copper mace rose and descended once more, and the machine fell with a clatter upon its side.

"My mental energy is greater than that of the Eternal One," the Mother piped in calm explanation. "I was able to interfere with its neural processes to cause paralysis." She looked about us suddenly.

"But smash the delicate parts of this machine that brought us here. So that if we have the good fortune to escape, they cannot soon bring us back. I know it is the only one they have, and it does not look as if it could be quickly repaired."

My club was busy again. Delicate coils were battered beneath it. Complex prisms and mirrors and lenses shattered. Delicate wires and grids in crystal shells, which must have been electron tubes, destroyed.

The three machines we had wrecked had been the only ones near. But a score or more of others were soon approaching across the metal-paved court, producing buzzing sounds as if of anger and excitement. Some of them were near before my work was done.

Too many of them to battle. We must attempt an escape.

I stooped, picked up the Mother's warm, downy body, and ran across the platform, toward the ring of approaching machine-beings. Near them, I leaped, as high and as far as I could.

The spring carried me over them, and a good many yards beyond. In a moment I was in the middle of a worn pavement of metal. The street, almost empty of the machines, ran between ancient and ugly buildings, toward a lofty wall of some material black and brilliant as obsidian.

I hastened desperately toward the wall, moving with great leaps. The Eternal Ones followed in humming, clattering confusion, falling swiftly behind.

They had been taken quite by surprise, of course. And, as the Mother had said, dependence upon the machine had not developed in them the ability to respond quickly to emergencies.

As we later discovered, some of the machines could travel much faster than could we. But, as I have remarked, the things were not of a standard design, all differing. And none of those behind us happened to be of the fastest type.

I do not doubt that they could easily have destroyed us, as we fled. But their object would have been defeated. They wanted the Mother alive.

We reached the shining black wall well ahead of our pursuers. Its surface was smooth and perpendicular; it was fully as high as the cliff up which I had leaped with the Mother. And there was no projecting ledge to save us if I fell short.

I paused, dropping the heavy mace.

"You could toss me up," the Mother suggested. "Then leap."

There was no time for delay. She coiled quickly up into a golden sphere. I hurled her upward, like a football. She vanished over the top of the wall. I lifted the mace, threw it up, and to one side, so it would not strike her.

The Eternal Ones were close behind. A mob-like group of grotesque machines. Buzzing angrily. One of them flung some missile. There was a crashing explosion against the black wall, a flare of green light. I realized the danger of being separated from the Mother, even as I leaped.

My spring carried me completely over the wall, which was only some five or six feet thick.

I descended into a luxuriant tangle of the green creepers. Foot-thick stems covered the ground in an unbroken network, feathery leaves rising from them higher than my head. I fell on my side in the delicate foliage, struggled quickly to my feet. The green fronds cut off my view in all directions, though I could see the top of the black wall above.

Before I struck the ground I had glimpsed a vast green plain lying away eastward to the horizon. In the north was a distant line of red mountains. The city of the Eternal Ones lay westward.

I saw nothing of the Mother; I could not, in truth, see a dozen feet through the exotic jungle.

"This way," her cautious whistling tones reached me in a moment. "Here is your weapon."

I broke through the masses of delicate fronds in the direction of the sound, found the Mother unharmed, coiled in a golden circle beside the copper bar. She glided silently away; I picked up the bar and followed as rapidly and quietly as I could.

Once I looked back, when we passed a narrow open space, and saw a little group of the Eternal Ones standing upon the black wall. They must have been looking after us, but I do not suppose they saw us.

For the rest of the day—it was early afternoon when we escaped—and all night when the jungle was weird and silvery in the earth light, and until late on the following day, we hastened on. We did not stop except to drink and bathe at a little stream, and to scrape the sweet white powder from a few of the great argent flowers we passed. We ate as we moved. The jungle of creepers was unbroken; we were always hidden in the luxuriant, delicate foliage.

At first I had been sure we would be followed. But as the hours passed and there was no sign of pursuit, my spirits rose. I doubted now that the Eternal Ones could follow the trail swiftly enough to overtake us. But I still carried the copper mace.

The Mother was less optimistic than I.

"I know they are following," she told me. "I feel them. But we may lose them. If they cannot repair the machine which you wrecked—and I am sure they cannot do it soon."

We had approached a rocky slope, and the Mother found a little cave, beneath an overhanging ledge, in which we rested. Totally exhausted, I threw myself down, and slept like a dead man.

It was early on the next morning when the Mother woke me. She lay coiled at the entrance of the cave, the frail mantles stiffened and flushed a little with rosy light, violet eyes grave and watchful.

"The Eternal Ones follow," she piped. "They are yet far-off. But we must go on."

CHAPTER VIII

An Earth Man Fights

Climbing to the top of the rocky slope, we came out upon a vast plateau, covered with green moss. The level surface was broken here and there by low hills; but no other vegetation was in view before us. At a distance, the plain resembled a weird desert covered with green snow.

It took six days to cross the moss-grown table-land. We finished the white powder we had carried with us on the fourth day; and we found no water on the fifth or sixth. Though, of course, those days were of only eighteen hours each, we were in a sorry plight when we descended into a valley green with the creepers, watered with a crystal stream whose water seemed the sweetest I had ever tasted.

We ate and rested for two nights and a day, before we went on—though the Mother insisted that the Eternal Ones still followed.

Then, for seventeen days, we followed down the stream, which was joined by countless tributaries until it became a majestic river. On the seventeenth day, the river flowed into a still greater one, which came down a valley many miles wide, covered with yellow thorn-brush and green creepers, and infested with thousands of the purple balloon-creatures, which I had learned to avoid by keeping to the green jungle, where they could not throw their webs with accuracy.

We swam the river, and continued down the eastern bank—it was flowing generally south. Five days later we came in view of a triple peak I well remembered.

Next morning we left the jungle, and climbed up to the little moss-carpeted plateau where I had left the machine. I had feared that it somehow would be gone, or wrecked. But it lay just as I had left it on the day after I landed on the moon. Bright, polished, window-studded wall of armor, between two projecting plates of gleaming copper.

We reached the door, the Mother gliding beside me.

Trembling with a great eagerness, I turned the knob and opened it. Everything was in order, just as I had left it. The oxygen cylinders, the batteries, the food refrigerator, the central control table, with the chart lying upon it.

In a week—if the mechanism worked as I hoped it would—I should be back upon the earth. Back on Long Island. Ready to report to my uncle, and collect the first payment of my fifty thousand a year.

Still standing on the narrow deck outside the door, I looked down at the Mother.

She was coiled at my feet. The blue plume upon her golden head seemed to droop. The white mantles were limp, dragging. Her violet eyes, staring up at me, somehow seemed wistful and sad.

Abruptly an ache sprang into my heart, and my eyes dimmed, so that the bright golden image of her swam before me. I had hardly realized what her companionship had come to mean to me, in our long days together. Strange as her body was, the Mother had come to be almost human in my thoughts. Loyal, courageous, kind—a comrade.

"You must go with me," I stammered, in a voice gone oddly husky. "Don't know whether the machine will ever get back to earth or not. But at least it will carry us out of reach of the Eternal Ones."

For the first time, the musical pipings of the Mother seemed broken and uneven, as if with emotion.

"No. We have been together long, Adventurer. And parting is not easy. But I have a great work. The seed of my kind is in me, and it must not die. The Eternal Ones are near. But I will not give up the battle until I am dead."

Abruptly she lifted her tawny length beside me. The limp, pallid mantles were suddenly bright and strong again. They seized my hands in a grasp convulsively tight. The Mother gazed up at my face, for a little time, with deep violet eyes—earnest and lonely and wistful, with the tragedy of her race in them.

Then she dropped, and glided swiftly away.

I looked after her with misty eyes, until she was half across the plateau. On her way to the sea, to find a home for the new race she was to rear. With a leaden heart, and an aching constriction in my throat, I climbed through the oval door, into the machine, and fastened it.

But I did not approach the control table. I stood at the little round windows, watching the Mother gliding away, across the carpet of moss. Going ahead alone . . . the last of her race. . . .

Then I looked in the other direction, and saw the Eternal Ones. She had said the machines were near. I saw five of them. They were moving swiftly across the plateau, the way we had come.

Five grotesque machines. Their bright metal cases were larger than those of the ones we had encountered in the city. And their limbs were longer. They stalked like moving towers of metal, each upon four jointed stilts. And long, flail-like limbs dangled from the case of each. Crystal domes crowned them, sparkling in the sunlight—covering, I knew, the feeble gray brains that controlled them. The Eternal Ones.

Almost at the edge of the plateau they were when I first saw them. I had time easily to finish sealing the door, to close the valve through which I had let out the excess air upon landing, and to drive up through the moon's atmosphere, toward the white planet.

But I did not move to do those things. I stood at the window watching, hands clenched so that nails cut into my palms, set teeth biting through my lip.

Then, as they came on, I moved suddenly, governed not by reason but by an impulse that I could not resist. I opened the door and clambered hastily out, picking up the great copper mace that I had left lying outside.

And I crouched beside the machine, waiting.

Looking across the way the Mother had gone, I saw her at the edge of the plateau. A tiny, distant form, upon the green moss. I think she had already seen the machines, and realizing the futility of flight had turned back to face them.

As the machine-things came by, I was appalled at their size. The metal stilts were fully six feet long, the vulnerable crystal domes eight feet above the ground.

I leaped up, and struck at the brain of the nearest, as it passed. My blow crushed the transparent shell and the soft brain within it. But the machine toppled toward me, and I fell with it to the ground, cruelly bruised beneath its angular levers.

One leg was fast beneath it, pinned against the ground, and its weight was so great that I could not immediately extricate myself. But I had clung to the copper bar, and when another machine bent down, as if to examine the fallen one, I seized the weapon with both hands, and placed another fatal blow.

The second machine fell stiffly beside me, an odd humming sound continuing within it, in such a position that it almost concealed me from the others. I struggled furiously to free my leg, while the other Eternal Ones gathered about, producing curious buzzing sounds.

At last I was free, and on my knees. Always slow in such an unexpected emergency, the machine-beings had taken no action, though they continued the buzzing.

One of them sprang toward me as I moved, striking a flailing blow at me with a metal arm. I leaped up at it, avoiding the sweeping blow, and struck its crystal case with the end of the copper bar.

The bar smashed through the crystal dome, and crushed the frail brain-thing within it. But the machine still moved. It went leaping away across the plateau, its metal limbs still going through the same motions as before I had killed the ruling brain.

I fell back to the ground, rolling over quickly to avoid its stalking limbs, and struggling to my feet, still holding grimly to the copper bar.

The remaining machine-beings rushed upon me, flailing out with metal limbs. Desperately, I leaped into the air, rising ten feet above their glistening cases. I came down upon the case of one, beside the crystal dome that housed its brain. I braced my feet and struck, before it could snatch at me with its hooked levers.

As it fell to the moss, humming, buzzing, and threshing about with bright metal limbs, I leaped from it toward the other, holding the bar before me. But I struck only the metal case, without harming it, and fell from it into the moss.

Before I could stir, the thing drove its metal limb down upon my body. It struck my chest with a force that was agonizing . . . For a moment, I think, I was unconscious. Then I was coughing up bloody foam.

I lay on the red moss, unable to move, the grim realization that I would die breaking over me in a black wave, that swept away even my pain. The metal limb had been lifted from me.

Then the Mother was beside me. She had come back.

Her warm smooth furry body was pressed against my side. I saw her violet eyes, misty, appealing. She laid the rose-flushed mantles over my side. The pain went suddenly from it. And I felt new strength, so I could get to my feet, though red mist still came from my nostrils, and I felt a hot stream of blood down my side.

The remaining machine-monster was bending, reaching for the Mother. I seized the copper mace again, struck a furious blow at the crystal shell that housed its brain. As it crashed down, beating about blindly and madly with its great metal limbs, my new strength went suddenly from me and I fell again, coughing once more.

A flailing limb struck the Mother a terrific blow, flinging her against the moss many yards away. She crept back to me, brokenly, slowly. Her golden fur was stained with crimson. Her mantles were limp and pale. There was agony in her eyes.

She came to where I lay, collapsed against my side. Very low, her musical tones reached my ears and died abruptly with a choking sound. She had tried to tell me something, and could not.

The last of the Eternal Ones that had followed was dead, and presently the machines ceased their humming and buzzing and threshing about upon the moss.

Through the rest of the day we lay there, side by side, both unable to move. And through the strange night, when the huge white disk of the earth bathed us in silver splendor, and in my delirium I dreamed alternately of my life upon it, and of my adventures upon this weird moon-world, with the Mother.

When the argent earth was low, and we were cold and drenched with dew, lying very close together to benefit from each other's warmth, the wild dreams passed. For a few minutes I was coldly sane. I looked back upon a life that had never had any great purpose, that had been lived carelessly, and impulsively. And I was not sorry that I had come to the moon.

I remained with the Mother until she stirred no more, and no effort on my part could rouse her to life. With tears in my eyes, I buried her beneath the green moss. Then stumbling to the ship I climbed in. Sealing the door and starting the machinery, I felt the ship lift quickly toward the distant beckoning earth.

———

When I began writing science fiction myself, I still had had no dates with girls and I made very little effort to deal with women in my stories (see *The Early Asimov*). I had, however, learned the power of the understated romance from "The Moon Era" and other, less remarkable stories.

There came a time when I used the device of an implicit love developed across an impossible gap, either social or biological, and underplayed it every time. "The Moon Era," even if unconsciously, influenced me in my short stories "Sally," "Lennie," and "The Ugly Little Boy," to say nothing of my novel *The Naked Sun*.

In September 1932, I entered Boys High School, but spent the first half of the tenth grade (or as we called it, "the third term," since my last year at junior high had embraced the first and second terms of high school) at Waverley Annex. This was a small, ramshackle school that served as a reservoir, intended to keep the student body at Boys High itself from overflowing its bounds.

The Annex contributed a column to the high school newspaper (a "news from Waverley" thing), and I volunteered to write it. I don't remember how many columns I did, but I do remember that on one occasion there was a mini-stir occasioned by the fact that I had naïvely reported that we had been let out early one day, when that had been done against the rules. (The head of the Annex found he had to do some explaining, and from then on he read my column before I was allowed to pass it on to the newspaper office.)

This column was the first occasion on which I had written anything for publication. It was the first time I had ever seen any words of my own in actual print with my own name on them. (In *The Early Asimov*, I said that an essay I had written in 1934 was my first published piece. That was wrong. I had forgotten about this earlier material, and it is only now, when I am rummaging about in the ancient lumber of my mental attic, that I have come across it.)

I had assumed when I was in the Annex that once I went to Boys High School itself, I would join the staff of the school paper. It seemed natural to me to do so, since I had no doubt of my writing ability at all. That, however, was never to come to pass.

For one thing, I found that working on the paper meant all kinds of after-school activity, and I *couldn't* work after school. I had to get back to the candy store. For another thing, the students on the staff of the paper were all considerably older than myself and seemed to my frightened self to be very cynical and worldly-wise. I was overawed and backed away.

The result is that I *never* worked on a school paper, either in high school or in college. My brother, Stanley, however, when it was his turn to be in his teens, was a much more self-possessed youngster. He worked on the papers, was eventually editor of a school paper, made newspapers his life-work, and is now Assistant Publisher of the Long Island *Newsday*. He is very highly thought of in the field.

I'm not sorry. I'd have made a rotten reporter and a rottener editor.

Part Four

1933

IN FEBRUARY 1933, I finally went to the main campus of Boys High. I had just passed my thirteenth birthday and was now in the "fourth term."

The main campus came, in one way, as a kind of shock. I had been the "smartest kid in class" and very probably the "smartest kid in school" all my school life, right down to and including the Waverley Annex. Now this was no longer so.

Boys High's reputation for scholastic excellence was deserved, and there were easily a dozen students there who consistently got higher marks than I did. One student averaged 98 per cent each term, whereas I was pleased if I got as much as a 93.

After the initial shock, however, I shrugged it off. All the rest were much older than I was, and besides, I had grown old enough to realize that "smartness" is not exactly or entirely equivalent to high marks. It was quite clear to me that some of the youngsters who did very well did so only at the cost of a great deal of sweating over their books. I, of course, continued to depend on what I could get by understanding-at-once and remembering-forever. I *had* to, as long as so much of my out-of-school time had to be spent in the candy store.

My cheerful self-appreciation (or my role as "monster of arrogance and conceit" if you'd rather) therefore continued undisturbed.

My father was far more annoyed than I was at my failure to be at the tiptop of the class. He was particularly irritated at my failure to be elected to the Arista, which was the school's honor society. Apparently, my school marks qualified me, but—very rightly—this was not enough. You had also to engage in extracurricular activity in order to show yourself a well-rounded person. This I could not do, because extracurricular activity meant staying after school and I *couldn't* stay after school. I had to go home and get behind that darned candy-store counter.

This I never explained to the school authorities, because I didn't want to seem to be begging to get in. I also never explained it to my father, since it would have saddened him without helping the situation in the least. The candy store *had* to come first.

In the course of the year, my father gave up his second candy store. It had seen us through the Hoover administration, and now he found a new, third candy store, at 1312 Decatur Street, in the Ridgewood section of Brooklyn, only a block and a half from the border of Queens. (This meant I could belong to both the Brooklyn Public Library *and* the Queens Public Library, and you can bet I made use of both.)

For the first time since we came to the United States ten years before, we moved out of the East New York section. We never returned, even for a visit.

I am sometimes asked whether I have ever gone back to visit this or that early scene in my life (even, sometimes, whether I have ever visited Petrovichi again), and the answer is always that I have not. I sometimes pass near the place out of business necessity but never out of sentimentality. I don't have that particular variety.

In any case, it is far too late to speak of returning to East New York on a nostalgia pilgrimage. The area is now depressed, I understand (though it wasn't terribly exalted in my day either), and is entirely unrecognizable.

In high school, I grew even lonelier as a science fiction reader. I continued to find no one else who shared my interest, of course, but in junior high school I had at least created an interest by retelling the stories I read. That didn't seem possible in the older and soberer atmosphere of a high school with scholastic pretensions.

(In those days, of course, there was no academic interest whatever in science fiction, and to study it in school would have been in the highest degree unthinkable. It would have been like taking a course in baseball cards. My daughter, however, when she was in high school, took a course in science fiction and was a celebrity because of her last name. Hah!)

Nor was it just that people didn't read science fiction. A person might not read detective stories or Westerns and yet not laugh at those who did. Science fiction reading, however, elicited laughter. "Do you really read that crazy stuff?" was the question.

Science fiction was escape literature, you see. It was more quintessentially escape than any other form of popular reading was, because it escaped you right out of this world. It seemed there was something contemptible about escape.

In that connection, though, I always remember "The Man Who Awoke," by Laurence Manning, which appeared in the March 1933 *Wonder Stories*.

THE MAN WHO AWOKE

by Laurence Manning

It was in all the newspapers for the entire month of September. Reports came in from such out-of-the-way places as Venezuela and Monte Carlo: "MISSING BANKER FOUND." But such reports always proved false. The disappearance of Norman Winters was at last given up as one of those mysteries that can only be solved by the great detectives Time and Chance. His description was broadcast from one end of the civilized world to the other: Five feet eleven inches tall; brown hair; grayish dark eyes; aquiline nose; fair complexion; age forty-six; hobbies: history and biology; distinguishing marks: a small mole set at the corner of the right nostril.

His son could spare little time for search, for just a month before his disappearance Winters had practically retired from active affairs and left their direction to his son's capable hands. There was no clue as to motive, for he had absolutely no enemies and possessed a great deal of money with which to indulge his dilettante scientific hobbies.

By October only the highly paid detective bureau that his son employed gave the vanished man any further thought. Snow came early that year in the Westchester suburb where the Winters estate lay and it covered the ground with a blanket of white. In the hills across the Hudson the bears had hibernated and lay sleeping under their earthen and icy blanket.

In the pond on the estate the frogs had vanished from sight and lay hidden in the mud at the bottom—a very miracle in suspended animation for biologists to puzzle over. The world went on about its winter business and gave up the vanished banker for lost. The frogs might have given them a clue—or the bears.

But even stranger than these was the real hiding place of Norman Winters. Fifty feet beneath the frozen earth he lay in a hollow chamber a dozen feet across. He was curled up on soft eiderdown piled five feet deep and his eyes were shut in the darkness of absolute night and in utter quiet.

During October his heart beat slowly and gently and his breast, had there been light to see by, might have been observed to rise and fall very slightly. By November these signs of life no longer existed in the motionless figure.

The weeks sped by and the snow melted. The bears came hungrily out of winter quarters and set about restoring their wasted tissues. The frogs made the first warm nights of spring melodious to nature-lovers and hideous to light sleepers.

But Norman Winters did not rise from his sleep with these vernal harbingers. Still—deathly still—lay his body and the features were waxy white. There was no decay and the flesh was clean and fresh. No frost penetrated to this great depth; but the chamber was much warmer than this mere statement would indicate. Definite warmth came from a closed box in one corner and had come from it all the winter. From the top of the chamber wall a heavy leaden pipe came through the wall from the living rock beyond and led down to this closed box. Another similar pipe led out from it and down through the floor. Above the box was a dial like a clockface in appearance. Figures on it read in thousands from one to one hundred and a hand pointed to slightly below the two thousand mark.

Two platinum wires ran from the box over to the still figure on its piled couch and ended in golden bands—one around one wrist and one circling the opposite ankle. By his side stood a cabinet of carved stone—shut and mysterious as anything in that chamber. But no light was here to see by, only darkness; the black of eternal night; the groping stifling darkness of the tomb. Here was no cheering life-giving radiation of any kind. The unchanging leaden metal sealed in the air from which the dust had settled completely, as it never does on the surface of our world, and had left it as pure and motionless as crystal—and as lifeless. For without change and motion there can be no life. A faint odor remained in the atmosphere of some disinfectant, as though not even bacteria had been permitted to exist in this place of death.

At the end of a month Vincent Winters (the son of the missing man) made a thorough examination of all the facts and possible clues that the detectives had brought to light bearing upon his father's disappearance. They amounted to very little. On a Friday, September 8th, his father had spent the day on his estate; he had dinner alone, read awhile in the library, had written a letter or two and retired to his bedroom early. The next morning he had failed to put in an appearance for breakfast and Dibbs the butler, after investigating, reported that his bed had not been slept in. The servants had, of course, all been minutely questioned even though their characters were such as almost to preclude suspicion. One only—and he the oldest and most loyal of them all—had acted and spoken in answer to questions in a fashion that aroused the curiosity of Vincent

Winters. This man was Carstairs, the gardener—a tall ungainly Englishman with a long sad-looking face. He had been for twelve years in the employ of Mr. Winters.

On Friday night, about midnight, he had been seen entering his cottage with two shovels over his shoulder—itself, perhaps, not an incriminating circumstance, but his explanation lacked credibility: he had, he said, been digging in the garden.

"But why *two* shovels, Carstairs?" asked Vincent for the hundredth time and received the same unvarying answer: "I'd mislaid one shovel earlier in the day and went and got another. Then I found the first as I started home."

Vincent rose to his feet restlessly.

"Come," he said, "show me the place you were digging."

And Carstairs paled slightly and shook his head.

"What, man! You refuse?"

"I'm sorry, Mr. Vincent. Yes, I must refuse to show you . . . *that*."

There were a few moments of silence in the room. Vincent sighed.

"Well, Carstairs, you leave me no choice. You are almost an institution on this place; my boyhood memories of the estate are full of pictures of you. But I shall have to turn you over to the police just the same," and he stared with hardening eyes at the old servitor.

The man started visibly and opened his mouth as if to speak, but closed it again with true British obstinacy. Not until Vincent had turned and picked up the telephone did he speak.

"Stop, Mr. Vincent."

Vincent turned in his chair to look at him, the receiver in his hand.

"I cannot show you the place I was digging, for Mr. Winters ordered me not to show it to anyone."

"You surely don't expect me to believe that!"

"You will still insist?"

"Most assuredly!"

"Then I have no choice. In case it were absolutely necessary to do so, I was to tell you these words. 'Steubenaur on Metabolism.'"

"What on earth does that mean?"

"I was not informed, sir."

"You mean my father told you to say that if you were suspected of his . . . er . . . of being connected with his disappearance?"

The gardener nodded without speaking.

"H'm . . . sounds like the name of a book . . ." and Vincent went into the library and consulted the neatly arranged card catalog. There was the book, right enough, an old brown leather volume in the biological section. As Vincent opened it wonderingly an envelope fell out and onto the floor.

He pounced upon this and found it addressed to himself in his father's handwriting. With trembling anxious fingers he opened and read:

"My dear son:

"It would be better, perhaps, if you were never to read this. But it is a necessary precaution. Carstairs *may* in some unforseen way be connected with my disappearance. I anticipate this possibility because it is true. He has in very fact helped me disappear and at my own orders. He obeyed these orders with tears and expostulation and was to the very end just what he has always been—a good and devoted servant. Please see that he is never in want.

"The discovery and investigation of the so-called 'cosmic' rays was of the greatest interest to us biologists, my son. Life is a chemical reaction consisting fundamentally in the constant, tireless breaking up of organic molecules and their continual replacement by fresh structures formed from the substance of the food we eat. Lifeless matter is comparatively changeless. A diamond crystal, for instance, is composed of molecules which do not break up readily. There is no change—no life—going on in it. Organic molecules and cells are termed 'unstable,' but why they should be so was neither properly understood nor explained until cosmic rays were discovered. Then we suspected the truth: The bombardment of living tissue by these minute high-speed particles caused that constant changing of detail which we term 'life.'

"Can you guess now the nature of my experiment? For three years I worked on my idea. Herkimer of Johns Hopkins helped me with the drug I shall use and Mortimer of Harvard worked out my ray-screen requirements. But neither one knew what my purpose might be in the investigations. Radiation cannot penetrate six feet of lead buried far beneath the ground. During the past year I have constructed, with Carstairs' help, just such a shielded chamber on my estate. Tonight I shall descend into it and Carstairs shall fill in the earth over the tunnel entrance and plant sod over the earth so that it can never be found.

"Down in my lead-walled room I shall drink my special drug and fall into a coma which would on the surface of the earth last (at most) a few hours. But down there, shielded from all change, I shall never wake until I am again subjected to radiation. A powerful X-ray bulb is connected and set in the wall and upon the elapse of my alloted time this will light, operated by the power generated from a subterranean stream I have piped through my chamber.

"The X-ray radiation will, I hope, awaken me from my long sleep and I shall arise and climb up through the tunnel to the world above. And I shall see with these two eyes the glory of the world that is to be when Mankind has risen on the steppingstones of science to its great destiny.

"Do not try to find me! You will marry and forget me in your new interests. As you know, I have turned over to you my entire wealth. You wondered why at the time. Now you know. By all means marry. Have healthy children. I shall see your descendants in the future, I hope, although I travel very far in time: One hundred and twenty generations will have lived and died when I awaken and the Winters blood will have had time to spread throughout the entire world.

"Oh my son, I can hardly wait! It is nine o'clock now and I must get started upon my adventure! The call is stronger than the ties of blood. When I awaken you will have been dead three thousand years, Vincent. I shall never see you again. Farewell, my son! Farewell!"

And so the disappearance of Norman Winters passed into minor history. The detective agency made its final report and received its last check with regret. Vincent Winters married the next year and took up his residence upon his father's estate. Carstairs aged rapidly and was provided with strong young assistants to carry on the work of the place. He approached Vincent one day, years later, and made the request that he might be buried on the estate at the foot of the mound covered with hemlock and rhododendrons. Vincent laughed at the suggestion and assured him that he would live many a year yet, but the old gardener was dead within a year and Vincent had the tomb dug rather deeper than is usual, peering often over the shoulder of the laborer into the depth of the grave. But he saw nothing there except earth and stones. He erected a heavy flat slab of reinforced concrete on the spot.

"Most peculiar, if you ask me," said old Dibbs to the housekeeper. "It's almost as if Mr. Vincent wanted Carstairs' stone to last a thousand years. Why, they cut the letters six inches deep in it!"

In due time Vincent Winters himself died and was buried beside the gardener at his earnest request. There remained no one on the earth who remembered Norman Winters.

CHAPTER II

Awakening—in What Year?

It was night and great blue sheets of flame lit the sky with a ghastly glare. Suddenly a blinding flash enveloped him—he felt a million shooting pains in every limb—he was lying on the ground helpless and suffering —he fell into a brief unconsciousness.

A dozen times he awakened and each time he shrieked with the pain in his whole body and opened his eyes upon a small room lit by a penetrating blue electric bulb. Numberless times he tried to move his right hand to shield his eyes but found he could not force his muscles to obey his will. Days must have passed, as he lay there, with sweat dotting his brow with the effort, and finally one day his hand moved up slowly. He lay a full minute recovering. He did not know where he was. Then from the depths of infinity a little memory came into his dulled brain; a memory with a nameless joy in it. And slowly his surroundings struck new meaning and a vast thrill coursed through him. He was awake! Had he succeeded? Was he really alive in the distant future?

He lay quiet a moment letting the great fact of his awakening sink in. His eyes turned to the stone cabinet beside his couch. Slowly his hand reached out and pulled softly at the handle and a compartment on the level of his face revealed two bottles of yellowish liquor. With gasping effort he reached one and dragged it over to him, succeeding in spilling a little of its contents but also in getting a mouthful which he swallowed. Then he lay quietly a full half hour, eyes purposefully shut and lips tightly pressed together in the agony of awakened animation, while the medicine he had taken coursed through his veins like fire and set nerves a-tingling in arms and legs and (finally) in very fingertips and toes.

When he again opened his eyes he was weak but otherwise normal. The stone cabinet now yielded concentrated meat lozenges from a metal box and he partook very sparingly from the second bottle of liquid. Then he swung his legs down from the eiderdown couch, now tight-compressed from its original five feet to a bare two feet of depth by his age-long weight, and crossed the chamber to the clock.

"Five thousand!" he read breathlessly, clasping his thin hands together in delight. But could it be true? He must get outside! He reached down to a valve in the leaden piping and filled a glass tumbler with cold water which he drank greedily and refilled and drank again. He looked about curiously to note the changes time had produced on his chamber, but he had planned well and little or nothing had deteriorated.

The lead pipe was coated with a few tiny cracks in its surface and particles of white dust lay in them, where the cold water had gathered the moisture of the air by condensation. But this could not have been helped, for the stream of water through this pipe was all that kept the tiny generator turning—that made possible the heated chamber and the final blaze of the specially constructed X-ray lamp that now filled his whole being with its life-restoring radiations.

Winters removed the cover from the power box and examined the motor and generator with great care. The chromium metal parts and the jewelled bearings showed no slightest sign of wear. Did that mean that only a few years had elapsed? He doubted his clock's accuracy. He replaced the covering and brushed off his hands, for everything was coated with dusty sediment. Next, Winters examined the heat elements and placed a glass container of water upon them to heat. With more of his meat concentrate he made a hot soup and drank it thankfully.

Now he went eagerly to the door in the lead wall and pulled at the locking lever. It resisted and he pulled harder, finally exerting all the strength he had in the effort. It was useless. The door was immovable! He leaned against it a moment, panting, then stooped and scrutinized the door-jamb. With a chill of dread he observed that the leaden chamberwall had become coated at the crack with a fine white dust. It had rusted the door into place! Had he awakened only to die here like a rat in a trap?

In his weakened condition he felt despair creep over his body and mind helplessly. He again sank back on his couch and stared desperately at the door. It was hours before the simple solution to his difficulties occurred to him. The locking lever—of course! It was of stainless steel and held to the door only by one bolt. A matter of a dozen turns loosened the nut on this bolt and the lever came away freely in his hands.

With this bar of stout metal as a crowbar he easily pried into the soft lead wall beside the door-jamb and, obtaining a fulcrum, put his frail weight on the end of the lever. The door gave inward an inch! In a few minutes his efforts were rewarded. The door groaned protestingly as it swung open and Winters looked up the ancient stone steps, half-lit by the room's illumination. But in the open doorway a chill draft blew on his ragged and time-tattered garments and he went back to the chamber and commenced unscrewing a circular cover set into the wall.

It came away heavily with a hiss of air, for it had enclosed a near-vacuum, and Winters pulled out clothes neatly folded. He was relieved to find a leather jacket still strong and perfect. It had been well oiled and was as supple as new. Some woolen things had not fared so well, but stout corduroy breeches of linen fibre seemed well preserved and he put these on. A tightly covered crock of glass filled with oil yielded up a pistol designed to shoot lead bullets under compressed air and a neat roll of simple tools: a small saw, a file, a knife and a hand-axe. These he thrust into the waist-band of his breeches, which had been slit around the belt to accommodate them.

Now with a last look around, Norman Winters started up the steps, guided only by the light from the chamber behind. He stumbled over fallen stones and drifted earth as he climbed and at the top came to a mat of tree-roots sealing him in. And now the axe was wielded delicately by those enfeebled arms and many minutes passed in severing one small piece at a time. The cap-stone which had originally covered the tunnel had been split and pressed to one side by the force of the growing tree and after the third large root had been severed a small cascade of earth and pebbles let down on him a blazing flood of sunlight.

He paused and forced himself to return to his chamber; filled a glass bottle with water and slung it to his belt; put a handful of concentrated food in his pocket, and left the chamber for good, closing the door behind him and turning off the light.

It took a few minutes only to squeeze his head and shoulders through the opening between the roots and he looked about him with pounding heart.

But what was this? He was in the middle of a forest!

Upon all sides stretched the trees—great sky-thrusting boles with here and there a clump of lesser growth, but set so evenly and spaced so regularly as to betray human oversight. The ground was softly deep in dead leaves and over them trailed a motley of vine-like plants. Winters recognized a cranberry vine and the bright wintergreen berries among many others he did not know. A pleasant sort of forest, he decided, and he set off rather hesitantly through the trees to see what he could find, his mind full of speculations as to how long it must have taken these trees to grow. To judge from the warmth it must be about noon of a midsummer's day but what year? Certainly many of the trees were over 100 years old!

He had not progressed more than a hundred yards before he came upon a clearing ahead and, passing beyond a fringe of shrubs he came into full view of a great highway. North and south it stretched and he stamped his feet upon the strange hard surface of green glass-like material. It was smooth in texture and extraordinarily straight and level. For miles he could look in both directions but, gaze as he might, no slightest sign of buildings could he detect.

Here was a poser indeed, where had the suburbs of New York gone? Had even New York itself joined the lost legion in limbo? Winters stood in indecision and finally started tramping northward along the road. About a mile further along had once been the town of White Plains. It was nearby and, even if no longer in existence, would make as good a starting point as any. His pace was slow, but the fresh air and bright sunshine set the blood coursing through his veins and he went faster as he felt his strength returning with each step. He had gone half an hour and seen no sign of human habitation when a man came out upon the glass roadway a hundred yards ahead of him. He was dressed in red and russet and held one hand over his eyes, peering at Winters, who hesitated and then continued to approach with a wild thrill surging through his veins.

The man seemed in some vague way different. His skin was dark and tanned; features full and rounded; and eyes (Winters observed as he got nearer) a soft brown. The supple body seemed alert and exuded the very breath of health, yet it was indefinably sensuous and indolent—graceful in movement. He could not for the life of him decide even what race this man of the future represented; perhaps he was a mixture of many. Then the man made a curious gesture with his left hand—a sort of circle waved in the air. Winters was puzzled, but believing it was meant for greeting imitated it awkwardly.

"Wassum! You have chosen a slow way to travel!"

"I am in no hurry," replied Winters, determined to learn all he could before saying anything himself. He had to repress his natural emotions of excitement and joy. He felt an urge to shout aloud and hug this stranger in his arms.

"Have you come far?"

"I have been travelling for years."

"Come with me and I will take you to our orig. No doubt you will want food and drink and walling." The words were drawled and his walk was slow: so much so that Winters felt a slight impatience. He was to feel this constantly among these people of the future.

The surprising thing, when he came to think about it, was that the man's speech was plain English, for which he was thankful. There were new words, of course, and the accent was strange in his ears—a tang of European broad As and positively continental Rs. He was wondering if radio and recorded speech had been the causes of this persistence of the old tongue when they came to a pleasant clearing lined with two-story houses of shiny brown. The walls were smooth as if welded whole from some composition plastic. But when he entered a house behind his guide he perceived that the entire wall admitted light translucently from outside and tiny windows were placed here and there purely for observation and air. He had little time to look around, for a huge dark man was eyeing him beneath bushy gray eyebrows.

"A stranger who came on foot," said his guide and (to Winters) "Our chief Forester." Then he turned abruptly and left them together, without the slightest indication of curiosity.

"Wassum, stranger! Where is your orig?" asked the Forester.

"My orig? I don't understand."

"Why, your village of course!"

"I have none."

"What! A trogling?"

"I don't understand."

"A wild man—a herman—don't you understand human speech?"

"Where I come from there were several forms of human speech, sir."

"What is this? Since the dawn of civilization two thousand years ago there has been one common speech throughout the world!"

Winters made an excited mental note of the date. Two thousand years then, at the least, had elapsed since he entered his sleeping chamber!

"I have come to learn, sir. I should like to spend several days in your village observing your life in . . . er . . . an elementary sort of way. For instance, how do you obtain your food here in the middle of a forest. I saw no farms or fields nearby."

"You are wassum to the walling, but farms—what are they? And fields!

You will travel many a mile before you find a field near here, thanks to our ancestors! We are well planted in fine forests."

"But your food?"

The Forester raised his eyebrows. "Food—I have just said we have fine forests, a hundred square kilos of them—food and to spare! Did you walk with your eyes shut?"

"Where I come from we were not used to finding food in forests, exactly. What sort of food do you get from them—remember I said I wanted elementary information, sir."

"Elementary indeed! Our chestnut flour for baking, naturally, our dessert nuts and our vegetables, like the locust bean, the Keawe, the Catalpea and a dozen others—all the food a man could desire. Then the felled logs bear their crops of mushrooms—we have a famous strain of beefsteak mushroom in this orig. And of course the mast-fattened swine for bacon and winter-fats and the pitch pines for engine oils—the usual forest crops. How can it be that you are ignorant of the everyday things which even schoolboys know?"

"Mine is a strange story, sir," replied Winters. "Tell me what I ask and I will tell you later anything you want to know about myself. Tell me things as though I were—oh, from another planet, or from the distant past," and Winters forced a laugh.

"This is a strange request!"

"And my story, when I tell it to you, will be stranger still—depend upon it!"

"Ha! Ha! It should prove amusing—this game! Well then, this afternoon I will spend showing you about and answering questions. After our meal tonight you shall tell me your story—but I warn you! Make it a good one —good enough to repay me for my time!"

They went out into the sunlight together. The village proved to be a gathering of about fifty large houses stretching for half a mile around a long narrow clearing. The background consisted of the huge trunks, gnarled branches and dark green of the forest. The Forester himself was a rather brisk old fellow, but the villagers seemed to strike again that vague chord of strangeness—of indolence—which he had noticed in his first acquaintance. Groups lay gracefully stretched out here and there under trees and such occasional figures as were in motion seemed to move with dragging feet, to Winters' business-like mind. It came upon him that these people were downright *lazy*—and this he afterwards observed to be almost invariably true. They accomplished the work of the village in an hour or two a day—and this time was actually begrudged and every effort was being made to reduce it. The chief effort of world-wide science was devoted to this end, in fact.

The people were dressed in bright colors and the green grass and the rich brown of the buildings made a background to the colorful picture. Everywhere he saw the same racial characteristics of dark, swarthy faces and soft, liquid, brown eyes. There was something strange about the eyes —almost as if they were not set straight in the face, but a trifle aslant. Very little attention was paid Winters, except for occasional glances of idle curiosity aroused by his unusual attire. He thought the women unusually attractive, but the men seemed somehow effeminate and too soft; not but that they were fine specimens of humanity physically speaking, but that their faces were too smooth and their bodies too graceful to suit his twentieth-century ideas of what vigorous manhood should look like. Their bodies suggested the feline—cat-like grace and lethargy combined with supple strength.

Winters was told that a thousand people usually formed an "orig." Just now there were several hundred extra inhabitants and a "colorig" had been prepared fifty miles to the north and trees had been growing for half a century there, making ready for the new colony.

"But why should you not simply make your village large enough to keep the extra people right here?"

"The forest supports just so many in comfort—we are having trouble now as it is."

"But are there no larger villages where manufacturing is done?"

"Of course. There are factory origs near the Great Falls in the north. Our airwheel goes there twice a week—a two-hours' flight. But there are only a few people there; just enough to tend the machines."

The people of the village seemed happy and very much contented with life, but most of the younger men and women seemed to Winters too serious. Their dark faces hardly ever showed a smile. He entered several of the houses: among others that of the guild of cloth-makers. He was greatly interested, as if seeing an old friend, to observe wood-pulp fed through a pipe into the thread-making tubes to be hardened in an acid bath. He recognized, of course, the rayon process—new in his youth, but here considered ancient beyond history.

"How many hours a day do you work here?" he asked of the elderly attendant.

"I have worked three hours every day for the past week getting cloth ready for the new colonists," he replied grumblingly. "Perhaps we shall have some peace in this orig when the youngsters are gone! At least there will be plenty of everything to go around once again!"

As he spoke, a young man, evidently his son, entered the thread room and stared at his father and the Forester with cold, supercilious eyes. "Wassum!" said the attendant, but the youth merely scowled in reply. He examined Winters silently and with distrust and went out again without speaking.

"Your son is a solemn chap!"

"Yes. So is his generation—they take life too seriously."

"But do they never enjoy themselves?"

"Oh yes! There is the hunting moon in fall. The young men track the deer on foot and race him—sometimes for days on end—then throw him with their bare hands. My son is a famous deer-chaser. He practises all year long for the Autumn season."

"But are there no . . . er . . . lighter pastimes?"

"There are the festivals. The next one is the festival of autumn leaves. At the time of the equinox the young people dress in russets and reds and gold and dance in a clearing in the woods which has been chosen for its outstanding autumn beauty of color. The young women compete in designing costumes."

"But the younger ones—the children?"

"They are at school until they are twenty years of age. School is the time of hard work and study. They are not permitted games or pastimes except such exercise as is needed to keep them in health. When they finish school, then they enter upon the rights and pleasures of their generation —a prospect which makes them work the harder to finish their schooling as soon as may be."

As they went out into the sunlight once more Winters observed a small airship settling down in the village campus. It was the airwheel, the Forester said, and would not leave again until dusk.

"I have never been in one," said Winters.

"You *are* a trogling," exclaimed the Forester. "Suppose we go up for a short flight, then?" and Winters eagerly agreed. They walked over to the machine which Winters examined curiously. Here, at least, three thousand years of improvements were amply noticeable. The enclosed cabin would seat about twenty persons. There were no wings at all, but three horizontal wheels (two in front and one in the rear) above the level of the cabin. A propeller projected from the nose and this was still idling when they arrived. The Forester explained his wishes to the pilot who asked which direction they should prefer to take.

"South to the water and back!" put in Winters, with visions of the thriving New York metropolitan area of his day running through his memory. They took their places and the airwheel rose gently and with only a faintly audible hum—it was practically silent flight and made at enormous speed.

In ten minutes the sea was in sight and Winters gazed breathless through the crystal windows upon several islands of varying sizes—

clothed in the green blanket of dense forest. Slowly he pieced out the puzzle: there was Long Island, evidently, and over there showed Staten Island. Beneath him then lay the narrow strip of Manhattan and the forest towered over everything alike.

"There are ruins beneath the trees," said the Forester, noting his interest. "I have been there several times. Our historians believe the people of ancient times who lived here must have been afraid of the open air, for they either lived beneath the ground or raised stone buildings which could be entered without going out-of-doors: There are tunnels, which they used for roadways, running all beneath the ground in every direction."

CHAPTER III

"He Has an Appendix!"

And now the airship turned about and as it did so Winters caught sight of one gray pile of masonry—a tower-tip—showing above the forest. Surely it must have taken thousands of years to accomplish this oblivion of New York! And yet, he thought to himself, even one century makes buildings old.

He scarcely looked out of the window on the way back, but sat engrossed in sad thoughts and mournful memories. They landed once more in the village clearing and he continued his tour under the Forester's guidance, but a recounting of this would be tedious. When the afternoon was over he had gathered a confusing mass of general information about life in the new age. Metals were carefully conserved and when a new colony was started its supply of metal utensils and tools was the final great gift of the parent villages. Farming was entirely unknown, and grain— which the Forester did not know except as "plant-seed"—was not used for food, although primitive races had once so used it, he said. Everything came from trees now, food, houses, clothing—even the fuel for their airships, which was wood alcohol.

The life of a villager was leisurely and pleasant, Winters decided. Hours of labor were short and the greater part of the day was devoted to social pleasures and scientific or artistic hobbies. There were artists in the village, mostly of some new faddist school whose work Winters could not in the least understand. (They painted trees and attempted to express emotions thereby.) But many beautiful pieces of sculpture were set about in some of the houses. Electric power was received through the air from the Great Falls, where it was generated, and each socket received its current without wiring of any sort. The village produced its own food and made its own clothes and building materials, paper, wood alcohol, turpentine and oils. And as this village lived, so apparently, did the rest of the world.

As Winters pictured this civilization, it consisted of a great number of isolated villages, each practically self-sufficient, except for metals. By taking the airwheel from one village to the next and there changing for another ship, a man could make a quick trip across the continents and oceans of the globe. But science and art were pursued by isolated individuals, the exchange of ideas being rendered easy by the marvellously realistic television and radio instruments.

At dusk they returned to the Chief Forester's house for dinner.

"I must apologize to you for the food," said he. "We are on slightly curtailed supplies, due to our population having grown faster than our new plantings. Oh, you will have a good meal—I do not mean to starve you, —but merely that you will be expected not to ask for a second service of anything and excuse the absence of luxuries from my table." His great body dropped into an upholstered chair.

"Is there no way to arrange things except by rationing yourselves while you wait for the new forests to bear crops?"

The Forester laughed a trifle bitterly. "Of course—but at a price. We could easily fell some trees for mushroom growing (they grow on dead logs) and also we could cut into the crop of edible pith-trees a little before maturity—and so all along the line. It would set us back in our plans a few years at the most, but there is no use talking about it. The Council of Youth has claimed the Rights of its Generation. The future is theirs, of course, and they object to our spending any of their resources now. We older people are a little more liberal in our views—not selfishly, but on a principle of common-sense. There have been some bitter words, I'm afraid, and the matter is by no means settled yet—for their attitude is almost fanatical and lacks all reason. But there is no need to bother you with our local affairs," and he turned the conversation into other channels.

He was forever using the expression "thanks to our ancestors," a point which Winters noted with surprise. So far one thing had eluded Winters completely: that was the history of the past ages during which all these drastic changes had come about. When the time came that he was bade tell his story, at the conclusion of the meal, he thought a moment as to how he might best obtain this information.

"I have travelled far," he said, "but in time—not in distance."

The Forester held a forkful of food poised in the air, eyebrows raised. "What nonsense is this?" he demanded.

"No nonsense . . . your mushrooms *are* delicious . . . I have succeeded in controlling the duration of a state of suspended animation. I went to sleep many years ago; woke up this morning."

The Forester was incredulous.

"How long do you pretend to have slept?"

"I don't know for sure," replied Winters. "My instruments showed a certain figure, but to be at all certain I should prefer that you tell me the history of the world. No need of anything but the rough outlines."

"Ha, ha! You promised me a story and you are most ingenious in fulfilling your promise, stranger!"

"I am, on the contrary, absolutely serious!"

"I cannot believe it—but it may be an amusing game. Let me see . . . Last year the first breadfruit trees bore in the lower temperate zones of the earth (that is a piece of it in your plate). It has greatly changed our mode of life and it may soon be unnecessary to grind chestnut flour for baking."

"Interesting," replied Winters. "But go back a thousand years more."

The Forester's eyes opened wide. Then he laughed delightedly. "Good! It is no lowly boaster, eh! A thousand years . . . That would be about the time of the great aluminum process. As you know, prior to that time the world was badly in need of metals. When Koenig perfected his method for producing aluminum from clay the economics of the world was turned topsy-turvy and . . . what! Farther back than a thousand years!"

"I think you might try two thousand."

The Forester exploded with laughter and then sobered at a sudden thought. He glanced shrewdly at his companion a moment, and a slight coldness appeared in his eyes.

"You are not by any slightest chance serious?" he asked.

"I am."

"It is absurd! In those days the human body still had an appendix—that was just after the Great Revolution when the Wasters were finally overthrown and True Economics lifted her torch to guide the world on its upward path. Two thousand years ago! Thence dates all civilized history! Such archaic customs as organized superstitions, money and ownership by private people of land and a division of humanity into groups speaking different languages—all ended at that time. That was a stirring period!"

"Well then, go back another five hundred years."

"The height of the false civilization of Waste! Fossil plants were ruthlessly burned in furnaces to provide heat, petroleum was consumed by the million barrels, cheap metal cars were built and thrown away to rust after a few years' use, men crowded into ill-ventilated villages of a million inhabitants—some historians say several million. That was the age of race-fights where whole countrysides raised mobs and gave them explosives and poisons and sent them to destroy other mobs. Do you pretend to come from that shameful scene?"

"That is precisely the sort of thing we used to do," replied Winters, "although we did not call it by the same set of names." He could barely repress his elation. There could no longer be the slightest doubt of it—he was alive in the year 5000! His clock had been accurate!

The Forester's face was growing red. "Timberfall! You have been amusing long enough—now tell me the truth: Where is your orig?"

"I don't understand. I have told you the truth."

"Stupid nonsense, I tell you! What can you possibly hope to gain from telling such a story? Even if people were such fools as to believe you, you could hardly expect to be very popular!"

"Why," said Winters in surprise, "I thought you were so thankful for all your ancestors had done for you? I am one of your ancestors!"

The Forester stared in astonishment. "You act well," he remarked drily. "But you are, I am sure, perfectly aware that those ancestors whom we thank were the planners for our forests and the very enemies of Waste. But for what should we thank the humans of three thousand years ago? For exhausting the coal supplies of the world? For leaving us no petroleum for our chemical factories? For destroying the forests on whole mountain ranges and letting the soil erode into the valleys? Shall we thank them, perhaps, for the Sahara or the Gobi deserts?"

"But the Sahara and the Gobi were deserts five thousand years before my time."

"I do not know what you mean by 'your' time. But if so, all the more reason you should have learned a lesson from such deserts. But come! You have made me angry with your nonsense. I must have some pleasant sort of revenge! Do you still claim to be a living human from the Age of Waste?"

Winters' caution bade him be silent. The Forester laughed mischievously: "Never mind! You *have already* claimed to be that! Well then, the matter is readily proved. You would in that case have an appendix and . . . yes . . . hair on your chest! These two characteristics have not appeared in the last two thousand years. You will be examined and, should you prove to have lied to me, a fitting punishment will be devised! I shall try to think of a reward as amusing as your wild lies have proved."

His eyes twinkled as he pressed a button hidden in his chair arm and a minute later two young men entered. Winters was in no physical condition to resist and was soon stripped of his clothing. He was not particularly hairy of chest, as men of his age went, but hair there was unquestionably and the Forester stepped forward with an incredulous exclamation. Then he hurriedly seized the discarded clothing and felt the material carefully —examining the linen closely in the light of the electric lamp concealed in the wall.

"To the health room with him!" he cried.

Poor Winters was carried helplessly down a corridor and into a room lined with smooth white glass and set about with apparatus of an evident surgical nature. The place was odiferous with germicide. He was held against a black screen and the Forester snapped on an X-ray tube and peered at his nude body through a mask of bluish glass. After a minute he left the room and returned again almost instantly with a book in his hands. He opened to a page of photographs and studied them carefully, once more peering at Winters through the mask. Finally he grunted in stupefaction and with close-pressed lips and puzzled eyes turned to the two attendants.

"He has an appendix—there can be no doubt of it! This is the most amazing thing I have ever imagined! The stranger you see before you claims to have survived from the ancient days—from the age of waste! And he has an appendix, young comrades! I must talk to the biologists all over the country—the historians as well! The whole world will be interested. Take him along with you and see that he is provided with walling for the night."

He turned to the door and Winters heard him in the next room talking excitedly over the radio-telephone. The two young attendants led him along the hall and as he passed he could observe that the Forester was speaking to a fat red-headed, red-faced man, whose features showed in the televisor—and who evidently was proving difficult to convince. Winters stared a minute for this was the first man he had seen whose face was anything except swarthy and slender.

Winters was led down the hall and permitted to resume his clothing. He was in an exalted mood. So his arrival in this new world was creating a stir after all! In the morning the airwheel would perhaps bring dozens of scientists to examine into his case. He was beginning to feel weak and fatigued after his exciting day, but this latest thrill gave a last flip to his nerves and gave him strength just long enough to prove his own undoing.

One of the attendants hurried out of sight as they left the house. The other guided him along the edge of the village.

"We young members of the village have a gathering tonight, sir. It is called the Council of Youth and at it we discuss matters of importance to our generation. Would it be too much to ask that you address our meeting and tell us something of your experiences?"

His vanity was stirred and he weakly agreed, tired and sleepy though he was. The meeting place was just a little distance away, explained his guide.

In the meantime the youth who had hastened on ahead had entered a small room off the assembly hall. The room contained only three persons and they looked up as the newcomer entered.

"It is as we thought, comrades, the Oldsters have brought him here for some purpose of their own. He pretends to have slept for three thousand years and to be a human relic of the Age of Waste!"

The others laughed. "What will they try on us next?" drawled one lazily.

"Stronghold is bringing him here," continued the latest arrival, "and will persuade him to speak to us in the meeting, if he can. You understand the intent?"

There was a wise nodding of heads. "Does he know the law of the Council?"

"Probably, but even so it is worth the attempt—you know I'm not certain myself but that he may be from the old days—at least he is a startling good imitation. The man has hair on his body!"

There was a chorus of shocked disbelief, finally silenced by a sober and emphatic assurance. Then a moment of silence.

"Comrades, it is some trick of the Oldsters, depend upon it! Let the man speak to the Council. If he makes a slip, even a slight one, we may be able to work on the meeting and arouse it to a sense of our danger. Any means is fair if we can only prevent our inheritance being spent! I hear that the order to fell the half-matured pith-trees will go out tomorrow unless we can stop it. We must see what we can do tonight—make every effort."

When Winters arrived at the hall the three young men stood on the platform to welcome him. The room was low-raftered and about fifty feet square. It was filled with swarthy young men and women. The thing that most impressed Winters was the luxury of the seating arrangements. Each person sat in a roomy upholstered arm-chair! He thought of the contrast that a similar meeting-hall in his own times would have afforded—with its small stiff seats uncomfortably crowded together and its stuffy hot atmosphere.

The lighting was by electricity concealed in the walls and gave at the moment a rosy tint to the room, though this color changed continually to others—now red or purple or blue—and was strangely soothing. There was a lull in the general conversation. One of the young leaders stepped forward.

"Comrades! This stranger is of another generation than ours. He is come especially to tell us of conditions in the ancient days—he speaks from personal experience of the Age of Waste, comrades, from which times he has survived in artificial sleep! The Forester of our orig, who is *old* enough to know the truth, has so informed us!" Winters missed the sarcasm. He was tired now and regretting that he had consented to come.

There was a stir of astonishment in the audience and a low growling laughter which should have been a warning, but Winters, full of fatigue, was thinking only of what he should say to these young people. He cleared his throat.

"I am not sure that I have anything to say that would interest you: Historians or doctors would make me a better audience. Still, you might wish to know how the changes of three thousand years impress me. Your life is an altogether simpler thing than in my day. Men starved then for lack of food and youth had no assurance of even a bare living—but had to fight for it." (Here there were a few angry cheers, much to Winters' puzzlement.) "This comfortable assurance that you will never lack food or clothing is, to my mind, the most striking change the years have brought."

He paused a moment uncertainly and one of the young leaders asked him something about "if we were perhaps trying to accomplish this assurance too quickly."

"I am not sure that I know what you mean. Your Chief Forester mentioned something today of a question of economics. I am not familiar with the facts. However, I understand you have a very poor opinion of my own times, due to its possibly unwise consumption of natural resources. We had even then men who warned us against our course of action, but we acted upon the belief that when oil and coal were gone mankind would produce some new fuel to take their place. I observe that in this we were correct, for you now use wood alcohol—an excellent substitute."

A young man leaped to his feet excitedly. "For that reason, comrades," he said in a loud voice, "this stranger of course believes his age was justified in using up all the oil and fuel in the world!"

There was a slow growling which ended in a few full-throated cries and an uneasy stirring about in the audience. Winters was growing dazed with his need for rest and could not understand what was going on here.

"What you say interests us very much," said another of the men on the platform beside him. "Was it very common to burn coal for its mere heat?"

"Yes. It burned in every man's house—in my house as well."

There was an ugly moving about in audience, as though the audience was being transformed into a mob. The mob, like some slow lumbering beast, was becoming finally aroused by these continual pin-pricks from the sharp tongues of its leaders.

"And did you also use petroleum for fuel?"

"Of course. We all used it in our automobiles."

"And was it usual to cut down trees just for the sake of having the ground clear of them?"

"Well . . . yes. On my own land I planted trees, but I must say I had a large stretch of open lawn as well."

Here Winters felt faint and giddy. He spoke quietly to the young man who had brought him. "I must lie down, I'm afraid. I feel ill."

"Just one more question will be all," was the whispered reply. Then aloud: "Do you think we of the Youth Council should permit our inheritance to be used up—even in part—for the sake of present comfort?"

"If it is not done to excess I can see nothing wrong in principle—you can always plant more trees . . . but I must say good night for I am. . . ."

CHAPTER IV

Revolt of the Youth

He never finished his sentence. A very fury of sound arose from the hall of the Council. One of the leaders shouted for silence.

"You have heard, comrades! You observe what sort of man has been sent to address us! We of Youth have a lesson to learn from the Age of Waste, it appears! At least the Oldsters think so! The crisis that has arisen is a small matter, but if we should once give in when will the thing stop? What must they think of our intelligence if they expect us to believe this three thousand-year sleep story? To send him here was sheer effrontery! And to send him here with *that* piece of advice passes beyond all bounds of toleration. Timberfall! There can be only one answer" (here he turned to glare at poor dazed Winters, stupefied by the effect of his long emaciation). "We must make such an example of this person as shall forever stamp our principles deep in the minds of the whole world!"

There were loud shouts and several young people rushed up on the platform and seized Winters.

"He has confessed to breaking the very basic laws of Economics!" shouted the leader. "What is the punishment?"

There were cries of "Kill him! Exile! Send him to the plains for life!" and over and over one group was chanting savagely "Kill him! Kill him!"

"I hear the sentence of death proposed by many of you," cried the leader. "It is true that to kill is to waste a life—but what could be more fitting for one who has wasted things all his life?" (Loud cries of furious approval) "To your houses, every one of you! We will confine this creature who claims to be three thousand years old in the cellar of this hall. In the morning we will gather here again and give these Oldsters our public answer! And comrades! A piece of news for your ears alone—Comrade Stronghold has heard that in the morning the Oldsters will issue a felling order on the immature pith-trees!"

And now was such a scene of rage and violence that the walls shook and Winters was dragged away with dizzy brain and failing feet and thrust upon a couch in a stone-walled room beneath the hall. He fell instantly in utter exhaustion and did not hear the tramp of departing feet overhead. His horror and fright had combined with his fatigue to render him incapable of further emotion. He lay unconscious, rather than asleep.

Above in the small room off the now empty hall three young men congratulated each other, their soft brown eyes shining exultantly, and chatted a few minutes in great joy that they had protected the rights of their generation, regardless of the means which had been used to this desirable end. They parted for the night with that peculiar circling movement of the hand that seemed to have taken the place of the ancient hand-shaking.

But while they talked (so swift does Treason run) a young man crouched in the shadows back of the Forester's house and fumbled with the latch of a small door on the forest side. As the young men were bidding each other good night, a voice was whispering swiftly in the ear of the Chief Forester, whose rugged face and bristling eyebrows betrayed in turn astonishment, indignation, anger and fierce determination.

Winters woke to watch a shaft of dawn-light lying upon the stone floor. His body was bruised from the rough handling he had received and his wasted muscles felt dull and deadened. But his brain was clear once again and he recalled the events of the meeting. What a fool he had been! How he had been led on to his own undoing! His eyes followed the shaft of light up to a grating set in the stone wall above his couch and he could see a little piece of sky softly blue there with a plump little cloud sailing in it, like a duck in a pond. There came upon him a wave of nostalgia. Oh to see a friendly face—or one homely thing, even a torn piece of newspaper lying on the cellar floor! But there was no use in such wishes. Thirty centuries lay between those things and himself—lay like an ocean between a shipwrecked sailor and his homeland.

And then came other thoughts, his natural fund of curiosity arising in him once again. After all, this age was a reaction against his own. There had been two extremes, that was all history would say of it. Truth lay in neither, but in some middle gentler path. Mankind would find the road in time—say another thousand years or more. But what difference to him now? In a few more hours he would be dead. Presently the young men would come for him and he would be their sacrifice for some fancied wrong. In his weakened condition the whole thing struck him as unutterably pathetic and tears welled into his eyes until they were brushed away as the bitter bracing humor of the situation dawned upon his mind. As he mused he was startled to notice a shadow pass across the window grating and he thought he heard low voices.

Now in an instant he was full of lively fears. He would not be taken to his death so tamely as this! He turned over on the couch to get upon his feet and felt a hard object beneath him. He felt and brought forth his revolver which he fell at once to examining—ears and senses attuned to hints of danger, though nothing further came. The weapon was an air-pistol firing .22 calibre lead slugs. It was deadly only at very close ranges —thirty feet or less, perhaps—and the extending lever compressed enough air for ten shots. It was something, at all events. Hastily he worked the lever, loaded and pulled the trigger to hear a satisfying "smack" of the lead against the stone wall.

Now his mind was working full tilt and he brought the file from his belt and turned to the grating above his couch. If he could sever the bars he could manage to squeeze through the window! To his amazement these bars proved to be of wood—and his heart lifted in hope. The saw was out of his belt and he was at work in an instant. By dint of much arm-ache he severed four of the bars in as many minutes. Day was now dawning apace and a panic of haste seized him; he brought the hand-axe into play and with three blows had smashed the remaining wood in the window. As he did so a shadow approached and a face was thrust forward, blocking out the light. Winters crouched below with pistol pointed, finger on trigger.

"Here he is!" said the face in shadow and Winters recognized the voice of the Chief Forester and held his fire.

"Take my hand, stranger, and climb up out of there. We have been looking for you half an hour. Oh, have no fear, we will not permit you to come to harm!"

But Winters was cautious. "Who will protect me?"

"Hurry, stranger! You have fallen afoul of our young hot-heads in the orig—I blame myself for not taking greater thought—but there are a hundred Oldsters here with me. You will be safe with us."

And now Winters permitted himself to be helped through the window and up into the full light of morning. He was surrounded by men who gazed at him with interest and respect. Their attitude calmed his last suspicions.

"We must hurry," said the Forester. "The younger men will resist us, I am afraid. Let us reach my own house as soon as possible."

The party started across the clearing and two young men appeared almost at once in the doorway of a building near by. At sight of Winters in the midst of the Oldsters they turned and raced off in separate directions, shouting some indistinguishable cry as they ran.

"We must go faster than this!"

A short fat man with a red face and reddish hair put his arms beneath Winters' shoulders and half carried him along. His face was familiar and Winters remembered the man he had seen in the televisor the day before. His strength was enormous and his energy indefatigable—a tie that drew Winters to him in this age of indolence. "I am Stalvyn of History at the next orig," he boomed at Winters as they hurried along. "You are so valuable to me that I hope you do not mind if I take a personal interest in your protection!"

They had a quarter of a mile to go and had half accomplished the distance when a mob of shouting youths burst from behind a house just ahead of them. There was a pause as though their natural disinclination to physical exertion might even yet prevent the clash. But their leaders were evidently urging them on and suddenly they charged down amid a shower of stones and waving of clubs. In an instant the shock was felt and a furious mêlee commenced—a primitive angry fight without science or direction.

Here two youths beat an elderly man senseless with clubs and sprang in unison upon the next victim. There some mature, full-muscled bull of a man ran berserk among striplings, crushing them in his great arms or flailing fist like hams at their onrushing faces. As they fought, they kept moving toward their objective and had gone almost another hundred yards before the youths retreated. The superior numbers of the older ones had swung the balance.

Fifty men, however, were all that remained around the Chief Forester. The others had either deserted the fight or been injured—perhaps killed, thought Winters, looking back at a score of still figures lying on the earth. The youths had retired only a hundred feet and still kept pace with the fugitives. Fresh bands of young men were hurrying from every direction and it would be a matter of minutes before the attack would recommence with the odds on the other side this time.

Winters and Stalvyn, his self-appointed bodyguard, had not taken part in the struggle, for they had been in the center of the rescue party. Now they worked to the front of the party where the Forester strode along determinedly. Winters showed his pistol. "With this thing I can kill them as they run there. Shall I use it, sir?"

The Forester grunted. "Kill them, then. They are coming now to kill you!"

As he spoke the mob of youths rushed upon them in a murderous fury. The elder men closed together in a compact mass and Winters shot into the front rank of the attackers, to see three of them topple over and thereby lessen the shock of the charge, for those who followed tripped over the fallen. And now Stalvyn and the Forester stepped forward, and around these immovable figures the fight raged. Winters crouched behind them, swiftly pulled back his lever, loaded bullets and pulled the trigger like an automaton in a nightmare. Cries of passion and pain mingled with the thud of blows and the panting gasps of the fighters. It was a savage scene, the more shocking because of the unfitness of these quiet people for such work.

Suddenly the attackers withdrew sullenly, bearing injured with them. Two dozen remaining Oldsters looked dazedly around—free now to proceed to shelter. Fifty or more figures lay about on the ground and the Forester called out to the watchers in the windows to come and give first aid to friend and foe alike. This work was commenced at once, but with characteristic slowness, and he led his little band to the door of his house and inside.

"Give the stranger some food and drink, Stalvyn," drawled a tall thin man with ungainly limbs, who proved to be the biologist from an orig nearly a thousand miles away. "If I know our Youth they would never have wasted sustenance on a man who was so soon to die!" and he smiled a lazy sardonic smile at Winters as he placed in his hands a tumbler full of brown liquid. "Drink it without fear. It will both stimulate and nourish."

Winters was in a state of collapse now and Stalvyn had to help him drink and then carried him over to a couch. The biologist spent a few minutes examining him. "He must rest," he announced. "There will be no questions asked him today. I will prepare some medicine for him." Whereupon everyone left the room and Winters swallowed more drink and dropped fathoms deep in slumber. A man was set to guard the door of his room and the biologist tended him day and night. For a full week he was not permitted to wake. He had vague impressions as he slept of being rolled over, bathed, fed, massaged and watched over—impressions that were as dreams in an ordinary sleep. Under such expert ministration the thin cheeks filled out and the wasted flesh became plump and smooth.

When Winters awoke it was late afternoon. His blood pulsed strongly through his body and he was wide awake the instant his eyes opened. There on a stool were set out his clothes, and he got to his feet and dressed. His belt still contained the pistol and hatchet as well as the smaller tools. Feeling like a new man he strode to the door and opened it, to be surrounded presently in another room by a swarthy group of a dozen of the greatest scientists in the world—for the news had by this time spread everywhere and there had been time for travel from the most distant points. And now there followed a long period of questions and examinations. Stalvyn and the historians plied him with posers as to the life and habits of his world; the biologists demanded the secret of his sleeping potion and control of the period of suspended animation; he was put before the fluoroscope and his appendix photographed; his measurements were taken and plaster moulds of his hand, foot and head were cast for a permanent record.

Through it all Winters had a feeling of consummation—this was one of the things he had planned when he set off on his voyage into the future. Here was sane intelligence taking advantage of his work and respecting him for his exploit. But one thing was lacking completely. He had no sense of belonging to these people. He had hoped to find gods in human form living in Utopia. Instead, here were men with everyday human passions and weaknesses. True, they had progressed since his day—but his insatiable curiosity itched to learn what the future might produce.

After an evening meal which all partook together, Winters retired to his room with the Chief Forester, the biologist and Stalvyn, and the four men sat talking lazily.

"What do you plan to do now?" drawled the biologist.

Winters sighed. "I don't know exactly."

"I would ask you to settle down in my orig here," remarked the Forester, "but most of our young people and many of the Oldsters who should know better hold you to blame for the recent troubles. I am helpless before them."

"Hold *me* to blame!" exclaimed Winters bitterly. "What had I to do with it?"

"Nothing, perhaps. But the principle of the rights of the new Generation is still unsettled. The Council of Youth is obstinate and must be brought to see the sensible side of the matter. Their leaders pretend you, in some way, have been brought here to persuade them to cut down trees right and left at the whim of the nearest Oldster. Where it will end, I cannot say."

Stalvyn laid a friendly hand on his shoulder. "Human nature is seldom reasonable. Of course there is no logic in their attitude. Forget it! We will get you quietly into an airship and you shall come away from here and live with me. Together we will review and rewrite the history of your times as it has never been done!"

"Stop a moment! Do you mean that I shall have to escape secretly from this village?"

The others looked sheepish and the Forester nodded his head. "I am helpless in the matter. I could get perhaps twenty or thirty men to do my bidding—but you see, most of the villagers will not concern themselves with your fate. It is too much trouble to bother about it at all."

"Are they afraid of the youngsters?"

"No, of course not! They greatly outnumber the youths. They merely are not willing to work beyond the village figure of one hour and fifty minutes a day so they say. I'm afraid you will not find any men to take your side except the four of us and a handful of my oldest men. That's the way the world is made, you know!" and he shrugged his shoulders expressively.

"It is a simple matter to escape from this house," suggested the biologist.

"Why not tour quietly around the globe and see our world entire before you decide upon your future plans?"

Winters shook his head wearily. "I thank you for your kindness, gentlemen. I would never find a place for myself in this age. I gave up my own age for the sake of an ideal. I am searching for the secret of happiness. I tried to find it here, but you do not know it any more than we did three thousand years ago. Therefore I shall say goodbye and—go on to some future period. In perhaps five thousand years I shall awaken in a time more to my liking."

"Can your body support another long period of emaciation?" drawled the biologist. "To judge from your appearance you have hardly aged at all during your last sleep—but . . . five thousand years!"

"I feel as if I were a little older than when I left my own times—perhaps a year or two. Thanks to your attention I am again in excellent health. Yes, I should be able to survive the ordeal once again."

"Man! Oh man!" groaned the red-headed Stalvyn. "I would give my right hand to take a place with you! But I have my duty to my own times."

"Is your hiding-place near here?" asked the Forester.

"Yes. But I prefer to tell no one where it is—not even you three. It is well hidden and you cannot help me."

"I can!" put in the biologist. "I studied your metabolism as you lay unconscious all this week and I have prepared a formula. From it I shall make a drink for you to take with you. When—or if—you wake from your long sleep you must swallow it. It will restore your vitality enormously in a few hours."

"Thank you," said Winters. "That might make all the difference between success and failure."

"How are you going to reach your hiding place? Suppose some youth sees you and follows—remembering old grudges as youth can?"

"I must leave here secretly just before dawn," said Winters thoughtfully. "I know in a general way where to go. By daylight I shall be close by and shall have hidden myself forever long before anyone in the village is awake."

"Well—let us hope so! When will you start?"

"Tomorrow morning!"

They parted for the night with many a last word of caution and advice. Winters lay down to sleep and it seemed only a few seconds before the Forester stood over him shaking him awake. He arose and made sure of such things as he was to take with him. Stalvyn and the biologist were on hand in the darkness (they did not dare show a light) and Winters took a light breakfast and said his goodbyes. The three friends watched his body show shadowy against the trees and vanish into the dark night.

Winters walked with great care along the hard-surfaced roadway for almost an hour. He was sure he had made no slightest sound. He felt he must be almost at the right spot and left the road for the woods where he waited impatiently for the graying east to brighten. He spent half an hour in the shrubbery beside the road before he could see clearly enough to proceed. Just before he turned away he glanced from his leafy hiding back along the stretch of highway. In the distance, to his horror, he observed two figures hurrying toward him!

With panting fear he slipped back into the woods and cruised over the ground looking for his one particular tree-trunk out of all those thousands. Seconds seemed like hours and his ears were strained back for some sign of his pursuers. Sweating, panting, heart pounding, he ran back and forwards in an agony of directionless movement.

Then he became frantic and hurried faster and faster until his foot caught over some piece of stone and sent him sprawling. He rose to his knees and stopped there, frozen, for he heard voices! They were still distant, but he dared not rise. His eyes fell upon the stone over which he had stumbled. It was flat and thick and rather square in outline. Some marks appeared on the top—badly worn by weather. He brushed aside a few dead leaves listlessly, hopelessly and before his startled eyes there leaped the following:

"Carstairs, a gardener lies here—faithful servant to the end—he was buried at this spot upon his own request."

Buried here at his own request—poor old Carstairs! Could it be? If this grave were directly above his underground chamber then there, only fifty feet to the south, must lie the entrance! He crawled with desperate hope over the soft ground and there, sure enough, was a familiar tree and a leaf-filled depression at its base! The voices were approaching now and he slithered desperately into the hole, pushing the drifted leaves before him with his feet. Then he gathered a great armful of leaves scraped from each side and sank out of sight, holding his screen in place with one hand. With the other hand he reached for some pieces of cut roots and commenced to weave a support for the leaves. He was half done when his heart stood still at the sound of voices close by. He could not make out the words and waited breathlessly second after second. Then he heard the voices again—receding!

Winter came and the frogs found their sleeping places beneath the mud of the little pond that lay where once was the lake. And with the next spring the great tree had commenced spreading a new mat of roots to choke forever the entrance to that lead-lined chamber where, in utter blackness, a still figure lay on a couch. The sleeper's last hazy thoughts had taken him back in his dreams to his own youth and the wax-white face wore a faint smile, as if Winters had at last found the secret of human happiness.

———————

Manning, like many science fiction writers, went through a spurt of production and stopped. There were fifteen stories between 1932 and 1935 and then nothing. Something similar happened in the cases of Meek and Tanner.

The trouble was, I'm sure, that science fiction in those days paid virtually nothing, and that nothing only after long delays. Naturally, then, people weren't going to spend time at it unless it was truly a labor of love.

Manning was one of those I particularly missed, and, in the days before I understood about the economics of writing, I kept wondering, querulously, why he wrote no more. And don't think "The Man Who Awoke" wasn't appreciated. It went through five installments in successive issues of the magazine, each one carrying Norman Winters further forward in time and into another strange society.

What I chiefly want to point out, though, is that in this first installment, Winters encountered a society that resented the consumption of coal and oil in reckless profusion by their ancestors, and that lived in a stringently cycled economy made necessary, in part, by ancestral waste.

In the 1970s, everyone is aware of, and achingly involved in, the energy crisis. Manning was aware of it forty years ago, and because he was, I was, and so, I'm sure, were many thoughtful young science fiction readers.

Escape?

It was a funny kind of escape literature that had the youngsters who read it concerned about the consequences of the waste of fossil fuels forty years before all the self-styled normal and sensible human beings felt it necessary to become interested.

I did not fail to notice, too, that Manning's view of the future involved not merely new inventions but new societies, new ways of thought, new modifications of language. I did not forget. When the time came for me to write my own time-travel novel, *The End of Eternity*, some twenty years later, I remembered.

———————

The year 1933 was further enlivened for me by the appearance of a sequel to "Tumithak of the Corridors." This was not unexpected. The story had been greeted with enthusiasm and a sequel had been demanded.

Tanner, however, did not write quickly, apparently, and it was a year and a half before the sequel—"Tumithak in Shawm"—appeared, in the June 1933 *Amazing Stories*.

TUMITHAK IN SHAWM

by Charles R. Tanner

FOREWORD

Five thousand years have passed since the shelks, leaving their home
planet of Venus, invaded the earth and drove mankind from the Surface
into the Pits and Corridors that were to be his home for twenty centuries.
When at last he did emerge, a new Heroic Age was born, and we of
today look back upon the leaders of that great rebellion as little less than
demi-gods.

And of all the distorted, exaggerated traditions, perhaps the one most
filled with magic and wonder is that of Tumithak of Loor. The first and
actually the greatest of a long list of Shelk-slayers, men have, from the
first, been tempted to attribute to him supernatural, or at least, superhuman powers, and to claim for him, even, the direct supervision of the
Deity.

However, by using the knowledge that we have gained through recent
archeological research, it is possible to roughly rebuild the life of that great
hero into a rational possible story. Shorn of its prophecies, its miracles
and its wonder, it becomes the tale of a young man who, inspired by
stories of the great deeds of the past, determined to risk his life to prove
that the shelks were vulnerable and could yet be conquered. The story
of how he proved that to his people, the writer has already presented to
the public—the story of the deeds that followed, he now presents in this
continuation of the adventures of "Tumithak of the Corridors."

CHAPTER I

Shawm

The long corridor stretched almost as far as eye could see its beautiful marble sides gleaming under the many varicolored lights which, carefully concealed in the walls, cast over the hall an effect of creamy mellowness. The pictures and geometrical figures that were carved in the soft white stone of which the walls were composed seemed to have been designed to co-operate with the lights to produce a single harmonious effect of surpassing beauty. Here and there, ornate doorways appeared, with great bronze doors on which scenes and figures had been cast that rivalled those of the walls for beauty. A few of the doorways lacked these doors, and these were covered instead with great drapes and tapestries, heavy with threads of gold and silver, and dyed with every color of the spectrum.

But the beauties of this splendid hallway were wasted, for in all its length not a human being appeared to appreciate them, and indeed, the thick dust that covered the floor and the many spider webs on the walls gave evidence of the months that must have elapsed since it had been deserted. Not for several years, in fact, had anyone entered this part of the corridor, not since one from far below had emerged from a well-like opening in one of the apartments and passed through this hall on his way to the Surface of the earth, far above. Even before his coming, the ponderous dwellers of this corridor had always feared this hall of the pit and avoided it, for it led to the pits of the "wild men," and in the sybaritic life of the Esthetts, the least suggestion of danger was a thing to shun. And so this hall, in spite of its exceptional beauty, was always utterly deserted.

But now, after so long a time, sounds were breaking into the silence of the corridor. Soft rustlings, guarded whispers and muttered ejaculations were coming from one of the apartments, and after a few moments, a savage face peered out of the doorway; then, seeing the hallway quite deserted, its owner stepped into view. He looked up and down the hallway as though fearing an attack by some unseen enemy, but, after looking searchingly through several of the apartments and convincing himself that the passage was really deserted, he sheathed the huge sword which he had held in his hand and returned to the door from which he had emerged.

The Interlopers of the Corridor

He was a huge, savage-looking fellow, this interloper, over six feet in height, with a great hairy chest and huge shoulders and with a chin that was covered with an immense growth of red beard. He wore a single garment, a rough burlap-like tunic that fell to his knees, into the cloth of which were sewn dozens of bits of metal and of bone, the latter stained in various colors, and worked into a crude pattern. His rusty-red hair was worn long and around his neck was a necklace made of dozens of human finger bones threaded on a thin strip of skin.

He stood for a moment longer before leaving the hallway and then, re-entering the apartment, he called softly.

He was answered by a low hoot and then another man joined him, a taller, younger man who was dressed quite differently. This newcomer wore a tunic made of cloth of the finest texture imaginable, sheer gauze that was dyed in the most delicate shades of nacreous pinks and greens and blues. It was not a new garment, but worn and torn and sewn, as though it were highly prized by the owner, who had determined to wear it until it fell apart from old age. It was caught up about the middle by a wide, many-pocketed belt with an enormous buckle, a belt from which dangled a sword and—strange anachronism—a pistol! Around the head of its wearer was a metal band not unlike a crown, a band such as was worn by the chiefs of those enemies of mankind, the shelks. Although this second man had not the other's tremendous strength and physical perfection, he was far above the average man in size and muscular power, and the poorest reader of character could tell at a glance that he was the more intellectual of the two. And one could feel, too, that together these two would make a combination capable of facing anything with a good chance of winning.

They stood silently staring up and down the passage for a while and then at last the second man spoke to his companion.

Tumithak of the Corridors

"What think you of the Halls of the Esthetts, Datto?" he asked. "Are they not as wonderful and as beautiful as I have described them?"

"They are truly wonderful, Tumithak," the other answered. "Though of what use these strange pictures can be, I cannot tell. Nor can I understand why the curtains of the doors should be so elaborate." He paused and then his eyes brightened as he went on: "But there is a splendid idea in those metal doors. We must carry some of them back to the lower corridors. With one of them in his doorway, a man might well defend himself against a hundred enemies."

"Our only enemies now are the shelks," reminded Tumithak. "And do not think that metal doors would keep those savage beasts out, Datto."

Datto grunted and continued his disparaging appraisal of the corridor.

It was obvious that he lacked the sense of beauty, that stirred, even though feebly, in Tumithak's breast.

"Which way leads to the Surface?" Datto asked, tersely, and when Tumithak pointed it out, he continued: "Let us call the others. No doubt they are waiting impatiently for the signal." Tumithak agreed, whereupon his companion re-entered the apartment and gave again the low call that he had given before. There was a pause, and then men began to emerge from the rear room, men who had been waiting eagerly at the bottom of the pit concealed in that room, and who now, at Datto's call hurried up the ladder to the level on which their leaders stood.

The first to emerge was a lean young man with a hawk-like face, a young man whose close-cropped hair and wide, pocketed belt marked him as a citizen of the same town as Tumithak. Nikadur, this young man's name was, and as Tumithak's boyhood companion, he had been the first to swear to follow the Shelk-slayer wherever he might lead. This young man was closely followed by another, and if Nikadur bore evidence of being a follower of Tumithak, this other as obviously showed a similar relationship to Datto. Thorpf was this one's name, and he was the nephew of Datto, and helped him to rule the halls of the city of Yakra far below the Surface.

And behind these two came many others: Tumlook, the father of Tumithak; Nennapuss, the chief of the city of Nonone, with his sons and nephews; and then man after man of lesser importance in the cities of the lower corridors, men who had never distinguished themselves, and whose only claim to fame lay in their undoubted loyalty to their chiefs. And here and there among them were members of a tribe upon whom the people of the lower corridors still looked askance: the savages of the dark corridors, their eyes wrapped in fold after fold of cloth, to keep out the brilliant light which was so painful to their sensitive optic nerves. These latter were slaves now, only recently subdued by the men of the lower corridors, but already the plenitude of food had made them willing servants.

Tumithak's Company of Warriors

In all, over two hundred men emerged from the pit and drew up in formation in the corridor, awaiting the word from Tumithak that was to start them on their raid on the Esthetts. They stood silent while Tumithak outlined to them briefly what he knew of the halls and corridors of this vicinity and then, at a softly spoken word, the entire party moved swiftly down the passage.

This raid on the Esthetts was the first of its kind that the people of the lower corridors had attempted. Since Tumithak had returned from the Surface to become their chief, two years before, he had spent most of his time in consolidating his government. There were some malcontents among the Yakrans and even among the Loorians and these had been made to feel the heavy hand of the new ruler, and, when the three cities were at last one in their allegiance, there were many little groups or "villages" in the side corridors that had to be brought under the Loorian's sway.

And when, at last, all the lower corridors unhesitatingly acknowledged Tumithak as their chief, the people had swept into the dark corridors, and in a short while the savages were conquered and enslaved, and all the pits below the Halls of the Esthetts bowed to the new leader.

It was then that Tumithak decided that the time was almost at hand to begin the raid on the halls of that race of ponderous artists that gave their worship and allegiance to the shelks. The Loorian was under no illusions as to what this meant. Although he failed to realize the exact relationship that existed between the Esthetts and the shelks, he knew that these obese creatures looked upon the shelks as their masters, and would not hesitate to call them to their aid if danger threatened. And Tumithak realized, therefore, that an attack on the Esthetts was equivalent to an attack on their masters.

The shelks had "domesticated" the Esthetts and used them as we do cattle, lulling their suspicions with hypocritical lies and flattery and breeding them for bovine stupidity and trustfulness.

A Raid on the Domesticated Esthetts

Tumithak had postponed this raid, therefore, until the entire lower corridors were united, but once that was accomplished, he saw no reason for hesitating longer. He called for two classes of volunteers, those who were brave enough to aid in an attack on these creatures of the shelks, and those who would follow wherever led, even to the Surface. Tumithak knew that a volunteer army was the only type that he could take with him, and so when, of the thousands of people in the lower corridors, only some two hundred warriors responded, he perforce satisfied himself with this group, and started on his way. Fortunately, it seemed to him, the two classes of volunteers were identical, almost to a man.

And now this dauntless two hundred were swarming through the Halls of the Esthetts, their swords bared and their war-cries trembling on their lips, waiting for the moment when Tumithak should give the word to attack. That leader, however, saw no cause for hurry, he led them on and on through the corridor, his chief desire being to get as close to the center of the town as he could before he was discovered. And then at last, satisfying himself that he was not far from the Great Square of the Esthetts, he gave the word, and, in a trice, pandemonium broke loose in the Halls of the Esthetts.

The Raid Was a Massacre

There is little need to describe the ensuing battle. After all, it was not a battle but a massacre and, were it not for the absolute necessity of it, Tumithak would have dispensed with fighting the Esthetts at all. But he remembered Lathrumidor, the artist who had attempted to betray him on his way to the Surface before, and so, realizing the treacherous nature of the huge Esthetts, he determined that they must die.

And die they did, to the last one; and when the band of victors assembled at the upper end of the Esthetts' corridor some forty hours later, it was a motley crew indeed. Many wore the delicate gauzes of the Esthetts, others still dressed in the rough tunic of their native halls. Some carried the swords they had brought with them, some carried other weapons, swords and spears that the Esthetts had fashioned, not indeed for weapons, but merely for their artistic beauty. And they were weapons now, as were many other of the creations of the artists. One man even held in his hand a delicate statuette of bronze, its end clotted with blood and hair where he had struck down some Esthett with it.

And to these men Tumithak spoke, and again told them of the necessity of immediately going on. The shelks often visited the Esthetts, he said. No one could tell at what moment they might come again. And rather than have the shelks surprise the pit-men, it were well if the pit-men at once moved to the Surface to surprise the shelks! "And so," he finished, "all who would follow me, be ready after the very next sleep, for then I intend to lead my party out to the attack." He dismissed the warriors and retired, himself, to try to secure a much needed rest.

After the sleep, Tumithak was pleasantly surprised to find that not more than ten men desired to remain in the Halls of the Esthetts. These he placed under the authority of Thurranen, a son of Nennapuss; and then, with nearly two hundred men following him, he set out for the Surface and—the shelks!

The Campaign Against the Shelks

They came at last to that narrow hallway of jet black stone that told Tumithak that they were perilously near to the Surface. He called his chiefs together and held a council of war. It was a momentous council, for this was the first time, probably, in nineteen hundred years or more, that men had deliberately planned a campaign against the shelks. The most important thing that the pit-men lacked, the council decided, was knowledge of the Surface and of the ways of the shelks. This lack of knowledge, they felt, must be overcome at once, or any chance of victory would be lost at the very start. It would undoubtedly be necessary to send scouts up to the Surface to find out what the conditions were up there.

At this suggestion (which had been offered by Nennapuss), Datto the Yakran laughed loud and scornfully. In two thousand years, he said, only a single man had been found brave enough to face the dangers of the Surface. And now Nennapuss talked of sending out scouts, as though they were about to raid another passage of the dark corridors! Would Nenna-puss suggest, perhaps, to whom he intended to offer this position of scout?

Nennapuss was about to reply with some heat, when Tumithak inter-rupted him.

"Datto," stated the Loorian, "when the people of one corridor invade the halls of another, the position of scout or spy is a dangerous one yet not overly important or honorable. But in this war of ours, the scout is all important, for not only our lives but the very future of man depends on what information he can bring up. Now, but one of all this body has ever looked upon the Surface, and if that one feels that he should surely lead the scouts that must go ahead of this army, can any one deny him the right?"

The lesser chiefs were astounded.

"But we need you to lead the army, Tumithak!" they protested. "Never before has a chief taken such chances of leaving his men leaderless. Why, if you should die, the whole of the Great Rebellion would collapse!"

Tumithak smiled.

"Call the army together then," he suggested, "and ask for volunteers to go on to the Surface, *ahead of me!*" The chiefs were silent. Even they, themselves, would not be willing to face the Surface alone, though they would have cheerfully died *following* Tumithak.

The Leader of the Scouts

The Shelk-slayer waited a moment and then spoke: "You see? It is clear that I must lead the scouts. And for the same reason it must be the chiefs, the leaders, that make up this party of scouts. It is from you my council that I must call for volunteers."

Instantly a dozen swords were thrust out, hilt first, toward Tumithak. Every member of the council willingly agreed to follow the Shelk-slayer, where not one had been willing to precede him. Tumithak hesitated and then picked out three men. Nikadur he chose, his boyhood companion, for he felt he knew this Loorian so well, that he could anticipate his reaction to any event. Then, too, Nikadur was an accomplished archer, and possessed the only weapon known to the pit-men that could slay at a distance. Datto he chose, and this for the Yakran's hard, practical sense and unfailing courage, as well as for his immense, untiring strength. And lastly he chose Thorpf, the nephew of Datto, for the same reasons that he chose the Yakran chief.

So, a few hours later, these four were moving up the narrow, black-walled corridor, swords in hand and packs on their backs; while behind them, the army, in charge of Tumlook and Nennapuss, waited anxiously for their return.

The Approach to the Surface

They came to the narrow flight of stairs, ascended it, and saw in the distance the opening that was the entrance to the Surface. But to Tumithak's surprise, no reddish light appeared, as it had on his previous visit. In fact no light at all shone down into the hall from the Surface! Tumithak was puzzled. He motioned the other three to wait there, and then crept softly to the opening that was the goal of the long trek through the corridors. Cautiously, the slayer of the shelk raised his eyes above the level of the pit and looked about him. It was true, as he had thought, all the Surface was in darkness! He felt a pang of fear. Had the shelks discovered the approach of his men and somehow plunged the Surface into darkness, he wondered. Were they even now in hiding, waiting for the men of the lower corridors to emerge, that they might slaughter them?

Involuntarily, Tumithak drew back into the corridor and there he stood, lashing his failing courage. Once again, as in the days when he had come this way alone, his cold, fanatic reasoning overcame his emotions, as he remembered that all the legends that he had ever heard of the shelks told of their hatred of the dark. Indeed, his wonderbook, that manuscript that he had found when a boy, had told him that the shelks had originally come from a land where there was never darkness and that story—combined with the vague legends of his tribe which said that no shelk would ever, from choice, do battle in the dark—convinced him that the darkness could not be of the shelk's contriving.

So, once again he returned to the pit, and, greatly daring, leapt out of it and stood upon the Surface!

The Great Darkness and the Stars

After a short while, it seemed as if his eyes began to adapt themselves to the darkness, and faintly he could see certain forms in the distance. The trees, those pillars whose tops were covered with strange green billows, he could see as dense black blobs against a background only slightly less dark. A few hundred feet away and directly in front of him, rose the homes of the shelks, obelisk-like towers, leaning at crazy angles, silhouetted against the sky. And, looking up into the sky, Tumithak was amazed to see that that ceiling, as he thought it, was covered with hundreds, yes, thousands of tiny pin-points of brilliance, twinkling and glittering unceasingly, yet giving off so little light that the dense darkness could hardly be said to be diminished at all by them.

For some time the Loorian stood there and then, as nothing happened to disturb the stillness and calm of the night, he returned to the pit and called to his friends. In a few minutes Datto emerged from the pit, closely followed by Thorpf and Nikadur. They looked around them, obviously worried by the darkness, but afraid to ask questions, for fear that the sound of their voices might betray them. So they stood, awaiting an order from Tumithak, until in sudden decision, the Shelk-slayer fell on his face and began to crawl slowly in the direction of the towers of the shelks, motioning them, as he did so, to do likewise.

The trip to the towers took some time, for the slightest whisper of wind in the trees would frighten the pit-men and cause them to lie motionless for many minutes at a time, but at last they arose and stood in the shadow of one of the towers. They were panting, not so much with the exertion of wallowing through the grass, as with the realization of the frightful danger they were facing, but after many minutes of tense listening, they grew bold enough to look around and take an interest in their surroundings. It was a strange building in whose shadow they found themselves, composed of some strong metal that was strange to the pit-men; a four-sided building that rose nearly a hundred feet high and was not more than fifteen feet square at the base. And it leaned at an angle of nearly twenty-five degrees in the direction from which the men had come. Towering over them, it seemed that at any moment it must fall and crush them, yet when they looked at its firm strong base, they realized that it might stand thus for centuries.

Having come this far, the waning courage of the men of the pit forbade their penetrating further into the town of the shelks, and so, undecided, they stood for many minutes, wondering what to do next. And though they stood in utter silence for long, in all that time they heard no sound of shelk, nor did they see a moving form.

But at last, Nikadur spoke softly in Tumithak's ear.

"Something is happening to the wall of the Surface on our right, Tumithak," he breathed. "It seems to be giving off a faint light."

Light on the Surface

Tumithak started. It was true! A faint, uneven light dimly shone in the sky at his right. Even as he gazed at it, he realized that the glow was penetrating all over the Surface. He could distinguish the faces of his comrades and make out details on the ground! And Datto and Thorpf were commenting softly on the amazing wonder of the trees, which were now sufficiently visible to be distinguished separately.

Tumithak addressed his comrades: "The light is returning, or another is being prepared. It is strange, for it is in the opposite side of the Surface from the light which I saw when I came here before."

"Soon it will be light enough for the shelks to be about," whispered Datto. "Had we better retire to the pit, Tumithak?"

The Loorian was about to reply in the affirmative when Thorpf gave a gasp and, trembling violently, pointed to a spot under the trees beyond the pit. There, faint forms were visible, moving toward the towers, and to them from the distance came the sound of clacking voices! A group of shelks were moving toward them!

In a moment, the terrible fear that was almost instinctive in man had seized the four. Panic-stricken, they looked about them for some means of flight. To return to the pit was impossible—already the group of spider-like creatures had passed it. To attempt to flee to the trees on either side was equally impossible—they could not fail to be seen almost immediately. But a single direction offered possible protection, and the hair of all four rose at the thought of taking that direction. Yet if they did not do so, and at once, discovery would be inevitable in another minute, so they fled around the side of the tower, further into the shelk-city, intent only on avoiding the present evil, and leaving the future to take care of itself. Even as they did so, rustling noises and here and there a clacking voice, told them that the city was beginning to awake. Utterly beside themselves with fear, they hugged the walls of the tower—and then, suddenly there was a door before them, an old, badly dilapidated wooden door, and Tumithak had pushed it open and was hustling them into the interior of the tower.

Had there been an enemy within, he might have easily slain them as they entered, for the transition from the rapidly increasing light without to the dismal interior gloom made the room seem dark as Erebus. But before long, their eyes adjusted themselves and soon they could distinguish faintly the details of the tower. And great was their relief as they realized that this could hardly be one of the inhabited homes of their enemies.

The Web of Ropes in the Tower

The floor was uncovered, just bare earth, queer, thickly packed dust that covered all the floor of the Surface; and there was no furniture of any description visible, unless a pile of straw in one corner might pass as a bed of sorts. But here and there about the room hung ancient frayed ropes, and looking aloft, Tumithak could notice dimly that these ropes led up to where, about twenty feet above, a great mass of twisted cables, ropes and cords crossed and recrossed the entire interior of the tower. It was a veritable nest of ropes, a *web*, he thought, as the similarity of the shelks to spiders again came to him. And, indeed, he was not far from wrong, for the shelks used the towers only as sleeping quarters and, at night, retired to the upper parts of them, where, in a bed made of hundreds of cables and ropes hanging criss-crossed from the sides, they slumbered the dark hours away. Fortunately, this tower in which Tumithak and his companions found themselves was an old one, no longer considered fit for occupancy by the builders, and the use to which they now put it, we shall soon see.

The frightened pit-men stood for several minutes in the narrow confines of the tower, and their hearts were just beginning to again take up their normal beat when once more there came the ominous clacking voice of a shelk, this time almost without the door. It grew louder and the men knew suddenly, without a doubt, that the shelks were approaching this tower! They glanced wildly about them for a place of concealment, but even as they looked they knew there could be but one, and an attempt to hide in the maze of ropes and cables above the small room on the ground seemed tantamount to voluntary surrender. Nevertheless, no other alternative was possible, so in a moment, they were scrambling up the ropes and losing themselves in the thick maze of twisted cords and cables above. The criss-crossed ropes were not numerous near the ground, but some ten feet beyond where they began, they were so thickly placed that it would have been impossible to detect anyone hiding in them, from below. So here the adventurers halted their climb, and reclining in the thick web, lay listening to the sounds that were now immediately without the door. Indeed, by parting the ropes that concealed him, Tumithak found that he had an almost unhindered view of the floor beneath. That they had not concealed themselves a moment too soon was evidenced by the fact that hardly were they comfortably fixed among the ropes when the door was opened and a strange party came into view.

CHAPTER II

The Hounds of Hun-Pna

A shelk was the first to enter and Tumithak felt the ropes, on which he and his companions lay, shake as the other pit-men trembled with fear at this, their first sight of one of the savage beasts from Venus. The creature was a fair representative of its kind; about four feet high, and ten long spider-like limbs and a head that, save for the fact that it was hairless and noseless, might have been that of a man. Held high in two of its limbs, as a man might hold a twig between thumb and forefinger, this shelk held a rod of metal, the tip of which glowed with a brilliant light. On its back was a queer-looking box, from which a hose emerged that was coiled up and ended in a long rod that was set into a sort of scabbard fastened on the box.

Following him came another, that might have been his twin, and bringing up the rear of this strange party were *two men!* And the strangeness of these men made the party above gasp with astonishment. The men were tall, taller even than Tumithak; in fact, the larger of the two must have been nearly seven feet in height. It was not their height though which astonished Tumithak and his friends; it was their incredible thinness and the savage look on their faces. Their legs and arms were long and stringy; their thighs, indeed, being little bigger around than Tumithak's arm. Their waists, too, were surprisingly narrow, their necks were lean; but their chests were enormous, as were their hands. Not that all these members were out of proportion, no, there was something about them that made one feel that for certain purposes, these men might be better proportioned than even Datto, that colossus of the corridors. But, in comparing the two, it would be evident that these men were of another race, just as it had been clear that the Esthetts were. If one should compare a picture of those ancient dogs of the Golden Age which were called greyhounds with our dogs of today, one would be able to understand the difference between the men of the corridors and these creatures of the shelks.

Tlot and Trak

These men were clad only in a single garment, a cloth wrapped around their middle and dropping to their knees; but over this cloth a belt was strapped, and from this belt dangled a sword. In their hands, each held a vicious-looking whip made from the hide of some animal; and, as if all this were not enough to distinguish them, their hair and their luxurious beards were *black!* The pit-men, who had never seen hair of any other color than their own fiery red (save the yellow of the Esthetts), would not have been more surprised if their hair had been green.

These men followed the shelks into the room and at once cast themselves down on the beds of straw. The shelks muttered something to them in a low clacking whisper, and then, extinguishing their lights, they turned and left the tower. The men remained, lying on the straw in a manner that clearly indicated fatigue. After a moment, one of them spoke languidly.

"I have seen real hunts in Kaymak, Tlot," he said, and there was a decided sneer in his voice. "I have known the time when three and even four of the wild ones would be bagged before night fell. You should see some of those hunts in the great city, Tlot."

The man called Tlot grunted.

"When you see a hunt in Shawm, Trak, you know that you are really flushing a wild one. Those so called wild ones that you hunt in Kaymak are domesticated, and bred for the purpose, and you know it."

Trak looked crestfallen and turning to his bed, produced a small jug from within the straw. He poured some oil from it into his hand and began to oil his whip. Presently he made bold to speak again.

"Not for nothing is Hun-Pna called the cautious one," he remarked. "Never have I seen a hunter proceed with such caution. One might almost think that he expected one of the wild ones to turn and kill us. We might have brought down that one we pursued and reached Shawm before dark last night, had it not been that he feared to let us out."

Tlot sat up in his straw, and looked across at his companion. It was obvious that he shared the other's opinion of the shelk that was their lord and master.

"When you have belonged to Hun-Pna as long as I have," he stated, "you will be more used to his ways." He rummaged in the straw, pulled out another larger jug, and after drinking from it noisily, went on: "I have seen him give up a chase and call us off after hours of pursuit, because the wild one showed fight when cornered!"

"Why, they always show fight when cornered, don't they?" asked Trak, who was evidently the younger man and deferred to the other's knowledge.

"Only about one in five really fights," answered the older one. "The others struggle weakly, but make no defense worth worrying about. They have sense enough to know that, if they showed signs of defeating us, the shelks would immediately finish them."

The speakers were silent again, for a while, and above them, four silent watchers wondered in perplexity over what they had heard. Presently the older man spoke again: "But I have seen quite pretty vicious battles put up by some of the wild ones. The women of the Tains are notorious for their fury. I am reminded of a hunt which I had about two years ago. That was the hardest battle I ever did have. It was a woman, too. But *she* didn't get away, like this one did, yesterday. Her scalp is decorating Hun-Pna's tower, right now."

Tlot looked interested.

"Tell me about it," he suggested.

A Great Hunt

"Well," began the other, and there was a certain boastfulness about his manner that infuriated the pit-men who were listening from above, "you see, Hun-Pna was having a great feast to celebrate the Conjunction, and half the shelks in Shawm were invited. Nearly a hundred shelks were there, even old Hakh-Klotta himself; and, of course, one of the main features of the feast was to be the sacrifice to the mother planet. They don't sacrifice Esthetts at the Conjunction Ceremonies as I suppose you know, and so we were taken out to see if we could get some wild ones alive.

"Well we decided to look for Tains; Hun-Pna always hunts Tains because their corridors are so near the Surface. To go down into some of the deeper corridors, would be too much like risking his head, to suit the cautious one. He just drove us into the entrance to the pit and sat down to wait until we flushed some of the wild ones and chased them out to him.

"So I, with two other Mogs, started down into the corridors of the Tains. I had a sword, of course, and my whip and so had each of the others, for that is plenty of protection against a Tain. They're smart, the Tains are; but they're afraid of their own shadows.

"Well, it wasn't long before one of the other Mogs had spied a Tain and soon had him running to the Surface, and just as they disappeared up the corridor, I ran across a woman with a baby in her arms. Now, that was some find, as you'll agree; the shelks are always pleased to have you capture a live cub. So I bore down on her, expecting to find her an easy prey, but she turned on me like a wolf. She had a club in her hand, and before I could raise my whip, she had struck me a dizzying blow on the neck and was off in a flash, running toward the Surface. She must have been beside herself with fright or she would never have taken that route, for there wasn't a side passage or a branching corridor, all the way to the Surface. I was stunned by her blow, and stood for a moment, gathering my wits, before I took after her.

"I followed her, without hurrying greatly, to the entrance. I expected the shelks would seize her the minute she appeared, but unfortunately they were busy with the male Tain that the other Mog had flushed; and when I reached the open, I saw, to my dismay, that she had cleared the crowd and was running like mad into the forest. I shouted to Hun-Pna for help, and dashed in pursuit, never once glancing back to see if they were following. Naturally, I supposed they were.

"Well, the Tain had quite a start on me, and you know how hilly and stony it is in the neighborhood of the Tain's pit. So it was that even my legs refused to carry me fast enough to catch up with her until she began to get winded. But at last she threw herself down by a rock on the hillside and faced me, snarling viciously. I approached her with care, for I still remembered that I must catch her alive, if possible. I turned to see how far behind the shelks were, and to my surprise, I found they were nowhere in sight! For a moment, I began to fear that I must give up my quarry, for none of us are used to fighting without a shelk at our back, you know, but at last I made a bold decision. I would attack and conquer this Tain single-handed. And so I approached her as diplomatically as possible.

The Single-Handed Attempt to Capture the Tain and Her Baby

"She stood there panting with fatigue and still clinging to her baby and as I approached her she began to swing her club about her in circles.

" 'Give up, you fool,' I said, 'I'm not going to kill you. I want to take you alive.'

" 'Alive!' she sneered. 'For what purpose? Mate or meat?'

"I didn't answer. What was the use? I wouldn't mate with one of those wild ones, if I died for not doing it, and if I told her I wanted her for the sacrifice, that wouldn't help any. So I lashed out with my whip, and the battle was on.

"And it was a battle, too! As we struggled there, minute after minute, I took more than one blow from that infernal club of hers, while she was a mass of blood from where my whip had cut her skin. At last an idea came to me, and I began to direct the blows of my whip not at her but at her child! After that, it seemed that my victory was going to be an easy one. She was so taken up with protecting her child that she had not time to devote to hurting me. Presently she began to sob, and to curse me. Said I was a demon, and that I didn't deserve the name of man. You know what I mean, you've heard the wild ones give the same kind of talk. Well, that sort of stuff has never bothered me. I was born a Mog, and a Mog I'll die. But I knew, when she began that, that she had almost reached the breaking point, and I began to have new hopes of bringing in the mother and the baby, both of them alive.

The Death of the Baby and Its Mother

"But just as I expected her to cower down and give in, she suddenly shouted 'No!'—and raising the child over her head, she dashed it to the ground and brained it with a club. Then she rushed at me in a fury, clawing, biting and spitting, until in sheer self-defense, I was forced to use the sword on her.

"I returned with nothing to show for my hunt but the scalp of the woman, but Hun-Pna hung it up among his trophies and it's there yet."

The speaker was silent at last, and, pulling some straw over him, apparently prepared himself for a nap. The other man, after a moment, evidently decided to follow his example, but his preparations were rudely interrupted by the decision that had been reached by the pit-men in the ropes above.

While this gruesome tale was being related, the watchers had listened in horror. That men could exist, so low and base as to hunt their own kind for the pleasure of the shelks, had never entered their heads. They had been prepared for the fact of the existence of the Esthetts by the story that Tumithak had told them, but here was a race of shelk-worshippers even lower in the scale of humanity than were the Esthetts!

As the tale progressed, the horror of these creatures grew in the minds of Tumithak and his companions, and as Tlot finished his story, the same thought showed clearly in the eyes of each of them. These creatures had surely lived far too long, they felt. Black, unreasoning anger choked the pit-men, and without a word, with only a questioning look from Datto and Thorpf and an affirmative nod from Tumithak, the four dropped suddenly to the ground in front of the astonished Mogs, intent on bringing an end to their foul existence.

There is no doubt but that the continued victories that had attended the men in the corridors had made them over-confident. The savages of the dark corridors had capitulated to the force of their arms, the Esthetts had succumbed without a struggle, and in the minds of the four was the idea that this would not be so much a battle as an execution. With the advantage of four to two and the added fact that the attack was a surprise they expected to dispatch the Mogs on the instant. But once on the ground, it took but a matter of seconds for them to realize their error. Almost before they knew it, the Mogs were standing back to back; swords in hand, were defending themselves so valiantly that the outcome of the battle seemed for a moment in doubt. And as they fought, the Mogs shouted— shouted loudly for their masters to come and help them!

The Folly of the Attack on the Mogs

Tumithak realized the folly of their attack almost as soon as it was accomplished, yet even in the realization, he could not help but feel that somehow they were justified. And, if they could but slay the Mogs, their lives would not be sacrificed in vain.

One of the tall, black-haired creatures was down now, and Thorpf pounced upon him and finished him with a vicious thrust at his throat; but in the brief moment that the attention of the other two was diverted by this, the other Mog turned and sped like a deer past Datto and out the door, still bellowing for the shelks.

Datto roared with anger and would have sped after him, but Tumithak laid a restraining hand on his shoulder.

"Quick, Datto, we must hide again!" he whispered excitedly. "Up the ropes! Quickly!"

Without an instant's hesitation, Nikadur leaped for the ropes and began to climb, and the other three immediately followed his example. Without, the clickings and clatterings of shelk-talk were rising higher and the Loorians were hardly well-concealed by the strands of cables when the Mog rushed into the room, followed closely by a group of shelks. The creatures were all armed, each carrying the box and hose such as the shelk had worn, which had entered before. Only now the long, queer nozzle had been removed from the scabbard and was carried in two of the limbs.

The shelks looked about them in amazement for a moment, and then one of them pointed aloft. The pit-men had not ceased their climbing, apparently the web of ropes continued to the top of the tower, and so they climbed on, intent only on getting as far as possible from the savage masters of the Surface. But escape was utterly impossible, they felt, and what tiny grains of hope remained to them was lost when two of the shelks sheathed their weapons and with incredible agility began to follow them up the ropes.

Above, the four desperate pit-men could see little to do but to continue their hopeless climbing and to pray for some miraculous means of escape. Nikadur continued to be in the lead, closely followed by the agile Tumithak; but the great bulks of Datto and his huge nephew were handicaps to them and they were several feet below the Loorians.

The mazy web of ropes and cables became thicker and thicker as the men ascended, until it was impossible to see the ground; but the sounds from below left no doubt that the shelks were rapidly drawing nearer. Suddenly there was a cry from below Tumithak—a human cry, a cry of agony. And then there was a wild thrashing, a sound of bodies tumbling through the ropes and a crash! Tumithak looked back, but the thick tangle of ropes obscured his view, until they suddenly parted and Datto's fierce face appeared, its deadly pallor contrasting oddly with the red of his beard and hair.

Thorpf and the Shelks

"Thorpf!" he cried, in agonized tones. "They've got him, Tumithak, my nephew, Thorpf! It was he who fell. They leaped upon him and tried to tear at his neck with their infernal fangs! He struck back, but he lost his hold and fell. But he took them with him! He took them with him! You are not the only Shelk-slayer now, O Lord of Loor!"

The huge Yakran was weeping as he climbed, for his nephew had meant much to him and would have been his successor as Lord of Yakra. Tumithak, too, felt an ache in his heart at the realization that Thorpf was gone, but he made no answer to Datto, reserving all of his remaining breath for the climb. And then, Nikadur, who had been lost to sight in the web above, gave a cry and momentarily, Tumithak's heart sank in increased despair. Was he to lose this friend, too? Had the shelks somehow attacked them from above? He hastened his climbing, wondering if he would reach his friend in time to aid him.

He parted the ropes above him, climbed higher, and saw a dim light filtering down through the web. A moment later and Nikadur's form came into view, dimly against this new light. The light shone from one of the walls, and as Tumithak drew himself up beside his friend he saw the reason for his cry.

The light came from a small circular window set in the very top of the tower, and Nikadur had cried out involuntarily as he had looked out and beheld his first view of the Surface in the full light of day. As Tumithak raised his eyes to the level of the window's ledge, it was all that he could do to keep from crying out himself.

The little window looked down upon the shelk-city, and from its ledge a cluster of strong ropes hung. The other end of each rope was fastened to the window of another tower; apparently the shelks used these ropes to go from tower to tower without returning to the ground. Below, Tumithak could see the bases of the other towers, and an ever-increasing crowd of shelks, with here and there a lean, hairy-faced Mog.

It was not the crowd below, nor the connecting cables, not even the vast view from the window that had caused Nikadur to cry out in surprise, however. It was his first view of the sun! Even in his desperate straits, that object had been the thing that most impressed him as he looked for the first time on the fully lighted Surface of the earth. And indeed, Tumithak, who had seen the sun before, was hardly less surprised. For the sun he had seen before had been a dully glowing ball of red, setting in the west, while this great orb, dazzling in its intense, white brilliance, hung in the exact opposite side of the heavens. For a moment, he was puzzled, but he quickly thrust his amazement to the back of his mind, and strove to concentrate on some means of escape.

The metal walls that fell away from the window's ledge were as smooth as the blown glassy walls of his own home corridor—there was no chance of escape there. Indeed, could he have clambered down the side of the tower, it would have availed nothing, for the crowd of shelks below had by now grown to such proportions as to cover the ground, and Tumithak could see them pointing and gesticulating, exactly as a crowd of humans would do under similar circumstances.

Datto Joins the Other Two

Datto suddenly drew himself up between the two Loorians, leaning his huge form upon the ledge of the window. His eyes were still filled with the tears that had sprung into them at the death of Thorpf, but he spoke nothing now of his grief. His mind, too, was filled with the problem of escape.

"They are coming, Tumithak," he said. "Other shelks are coming up through the ropes. What shall we do now? Turn and fight them?"

The Loorian's heart felt a glow as he realized Datto's willingness to fight the shelks. This was one man, at least, who had learned the lesson that Tumithak had preached so long and earnestly to the pit-men. He shook his head at Datto's proposal, however, and continued to look out of the window. There did seem one course of escape left, but so small was it that Tumithak was loath to suggest it. At last, however, he heard sounds not far beneath him, and knowing that the pursuing shelks would soon reach the window, he determined to put his desperate plan into execution.

The far ends of the cables that hung from the window ledge, extended to towers that were, most of them, inhabited. Tumithak could see the faces of shelks at the windows, and in one, even, the hairy face of a Mog was visible. But two of the windows were empty and toward the nearer of these, Tumithak pointed.

"It is our only chance," he said, and tried to conceal the despair in his voice. "It is a slim chance, but perhaps we can get across and escape some way out of that other tower."

Nikadur, who held the best position at the window, seized upon the idea at once and, climbing into the window's opening, swung out upon the cable. Hand over hand he passed out on the rope, and Tumithak motioned to Datto to follow him. The big Yakran shook his head.

"This is no time for heroics, Lord of Loor," he said. "The lower corridors need you far more than me. The chances are slim enough for escape now, without increasing them. Go you, and I will follow and guard from the rear."

This arrangement was hardly to Tumithak's liking and for a moment, he felt inclined to argue, but the increasing danger made him realize that time was precious and so he took his place at the window and followed Nikadur hand over hand across the cable.

The Escape from the Tower—Datto's Sacrifice

Tumithak gave one look down as he swung ape-like along the rope but the vertigo that immediately resulted caused him to look hastily upward again. He found himself not far behind Nikadur and hesitated in his crawling pace long enough to look back to see if Datto was following him. The sight he saw in the brief glimpse he had was something that remained in his memories for years.

The shelks had arrived at the window's opening and Datto had been forced to turn and face them. As Tumithak looked, he saw the huge chief of Yakra, with one shelk clawing desperately at him from behind, pick up another and hurl him, clattering and squeaking from the window. Then he drew his sword and called to Tumithak.

"They have me, Tumithak," he cried, "I can't hold them off. There are many——" he hesitated and then, as if an idea had suddenly occurred to him: "Hold fast the rope, Tumithak!"

The Loorian chief gazed in puzzled despair as Datto swung his sword. Again the Yakran cried: "Hold fast the rope!" and then the blade struck down the cable, half severing it. Fearful, at a loss to understand Datto's reason for his actions, Tumithak gripped the cable even tighter, and then the sword struck again, cleanly cutting the cable from its fastening at the window.

Tumithak caught a single glimpse of Datto being jerked back into the tower, even as he struck; and then the Loorians were falling away from the tower. Nothing but death was in Tumithak's mind, yet some inward instinct made him obey Datto's last command and cling like grim death to the rope. He saw the ground approaching with terrible swiftness, saw that they were swinging toward the tower to which the other end of the cable was fastened; and then there was a terrific jolt, and beyond, he heard Nikadur scream fearfully. The rope had swung past the leaning tower, its end, weighted with the Loorians, acting as a huge pendulum and then the ground, which had approached with sickening closeness, was dropping away again!

Dimly conscious that they had somehow escaped death, the two had hardly realized it when Tumithak's precarious grip on the rope began to slip. He grabbed at the nearest object, which happened to be Nikadur's leg; heard his companion scream again, and then they were turning over and over in the air, to land, a second later, in the branches of a huge tree that stood beyond the group of towers.

Their Landing

Dazed and bruised though they were by the fall, the Loorians, nevertheless, hesitated not a moment in taking advantage of the opportunity for escape that had come to them. Instantly they were tumbling through the leafy branches, and although Tumithak wondered vaguely at the strange object in which he found himself, the fact that it was not inimical was sufficient to enable him to ignore it and to focus his attention on the business of fleeing from his enemies.

That the shelks had been amazed by the quick succession of events was obvious from the fact that they did not at once attempt pursuit. The Loorians were out of the tree, in fact, before the cries and clatters from the towers told them that the shelks had organized a pursuit. They looked about them, vainly hoping to spy their own pit, but it was far to the right, and hidden by the trees; so, calling to Nikadur to follow him, Tumithak plunged deeper into the forest, away from Shawm.

Breathless, bruised, with the brave thoughts of conquest utterly driven from their minds, like rabbits through the brush the two pit-men fled, while behind them, ever louder, sounded the tumult of the pursuit.

CHAPTER III

Tholura the Tain

It is hard for a writer of the present age to attempt to reproduce the thoughts that passed through the heads of the Loorians as they fled in hopeless panic through the woods. Three thousand years separate those heroes from the world of today, years of almost continued change and progress, and, in the safe, almost uneventful life that we lead, there is little to enable us to reproduce their overwhelming emotions. We can, of course, easily understand that fear, black, unreasoning fear, such as comes to us sometimes in nightmares, was probably uppermost in their minds. But there must have been other sensations, other feelings, too.

What, for instance, did they think of the trees that rose around them in such abundance? Strange forms of life, indeed, these must have been to those creatures of the underworld, in whose lives there had never been so much as a legend of vegetation. What did they think of the frightened cries of the birds, or of the sudden appearance, perhaps, of a rabbit, startled by their crashing flight? What would their reaction be to the sight of a brook or a thicket of brambles that clutched and tore at their clothes? Or to the great round sun that shone through the trees, glowing ever brighter and rising ever higher over their heads? We can well imagine that all these made but little impression on the Loorians in their flight, but that they had some effect was undeniable. And rising over all the tumbled thoughts of their minds were the sounds of the pursuing shelks, ever growing closer.

It was fortunate, indeed, for the Loorians that the shelks were too amazed to follow them quickly. By the time that the party of pursuit was organized the pit-men were lost in the deeply-wooded section just beyond the edge of the town and it was fully five minutes before the Mogs, which the shelks called out, had picked up their trail and started after them. By this time Tumithak and his companion had climbed the stony, gradually rising hillside that rose in front of them and were descending down the other side.

They fled in the last stages of terror, fled without thinking, the one idea in their minds was to put as much distance as possible between themselves and the town of their enemies. The trees thinned out on this side of the hill, but as they descended, it became increasingly difficult to make any progress, due to the tall grasses and bushes which grew here. Had they known the contour of the country, they would have realized that they were now in the valley of a broad shallow river that flowed not far from Shawm. This river was normally but a few hundred feet wide and several feet deep, but the spring rains had come and for a few days it would be a tumbling, turgid torrent that cut a deep curve through the valley on its way to the sea.

Toward this stream the Loorians were speeding, and before long, they dashed into the thick growth of willows and alders that grew along its banks, hoping against hope that the dense vegetation would conceal them from their pursuers.

The Fugitives Are Seen

As they entered the brush, Tumithak was bold enough to cast a hurried glance behind him. Far up the hill, he could see the pursuing party already rising over the top and rushing down into the valley. There were at least a dozen shelks, the majority of which carried the strange boxes with the hoses attached, and in the forepart of the band, he saw a group of the hairy-faced hunting men, the Mogs.

Even as he looked, one of the Mogs spied him, and with a hoarse bellow, called the attention of the others to the quarry.

Despair was in Tumithak's heart, for never, since he had begun his adventuring, had the Loorian been in such a dangerous predicament as this. And had you told him that the situation could be worse, he would not have believed it. Yet even as he turned and plunged into the deep thicket of willows, he heard Nikadur, ahead of him, give a cry of startled dismay! He pushed hurriedly forward, wondering what new disaster had befallen, and saw that his companion had stopped his flight. Stopped because he had come to the brink of the river and could go no farther!

To the despairing men of the corridors, this was the last straw. The two saw no escape at all, for the river swung in a curve around the point on which they stood, and there was no possibility of fleeing to either the right or the left. And at their back, they could hear the bellowing of the Mogs and the strange, inhuman voices of the shelks.

Never, in all man's history, was there a time when the phrase "between the devil and the deep sea" was more truly applicable.

On the River's Edge

Like some small animal cornered at last by a beast of prey, Nikadur cowered on the bank and buried his face in his arms. Tumithak would have given anything for the ability to surrender and feel the relief of utter resignation which he knew that Nikadur felt, but some inner part of him urged him to die fighting. He drew his pistol, with the three precious bullets that still remained from the day when he had slain his shelk; in his mind the consoling thought that if he must die, at least he could die fighting the enemies of man, an honor not often accorded to a Loorian.

Had the two but known it, though, neither was destined to die in this way for many long years. For several days before they arrived at this spot, Nature had been preparing the way for their escape; for the spot on which they stood was a few feet above the level of the river, it was a high, crumbling bank and the waters of the spring flood had washed away at it until the spot on which the two stood overhung the water by several feet. The added weight of the Loorians had weakened it until the slightest jar would be sufficient to break it off and hurl it into the flood. And even as they stood there, as the shelks and their hunting men began to push through the thicket to take them a huge log that had been caught in an eddy and swept shoreward, struck the bank a resounding thump—and the work of erosion was completed! Tumithak felt the ground dropping suddenly from beneath his feet; the whole world, it seemed, rocked crazily about him; and then he had splashed into the icy-cold water and was gasping and struggling and apparently certain of drowning. He still held his pistol with a deadly grip, some strange, sublimated idea of self-preservation causing him to cling to it tightly through all the strange events that followed.

In the Icy-Cold Water

When Tumithak rose to the surface of the water after that first chilling splash, his arms struck out in an instinctive attempt to keep from sinking. He knew nothing of swimming, in fact in all his life he had never before seen enough water to swim in, but some deep instinct caused him to thrash about, and in so doing his hand struck the log which had been the cause of his sudden advent into this amazing world of water. He grasped the log, threw an arm over it, and drew himself up on it. The hand that held his pistol struck a wet red-haired head and to his surprise, his eyes met the pallid, fear-stricken face of Nikadur, who had apparently managed to seize the log and raise himself to the other side.

By the time the two Loorians had ceased to gasp and sputter and had gained sufficient control of themselves to take notice of their surroundings, they found that the log had left the eddy into which it had drifted and was again floating down the stream and getting farther from the shore every minute. For a moment, hope rose in their breast—they were no longer in immediate danger of death from the shelks—but a brief reflection made them realize that they were no better off here; indeed, what might have been sudden, merciful extinction now threatened to be a death that was long and lingering. Yet they continued to cling to the log desperately, though it was only the instinct of self-preservation that kept them fighting at all.

They watched the shore with apathetic eyes as they were washed farther and farther away from it, and when they had almost reached the center of the stream, Nikadur gave an inarticulate cry and pointed to the spot where they had been precipitated into the water. The shelks had emerged from the thicket and stood in amazement, wondering where the pit-men had gone. Presently a Mog spied them and shouted the news to his masters. Tumithak saw the shelks unlimber the strange hoses with the long nozzles and point them in his direction. Little spurts of steam leaped from the water about a dozen yards from him but apparently the range was already too great for the weapons to do much harm. Once, indeed, he felt a fiery breath, as though from a furnace, beat upon his face, but it was no more than a passing discomfort, and, shortly after, the shelks gave up their attempt and stood watching until the Loorians had disappeared around the bend in the river.

The Escape

As they continued to be washed along in the main current, the Loorians found time to look about them and to observe the amazing details of this new world in which they found themselves. The current was fairly swift; yet as they moved along with it, its swiftness was not noticeable to them; in fact, the only discomfort they felt was the gradually increasing fatigue in their arms. They watched the shore, marvelling at the trees and bushes that seemed to stretch endlessly along the banks, and wondering how they would ever be able to find a way through their seeming impenetrability, if they should swim to the shore. They gazed at the sky, and were amazed at the clouds, which they were now able to study for the first time. And most of all, they were amazed at the sun, which by this time had reached the zenith, leaving no doubt in their minds that this astounding light of the Surface really did move slowly across the sky.

An hour passed, and still the pit-men were floating down the river with the floating log, and still the problem of reaching the shore was as unsolved as ever. Tumithak had attempted to climb up on the log and sit astride it; but at his first attempt, he had almost lost his companion when the log suddenly turned, so he had abandoned the idea at once and now continued to cling with weary arms, as he had since he had first been precipitated into the stream.

Another hour passed and with aching arms and water-soaked bodies, the Loorians were beginning to feel that even flight from the shelks might be preferred to this. Tumithak was beginning to wonder what would happen if he let go the log when he felt his feet touch something, float off and then touch it again! He released his grip on the log a little, and knew that it was the bottom of the river that he touched. The log had reached another huge bend in the stream, and unnoticed had approached the shore at a spot where a sand bank stretched out into the river. Tumithak cautiously released himself, sank slightly, and stood up to his neck in the water. He looked about him, and seeing the shore so near, let go of the log entirely and, calling out to Nikadur to do likewise, turned and waded to the shore. His companion followed his example, and in a few moments the two staggered across the sand-bar and fell, fatigued and water-worn, into the brush beyond.

On Land Again

Once concealed in the weeds and willows, they bent every effort to discern whether they were followed. They looked out over the broad river for long, and jumped with fright at every small sound that came from the woods behind them. But as time went on and no savage shelk appeared to slaughter them, nor did the clacking cries come to their ears, they at last decided that they had succeeded in evading their pursuers. Then it was that their over-taxed bodies began an insistent clamor for rest, and so, unable to resist further, they gave in to exhausted nature and in a few moments were asleep.

"The sleep of utter exhaustion" is a phrase that is often used to denote sound, undisturbable slumber. That afternoon, the Loorians were to learn what anyone who has ever been utterly exhausted can tell, that the sleep of an extremely tired person is anything but sound. Time and again, one or the other of the Loorians would start into wakefulness as some wood-sound startled them; time and again, their over-wrought nerves would tense, and they would find themselves sitting up and staring into the woods with throbbing alertness, and at last, toward evening, when they did begin to find some slumber, dream after nightmarish dream kept their minds in a turmoil. But rest came to them at last, and when the next morning came, it was a refreshed and vigorous Tumithak that opened his eyes and looked about upon the world which had recently shown him so much terror.

The sun was just rising and its light was reflected gloriously upon the swollen river; the birds were beginning to sing; and over Tumithak's head, the branches of a huge old pear tree showered down a million petals. A morning breeze was blowing, and rosy clouds scudded before it in the east; it was a perfect spring morning, but its beauty was lost upon Tumithak, for his mind was taken up almost entirely with wondering which of these many things might prove to be inimical, and just when he might expect them to become dangerous. At last, he turned and awakened Nikadur. The latter sat up, looked about him and then sank down again in despair.

It Seemed Like a Dream of Terror

"I had thought it was all a dream, Tumithak," he said mournfully.

Tumithak smiled and shrugged his shoulders.

"Unfortunately it was not," he said half-bitterly. "We are far from the safety of Loor, Nikadur."

He had removed the pack that was still strapped to his back as he spoke, and now he seated himself and removed from it a packet of food-cubes. He offered half of them to Nikadur, and for a while the two were silent as they partook of their simple breakfast, the first meal that they had eaten since emerging from the pit.

The meal finished, they fell to examining the details of the wonderful place in which they found themselves. The soil interested them most for a while, for they were unable to decide whether it was a thick coarse dust that had settled here or whether the original rock floor had crumbled and decayed. The question was abandoned, however, in the light of further mysteries; for wherever they looked they found new wonders to occupy their minds. A bird flew overhead, and although they were familiar with bats in the corridors, they wondered at the strangeness of this Surface creature, and at the perfection of its flight.

The flowers that were scattered in profusion through the woods excited their admiration now, but even as yet, they could not account for the fact that though these things certainly appeared to be living creatures, yet they were harmless and unable to move about. Twice they spied small animals, one of which fled from them, while the other peered curiously at them from a hole beneath a rock; but Tumithak had reached a point where he had some control of his fear, and he felt that he was at least the master of these small Surface creatures.

They had been examining this amazing world for over an hour when Nikadur voiced a thought that had been bothering Tumithak for some time.

"How are we to get back to our corridors, Tumithak?" he asked. "Have you given any thought to which way we must go?"

Tumithak considered. "If we could walk in the direction from which we were carried by the hurrying of the water, we should find ourselves near enough to the shelk-city to enable us to search for home. But perhaps the shelks are still seeking us. Do you feel that you could brave the dangers of Shawm again?"

The Duty of the Pit-Men Waiting in the Hall of the Esthetts

Nikadur trembled, but his answer showed Tumithak that the events of the past two days had somehow revived in Nikadur some trace of the ancient spirit of courage, for he answered bravely: "Nennapuss and our warriors wait in the Halls of the Esthetts. Is it not our duty to try to return to them?"

The Shelk-slayer smiled, and clapped his comrade on the back.

"Come then," he said, and they arose and started on their journey, keeping as close as they could to the banks of the river and praying that no new and unknown danger would confront them. They had not gone far, however, when it began to be increasingly evident that it would not be possible to follow the stream for long. The banks grew steeper and the vegetation grew denser and denser, until at last the Loorians gave up the attempt to remain close to the river, and struck off into the woods in the hope of finding a more open section. They had gone but a few dozen yards when they came to a well-marked trail leading in the very direction in which they wished to go. So ignorant were they of wood-craft or any similar art that the idea that this was a path made by the shelks never entered their heads. They at once turned into the path and continued on their way, sublimely unconscious of their increased danger.

For over a mile, they walked on without incident to distract their minds. A dozen times they congratulated themselves on the fortunate discovery of the path, and their hopes were beginning to run high that they might succeed in reaching their pit again, after all, when suddenly, as they topped a slow rise, they heard a distinct commotion in the little vale beyond. They at once darted into the brush, and froze into silence; then after a little while, they crawled slowly to the hill top and, lying there on their faces, looked upon an amazing scene.

A Fight Between Humans Watched by the Shelks

It was the scene of a battle—and just such a battle as they had heard described by Tlot, the Mog, when they had hidden in the ropes and cables of the shelk tower. There were seven figures in the little vale, three of which were shelks and four, humans. Three of the humans were Mogs, armed with short, heavy javelins not unlike the ancient Roman *pilum*; the other was a woman—a woman whose back was against the bole of a great tree, and who lashed out furiously at the Mogs with a long, needle-like sword that was, apparently quite capable of protecting her from the savage three. And the sight of three broken whips that lay at her feet showed that the battle had already occupied some time, and was evidence that the girl had been giving good account of herself.

The three shelks were taking no part in the fight; they stood well back and encouraged the Mogs with sardonic, clucking chatter. Two of them appeared to be unarmed, the other carried the now familiar box and hose, the long nozzle of which he held between two of his limbs, as a man might hold a pencil between his thumb and forefinger. He was watching the combat closely, and Tumithak knew that if the battle seemed to favor the brave girl too greatly, he could bring it to an end at once by slaying her.

Behind the shelks was a queer vehicle, a long, narrow, two-wheeled car that balanced strangely on its wheels, and that had a high, V-shaped transparent shield in front of it, behind which were a bewildering number of controls. Apparently the shelks and their attendant Mogs had been traveling some place in this car and had stopped long enough to enjoy the slaying of this girl.

The Strange Vehicle—The Fight—The Arrow of Nikadur

Tumithak's brief survey of the machine noted also a box that sat on the rear of the machine, a box with a number of white and shining rods of metal in it. These rods, it seemed, were made of a metal similar to that of the plates that illuminated the corridors. That they were not exactly the same was apparent from the fact that their light was not brilliant as was that of the plates, in fact, it was little more than a luminescence.

Tumithak's interest in the vehicle was but a passing one, just a single hurried glance, yet when his eyes returned to the fight, his heart leaped to his throat—for he saw that one of the Mogs had struck the girl's sword a particularly vicious blow, and before she could return to the defense, another Mog brought down his sword weapon, and then—There was a swish in the air, close to Tumithak's head, and before the Mog could finish his blow, he jerked violently forward and fell to the ground with an arrow in his heart!

Tumithak turned to see Nikadur, risen to his knees in the grass and already fitting another arrow to his bow. He comprehended instantly what his comrade had done, and chuckling in mingled amazement and delight at Nikadur's new-found courage, he drew his pistol and turned his face again to the battle. The shelks were filled with amazement at the sudden, unaccountable death of the hunting man, and the instant in which they stood in puzzled confusion had sufficed to give the Loorians that half second necessary to win. As Tumithak turned, he saw the armed shelk already raising his long-nozzled hose—and then to his surprise, the bushes to the right of him, at which the nozzle pointed, burst into flames!

The Marvelous Hose of the Dying Shelk

Instantly Tumithak's pistol spat, and, miraculously enough, the bullet struck the shelk squarely in the body. It gave a peculiar cry, its limbs went limp, and it collapsed on the ground, the hose dropping from its grip. As the hose fell, Tumithak became aware of a marvelous thing. The hose's long nozzle, in falling, described a vertical circle, and wherever it pointed, the vegetation immediately burst into flames! To the left, and high in the trees swung the flaming path, over their heads and back beyond the shelks; and then, as the nozzle came to rest on the ground, a long streak of blackened earth appeared, starting at the nozzle's mouth and stretching away into the forest. Somewhere a huge branch, severed from its trunk by the heat ray, fell crashing to the ground, and then Tumithak jerked his mind back to the scene of the battle, just as another of the shelks reached for the hose. Again Tumithak fired his revolver—and missed! He was about to fire his last remaining bullet when he again heard the twang of Nikadur's bow, and the second shelk fell to the ground, its limbs feebly twitching and attempting to claw at the arrow that had pierced its body.

Only two Mogs and a single shelk remained now, and the advantage was still with the Loorians. The remaining shelk made a dash for the weapon of its dead brother, but even as it did so, Tumithak and Nikadur, flushed with the fever of battle, dashed forward to prevent its reaching it. Halfway down the hill, both stopped to discharge their weapons, and when they reached their destination they found but a single Mog to oppose them. For the two hunting men had been so intent upon the battle with the girl that they had hardly been aware of the events going on behind them, and just as Tumithak and Nikadur reached the bottom of the hill, the girl, with a lucky stroke, had dispatched the second Mog and so the remaining one had turned to appeal to his masters. The sight of them stretched upon the ground was quite enough for the astounded Mog; with a howl, he abandoned the battle and fled.

Tumithak was at first inclined to let him go, but a second thought brought to him the memory of that other Mog who had escaped, in the shelk-tower in Shawm; and so he gave a quick order to Nikadur, and a swift arrow sped forward and overtook the hunting man, silenced his howling forever. Then the Loorians turned and approached the girl.

She still stood with her back to the tree, her chest was still rising and falling with the exertion of the battle, and her long hair, which was as black as that of any Mog, was tumbled about her shoulders and was damp with the perspiration brought out by the fight. Her dress was a long tunic, not unlike the belted dresses of the Loorian women, save that her people apparently possessed the secret of some dye, for its color was a brilliant blue. Tumithak felt that he had never before seen any woman with half the animation, half the determination shown by this strange girl. The Shelk-slayer, Tumithak, approached her diffidently, for the first time in his life consciously bashful before a woman. He spoke not at all; in fact it was Nikadur who finally broke the silence.

Addressing the Girl in Friendship

"We are friends," he said, and indeed, it was well that he said it, for the girl was holding her sword at the guard, uncertain of how she would be treated by these newcomers. At Nikadur's words, she lowered her sword slightly and relaxed her tense pose.

"Who are you?" she asked, and there was a touch of amazement in her voice. "Who are you who slay shelks and Mogs alike with strange weapons of thunder?"

Tumithak struck his chest importantly. He had regained his composure, and at the girl's words, that queer vanity of his again swelled within him. "I am Tumithak, slayer of shelks!" he announced. "Tumithak Lord of Loor chief of Yakra and Nonone, Master of the Dark Corridors and of the Halls of the Esthetts! I have come to the Surface to slay shelks, and to teach Man to again battle for his ancient heritage! This companion of mine is Nikadur—who also slays shelks," and as he spoke, it seemed to dawn on Tumithak for the first time that he was no longer "*The* Shelk-slayer," that now this honor was one that must be shared with his comrade. He turned to Nikadur and clasping him by the shoulders, kissed him on the cheek.

"You, too, are a Shelk-slayer now, old friend," he said. "Quick, take the heads, that we may show them to our friends, when we return to our corridors." And so, as Nikadur, obeying, turned and busied himself with the bodies of the shelks, Tumithak returned to the now friendly girl.

Tumithak and the Girl Now Friends—The Tains

"These places of which you speak," she said, as she thrust her sword through a ring at her belt, "I have never heard of them before. Can it be that you come from some other pit?"

This explanation seemed plausible enough for Tumithak, for never, in his own pit, had he seen anyone with hair colored as was this girl's. "I suppose you are right," he answered. "What do they call your pit, and what is your name?"

"I am Tholura the Tain, and my pit is the pit of the Tains," and the girl pointed to her throat, where a blue, six-pointed star was cleverly tattooed. "This is the mark of all the Tains," she said.

"But what are you doing on the Surface?" asked Tumithak. "Do your people often dare to come out on the Surface, and face the shelks?"

There was a world of scorn in the girl's voice as she replied.

"Never in my life have I heard of a Tain who would voluntarily face even a Mog," she replied. "The Tains are a race of rabbits! They cower in fear, deep in the lowest corridors of our pit, and when the shelks and foul Mogs come hunting them, they either flee in panic, or sacrifice one of their own people, that the rest may live."

"But you—" insisted Tumithak. "How did you have the courage to leave the pit? How do you happen to be on the Surface?"

"I do not know," Tholura answered, vaguely. "I have always been a little different from the other Tains. It has seemed to me a most degrading thing to flee ever from one's enemies. Many of my people have thought me mad because I believed that it would be nobler to die than to flee. But even I never dreamed of venturing upon the Surface until three days ago, when a party of hunting Mogs raided our part of the corridors and slew my sister.

The Death of Tholura's Sister—Her Revenge

"I tried to induce my father and my brothers to follow them for I felt sure that they could be overtaken before they left our pit. But like the craven cowards that all the Tains are they cowered in our apartment and told me I was mad to think of such a thing. Perhaps I was, for I took up my father's sword and turned my face toward the Surface vowing that I would follow and never return until I had taken vengeance on the murderers of my sister."

She paused as Nikadur drew near and threw the heads of the shelks at Tumithak's feet. She glanced at them for a moment in fascinated curiosity and then with a little feminine grimace of disgust she turned her head and went on: "I pursued my way to the entrance of the pit but saw no more of the Mogs who had slain my sister. So I continued my way out to the Surface and to-day after wandering for a long, long way, I came upon this other party. I might have tried to avoid them, but they spied me before I could hide. So I faced them, hoping only that I might slay a Mog or two before I died.

"But I little dreamed that a hero existed who would not only prevent my slaughter at the hands of the Mogs, but would slay their savage masters, too," and the look she gave Tumithak, as she finished speaking, caused Nikadur to smile discreetly and to turn away and busy himself with studying the various possessions of the shelks.

CHAPTER IV

The White and Shining Rods

For some time, Tumithak and Tholura sat conversing beneath the great tree, telling each other of the lives they had lived in the corridors. Tumithak was filled with wonder at the idea of finding this girl whose mind was such a strange parallel to his own and he plied her with dozens of questions concerning her past. And of course, she questioned him, too, and Tumithak recounted the great adventure which had first brought him to the Surface from his home corridors, so far below, and you may be sure the story lost nothing in the telling.

Nikadur, meanwhile, had made several discoveries that interested him greatly. The weapon which cast the ray of heat still lay where it had fallen, and now the line of burnt and blackened earth which streaked from the nozzle had begun to glow redly with the intensity of the heat. And some distance away dense smoke arose, where the green vegetation smoldered and burned. Nikadur approached the shelk-weapon diffidently, wondering how it could be possible for such a cool thing as the hose appeared to be to give out such intense heat. But this was a puzzle far beyond his intellect and so, placing it in his mind simply as a shelk wonder, not to be understood by men, he turned his attention to the long narrow car.

The machine was about twenty feet long, low and stream-lined and made of some strange yellow metal. It still stood balanced on its two wheels, and as Nikadur drew near to it he could hear from within it a subdued, throbbing hum. He inspected the controls, but was unable to comprehend them and so he turned to the rear of the car where lay the box of white and shining rods. He stooped over them, half-expecting them to be white-hot, but feeling no glow of heat from them, he finally picked up enough courage to take one of them in his hand and found out to his surprise that it was quite cool.

Nikadur examined it curiously. About four feet long it was, and a little over half an inch in diameter, and as he swung it about his head, Nikadur was struck with a brilliant idea. These rods of metal would make excellent ax handles. He thought of how proud he would be to possess such a beautiful weapon. And then, at the thought of the word weapon, his eyes instantly returned to the box and hose lying to the right of him. There, indeed, he thought, would be a real weapon, if a way could only be found to control the heat or to turn it off and on as the shelks apparently could. For the first time it dawned on Nikadur that this weapon in the hands of a man might be as dangerous to a shelk as it had hitherto been to humans. It was an epoch-making thought, and Nikadur must be given full credit for it. He turned to where Tumithak and the girl sat, still talking, and called to the Loorian chief.

"What shall we do with the shelk weapon, Tumithak?" he asked. "Think you there is some way to stop this terrific blast of heat as the shelks do? Perhaps we might find a way to control it and to keep the weapon for our own."

Tumithak was about to answer when Tholura gave a vexed little laugh and started for the weapon.

"How silly of me," she exclaimed, "I should have noticed it before." And picking up the long nozzle, she snapped back a small lever—and the weapon was harmless! The Loorians gasped.

"You know how to operate such a weapon?" cried Tumithak. "Where did you learn? What else do you know of the ways of the shelks?"

The girl smiled. "I know little of the ways of the shelks," she answered. "But of the ways of our ancient ancestors, I think I know far more than you. What you have been telling me of Loor and of your corridors shows that you have little or no knowledge of the wisdom of the ancient ones. There, at least, the Tains excel. For many hundreds of years, they have kept the traditions of the great wisdom of our wise ancestors, and in our museums, which are also our worshipping places, we have many tools and machines that were once used by those wise ancestors, and they are always kept in perfect repair by the priests. But alas; the fuel, the power that makes them operate, is unobtainable, and so the Tains are no better off than the most ignorant of those blind savages of which you have been telling me. Yet if the day should come when we again learn the secret of that lost power—" Tholura paused, her eyes shining. "There is something to which you might well devote your life, O Shelk-slayer!" she cried. "Could we but find the secret of that lost power, we might face the shelks on equal terms. And then—"

"And then," cried Tumithak, catching her enthusiasm and grasping the shelk weapon from her, "a raid on that stinking shelk-hole of Shawm! Fire-hoses blasting down tower after tower! Foul Mog and savage shelk alike fleeing in screaming terror to the woods!"

A Sudden Alarm from the Distance

He was not finished with his fantastic dreaming, yet he stopped suddenly as a sound came to him distantly from the woods in the direction of Shawm. Nikadur heard it too, and laid a warning hand upon his arm. The three were instantly silent, straining every ear, listening. Unmistakably, from afar came the faint clattering of an approaching band of shelks, and quite clearly it was no small party. From the heights of their dreams,

Tumithak and Tholura crashed to the depths of reality. Their human natures betrayed them and instinctively they turned to flee in the direction opposite to that from which came the sound of the voices. Strangely enough, it was Nikadur who caused them to hesitate. He had not yet brought to Tumithak's attention the white and shining rods that he had discovered, and a certain tenacity of purpose, that was characteristic of him, made him determined to take some of them with him as he fled. So he seized Tumithak by the arm and restrained his flight.

"Are you going to leave without taking the shelks' heads, Tumithak?" he asked. "And wouldn't these rods make excellent ax handles? Let us at least take a few of these rods with us, back to our pit."

Tumithak paused at once, rather ashamed of his sudden panic. He picked up two of the shelk heads and fastened them to his belt, while Nikadur picked up the other. Then he approached the car and for the first time, took a good look at it and at its contents. He was struck at once, as Nikadur had been, with the beauty as well as the utility of the shining rods of metal. So each of the Loorians took up about a dozen of the rods, and then Tholura, with a practical eye to the future, carried the remaining rods some distance away from the path and buried them in a pile of leaves. Then the three fled, leaving the path and running in a direction pointed out by Tholura.

"This way lies the pit of the Tains," explained the girl. "You could not now return to your own corridors without passing around the party of shelks which we hear approaching, and that would be a heedless and unnecessary danger. And perhaps, in their own pit you can, by example, instill some courage into those craven cowards, the Tains."

Tumithak's Caution in the Face of Danger

Tumithak was anxious to return to his own pit, but in spite of all his brave and boastful talk, he still retained enough instinctive caution to wish to avoid contact with a large group of shelks. He was no superman, he well knew, and just at present it seemed the better part of valor to seek safety some place below the ground where conditions would be more familiar to him than they were in this amazing Surface world. His companions back in the pit of Loor could probably take care of themselves for another day or two, without his help; in fact, it was most probable that they had already given him up for dead and returned to their own cities. So it was that Tumithak decided to turn and direct his footsteps toward the pit of the Tains.

For a while, the three ran swiftly through the trees while the sound of the shelks' voices came to them ever more distantly. At last they could be heard no longer and the adventurers slowed down their pace to a hurried walk. The Loorians took time now to make a pack of the shining rods and to fasten them on their backs so that their hands might be free. Tumithak also fastened the shelk's fire-hose to his back, and then they continued their journey in high spirits, for well they knew that in this day they had already accomplished more than any other man had accomplished in a dozen preceding centuries.

The Afternoon Rest—The Alarm Is Over

By mid-afternoon, they had covered quite a distance and the party of shelks was almost forgotten. Tumithak amused himself by familiarizing himself with the operation of the fire-hose, and many a sapling and small bush burst into flame as he directed the heat-ray upon it. Presently the forest thinned and was replaced by a park-like expanse, thinly wooded, through which they were able to make much better time. At last the trees disappeared entirely and they came to a broad shallow valley of meadow land, and here, by the side of a great glacial boulder nearly eight feet high, the three sat down to rest and to eat from Tumithak's diminishing supply of food-cubes. They munched their food in silence for a while and then Tholura spoke softly: "Much may be accomplished with the shelk weapon we have, Tumithak. I think we had better consult about it with Zar-Emo, the leader of the priests of the Tains. He is very wise in the wisdom of the ancients, and he can advise us how we may best use the power that has fallen into our hands. We should go to him at once when we reach the pit that is my home."

Tumithak agreed and again they fell into silence. They were tired from their long walk, the warm afternoon sun fell on their faces, and in the fresh spring air, there was a drowsiness that seemed to soak into them and permeate their very souls. Their heads drooped and Tholura, who had slept very little if any, the night before, had even fallen into a little nap when suddenly Tumithak sat up, every sense alert, his finger to his lips to caution Nikadur to silence. Unmistakably, from the other side of the boulder had come a familiar scratching sound! Some creature had moved, on the other side of the rock; was it shelk, man or some lesser animal?

Silently, the two Loorians stood there, immovable, until the sound was repeated. Evidently the creature of creatures had just arrived and had no knowledge of the party on the other side of the rock, for they were making no effort to avoid producing a noise. Tumithak unloosed the shelk weapon which he had on his back, took the nozzle in his hand and tiptoed to the side of the rock. Reaching the edge of it, he cautiously lowered his head and slowly, slowly peered around the corner. There was a sizzling spit, Tumithak jerked his head violently, and the grass a few feet beyond him burst into flames. Tumithak clapped his hand to his head, where a great singed spot of hair bore witness to the narrowness of his escape. Before he could speak or so much as warn the others, a shelk leaped into view, a fire-hose in its claws and a look of savage fury in its cold eyes!

A Shelk Attacks Tumithak

Now there is no doubt at all that if such a meeting as this one had occurred a dozen or so years later, when Tumithak as Lord of Kaymak had made his name a name of wonder and hate throughout shelkdom, there would have been better chance for the Loorian chief. But at this early day, the shelks were still the lords of all the earth and the idea of a man being on equal terms with a shelk was unthinkable. Therefore, the shelk, seeing Tumithak dodge behind the stone, thought of nothing but the sport of killing a man, and so immediately gave chase. It exhibited no caution in pursuing him, it probably felt that at most he could only be armed with a sword or perhaps a bow and arrows, and so it leaped around the edge of the rock—swinging its heat-ray, it leaped—straight in front of the fire-hose that Tumithak held in his hand. The Loorian snapped the lever, there was a hissing crackle of sound, a clattering cry, and the shelk was no more, another enemy of man had gone to join its fathers in that legendary land upon the mother planet.

Tumithak's mind was calm, yet it was functioning rapidly. Almost immediately, he decided that his best course was to pursue the advantage he had gained, and suiting the action to the thought, he again started around the rock, his weapon, this time, playing before him. He rounded the edge of the huge stone, half expecting to see the entire party that they had heard earlier in the day, but instead, the sight that met his eyes caused him to smile broadly and to mentally give himself several pats on the back. There were no more shelks, but about a hundred yards away, two Mogs were fleeing rapidly, dodging from tree to tree; while on the ground lay two strange cocoon-like bundles, quite evidently abandoned by the hunting men when they had seen the death of their master.

Tumithak Frees the Captured Datto and Thorpf

Tumithak turned and motioned his two companions to follow him and then, seeing that the two fleeing Mogs had already fled beyond the range of the fire-hose, he ignored them and approached the strange bundles. He eyed them carefully, their size and peculiar shape making him decidedly suspicious of what their contents might be. Halfway toward them, he stopped fearfully—he had caught a glimpse of a human face on the far side of one of them—he was right, there were men in these bundles! And then almost immediately, his half-uttered cry of alarm turned to one of surprise and delight and rushing to the bundles, he began to hack at their binding threads and cords like a madman.

Nikadur and Tholura, timidly following Tumithak round the boulder, heard his cry and started back, then, realizing that it was not a cry of fear they heard, hastened to see what had caused their leader such surprise. They had hardly come within sight when Tumithak called: "Nikadur! Come and help me!" and Nikadur, drawing his sword, rushed forward just as Tumithak cut the last of the binding cords from the body of— Datto, the Yakran!

For a dozen seconds, Nikadur's mind was a hodgepodge of jumbled thought. Tumithak had found the Yakrans! How did they come be be here? Were they alive or dead? Why had the shelks brought them here? He was recalled from his amazement by the voice of Tumithak: "Unbind Thorpf, Nikadur! They are weak from the tight bindings of the cords. They will be all right in a few minutes."

Nikadur hastened to obey and shortly the Yakrans were freed of their bonds and Tholura was pouring water down their throats, while Tumithak and Nikadur rubbed their limbs to restore the circulation. It was a long while before the Yakrans showed any signs of interest in their surroundings, indeed they seemed to be in a semi-conscious daze, but at last Thorpf, sitting up and beginning to rub his own arms, said in a comically solemn tone:

"There are those in Loor and Yakra, Tumithak, who hold that you are a superman. Never before today have I thought as they do, but how else your presence here, with shelk heads at your belt and shelk weapons in your hands, can be explained, I do not know. Tell me quickly how you came here, ere I suspect you of being a god."

Tumithak Tells His Story to His Rescued Companions

Tumithak laughed. There was nothing more pleasing to that strange vanity of his than such a speech as this, but he had no intention of adding to his prowess by making himself into a mystery. So he answered at once, giving the Yakrans a fairly detailed account of his adventures and introducing Tholura as he did so. Datto and Thorpf were amazed at the idea of another pit, this being one idea that had never entered their heads before. To them, the world had been the pits of Loor and Yakra, which, so legend said, opened to the Surface, and the Surface, to their minds, was merely a larger and roomier pit with more conveniences and luxuries. But when they heard of the pit of the Tains, they agreed at once that the best thing for all concerned would be a visit to that pit and an attempt to form an alliance with its people. The Loorians and Tholura were anxious to start, but the Yakrans were so stiff and sore from the hours that they had spent wrapped with the binding cords, that they implored the others to give them a few minutes at least to rest and restore their strength.

So it was agreed to wait awhile and as they rested, Tumithak suggested that the Yakrans tell how they had come to be in this place, for of course the Loorians were as amazed at the Yakrans' presence here as the latter had been at theirs.

The Two Yakrans Tell Their Story

Datto, who seemed to be feeling a little better than Thorpf, acted as spokesman. "When I severed the rope that you were swinging on, Tumithak, I had no chance to see whether I had saved your life or only brought you to a more merciful death, for the shelks were swarming over me, and though I fought with all my strength, it was sheer numbers that overcame me. They were not able to use their weapons among the ropes and cables where we clung, and to that I attribute the fact that they did not kill me at once.

"But when they had brought me to the ground, they had apparently thought the matter over and decided that they would not kill me until they had given their chief a chance to see me. I was amazed and overjoyed to see Thorpf alive and but little hurt, standing before me, when I reached the ground, held hand and foot by four Mogs. I was at once put in the care of four more Mogs, and, at a command from the shelks, we all left the tower and proceeded to the center of the city.

"You may be sure I looked about for signs of you as soon as we reached the outer air, but there was nothing at first to tell what had become of you. One of the Mogs, however, was evidently aware of your escape for he showed me a large party of shelks, armed and rushing away from the scene of our battle, and he pointed out the direction in which they were going.

"'They pursue your friends, Wild Man,' he said, with a sneer. 'Your friends will soon rejoin you. Half of Shawm is pursuing them, even now.' I didn't answer him, Tumithak, for I thought in my heart that he was right, that it was only a matter of time until you, too, would be with me.

"And so, after a while, we came to a tower that was taller than the rest and made of a different metal. We were brought inside and sat down on the ground, and presently a shelk dropped from the ropes above, a shelk who wore upon his head a crown such as you wear, Tumithak, and from that I knew him to be the leader of this city of shelks. The group of shelks who had captured me spoke to him and for a while they talked back and forth in their vile shelk speech, and I knew nothing of what they said. Then the chief shelk spoke to Tlot the Mog, whom we had fought with.

"'Tlot,' he said, 'I am told that one of these wild men, who is now being hunted in the woods, wore a crown such as mine. Is that the truth?' The Mog cringingly admitted that it was.

"'Is it also true that it wore clothes such as the Esthetts wear?' The Mog nodded another affirmative, and the anger of the chief shelk was terrible to see. He turned to Thorpf and me.

The Death of the Governor-Inferior of Shawm

"'Three years ago,' he said, in his clucking voice, 'the Governor-Inferior of the town of Shawm was slain at the entrance to a man-pit and his head cut off and carried away. Certain superstitious shelks claimed that it was done by a wild man from the depths of the pit, but they were laughed into silence. No man, we felt, had ever been born with the courage to do that. It seems now that they were right and we were wrong. Whence came you, wild men? Tell us the way to your pit, that we may wipe out the menace that confronts us.'

"I was about to answer him, Tumithak, for I was trembling with fear and terribly afraid that I would die, but suddenly it seemed that a courage was born of my very desperation. I must die anyhow, I thought, should I die giving my enemies aid in slaughtering my relatives and my friends? I answered the shelk and I must have surprised him mightily with my answer, for I surprised even myself.

"'Foul spider,' I said, 'too long have my people quailed and fled before you! If I choose not to answer your question, how can you force an answer? Go and ask of your Esthetts whence came the doom that has befallen them! Perhaps they will satisfy your curiosity.'"

Tumithak burst into laughter as did Nikadur, and Tholura looked as if she could not believe her ears.

"You told him *that?*" chuckled Tumithak, as his laughter died. "What did he then, Datto?"

The Anger of the Shelk at Datto's Rejoinder

"His anger, if possible, grew even greater. He clacked out an order, and several shelks left the room, hastening, I doubt not, to see what had happened to the Esthetts. Then he gave another order, but with this order several of the other shelks seemed to disagree. For some time they talked, and one of the foul Mogs, to frighten me I suppose, explained that the chief shelk, whom he called Hakh-Klotta, desired to slay me at once, while the others believed that we should both be sent to a place called Kaymak, the great town of this part of the Surface, for here there were shelks that could force us to divulge all that we knew, even though we would rather die than tell. And at last these shelks prevailed over old Hakh-Klotta and we were taken from the great tower and thrown into another, with a shelk and a dozen Mogs to watch over us.

"We stayed there for many hours, and the dark time came again, and while the shelk slept, the Mogs took turns at watching over us. When again the light came, Thorpf and I were led out and brought before the great tower again. We waited awhile and then there appeared a great wonder—a huge machine that flew in the air like a bat, Tumithak! It came over the shelk towers and settled down on the ground near us and then the door opened and we were hurried toward it. Shelks emerged from it and dragged us in, and then, to our horror, the machine again rose into the air and flew away with us!

The Flying Machine Brought Down by the Captured Datto

"We had not flown very far when Thorpf noticed a wonderful thing. One of the shelks sat in the front of the little cabin in which we were and he looked constantly out of a window in the front. In his claws he held the end of a little stick, the other end of which disappeared in the top of a box set by the window. When he moved this stick to the right or left, the flying machine turned as he moved it. And when he pushed the stick down, the machine went down also! Thorpf called my attention to this fact and a desperate plan came to me. Without even acquainting Thorpf with the details of my plan, I gave a sudden lunge that tore me from the grasp of the Mogs that held me and threw myself upon the shelk that held the stick.

"As he fell with me on top of him I seized the stick and pushed it downward as far as it would go. The shelks screeched with fear and all leaped upon me, I rose to my feet, hurling them right and left and then there was a crash and I knew no more. . . . When I recovered my senses, I was tied up as you saw me and the Mogs were carrying Thorpf and me through the forest. Then you came, and the rest you know."

"The flying machine was wrecked so that it was useless," spoke up Thorpf, who apparently had seen more of the crash than Datto had. "Two Mogs were killed and three shelks, leaving only one shelk and the two Mogs that escaped from you. The remaining shelk must have decided to return to Shawm and await the coming of another flying machine, for he gave orders to the Mogs to carry us back to the city. They tied us up thoroughly, to make certain that we could do no more harm and then the shelk gave orders to them to begin the march. We had marched about four hours, I think, when, tired and worn out from carrying such heavy loads, the Mogs insisted that they take a rest beside this huge rock, where you found us."

"Did you learn much of the customs of the shelks?" asked Tumithak. "How they operate their strange machines, or what other weapons they have? How they live, or what they eat? More and more I feel that the greatest handicap that men have is the lack of knowledge of our enemies."

Datto's Story About the Shelks

Datto hesitated. "I learned little enough about them, O Lord of Loor," he answered. "But one thing I noticed that may help us in the future. Do you remember how silent and deserted the town seemed to us when we first saw it? And how with the coming of the light, the town at once awoke? Well, when the light of the Surface again sank below the floor, and darkness came, a silence again came over the city. For a while, Thorpf and I were at a loss to understand what had brought that silence, and then at last we understood. These dark periods, Tumithak, are used by the shelks as sleeping times, and all the shelks in the town go to sleep until the light returns, save only a few who remain awake as guards. If ever the time comes when we return to our own pit, and can attack the shelks, we must be sure to attack them during the time of darkness."

"A discovery that may prove of value, too," said Tumithak, and was about to make some further remark when Tholura interrupted him.

"These discussions, Tumithak," she said, "could they not be continued later? The light sinks toward the Floor, and we are still some distance from the pit of the Tains. Let us be going."

Tumithak saw the wisdom of her suggestion and in a few moments the party was moving off across the broad plain that led to the foot-hills in the distance. Nikadur had armed himself with the fire-hose of the slain shelk, and had given his bow to Thorpf, who was no mean archer, while

Datto had taken up a short sword which had been dropped by one of the Mogs in his hasty departure.

On the Way to the Pit of the Tains—An Interruption by the Shelks

They traveled for several hours and were, according to Tholura, within a very short distance of the pit's opening when Thorpf gave a cry of fear.

"Look behind, Tumithak!" he cried. "We are pursued!"

Sure enough, in the distance behind them was a large band of shelks, a band that was rapidly drawing closer. The pit-men were amazed at the speed with which the beasts approached. They did not run, but came on in great springy leaps that carried them over the ground at a terrific speed. There was little doubt that it was the same party that they had heard earlier in the day, probably turned from their original journey by the Mogs who had escaped during the fight at the rock. There was no doubt that the shelks were pursuing them. Tumithak uttered an exclamation of vexation and despair and half turned to face them, but Tholura dragged him on.

"Quickly!" she cried. "We are almost to the entrance to the pit. We can make it, and once in the pit, perhaps we can elude them in its maze of corridors."

So they turned and fled into the low foot-hills, and for half an hour they ran wildly behind the girl in blue. But ever, as they glanced behind them, they saw the shelk party drawing nearer. At last, when it became evident to Tumithak that they must either turn and face the shelks or die fleeing, the girl suddenly stopped.

"Quick! Behind this stone!" she exclaimed, and looking where she pointed, Tumithak saw a narrow cleft between two rocks, "Inside," she panted. "Perhaps we can yet elude them."

But Tumithak knew that any attempt to escape facing the shelks was now hopeless. The spidery creatures were not a hundred yards away, and already, as the party leaped into the pit, he saw the fire-hose in the claws of the foremost shelk point in his direction. He raised his own hose, sent a blast of heat toward the shelks and then sped into the cave-like pit-mouth himself.

The Party Ordered to Divide at the Tains' Pit

"We are too close to them," he called to Tholura. "Datto, Thorpf and you must take Tholura on, to her people. Nikadur, you and I are armed with shelk weapons; we must stay here and attempt to drive off this party of shelks. If we all fled now they would follow us to the town and wipe out the whole city of the Tains. Come, Nikadur," and Tumithak stepped back toward the entrance.

For a moment, the others hesitated. Then Nikadur stepped to his chief's left, his fire-hose ready in his hand. And to Tumithak's surprise, Tholura took her place at his other side.

"I cannot leave you, Tumithak," she said, "not while you prepare to die for me and my people."

Tumithak gave a gesture of impatience. "I am not so foolish as to die for a city of people of whom I know nothing, Tholura. This will not be as hard as you think. I am well protected, here in the entrance, and am armed as well as they; while they are in the open and are ignorant of the fact that I possess and can operate one of their fire-hoses. See, I will soon wipe them out."

He raised his fire-hose as he spoke, and sent a blast out of the pit mouth. A clattering screech of surprise broke from the shelks without, and Tholura, glancing over his shoulder, saw them suddenly break for shelter. Three of them already lay upon the ground, one quite dead, the others hopelessly burned. Tumithak laughed, and again his fire-hose spat its invisible ray toward them. A fourth shelk dropped, and then he darted back, and the wall at one side of the cave glowed for a second and hot splinters of rock flew off and scattered about them. When they ventured to look out again, the shelks had managed to conceal themselves behind rocks and trees, and the battle settled down into a game of waiting. Presently Nikadur uttered a soft pleased ejaculation and raised his hose. One of the huge trees began to splutter, close to the ground, where his heat-ray touched it, and then, with a clacking cry of anguish, a shelk sped from the shelter which the heat had made untenable and fled for a nearby rock. Halfway there, Nikadur's ray met him, and he fell, an unrecognizable cinder.

The Loorians' Laughter as They Fight the Shelks

The Loorians laughed again. So successful had the day's fighting been that they were beginning to underestimate the shelks, beginning to believe that these enemies were not as dangerous as they seemed. But now something was to happen that was to revive their respect for the shelks, to make them realize that after all they knew little of the uses of the shelk weapons, and that it would be many a day before they could really meet the savage beasts on even terms.

The first knowledge they had of anything strange happening was when

Tholura pointed to the roof of the cave. It was glowing, a dull red, where the fire-hose of some invisible shelk was playing on it. There was little danger to them, Tumithak thought, for it was several feet above their heads, but nevertheless the shelk persisted in his burning of the roof. And then—Tholura screamed, and seizing Tumithak by the shoulder dragged him backward into the cave.

"Back, Loorians, quickly," she shouted to the others, and it was only the old instinctive timidity in them that enabled them to rush back quickly enough. With a crash and a roar that almost deafened them in the closely confined corridor, the entire entrance collapsed and fell inward. Had they been but a second later, they must have all been crushed beneath the rock as it came tumbling down.

CHAPTER V

The Wisdom of Zar-Emo

The narrowness of their escape temporarily shook the entire party. Thorpf and Nikadur both had several small cuts where flying bits of rock had struck them, and for a little while, Tumithak was frankly dazed. Presently Tholura gave a trembling little laugh.

"We still live, Loorians," she said. "Truly, I am beginning to believe, Tumithak, that you really do bear a charmed life. The shelks evidently meant to crush us beneath the rock of the entrance, but they have defeated their own ends. We are not only alive and almost unhurt, but we have escaped from them, at least for the present."

The men made no reply to this. They did not share the relief of Tholura, for they realized that even if they were cut off from the shelks, they were also effectively cut off from their return home; marooned in a corridor whose occupants might even yet prove to be inimical. Presently, Tholura turned and began the descent of the corridor. The others followed in silence, still shaken from their recent adventure, but presently they began to observe the corridors that they were passing through. Such a maze of blind alleys and false apartments, Tumithak had never seen, and his head was soon spinning with the attempt to remember the way that he had come. They had walked for but little more than an hour when they began to notice signs of occupancy of the apartments. Tumithak was amazed. He had heard, first from the conversation of the Mogs in the tower, and later from Tholura herself, that the pit of the Tains was very shallow; but that people would be living only an hour's walk or so from the Surface seemed foolhardy in the extreme. No wonder the shelks preferred to hunt in the pit of the Tains. Compared with a hunt in this pit, a raid on Yakra would take on the appearance of an extended expedition.

In the Pit of the Tains—The Great City

However, Tumithak was to learn that the Tains had some small protection at least, in this labyrinthine maze of corridors. Tholura led them for at least two more miles through a series of pits and corridors that left them hopelessly puzzled. At last she paused as they reached the bottom of a ladder that led into a long, broad corridor.

"Here begins the city of the Tains, Tumithak," she said. "I think I had better go on ahead to tell of your coming. You wait here until——" She broke off with a gasp as a figure suddenly burst from a near-by apartment and hurled itself upon Tumithak. It was a boy, a youngster of perhaps sixteen, armed only with a short sword, but so fierce was his attack that for a moment Tumithak was hard put to defend himself.

"Flee, Tholura," cried the lad, his sword sweeping and darting through the air with amazing skill, "flee while I can hold them from you!" And then to the Loorians: "Foul Mogs! You shall never touch my sister while I live! Defend yourselves before I slay you!"

Datto was about to smite the boy with his sword, his only thought to protect Tumithak; but Tholura stopped him with her next words.

"Stop, Luramo," she cried. "Stop, I say! These are friends!" And then to Tumithak: "Oh, don't hurt him! He is my brother!"

Tumithak and Datto dropped their swords, and after a moment, the boy followed their example, a sheepish half-smile coming to his lips.

"This is my brother Luramo," announced Tholura, placing her arm about the youth's shoulder. "He is the youngest of my brothers, but I think he is also the bravest."

Luramo grinned happily.

"You bring strange friends, Tholura," he exclaimed. "These are not Tains, nor are they Mogs, I see now. Tell me, who are they?"

"Greater than Tains or Mogs are the ones that are here," answered Tholura. "This is Tumithak, Slayer of Shelks, and his companions, who have also slain shelks! I was out upon the Surface, Luramo, and there I was beset by three Mogs and three shelks! And while I fought with the Mogs Tumithak, with but one of his friends to help him, slew all six of them and saved me! Behold the evidence of his greatness!" and she turned Tumithak around that Luramo might see the shelk's head that hung from his belt.

Luramo stared in awe. For fully a minute he stared, and his thoughts can better be imagined than written. Then slowly he held his sword out to Tumithak in the age-old symbol of allegiance. Tumithak smiled a little and touching the sword lightly accepted the boy's fealty. Though he thought little of that act at the time, in after years he was to value that allegiance over almost any other's, and Luramo became one of Tumithak's bravest warriors.

The Allegiance of the Boy, Luramo

And now Tholura was looking at Luramo anxiously. "What was it, brother," she asked, suddenly, "that brought you here to the edge of the city? Is all well with them at home?"

"Well enough, I suppose," answered Luramo, scornfully. "Father still cowers in his apartment and bemoans the fact that his two daughters have died at the hands of the Mogs, for of course he thinks you dead, too. And Luragar and Bathlura try to comfort him, and swear that you will be avenged if the Mogs ever come to the city again. But they make no attempt to follow you, though they know that when you left the pit you went to almost certain death.

"I spent many hours trying to stir them up to go in search of you, Tholura; but they found one excuse after another to remain at home, and so at last I decided to find you myself. You see," he made his confession somewhat shamefacedly, "I didn't dream that you would actually go all the way to the Surface. I thought you might wander here in the corridors and that here I would find you. I—I think I would have been afraid to venture on the Surface by myself."

Tumithak suddenly laughed and gripped the lad's hand in his.

"Luramo," he said, in a delighted tone, "surely I have found two after my own heart, in you and your wonderful sister. Do not be ashamed of what you have not done. I doubt if there is another man, in all the city of the Tains, who would be bold enough to do as much as you have."

Luramo smiled a trifle proudly, and as Tholura turned to resume the interrupted journey, he sheathed his sword and fell in behind Tumithak, taking his place with the Yakrans and Nikadur. After a while, Tholura called to him and said: "It would be well, Luramo, if you were to hurry ahead of us, to inform the people that we are coming. If you do not, some one else may make the same mistake you did and trouble may ensue."

So Luramo ran ahead, and in a few minutes disappeared from sight around a bend in the passage. Some fifteen minutes elapsed, during which the party strolled slowly down the corridor, and then Luramo was seen approaching at the head of a great crowd of people. The crowd moved cautiously, half fearfully as was the custom with men, but one could see that they were very curious, and all excited at the new wonder of which Luramo had told them. In the midst of them, an old man strode, a man dressed in a tunic all of white, and whose long, thin beard reached almost to his waist.

"Zar-Emo," whispered Tholura pointing at him, "there is the priest of the Tains, the wisest of all the Tains in the wisdom of our wise ancestors."

The High-Priest, Zar-Emo

He came, his right hand extended upward and outward, a sign of peace which Tumithak recognized and returned. The party of Tains halted a short distance away, and for a while the two groups stood, appraising one another. Then Tholura spoke.

"I have been to the Surface, Zar-Emo, and I return bringing guests. No doubt Luramo has already told you of how these men saved me, slaying shelk and Mog alike with their strange weapons. This one is Tumithak, their chief and the greatest Shelk-slayer, behind him stand Nikadur, Datto and Thorpf."

Zar-Emo acknowledged the introductions and then said: "Welcome to the city of the Tains, strange ones. It is many generations since one came here from without, other than foul Mogs and savage shelks. Yet we have had for long a prophecy that some day a hero would come from the Surface to teach us again the use of our ancestors' mighty weapons. Is it possible that you are he?"

Tumithak shook his head ruefully.

"No, Zar-Emo. I have heard of our wise ancestors' great wisdom, but I know far less of it than you do, if what Tholura tells me is true. Nevertheless, by a lucky chance, I have with me this shelk weapon. Perhaps from it you can learn something of the machines and weapons of old."

He unstrapped the fire-hose as he spoke and held it out to the old priest. The latter was about to take it, when his eyes fell upon the white and shining rods that Tumithak still carried strapped to his back. As he looked at them, the priest's eyes grew large with wonder, and his hands which had been extended for the fire-hose, dropped empty to his sides. He was silent with a sort of awe, and then at last he spoke.

The Story of the Rods Found in the Car

"There is something that you carry, O Shelk-slayer, that is mightier and more potent than either the shelk's head or the fire-hose! Whence did you get those white and shining rods?"

Tumithak told him briefly of the battle that had resulted in Tholura's rescue, and of the finding of the rods in the car, after their victory. Zar-Emo nodded.

"I do not think I can be wrong," he said, a trifle dubiously, and then, taking the fire-hose from Tumithak's still extended hand, he turned the screw in the long nozzle, opened a cap at its end—and drew out from its interiors the half consumed end of one of the white rods!

"Behold the Power!" he cried, dramatically. "The fuel by which the shelks operate their machines! And you, O Tumithak, are truly the one spoken of in our prophecy, for you have brought the one thing needed to enable us to operate the many machines that we have in our museums!"

As he spoke, his many followers bowed their heads in worship and in awe, and Zar-Emo stood, waving the stub of the rod at Tumithak while he continued in almost a frenzy of fanaticism: "With these can the Tains power the fire-hoses which we keep in our museums! With these, we can power the strange machines that blast the corridors into the ground! We may make new corridors, far deeper than the ones we now live in, corridors so deep that the shelks and foul Mogs will never reach us! With these the Tains will know safety at last."

"With these," interrupted Tumithak, waving the priest to silence, "we will teach the savage shelks that man still knows his destiny! With these, we shall drive the shelks from their stinking towers at Shawm, and with these, at the last, we shall slay, to the last one, the beasts that have for so long attempted to rule the earth!"

Behind him, the boy Luramo gave a cheer. Datto slapped his chief resoundingly on the back, while Tholura nodded her head eagerly in approval. Zar-Emo and the other Tains looked as if they could scarcely believe their ears. Tumithak decided that now was a favorable time to convert them to his beliefs, and so he launched into a speech, much as he had done many times before in Loor and Yakra.

Tumithak's Speech

He told of his own life, and of his mission; he told of his first long journey through the corridors; and lastly he told of how he had slain his first shelk and of his subsequent elevation to the lordship of the lower corridors. Then he begged the Tains to look at him, to realize that he was but an ordinary man, and that what he had done, any man could do. And in the end, the result of his speech was just as it had always been. The Tains looked upon him as something more than human; from Zar-Emo down, they swore allegiance to him; but almost to a man, they refused to believe that it was possible for them to even attempt to fight against the shelks.

At last Tumithak turned to the old priest and asked that he be assigned an apartment.

"I shall probably be here for some time," he said. "For the road to the Surface is blocked and I see no way to return to my own people until it is opened again. And it will be many sleeps before that can be accomplished."

"Perhaps less than you think," answered the priest. "I do not want to raise your hopes, but there may be a way to your corridors without returning to the Surface. I shall tell you more when I am sure of it," and turning, Zar-Emo led the way into the inhabited corridors.

For a period equal to three days, Tumithak lived in the city and the Tains lavished upon him their hospitality. He was astounded at their food, for the Tains had preserved the method of making their synthetic food-cubes *taste,* and for the first time in his life, Tumithak found that eating could be a pleasure, rather than a mere dull duty. Indeed, not only he, but Datto, Nikadur and Thorpf as well, were in danger of stuffing themselves into a state of indigestion.

Life Among the Tains

Most of the time when not employed in eating or sleeping, Tumithak and his companions spent in the great temple or museum corridor, studying the wonderful machines that had been built by the ancestors of the Tains. The Tains had kept them in perfect condition, and they were all in perfect working order, even after so many hundreds of years. Zar-Emo powered a fire-hose and a disintegrating machine, and showed the party how well they still worked. These two machines were of especial interest to Tumithak, for the one he knew how to operate and the other had been mentioned frequently in that famous book that he had found, so long ago, in the deserted corridor in Loor.

But these were not the only machines that the Tains had preserved, or that Zar-Emo knew the use or meaning of. The priest showed the strangers marvellous weapons that slew with shrill sounds; others that, so he said, turned the very air into a deadly poison that killed all who breathed it; and then, too, there were machines that helped man, among these being the machines that made the cool white lights that illuminated these corridors.

And all of these could now be used again although sparingly, for even the rods that the Loorians had brought with them could not last forever. These rods were composed of a metal that had been activated by treatment which caused its atoms to break down at a terrific rate. And when it was exposed to a certain ray created in the machines its collapse into energy was greatly increased. But, although this method of securing energy allowed an enormous amount of fuel to be stored in a very small space, eventually even the white rods were burned up and gone. So Tumithak decided that he must have a talk with Zar-Emo concerning the best use that the rods might be put to, in order that the greatest advantage might accrue. He suggested to the priest that he and his companions arm themselves with fire-hoses and attempt a return to their pit. Zar-Emo shook his head.

A Possible Alliance Suggested

"It would be a great danger to attempt to fight your way back to the pit from which you came, Tumithak," he said gravely. "I think I can help you in a way that will not only remove all the danger, but will bring your people and mine into an alliance that will be closer than you have dreamed."

Puzzled, Tumithak asked the Tain to explain himself, but Zar-Emo only shook his head.

"I am not at all sure that I can do what I hope to do," he explained, "and until I am, I prefer not to raise hopes that I may not be able to gratify."

But the next day, the old man called Tumithak and Nikadur to him and led them to a deserted corridor where a strange machine was set up. It was a machine far too complicated for Tumithak to understand. In appearance it was a metal box five feet high with a number of strange transparent tubes on the top of it, inside of which tubes there glowed strange lights. Out of the side of this metal box extended a long arm, at the end of which a great soft pad was fastened, apparently by suction, to the wall of the corridor. Zar-Emo pointed down the corridor, and there, approximately a hundred yards away, was another machine, identical in every respect to this one.

One of Zar-Emo's lesser priests was seated on a little stool that was fastened on the side of the metal box, and now, at a word from his master, reached up and placed on his head a strange piece of apparatus that entirely covered his ears. Then he turned a small knob on the box, and turning, called to the man that controlled the farther machine. The latter also placed the strange headgear on his head, and brought his own machine into play.

Trying a Sounding Machine in the Corridors

For several minutes, the two turned and twisted the little knobs and at each twist they listened intently, as though they could hear some distant sound that was inaudible to the others. Then the nearer of them turned to Zar-Emo.

"There is a different tune here, Zar-Emo," he said. "How are we to tell what it represents?"

The priest motioned him to get up from his seat, and then told Tumithak to take his place. Hesitatingly, the Loorian did as he was requested, and gingerly put the headpiece over his ears. As he did so a strange tone suddenly filled his ears, a continuous monotonous hum. Tumithak took the headpiece off and looked at the chief priest inquiringly.

"The machine, Tumithak," explained Zar-Emo, seeing the puzzled look in Tumithak's eyes, "was used by our ancestors to detect underground veins of metal, or water or even underground caverns. It is based on the principle of the echo. One part of this arm which is fastened to the corridor wall sends out a sound into the rock, a sound of so high a pitch that human ears cannot detect it. This sound travels through the rock until it strikes some different substance and there a portion of it is reflected back to another part of the arm, a receiver which picks it up and so alters it that it can be heard in the earpieces fastened on Coritac's head.

"Now this sound is not like the sounds that we are used to thinking of. As I have said, it is far too shrill to be heard by human ears, and such sounds act quite differently from common sounds. In the first place, these sound waves can be sent in a beam, as light waves are; and in the second place, they are slightly altered by the density of the material that reflects them. Thus it is possible to tell in just what direction the reflecting material is, and whether it is liquid, solid, or, say, a cavern or hole.

"Now it has been my thought, Tumithak, that if with this we could discover a long straight cavern running through the ground we could be fairly sure that it would be your home corridors and thus we would know in just what direction they lie. And by the help of another machine, some distance away, we could tell the exact distance of your corridors from here."

Locating the Loorian Corridors by Sound

Tumithak had listened in a daze. Vaguely he had understood some part of what the Tain had said, but this last was too much for him. It was necessary for Zar-Emo to explain to him the mystery of the two angles and an included side in great detail before he finally saw how it would be possible to measure the distance to his home from this far-off corridor. And when he did understand his wonder was increased.

"Truly, Zar-Emo," he cried, "the wonders of our ancestors were unending. But tell me, why have you gone to all this trouble to locate my home corridors?"

The Tain smiled proudly as he moved to take his place on the seat from which Tumithak, in his excitement, had moved.

"Have you forgotten the disintegrating machine?" he asked. "Tumithak, I intend to drive a new corridor from the pit of the Tains to the pit of the Loorians!"

The hours that followed were exciting ones. Time and again, the workers thought they had discovered the distant corridor, only to find on further examination, that their discovery was only one small cavern or underground stream. But at last they detected what, from its straightness and regularity, could be nothing other than a man-made corridor. Then Zar-Emo and his men began a series of tests and problems that ended, at last, with the verification of the exact distance and direction of Tumithak's home corridor.

The party returned to the inhabited portion of the pit and jubilantly prepared for the work of the next day. The disintegrating machine was taken to the spot where the detectors had been and there set up, a queer, monstrous thing with a great trumpet-shaped ray projector in front, and with three seats on the back of it to accommodate the men that worked it. Zar-Emo left his men working over it and, taking Tumithak with him, returned to the city for supper.

"I feel that you should be one of the men to take the machine through the rock, Tumithak," he told the Loorian, as they finished the meal. "Not only because the honor surely belongs to you, but because it may be necessary to have someone to convince your friends that our mission is friendly. You will have little to do with the operation of the machine and that little will not be hard to learn."

So, after the time of sleep was over, the party assembled in the hall that contained the disintegrating ray machine. Nikadur and the Yakrans, who planned to follow Tumithak as quickly as possible, were each given one of the ancient fire-hoses, as was the boy Luramo, who insisted that he be considered one of Tumithak's party. And to Tumithak's surprise, another insisted that she, too, be considered a warrior—none other than Tholura, who declared that she would not let her new friends go forth to any danger without also going along. So at last it was decided to let her go with them, and then Zar-Emo approached Tumithak, who already was at his seat on the machine, and proceeded to instruct him in his duties.

The Operation of the Machine

"See here, Loorian," explained the priest. "Behind you on this wall is a large white cross. Looking through this eyepiece in front of you, you will see another cross painted on this mirror in which you will also see a reflection of the first cross. As long as the reflected cross is superimposed on the other, your machine is going in the right direction. Should it vary by even so much as a hair's breadth, you must at once call it to the attention of these other men who work the machine. That is all that is necessary; my men will attend to all the rest. Your party will follow you as soon as the rock becomes cool enough to walk on. Good-bye, and let us hope that everything turns out as we have planned it."

He turned as he spoke and gave an order to the men seated with Tumithak. One of them turned a lever, there was a blinding flash of light, and as it dulled to a faint violet glow, Tumithak saw a great hole appear in the side of the wall toward which the trumpet-like projector pointed. The other man now pulled back on his lever, pushed a button of some kind, and the great machine moved slowly into the hole it had made. As it moved the hole grew deeper, and a hot gust of queer-smelling air swept out of it. Again the machine pushed into the hole, and again the further wall retreated. Tumithak and his friends were successfully engaged in an act that had not been performed by men for nearly two thousand years!

Boring the Tunnel

For hours thereafter, Tumithak kept his eyes fixed to the eye-pieces of the machine. It was tedious work, for it was not often that the machine varied from the straight path on which it had been set. Once in a while, it would strike some new vein of rock, and this might cause it to change its direction slightly, but then Tumithak would call this to the attention of the others and the fault would be at once corrected.

The huge white cross which Zar-Emo had painted on the back corridor wall grew smaller and smaller as the machine crept away from it, but when Tumithak could no longer see it clearly he focused the center of his own cross on the distant mouth of the new corridor and the machine continued on its way.

The heat was terrific. Sweat was soon streaming down Tumithak's face and the faces of the two priests. At last after what seemed to be hours of continuous moving they unanimously agreed that they must call a temporary halt. The machine was stopped and all three lay back in their seats for a much-needed rest.

After about an hour they started the machine again. "We are probably more than half-way there," said one of the priests, "but this second half will seem much worse than the first. It is not so easy for the heat to escape now as it was when we were close to the city."

He was right. Never had Tumithak felt such heat before, and never had time dragged so. It seemed days, days of scorching merciless misery before one of the men announced that they were at last nearing their goal. Tumithak became eager now, and so, of course, the time began to pass more rapidly. And then, at last, a strange hollow roar began to sound from the rock in front of them, and in a moment, a small hole appeared that rapidly widened and as the priests hastened to shut off the power of the machine, Tumithak leaped from his seat and found himself in an old familiar corridor.

A Corridor Familiar to Tumithak—A Letter from His Father Scratched on the Wall

He stood in a section of that roughly unfinished corridor that lay between the Surface and the Halls of the Esthetts. Not far from here, he had once watched a group of shelks slay a group of Esthetts, and trembling with horror, had wondered why they did so. And not more than two miles down this corridor, if memory served him right, his band of warriors should be waiting. "Were they still there," he wondered, "or had they given his party up for dead and returned to Loor and Yakra? Or had the shelks discovered them and slain them all?" Tumithak remembered with sudden misgivings the fact that Datto had told him of boasting to the shelk chief of having raided the Halls of the Esthetts. And the shelk chief had ordered an investigation! Unable to control his anxiety, thinking of a thousand and one things that might have happened, he beckoned to the two priests to follow him, and sped down the corridor.

As he neared the spot where his party should be, his anxiety increased, for a silence reigned that told him that the corridor was deserted. At last, he reached the place where his men should have been, to find that his fears were verified. But on one side of the wall a message had been scrawled, a message from his father:

"Tumithak," it read, "Our guards have reported the approach of a band of shelks. The savages of the dark corridors have offered to conceal us in the clefts and caverns of their home, and so we are leaving this place. If you ever return, seek for us in the dark corridors.

Tumlook."

Tumithak, at first, was for starting for the dark corridors at once, but on second thought he decided to wait until the coming of the party that would soon be arriving from the city of the Tains, for he knew that they would follow as closely as possible. So he and the two priests sat down and ate some of the food they had brought with them and then, entering a concealing apartment, they prepared to take a much-needed sleep.

The Meeting

They were awakened by sounds in the corridor without, and emerged to find Nikadur, Tholura and all the others who had arrived while they slept and had been much worried over their disappearance. Nikadur had discovered Tumlook's message, at last, and was about to make the attempt to lead the party down into the dark corridors when Tumithak and his companions were discovered. The party, reunited now, decided to begin at once the attempt to find Nennapuss and the other warriors, and so they began the descent; but they had not gone a mile when they came upon the entire party, warily returning to their former camping place. They had hidden in the dark corridors while the shelks held an investigation in the corridors above, and when they felt sure that the latter had again returned to the Surface, they had boldly set out to return to the Halls of the Esthetts.

Nennapuss and Tumlook, who were leading them, were overjoyed to see their comrades safe again, and they eagerly plied them with questions. Tumithak related their story briefly and told of the wonderful machines that they had managed to procure. The enthusiasm of the Loorians and Yakrans knew no bounds; they even so far forgot themselves as to give a cheer that echoed again and again through the corridors. And then the leaders sat down and began to formulate a plan of attack upon the city of Shawm.

CHAPTER VI

The Whelming of Shawm

The ensuing hundred hours were busy ones for the people of the pits. The six or seven miles of new corridor became a teeming thoroughfare, through which Tains, Loorians and Yakrans hurried busily back and forth, trading the captured beauties of the Esthetts for the wonderful food that was the secret of the Tains, and for the ancient weapons that were now so precious.

Tumithak returned to the city of the Tains and brought Zar-Emo through the new corridor to confer with his other chiefs on the possibility of attacking Shawm. For several days they plotted and planned, and at last a feasible method was devised. Nikadur, with Tumlook, Nennapuss and the Loorians and the Nononese, would remain in the home corridor, while Tumithak, with Datto, Thorpf and the Yakrans, was to go through the corridor and the pit of the Tains, and, returning over the Surface, was to attack the town from the other side.

The ones who remained in the pit were to wait for fifty hours, and then, in the third hour of the night following the expiration of the fifty hours, they were to attack. Thus if their plans went well the two attacks would be simultaneous, unexpected and, they hoped, overwhelming. The shelks would be caught between two fires and, so the pit-men hoped, wiped out to the last one. The city of Shawm would be in the hands of men, together with all its wonderful engines and machines, and man would again have a place in the sun, on the Surface of the world.

It was a proud Tumithak that led his bravely singing Yakrans through the city of the Tains and up the labyrinthine corridors to the place where the entrance had been blasted shut by the shelks. They paused for a time, while a Tain with a small disintegrating machine opened the way for them again, and then they resumed their march, out over the Surface. And here Tumithak was halted by a party of Tains who had followed them up the corridor. There were about ten of them and leading them was the boy, Luramo.

"Wait, Tumithak," he called, "here are a few more warriors to go with you. Not all the Tains are the cowards you seem to think them." He turned and beckoned the party to advance, and Tumithak perceived that the majority of them were mere boys, youths who had not yet completely developed the terrible fear that was so much more noticeable in the older folk. His eyes roved over the group and suddenly halted in surprise.

"You, Tholura?" he exclaimed in amazement. "You are going with these warriors? I fear this war party is no place for a woman, Tholura."

The girl answered him indignantly.

"I hope you spoke without thinking, Tumithak," she said. "Surely, if you but think, you will remember that of all the Tains, I was the first to dare look upon the Surface. Have you forgotten how you said that I was one after your own heart? And would such a one cower in the corridors while others went to fight the enemies of man?"

Tholura Is to Fight with the Warriors

Tumithak smiled. The girl had convicted him by his own words, and now that he stopped to think, he wondered why he had suggested that she remain behind. He only knew that he felt a sudden unexplainable feeling that it would be terrible to live in this world if Tholura were slain in the fight. He had sought to protect her in the easiest way—by ordering her back to the corridors.

But now he knew this was impossible, and so, with a shrug, he motioned her to take a place beside him, along with Datto and Thorpf.

The party left the foothills and marched across the grassy plain without incident or adventure. Once in the forest, Tumithak felt safer, especially as night was approaching and he knew that, although this would make marching much slower, nevertheless, there would be practically no danger at all from the enemy. Dawn found them close to the spot where the other white and shining rods had been hidden, and soon after, to their great delight, they came upon them, still hidden in the leaves where Tholura had concealed them.

They realized that they could not be far from the city of Shawm now, and it was a cautious group of warriors that moved slowly behind Tumithak as he darted from tree to tree or crept along through the underbrush, whenever it was thick enough to conceal him. At last, they reached the summit of a rocky, sparsely wooded hill and looked down across the wood at its base to see the towers of Shawm in the distance.

The needle-like towers, with their connecting cables and gleaming metal sides presented a strange appearance to the pit-men, but the day had been so full of strange appearances that the only feeling they had was one of satisfaction that here was their goal. Tumithak continued to look out over the towers as if in search of something, and presently uttered a pleased cry.

The Entrance Opening to Loor

"Look there, Datto!" he cried. "See there, the opening to our pit?" and sure enough, beyond the group of towers could be faintly distinguished the shallow hole that held the opening to the vast corridors that led to Loor. Somewhere, not far below, Tumlook and Nennapuss waited with their army for the moment to arrive when they could sweep out and begin the conquest of Shawm.

Tumithak pointed out the pit-mouth to the others, Tholura and Luramo being especially interested in the location of the hole. While they were still looking at it, a cry arose from one of the Tains and turning, Tumithak saw him pointing up into the sky. The Loorian looked and gave a cry of fear, for sweeping down on them was one of the shelks' flying machines, a huge one, one that must have, concealed within it, at least a dozen shelks!

In a moment, the scene was one of indescribable confusion. Gone were the brave thoughts of conquest, the minds of the men were taken up only with the great hereditary fear that had for so many generations oppressed them. The Tains, and indeed most of the braver Yakrans, broke from the group and fled, vainly trying to hide themselves behind rocks, trees, bushes or whatever seemed to promise shelter. Ere two minutes had passed, the only ones who remained with Tumithak were Datto, Thorpf, Tholura, the boy Luramo and three other Yakrans. These, all of whom were armed with fire-hoses, stood their ground and watched the oncoming flyer. Like a huge bird, its wings outspread, the machine hovered for a moment and then sank to the ground. A door in its side opened—and Tumithak sent a blast from his fire-hose into the opening! There was a clattering cry and the door closed again. Tumithak smiled grimly and motioned the rest of the party back. A large rock stood about twenty yards away, and to this he led them hurriedly, taking a position behind it and awaiting further movement from the shelks.

Now it was fortunate for Tumithak that this flyer was a freighter and as such was not equipped for fighting. Several of the shelks within it were armed, of course, but there were no guns mounted on the outside, nor was it possible to use a fire-hose from within, when the doors were closed. So the shelks could not attack the men from within, and, strange as it may seem, it never dawned on either Tumithak or his companions that the plane was absolutely at their mercy. For so many years had the weapons of man been directed only at their enemies, that the idea of destroying the shelks by burning down flyer and all never entered Tumithak's head. And so the battle seemed to have reached a deadlock.

The Flying Machine Captures Tholura and Two Others

And then, suddenly, as though a decision had been reached within, the shelk flyer rose about fifty feet and swung above the rock that concealed the little party. It hung there for a moment, and then from beneath its hull, a huge claw-like hand of metal reached out, the car dropped with dizzying suddenness, and the claw closed over three of the party and swept them aloft! Tumithak gave a wild cry, as did the others, for one of the three who were seized was Tholura!

The thoughts that swept over Tumithak as he watched the flyer swing aloft again were puzzling in the extreme. He saw, in his mind's eye, the battle in which he met Tholura; he remembered her bravery and her beauty; he thought of how dull and uninteresting his world would be if she were suddenly taken out of it—and then, suddenly, he realized that he loved her. And she was being taken from him! Madly he cast about in his mind for some method whereby he might save her. Now the idea of blasting the flyer with his fire-hose came belatedly to him, but already it was so high that if he attempted this, Tholura was almost certain to be killed in the crash. While he sought some means of rescuing her, he saw the flyer sweep down over the forest and disappear among the towers of Shawm. Tholura, if not already dead, was a prisoner of the shelks!

For a while, Tumithak gave way to grief. Little Luramo came up to him and took his hand, and Tumithak saw great tears in the lad's eyes, yet when the Loorian looked at him, the boy forced a smile and said bravely: "There is still work for us, Tumithak. Let us mourn my sister after we have avenged her."

The brave words gave Tumithak a new grip on himself. Luramo, he knew, truly loved his sister, yet the lad remembered their mission was one that called for sacrifices even greater than this, if possible. It behooved Tumithak to remember it also.

Tumithak's Grief and His Recovery to Fight

So, a few minutes later, Tumithak was his old self again; and calling back to him such of the Yakrans and Tains as could be found, he berated them roundly for their cowardice and urged them to redeem themselves as well as they might in the coming battle. Then he called to Luramo, and pointing to the distantly seen pit-mouth of the Loorian pit, he asked: "Do you think that you could find your way through the forest to the pit-mouth, Luramo?" And when the lad answered in the affirmative, he went on: "You must go straightway and inform Nikadur that the attack must begin at once. The shelks in the flyer will surely warn Shawm of our presence, and so we can no longer delay the attack. Meanwhile, we who are here will attack at once. So hurry, Luramo!"

The little Tain sped off down the hill, and in a moment, disappeared into the wood at its base. Then Tumithak gave the command and the party moved to the attack of Shawm.

Strange events had been happening in the shelk-city of Shawm. It was not a large town, nor an old one, as towns go; it was little more than a recent settlement in this wild unsettled land, which had for many centuries been abandoned by the shelks. Yet in all the history of the town, nothing similar to these recent events had been heard of. From somewhere deep in the corridors, a race of men had made their appearance that were apparently wild and decidedly vicious. First had come the strange slaughter of a Mog with the accompanying pursuit and escape of the creatures that slew him; then close on the heels of that strange catastrophe had come the news that a party of shelks and Mogs had been slain by their own weapons in the woods beyond Shawm. The party that went to investigate had been wiped out almost to the last one, those who escaped returning to tell of men armed with fire-hoses, who had fled into the pit of the Tains. And this was most puzzling, for one of the wild men, who had been captured and supposedly sent to Kaymak, had intimated, while captured, that he had come from the pit that held the Halls of the Esthetts.

The shelks had at last begun to make preparations to invade both of the pits and make certain of their safety by completely wiping out all traces of men in them, when a flyer arrived in the city, telling of a large force of men armed with heat-rays, which were near the city, and bringing three armed specimens, in its claw, for proof.

At once the wildest excitement prevailed. The shelks rushed hither and thither, arming themselves, taking posts in various portions of the city where a watch was maintained on that part of the wood from which the danger might be expected to appear, and getting ready all the strange weapons that the little town could boast. Hakh-Klotta, the Governor-Inferior, unable to believe that men could actually be intelligent enough to use heat-rays, called together a group of trained hunting men, and sent them off in the direction from which the flyer had come. He watched them from a tower as they crossed the cleared space between the towers and the trees, and smiled a savage smile as he noticed them near the trees in safety. Certainly, if there had been any wild men in the woods they would have burned down the Mogs before the latter reached the comparative protection of the trees, he thought. But hardly had these thoughts taken form in his mind before he saw a burst of smoke from the ground in front of the Mogs, and then another, and another; and before his very eyes, his Mogs fell to the ground, and slowly burned to cinders beneath the heat-rays directed on them from the forest.

A Real Danger Threatens the City

This convinced Hakh-Klotta that the danger was a very real one, and made him more cautious in his movements. He began to wonder if it would be possible to attack these strange men at all, seeing that they were hiding among the trees at a distance beyond the reach of the heat-rays. He knew that the pit-men dared not to leave the shelter of the trees, but then, the shelks dared not leave the shelter of the towers. And so it began to seem as if the battle might take on the appearance of a siege.

But, meanwhile, the idea of a siege was very far from Tumithak's mind. He knew that he would be unable to approach Shawm from this point, for there was a broad open space of nearly four hundred yards between the forest and the towers; but the Loorian remembered that at the point where he had first escaped from Shawm, the trees had approached almost to the towers, and so, leaving a detachment of men under Datto and Thorpf to besiege this portion of the town, Tumithak, with a dozen others, set off to attack the town on that side where the trees were closest to it.

The Attack

It was fortunate for Tumithak that he formed the idea when he did, for the mind of old Hakh-Klotta was not slow and the thought of this danger came to him almost as soon as it came to Tumithak. As soon as he thought of it, he immediately dispatched a group of shelks to defend the spot, and so, as Tumithak and his warriors approached through the trees, they saw the shelks wending their way through the towers.

Instantly, Tumithak called his men to attack, while at the same moment, several blasts of heat flashed at him from the party of shelks. He darted behind a tree, calling to his men to likewise conceal themselves, and then, turning on his fire-hose, he directed its beam at one of the towers beneath which the shelks were cowering.

The shelks at once turned their rays upon the bases of the trees behind which the men were concealed, their idea obviously being to burn down each tree and then strike the man behind it. But Tumithak had been seized with a better idea, and so he called softly to his men to direct their fire at the towers to the right and left of the shelks, burning only those sides that were nearest the group. The others grasped his idea and at once began to carry it out. The trees were filled with the sap of early spring and so they heated slowly, but metal towers absorbed the heat rapidly and before the heat-rays could burn through the trees, Tumithak's object had been accomplished. Two of the towers, one to the right and one to the left of the shelks, suddenly collapsed, their foundations melting beneath them, and down they came with a crash, burying the entire group of shelks beneath them. Most of the shelks were killed outright, others were seriously injured, and the only one that was apparently unhurt, turned and sped like lightning farther into the city. The men looked on in amazement, unable to believe their eyes. Yet, incredible as the fact was, they were actually looking at a shelk, fleeing from a group of men. For a space, they stared in wonder and then it dawned on them that their brush with this party of shelks had been successful. The defenders were all dead or dying, and the way into Shawm was opened!

It was not the plan of Tumithak to dash recklessly into the city, however. He at once gave orders that began a steady, methodical burning of the towers in this portion of Shawm. One after another the towers crashed to the ground, their foundations blasted away by the terrific heat of the fire-hoses in the hands of the Yakrans.

The Towers Fallen, the City Exposed

And as the towers fell, the pit-men moved forward into the ruins, and, concealing themselves, began the destruction of towers farther within the city. But they were not to continue their work of destruction for many minutes. Before a half dozen towers were destroyed, they found new parties of shelks opposing them, and in a moment of carelessness, two of the Yakrans were slain before they could properly conceal themselves.

Within the city, now, the men from the pit were at an advantage. The shelks, however desperate, did their best to slay their enemies without destroying their homes, while the men had no such compunction, and would have gladly destroyed all Shawm to kill a single shelk. And so, in spite of a number of casualties, Tumithak and his men moved forward until he reached a spot where he could attack, from a little elevation, the party that was defending the town from Datto and his men.

Then the huge Yakran chief, his even huger nephew, and their savage warriors, dashed across the open space before the city and in a moment were in the town. With wild cries, they attacked the shelks, forgetful, now that they were at close grips with the creatures, of either fire-hose or disintegrating ray. And indeed, at such close quarters, the rays became double-edged weapons, liable to slay friend and foe alike, and even the shelks seemed to realize their danger and ceased to use them. Strange knife-like weapons appeared in their claws, sharp disks of steel mounted on sticks and rotating rapidly, like a child's pinwheel; dangerous weapons, indeed, for whenever they touched an arm or leg or head, it was sheered off instantly.

And so the battle raged in hand-to-hand conflict, like the battles of the ancient world, before the dawn of modern knowledge. For the first time in nearly two thousand years, Man was facing his enemies on equal ground, and a good showing he was making, too. The shelks already were yielding ground to the men, when a cry from beyond them told Tumithak that Nikadur and the Loorians had emerged from the pit. He gave a triumphant answering cry and attacked the shelks with renewed vigor.

To tell all the details of the battle would require a story longer than all of this one. It had become a vast series of individual encounters, and in such a fight, heroes are made by the dozen. Thurranen of Nonone first distinguished himself in this fight, as did several others, who were afterward to become famous knights in Tumithak's kingdom; Luramo verified Tumithak's belief in him; while the others, Datto, Nikadur, Thorpf, Nennapuss and Tumlook and their ilk showed added prowess by the fearful way in which they brought down shelk after shelk.

The Battle Reaching Its End

Twice Tumithak faced old Hakh-Klotta himself; twice lesser shelks bravely died to allow the old governor a chance to avoid the leader of the pit-men. It was astounding to Tumithak to see how willing the shelks were to die defending this old ruler. It was his first contact with that strange social instinct that was afterward to enable him to gain such great advantages over the shelks. He was in after years to learn that a battle with the shelks was somewhat like a game of chess—capture the king and you capture all.

But now the Loorian was ignorant of this fact and so when Hakh-Klotta avoided him he was content to attack some lesser shelk. And the battle continued, while shelk after shelk died in a manner that must have seemed strange beyond telling, to them. Imagine a man dying in a battle with sheep and hogs, with sheep and hogs that used guns, knives and that united together to destroy a village! That is probably as close an analogy to this strange raid as we of today can conceive.

We must not suppose that the battle was entirely with the pit-men. In places the shelks would be temporarily victorious and dozens of men would die under the whirling knives of the shelks. In places, too, men would be isolated from the main battle, and then a fire-hose, wielded by some shelk, would blast them to cinders before they could flee.

But for every man that died beneath the shelks' whirling knives, two shelks would perish beneath the swords or the arrows of the men; and for every group that died under the fire-hoses of the shelks, another perished beneath the fire-hoses of the men of the pits.

Retreat to the Flying Machine

Until at last, as the sun sank low in the heavens, the last group of shelks gathered close to the huge flying machine that lay in the center of the village, and attempted to make a last stand. They had hoped, much earlier in the day, to enter the flyer and escape, in order to bring help from the large city of Kaymak, some distance away; but Tumithak had forestalled them by ordering one of his men to play a fire-hose across the entrance from the protection of a near-by tower. And so they had been balked of their desire. They had made their last stand here however, hoping that some last minute accident would enable them to enter the flyer and escape.

It seemed that there would be little chance for them now. It would be but a moment until they were cut down. And then the Loorian, who had been guarding the entrance to the flyer, gave a cry and fell backward, his head burned to a cinder by the heat-ray of some concealed shelk sniper. Nikadur immediately directed his own fire-hose in the direction from which the ray had come, and had the satisfaction of seeing a burned shelk tumble screaming from the window of the tower, but the few seconds during which the door of the flyer was unguarded enabled fully half of the remaining shelks to enter the flyer and swing shut the door. Hakh-Klotta was the first to enter, needless to say, and then, as the door swung shut, the few remaining shelks died instantly under the rays of the Yakrans. Tumithak was just about to order the fire-hoses to blast the flyer to molten metal when a terrifying thought came to him. Tholura and the two captured Yakrans had not been seen in any part of Shawm during the fight. Was it possible that they were still in the flyer? If they were, to blast the flyer would mean their certain death. Tumithak turned sick at the thought of how close he had come to giving the order that would have slain them. He ordered his men back from the flyer and waited in anxiety to see if it would rise, bearing away with it the shelk chief and the one in all the world that Tumithak loved most. But as moment after moment passed, and the flyer did not move, he gained renewed hope. Perhaps the flyer was injured in some way, and could not rise.

Tholura Is Now a Slayer of Shelks

Perhaps the shelks were so seriously wounded that they could not operate the machine. And then, just as he was about to give an order to attack the machine and try to get within it, the door of the flyer flew open and a disheveled, white-faced figure stood in the doorway. It was Tholura; and on her head was a golden band such as the Governor-Inferior of Shawm had worn. And in her hand was a charred and dripping head—the head of Hakh-Klotta of Shawm!

"Tumithak!" she called weakly, and then, spying him rushing toward her: "Tumithak," she cried. "Take me. I love you and now I am worthy of you . . . and I too am a slayer of shelks."

CHAPTER VII

The Walls of Shawm

Tholura's story was soon told. As the flyer had swept toward Shawm, she and the two Yakrans had been drawn up into the body of the machine, disarmed, and thrown unceremoniously into a corner, where they had cowered in terror, wondering what was coming next. The excitement caused by the news which the shelks in the flyer told on their arrival, and the tumult of the battle which immediately followed, evidently caused the shelks to entirely forget them; and so they remained locked in the flyer all during the fight. Toward the last, Tholura so far regained her courage as to begin a search of the flyer. She went looking around here and there, examined the controls and decided that they were too complicated to experiment with, looked here, there and everyplace in search of some sort of a weapon, and finally, to her surprise and delight, found the very arms which had been taken from them earlier in the day. The shelks had evidently tossed them carelessly into a chest used for storing baggage, and it was here that the girl found them. It was obvious that here, as all through the battle without, the shelks had underestimated the intelligence of the men against whom they were fighting, and here, as in the fighting without, they were to pay dearly for their mistake.

Grimly, Tholura strapped the box to her back and sat down at the entrance to await the return of the shelks. When the door opened, she hid herself until the entire party was safely within the cabin, and then she opened fire on them with the heat-ray. The shelks did not have a chance, but in her excitement, Tholura forgot how the use of the fire-hose in such confined quarters would raise the surrounding temperature. She and the two Yakrans also had almost been overcome by the heat, before they could manage to get the door open and escape to the cooler air of the outside.

The Battle Was Ended—The Last Shelk Was Killed

But now the battle was over, the shelks were dead to the last one, Tumithak and Tholura were united again, and the pit-men had cheered themselves hoarse when Tumithak announced his intention of marrying Tholura at the earliest opportunity.

Then Tumithak, at Datto's suggestion, allowed the warriors to disband and turned the city over to them for looting; while he gathered together his officers to discuss ways and means of properly protecting the city proper.

Next morning Nennapuss approached the Loorian chief with a very business-like air and asked permission to read a list he had compiled. Tumithak nodded permission and the Nononese cleared his throat, and, in the oratorical voice that was so characteristic of him began:

"This is a list of all the engines and machines that have been captured in the taking of the city. I took the liberty of ordering all men who had obtained these machines to make a report of them, and the following is a summation of their reports. We have secured twenty-seven fire-hoses, which, added to the forty-four which the Tains provided, makes seventy-one in all. We have two hundred and fifty rods of the power metal, a cache of which was found in the tower of the chief shelk. Twenty-six small machines of the type that makes nothing of things, four strange going-machines which no one can make to go, one machine with strong arms that seems to be made for lifting large objects, one machine to fly through the air, and seventy-two machines of which at present we know not the use."

Tumithak smiled at the formidable list which the chief of Nonone had so carefully compiled, and then considered seriously for a moment.

"The fire-hoses," he announced at last, "and the rods of metal may become the property of those who found them. The machines of which we know not the use shall remain in the possession of those who have them until we find out their use. But the disintegrating machines shall become the property of the council, to be used for the protection of the city. Tell Datto and Zar-Emo to report to me."

The two chiefs came and Tumithak laid before them the plan which he had conceived for the protection of the city. Enthusiastically, Zar-Emo and Datto departed and busied themselves in setting up the disintegrating machines in the manner agreed upon. A huge circle was drawn on the ground all about Shawm and then, at equal intervals about this circle, the machines were set up, and Tains spent some time teaching the use of them to warriors who were assigned to operate them.

For a guard, one of the many that Tumithak had placed in the towers and on the higher elevations of land beyond the city, came rushing to the chief to announce, in a voice laden with terror, that a number of great bird-like shapes had appeared on the distant horizon, and were moving rapidly toward Shawm.

"They are shelk-flyers, Tumithak!" he cried in fear. "Let us flee to the pits at once, Tumithak."

The Shelk-slayer silenced him with a stern gesture, and, turning, ordered a messenger to summon the other chiefs. When they arrived he began at once to give them instructions for the defense of the city. Messengers were sent rushing to the guards who maintained a constant watch at the disintegrating machines, others assembled the possessors of fire-hoses in the center of the city, while still others busied themselves with the work of herding the women and children into the pits, that they might be safe in the event that the battle went against the defenders.

By the time that all these preparations were completed, the shelk fleet (which, although Tumithak could not know it, was probably little more than a group of freighters, ignorant of the conquest of Shawm, which were bringing supplies to the little city from some larger metropolis), had reached a point not over a few miles from the town. Standing on the little elevation near the center of Shawm, Tumithak, with Tholura at his side and his chiefs behind him, watched its approach. The shelk-flyers were ornithopters and the lazy flap-flap of the metal wings caused them to flash intermittently in the sun.

On they came, suspecting nothing, until they reached a point but a few hundred yards away from the city, and then they began to descend. The clattering hum of their engines could be heard plainly now, and Tumithak began to look anxiously toward the ground beyond the city. Would his plan work, or were the pit-men about to participate in a desperate battle that would question their very existence?

The End of the Fleet

And then, just when the Loorian had given up hope, came the event that he had been waiting for. There came a splitting roar from the foremost of the flyers, it gleamed momentarily with a brilliant, a dazzling light —and then it was gone! There was a clap of thunder as the sound of air rushing in to take the place of that destroyed by the ray reached their ears, and that was all.

Tumithak smiled a relieved smile and turned to Tholura.

"The disintegrating machines," he explained. "They have been set up so as to form a huge cone of rays over Shawm through which nothing can pass until we shut off our machines. There is a watch over the machines, day and night, and whenever anything strange appears in the sky, the power is immediately turned on."

He turned and watched the remaining flyers. The main body of the machines, about seven of them, had been flying immediately behind the leader, and had not attempted to stop when the leader was struck. They had no cause to believe that the machine had been attacked from the ground, and apparently those who noticed its collapse credited it to some accident within the flyer.

And so, before they could help themselves, they, too, had moved on within reach of the rays and in less than a minute they, too, had roared into oblivion. One straggler, indeed, managed to avoid the general fate for a few moments, and Tumithak watched it anxiously, fearful that it might succeed in escaping entirely, and reach some distant shelk center from which it could bring an army that would wipe out the pit-men entirely. But fortunately this was not to happen, the men who controlled the disintegrators, considering it a point of honor to completely wipe out the entire shelk fleet, directed the whole battery of sixteen machines against it and under such a barrage escape was impossible. The last flyer exploded noisily (the disintegrating rays were weak at that distance) and a fine rain of dust over the forest marked the last of the fleet.

The breeze that had sprung up at the moment of the turning on of the disintegrators, and which had grown until it was a brisk wind, died down now, and Tumithak turned to Tholura and gave her a kiss of triumph. Then he gave a sigh of fervent relief, for he had been uncertain as to how this method of defense was going to work.

"We have triumphed once more," he said softly, and then: "But they will come again, Tholura, they will surely come again. . . . But when they do, we will be ready for them."

I continue to be amazed at Tanner's realism. In the battle between the Mog and the woman, there was no last-minute rescue of the woman or any last-minute conversion of the Mog. It is clear that further sequels were in Tanner's mind, but they did not appear.

Nine years later, in the November 1941 issue of *Super Science Stories,* there was indeed a third story in the series, "Tumithak of the Towers of Fire." I never read it, however. Perhaps I ought not; it might be a disappointment.

The battle between human beings and the shelks remained with me, of course, and influenced me in my description of the battle (on a large scale) between human beings and the Lhasinu in *The Black Friar of the Flames.*

The Great Depression had reached its low point in 1933 just before Franklin D. Roosevelt was inaugurated president. The science fiction magazines felt the pinch. There was a general withering.

Worst off was *Astounding Stories.* Actually, of the three, it was the most successful from the standpoint of circulation and earnings (I believe), but the publishers were having Depression-born troubles, and when the heart died, the limbs withered.

The June 1932 issue of *Astounding Stories* was the thirtieth and last of the monthly issues. Thereafter, the magazine came out at two-month intervals. It staggered on, in this way, for four more issues, and with the March 1933 issue, the Clayton *Astounding* was dead.

I was not greatly distressed at the loss of the Clayton *Astounding*, for I had never liked it. However, it was clear that its end was symptomatic of more general difficulties in the field, and as 1933 wore on, the evidence grew stronger and stronger that there might soon be no science fiction at all to read.

After the June 1933 issue, *Wonder Stories* became bimonthly too, and with the November 1933 issue, it returned to the pulp size—this time permanently. *Wonder Stories Quarterly*, after fourteen successive issues at three-month intervals (the first three having been called *Science Wonder Quarterly*) came to a final end with the winter 1933 issue.

As before, *Amazing Stories* held out best, but even there, there were signs of trouble. For one thing, it changed its appearance.

Ever since it had begun publication, the phrase "Amazing Stories" had appeared on its cover as a series of block letters, with a giant initial *A* followed by the other letters in rapidly and progressively diminishing size. In 1933, that vanished, and, in an apparent attempt to gain readership by a greater appearance of respectability, "Amazing Stories" became a series of equal-sized letters printed diagonally across the cover. The cover illustrations became more nearly monochrome and more nearly modernistic.

I hated it at the time, and when I received the issue containing "Tumithak in Shawm" from Sam Moskowitz and found that it had such a cover, I hated it all over again.

Then, in mid-1933, *Amazing Stories* skipped an issue for the first time in its seven-and-one-half-year history. It put out an August–September 1933 issue. This did not mean a shift to regular bimonthly publication, however. With the October 1933 issue, *Amazing Stories* was on a monthly basis again, but it, too, had now gone pulp size. By the end of 1933, then, the large-size science fiction magazines were gone. (In later years, there were several attempts to produce science fiction magazines in large size again, but they were uniformly unsuccessful.)

As for *Amazing Stories Quarterly*, that was coming out with increasing irregularity. There were only three issues in 1932, only two in 1933, and one, last issue in 1934.

Amid all this disaster, there were signs of hope. *Wonder Stories*, having gone pulp size, also restored itself to a monthly schedule. And as for *Astounding Stories*, it was, surprisingly, reborn.

What happened was that Street & Smith Publications, Inc., bought *Astounding Stories* from the bankrupt Clayton people and began to publish it themselves, the first issue under the new regime being that of October 1933.

At first, it didn't seem that this meant much. The first issues used up the stories that had been at hand before the Clayton *Astounding* had died, and they did not please me, either.

But the new editor, F. Orlin Tremaine, was to be in charge for four and a half years (the period of the so-called "Tremaine *Astounding*"), and he had bold ideas. The result was to become apparent soon.

Part Five

1934

Part Five

IN February 1934, I entered "sixth term" at Boys High. As a startling innovation, the school offered a special course in creative writing for those
who chose to take it, and I jumped at the chance. I had been writing, on
and off, ever since I had worked on the Greenville Chums. I don't remember any of the details at all, except that I remember being occasionally
driven to attempt to write poetry.

Now there seemed a chance for me to demonstrate my literary prowess.
(Somehow I saw the class only as a chance to shine. It never occurred to
me that I might learn something. I felt I already *knew* how to write.)

The result was utter fiasco. Surely few young men have had so marvelous a chance to make fools of themselves and then took advantage of
the chance as liberally as I did. Everything I wrote was laughable, and it
was all laughed at thoroughly, both by the teacher and the other students.

I mentioned this in *The Early Asimov* and mentioned further that the
one useful result of the course was that I wrote a humorous essay entitled
"Little Brothers," which was published in the Boys High School literary
semi-annual.

Until I mentioned the essay, I had never thought of it particularly, but
once *The Early Asimov* appeared, I began to wonder if I ought to try to
get a copy. In February 1973, I gave a talk to a group of librarians from
the New York metropolitan area, and attending was the present librarian
of Boys High School. When she introduced herself, I asked at once if there
was any chance she might perhaps locate a copy of the literary semi-annual
in some of the dusty storage bins of the school.

In June 1973, she succeeded, and sent me a copy. This book had already
been put together but was still in an early stage of production, so I could
make the necessary revision.

When the magazine came—its name was *Boys High Recorder*, incidentally, and the issue was spring 1934—I turned to "Little Brothers" at

once and read it eagerly. I was sure I would find in it the clear signs of writing talent.

Alas, I didn't. It sounds exactly as any essay would that was written by a precocious fourteen-year-old. How disappointing! And yet, in order to keep the record complete and to prevent myself from receiving a horde of letters demanding to see it (presumably in order that all my readers have the same chance to laugh at me that the members of the damnable writing class did), here it is:

LITTLE BROTHERS

My mission in life right now is to express the venomous feelings that we "big" brothers have for the bane of our lives, the "little" brothers.

When I first received the news that I had a little brother, on July 25, 1929, I felt slightly uncomfortable. As for myself, I knew nothing about brothers, but many of my friends had related at great length the inconveniences (to say the least) of attending babies.

On August 3, my little brother came home. All I could see was a little bundle of pink flesh, with apparently no ability to do the slightest mischief.

That night, I suddenly sprang out of bed with gooseflesh all over me and my hair on end. I had heard a shriek apparently made by no earthly being. In response to my frenzied questions, my mother informed me in a commonplace manner that it was just the baby. Just the baby! I was almost knocked unconscious. A puny, nine-pound baby, 10 days old, to make such a scream! Why, I was convinced that no less than three men together could have strained their vocal cords to such an extent.

But this was only the beginning. When he began teething, the real torture came. I did not sleep a wink for two months. I only existed by sleeping with my eyes open in school.

And still it wasn't all. Easter was coming, and I was feeling joyous at the prospect of a trip to Rhode Island, when that kid brother of mine got the measles and everything went up like smoke.

Soon he reached the age where his teeth were already cut and I hoped to obtain a little peace, but no, that could not be. I had yet to learn that when a child learns to walk, and talk baby-language, he is rather more of an inconvenience than a cyclone, with a hurricane thrown in for good measure.

His favorite recreation was that of falling down the stairs, hitting each step with a resounding bump. This occurred on the average of once every other minute and always brought on a scolding from my mother (not for him, but for me for not taking care of him).

This "taking care" of him is not as easy as it sounds. The baby usually shows his devotion by grabbing generous fistfuls of hair and pulling with a strength that you would never have thought possible in a one-year-old.

When, after a few minutes of excruciating torture, you persuade him to let go, he seeks diversion in hitting your shins with a heavy piece of iron, preferably a sharp or pointed one.

Not only is a baby a pest when awake, but is doubly so when taking his daily nap.

This is a typical scene. I am sitting in a chair next to the carriage, deeply immersed in *The Three Musketeers* and my little brother is apparently sleeping peacefully; but he really isn't. With an uncanny instinct, in spite of his closed eyes and inability to read, he knows exactly when I reach an exciting point and with a malicious grin selects that very moment to awake. With a groan I leave my book and rock him till my arms feel as if they will fall off any minute. By the time he does go back to sleep, I have lost interest in the famous trio and my day is ruined.

Now my little brother is 4½ years old and most of these aggravating habits have disappeared, but I feel in my bones that there is more to come. I shudder to think of the day when he'll enter school and place a new burden upon my shoulders. I feel absolutely sure that not only will I be afflicted with the homework which my hard-hearted teachers will give me, but I will also be responsible for my little brother's.

I wish I were dead!

Needless to say, this essay is completely fictional except that the dates of my little brother's birth and his arrival home are correct. Actually, my brother Stan was a model child, who gave me very little trouble. I did wheel him about in his carriage an awful lot, but that was always with a book open on the handlebar, so it didn't matter to me. I also sat by the carriage when he was sleeping, but again I invariably read—and he rarely disturbed me. What's more, he always did his own homework when it came time for that.

I am most thunderstruck by my reference to "the prospect of a trip to Rhode Island." What a lie! There was never a prospect of a trip anywhere. Never! Not while we had the candy store.

One more thing about the *Boys High Recorder*: All through the four decades since that writing class, I have wondered about the kids who laughed at me in that class. Are any of them aware that they laughed at the wrong person? That I was destined to become a successful and prolific writer? And what have *they* accomplished? Anything? (Don't get me wrong. I don't hold a grudge. It's only forty years. Any decade now, I'll forget.)

Unfortunately I didn't remember any of the youngsters in the class, and I decided, rather uneasily, that I had better not try to find out. For all

I knew, their names would now be recognizable to me as those of great writers. For all I knew, for instance, men of the caliber of Norman Mailer had been in that class. (Not Norman Mailer himself, of course. He was only eleven at the time.)

When I got the *Boys High Recorder*, therefore, I looked at the title page, all set to wince badly. Every piece had been written by members of that class and only the best had been taken. . . . So I went down the list and not one name was familiar to me. Not one! Except my own, of course.

What a relief!

What I wrote in that traumatic creative-writing class, by the way, was never science fiction, and a good thing, too. Had I written science fiction and been laughed at, it might conceivably have inhibited me from writing more of it for a long time.

What saved me was that I still didn't think I was capable of writing science fiction. At the age of fourteen I might have dreamed of writing at the old *Amazing/Wonder* level, but the Tremaine *Astounding* in its first astonishing half year had kicked matters far out of my reach again.

In that half year, *Astounding Stories* took a clear lead over the other two magazines, which were now fellow pulps. With the backing of the affluent Street & Smith chain of magazines, *Astounding Stories* flourished and expanded, while *Amazing Stories* and *Wonder Stories* were visibly stagnating.

Astounding Stories had the best stories, the most interesting artwork, the liveliest letters column. With the March 1934 issue, it increased the number of its pages from 144 to 160, so it became the largest of the magazines, and it charged only twenty cents, to the twenty-five cents of the others.

This all had its effect on me. After five years of allegiance to *Amazing Stories* as the best of the magazines, I switched instantly and massively to *Astounding Stories* and so did nearly everyone else. Beginning in early 1934, *Astounding Stories* became the dominating magazine in science fiction and has remained so, through a couple of changes in name, a couple of changes in editor, and many changes in competition, for forty years.

One thing Tremaine introduced was what he called "Thought-Variant" stories. These were stories that advanced new ideas, unlike any that had been seen in science fiction before (or, at least, any that had become clichés). In general, the thought-variants pleased me and pleased other readers as well.

Consider "Colossus," by Donald Wandrei, for instance.

COLOSSUS

by Donald Wandrei

"Their (certain astronomers) picture is the picture of an *expanding universe*. The supersystem of the galaxies is dispersing as a puff of smoke disperses. Sometimes I wonder whether there may not be a greater scale of existence of things, in which it *is* no more than a puff of smoke."—Sir Arthur Eddington, *The Expanding Universe;* Macmillan & Co., 1933.

Like a flame in the sky, the golden-red stratoplane circled Mount Everest and dipped toward its crest. Not so many years ago that peak had been unclimbed, almost unknown, a challenge to man. Wintry gales tore across this top of the world, and cold rivaled precipices to defeat assault. The bitter winds still blew, but a man-made tower rose higher than the old peak, and a landing field which was a triumph of engineering audacity and genius stretched over sheer space beside the tower.

The circling stratoplane landed and rolled to a stop. The man who climbed out—Duane Sharon—seemed distinctive even in his heavy flying clothes.

His hands were powerful. No one would have admired any single feature of his, the hair of casual brown, a weathered face, a nose far from classic, and eyes of gray that glittered or softened as occasion required. But the general effect was good. He had a kind of loose rhythm, and a genial personality.

He sauntered toward the great observatory of the WLAS—World League for the Advancement of Science. Fifteen years had been required to build and equip this observatory which had been planned as long ago as 1960.

Once inside the tower, he identified himself and tossed a cheery word to the guard before sauntering into the observation room.

Probably the 400-inch reflector of Mount Everest Observatory would never be surpassed. Man, on Earth, could go no further toward conquering the limitations of atmosphere, metals, and optics. Through this gigantic mirror, underlying a telescope in whose construction the efforts of dozens of great minds had been united for years to produce an instrument of un-rivaled accuracy, intricacy, and range, equipped with every device desired by and known to astronomers, study of the universe had reached a climax.

A man of ascetic features was studying the reflector. His speculation must be idle, since the Sun had not set. Calculations and symbols, equations and reductions covered a blackboard near him. A sheaf of scribbled pages lay on a table beside a heap of photographs, charts, and books. Professor Dowell had his own quarters, but he usually worked in the observation room itself. Here the temperature always remained constant, at thirty below zero, but special clothing warmed him and nonfrosting goggles permitted vision.

Dowell did not look up until Duane stood beside him. Even then, consciousness of another's presence was slow to dawn.

"Hello! Am I intruding?" Duane asked.

Dowell blinked. A far-away look in his eyes faded. "Not at all; I'm glad you came. Here, have a chair—sit down!"

"Thanks, but I've been sitting in a plane for the last hour. I'd rather stand around for a while. Anything new? What's on your mind?"

The astronomer motioned toward the calculations. "You remember when you were here the day before yesterday? And I showed you photographs we made of the thirty-first magnitude nebulæ in the Orion group?"

"Of course! You said they marked a milepost in astronomy."

"Did I? Yes, yes; to be sure. Just to think that only eighteen magnitudes were visible until we built this telescope, and now there are thirty-one, while the known universe has been expanded to nearly a billion light-years."

"Don't!" protested Duane. "That's too much!"

The professor did not hear him. "I'm puzzled about a phenomenon of the thirty-second magnitude."

"What is it?"

"There is no thirty-second magnitude!"

Duane reflected, lit a cigarette. "That's very interesting," he remarked. "I don't understand."

Dowell fretted. "Neither do I. Several nights ago, we photographed nebulæ of the thirty-first magnitude. According to Jeans' theory and Valma's equations of the expanding universe, there should be nebulæ up to about the fortieth magnitude."

"And there aren't?"

"Right."

"What's the reason?"

"I don't know. There are only two possible answers. Either Valma made an error, which is inconceivable, or our whole theory of the universe is wrong."

Duane thought this over. "How?"

Dowell paced back and forth nervously. "You know the three main theories of the universe, of course. There's the old one that space is limitless and extends forever in all directions. There is the theory elaborated by Einstein early this century, that space is affected with a curvature which makes it return upon itself. After Einstein, a group headed by Jeans advanced the idea of an expanding universe which might be said to create space as it expanded."

"Yes, I'm familiar with them and some others," Duane commented.

"No doubt. But nebulæ and dark spots from the thirty-first to fortieth magnitudes do not exist, though they should. That may mean any of several possible explanations. Perhaps the universe has stopped expanding. Perhaps it is stationary, or even contracting now. Or if Einstein was right, perhaps the outer star-clusters have swerved through the curvature of space so that they are now approaching us instead of receding. That would account for the surprising number of aggregates in the twenty-ninth to thirty-first magnitudes. Possibly the oldest theory is correct, but some unknown set of factors prevents us from seeing galaxies beyond the thirty-first order. There are other possibilities."

"What's your guess?"

"I don't know," Dowell replied querulously. "But there is a fourth alternative that has almost driven me mad just to think about."

"So? What's this one?"

Dowell polished his glasses. "I don't know whether I can explain it, the concept is so gigantic. Well, here goes: You are familiar with the atomic theories. Has it ever occurred to you that all the billions of stars that form all the millions of nebulæ and galaxies of our whole universe might be only the electrons of a superatom upon which vast beings might exist as we dwell upon the surface of Earth? That concept would explain the absence of nebulæ beyond the thirty-first magnitude.

"From there on would be an outer shell, or an invisible plane of energy and tension that incloses our universe but is substantial enough for beings to live on. There is no such thing as solid earth. The apparently solid matter we are standing on is, ultimately, atoms, electrons, vibration, with spaces between each particle comparatively as great as those between the stars and galaxies."

The voice of the astronomer trembled in presenting this tremendous theme. "Think what might happen if some one from Earth could burst through that superatom!"

Duane pondered. "It's a staggering conception. If you carry it out to its limit, that giant atom might be only one of billions of other atom-worlds on a scale we can't even begin to imagine, and all that super-universe form-ing—what?"

"A molecule! And there might be on that still vaster universe still more tremendous beings! And that molecule might be only one of billions of other molecules sown through trillions of trillions of light-years of space and forming even——"

"Don't!" Duane cried. "It's too big! I can hardly grasp it!"

He stared at the reflector. When sunset came, its vast disk would gather the light of stars from far places, light that had been traveling since land boiled out of steaming seas and formed continents on young Earth. Lights of infinity, the stars would record their being upon plates for men like Dowell to analyze.

In the old days, the prophets had looked at the night sky and bowed to God who made Earth the center of the universe of fixed stars. Then the scientists had come to prove that the Sun was the center only of a plane-tary system that moved in a universe. Then the astronomers had shown that a spiral haze in Andromeda was a galactic universe 800,000 light-years away, and that the whole Milky Way was only a galaxy among thou-sands.

So the roll of star-fields mounted, and the boundaries swept outward, and men's imaginations, roving afar, found new glory while the universe expanded and its depth staggered understanding. Beyond the stars lay nebulæ, gaseous and spiral and helical, with vast voids between; until by 1933, some 30,000,000 galaxies were identified in a range of 200,000,000 light-years; and by Duane's time, with the Mount Everest telescope, the range had risen to over 800,000,000 light-years, comprising 150,000,000 galaxies, each composed of millions of stars.

"Tell me," Dowell requested, "how is the *White Bird* coming along? Is she about ready? It was stupid of me to bore you with my guesswork."

"Don't mention it," Duane answered. "It wasn't dull. The mere idea of limitless space is as exciting as life itself. As for the *White Bird,* she'll be done by October. The power-converters are being installed now. I think that a preliminary test can be made in September."

"I see. Perhaps you'll have the honor of informing us astronomers what the other universe really is like!"

Duane retorted: "Long before then, you'll have worked out the one theory that my voyage will only prove to be true. I still wonder if the theory you mentioned a while ago could be right. And what would happen if the *White Bird* could carry us through?"

"If there were beings on that giant atom, they would never see you, so infinitesimal would you be. We have never seen an electron, let alone anything that might be on an electron. And you could never get there in a million lifetimes even at the speed of light."

"True," Duane answered thoughtfully, "but I haven't told you the whole story. The *White Bird* draws on intra-spatial emanations and radiations. It has unlimited power. It should be able to reach a maximum velocity of thousands of light-years, *per second!*"

"What!" shrilled Dowell, his face shining with excitement. "Do you realize what that means? You and the *White Bird* would extend in the direction of flight until you were as tenuous as a gas and elongated to thousands or even millions of times your first proportion! The ship would swell sidewise as well from the transverse energy-pull of the universe! You might become huger than Earth, or the solar system, or even our galaxy! You would be Colossus himself! And you would never realize any change because you would have nothing for comparison! Duane, if you do it, you may burst through to that giant atom, and you *would* be visible to, and you *could* perceive, whatever was on it!"

Duane, overwhelmed, looked dreamy-eyed. "Vast concepts!" he murmured. "They're too much for my brain."

"Colossus!" Dowell half whispered, as though this vision, this apex of cosmic conjecture, dominated his mind and exerted a hypnotic fascination. "Colossus of time, space, and matter!"

"Even the mention of such a journey appalls me."

"I wish I could go with you."

"Nothing would please me better."

"I know, but if Anne is along—by the way, I suppose you would like to see Anne?"

Duane, the chain of cosmic theory broken, made gestures of mock deprecation, "Oh, my, no! Anne? Why, I merely came from America to make sure that Mount Everest was still standing."

"I like that!" A musical but at the moment sarcastic voice broke in. "So it's Mount Everest you're here to see and not me? Well, you can have Mount Everest." With truly feminine pique, the girl who had entered banged the door as she went out.

Anne was not a beauty in the sense of Mona Lisa or a movie star. She had above all animation of expression, clearness of thought, and more than average appeal. Her dynamic qualities were masculine wit, reason, energy, originality. Her æsthetic characteristics were feminine changeability, the figure of a patrician, Nordic features with mahogany-colored hair, a rhythmic stride and beauty of motion.

Probably she was most effective when annoyed as at present, for the triumph of emotion over reason lent her face a kind of hectic charm, and she made a study of strength and weakness.

Duane turned to Dowell. "If you will excuse me, I'll try to make my peace. I——"

"Go right ahead!"

It took little time to find Anne. It required patience to pacify her. He need not have done so, but he found delight in playing up to her mood. The game of pursuit and the world of pretense would never change, however long Earth wore away to old age.

II.

The holidays of August drew to a close. September came in with a burst of riotous colors through forest and hills. Work on the *White Bird* came to an end. Professor Dowell knew of its imminent launching. So did Anne. The world did not. Duane figured that there would be ample time to tell the world after, of success or failure.

It was a windless evening whose chill approached frost when he and Anne stood beside the *White Bird* at Havenside, north of New York.

"Almost anything can happen," Duane said gravely. "The ship may not work, something might go wrong, or we might run into dangers beyond our knowledge. Do you know what you are letting yourself in for?"

Anne looked at him with slightly disgusted eyes. "I'm not a child. Forget this protective business. Let's go."

Duane sighed. Anne's realism was disconcerting.

The girl's eyes sparkled as she looked at the *White Bird*. "Only you could have built such a thing of beauty," she said and impulsively clung to Duane. She darted off as he made a futile grab and laughed at him, teasing, "That wasn't an invitation, Duane!"

"The devil it wasn't!" Duane shouted in exasperation and dived after the fleet-footed girl. Breathless they came to the *White Bird's* entrance.

The ship lay long and low in the light of the full moon. It shone with a glow like phosphorus. A hundred feet in length, the cylinder, never more than ten feet thick, tapered to points. Crystalite composed its shell—crystalite, that strange element numbered ninety-nine. Invented by chemists, it had the transparency of glass, the color of platinum, and a higher tensile strength than any other metal, combined with a melting point above 6,000° C.

The *White Bird's* interior contained only essentials: a pilot room; a cabin; a supply room; and the front and rear power compartments. The torpedo looked bizarre, for its shell was transparent, but the inner walls dividing room from room were of vanachrome, that thin, rubbery steel which was virtually indestructible.

To look at the *White Bird* was to look into a house like a glass cylinder and see the rooms within, though, from within, no room could be seen from any other room.

"I'll never get over this funny arrangement," Anne remarked as they entered. "The whole world can look inside, but I have to walk from room to room to see what's there."

"Not a bad idea," Duane answered cheerfully. Anne's eyelids went down. Duane fidgeted. He suddenly stated, "Let's go!" and pushed a button.

The *White Bird* curved up from the ground like a real bird soaring after a dive.

"Oh!" exclaimed Anne. "You should have warned me!" Her face sobered. The great adventure had begun. "Isn't it strange?" she asked in a very small voice and with very big eyes.

"It's a miracle," Duane answered. His fingers caressed the dials as he spoke. "Just to think that a simple condenser-transformer picks up cosmic radiations all around us, turns them to power and drives us on. Power by radio, more power than we could ever use, out of thin air!"

Anne emerged from her awe, but she seemed a different girl with more of the poetic about her. There was indeed a new luminous quality to her face while she took in the impressive spectacle of the skies.

The *White Bird*, at steadily mounting speed, passed beyond the stratosphere.

Above them, the sky darkened and blackened. Stars brightened to a brilliance that dazzled the eyes.

Then the Sun of the solar system became visible beyond Earth, and the light of the Sun and its reflected glare from Earth and Moon bathed the *White Bird* in a flood of radiance so bright that Duane and Anne donned goggles, and the craft's interior became perceptibly warmer in spite of the crystalite hull.

There was a glory to the skies, a spacious sweep, an infinite majesty of stars that ranged from brilliant white to faint and far-away orange, from pale blue to flame red and emerald green, which silenced the voyagers by its cosmic beauty.

It was long before either traveler spoke, and steadily the *White Bird* fled outward, erasing the way to the Moon in ever faster time.

Anne broke the reverie. She waved her hand toward the universe. "If all this affects us so much," she said simply, "what would we feel out there?" She pointed toward the faintest star, out where the spiral nebulæ began in Andromeda.

"When I go there, perhaps I can answer then," Duane replied.

A dreamy look entered Anne's eyes, and they shone with an almost mystical fervor. "I have a queer idea, Duane. Maybe it wouldn't be so different from Earth. Back home, everything is related to something else. The same trees grow every spring. The same Sun rises and the days are always alike. Don't look so skeptical—you know what I mean. Of course they aren't the same trees, and the days are separated by time, and there aren't any two persons alike, but, just the same, nature repeats herself, and there seems to be some sort of pattern to everything, a pattern that unites everything and recurs again and again." She ended with a breathless rush of words.

"I think you're right," Duane mused, "but who knows? I don't. I don't suppose any one will ever know, unless he can go out there, where the stars end."

"Why don't we?" A hectic note heightened Anne's voice, and her cheeks flushed with excitement.

"Why don't we?" Duane echoed. "Why—I mentioned it to Professor Dowell and we joked about it, but I never really expected to go beyond the planets."

Mysterious raptures burned in Anne's eyes. "I wonder what's beyond the stars?"

That question which the wisest philosophers never have been able to answer, and the most learned astronomers have fretted in vain to solve, brought only reflective silence from Duane for a long period.

"I don't know," he said at last. "Professor Dowell thinks I might break through and discover that our whole universe is just an atom, and the great atom might be only one world among billions forming a still more gigantic molecule. Why, Anne, if he's right——"

Anne looked dazed. "What an idea! You'll go mad thinking about it. Why, it gives me the creeps!"

"I don't wonder!"

"I once took a course in biology. If we are essentially like matter, then electrons make atoms that form cells that compose organs which are part of a body. If that's so, Duane, and you got on the giant atom-world, and could go still farther, you might eventually come out on a vast living organism of which Earth is merely part of a single cell."

"Now you're giving me the creeps! Don't think about it. The idea is maddening. It's all I can do just to picture the giant atom!"

Anne went on recklessly, with morbid mischief, "Darling, maybe some one like you on one of those invisible particles inside you is traveling outward now on a space ship and is going to burst through on a cell——"

"Anne!"

"—and you'll feel just a little twitch in your side, and maybe he'll keep on going and pop out of your brain finally and——"

Duane stopped this merciless and all-too-vivid description by the simple process of kissing Anne's inviting lips.

"Oh!" She broke away. "What a man! Is that all you think about?"

"Sure, when I'm with you!" he answered candidly; and then, serious again: "But don't forget, Anne, that the world is a powder mine right now. If war comes, all trips are off."

"War!" she blazed. "You would agree to murder and give up the pursuit of something that will mean more than all the wars in history? I will never love you for that!"

Duane kept a thoughtful silence.

Visions beyond infinity and past eternity changed gradually to speculation about the Moon, which loomed ever larger overhead. The buoyant feeling that Duane and Anne should have experienced as they drew away from the attraction of gravitation did not materialize, since the speed of the *White Bird* counteracted it.

The Moon swelled, cut off a fiftieth, a tenth, a fifth of the sky above. Their viewpoint modified. Instead of flying upward, they found themselves falling. The new perspectives of space gave rise to new experiences and unfamiliar sensations. They had been shooting upward from Earth. Now they were descending toward the Moon.

Duane cut off their power. The *White Bird* fell at furious speed. He turned on the forward repellers, unloosing upon the Moon's surface an invisible bombardment of energy that almost counterbalanced their speed.

The *White Bird* plunged less rapidly, slowed, and finally hung a few thousand feet above the Moon.

"Only Doré could have dreamed it!" exclaimed Anne.

Great craters pitted its surface. Masses of slag and lava flowed down the sides of extinct mountains, and fissures like the marks of giants' swords marred its lowlands.

Dead sea bottoms and barren continents alone suggested life of long ago; these, and certain clusters that might have been cities; masses of granite, blocks of marble and basalt, quartz, and silica, arranged in geometric formations. Were these ruinous heaps the remains of cities? Had a civilization flourished here, of a race that had perished, leaving only its works to crumble beneath the everlasting encroachments of time? What legends and records, achievements and histories might lie beneath those shards?

Duane drew a deep breath. The answer would never be known to men. Great as the curiosity was that impelled him to study the riddles of the Moon, the dangers were greater, and greater still the goal of his dream.

There was a mystery to all the universe. What lay beyond? Where would the end be, if one started off and traveled at random in any direction for as long as space lasted or life permitted?

"Let's land!" cried Anne. "Just imagine—walking on the Moon! And we can do it with your space suits!"

"Not now. We ought to be returning to Earth. There is little to be gained by landing, and a lot that we might lose."

Anne looked hurt. "All this way, all this trouble, and we don't find out what's on the Moon?"

Duane, exasperated, cursed inwardly this plague of woman's desire, this wish to exhaust the moment. Aloud, he answered: "We can always come. I've proved what I wanted—the *White Bird's* capacity. Let's head home. Our next trip will take us—well, wait and see."

"Where will we go?"

"Outside. Away to the end of things, whatever that may be. The *White Bird* can do it, and I'm going to where space ends. Whatever lies beyond the universe, empty and endless space or giant atom, I'll find—with you."

Anne's eyes shone. She held the breathless appearance of a mystic to whom a vision of glory comes. The dream transfigured her face as she gazed at infinity and saw the far places. Sappho might have had so lovely and rapturous an aspect when she stood on a cliff of Lesbos and looked at the sweep of sky and wine-dark sea. Never before, and never again, did Anne's expression achieve such beauty. And Duane, as he watched her, absorbed something of her mood, that supernal wonder which the old philosophers and the great poets and the prophets have been gifted with.

Alexander, wishing for more worlds to conquer; Marco Polo, wending his way across lands of legend; Columbus, sailing upon unknown waters; Peary, assaulting the roof of the world; Lindbergh, winging through the skies—the ghosts of all the master explorers and travelers of the past haunted him, and he felt an invisible presence urging him on to that voyage for which history, and almost thought, had no counterpart. An exaltation of spirit possessed the two, and spontaneously they leaned together in unity of mood and vision.

"The way is homeward," said Duane at last.

"And outward," echoed Anne. She lifted her hazel eyes to his, and even he, well as he knew her, was startled by the unfathomable depths that they showed.

Almost regretfully, he sent the *White Bird* flying Earthward, and the crag-strewn, jagged, white ruin of the Moon's surface fell swiftly away, paled into softer outline, until once again, like a silver disk in the sky, it floated glowing and lovely and bathed in soft radiance. Then the majesty of stars and the procession of the Milky Way; and Earth looming larger. A buoyancy of spirit raised Duane to a peak of mental intoxication.

Here, in open space, he felt a sense of freedom such as he had never before known. Was it the nearness of Anne, whose mere presence influenced him strangely? His partial escape from the attraction of gravitation? Or a headiness that came inevitably from this preliminary voyage? He looked at the Moon and Earth, Sun and stars, the great void beyond, and then back to Anne. Anne's eyes were refreshing. Especially when they were as large and reliant as now. Duane parked her beside him on the way back. There was a mutual need for physical reality in the presence of space rampant.

III.

September marched into October; and the maples vied with the oaks in colors of russet and tawny and flame. Earth throbbed with the activity that was industrializing Africa, tapping energy from the Gulf Stream, capitalizing power from the Sun. Socialized Russia in the eastern hemisphere stood powerful and defiant against the yellow menace that rolled over northern Asia. The proscripted United States, operating under dictatorship with industrial and capitalistic socialism, wealthier and stronger than ever before, with the unfit retired, the insane eliminated by euthanasia, and the criminal sterilized, surged on to dominance of the western world.

Economic rivalry in the new market of Africa created estrangement between England and the United States. The ugly undercurrents of competition and diplomatic folly were repeating themselves in the World War. Russia and the United States against Japan and England seemed to be the coming line-up of Titans, with the rest of the world involved in a holocaust that would undoubtedly mark the end of civilization.

Duane looked at a news sheet. "Japan Creates Secondary Militia of Women; British Claim New Germ That Kills Millions," ran the headlines.

"The world goes mad," he mused. "I only hope that all this slaughter will be over by the time I return."

For the remodeling of the *White Bird* went on swiftly. Adjustments of the delicate power controls to give the ship greater drive, corrections in its sensitive hull so that it might make the utmost of cosmic rays, gravity attractions, and atomic repulsions, correction of instruments to accuracy—these were changes that must be made before the *White Bird* could start upon that tremendous voyage to the end of the universe.

The work ran on, and the world raced ahead to disaster. The looming clouds of war grew blacker, and Duane fretted. What did the bickerings of mankind matter when so vast a project neared fruition?

October nineteenth. Mist opened the day at Havenside. By noon, a fine rain was falling, and the skies were solid gray. Duane roved restlessly around. To-night was the night of launching. The *White Bird* would set out to the ends of the universe, in an effort to solve one of the greatest riddles that confronted man—the mystery of space.

Twelve o'clock brought an ominous note. Duane, as always when he felt nervous, sat down at his light-piano and rippled off phrases of his favorites—a Bach fugue, the frantic monotone of Ravel's *Bolero*, Lecuona's wild *Malagueña*, a few bars from the *Peer Gynt* suite of Grieg. And while he played, upon a panel in front of him, wizardry of supersonics transformed sound to light and color that wove a visible symphony.

Duane had reached an impressive passage from *The Hall of the Mountain King* when the televisor broke forth: "Count Katsu Irohibi, Minister of War for Japan, announced at 11:55 a. m. to-day that Japan was prepared to drop bombs of a new nature upon any part of the world by remote control unless Russian aggression in Central Asia ceased immediately, and unless the United States and England permitted her to compete with them in the development of Africa."

Duane felt a growing tightness. He anxiously wanted to fly immediately to Everest and bring Anne back, but she would not be ready until two, by which time Professor Dowell and she would have analyzed the previous night's photographs—their final effort to riddle the stars and uncover the secret of perplexing vacua beyond the thirty-first magnitude nebulæ.

He rambled through sonatas and fugues, fragments of symphonies. The drizzle turned to a sodden downpour, and the oaks and poplars shook with sodden groans.

About twelve thirty, the televisor erupted: "Russia replied to Japan's ultimatum at 12:25 p. m., to the effect that she was not the aggressor, and that her territorial rights would be fully protected in Central Asia. The British and American governments simultaneously issued a redeclaration of African policy, denying the right of interference to any third party.

"Russia's defenses and offenses are already fully mobilized, as are Japan's, according to unconfirmed report. England is expected to issue a proclamation of national peril at any moment. John L. Caverhill, dictator of America, will declare our position shortly, according to reports from Washington. The situation has grown tense. Analysts fear a recurrence of the World War upon a more serious scale. Every effort is being made to avoid armed conflict, but—" the voice droned on.

Prophetic clouds of war! Events were moving far too swiftly in a world of delicate economic adjustments. Duane turned away from the speaker's image and strode toward his stratoplane.

Rain beat upon him and ran in rapid trickles down the slicker he had donned, a sullen, heavy, steady rain splashing from skies of slate. Nations plunged toward disaster. Darker than any clouds loomed the threat of war. Mass murder might come by nightfall—and his dream would be ended. Duane had no illusions. If war came, he knew that he would plunge blindly in at the draught like millions of other pawns in the game of economic kings. He would serve for loyalty, patriotism, many reasons, but he would serve unwillingly because a greater goal lay at stake.

He climbed in his stratoplane, headed toward Tibet. Anne should be ready by the hour of his arrival. The voyage through infinity would begin at sunset—unless war intervened.

Skies of blue steel overhung Everest. The quarrels of nations seemed something alien and apart from this austere summit of Earth. The sky-ward pointing finger of the observatory rose like a timeless tower, a thing of perpetual beauty, a challenge above the assaults of weather and war, age and decay.

But the televisor gave pictures and words of ugly meaning: "War Minister Irohibi issued a proclamation at 1:10 interning all Russian ships lying in Japanese ports. The order will remain in effect until Russia makes a satisfactory explanation and settlement for the mysterious explosion that wrecked the Japanese embassy in Stalingrad yesterday. It is reported that a great concentration of all Russian aircraft is now taking place outside of Stalingrad.

"Simultaneously, a second note was received at Washington demanding unrestricted colonization privileges for Japanese in the recently formed Anglo-American territory of Tanesia in Southeast Africa. The state department has made no official reply as yet; but a bulletin issued at noon to-day announced the perfection of a new instrument of war. Short-waves are sent by remote control to cause the collapse by vibration of buildings at any given spot. The situation is critical. Mobilization may be ordered by nightfall."

Suppressing the anxiety and weariness he felt over this danger that loomed, Duane landed his ship and walked into the observatory.

Professor Dowell was striding back and forth irritably, his sandy mustache bristling. "War! War!" he choked. "They want me to work out formulæ for the flight of projectiles! They want me to tell them just how to shoot at a point a thousand miles off and kill every one within a mile radius. Me? And there is work to be done on those!" He waved thin fingers toward the sky whose stars were hidden by day.

"I know; I'm worried, too. It looks like the end."

The astronomer raved: "They want to store munitions here! Make this a mere depot! This, the finest observatory ever built!"

Duane tried to soothe him. "War has not been declared yet. Every one knows that it will be the end if it comes. It will be the last war and maybe the last of civilization. But where's Anne? I took out the license this morning. We're to be married at three, and I've advanced the take-off to three-ten."

The professor bristled in one of those swift changes of mood that make the individual both fantastic and human. "Running away, eh? On the eve of battle, as the historians would say?"

"No," Duane replied steadily. "I've got a goal. A tremendous goal. Something that may enrich man's life more than the last two thousand years. I have a mission. If I fail, what is one life lost? If I succeed, the rewards will be beyond guessing. If I stay here—what? Whether I am killed or not, nothing is gained. Therefore, I go. If that is cowardice, then I am glad to be a coward. If war is declared, I will serve. Frankly, I am trying to get started before war begins."

Dowell stalked around. "Madness, all is madness. Let war come. Science must push on. There may never be another opportunity to find out what lies at the end of the universe. Electrons and atoms. Giant atom universes in a vaster molecule." He paused and stared owlishly a long minute through thick glasses at Duane. "Go away!" he commanded. "I'm upset. I do not know what I say. Find Anne and take her with you, my blessings upon you both!" He snorted and trod about in nervous circles, weighing —who knows what?

Duane turned away from this spectacle of a fine mind sent askew by the forces of disaster.

Anne was laboring over photographs. She glanced up as he entered her workroom. "Hello!" she greeted him. "I'm fine, thanks, even if you didn't ask."

"Now, Anne——"

"I know the rest. These photographs are more important. Nothing beyond thirty-one."

"Listen, lady——"

"And what's more——"

Anne never finished the sentence. She suddenly found herself picked up and carried out. She did not seem to mind.

"Hello!" exclaimed Professor Dowell, surprised. "And good-by!"

"See you when I return!" Duane called.

"Good luck!"

Duane deposited Anne in the cockpit beside him and headed home-ward. She leaned back, stretched in a most unfeminine but natural fash-ion. "So we get married today?" she remarked casually.

"So it would seem, but don't let that bother you. You'll get over it and—"

The televisor cut in: "Emergency announcement! Japan declared war against Russia at two-five to-day. The Bank of England has just issued a call for the loan of one billion pounds by popular subscription. The department of war of the United States has evoked the compulsory clause of the war code of 1943. All males registered as voters are required to report at their district military station before sundown."

Duane stepped up the speed of his stratoplane to the limit.

"That means—what?" Anne queried.

"The end," replied Duane grimly, "unless we leave sooner."

The stratoplane bored westward high above the Atlantic. New York City curved into view, a vague blur looking like some fantastic toy with its towers and megaliths, its setbacks and hanging gardens and sky palaces showing as a sodden blur through the rain that still fell.

Duane headed north of the city and landed at Havenside. Standing beside the hangar that housed the *White Bird,* with rain pouring down his face and oilskins, he smiled at his bride-to-be. Casual though they had been thus far, he felt the stir of vast, sinister forces that menaced life, and felt, too, a surge of emotion that was novel.

A small blue plane darted from leaden skies toward them. "That must be the official minister and the National Marriage Bureau's representative," Duane speculated.

Anne, looking suddenly flustered and with heightened color, decided: "Say, darling, I'll go straighten myself up a bit if you don't mind," and turned toward Duane's bungalow. "What a rotten day!" The steady downpour had soaked fields and trees, and pools gathered in every hollow.

A blast of sound, an explosion like thunder smote the air! The stratoplane's televisor crackled: "A terrific explosion has just occurred in New York City. The explosion was preceded by a shrill whine. It is believed that this is the unofficial opening of war. It will be recalled that Japan announced the possession of a new explosive that could be dropped in bomb form on any part of the globe by remote control. Stand by! A second whine has come——"

Out of the televisor came a roar that deafened. Then silence. And out of the south swept a second blast. Duane looked up. The blue plane rocked wildly in violent currents of air. Rushing winds caught it, flung it upward, sent it spinning to earth. Flames licked it up; the wreck became a funeral pyre. The rain eddied in mad gusts.

Duane's face was gray. "It is war," he said coldly and swiftly. "Get anything you want. We're leaving now!"

Anne flung her arms around him like a child, her wet face pressed to his. She kissed him quickly and ran toward the house, after a promise, "I'll be right back—by the time you're ready."

Duane entered the hangar, and moved his space ship outside. Resting on automatic rolling supports, the *White Bird* glistened with silvery transparency. Her mechanism in the fore and aft compartments was of provocative design and strangeness. All possible essentials piled the supply room amidship. Behind it lay sleeping quarters. Controls occupied the room behind the fore power chamber. A door, so finely fitted that it was unnoticeable, supplied the only entrance midway between stem and tail.

Duane surveyed everything in a quick appraisal. The long streamlined hull, pointed at each end, passed his inspection. He waited anxiously, peered through mist and water toward his bungalow. He felt relieved when Anne appeared, running through the doorway.

Something screamed from afar. Duane paled. "Hurry!" he called.

A blast of flame roared up beyond his home, colossal gouts of soil and rock belched skyward, and his home flattened from a hurricane wind. Rain drove at him like needles. The explosion blew him down and swept the *White Bird* from her supports.

"Duane!"

That faint cry brought him out of his daze as nothing else could have. He staggered toward the spot where he had last seen Anne. He threw boards and planks aside with incredible strength. The rain beat down, but the darker rain of debris ceased.

Somehow, he clawed and dug his way to Anne, all the while cursing fate and the gods of war who had mocked him. A great dead quiet overhung the world. Only the endless rain dripped while riven oaks and blasted bushes gave the dreary, sloshy sound of wet vegetation.

Anne was dying.

The realization of that fact was the most heartbreaking moment in his life. He stared dumbly at the face, lovely and white and calming, with whose repose would go half the driving desire of his life. And with that love lost, the trip became as nothing.

Anne's eyes opened tiredly. Her lips moved. "Go," she whispered. "I'll be with you, darling. Remember what I said when we were coming back from Everest a few weeks ago? There is no beginning or end to anything. All goes on and on, and so will you and I."

A moody look misted her eyes, they grew ghostly with something that only a mystic could interpret. If this were death, then death were ecstasy. The effort to speak exhausted her. Duane bent over as her lips moved, and her voice came to him from infinite distances with a last command, faint and barely audible: "Go!" Longing and love, peace and dreams, were in her eyes.

The embrace that she asked for, the kiss he gave, was the seal of death and the token that parted.

Beginning, and end. End, or beginning? The words danced a monotonous refrain in his thoughts when he raised himself and stared bitterly ahead, a queer, hurt look warping his expression, as though he tried to understand some simple fact that continued to elude him.

Why go? Where to? War ran a red smear around the globe. He would be needed. But war had taken Anne from him. Hatred of man and his savage works seethed through his mind, a crimson background to the black tapestry of his thoughts. Go—go—go—that was Anne's request.

In the distance, the eerie whine of radio projectiles shrilled anew. Earth shook with blasts and detonations. Fumes of acrid and pungent odor bit into his lungs.

The air itself was now becoming poisoned.

The glare of a great conflagration or explosion reddened the sky above New York City, turned the wall of rain into smoky scarlet. His mind was made up. He entered the *White Bird*.

The door closed behind him. Burned energy shot from the three rear projectors. The craft swooshed away and up in a great arc and disappeared like a ghost amid rain and gloom, while giant flashes of flame roared up where cities had stood.

IV.

The sweep of infinity, so impressive, so implicative of mysteries that mind never had solved, helped to relieve Duane of his misery. He would never forget, wholly; but there were splendor and cosmic riddles all around, and beyond the end—would there be another beginning? What lay out there, past the ultimate stars? Was Dowell correct, and did the circling stars represent only vibrating electrons of a giant atom? And if the extension and expansion of the *White Bird* took place as predicted, would Dowell follow his progress, watching him grow ever larger and dimmer as he sundered space, until he became invisible because of distance and attenuation?

Sunlight flooded the *White Bird,* and the Sun hung radiant and the Moon gleamed, but the skies were a blackness fretted with hordes of stars, not only above, but below, and in every direction; and the traveler felt again the overwhelming strangeness of things, the crushing magnitude of the universe, as Earth dropped away.

Go he must. All his dreams lay buried upon Earth. As if to symbolize his flight—or was it pursuit?—he stepped up the cosmic-ray power in successive jerks that hurled the *White Bird* at ever-accelerating velocity toward the constellation Cygnus. Any constellation would serve, but Cygnus, the Swan, was overhead when he burst from the air blanket of Earth, and toward Cygnus he shot.

Power he would never lack. Space was filled with more power than he could use. Light rays, cosmic rays, infra-red rays, radiations of countless kinds were all picked up by his driving mechanism, much as a radio picks up waves, and were transformed into energy that bombarded all matter lying behind his line of flight with a force that hurtled him forward. There was only a theoretical limit to the speed he could attain—whatever limit the nature of things imposed.

He had not yet, even in his experimental runs, tested the *White Bird's* capacity, but he knew that she could exceed the velocity of light. He knew, too, that a metamorphosis would occur when he passed the speed of light rays. According to the law propounded decades ago by Einstein, the *White Bird*, all its contents, and he himself would undergo a change, lengthening in the direction of flight. How great that extension would be depended upon the velocity itself.

He could estimate it in advance, but he could never realize it as an experience, simply because he could have nothing for comparison excepting the stars. And expansion would accompany that elongation; enlargement, to a degree beyond computation, along the planes of both the long and the short axes of the *White Bird*.

The planets of Saturn, Uranus, Neptune, and Pluto passed behind. Ahead lay a great void of four light-years until the myriad stars of the solar system's galaxy began with Alpha Centauri. The solar system diminished to a mere point. The bright illumination in the *White Bird* faded to a glow which was all that the stars provided. Duane did not turn on the interior lights. He preferred this shadowy and soft luminance.

There was nothing to do, little to calculate, nothing to expect until he approached his goal. The danger of collision remained ever present, but automatic safeguards could be depended upon to swing the *White Bird* around any important mass that loomed ahead. Later, at the ultimate enormous speed he hoped to attain, scarcely any mass smaller than the Sun would disturb his cruiser. Its attenuation and expansion would be so great, its elongation and atomic separation so tremendous, that it would approximate the nature of a gas and literally pass through intervening bodies.

Stars paraded. Constellations swung behind. Cygnus vanished, the Big Dipper changed its outlines, the evening star became faint, Betelgeuse and Antares flamed away, second and third-brilliance suns loomed as bright as the old first-magnitude stars. His speed pyramided. He achieved the velocity of light and outdid it. The *White Bird* swept onward with cyclonic fury. It tore outward in tens, hundreds, and thousands of times the speed of light.

It streamed beyond the eighth, ninth, and tenth-magnitude stars. Always its velocity increased. The man who watched the controls had a demon's set expression. He seemed to take a bitter pleasure in increasing the *White Bird's* velocity to a pitch that imagination itself could hardly grasp.

Eight hundred million light-years formed the distance to the farthest nebula. Even if he hurtled at a million times the rate of light, it would require eight hundred years for him to reach the outpost. Even at a light-year per second, more than twenty years would lapse before he achieved the goal. So he continued to draw on universal energy in a steady acceleration that ripped the *White Bird* through space at a blasting and frightful velocity now mounting toward dozens and hundreds of light-years per second.

Duane, exhausted, dropped into a dreamless slumber at some point of his journey. The automatic controls were set. Whether they worked he hardly cared. His accumulated hopes, tragedy, and undertaking of the day were above rational analysis.

The eternal procession continued. He wakened to find stars and suns hurtling past in linear streaks. All the heavens were strange. Not one body did he recognize. Star-point far ahead, streaks parallel with his plane, dwarfing maze of light flecks remotely to his rear—these were intangible realities.

Blackness deepened ahead. The Milky Way and its spectacular infinitude of suns became as a dream. He bored out of this galaxy in a haze of vaporous extension, burst through eternal voids. Now space was a misty immensity where the nebulæ, the island universes, sown afar on a lavish scale, rushed toward him out of the cosmic depth, with glow of birth and procession of star-field units, and blaze of youth and parade of creation. He was a star treader, a traveler who used the starry galaxies for fleet stepping points toward the outer blackness.

Days and nights passed, but there were no days and nights, only the ceaseless gyration of stars, passing of constellations, traversing of nebulæ and clusters and great gaseous patches, in whose center cosmic birth or death might be taking place.

The *White Bird's* speed still increased. That vast gap between the solar system and Alpha Centauri, a distance so enormous that light required four years to cross it, represented a fraction of a second at his present velocity. The fastest lens, the quickest eye, could not have seen his passing. The *White Bird* fled swifter than a dream, winged through infinity almost as instantly as the mind itself could think of the spaces outward.

A cyclone stood still compared to the *White Bird*. The flight of bullets, the flight of meteors, the flight of light, were snails in relation to him. He annihilated the far reaches of the universe at hundreds and thousands of light-years per second. A flash in infinity, a silvery bolt through the black, a ghost that was gone more quickly than the messengers of death, the *White Bird* bored the known universe, and went on.

Great constellations, Cygnus itself, which had loomed large ahead, had resolved themselves into streaks shooting by all around him, and had then faded behind to a cluster, a point, a mote, were now nothingness. He hurtled stars and clusters and nebulæ, plunged wildly across voids, leaped infinitudes. His galaxy had utterly disappeared.

And all the while, according to theory, the *White Bird* underwent a transformation, became longer, stretched away farther and farther as the speed mounted, but Duane would never know, for he was part of that change.

The *White Bird* by Earth measurements must be hundreds, perhaps thousands, of miles in length, so attenuated as to be almost vaporous, so nebulous and distorted as to appear like a mist. According to calculation, he must also be annihilating time, for his whole relation to the cosmos had been profoundly altered, and what he perceived as a thousand miles was in reality a thousand light-years, and what seemed to him a second must actually be centuries of Earth time.

If Dowell were watching, he must have seen the *White Bird* become as a meteor, a vaporous fog, a gigantic haze, hurtling and expanding toward infinity, until it vanished, since it exceeded the speed of light, and light-rays from it would require hours or years to reach Dowell's reflector.

Now it mattered not whether he pierced suns or struck planets. Automatic controls veered the *White Bird;* but, in theory, at this frightful velocity, and with this vaporous extension, he should pass through apparent solids, much as air blows through a sponge. Power? All space held invisible power. He had not begun to tap the inexhaustible store, but greater speed he feared to achieve lest the *White Bird* pass completely out of control.

The crystalite cruiser traversed voids and eons in moments. Nebulæ of the twentieth magnitude streaked past. White suns and blue, pale-orange and apple-green stars, colossal tapestry of night blazing with eternal jewels, the procession approached and receded. Blackness deepened ahead. The hordes of star systems grew fewer. The spiral nebulæ and the black gas clouds, the island universes and the chaoses of flaming birth decreased. He was nearing the end.

By only one comparison could he sense the change that was occurring. At first, the galaxies had seemed gigantic, flaming constellations and aggregates of billions of stars. Now they looked like dim and hazy disks of mist; and, by that diminution alone, Duane guessed that his extension and expansion had progressed on an unbelievable scale of magnitude. Had the *White Bird* surpassed in size the Earth or the solar system or even his galaxy? He would never accurately know, though he were Colossus beyond measurement.

What would he find? Some scientists held that the universe was expanding and that space was created with this expansion. What would happen if this were true, and if the *White Bird* at its present velocity passed beyond the limit? Other astronomers held that space was infinite in all

directions. Must he go on till death overtook him while he tried to find
an end when there was no end?

Still other prophets suggested that all the bodies of the universe might
be only the myriad components of a superatom, beyond which lay a greater
universe; and if these proved true, would that superuniverse be only a
stepping-stone, only a larger atom in a yet more gigantic cosmos? Where
did the end lie? And if those speculative mathematicians were correct who
thought that space was subject to a curvature which made it return to
its beginnings——

Duane's head ached. So vast the possibilities, and so limited his ability
to understand! Life so short, and truth so hard to learn! And this the attempt to solve a problem above even the deepest inquiries of mind, exceeding the oldest attempts that thought had made to fathom!

"Thus far shall ye go, and no farther." A phrase from dimly remembered teachings drifted through his brain. "Seek, and ye shall find." What?
He wondered. "Men are deceived in their conceits beneath the Moon,
and have sought in vain for any patent from oblivion above the Sun!"
So a mystic had said.

Who had guessed closest to truth? Dowell, with his theory about a giant
atom-world composed of electronic vibrations represented by all the stars
of all the galaxies of all the universe known to man? Einstein? Jeans?
Or some obscure prophet? Duane shook his head as though to free it of
oppressive weight. These were thoughts too complex and inconceivable
for mortal mind, too dangerous for sanity.

Now the last stars shone close, and streaked by, and one emerald sun
marked the outpost of space.

Remotely ahead came blackness, solid, absolute blackness. Behind lay
Earth and Sun, stars and constellations, galaxies and star-fields, a hundred
million strong, billions of billions of stars, trillions of trillions of miles,
enormity comprehensible solely in terms of the stellar mathematics of
astrophysics. The young emerald sun, flaming in the radiant beauty of
birth, swirled by and became one with the billions of billions of stars
behind. Duane looked back. There was a vast and dwindling conglomeration of points of light that receded to haze, to a vague luminousness, and
that mysteriously was blotted out. The phenomenon puzzled him until
he thought of one explanation—light rays had not yet penetrated thus far!

No loneliness, no fear of darkness, no feeling of utter helplessness in
the grip of frightful forces and in the presence of far places and alien
lands, no longing for the sweet companionship of Anne, such as now overwhelmed him, had ever before combined to appall in such magnitude any
mortal creature. The blackness everywhere was solid, so complete that his

eyes ached, and not one part of his ship could he discern, not one object, not even the hand that he held before his eyes.

A horror of that infinite blackness, that absolute void, gripped him, and he stumbled about with something akin to blind panic in an effort to find the interior-lighting controls. The glow comforted him, until he looked at his velocity dial. The speed of the *White Bird* was falling off swiftly!

Was this immensity so vacant that there were not even cosmic radiations to supply him with power? Or was some unknown but terrific drag slowing him down? Would the *White Bird* come to inertia and he to death in this black void? What forces prevailed here?

And what was the nature of that dim and shadowy glow, like a pale fog, that gradually appeared in place of a void blacker than coal?

Hope surged anew through the voyager, an uncontrollable excitement gripped him, he stared with painful intensity at the far-away mist. Had he followed a curvature of space and did he now approach his own universe? Had the *White Bird* leaped some titanic chasm to a new universe? Did he plunge toward that enormous atom imagined by Dowell? Was he now Colossus, exceeding man's deepest dream of giantism?

Colossal speculations of a colossal journey!

The mist drew closer. The *White Bird's* velocity fell to thousands, hundreds, and now only tens of light-years per second. Duane experienced a curious buoyancy and dizziness. He felt as if unfamiliar power and forces were gathering him in. Weakness overcame him. The play of foreign laws inclosed him. His sensations baffled analysis. His mind, governed still by Earth principles, could not understand what was happening. A whirling confusion as though his brain were an eddying mist enveloped him. Darkness and light divided his course. He sensed a shudder and a trembling of the *White Bird* as if it were a deep-sea creature caught in tides and forced toward the surface.

A shock followed by a violent jolt stunned him.

He had literally burst space.

V.

When Duane's dazed faculties began to function again, it was with a feeling of the deepest awe that he stared around and tried to comprehend what had happened. Realization came slowly, and he found it difficult even to decipher his surroundings.

Light flooded his compartment, bright white light that was curiously restful and soothing to his eyes, unlike the glare of the Sun. The *White Bird* rested on a flat plain of what looked like glass, perhaps a hundred yards long and ten wide. Far below him he saw a second plain, mahogany-colored, which swept away in the distance, then stopped at a sheer cliff that fell an unknown distance down toward the blur of what seemed to be solid ground. From the second level rose two brasslike towers that supported the glassy oblong upon which the *White Bird* rested.

What did this mean?

He looked upward. What was that giant circle overhead?

He peered out. What were those colossal and serrated monuments that looked like the mechanism of giants and possessed eerie illusions of a four-dimensional geometry? What were those other massive bulks that towered toward the spaces above?

Understanding, and fright paralyzed him in a flash of intuition.

The White Bird reposed on the slide of a microscope! The second plain was a table top, the third plain a floor. The geometric metallic mountains were apparatus and machines. The towering things were living beings. He had burst through the atom that was his universe and had emerged on a planet of a greater universe, a superuniverse!

The vastness and spaciousness around, the acres and leagues of ground, staggered him. Everything was on a giant scale to which it was hard for him to become accustomed. And yet it was not until he looked intently upward that the full magnitude of his surroundings impressed themselves upon him.

At what seemed the horizon, and seen as through a light haze, beyond plains and mountains that were only tables and machinery, rose walls more towering than the peaks of the Himalayas or the cliffs of the Moon, walls that curved gigantically zenithward where lay an opening toward which pointed a monstrous tube whose length must have been miles.

Around this tube stood two of the alien beings, and at a table far to one side sat a third, and a fourth faced a complicated mass of blue-white metal apparatus whose nature was beyond conjecture, while a fifth leaned beside the great microscope.

Duane at long last understood completely. This vast region of bare surfaces and precipitous descents was only a single room, an observatory, and the beings were astronomers studying whatever skies lay above!

Still dazed by his pilgrimage, he experienced a new awe. Dowell had guessed the truth in his amazing theory! All the universe that he had traversed was only an atom, perhaps drifting in the air around him, perhaps part of the slide, perhaps the whole interior of this world. He would never know where, for it was as lost to him as the treasures of Atlantis. But that universe, with its scope and sweep and myriad components, formed only the least part of this sphere. There must be other worlds, an entire new universe of stars and suns and comets! And beyond these—

what? His mind, numb from the exhaustion of mere speculation upon so stupendous a scale, turned wearily to the beings.

They were Titans. Compared to Duane, the Colossus of Rhodes was infinitely less than the tiniest particle of matter. Compared to the Titans, Duane stood as lowly as a worm!

Anthropomorphic in general appearance, they possessed both strikingly human characteristics and alien traits. They reminded Duane—but on how gigantic a size!—of the Easter Island sculptures, for these Titans had flat-backed heads, high, slanting foreheads, deep-set eyes, the noses of kings, and thin, ascetic lips above a jutting jaw. No race of conquerors ever before gave such an impression of strength, austerity, intelligence, and power.

Godlike, the incarnation of supremacy, these giants gained added impressiveness from the radiant texture of their skin, which was as clear and cold as the glint of ice or the sparkle of a blue-white diamond, and as smooth. Had some dim awareness of these entities filtered through the minds of the races of Earth and helped to develop the concept of deity? Were these the prototypes that served the sculptors of Easter Island?

Duane, moody and tired, longed for the companionship of Anne, for the presence of one human being to accompany him in this Odyssey that vanquished space, only to plunge him into the beginning of new mystery.

Far, far overhead towered the Titans, league-long, massive creations overshadowing even the inhabitants of Brobdingnag. The reddish tunics that they wore formed a splash of color against the brightness of their Cyclopean bodies.

They were talking among themselves, the Earth man observed by the motion of their lips, and curiosity overcame fear. He stealthily opened the *White Bird's* door. A Titan, peering through the telescope, spoke. In the vast but clear resonance of that voice, Duane distinguished a syllable wholly foreign to the tongues of Earth. The Titan by the mechanisms pushed a lever, and from the machine came five strokes of a gong. The first Titan peered through the telescope and spoke again, a different syllable. The mechanism rang once.

Understanding flashed through Duane. The first Titan, evidently an astronomer, was studying a body in the skies and reading its position to his companion who registered the figure. The first word, then, meant "five," and the second word, "one." He jotted down the syllables as accurately as he remembered them.

The astronomer spoke again, the recorder pressed a level, but no gong resounded. "Nothing, or zero," Duane wrote. The last number was "nine."

Silence descended, and now the intruder made out, upon a great mirror beside the recorder, a reflection of star fields, and guessed that the Titans were studying one among that horde. The astronomer called out, and the recorder raised his head. Duane wrote two words as the name of the recorder who played with intricate mechanisms.

Then the star fields began an apparent march, drawing ever nearer, until one bright sun or planet loomed largest in the mirror's center. The astronomer uttered a command, the reflection became motionless, and Duane wrote the phonetic transcription for "stop."

All this while his fear of discovery had been lessening since the attention of the giants was centered elsewhere, but his curiosity was mounting. Why were the great ones so interested in this star or planet? Who were they and how did their apparatus function? He wished that he could understand every word they spoke; given time enough, he would, for already he had a fair list of primary words: several mathematical numbers, the concept "zero," a few verbs, including "stop," "continue" or "go," and "to be," the names of three of the Titans, and several adjectives of whose meaning he was uncertain but had an approximate understanding.

The star cluster swam closer until only one body filled the mirror. The recorder played with dials and levers, and the one sphere, now discernible as a planet, and approaching rapidly, expanded beyond the reflector's sides.

The Titans gathered around the mirror. The surface of the satellite raced toward them. Continents became visible, outlined by seas. Dark masses of forests and mountain ranges contrasted with units that looked like villages or cities. Paths, trees, huts, and lakes were visible. At last the recorder adjusted whatever mechanism controlled this optical marvel, and the picture again became stationary.

There on the Gargantuan panel, a forest glade showed clearly to the last detail. Strange and exotic trees, not unlike those of Earth's carboniferous era, raised great conical leaves and flower buds and full blooms to the sky. The ground was riotous with ferns and glossy flowers, orchidaceous cups and blossoms of wallflower brown.

Dawn was breaking and blue-white light filtered through the vegetation. Shadows shortened. Moths fluttered, and birds of brilliant plumage soared up with lyrical morning songs. A creature similar to a deer crossed with a rabbit bounded away in search of breakfast. Another beast, resembling a huge squirrel, but with a glossy coat and the membranes of a bat, flitted to the edge of a pool and, after drinking greedily, frolicked away through the forest.

A path led to the pool. While the Titans and Duane looked on, a girl danced into view.

Nothing that he had experienced in these hectic weeks affected Duane as profoundly as the sight of that girl. She differed from the women of Earth, and yet she possessed a similarity. He thought that she looked like Anne—or was his impression only a wish fulfillment? In the quiet of dawn, she danced along. She wore no garments. Her supple figure, tawny as ripe wheat, pirouetted around trees, and her light feet dipped across mosses. She had hair of emerald, that floated lightly around her, and liquid, beguiling eyes of amber. A glow the color of goldenrod pollen enriched her face. Her fingers seemed boneless, so tapering were they, and flexible as she cupped them and wove them in supplication to the dawn.

The scene held beauty of an exquisite kind, from the lush petals of flowers and mossy carpet to the exotic trees; from the young girl dancing in the glow of sunrise to the light that shimmered through branch and leaf and formed patterns of divided darkness upon the ground.

Then the girl flung her arms skyward and lifted her face to greet the sun. In the forest glade she seemed lovelier than a naiad out of legend. Her lips parted, and Duane could almost hear the rapturous song that she caroled. Then she danced again in carefree abandon, swirling toward the edge of the pool, and there she flung herself down and laughed at her own drowning image in the waters.

From the poetry and enchantment of the idyll, Duane's attention was gradually turned to a crescendo whose volume reverberated through the air. The Titans were talking excitedly, one Titan apparently scoffing at the others who ringed him. Judging by his gestures, he was discounting the truth of the visualization which had occurred upon the mirror. He strode from the circle and in a few Gargantuan steps was beside the microscope to resume whatever investigation he had interrupted.

His peril engraved itself on Duane's mind in a second that saw him frantically spin the door to the *White Bird*. His action came too late. The door was only partly sealed when a vast cry issued from the throat of the giant. The others looked over and began approaching him. Two fingers the size of barrels appeared at the edges of the slide and lifted it in a wild swoop skyward!

VI.

That curving sweep, almost vertical, which carried him a mile upward in a mere second, was more sickening than a plunge, but Duane quaked at a simple but terrifying incident that followed. The Titan raised him to eye level and scrutinized him with cold appraisal. His eye, huge as a room, with fathomless depths of black in it and a piercing, hypnotic pupil, overwhelmed Duane with its conviction of dynastic power and its attitude of unhuman, solely scientific analysis. No worm in alcohol, no microbe under the lens, could have felt more lowly than he, under the glare of that tremendous orb.

Duane was trapped and he knew it. One squeeze of colossal fingers and he would be pulp in the flattened shards of his stratoplane. It might have been fear, it might have been courage, that prompted him. He opened the *White Bird's* door and stepped out onto the slide.

The great eye widened and its black depths stirred. The four other Titans gathered around like shining angels of doom, their stern, conquerors' faces staring at him with more interest, but no more personal feeling than they would have studied a fly. They talked rapidly, the cruel lips forming thunder that deafened at this close range. Duane gesticulated, and they became silent, looking at him and at each other with questioning glances. Using all the power he could muster, he shouted out the microscopist's name.

The effect was electrical. The Titan almost dropped the slide. He broke into a flood of questions, but the Earth man shook his head and shouted the syllable for "nothing."

The Titan understood—Duane did not know the questions. Walking toward a mechanism of abstruse nature, the astronomer set his captive on a table and placed upon his head a cap of metal with a skein of fine wires terminating in what resembled a telephone switchboard beside a smooth panel. He placed a similar cap on the table and indicated that Duane touch it with his head. It looked like the crown of an observatory, this hemisphere of the gods. A tingling flux ebbed through his body upon contact.

In the mirror appeared an image of the astronomer with his name underneath. Duane comprehended. This miraculous apparatus transformed thought currents into pictures and made ideas visible. Duane thought of his portrait and his name. Promptly they flashed upon the panel. In this novel manner, with the start he already had in finding something of their speech and language, he had little difficulty in carrying on a silent conversation.

"Did you come from Valadom—the planet in the reflector? Are you one of the little creatures?"

"No."

The Earth man's reply obviously surprised them. The scientists conferred, as if deciding whether he was giving truthful answers.

"Whence came you?"

Duane hesitated. Would they believe him if he told the truth? Should he rescind his first answer and assert that he was one of the "little creatures"? These were giants of intellect as well as Titans of body. It would be wiser to answer truthfully even if they scoffed. "I came from an atom under your microscope," he answered.

His reply raised a tempest, but not the skepticism that he had expected. The astronomer talked with new animation as though he had found support for a theory, and the mind reflector became a crazed confusion of mathematical symbols, concepts involving energy and matter, and hypotheses of atoms.

Appearances indicated that he had once set forth a theory that each particle of matter was as complex as the universe, and that submicroscopic parts might be star fields as elaborate as those visible above, and with life on a proportionately most infinitesimal scale, a theory which his associates must have decided against. The very concept taxed Duane's faculties. His universe an atom forming this sphere; this globe a planet in the superuniverse; and what if that billion-bodied unit was, as Dowell had suggested, only the molecule of a cosmos still more far-flung, above and beyond and outside? Conversely, were there universes within the atoms of the Earth he had left? Where did the cycle begin or end?

His gangling figure, in which tenseness fought his desire to relax, must have presented a study in contrasts. The cathedralesque majesty of this one hall that formed an arena as large as the ground and the heavens and the horizons of Earth was in itself a thing of wonder, but the lordly dwellers added the emotional burdens of awe and fear and inferiority, so massive were their statures, so radiant, so stern, so implacable, and godlike. And to the weight of these visible things was piled on concepts to stagger the brain of genius, or the universal mind, if such existed, or the intrauniversal intellect. Yet the general patterns of nature as he knew it seemed to recur here. Where lay the beginning and whither the end? To what purpose? He drifted back from mental fog to find the Titans questioning him anew.

"Can you return to your universe, your atom?"

"No," Duane replied.

"Why not?"

"I do not know where it is. I would not know how to find it. If I could find it, I would not be able to enter. Something happened, when I burst through. I am bigger than my whole universe was. I cannot shrink down. Besides, millions of years have passed back there since I departed. I do not even know whether Earth, my planet, still exists."

The sages nodded gravely, accepting his statement, and evidently understanding far better than he did what had happened.

"What is the principle of your tiny ship, little one?"

Duane bristled and his lank joints stiffened. The *White Bird* a "tiny ship"? He, Colossus, called a "little one"? He swore angrily, and a flock of "damns" appeared on the mind reflector. The Titans stared without feeling at these strange words, asked him to elaborate. Swallowing his indignation, he tried to pictorialize the building of the *White Bird*, and how it harnessed universal radiations for its energy. The Titans watched, attentive and impassive as before. And yet Duane sensed an extraordinary in-

terest in his ideas; and by careful observation came to the conclusion that
they had only recently built this laboratory with a scientific knowledge
far in advance of that of the human race.

They, too, had discovered how to tap perpetual power. Already exploration of the great spaces, the outer abysses, the chasms and voids and
illimitable depths, was under way. They were plainly amazed that any
creature as minute as he could have progressed so far; and still more eagerness accompanied their absorption in his story of the submicroscopic electrons which, to beings as small as he once had been, yet represented a
mysterious, enormous, and complex universe of inconceivable magnitude.

Duane felt his prestige rising. He thought it his turn to watch mind
pictures and obtain some understanding of his journey's end.

"Who are you? Where am I?" he began.

The astronomer reflected soberly, as though weighing whether this mite
could possibly grasp the ideas that might be presented. Then, upon the
panel, flowed a stream of images: Qthyalos, a giant world in its ripe maturity, inhabited by Titans of deific knowledge and power, whose intellects
rivaled in proportion the girth of their bodies; mind supreme in supreme
and vital matter whose life-span averaged thousands of years.

Duane's eyes ached when he saw their cities, how Cyclopean they were,
and their works, how passing strange, and their arts, how alien and
bizarre. Their structures baffled him with their apparent fluxes and pro-
cessional changes, their tenuous and unreal unstability, combining with
solid attributes. Had they a four-dimensional basis that warped straight
lines into helical spirals, and cubes into weirdly shimmering pyramids?

What was the gleaming stuff that composed these megalithic metropolises which shone with blinding color and yet whose incandescence was
underlain with the shadow and ambiguity and shifting forms of a geometry that eluded him? Whether he understood or not, the résumé flowed
on, and now he found why they were examining Valadom with such interest when he came. He translated the series of images into words.

"One of our exploring flyers reported that he thought he saw signs of
life on a small planet of our system." Here the consecutive pictures broke,
and a sight of the giant globe Qthyalos flashed forth alone, then the image
of its sun and hundreds of large and small planets that made a solar system upon a huge scale; then the great sweep of a galaxy, and beyond this
island universe—nebula after nebula, star-field on star-field, flaming gas
and black voids, soaring outward and deepening afar toward infinity,
the eternal abyss.

Duane, humble in the presence of this immensity so like his own universe but of so immeasurably a more stupendous range, watched with almost glazed eyes the resumption of the story.

"Only recently have we controlled optical and intra-spatial laws to such a degree that we could bring any planet of our system into as close focus as we wished. We have been studying one planet or more nightly for the past year, but discovered no signs of life until the explorer reported today on Valadom, which we studied through a telescope a while ago.

"We had intended to send scientists there to obtain specimens of these curious little creatures, who seem to be much like us, for laboratory study and analysis. There are several difficulties in the way. One is their tiny size. Judging by the one we saw, they can be no larger than you. Consequently, if we landed, they would probably be so paralyzed by fright that they would run away and hide. We might step on thousands of them without ever realizing it. Great pains would be needed to capture even one, and he would be likely to be badly damaged or fear-filled so as to be useless to us.

"We could not camp there. It is doubtful if we could live on that small asteroid. The air blanket would extend, perhaps, no higher than our heads. Even if we took advantage of all our wisdom, conditions would be most unfavorable for observation. Our purpose would not be wholly answered by observation from here. We can watch actions, but we cannot discover their past, interpret their thoughts, examine their true nature, or obtain more than a general idea of their life."

This long sequence, much of it obscure and only guessed at by Duane because of the abstract quality of the pictures which resulted from the Titan's attempt to visualize concepts, seemed to be leading up to a definite end.

The five conferred among themselves, their miens dignified and stately with an austerity that ascetics would have envied. Like sculpture of gods, like the chiseled, enigmatic heads of Easter Island, like uncrowned rulers debating the fate of empires, and with expressions immobile to a degree that seemed stony, the Cyclopean beings conversed in voices that quaked like thunder, roaring in Duane's ears, cataclysmic volumes of resonance. From this table top, now that the shining giants stood erect, they looked like figures of hewn marble slashed from mountains.

Fleetingly, he thought of plunging into the *White Bird* and rocketing off, but he knew the gamble would not win. The heads in conclave miles above, the horizon-reaching sweep of floor and apparatus and devices, the seemingly boundless space overhead, offered no hope of escape. Then the stone-hard, mercury-glistening head of the astronomer bent toward him in a rush that sent violent currents of air whirling across the table, and the lordly entity spoke words that he could not understand, but whose import was translated by the mind panel.

"Since it is unwise to explore Valadom, and difficult to obtain a little creature, we have decided to dissect you, instead, and discover how you work, what you are made of, and how you react."

The Titan enunciated doom as if he conferred an honor. His expression was imperturbable. Why he should have announced to the victim his purpose remained a riddle, unless he had access to power beyond Duane's knowledge, or unless the fervor of scientific inquiry obsessed him, and he saw goals but forgot intermediaries.

Whatever the reason, it mattered little to Duane. His life hung at stake. He was no more than a germ, an insect, a minute creature, a worm, to these Titans. There was neither cruelty, enmity, nor any other emotion in the statement. To them, it was a simple fact. Here stood a little creature who stimulated their curiosity. He would make a splendid laboratory specimen. They did not like him or resent him. They had no feeling about him. The cause of knowledge would be far advanced by the dissection and analysis of this specimen of a new species.

The Earth exile, the chill of horror overcoming him at his prospective fate, strove to think. Was this to be the reward of his stellar Odyssey? This bitter death in foreign places to be the last goal? This going out, not in glory, but ignominiously, with not so much quickness and almost as little distinction as the lowliest insect?

He would make a run for it at the end, a dash that at least would win him fast oblivion in a snap of those monstrous fingers. Better to be slapped into pulp than to linger under the knife. But these were Titans dominated wholly by mind and its pursuits. If he could only appeal to their rational nature!

Upon the reflector appeared the ideas set up by his chain of thought, the appeal and defense that he mentally projected:

"Titans! I am not one of the little creatures of Valadom! You may put me under the microscope and the knife, but you will still know nothing of how the little creatures work!"

The master of the microscope lowered the mammoth and marmoreal sculpture of his flat-backed head, donned a metal cap, and with brooding visage replied through thought-presentation: "It does not matter. We find out how you work, and later how the little creatures work, as well."

Disheartened, Duane tried again. "My death will not serve you, Titans! You will discover what I am made of, but only that, and you know little of my life!"

He had made a bad mistake, a tactical blunder, and he realized it the instant he spoke. Sweat oozed out on his forehead. The biologist-Titan destroyed his plea with: "We do not plan to end you for some time. We will keep you under observation for experiments in the laboratory for as long as may be necessary until we have exhausted your animate being. Then we will take you apart."

Only the aims of high endeavor lightened the black, enormous eyes. No feeling marred their serenity and repose as the sentence of death remained.

Discouraged, but with will indomitable while life lasted, and with wits sharpened by this intellectual battle for preservation, Duane made a new shift in the game. "Titans! I am like you. I think, I feel, I am as you are! Why then dissect me? I differ principally in size from you! Would you dismember one of your own race?"

"We have taken apart enough beings among ourselves to find out what causes us to be what we are," came the unexpected and disillusioning response. "You resemble us, but exact study of everything in you will be necessary to prove the similarities and differences between us. Your head has a strange shape. Thus your brain cannot function quite like ours."

The web tightened. They closed each argument as quickly as he advanced it. His sole comfort was their consent to listen, dispassionately, detached, impersonal, weighing his reasons for their intrinsic validity. He had one chance left, short of a fatal dash, and he put all his persuasive mental resources into the gamble.

"Titans! I will make a bargain with you! Let me enter my cosmocraft and depart. I will go to Valadom! I will live among the little people. I will stay there for a year. I will learn their language, study their customs and history, interpret their life. At the end of a year, I will return and give you all the knowledge I have obtained. Furthermore, I will bring back at least one dead specimen of the little people for you to examine. All this I promise, Titans, in return for two conditions—you will agree not to harm me when I return, and you will agree not to harm the little people of Valadom."

The five grave giants, like judges studying evidence, considered his proposal. He sensed the biologist arguing against him, and in favor of immediate experimentation, since specimens of the little creatures might be obtained later. The astronomer favored his case, for he would enable them without trouble to obtain a complete record of Valadom, and in the year intervening they could pursue researches into other parts of the universe. The three remaining giants appeared to show little preference which way the discussion ended.

Duane, tense and drawn, waited for their decision. There was a grotesque quality to this situation, something both superhuman and supernormal, something both familiar and foreign, something gigantically dissimilar between these Cyclopean conquerors with their minds that thirsted for knowledge alone, and he himself, a mite to them, but pleading for his existence—he, who in his own search for the answer to the mystery of things had performed the feat of bursting through a universe and leaving it but an atom behind. Colossus though he had become, he was only an insect to them! Titanic though they seemed, were they only submicroscopic, submeasurable motes in the fathomless molecule beyond?

The astronomer prepared to reply, and Duane's eyes hovered on the reflector; a lone, small figure against fate and the gods, he watched judgment.

"Little creature, we have decided that the cause of knowledge will be furthered better and quicker by your going to Valadom and returning here, than by our analyzing you now. We will allow you to proceed on your way, but you must return according to your agreement in a year. Go!"

Shaking in the nervous let-down that followed reprieve, he said: "I thank you, Titans. What pledge will you have?"

"Pledge? Truth showed in your thoughts. If it had not, we would not let you depart. Do you know the way to Valadom?"

"No."

The astronomer flashed upon the screen picture after picture of the skies, the principal stars, Valadom and Qthyalos and their system, until Duane had the necessary directions. Then he bowed to those great beings, who, incalculable, thinking thoughts beyond his grasp, and preserving a silence more stately than the repose of a deserted cathedral, watched him depart.

Neither well-wishing nor friendly farewell attended his going. The flat-backed heads of sloping brow, the stern lips, the chins and noses of deific disdain, the cheek bones of godlike pride, the faces of sexless radiance, the black, tremendous eyes from whose wells shone the vision of destroying angels, these betrayed unhuman, abstract interest, and nothing more.

The *White Bird* soared skyward in a beautiful arc. The heads of the Titans dropped away. The horizon-sweeping immensity of the observatory fell behind, and became like an ordinary room, with beings of generally anthropomorphic nature standing amid devices and structures of puzzling design. The austere faces of the giants blurred to points as the wanderer of infinity rocketed outward through the open roof in a trajectory that followed the league-long telescope.

It gave him a queazy sensation to realize that he himself, could he see himself with the eyes of man, must be Colossus multi-magnified as a result of the transmutation that had occurred when he annihilated space and sundered his universe, yet only a thumbnail pygmy to them, who were nothing compared with the molecule beyond!

His last impression of the lordly dwellers on Qthyalos was one of profound reverence mingled with fruitless speculation. Who they were and what their nature remained almost as insoluble conjectures as when he first saw them. Then darkness enfolded him and he burst through the dome where it lay open for the telescope.

VII.

Now there were star-fields again, and the ceaseless throngs shone above, and the skies hung strange and alien, ablaze with infinite brilliant jewels. On the rim of the northern horizon sank a pale-gray moon, and on the edge of a southern sea sank a moon of orange.

As the *White Bird* soared, Duane looked back. The surface of Qthyalos, in the shadow of night and under the canopy of stars, stretched vast, dim, and mysterious. There were mountain ranges striking stark and bold five thousand miles and more into the citadels of space, peaks of terrific bleakness until their ice-crowns of naked and blue-white grandeur blocked the skies beyond them.

The observatory itself stood on a precipice whose sides were chasms plunging sheer through sooty gulfs. There were cities on the plains and in the valleys, monstrous metropolises, dark towers out of fable, erections on titanic scale that tortured vision with illusions of a new geometry, dream cities as unreal as the domes of Xanadu, and assaulting the skies themselves with their topmost and almost topless towers.

There were lakes as large as seas, and seas that curved like the arc of heaven. There were islands the size of continents, and continents of unguessable extent.

Colossal lords of a colossal planet! Qthyalos, a single planet huger than the universe, faded, with all its mysteries and all its visionary wonder, farther and ever farther behind. Its mass became a dark puzzle, but its rim brightened sharply and the edge of a dazzling sun crept out.

The *White Bird* sped on, and the central sun emerged into the radiant glory, a white-hot orb that compared with Qthyalos as a balloon to a ball-bearing. There were great planets and multiple moons and a host of asteroids behind, on the opposite side of this system; and ahead shone other planets and moons against the tapestry of space; and among them glimmered Valadom, a mere asteroid to Titan, a sphere as big as Earth to Duane's sense of values.

The *White Bird* winged onward in accelerating tempo that shot her toward her goal. Scarcely an hour could have lapsed as his senses recorded time before Valadom became discernible as a tiny globe. Beyond it, the enormous sweep of constellations sprinkled infinity; and beyond the riotous blaze glowed the haze of nebulæ where the celestial parade began of outward-flung galaxies in the remote depths and recesses of this cosmos. Twin stars and suns of purple and white and gold, myriad moons and planets of silvery splendor, space and night held unrivaled beauty, majesty, and glory, a spectacular display that challenged the scope of imagination, and the *White Bird* only a streaming blur amid the immensities and infinitudes.

He felt tempted to trick the Titans; to blast his way outward and discover the final organism or farthest megacosmos, to test Dowell's theory in its ultimate scope. His pledge to the Titans prevailed.

Yet it was with a sense of cosmic weariness that Duane approached Valadom. The everlasting procession of stars and galactic universes began to pall. Who could say what lay beyond the utmost outpost? Beyond this cosmos—another atom on a larger scale? A cell or molecule? Or night eternal? Or mysterious limitations where space finally ceased? His mind withdrew from visions too vast, speculations where madness lay.

Oddly, he felt a gladness as Valadom loomed large, the gladness of the wanderer homeward bound from voyages afar. The blinding sun shone remotely behind, yet still far larger than the Sun of Earth; and to one side hung Qthyalos, abode of Titans; and, in relation to them, Valadom seemed hardly so much as a pin point, but it loomed fully the size of Earth.

Duane's thoughts recurred to Anne with a kind of sad longing for her companionship. So well she would have changed the loneliness of his travels! So sweet a comfort she would have been! But irrecoverable years in a universe more distant than Carcosa and Hali divided him from the dead dream of love.

Valadom swept close. Moody, the expression of an old man in his youthful eyes, Duane watched the harbor draw nigh. He could not rid himself of the feeling that the Titans watched his progress through their telescopic and ultra-optical equipment; and the sense of their invisible presence billions of miles behind was a depressant only partly relieved by his impression of another presence, ghostly, intangible, elusive.

But over Valadom lay quiet; the quiet of dawn above the seas and continents toward which he dropped; and peace became part of his mood. His thoughts drifted to the lovely and forlorn creature he had watched make her obeisance to the morning. Did she still recline beside the pool? Or had she danced her way back to lover or family or mate? Duane was startled by his interest and resentment. Preposterous! He did not even know the nature of this child of Valadom, and might never find her, yet he dreamed while the planet rushed near.

Seas outlined themselves against land masses. He recognized the topography as he recalled it in the Titans' reflector. Swiftly the *White Bird* settled, too swiftly. He unloosed the triple fore projectors to break his fall. The *White Bird* leveled away high over a tossing sea, and headed westward until the coasts of a continent swam out of azure mist.

There were dots on the ocean below—atolls or flotsam or small craft?

He could not tell and did not pause. The ramparts of a village or city rose on a bay. Civilization? Or savagery? Did it indicate rising culture and progress, or decline from a peak surpassed? Time might answer; now, he had only a desire, curiously compelling, to reach the glade he had seen. The village flowed underneath, its architecture analogous to that of the Greeks—temple and dwelling, shrine and inn, lying white and pagan in the dawn.

The *White Bird* dipped toward the surrounding forest, for here should lie the haven he sought. The dark thread of a river wound its way seaward in the distance. The forest rushed up. The *White Bird* settled toward a greensward between two ridges, which he recognized immediately as the vista he had scrutinized from Qthyalos. Here lay the pool, a disk of emerald.

The *White Bird* came to rest upon grasses and lush flowers amid trees of fantastic shape. The loose-jointed figure of the Earth man slouched out.

Morning had broken. The sun stood high, Qthyalos a sphere of misty beauty beside it. A soft wind blew, and he breathed deeply of that fresh, fragrant elixir. Sounds came from the forest, strange songs of unknown birds and cries of hidden beasts. Moths of brilliant coloring made splashes of cerise and green-gold, lemon and indigo and ebony; one long-beaked bird, imperial purple with markings of pomegranate red, flew past, a lovely thing until it croaked harshly.

Everywhere rose curious vegetation; flower-capped stalks; ferns of feathery grace; lichens and great single leaves; coniferous trees; weird trunks and stems from which clusters of berries, fruit, nuts, and blossoms hung; buds like bursting seed pods; thick moss. The ground was a carpet where green grew the grasses, and over them wealth of blooms; orchids that lifted hot faces to the sun; petals of silver freaked with black, and of turquoise, of cinnamon, of pistachio, and blood; a hectic riot wherein colors of fever and tones of coolness splashed the landscape.

The wanderer, amid this drowsy paradise, where dreams faded and aspirations vanished in the presence of nature's extravagance, trod his way toward the pool. Through foliage and frondage and leafy patch, with sunlight fretting arabesques of light and shadow athwart his path, he sauntered on, wearily, hesitantly, but with active curiosity.

There was never so exquisite a peace as this, so ineffable a haven, and the rising music of birds became a choir that only deepened the repose. Then a voice caroled, a rich, glad hymn to the sun, soaring and falling, deepening with ecstasy and dreamful of rapture. His mood responded to the song and the invisible singer. As he wove his way through the forest, the recollection of Anne rose like a specter hovering behind the lyrical and golden-throated phrases.

Then he came to the edge of the glade and saw the girl. She stood beside the pool. She laughed at the sky and the sun, the land and the waters. Her young face flushed in the bloom of youth. Her emerald hair hung silken around her throat and shoulders. She sang for the glory of living, the breathless adoration of being, and her voice warbled gladness. She whirled in light abandon, and the hair rippled across her back and shimmered against the glow of her skin.

For a long minute, Duane dwelt on the beauty of her figure and her dance, the grace of her rhythm, before he stepped out.

Exile from Earth and child of Valadom, they faced each other. The dance came to an abrupt end. Her amber eyes grew wide and startled, questioning the intruder. Hesitantly, he stepped a pace forward and greeted the girl with hands spread in token of peace.

Her lips parted and her eyes, showing neither the fear nor the mistrust that he might have expected, shone of something secret, as if to greet some dimly remembered and half-forgotten friend of long ago.

What made "Colossus" a thought-variant was its reversal of a cliché. Plots had frequently involved the shrinking of a hero to the level where ordinary atoms became solar systems, but here the hero rose to the level where the whole Universe was an atom (inspired by the Eddington quotation with which the story begins).

The story was very successful,* and the readers demanded a sequel. Wandrei had clearly planned for one in writing the story, and the sequel appeared as "Colossus Eternal," in the December 1934 issue of *Astounding Stories*.

Yet, although I liked "Colossus" and remembered it well enough to want to include it here, I had begun to refuse to accept stories that did not meet my stiffening standards of scientific accuracy. I knew that, according to Einstein's theory of relativity, the speed of light could not be surpassed, and already, by the age of fourteen, I was not ready to accept the vast speeds so easily attained by the hero's vessel. I also knew that while the mass of any object increased with speed relative to the Universe generally, the volume did not. In fact, by the Lorentz-Fitzgerald contraction, the volume actually decreased.

* "Colossus" has, as I look back on it now, an interestingly distorted preview of World War II, which was to start five and a half years after its appearance. Japan was the aggressor, launching war with a sneak attack—after all, it was already invading China at the time the story was written—and there is a curious mention of Stalingrad. There is, however, no reference at all to Germany, and Great Britain is on Japan's side—as, indeed, it seemed to be in the early 1930s.

"Colossus," "Colossus Eternal," and additional stories are to be included (in revised versions) in a book now being planned, Wandrei tells me. Such a book should help call back to the public mind an unjustly neglected author.

Nevertheless, the thought-variants (however noticeable their errors in science to my increasingly hypercritical self) affected me profoundly. They struck me as science fiction par excellence, and by the time I began to write science fiction myself, I yearned to write thought-variants, even though the use of the term vanished with Tremaine.

My story "Nightfall" was consciously written as a thought-variant, and so was my story "The Last Question." Even my recent novel *The Gods Themselves* had thought-variant qualities.

Donald Wandrei was a Tremaine author. He had never appeared in *Amazing Stories* or *Wonder Stories,* and only once in a late issue of the Clayton *Astounding.* He appeared about seventeen times in the Tremaine *Astounding,* however, then faded out when Tremaine left.

Tremaine, however, did more than develop new writers. The fact that he paid higher fees more promptly attracted the older writers to him. Jack Williamson, one of the best of them (consider his "The Moon Era"), now switched to *Astounding Stories* and, indeed, even survived Tremaine and continued to be a major contributor to *Astounding* in the Golden Age itself.

Williamson contributed one of the most startling of the thought-variants, "Born of the Sun," in the March 1934 *Astounding Stories.*

BORN OF THE SUN

by Jack Williamson

The deep song of a wide-open motor throbbed into the huge mahogany library—the first faint note of rising menace. Foster Ross, busy over a great table in the end of the room, glanced up abstractedly at a frost-rimed window. Gaunt trees, outside, flung bare, skeletal branches against the gray gloom of an early December dusk; the moaning wind carried a few flakes of snow.

Listening, Foster Ross wondered briefly the reason for such suicidal haste over the icy highways, before his attention went back to the experiment that had engrossed him for two hard years.

He was alone in the great, rambling stone mansion his father had left him, secluded upon a lonely, wooded Pennsylvania hilltop. No visitors were expected—the house was being closed for the winter. The few servants had departed that afternoon. Foster, himself, planned to leave at midnight for sunny Palm Beach to meet June Trevor.

A lean, muscular giant, he was whistling absently as he bent over the immense mahogany table. It was littered with electrical apparatus. In the center of it, shimmering under brilliant light, was a little aluminum sphere, trailing two fine platinum wires.

Foster tightened a last connection. He stepped back a little eagerly brushing a wisp of copper-colored hair out of his eyes.

"Now!" he whispered. "It should go up. As the first space ship will go up toward the Moon! It should be——"

Nervously watching the toylike sphere, he snapped down a key. Anxiously, he waited, as coils whined angrily, and violet discharges flickered about bright contacts.

The tiny globe did not move. A moment he stared at it, sighing wearily. Then he shrugged, grinned at himself.

"Fifty thousand, that makes," he muttered to himself. "Fifty thousand dollars, for a pipe dream! I could have sowed a lot of wild oats for that. What a fool I am, to be fussing with this infernal thing like an old crank, when I might be lounging on the beach with June!"

But something flashed, then, in his level blue eyes; his wide shoulders squared.

"It can be done!" he insisted under his breath. "I might try a conegrid. Or alloy the cathode element with titanium. The motor-tube——"

He heard, then, the insistent doorbell and frantic knocking at the front door. Foster hurried down the gloomy hall.

Still he could hear the racing car, a deep-toned, ominous roll, that grew swiftly louder. It slackened momentarily, was renewed.

"It has turned in the drive," he thought. "Two unexpected guests, and both in a hurry!"

He flung the door open upon wintry gloom; the bitter wind whirled snow into his face.

A cab was standing in front of the door, yellow lights stabbing feebly into the swirling snow. It glided away as he appeared. And Foster saw the man who had rung, a small figure, muffled in an enormous gray coat, crouching against the wall.

He sprang toward the opening door, gasping: "Quick! Inside! The other car——"

Powerful lights probed through the snow; the second machine came roaring up the drive, behind the departing cab. Skidding recklessly, it swerved toward the door.

Terrific reports crashed in Foster's ears; yellow flame jetted from a black automatic in the little man's hand. He was shooting into the skidding sedan.

A thin sword of blinding orange light stabbed back from the machine, as it thundered past. The ray seemed to touch the little man. He whirled, as his gun exploded a last time, fell inside the door.

The black car paused, plunged forward again. Its headlights rested a moment on the cab, swept past it. It vanished down the drive.

Bewildered, Foster slammed the door, locked it. He bent over the little man on the floor. A gasping breath greeted him, then a faint chuckle.

A low voice spoke, oddly calm: "We score one, Foster!"

"You aren't hurt, sir? You fell, when the orange light——"

"No. I dropped in time."

Foster was helping him to rise.

"But it's a deadly thing. The poison flame, they call it. It's an actinic radiation, I believe, that splits proteins. It forms poison in the blood."

The little man bent for his automatic. Deliberately, he removed the empty cartridge clip, snapped another into place, slipped the heavy weapon back into the pocket of his gray coat.

"Won't you come in where it's warmer?" Foster invited. "And if you don't mind explaining——"

"Of course, Foster."

His strange guest followed him through the shadowy hall, into the brightly lighted library. Foster turned, when they came into the light, to survey the other.

"You seem to know my name," he remarked. Recognition flashed then, in his level blue eyes. "Uncle Barron!" he exclaimed. "I hadn't recognized you!" He offered his hand cordially.

Barron Kane was a small man. His chest was flat; his drooping shoulders were thin as a boy's; his arms were lean and stringy. Yet the serene patience of the scientist lighted his weary face with a radiance of power. In his calm gray eyes was confidence, and beside it, strangely, the shadow of a devouring dread.

"You surprised me," said Foster. "I thought, you know, that you must be—dead. It's years since any one has heard from you. My father tried to locate you."

"I've been in Asia," said the little sun-browned man, "at an oasis in the Gobi, that you won't find on the maps. I was completely cut off from civilization. And there's a power, you see, that would cut me off forever."

He nodded in the direction the racing car had gone.

"I remember when you were fitting out your last expedition," recalled Foster. "Twelve years ago—I was in high school. You were so mysterious about where you were headed. And I was wild to go along, for the adventure of it, trying to talk dad out of the idea that I was destined to run the steel business.

"But sit down. Do you care for a drink?"

Barron Kane shook a brown, bald head—he had arrived without a hat. "But I must talk to you, Foster."

"I'm keen to know all about it," Foster assured him. "All this is—well, interesting."

"We might be interrupted," said Barron Kane. "Do you mind fastening the doors and windows and drawing the blinds?"

"Of course not. Do you think—they will come back?"

"There is a power," said Barron Kane, his low voice still oddly calm, "that will not rest without positive proof that I am dead."

Foster locked the door, went to secure the windows. He came back to find his uncle curiously examining the little silver model on the table.

"I read your monograph last month in the *Science Review*," he said. "About the omicron-effect and your motor-tube. That's why I've come to you, Foster. You've hit on a tremendous thing——"

"Not yet," denied Foster, with a weary little smile. "I've spent two years of time and a good deal of money on the motor-tube. And still it won't lift its own weight."

"But you're still trying?" The low voice was edged with a strange anxiety.

"I was working to-day." Foster touched the little aluminum globe. "This is a model of the space machine. The motor-tube is inside, connected with these platinum wires. The real ship, of course, would have all this other apparatus aboard. The living accommodations and she——"

He stopped himself, shook his head bitterly.

"But it's just a dream!" he muttered. "A crazy dream—I'm not going to waste my life on it." His blue eyes flashed at Barron Kane defiantly. "I'm leaving for Palm Beach, to-night, to meet June Trevor." He explained: "We're engaged. We'll be married New Year's. Barron, June's simply—wonderful!"

"You can't do that!" protested Barron Kane. Gripping Foster's arm, he spoke with a puzzling urgency. "You must stick to the space machine. You must finish it, Foster, to save the human race."

"Eh!" Grunting with astonishment, Foster stepped back from him. "What do you mean?"

"Just that," Barron Kane told him, in the same quiet voice that was emphatic for its very lack of emphasis. "I've come to tell you a dreadful thing, Foster. A thing I learned in Asia. A thing that a terrible power is bent upon keeping me from telling."

Foster stared at him, demanded: "What's that?"

"The planet is doomed to destruction," said Barron Kane, still grimly calm. "And the human race with it—unless you can save a handful of humanity. You are the one man who has even the ghost of a chance, Foster, with your steel mills and your invention of the motor-tube."

Amazed, a little shaken, despite himself, at the chill touch of alien fear, Foster watched his uncle.

Had the man gone mad in the twelve years since he vanished? He always had been famous for an eccentricity of character no less than his ability as geologist and astrophysicist. No, Foster decided, his manner was sane enough. And the car from which the orange ray had flamed had been no mad delusion. It had been very real.

Foster took Barron Kane by the shoulder, marched him to a great leather chair and seated him in it. Standing over him, he demanded:

"Now tell me exactly what this is all about?"

Grave humor momentarily banished the haunting shadow of dread from those calm gray eyes.

"No, Foster," the quiet voice said; "I'm afraid that I'm perfectly sane."

Barron Kane laced his thin brown fingers together, stared at them meditatively.

"You cannot have heard of the Cult of the Great Egg," he began. "You can't, because even the name of it is almost completely unknown outside. But it is a fanatical religious sect, whose temple is hidden in an unknown oasis in the Gobi.

"Nearly ten years ago, Foster, I became a member of that sect. It was not easily done. And afterward I had to endure ordeals that were—well, trying. After seven years I was fully initiated. From the lips of the head of the order—a human demon named L'ao Ku—I heard the dreadful secret that I had gone to Asia to learn.

"That was three years ago. L'ao Ku must have suspected me. I was very closely watched. Two years I had to wait, even for the chance to escape. Since, I've been hunted across the world by the agents of L'ao Ku. It's almost another year.

"I thought I'd given them the slip in Panama. I saw your article about the motor-tube and came to you, Foster. You, as I say, are the only man—— But they've somehow picked up the trail again. I'm afraid I've sentenced you to death."

"Sentenced me?" asked Foster. "How?"

"L'ao Ku wants his secret kept. Three men have died very soon after talking with me, mysteriously."

Foster was still planted in front of Barron Kane, wonder and incredulity struggling in his mind. His chin tightened with determination to find some rational order in these bewildering incidents.

"This secret?" he demanded. "What is it? What's this about the end of the world?"

Again Barron Kane thoughtfully studied the tips of his laced fingers. "I'll begin, I think," he said, "by asking you a question—by asking you, Foster, the greatest riddle in the world. What is the Earth?"

Startled, Foster searched the weary, patient face. He studied the gray eyes, calm, yet shadowed with brooding horror. He shook his head. Barron Kane was an enigma.

"All right, what *is* the Earth?"

"I've a very astounding thing to tell you," went on Barron Kane, "a very terrible thing. It will be hard for you to accept, for it is contrary to a lot of our unthinking dogma that is older than science.

"The idea is so strange, so terrible, Foster, that no western mind could have conceived it. We owe a debt, after all, to the Cult of the Great Egg. The oriental mentality, working with the secret science of the order, saw a thing that we should never have been able to see, in spite of all the evidence in front of our eyes.

"But I can make it easier for you to accept the thing, Foster, by recalling a few notorious gaps in scientific knowledge. And you *must* accept it, Foster. The very life of humanity depends upon you."

Foster dropped into a chair directly before Barron Kane. Sitting bolt upright, he waited silently.

"We live in appalling ignorance of the planet beneath us," the same calm voice spoke on, edged still with a terrible intensity. "Out of four thousand miles to the center of the Earth, how far have we penetrated? Not four miles!

"What lies beyond? What, really, is the thing whose tremors we call earthquakes? What lies beneath the thin shell of solid rock we live upon? What is it whose heat causes our volcanoes? I could cite you a thousand vague, conflicting theories, guesses, about the nature of the Earth's interior —but hardly one proved fact. We know actually as little of the Earth, Foster, as a fly, crawling on an egg, knows of the mystery of embryonic life within.

"And how much less we know of the other planets! What scientist can tell you even how they came to be? Oh, there've been fine theories enough, since Laplace. We have the planetesimal hypothesis, the nebular hypothesis, the gaseous hypothesis, the meteoritic hypothesis—this hypothesis and that. The most remarkable thing about each one is that it successfully contradicts all the others.

"Think of the puzzle of the lost planet! According to Bode's Law, you know, there should be another planet in the gap between Mars and Jupiter, where the asteroids are. The asteroids and the comets and the meteor swarms apparently are fragments of it—but, altogether, they account for no more than a tenth of the bulk it should have had. What unthinkable cataclysm shattered the lost planet, Foster? And, tell me, what became of the nine-tenths of it that is gone?

"Take another cosmic enigma! What is the Sun itself, upon which our very lives depend? What is the life story of a sun, any sun? How does it acquire its matter and its motion and its heat? What is the purpose in existence of a sun? When you look at the stars on a winter night, Foster, can you conceive them without any end in being?

"Consider the riddle of entropy! There is a force of death that pervades the universe. Stars grow cold and die; star dust is scattered; radiation is diffused and lost. Our cosmogonists say the universe is running down. But must there not also be a force of life, of growth, of creation?

"How can death be, Foster, without life before it?

"Did you never wonder, Foster, why the Sun, like other variable stars, expands and contracts in the rhythm of the sun-spot cycle, with a beat like the pulse of a living thing?"

Barron Kane leaned forward. His gray eyes—the shadow of haunting horror was deeper in them, now—fixed upon Foster's face with a desperate, appealing earnestness.

"Foster," he went on, "I know what the Earth is!

"Years ago, struggling with the failures and the contradictions of our western science, I vaguely guessed the thing. Twelve years ago, from a chance faint rumor, I inferred that oriental insight had seen the truth hidden from our dogmatic western minds.

"I went, as I say, into the Gobi. I found the secret sect. After seven years of effort and endurance, I reached the inner mystery. L'ao Ku confirmed my terrible inference.

"I learned from him things I had not dared even to guess. I learned that the Earth—the entire solar system—is destined to break up within a very short time. We shall see the end, Foster—unless the secret agents of L'ao Ku make away with us first.

"We must not forget him, Foster, in the greater danger. The man is inhuman, fanatic, diabolical; but he is a genius. And all his power, all the secret science that produced the poison ray, is bent upon our destruction."

The calm voice paused. Quiet hung in the wide library, strained, electric. And Foster whispered, incredulous:

"The end of the world!"

"The end," repeated Barron Kane, with the same compelling calm. "I had hoped we might have—years. But I know to-night, from an item in the evening paper, that the change has already begun."

Foster Ross surged back to his feet, towered over the little brown man. "Tell me," he implored, "just what are you getting at?"

Barron Kane told him, leaning forward, his low voice sunk almost to a whisper. Foster listened silently, still standing. Unbelieving wonder was first in his blue eyes. It gave way slowly to the dawn of a terrible fear.

II.

An hour later, it was, when the grave little scientist finished and leaned back in the huge leather chair lacing his thin brown fingers together again.

Without speaking, Foster strode to a tall window. He put up the blind and stared out into the early-winter night. The bare trees were a ghostly rank of skeletons on fields of snow that shimmered faintly under the dark sky. Flakes of snow gleamed white in the flood of light from the window. The bitter wind moaned bleakly against the ancient stone walls.

"Please draw the blind," requested Barron Kane, with that same calm that nothing disturbed. "The agents of L'ao Ku might be watching. The poison ray——"

Foster snatched down the blind. He strode back to his uncle, tense, trembling a little. "Sorry!" he muttered. "I forgot."

"The idea is a peculiarly difficult one for the western mind to receive," said Barron Kane sympathetically. "It would drive most westerners mad, I suspect, to be forced to believe it. But, if you will try to grasp it with something of the oriental fatalism——"

Foster seemed unconscious of him. He strode up and down the vast, dark-paneled room. He paused, once, to touch the little aluminum model of the space ship on the table. He took a photograph of dark-eyed June Trevor from the mantel, and studied her demure, classic loveliness for a moment and replaced it very carefully. He strode back to his uncle.

"The Earth—that!" he rasped. "I can't believe it! It's too—monstrous!"

Barron Kane rose and came to him eagerly. "You must believe me, Foster," his low voice pleaded. "Because only you have the means to save the seed of humanity. And you must begin the work at once—to-night!"

"To-night?" echoed Foster, in dull surprise.

"You must realize, Foster, that we've only months. Half a year, at most. And the undertaking is—terrific. We must set up a laboratory to rush the development of your motor-tube. Your steel mills must begin fabricating parts for the—the ark of space.

"We've a thousand problems to solve in every branch of engineering. And the thing must be finished in less time than was ever taken for a similar construction. Much less time!"

"There has been no similar construction," Foster said. "Even a battle ship is a simple toy compared to the space machine. It would take a lifetime to launch the thing.

"Besides," he protested vaguely, still lost in wonderment, "I'm going to Palm Beach. I promised June that I——"

"Then you must break your promise," cut in Barron Kane imperatively. "Both of us must give every second to the job. Even then, the time is fearfully short. And we must look out for L'ao Ku with his poison ray."

"Really, you see, I can't—can't quite believe." Foster's blue eyes looked soberly at Barron Kane. "The thing's too damnably fantastic!"

"You must try to grasp it with the oriental viewpoint," urged his uncle. "The eastern fatalism——"

"I'm no Chinaman," said Foster. "But I do love June Trevor—more than anything. Even if you're right—if the next six months will be the last—I'd rather spend them with her."

"Don't you see?" whispered Barron Kane. He gripped Foster's arm with thin fingers. "If you love June Trevor, you must build the space machine to save her. Would you want to see her die, Foster, with the rest of the human race, like—like vermin in a burning house? Wiped out—annihilated?"

"No!" exclaimed Foster. "No! But I can't believe——"

"You must!" insisted Barron Kane. "There's proof, I tell you. To-night, in the evening paper, is an item that heralds the disruption of the solar system."

"Proof?" cried Foster incredulously. "Proof of—that?"

"Have you an evening paper?"

"It's here somewhere. I had no time to look at it. The experiment, you know."

He found the paper, unfolded it curiously. His eye sought the chief headline, saw that it concerned merely a new disclosure of political corruption.

Barron Kane's thin, eager hands took the paper from him, pointed out an obscurely headed item at the bottom of the page.

SAVANTS PUZZLED

Doctor Lynn Poynter, of the Mount Wilson Observatory, reported this morning that the planet Pluto has left its orbit and is wandering away from the Sun on an erratic and inexplicable path. The planet's color, Doctor Poynter also stated, has changed from yellowish to vivid green.

He is unable, Doctor Poynter says, to give any explanation of the phenomenon. He refuses to make any further comments upon it, except to say that other astronomers, in all parts of the world, are being requested to check his observations.

Foster's face set grimly as he read the brief paragraphs. His fingers, trembling, closed unconsciously upon the newspaper, tore it slowly in two. Into his blue eyes, when he looked back at Barron Kane, had come a new, consuming horror. Huskily, he spoke:

"So Pluto is already—gone? Already, the solar system is breaking up!"

He gazed down at the torn paper in his hands.

"We'll go down to the mill in the morning, Barron," he said, "to begin."

Silently, the little brown man gripped his hand, mutely thankful.

"Now," said Foster, "I must telephone June."

"It's you, Foster!" came the girl's clear voice over the wire, eager with anticipation. "You're coming down to-morrow? I'll drive to meet you——"

Foster was picturing her staid, brown-eyed charm; he saw her as she would sit at the wheel, tall, slender: a gay, childish eagerness beneath her sedate reserve. And he was faint, suddenly, with a sick regret that he could not go to her.

"No," he was saying, trying to keep the pain from his voice; "I'm afraid I can't come down."

He sensed the quick anxiety in her reply:

"Is something—wrong?"

"A thing has come up," he stumbled, searching for words not too alarming. "A job that I must do. It's tremendously important. I must stay——"

"Oh!" In her voice was a little catch of agony. "Will it keep you—past the New Year?"

"Yes," he said. "We'll have to name a new wedding day."

"Oh!" It was a gasp of pain: Foster was sick with pity for her. "Can't you tell me what it is?"

"No; not over the phone. But I want you to come to me, June, as soon as you can. I'll explain."

"I've a lot of engagements," she protested. "And you seem so—strange!"

"It's really important," he urged. "Please come! I need you, really. Oh, June—please——"

A moment of silence; then she spoke decisively:

"All right, Foster, I'll be there—let's see—Monday."

"Thanks, dear!" he said gratefully. "When you understand——"

"Atta boy!" she cried, almost gayly. "Get some sunshine in your voice! You were talking as if the world were going to end! I'll be there Monday."

Dear June, the same good sport, he was thinking, as she hung up. Gay and unselfish as ever. She always understood. And he would, he must, finish the space machine in time to carry her away from this unbelievable terror that Barron Kane promised.

That night Barron Kane and Foster Ross did not go to bed. They stayed in the long library, beside the little aluminum model of the space machine, planning how to transform the dream of it into reality. Foster ventured to the kitchen at midnight and brought bread and cold ham and a bottle of milk and set them beside the toy ship.

At dawn he began packing into a brief case the model and the sheets they had covered with plans, to carry down to the mill.

"There's a danger, remember," warned Barron Kane. "The men who followed me won't be far away. They won't go back without proof that I am dead."

"I'll call the mill," said Foster, "have a few men sent out."

But the line, he discovered, was dead.

"The wires are down," he said. "The storm——"

"L'ao Ku's men have cut them," whispered Barron Kane. "They are waiting for us."

"We'd better make a dash for it, then," Foster suggested, "while we can."

Barron Kane nodded. "We'll have to fence ourselves in if we do get to the mill," he said. "For we'll be fighting L'ao Ku, to the end, as well as fighting against time. It is the basis of the secret sect that all life must perish when the Earth breaks up. Any attempt to save even a single human life breaks the first tenet of their fantastic dogma."

Leaving the lights burning in the library, the two slipped out through the rear of the old mansion. The grounds were ghostly white with snow. Dense clouds hid the sky, ice-gray with the first glow of dawn. Mysterious shadows were clotted against trees and buildings.

Foster carried his priceless model. Barron Kane had drawn his heavy automatic, snapped off the safety. At a half run, they crunched through thick snow to the garage. Foster unlocked the doors, flung them back.

A thin orange ray, bright as a blade of incandescent metal, flamed silently out of the gloomy doorway. It struck Barron Kane's arm. His automatic spoke once in reply. Then, gasping with agony, he crumpled down on the snow.

Foster caught his breath. His lean body catapulted instantly into the black corner from which the silent ray had come.

His groping hand closed over a talonlike hand that held a light metal tube. His shoulder struck a lithe, powerful body, flung it heavily against the wall. Another lean hand closed on his throat. He caught a sinewy wrist, forced it back.

The two recoiled from the wall, thudded on the concrete floor. Foster had heard a guttural grunt of surprise. That was the only sound from his unseen opponent. The battle was finished in silence and darkness.

A doubled knee drove into Foster's groin. As he writhed in agony, hard fingers twitched under his. A blinding finger of yellow light stabbed from the little tube. It wavered across the wall of the garage. Slowly it came down.

The poison ray! If it touched him, to make a deadly venom of his own blood——

Intolerable agony burst suddenly from the tortured wrist of his resisting arm. He trembled with the pain of effort. Hot sweat burst out on his face.

The orange ray touched the floor, trembled toward his shoulder. The talons that moved it were hard as steel.

Foster was giddy with the unbearable pain from his twisted arm. The world spun; a wave of blackness rose. Then, in the moment of defeat, a queer something happened to him, a blinding revelation. In a moment of crystal vision, he saw himself not as one man fighting for his own life, but the champion of humanity, battling for ultimate survival.

A new strength came oddly with the vision; deathless purpose flowed into him like a strange tide.

He straightened his tortured arm. Red agony flamed in it. But the orange needle flickered away. The hard body against him knotted with exertion;

the ray flashed back. Faint and dizzy, Foster drew on his new strength to the utmost.

He heard the dull snap of a breaking bone. The steel talons in his grasp turned to limp flesh. The orange blade described a sudden arc, that touched the head of the other man. Then the little tube crashed against the wall, the ray went out.

The other was already dead from his own weapon when Foster staggered to his feet.

Barron Kane lay still on the snow outside, a small gray huddle in the pale dawn light. Foster ran to him, heard his faint whisper:

"The poison ray—my wrist—a tourniquet at the elbow—bleed it."

Foster pushed up the sleeve on the thin brown arm. He whipped his handkerchief around the right elbow, twisted it tight with a spanner he snatched from the wall. On the lean, stringy wrist he saw a swelling, lividly purple, swiftly increasing in size. He dug a keen penknife out of his vest pocket, slashed deep into it, put his own lips to the wound to draw out the poison.

"That will do," whispered Barron Kane at last, his voice a little stronger. "Guess I'm done for, anyhow. Just hope I live to see you win, Foster. No matter. I've done my part. It's up to you, now, to save the seed of mankind."

"I—I'll do my best," Foster promised him, choking. He was still strong with the strange self-forgetful resolution that had come to him in the fight.

"Drive on," whispered Barron Kane, "to the mill!"

Foster lifted him into the roadster. When he switched on the lights he paused a moment to look down at the dead man on the floor. His face was yellow, Mongoloid, with a hawklike thinness. It was set, now, in the fearful, derisive grin of death.

"Open his clothing, Foster," commanded Barron Kane. "Look on his body, under the left arm."

Foster obeyed. Under the man's arm, on the yellow skin stretched like parchment over the ribs, was a scarlet mark, like a large O.

"He's branded!" he cried. "With a red circle!"

"That is the emblem of the secret cult," whispered Barron Kane. "He came from L'ao Ku."

Foster leaped in beside Barron Kane. The stiff motor came to bellowing life. The roadster lunged forward, swerved past the dead man, skidded out upon the icy drive.

The leaden, frigid day had come when they drove into the grimy mill town. Gaunt, ugly, the little buildings of the workers huddled over hillsides gray with snow and soot. The mill stood in the level valley; gigantic blast furnaces marched, like a grim army of black steel monsters, against the gloomy clouds.

Foster drove straight through the gates to the emergency hospital. He carried Barron Kane to a cot inside.

"The doctors will soon be here," he promised.

"Don't worry about me," the little man whispered. "You have work to do. I'm going to try to live to see you finish it."

III.

Three months later, a new fence surrounded the steel mill. It was twenty feet high, and the first ten were bullet-proof concrete and steel. The top of it was wired to powerful generators. At hundred-foot intervals it was studded with rotating turrets of steel and bullet-proof glass, in which sentries watched always, behind frowning machine guns.

Inside the fence, on a huge pier of reënforced concrete, the space machine was building.

Its hull was already completed—a feat unprecedented in engineering. A colossal sphere, nearly five hundred feet in diameter, it dwarfed to insignificance the flanking armies of blast furnaces. The top of its gray bulk was visible for many miles across the low Pennsylvania hills, that now, in March, were green with the last spring of Earth.

Much, however, remained to be done in perfecting the interior arrangements, by which human life was to be sustained indefinitely in the sunless void. Greatest lack of all, the motor-tube, which was to utilize Foster Ross' omicron-effect to propel the machine, was still unperfected.

"The rest will be finished in a month," Foster promised Barron Kane, one windy spring day. "But a lot of good that will be if the motor-tube won't work. A million tons of steel and glass! We have no way to move it an inch, unless——"

They were in a room in the emergency hospital, from the windows of which the sick man could watch the tremendous gray-painted sphere of steel, looming against pale-green hills and wind-torn sky.

Barron Kane was still on his back. The venom formed by the orange ray had affected spinal nerve centers; he was unable to walk, even his hands were partially paralyzed. But his brain remained keen as ever; despite his helplessness and pain, he had helped the solution of many a problem in the building of the space machine.

"Unless?" he whispered. "You're trying something else?"

"We began this morning to work out a new design. We started from a new beginning, suggested by the equations of the omicron-effect. We don't know that it will be any better. Even if it works, the installation will take six weeks."

"Six weeks?" breathed Barron Kane, in weary alarm. "We may not have that long before the Earth breaks up!"

His gray eyes stared at Foster from the pillow, calm, yet dark with dread.

"The moon of Neptune, you know," he whispered, "left its orbit last week. It turned greenish and followed Pluto off into space. And there's another thing——"

His shrunken, half-useless hands fumbled for the newspaper on the blanket beside him.

"What is it?" asked Foster.

"In the morning paper. Still no one sees what's coming. They have the story hidden on an inside page—nobody saw what it meant. But it's about the most important thing they ever printed. Here it is!"

Foster read the item:

QUAKES SHOW RHYTHM

A new series of tremors is shaking the earth, announced Doctor Madison Kline, noted English seismologist, speaking to-day before an international convention of geologists.

These recently observed earth tremors occur at regular intervals of about thirty-one minutes, said Doctor Kline. He believes they reflect some rhythmic disturbance deep within the planet.

Doctor Kline and his associates, he stated, have had the phenomenon under observation for several weeks, during which time it has steadily and markedly increased.

No conclusively definite explanation can yet be offered, Doctor Kline said, though he believes that the period of the vibration corresponds to the natural fundamental frequency of the planet.

Foster's hands closed until the knuckles went white. "That means," he muttered huskily, "that we're near—the finish."

"You see," whispered Barron Kane, "you must rush the installation of the new motor-tube."

"We will!" Foster promised. "Though the thing may not work, when it's done. We're trying, you see, to compress a generation of scientific progress into four months."

"There are other things," Barron Kane reminded him. "We must be ready to cut all connection with civilization."

"Our supplies are mostly on board, already," Foster informed him. "And our people are moving into the machine as fast as the quarters are ready. Six hundred picked men, representing every race and every craft and every creed, with their wives and children. Two thousand, all told—and the very cream of humanity."

"The laboratories?" queried Barron Kane.

"Oh, they'll be finished in time," Foster assured him. "In a month, Barron, we'll have our own artificial air and our own synthetic food, made on board from the refined elements of the waste.

"Once out in space," he went on, a ring of enthusiasm in his voice, "we'll be independent. Our generators will tap the limitless energy of the cosmic ray. They will supply warmth and light and power, the means for the manufacture of oxygen and food, and current for the motor-tube.

"The machine can sail on forever, Barron. It's a little world, itself, independent of the Sun——"

Foster stopped himself, bit his lips. "Here I am," he muttered sheepishly, "ranting about the thing! When I couldn't move it an inch, to save my soul! So long, Barron. I must get back to the shops."

"Wait!" whispered the sick man. "There's another thing. Where is your fiancée?"

"Why," Foster told him, "June has gone back to Florida for a short visit with some friends. I want her to forget, as much as she can, what's coming. It's so terrible, for a girl like her——"

"Have her come back," advised Barron Kane. "Have her move on board with us."

"There's danger?" demanded Foster. "Already?"

"The first quiver of the Earth's crust will be enough to shatter the thing we call civilization," whispered the little man. "She must be here before that happens. And there's another danger."

"What's that?"

"L'ao Ku hasn't shown his power, Foster. But don't forget that he has a power. He's just waiting, getting ready. Don't be deceived; don't let down your guard."

"Oh!" breathed Foster, relieved. "I thought you meant some danger to June."

"I do," whispered Barron Kane.

Foster leaned over him, tense with alarm.

"In that temple in the Gobi is an altar erected to the Great Egg. Above it is an image, cut from black stone. The image is a globe, with the outlines of the continents engraved on it, so you can see that it represents the Earth. It is split, and a thing is emerging. A thing obscenely monstrous!

"Regular ceremonies are held in the temple, Foster. On that altar, under the image of that unthinkable obscenity breaking from the earth, L'ao Ku offers sacrifices. The victims are always women. When possible, they are heretics or members of their families.

"It is possible, Foster, that June Trevor might—suffer, just because you plan to save her."

Foster's face was gray, drawn. Hoarsely, he rasped: "I'll send for her to come on board. Right away!"

The scientific world was stunned from the first. The aberration of Pluto shattered the whole painfully built structure of western science. The pulselike tremors of the earth, which soon became violent enough to be felt as one walked in the street, received no adequate explanation.

Scientists, for a time, took refuge in pitiful charges of inaccurate observation. But they could not long deny that the solar system was breaking up. The planet Neptune shifted unaccountably from its calculated position. One by one, the greater moons of Saturn and Uranus assumed a greenish color and departed from their orbits. The change, spreading inward through the solar system, overtook the four large moons of Jupiter.

The very universe of science collapsed.

The common man, however, at first was only slightly concerned. Business went on as usual; the public attention centered in turn upon unemployment, the stabilized dollar, the sensational murder of a Hollywood actress. There was no real panic, even when the "Earth-beat," as the newspapers termed the oddly rhythmic tremors of the planet, became a chief topic of conversation.

Real panic began only with loss of life. Late in March a series of terrific earthquakes and accompanying tidal waves overwhelmed, one by one, Tokyo, Bombay, Rio de Janeiro, and Los Angeles. The cataclysms were progressively more violent. Hardly a paper, so long as papers were printed, lacked its story of a new holocaust.

Even then, the old order did not immediately fall. "Business as usual" was a catchword, though prices rocketed, governments and corporations crashed, and crime ran wild.

New leaders, radical movements, fantastic fads, won tremendous support. New religions, in particular, were widely and feverishly embraced. Ten thousand new prophets rose and were acclaimed; but the greatest following was won by the disciples of that strange oriental sect, the Cult of the Great Egg.

They, alone, professed to understand the change. They, alone, could offer bewildered humanity a rational, if fantastic, key to the astounding riddle of the crumbling solar system. Even though he promised only grim death—death as a sacred duty—L'ao Ku became the master of fanatic millions.

The mad tide of his increasing power, Barron Kane and Foster Ross recognized from the beginning, was sure to be turned against them. They had made a fortress of the steel mill. They hastened the construction of the space machine to the utmost. They could do no more.

IV.

The crisis came on the night of April 23rd. The Moon was full. The skies, often of late strangely clouded, were clear over most of North America. Horror-stricken millions, that night, watched the change overtake the Moon. Few, having seen it, were ever completely sane again.

It was the madness born of that incredible vision of mind-breaking horror, guided by the fanatic genius of L'ao Ku, that led to the mass attacks on the space machine.

The *Planet*—so June Trevor had named the space machine, since it was to be the sole future home of humanity—lay still upon the concrete pier, inside the fence. And still it could not be moved; the motor-tube was yet incomplete.

Atop the gray, colossal sphere of steel was a little domed space roofed with crystal panels. It was reached by a short stair from a door below. Gleaming mechanisms crowded it, the intricate instruments designed for the control and navigation of the space machine.

On that fatal night, Foster Ross and June Trevor came into the little control room, Foster carrying Barron Kane in his arms. They made the wrecked body of the little scientist as comfortable as possible in an invalid chair amid the shining instruments.

"Last night," Foster said, "observers saw cracks spreading across the Moon. Its crust is splitting. Beneath is something—— It is greenish, incandescent. To-night, we shall see the end of the Moon!

"Watching the Moon, we can see the thing that, in a day or so, is going to happen to the Earth!"

June Trevor moved, quickly, anxiously, to his side. June was a tall girl, dark-eyed, with a grave, classic beauty. She smiled at Foster—it was a wan, anxious little smile. Apprehensive, she slipped her hand into his.

"Foster," she whispered, "will it be very—terrible?"

"The terror of it," he told her, "will not be in what we see. It will be in what it means. In the fate of the Moon, we see the fate of the Earth, of human civilization. But try, dear, not to be afraid."

"I'm not—not exactly afraid," she whispered, shivering a little. "But it's dreadful to think of so many—perishing——"

Foster's hand tightened on her own. "June," he said huskily, "you must try not to think of that. We've each other, remember. Without you, I—I'd go mad!"

"And there's a bigger thing," she breathed. "We've a duty. To save the race!"

Foster turned out the lights, then, in the tiny room. They looked upward through the panels of heavy fused quartz. Flooded with moonlight, the sky was silver-gray; in the south were white, luminous feathers of cloud. The Moon was high in the east, a supernal disk of mottled gold.

They stared at it. June Trevor quivered; she pressed close against Foster's lean body.

"There *are* cracks!" she murmured, breathless. "I see them! Like a net of wire."

"They're spreading," muttered Foster. "And—I see a green something, breaking through."

From his pillow came the queer, voiceless whisper of the paralyzed scientist: "The being is emerging."

Breathless, speechless with fearful awe, the three watched the Moon —as maddened millions were watching it over all the continent.

They saw the familiar seas and ring craters of the lunar topography dissolve in a network of cracks, black and shining green. They saw the face of the Moon, for the first time in human memory, misty with clouds of its own.

They saw a thing come out of the riven planet—an unthinkable head appeared——

It broke through, in the region of the great crater Tycho. It was monstrously weird. Colossal, triangular, a beak came first, green and shining. Behind it were two ovoid, enormous patches, like eyes, glowing with lambent purple. Between and above them was an enigmatic organ, arched, crested; it was an unearthly spray of crimson flame.

Incredible wings—reaching out—stretching——

They pushed through the shattered, crumbling shell, which already had lost all likeness to the Moon of old. Wings, alone, could human beings term them. Yet, Foster thought, they were more than anything else like the eldritch, gorgeous streamers of the Sun's corona, which is seen only at the moment of total eclipse, spreading from the black disk like two wings of supernal light. They were sheets of green flame. They shimmered with slow waves of light, that faded indistinctly at the edges, like the uncanny fans of the aurora. They were finely veined with bright silver.

A body, both horrible and beautiful——

It came into view, when the slowly expanding, supernal wings pushed back the cosmic debris that had been the Moon's crust. It uncoiled into a sinuous loveliness, long and slender, delicately tapering. It was green as emerald, bright as flame, and strangely marked with silver and black.

The color of all the sky changed appallingly from silver-gray to green, with the fearful radiation of the thing. The shadows it cast, inky-black, green-fringed, were uncanny—dreadful.

It hung for a time in the sky where the Moon had been, nearly motionless. Monstrous appendages like serpents of blue flame reached out of its head, beneath the purple ovoids. They writhed over its slender, terrible body and its diaphanous wings.

It preened itself.

Amazingly, then, it wheeled across the sky. Its fantastic shadows crept like living things. With luminous waves, like some strange force, pulsing outward through the wondrous sheets of flame that were like wings, it flew away. The dread green illumination faded from the sky, and the terrible shadows died, and the thing became a minute fleck of emerald light, dwindling beside white Vega.

"The Moon is gone!" breathed Foster, dazed with wonder.

"As the Earth will go," came the voiceless whisper of Barron Kane, "in a few days, now."

"Beautiful!" gasped June Trevor, in a queer, shaken little voice. "It was lovely—and horrible——"

She shuddered, and Foster was surprised to find her firm, warm, straight body in his arms. Unconsciously she nestled against him, instinctively seeking comfort; and his arm tightened, before he released her.

"Our world must go—that way, dear——" he breathed; and her shivery, tiny whisper finished: "But we have—each other——"

Barron Kane was still looking out through the crystal dome. Since the going of the Moon, the sky was a dome of splendid stars. The low, rolling Pennsylvania hills loomed dark under it, picked out with tiny, winking lights of house and motor. The lights of the mill town, under the towering bulk of the *Planet*, were little bright rectangles in the blackness.

"There are too many lights on the roads," said Barron Kane, and his whisper was edged with alarm. "Cars and torches and swinging lanterns. They are all coming toward the *Planet!*"

Foster and June looked down from the lofty windows. Over the dark hills they saw the rivers of dancing, flickering light, flowing toward them.

Foster rasped a single bitter word: "Mobs!"

"Mobs?" echoed June wonderingly. "Why?"

"People aren't human beings any longer," Foster told her grimly. "They are animals—frightened animals. They are mad with fear, since they've seen the break-up of the Moon. They're driven to fight, like any fear-crazed thing. We can't blame them—but we must defend the *Planet*."

Tenderly, he put the girl from him.

"I must go down to warn the guard," he said, "and to help the men in the power rooms. They're installing the motor-tube."

"When," rustled the anxious whisper of Barron Kane, "when will you be able to move the *Planet?*"

"The castings came this morning from the foundry," Foster informed him. "It will take a day to put them in. Then—if the mob hasn't wiped us out!—we can see whether the *Planet* will move. Whether the human race is to live—or to die with the Earth."

"A day?" breathed Barron Kane despairingly. "Our fence won't hold them back so long."

"It will take that long," Foster told him, tight-lipped. "Twenty hours, at the very least. We'll save every second, of course. And the entrance valve is ready to close. We'll make an inner fort of the *Planet*, itself. But I must go!" He squeezed June's hand and ran out of the little room.

The girl and Barron Kane waited there, amid the gleaming instruments that were to navigate the space machine—if it ever moved. The sick man was whispering orders into a telephone mouthpiece, to help organize the defense.

Impatiently, June waited; at last she demanded fearfully:

"Is there much—danger? The people are mad with fear; I understand that. But why should they attack us?"

"The priests of a fanatic religion have stirred them up against us," grimly whispered Barron Kane. "In Asia, the priests of a secret sect foresaw the doom. They based their faith on it, and on the duty of man to die. In their eyes, we are heretics. They seek to destroy us.

"To destroy us," the dread-chilled whisper went on, "and perhaps to sacrifice some of us, for atonement, at the ceremonial altar of the Great Egg, in the temple in the Gobi."

June shuddered, as if with a premonition of horror.

"I'm going after Foster," she cried, fighting to keep a thin edge of hysteria out of her voice. "I want to be with him."

"You had better wait here," Barron Kane advised her. "Or rest in your room, just below. Foster is very busy." And he added grimly: "You will be safer here—you are in the greatest danger."

"I'm not afraid!" she burst out, wild-voiced. Then calmness came back; she went on quietly: "Not for myself, I mean. It's the terror of it, the thought that so many must die. And the awful, awful thing we saw, that came out of the Moon! I want to be with Foster. But I'll stay, if you think best."

And she sank on a seat, face buried in her hands, and fought to control her sobs.

All the terrible night, June remained in the little room. The mob still increased; ten thousand small fires flickered upon the hillsides; swinging lights crept here and there. The voice of the mob was a ceaseless, menacing murmur; again and again she heard a rattle of shots.

Barron Kane slept, in his invalid chair, at dawn. June covered him and watched a while. Then the loneliness, the strain, became so terrible that she went down to her own room and tried to sleep. But she could not, and before noon she came back into the bridge. The sick man was awake again.

He gazed at her.

"How is—everything?" her anxious question greeted him.

"They attacked three times in the night," the little man whispered. "The wall held them back; many were killed, by the charge on the wall, and by the guns. But a thousand more poor wretches have come, for every one that died."

His quiet gray eyes looked out through the thick quartz panels, down upon hillsides that were brown and swarming with the horde.

"There must be a million," his voiceless whisper went on. "They came every way you could imagine. On foot, on bicycles and trucks and freight cars, in cars and airplanes.

"You can't help pitying them, so frightened, so soon to die. A great many of them seem to be ragged and cold; they can't have brought food enough. Most of them didn't bring any weapons.

"But the disciples of L'ao Ku have taken them over. You can see rings of them gathered around the priests, who are fanning their hate against us. You can see them marching, drilling. And some of them are unloading explosive and weapons that came this morning on the railroad. L'ao Ku is making an army out of the mob."

Wearily nervous, June was peering with sleepless eyes through the heavy panels.

"I see a plane!" she cried suddenly. "Flying low over the hills. It's going to land!" She watched it, adding: "It's a huge ship, black, and it has scarlet circles on the wings and the fuselage."

Grimly Barron Kane whispered: "That is L'ao Ku's own ship. He has come to direct the attack in person. And, perhaps, to take one of us back——"

Silently, biting her lips until they bled, clenching her small hands, June Trevor watched—until the mob rolled toward the *Planet*, a resistless wave of fanatic, terror-mad hate.

Flashing like golden blades, the narrow blinding jets of the poison ray silenced the machine guns in the armored turrets. Bombs of high explosive, hurled from cunningly improvised catapults, demolished the electrified wall. A million men, commanded by a pitiless fanaticism and armed by a secret science, stormed the great steel valve of the *Planet*.

Racked with an agony of suspense, June waited in the bridge room, until her straining ears caught the dull crash of a heavy explosion, and then the sharp rattle of gunfire—inside the *Planet!*

"They've taken the valve!" she whispered, then, forcing the words through a black haze of despair: "They're coming on board. I must go to find Foster."

Barron Kane began some protest; she stopped him with a fierce gesture. "I'm not—not afraid," she gasped. "But the—finish has come. I want to be with Foster."

She ran out of the room and hastened down toward the sound of desperate battle.

In the exact center of the great steel globe of the *Planet* was a sixty-foot, spherical chamber. In that chamber, mounted in hugely massive gimbals, was an immense tube of fused quartz and steel, fifty feet long.

Foster Ross, with a score of other grimy, haggard, red-eyed men, was laboring to complete the assembly of that tube. A manhole was open in the top of the tube. With hoisting tackle, they were lifting a four-ton casting of a new alloy, to lower it through the manhole.

The confused, terrible roar of fighting burst suddenly into the chamber. "They've stormed the valve!" came a terror-laden shout; and consternation shook the men.

"Wait, men!" implored Foster desperately. "We can't quit the job. A few more minutes, and we'll have it done. We can take off into space. Come on——"

But some one, in his fright, had left his post. The tackle slipped. The great casting swung; it toppled out of the creaking sling and crashed to the floor. A man's legs were pinned under it. He made a low cry, thin, dreadful, and then began to whimper like a child.

Some of the men started a rush to leave the chamber.

Faint, himself, with the shock of unexpected disaster, Foster struggled grimly to keep his self-command.

"Here, boys!" he shouted, forcing a show of unfelt confidence. "Let's try again! Yet, we may have time to get——"

The panic-stricken men hesitated. Foster seized a bar, and struggled to lift the casting off the legs of the trapped man. The others came back to help. The man was freed, and the tackle quickly adjusted to the casting again.

The four-ton mass of metal was lifted, and lowered, this time safely through the manhole. It was being bolted into place, when the mob, howling with maniacal fanaticism and led by yellow-visaged demons armed with the weapons of a secret science, stormed the room.

Foster's recollection, after that, was a red haze of horror.

He led the resistance of the doomed defenders. He made a fortress of every angle of the corridors, of every door and bulkhead, of every stair and elevator shaft. To the last, he guarded the way to the bridge, because he thought June Trevor was still there with Barron Kane.

His six hundred men fought with the courage that became the flower of the race. Their six hundred women stood beside them. Even the children gave the aid they could. And the *Planet* had been well-armed; each new position was a fresh arsenal. Yet the conclusion was inevitable.

Foster made the last stand on the little stair beneath the bridge. He staggered back to it, with four others—three men and a woman, all of them wounded. They had a machine gun. With that, until the last ammunition drum was empty, they kept the howling, triumphant mob at bay.

Then they contested the way with bayonets, with clubbed rifles, with pistols, even with bare hands. One of the men, dying, leaped forward and cleared the stair as he went down. The woman fell. Another man was dragged down by the mob, eviscerated, dismembered. Foster's last comrade shrieked and collapsed before the stabbing orange blade of a poison ray.

Foster dragged himself, then, to the top of the stair, to make the last defense. He looked about the tiny room for June and saw that she was gone. Sickness of utter despair rolled in a black flood over him at the discovery. Strength left him; he felt, for the first time, his many wounds and fell senseless.

Only Barron Kane was left, lying helpless in his invalid chair. Clumsily, his half-useless hands raised his big automatic and shot down the first grim-faced Asiatic who leaped into the room over Foster's still body.

That was the end of the defense.

L'ao Ku's black plane with the scarlet circles rose, an hour later, and fled into the flaming sunset, toward the temple of the Great Egg, in the Gobi.

V.

Foster Ross came to himself, lying on the bloodstained floor of the wrecked bridge room. His body was a stiff mass of cuts and bruises; dull agony throbbed from a swollen wound in his temple; a lock of his hair was stiffly cemented to his forehead with dried blood.

He stood up, reeling with a sudden sickness, biting his salty, blood-crusted lip to keep back a cry of pain. The smashed room, littered with broken instruments, swam before his darkened sight. For a moment he had no memory.

"Foster!" Barron Kane's faint, heartsick whisper brought him a shock of dim surprise. "L'ao Ku told me he was leaving you alive. I thought he lied, to torture me."

"L'ao Ku!" It was a dry, harsh gasp, from Foster's burning throat. "He was here?"

"He came," whispered Barron Kane, "when we all were helpless. He left us alive, he told me, because our sin is too great to be punished by the hand of man. He wanted us to live, he said, to know that we had failed, and then to die from the opening of the Great Egg."

"June?" rasped Foster's dusty voice. "Where is she?"

"I don't know," the weary, hopeless whisper answered. "She went to look for you, when they stormed the valve. I don't know——"

"Did L'ao Ku take her?" Agony leaped in Foster's heart.

"It may be," admitted Barron Kane. "L'ao Ku went back, in the black plane. He may have taken her. That, or else she will be—among the bodies——"

Foster reeled dizzily toward the stairway. "I'm going to look," he rasped. "If I don't find her, I'll finish the motor-tube and fly the *Planet* to the Gobi and take her back from L'ao Ku!" A glare of terrible madness flickered in his blue eyes.

"You couldn't do that," whispered Barron Kane. "It's just two days, L'ao Ku told me, until the Earth will break up. And we may not live even that long."

"Eh?" said Foster, with a staring blankness on his blood-caked face.

"A tidal wave is coming from the Atlantic," Barron Kane informed him. "It has overwhelmed the coastal cities. New York is gone and Boston and Washington. It will reach us to-night—a terrible rushing wall of sea water, a hundred feet high."

Foster did not seem to be listening. He reeled, and stumbled against the standard of a broken telescope; he gripped it with both his bruised hands, as if making a terrible effort to keep upright; his dry lips murmured: "I'll finish the motor-tube and look for June."

"Lie down again, Foster," advised Barron Kane. "You'll faint."

Foster paid him no heed, and the dull whisper ran on:

"Even if you finished the motor-tube, the *Planet* couldn't fly. L'ao Ku told me that. They blew the entrance valve open with explosive. It was wrecked, so it can't be sealed any more. If we got off into space, the air would leak out, and we should die."

"I'm going to find June," Foster muttered faintly.

His gripping hands slipped off the standard. Beneath its stain of grime and blood, his lean face whitened. He fell heavily, at full length, on the floor.

It was twenty hours later, when Foster went down to close the valve.

Some strength had come back, as he lay unconscious on the floor; the throbbing agony in his temple had become more endurable. He had washed his wounds, when he woke and bandaged the worst of them; he had found a little food for himself and Barron Kane.

His first trip had been to search for June.

"I've looked at all the dead," he informed Barron Kane grimly, when he came back to the bridge. "I didn't find—her."

"Then," the sick man whispered, "the black plane must have taken her to L'ao Ku's altar."

"I'm going after her," Foster told him, with the quietness of a terrible fatigue and of a determination that was invincible. And he said in a tired voice that held no triumph:

"The motor-tube is finished. We had the elements in place before the mob came. I stopped to make the connections, and seal the manhole, and start the pumps to evacuate it. In ten hours, it will be ready."

"Still," protested the hopeless whisper of Barron Kane, "we cannot seal the valve. We can't live, in outer space——"

"I'm going down, now," Foster told him, "to close the valve. Then, we'll look for June."

"It was two days," the sick man reminded him, "until the end. And one has gone. It is killing me, Foster, to give up. But we can only die."

"The water is rising," Foster told him. "I must hurry."

And he went down to close the valve.

The tidal wave had come, as he lay unconscious—the same racing wall of the advancing ocean, gray, dreadful, that had drowned the coastal cities. It had routed the triumphant mob, at the very moment of victory, before they had plundered the ship; it had overcome them as they fled.

A tremendous blow, it had struck the gray, steel side of the *Planet*; a stormy sea still crashed against the concrete pier beneath the space machine. The green surrounding hills of yesterday now were barren, rocky islets, drenched with spray.

The huge steel entrance valve had been torn open with a charge of high explosive. The hinges were twisted, the lock demolished.

Grimly, Foster surveyed the damage. The massive steel disk of the door itself, he decided, was not much injured. If he could straighten the hinges, to allow it to fit, and then find some way to fasten it——

He dragged himself to the machine shops and staggered back with hammers and wrenches and lifting tackle; he went again for a portable welding torch. Grimly deliberate, he set about heating the massive hinges and straightening them, so that the valve could close.

The massive concrete pier trembled constantly beneath him, as the whole Earth trembled. At thirty-minute intervals, it rocked and swayed dizzily beneath him—as the whole planet yielded to the ever-stronger pulse of the awakening thing within.

The mad waves of the conquering sea thundered endlessly against the great pier. Spray kept Foster drenched; sometimes it put out his torches. The wild waters came up, as he worked—he was sick with fear that the valve would be covered before he could close it.

Paroxysms of a tortured, outraged nature threatened his life, moment by moment. A weary, naked pygmy, wounded, scalded, blistered. Foster worked doggedly on, pitting his puny efforts against the convulsions of a dying giant.

A pall of dreadful gloom had covered the sky, that did not change when day should have come. It was crimson with dull volcanic light. Gray cinders showered out of it intermittently; and huge drops of boiling volcanic mud. Hot winds parched his skin, suffocated him with the reek of sulphur.

Thunder boomed endlessly above the chaos of a world in the agony of death; blue lightning stabbed in an endless blinding torrent against the top of the sphere, as if the heavens themselves had conspired against mankind.

Sometimes Foster left his tools a moment, to look down into the black, crashing waves, that were always higher. Under the red, uncanny gloom that did not change between night and day, in the violet, sudden glare of lightning, he saw the débris of a lost world. Remains of men were flung past him, shattered, twisted. Sometimes he shuddered to the horror of a drowned face, gray and bloated and pulped.

Despair, then, would overcome him. He would drop wearily upon the brine-drenched pier and gaze hopelessly into the red, mad gloom of the disintegrating world.

But then a picture would always come to him—a picture of June Trevor, tall and grave-eyed and beautiful, about to die on an altar before an image of the Earth and an obscene monstrosity emerging. That picture always banished his sense of helpless futility and brought back that strange, impersonal, self-forgetful resolution that had come to him first in the fight in the garage, so long ago.

Moved by a purpose that was racial, above anything of himself, he would pick up his tools again.

Numb with exhaustion, dull-brained for want of sleep, Foster came at last into the little bridge room again.

"The valve is sealed," he announced in a voice heavy and faint with unutterable weariness. "Now I can start the generators, and see if the motor-tube will work——"

He stopped, for his haggard, bloodshot eyes had seen that Barron Kane was sleeping. He tried a little to wake him, and make him eat—he had paused, on the way up, to snatch a little food from the storerooms, oranges, a can of broth, and crackers. But the frail little man did not stir. He had fever, Foster decided, and his pulse was fluttering irregularly.

"He wanted so to live to see us win," Foster breathed to himself. "But I think he won't wake up. Anyhow, he still—hoped——"

Then, moving in his great weariness like a slow mechanism, he turned to the half-wrecked instruments. His first glance at a chronometer shocked him with horror and despair.

Twenty-two hours had passed, while he labored with the valve. The second day had almost gone. In hours, now, would come—ultimate cataclysm——

He reeled drunkenly, as if from a blow, and stumbled back to the wall.

For a time he leaned there, lifeless with the shock of it. His red-rimmed eyes, dull and stupid, gazed fixedly out through the heavy quartz panels. The sky was a sullen mask of crimson gloom. Lightning ripped out of it in a fearful cascade of violet fire. Brown, boiling liquid mud fell against the steel hull of the *Planet* with a continual booming roar that drowned the thunder. The tempestuous black sea had risen over the hills; now it covered the pier, and its gigantic breakers hammered against the *Planet* itself. Littered with tiny, pitiful fragments of human wreckage, its wild dark surface reached to horizons of red, chaotic gloom.

Even as his blank eyes were staring aimlessly out, a fresh quake shook the space machine, so violent that it sent him staggering across the room. And a second tidal wave, a gray-crested, tremendous black wall, thundering with incredible velocity out of the advancing Atlantic, struck the *Planet* resistlessly.

Like a chip, it tossed the million tons of the space machine away from her cradle; she was carried away upon the mad sea.

The impact stirred Foster from his daze. He remembered June Trevor. And that lofty purpose, that was a thing not of himself but of the race, came back.

With a weary patience, he set to work to repair the controls and then to start the generators and transformers and otherwise prepare the *Planet* for flight. Her machinery was automatic, so that one man could drive her from the bridge. But the mob had broken half the instruments.

The space machine, as he worked, was tossed and battered by the mad-dened elements. Terrific waves thundered against her steel sides; floating wreckage hammered her; she floated at last against a new reef and was driven against it, crushingly, again and again, until Foster was despairingly certain that her hull must yield.

He toiled on.

And at last the thing was done, and still she floated. Foster turned the current into the motor-tube, his aching hands trembling with anxiety. He stepped it quickly up. Then he stumbled back—waiting—waiting——"

The *Planet* lay on the black, terrible sea, beside the gray fury of the manacing reef. Out of the crimson gloom of the sky poured livid lightning and clattering fragments of volcanic rock. Furious winds drove at her with a force that rivaled that of the insurgent sea.

She was swinging back toward the hidden fangs of the reef; and Foster knew her hull could not endure another blow. Would the motor-tube lift her? Would it——

He ceased to breathe. His teeth ground together. He reeled heavily against a chair, and his bruised hands fixed themselves upon it with a grip like that of a dying man. His glaring, dark-rimmed eyes alternately watched the instruments and looked out into the fearful red gloom of the dying world.

The *Planet* lifted! She rose off the dark, furious sea, into the scarlet darkness of the sky. She rose, through mighty winds, through rain of volcanic mud and cinders, through blazing sheets of purple lightning. At a great altitude, the rain gave way to thundering hail.

And the space machine, at last, came through the clouds; and Foster saw the stars.

He was full of a great serenity. A kind of lofty elation had come with the rising of the space machine. It was a sense of triumphant power that lifted him far above any human concern.

His great weariness had slipped from him. He felt, no longer, his mind-deadening want of sleep, or even the dull throbbing of the wound in his temple. For a moment he attained the supreme tranquillity of a god.

It was sublime, awful Nirvana. He had forgotten even June.

It was night, and the stars flamed at Foster. As the *Planet* came above the turbulent atmosphere, they burst into a greater splendor than any man had ever seen. In an emptiness that was utterly black, they burned motionless and ghostly, more brilliant than jewels. They were infinitely tiny, infinitely bright. Mysterious and eternal, they flamed in the black void.

Foster stared at them, transfixed with the strange wonder that came from the knowledge that each of them was a sentient thing.

And still the *Planet* rose, on a high, swift arc, toward the living stars. Foster felt himself one with them; he was no more a puny man, but a serene and deathless entity, of supernal power and supernal vision.

Then Barron Kane's frail body moved, uneasily, in its feverish sleep. And Foster was abruptly a man again and filled with pity. He tried again to wake his uncle—once more in vain. He smoothed the pillow under his head and drew the blanket close about him.

He went back, then, to the controls. He remembered June again and her frightful danger. His purpose had come back, even stronger for its lapse as he first soared toward the stars. He was moved as if by some vast power without, as if he were simply a puppet in the hands of a racial will, itself as sublime and eternal as the undying stars he had looked upon.

Still, he grimly realized the multiplied odds against him. In the universal, cataclysmic storm that raged about the whole Earth, he might be unable to find the lost oasis in the Gobi—in time. If he did, he would be only one man, battling hundreds. He might, the fear pierced him like a cold blade, find the sacrifice already consummated. Or he might—to judge from what he had seen, it was even probable—find that the temple and all in it had already been overwhelmed by storm or earthquake or volcano or the terror of the rising sea.

Yes, bitter realization came, the chances against him were hopelessly great. It was useless to go. But that blind, sublime purpose, that was like an external force, moved him to drop the *Planet* back into the dark, furiously agitated clouds that totally obscured the face of the disintegrating globe.

Down sank the space machine, through terrible crimson gloom, through the furious chaos of a tortured, disrupting world. Hurricanes tore at the steel ball; it was bombarded with volcanic débris, struck with flaming lightning, sluiced with boiling mud.

Foster, watching through mudstained crystal panels, at last saw the surface of the earth where the Gobi had been—and it was a black and fearful sea.

The temple of the fanatic cult was gone, and June Trevor—— And with the girl, all the meaning was gone out of his life and out of his superhuman struggle to live. The sublime purpose that had so long sustained him flowed out of him utterly; it left him a lonely, weary, haggard wreck. He had been more than human; now he was less—sick and old and useless.

June was gone. The thought beat through his tired, dull brain, a refrain of despair. *June, gone!* Only he and Barron Kane were left, two useless, aimless men, with nothing to live for; and nothing to hope for but death.

And Barron Kane was obviously dying. Soon he, Foster, would be alone —more alone than a human being had ever been. He would be alone in the void of space. He would know that the Earth was gone, that there was no other man or woman anywhere.

He would be alone, with the living, mocking stars!

A frantic terror grasped Foster's throat, at the thought, with icy fingers that choked him; he was faint with the most dreadful fear he had ever known.

Sick with it, trembling convulsively, he tried desperately to wake Barron Kane. He shook the little man's shrunken shoulder and dashed water into his face. He wanted terribly to speak to a human being again, to listen again to a human voice not his own—even the voiceless whisper of the dying man.

Barron Kane gasped in his sleep, he breathed strangely, a sudden spasmodic trembling disturbed his thin limbs. But he would not wake. Aching with a pity deeper than he had ever known, Foster covered the slight, drawn body again.

He looked out again at the scarlet, lightning-split darkness of the sky, at the black, wildly heaving plain of the sea that had swept away the secret temple and all the essence of his life.

VI.

The sea was riven, as Foster looked. It was cleft, as if by a Titan's blade. The two dark halves of it were thrust miles apart. Stupendous, unthinkable, an abysmal gulf yawned between them, with black water plunging into it from either side, like a million Niagaras.

The world had parted.

Hanging in that dark storm sky of lurid and dreadful red, Foster stared with horror-glazed eyes down into the new gulf. Mile upon mile, incredibly, fell the jagged walls of the broken Earth crust, crumbling, splashed with dark sheets of the oceanic cataracts.

Below—scores of miles below—was a smooth, shimmering surface of green, bright as flame, marked strangely with silver and black. It was moving with weird paroxysms. It was the body of the Earth entity, struggling in the agony of birth.

Foster watched it, dazed with astounded horror.

The two halves of the split sea were thrust back, with a fearful quickness, until they were lost under the dark sky, which now was changing from dull red to a terrible, ominous, reflected green. The space machine hung between the menacing pall of the sky and the bright surface of that dreadful body that was struggling to life within the Earth.

Foster's mind perceived the new danger. But in the lifeless, purposeless, hopeless apathy that had settled upon him he felt no alarm; he didn't care, nothing mattered, now, since June was gone.

The wind struck. The atmosphere, disturbed by the movements of the waking thing, drove against the *Planet* with the solid, battering impact of an avalanche. With a force no hurricane had ever equaled, it hurled the steel globe down toward the green body, helpless as a toy balloon.

Foster's blue eyes, sick with an agony unutterable, looked dully, without panic and without hope, at the eldritch doom ahead. All aim and direction had left him. His life had become a bitter joke, fantastic as the fate of humanity.

It was only the blind instinct to live that kept him wearily at the controls. His mind sat back, a weary, disinterested spectator, as his bruised, aching fingers moved automatically, and the *Planet* battled to survive.

The steel ball was drawn down, resistlessly, toward the fantastic markings on the side of that unbelievable body. Foster watched with lackluster eyes that held no fear, while his automatic fingers flung on the full power of the motor-tube to fight that freakish, fiendish wind.

He felt no triumph when the machine broke free; he had no elation as it drove upward through mad, torn cloud masses that were fearfully illuminated with green. He stared out, through the heavy crystal panels, still beyond panic and beyond hope.

Above the green clouds, he came; above the air and into the freedom of space. The sky was a hollow globe of darkness, pierced with a million, many-hued points of light—each of them, he knew, a thing alive.

The earth hung below—a huge, swollen globe, dark and fantastically patched with green.

A wing broke through the clouds—a stupendous sheet of supernal fire; a shield of green flame, wondrous as the aurora of the solar corona, and veined with bright silver. With its first, uncertain unfolding, it brushed close to the *Planet*—a blade of amazing death.

Foster's instinctive fingers flung the space machine away, and the glorious, dreadful wing passed beneath, harmlessly. And the *Planet* drove on away into space, on her voyage that had no destination.

The Earth fell away behind.

And a thing emerged from the shattered crust of it that was like the creature that had come from the Moon. The beaked head was crested with a spray of crimson flame; it was marked with two ovoid patches, glowing lividly purple, that were like dread eyes. Flame-green, its body was slender and tapering and marked weirdly with black and silver. Slow, shining waves shimmered through its wings, that were like green fans of the aurora and veined with burning white.

It moved uncertainly in the void, as if to test its members. It preened itself with thin blue appendages that were thrust from the head. Then, with a beat of strange luminous force in its wings, it wheeled away from the Sun, and drove outward into the void of space.

Mercury and Venus, the two inner planets, Foster saw, had also changed; they had become winged, greenish motes, drifting away from the Sun. And the light of the Sun itself, he fancied, was already dimming, fading slowly toward crimson, toward ultimate darkness.

"The Sun is dying," his dry lips muttered the thought from his disinterested, dully observant brain. "It's the end! The mad finish of man's universe——"

"You see?" Foster was startled to hear the faint whisper of Barron Kane, awake again on his invalid chair. "We are seeing the solution of the last riddle, Foster—the riddle of the suns! We are watching one die. We have seen many born."

Foster hurried to him and lifted his head higher on the pillow so that he could see the room and look out through the crystal panels. And he spoke to the sick man of food, but Barron Kane did not seem to notice him. The small whisper ran on:

"The planets were the seed of the Sun. Strange life developed in them, through the ages, under solar radiation. The Sun will die, now; its work is done. And the new creatures have gone forth, to feed themselves upon the star dust, to absorb diffuse radiation and the cosmic rays, to consume perhaps, fragments of old suns, until they themselves are suns, spawning planets, and the cycle of their life is complete.

"And there you have the answer, Foster, to many a problem that has baffled science. We've won, Foster!" There was a vague triumph in the muted whisper. "Even if we die to-day—we're on our own!"

"What's the good of it?" muttered Foster, too weary, too hopeless to be bitter. "We're—alone," he went on dully. "Soon we'll be—dead. The *Planet* will drift on, perhaps forever. A little world, with all that life needs, but dead——

"Listen!"

Foster stopped speaking, suddenly, and a fearful silence hung in the room, grimly deep, haunted only with the sounds of their breath.

"Listen!" A wild, strange ring of madness had come into his voice. "There's no sound—no other voice! We're alone, Barron; we're the last men. There can't be another voice anywhere! Think what it means—not ever to hear any one speak again! When we are dead——"

His voice dropped again abruptly, for his straining ears had caught the pad of human footsteps.

He rushed, trembling with incredulous hope and a fear born with it, down the steps to the door of the bridge room. He flung it open and stood swaying in it, gazing wildly, unbelievingly, at June Trevor.

She was grimy, bedraggled; her clothing was black with something thick and viscid and dripping; her hair was plastered against her head with it; her face was scratched, and a blue bruise was on her forehead. Yet he saw still a beauty in her tall, straight form; in her clear brown eyes was a dawning, luminous joy.

They stood a moment face to face.

Foster wet his lips. "June?" he whispered. "June——"

She reeled a little, and he started forward to catch her.

"Don't touch me," she gasped weakly and swayed back from him. "I'm all soaked with oil—I was in a tank. You'll get covered with it."

"You poor kid!" he breathed, and something made him laugh a little.

He slipped his arm around her grimy shoulders, held her up. And she clung to him suddenly, ignoring the oil. In turn, she laughed—a shaky, happy little laugh of relief.

"Oh, Foster!" she cried. "I'm so—so glad—that you're here. I thought I was the only person alive. And I was so miserably soaked with oil."

"How did you get here?" Foster asked as he helped her into the bridge room and made her sit down beside him. "When you were gone, we thought that L'ao Ku must have taken you—to his temple."

"L'ao Ku?" she breathed, in weary surprise. "No; I didn't see him. You see, I went to look for you, Foster, when the mob was coming. I asked the men where to find you. They sent me from one place to another, until I was down in the generator rooms. I couldn't find you anywhere."

She had relaxed, happily, against his great shoulder; unconsciously her hand had caught his arm, as if she feared that something might take him from her.

"What then?" Foster asked. "How'd you get away from the mob?"

"I was down in the generator room," her tired voice went on. "I couldn't find you. All of a sudden, there were shots and screams. The mob was killing the enginemen.

"One of the enginemen ran to me. 'The damn' chinks have come, miss,' he said. 'But I'll put you where they won't find you.' And he made me come to a tank, and opened a lid, and made me climb down a ladder in it. It was full of oil—it came up to my chin. And he let the lid back down on me.

"I waited. It was dark in the tank. And the fumes of the oil made me sick. I nearly fell off the ladder. For a while I could hear shots and roaring voices. Then—silence.

"Nobody came to lift the lid, and I tried to get out. I was faint. And the lid was so heavy I couldn't lift it. I worked until I couldn't move. Then I rested, and tried again. At last I found a way, standing on the top of the ladder, and using my back."

"You poor, game kid!" whispered Foster, and patted her shoulder.

She shuddered; her brown eyes seemed not to see him—they were dull with remembered horror.

"I came out," she went on grimly. "And every one was—was dead. The floors were all covered with blood and—bodies. And the quiet—it was terrible. You know how still it was, Foster. I couldn't hear a voice. Not a sound! I thought I was the only one alive."

"Why didn't you come back here?" asked Foster. "Barron was here."

"I did," she whispered. "I looked in and saw him lying there—so still. I spoke, and he didn't move. I thought he was dead, like all the rest. I thought I was the only one still living——"

"You must forget all that," Foster urged her. "But where have you been?"

"I was—looking"—she paused, shuddering—"looking—among—the bodies for—for you, Foster."

He held her trembling body close; for a moment she did not speak.

"I thought I was the—the last," she went on jerkily, with an effort. "I thought I was—alone—alone with all the dead. I was looking for you, Foster, so that we could be together. And then——"

The sick horror ebbed slowly from her brown eyes; she smiled a little, wearily.

"Then I felt the machine moving, Foster. I had been asleep—I was so weary from searching and so grimy with oil. I woke and felt that we were moving. I knew, then, there was some one——"

Her brown eyes shone bravely into Foster's blue ones, alight with hope and joy and new confidence. Then they closed; her body relaxed in his arms; she had gone to sleep. Her lips parted, and she smiled a weary little smile, in her sleep.

"She's worn out, the nervy little kid," Foster told Barron Kane. "I'm going to take her down to her room, where she can rest. I'll come back in a minute, to help you down——"

"No, Foster," the little man whispered. "I want to look out—at the stars."

Foster lifted him a little, propped up his head with the pillow. "Men can carry on, now, Barron," he said. "We can make a new beginning."

Foster took up the girl's quietly breathing body and started toward the door.

"Yes, Foster," the sick man whispered after him, "we've really won."

The scientist's gray calm eyes watched Foster until he had vanished down the little stairs. Then he looked back at the motionless, splendid stars. They were tiny and unmoving and many-colored, swung eternal in black space.

"We've won," he whispered again to himself. "I had hoped to live—for this. Men will now be small parasites no longer, to be crushed like vermin by any chance tremor of the beast that bears them. In the *Planet*, men are free, on their own."

He seemed to like the phrase, for he whispered it again: "On their own."

He lay still for a time, musing.

"We're off in the *Planet*, to a new beginning. And it's just a beginning."

His serene quiet eyes stared at the mocking points of the stars, and he whispered to them:

"You're alive, all of you. We owe our lives to you—we've been parasites on your kind. But we aren't any longer. We're beginning all over again, on our own."

His dying breath whispered a last prophecy:

"There will be many *Planets*, and greater ones. The new, free race will be greater than the old. The children of Foster and June will conquer space, to the farthermost one of you!"

A joy seemed to linger in his tranquil eyes, that still looked out at the stars.

For me, the story holds up. I read it for the first time in nearly forty years in preparing this anthology, and it is *still* exciting to me, even though I remembered the point of the plot. The love interest is a little clumsy perhaps, and the Fu Manchu attitude toward the Chinese is now dated, but, by and large, it moves quickly, and Williamson keeps the wild plot plausible.

As I read it, however, I was uncomfortably struck by the scene in which religious cultists attack the scientific center that was trying to save a fragment of the human race. I had forgotten that. The question is, though, had I forgotten it at the time I wrote *Nightfall*, only seven years later? Even if I had, surely the influence of "Born of the Sun" must have been there just under the surface, for *Nightfall* had a similar scene.

Even longer in the field than Williamson was Murray Leinster (the pseudonym of Will F. Jenkins). He had a story, "The Runaway Skyscraper," in the June 1926 *Amazing Stories*, the third issue of that magazine, and he had been publishing for some years before that.* Tremaine added him to his stable and Leinster contributed the thought-variant "Sidewise in Time," in the June 1934 *Astounding Stories*.

* He remained active for decades afterward and is still alive today, the acknowledged dean of science fiction writers.

SIDEWISE IN TIME

by Murray Leinster

FOREWORD.

Looking back, it seems strange that no one but Professor Minott figured the thing out in advance. The indications were more than plain. In early December of 1934 Professor Michaelson announced his finding that the speed of light was not an absolute—could not be considered invariable. That, of course, was one of the first indications of what was to happen.

A second indication came on February 15th, when at 12:40 p.m., Greenwich mean time, the sun suddenly shone blue-white and the enormously increased rate of radiation raised the temperature of the earth's surface by twenty-two degrees Fahrenheit in five minutes. At the end of the five minutes, the sun went back to its normal rate of radiation without any other symptom of disturbance.

A great many bids for scientific fame followed, of course, but no plausible explanation of the phenomenon accounted for a total lack of after disturbances in the sun's photosphere.

For a third clear forerunner of the events of June, on March 10th the male giraffe in the Bronx Zoölogical Park, in New York, ceased to eat. In the nine days following, it changed its form, absorbing all its extremities, even its neck and head, into an extraordinary, egg-shaped mass of still-living flesh and bone which on the tenth day began to divide spontaneously and on the twelfth was two slightly pulsating fleshy masses.

A day later still, bumps appeared on the two masses. They grew, took form and design, and twenty days after the beginning of the phenomenon were legs, necks, and heads. Then two giraffes, both male, moved about the giraffe inclosure. Each was slightly less than half the weight of the original animal. They were identically marked. And they ate and moved and in every way seemed normal though immature animals.

An exactly similar occurrence was reported from the Argentine Republic, in which a steer from the pampas was going through the same extraordinary method of reproduction under the critical eyes of Argentine scientists.

Nowadays it seems incredible that the scientists of 1935 should not have understood the meaning of these oddities. We now know something of the type of strain which produced them, though they no longer occur. But between January and June of 1935 the news services of the nation were flooded with items of similar import.

For two days the Ohio River flowed upstream. For six hours the trees in Euclid Park, in Cleveland, lashed their branches madly as if in a terrific storm, though not a breath of wind was stirring. And in New Orleans, near the last of May, fishes swam up out of the Mississippi River through the air, proceeded to "drown" in the air which inexplicably upheld them, and then turned belly up and floated placidly at an imaginary water level some fifteen feet above the pavements of the city.

But it seems clear that Professor Minott was the only man in the world who even guessed the meaning of these—to us—clear-cut indications of the later events. Professor Minott was instructor in mathematics on the faculty of Robinson College in Fredericksburg, Va. We know that he anticipated very nearly every one of the things which later startled and frightened the world, and not only our world. But he kept his mouth shut.

Robinson College was small. It had even been termed a "jerkwater" college without offending anybody but the faculty and certain sensitive alumni. For a mere professor of mathematics to make public the theory Minott had formed would not even be news. It would be taken as stark insanity. Moreover, those who believed it would be scared. So he kept his mouth shut.

Professor Minott possessed courage, bitterness, and a certain cold-blooded daring, but neither wealth nor influence. He had more than a little knowledge of mathematical physics and his calculations show extraordinary knowledge of the laws of probability, but he had very little patience with problems in ethics. And he was possessed by a particularly fierce passion for Maida Haynes, daughter of the professor of Romance languages, and had practically no chance to win even her attention over the competition of most of the student body.

So much of explanation is necessary, because no one but just such a person as Professor Minott would have forecast what was to happen and then prepare for it in the fashion in which he did.

We know from his notes that he considered the probability of disaster as a shade better than four to one. It is a very great pity that we do not have his calculations. There is much that our scientists do not understand even yet. The notes Professor Minott left behind have been invaluable, but there are obvious gaps in them. He must have taken most of his notes—and those the most valuable—into that unguessed at place where he conceivably now lives and very probably works.

He would be amused, no doubt, at the diligence with which his most unconsidered scribble is now examined and inspected and discussed by the greatest minds of our time and space. And perhaps—it is quite probable—he may have invented a word for the scope of the catastrophe we escaped. We have none as yet.

There is no word to describe a disaster in which not only the earth but our whole solar system might have been destroyed; not only our solar system but our galaxy; not only our galaxy but every other island universe in all of the space we know; more than that, the destruction of all space as we know it; and even beyond that the destruction of time, meaning not only the obliteration of present and future but even the annihilation of the past so that it would never have been. And then, besides, those other strange states of existence we learned of, those other universes, those other pasts and futures—all to be shattered into nothingness. There is no word for such a catastrophe.

It would be interesting to know what Professor Minott termed it to himself, as he coolly prepared to take advantage of the one chance in four of survival, if that should be the one to eventuate. But it is easier to wonder how he felt on the evening before the fifth of June, in 1935. We do not know. We cannot know. All we can be certain of is how we felt—and what happened.

I.

It was half past seven a. m. of June 5, 1935. The city of Joplin, Missouri, awaked from a comfortable, summer-night sleep. Dew glistened upon grass blades and leaves and the filmy webs of morning spiders glittered like diamond dust in the early sunshine. In the most easterly suburb a high-school boy, yawning, came somnolently out of his house to mow the lawn before schooltime. A rather rickety family car roared, a block away. It back-fired, stopped, roared again, and throttled down to a steady, waiting hum. The voices of children sounded among the houses. A colored washer-woman appeared, striding beneath the trees which lined this strictly residential street.

From an upper window a radio blatted: "—one, two, three, four! Higher, now!—three, four! Put your weight into it!—two, three, four!" The radio suddenly squawked and began to emit an insistent, mechanical shriek which changed again to a squawk and then a terrific sound as of all the static of ten thousand thunderstorms on the air at once. Then it was silent.

The high-school boy leaned mournfully on the push bar of the lawn mower. At the instant the static ended, the boy sat down suddenly on the dew-wet grass. The colored woman reeled and grabbed frantically at the nearest tree trunk. The basket of wash toppled and spilled in a snowstorm of starched, varicolored clothing. Howls of terror from children. Sharp shrieks from women. *"Earthquake! Earthquake!"* Figures appeared running, pouring out of houses. Some one fled out to a sleeping porch, slid down a supporting column, and tripped over a rosebush in his pajamas. In seconds, it seemed, the entire population of the street was out-of-doors.

And then there was a queer, blank silence. There was no earthquake. No house had fallen. No chimney had cracked. Not so much as a dish or windowpane had made a sound in smashing. The sensation every human being had felt was not an actual shaking of the ground. There had been movement, yes, and of the earth, but no such movement as any human being had ever dreamed of before. These people were to learn of that movement much later. Now they stared blankly at each other.

And in the sudden, dead silence broken only by the hum of an idling car and the wail of a frightened baby, a new sound became audible. It was the tramp of marching feet. With it came a curious clanking and clattering noise. And then a marked command, which was definitely not in the English language.

Down the street of a suburb of Joplin, Missouri, on June 5, in the year of our Lord 1935, came a file of spear-armed, shield-bearing soldiers in the short, skirtlike togas of ancient Rome. They wore helmets upon their heads. They peered about as if they were as blankly amazed as the citizens of Joplin who regarded them. A long column of marching men came into view, every man with shield and spear and the indefinable air of being used to just such weapons.

They halted at another barked order. A wizened little man with a short sword snapped a question at the staring Americans. The high-school boy jumped. The wizened man roared his question again. The high-school boy stammered, and painfully formed syllables with his lips. The wizened man grunted in satisfaction. He talked, articulating clearly if impatiently. And the high-school boy turned dazedly to the other Americans.

"He wants to know the name of this town," he said, unbelieving his own ears. "He's talking Latin, like I learn in school. He says this town isn't on the road maps, and he doesn't know where he is. But all the same he takes possession of it in the name of the Emperor Valerius Fabricius, emperor of Rome and the far corners of the earth." And then the school-boy stuttered: "He—he says these are the first six cohorts of the Forty-second

Legion, on garrison duty in Messalia. That—that's supposed to be two days' march up that way."

He pointed in the direction of St. Louis.

The idling motor car roared suddenly into life. Its gears whined and it came rolling out into the street. Its horn honked peremptorily for passage through the shield-clad soldiers. They gaped at it. It honked again and moved toward them.

A roared order, and they flung themselves upon it, spears thrusting, short swords stabbing. Up to this instant there was not one single inhabitant of Joplin who did not believe the spear-armed soldiers were motion-picture actors, or masqueraders, or something else equally insane but credible. But there was nothing make-believe about their attack on the car. They assaulted it as if it were a strange and probably deadly beast. They flung themselves into battle with it in a grotesquely reckless valor.

And there was nothing at all make-believe in the thoroughness and completeness with which they speared Mr. Horace B. Davis, who had only intended to drive down to the cotton-brokerage office of which he was chief clerk. They thought he was driving this strange beast to slaughter them, and they slaughtered him instead. The high-school boy saw them do it, growing whiter and whiter as he watched. When a swordsman approached the wizened man and displayed the severed head of Mr. Davis, with the spectacles dangling grotesquely from one ear, the high-school boy fainted dead away.

II.

It was sunrise of June 5, 1935. Cyrus Harding gulped down his breakfast in the pale-gray dawn. He had felt very dizzy and sick for just a moment, some little while since, but he was himself again now. The smell of frying filled the kitchen. His wife cooked. Cyrus Harding ate. He made noises as he emptied his plate. His hands were gnarled and work-worn, but his expression was of complacent satisfaction. He looked at a calendar hung on the wall, a Christmas sentiment from the Bryan Feed & Fertilizer Co., in Bryan, Ohio.

"Sheriff's goin' to sell out Amos to-day," he said comfortably. "I figger I'll get that north forty cheap."

His wife said tiredly: "He's been offerin' to sell it to you for a year."

"Yep," agreed Cyrus Harding more complacently still. "Comin' down on the price, too. But nobuddy'll bid against me at the sale. They know I want it bad, an' I ain't a good neighbor to have when somebuddy takes somethin' from under my nose. Folks know it. I'll git it a lot cheaper'n

Amos offered it to me for. He wanted to sell it t'meet his int'rest an' hol' on another year. I'll git it for half that."

He stood up and wiped his mouth. He strode to the door.

"That hired man shoulda got a good start with his harrowin'," he said expansively. "I'll take a look an' go over to the sale."

He went to the kitchen door and opened it. Then his mouth dropped open. The view from this doorway was normally that of a not especially neat barnyard, with beyond it farmland flat as a floor and cultivated to the very fence rails, with a promising crop of corn as a border against the horizon.

Now the view was quite otherwise. All was normal as far as the barn. But beyond the barn was delirium. Huge, spreading tree ferns soared upward a hundred feet. Lacy, foliated branches formed a roof of incredible density above sheer jungle such as no man on earth had ever seen before. The jungles of the Amazon basin were parklike by comparison with its thickness. It was a riotous tangle of living vegetation in which growth was battle, and battle was life, and life was deadly, merciless conflict.

No man could have forced his way ten feet through such a wilderness. From it came a fœtid exhalation which was part decay and part lush, rank, growing things, and part the overpowering perfumes of glaringly vivid flowers. It was jungle such as palæobotanists have described as existing in the Carboniferous period; as the source of our coal beds.

"It—it ain't so!" said Cyrus Harding weakly. "It—ain't so!"

His wife did not reply. She had not seen. Wearily, she began to clean up after her lord and master's meal.

He went down the kitchen steps, staring and shaken. He moved toward this impossible apparition which covered his crops. It did not disappear as he neared it. He went within twenty feet of it and stopped, still staring, still unbelieving, beginning to entertain the monstrous supposition that he had gone insane.

Then something moved in the jungle. A long, snaky neck, feet thick at its base and tapering to a mere sixteen inches behind a head the size of a barrel. The neck reached out the twenty feet to him. Cold eyes regarded him abstractedly. The mouth opened. Cyrus Harding screamed.

His wife raised her eyes. She looked through the open door and saw the jungle. She saw the jaws close upon her husband. She saw colossal, abstracted eyes half close as the something gulped, and partly choked, and swallowed—— She saw a lump in the monstrous neck move from the relatively slender portion just behind the head to the feet-thick section projecting from the jungle. She saw the head withdraw into the jungle and instantly be lost to sight.

Cyrus Harding's widow was very pale. She put on her hat and went out of the front door. She began to walk toward the house of the nearest neighbor. As she went, she said steadily to herself:

"It's come. I'm crazy. They'll have to put me in an asylum. But I won't have to stand him any more. I won't have to stand him any more!"

It was noon of June 5, 1935. The cell door opened and a very grave, whiskered man in a curious gray uniform came in. He tapped the prisoner gently on the shoulder.

"I'm Dr. Holloway," he said encouragingly. "Suppose you tell me, suh, just what happened t'you? I'm right sure it can all be straightened out."

The prisoner sputtered: "Why—why—dammit," he protested, "I drove down from Louisville this morning. I had a dizzy spell and—well—I must have missed my road, because suddenly I noticed that everything around me was unfamiliar. And then a man in a gray uniform yelled at me, and a minute later he began to shoot, and the first thing I knew they'd arrested me for having the American flag painted on my car! I'm a traveling salesman for the Uncle Sam Candy Bar Co! Dammit, it's funny when a man can't fly his own country's flag——"

"In your own country, of co'se," assented the doctor comfortingly. "But you must know, suh, that we don't allow any flag but ouah own to be displayed heah. You violated ouah laws, suh."

"Your laws!" The prisoner stared blankly. "What laws? Where in the United States is it illegal to fly the American flag?"

"Nowheah in the United States, suh." The doctor smiled. "You must have crossed ouah border unawares, suh. I will be frank, an' admit that it was suspected you were insane. I see now that it was just a mistake."

"Border—United——" The prisoner gasped. "I'm not in the United States? I'm not? Then where in hell am I?"

"Ten miles, suh, within the borders of the Confederacy," said the doctor, and laughed. "A queer mistake, suh, but theah was no intention of insult. You'll be released at once. Theah is enough tension between Washington an' Richmond without another border incident to upset ouah hotheads."

"Confederacy?" The prisoner choked. "You can't—you don't mean the Confederate States——"

"Of co'se, suh. The Confederate States of North America. Why not?"

The prisoner gulped. "I—I've gone mad!" he stammered. "I must be mad! There was Gettysburg—there was——"

"Gettysburg? Oh, yes!" The doctor nodded indulgently. "We are very proud of ouah history, suh. You refer to the battle in the war of separation, when the fate of the Confederacy rested on ten minutes' time. I have often wondered what would have been the result if Pickett's charge had been driven back. It was Pickett's charge that gained the day for us, suh.

England recognized the Confederacy two days later, France in another week an' with unlimited credit abroad we won out. But it was a tight squeeze, suh!"

The prisoner gasped again. He stared out of the window. And opposite the jail stood an unquestionable courthouse. Upon the courthouse stood a flagpole. And spread gloriously in the breeze above a government building floated the Stars and Bars of the Confederacy!

It was night of June 5, 1935. The postmaster of North Centerville, Massachusetts, came out of his cubby-hole to listen to the narrative. The pot-bellied stove of the general store sent a comfortable if unnecessary glow about. The eyewitness chuckled.

"Yeah. They come around the cape, thirty or forty of 'em in a boat all o' sixty feet long with a crazy square sail drawin'. Round things on the gunnel like—like shields. An' rowin' like hell! They stopped when they saw the town an' looked s'prised. Then they hailed us, talkin' some lingo that wa'n't American. Ole Peterson, he near dropped his line, with a fish on it, too. Then he tried to talk back. They hadda lotta trouble understandin' him, or made out to. Then they turned around an' rowed back. Actors or somethin', tryin' to play a joke. It fell flat, though. Maybe some of those rich folks up the coast pullin' it. Ho! Ho! Ole says they was talkin' a funny, old-fashioned Skowegian. They told him they was from Leifsholm, or somethin' like that, just up the coast. That they couldn't make out how our town got here. They'd never see it before! Can y'imagine that? Ole says they were wikin's, an' they called this place Winland, an' says— What's that?"

A sudden hubbub arose in the night. Screams. Cries. A shotgun boomed dully. The loafers in the general store crowded out on the porch. Flames rose from half a dozen places on the water front. In their light could be seen a full dozen serpent ships, speeding for the shore, propelled by oars. From four of their number, already beached, dark figures had poured. Firelight glinted on swords, on shields. A woman screamed as a huge, yellow-maned man seized her. His brazen helmet and shield glittered. He was laughing. Then a figure in overalls hurtled toward the blond giant, an ax held threateningly.

The giant cut him down with an already dripping blade and roared. Men rushed to him and they plunged on to loot and burn. More of the armored figures leaped to the sand from another beached ship. Another house roared flames skyward.

III.

And at half past ten a. m. on the morning of June 5th, Professor Minott turned upon the party of students with a revolver in each hand. Gone was the appearance of an instructor whose most destructive possibility was a below-passing mark in mathematics. He had guns in his hands now, instead of chalk or pencil, and his eyes were glowing even as he smiled frostily. The four girls gasped. The young men, accustomed to seeing him only in a classroom, realized that he not only could use the weapons in his hands, but that he would. And suddenly they respected him as they would respect, say, a burglar or a prominent kidnaper or a gang leader. He was raised far above the level of a mere mathematics professor. He became instantly a leader, and, by virtue of his weapons, even a ruler.

"As you see," said Professor Minott evenly, "I have anticipated the situation in which we find ourselves. I am prepared for it, to a certain extent. At any moment not only we, but the entire human race may be wiped out with a completeness of which you can form no idea. But there is also a chance of survival. And I intend to make the most of my survival—if we do live."

He looked steadily from one to another of the students who had followed him to explore the extraordinary appearance of a sequoia forest north of Fredericksburg.

"I know what has happened," said Professor Minott. "I know also what is likely to happen. And I know what I intend to do about it. Any of you who are prepared to follow me, say so. Any of you who object—well—I can't have mutinies! I'll shoot him!"

"But—professor," said Blake nervously, "we ought to get the girls home——"

"They will never go home," said Professor Minott calmly. "Neither will you, nor any of us. As soon as you're convinced that I'm quite ready to use these weapons, I'll tell you what's happened and what it means. I've been preparing for it for weeks."

Tall trees rose around the party. Giant trees. Magnificent trees. They towered two hundred and fifty feet into the air, and their air of venerable calm was at once the most convincing evidence of their actuality, and the most improbable of all the things which had happened in the neighborhood of Fredericksburg, Virginia. The little group of people sat their horses affrightedly beneath the monsters of the forest. Minott regarded them estimatingly—these three young men and four girls, all students of

Robinson College. Professor Minott was now no longer the faculty member in charge of a party of exploration, but a definitely ruthless leader.

At half past eight a. m. on June 5, 1935, the inhabitants of Fredericksburg had felt a curious, unanimous dizziness. It passed. The sun shone brightly. There seemed to be no noticeable change in any of the facts of everyday existence. But within an hour the sleepy little town was buzzing with excitement. The road to Washington—Route One on all road maps —ceased abruptly some three miles north. A colossal, a gigantic forest had appeared magically to block the way.

Telegraphic communication with Washington had ceased. Even the Washington broadcasting stations were no longer on the air. The trees of the extraordinary forest were tall beyond the experience of any human being in town. They looked like the photographs of the giant sequoias on the Pacific Coast, but—well, the thing was simply impossible.

In an hour and a half, Professor Minott had organized a party of sightseers among the students. He seemed to pick his party with a queer definiteness of decision. Three young men and four girls. They would have piled into a rickety car owned by one of the boys, but Professor Minott negatived the idea.

"The road ends at the forest," he said, smiling. "I'd rather like to explore a magic forest. Suppose we ride horseback? I'll arrange for horses."

In ten minutes the horses appeared. The girls had vanished to get into riding breeches or knickers. They noted appreciatively on their return that besides the saddles, the horses had saddlebags slung in place. Again Professor Minott smiled.

"We're exploring," he said humorously. "We must dress the part. Also, we'll probably want some lunch. And we can bring back specimens for the botanical lab to look over."

They rode forth; the girls thrilled, the young men pleased and excited, and all of them just a little bit disappointed at finding themselves passed by motor cars which whizzed by them as all Fredericksburg went to look at the improbable forest ahead.

There were cars by hundreds where the road abruptly ended. A crowd stared at the forest. Giant trees, their roots fixed firmly in the ground. Undergrowth here and there. Over it all, an aspect of peace and utter serenity —and permanence. The watching crowd hummed and buzzed with speculation, with talk. The thing they saw was impossible. It could not have happened. This forest could not possibly be real. They were regarding some sort of mirage.

But as the party of riders arrived, half a dozen men came out of the forest. They had dared to enter it. Now they returned, still incredulous of their own experience, bearing leaves and branches and one of them certain small berries unknown on the Atlantic coast.

A State police officer held up his hand as Professor Minott's party went toward the edge of the forest.

"Look here!" he said. "We' been hearin' funny noises in there. I'm stoppin' anybody else from goin' in until we know what's what."

Professor Minott nodded. "We'll be careful. I'm Professor Minott of Robinson College. We're going in after some botanical specimens. I have a revolver. We're all right."

He rode ahead. The State policeman, without definite orders for authority, shrugged his shoulders and bent his efforts to the prevention of other attempts to explore. In minutes, the eight horses and their riders were out of sight.

That was now three hours past. For three hours, Professor Minott had led his charges a little south of northeast. In that time they saw no dangerous animals. They saw some—many—familiar plants. They saw rabbits in quantity, and once a slinking gray form which Tom Hunter, who was majoring in zoölogy, declared was a wolf. There are no wolves in the vicinity of Fredericksburg, but neither are there sequoias. And the party had seen no signs of human life, though Fredericksburg lies in farming country which is thickly settled.

In three hours the horses must have covered between twelve and fifteen miles, even through the timber. It was just after sighting a shaggy beast which was unquestionably a woodland buffalo—extinct east of the Rockies as early as 1820—that young Blake protested uneasily against further travel.

"There's something awfully queer, sir," he said awkwardly. "I don't mind experimenting as much as you like, sir, but we've got the girls with us. If we don't start back pretty soon, we'll get in trouble with the dean."

And then Minott drew his two revolvers and very calmly announced that none of them would ever go back. That he knew what had happened and what could be expected. And he added that he would explain as soon as they were convinced he would use his revolvers in case of a mutiny.

"Call us convinced now, sir," said Blake.

He was a bit pale about the lips, but he hadn't flinched. In fact, he'd moved to be between Maida Haynes and the gun muzzle.

"We'd like very much to know how all these trees and plants, which ought to be three thousand miles away, happen to be growing in Virginia without any warning. Especially, sir, we'd like to know how it is that the topography underneath all this brand-new forest is the same. The hills trend the same way they used to, but everything that ever was on them has vanished, and something else is in its place."

Minott nodded approvingly. "Splendid, Blake!" he said warmly. "Sound observation! I picked you because you're well spoken of in geology, even though there were—er—other reasons for leaving you behind. Let's go on over the next rise. Unless I'm mistaken, we should find the Potomac in view. Then I'll answer any questions you like. I'm afraid we've a good bit more of riding to do to-day."

Reluctantly, the eight horses breasted the slope. They scrambled among underbrush. It was queer that in three hours they had seen not a trace of a road leading anywhere. But up at the top of the hill there was a road. It was a narrow, wandering cart track. Without a word, every one of the eight riders turned their horses to follow it. It meandered onward for perhaps a quarter of a mile. It dipped suddenly. And the Potomac lay before and below them.

Then seven of the eight riders exclaimed. There was a settlement upon the banks of the river. There were boats in harbor. There were other boats in view beyond, two beating down from the long reaches upstream, and three others coming painfully up from the direction of Chesapeake Bay. But neither the village nor the boats should have been upon the Potomac River.

The village was small and mud-walled. Tiny, blue-clad figures moved about the fields outside. The buildings, the curving lines of the roofs, and more especially the unmistakable outline of a sort of temple near the center of the fortified hamlet—these were Chinese. The boats in sight were junks, save that their sails were cloth instead of slatted bamboo. The fields outside the squat mud walls were cultivated in a fashion altogether alien. Near the river, where marsh flats would be normal along the Potomac, rice fields intensely worked spread out instead.

Then a figure appeared near by. Wide hat, wadded cotton-padded jacket, cotton trousers, and clogs—it was Chinese peasant incarnate, and all the more so when it turned a slant-eyed, terror-stricken face upon them and fled squawking. It left a monstrously heavy wooden yoke behind, from which dangled two buckets filled with berries it had gathered in the forest.

The riders stared. There was the Potomac. But a Chinese village nestled beside it, Chinese junks plied its waters.

"I—I think," said Maida Haynes unsteadily, "I—think I've—gone insane. Haven't I?"

Professor Minott shrugged. He looked disappointed but queerly resolute.

"No," he said shortly. "You're not mad. It just happens that the Chinese happened to colonize America first. It's been known that Chinese junks touched the American shore—the Pacific coast, of course—long before Columbus. Evidently they colonized it. They may have come all the way overland to the Atlantic, or maybe around by Panama. In any case, this is a Chinese continent now. This isn't what we want. We'll ride some more."

The fleeing, squawking figure had been seen from the village. A huge, discordant gong began to sound. Figures fled toward the walls from the fields round about. The popping of firecrackers began, with a chorus of most intimidating yells.

"Come on!" said Minott sharply. "We'd better move!"

He wheeled his horse about and started off at a canter. By instinct, since he was the only one who seemed to have any definite idea what to do, the others flung after him.

And as they rode, suddenly the horses staggered. The humans on them felt a queer, queasy vertigo. It lasted only for a second, but Minott paled a little.

"Now we'll see what's happened," he said composedly. "The odds are still fair, but I'd rather have had things stay as they were until we'd tried a few more places."

IV.

That same queasy vertigo affected the staring crowd at the end of the road leading north from Fredericksburg. For perhaps a second they felt an unearthly illness, which even blurred their vision. Then they saw clearly again. And in an instant they were babbling in panic, starting their motor cars in terror, some of them fleeing on foot.

The sequoia forest had vanished. In its place was a dreary waste of glittering white; stumpy trees buried under snow; rolling ground covered with a powdery, glittering stuff.

In minutes dense fog shut off the view, as the warm air of a Virginia June morning was chilled by that frigid coating. But in minutes, too, the heavy snow began to melt. The cars fled away along the concrete road, and behind them an expanding belt of fog spread out—and the little streams and runlets filled with a sudden surplus of water, and ran more swiftly, and rose.

The eight riders were every one very pale. Even Minott seemed shaken but no less resolute when he drew rein.

"I imagine you will all be satisfied now," he said composedly. "Blake, you're the geologist of the party. Doesn't the shore line there look familiar?"

Blake nodded. He was very white indeed. He pointed to the stream.

"Yes. The falls, too. This is the site of Fredericksburg, sir, where we were this morning. There is where the main bridge was—or will be. The main highway to Richmond should run"—he licked his lips—"it should run where that very big oak tree is standing. The Princess Anne Hotel should be on the side of that hill. I—I would say, sir, that somehow we've gone back in time or else forward into the future. It sounds insane, but I've been trying to figure it out——"

Minott nodded coolly. "Very good! This is the site of Fredericksburg, to be sure. But we have not traveled forward or back in time. I hope that you noticed where we came out of the sequoia forest. There seems to be a sort of fault along that line, which it may be useful to remember." He paused. "We're not in the past or the future, Blake. We've traveled sidewise, in a sort of oscillation from one time path to another. We happen to be in a—well, in a part of time where Fredericksburg has never been built, just as a little while since we were where the Chinese occupy the American continent. I think we better have lunch."

He dismounted. The four girls tended to huddle together. Lucy Blair's teeth chattered.

Blake moved to their horses' heads. "Don't get rattled," he said urgently. "We're here, wherever it is. Professor Minott is going to explain things in a minute. Since he knows what's what, we're in no danger. Climb off your horses and let's eat. I'm hungry as a bear. Come on, Maida!"

Maida Haynes dismounted. She managed a rather shaky smile. "I'm —afraid of—him," she said in a whisper. "More than—anything else. Stay close to me, please!"

Blake frowned.

Minott said dryly: "Look in your saddlebags and you'll find sandwiches. Also you'll find firearms. You young men had better arm yourselves. Since there's now no conceivable hope of getting back to the world we know, I think you can be trusted with weapons."

Blake stared at him, then silently investigated his own saddlebags. He found two revolvers, with what seemed an abnormally large supply of cartridges. He found a mass of paper, which turned out to be books with their cardboard backs torn off. He glanced professionally at the revolvers and slipped them in his pockets. He put back the books.

"I appoint you second in command, Blake," said Minott, more dryly than before. "You understand nothing, but you wait to understand. I made no mistake in choosing you despite my reasons for leaving you behind. Sit down and I'll tell you what happened."

With a grunt and a puffing noise, a small black bear broke cover and fled across a place where only that morning a highly elaborate filling station had stood. The party started, then relaxed. The girls suddenly started to giggle foolishly, almost hysterically. Minott bit calmly into a sandwich and said pleasantly:

"I shall have to talk mathematics to you, but I'll try to make it more palatable than my classroom lectures have been. You see, everything that has happened can only be explained in terms of mathematics, and more especially certain concepts in mathematical physics. You young ladies and gentlemen being college men and women, I shall have to phrase things very simply, as for ten-year-old children. Hunter, you're staring. If you actually see something, such as an Indian, shoot at him and he'll run away. The probabilities are that he never heard the report of a firearm. We're not on the Chinese continent now."

Hunter gasped, and fumbled at his saddlebags. While he got out the revolvers, Minott went on imperturbably:

"There has been an upheaval of nature, which still continues. But instead of a shaking and jumbling of earth and rocks, there has been a shaking and jumbling of space and time. I go back to first principles. Time is a dimension. The past is one extension of it, the future is the other, just as east is one extension of a more familiar dimension and west is its opposite.

"But we ordinarily think of time as a line, a sort of tunnel, perhaps. We do not make that error in the dimensions about which we think daily. For example, we know that Annapolis, King George courthouse, and—say— Norfolk are all to the eastward of us. But we know that in order to reach any of them, as a destination, we would have to go not only east but north or south in addition. In imaginative travels into the future, however, we never think in such a common-sense fashion. We assume that the future is a line instead of a coördinate, a path instead of a direction. We assume that if we travel to futureward there is but one possible destination. And that is as absurd as it would be to ignore the possibility of traveling to eastward in any other line than due east, forgetting that there is northeast and southeast and a large number of intermediate points."

Young Blake said slowly: "I follow you, sir, but it doesn't seem to bear——"

"On our problem? But it does!" Minott smiled, showing his teeth. He bit into his sandwich again. "Imagine that I come to a fork in a road. I flip a coin to determine which fork I shall take. Whichever route I follow, I shall encounter certain landmarks and certain adventures. But they will not be the same, whether landmarks or adventures.

"In choosing between the forks of the road I choose not only between two sets of landmarks I could encounter, but between two sets of events. I choose between paths, not only on the surface of the earth, but in time. And as those paths upon earth may lead to two different cities, so those paths in the future may lead to two entirely different fates. On one of them may lie opportunities for riches. On the other may lie the most prosaic of hit-and-run accidents which will leave me a mangled corpse, not only upon one fork of a highway in the State of Virginia, but upon one fork of a highway in time.

"In short, I am pointing out that there is more than one future we can encounter, and with more or less absence of deliberation we choose among them. But the futures we fail to encounter, upon the roads we do not take, are just as real as the landmarks upon those roads. We never see them, but we freely admit their existence."

Again it was Blake who protested: "All this is interesting enough, sir, but still I don't see how it applies to our present situation."

Minott said impatiently: "Don't you see that if such a state of things exists in the future, that it must also have existed in the past? We talk of three dimensions and one present and one future. There is a theoretic necessity—a mathematical necessity—for assuming more than one future. There are an indefinite number of possible futures, any one of which we would encounter if we took the proper 'forks' in time.

"There are any number of destinations to eastward. There are any number to futureward. Start a hundred miles west and come eastward, choosing your paths on earth at random, as you do in time. You may arrive here. You may arrive to the north or south of this spot, and still be east of your starting point. Now start a hundred years back instead of a hundred miles west."

Groping, Blake said fumblingly: "I think you're saying, sir, that—well, as there must be any number of futures, there must have been any number of pasts besides those written down in our histories. And—and it would follow that there are any number of what you might call 'presents.'"

Minott gulped down the last of his sandwich and nodded. "Precisely. And to-day's convulsion of nature has jumbled them and still upsets them from time to time. The Northmen once colonized America. In the sequence of events which mark the pathway of our own ancestors through time, that colony failed. But along another path through time that colony throve and flourished. The Chinese reached the shores of California. In the path our ancestors followed through time, nothing developed from the fact. But this morning we touched upon the pathway in which they colonized and conquered the continent, though from the fear that one peasant we saw displayed, they have not wiped out the Indians.

"Somewhere the Roman Empire still exists, and may not improbably rule America as it once ruled Britain. Somewhere, not impossibly, the conditions causing the glacial period still obtain and Virginia is buried under a mass of snow. Somewhere even the Carboniferous period may exist. Or to come more closely to the present we know, somewhere there is a path through time in which Pickett's charge at Gettysburg went desperately home, and the Confederate States of America is now an independent nation with a heavily fortified border and a chip-on-the-shoulder attitude toward the United States."

Blake alone had asked questions, but the entire party had been listening open-mouthed.

Now Maida Haynes said: "But—Professor Minott, where are we now?"

"We are probably," said Minott, smiling, "in a path of time in which America has never been discovered by white men. That isn't a very satisfactory state of things. We're going to look for something better. We wouldn't be comfortable in wigwams, with skins for clothing. So we shall hunt for a more congenial environment. We will have some weeks in which to do our searching, I think. Unless, of course, all space and time are wiped out by the cause of our predicament."

Tom Hunter stirred uncomfortably. "We haven't traveled backward or forward in time, then?"

"No," repeated Minott. He got to his feet. "That odd nausea we felt seems to be caused by travel sidewise in time. It's the symptom of a time oscillation. We'll ride on and see what other worlds await us. We're a rather well-qualified party for this sort of exploration. I chose you for your trainings. Hunter, zoölogy. Blake, engineering and geology. Harris"—he nodded to the rather undersized young man, who flushed at being noticed —"Harris is quite a competent chemist, I understand. Miss Ketterling is a capable botanist. Miss Blair——"

Maida Haynes rose slowly. "You anticipated all this, Professor Minott, and yet you brought us into it. You—you said we'll never get back home. Yet you deliberately arranged it. What—what was your motive? What did you do it for?"

Minott climbed into the saddle. He smiled, but there was bitterness in his smile. "In the world we know," he told her, "I was a professor of mathematics in a small and unconsidered college. I had absolutely no chance of ever being more than a professor of mathematics in a small and unconsidered college. In this world I am, at least, the leader of a group of reasonably intelligent young people. In our saddlebags are arms and ammunition and—more important—books of reference for our future activities. We shall hunt for and find a world in which our technical knowledge is at a premium. We shall live in that world—if all time and space is not destroyed—and use our knowledge."

Maida Haynes said: "But again—what for?"

"To conquer it!" said Minott in sudden fierceness. "To conquer it! We eight shall rule a world as no world has been ruled since time began! I promise you that when we find the environment I seek, you will have wealth by millions, slaves by thousands, every luxury, and all the power human beings could desire!"

Blake said evenly: "And you, sir? What will you have?"

"Most power of all," said Minott steadily. "I shall be the emperor of the world! And also"—his tone changed indescribably as he glanced at Maida —"also I shall have a certain other possession that I wish."

He turned his back to them and rode off to lead the way. Maida Haynes was deathly pale as she rode close to Blake. Her hand closed convulsively upon his arm.

"Jerry!" she whispered. "I'm—frightened!"

And Blake said steadily: "Don't worry! I'll kill him first!"

V.

The ferryboat from Berkeley plowed valorously through the fog. Its whistle howled mournfully at the regulation intervals.

Up in the pilot house, the skipper said confidentially: "I tell you, I had the funniest feelin' of my life, just now. I was dizzy an' sick all over, like I was seasick an' drunk all at the same time."

The mate said abstractedly: "I had somethin' like that a little while ago. Somethin' we ate, prob'ly. Say, that's funny!"

"What?"

"Was a lot o' traffic in the harbor just now, whistlin'. I ain't heard a whistle for minutes. Listen!"

Both men strained their ears. There was the rhythmic shudder of the vessel, itself a sound produced by the engines. There were fragmentary voice noises from the passenger deck below. There was the wash of water by the ferryboat's bow. There was nothing else. Nothing at all.

"Funny!" said the skipper.

"Damn funny!" agreed the mate.

The ferryboat went on. The fog cut down all visibility to a radius of perhaps two hundred feet.

"Funniest thing I ever saw!" said the skipper worriedly. He reached for the whistle cord and the mournful bellow of the horn resounded. "We're near our slip, though. I wish——"

With a little chugging, swishing sound a steam launch came out of the mist. It sheered off, the men in it staring blankly at the huge bulk of the ferry. It made a complete circuit of the big, clumsy craft. Then some one stood up and bellowed unintelligibly in the launch. He bellowed again. He was giving an order. He pointed to the flag at the stern of the launch— it was an unfamiliar flag—and roared furiously.

"What the hell's the matter of that guy?" wondered the mate.

A little breeze blew suddenly. The fog began to thin. The faintly brighter spot which was the sun overhead grew bright indeed. Faint sunshine struggled through the fog bank. The wind drove the fog back before it, and the bellowing man in the steam launch grew purple with rage as his orders went unheeded.

Then, quite abruptly, the last wisps of vapor blew away. San Francisco stood revealed. But—San Francisco? This was not San Francisco! It was a wooden city, a small city, a dirty city with narrow streets and gas street lamps and four monstrous, barracklike edifices fronting the harbor. Nob Hill stood, but it was barren of dwellings. And——

"Damn!" said the mate of the ferryboat.

He was staring at a colossal mass of masonry, foursquare and huge, which rose to a gigantic spiral fluted dome. A strange and alien flag fluttered in the breeze above certain buildings. Figures moved in the streets. There were motor cars, but they were clumsy and huge.

The mate's eyes rested upon a horse-drawn carriage. It was drawn by three horses abreast, and they were either so trained or so checkreined that the two outer horses' heads were arched outward in the fashion of Tsarist Russia.

But that was natural enough. When an interpreter could be found, the mate and skipper were savagely abused for entering the harbor of Novo Skevsky without paying due heed to the ordinances in force by the ukase of the Tsar Alexis of all the Russias. These rules, they learned, were enforced with special rigor in all the Russian territory in America, from Alaska on the south.

The boy ran shouting up to the village. "Hey, grandpa! Hey, grandpa! Lookit the birds!" He pointed as he ran.

A man looked idly, and stood transfixed. A woman stopped, and stared. Lake Superior glowed bluely off to westward, and the little village most often turned its eyes in that direction. Now, though, as the small boy ran shouting of what he had seen, men stared, women marveled, and children ran and shouted and whooped in the instinctive excitement of childhood at anything which entrances grown-ups.

Over the straggly pine forests birds were coming. They came in great dark masses. Not by dozens, or by hundreds, or even by thousands. They came in millions, in huge dark clouds which obscured the sky. There were two huge flights in sight at the boy's first shouting. There were six in view before he had reached his home and was panting a demand that his elders come and look. And there were others, incredible numbers of others, sweeping onward straight over the village.

Dusk fell abruptly as the first flock passed overhead. The whirring of wings was loud. It made people raise their voices as they asked each other what such birds could possibly be. Daylight again, and again darkness as the flocks poured on. The size of each flock was to be measured not in feet or yards, but in miles of front. Two, three miles of birds, flying steadily in a single enormous mass some four miles deep. Another such mass, and another, and another.

"What are they, grandpa? There must be millions of 'em!"

Somewhere, a shotgun went off. Small things dropped from the sky.

Another gunshot, and another. A rain of bird shot went up from the village into the mass of whirring wings. And crazily careening small bodies fell down among the houses.

Grandpa examined one of them, smoothing its rumpled plumage. He exclaimed. He gasped in excitement. "It's a wild pigeon! What they used to call passenger pigeons! Back in '78 there was these birds by billions. Folks said a billion was killed in Michigan that one year! But they're gone now. They're gone like the buffalo. There ain't any more."

The sky was dark with birds above him. A flock four miles wide and three miles long made lights necessary in the village. The air was filled with the sound of wings. The passenger pigeon had returned to a continent from which it had been absent for almost fifty years.

Flocks of passenger pigeons flew overhead in thick, dark masses equaling those seen by Audubon in 1813, when he computed the pigeons in flight above Kentucky at hundreds of billions in number. In flocks that were innumerable they flew to westward. The sun set, and still the air was filled with the sound of their flying. For hours after darkness fell, the whirring of wings continued without ceasing.

VI.

A great open fire licked at the rocks against which it had been built. The horses cropped uneasily at herbage near by. The smell of fat meat cooking was undeniably savory, but one of the girls blubbered gustily on a bed of leaves. Harris tended the cookery. Tom Hunter brought wood. Blake stood guard a little beyond the firelight, revolvers ready, staring off into the blackness. Professor Minott pored over a topographical map of Virginia. Maida Haynes tried to comfort the blubbering girl.

"Supper's ready," said Harris. He made even that announcement seem somehow shy and apologetic.

Minott put down his map. Tom Hunter began to cut great chunks of steaming meat from the haunch of venison. He put them on slabs of bark and began to pass them around. Minott reached out his hand and took one of them. He ate with obvious appetite. He seemed to have abandoned his preoccupation the instant he laid down his map. He was displaying the qualities of a capable leader.

"Hunter," he observed, "after you've eaten that stuff, you might relieve Blake. We'll arrange reliefs for the rest of the night. By the way, you men mustn't forget to wind your watches. We'll need to rate them, ultimately."

Hunter gulped down his food and moved out to Blake's hiding place. They exchanged low-toned words. Blake came back to the fire. He took the food Harris handed him and began to eat it. He looked at the blubbering girl on the bed of leaves.

"She's just scared," said Minott. "Barely slit the skin on her arm. But it is upsetting for a senior at Robinson College to be wounded by a flint arrowhead."

Blake nodded. "I heard some noises off in the darkness," he said curtly. "I'm not sure, but my impression was that I was being stalked. And I thought I heard a human voice."

"We may be watched," admitted Minott. "But we're out of the path of time in which those Indians tried to ambush us. If any of them follow, they're too bewildered to be very dangerous."

"I hope so," said Blake.

His manner was devoid of cordiality, yet there was no exception to be taken to it. Professor Minott had deliberately got the party into a predicament from which there seemed to be no possibility of escape. He had organized it to get it into just that predicament. He was unquestionably the leader of the party, despite his action. Blake made no attempt to undermine his leadership.

But Blake himself had some qualifications as a leader, young as he was. Perhaps the most promising of them was the fact that he made no attempt to exercise his talents until he knew as much as Minott of what was to be looked for, what was to be expected.

He listened sharply and then said: "I think we've digested your lesson of this morning, sir. But how long is this scrambling of space and time to continue? We left Fredericksburg and rode to the Potomac. It was Chinese territory. We rode back to Fredericksburg, and it wasn't there. Instead, we encountered Indians who let loose a flight of arrows at us and wounded Bertha Ketterling in the arm. We were nearly out of range at the time, though."

"They were scared," said Minott. "They'd never seen horses before. Our white skins probably upset them, too. And then our guns, and the fact that I killed one, should have chased them off."

"But—what happened to Fredericksburg? We rode away from it. Why couldn't we ride back?"

"The scrambling process has kept up," said Minott dryly. "You remember that queer vertigo? We've had it several times to-day, and every time, as I see it, there's been an oscillation of the earth we happened to be on. Hm! Look!"

He got up and secured the map over which he had been poring. He brought it back and pointed to a heavy penciled line. "Here's a map of Virginia in our time. The Chinese continent appeared just about three miles north of Fredericksburg. The line of demarcation was, I consider, the line along which the giant sequoias appeared. While in the Chinese time we felt that giddiness and rode back toward Fredericksburg. We came out of the sequoia forest at the same spot as before. I made sure of it. But the continent of our time was no longer there.

"We rode east and—whether you noticed it or not—before we reached the border of King George County there was another abrupt change in the vegetation—from a pine country to oaks and firs, which are not exactly characteristic of this part of the world in our time. We saw no signs of any civilization. We turned south, and ran into that heavy fog and the snow beyond it. Evidently, there's a section of a time path in which Virginia is still subject to a glacial climate."

Blake nodded. He listened again. Then he said:

"You've three sides of an—an island of time marked there."

"Just so," agreed Minott. "Exactly! In the scrambling process, the oscillating process, there seem to be natural 'faults' in the surface of the earth. Relatively large areas seem to shift back and forth as units from one time path to another. In my own mind, I've likened them to elevators with many stories.

"We were on the Fredericksburg 'elevator,' or that section of our time path, when it shifted to another time. We rode off it onto the Chinese continent. While there, the section we started from shifted again, to another time altogether. When we rode back to where it had been—well, the town of Fredericksburg was in another time path altogether."

Blake said sharply: "Listen!"

A dull mutter sounded far to the north. It lasted for an instant and died away. There was a crashing of bushes near by and a monstrous animal stepped alertly into the firelight. It was an elk, but such an elk! It was a giant, a colossal creature. One of the girls cried out affrightedly, and it turned and crashed away into the underbrush.

"There are no elk in Virginia," said Minott dryly.

Blake said sharply again: "Listen!"

Again that dull muttering to the north. It grew louder, now. It was an airplane motor. It increased in volume from a dull mutter to a growl, from a growl to a roar. Then the plane shot overhead, the navigation lights on its wings glowing brightly. It banked steeply and returned. It circled overhead, with a queer effect of helplessness. And then suddenly it dived down.

"An aviator from our time," said Blake, staring toward the sound. "He saw our fire. He's going to try to make a crash landing in the dark."

The motor cut off. An instant in which there was only the crackling of the fire and the whistling of wind around gliding surfaces off there in the night. Then a terrific thrashing of branches. A crash——

Then a flare of flame, a roaring noise, and the lurid yellow of gasoline flames spouting skyward.

"Stay here!" snapped Blake. He was on his feet in an instant. "Harris, Professor Minott! Somebody has to stay with the girls! I'll get Hunter and go help!"

He plunged off into the darkness, calling to Hunter. The two of them forced their way through the underbrush. Minott scowled and got out his revolvers. Still scowling, he slipped out of the firelight and took up the guard duty Hunter had abandoned.

A gasoline tank exploded, off there in the darkness. The glare of the fire grew intolerably vivid. The sound of the two young men racing through undergrowth became fainter and died away.

A long time passed—a very long time. Then, very far away, the sound of thrashing bushes could be heard again. The gasoline flare dulled and dimmed. Figures came slowly back. They moved as if they were carrying something very heavy. They stopped beyond the glow of light from the camp fire. Then Blake and Hunter reappeared, alone.

"He's dead," said Blake curtly. "Luckily, he was flung clear of the crash before the gas tanks caught. He came back to consciousness for a couple of minutes before he—died. Our fire was the only sign of human life he'd seen in hours. We brought him over here. We'll bury him in the morning."

There was silence. Minott's scowl was deep and savage as he came back to the firelight.

"What—what did he say?" asked Maida Haynes.

"He left Washington at five this afternoon," said Blake shortly. "By our time, or something like it. All of Virginia across the Potomac vanished at four thirty, and virgin forest took its place. He went out to explore. At the end of an hour he came back, and Washington was gone. In its place was a fog bank, with snow underneath. He followed the Potomac down and saw palisaded homesteads with long, oared ships drawn up on shore."

"Vikings, Norsemen!" said Minott in satisfaction.

"He didn't land. He swept on down, following the edge of the bay. He looked for Baltimore. Gone! Once, he's sure, he saw a city, but he was taken sick at about that time and when he recovered, it had vanished. He was heading north again and his gasoline was getting low when he saw our fire. He tried for a crash landing. He'd no flares with him. He crashed —and died."

"Poor fellow!" said Maida shakenly.

"The point is," said Blake, "that Washington was in our present time at about four thirty to-day. We've got a chance, though a slim one, of getting back! We've got to get to the edge of one of these blocks that go swinging through time, the edge of what Professor Minott calls a 'time fault,' and watch it! When the shifts come, we explore as quickly as we can. We've no great likelihood, perhaps, of getting back exactly to our own period, but we can get nearer to it than we are now! Professor Minott said that somewhere the Confederacy exists. Even that, among people of our own race and speaking our own language, would be better than to be marooned forever among Indians, or among Chinese or Norsemen."

Minott said harshly: "Blake, we'd better have this out right now! I give the orders in this party! You jumped quickly when that plane crashed, and you gave orders to Harris and to me. I let you get away with it, but we can have but one leader. I am that leader! See you remember it!"

Blake swung about. Minott had a revolver bearing on his body.

"And you are making plans for a return to our time!" he went on savagely. "I won't have it! The odds are still that we'll all be killed. But if I do live, I mean to take advantage of it. And my plans do not include a return to a professorship of mathematics at Robinson College."

"Well?" said Blake coolly. "What of it, sir?"

"Just this! I'm going to take your revolvers. I'm going to make the plans and give the orders hereafter. We are going to look for the time path in which a viking civilization thrives in America. We'll find it, too, because these disturbances will last for weeks yet. And once we find it, we will settle down among those Norsemen, and when space and time are stable again I shall begin the formation of my empire! And you will obey orders or you'll be left afoot while the rest of us go on to my destiny!"

Blake said very quietly indeed: "Perhaps, sir, we'd all prefer to be left to our own destinies rather than be merely the tools by which you attain to yours."

Minott stared at him an instant. His lips tensed. "It is a pity," he said coldly. "I could have used your brains, Blake. But I can't have mutiny. I shall have to shoot you."

His revolver came up remorselessly.

VII.

To determine the cause of various untoward events, the British Academy of Sciences was in extraordinary session. Its members were weary; bleary-eyed, but still conscious of their dignity and the importance of their task. A venerable, whiskered physicist spoke with fitting definiteness and solemnity.

"And so, gentlemen, I see nothing more that remains to be said. The extraordinary events of the past hours seem to follow from certain facts about our own closed space. The gravitational fields of 10^{79} particles of matter will close space about such an aggregation. No cosmos can be larger. No cosmos can be smaller. And if we envision the creation of such a cosmos we will observe its galaxies vanish at the instant the 10^{79}th particle adds its own mass to those which were present before it.

"However, the fact that space has closed about such a cosmos does not imply its annihilation. It means merely its separation from its original space, the isolation of itself in space and time because of the curvature of space due to its gravitational field. And if we assume the existence of more than one area of closed space, we assume in some sense the existence of a hyper-space separating the closed spaces; hyper-spatial coördinates which mark their relative hyper-spatial positions; hyper-spatial——"

A gentleman with even longer and whiter whiskers than the speaker said in a loud and decided voice: "Fiddlesticks! Stuff and nonsense!"

The speaker paused. He glared. "Sir! Do you refer——"

"I do!" said the gentleman with the longer and whiter whiskers. "It is stuff and nonsense! Next you'd be saying that in this hyper-space of yours the closed spaces would be subject to hyper-laws, revolve about each other in hyper-orbits regulated by hyper-gravitation, and undoubtedly at times there would be hyper-earth tides or hyper-collisions, producing decidedly hyper-catastrophes."

"Such, sir," said the whiskered gentleman on the rostrum, quivering with indignation, "such is the fact, sir!"

"Then the fact," rejoined the scientist with the longer and whiter whiskers, "sir, makes me sick!"

And as if to prove it, he reeled. But he was not alone in reeling. The entire venerable assembly shuddered in abrupt, nauseating vertigo. And then the British Academy of Sciences adjourned without formality and in a panic. It ran away. Because abruptly there was no longer a rostrum nor an end to its assembly hall. Where their speaker had been was open air. In the open air was a fire. About the fire were certain brutish figures incredibly resembling the whiskered scientists who fled from them. They roared at the fleeing, venerable men. Snarling, wielding crude clubs, they plunged into the hall of the British Academy of Sciences. It is known that they caught one person—a biologist of highly eccentric views. It is believed that they ate him.

But it has long been surmised that some, at least, of the extinct species of humanity, such as the Piltdown and Neanderthal men, were cannibals. If in some pathway of time they happened to exterminate their more intelligent rivals—if somewhere *pithecanthropus erectus* survives and *homo sapiens* does not—well, in that pathway of time cannibalism is the custom of society.

VIII.

With a gasp, Maida Haynes flung herself before Blake. But Harris was even quicker. Apologetic and shy, he had just finished cutting a smoking piece of meat from the venison haunch. He threw it swiftly, and the searing mass of stuff flung Minott's hand aside at the same instant that it burned it horribly.

Blake was on his feet, his gun out. "If you pick up that gun, sir," he said rather breathlessly but with unquestionable sincerity, "I'll put a bullet through your arm!"

Minott swore. He retrieved the weapon with his left hand and thrust it in his pocket. "You young fool!" he snapped. "I'd no intention of shooting you. I did intend to scare you thoroughly. Harris, you're an ass! Maida, I shall discuss your action later. The worst punishment I could give the lot of you would be to leave you to yourselves."

He stalked out of the firelight and off into the darkness. Something like consternation came upon the group. The glow of fire where the plane had crashed flickered fitfully. The base of the dull red light seemed to widen a little.

"That's the devil!" said Hunter uneasily. "He does know more about this stuff than we do. If he leaves us we're messed up!"

"We are," agreed Blake grimly. "And perhaps if he doesn't."

Lucy Blair said: "I—I'll go and talk to him. He—he used to be nice to me in class. And—and his hand must hurt terribly. It's burned."

She moved away from the fire, a long and angular shadow going on before her.

Minott's voice came sharply: "Go back! There's something moving out here!"

Instantly after, his revolver flashed. A howl arose, and the weapon flashed again and again. Then there were many crashings. Figures fled.

Minott came back to the firelight, scornfully. "Your leadership is at fault, Blake," he commented sardonically. "You forgot about a guard. And you were the man who thought he heard voices! They've run away now, though. Indians, of course."

Lucy Blair said hesitantly: "Could I—could I do something for your hand? It's burned——"

"What can you do?" he asked angrily.

"There's some fat," she told him. "Indians used to dress wounds with bear fat. I suppose deer fat would do as well."

He permitted her to dress the burn, though it was far from a serious one. She begged handkerchiefs from the others to complete the job. There was distinct uneasiness all about the camp fire. This was no party of adventurers, prepared for anything. It had started as an outing of undergraduates.

Minott scowled as Lucy Blair worked on his hand. Harris looked as apologetic as possible, because he had made the injury. Bertha Ketterling blubbered—less noisily, now, because nobody paid her any attention. Blake frowned meditatively at the fire. Maida Haynes tried uneasily not to seem conscious of the fact that she was in some sense—though no mention had been made of it—a bone of contention.

The horses moved uneasily. Bertha Ketterling sneezed. Maida felt her eyes smarting. She was the first one to see the spread of the blaze started by the gas tanks of the airplane. Her cry of alarm roused the others.

The plane had crashed a good mile from the camp fire. The blazing of its tanks had been fierce but brief. The burning of the wings and chassis fabric had been short, as well. The fire had died down to seeming dull embers. But there were more than embers ablaze out there now.

The fire had died down, to be sure, but only that it might spread among thick and tangled underbrush. It had spread widely on the ground before some climbing vine, blazing, carried flames up to resinous pine branches overhead. A small but steady wind was blowing. And as Maida looked off to see the source of the smoke which stung her eyes, one tall tree was blazing, a long line of angry red flames crept along the ground, and then at two more, three more, then at a dozen points bright fire roared upward toward the sky.

The horses snorted and reared.

Minott snapped: "Harris! Get the horses! Hunter, see that the girls get mounted, and quickly!"

He pointedly gave Blake no orders. He pored intently over his map as more trees and still more caught fire and blazed upward. He stuffed it in his pocket. Blake calmly rescued the haunch of venison, and when Minott sprang into the saddle among the snorting, scared horses, Blake was already by Maida Haynes' side, ready to go.

"We ride in pairs," said Minott curtly. "A man and a girl. You men, look after them. I've a flashlight. I'll go ahead. We'll hit the Rappahannock River sooner or later, if we don't get around the fire first—and if we can keep ahead of it."

They topped a little hillock and saw more of the extent of their danger. In a half mile of spreading, the fire had gained three times as much breadth. And to their right the fire even then roared in among the trees of a forest so thick as to be jungle. The blaze fairly raced through it as if the fire made its own wind; which in fact it did. To their left it crackled fiercely in underbrush which, as they fled, blazed higher.

And then, as if to add mockery to their very real danger, a genuinely brisk breeze sprang up suddenly. Sparks and blazing bits of leaves, fragments of ash and small, unsubstantial coals began to fall among them. Bertha Ketterling yelped suddenly as a tiny live coal touched the flesh of her cheek. Harris' horse squealed and kicked as something singed it. They galloped madly ahead. Trees rose about them. The white beam of Minott's flashlight seemed almost ludicrous in the fierce red glare from behind, but at least it showed the way.

IX.

Something large and dark and clumsy lumbered cumbersomely into the space between Grady's statue and the post-office building. The arc lights showed it clearly, and it was not anything which should be wandering in the streets of Atlanta, Georgia, at any hour of the day or night. A taxicab chauffeur saw it and nearly tore off a wheel in turning around to get away. A policeman saw it, and turned very pale as he grabbed at his beat telephone to report it. But there had been too many queer things happening this day for him to suspect his own sanity, and the *Journal* had printed too much news from elsewhere for him to disbelieve his own eyes.

The thing was monstrous, reptilian, loathesome. It was eighty feet long, of which at least fifty was head and tail and the rest flabby-fleshed body. It may have weighed twenty-five or thirty tons, but its head was not much larger than that of a large horse. That tiny head swung about stupidly. The thing was bewildered. It put down a colossal foot, and water gushed up from a broken water main beneath the pavement. The thing did not notice. It moved vaguely, exhaling a dank and musty odor.

The clang of police-emergency cars and the scream of fire-engine sirens filled the air. An ambulance flashed into view—and was struck by a balancing sweep of the mighty tail. The ambulance careened and crashed.

The thing uttered a plaintive cry, ignoring the damage its tail had caused. The sound was like that of a bleat, a thousand times multiplied. It peered ceaselessly around, seeming to feel trapped by the tall buildings about it, but it was too stupid to retrace its steps for escape.

Somebody screamed in the distance as police cars and fire engines reached the spot where the first thing swayed and peered and moved in quest of escape. Two other things, smaller than the first, came lumbering after it. Like it, they had monstrous bodies and disproportionately tiny heads. One of them blundered stupidly into a hook-and-ladder truck. Truck and beast went down, and the beast bleated like the first.

Then some fool began to shoot. Other fools joined in. Steel-jacketed bullets poured into the mountains of reptilian flesh. Police sub-machine guns raked the monsters. Those guns were held by men of great daring, who could not help noting the utter stupidity of the things out of the great swamp which had appeared where Inman Park used to be.

The bullets stung. They hurt. The three beasts bleated and tried bewilderedly and very clumsily to escape. The largest tried to climb a five-story building, and brought it down in sheer wreckage.

Before the last of them was dead—or rather, before it ceased to move its great limbs, because the tail moved jerkily for a long time and its heart was still beating spasmodically when loaded on a city dump cart next day—before the last of them was dead they had made sheer chaos of three blocks of business buildings in the heart of Atlanta, had killed seventeen men, and the best testimony is that they made not one attempt to fight. Their whole and only thought was to escape. The destruction they wrought and the deaths they caused were due to their clumsiness and stupidity.

X.

The leading horses floundered horribly. They sank to their fetlocks in something soft and very spongy. Bertha Ketterling squawked in terror as her mount's motion changed.

Blake said crisply in the blackness: "It feels like plowed ground. Better use the light again, Professor Minott."

The sky behind them glowed redly. The forest fire still trailed them. For miles of front, now, it shot up sparks and flame and a harsh red glare which illumined the clouds of its own smoke.

The flashlight stabbed at the earth. The ground was plowed. It was softened by the hands of men. Minott kept the light on as little gasps of thankfulness arose.

Then he said sardonically: "Do you know what this crop is? It's lentils. Are lentils grown in Virginia? Perhaps! We'll see what sort of men these may happen to be."

He swung to follow the line of the furrows.

Tom Hunter said miserably: "If that's plowed ground, it's a damn shallow furrow. A one-horse plow'd throw up more dirt than that."

A light glowed palely in the distance. Every person in the party saw it at the same instant. As if by instinct, the head of every horse swerved for it.

"We'll want to be careful," said Blake quietly. "These may be Chinese, too."

The light was all of a mile distant. They moved over the plowed ground cautiously.

Suddenly the hoofs of Lucy Blair's horse rang on stone. The noise was startlingly loud. Other horses, following hers, clattered thunderously.

Minott flashed down the light again. Dressed stone. Cut stone. A roadway built of dressed-stone blocks, some six or eight feet wide. Then one of the horses shivered and snorted. It pranced agitatedly, edging away from something on the road. Minott swept the flashlight beam along the narrow way.

"The only race," he said dryly, "that ever built roads like this was the Romans. They made their military roads like this. But they didn't discover America that we know of."

The beam touched something dark. It came back and steadied. One of the girls uttered a stifled exclamation. The beam showed dead men. One was a man with a shield and sword and a helmet such as the soldiers of ancient Rome are pictured as having worn. He was dead. Half his head had been blown off. Lying on top of him there was a man in a curious gray uniform. He had died of a sword wound.

The beam searched around. More bodies. Many Roman-accoutered figures. Four or five men in what looked remarkably like the uniform that might be worn by soldiers of the Confederate Army—if a Confederate Army could be supposed to exist.

"There's been fighting," said Blake composedly. "I guess somebody from the Confederacy—that time path, say—started to explore what must have seemed a damned strange happening. And these Romans—if they are Romans—jumped them."

Something came shambling through the darkness. Minott threw the flash beam upon it. It was human, yes. But it was three parts naked, and it was chained, and it had been beaten horribly, and there were great sores upon its body from other beatings. It was bony and emaciated. The insensate ferocity of sheer despair marked it. It was brutalized by its sufferings until it was just human, barely human, and nothing more.

It squinted at the light, too dull of comprehension to be afraid.

Then Minott spoke, and at his words it groveled in the dirt. Minott spoke harshly, in half-forgotten Latin, and the groveling figure mumbled words which had been barbarous Latin to begin with, and through its bruised lips were still further mutilated.

"It's a slave," said Minott coldly. "Strange men—Confederates, I suppose —came from the north to-day. They fought and killed some of the guards at this estate. This slave denies it, but I imagine he was heading north in hopes of escaping to them. When you think of it, I suppose we're not the only explorers to be caught out of our own time path by some shift or another."

He growled at the slave and rode on, still headed for the distant light.

"What—what are you going to do?" asked Maida faintly.

"Go on to the villa yonder and ask questions," said Minott dryly. "If

Confederates hold it, we'll be well received. If they don't, we'll still manage to earn a welcome. I intend to camp along a time fault and cross over whenever a time shift brings a Norse settlement in sight. Consequently, I want exact news of places where they've been seen, if such news is to be had."

Maida Haynes pressed close to Blake. He put a reassuring hand on her arm as the horses trudged on over the soft ground. The firelight behind them grew brighter. Occasional resinous, coniferous trees flared upward and threw fugitive red glows upon the riding figures. But gradually the glare grew steadier and stronger. The white walls of a rambling stucco house became visible—outbuildings—barns. A monstrous structure which looked startlingly like a barracks.

It was a farm, an estate, a Roman villa transplanted to the very edge of a wilderness. It was—Blake remembered vaguely—like a picture he had once seen of a Roman villa in England, restored to look as it had been before Rome withdrew her legions from Britain and left the island to savagery and darkness. There were small mounds of curing hay about them, through which the horses picked their way. Blake suddenly wrinkled his nostrils suspiciously. He sniffed.

Maida pressed close to him. Her lips formed words. Lucy Blair rode close to Minott, glancing up at him from time to time. Harris rode beside Bertha Ketterling, and Bertha sat her horse as if she were saddle sore. Tom Hunter clung close to Minott as if for protection, leaving Janet Thompson to look out for herself.

"Jerry," said Maida, "what—what do you think?"

"I don't like it," admitted Blake in a low tone. "But we've got to tag along. I think I smell——"

Then a sudden swarm of figures leaped at the horses—wild figures, naked figures, sweaty and reeking and almost maniacal figures, some of whom clanked chains as they leaped. A voice bellowed orders at them from a distance, and a whip cracked ominously.

Before the struggle ended, there were just two shots fired. Blake fired them both and wheeled about. Then a horse streaked away, and Bertha Ketterling was bawling plaintively, and Tom Hunter babbled hysterically, and Harris swore with a complete lack of his customary air of apology.

Minott seemed to be buried under a mass of foul bodies like the rest, but he rasped at his captors in an authoritative tone. They fell away from him, cringing as if by instinct. And then torches appeared suddenly and slaves appeared in their light—slaves of every possible degree of filth and degradation, of every possible racial mixture, but unanimous in a desperate abjectness before their master amid the torchbearers.

He was a short, fat man, in an only slightly modified toga. He drew it close about his body as the torchbearers held their flares close to the captives. The torchlight showed the captives, to be sure, but also it showed the puffy, self-indulgent and invincibly cruel features of the man who owned these slaves and the villa. By his pose and the orders he gave in a curiously corrupt Latin, he showed that he considered he owned the captives, too.

XI.

The deputy from Aisne-le-Sur decided that it had been very wise indeed for him to walk in the fresh air. Paris at night is stimulating. That curious attack of vertigo had come of too much champagne. The fresh air had dispelled the fumes. But it was odd that he did not know exactly where he was, though he knew his Paris well.

These streets were strange. The houses were unlike any that he remembered ever having seen before. In the light of the street lamps—and they were unusual, too—there was a certain unfamiliar quality about their architecture. He puzzled over it, trying to identify the peculiar *flair* these houses showed.

He became impatient. After all, it was necessary for him to return home some time, even though his wife—— The deputy from Aisne-le-Sur shrugged. Then he saw bright lights ahead. He hastened his steps. A magnificent mansion, brilliantly illuminated.

The clattering of many hoofs. A cavalry escort, forming up before the house. A pale young man emerged, escorted by a tall, fat man who kissed his hand as if in an ecstasy of admiration. Dismounted cavalrymen formed a lane from the gateway to the car. Two young officers followed the pale young man, ablaze with decorations. The deputy from Aisne-le-Sur noted subconsciously that he did not recognize their uniforms. The car door was open and waiting. There was some oddity about the car, but the deputy could not see clearly just what it was.

There was much clicking of heels—steel blades at salute. The pale young man patiently allowed the fat man to kiss his hand again. He entered the car. The two bemedaled young officers climbed in after him. The car rolled away. Instantly, the cavalry escort clattered with it, before it, behind it, all around it.

The fat man stood on the sidewalk, beaming and rubbing his hands together. The dismounted cavalrymen swung to their saddles and trotted briskly after the others.

The deputy from Aisne-le-Sur stared blankly. He saw another pedestrian, halted like himself to regard the spectacle. He was disturbed by the fact that this pedestrian was clothed in a fashion as perturbingly unfamiliar as these houses and the spectacle he had witnessed.

"Pardon, m'sieu'," said the deputy from Aisne-le-Sur, "I do not recognize my surroundings. Would you tell me——"

"The house," said the other caustically, "is the hotel of Monsieur le Duc de Montigny. Is it possible that in 1935 one does not know of Monsieur le Duc? Or more especially of Madame la Duchesse, and what she is and where she lives?"

The deputy from Aisne-le-Sur blinked. "Montigny? Montigny? No," he admitted. "And the young man of the car, whose hand was kissed by——"

"Kissed by Monsieur le Duc?" The stranger stared frankly. "*Mon dieu!* Where have you come from that you do not recognize Louis the Twentieth? He has but departed from a visit to madame his mistress."

"Louis—Louis the Twentieth!" stammered the deputy from Aisne-le-Sur. "I—I do not understand!"

"Fool!" said the stranger impatiently. "That was the king of France, who succeeded his father as a child of ten and has been free of the regency for but six months—and already ruins France!"

The long-distance operator plugged in with a shaking hand. "Number please. . . . I am sorry, sir, but we are unable to connect you with Camden. . . . The lines are down. . . . Very sorry, sir." She plugged in another line. "Hello. . . . I am sorry, sir, but we are unable to connect you with Jenkinstown. The lines are down. . . . Very sorry, sir."

Another call buzzed and lighted up.

"Hello. . . . I am sorry, sir. We are unable to connect you with Dover. The lines are down. . . ." Her hands worked automatically. "Hello. . . . I am sorry, but we are unable to connect you with New York. The lines are down. . . . No, sir. We cannot route it by Atlantic City. The lines are down. . . . Yes, sir, I know the telegraph companies cannot guarantee delivery. . . . No, sir, we cannot reach Pittsburgh, either, to get a message through. . . ." Her voice quivered. "No, sir, the lines are down to Scranton. . . . And Harrisburg, too. Yes, sir. . . . I am sorry, but we cannot get a message of any sort out of Philadelphia in any direction. . . . We have tried to arrange communication by radio, but no calls are answered. . . ."

She covered her face with her hands for an instant. Then she plugged in and made a call herself:

"Minnie! Haven't they heard anything? . . . Not anything? . . . What? They phoned for more police? . . . The—the operator out there says there's fighting? She hears a lot of shooting? . . . What is it, Minnie? Don't they even know? . . . They—they're using the armored cars from the banks to fight with too? . . . But what are they fighting? What? . . . My folks are out there, Minnie! My folks are out there!"

The doorway of the slave barracks closed and great bars slammed against its outer side. Reeking, foul, unbreathable air closed about them like a wave. Then a babbling of voices all about. The clanking of chains. The rustling of straw, as if animals moved. Some one screeched; howled above the others. He began to gain the ascendancy. There was almost some attention paid to him, though a minor babbling continued all about.

Maida said in a strained voice: "I—I can catch a word here and there. He's—telling these other slaves how we were captured. It's—Latin, of sorts."

Bertha Ketterling squalled suddenly, in the absolute dark. "Somebody touched me!" she bawled. "A man!"

A voice spoke humorously, somewhere near. There was laughter. It was the howled laughter of animals. Slaves were animals, according to the Roman notion. A rustling noise, as if in the noisome freedom of their barracks the utterly brutalized slaves drew nearer to the newcomers. There could be sport with new-captured folk, not yet degraded to their final status.

Lucy Blair cried out in a stifled fashion. There was a sharp, incisive *crack*. Somebody fell. More laughter.

"I knocked him out!" snapped Minott. "Harris! Hunter! Feel around for something we can use as clubs! These slaves intend to haze us, and in their own den there's no attempt to control them. Even if they kill us they'll only be whipped for it. And the women will——"

Something, snarling, leaped for him in the darkness. The authoritative tone of Minott's voice was hateful. A yapping sound arose. Other figures closed in. Reduced to the status of animals, the slaves of the Romans behaved as beasts when locked in their monster kennel. The newcomers were hateful if only because they had been freemen, not slaves. The women were clean and they were frightened—and they were prey. Chains clanked ominously. Foul breaths tainted the air. The reek of utter depravity, of human beings brought lower than beasts, filled the air. It was utterly dark.

Bertha Ketterling began to blubber noisily. There was the sudden savage sound of a blow meeting flesh. Then pandemonium and battle, and the sudden terrified screams of Lucy Blair. The panting of men who fought. The sound of blows. A man howled. Another shrieked curses. A woman screamed shrilly.

Bang! Bang! Bang-bang! Shots outside, a veritable fusillade of them. Running feet. Shouts. The bars at the doorway fell. The great doors opened, and men stood in the opening with whips and torches, bellowing for the slaves to come out and attack something yet unknown. They were being called from their kennel like dogs. Four of the whip men came inside, flogging the slaves out, while the sound of shots continued. The slaves shrank away, or bounded howling for the open air. But there were three of them who would never shrink or cringe again.

Minott and Harris stood embattled in a corner of the slave shed. Lucy Blair, her hair disheveled, crouched behind Minott, who held a heavy beam in desperate readiness for further battle. Harris, likewise, held a clumsy club. With torchlight upon him, his air of savage defiance turned to one of quaint apology for the dead slave at his feet. And Hunter and two of the girls competed in stark panic for a position behind him. Maida Haynes, dead white, stood backed against a wall, a jagged fragment of gnawed bone held daggerwise.

The whips lashed out at them. Voices snarled at them. The whips again. Minott struck out furiously, a huge welt across his face.

And revolvers cracked at the great door. Blake stood there, a revolver in each hand, his eyes blazing. A torchbearer dropped, and the torches flared smokily in the foul mud of the flooring.

"All right," said Blake fiercely. "Come on out!"

Hunter was the first to reach him, babbling and gasping. There was sheer uproar all about. A huge grain shed roared upward in flames. Figures rushed crazily all about it. From the flames came another explosion, then two, then three more.

"Horses over here by the stables," said Blake, his face white and very deadly indeed. "They haven't unsaddled them. The stable slaves haven't figured out the cinches yet. I put some revolver bullets in the straw when I set fire to that grain shed. They're going off from time to time."

A figure with whip and dagger raced around an outbuilding and confronted them. Blake shot him down.

Minott said hoarsely: "Give me a revolver, Blake! I want to——"

"Horses first!" snapped Blake.

They raced into a courtyard. Two shots. The slaves fled, howling. Out of the courtyard, bent low in the saddle. They swept close to the villa itself. On a little raised terrace before it, a stout man in an only slightly modified toga raged. A slave groveled before him. He kicked the abject figure and strode out, shouting commands in a voice that cracked with fury. The horses loomed up and he shook his fists at the riders, purple with wrath, incapable of fear because of his beastly rage.

Blake shot him dead, swung off his horse, and stripped the toga from him. He flung it to Maida.

"Take this!" he said savagely. "I could kill——"

There was now no question of his leadership. He led the retreat from the villa. The eight horses headed north again, straight for the luridly flaming forest.

They stopped once more. Behind them, another building of the estate had caught from the first. Sheer confusion ruled. The slaughter of the master disrupted all organization. The roof of the slave barracks caught: Screams and howls of pure panic reached even the fugitives. Then there were racing, maddened figures rushing here and there in the glare of the fires. Suddenly there was fighting. A howling ululation arose.

Minott worked savagely, stripping clothing from the bodies slain in that incredible, unrecorded conflict of Confederate soldiers and Roman troops, in some unguessable pathway of space and time. Blake watched behind, but he curtly commanded the salvaging of rifles and ammunition from the dead Confederates—if they were Confederates.

And as Hunter, still gasping hysterically, took the load of yet unfamiliar weapons upon his horse, the eight felt a certain incredible, intolerable vertigo and nausea. The burning forest ahead vanished from their sight. Instead, there was darkness. A noisome smell came down wind; dampness and strange, overpowering perfumes of strange, colored flowers. Something huge and deadly bellowed in the space before them which smelled like a monstrous swamp.

The liner *City of Baltimore* plowed through the open sea in the first pale light of dawn. The skipper, up on the bridge, wore a worried frown. The radio operator came up. He carried a sheaf of radiogram forms. His eyes were blurry with loss of sleep.

"Maybe it was me, sir," he reported heavily. "I felt awful funny for a while last night, and then all night long I couldn't raise a station. I checked everything and couldn't find anything wrong. But just now I felt awful sick and funny for a minute, and when I come out of it the air was full of code. Here's some of it. I don't understand how I could have been sick so I couldn't hear code, sir, but——"

The skipper said abruptly: "I had that sick feeling, too—dizzy. So did the man at the wheel. So did everybody. Give me the messages."

His eyes ran swiftly over the yellow forms.

"News flash: Half of London disappeared at 2:00 a. m. this morning. . . . S.S. *Manzanillo* reporting. Sea serpent which attacked this ship during the night and seized four sailors returned and was rammed five minutes ago. It seems to be dying. Our bow badly smashed. Two forward compartments flooded. . . . Warning to all mariners. Pack ice seen floating fifty miles off New York harbor. . . . News flash: Madrid, Spain, has undergone inexplicable change. All buildings formerly known now unrecognizable from the air. Air fields have vanished. Mosques seem to have taken the place of churches and cathedrals. A flag bearing the crescent floats. . . . European population of Calcutta seems to have been massacred. S.S. *Carib* reports harbor empty, all signs of European domination vanished, and hostile mobs lining shore. . . ."

The skipper of the *City of Baltimore* passed his hand over his forehead. He looked uneasily at the radio operator. "Sparks," he said gently, "you'd better go see the ship's doctor. Here! I'll detail a man to go with you."

"I know," said Sparks bitterly. "I guess I'm nuts, all right. But that's what come through."

He marched away with his head hanging, escorted by a sailor. A little speck of smoke appeared dead ahead. It became swiftly larger. With the combined speed of the two vessels, in a quarter of an hour the other ship was visible. In half an hour it could be made out clearly. It was long and low and painted black, but the first incredible thing was that it was a paddle steamer, with two sets of paddles instead of one, and the after set revolving more swiftly than the forward.

The skipper of the *City of Baltimore* looked more closely through his glasses and nearly dropped them in stark amazement. The flag flying on the other ship was black and white only. A beam wind blew it out swiftly. A white death's-head, with two crossed bones below it—the traditional flag of piracy!

Signal flags fluttered up in the rigging of the other ship. The skipper of the *City of Baltimore* gazed at them, stunned.

"Gibberish!" he muttered. "It don't make sense! They aren't international code. Not the same flags at all!"

Then a gun spoke. A monstrous puff of black powder smoke billowed over the other ship's bow. A heavy shot crashed into the forepart of the *City of Baltimore*: An instant later it exploded.

"I'm crazy, too!" said the skipper dazedly.

A second shot. A third and fourth. The black steamer sheered off and started to pound the *City of Baltimore* in a businesslike fashion. Half the bridge went overside. The forward cargo hatch blew up with a cloud of smoke from an explosion underneath.

Then the skipper came to. He roared orders. The big ship heeled as it came around. It plunged forward at vastly more than its normal cruising speed. The guns on the other ship doubled and redoubled their rate of fire. Then the black ship tried to dodge. But it had not time.

The *City of Baltimore* rammed it. But at the very last moment the skipper felt certain of his own insanity. It was too late to save the other ship then. The *City of Baltimore* cut it in two.

XII.

The pale gray light of dawn filtered down through an incredible thickness of foliage. It was a subdued, a feeble twilight when it reached the earth where a tiny camp fire burned. That fire gave off thick smoke from water-soaked wood. Hunter tended it, clad in ill-assorted remnants of a gray uniform.

Harris worked patiently at a rifle, trying to understand exactly how it worked. It was unlike any rifle with which he was familiar. The bolt action was not really a bolt action at all, and he'd noticed that there was no rifling in the barrel. He was trying to understand how the long bullet was made to revolve. Harris, too, had substituted Confederate gray for the loin cloth flung him for sole covering when with the others he was thrust into the slave pen of the Roman villa. Minott sat with his head in his hands, staring at the opposite side of the stream. On his face was all bitterness.

Blake listened. Maida Haynes sat and looked at him. Lucy Blair darted furtive, somehow wistful, glances at Minott. Presently she moved to sit beside him. She asked him an anxious question. The other two girls sat by the fire. Bertha Ketterling was slouched back against a tree-fern trunk. Her head had fallen back. She snored. With the exception of Blake, all of them were barefoot.

Blake came back to the fire. He nodded across the little stream. "We seem to have come to the edge of a time fault," he observed. "This side of the stream is definitely Carboniferous-period vegetation. The other side isn't as primitive, but it isn't of our time, anyhow. Professor Minott!"

Minott lifted his head. "Well?" he demanded bitterly.

"We need some information," said Blake. "We've been here for hours, and there's been no further change in time paths that we've noticed. Is it likely that the scrambling of time and space is ended, sir? If it has, and the time paths stay jumbled, we'll never find our world intact, of course, but we can hunt for colonies, perhaps even cities, of our own kind of people."

"If we do," said Minott bitterly, "how far will we get? We're practically unarmed. We can't——"

Blake pointed to the salvaged rifles. "Harris is working on the arms problem now," he said dryly. "Besides, the girls didn't take the revolvers from their saddlebags. We've still two revolvers for each man and an extra pair. Those Romans thought the saddlebags were decorations, perhaps, or they intended to examine the saddles as a whole. We'll make out. What I want to know is, has the time-scrambling process stopped?"

Lucy Blair said something in a low tone. But Minott glanced at Maida Haynes. She was regarding Blake worshipfully.

Minott's eyes burned. He scowled in surpassing bitterness. "It probably hasn't," he said harshly. "I expect it to keep up for probably two weeks or more of—of duration. I use that term to mean time elapsed in all the time paths simultaneously. We can't help thinking of time as passing on our particular time path only. Yes. I expect disturbances to continue for two weeks or more, if everything in time and space is not annihilated."

Blake sat down.

Insensibly Maida Haynes moved closer to him. "Could you explain, sir?

We can only wait here. As nearly as I can tell from the topography, there's a village across this little stream in our time. It ought to be in sight if our time path ever turns up in view, here."

Minott unconsciously reassumed some of his former authoritative manner. Their capture and scornful dismissal to the status of slaves had shaken all his self-confidence. Before, he had felt himself not only a member of a superior race, but a superior member of that race. In being enslaved he had been both degraded and scorned. His vanity was still gnawed at by that memory, and his self-confidence shattered by the fact that he had been able to kill only two utterly brutalized slaves, without in the least contributing to his own freedom. Now, for the first time, his voice took on a semblance of its old ring.

"We—we know that gravity warps space," he said precisely. "From observation we have been able to discover the amount of warping produced by a given mass. We can calculate the mass necessary to warp space so that it will close in completely, making a closed universe which is unreachable and undetectable in any of the dimensions we know. We know, for example, that if two gigantic star masses of a certain combined mass were to rush together, at the instant of their collision there would not be a great cataclysm. They would simply vanish. But they would not cease to exist. They would merely cease to exist in our space and time. They would have created a space and time of their own."

Harris said apologetically, "Like crawling in a hole and pulling the hole in after you. I read something like that in a Sunday supplement once, sir."

Minott nodded. He went on in a near approach to a classroom manner. "Now, imagine that two such universes have been formed. They are both invisible from the space and time in which they were formed. Each exists in its own space and time, just as our universe does. But each must also exist in a certain—well, hyper-space, because if closed spaces are separated, there must be some sort of something in between them, else they would be together."

"Really," said Blake, "you're talking about something we can infer, but ordinarily can't possibly learn anything about by observation."

"Just so." Minott nodded. "Still, if our space is closed, we must assume that there are other closed spaces. And don't forget that other closed spaces would be as real—are as real—as our closed space is."

"But what does it mean?" asked Blake.

"If there are other closed spaces like ours, and they exist in a common medium—the hyper-space from which they and we alike are sealed off— they might be likened to, say, stars and planets in our space, which are separated by space and yet affect each other through space. Since these various closed spaces are separated by a logically necessary hyper-space, it is at least probable that they should affect each other through that hyper-space."

Blake said slowly: "Then the shiftings of time paths—well, they're the result of something on the order of tidal strains. If another star got close to the sun, our planets would crack up from tidal strains alone. You're suggesting that another closed space has got close to our closed space in hyper-space. It's awfully confused, sir."

"I have calculated it," said Minott harshly. "The odds are four to one that space and time and universe, every star and every galaxy in the skies, will be obliterated in one monstrous cataclysm when even the past will never have been. But there is one chance in four, and I planned to take full advantage of it. I planned—I planned——"

Then he stood up suddenly. His figure straightened. He struck his hands together savagely. "By Heaven, I still plan! We have arms. We have books, technical knowledge, formulas—the cream of the technical knowledge of earth packed in our saddlebags! Listen to me! We cross this stream now. When the next change comes, we strike across whatever time path takes the place of this. We make for the Potomac, where that aviator saw Norse ships drawn up! I have Anglo-Saxon and early Norse vocabularies in the saddlebags. We'll make friends with them. We'll teach them. We'll lead them. We'll make ourselves masters of the world and——"

Harris said apologetically: "I'm sorry, sir, but I promised Bertha I'd take her home, if it was humanly possible. I have to do it. I can't join you in becoming an emperor, even if the breaks are right."

Minott scowled at him.

"Hunter?"

"I—I'll do as the others do," said Hunter uneasily. "I—I'd rather go home."

"Fool!" snarled Minott.

Lucy Blair said loyally: "I—I'd like to be an empress, Professor Minott."

Maida Haynes stared at her. She opened her mouth to speak. Blake absently pulled a revolver from his pocket and looked at it meditatively as Minott clenched and unclenched his hands. The veins stood out on his forehead. He began to breathe heavily.

"Fools!" he roared. "Fools! You'll never get back! Yet you throw away——"

Swift, sharp, agonizing vertigo smote them all. The revolver fell from Blake's hands. He looked up. A dead silence fell upon all of them.

Blake stood shakily upon his feet. He looked, and looked again. "That——" He swallowed. "That is King George courthouse, in King George County, in Virginia, in our time I think—— Hell! Let's get across that stream."

He picked up Maida in his arms. He started.

Minott moved quickly and croaked: "Wait!"

He had Blake's dropped revolver in his hand. He was desperate, hunted; gray with rage and despair. "I—I offer you, for the last time—I offer you riches, power, women and——"

Harris stood up, the Confederate rifle still in his hands. He brought the barrel down smartly upon Minott's wrist.

Blake waded across and put Maida safely down upon the shore. Hunter was splashing frantically through the shallow water. Harris was shaking Bertha Ketterling to wake her. Blake splashed back. He rounded up the horses. He loaded the salvaged weapons over a saddle. He shepherded the three remaining girls over. Hunter was out of sight. He had fled toward the painted buildings of the courthouse. Blake led the horses across the stream. Minott nursed his numbed wrist. His eyes blazed with the fury of utter despair.

"Better come along," said Blake quietly.

"And be a professor of mathematics?" Minott laughed savagely. "No! I stay here!"

Blake considered. Minott was a strange, an unprepossessing figure. He was haggard. He was desperate. Standing against the background of a carboniferous jungle, in the misfitting uniform he had stripped from a dead man in some other path of time, he was even pitiable. Shoeless, unshaven, desperate, he was utterly defiant.

"Wait!" said Blake.

He stripped off the saddlebags from six of the horses. He heaped them on the remaining two. He led those two back across the stream and tethered them.

Minott regarded him with an implacable hatred. "If I hadn't chosen you," he said harshly, "I'd have carried my original plan through. I knew I shouldn't choose you. Maida liked you too well. And I wanted her for myself. It was my mistake, my only one."

Blake shrugged. He went back across the stream and remounted.

Lucy Blair looked doubtfully back at the solitary, savage figure. "He's —brave, anyhow," she said unhappily.

A faint, almost imperceptible, dizziness affected all of them. It passed. By instinct they looked back at the tall jungle. It still stood. Minott looked bitterly after them.

"I've—I've something I want to say!" said Lucy Blair breathlessly. "D-don't wait for me!"

She wheeled her horse about and rode for the stream. Again that faint, nearly imperceptible, dizziness. Lucy slapped her horse's flank frantically.

Maida cried out: "Wait, Lucy! It's going to shift——"

And Lucy cried over her shoulder: "That's what I want! I'm going to stay——"

She was halfway across the stream—more than halfway. Then the vertigo struck all of them.

XIII.

Every one knows the rest of the story. For two weeks longer there were still occasional shiftings of the time paths. But gradually it became noticeable that the number of time faults—in Professor Minott's phrase—were decreasing in number. At the most drastic period, it has been estimated that no less than twenty-five per cent of the whole earth's surface was at a given moment in some other time path than its own. We do not know of any portion of the earth which did not vary from its own time path at some period of the disturbance.

That means, of course, that practically one hundred per cent of the earth's population encountered the conditions caused by the earth's extraordinary oscillations sidewise in time. Our scientists are no longer quite as dogmatic as they used to be. The dialectics of philosophy have received a serious jolt. Basic ideas in botany, zoölogy, and even philology have been altered by the new facts made available by our travels sidewise in time.

Because of course it was the fourth chance which happened, and the earth survived. In our time path, at any rate. The survivors of Minott's exploring party reached King George courthouse barely a quarter of an hour after the time shift which carried Minott and Lucy Blair out of our space and time forever. Blake and Harris searched for a means of transmitting the information they possessed to the world at large. Through a lonely radio amateur a mile from the village, they sent out Minott's theory on short waves. Shorn of Minott's pessimistic analysis of the probabilities of survival, it went swiftly to every part of the world then in its proper relative position. It was valuable, in that it checked explorations in force which in some places had been planned. It prevented, for example a punitive military expedition from going past a time fault in Georgia, past which a scalping party of Indians from an uncivilized America had retreated. It prevented the dispatch of a squadron of destroyers to find and seize Leifsholm, from which a viking foray had been made upon North Centerville, Massachusetts. A squadron of mapping planes was recalled from reconnaissance work above a carboniferous swamp in West Virginia, just before the time shift which would have isolated them forever.

Some things, though, no knowledge could prevent. It has been estimated that no less than five thousand persons in the United States are missing from their own space and time, through having adventured into the strange landscapes which appeared so suddenly. Many must have perished. Some, we feel sure, have come in contact with one or another of the distinct civilizations we now know exist.

Conversely, we have gained inhabitants from other time paths. Two cohorts of the Twenty-second Roman Legion were left upon our soil near Ithaca, New York. Four families of Chinese peasants essayed to pick berries in what they considered a miraculous strawberry-patch in Virginia, and remained there when that section of ground returned to its proper *milieu.*

A Russian village remains in Colorada. A French settlement in the— in their time undeveloped—Middle West. A part of the northern herd of buffalo has returned to us, two hundred thousand strong, together with a village of Cheyenne Indians who had never seen either horses or fire-arms. The passenger pigeon, to the number of a billion and a half birds, has returned to North America.

But our losses are heavy. Besides those daring individuals who were carried away upon the strange territories they were exploring, there are the overwhelming disasters affecting Tokyo and Rio de Janeiro and Detroit. The first two we understand. When the causes of oscillation sidewise in time were removed, most of the earth sections returned to their proper positions in their own time paths. But not all. There is a section of Post-Cambrian jungle left in eastern Tennessee. The Russian village in Colorado has been mentioned, and the French trading post in the Middle West. In some cases sections of the oscillating time paths remained in new positions, remote from their points of origin.

That is the cause of the utter disappearance of Rio and of Tokyo. Where Rio stood, an untouched jungle remains. It is of our own geological period, but it is simply from a path in time in which Rio de Janeiro never happened to be built. On the site of Tokyo stands a forest of extraordinarily primitive type, about which botanists and paleontologists still debate. Somewhere, in some space and time, Tokyo and Rio yet exist and their people still live on. But Detroit——

We still do not understand what happened to Detroit. It was upon an oscillating segment of earth. It vanished from our time, and it returned to our time. But its inhabitants did not come back with it. The city was empty—deserted as if the hundreds of thousands of human beings who lived in it had simply evaporated into the air. There have been some few signs of struggle seen, but they may have been the result of panic. The city of Detroit returned to its own space and time untouched, unharmed, unlooted, and undisturbed. But no living thing, not even a domestic animal or a caged bird, was in it when it came back. We do not understand that at all.

Perhaps if Professor Minott had returned to us, he could have guessed at the answer to the riddle. What fragmentary papers of his have been shown to refer to the time upheaval have been of inestimable value. Our whole theory of what happened depends on the papers Minott left behind as too unimportant to bother with, in addition, of course, to Blake's and Harris' account of his explanation to them. Tom Hunter can remember little that is useful. Maida Haynes has given some worth-while data, but it covers ground we have other observers for. Bertha Ketterling also reports very little.

The answers to myriad problems yet elude us, but in the saddlebags given to Minott by Blake as equipment for his desperate journey through space and time, the answers to many must remain. Our scientists labor diligently to understand and to elaborate the figures Minott thought of trivial significance. And throughout the world many minds turn longingly to certain saddlebags, loaded on a led horse, following Minott and Lucy Blair through unguessable landscapes, to unimaginable adventures, with revolvers and textbooks as their armament for the conquest of a world.

"Sidewise in Time" was one of those stories that had a long-term effect on my thinking. It made me always conscious of the "ifs" of history, and this showed up not only in my science fiction, as in *The Red Queen's Race*, but in my serious books on history as well. I also used the alternate-history theme, in enormous complexity, in my novel *The End of Eternity*.

Science fiction itself advanced with time. When a new concept arose which clearly, in its sophistication and truth, replaced an older and cruder one, it was almost invariably recognized at once by the readers. And while the older and cruder concept did not entirely disappear (what ever entirely disappears?), it was relegated to the less important corners of the field.

For instance, H. G. Wells had written the first science fiction story ever to deal realistically with intelligent organisms of another world. That story was *The War of the Worlds* published in 1898, and the organisms were Martians. From the title alone, you can guess that the Martians came to Earth in order to take it over, which was a natural thought at the time, since that was what Europeans were doing to Africa.

Wells's influence was forceful, and for forty years extraterrestrial invasion was a common theme for science fiction stories. Extraterrestrials were always intent on conquest, cared nothing for human life, and displayed no interest in human culture. Among the stories in this volume, "Tetrahedra of Space" and the Tumithak stories are examples, with invaders from Mercury and Venus, respectively.

Occasionally another view was presented, as in the sympathetic portrait of the Mother in Williamson's "The Moon Era," but it weighed little in comparison. In the December 1934 issue of *Astounding Stories*, however, Raymond Z. Gallun had a story, "Old Faithful," that really forced a change.

OLD FAITHFUL

by Raymond Z. Gallun

If Number 774 had been a human being, he might have cursed bitterly or he might have wept. Certainly he had reason to do so. But Number 774 was not a human being. His fragile form bore not the slightest resemblance to that of a man; he knew nothing of smiles or frowns or tears, and whatever emotions passed within his cool, keen mind were hidden even to members of his own race.

The two messengers who had come to his workshop that afternoon had not seen into his heart, and he received their message with the absolute outward calm that was characteristic of his kind—at the end of forty days Number 774 must die. He had lived the allotted span fixed by the Rulers.

With food and water as scarce as they were, no one had the right to live longer unless he had proved through the usefulness of his achievements that it was for the good of all that he be granted an extension. Otherwise the young and strong must always replace the old and weak.

In the opinion of the Rulers the work of Number 774 was not useful; it was without value and was even wasteful. An extension of life-span could not be considered; Number 774 must die.

Having imparted this information the messengers had crept into the streamlined hull of their ornithopter. Silvery wings had flapped, and the weird craft had lifted lightly, circled the great isolated workshop once in parting salute, and then had sped off into the west toward a distant city.

In obedience to some impulse Number 774 had ascended to a high-placed window in the towering wall of his domicile, to watch the ornithopter go. But long after the glinting metallic speck of its form had vanished into the sunset, Number 774 continued to stare out toward the west. Pools of purple shade swelled and broadened in the hollows between the dunes of the Martian desert that stretched in undulating flatness to the far horizon.

The sun sank out of sight, leaving only a faint reddish glow that quickly faded out at the rim of the world. The Martian sky, deep purple and shot with stars even during the day, became almost black, and the stars, veiled by an atmosphere only one-sixth as dense as that of Earth, gleamed with a steady and eerie brilliance that is never seen by terrestrial observers.

It was a strange, beautiful sight, and perhaps in other circumstances something fine and paradoxically human in Number 774's being might have appreciated its wild and lonely grandeur. But natural splendors could scarcely have interested him now, for his mind was too full of other things.

In the sky was a tiny gray-green streak which he knew marked the position of an approaching comet. For a long moment he stared at it; and then his gaze wandered up among the welter of stars and sought out a greenish silver speck far brighter than any of its fellows.

For many minutes his attention clung unwavering to that brilliant point of light. He knew more about that planet than any other inhabitant of Mars. He had never heard its name, nor in fact did he have a vocal name of his own for it. To him it was just the world which held the third orbital position in order from the sun. And yet, for him, there was concentrated in it all the hopes and all the fascination of a lifetime of painstaking work and effort.

Gradually, by patient, methodical observation, he had wrested a few of its secrets from it. He had learned the composition of its atmosphere; he could describe its climates accurately; he even knew something about its soil. But beyond such superficial information for a long time it seemed that he could never go.

And then one night when, with stoical resignation, he had all but laid aside his fondest dream, a sign had come. The third planet, Earth, was inhabited by thinking beings. It was not a spectacular sign; neither was his conclusion guesswork. Number 774's telescope had revealed, on the darkened side of Earth, between the limbs of its crescent, a barely discernible flicker of light flashes, evenly spaced, and repeated at perfectly regular intervals. Only a high order of intelligence could have produced such signals.

Dominated by a new zeal, Number 774 had constructed a gigantic apparatus and had duplicated the Earthian signals flash for flash. Immediately he had been answered. Then he had tried a new arrangement of flashes, and the unknown beings on Planet Three had seen, for they had repeated his signals perfectly.

For five Martian years, the equivalent of nearly ten passages of the Earth around the sun, he and the unimaginable entities on that other world, hardly ever less than thirty-five million miles away, had labored on the colossal problem of intelligent communication.

The results of their efforts had been small and discouraging; yet in ten or twenty years even that gigantic enigma might have yielded to persistence, ingenuity, and the indomitable will to do. But now no such thing could be. In forty days Number 774 would no longer exist. Nor would there be another to carry on his work.

Study of the third world could not produce more food or make water more plentiful. The Rulers would dismantle all the marvelous equipment that he had assembled to aid him in his quest for useless and impractical knowledge. The veil of mystery would remain drawn over Planet Three for many thousands of years, perhaps forever.

But it was the Rulers' privilege to command and to expect unquestioning obedience. Never once in a millennium had their authority been disputed; for the very existence of the dominant race of Mars, a world aged almost to the limit of its ability to support life, depended on absolute spartan loyalty and discipline. Revolt now was unheard of; it could not be.

Did Number 774 feel resentment over his fate? Or did he accept his sentence with the stoicism of a true child of Mars? There was no way of telling. His position was almost unduplicated in the annals of the Red Planet, and, in consequence, his reactions may have been out of the ordinary. Almost never before had a creature of his kind wandered so far along the road of impractical knowledge, or had received the notice of the termination of life-span so inopportunely.

And so Number 774 continued to gaze up at the green star that had been included in every dream and effort of his existence. Thoughts and feelings must have tumbled in riotous confusion inside his brain.

After a while Phobos, the nearer moon, mounted up over the western* horizon and began its rapid march among the stars. Its pallid radiance converted everything into a half-seen fairyland of tarnished silver and ebony, the dunes of the lonely desert extending mile on mile in every direction, the low, fortlike walls of Number 774's workshop, the great shining dome of metal that capped it. Nothing was clearly discernible, nothing seemed real.

The coming of Phobos aroused Number 774 from his lethargy. It may be that he realized that time was fleeting, and that an hour could ill be spared from the forty days of life that still remained to him. At a deft touch the crystal pane that glazed the window before him slipped aside,

---

* Mars rotates on its axis in 24 hours, 37 minutes, 22.67 seconds. Phobos, the nearer Moon, which is only 3,700 miles distant from Mars, completes its orbit in only 7 hours, 39 minutes, thus circling its primary more than three times in every Martian day. Since Phobos follows its path in the same direction that the planet rotates, it is evident that to an observer on Mars, it would appear to rise in the west and set in the east.

and a faint night breeze, arid and chilled far below zero, blew in upon him.

Edging his strange form forward, he leaned far out of the window and seemed intent upon creeping headlong down the rough stone wall. Long slender portions of his anatomy clutched the sill, and he hung inverted like a roosting bat of Earth. But otherwise there was not the remotest resemblance between Number 774 and a winged terrestrial mammal.

If, by means of some miraculous transition, an Earthman had suddenly found himself standing there on the desert and looking up at the wall of the workshop close above, he might not even have recognized Number 774 as a living creature in the shifting, uncertain moonlight. Amid the fantastic jumble of light and shade he would have seen only a blob of rusty brown color that might have been just the distorted shadow of one of the stone projections that jutted from the wall.

If he had looked closer he might have believed that the thing he saw was a small bundle of ancient and rotten rags dangling from the window ledge, with long, loose tatters stirring idly in the faint breeze. Still, the glint of bright metal from Number 774's equipment would have puzzled him, and perhaps his flesh would have tingled slightly at the suggestively gruesome aspect of this unknown and poorly illuminated object.

From his dangling position Number 774 sucked a great breath of cold air into his complex breathing organs. The frigid tang of the night refreshed him and seemed to endow him with new life. One last glance he cast toward the glory of the Martian heavens. At sight of Earth and the threadlike speck of the comet, his great eyes, dark and limpid and more nearly human than anything else about him, flashed briefly with a vague, slumberous suggestion of something pent up behind a barrier that was none too strong to hold it back. Then Number 774 drew himself up into the window.

Three jointed rods of metal unfolded themselves from the complicated arrangement of mechanisms that was fastened to his fragile body, and in a moment he was striding along on them like a man, down a green-lighted cylindrical passage that extended off into misty obscurity. A faint and regular clicking came from the device, but Number 774 did not hear it. He knew of sound only as a vibration detectable by his keen sense of touch, and as a phenomenon registered by his scientific instruments, for Number 774 had no organs of hearing.

His steps seemed hurried and feverish. Perhaps some un-Martian plan was already half formulated in his restless and troubled mind.

The tunnel debouched at last into a colossal chamber where gigantic flying buttresses swept up and up through a misty green glow to meet the sides of an enormous rotunda of white metal that roofed the room. Enigmatic forms of weird apparatus crowded in bewildering complexity against the walls. Tipped at a steep angle at the center of the floor was a vast cylinder of webby girders. Piercing the dome, opposite the upper end of the cylinder, was a circular opening through which a portion of the starlit sky was visible; and at the base of the cylinder a great bowl rotated rapidly, like a huge wheel.

Here was the observatory of Number 774, housing his telescope, and here were the controlling mechanisms of his signaling apparatus. He hurried up a steep ramp, from the upper end of which he could look down into the interior of the great rotating bowl. His eyes glanced critically over the device, searching for any possible slight disorder in its function. But there was none.

To an Earthman acquainted with astronomical equipment, the purpose of the rotating bowl would have been at once apparent, and he would have marveled at the simple cleverness of this piece of Martian ingenuity.

The bowl contained mercury. As the container spun on its perfectly balanced axis, centrifugal force caused the mercury to spread in a thin, precisely distributed layer over the inside of the bowl, forming a convex surface that acted admirably as a mirror for Number 774's gigantic reflecting telescope. Its area, and its consequent light-collecting capacity, was many times greater than any rigid mirror that could have been constructed without flaws.

Satisfied with his inspection, Number 774 hoisted himself nimbly to a small platform, placed high among the spidery girders of the chamber. His movements were quick and catlike, yet coolly efficient, and he seemed bent upon making use of every moment of life that remained to him.

His eyes almost lambent with eagerness, he stared into the large crystal sphere which the platform supported. From a prismatic arrangement fixed to the telescope arrangement above, an invisible beam of light came down, impinging on the sphere and causing the picture which Number 774 was so intent upon to appear.

In the depths of the crystal was an image of the third world, Earth. Since it was to sunward and nearing inferior conjunction with Mars, most of its surface that was turned to the Red Planet was in shadow and could not be seen. Only a thin curve of light fringed one hemisphere.

Visible in the crescent were mottled areas of gray and green and brown, which Number 774 knew were oceans, continents, deserts, and verdant countryside. The shifting blurs of clouds, the winding rivers, and the snow-capped mountain chains, he could recognize and understand, too; but there was so much that distance and the distorting effects of two atmospheres left hidden and seemingly unattainable—things about which he had longed so passionately to see and to know.

A delicate bundle of pink filaments that terminated one of Number 774's stalklike limbs rested on a tiny lever before him. The threadlike tentacles, marvelously adapted and trained for the finest and most accurate sort of work, moved the lever slightly to the right.

Immediately there was responding movement in the heavy parts of the huge telescope, and the image of Planet Three in the crystal globe began to grow. Mountains loomed larger; seas and continents swelled until the whole of the image of the terrestrial sphere could not occupy the globe, and all that could be seen was a small part of the illuminated crescent.

For a while, as the increase in magnification went on, details on Planet Three were brought more clearly into view; but presently, as the picture grew larger and larger, it began to tremble and to undulate, as if it were seen through a million atmospheric heat waves.

As the power of the telescope was increased still further, the flickering, jumping, shifting luminescence that appeared in the vision globe became totally incoherent and meaningless and bore no slight relationship to an Earthly scene. Number 774's huge optical instrument was failing before one of the same obstacles to magnification that terrestrial observers have noted in their telescopes.

The gaseous envelopes of Earth and Mars, with their countless irregular air currents and varying indices of refraction due to differences in temperature and humidity, were distorting the image-bearing rays of light coming from Earth across fifty million miles of space and rendering magnification beyond a certain point useless. The telescope of Number 774 still had many Martian units of magnification in reserve, but for probing into the mysteries of Planet Three that reserve was of not the least value.

Still, Number 774 often gave his instrument full power in the vain hope, perhaps, that some day, by some trick of fate, the atmospheres of the two worlds would be quiet enough and clear enough to give him a momentary glimpse into the unknown. But the opportunity for such a glimpse had never come.

Cool and collected, Number 774 brought his telescope back to the limit of effective magnification. In response to the manipulation of some instrument, the image of Planet Three shifted so that no portion of the crescent was visible. The crystal globe was dark, but Number 774 knew that the third world was within the field of view.

Unerringly, guided by his instruments, he fixed his telescope on a certain spot on the dark side of Planet Three. He knew that shrouded in the shadows of the night hemisphere of that distant world there was a great continent extending broad and diversified, between two vast oceans. It had lofty ranges of snow-crowned mountains, extensive plains green with an unknown vegetation, great lakes, and winding rivers. In the southwestern portion of that continent was a desert, and near the edge of that desert was the Place of the Light—the light that was the voice of the friend he had never seen, and whose form was unimaginable to him, much though he might imagine and long to know.

The light was not there now; only the vague, white blurs of Earthly cities dotting the darkened continent, adding the mystery of their existence to the enigma of Planet Three. But Number 774 was not troubled by the absence of the light, for he had faith in it. When he had signaled, it had always appeared in answer; it would appear this time, too.

At his touch a vast mechanism in a room far beneath the chamber of the telescope began to function silently and efficiently, building up power. Feeble and delicate and hideous though Number 774 was by Earthly standards, at a mere gesture he could evoke forces that were worthy of the gods.

Number 774 watched a Martian version of a potentiometer. It was not like a terrestrial potentiometer. It had no graduated scale, no nervous pointer. It was just a globe of something that looked like frosted glass, from which a soft luminescence proceeded.

First, Number 774 saw in its depths a slumberous glow of a beautiful shade, quite unknown and unseeable to human eyes. It was what is called infrared on Earth. The color, being invisible to men, was of course quite indescribable, but to Number 774 it was as common as blue or yellow, for his eyes, like the eyes of some of the lower forms of Earth, were constructed to see it.

In addition, like all Martians, he was able to distinguish the slightest difference between one shade of color and another.

It is upon this fact that Martians depend for the accurate reading of instruments which, among men, would ordinarily have pointers and graduated scales. In any Martian meter, infrared, and of course the various shades of infrared, in their order of appearance in the spectrum, means a low reading. Red, and the shades of red, advancing toward orange, constitute somewhat higher readings. Orange, yellow, green, blue, and violet are progressively higher; while the shade at the extreme outer end of the ultraviolet band, which Martian eyes can also see, represents the highest reading.

In short, light of various wavelengths is used in practically all Martian meters to designate readings. Low readings are represented by long wavelengths near the infrared end of the spectrum; while high readings are designated by short wavelengths near the ultraviolet end of the spectrum.

Number 774 waited until the changing kaleidoscope of ordinary colors had passed and the delicate hue of ultraviolet had reached its maximum in the globe of the potentiometer before he made any further move. Then his tense body swayed forward, closing a complicated switch.

The result was instantaneous. Through the circular opening in the rotunda, at which the muzzle of the telescope was pointed, a dazzling blaze of incandescence was visible in a sudden tremendous flash. The detonation that accompanied it was of a magnitude which one would have scarcely believed the rarefied atmosphere of old Mars capable of transmitting. The whole building, solidly constructed though it was, trembled with the concussion.

For a moment the Martian night, within a radius of twenty miles or more of Number 774's workshop, became brighter than midday, as an enormous store of energy, released from the outer surface of the metal dome which capped the observatory, poured suddenly into the atmosphere, thus forming above the workshop a vast canopy of cold light, far more intense than any aurora borealis of Earth.

But the sudden flare died out as quickly as it had come; the echoes of the crash faded, and the calm of lonely desert and stars reasserted itself. Some eerie monster, which had unwittingly buried itself in the sand too close to the lair of Number 774, scrambled out of its warm sleeping place amid a cloud of dust and on gauzy wings sped hurriedly away from the zone of the thunder that had terrified it. As it flew, its fantastic shadow bobbed crazily over the moonlit sand.

But Number 774 was quite oblivious of any fears his experiments might arouse in the creatures of Mars. As far as his mind was concerned, for the time being things Martian had almost ceased to exist for him. Earth, Planet Three, claimed all his attention, and there was room for nothing else. He had given his sign; now he would wait for the answer that was sure to come.

It would take approximately nine minutes for Earth to get signals back to him. For that was the time which light, traveling at a speed of 186,000 miles per second, required to bridge twice the fifty-million-mile void lying between the two planets.

Number 774's weird, fragile body hunched eagerly forward on the small mat on which he squatted. His great eyes burned with the same fire of fascination which they had held when, a little while ago, he had gazed up at Earth and the approaching comet from the window in the wall of his workshop. Unwaveringly they were fixed on the spot in the darkened vision globe where the light would appear.

Sometimes that light was too dim for his trained and sensitive eyes to see; but arranged and hooded on a carefully shaded portion of the vision globe was a Martian photoelectric cell which would pick up the faintest of light signals and convert them into electrical impulses which would be amplified and relayed to an instrument close beside Number 774.

This instrument would reproduce the signals just as they came from Earth, but bright enough to be easily watched. Another device would record each flash for later study.

II

The body of Number 774 tensed suddenly. There was the first signal, flickering faint and feeble across the millions of miles of space; yet on the desert of Earth it doubtless represented flashes almost comparable with those which Number 774's powerful sending equipment produced.

Number 774 could barely see them in his vision globe, but the little glass bulb of the reproducing apparatus flickered them out plain and clear—long flashes, short flashes, representing the dots and dashes of the Morse code of Earth.

Flash—flash—flash—flash——

"Hello, Mars! Hello, Mars! Hello, Mars! Earth calling. Earth calling. Earth calling," the message spelled, and Number 774 was grimly in the midst of the colossal task he had set for himself.

Lurking in the back of his mind was the realization that his death was decreed and that soon, unless something unprecedented happened, all this work of his, and of his friend of the light, must end, unfinished, before the intelligences of two worlds could really meet and exchange ideas freely. But it did not divert him or make his attention to the task in hand less keen. In fact it seemed to sharpen his wits and to add pressure to his determination.

Still, his mind seemed divided into two parts, one of which was cool and logical and scientific, the other in a turmoil, fighting with itself and its loyalty to time-honored traditions.

"Hello, Mars! Hello, Mars! Earth calling. Man of Mars is late—late—late—late—— One, two, three, four, five, six, seven, eight, nine, ten. Four and five are nine. Two times three is six. Man of Mars is late—late—late—late—"

How much of this queer jangle of light flashes, spelling out Earth words and numbers in the Morse code did Number 774 understand? How much could he understand?

Intelligent comprehension of anything new is almost always based on an understanding of similar things previously in the experience of the individual in question. The mind of Number 774 was brilliantly clever and methodical, but what can an Earthman and a Martian have in common? Many points of contact exist, it is true, but for two entities so far removed from one another in physical form, senses, environment, and modes of living, with not the vaguest conception of what the other upon the distant world is like, such similarities of experience are extremely hard to find.

In the first place, the messages that were coming to Number 774 were the code representations of alphabetical letters standing for various sounds which, when taken in groups, made up words of vocal speech.

As previously stated, Number 774 had no idea of sound except as an interesting phenomenon recorded by his scientific instruments, and as a vibration detectable by his touch sense in the same way that human beings can feel sound vibrations in solid objects. He had no ears; neither did he have well-developed vocal organs.

Strange as it may seem to us, prior to his experience with the light, he had not the faintest idea of what a word was, either a vocal word or a written word, or a word represented in the form of a group of signals. Because Martian methods of communicating with one another, and of recording knowledge, are so different from ours that a word would have been as great a mystery to him as it would have been to a newborn kitten.

Describing sound to him, as we know it through our sense of hearing, would have been as hopeless a task as describing red to a man who has been stone-blind since birth. It simply could not be done. He might know that sound and vocal speech existed, but short of trading actual sensations with an Earthman, he could never fully comprehend. Neither could he have told us in any way how the color of ultraviolet or infrared looked, for such things are totally out of our experience.

In the face of these enormous handicaps, in spite of his intelligence and scientific knowledge, he had been like a little child, humbly and intensely eager to learn, yet bungling and quick to make mistakes which, from an Earthman's point of view, would often have seemed more than childish.

Once he had tried a method of his own of establishing communication. If Earth had been peopled by a race physically and psychologically similar to the Martians, quick success might have been expected; but his efforts had evoked only a, to him, meaningless jumble of flashes from the light. Realizing that his method was not suited to Earthmen, he had given up trying to be teacher and had assumed instead the rôle of conscientious pupil.

"Hello, Mars!" Those two groups of symbols had always been the beginning of every message flashed by the light; but except for seeing the unmistakable evidence of intelligence in the oft-repeated and unvarying signal, Number 774 had been quite unable at first to grasp in it any thread of meaning.

A greeting phrase was, if possible, even more incomprehensible to him than a word itself. Try as he might, he could not understand. On Mars, where speech is not the mode of communication, greeting phrases did not exist.

Then Earthly genius, doubtless assisted a great deal by chance, had come to his aid. Number 774 had no difficulty in separating the twenty-six alphabetical symbols of the Morse code. Nor when the Earth entities, controlling the flickerings of the light, had sent out code symbols for numerals in a sequence of 0, 1, 2, 3, 4, 5, and so on, did he have any trouble in recognizing and cataloguing each separate signal, though their meanings were still entirely unfathomable to him.

It was when the counting proceeded above nine, and numbers of more than one digit appeared, that Number 774, after a long period of association with the riddle, had received his first faint glimmer of understanding. No; it was not really understanding yet; just a vague, intuitive intimation that something concrete and graspable was not far off.

He had noted that there were but ten separate signals in this strange system, which was apparently quite distinct from that other mysterious system of twenty-six symbols, for the two had never yet been mixed in one signal group or word; and that, as the flashing of the signals proceeded, each symbol seemed to bear a definite relationship to the others.

They always were in fixed sequence. 1 was followed by 2, 2 by 3, and so on through a sequence of ten. The first symbol of a two-digit number was always repeated ten times as the counting went on, while the second symbol changed according to the fixed rule which he had already noted.

Perhaps Number 774 already had a dim notion of the terrestrial numeral system, when his friend of the light conceived the plan of sending simple problems of arithmetic. Obviously, one plus one of anything is two on the planet Mars just as certainly as it is on Earth.

There was the real beginning. Number 774 had studied carefully the simple equations that had come to him, and at length he had been able to grasp what was meant. In a message like "3 and 3 are 6" he was presently able to see the relationship between the numeral signals. The last in the group was the sum of the preceding two.

Finally he understood. Here was some quaint terrestrial method of expressing the unit quantity of anything. The first point of contact between Earth and Mars had been established.

Flushed with success, Number 774 had made rapid progress for a while after he had learned about the terrestrial decimal system. If 3 and 3 are 6, and 2 and 5 are 7, then 4 and 5 are 9. Reproducing faithfully, though without clear comprehension, the intermediate letter groups of the Earthly equation he had invented, "a-n-d" and "a-r-e," he had flashed the equation to his friend of the light: "4 and 5 are 9."

And the answering flicker of the light seemed to dance with an eager exultation: "4 and 5 are 9. 4 and 5 are 9. Yes, yes, yes. 5 and 5 are 10. 8 and 4 are 12. 9 and 7 are? 9 and 7 are?"

Keyed to a high pitch, Number 774 had sensed immediately what was required of him. Answers were wanted. Though two-digit numbers were still something of a mystery to him, making his reply partly guesswork, he lit upon the correct representation of the sum: "9 and 7 are 16."

Through the succeeding months, during which the positions of the two planets were favorable for astronomical observation of each other, the work had gone on, various methods being employed. Sometimes Number 774 presented his own problems of addition, giving the answers. If his answer was correct, the light invariably flashed "Yes, yes, yes," exultantly, and repeated the equation.

On those rare occasions when the problems became more complex, Number 774 made mistakes, the answering message was "No, no, no," and the correction was made.

Thus Number 774 had gained his first knowledge of words, as represented by the twenty-six letter code alphabet. "Yes, yes, yes," meant that he was right, and "no, no, no," meant that he was wrong. It trickled into his mind that each group of alphabetical symbols represented, in its crude way, some definite idea. "And" and "are" in a simple addition problem, showed certain relationships between the numbers; and those relationships were different from the ones expressed by other words.

A mistake he had once made had clearly demonstrated this fact to him. It was in the transition from addition problems to problems of multiplication. 10 and 2 was different from 10 times 2. 10 and 2 made 12, while 10 times 2 made 20. "Times" represented a different relationship between numbers than "and." One indicated that the sum was to be taken, while the other indicated that the two were to be multiplied together.

In a similar way he found out what "divided by," "plus," "minus," and other words meant by noting the relationship of the numbers of the equation to the final answer.

Once understanding simple division as it is done on Earth, Number 774 quickly grasped the decimal-position system of representing fractions. In an equation like $36 \div 5$ equals 7.2, he could substitute Martian methods of representing values and division and correlate them with terrestrial methods. In the Martian way he knew what $36 \div 5$ was, and of course his answer thus obtained might just as well be represented by the Earthly 7.2, for they were the same.

Number 774 had found in the number 3.1416, part of which was a decimal fraction, the relationship of the circumference of a circle to its diameter, and so the oft-repeated message of the light, "Diameter times 3.1416 equals the circumference of a circle," had a certain vague meaning for him that was not by any means completely understandable at once.

"Earth, Planet 3, Mars, Planet 4," was a message he was able to guess the meaning of correctly because in the Martian system numbers were used to designate planets in their order from the sun. Aided by the message, "Earth Planet 3, has 1 moon. Mars, Planet 4, has 2 moons," he had been half able to clinch his guess.

Stumblingly, yet reproducing the Earth words with the faithfulness of a good mimic, he had flashed: "Planet 1 has 0 moon. Planet 2 has 0 moon. Earth, Planet 3, has 1 moon. Mars, Planet 4, has 2—"

And an enthusiastic "yes, yes, yes" had come from the light, and the dim flickering glow had gone on to tell that: "Mercury, Planet 1, has no moon. Venus, Planet 2, has no moon. Jupiter, Planet 5, has 9 moons. Saturn, Planet 6, has 10 moons—" And so on out to Pluto, Planet Nine, beyond Neptune.

Thus Number 774 had learned the names of the planets and the meaning of the words "moon" and "planet." In the same way he received a dim idea of such simple verbs as "has."

And so the process of his Earthly education had gone on, slowly, depending to a large extent upon brilliant though not very certain guesswork, and demanding a degree of patience in instructor and pupil for which teaching a person to talk who has been deaf, blind, and dumb since birth is but a feeble and inadequate analogy.

Number 774 had certain knowledge of a few Earthly words and the privilege of guessing more or less accurately on a number of others. Words like "snow," "clouds," or "storm," he could perhaps gather the general sense of fairly well. For whenever a great atmospheric disturbance appeared over the continent of the light, disturbing observations, the light repeated these words over and over again.

He knew a little about the structure of the simplest of verbs and perhaps somewhat more about the forming of the plurals of nouns by the addition of an "s" symbol. "Hello!" in the phrase "Hello, Mars!" still was beyond him. He could answer it correctly with "Hello, Earth!" knowing that this was the Earthly way; but the human sentiment of the greeting eluded him completely. And of course he had no sound values to give to those Earthly words which he did understand.

Progress had been made, but the forms which the intelligences of Planet Three inhabited, their manner of living, their machines and their accomplishments, were still as much of an enigma as ever. Consummation of the great dream of intelligent communication still belonged to the future, and now there would be no future—only death and a mighty prophecy unfulfilled.

That prophecy had been, and still was, the essence of Number 774's life. In the face of defeat he still worked on the fulfillment of it now, as though a thousand years of usefulness still lay ahead of him. It was habit, perhaps; and meanwhile his mind smoldered with thoughts which we of Earth can only guess at.

"You are late, Man of Mars. Late, late, late," the dim flicker in the vision globe, and the brighter light in the reproducer bulb beside him, spelled; and Number 774 bent to his task.

He understood sketchily most of the message. He knew that the light referred to him as "Man of Mars." He knew that "you are" should be followed by a group of signals describing him. Only "late," the essence of the sentence, the word which gave it sense, was new. What could "late" mean?

Intuition told him that some circumstances which existed only for the present had combined to make him "late," since he had never been called that before. What were those circumstances? He racked his brain over the question. Perhaps the light wished to indicate that he had been delayed in sending out his flash call-signal. But this was only a guess which could be right or wrong.

Still, perhaps it could be clinched. Some other day he might be purposely several minutes behind in sending out his call; then, by way of beginning he could admit that he was "late" and, if his surmise had been correct, the light would confirm it.

But the matter of this new combination of signals could wait now. Number 774 must watch for other, possibly intelligible, things which the light might flash.

"Comet coming. Comet coming. Comet coming," the flicker in the reproducer bulb spelled. "Comet coming toward sun, Mars, and Earth. Comet coming. Comet coming. Comet coming."

If Number 774 had been a man, he might have given a sudden start. And it was not the message itself that would have been responsible, even though he caught some of its meaning. "Comet" was not a word that was new in his experience; for on several occasions when one of those long-tailed wanderers had come back into the solar system, after taking its long dive out toward interstellar space, the light had flashed the information: "Comet coming."

Number 774 knew what "comet" meant, and he could differentiate vaguely between "comet coming" and "comet going," for one indicated that the celestial visitor was entering the solar system, and the other that it was leaving. For several evenings the light had been telling him that a comet was arriving, and he had accepted the information as nothing particularly startling or new; he had been puzzled only at the significance of the other words of the message, "toward," for instance. So far he had not been quite able to grasp "toward."

No; it was not the message itself that was so startling to Number 774. Somehow, tonight, the flashing of the distant light on Earth, telling in its cryptic way of the arrival of the visitor, bridged a gap between two of Number 774's thoughts and furnished him with an inspiration—a colossal inspiration which only genius, backed up by a knowledge considerably in excess of that of mankind, and a wonder-deadening familiarity with marvelous scientific triumphs, would have dreamed possible of fulfillment.

In one timeless instant, all of Number 774's dreams and hopes became linked together with the comet. Might he not still be guilty of revolt against the age-honored conventions of old Mars?

III

Something almost electrical seemed suddenly to take possession of Number 774. His cold eyes, fixed on the reproducer bulb, glittered with impatience. The flickering message, which a moment before would have held the complete attention of his every deductive faculty, had little interest for him now. He translated the signals perfunctorily, gathering what little meaning he could from them and not bothering to puzzle over what was new. He waited with tense eagerness for the moment when the light would go out, and it would be his turn to speak. There was something which he *must* tell his friend of Planet Three, and he *must* tell it so that it would be understood. But how? How could he direct those strange, clumsy signals, of which he knew so very little, so that the information he wished to convey would be received and properly understood?

There! The closing phrase of the message from Planet Three was coming: "Earth standing by for Mars. Earth standing by—" The scarcely noticeable speck of light in the vision globe of the telescope disappeared; the pulsating purple glow in the reproducer bulb faded out, and the darkness there seemed tense with expectancy and eager waiting. It seemed to fling an insurmountable challenge at the intellect and ingenuity of Number 774.

In their present relative positions, Earth and Mars were about fifty million miles, or four and a half light-minutes, apart. Thus any message depending on light would of course take four and a half minutes to travel from Earth to Mars, or vice versa.

To avoid confusion in exchanging their communications, Number 774 and his friend of Planet Three had worked out a system whereby each would send out his signals for two minutes, with an intervening pause of two minutes, during which the other could answer. This Earthly time interval Number 774 had learned to recognize and to interpret in terms of the Martian method of measuring time.

It was his turn now; and though he had something far more important to say than ever before, he hesitated, all his cleverness seemingly checkmated by the immensity of his problem. But the lagging, slipping moments lashed his mind, driving it by sheer tenseness of determination to a higher pitch of keenness, almost, than ever before. At least he could try. He could guess, and he could stumble, but he could try.

The little lever of the signaling mechanism trembled in his grasp, and in response to its feeble movements the signals thundered and flared from the outer surface of the dome overhead. For a full three minutes, violating the rule, Number 774 continued to send, repeating the same phrase over and over again, changing certain words each time, in the hope of hitting the right combination that would convey his meaning.

He did not wait for a reply. Earth had already sunk low in the west, and before a reply could come the flashes arriving from the feeble station on Earth would be rendered too dim and wavering and uncertain by the almost imperceptible haze of the Martian horizon to be properly recorded. Besides, he had so little time and so much to do.

Ponderously, under his guidance, the great telescope tube swung into line with the comet, which still rode high up in the west. The circular opening in the dome shifted automatically with the telescope, keeping opposite to its muzzle.

The huge form of the comet's head filled the vision globe, spreading brilliant and silvery and tenuous around the more solid spot of the glowing central nucleus.

Delicate instruments came into play, recording and measuring speeds, distances, and densities. But this was no mere quest for abstract scientific knowledge. His eyes smoldered with a grimly definite purpose, in which the shadow of death was very near.

But toward death Number 774's reactions were hardly human. In the torrent of his thoughts one thing shone out clear—the comet would pass close to Mars, and it would also pass close to Earth. That fact offered a slender and stupendous possibility. But in ten days the comet would pass and his chance would be gone. Unless he could cram into that brief time more work than anything human or Martian had ever before been called upon to do, his opportunity would be gone forever.

He finished his measurements quickly and efficiently. Switches clicked, and great mechanisms, and incredibly delicate and sensitive instruments, ceased functioning. The circular opening in the rotunda closed, hiding the stars and the comet. The observatory was at rest, for its eerie, fragile master needed it no more.

Number 774 was hurrying down a passage, the stalky limbs of the machine that carried him making a regular, clicking sound.

He came to a great wall that tumbled away in a murky, green-lighted haze, far beneath. Without hesitation he leaped into it and, seemingly supported and retarded in his fall by the emerald substance of the glow from the metal walls, he floated downward as gently and securely as a feather in the heavy atmosphere of Earth.

At the bottom of the well another vast, low-ceiled chamber spread out, its remote walls lost in the luminescent emerald murk, through which the burnished forms of gigantic machines gleamed elfinly.

This was Number 774's workroom, and here, now, he set to work, laboring with cool, unhurried efficiency, so characteristic of the children of dying Mars.

Many times before he had struggled with the same problem which now held his attention, and he had learned much concerning it, yet the technical difficulties he had encountered had convinced him that the solution of that problem still lay many years in the future.

But now something had happened. An unforeseen chance had come—a chance which might or might not be possible. It was all a gamble.

There was no time for further experiments. Perhaps with this new opportunity there was no need for further experiments, for Number 774 grasped the underlying principles. He must plan and build; above all he must be quick and sure.

He was thinking of a certain barren valley far out in the desert. In a thousand years, perhaps, no one had visited it except him. Aircraft hardly ever flew over that waterless sand pocket set amid the arid hills of Mars. There would be the ideal spot for the completion of his task, for here in his workshop he knew that he dared not stay.

Delicate electrical impulses transmitted his commands, and in response five giant shapes, paradoxically human travesties wrought in shining metal, rose from their resting places to do his bidding. Under his guidance they made preparation for the exodus, gathering instruments, tools, and other paraphernalia, and packing them in metal cases; binding long arms of metal into great sheafs that would be easy to carry. Meanwhile Number 774 busied himself with a complicated Martian calculating machine.

Thus the night passed. In the almost momentary twilight that preceded the dawn, the strange caravan set out. Number 774 had changed his identity; instead of being only a fragile lump of living protoplasm, he was now a giant of metal, like the five automatons that served him, for the powerful machine he rode was so versatile, and so quick and accurate in its responses to his every guiding gesture, that it was to all intents and purposes his body.

A pair of wings of metal fabric disengaged themselves from the intricacies of his machine and began to flap ponderously. Number 774 soared upward on them, over his servitors that plodded along on the ground, bearing their heavy burdens. His gaze darted back briefly toward the silvery dome of his workshop and at its dusty walls, matching the slightly ocher-tinged dun color of the desert.

But the fact that he had lived in that structure most of his life, and that he was now leaving it forever, aroused no sentiment in his mind. He had no time for sentiment now, for time was precious. Besides, he was looking forward to the trials and dangers that were certain to come soon and to the triumphs that might come with them.

He swung and turned in the air, scanning the terrain with wary watchfulness, on guard for any possible approaching aircraft. It would not be well if he were seen, and if a flier should appear he must take cover. But there was really little danger to face as far as his own people were concerned.

Avoidance of the death sentence imposed by the Rulers was practically without precedent. For thousands of years Martians had obeyed their Rulers' commands so implicitly that now prisons for the detention of the condemned were unknown. When the order came, the people of Mars went to their deaths willingly and without a guard. And so it was unlikely that any one would suspect that Number 774 had intentions of escaping execution now.

It is hardly likely that Number 774 felt triumphant over his revolt against ancient law—possibly he even felt guilty—but his earnest eagerness to learn things that he did not know, and to give himself to the cause to which his life had been pledged, was an urge that surpassed and defied even age-old code and tradition.

The stars, and leisurely Deimos, the farther moon, shone on an ashen haze that obscured the horizon in every direction. A mounting breeze, keen and cutting for all its thinness, blew out of the west. When the sun rose, it changed the haze of the dust-laden air to a tumultuous, fiery murk that flung long, ominous streamers of orange and red across the sky. Number 774 knew what was coming and knew the hazards that it brought.

The wind became more and more violent, increasing by puffs and gusts, and at last settling down to a steady powerful blast of the proportions of a terrestrial hurricane. If human ears had been there to hear, they would have detected the mounting whisper and rustle of millions of flying sand particles, rubbing and sliding over each other, making a blurred and soothing purr of sound.

As the streaming, flame-hued trains of sand thickened and mounted higher in the atmosphere, the sun dimmed to a red bubble floating in the murk, and only a bloody reminder of its normal brilliance reached the ground.

Number 774 had descended to join his robots in their march on the ground. He had seen many of these fierce dust storms of Mars, and he accepted them as a matter of course, just as an experienced old mariner of Earth accepts tempests at sea. He himself was safely incased in an airtight glass cage atop the machine he rode; he was breathing pure filtered air.

The chief dangers were that the filtering equipment which fed oxygen to the engines of his automatons would become clogged, or that he would accidentally be engulfed in some newly formed bed of quicksand, hidden

beneath the clouds of dust that swirled about him. But these were un-
avoidable dangers which must be faced.

Under the pressure of necessity, Number 774 urged his robots to the
fastest pace they could attain in the shifting desert soil. The metal giants'
long, webby limbs swung on and on steadily, into the east, breasting sand
and wind, and climbing several steep rocky ridges they encountered with
agile ease, in spite of their great bulk and the weight of the burdens they
carried.

Twice they crossed deep, twenty-mile-wide artificial gorges, which on
Earth have earned the not entirely correct name of "canals." Now and
then during each crossing, the dry and lifeless stalks of some weird Martian
vegetation would loom dimly through the storm like grotesque totem poles.
The canals were as desolate as the desert itself, for it was very early in
the spring, and the water from the melting polar snowcaps had not yet
come down through the network of conduits and perforated pipettes buried
beneath the canal bed.

When the water did appear, vegetation would spring up in rapid growth
along the bottoms of the hundreds of straight scars that had been dredged
across the barren desert ages before. But as yet there was no sign
of the great Martian planting machines, for it was still too early in the
season even for them.

Number 774's wariness in crossing seemed completely unnecessary, for
his eyes caught no sign of his own kind, or, in fact, of any living creature.
He was as completely alone in the flat expanses of the canals as he was
in the desert proper.

Late in the afternoon he arrived at his destination. By sunset the wind
had subsided and the air was clearing. The work was already underway.
Two of the robots, equipped now with great scooplike claws, had excavated
a vast hole in the sand. Feverishly active, the other two were assisting
Number 774 with other tasks. Rods were being arranged around the pit.
Something of a strange, dark substance was taking form. A stream of
molten metal was pouring from a broad, squat mechanism. A thin trickle
of white vapor trailed up in the quiet air.

At dusk Number 774 paused to look up, over the rounded hills that
ringed the valley, at Planet Three that hung in the western sky, gleaming
regally amid its retinue of stars. The light on that distant world would
flicker in vain tonight, calling eagerly to the Man of Mars. There would
be no answer. Higher up, fainter and less conspicuous, was the silvery
dart of the comet.

Perhaps Number 774 was trying to imagine what his unknown friend
of the light would think when no replying flicker appeared on the disk
of Mars. Perhaps he was trying to imagine, as he had done so often before,

what his friend of the light was like. Maybe he was wondering whether he should soon know.

His pause was only momentary. There was much to do, for in effect he was racing with the comet. Martians need very little sleep, and it was certain that Number 774 would get no sleep this night, nor the next, nor the next.

IV

Young Jack Cantrill cast a brief glance at the big diesel engine he had been inspecting, and then, with an air of finality, wiped his grease-blackened hands on a fistful of cotton waste. The outfit was functioning perfectly. Ordinarily he might have paused for a moment to admire the easy strength and motion of the machinery to which he played nursemaid, but, lover of machines though he certainly was, he had no time now.

His eyes did not linger on the reflection of the glowing electric light-bulbs mirrored on the polished circumference of the spinning flywheel, as they usually did; nor did his attention wander to the sparks that purred blue and steady on the brushes of the gigantic dynamo attached to the engine.

He had something far more interesting to occupy his mind, and besides, a rather astounding idea had just occurred to him. Old Doc Waters and Yvonne might laugh at the notion; and then again they might be struck by it just as he had been. He'd have to try it out on them right away.

He tossed the handful of waste carelessly into a metal box, then made a perfunctory reading of the meters and instruments banked close and bewilderingly on the switchboard. He adjusted a small rheostat and jotted something down on a chart on the wall with a red crayon. Then, heedless of his light clothing and his perspiring condition, he hurried out into the frosty desert night.

The breeze, cold and untainted by the smell of burning fuel oil, chilled his damp body uncomfortably, but he did not heed it. The steady thud of the exhaust of the high-compression motor in the iron shack receded rapidly behind him as he ran up a path which led to the summit of a low hill.

On the crest of a neighboring knoll, a broad patch of dazzling light winked on and off regularly, where scores of huge searchlights poured their billions of candlepower toward the twinkling stars, in systematically arranged long and short spurts. Jack Cantrill's glance toward them was brief but intense. His lips moved as though he were counting to himself.

The door of the domed observatory building at the top of the hill opened at his touch. He passed through a small lean-to and entered the brick-lined circular chamber that housed the telescope. Here a single shaded lamp cast a subdued glow over a big desk on which various opened notebooks and papers were scattered. Amid the litter an astronomer's chronometer ticked loudly in shadowed stillness. The gloom was eerie and soft and strange.

Jack Cantrill made his way quietly to the low platform under the eyepiece of the telescope, where the other two occupants of the room stood.

The girl was pretty in a blond, elfin sort of way. She smiled briefly at Jack's approach.

"Any luck, folks?" he inquired.

He was trying to make his voice sound calm and casual, but a tense and excited huskiness crept into his words and spoiled his bluff.

Professor Waters looked up from the eyepiece of the big instrument. The glow coming from the nearby lamp accentuated the tired lines of his face, making him look almost haggard. He grinned wearily.

"Not yet, boy," he said. "It seems as though Old Faithful has deserted us completely. It's funny, too, when you remember that when conditions were at all favorable for observation, he hasn't failed me once in nine years. And yet this is the second night that he hasn't given us a sign. The shaded side of Mars hasn't shown a single flicker that you can see, and even the photoelectric cell doesn't detect anything."

The young man glanced uncertainly at the girl and then back at her father. The fingers of one of his hands crept slowly through his curly red hair. With the air of a small schoolboy about to make his first public address, he was fumbling with a soiled sheet of paper he had taken from his pocket. He felt rather sheepish about that idea he had thought of.

"Yvonne— Doc—" he said almost plaintively, in an awkward attempt to get their undivided attention centered on what he was going to say. "I'm not much of a scientist, and maybe I'm a darned fool; but—well, this message—the final one we received the night before last—we thought it was just a jumble but, when you read it, it almost has meaning. Here, listen to it once."

Clearing his throat he proceeded to read from the sheet of paper: "Comet coming. Yes. Comet coming. Yes. Comet coming of Man of Mars. Comet Man of Mars coming toward Earth. Comet coming Man of Mars. Man of Mars. Comet. Man of Mars. Comet. Man of Mars. Comet. Yes, yes, yes. Man of Earth. Yes, yes, yes. Signing off. Signing off."

Jack Cantrill's thin cheeks were flushed when he stopped reading.

"Get it?" he asked in a husky whisper. "Get any sense out of that?"

Yvonne Waters' pretty face had paled slightly. "You mean, Jack—you mean that he wanted to say that he was coming *here*, across fifty million miles of emptiness? He can't do that! He can't! It's too far and too impossible!"

Her concerned manner bolstered up the youth's confidence in his idea. "You caught on to exactly what I thought of," he said.

Professor Waters did not betray any outward excitement. His manner was musing, and he rubbed his cheek reflectively. "I thought of that, too," he admitted after a moment. "But it seemed too wild for serious consideration. Still there's a chance—that you are right."

The thought put into words seemed suddenly to startle the old man. "Gad, boy!" he exploded suddenly. "Supposing it *is* the truth! Old Faithful signaled about the comet. If there's anything to this at all, the comet must be tied up with his coming. And for all we know the comet might help. It passes close to both Earth and Mars. If in some way he could fall into its gravitation field, it would drag him almost all the way. That's it! It would save an enormous energy. It would put his trip, otherwise still impossible, into the realm of possibility!"

"You get me at last, doc," Jack said quickly. "And when you say, 'Supposing it's the truth,' think of what it means! The navigation of interplanetary space, maybe! Commerce between Earth and Mars! A new and wonderful era, with the minds of one world exchanging ideas with the minds of another."

Unconsciously Jack Cantrill had taken Yvonne Waters' hand. Her eyes were starry.

"If it did happen we'd all be heroes, Jack," she said. "Dad and you and I. We'd be the ones to get the credit."

"We would, Yvonne," Jack admitted with a chuckle.

It was the professor's turn to smile. "You two have got the whole business nicely ready-made, haven't you?" he chided. Then his face sobered as he went on: "The gap is pretty wide between Earthman and Martian; and in consequence yours may be very far off, even if that guess of ours about the message is right.

"We don't know that Martians are human beings. The chances are a million to one that they aren't. It is very unlikely that evolution, operating on so different a planet, could produce a being even remotely resembling a man. We don't even know that the people of Mars use speech as we use it. Old Faithful certainly is very intelligent, yet the way he has fumbled blunderingly with our code seems to indicate that even a faint conception of vocal speech is something new and strange to him.

"Those are some of the gaps, but there may be sinister similarities between Earthmen and Martians.

"Who knows but that something darker lies behind what we think is friendly interest in us? Sometimes conquest is more satisfying than commerce. We can't tell." Professor Waters paused.

"Making it extra strong, aren't you, doc?" Jack put in.

"I guess I am, and now I think I'll do a little news-spreading." The professor strode to the desk.

"Human or not, I hope the Martians are handsome," Yvonne confided impishly to Jack.

"And I hope they're not, darling," he replied, putting his arm affectionately about her waist. He was about to add something more when what the girl's father was saying into the telephone riveted their attention.

"Long distance? I'm calling Washington. I want to speak directly to Mr. Grayson, the Secretary of War. Strange call? Perhaps. But put it through."

Before dawn all the observatories of Earth had begun their watch.

V

Far away on the Red Planet, the work of Number 774 went steadily forward. Then came the night when all was ready except for one thing. A powerful urge, the roots of which are deeply implanted in the dominant forms of life on both Earth and Mars, and perhaps the whole universe, was calling him to a city at the joining place of four canals, far to the east. In that urge there was a pathetic something, perfectly understandable by human standards.

The bright stars reeled dizzily before Number 774 as he swooped out over the desert on the wings of the ornithopter that bore him and sped eastward. He must be cautious, but above all he must hurry.

An hour or so slipped by. The Martian's big eyes, keen and catlike, picked out in the broad cleft of a canal a gigantic angular shape, looming dim and uncertain in the gloom. Inconspicuous as a drifting shadow, he settled toward it. The talons of his automaton found a metal panel that slipped aside at a touch. The green glow of the immense well thus revealed dropped away into deserted obscurity. In a moment he was floating down it, past myriads of openings, from which radiated the labyrinthine tunnels of the buried Martian city.

He entered one of these passages and followed it for perhaps a mile, until he came to a vast chamber, pervaded by a moist, humid heat. The floor was covered with thousands of boxes of clear crystal; and in each box was a purple gob of something feeble and jellylike and alive.

Aided perhaps by some Martian numeral system, Number 774 found his way to the box he sought. At his touch the lid opened. He had dismounted from his automaton, and now, creeping forward, he thrust a slender appendage into the crystal case.

A score of nerve filaments, fine, almost, as human hair, darted out from the chitinous shell that protected them and roved caressingly over the lump of protoplasm. Immediately it responded to the gentle touch of the strange creature that had sired it. Its delicate integument quivered, and a thin pseudopod oozed up from its jellylike form and enveloped the nerve filaments of Number 774. For minutes the two remained thus, perfectly motionless.

It was a bizarre travesty of a touching and perfectly human situation; yet its utter strangeness by Earthly standards robbed it of some of its pathos. No words were spoken, no sign of affection that a terrestrial being could interpret was given; and yet perhaps the exchange of feeling and thought and emotion between parent and offspring was far more complete than anything of the kind possible on Earth.

Number 774 did not forget caution. Perhaps it was intuition that informed him that someone was coming. Quickly, yet without haste, he regained his automaton, replaced the lid on the crystal box, and slipped quietly away into the luminescent obscurity of the tunnel. In a few minutes he had safely reached the open of the canal bed. Broad wings flapped, and the starlit night swallowed him up.

As he hurried back toward his hidden valley, he saw the silvery green speck of Earth dip beneath the western horizon. The sight of it must have aroused a turmoil of forebodings within him; for absently, as if he were already facing unknown horrors in mortal combat, he moved a small switch, and in response a jagged flash of flame leaped from an apparatus carried on a long arm of his flying automaton. Where the bolt struck, the desert sand turned molten.

Above, the comet glowed, pallid and frosty and swollen. It was very near to Mars now.

Having reached his valley, Number 774 descended into the pit. A silvery thing that was illy defined in the uncertain light loomed over him. A door opened and closed, and Number 774 was alone and busy amid a bewildering array of machinery.

There came a blinding flash of incandescence, and a roar that sounded like the collision of two worlds; then a shrill, tortured, crackling whistle. The pit glowed white-hot, and the silvery thing was gone. Above the pit, towering many miles into the sky, was an immense jetted plume of vapor, shining rosy with heat. It would be many minutes before that huge gaseous cloud would cool sufficiently to be invisible.

The body of Number 774 was battered and torn and broken; the terrific acceleration was crushing him; consciousness was slipping, even though he was exerting a tremendous effort of will to cling to it. In a few minutes it would not matter if he did go out, but now there were controls to watch and to handle. If they were not manipulated properly everything he had done was for naught.

But the blackness of oblivion was closing in. He struggled valiantly

to master himself and to fight through the gathering gloom that was mist-
ing his vision and clouding his mind. Though his whole being cried out
for a cessation of torturing effort, still he kept fiercely at his task. There
was too much at stake. That little globe there—it was glowing red when
it should glow violet. It must be attended to. The craft was wobbling,
and it must not wobble. A trifling adjustment of delicate stabilizers would
fix that, if he could only somehow make the adjustment.

A dribble of sticky, oozy fluid welled from a wound in Number 774's
side. His limbs, some of them broken, fumbled awkwardly and inefficiently
with the complicated controls. He was gasping, and all the while his glazing eyes remained fixed grimly on the form of the comet, toward which
he and the strange craft he had built were hurtling. Could he reach it?
He must!

VI

On Earth, Professor Waters, his daughter, and his young engineer,
watched and waited. It was a tense, grueling task, heavy-laden with
monotony, a thousand weird imaginings, and a horde of questions, none
of which could be answered with any certainty.

They were uncertain whether to be fearful of the unknown thing whose
approach they sensed, or to be exultant. They did not even know whether
their vigil was just a huge nerve-racking practical joke which their fancies
had played upon them.

Time dragged with torturing slowness. Tardy seconds became minutes,
tedious minutes were built up into hours, and hours became days that
seemed like centuries. And over the rest of the world, the vigil was much
the same.

On the ninth day after the last flickering message had come from Mars,
Professor Waters had seen through his telescope, on the surface of the
Red Planet, a fine dot of white light that, after its sudden appearance,
faded quickly to red, and then, after a few minutes, disappeared altogether.
A few hours later he thought he detected a slight and momentary ripple
in the gaseous substance of the comet's head, which then had just passed
Mars on its sunward journey.

Newspaper reporters who had come many miles to this lonely spot in
the desert were constantly seeking interviews. The three watchers supplied
them with all the information they knew; and at last, tiring of the additional strain of being constantly hounded by these persistent seekers after
sensational news, they refused even to grant them admittance into the
barbed-wire stockade of the camp.

At last the comet reached its point of closest approach to the Earth.

Faint and ashy though it was, low down in the sunlit afternoon heavens, still it was an awesome, impressive object, with its colossal, fan-shaped head and the vast curved sweep of its gigantic ghost-silver tail.

When the desert dusk settled, the visiting wanderer increased a score of times in brilliance and glory. It had now passed the line and was hurtling away. And as yet nothing that would satisfy the eager hopes and fears of the watchers had happened.

The three were standing on the veranda of the little adobe house they inhabited. All of a sudden Doctor Waters' haggard face relaxed. He sighed heavily.

"I guess that it has been proved that we are all of us fools," he said wearily. "There hasn't been much of anything to reward us for our pains." His glance toward Jack Cantrill was slightly apologetic. "I think I'll go to bed," he added abruptly.

Jack's rather good-looking face twisted into a rueful smile. "Bed isn't at all a bad idea," he admitted. "I feel as though I could snooze a week straight without waking up. Well, anyway, if we're fools, I'm the biggest one, because I started all this." He looked at the old man and then at the girl. "Forgive me, Yvonne?" he queried good-humoredly.

"No," she replied with mock seriousness. "Making me lose so much of my beauty sleep like this! You ought to be ashamed of yourself." Her little speech was terminated by a faintly amused chuckle, and she pinched his cheek impishly.

It was some hours after they had retired that a faint soughing noise began from somewhere, apparently at a great distance. It was like the sound of a suddenly stiffening night breeze, sweeping through a grove of pine trees. Something that glowed rosy with the heat of atmospheric friction swept in hurtling flight across the sky. A mile or so beyond the camp, broad thin flanges of metal shot out from it, and it made a feeble attempt to steady itself and check its almost meteoric speed. It wobbled, then fluttered down weakly. A cloud of dust and sand rose where it smashed into the ground. But there was no human eye to see. For an hour or more it gave no further sign of life or motion.

Yvonne Waters was a light sleeper. Unusual night noises ordinarily aroused her. The momentary soughing rustle caused her to stir, but she did not awaken. Then, toward four in the morning, another disturbance came. It was a faint stretching, creaking, straining sound, that nevertheless held a suggestion of powerful forces acting stealthily.

Instantly Yvonne was wide awake. She sat up in bed, listening. What she heard produced quick and accurate associations in her nimble and cool young mind. A barbed-wire fence would make a creaking, straining noise like that, if something big and powerful were seeking tentatively to force an entrance. The stockade!

Yes; she was right. Presently there came the sharp snap and snarl that told of the sudden parting of a taut wire. Four times the sound was repeated.

Yvonne Waters had bounded out of her bunk and had rushed to a window. It was still very dark, but outlined against the stars she saw a vague shape that swayed and moved. The girl's hand groped quickly into the drawer of a small stand beside her and drew out a heavy automatic pistol. Then she hurried to the door and across the hallway.

"Dad! Jack!" she called in a husky whisper. "I've seen something big. It's coming toward the house!"

The young man responded quickly, his unshod feet thudding across the floor. His eyes narrowed when he leaned out of the window. There the thing stood, statuesquely now, not fifty paces away. It was not clearly defined in the darkness, but Jack Cantrill knew at once that it was something completely out of his experience. It seemed to have an upright, cylindrical body that rose perhaps fifteen feet above the ground. Leverlike limbs projected grotesquely from the upper end of this torso, and at the lower end there were shadowy suggestions of other limbs, long and spidery. An angular object surmounted the cylinder, and in its present position it was an outlandish travesty of the head of a man, cocked to one side, listening.

A minute passed. Obeying what must have been an automatic impulse, Yvonne Waters drew on her boots. About the camp she always dressed like the men, and during the last few nights, anticipating sudden developments, they had all slept in their clothing.

Jack Cantrill, crouching by the window, felt the short hairs at the nape of his neck stiffen. Doctor Waters' hand was on the young man's shoulder. The fingers were trembling slightly.

It was Jack who first put into words what they were all sure was the truth: "Old Faithful, I think," he whispered, without any apparent excitement.

He paused for a moment, during which neither of his companions made any comment, for even a slight sound, as far as they knew, might be heard, with disastrous consequences.

The young man was thinking fast. Something had to be done and done quickly, and it was perhaps very easy to do the wrong thing.

"Flashlight!" he whispered presently, taking command of the situation, and the girl, responding quickly to his leadership, slipped her big electric torch into his hand.

"Now out into the open—all of us," he ordered. "Armed?"

Each carried a pistol. They slipped around to the side of the house, with Cantrill in the lead. The weird giant stood as before, rigid and perfectly still.

Jack raised the flashlight. Working the flash button with his thumb, he proceeded to signal out in the Morse code, a familiar message: "Hello, Man of Mars! Hello, Man of Mars! Hello, Man of Mars!"

And the answer came immediately, flickering from a small spot of green light on the angular "head" of the automaton: "Hello, Man of Earth! Hello, Man of Earth! Comet. Comet. Comet. Comet." The message was clear enough, but there was an unusual halting, stumbling hesitancy in the way it was given. Old Faithful had always been precise and quick in the messages he had flashed from Mars.

As the three watchers stood spellbound, the great quasi-human machine started forward toward the house. Its movements were powerful, but drunken and unsteady. It seemed to be little more than an insensate mechanism running amuk. The intelligence that was guiding it was losing its hold. Nothing could avert an accident.

The robot struck the side of the house with a heavy thud, lurched forward, stumbled, and fell with a clatter and clang of metal across the low roof that collapsed under its weight and the force of its overthrow. Prostrate though it was, its lower limbs continued to simulate the movements of walking.

Its arms sprawled wide, and from a metal knob at the tip of one a torrent of blue sparks began to pour into the earth, causing the patch of sand it struck to turn molten and boil away in a cloud of incandescent vapor. A minute must have passed before the sparks burned out and the appendages of the machine ceased their ponderous thrashing.

Meanwhile the three watchers had been staring at the weird and inspiring sight, not knowing just what to do. But now, when quiet was restored, they edged cautiously toward the fallen machine. Jack Cantrill's flashlight beam played over the wreckage and halted upon the flattened "head" of the robot. It was pyramidal in form and had been supported by a flexible pillar of pointed metal. There was an opening in one side, and from it something had tumbled. A shadow veiled it, so that the watchers could not immediately see what it was. Then Jack leaped to a different position and poured the beam of the flashlight full upon it.

The effect of its strangeness did not come upon them right away, for they did not at once realize its true nature. It seemed at first only a sprawling mass of drab gray, as large, perhaps, as the open top of an ordinary umbrella. It might have been nothing more than a large lump of wet mud, flattened out by being dropped.

Then, after a moment, the three took note of the ragged tendrils that radiated out from the oblate form somewhat in the manner of the arms of a starfish. The ends of some of those tendrils were slender and stalklike and were terminated by incredibly fine filaments of coral pink. Those filaments were twitching convulsively.

Yvonne Waters was the first to find her voice. It was choking and tremulous: "The thing's alive!" she cried. "Dad! Jack! It's alive!"

Obscure primal instincts had taken possession of them. Like wary alley curs they inched their way forward, craning their necks to look closer at the creature, in which, for them, both fascination and fear were combined.

It was then they saw that the central lump of the thing was contracting in painful, jerky spasms. It was breathing, or gasping, rather. Feathery pink palps around a cone-shaped orifice that resembled the inside of a funnel coiled in agony. They could hear the monster's breath whistle through the opening in long, rasping sighs.

But the creature's eyes, fixed to the ends of two tentacular appendages that protruded from beneath the outer folds of its flattened body, regarded them with what seemed to be an interest which could not be dimmed by physical pain and suffering. They were very large eyes, three inches across, and there was in their alien, brooding intensity, slightly veiled now by the film of approaching death, a suggestion of an intelligence in this monstrous, inhuman body that was more than human.

Yvonne Waters had taken note of these things almost in the space of a moment. She saw the hideous festering gashes of wounds that must have been several days old on the body of the visiting being, and she saw that several of its limbs were shattered. Some of them seemed to be partly knit, but others were evidently recent injuries. From the fresh wounds bright red blood oozed, giving evidence of a very high hemoglobin content, which would be necessary for a creature accustomed to breathing an atmosphere much more rarefied than that of Earth.

Maybe it was because Yvonne Waters was a woman that she bridged the gap between Earthman and Martian more quickly than her companions.

"He's hurt!" she gasped suddenly. "We've got to help him some way! We ought to—ought to—get a doctor." She halted a little in expressing this last idea. It seemed so totally wild and fantastic.

"A doctor for that horror?" Jack Cantrill asked, a trifle dazed.

"Yes! Well, maybe no," the girl amended. "But still we must do something. We've got to! He's human, Jack—human in everything but form. He has brains; he can feel pain like any human being. Besides, he has courage of the same kind that we all worship. Think of the pluck it took to make the first plunge across fifty million miles of cold, airless void! That's something to bow down to, isn't it? And, besides, this is our friend, Old Faithful!"

"By the gods, Yvonne, you're right!" the young man exploded with sudden realization. "And here I am, wasting time like a dumb fool!"

He dropped to his knees beside the injured Martian, and his big hands poised, ready and willing, but still uncertain how to help this bizarre entity of another world.

Doctor Waters had by this time shaken the fog of sleep from his older and less agile faculties, and he was now able to grasp the situation. With a brief and crisp, "I'll get the first-aid kit!" he hurried into the partially wrecked house, across the roof of which sprawled Old Faithful's automaton.

Conquering her natural revulsion, Yvonne brought herself to touch the dry, cold flesh of the Martian, and to try as best she might to ease its suffering. Presently the three of them were working over their weird patient, disinfecting and bandaging its wounds. But there was small hope that their efforts would be of any avail.

At their first touch, Old Faithful had started convulsively, as though in fear and repugnance of these, to him, horrid monsters; and a low, thick cry came from the opening in his body. But he must have realized that their intentions were harmless, for he had relaxed immediately. His breath, however, was rapidly growing weaker and more convulsive, and his eyes were glazing.

"We're dumb!" Jack stated with sudden vehemence. "He's badly hurt, but that's not all. This atmosphere is six times too dense for him. He's smothering in it—drowning! We've got to get him somewhere where the pressure won't be crushing him!"

"We'll rig up a vacuum tank down in the engine shed," said Doctor Waters. "It won't take but a minute."

It was done. However, when they were lifting Old Faithful onto the litter they had improvised, his body stiffened, shuddered, and grew suddenly limp. They knew that Old Faithful—Number 774—was gone. Still, to aid the remote possibility that he would revive, they placed him in the vacuum tank and exhausted most of the air so that the pressure inside duplicated that of the rarefied Martian atmosphere. Fresh air was admitted slowly through the pet cock. But within an hour Old Faithful's flesh had become stiff with *rigor mortis*. He was dead.

Much must have passed through the devious channels of his Martian mind during those brief hours on Planet Three. He must have felt satisfied that his eagerness to penetrate the unknown was partly rewarded, his ambition partly fulfilled. He had learned what lay back of, and what had guided, the flickerings of the light. He had seen the people of Planet Three. Perhaps, at the last, he had thought of Mars, his home, and the sorry plight of his race.

Maybe he thought of his growing offspring in that buried nursery chamber, fifty million miles away. Maybe the possibilities of Earth, as a means of aiding dying Mars, occurred to him, if it had not come into his mind before, and it is quite likely that his ideas in that direction were not alto-gether altruistic toward mankind.

Certainly he hoped that his friend of the light would find his space car and what it contained, out there in the desert, and that they would study and understand.

Dawn came, with the eastern sky sprinkled with a few pink feathery clouds that the bright sun would soon dissipate.

In one of the various corrugated iron sheds of the camp, Yvonne, Jack, and the doctor were bending over the body of Old Faithful, which lay stiff and lifeless on a long table.

"Kind of heartless to be preparing this intelligent being for immersion in a preservative spirit bath so that a lot of curious museum-goers can have a thrill, don't you think, folks?" Jack was complaining with make-believe gruffness. "How would you like it if the situation was reversed—if we were stiffs with the curious of Mars looking at us?"

"I wouldn't mind if I was dead." The girl laughed. "It would be an honor. Oh, look, Jack—the funny little mark on Old Faithful's skin—it's tattooed with red ink. What do you suppose it means?"

Jack had already seen the mark. It was a circle with a bar through the center and was, as the girl had said, an artificial decoration or symbol. Jack shrugged. "Search me, honey!" He chuckled. "Say, doc, do you suppose that space car is around here somewhere?"

The doctor nodded. "It must be."

"Well, come on! Let's look for it, then! This can wait."

After a very hasty and sketchy breakfast, they made their way on horse-back out into the desert, following the tracks the Martian robot had made.

At the summit of a rocky ridge they found what they sought—a long cylinder of metal deeply imbedded in sand that seemed literally to have splashed like soft mud around it. The long fins of the space car were crum-pled and broken and covered with the blue-gray ash of oxidation. Here and there a fragment had peeled away, revealing bright metal beneath.

The nose of the shell had become unscrewed, exposing burnished threads that glistened in the sun. Into the shadowed interior they made their way, rummaging gingerly among the bewildering maze of Martian instruments. The place reeked with a scorched, pungent odor.

At the rear of the cylindrical compartment they found a great round drum of metal, fitting snugly into the interior of the shell. Sleepily they wondered what was in it and made several weary attempts to move it. At nine o'clock the police guard that Doctor Waters had sent for arrived.

"Tell those damned reporters who are trying to crash in on us to go to hell," Jack Cantrill told the lieutenant in charge, as he and his two com-panions were starting wearily back toward camp. "We've got to snooze."

Several weeks had passed. In a hotel room in Phoenix, Arizona, Doctor Waters was speaking to Mr. and Mrs. Cantrill, who had just arrived.

"I'm turning the camp and the signaling apparatus over to Radeau and his associates," he was saying. "No more signals from Mars, somehow, and I don't feel very much like continuing there anyway. There are a lot more interesting things on the horizon.

"That drum which Old Faithful brought us—it contained models and many charts and sheets of parchment with drawings on them. I'm beginning to see light through the mystery at last. There are suggestions there for constructing a spaceship. I'm going to work on that problem as long as I live.

"Maybe I'll succeed with the help of Old Faithful. Human ingenuity will have to be called on, too, of course. I don't think that the Martians have the problem completely solved themselves. Old Faithful used the comet, you know."

The doctor's smile broadened as he went on: "Children, how would you like to go to Mars with me some day?"

"Don't ask silly questions, dad," said Yvonne. "We'd go in a minute!"

The young man nodded seriously. "What a honeymoon that would make, if we could have it now!" he enthused.

"A million times better than going to Seattle," the girl agreed.

The doctor grinned faintly. "Even if you were treated like poor Old Faithful—pickled and put in a museum?"

"Even if!"

Jack Cantrill's eyes narrowed and seemed to stare far away into nothing. His lips and his gaunt sunburned cheeks were stern. Perhaps he was looking into the future toward adventures that might or might not come.

Something of the same rugged spirit seemed suddenly to have infused itself into the strong, bronzed beauty of the girl at his side. They both loved adventure; they both knew life in the rough.

At the door Yvonne kissed her father good-bye. "Just a little run up to Seattle, dad," she explained cheerily, "two or three weeks, maybe. Then both of us back with you—to work."

"Old Faithful" made a deep impression on the readers. One demonstration of that showed itself, inevitably, in the fact that Gallun was pushed into writing a sequel, "The Son of Old Faithful," which appeared in the July 1935 issue of *Astounding Stories*.

More important was the fact that sympathetic portraits of extraterrestrials became common after "Old Faithful," particularly among the more sophisticated writers. The old picture of extraterrestrial as mindless villain receded into the more primitive byways.

One might say, of course, that Gallun was not fundamentally responsible for this, but that he, and everyone else, were unavoidably affected by trends and events of the times. In January 1933, Adolf Hitler had come to power in Germany, and, in the United States at least, he was making racism unpopular. Whatever the private feelings of individual Americans, it became difficult to express anything in print that might resemble the Nazi doctrine.

The easy assumption of early science fiction writers that Nordic whites were the natural heroes and the darker the complexion the more villainous the character, had to disappear. And inasmuch as the easy assumption of villainous extraterrestrials was a kind of reflection of terrestrial racism, that, too, began to fade.

But if the trend was inevitable, Gallun nevertheless was the first to take advantage of it in a really effective manner.

I eventually wrote stories in which I had a rather primitive view of extraterrestrials bent single-mindedly on conquest, as in "The Black Friar of the Flame," "C-Chute," and "In a Good Cause . . . ," though in each case I believe I made some small attempt at presenting their side.

On the whole, though, I avoided extraterrestrials, because I did not want to be more or less forced into treating them as simple villains (see *The Early Asimov*). When they did appear, I sometimes applied the example of such writers as Gallun and treated them sympathetically, as in my stories "Hostess" and "Blind Alley."

Finally, when I decided at last, quite deliberately, to go all out on the extraterrestrial theme (partly out of annoyance at suggestions that I avoided them because I couldn't handle them), I produced the second part of my novel *The Gods Themselves*. There I treated them on their own terms and viewed through their own eyes, as Gallun had done in "Old Faithful," and Dua, my heroine, may even have traced back in my mind to Williamson's "Mother" in "The Moon Era."

It was chiefly because of this second part, I think, that *The Gods Themselves* was awarded a Nebula as the "Best Science Fiction Novel of 1972" by the Science Fiction Writers of America and a Hugo at the 31st World Science Fiction Convention at Toronto, on September 3, 1973.

Part Six

1935

IN THE SPRING of 1935, I completed my high school education, and in June I graduated. The Boys High librarian who hunted successfully for the *Boys High Recorder* of Spring 1934 also came up with a copy of the *Senior Recorder* for the class of June 1935, and it is now one of my proud possessions.

You might ask me why I didn't have my own copy (and also a copy of the *Recorder*), saved these last nearly forty years—but I told you I don't have that kind of sentimentality. I started keeping a diary on January 1, 1938, and I save that for reference. I also save the various publications in which my material appears (one of each), also as reference. Anything else —no.

Back in 1966, when Boston University decided to collect all my papers and got in touch with me for that purpose (and went to considerable trouble to convince me that they, or anyone, could indeed possibly want those papers), I gave them what I had, which was very little.

"Is this all?" they asked.

"Yes," I answered indifferently.

"Where is the rest?" they asked.

"I've been burning it," I said—creating the utmost despondency in the poor gentlemen of the library.

Of course, they now get everything. It doesn't matter to me whether I get rid of it by way of a fireplace or of a library vault, as long as I'm not expected to keep it.

If they had asked for my papers back in 1935, they would have gotten my copy of the yearbook; as it is, it doesn't exist.

At any rate, when I looked at the yearbook, I found the photograph of an incredibly young (fifteen), incredibly skinny (150 pounds), incredibly toothy Isaac Asimov staring back at me. Actually, I remembered the picture, because my father saved a print for some reason and had it in the mirror over the bureau in his bedroom. Otherwise, I simply wouldn't have recognized it.

The small caption appended to the photo recorded that I was planning to go to Columbia, which was true, and that I intended to be a surgeon. Well, as I said, my parents expected me to go to medical school and I had accepted their ambitions for me since I had never had it made clear to me that children were allowed to have ambitions for themselves. But *surgeon?* Where the devil did I get the idea that I wanted to be a surgeon? I cannot think of any profession more repellent, except possibly that of a professional literary critic.

Each photograph of each student had something written underneath in italics by some anonymous wit who probably did not survive the strain and who perished to universal applause. Underneath mine, the villain had written: "When he looked at the clock, not only did it stop, but it started going backwards." This is an allegation I repel with the scorn and contumely it deserves.

Incidentally, you yourself will have the chance to see the photograph, since I persuaded Doubleday & Company to use it on the book jacket.

Alas, the photograph and its accompanying caption are the only indication anywhere in the *Senior Recorder* that I attended Boys High. I am not mentioned in any of the listings of Halls of Fame, in any of the historical items, in any of the statistics. Nowhere.

On page 54 of the *Senior Recorder* is a list headed "Class Statistics," which includes the best this and the best that. The Best Literary Man is listed as Martin Lichterman.

Oh, well.

Unlike my junior high school graduation, which I remember, I do not remember my high school graduation at all. I'm not sure what that proves, if anything.

Have I ever gone back to Boys High since my graduation in June 1935? You know the answer to that: I haven't. I understand that it is now a ghetto school, almost entirely Black and Puerto Rican, as far as its student body is concerned.

During my last months in Boys High I discovered Stanley G. Weinbaum and his science fiction stories—a half year too late.

The trouble was, you see, that *Wonder Stories* and *Amazing Stories* were declining steadily in 1934, and neither was received regularly at my father's newsstand. On the other hand, *Astounding Stories* grew so great in 1934 that it had begun to absorb me utterly. I made no effort to get any copies of *Wonder Stories* and *Amazing Stories* that I might miss as long as I got every single copy of *Astounding Stories*.

The result was that I missed the July 1934 *Wonder Stories* and did not read Stanley G. Weinbaum's "A Martian Odyssey" when it came out. Some years later I read it, of course, but by that time I lost the chance to participate in the effect it (and several other stories of his that appeared in later issues of *Wonder Stories*) had on everyone.

Weinbaum was the most tragic figure in the history of magazine science fiction. "A Martian Odyssey" was his first science fiction story to be published (he was then thirty-four years old) and it established him at once (*at once!*) as a leading writer. His easy style and his realistic description of extraterrestrial scenes and life-forms were better than anything yet seen, and the science fiction reading public went mad over him.

Nothing as unanimously and instantly enthusiastic had taken place since the first story by E. E. Smith, six years earlier. Nothing like it was to take place again till the first stories of Robert A. Heinlein, six years later.

Weinbaum, though we didn't know it at the time, was a Campbell author before Campbell had begun to mold a whole group of them. He was the one author to achieve Campbell stature without Campbell. Had he continued to write in the field (as, for instance, Smith and Heinlein did) for decades, there might have been less need of Campbell.

But he didn't live. For a year and a half he continued to publish stories in rapid succession and with steadily rising enthusiasm on the part of the readers. Then, in early 1936, he died of cancer, and it was all over.

But he has never been forgotten. In the myriads of science fiction anthologies that have appeared since World War II, relatively few stories published prior to 1938 (that is, before the Coming of Campbell) are to be found. "A Martian Odyssey" is the most important exception.

In 1970, thirty-six years after publication, the Science Fiction Writers of America voted on the best short science fiction stories of all time, and "A Martian Odyssey" finished in second place. In all the time since, only one story had been written that was considered to have surpassed it.*

Had I read "A Martian Odyssey" when it first appeared, its effect on me would surely have been such that I would have had to include it in this anthology. However, I did not read Weinbaum till his first appearance in *Astounding Stories*, with his "Flight on Titan," in the January 1935 issue.

I liked it, of course, but "The Parasite Planet," in the very next issue, was what hit me with the force of a pile driver and turned me instantly into a Weinbaum idolater.

* My cheerful self-appreciation simply won't let me pass up this chance. That one story that was considered to have surpassed it was "Nightfall," by Isaac Asimov.

THE PARASITE PLANET

by Stanley G. Weinbaum

Luckily for "Ham" Hammond it was mid-winter when the mudspout
came. Mid-winter, that is, in the Venusian sense, which is nothing at all
like the conception of the season generally entertained on Earth, except
possibly, by dwellers in the hotter regions of the Amazon basin, or the
Congo.

They, perhaps, might form a vague mental picture of winter on Venus
by visualizing their hottest summer days, multiplying the heat, discomfort
and unpleasant denizens of the jungle by ten or twelve.

On Venus, as is now well known, the seasons occur alternately in opposite hemispheres, as on the Earth, but with a very important difference.
Here, when North America and Europe swelter in summer, it is winter
in Australia and Cape Colony and Argentina. It is the northern and southern hemispheres which alternate their seasons.

But on Venus, very strangely, it is the eastern and western hemispheres,
because the seasons of Venus depend, not on inclination to the plane of
the ecliptic, but on libration. Venus does not rotate, but keeps the same
face always toward the Sun, just as the Moon does toward the earth. One
face is forever daylight, and the other forever night, and only along the
twilight zone, a strip five hundred miles wide, is human habitation possible, a thin ring of territory circling the planet.

Toward the sunlit side it verges into the blasting heat of a desert where
only a few Venusian creatures live, and on the night edge the strip ends
abruptly in the colossal ice barrier produced by the condensation of the
upper winds that sweep endlessly from the rising air of the hot hemisphere
to cool and sink and rush back again from the cold one.

The chilling of warm air always produces rain, and at the edge of the
darkness the rain freezes to form these great ramparts. What lies beyond,
what fantastic forms of life may live in the starless darkness of the frozen

Copyright 1935 by Street & Smith Publications, Inc.

face, or whether that region is as dead as the airless Moon—those are mysteries.

But the slow libration, a ponderous wabbling of the planet from side to side, does produce the effect of seasons. On the lands of the twilight zone, first in one hemisphere and then the other, the cloud-hidden Sun seems to rise gradually for fifteen days, then sink for the same period. It never ascends far, and only near the ice barrier does it seem to touch the horizon; for the libration is only seven degrees, but it is sufficient to produce noticeable fifteen-day seasons.

But such seasons! In the winter the temperature drops sometimes to a humid but bearable ninety, but, two weeks later, a hundred and forty is a cool day near the torrid edge of the zone. And always, winter and summer, the intermittent rains drip sullenly down to be absorbed by the spongy soil and given back again as sticky, unpleasant, unhealthy steam.

And that, the vast amount of moisture on Venus, was the greatest surprise of the first human visitors; the clouds had been seen, of course, but the spectroscope denied the presence of water, naturally, since it was analyzing light reflected from the upper cloud surfaces, fifty miles above the planet's face.

That abundance of water has strange consequences. There are no seas or oceans on Venus, if we expect the probability of vast, silent, and eternally frozen oceans on the sunless side. On the hot hemisphere evaporation is too rapid, and the rivers that flow out of the ice mountains simply diminish and finally vanish, dried up.

A further consequence is the curiously unstable nature of the land of the twilight zone. Enormous subterranean rivers course invisibly through it, some boiling, some cold as the ice from which they flow. These are the cause of the mud eruptions that make human habitation in the Hotlands such a gamble; a perfectly solid and apparently safe area of soil may be changed suddenly into a boiling sea of mud in which buildings sink and vanish, together, frequently, with their occupants.

There is no way of predicting these catastrophes; only on the rare outcroppings of bed rock is a structure safe, and so all permanent human settlements cluster about the mountains.

Ham Hammond was a trader. He was one of those adventurous individuals who always appear on the frontiers and fringes of habitable regions. Most of these fall into two classes; they are either reckless daredevils pursuing danger, or outcasts, criminal or otherwise, pursuing either solitude or forgetfulness.

Ham Hammond was neither. He was pursuing no such abstractions, but the good, solid lure of wealth. He was, in fact, trading with the natives for the spore-pods of the Venusian plant *xixtchil*, from which terrestrial chemists would extract trihydroxyl-tertiary-tolunitrile-beta-anthraquinone, the xixtline or triple-T-B-A that was so effective in rejuvenation treatments.

Ham was young and sometimes wondered why rich old men—and women—would pay such tremendous prices for a few more years of virility, especially as the treatments didn't actually increase the span of life, but just produced a sort of temporary and synthetic youth.

Gray hair darkened, wrinkles filled out, bald heads grew fuzzy, and then, in a few years, the rejuvenated person was just as dead as he would have been, anyway. But as long as triple-T-B-A commanded a price about equal to its weight in radium, why, Ham was willing to take the gamble to obtain it.

He had never really expected the mudspout. Of course it was an ever-present danger, but when, staring idly through the window of his shack over the writhing and steaming Venusian plain, he had seen the sudden boiling pools erupting all around, it had come as a shocking surprise.

For a moment he was paralyzed; then he sprang into immediate and frantic action. He pulled on his enveloping suit of rubberlike transkin; he strapped the great bowls of mudshoes to his feet; he tied the precious bag of spore-pods to his shoulders, packed some food, and then burst into the open.

The ground was still semisolid, but even as he watched, the black soil boiled out around the metal walls of the shack, the cube tilted a trifle, and then sank deliberately from sight, and the mud sucked and gurgled as it closed gently above the spot.

Ham caught himself. One couldn't stand still in the midst of a mudspout, even with bowl-like mudshoes as support. Once let the viscous stuff flow over the rim and the luckless victim was trapped; he couldn't raise his foot against the suction, and first slowly, then more quickly, he'd follow the shack.

So Ham started off over the boiling swamp, walking with the peculiar sliding motion he had learned by much practice, never raising the mud-shoes above the surface, but sliding them along, careful that no mud topped the curving rim.

It was a tiresome motion, but absolutely necessary. He slid along as if on snowshoes, bearing west because that was the direction of the dark side, and if he had to walk to safety, he might as well do it in coolness. The area of swamp was unusually large; he covered at least a mile before he attained a slight rise in the ground, and the mudshoes clumped on solid, or nearly solid, soil.

He was bathed in perspiration, and his transkin suit was hot as a boiler room, but one grows accustomed to that on Venus. He'd have given half his supply of xixtchil pods for the opportunity to open the mask of the suit, to draw a breath of even the steamy and humid Venusian air, but that was impossible; impossible, at least, if he had any inclination to continue living.

One breath of unfiltered air anywhere near the warm edge of the twilight zone was quick and very painful death; Ham would have drawn in uncounted millions of the spores of those fierce Venusian molds, and they'd have sprouted in furry and nauseating masses in his nostrils, his mouth, his lungs, and eventually in his ears and eyes.

Breathing them wasn't even a necessary requirement; once he'd come upon a trader's body with the molds springing from his flesh. The poor fellow had somehow torn a rip in his transkin suit, and that was enough.

The situation made eating and drinking in the open a problem on Venus; one had to wait until a rain had precipitated the spores, when it was safe for half an hour or so. Even then the water must have been recently boiled and the food just removed from its can; otherwise, as had happened to Ham more than once, the food was apt to turn abruptly into a fuzzy mass of molds that grew about as fast as the minute hand moved on a clock. A disgusting sight! A disgusting planet!

That last reflection was induced by Ham's view of the quagmire that had engulfed his shack. The heavier vegetation had gone with it, but already avid and greedy life was emerging, wriggling mud grass and the bulbous fungi called "walking balls." And all around a million little slimy creatures slithered across the mud, eating each other rapaciously, being torn to bits, and each fragment re-forming to a complete creature.

A thousand different species, but all the same in one respect; each of them was all appetite. In common with most Venusian beings, they had a multiplicity of both legs and mouths; in fact some of them were little more than blobs of skin split into dozens of hungry mouths, and crawling on a hundred spidery legs.

All life on Venus is more or less parasitic. Even the plants that draw their nourishment directly from soil and air have also the ability to absorb and digest—and, often enough, to trap—animal food. So fierce is the competition on that humid strip of land between the fire and the ice that one who has never seen it must fail even to imagine it.

The animal kingdom wars incessantly on itself and the plant world; the vegetable kingdom retaliates, and frequently outdoes the other in the production of monstrous predatory horrors that one would even hesitate to call plant life. A terrible world!

In the few moments that Ham had paused to look back, ropy creepers had already entangled his legs; transkin was impervious, of course, but he had to cut the things away with his knife, and the black, nauseating juices that flowed out of them smeared on his suit and began instantly to grow furry as the molds sprouted. He shuddered.

"Hell of a place!" Ham growled, stooping to remove his mudshoes, which he slung carefully over his back.

He slogged away through the writhing vegetation, automatically dodging the awkward thrusts of the Jack Ketch trees as they cast their nooses hopefully toward his arms and head.

Now and again he passed one that dangled some trapped creature, usually unrecognizable because the molds had enveloped it in a fuzzy shroud, while the tree itself was placidly absorbing victim and molds alike.

"Horrible place!" Ham muttered, kicking a writhing mass of nameless little vermin from his path.

He mused; his shack had been situated rather nearer the hot edge of the twilight zone; it was a trifle over two hundred and fifty miles to the shadow line, though of course that varied with the libration. But one couldn't approach the line too closely, anyway, because of the fierce, almost inconceivable, storms that raged where the hot upper winds encountered the icy blasts of the night side, giving rise to the birth throes of the ice barrier.

So a hundred and fifty miles due west would be sufficient to bring coolness, to enter a region too temperate for the molds, where he could walk in comparative comfort. And then, not more than fifty miles north, lay the American settlement Erotia, named, obviously, after that troublesome mythical son of Venus, Cupid.

Intervening, of course, were the ranges of the Mountains of Eternity, not those mighty twenty-mile-high peaks whose summits are occasionally glimpsed by Earthly telescopes, and that forever sunder British Venus from the American possessions, but, even at the point he planned to cross, very respectable mountains indeed. He was on the British side now; not that any one cared. Traders came and went as they pleased.

Well, that meant about two hundred miles. No reason why he couldn't make it; he was armed with both automatic and flame-pistol, and water was no problem, if carefully boiled. Under pressure of necessity, one could even eat Venusian life—but it required hunger and thorough cooking and a sturdy stomach.

It wasn't the taste so much as the appearance, or so he'd been told. He grimaced; beyond doubt he'd be driven to find out for himself, since his canned food couldn't possibly last out the trip. Nothing to worry about, Ham kept telling himself. In fact, plenty to be glad about; the xixtchil pods in his pack represented as much wealth as he could have accumulated by ten years of toil back on Earth.

No danger—and yet, men had vanished on Venus, dozens of them. The molds had claimed them, or some fierce unearthly monster, or perhaps one of the many unknown living horrors, both plant and animal.

Ham trudged along, keeping always to the clearings about the Jack

Ketch trees, since these vegetable omnivores kept other life beyond the reach of their greedy nooses. Elsewhere progress was impossible, for the Venusian jungle presented such a terrific tangle of writhing and struggling forms that one could move only by cutting the way, step by step, with infinite labor.

Even then there was the danger of Heaven only knew what fanged and venomous creatures whose teeth might pierce the protective membrane of transkin, and a crack in that meant death. Even the unpleasant Jack Ketch trees were preferable company, he reflected, as he slapped their questing lariats aside.

Six hours after Ham had started his involuntary journey, it rained. He seized the opportunity, found a place where a recent mudspout had cleared the heavier vegetation away, and prepared to eat. First, however, he scooped up some scummy water, filtered it through the screen attached for that purpose to his canteen, and set about sterilizing it.

Fire was difficult to manage, since dry fuel is rare indeed in the Hotlands of Venus, but Ham tossed a thermide tablet into the liquid, and the chemicals boiled the water instantly, escaping themselves as gases. If the water retained a slight ammoniacal taste—well, that was the least of his discomforts, he mused, as he covered it and set it by to cool.

He uncapped a can of beans, watched a moment to see that no stray molds had remained in the air to infect the food, then opened the visor of his suit and swallowed hastily. Thereafter he drank the blood-warm water and poured carefully what remained into the water pouch within his transkin, where he could suck it through a tube to his mouth without the deadly exposure to the molds.

Ten minutes after he had completed the meal, while he rested and longed for the impossible luxury of a cigarette, the fuzzy coat sprang suddenly to life on the remnants of food in the can.

II.

An hour later, weary and thoroughly soaked in perspiration, Ham found a Friendly tree, so named by the explorer Burlingame because it is one of the few organisms on Venus sluggish enough to permit one to rest in its branches. So Ham climbed it, found the most comfortable position available, and slept as best he could.

It was five hours by his wrist watch before he awoke, and the tendrils and little sucking cups of the Friendly tree were fastened all over his transkin. He tore them away very carefully, climbed down, and trudged westward.

It was after the second rain that he met the doughpot, as the creature is called in British and American Venus. In the French strip, it's the *pot à colle*, the "paste pot"; in the Dutch—well, the Dutch are not prudish, and they call the horror just what they think it warrants.

Actually, the doughpot is a nauseous creature. It's a mass of white, doughlike protoplasm, ranging in size from a single cell to perhaps twenty tons of mushy filth. It has no fixed form; in fact, it's merely a mass of de Proust cells—in effect, a disembodied, crawling, hungry cancer.

It has no organization and no intelligence, nor even any instinct save hunger. It moves in whatever direction food touches its surfaces; when it touches two edible substances, it quietly divides, with the larger portion invariably attacking the greater supply.

It's invulnerable to bullets; nothing less than the terrific blast of a flame-pistol will kill it, and then only if the blast destroys every individual cell. It travels over the ground absorbing everything, leaving bare black soil where the ubiquitous molds spring up at once—a noisome, nightmarish creature.

Ham sprang aside as the doughpot erupted suddenly from the jungle to his right. It couldn't absorb the transkin, of course, but to be caught in that pasty mess meant quick suffocation. He glared at it disgustedly and was sorely tempted to blast it with his flame-pistol as it slithered past at running speed. He would have, too, but the experienced Venusian frontiersman is very careful with the flame-pistol.

It has to be charged with a diamond, a cheap black one, of course, but still an item to consider. The crystal, when fired, gives up all its energy in one terrific blast that roars out like a lightning stroke for a hundred yards, incinerating everything in its path.

The thing rolled by with a sucking and gulping sound. Behind it opened the passage it had cleared; creepers, snake vines, Jack Ketch trees—everything had been swept away down to the humid earth itself, where already the molds were springing up on the slime of the doughpot's trail.

The alley led nearly in the direction Ham wanted to travel; he seized the opportunity and strode briskly along, with a wary eye, nevertheless, on the ominous walls of jungle. In ten hours or so the opening would be filled once more with unpleasant life, but for the present it offered a much quicker progress than dodging from one clearing to the next.

It was five miles up the trail, which was already beginning to sprout inconveniently, that he met the native galloping along on his four short legs, his pincerlike hands shearing a path for him. Ham stopped for a palaver.

"*Murra*," he said.

The language of the natives of the equatorial regions of the Hotlands is a queer one. It has, perhaps, two hundred words, but when a trader has learned those two hundred, his knowledge of the tongue is but little greater than the man who knows none at all.

The words are generalized, and each sound has anywhere from a dozen to a hundred meanings. *Murra*, for instance, is a word of greeting; it may mean something much like "hello," or "good morning." It also may convey a challenge—"on guard!" It means besides, "Let's be friends," and also, strangely, "Let's fight this out."

It has, moreover, certain noun senses; it means peace, it means war, it means courage, and, again, fear. A subtle language; it is only very recently that studies of inflection have begun to reveal its nature to human philologists. Yet, after all, perhaps English, with its "to," "too," and "two," its "one," "won," "wan," "wen," "win," "when," and a dozen other similarities, might seem just as strange to Venusian ears, untrained in vowel distinctions.

Moreover, humans can't read the expressions of the broad, flat, three-eyed Venusian faces, which in the nature of things must convey a world of information among the natives themselves.

But this one accepted the intended sense. "*Murra*," he responded, pausing. "*Usk?*" That was, among other things, "Who are you?" or "Where did you come from?" or "Where are you bound?"

Ham chose the latter sense. He pointed off into the dim west; then raised his hand in an arc to indicate the mountains. "Erotia," he said. That had but one meaning, at least.

The native considered this in silence. At last he grunted and volunteered some information. He swept his cutting claw in a gesture west along the trail. "*Curky*," he said, and then, "*Murra*." The last was farewell; Ham pressed against the wriggling jungle wall to permit him to pass.

Curky meant, together with twenty other senses, trader. It was the word usually applied to humans, and Ham felt a pleasant anticipation in the prospect of human company. It had been six months since he had heard a human voice other than that on the tiny radio now sunk with his shack.

True enough, five miles along the doughpot's trail Ham emerged suddenly in an area where there had been a recent mudspout. The vegetation was only waist-high, and across the quarter-mile clearing he saw a structure, a trading hut. But far more pretentious than his own iron-walled cubicle; this one boasted three rooms, an unheard-of luxury in the Hotlands, where every ounce had to be laboriously transported by rocket from one of the settlements. That was expensive, almost prohibitive. Traders took a real gamble, and Ham knew he was lucky to have come out so profitably.

He strode over the still spongy ground. The windows were shaded against the eternal daylight, and the door—the door was locked. This was a violation of the frontier code. One always left doors unlocked; it might mean the salvation of some strayed trader, and not even the most dishonorable would steal from a hut left open for his safety.

Nor would the natives; no creature is as honest as a Venusian native, who never lies and never steals, though he might, after due warning, kill a trader for his trade goods. But only after a fair warning.

Ham stood puzzled. At last he kicked and tramped a clear space before the door, sat down against it, and fell to snapping away the numerous and loathsome little creatures that swarmed over his transkin. He waited.

It wasn't half an hour before he saw the trader plowing through the clearing—a short, slim fellow; the transkin shaded his face, but Ham could make out large, shadowed eyes. He stood up.

"Hello!" he said jovially. "Thought I'd drop in for a visit. My name's Hamilton Hammond—you guess the nickname!"

The newcomer stopped short, then spoke in a curiously soft and husky voice, with a decidedly English accent. "My guess would be 'Boiled Pork,' I fancy." The tones were cold, unfriendly. "Suppose you step aside and let me in. Good day!"

Ham felt anger and amazement. "The devil!" he snapped. "You're a hospitable sort, aren't you?"

"No. Not at all." The other paused at the door. "You're an American. What are you doing on British soil? Have you a passport?"

"Since when do you need a passport in the Hotlands?"

"Trading, aren't you?" the slim man said sharply. "In other words, poaching. You've no rights here. Get on."

Ham's jaw set stubbornly behind his mask. "Rights or none," he said, "I'm entitled to the consideration of the frontier code. I want a breath of air and a chance to wipe my face, and also a chance to eat. If you open that door I'm coming in after you."

An automatic flashed into view. "Do, and you'll feed the molds."

Ham, like all Venusian traders, was of necessity bold, resourceful, and what is called in the States "hard-boiled." He didn't flinch, but said in apparent yielding:

"All right; but listen, all I want is a chance to eat."

"Wait for a rain," said the other coolly and half turned to unlock the door.

As his eyes shifted, Ham kicked at the revolver; it went spinning against the wall and dropped into the weeds. His opponent snatched for the flame-pistol that still dangled on his hip; Ham caught his wrist in a mighty clutch.

Instantly the other ceased to struggle, while Ham felt a momentary surprise at the skinny feel of the wrist through its transkin covering.

"Look here!" he growled. "I want a chance to eat, and I'm going to get it. Unlock that door!"

He had both wrists now; the fellow seemed curiously delicate. After a moment he nodded, and Ham released one hand. The door opened, and he followed the other in.

Again, unheard-of magnificence. Solid chairs, a sturdy table, even books, carefully preserved, no doubt, by lycopodium against the ravenous molds that sometimes entered Hotland shacks in spite of screen filters and automatic spray. An automatic spray was going now to destroy any spores that might have entered with the opening door.

Ham sat down, keeping an eye on the other, whose flame-pistol he had permitted to remain in its holster. He was confident of his ability to outdraw the slim individual, and, besides, who'd risk firing a flame-pistol indoors? It would simply blow out one wall of the building.

So he set about opening his mask, removing food from his pack, wiping his steaming face, while his companion—or opponent—looked on silently. Ham watched the canned meat for a moment; no molds appeared, and he ate.

"Why the devil," he rasped, "don't you open your visor?" At the other's silence, he continued: "Afraid I'll see your face, eh? Well, I'm not interested; I'm no cop."

No reply.

He tried again. "What's your name?"

The cool voice sounded: "Burlingame. Pat Burlingame."

Ham laughed. "Patrick Burlingame is dead, my friend. I knew him." No answer. "And if you don't want to tell your name, at least you needn't insult the memory of a brave man and a great explorer."

"Thank you." The voice was sardonic. "He was my father."

"Another lie. He had no son. He had only a——" Ham paused abruptly; a feeling of consternation swept over him. "Open your visor!" he yelled.

He saw the lips of the other, dim through the transkin, twitch into a sarcastic smile.

"Why not?" said the soft voice, and the mask dropped.

Ham gulped; behind the covering were the delicately modeled features of a girl, with cool gray eyes in a face lovely despite the glistening perspiration on cheeks and forehead.

The man gulped again. After all, he was a gentleman despite his profession as one of the fierce, adventurous traders of Venus. He was university-educated—an engineer—and only the lure of quick wealth had brought him to the Hotlands.

"I—I'm sorry," he stammered.

"You brave American poachers!" she sneered. "Are all of you so valiant as to force yourselves on women?"

"But—how could I know? What are you doing in a place like this?"

"There's no reason for me to answer your questions, but"—she gestured toward the room beyond—"I'm classifying Hotland flora and fauna. I'm Patricia Burlingame, biologist."

He perceived now the jar-inclosed specimens of a laboratory in the next chamber. "But a girl alone in the Hotlands! It's—it's reckless!"

"I didn't expect to meet any American poachers," she retorted.

He flushed. "You needn't worry about me. I'm going." He raised his hands to his visor.

Instantly Patricia snatched an automatic from the table drawer. "You're going, indeed, Mr. Hamilton Hammond," she said coolly. "But you're leaving your xixtchil with me. It's crown property; you've stolen it from British territory, and I'm confiscating it."

He stared. "Look here!" he blazed suddenly. "I've risked all I have for that xixtchil. If I lose it I'm ruined—busted. I'm not giving it up!"

"But you are."

He dropped his mask and sat down. "Miss Burlingame," he said, "I don't think you've nerve enough to shoot me, but that's what you'll have to do to get it. Otherwise I'll sit here until you drop of exhaustion."

Her gray eyes bored silently into his blue ones. The gun held steadily on his heart, but spat no bullet. It was a deadlock.

At last the girl said, "You win, poacher." She slapped the gun into her empty holster. "Get out, then."

"Gladly!" he snapped.

He rose, fingered his visor, then dropped it again at a sudden startled scream from the girl. He whirled, suspecting a trick, but she was staring out of the window with wide, apprehensive eyes.

Ham saw the writhing of vegetation and then a vast whitish mass. A doughpot—a monstrous one, bearing steadily toward their shelter. He heard the gentle *clunk* of impact, and then the window was blotted out by the pasty mess, as the creature, not quite large enough to engulf the building, split into two masses that flowed around and remerged on the other side.

Another cry from Patricia. "Your mask, fool!" she rasped. "Close it!"

"Mask? Why?" Nevertheless, he obeyed automatically.

"Why? That's why! The digestive acids—look!"

She pointed at the walls; indeed, thousands of tiny pinholes of light were appearing. The digestive acids of the monstrosity, powerful enough to attack whatever food chance brought, had corroded the metal; it was porous; the shack was ruined. He gasped as fuzzy molds shot instantly from the remains of his meal, and a red-and-green fur sprouted from the wood of chairs and table.

The two faced each other.

Ham chuckled. "Well," he said, "you're homeless, too. Mine went down in a mudspout."

"Yours would!" Patricia retorted acidly. "You Yankees couldn't think of finding shallow soil, I suppose. Bed rock is just six feet below here, and *my* place is on pilons."

"Well, you're a cool devil! Anyway, your place might as well be sunk. What are you going to do?"

"Do? Don't concern yourself. I'm quite able to manage."

"How?"

"It's no affair of yours, but I have a rocket call each month."

"You must be a millionaire, then," he commented.

"The Royal Society," she said coldly, "is financing this expedition. The rocket is due——"

She paused; Ham thought she paled a little behind her mask.

"Due when?"

"Why—it just came two days ago. I'd forgotten."

"I see. And you think you'll just stick around for a month waiting for it. Is that it?"

Patricia stared at him defiantly.

"Do you know," he resumed, "what you'd be in a month? It's ten days to summer and look at your shack." He gestured at the walls, where brown and rusty patches were forming; at his motion a piece the size of a saucer tumbled in with a crackle. "In two days this thing will be a caved-in ruin. What'll you do during fifteen days of summer? What'll you do without shelter when the temperature reaches a hundred and fifty—a hundred and sixty? I'll tell you—you'll die."

She said nothing.

"You'll be a fuzzy mass of molds before the rocket returns," Ham said. "And then a pile of clean bones that will go down with the first mud-spout."

"Be still!" she blazed.

"Silence won't help. Now I'll tell you what you can do. You can take your pack and your mudshoes and walk along with me. We can make the Cool Country before summer—if you can walk as well as you talk."

"Go with a Yankee poacher? I fancy not!"

"And then," he continued imperturbably, "we can cross comfortably to Erotia, a good American town."

Patricia reached for her emergency pack, slung it over her shoulders. She retrieved a thick bundle of notes, written in aniline ink on transkin, brushed off a few vagrant molds, and slipped it into the pack. She picked up a pair of diminutive mudshoes and turned deliberately to the door.

"So you're coming?" he chuckled.

"I'm going," she retorted coldly, "to the good British town of Venoble. Alone!"

"Venoble!" he gasped. "That's two hundred miles south! And across the Greater Eternities, too!"

III.

Patricia walked silently out of the door and turned west toward the Cool Country. Ham hesitated a moment, then followed. He couldn't permit the girl to attempt that journey alone; since she ignored his presence, he simply trailed a few steps behind her, plodding grimly and angrily along.

For three hours or more they trudged through the endless daylight, dodging the thrusts of the Jack Ketch trees, but mostly following the still fairly open trail of the first doughpot.

Ham was amazed at the agile and lithe grace of the girl, who slipped along the way with the sure skill of a native. Then a memory came to him; she *was* a native, in a sense. He recalled now that Patrick Burlingame's daughter was the first human child born on Venus, in the colony of Venoble, founded by her father.

Ham remembered the newspaper articles when she had been sent to Earth to be educated, a child of eight; he had been thirteen then. He was twenty-seven now, which made Patricia Burlingame twenty-two.

Not a word passed between them until at last the girl swung about in exasperation.

"Go away," she blazed.

Ham halted. "I'm not bothering you."

"But I don't want a bodyguard. I'm a better Hotlander than you!"

He didn't argue the point. He kept silent, and after a moment she flashed:

"I hate you, Yankee! Lord, how I hate you!" She turned and trudged on.

An hour later the mudspout caught them. Without warning, watery muck boiled up around their feet, and the vegetation swayed wildly. Hastily, they strapped on their mudshoes, while the heavier plants sank with sullen gurgles around them. Again Ham marveled at the girl's skill; Patricia slipped away across the unstable surface with a speed he could not match, and he shuffled far behind.

Suddenly he saw her stop. That was dangerous in a mudspout; only an emergency could explain it. He hurried; a hundred feet away he perceived the reason. A strap had broken on her right shoe, and she stood helpless, balancing on her left foot, while the remaining bowl was sinking slowly. Even now black mud slopped over the edge.

She eyed him as he approached. He shuffled to her side; as she saw his intention, she spoke.

"You can't," she said.

Ham bent cautiously, slipping his arms about her knees and shoulders. Her mudshoe was already embedded, but he heaved mightily, driving the rims of his own dangerously close to the surface. With a great sucking gulp, she came free and lay very still in his arms, so as not to unbalance him as he slid again into careful motion over the treacherous surface. She was not heavy, but it was a hairbreadth chance, and the mud slipped and gurgled at the very edge of his shoe-bowls. Even though Venus has slightly less surface gravitation than Earth, a week or so gets one accustomed to it, and the twenty per cent advantage in weight seems to disappear.

A hundred yards brought firm footing. He sat her down and unstrapped his mudshoes.

"Thank you," she said coolly. "That was brave."

"You're welcome," he returned dryly. "I suppose this will end any idea of your traveling alone. Without both mudshoes, the next spout will be the last for you. Do we walk together now?"

Her voice chilled. "I can make a substitute shoe from tree skin."

"Not even a native could walk on tree skin."

"Then," she said, "I'll simply wait a day or two for the mud to dry and dig up my lost one."

He laughed and gestured at the acres of mud. "Dig where?" he countered. "You'll be here till summer if you try that."

She yielded. "You win again, Yankee. But only to the Cool Country; then you'll go north and I south."

They trudged on. Patricia was as tireless as Ham himself and vastly more adept in Hotland lore. Though they spoke but little, he never ceased to wonder at the skill she had in picking the quickest route, and she seemed to sense the thrusts of the Jack Ketch trees without looking. But it was when they halted at last, after a rain had given opportunity for a hasty meal, that he had real cause to thank her.

"Sleep?" he suggested, and as she nodded: "There's a Friendly tree."

He moved toward it, the girl behind.

Suddenly she seized his arm. "It's a Pharisee!" she cried, jerking him back.

None too soon! The false Friendly tree had lashed down with a terrible stroke that missed his face by inches. It was no Friendly tree at all, but an imitator, luring prey within reach by its apparent harmlessness, then striking with knife-sharp spikes.

Ham gasped. "What is it? I never saw one of those before."

"A Pharisee! It just looks like a Friendly tree."

She took out her automatic and sent a bullet into the black, pulsing trunk. A dark stream gushed, and the ubiquitous molds sprang into life about the hole. The tree was doomed.

"Thanks," said Ham awkwardly. "I guess you saved my life."

"We're quits now." She gazed levelly at him. "Understand? We're even."

Later they found a true Friendly tree and slept. Awakening, they trudged on again, and slept again, and so on for three nightless days. No more mudspouts burst about them, but all the other horrors of the Hotlands were well in evidence. Doughpots crossed their path, snake vines hissed and struck, the Jack Ketch trees flung sinister nooses, and a million little crawling things writhed underfoot or dropped upon their suits.

Once they encountered a uniped, that queer, kangaroolike creature that leaps, crashing through the jungle on a single mighty leg, and trusts to its ten-foot beak to spear its prey.

When Ham missed his first shot, the girl brought it down in mid-leap to thresh into the avid clutches of the Jack Ketch trees and the merciless molds.

On another occasion, Patricia had both feet caught in a Jack Ketch noose that lay for some unknown cause on the ground. As she stepped within it, the tree jerked her suddenly, to dangle head down a dozen feet in the air, and she hung helplessly until Ham managed to cut her free. Beyond doubt, either would have died alone on any of several occasions; together they pulled through.

Yet neither relaxed the cool, unfriendly attitude that had become habitual. Ham never addressed the girl unless necessary, and she in the rare instances when they spoke, called him always by no other name than Yankee poacher. In spite of this, the man found himself sometimes remembering the piquant loveliness of her features, her brown hair and level gray eyes, as he had glimpsed them in the brief moments when rain made it safe to open their visors.

At last one day a wind stirred out of the west, bringing with it a breath of coolness that was like the air of heaven to them. It was the underwind, the wind that blew from the frozen half of the planet, that breathed cold from beyond the ice barrier. When Ham experimentally shaved the skin from a writhing weed, the molds sprang out more slowly and with encouraging sparseness; they were approaching the Cool Country.

They found a Friendly tree with lightened hearts; another day's trek might bring them to the uplands where one could walk unhooded, in safety from the molds, since these could not sprout in a temperature much below eighty.

Ham woke first. For a while he gazed silently across at the girl, smiling at the way the branches of the tree had encircled her like affectionate arms. They were merely hungry, of course, but it looked like tenderness. His smile turned a little sad as he realized that the Cool Country meant parting, unless he could discourage that insane determination of hers to cross the Greater Eternities.

He sighed, and reached for his pack slung on a branch between them, and suddenly a bellow of rage and astonishment broke from him.

His xixtchil pods! The transkin pouch was slit; they were gone.

Patricia woke startled at his cry. Then, behind her mask, he sensed an ironic, mocking smile.

"My xixtchil!" he roared. "Where is it?"

She pointed down. There among the lesser growths was a little mound of molds.

"There," she said coolly. "Down there, poacher."

"You——" He choked with rage.

"Yes. I slit the pouch while you slept. You'll smuggle no stolen wealth from British territory."

Ham was white, speechless. "You damned devil!" he bellowed at last. "That's every cent I had!"

"But stolen," she reminded him pleasantly, swinging her dainty feet.

Rage actually made him tremble. He glared at her; the light struck through the translucent transkin, outlining her body and slim rounded legs in shadow. "I ought to kill you!" he muttered tensely.

His hand twitched, and the girl laughed softly. With a groan of desperation, he slung his pack over his shoulders and dropped to the ground.

"I hope—I hope you die in the mountains," he said grimly, and stalked away toward the west.

A hundred yards distant he heard her voice.

"Yankee! Wait a moment!"

He neither paused nor glanced back, but strode on.

Half an hour later, glancing back from the crest of a rise, Ham perceived that she was following him. He turned and hurried on. The way was upward now, and his strength began to outweigh her speed and skill.

When next he glimpsed her, she was a plodding speck far behind, moving, he imagined, with a weary doggedness. He frowned back at her; it had occurred to him that a mudspout would find her completely helpless, lacking the vitally important mudshoes.

Then he realized that they were beyond the region of mudspouts, here in the foothills of the Mountains of Eternity, and anyway, he decided grimly, he didn't care.

For a while Ham paralleled a river, doubtless an unnamed tributary of the Phlegethon. So far there had been no necessity to cross watercourses, since naturally all streams on Venus flow from the ice barrier across the twilight zone to the hot side, and therefore had coincided with their own direction.

But now, once he attained the table-lands and turned north, he would encounter rivers. They had to be crossed either on logs or, if opportunity offered and the stream was narrow, through the branches of Friendly trees. To set foot in the water was death; fierce fanged creatures haunted the streams.

He had one near catastrophe at the rim of the table-land. It was while he edged through a Jack Ketch clearing; suddenly there was a heave of white corruption, and tree and jungle wall disappeared in the mass of a gigantic doughpot.

He was cornered between the monster and an impenetrable tangle of vegetation, so he did the only thing left to do. He snatched his flame-pistol and sent a terrific, roaring blast into the horror, a blast that incinerated tons of pasty filth and left a few small fragments crawling and feeding on the debris.

The blast also, as it usually does, shattered the barrel of the weapon. He sighed as he set about the forty-minute job of replacing it—no true Hotlander ever delays that—for the blast had cost fifteen good American dollars, ten for the cheap diamond that had exploded, and five for the barrel. Nothing at all when he had had his xixtchil, but a real item now. He sighed again as he discovered that the remaining barrel was his last; he had been forced to economize on everything when he set out.

Ham came at last to the table-land. The fierce and predatory vegetation of the Hotlands grew scarce; he began to encounter true plants, with no power of movement, and the underwind blew cool in his face.

He was in a sort of high valley; to his right were the gray peaks of the Lesser Eternities, beyond which lay Erotia, and to his left, like a mighty, glittering rampart, lay the vast slopes of the Greater Range, whose peaks were lost in the clouds fifteen miles above.

He looked at the opening of the rugged Madman's Pass where it separated two colossal peaks; the pass itself was twenty-five thousand feet in height, but the mountains out-topped it by fifty thousand more. One man had crossed that jagged crack on foot—Patrick Burlingame—and that was the way his daughter meant to follow.

Ahead, visible as a curtain of shadow, lay the night edge of the twilight zone, and Ham could see the incessant lightnings that flashed forever in this region of endless storms. It was here that the ice barrier crossed the ranges of the Mountains of Eternity, and the cold underwind, thrust up by the mighty range, met the warm upper winds in a struggle that was one continuous storm, such a storm as only Venus could provide. The river Phlegethon had its source somewhere back in there.

Ham surveyed the wildly magnificent panorama. To-morrow, or rather, after resting, he would turn north. Patricia would turn south, and, beyond doubt, would die somewhere on Madman's Pass. For a moment he had a queerly painful sensation, then he frowned bitterly.

Let her die, if she was fool enough to attempt the pass alone just because she was too proud to take a rocket from an American settlement. She deserved it. He didn't care; he was still assuring himself of that as he prepared to sleep, not in a Friendly tree, but in one of the far more friendly specimens of true vegetation and in the luxury of an open visor.

The sound of his name awakened him. He gazed across the table-land to see Patricia just topping the divide, and he felt a moment's wonder at how she had managed to trail him, a difficult feat indeed in a country where the living vegetation writhes instantly back across one's path. Then he recalled the blast of his flame-pistol; the flash and sound would carry for miles, and she must have heard or seen it.

Ham saw her glancing anxiously around.

"Ham!" she shouted again—not Yankee or poacher, but "Ham!"

He kept a sullen silence; again she called. He could see her bronzed and piquant features now; she had dropped her transkin hood. She called again; with a despondent little shrug, she turned south along the divide, and he watched her go in grim silence. When the forest hid her from view, he descended and turned slowly north.

Very slowly; his steps lagged; it was as if he tugged against some invisible elastic bond. He kept seeing her anxious face and hearing in memory the despondent call. She was going to her death, he believed, and, after all, despite what she had done to him, he didn't want that. She was too full of life, too confident, too young, and above all, too lovely to die.

True, she was an arrogant, vicious, self-centered devil, cool as crystal, and as unfriendly, but—she had gray eyes and brown hair, and she was courageous. And at last, with a groan of exasperation, he halted his lagging steps, turned, and rushed with almost eager speed into the south.

Trailing the girl was easy here for one trained in the Hotlands. The vegetation was slow to mend itself, here in the Cool Country, and now and again he found imprints of her feet, or broken twigs to make her path. He found the place where she had crossed the river through tree branches, and he found a place where she had paused to eat.

But he saw that she was gaining on him; her skill and speed outmatched his, and the trail grew steadily older. At last he stopped to rest; the table-land was beginning to curve upward toward the vast Mountains of Eternity, and on rising ground he knew he could overtake her. So he slept for a while in the luxurious comfort of no transkin at all, just the shorts and shirt that one wore beneath. That was safe here; the eternal underwind, blowing always toward the Hotlands, kept drifting mold spores away, and any brought in on the fur of animals died quickly at the first cool breeze. Nor would the true plants of the Cool Country attack his flesh.

He slept five hours. The next "day" of traveling brought another change in the country. The life of the foothills was sparse compared to the tablelands; the vegetation was no longer a jungle, but a forest, an unearthly forest, true, of treelike growths whose boles rose five hundred feet and then spread, not into foliage, but flowery appendages. Only an occasional Jack Ketch tree reminded him of the Hotlands.

Farther on, the forest diminished. Great rock outcroppings appeared, and vast red cliffs with no growths of any kind. Now and then he encountered swarms of the planet's only aerial creatures, the gray, mothlike dusters, large as hawks, but so fragile that a blow shattered them. They darted about, alighting at times to seize small squirming things, and tinkling in their curiously bell-like voices. And apparently almost above him, though really thirty miles distant, loomed the Mountains of Eternity, their peaks lost in the clouds that swirled fifteen miles overhead.

Here again it grew difficult to trail, since Patricia scrambled often over bare rock. But little by little the signs grew fresher; once again his greater strength began to tell. And then he glimpsed her, at the base of a colossal escarpment split by a narrow, tree-filled canyon.

She was peering first at the mighty precipice, then at the cleft, obviously wondering whether it offered a means of scaling the barrier, or whether it was necessary to circle the obstacle. Like himself, she had discarded her transkin and wore the usual shirt and shorts of the Cool Country, which, after all, is not very cool by terrestrial standards. She looked, he thought, like some lovely forest nymph of the ancient slopes of Pelion.

He hurried as she moved into the canyon. "Pat!" he shouted; it was the first time he had spoken her given name. A hundred feet within the passage he overtook her.

"You!" she gasped. She looked tired; she had been hurrying for hours, but a light of eagerness flashed in her eyes. "I thought you had—I tried to find you."

Ham's face held no responsive light. "Listen here, Pat Burlingame," he said coldly. "You don't deserve any consideration, but I can't see you walking into death. You're a stubborn devil, but you're a woman. I'm taking you to Erotia."

The eagerness vanished. "Indeed, poacher? My father crossed here. I can, too."

"Your father crossed in midsummer, didn't he? And midsummer's to-day. You can't make Madman's Pass in less than five days, a hundred and twenty hours, and by then it will be nearly winter, and this longitude will be close to the storm line. You're a fool."

She flushed. "The pass is high enough to be in the upper winds. It will be warm."

"Warm! Yes—warm with lightning." He paused; the faint rumble of thunder rolled through the canyon. "Listen to that. In five days that will be right over us." He gestured up at the utterly barren slopes. "Not even Venusian life can get a foothold up there—or do you think you've got brass enough to be a lightning rod? Maybe you're right."

Anger flamed. "Rather the lightning than you!" Patricia snapped, and then as suddenly softened. "I tried to call you back," she said irrelevantly.

"To laugh at me," he retorted bitterly.

"No. To tell you I was sorry, and that——"

"I don't want your apology."

"But I wanted to tell you that——"

"Never mind," he said curtly. "I'm not interested in your repentance. The harm's done." He frowned coldly down on her.

Patricia said meekly: "But I——"

A crashing and gurgling interrupted her, and she screamed as a gigantic doughpot burst into view, a colossus that filled the canyon from wall to wall to a six-foot height as it surged toward them. The horrors were rarer in the Cool Country, but larger, since the abundance of food in the Hot-lands kept subdividing them. But this one was a giant, a behemoth, tons and tons of nauseous, ill-smelling corruption heaving up the narrow way. They were cut off.

Ham snatched his flame-pistol, but the girl seized his arm.

"No, no!" she cried. "Too close! It will spatter!"

IV.

Patricia was right. Unprotected by transkin, the touch of a fragment of that monstrosity was deadly, and, beyond that, the blast of a flame-pistol would shower bits of it upon them. He grasped her wrist and they fled up the canyon, striving for vantage-way enough to risk a shot. And a dozen feet behind surged the doughpot, traveling blindly in the only direction it could—the way of food.

They gained. Then, abruptly, the canyon, which had been angling southwest, turned sharply south. The light of the eternally eastward Sun was hidden; they were in a pit of perpetual shadow, and the ground was bare and lifeless rock. And as it reached that point, the doughpot halted; lacking any organization, any will, it could not move when no food gave it direction. It was such a monster as only the life-swarming climate of Venus could harbor; it lived only by endless eating.

The two paused in the shadow.

"Now what?" muttered Ham.

A fair shot at the mass was impossible because of the angle; a blast would destroy only the portion it could reach.

Patricia leaped upward, catching a snaky shrub on the wall, so placed that it received a faint ray of light. She tossed it against the pulsing mass; the whole doughpot lunged forward a foot or two.

"Lure it in," she suggested.

They tried. It was impossible; vegetation was too sparse.

"What will happen to the thing?" asked Ham.

"I saw one stranded on the desert edge of the Hotlands," replied the girl. "It quivered around for a long time, and then the cells attacked each other. It ate itself." She shuddered. "It was—horrible!"

"How long?"

"Oh, forty or fifty hours."

"I won't wait *that* long," growled Ham. He fumbled in his pack, pulling out his transkin.

"What will you do?"

"Put this on and try to blast that mass out of here at close range." He fingered his flame-pistol. "This is my last barrel," he said gloomily, then more hopefully: "But we have yours."

"The chamber of mine cracked last time I used it, ten or twelve hours ago. But I have plenty of barrels."

"Good enough!" said Ham.

He crept cautiously toward the horrible, pulsating wall of white. He thrust his arm so as to cover the greatest angle, pulled the trigger, and the roar and blazing fire of the blast bellowed echoing through the canyon. Bits of the monster spattered around him, and the thickness of the remainder, lessened by the incineration of tons of filth, was now only three feet.

"The barrel held!" he called triumphantly. It saved much time in recharging.

Five minutes later the weapon crashed again. When the mass of the monstrosity stopped heaving, only a foot and a half of depth remained, but the barrel had been blown to atoms.

"We'll have to use yours," he said.

Patricia produced one, he took it, and then stared at it in dismay. The barrels of her Enfield-made weapon were far too small for his American pistol stock!

He groaned. "Of all the idiots!" he burst out.

"Idiots!" she flared. "Because you Yankees use trench mortars for your barrels?"

"I meant myself. I should have guessed this." He shrugged. "Well, we have our choice now of waiting here for the doughpot to eat himself, or trying to find some other way out of this trap. And my hunch is that this canyon's blind."

It was probable, Patricia admitted. The narrow cleft was the product of some vast, ancient upheaval that had split the mountain in halves. Since it was not the result of water erosion, it was likely enough that the cleft ended abruptly in an unscalable precipice, but it was possible, too, that somewhere those sheer walls might be surmountable.

"We've time to waste, anyway," she concluded. "We might as well try it. Besides——" She wrinkled her dainty nose distastefully at the doughpot's odor.

Still in his transkin, Ham followed her through the shadowy half dusk. The passage narrowed, then veered west again, but now so high and sheer were the walls that the Sun, slightly south of east, cast no light into it. It was a place of shades like the region of the storm line that divides the twilight zone from the dark hemisphere, not true night, nor yet honest day, but a dim middle state.

Ahead of him Patricia's bronzed limbs showed pale instead of tan, and when she spoke her voice went echoing queerly between the opposing cliffs. A weird place, this chasm, a dusky, unpleasant place.

"I don't like this," said Ham. "The pass is cutting closer and closer to the dark. Do you realize no one knows what's in the dark parts of the Mountains of Eternity?"

Patricia laughed; the sound was ghostly. "What danger could there be? Anyway, we still have our automatics."

"There's no way up here," Ham grumbled. "Let's turn back."

Patricia faced him. "Frightened, Yankee?" Her voice dropped. "The natives say these mountains are haunted," she went on mockingly. "My father told me he saw queer things in Madman's Pass. Do you know that if there is life on the night side, here is the one place it would impinge on the twilight zone? Here in the Mountains of Eternity?"

She was taunting him; she laughed again. And suddenly her laughter was repeated in a hideous cacophony that hooted out from the sides of the cliffs above them in a horrid medley.

She paled; it was Patricia who was frightened now. They stared apprehensively up at the rock walls where strange shadows flickered and shifted.

"What—what was it?" she whispered. And then: "Ham! Did you see that?"

Ham had seen it. A wild shape had flung itself across the strip of sky, leaping from cliff to cliff far above them. And again came a peal of hooting that sounded like laughter, while shadowy forms moved, flylike, on the sheer walls.

"Let's go back!" she gasped. "Quickly!"

As she turned, a small black object fell and broke with a sullen pop before them. Ham stared at it. A pod, a spore-sac, of some unknown variety. A lazy, dusky cloud drifted over it, and suddenly both of them were choking violently. Ham felt his head spinning in dizziness, and Patricia reeled against him.

"It's—narcotic!" she gasped. "Back!"

But a dozen more *plopped* around them. The dusty spores whirled in dark eddies, and breathing was a torment. They were being drugged and suffocated at the same time.

Ham had a sudden inspiration. "Mask!" he choked, and pulled his transkin over his face.

The filter that kept out the molds of the Hotlands cleaned the air of these spores as well; his head cleared. But the girl's covering was somewhere in her pack; she was fumbling for it. Abruptly she sat down, swaying.

"My pack," she murmured. "Take it out with you. Your—your——" She broke into a fit of coughing.

He dragged her under a shallow overhang and ripped her transkin from the pack. "Put it on!" he snapped.

A score of pods were popping.

A figure flitted silently far up on the wall of rock. Ham watched its progress, then aimed his automatic and fired. There was a shrill, rasping scream, answered by a chorus of dissonant ululations, and something as large as a man whirled down to crash not ten feet from him.

The thing was hideous. Ham stared appalled at a creature not unlike a native, three-eyed, two-handed, four-legged, but the hands, though two-fingered like the Hotlanders', were not pincerlike, but white and clawed. And the face! Not the broad, expressionless face of the others, but a slanting, malevolent, dusky visage with each eye double the size of the natives'. It wasn't dead; it glared hatred and seized a stone, flinging it at him with weak viciousness. Then it died.

Ham didn't know what it was, of course. Actually it was a *triops noctivivans*—the "three-eyed dweller in the dark," the strange, semi-intelligent being that is as yet the only known creature of the night side, and a member of that fierce remnant still occasionally found in the sunless parts of the Mountains of Eternity. It is perhaps the most vicious creature in the known planets, absolutely unapproachable, and delighting in slaughter.

At the crash of the shot, the shower of pods had ceased, and a chorus of laughing hoots ensued. Ham seized the respite to pull the girl's transkin over her face; she had collapsed with it only half on.

Then a sharp crack sounded, and a stone rebounded to strike his arm. Others pattered around him, whining past, swift as bullets. Black figures flickered in great leaps against the sky, and their fierce laughter sounded mockingly. He fired at one in mid air; the cry of pain rasped again, but the creature did not fall.

Stones pelted him. They were all small ones, pebble-sized, but they were flung so fiercely that they hummed in passage, and they tore his flesh through his transkin. He turned Patricia on her face, but she moaned faintly as a missile struck her back. He shielded her with his own body.

The position was intolerable. He must risk a dash back, even though the doughpot blocked the opening. Perhaps, he thought, armored in transkin he could wade through the creature. He knew that was an insane idea; the gluey mass would roll him into itself to suffocate—but it had to be faced. He gathered the girl in his arms and rushed suddenly down the canyon.

Hoots and shrieks and a chorus of mocking laughter echoed around him. Stones struck him everywhere. One glanced from his head, sending him stumbling and staggering against the cliff. But he ran doggedly on; he knew now what drove him. It was the girl he carried; he *had* to save Patricia Burlingame.

Ham reached the bend. Far up on the west wall glowed cloudy sunlight, and his weird pursuers flung themselves to the dark side. They couldn't stand daylight, and that gave him some assistance; by creeping very close to the eastern wall he was partially shielded.

Ahead was the other bend, blocked by the doughpot. As he neared it, he turned suddenly sick. Three of the creatures were grouped against the mass of white, eating—actually eating!—the corruption. They whirled, hooting, as he came; he shot two of them, and as the third leaped for the wall, he dropped that one as well, and it fell with a dull gulping sound into the doughpot.

Again he sickened; the doughpot drew away from it, leaving the thing lying in a hollow like the hole of a giant doughnut. Not even that monstrosity would eat these creatures.*

* Note: It was not known then that while the night-side life of Venus can eat and digest that of the day side, the reverse is not true. No day-side creature can absorb the dark life because of the presence of various metabolic alcohols, all poisonous.

But the thing's leap had drawn Ham's attention to a twelve-inch ledge. It might be—yes, it was possible that he could traverse that rugged trail and so circle the doughpot. Nearly hopeless, no doubt, to attempt it under the volley of stones, but he must. There was no alternative.

He shifted the girl to free his right arm. He slipped a second clip in his automatic and then fired at random into the flitting shadows above. For a moment the hail of pebbles ceased, and with a convulsive, painful struggle, Ham dragged himself and Patricia to the ledge.

Stones cracked about him once more. Step by step he edged along the way, poised just over the doomed doughpot. Death below and death above! And little by little he rounded the bend; above him both walls glowed in sunlight, and they were safe.

At least, *he* was safe. The girl might be already dead, he thought frantically, as he slipped and slid through the slime of the doughpot's passage. Out on the daylit slope he tore the mask from her face and gazed on white, marble-cold features.

It was not death, however, but only drugged torpor. An hour later she was conscious, though weak and very badly frightened. Yet almost her first question was for her pack.

"It's here," Ham said. "What's so precious about that pack? Your notes?"

"My notes? Oh, no!" A faint flush covered her features. "It's—I kept trying to tell you—it's your xixtchil."

"What?"

"Yes. I—of course I didn't throw it to the molds. It's yours by rights, Ham. Lots of British traders go into the American Hotlands. I just slit the pouch and hid it here in my pack. The molds on the ground were only some twigs I threw there to—to make it look real."

"But—but—why?"

The flush deepened. "I wanted to punish you," Patricia whispered, "for being so—so cold and distant."

"I?" Ham was amazed. "It was you!"

"Perhaps it was, at first. You forced your way into my house, you know. But—after you carried me across the mudspout, Ham—it was different."

Ham gulped. Suddenly he pulled her into his arms. "I'm not going to quarrel about whose fault it was," he said. "But we'll settle one thing immediately. We're going to Erotia, and that's where we'll be married, in a good American church if they've put one up yet, or by a good American justice if they haven't. There's no more talk of Madman's Pass and crossing the Mountains of Eternity. Is that clear?"

She glanced at the vast, looming peaks and shuddered. "Quite clear!" she replied meekly.

After Weinbaum's coming, there was a period when it seemed that every writer was turning out stories of strange life-forms. Stories became extraterrestrial travelogues, though no one ever did it as well as Weinbaum. When I began writing science fiction, I was not immune either. Even though I concentrated on human beings for the most part, I occasionally ventured into the Weinbaum-like bit, as in "Christmas on Ganymede."

My most Weinbaum-like story and, in fact, a conscious imitation of the spirit of "The Parasite Planet" was my juvenile novel *Lucky Starr and the Oceans of Venus*, written twenty years after the story that inspired it. (Don't worry. I hadn't forgotten.) What a pity that increasing astronomical knowledge concerning Venus has completely eliminated the possibility of its being a tropical, watery world and has made both "The Parasite Planet" and *Lucky Starr and the Oceans of Venus* ludicrously obsolete.

Science-fiction stories were steadily paying more attention to science. In "Colossus" the speed-of-light limitation was ignored. In a later story, "Proxima Centauri," by Murray Leinster, in the March 1935 *Astounding Stories*, it was not. The journey to the nearest star was described as a many-year trip.

PROXIMA CENTAURI

by Murray Leinster

The *Adastra*, from a little distance, already shone in the light of the approaching sun. The vision disks which scanned the giant space ship's outer skin relayed a faint illumination to the visiplates within. They showed the monstrous, rounded bulk of the metal globe, crisscrossed with girders too massive to be transported by any power less than that of the space ship itself. They showed the whole, five-thousand-foot globe as an ever so faintly glowing object, seemingly motionless in mid-space.

In that seeming, they lied. Monstrous as the ship was, and apparently too huge to be stirred by any conceivable power, she was responding to power now. At a dozen points upon her faintly glowing side there were openings. From those openings there flowed out tenuous purple flames. They gave little light, those flames—less than the star ahead—but they were the disintegration blasts from the rockets which had lifted the *Adastra* from the surface of Earth and for seven years had hurled it on through interstellar space toward Proxima Centauri, nearest of the fixed stars to humanity's solar system.

Now they hurled it forward no more. The mighty ship was decelerating. Thirty-two and two-tenths feet per second, losing velocity at the exact rate to maintain the effect of Earth's gravity within its bulk, the huge globe showed. For months braking had been going on. From a peak-speed measurably near the velocity of light, the first of all vessels to span the distance between two solar systems had slowed and slowed, and would reach a speed of maneuver some sixty million miles from the surface of the star.

Far, far ahead, Proxima Centauri glittered invitingly. The vision disks that showed its faint glow upon the space ship's hull had counterparts which carried its image within the hull, and in the main control room it appeared enlarged very many times. An old, white-bearded man in uniform regarded it meditatively. He said slowly, as if he had said the same thing often before:

"Quaint, that ring. It is double, like Saturn's. And Saturn has nine moons. One wonders how many planets this sun will have."

The girl said restlessly: "We'll find out soon, won't we? We're almost there. And we already know the rotation period of one of them! Jack said that——"

Her father turned deliberately to her. "Jack?"

"Gary," said the girl. "Jack Gary."

"My dear," said the old man mildly, "he seems well-disposed, and his abilities are good, but he is a Mut. Remember!"

The girl bit her lip.

The old man went on, quite slowly and without rancor: "It is unfortunate that we have had this division among the crew of what should have been a scientific expedition conducted in the spirit of a crusade. You hardly remember how it began. But we officers know only too well how many efforts have been made by the Muts to wreck the whole purpose of our voyage. This Jack Gary is a Mut. He is brilliant, in his way. I would have brought him into the officers' quarters, but Alstair investigated and found undesirable facts which made it impossible."

"I don't believe Alstair!" said the girl evenly. "And, anyhow, it was Jack who caught the signals. And he's the one who's working with them, officer or Mut! And he's human, anyhow. It's time for the signals to come again and you depend on him to handle them."

The old man frowned. He walked with a careful steadiness to a seat. He sat down with an old man's habitual and rather pathetic caution. The *Adastra*, of course, required no such constant vigilance at the controls as the interplanetary space ships require. Out here in emptiness there was no need to watch for meteors, for traffic, or for those queer and yet inexplicable force fields which at first made interplanetary flights so hazardous.

The ship was so monstrous a structure, in any case, that the tinier meteorites could not have harmed her. And at the speed she was now making greater ones would be notified by the induction fields in time for observation and if necessary the changing of her course.

A door at the side of the control room opened briskly and a man stepped in. He glanced with conscious professionalism at the banks of indicators. A relay clicked, and his eyes darted to the spot. He turned and saluted the old man with meticulous precision. He smiled at the girl.

"Ah, Alstair," said the old man. "You are curious about the signals, too?"

"Yes, sir. Of course! And as second in command I rather like to keep an eye on signals. Gary is a Mut, and I would not like him to gather information that might be kept from the officers."

"That's nonsense!" said the girl hotly.

"Probably," agreed Alstair. "I hope so. I even think so. But I prefer to leave out no precaution."

A buzzer sounded. Alstair pressed a button and a vision plate lighted. A dark, rather grim young face stared out of it.

"Very well, Gary," said Alstair curtly.

He pressed another button. The vision plate darkened and lighted again to show a long corridor down which a solitary figure came. It came close and the same face looked impassively out. Alstair said even more curtly:

"The other doors are open, Gary. You can come straight through."

"I think that's monstrous!" said the girl angrily as the plate clicked off. "You know you trust him! You have to! Yet every time he comes into officers' quarters you act as if you thought he had bombs in each hand and all the rest of the men behind him!"

Alstair shrugged and glanced at the old man, who said tiredly:

"Alstair is second in command, my dear, and he will be commander on the way back to Earth. I could wish you would be less offensive."

But the girl deliberately withdrew her eyes from the brisk figure of Alstair with its smart uniform, and rested her chin in her hands to gaze broodingly at the farther wall. Alstair went to the banks of indicators, surveying them in detail. The ventilator hummed softly. A relay clicked with a curiously smug, self-satisfied note. Otherwise there was no sound.

The *Adastra*, mightiest work of the human race, hurtled on through space with the light of a strange sun shining faintly upon her enormous hull. Twelve lambent purple flames glowed from holes in her forward part. She was decelerating, lessening her speed by thirty-two point two feet per second per second, maintaining the effect of Earth's gravity within her bulk.

Earth was seven years behind and uncounted millions of billions of miles. Interplanetary travel was a commonplace in the solar system now, and a thriving colony on Venus and a precariously maintained outpost on the largest of Jupiter's moons promised to make space commerce thrive even after the dead cities of Mars had ceased to give up their incredibly rich loot. But only the *Adastra* had ever essayed space beyond Pluto.

She was the greatest of ships, the most colossal structure ever attempted by men. In the beginning, indeed, her design was derided as impossible of achievement by the very men who later made her building a fact. Her framework beams were so huge that, once cast, they could not be moved by any lifting contrivance at her builders' disposal. Therefore the molds for them were built and the metal poured in their final position as a part of the ship. Her rocket tubes were so colossal that the necessary supersonic vibrations—to neutralize the disintegration effect of the Caldwell field—had to be generated at thirty separate points on each tube, else the disintegration of her fuel would have spread to the tubes themselves and the big ship afterward, with even the mother planet following in a burst of lambent purple flame. At full acceleration a set of twelve tubes disintegrated five cubic centimeters of water per second.

Her diameter was a shade over five thousand feet. Her air tanks carried a reserve supply which could run her crew of three hundred for ten months without purification. Her stores, her shops, her supplies of raw and finished materials, were in such vast quantities that to enumerate them would be merely to recite meaningless figures.

There were even four hundred acres of food-growing space within her, where crops were grown under sun lamps. Those crops used waste organic matter as fertilizer and restored exhaled carbon dioxide to use, in part as oxygen and in part as carbohydrate foodstuffs.

The *Adastra* was a world in herself. Given power, she could subsist her crew forever, growing her food supplies, purifying her own internal atmosphere without loss and without fail, and containing space within which every human need could be provided, even solitude.

And starting out upon the most stupendous journey in human history, she had formally been given the status of a world, with her commander empowered to make and enforce all needed laws. Bound for a destination four light-years distant, the minimum time for her return was considered to be fourteen years. No crew could possibly survive so long a voyage undecimated. Therefore the enlistments for the voyage had not been by men, but by families.

There were fifty children on board when the *Adastra* lifted from Earth's surface. In the first year of her voyage ten more were born. It had seemed to the people of Earth that not only could the mighty ship subsist her crew forever, but that the crew itself, well-nourished and with more than adequate facilities both for amusement and education, could so far perpetuate itself as to make a voyage of a thousand years as practicable as the mere journey to Proxima Centauri.

And so it could, but for a fact at once so needless and so human that nobody anticipated it. The fact was tedium. In less than six months the journey had ceased to become a great adventure. To the women in particular, the voyage of the big ship became deadly routine.

The *Adastra* itself took on the semblance of a gigantic apartment house without newspapers, department stores, new film plays, new faces, or even the relieving annoyances of changeable weather. The sheer completeness of all preparations for the voyage made the voyage itself uneventful. That meant tedium.

Tedium meant restlessness. And restlessness, with women on board who had envisioned high adventure, meant the devil to pay. Their husbands no longer appeared as glamorous heroes. They were merely human beings. The men encountered similar disillusionments. Pleas for divorce flooded the commander's desk, he being legally the fount of all legal action. During the eighth month there was one murder, and in the three months following, two more.

A year and a half out from Earth, and the crew was in a state of semi-mutiny originating in sheer boredom. By two years out, the officers' quarters were sealed off from the greater part of the *Adastra's* interior, the crew was disarmed, and what work was demanded of the mutineers was enforced by force guns in the hands of the officers. By three years out, the crew was demanding a return to Earth. But by the time the *Adastra* could be slowed and stopped from her then incredible velocity, she would be so near her destination as to make no appreciable difference in the length of her total voyage. For the rest of the time the members of the crew strove to relieve utter monotony by such vices and such pastimes as could be improvised in the absence of any actual need to work.

The officers' quarters referred to the underlings by a term become habitual, a contraction of the word "mutineers." The crew came to have a queer distaste for all dealing with the officers. But, despite Alstair, there was no longer much danger of an uprising. A certain mental equilibrium had—very late—developed.

From the nerve-racked psychology of dwellers in an isolated apartment house, the greater number of the *Adastra's* complement came to have the psychology of dwellers in an isolated village. The difference was profound. In particular the children who had come to maturity during the long journey through space were well-adjusted to the conditions of isolation and of routine.

Jack Gary was one of them. He had been sixteen when the trip began, son of a rocket-tube engineer whose death took place the second year out. Helen Bradley was another. She had been fourteen when her father, as designer and commanding officer of the mighty globe, pressed the control key that set the huge rockets into action.

Her father had been past maturity at the beginning. Aged by responsibility for seven uninterrupted years, he was an old man now. And he knew, and even Helen knew without admitting it, that he would never survive the long trip back. Alstair would take his place and the despotic authority inherent in it, and he wanted to marry Helen.

She thought of these things, with her chin cupped in her hand, brooding in the control room. There was no sound save the humming of the ventilator and the infrequent smug click of a relay operating the automatic machinery to keep the *Adastra* a world in which nothing ever happened.

A knock on the door. The commander opened his eyes a trifle vaguely. He was very old now, the commander. He had dozed.

Alstair said shortly, "Come in!" and Jack Gary entered.

He saluted, pointedly to the commander. Which was according to regulations, but Alstair's eyes snapped.

"Ah, yes," said the commander. "Gary. It's about time for more signals, isn't it?"

"Yes, sir."

Jack Gary was very quiet, very businesslike. Only once, when he glanced at Helen, was there any hint of anything but the formal manner of a man intent on his job. Then his eyes told her something, in an infinitely small fraction of a second, which changed her expression to one of flushed content.

Short as the glance was, Alstair saw it. He said harshly:

"Have you made any progress in deciphering the signals, Gary?"

Jack was setting the dials of a panwave receptor, glancing at penciled notes on a calculator pad. He continued to set up the reception pattern.

"No, sir. There is still a sequence of sounds at the beginning which must be a form of call, because a part of the same sequence is used as a signature at the close. With the commander's permission I have used the first part of that call sequence as a signature in our signals in reply. But in looking over the records of the signals I've found something that looks important."

The commander said mildly: "What is it, Gary?"

"We've been sending signals ahead of us on a tight beam, sir, for some months. Your idea was to signal ahead, so that if there were any civilized inhabitants on planets about the sun, they'd get an impression of a peaceful mission."

"Of course!" said the commander. "It would be tragic for the first of interstellar communications to be unfriendly!"

"We've been getting answers to our signals for nearly three months. Always at intervals of a trifle over thirty hours. We assumed, of course, that a fixed transmitter was sending them, and that it was signaling once a day when the station was in the most favorable position for transmitting to us."

"Of course," said the commander gently. "It gave us the period of rotation of the planet from which the signals come."

Jack Gary set the last dial and turned on the switch. A low-pitched hum arose, which died away. He glanced at the dials again, checking them.

"I've been comparing the records, sir, making due allowance for our approach. Because we cut down the distance between us and the star so rapidly, our signals to-day take several seconds less to reach Proxima Centauri than they did yesterday. Their signals should show the same shortening of interval, if they are actually sent out at the same instant of planetary time every day."

The commander nodded benevolently.

"They did, at first," said Jack. "But about three weeks ago the time interval changed in a brand-new fashion. The signal strength changed, and the wave form altered a little, too, as if a new transmitter was sending. And the first day of that change the signals came through one second earlier than our velocity of approach would account for. The second day they were three seconds earlier, the third day six, the fourth day ten, and so on. They kept coming earlier by a period indicating a linear function until one week ago. Then the rate of change began to decrease again."

"That's nonsense!" said Alstair harshly.

"It's records," returned Jack curtly.

"But how do you explain it, Gary?" asked the commander mildly.

"They're sending now from a space ship, sir," replied Jack briefly, "which is moving toward us at four times our maximum acceleration. And they're flashing us a signal at the same interval, according to their clocks, as before."

A pause. Helen Bradley smiled warmly. The commander thought carefully. Then he admitted:

"Very good, Gary! It sounds plausible. What next?"

"Why, sir," said Jack, "since the rate of change shifted, a week ago, it looks as if that other space ship started to decelerate again. Here are my calculations, sir. If the signals are sent at the same interval they kept up for over a moment, there is another space ship headed toward us, and she is decelerating to stop and reverse and will be matching our course and speed in four days and eighteen hours. They'll meet and surprise us, they think."

The commander's face lighted up. "Marvelous, Gary! They must be far advanced indeed in civilization! Intercourse between two such peoples, separated by four light-years of distance! What marvels we shall learn! And to think of their sending a ship far beyond their own system to greet and welcome us!"

Jack's expression remained grim.

"I hope so, sir," he said dryly.

"What now, Gary?" demanded Alstair angrily.

"Why," said Jack deliberately, "they're still pretending that the signals come from their planet, by signaling at what they think are the same times. They could exchange signals for twenty-four hours a day, if they chose, and be working out a code for communication. Instead, they're trying to deceive us. My guess is that they're coming at least prepared to fight. And if I'm right, their signals will begin in three seconds, exactly."

He stopped, looking at the dials of the receptor. The tape which photographed the waves as they came in, and the other which recorded the modulations, came out of the receptor blank. But suddenly, in just three seconds, a needle kicked over and tiny white lines appeared on the rushing tapes. The speaker uttered sounds.

It was a voice which spoke. So much was clear. It was harsh yet sibilant, more like the stridulation of an insect than anything else. But the sounds it uttered were modulated as no insect can modulate its outcry. They formed what were plainly words, without vowels or consonants, yet possessing expression and varying in pitch and tone quality.

The three men in the control room had heard them many times before, and so had the girl. But for the first time they carried to her an impression of menace, of threat, of a concealed lust for destruction that made her blood run cold.

II.

The space ship hurtled on through space, her rocket tubes sending forth small and apparently insufficient purple flames which emitted no smoke, gave off no gas, and were seemingly nothing but small marsh fires inexplicably burning in emptiness.

There was no change in her outer appearance. There had been none to speak of in years. At long, infrequent intervals men had emerged from air locks and moved about her sides, bathing the steel they walked on and themselves alike with fierce glares from heat lamps lest the cold of her plating transmit itself through the material of the suits and kill the men like ants on red-hot metal. But for a long time no such expedition had been needed.

Only now, in the distant faint light of Proxima Centauri, a man in a space suit emerged from such a tiny lock. Instantly he shot out to the end of a threadlike life line. The constant deceleration of the ship not only simulated gravity within. Anything partaking of its motion showed the same effect. The man upon its decelerating forward side was flung away from the ship by his own momentum, the same force which, within it, had pressed his feet against the floors.

He hauled himself back laboriously, moving with an exaggerated clumsiness in his bloated space suit. He clung to handholds and hooked himself in place, while he worked an electric drill. He moved still more clumsily to another place and drilled again. A third, and fourth, and fifth. For half an hour or more, then, he labored to set up on the vast steel surface, which seemed always above him, an intricate array of wires and framework. In the end he seemed content. He hauled himself back to the air lock and climbed within. The *Adastra* hurtled onward, utterly unchanged save for a very tiny fretwork of wire, perhaps thirty feet across, which looked more like a microscopic barbed-wire entanglement than anything else.

Within the *Adastra*, Helen Bradley greeted Jack warmly as he got out of his space suit.

"It was horrible!" she told him, "to see you dangling like that! With millions of miles of empty space below you!"

"If my line had parted," said Jack quietly, "your father'd have turned the ship and caught up to me. Let's go turn on the inductor and see how the new reception grid works."

He hung up the space suit. As they turned to go through the doorway their hands touched accidentally. They looked at each other and faltered. They stopped, Helen's eyes shining. They all unconsciously swayed toward each other. Jack's hands lifted hungrily.

Footsteps sounded close by. Alstair, second in command of the space ship, rounded a corner and stopped short.

"What's this?" he demanded savagely. "Just because the commander's brought you into officers' quarters, Gary, it doesn't follow that your Mut methods of romance can come, too!"

"You dare!" cried Helen furiously.

Jack, from a hot dull flush, was swiftly paling to the dead-white of rage.

"You'll take that back," he said very quietly indeed, "or I'll show you Mut methods of fighting with a force gun! As an officer, I carry one, too, now!"

Alstair snarled at him.

"Your father's been taken ill," he told Helen angrily. "He feels the voyage is about over. Anticipation has kept up his strength for months past, but now he's——"

With a cry, the girl fled.

Alstair swung upon Jack. "I take back nothing," he snapped. "You're an officer, by order of the commander. But you're a Mut besides, and when I'm commander of the *Adastra* you don't stay an officer long! I'm warning you! What were you doing here?"

Jack was deathly pale, but the status of officer on the *Adastra*, with its consequent opportunity of seeing Helen, was far too precious to be given up unless at the last extremity. And, besides, there was the work he had in hand. His work, certainly, could not continue unless he remained an officer.

"I was installing an interference grid on the surface," he said, "to try to discover the sending station of the messages we've been getting. It will also act, as you know, as an inductor up to a certain range, and in its range is a good deal more accurate than the main inductors of the ship."

"Then get to your damned work," said Alstair harshly, "and pay full attention to it and less to romance!"

Jack plugged in the lead wire from his new grid to the pan-wave receptor. For an hour he worked more and more grimly. There was something very wrong. The inductors showed blank for all about the *Adastra*. The interference grid showed an object of considerable size not more than two million miles distant and to one side of the *Adastra's* course. Suddenly, all indication of that object's existence blanked out. Every dial on the pan-wave receptor went back to zero.

"Damnation!" said Jack under his breath.

He set up a new pattern on the controls, calculated a moment and deliberately changed the pattern on the spare bank of the main inductors, and then simultaneously switched both instruments to their new frequencies. He waited, almost holding his breath, for nearly half a minute. It would take so long for the inductor waves of the new frequency to reach out the two million miles and then collapse into the analyzers and give their report of any object in space which had tended to deform them.

Twenty-six, twenty-seven, twenty-eight seconds. Every alarm bell on the monstrous ship clanged furiously! Emergency doors hissed into place all over the vessel, converting every doorway into an air lock. Seconds later, the visiplates in the main control room began to flash alight.

"Reporting, Rocket Control!" "Reporting, Air Service!" "Reporting, Power Supply."

Jack said crisply: "The main inductors report an object two million miles distant with velocity in our direction. The commander is ill. Please find Vice Commander Alstair."

Then the door of the control room burst open and Alstair himself raged into the room.

"What the devil!" he rasped. "Ringing a general alarm? Have you gone mad? The inductors——"

Jack pointed to the main inductor bank. Every dial bore out the message of the still-clanging alarms. Alstair stared blankly at them. As he looked, every dial went back to zero.

And Alstair's face went as blank as the dials.

"They felt out our inductor screens," said Jack grimly, "and put out some sort of radiation which neutralized them. So I set up two frequencies, changed both, and they couldn't adjust their neutralizers in time to stop our alarms."

Alstair stood still, struggling with the rage which still possessed him. Then he nodded curtly.

"Quite right. You did good work. Stand by."

And, quite cool and composed, he took command of the mighty space ship, even if there was not much for him to do. In five minutes, in fact, every possible preparation for emergency had been made and he turned again to Jack.

"I don't like you," he said coldly. "As one man to another, I dislike you intensely. But as vice commander and acting commander at the moment, I have to admit that you did good work in uncovering this little trick of our friends to get within striking distance without our knowing they were anywhere near."

Jack said nothing. He was frowning, but it was because he was thinking of Helen. The *Adastra* was huge and powerful, but she was not readily maneuverable. She was enormously massive, but she could not be used for ramming. And she possessed within herself almost infinite destructiveness, in the means of producing Caldwell fields for the disintegration of matter, but she contained no weapon more dangerous than a two-thousand-kilowatt vortex gun for the destruction of dangerous animals or vegetation where she might possibly land.

"What's your comment?" demanded Alstair shortly. "How do you size up the situation?"

"They act as if they're planning hostilities," replied Jack briefly, "and they've got four times our maximum acceleration so we can't get away. With that acceleration they ought to be more maneuverable, so we can't dodge them. We've no faintest idea of what weapons they carry, but we know that we can't fight them unless their weapons are very puny indeed. There's just one chance that I can see."

"What's that?"

"They tried to slip up on us. That looks as if they intended to open fire without warning. But maybe they are frightened and only expected to examine us without our getting a chance to attack them. In that case, our only bet is to swing over our signaling beam to the space ship. When they realize we know they're there and still aren't getting hostile, they may not guess we can't fight. They may think we want to be friendly and they'd better not start anything with a ship our size that's on guard."

"Very well. You're detailed to communication duty," said Alstair. "Go ahead and carry out that program. I'll consult the rocket engineers and see what they can improvise in the way of fighting equipment. Dismiss!"

His tone was harsh. It was arrogant. It rasped Jack's nerves and made him bristle all over. But he had to recognize that Alstair wasn't letting his frank dislike work to the disadvantage of the ship. Alstair was, in fact, one of those ambitious officers who are always cordially disliked by everybody, at all times, until an emergency arises. Then their competence shows up.

Jack went to the communications-control room. It did not take long to realign the transmitter beam. Then the sender began to repeat monotonously the recorded last message from the *Adastra* to the distant and so far unidentified planet of the ringed star. And while the signal went out, over and over again, Jack called on observations control for a sight of the strange ship.

They had a scanner on it now and by stepping up illumination to the utmost, and magnification to the point where the image was as rough as an old-fashioned half-tone cut, they brought the strange ship to the visiplate as a six-inch miniature.

It was egg-shaped and perfectly smooth. There was no sign of external girders, of protruding atmospheric-navigation fins, of escape-boat blisters. It was utterly featureless save for tiny spots which might be portholes, and rocket tubes in which intermittent flames flickered. It was still decelerating to match the speed and course of the *Adastra*.

"Have you got a spectroscope report on it?" asked Jack.

"Yeh," replied the observations orderly. "An' I don't believe it. They're using fuel rockets—some organic compound. An' the report says the hull of that thing is cellulose, not metal. It's wood, on the outside."

Jack shrugged. No sign of weapons. He went back to his own job. The space ship yonder was being penetrated through and through by the message waves. Its receptors could not fail to be reporting that a tight beam was upon it, following its every movement, and that its presence and probable mission were therefore known to the mighty ship from out of space.

But Jack's own receptors were silent. The tape came out of them utterly blank. No—a queer, scrambled, blurry line, as if the analyzers were unable to handle the frequency which was coming through. Jack read the heat effect. The other space ship was sending with a power which meant five thousand kilowatts pouring into the *Adastra*. Not a signal. Grimly, Jack heterodyned the wave on a five-meter circuit and read off its frequency and type. He called the main control.

"They're pouring short stuff into us," he reported stiffly to Alstair. "About five thousand kilowatts of thirty-centimeter waves, the type we use on Earth to kill weevils in wheat. It ought to be deadly to animal life, but of course our hull simply absorbs it."

Helen. Impossible to stop the *Adastra*. They'd started for Proxima Centauri. Decelerating though they were, they couldn't check much short of the solar system, and they were already attacked by a ship with four times their greatest acceleration. Pouring a deadly frequency into them—a frequency used on Earth to kill noxious insects. Helen was——

"Maybe they think we're dead! They'll know our transmitter's mechanical."

The G. C. phone snapped suddenly, in Alstair's voice.

"Attention, all officers! The enemy space ship has poured what it evidently considers a deadly frequency into us, and is now approaching at full acceleration! Orders are that absolutely no control of any sort is to be varied by a hair's breath. Absolutely no sign of living intelligence within the *Adastra* is to be shown. You will stand by all operative controls, prepared for maneuver if it should be necessary. But we try to give the impression that the *Adastra* is operating on automatic controls alone! Understood?"

Jack could imagine the reports from the other control rooms. His own receptor sprang suddenly into life. The almost hooted sounds of the call signal, so familiar that they seemed words. Then an extraordinary jumble of noises—words in a human voice. More stridulater sounds. More words in perfectly accurate English. The English words were in the tones and accents of an officer of the *Adastra,* plainly recorded and retransmitted.

"Communications!" snapped Alstair. "You will not answer this signal! It is an attempt to find out if we survived their ray attack!"

"Check," said Jack.

Alstair was right. Jack watched and listened as the receptor babbled on. It stopped. Silence for ten minutes. It began again. The *Adastra* hurtled on. The babble from space came to an end. A little later the G. C. phone snapped once more:

"The enemy space ship has increased its acceleration, evidently convinced that we are all dead. It will arrive in approximately four hours. Normal watches may be resumed for three hours unless an alarm is given."

Jack leaned back in his chair, frowning. He began to see the tactics Alstair planned to use. They were bad tactics, but the only ones a defenseless ship like the *Adastra* could even contemplate. It was at least ironic that the greeting the *Adastra* received at the end of a seven-years' voyage through empty space be a dose of a type of radiation used on Earth to exterminate vermin.

But the futility of this attack did not mean that all attacks would be similarly useless. And the *Adastra* simply could not be stopped for many millions of miles, yet. Even if Alstair's desperate plan took care of this particular assailant and this particular weapon, it would not mean—it could not!—that the *Adastra* or the folk within had any faintest chance of defending themselves. And there was Helen——

III.

The visiplates showed the strange space ship clearly, now, even without magnification. It was within five miles of the *Adastra* and it had stopped. Perfectly egg-shaped, without any protuberance whatever except the rocket tubes in its rear, it hung motionless with relation to the Earth ship, which meant that its navigators had analyzed her rate of deceleration long since and had matched all the constants of her course with precision.

Helen, her face still tear-streaked, watched as Jack turned up the magnification, and the illumination with it. Her father had collapsed very suddenly and very completely. He was resting quietly now, dozing almost continuously, with his face wearing an expression of utter contentment.

He had piloted the *Adastra* to its first contact with the civilization of another solar system. His lifework was done and he was wholly prepared to rest. He had no idea, of course, that the first actual contact with the strange space ship was a burst of short waves of a frequency deadly to all animal life.

The space ship swelled on the visiplate as Jack turned the knob. He brought it to an apparent distance of a few hundred yards only. With the illumination turned up, even the starlight on the hull would have been sufficient to show any surface detail. But there was literally none. No rivet, no bolt, no line of joining plates. A row of portholes were dark and dead within.

"And it's wood!" repeated Jack. "Made out of some sort of cellulose which stands the cold of space!"

Helen said queerly: "It looks to me as if it had been grown, rather than built."

Jack blinked. He opened his mouth as if to speak, but the receptor at his elbow suddenly burst into the hootlike stridulations which were the signals from the egglike ship. Then English words, from recordings of previous signals from the *Adastra*. More vowelless, modulated phrases. It sounded exactly as if the beings in the other space ship were trying urgently to open communication and were insisting that they had the key to the *Adastra's* signals. The temptation to reply was great.

"They've got brains, anyhow," said Jack grimly.

The signals were cut off. Silence. Jack glanced at the wave tape. It showed the same blurring as before.

"More short stuff. At this distance, it ought not only to kill us, but even sterilize the interior of the whole ship. Lucky our hull is heavy alloy with a high hysteresis-rate. Not a particle of that radiation can get through."

Silence for a long, long time. The wave tape showed that a terrific beam of thirty-centimeter waves continued to play upon the *Adastra*. Jack suddenly plugged in observations and asked a question. Yes, the outer hull was heating. It had gone up half a degree in fifteen minutes.

"Nothing to worry about in that," grunted Jack. "Fifteen degrees will be the limit they can put it up, with this power."

The tape came out clear. The supposed death radiation was cut off. The egg-shaped ship darted forward. And then for twenty minutes or more Jack had to switch from one outside vision disk to another to keep it in sight. It hovered about the huge bulk of the *Adastra* with a wary inquisitiveness. Now half a mile away, now no more than two hundred yards, the thing darted here and there with an amazing acceleration and as amazing a braking power. It had only the rocket tubes at the smaller end of its egg-shaped form. It was necessary for it to fling its whole shape about to get a new direction, and the gyroscopes within it must have been tremendously powerful. Even so, the abruptness of its turns were startling.

"I wouldn't like to be inside that thing!" said Jack. "We'd be crushed to a pulp by their normal navigation methods. They aren't men like us. They can stand more than we can."

The thing outside seemed sentient, seemed alive. And by the eagerness of its movements it seemed the more horrible, flitting about the gigantic space ship it now believed was a monstrous coffin.

It suddenly reversed itself and shot back toward the *Adastra*. Two hundred yards, one hundred yards, a hundred feet. It came to a cushioned stop against the surface of the Earth vessel.

"Now we'll see something of them," said Jack crisply. "They landed right at an air lock. They know what that is, evidently. Now we'll see them in their space suits."

But Helen gasped. A part of the side of the strange ship seemed to swell suddenly. It bulged out like a blister. It touched the surface of the *Adastra*. It seemed to adhere. The point of contact grew larger.

"Good Lord!" said Jack blankly. "Is it alive? And is it going to try to eat our ship?"

The general-communication phone rasped sharply:

"Officers with arms to the air lock GH41 immediately! The Centaurians are opening the air lock from the outside. Wait orders there! The visiplate in the air lock is working and you will be informed. Go ahead!"

The phone clicked off. Jack seized a heavy gun, one of the force rifles which will stun a man at anything up to eighteen hundred yards and kill at six, when used at full power. His side arm hung in its holster. He swung for the door.

"Jack!" said Helen desperately.

He kissed her. It was the first time their lips had touched, but it seemed the most natural thing in the world, just then. He went racing down the long corridors of the *Adastra* to the rendezvous. And as he raced, his thoughts were not at all those of a scientist and an officer of Earth's first expedition into interstellar space. Jack was thinking of Helen's lips touching his desperately, of her soft body pressed close to him.

A G. C. speaker whispered overhead as he ran:

"They're inside the air lock. They opened it without trouble. They're testing our air, now. Apparently it suits them all."

The phone fell behind. Jack ran on, panting. Somebody else was running ahead. There were half a dozen, a dozen men grouped at the end of the corridor. A murmur from the side wall.

". . . rking at the inner air-lock door. Only four or five of them, apparently, will enter the ship. They are to be allowed to get well away from the air lock. You will keep out of sight. When the emergency locks go on it will be your signal. Use your heavy force guns, increasing power from minimum until they fall paralyzed. It will probably take a good deal of power to subdue them. They are not to be killed if it can be avoided. Ready!"

There were a dozen or more officers on hand. The fat rocket chief. The lean air officer. Subalterns of the other departments. The rocket chief puffed audibly as he wedged himself out of sight. Then the clicking of the inner air-lock door. It opened into the anteroom. Subdued, muffled hootings came from that door. The Things—whatever they were—were inspecting the space suits there. The hootings were distinctly separate and distinctly intoned. But they suddenly came as a babble. More than one Thing was speaking at once. There was excitement, eagerness, an extraordinary triumph in these voices.

Then something stirred in the doorway of the air-lock anteroom. A shadow crossed the threshold. And then the Earthmen saw the creatures who were invading the ship.

For an instant they seemed almost like men. They had two legs, and two dangling things—tentacles—which apparently served as arms and tapered smoothly to ends which split into movable, slender filaments. The tentacles and the legs alike seemed flexible in their entire lengths. There were no "joints" such as men use in walking, and the result was that the Centaurians walked with a curiously rolling gait.

Most startling, though, was the fact that they had no heads. They came wabbling accustomedly out of the air lock, and at the end of one "arm" each carried a curious, semicylindrical black object which they handled as if it might be a weapon. They wore metallic packs fastened to their bodies. The bodies themselves were queerly "grained." There was a tantalizing familiarity about the texture of their skin.

Jack, staring incredulously, looked for eyes, for nostrils, for a mouth. He saw twin slits only. He guessed at them for eyes. He saw no sign of any mouth at all. There was no hair. But he saw a scabrous, brownish substance on the back of one of the Things which turned to hoot excitedly at the rest. It looked like bark, like tree bark. And a light burst upon Jack. He almost cried out, but instead reached down and quietly put the lever of his force gun at full power at once.

The Things moved on. They reached a branching corridor and after much arm waving and production of their apparently articulated sounds they separated into two parties. They vanished. Their voices dwindled.

The signal for an attack upon them had not yet been given. The officers, left behind, stirred uneasily. But a G. C. phone whispered.

"Steady! They think we're all dead. They're separating again. We may be able to close emergency doors and have each one sealed off from all the rest and then handle them in detail. You men watch the air lock!"

Silence. The humming of a ventilator somewhere near by. Then, suddenly, a man screamed shrilly a long distance off, and on the heels of his outcry there came a new noise from one of the Things. It was a high-pitched squealing noise, triumphant and joyous and unspeakably horrible.

Other squealings answered it. There were rushing sounds, as if the other Things were running to join the first. And then came a hissing of compressed air and a hum of motors. Doors snapped shut everywhere, sealing off every part of the ship from every other part. And in the dead silence of their own sealed compartment, the officers on guard suddenly heard inquiring hoots.

Two more of the Things came out of the air lock. One of the men moved. The Thing saw him and turned its half-cylindrical object upon him. The man—it was the communications officer—shrieked suddenly and leaped convulsively. He was stone dead even as his muscles tensed for that incredible leap.

And the Thing emitted a high-pitched triumphant note which was exactly like the other horrible sound they had heard, and sped eagerly toward his body. One of the long, tapering arms lashed out and touched the dead man's hand.

Then Jack's force gun began to hum. He heard another and another open up. In seconds the air was filled with a sound like that of a hive of angry bees. Three more of the Things came out of the air lock, but they dropped in the barrage of force-gun beams. It was only when there was a sudden rush of air toward the lock, showing that the enemy ship had taken alarm and was darting away, that the men dared cease to fill that doorway with their barrage. Then it was necessary to seal the air lock in a hurry. Only then could they secure the Things that had invaded the *Adastra*.

Two hours later, Jack went into the main control room and saluted with an exact precision. His face was rather white and his expression entirely dogged and resolved. Alstair turned to him, scowling.

"I sent for you," he said harshly, "because you're likely to be a source of trouble. The commander is dead. You heard it?"

"Yes, sir," said Jack grimly. "I heard it."

"In consequence, I am commander of the *Adastra*," said Alstair provocatively. "I have, you will recall, the power of life and death in cases of mutinous conduct, and it is also true that marriage on the *Adastra* is made legal only by executive order bearing my signature."

"I am aware of the fact, sir," said Jack more grimly still.

"Very well," said Alstair deliberately. "For the sake of discipline, I order you to refrain from all association with Miss Bradley. I shall take disobedience of the order as mutiny. I intend to marry her myself. What have you to say to that?"

Jack said as deliberately: "I shall pay no attention to the order, sir, because you aren't fool enough to carry out such a threat! Are you such a fool that you don't see we've less than one chance in five hundred of coming out of this? If you want to marry Helen, you'd better put all your mind on giving her a chance to live!"

A savage silence held for a moment. The two men glared furiously at each other, the one near middle age, the other still a young man, indeed. Then Alstair showed his teeth in a smile that had no mirth whatever in it.

"As man to man I dislike you extremely," he said harshly. "But as commander of the *Adastra* I wish I had a few more like you. We've had seven years of routine on this damned ship, and every officer in quarters is rattled past all usefulness because an emergency has come at last. They'll obey orders, but there's not one fit to give them. The communications officer was killed by one of those devils, wasn't he?"

"Yes, sir."

"Very well. You're brevet communications officer. I hate your guts, Gary, and I do not doubt that you hate mine, but you have brains. Use them now. What have you been doing?"

"Adjusting a dictawriter, sir, to get a vocabulary of one of these Centaurian's speech, and hooking it up as a two-way translator, sir."

Alstair stared in momentary surprise, and then nodded. A dictawriter, of course, simply analyzes a word into its phonetic parts, sets up the analysis and picks out a card to match its formula. Normally, the card then actuates a printer. However, instead of a type-choosing record, the card can contain a record of an equivalent word in another language, and then operates a speaker.

Such machines have been of only limited use on Earth because of the need for so large a stock of vocabulary words, but have been used to some extent for literal translations both of print and speech. Jack proposed to record a Centaurian's vocabulary with English equivalents, and the dictawriter, hearing the queer hoots the strange creature uttered, would pick out a card which would then cause a speaker to enunciate its English synonym.

The reverse, of course, would also occur. A conversation could be carried on with such a prepared vocabulary without awaiting practice in understanding or imitating the sounds of another language.

"Excellent!" said Alstair curtly. "But put some one else on the job if you can. It should be reasonably simple, once it's started. But I need you for other work. You know what's been found out about these Centaurians, don't you?"

"Yes, sir. Their hand weapon is not unlike our force guns, but it seems to be considerably more effective. I saw it kill the communications officer."

"But the creatures themselves!"

"I helped tie one of them up."

"What do you make of it? I've a physician's report, but he doesn't believe it himself!"

"I don't blame him, sir," said Jack grimly. "They're not our idea of intelligent beings at all. We haven't any word for what they are. In one sense they're plants, apparently. That is, their bodies seem to be composed of cellulose fibers where ours are made of muscle fibers. But they are intelligent, fiendishly intelligent.

"The nearest we have to them on Earth are certain carnivorous plants, like pitcher plants and the like. But they're as far above a pitcher plant as a man is above a sea anemone, which is just as much an animal as a man is. My guess, sir, would be that they're neither plant nor animal. Their bodies are built up of the same materials as earthly plants, but they move about like animals do on Earth. They surprise us, but we may surprise them, too. It's quite possible that the typical animal form on their planet is sessile like the typical plant form on ours."

Alstair said bitterly: "And they look on us, animals, as we look on plants!"

Jack said without expression: "Yes, sir. They eat through holes in their arms. The one who killed the communications officer seized his arm. It seemed to exude some fluid that liquefied his flesh instantly. It sucked the liquid back in at once. If I may make a guess, sir——"

"Go ahead," snapped Alstair. "Everybody else is running around in circles, either marveling or sick with terror."

"The leader of the party, sir, had on what looked like an ornament. It was a band of leather around one of its arms."

"Now, what the devil——"

"We had two men killed. One was the communications officer and the other was an orderly. When we finally subdued the Centaurian who'd killed that orderly, it had eaten a small bit of him, but the rest of the orderly's body had undergone some queer sort of drying process, from chemicals the Thing seemed to carry with it."

Alstair's throat worked as if in nausea. "I saw it."

"It's a fanciful idea," said Jack grimly, "but if a man was in the position of that Centaurian, trapped in a space ship belonging to an alien race, with death very probably before him, well, about the only thing a man would strap to his body, as the Centaurian did the dried, preserved body of that orderly——"

"Would be gold," snapped Alstair. "Or platinum, or jewels which he would hope to fight clear with!"

"Just so," said Jack. "Now, I'm only guessing, but those creatures are not human, nor even animals. Yet they eat animal food. They treasure animal food as a human being would treasure diamonds. An animal's remains—leather—they wear as an ornament. It looks to me as if animal tissue was rather rare on their planet, to be valued so highly. In consequence——"

Alstair stood up, his features working. "Then our bodies would be the same as gold to them! As diamonds! Gary, we haven't the ghost of a chance to make friends with these fiends!"

Jack said dispassionately: "No; I don't think we have. If a race of beings with tissues of metallic gold landed on Earth, I rather think they'd be murdered. But there's another point, too. There's Earth. From our course, these creatures can tell where we came from, and their space ships are rather good. I think I'll put somebody else on the dictawriter job and see if I can flash a message back home. No way to know whether they get it, but they ought to be watching for one by the time it's there. Maybe they've improved their receptors. They intended to try, anyhow."

"Men could meet these creatures' ships in space," said Alstair harshly, "if they were warned. And guns might answer, but if they didn't handle these devils Caldwell torpedoes would. Or a suicide squad, using their bodies for bait. We're talking like dead men, Gary."

"I think, sir," said Jack, "we are dead men." Then he added: "I shall put Helen Bradley on the dictawriter, with a guard to handle the Centaurian. He'll be bound tightly."

The statement tacitly assumed that Alstair's order to avoid her was withdrawn. It was even a challenge to him to repeat it. And Alstair's eyes glowed and he controlled himself with difficulty.

"Damn you, Gary," he said savagely, "get out!"

He turned to the visiplate which showed the enemy ship as Jack left the control room.

The egg-shaped ship was two thousand miles away now, and just decelerating to a stop. In its first flight it had rocketed here and there like a mad thing. It would have been impossible to hit it with any projectile, and difficult in the extreme even to keep radiation on it in anything like a tight beam. Now, stopped stock-still with regard to the *Adastra*, it hung on, observing, very probably devising some new form of devilment. So Alstair considered, anyhow. He watched it somberly.

The resources of the *Adastra*, which had seemed so vast when she took off from Earth, were pitifully inadequate to handle the one situation which had greeted her, hostility. She could have poured out the treasures of man's civilization to the race which ruled this solar system. Savages, she could have uplifted. Even to a race superior to men she could have offered man's friendship and eager pupilage. But these creatures that——

The space ship stayed motionless. Probably signaling back to its home planet, demanding orders. Reports came in to the *Adastra's* main control room and Alstair read them. The Centaurians were unquestionably extracting carbon dioxide from the air. That compound was to their metabolism what oxygen is to men, and in pure air they could not live.

But their metabolic rate was vastly greater than that of any plant on Earth. It compared with the rate of earthly animals. They were not plants by any definition save that of constitution, as a sea anemone is not an animal except by the test of chemical analysis.

The Centaurians had a highly organized nervous system, the equivalent of brains, and both great intelligence and a language. They produced sounds by a stridulating organ in a special body cavity. And they felt emotion.

A captive creature when presented with various objects showed special interest in machinery, showing an acute realization of the purpose of a small sound recorder and uttering into it an entire and deliberate series of sounds. Human clothing it fingered eagerly. Cloth it discarded, when of cotton or rayon, but it displayed great excitement at the feel of a woolen shirt and even more when a leather belt was given to it. It placed the belt about its middle, fastening the buckle without a fumble after a single glance at its working.

It unraveled a thread from the shirt and consumed it, rocking to and fro as if in ecstasy. When meat was placed before it, it seemed to become almost delirious with excitement. A part of the meat it consumed instantly, to ecstatic swayings. The rest it preserved by a curious chemical process, using substances from a small metal pack it had worn and for which it made gestures.

Its organs of vision were behind two slits in the upper part of its body, and no precise examination of the eyes themselves had been made. But the report before Alstair said specifically that the Centaurian displayed an avid eagerness whenever it caught sight of a human being. And that the eagerness was not of a sort to be reassuring.

It was the sort of excitement—only much greater—which it had displayed at the sight of wool and leather. As if by instinct, said the report, the captive Centaurian had several times made a gesture as if turning some weapon upon a human when first it sighted him.

Alstair read this report and others. Helen Bradley reported barely two hours after Jack had assigned her to the work.

"I'm sorry, Helen," said Alstair ungraciously. "You shouldn't have been called on for duty. Gary insisted on it. I'd have left you alone."

"I'm glad he did," said Helen steadily. "Father is dead, to be sure, but he was quite content. And he died before he found out what these Centaurians are like. Working was good for me. I've succeeded much better than I even hoped. The Centaurian I worked with was the leader of the party which invaded this ship. He understood almost at once what the dictawriter was doing, and we've a good vocabulary recorded already. If you want to talk to him, you can."

Alstair glanced at the visiplate. The enemy ship was still motionless. Easily understandable, of course. The *Adastra's* distance from Proxima Centauri could be measured in hundreds of millions of miles, now, instead of millions of billions, but in another terminology it was light-hours away still. If the space ship had signaled its home planet for orders, it would still be waiting for a reply.

Alstair went heavily to the biology laboratory, of which Helen was in charge, just as she was in charge of the biological specimens—rabbits, sheep, and a seemingly endless array of small animals—which on the voyage had been bred for a food supply and which it had been planned to release should a planet suitable for colonizing revolve about the ringed star.

The Centaurian was bound firmly to a chair with a myriad of cords. He —she—it, was utterly helpless. Beside the chair the dictawriter and its speaker were coupled together. From the Centaurian came hooted notes which the machine translated with a rustling sound between words.

"You—are—commander—this—ship?" the machine translated without intonation.

"I am," said Alstair, and the machine hooted musically.

"This—woman—man—dead," said the machine tonelessly again, after more sounds from the extraordinary living thing which was not an animal.

Helen interjected swiftly: "I told him my father was dead."

The machine went on: "I—buy—all—dead—man—on—ship—give—metal —gold—you—like——"

Alstair's teeth clicked together. Helen went white. She tried to speak, and choked upon the words.

"This," said Alstair in mirthless bitterness, "is the beginning of the interstellar friendship we hoped to institute!"

Then the G. C. phone said abruptly:

"Calling Commander Alstair! Radiation from ahead! Several wave lengths, high intensity! Apparently several space ships are sending, though we can make out no signals!"

And then Jack Gary came into the biology laboratory. His face was set in grim lines. It was very white. He saluted with great precision.

"I didn't have to work hard, sir," he said sardonically. "The last communications officer had been taking his office more or less as a sinecure.

We'd had no signals for seven years, and he didn't expect any. But they're coming through and have been for months.

"They left Earth three years after we did. A chap named Callaway, it seems, found that a circularly polarized wave makes a tight beam that will hold together forever. They've been sending to us for years past, no doubt, and we're getting some of the first messages now.

"They've built a second *Adastra*, sir, and it's being manned—hell, no! It was manned four years ago! It's on the way out here now! It must be at least three years on the way, and it has no idea of these devils waiting for it. Even if we blow ourselves to bits, sir, there'll be another ship from Earth coming, unarmed as we are, to run into these devils when it's too late to stop——"

The G. C. phone snapped again:

"Commander Alstair! Observations reporting! The external hull temperature has gone up five degrees in the past three minutes and is still climbing. Something's pouring heat into us at a terrific rate!"

Alstair turned to Jack. He said with icy politeness:

"Gary, after all there's no use in our continuing to hate each other. Here is where we all die together. Why do I still feel inclined to kill you?"

But the question was rhetorical only. The reason was wholly clear. At the triply horrible news, Helen had begun to cry softly. And she had gone blindly into Jack's arms to do it.

IV.

The situation was, as a matter of fact, rather worse than the first indications showed. The external hull temperature, for instance, was that of the generalizing thermometer, which averaged for all the external thermometers. A glance at the thermometer bank, through a visiphone connection, showed the rearmost side of the *Adastra* at practically normal. It was the forward hemisphere, the side nearest Proxima Centauri, which was heating. And that hemisphere was not heating equally. The indicators which flashed red lights were closely grouped.

Alstair regarded them with a stony calm in the visiplate.

"Squarely in the center of our disk, as they see it," he said icily. "It will be that fleet of space ships, of course."

Jack Gary said crisply: "Sir, the ship from which we took prisoners made contact several hours earlier than we expected. It must be that, instead of sending one vessel with a transmitter on board, they sent a fleet, and a scout ship on ahead. That scout ship has reported that we laid a trap for some of her crew, and consequently they've opened fire!"

Alstair said sharply into a G. C. transmitter:

"Sector G90 is to be evacuated at once. It is to be sealed off immediately and all occupants will emerge from air locks. Adjoining sectors are to be evacuated except by men on duty, and they will don space suits immediately."

He clicked off the phone and added calmly: "The external temperature over part of G90 is four hundred degrees now. Dull-red heat. In five minutes it should melt. They'll have a hole bored right through us in half an hour."

Jack said urgently: "Sir! I'm pointing out that they've attacked because the scout ship reported we laid a trap for some of its crew! We have just the ghost of a chance——"

"What?" demanded Alstair bitterly. "We've no weapons!"

"The dictawriter, sir!" snapped Jack. "We can talk to them now!"

Alstair said harshly: "Very well, Gary. I appoint you ambassador. Go ahead!"

He swung on his heel and went swiftly from the control room. A moment later his voice came out of the G. C. phone: "Calling the Rocket Chief! Report immediately on personal visiphone. Emergency!"

His voice cut off, but Jack was not aware of it. He was plugging in to communications and demanding full power on the transmission beam and a widening of its arc. He snapped one order after another and explained to Helen in swift asides.

She grasped the idea at once. The Centaurian in the biology laboratory was bound, of course. No flicker of expression could be discovered about the narrow slits which were his vision organs. But Helen—knowing the words of the vocabulary cards—spoke quietly and urgently into the dictawriter microphone. Hootlike noises came out of the speaker in their place, and the Centaurian stirred. Sounds came from him in turn, and the speaker said woodenly:

"I—speak—ship—planet. Yes."

And as the check-up came through from communications control, the eerie, stridulated, unconsonanted noises of his language filled the biology laboratory and went out on the widened beam of the main transmitter.

Ten thousand miles away the Centaurian scout ship hovered. The *Adastra* bored on toward the ringed sun which had been the goal of mankind's most daring expedition. From ten thousand miles she would have seemed a mere dot, but the telescopes of the Centaurians would show her every detail. From a thousand miles she would seem a toy, perhaps, intricately crisscrossed with strengthening members.

From a distance of a few miles only, though, her gigantic size could be realized fully. Five thousand feet in diameter, she dwarfed the hugest of those distant, unseen shapes in emptiness which made up a hostile fleet now pouring deadly beams upon her.

From a distance of a few miles, too, the effect of that radiation could be seen. The *Adastra's* hull was alloy steel; tough and necessarily with a high hysteresis rate. The alternating currents of electricity induced in that steel by the Centaurian radiation would have warmed even a copper hull. But the alloy steel grew hot. It changed color. It glowed faintly red over an area a hundred feet across.

A rocket tube in that area abruptly ceased to emit its purple, lambent flame. It had been cut off. Other rockets increased their power a trifle to make up for it. The dull red glow of the steel increased. It became carmine. Slowly, inexorably, it heated to a yellowish tinge. It became canary in color. It tended toward blue.

Vapor curled upward from its surface, streaming away from the tortured, melting surface as if drawn by the distant sun. That vapor grew thick; dazzlingly bright; a veritable cloud of metallic steam. And suddenly there was a violent eruption from the center of the *Adastra's* lighted hemisphere. The outer hull was melted through. Air from the interior burst out into the void, flinging masses of molten, vaporizing metal before it. It spread with an incredible rapidity, flaring instantly into the attenuated, faintly glowing mist of a comet's tail.

The visiplate images inside the *Adastra* grew dim. Stars paled ahead. The Earth ship had lost a part of her atmosphere and it fled on before her, writhing. Already it had spread into so vast a space that its density was immeasurable, but it was still so much more dense than the infinite emptiness of space that it filled all the cosmos before the *Adastra* with a thinning nebulosity.

And at the edges of the huge gap in the big ship's hull, the thick metal bubbled and steamed, and the interior partitions began to glow with an unholy light of dull-red heat, which swiftly went up to carmine and began to turn faintly yellow.

In the main control room, Alstair watched bitterly until the visiplates showing the interior of section G90 fused. He spoke very calmly into the microphone before him.

"We've got less time than I thought," he said deliberately. "You'll have to hurry. It won't be sure at best, and you've got to remember that these devils will undoubtedly puncture us from every direction and make sure there's absolutely nothing living on board. You've got to work something out, and in a hurry, to do what I've outlined!"

A half-hysterical voice came back to him.

"But sir, if I cut the sonic vibrations in the rockets we'll go up in a flare! A single instant! The disintegration of our fuel will spread to the tubes and the whole ship will simply explode! It will be quick!"

"You fool!" snarled Alstair. "There's another ship from Earth on the way! Unwarned! And unarmed like we are! And from our course these devils can tell where we came from! We're going to die, yes! We won't die pleasantly! But we're going to make sure these fiends don't start out a space fleet for Earth! There's to be no euthanasia for us! We've got to make our dying do some good! We've got to protect humanity!"

Alstair's face, as he snarled into the visiplate, was not that of a martyr or a person making a noble self-sacrifice. It was the face of a man over-awing and bullying a subordinate into obedience.

With a beam of radiation playing on his ship which the metal hull absorbed and transformed into heat, Alstair raged at this department and that. A second bulkhead went, and there was a second eruption of vaporized metal and incandescent gas from the monster vessel. Millions of miles away, a wide-flung ring of egg-shaped space ships lay utterly motionless, giving no sign of life and looking like monsters asleep. But from them the merciless beams of radiation sped out and focused upon one spot upon the *Adastra's* hull, and it spewed forth frothing metal and writhing gases and now and again some still recognizable object which flared and exploded as it emerged.

And within the innumerable compartments of the mighty ship, human beings reacted to their coming doom in manners as various as the persons themselves. Some screamed. A few of the more sullen members of the crew seemed to go mad, to become homicidal maniacs. Still others broke into the stores and proceeded systematically but in some haste to drink themselves comatose. Some women clutched their children and wept over them. And some of them went mad.

But Alstair's snarling, raging voice maintained a semblance of discipline in a few of the compartments. In a machine shop men worked savagely, cursing, and making mistakes as they worked which made their work useless. The lean air officer strode about his domain, a huge spanner in his hand, and smote with a righteous anger at any sign of panic. The rocket chief, puffing, manifested an unexpected genius for sustained profanity, and the rockets kept their pale purple flames out in space without a sign of flickering.

But in the biology laboratory the scene was one of quiet, intense concentration. Bound to helplessness, the Centaurian, featureless and inscrutable, filled the room with its peculiar form of speech. The dictawriter rustled softly, senselessly analyzing each of the sounds and senselessly questing for vocabulary cards which would translate them into English wordings. Now and again a single card did match up. Then the machine translated a single word of the Centaurian's speech.

"——ship——" A long series of sounds, varying rapidly in pitch, in intensity, and in emphasis. "——men——" Another long series. "——talk men——"

The Centaurian ceased to make its hootlike noises. Then, very carefully, it emitted new ones. The speaker translated them all. The Centaurian had carefully selected words recorded with Helen.

"He understands what we're trying to do," said Helen, very pale.

The machine said: "You—talk—machine—talk—ship."

Jack said quietly into the transmitter: "We are friends. We have much you want. We want only friendship. We have killed none of your men except in self-defense. We ask peace. If we do not have peace, we will fight. But we wish peace."

He said under his breath to Helen, as the machine rustled and the speaker hooted: "Bluff, that war talk. I hope it works!"

Silence. Millions of miles away, unseen space ships aimed a deadly radiation in close, tight beams at the middle of the *Adastra's* disk. Quaintly enough, that radiation would have been utterly harmless to a man's body. It would have passed through, undetected.

But the steel of the Earth ship's hull stopped and absorbed it as eddy currents. The eddy currents became heat. And a small volcano vomited out into space the walls, the furnishing, the very atmosphere of the *Adastra* through the hole that the heat had made.

It was very quiet indeed in the biology laboratory. The receptor was silent. One minute. Two minutes. Three. The radio waves carrying Jack's voice traveled at the speed of light, but it took no less than ninety seconds for them to reach the source of the beams which were tearing the *Adastra* to pieces. And there was a time loss there, and ninety seconds more for other waves to hurtle through space at one hundred and eighty-six thousand miles each second with the reply.

The receptor hooted unmusically. The dictawriter rustled softly. Then the speaker said without expression:

"We—friends—now—no—fight—ships—come—to—take—you—planet."

And simultaneously the miniature volcano on the *Adastra's* hull lessened the violence of its eruption, and slowly its molten, bubbling edges ceased first to steam, and then to bubble, and from the blue-white of vaporizing steel they cooled to yellow, and then to carmine, and more slowly to a dull red, and more slowly still to the glistening, infinitely white metallic surface of steel which cools where there is no oxygen.

Jack said crisply into the control-room microphone: "Sir, I have communicated with the Centaurians and they have ceased fire. They say they are sending a fleet to take us to their planet."

"Very good," said Alstair's voice bitterly, "especially since nobody seems able to make the one contrivance that would do some good after our death. What next?"

"I think it would be a good idea to release the Centaurian here," said

Jack. "We can watch him, of course, and paralyze him if he acts up. It would be a diplomatic thing to do, I believe."

"You're ambassador," said Alstair sardonically. "We've got time to work, now. But you'd better put somebody else on the ambassadorial work and get busy again on the job of sending a message back to Earth, if you think you can adapt a transmitter to the type of wave they'll expect."

His image faded. And Jack turned to Helen. He felt suddenly very tired.

"That is the devil of it," he said drearily. "They'll expect a wave like they sent us, and with no more power than we have, they'll hardly pick up anything else! But we picked up in the middle of a message and just at the end of their description of the sending outfit they're using on Earth. Undoubtedly they'll describe it again, or rather they did describe it again, four years back, and we'll pick it up if we live long enough. But we can't even guess when that will be. You're going to keep on working with this—creature, building up a vocabulary?"

Helen regarded him anxiously. She put her hand upon his arm.

"He's intelligent enough," she said urgently. "I'll explain to him and let somebody else work with him. I'll come with you. After all, we—we may not have long to be together."

"Perhaps ten hours," said Jack tiredly.

He waited, somberly, while she explained in carefully chosen words—which the dictawriter translated—to the Centaurian. She got an assistant and two guards. They released the headless Thing. It offered no violence. Instead, it manifested impatience to continue the work of building up in the translator files a vocabulary through which a complete exchange of ideas could take place.

Jack and Helen went together to the communications room. They ran the Earth message, as received so far. It was an extraordinary hodgepodge. Four years back, Earth had been enthusiastic over the thought of sending word to its most daring adventurers. A flash of immaterial energy could travel tirelessly through uncountable millions of billions of miles of space and overtake the explorers who had started three years before. By its text, this message had been sent some time after the first message of all. In the sending, it had been broadcast all over the Earth, and many millions of people undoubtedly had thrilled to the thought that they heard words which would span the space between two suns.

But the words were not helpful to those on the *Adastra*. The message was a "cheer-up" program, which began with lusty singing by a popular quartet, continued with wisecracks by Earth's most highly paid comedian —and his jokes were all very familiar to those on the *Adastra*—and then a congratulatory address by an eminent politician, and other drivel. In short, it was a hodgepodge of trash designed to gain publicity by means of the Earth broadcast for those who took part in it.

It was not helpful to those on the *Adastra*, with the hull of the ship punctured, death before them, and probably destruction for the whole human race to follow as a consequence of their voyage.

Jack and Helen sat quietly and listened. Their hands clasped unconsciously. Rather queerly, the extreme brevity of the time before them made extravagant expressions of affection seem absurd. They listened to the unspeakably vulgar message from Earth without really hearing it. Now and again they looked at each other.

In the biology laboratory the building-up of a vocabulary went on swiftly. Pictures came into play. A second Centaurian was released, and by his skill in delineation—which proved that the eyes of the plant men functioned almost identically with those of Earth men—added both to the store of definitions and equivalents and to knowledge of the Centaurian civilization.

Piecing the information together, the civilization began to take on a strange resemblance to that of humanity. The Centaurians possessed artificial structures which were undoubtedly dwelling houses. They had cities, laws, arts—the drawing of the second Centaurian was proof of that —and sciences. The science of biology in particular was far advanced, taking to some extent the place of metallurgy in the civilization of men. Their structures were grown, not built. Instead of metals to shape to their own ends, they had forms of protoplasm whose rate and manner of growth they could control.

Houses, bridges, vehicles—even space ships were formed of living matter which was thrown into a quiescent nonliving state when it had attained the form and size desired. And it could be caused to become active again at will, permitting such extraordinary features as the blisterlike connection that had been made by the space ship with the hull of the *Adastra*.

So far, the Centaurian civilization was strange enough, but still comprehensible. Even men might have progressed in some such fashion had civilization developed on Earth from a different point of departure. It was the economics of the Centaurians which was at once understandable and horrifying to the men who learned of it.

The Centaurian race had developed from carnivorous plants, as men from carnivorous forebears. But at some early date in man's progression, the worship of gold began. No such diversion of interest occurred upon the planets of Proxima Centauri. As men have devastated cities for gold, and have cut down forests and gutted mines and ruthlessly destroyed all things for gold or for other things which could be exchanged for gold, so the Centaurians had quested animals.

As men exterminated the buffalo in America, to trade his hide for gold, so the Centaurians had ruthlessly exterminated the animal life of their planet. But to Centaurians, animal tissue itself was the equivalent of gold. From sheer necessity, ages since, they had learned to tolerate vegetable foodstuffs. But the insensate lust for flesh remained. They had developed methods for preserving animal food for indefinite periods. They had dredged their seas for the last and smallest crustacean. And even space travel became a desirable thing in their eyes, and then a fact, because telescopes showed them vegetation on other planets of their sun, and animal life as a probability.

Three planets of Proxima Centauri were endowed with climates and atmospheres favorable to vegetation and animal life, but only on one planet now, and that the smallest and most distant, did any trace of animal life survive. And even there the Centaurians hunted feverishly for the last and dwindling colonies of tiny quadrupeds which burrowed hundreds of feet below a frozen continent.

It became clear that the *Adastra* was an argosy of such treasure—in the form of human beings—as no Centaurian could ever have imagined to exist. And it became more than ever clear that a voyage to Earth would command all the resources of the race. Billions of human beings! Trillions of lesser animals! Uncountable creatures in the seas! All the Centaurian race would go mad with eagerness to invade this kingdom of riches and ecstasy, the ecstasy felt by any Centaurian when consuming the prehistoric foodstuff of his race.

V.

Egg-shaped, featureless ships of space closed in from every side at once. The thermometer banks showed a deliberate, painstaking progression of alarm signals. One dial glowed madly red and faded, and then another, and yet another, as the Centaurian ships took up their positions. Each such alarm, of course, was from the momentary impact of a radiation beam on the *Adastra's* hull.

Twenty minutes after the last of the beams had proved the *Adastra's* helplessness, an egglike ship approached the Earth vessel and with complete precision made contact with its forward side above an air lock. Its hull bellied out in a great blister which adhered to the steel.

Alstair watched the visiplate which showed it, his face very white and his hands clenched tightly. Jack Gary's voice, strained and hoarse, came from the biology-laboratory communicator.

"Sir, a message from the Centaurians. A ship has landed on our hull and its crew will enter through the air lock. A hostile move on our part, of course, will mean instant destruction."

"There will be no resistance to the Centaurians," said Alstair harshly. "It is my order! It would be suicide!"

"Even so, sir," said Jack's voice savagely, "I still think it would be a good idea!"

"Stick to your duty!" rasped Alstair. "What progress has been made in communication?"

"We have vocabulary cards for nearly five thousand words. We can converse on nearly any subject, and all of them are unpleasant. The cards are going through a duplicator now and will be finished in a few minutes. A second dictawriter with the second file will be sent you as soon as the cards are complete."

In a visiplate, Alstair saw the headless figures of Centaurians emerging from the entrance to an air lock in the *Adastra's* hull.

"Those Centaurians have entered the ship," he snapped as an order to Jack. "You're communications officer! Go meet them and lead their commanding officer here!"

"Check!" said Jack grimly.

It sounded like a sentence of death, that order. In the laboratory he was very pale indeed. Helen pressed close to him.

The formerly captive Centaurian hooted into the dictawriter, inquiringly. The speaker translated.

"What—command?"

Helen explained. So swiftly does humanity accustom itself to the incredible that it seemed almost natural to address a microphone and hear the hoots and stridulations of a nonhuman voice fill the room with her meaning.

"I—go—also—they—no—kill—yet."

The Centaurian rolled on before. With an extraordinary dexterity, he opened the door. He had merely seen it opened. Jack took the lead. His side-arm force gun remained in its holster beside him, but it was useless. He could probably kill the plant man behind him, but that would do no good.

Dim hootings ahead. The plant man made sounds—loud and piercing sounds. Answers came to him. Jack came in view of the new group of invaders. There were twenty or thirty of them, every one armed with half-cylindrical objects, larger than the first creatures had carried.

At sight of Jack there was excitement. Eager trembling of the armlike tentacles at either side of the headless trunks. There were instinctive, furtive movements of the weapons. A loud hooting as of command. The Things were still. But Jack's flesh crawled from the feeling of sheer, carnivorous lust that seemed to emanate from them.

His guide, the former captive, exchanged incomprehensible noises with the newcomers. Again a ripple of excitement in the ranks of the plant men.

"Come," said Jack curtly.

He led the way to the main control room. Once they heard someone screaming monotonously. A woman cracked under the coming of doom. A hooting babble broke the silence among the ungainly Things which followed Jack. Again an authoritative note silenced it.

The control room. Alstair looked like a man of stone, of marble, save that his eyes burned with a fierce and almost maniacal flame. A visiplate beside him showed a steady stream of Centaurians entering through a second air lock. There were hundreds of them, apparently. The dictawriter came in, under Helen's care. She cried out in instinctive horror at sight of so many of the monstrous creatures at once in the control room.

"Set up the dictawriter," said Alstair in a voice so harsh, so brittle that it seemed pure ice.

Trembling, Helen essayed to obey.

"I am ready to talk," said Alstair harshly into the dictawriter microphone. The machine, rustling softly, translated. The leader of the new party hooted in reply. An order for all officers to report here at once, after setting all controls for automatic operation of the ship. There was some difficulty with the translation of the Centaurian equivalent of "automatic." It was not in the vocabulary file. It took time.

Alstair gave the order. Cold sweat stood out upon his face, but his self-control was iron.

A second order, also understood with a certain amount of difficulty. Copies of all technical records, and all—again it took time to understand —all books bearing on the construction of this ship were to be taken to the air lock by which these plant men had entered. Samples of machinery, generators, and weapons to the same destination.

Again Alstair gave the order. His voice was brittle, was even thin, but it did not falter or break.

The Centaurian leader hooted an order over which the dictawriter rustled in vain. His followers swept swiftly to the doors of the control room. They passed out, leaving but four of their number behind. And Jack went swiftly to Alstair. His force gun snapped out and pressed deep into the commander's middle. The Centaurians made no movement of protest.

"Damn you!" said Jack, his voice thick with rage. "You've let them take the ship! You plan to bargain for your life! Damn you, I'm going to kill you and fight my way to a rocket tube and send this ship up in a flare of clean flame that'll kill these devils with us!"

But Helen cried swiftly: "Jack! Don't! I know!"

Like an echo her words—because she was near the dictawriter microphone—were repeated in the hooting sounds of the Centaurian language. And Alstair, livid and near to madness, nevertheless said harshly in the lowest of tones:

"You fool! These devils can reach Earth, now they know it's worth reaching! So even if they kill every man on the ship but the officers—and they may—we've got to navigate to their planet and land there." His voice dropped to a rasping whisper and he raged almost soundlessly: "And if you think I want to live through what's coming, shoot!"

Jack stood rigid for an instant. Then he stepped back. He saluted with an elaborate, mechanical precision.

"I beg your pardon, sir," he said unsteadily. "You can count on me hereafter."

One of the officers of the *Adastra* stumbled into the control room. Another. Still another. They trickled in. Six officers out of thirty.

A Centaurian entered with the curious rolling gait of his race. He went impatiently to the dictawriter and made noises.

"These—all—officers?" asked the machine tonelessly.

"The air officer shot his family and himself," gasped a subaltern of the air department. "A bunch of Muts charged a rocket tube and the rocket chief fought them off. Then he bled to death from a knife in his throat. The stores officer was——"

"Stop!" said Alstair in a thin, high voice. He tore at his collar. He went to the microphone and said thinly: "These are all the officers still alive. But we can navigate the ship."

The Centaurian—he wore a wide band of leather about each of his arms and another about his middle—waddled to the G. C. phone. The tendrils at the end of one arm manipulated the switch expertly. He emitted strange, formless sounds—and hell broke loose!

The visiplates all over the room emitted high-pitched, squealing sounds. They were horrible. They were ghastly. They were more terrible than the sounds of a wolf pack hard on the heels of a fear-mad deer. They were the sounds Jack had heard when one of the first invaders of the *Adastra* saw a human being and killed him instantly. And other sounds came out of the visiplates, too. There were human screams. There were even one or two explosions.

But then there was silence. The five Centaurians in the control room quivered and trembled. A desperate bloodlust filled them, the unreasoning, blind, instinctive craving which came of evolution from some race of carnivorous plants become capable of movement through the desperate need for food.

The Centaurian with the leather ornaments went to the dictawriter again. He hooted in it:

"Want—two—men—go—from—ship—learn—from—them—now."

There was an infinitely tiny sound in the main control room. It was a drop of cold sweat, falling from Alstair's face to the floor. He seemed to have shriveled. His face was an ashy gray. His eyes were closed. But Jack looked steadily from one to the other of the surviving officers.

"That will mean vivisection, I suppose," he said harshly. "It's certain they plan to visit Earth, else—intelligent as they are—they wouldn't have wiped out everybody but us. Even for treasure. They'll want to try out weapons on a human body, and so on. Communications is about the most useless of all the departments now, sir, I volunteer."

Helen gasped: "No, Jack! No!"

Alstair opened his eyes. "Gary has volunteered. One more man to volunteer for vivisection." He said it in the choked voice of one holding to sanity by the most terrible of efforts. "They'll want to find out how to kill men. Their thirty-centimeter waves didn't work. They know the beams that melted our hull wouldn't kill men. I can't volunteer! I've got to stay with the ship!" There was despair in his voice. "One more man to volunteer for these devils to kill slowly!"

Silence. The happenings of the past little while, and the knowledge of what still went on within the *Adastra's* innumerable compartments, had literally stunned most of the six. They could not think. They were mentally dazed, emotionally paralyzed by the sheer horrors they had encountered.

Then Helen stumbled into Jack's arms. "I'm—going, too!" she gasped. "We're—all going to die! I'm not needed! And I can—die with Jack."

Alstair groaned. "Please!"

"I'm—going!" she panted. "You can't stop me! With Jack! Whither thou goest——"

Then she choked. She pressed close. The Centaurian of the leather belts hooted impatiently into the dictawriter.

"These—two—come."

Alstair said in a strange voice: "Wait!" Like an automaton, he moved to his desk. He took up an electropen. He wrote, his hands shaking. "I am mad," he said thinly. "We are all mad. I think we are dead and in hell. But take this."

Jack stuffed the official order slip in his pocket. The Centaurian of the leather bands hooted impatiently. He led them, with his queer, rolling gait, toward the air lock by which the plant men had entered. Three times they were seen by roving Things, which emitted that triply horrible shrill squeal. And each time the Centaurian of the leather bands hooted authoritatively and the plant men withdrew.

Once, too, Jack saw four creatures swaying backward and forward about something on the floor. He reached out his hands and covered Helen's eyes until they were past.

They came to the air lock. Their guide pointed through it. The man and the girl obeyed. Long, rubbery tentacles seized them and Helen gasped and was still. Jack fought fiercely, shouting her name. Then something struck him savagely. He collapsed.

He came back to consciousness with a feeling of tremendous weight upon him. He stirred, and with his movement some of the oppression left him. A light burned, not a light such as men know on Earth, but a writhing flare which beat restlessly at the confines of a transparent globe which contained it. There was a queer smell in the air, too, an animal smell. Jack sat up. Helen lay beside him, unconfined and apparently unhurt. None of the Centaurians seemed to be near.

He chafed her wrists helplessly. He heard a stuttering sound and with each of the throbs of noise felt a momentary acceleration. Rockets, fuel rockets.

"We're on one of their damned ships!" said Jack coldly. He felt for his force gun. It was gone.

Helen opened her eyes. She stared vaguely about. Her eyes fell upon Jack. She shuddered suddenly and pressed close to him.

"What—what happened?"

"We'll have to find out," replied Jack grimly.

The floor beneath his feet careened suddenly. Instinctively, he glanced at a porthole which until then he had only subconsciously noted. He gazed out into the utterly familiar blackness of space, illumined by very many tiny points of light which were stars. He saw a ringed sun and points of light which were planets.

One of those points of light was very near. Its disk was perceptible, and polar snow caps, and the misty alternation of greenish areas which would be continents with the indescribable tint which is ocean bottom when viewed from beyond a planet's atmosphere.

Silence. No hootings of that strange language without vowels or consonants which the Centaurians used. No sound of any kind for a moment.

"We're heading for that planet, I suppose," said Jack quietly. "We'll have to see if we can't manage to get ourselves killed before we land."

Then a murmur in the distance. It was a strange, muted murmur, in nothing resembling the queer notes of the plant men. With Helen clinging to him, Jack explored cautiously, out of the cubby-hole in which they had awakened. Silence save for that distant murmur. No movement anywhere. Another faint stutter of the rockets, with a distinct accelerative movement of the whole ship. The animal smell grew stronger. They passed through a strangely shaped opening and Helen cried out:

"The animals!"

Heaped higgledy-piggledy were cages from the *Adastra,* little compartments containing specimens of each of the animals which had been bred from for food, and which it had been planned to release if a planet suitable for colonization revolved about Proxima Centauri. Farther on was an indescribable mass of books, machines, cases of all sorts—the materials ordered to be carried to the air lock by the leader of the plant men. Still no sign of any Centaurian.

But the muted murmur, quite incredibly sounding like a human voice, came from still farther ahead. Bewildered, now, Helen followed as Jack went still cautiously toward the source of the sound.

They found it. It came from a bit of mechanism cased in with the same lusterless, dull-brown stuff which composed the floor and walls and every part of the ship about them. And it was a human voice. More, it was Alstair's, racked and harsh and half hysterical.

"—you must have recovered consciousness by now, dammit, and these devils want some sign of it! They cut down your acceleration when I told them the rate they were using would keep you unconscious! Gary! Helen! Set off that signal!"

A pause. The voice again:

"I'll tell it again. You're in a space ship these fiends are guiding by a tight beam which handles the controls. You're going to be set down on one of the planets which once contained animal life. It's empty now, unoccupied except by plants. And you and the space ship's cargo of animals and books and so on are the reserved, special property of the high arch-fiend of all these devils. He had you sent in an outside-controlled ship because none of his kind could be trusted with such treasure as you and the other animals!

"You're a reserve of knowledge, to translate our books, explain our science, and so on. It's forbidden for any other space ship than his own to land on your planet. Now will you send that signal? It's a knob right above the speaker my voice is coming out of. Pull it three times, and they'll know you're all right and won't send another ship with preservatives for your flesh lest a priceless treasure go to waste!"

The tinny voice—Centaurian receptors were not designed to reproduce the elaborate phonetics of the human voice—laughed hysterically.

Jack reached up and pulled the knob, three times. Alstair's voice went on:

"This ship is hell, now. It isn't a ship any more, but a sort of brimstone pit. There are seven of us alive, and we're instructing Centaurians in the operation of the controls. But we've told them that we can't turn off the rockets to show their inner workings, because to be started they have to have a planet's mass near by, for deformation of space so the reaction can be started. They're keeping us alive until we've shown them that. They've got some method of writing, too, and they write down everything we say, when it's translated by a dictawriter. Very scientific——"

The voice broke off.

"Your signal just came," it said an instant later. "You'll find food somewhere about. The air ought to last you till you land. You've got four more days of travel. I'll call back later. Don't worry about navigation. It's attended to."

The voice died again, definitely.

The two of them, man and girl, explored the Centaurian space ship. Compared to the *Adastra*, it was miniature. A hundred feet long, or more, by perhaps sixty feet at its greatest diameter. They found cubby-holes in which there was now nothing at all, but which undoubtedly at times contained the plant men packed tightly.

These rooms could be refrigerated, and it was probable that at a low temperature the Centaurians reacted like vegetation on Earth in winter and passed into a dormant, hibernating state. Such an arrangement would allow of an enormous crew being carried, to be revived for landing or battle.

"If they refitted the *Adastra* for a trip back to Earth on that basis," said Jack grimly, "they'd carry a hundred and fifty thousand Centaurians at least. Probably more."

The thought of an assault upon mankind by these creatures was an obsession. Jack was tormented by it. Womanlike, Helen tried to cheer him by their own present safety.

"We volunteered for vivisection," she told him pitifully, the day after their recovery of consciousness, "and we're safe for a while, anyhow. And —we've got each other——"

"It's time for Alstair to communicate again," said Jack harshly. It was nearly thirty hours after the last signing off. Centaurian routine, like Earth discipline on terrestrial space ships, maintained a period equal to a planet's daily rotation as the unit of time. "We'd better go listen to him."

They did. And Alstair's racked voice came from the queerly shaped speaker. It was more strained, less sane, than the day before. He told them of the progress of the Things in the navigation of the *Adastra*. The six surviving officers already were not needed to keep the ship's apparatus functioning. The air-purifying apparatus in particular was shut off, since in clearing the air of carbon dioxide it tended to make the air unbreathable for the Centaurians.

The six men were now permitted to live that they might satisfy the insatiable desire of the plant men for information. They lived a perpetual third degree, with every resource of their brains demanded for record in the weird notation of their captors. The youngest of the six, a subaltern of the air department, went mad under the strain alike of memory and of anticipation. He screamed senselessly for hours, and was killed and his body promptly mummified by the strange, drying chemicals of the Centaurians. The rest were living shadows, starting at a sound.

"Our deceleration's been changed," said Alstair, his voice brittle. "You'll land just two days before we settle down, on the planet these devils call home. Queer they've no colonizing instinct. Another one of us is about to break, I think. They've taken away our shoes and belts now, by the way. They're leather. We'd take a gold band from about a watermelon, wouldn't we? Consistent, these——"

And he raged once, in sudden hysteria:

"I'm a fool! I sent you two off together while I'm living in hell! Gary, I order you to have nothing to do with Helen! I order that the two of you shan't speak to each other! I order that——"

Another day passed. And another. Alstair called twice more. Each time, by his voice, he was more desperate, more nerve-racked, closer to the bounds of madness. The second time he wept, the while he cursed Jack for being where there were none of the plant men.

"We're not interesting to the devils, now, except as animals. Our brains don't count! They're gutting the ship systematically. Yesterday they got the earthworms from the growing area where we grew crops! There's a guard on each of us now. Mine pulled out some of my hair this morning and ate it, rocking back and forth in ecstasy. We've no woolen shirts. They're animal!"

Another day still. Then Alstair was semihysterical. There were only three men left alive on the ship. He had instructions to give Jack in the landing of the egg-shaped vessel on the uninhabited world. Jack was supposed to help. His destination was close now. The disk of the planet which was to be his and Helen's prison filled half the heavens. And the other planet toward which the *Adastra* was bound was a full-sized disk to Alstair.

Beyond the rings of Proxima Centauri there were six planets in all, and the prison planet was next outward from the home of the plant men. It was colder than was congenial to them, though for a thousand years their flesh-hunting expeditions had searched its surface until not a mammal or a bird, no fish or even a crustacean was left upon it. Beyond it again an ice-covered world lay, and still beyond there were frozen shapes whirling in emptiness.

"You know, now, how to take over when the beam releases the atmospheric controls," said Alstair's voice. It wavered as if he spoke through teeth which chattered from pure nerve strain. "You'll have quiet. Trees and flowers and something like grass, if the pictures they've made mean anything. We're running into the greatest celebration in the history of all hell. Every space ship called home. There won't be a Centaurian on the planet who won't have a tiny shred of some sort of animal matter to consume. Enough to give him that beastly delight they feel when they get hold of something of animal origin.

"Damn them! Every member of the race! We're the greatest store of treasure ever dreamed of! They make no bones of talking before me, and I'm mad enough to understand a good bit of what they say to each other. Their most high panjandrum is planning bigger space ships than were ever grown before. He'll start out for Earth with three hundred space ships, and most of the crews asleep or hibernating. There'll be three million devils straight from hell on those ships, and they've those damned beams that will fuse an earthly ship at ten million miles."

Talking helped to keep Alstair sane, apparently. The next day Jack's and Helen's egg-shaped vessel dropped like a plummet from empty space into an atmosphere which screamed wildly past its smooth sides. Then Jack got the ship under control and it descended slowly and ever more slowly and at last came to a cushioned stop in a green glade hard by a forest of strange but wholly reassuring trees. It was close to sunset on this planet, and darkness fell before they could attempt exploration.

They did little exploring, however, either the next day or the day after. Alstair talked almost continuously.

"Another ship coming from Earth," he said, and his voice cracked. "Another ship! She started at least four years ago. She'll get here in four years more. You two may see her, but I'll be dead or mad by to-morrow night! And here's the humorous thing! It seems to me that madness is nearest when I think of you, Helen, letting Jack kiss you! I loved you, you know, Helen, when I was a man, before I became a corpse watching my ship being piloted into hell. I loved you very much. I was jealous, and when you looked at Gary with shining eyes I hated him. I still hate him, Helen! Ah, how I hate him!" But Alstair's voice was the voice of a ghost, now, a ghost in purgatory. "And I've been a fool, giving him that order."

Jack walked about with abstracted, burning eyes. Helen put her hands on his shoulders and he spoke absently to her, his voice thick with hatred. A desperate, passionate lust to kill Centaurians filled him. He began to hunt among the machines. He became absorbed, assembling a ten-kilowatt vortex gun from odd contrivances. He worked at it for many hours. Then he heard Helen at work, somewhere. She seemed to be struggling. It disturbed him. He went to see.

She had just dragged the last of the cages from the *Adastra* out into the open. She was releasing the little creatures within. Pigeons soared eagerly above her. Rabbits, hardly hopping out of her reach, munched delightedly upon the unfamiliar but satisfactory leafed vegetation underfoot.

She browsed. There were six of them besides a tiny, wabbly-legged lamb. Chickens pecked and scratched. But there were no insects on this world. They would find only seeds and green stuff. Four puppies rolled ecstatically on scratchy green things in the sunlight.

"Anyhow," said Helen defiantly. "They can be happy for a while! They're not like us! We have to worry! And this world could be a paradise for humans!"

Jack looked somberly out across the green and beautiful world. No noxious animals. No harmful insects. There could be no diseases on this planet, unless men introduced them of set purpose. It would be a paradise.

The murmur of a human voice came from within the space ship. He went bitterly to listen. Helen came after him. They stood in the strangely shaped cubby-hole which was the control room. Walls, floors, ceiling, instrument cases—all were made of the lusterless dark-brown stuff which had grown into the shapes the Centaurians desired. Alstair's voice was strangely more calm, less hysterical, wholly steady.

"I hope you're not off exploring somewhere, Helen and Gary," it said from the speaker. "They've had a celebration here to-day. The *Adastra's* landed. I landed it. I'm the only man left alive. We came down in the center of a city of these devils, in the middle of buildings fit to form the headquarters of hell. The high panjandrum has a sort of palace right next to the open space where I am now.

"And to-day they celebrated. It's strange how much animal matter there was on the *Adastra*. They even found horsehair stiffening in the coats of our uniforms. Woolen blankets. Shoes. Even some of the soaps had an animal origin, and they 'refined' it. They can recover any scrap of animal matter as cleverly as our chemists can recover gold and radium. Queer, eh?"

The speaker was silent a moment.

"I'm sane, now," the voice said steadily. "I think I was mad for a while. But what I saw to-day cleared my brain. I saw millions of these devils dipping their arms into great tanks, great troughs, in which solutions of all the animal tissues from the *Adastra* were dissolved. The high panjandrum kept plenty for himself! I saw the things they carried into his palace, through lines of guards. Some of those things had been my friends. I saw a city gone crazy with beastly joy, the devils swaying back and forth in ecstasy as they absorbed the loot from Earth. I heard the high panjandrum hoot a sort of imperial address from the throne. And I've learned to understand quite a lot of those hootings.

"He was telling them that Earth is packed with animals. Men. Beasts. Birds. Fish in the oceans. And he told them that the greatest space fleet in history will soon be grown, which will use the propulsion methods of men, our rockets, Gary, and the first fleet will carry uncountable swarms of them to occupy Earth. They'll send back treasure, too, so that every one of his subjects will have such ecstasy, frequently, as they had to-day. And the devils, swaying crazily back and forth, gave out that squealing noise of theirs. Millions of them at once."

Jack groaned softly. Helen covered her eyes as if to shut out the sight her imagination pictured.

"Now, here's the situation from your standpoint," said Alstair steadily, millions of miles away and the only human being upon a planet of blood-lusting plant men. "They're coming here now, their scientists, to have me show them the inside workings of the rockets. Some others will come over to question you two to-morrow. But I'm going to show these devils our rockets. I'm sure—perfectly sure—that every space ship of the race is back on this planet.

"They came to share the celebration when every one of them got as a free gift from the grand panjandrum as much animal tissue as he could hope to acquire in a lifetime of toil. Flesh is a good bit more precious than gold, here. It rates, on a comparative scale, somewhere between plati-num and radium. So they all came home. Every one of them! And there's a space ship on the way here from Earth. It'll arrive in four years more. Remember that!"

An impatient, distant hooting came from the speaker.

"They're here," said Alstair steadily. "I'm going to show them the rock-ets. Maybe you'll see the fun. It depends on the time of day where you are. But remember, there's a sister ship to the *Adastra* on the way! And Gary, that order I gave you last thing was the act of a madman, but I'm glad I did it. Good-by, you two!"

Small hooting sounds, growing fainter, came from the speaker. Far, far away, amid the city of fiends, Alstair was going with the plant men to show them the rockets' inner workings. They wished to understand every aspect of the big ship's propulsion, so that they could build—or grow—ships as large and carry multitudes of their swarming myriads to a solar system where animals were to be found.

"Let's go outside," said Jack harshly. "He said he'd do it, since he couldn't get a bit of a machine made that could be depended on to do it. But I believed he'd go mad. It didn't seem possible to live to their planet. We'll go outside and look at the sky."

Helen stumbled. They stood upon the green grass, looking up at the firmament above them. They waited, staring. And Jack's mind pictured the great rocket chambers of the *Adastra*. He seemed to see the strange procession enter it; a horde of the ghastly plant men and then Alstair, his face like marble and his hands as steady.

He'd open up the breech of one of the rockets. He'd explain the disintegration field, which collapses the electrons of hydrogen so that it rises in atomic weight to helium, and the helium to lithium, while the oxygen of the water is split literally into neutronium and pure force. Alstair would answer hooted questions. The supersonic generators he would explain as controls of force and direction. He would not speak of the fact that only the material of the rocket tubes, when filled with exactly the frequency those generators produced, could withstand the effect of the distintegration field.

He would not explain that a tube started without those generators in action would catch from the fuel and disintegrate, and that any other substance save one, under any other condition save that one rate of vibration, would catch also and that tubes, ship, and planet alike would vanish in a lambent purple flame.

No; Alstair would not explain that. He would show the Centaurians how to start the Caldwell field.

The man and the girl looked at the sky. And suddenly there was a fierce purple light. It dwarfed the reddish tinge of the ringed sun overhead. For one second, for two, for three, the purple light persisted. There was no sound. There was a momentary blast of intolerable heat. Then all was as before.

The ringed sun shone brightly. Clouds like those of Earth floated serenely in a sky but a little less blue than that of home. The small animals from the *Adastra* munched contentedly at the leafy stuff underfoot. The pigeons soared joyously, exercising their wings in full freedom.

"He did it," said Jack. "And every space ship was home. There aren't any more plant men. There's nothing left of their planet, their civilization, or their plans to harm our Earth."

Even out in space, there was nothing where the planet of the Centaurians had been. Not even steam or cooling gases. It was gone as if it had never existed. And the man and woman of Earth stood upon a planet which could be a paradise for human beings, and another ship was coming presently, with more of their kind.

"He did it!" repeated Jack quietly. "Rest his soul! And we—we can think of living, now, instead of death."

The grimness of his face relaxed slowly. He looked down at Helen. Gently, he put his arm about her shoulders.

She pressed close, gladly, thrusting away all thoughts of what had been. Presently she asked softly: "What was that last order Alstair gave you?"

"I never looked," said Jack.

He fumbled in his pocket. Pocketworn and frayed, the order slip came out. He read it and showed it to Helen. By statutes passed before the *Adastra* left Earth, laws and law enforcement on the artificial planet were intrusted to the huge ship's commander. It had been specially provided that a legal marriage on the *Adastra* would be constituted by an official order of marriage signed by the commander. And the slip handed to Jack by Alstair, as Jack went to what he'd thought would be an agonizing death, was such an order. It was, in effect, a marriage certificate.

They smiled at each other, those two.

"It—wouldn't have mattered," said Helen uncertainly. "I love you. But I'm glad!"

One of the freed pigeons found a straw upon the ground. He tugged at it. His mate inspected it solemnly. They made pigeon noises to each other. They flew away with the straw. After due discussion, they had decided that it was an eminently suitable straw with which to begin the building of a nest.

The thing I remember most clearly over the years about "Proxima Centauri" is the peculiar horror I felt at the thought of a race of intelligent plants that lusted after animal food. It is almost an unfailing recipe for a startling science fiction story to begin by inverting some thoroughly accepted situation, something so ordinary as to be almost disregarded. Of course, animals eat plants, and of course, animals are quick and more or less intelligent, while plants are motionless and utterly passive (except for a few insect-eating plants, which can be disregarded). But what if intelligent and carnivorous plants fed on animals, eh?

I did not forget the lesson, and sometimes I tried to make use of it. In my first full-length novel, *Pebble in the Sky*, I pitted Earth against the galaxy—but made *Earth* the villain. (John Campbell, to whom Earth was always the hero, rejected *Pebble in the Sky* in an early version, though I wouldn't say that was his only reason for rejecting it.)

I can't, by the way, speak for influences on other authors. I, myself, can judge whether in my own story creations I remembered and was influenced, either consciously or unconsciously, by the stories of other authors I had read and admired.

How can I say, however, on the basis of some superficial resemblance, that some other author has been influenced by an earlier story, which, for all I know, he has never read?

Yet, this one time, I cannot resist. As I reread "Proxima Centauri" in the course of the preparation of this anthology, I was forcibly reminded of Robert A. Heinlein's "Universe," which appeared six years later, in the May 1941 *Astounding Stories*. So aware was I of the similarities between the two that when Jack Gary, in "Proxima Centauri," was described as a "Mut," I instantly assumed that he was a "Mutant," as he would have been in "Universe," and was astonished to find that it stood for "Mutineer."

As I said, however, the similarities may be coincidence. Heinlein may never have read "Proxima Centauri."

Yet I had better point out that, when speaking of "influences," I mean only that. If Heinlein was indeed inspired by some of the notions in "Proxima Centauri," he clearly developed those notions in his own fashion and in his own direction and produced "Universe," which, in my opinion (and probably in that of most science fiction readers), was clearly and considerably superior to "Proxima Centauri."

In the same way, I must warn readers that although I am carefully and liberally pointing out influences on my own writing in this book, I carried all influences outward in my own particular fashion and in my own particular direction and made out of them something entirely my own.

As I said earlier, I had decided to go to Columbia for my college education. It was, after all, in Manhattan, and there was no question of leaving the city. College or not, I had to continue working in the candy store.

Wanting to go to Columbia was the least of it, however. The important questions were, first, whether the family could afford the tuition, and second, whether Columbia wanted me.

About the tuition, there was no way of being certain. If we had to, we would find some way. As to the question of Columbia's wishes, that would be determined. I had applied for entrance, and a date had been fixed for an interview. It was April 10, 1935. (This was nearly three years before I started the diary that helped me so with *The Early Asimov*, but I remember that day for a reason I will explain later.)

I was still only fifteen at the time and had never gone to Manhattan alone. My father, I think, had visions of me ruining my chance of getting into Columbia by getting lost in the confusing subway system and arriving late for the interview—or not arriving at all. He therefore actually abandoned the store to my mother and came with me. Naturally, he waited outside the building I was supposed to enter, because he didn't want to ruin my chances by having me appear to be a baby who could not be trusted to travel on his own.

He might have saved himself the trouble. I ruined my chances entirely on my own. I made a very poor impression. I was bound to. I don't think that I ever made a good first impression on anyone in my life until such time as my name had become impressive on its own. After that, of course, there is no such thing as a first impression.

The trouble is, and always has been, that at any first interview, I am too eager, too talkative, too lacking in poise and self-assurance, too obviously immature (even *now*). And in my teens, to add to it all, I suffered from acne. This is a common complaint and it is no great crime to be pimply, but it is no great honor either and doesn't improve the impression you make.

All in all, then, the poor man who had to face me and decide if I was Columbia material didn't have a difficult job at all. I have never held it against him (whoever he was, for I don't remember) that he decided against me.

As far as Columbia *College* was concerned, that is. I was so naïve in those days that I knew nothing beyond the mere name "Columbia." I did not realize that Columbia *University* was a huge establishment of which Columbia *College*, the elite undergraduate school, was but a small part. However, I found this out in the course of the interview.

My interviewer may have been impressed by my scholastic record and (I hope) by the intelligence that must have been apparent even through my obvious adolescent uneasiness. He therefore suggested I attend Seth Low Junior College.* This was another undergraduate college of Columbia University and was by no means elite. I had never heard of it at the time, and, in my entire life since, I have never met anyone who had heard of it (unless he had been a student there).

It was in Brooklyn and had the same scholastic standards as Columbia College (the interviewer said), and in the third and fourth years I would be allowed to take courses with the Columbia College students. What he didn't say, but what I eventually found to be the case, was that the Seth Low student body was heavily Jewish and Italian, so the school served to give bright youngsters a Columbia education without too badly contaminating the elite young men of the College itself. Those were the days when racial quotas were as American as apple pie.

Seth Low Junior College was not what I wanted, but what could I do? I nodded as cheerfully as I could manage and said, "All right."

I tried to put a good face on it to my father when I came out of the building and stoutly maintained that Seth Low "was just as good" and my father stoutly said it was. I didn't believe it, though, and neither did he.

We went home glumly, and my father took advantage of one of his

---

* It was named for the president of Columbia University in the 1890s, who before that had been mayor of the independent city of Brooklyn and after that the mayor of the conglomerated city of Greater New York.

rare absences from the store to stop in to see a movie with me. I even remember what it was: *Richelieu,* with George Arliss, Edward Arnold, and Cesar Romero.

We also stopped in at a museum (I *think* it was the Metropolitan Museum of Art but it may not have been). There we saw Albert Einstein, who happened to be looking at the exhibits also. He was unmistakable, and everywhere he went a small crowd of the curious followed, my father and I among them, all maintaining a respectful distance. Einstein, undoubtedly used to this, paid no attention. It was the only time I ever saw him, and it is for his sake more than for my Columbia interview that I remember the day.

My failure at Columbia rather cast a damper on my high school graduation, but there was always science fiction, and about that time I even made a trifling advance in the direction of involving myself in the field beyond the stage of my role as a merely passive reader.

In the mid-1930s, science fiction clubs were springing up around the country, and *Wonder Stories,* at least, was sponsoring them as one way of drumming up circulation, I suppose. There were clubs in the New York area, too, in which Sam Moskowitz was active, for instance, and in which great science fiction writers and editors of the future, such as Frederik Pohl and Donald A. Wollheim, spent their teen years.

It was not in that direction that my own activities tended. I had no knowledge of such things, and if I had known, it would probably have done me no good. To have been active in a science fiction club would have required an investment of several hours a week, and between school and the candy store, I didn't have those hours.

Yet there was a more modest advance I could make. The various science fiction magazines, in those days, had long letters columns in microscopic print at the back of each issue. They represented pages they could fill without payment, and the readers found them fascinating. (So did the writers, who valued the readers' comments—especially when those comments were enthusiastic.)

In 1935, I tried, for the first time, to write to one of the magazines—*Astounding Stories,* of course. It must have been a handwritten letter, for in 1935 I didn't know how to type and, for that matter, I had no access to a typewriter. Just the same, the letter was published. It was a perfectly ordinary letter. I commented on the most recent issue of *Astounding Stories* I had read, praising and denouncing stories and authors with the usual lordly condescension of the critic, and asked for trimmed edges.

Despite my success in achieving a published letter and seeing my name in print, I did not try again for three years. In fact, I forgot I had ever written the letter.

When, many years later, however, "First Fandom" was being organized, with membership extended to those who had been active in the field before the Campbell era opened, in 1938, the organizers approached me. Sadly, I said that although I had read science fiction avidly for years before 1938, I had not been active. And at once they came up with that 1935 letter in *Astounding Stories* and said that in my case that was qualification enough.*

And there were stories, too. I could console myself, for instance, with Edmond Hamilton's "The Accursed Galaxy," in the July 1935 *Astounding Stories*.

* This book is dedicated to First Fandom, you may have noticed, and I hope it qualifies me, ex post facto, for membership more than that letter ever did.

THE ACCURSED GALAXY

by Edmond Hamilton

A thin, tearing sound like the ripping of thousands of sheets of paper grew with lightning speed to a vibrant roar that brought Garry Adams to his feet in a jump.

He leaped to the door of his cabin and as he flung it open, he saw a sword of white fire cleave the night vertically and heard an abrupt ear-shattering crash from the distant darkness.

Then all was dark and still again, but down in the dimly starlit valley he could see clouds of smoke slowly rising.

"Good heavens, a meteorite!" Garry exclaimed. "And it's fallen right into my lap."

His eyes suddenly lighted. "Will this make a story! Reporter Sole Witness of Meteor's Fall——"

He grabbed a flashlight from the shelf by the door and the next minute was hurrying down the rude path that twisted from his hilltop cabin down the wooded slope to the valley.

Garry Adams was for fifty weeks of each year a reporter on one of the more sensational New York dailies. But two weeks each summer he spent in this lonely cabin in the northern Adirondacks and washed the taste of slayings, scandals and corruption out of his mind.

"Hope there's something left of it," he muttered as he tripped over a root in the dark. "It would rate a three-column picture."

Stopping for a moment at a place where the rude path emerged from the trees, he scanned the darkness of the valley. He spotted the place where faint wisps of smoke were still rising and plunged unhesitatingly in that direction through the woods.

Briers tore Garry's trousers and scratched his hands, and boughs whipped and stung his face as he struggled ahead. He dropped the flashlight once and had a hard time getting it. But before long he heard a crackle of small flames and smelled smoke. He emerged a few minutes later into a hundred-foot circle crushed flat by the impact of the meteorite.

Brush and grass, set afire by the heat of impact, were burning feebly, several places around the edge of this circle, and smoke got into Garry's eyes. He stood blinking, then saw the meteorite.

It was not an ordinary meteorite at all. He saw that at the first glance, even though the thing was half buried in the soft earth which it had flung up around itself. It was a glowing polyhedron ten feet in diameter, its surface a multitude of small flat facets, perfectly geometrical in shape. An artificial polyhedron that had fallen from outer space.

Garry Adams stared, and as he stared the visioned news headings in his mind expanded into black headlines.

"Meteorite Proves Shot from Space! Reporter Finds Shell from Space that Contains——"

What *did* the thing contain? Garry took a step toward it, cautiously because of the heat the white glow of it betokened. To his surprise, he found that the polyhedron was not hot at all. The ground under his feet was hot from the impact but the faceted thing before him was not. Its glow, whatever it was, was not of heat.

Garry stared, his black brows concentrated into a frown beneath which his brain worked excitedly. It must be, he argued, a thing made by intelligent beings, somewhere out in space.

It could hardly contain living beings, for they could not have survived its fall. But there might be books, machines, models——

Garry came to a sudden decision. This story was too big for him to handle alone. He knew the man he needed here. He turned around and struggled back through the woods to the path, then followed it, not back up to the cabin but on down the valley until it joined a narrow, rude dirt road.

An hour of walking on this brought him to a somewhat better dirt road, and an hour more on this brought him, tired but still vibrant with excitement, into a dark, sleeping little village.

Garry pounded on the door of the general store until a querulous, sleepy storekeeper came down in his nightshirt and let him in. He made straight for the telephone.

"I want to call a Dr. Peters, Dr. Ferdinand Peters of Manhattan University Observatory, in New York," he said to the operator. "And keep ringing until you get him."

Ten minutes later the astronomer's sleepy, irritated voice greeted his ears. "Well, who's this?"

"It's Garry Adams, doctor," Garry said rapidly. "You remember, the reporter who wrote up your solar researches last month?"

"I remember that your story contained no less than thirty errors," Dr.

Peters answered acidly. "What in the devil do you want at this time of night?"

Garry talked steadily for five minutes, and when he had finished there was so long a silence that he shouted into the transmitter, "Did you hear me? Are you there?"

"Of course I'm here—don't yell so loud," retorted the astronomer's voice. "I was just considering." He began to speak rapidly. "Adams, I'm coming up to that village of yours on the dot, by plane if possible. You wait there for me and we'll go out and look at the thing together. If you're telling me the truth, you've got a story that will make you famous forever. If you're hoaxing me, I'll flay you alive if I have to chase you around the world to do it."

"Don't let anyone else know about it, whatever you do," cautioned Garry. "I don't want any other paper to get it."

"All right, all right," said the scientist. "A lot of difference it makes to me whether any of your filthy rags get it."

Four hours later Garry Adams saw a plane buzzing earthward through the dawn mists east of the village. He waited, and in another half hour the astronomer tramped into the place.

Dr. Peters saw Garry and came straight toward him. Peters' keen, spectacled black eyes and ascetic, shaven face wore an expression in which were mixed doubt and repressed excitement.

Characteristically, he wasted no time in greetings or preliminaries. "You're sure the thing is a geometrical polyhedron? Not just a natural meteorite with some resemblance to that shape?" he queried.

"Wait till you see it for yourself," Garry told him. "I've rented a car that will take us almost there."

"Drive out to my plane first," the doctor ordered. "I've brought some equipment that may prove useful."

The equipment consisted of bars, tools and wrenches of fine steel and a complete oxy-acetylene torch outfit, with the necessary tanks. They stowed it into the back of the car and then bumped and rattled over the uncertain mountain roads until they reached the beginning of the path.

When Dr. Peters emerged with the reporter into the clearing where lay the half-buried, glowing polyhedron, he stared at it for some moments in silence.

"Well?" asked Garry impatiently.

"It's not a natural meteorite, that's sure."

"But what is it?" Garry exclaimed. "A projectile from another world? What's in it?"

"We'll know that when we've opened it," Peters answered coolly. "The first thing is to dig away the dirt so that we can examine it."

Despite the astronomer's calmness, Adams saw a glitter in his eyes as they lugged the heavy equipment from the automobile to the clearing. And the driving energy with which Dr. Peters worked was further index of the intensity of his interest.

They started at once digging away the earth around the thing. Two hours of hard work did it, and the whole polyhedron stood naked before them, still glowing whitely in the morning sunlight. The scientist then made minute examination of the substance of the glowing thing. He shook his head.

"It's not like any terrestrial substance ever heard of. Is there any sign of a door or opening?"

"Not a trace of one," Garry answered, then added suddenly, "But here's something on one of the facets, a sort of diagram."

Dr. Peters hurried quickly to his side. The reporter pointed to what he had discovered, a curious and complex sign graven deep on a facet half-way up the side of the polyhedron.

The diagram represented a small, spiral-shaped swarm of densely crowded dots. A little out from this central swarm were other little swarms of graven dots, mostly spiral-shaped also. Above this curious diagram was a row of grotesque, interlinked symbols.

"By heaven, it's writing of some sort, an inscription!" Garry cried. "I wish we had a photographer here."

"And a pretty girl to sit with her knees crossed and give the picture sex-appeal," Peters observed caustically. "You can think of your dirty sheet in the presence of—this."

His eyes were brilliant with controlled excitement. "The symbols, we can't guess what they mean, of course. Undoubtedly they tell something about this thing's contents. But the diagram——"

"What do you think the diagram means?" Garry asked excitedly as the astronomer paused.

"Well, those swarms of dots seem intended to represent galaxies of stars," Peters said slowly. "The central one, no doubt, symbolizes our own galaxy, which has just such a spiral shape, and the other swarms stand for the other galaxies of the cosmos.

"But they're too close to ours, those others—too close. If they were actually that close when this thing was made, it means that the thing was made back when the universe first started to expand!"

He shook off his abstracted ponderings and turned briskly toward the pile of tools and equipment.

"Come on, Adams, we'll try to open it up on the side opposite the inscription. If the bars won't do it, the torch will."

Two hours later Garry and Dr. Peters, exhausted, sweating and baffled, stood back and gazed at each other in wordless futility. All of their efforts to open the mysterious polyhedron had utterly failed.

Their sharpest tools made not the slightest scratch on the glowing walls. The oxy-acetylene torch had not the least bit more effect, its flame not even seeming to heat the substance. And even a variety of acids which Dr. Peters had brought with him had no effect.

"Whatever it is," Garry panted, "I'll say it's the hardest and most intractable matter I ever heard of."

The astronomer nodded slowly. "If it is matter at all," he said.

Garry stared. "If it is matter? Why, we can see the thing's matter; it's solid and real as we are."

"It's solid and real," Peters agreed, "but that does not prove that it is matter. Adams, I think that it is force of some kind, crystallized in some superhuman and unknown way into a solid-seeming polyhedron. Frozen force!

"And I don't think we'll ever open it with ordinary tools. They would work with ordinary matter, but not with this thing."

The reporter looked perplexedly from him to the glowing mystery. "Frozen force? Then what are we going to do?"

Peters shook his head. "The thing's beyond me. There isn't a way in the world that I can think of to——"

He stopped suddenly. Garry, looking up sharply at the interruption in his words, saw that an odd listening expression had fallen upon the scientist's face.

It was at the same time an expression of surprise, as though some part of his mind were surprised at something another part told it.

Dr. Peters spoke in a moment, and with the same surprise in his voice.

"Why, what am I talking about? Of course we can open the thing. A way just occurred to me—— The thing is made of crystallized force. Well, all we need to do is to de-crystallize that force, to melt it away by the application of other forces."

"But surely it's beyond your scientific knowledge how to do a thing like that!" the reporter said.

"Not at all; I can do it easily but I'll need more equipment," the scientist said.

He fished an envelope and pencil from his pocket and hastily jotted down a list of items. "We'll go into the village and I'll telephone New York to have these things rushed up."

Garry waited in the village store while the astronomer read his list into the telephone. By the time this was done and they returned to the clearing in the valley woods, darkness had fallen.

The polyhedron was glowing weirdly in the night, a shimmering, faceted enigma. Garry had to tear his companion away from his fascinated inspection. He finally did so and they climbed to the cabin and cooked and ate a sketchy supper.

The two sat after supper and tried to play cards by the light of the kerosene lamp. Both men were silent except for the occasional monosyllables of the game. They made error after error, until at last Garry Adams flung the cards down.

"What's the use of this? We're both too wrought up over that darned thing down there to give a thought to anything else. We might as well admit that we're dying with curiosity. Where did the thing come from and what's in it? What do those symbols on it mean, and that diagram you said represented the galaxies? I can't get it all out of my head."

Peters nodded thoughtfully. "Such a thing doesn't come to earth every day. I doubt if such a thing has ever come to earth before."

He sat staring into the soft flame of the lamp, his eyes abstracted and his ascetic face frowning in intense interest and disturbed perplexity.

Garry remembered something. "You said when we looked at that queer diagram on it that it might mean the polyhedron was made when the universe first started expanding. What the devil did you mean by that? *Is* the universe expanding?"

"Of course it is. I thought everyone was aware of the fact," Dr. Peters said irritably.

Then he smiled suddenly. "But I keep forgetting, since I associate almost always with fellow scientists, how completely ignorant most people are of the universe in which they live."

"Thanks for the compliment," Garry said. "Suppose you enlighten my ignorance a little on this point."

"Well," said the other, "you know what a galaxy is?"

"A swarm of stars like our sun, isn't it—a whole lot of them?"

"Yes, our sun is only one of billions of stars gathered together in a great swarm which we call our galaxy. We know that the swarm has a roughly spiral shape and that as it floats in space the whole spiral swarm is rotating on its center.

"Now, there are other galaxies in space beside our own, other great swarms of stars. It is estimated, indeed, that their number runs into billions and each of them, of course, contains billions of stars. But—and this has seemed to astronomers a curious thing—our own galaxy is definitely larger than any of the others.

"Those other galaxies lie at enormous distances from our own. The nearest is more than a million light years away and the others are much farther. And all of them are moving through space, each star cloud sweeping through the void.

"We astronomers have been able to ascertain the speed and direction of their movements. When a star, or a swarm of stars, is moving in the line of sight of the observer, the movement has a definite effect upon its spectrum. If the swarm is moving away from the observer, the lines in its spectrum will shift toward the red end of the spectrum. The faster it is moving away, the greater will be the shift toward the red.

"Using this method, Hubble, Humason, Slipher and other astronomers have measured the speed and direction of movement of the other galaxies. They have found an amazing thing, a thing that has created a tremendous sensation in astronomical circles. They have found that those other galaxies are all running away from our own!

"It is not just a few of them that are moving away from our own but all of them. In every side, every galaxy in the cosmos is hurtling away from our own galaxy! And they are doing so at speeds as high as fifteen thousand miles a second, which is almost a tenth the speed of light itself.

"At first astronomers could not believe their own observations. It seemed incredible that all other galaxies should be fleeing from our own, and for a time it was thought that certain of the nearer ones were not receding. But that has been seen to be an observational error and we now accept the incredible fact that all other galaxies are flying away from our own.

"What does that mean? It means that there must once have been a time when all those outward-speeding galaxies were gathered with our own into a single giant supergalaxy that contained all the stars in the universe. By calculating back from their present speeds and distances, we find that that time was about two billion years ago.

"Then something made that supergalaxy suddenly break up, and all its outer portions went flying off into space in all directions. The portions that flew off are the galaxies that are still flying away from us. Our own is without doubt the center or core of the original supergalaxy.

"What caused that break-up of the gigantic supergalaxy? That we do not know, though many theories have been advanced. Sir Arthur Eddington believes that the break-up was caused by some unknown principle of repulsion in matter which he calls the cosmical constant. Others have suggested that space itself started expanding, an even more incredible explanation. Whatever the cause, we know that that supergalaxy did break up and that all the other galaxies formed by its break-up are flying away from our own at tremendous speeds."

Garry Adams had listened intently to Dr. Peters as the astronomer spoke in quick, nervous fashion.

His own lean, newly tanned face was serious in the glow of the lamp. "It seems strange, at that," he commented. "A cosmos in which all the other galaxies are fleeing from us. But that diagram on the side of the polyhedron—you said that indicated the thing was made when the expansion first started?"

"Yes." Peters nodded. "You see, that diagram was made by intelligent or superintelligent beings, for they knew our own galaxy is spiral-shaped and so depicted it.

"But they depicted the other galaxies as almost touching our own. In other words, that diagram must have been made when the giant super-galaxy first started breaking up, when the other galaxies first started running away from our own. That was some two billion years ago, as I said. Two thousand million years. So you see, if the polyhedron was actually made that long ago it——"

"I see enough to feel that I'm going crazy with speculation," Garry Adams said, getting to his feet. "I'm going to bed, whether I'm able to sleep or not."

Dr. Peters shrugged. "I suppose we might as well. The equipment I sent for won't be out until morning."

Garry Adams lay thinking in the darkness after he had retired to the upper of the two bunks in the cabin. What was this visitant from outer space and what would they find in it when they opened it?

His wonderings merged into sleep mists out of which he suddenly awoke to find the cabin bright with morning sunshine. He woke the scientist and after a hasty breakfast they hurried down to the point on the dirt road where Dr. Peters had directed the ordered equipment to be brought.

They had waited there but a half hour when the sleek high-speed truck came humming along the narrow road. Its driver halted it at sight of them, and they helped him unload the equipment it carried. Then he drove back the way he had come.

Garry Adams surveyed the pile of equipment dubiously. It looked too simple to him, consisting only of a dozen or so sealed containers of chemicals, some large copper and glass containers, a pile of copper strips and wiring, and some slender ebonite rods.

He turned to Dr. Peters, who was also gazing at the pile.

"This sure looks like a lot of junk to me," the reporter said. "How are you going to use this stuff to de-crystallize the frozen force of the polyhedron?"

Dr. Peters turned to him a blank, bewildered stare. "I don't know," he answered slowly.

"You don't know?" Garry echoed. "Why, what do you mean? Yesterday there at the polyhedron you said it was quite clear to you how to do it. You must have known, to order all this stuff."

The astronomer seemed even more bewildered. "Garry, I remember that I did know how then, when I jotted down the list of these things. But I don't now. I haven't the slightest idea of how they could be used on the polyhedron."

Garry dropped his arms, stared unbelievingly at his companion.

He started to say something, but as he saw the other's evident mental distress he checked himself.

"Well, we'll take the stuff over to the polyhedron now," he said calmly. "Maybe by that time you'll remember the plan you've forgotten."

"But I've never before forgotten anything in this way," Peters said dazedly as he helped pick up the mass of things. "It's simply beyond my understanding."

They emerged into the crushed clearing where the enigmatic polyhedron still glowed and shimmered. As they set down their burdens beside the thing, Peters burst suddenly into a laugh.

"Why, of course I know how to use this stuff on the polyhedron. It's simple enough."

Garry stared at him again. "You've remembered?"

"Of course," the scientist answered confidently. "Hand me that biggest box marked barium oxide, and two of those containers. We'll soon have the polyhedron open."

The reporter, his jaw hanging in surprise, watched Peters start confidently to work with the supplies. Chemicals foamed together in the containers as rapidly as he mixed them.

He worked swiftly, smoothly, without asking any aid of the reporter. He had an utter efficiency and utter confidence, so dissimilar to his attitude of a few minutes before, that an incredible idea was born and grew in Garry Adams' mind.

He said suddenly to Peters, "Doctor, you know completely what you're doing now?"

Peters looked up impatiently. "Of course I do," he replied sharply. "Doesn't it look like it?"

"Will you do something for me?" asked Garry. "Will you come back with me to the road where we unloaded the supplies?"

"Why in the world do that?" demanded the scientist. "I want to get this finished."

"Never mind; I'm not asking for fun but because it's important," Garry said. "Come on, will you?"

"Oh, damn such foolishness, but I'll go," the scientist said, dropping his work. "It'll lose us half an hour."

Fuming over this, he tramped back with Garry to the dirt road, a half mile from the polyhedron.

"Now what do you want to show me?" he snapped, looking around.

"I only want to ask you something," Garry said. "Do you still know how to open the polyhedron?"

Dr. Peters' expression showed pure anger. "Why, you time-wasting young fool! Of course I——"

He stopped suddenly, and abruptly panic fell on his face, blind terror of the unknown.

"But I don't!" he cried. "I did there a few minutes ago but now I don't even know just what I was doing there!"

"I thought so," said Garry Adams, and though his voice was level there was a sudden chill along his spine. "When you're at the polyhedron, you know well enough how to go about a process that is completely beyond present-day human science.

"But as soon as you go some distance away from the polyhedron, you know no more about it than any other scientist would. Do you see what it means?"

Peters' face showed astounded comprehension. "You think that something—something about that polyhedron, is putting into my mind the way to get it open?"

His eyes widened. "It seems incredible, yet at that it may be true. Neither I nor any other scientist of earth would know how to melt frozen force. Yet when I'm there at the polyhedron I *do* know how to do it!"

Their eyes met. "If something wants that open," Garry said slowly, "it's something inside the polyhedron. Something that can't open it from the inside, but is getting you to do so from the outside."

For a space of seconds they stood in the warm morning sunlight looking at each other. The woods around them gave off a smell of warm leaves, a sleepy hum of insects. When the reporter spoke again, his voice was unconsciously lower than it had been.

"We'll go back," he said. "We'll go back, and if you know how again when we're at the thing, we'll know that we're right."

They walked silently, hesitatingly, back toward the polyhedron. Though he said nothing, the hair rose on Garry Adams' neck as they entered the clearing and approached the glowing thing.

They went closer until they stood again beside the thing. Then Peters suddenly turned a white face toward the reporter.

"You were right, Garry!" he said. "Now that I'm back here beside the thing, I suddenly know how to open it!

"Something inside must be telling me, as you said. Something that ages ago was locked up in this and that wants—freedom."

A sudden alien terror fell upon them both, chilling them like a gelid breath from the unknown. With a common impulse of panic they turned hastily.

"Let's get away from it!" Garry cried. "For Heaven's sake, let's get out of here!"

Four steps only they ran when a thought sounded in Garry's brain, clear and loud.

"Wait!"

The word, the pleading request, was as strong in his mind as though his ears had heard it.

Peters looked at him with wide eyes as they unconsciously stopped.

"I heard it, too," he whispered.

"Wait, do not go!" came the rapid thought message into their minds. "Hear me at least, let me at least explain to you, before you flee!"

"Let's go while we can!" Garry cried to the scientist. "Peters, whatever's in that thing, whatever is talking to our minds, isn't human, isn't of earth. It came from outside space, from ages ago. Let's get away from it!"

But Dr. Peters was looking fascinatedly back at the polyhedron. His face was twisted by conflicting emotions.

"Garry, I'm going to stay and listen to it," he said suddenly. "I've got to find out what I can about it—if you were a scientist you'd understand! You go on and get away; there's no reason for your staying. But I'm going back."

Garry stared at him, then grinned crookedly though he was still a little white beneath his tan. He said, "Just as a scientist is ridden by his passion, doctor, so is a reporter by his. I'm going back with you. But for Heaven's sake don't touch that equipment; don't try to open the polyhedron, until we at least have some idea as to what kind of thing is inside!"

Dr. Peters nodded wordlessly and then slowly they moved back to the glowing polyhedron, feeling as though the ordinary sunlit noonday world had suddenly become unreal. When they neared the polyhedron, the thoughts from within it beat more strongly into their minds.

"I sense that you have stayed. Come closer to the polyhedron—it is only by immense mental effort that I can force my thoughts through this insulating shell of force at all."

Numbly they stepped closer until they were at the very side of the faceted, glowing thing.

"Remember," Garry whispered hoarsely to the scientist, "no matter what it tells us, what it promises, don't open it yet!"

The scientist nodded unsteadily. "I'm as afraid of opening it as you are."

The thought messages came clearer into their brains now from the polyhedron.

"I am a prisoner in this shell of frozen force, as you have guessed. For a time almost longer than you can comprehend, I have been prisoned in it. My prison has at last been cast on your world, wherever that may be. I want your help now and I sense that you are too afraid to help me. If I disclose to you who I am and how I came to be here, you will not then be so afraid. That is why I wish now to tell you these things."

Garry Adams felt as though he stood in a strange dream as the thoughts from the polyhedron beat into his brain.

"Not in mere thought messages will I tell you what I wish to tell, but visually by thought pictures that you can understand better. I do not know the capacity of your mental systems for reception of such pictures, but I will try to make them clear.

"Do not try to think about what you see but merely allow your brains to remain in receptive condition. You will see what I wish you to see and will understand at least partially because my thoughts will accompany the visual impressions."

Garry felt sudden panic as the world seemed suddenly to vanish from around him. Dr. Peters, the polyhedron, the whole noonday sunlit scene, disappeared in an instant. Instead of standing in the sunlight, Garry seemed now to himself to be hanging suspended in the black vault of the cosmos—a lightless, airless void.

Everywhere about him was only that empty blackness, save below him. Below him, far, far below, there floated a colossal cloud of stars shaped like a flattened globe. Its stars could be counted only by the millions of millions.

Garry knew that he looked on the universe as it was two billion years ago. He knew that this below him was the giant supergalaxy in which were all the stars in the cosmos. Now he seemed to rocket down toward the mighty swarm with the swiftness of thought, and now he saw that the worlds of its swarming suns were inhabited.

Their inhabitants were volitient beings of force, each one like a tall, disk-crowned pillar of blue-brilliant light. They were immortal; they needed no nourishment; they passed through space and matter at will. They were the only volitient beings in the whole supergalaxy and its inert matter was almost entirely at their command.

Now Garry's viewpoint shifted to a world near the center of the super-galaxy. There he saw a single force creature who was engaged in a new experiment upon matter. He was seeking to build new forms of it, combining and re-combining atoms in infinite permutations.

Suddenly he came upon a combination of atoms that gave strange results. The matter so formed moved of its own accord. It was able to receive a stimulus and to remember it and act upon it. It was able also to assimilate other matter into itself; and so to grow.

The force creature experimenter was fascinated by this strange disease of matter. He tried it on a larger scale and the diseased matter spread out and assimilated more and more ordinary matter. He named this disease of matter by a name that reproduced itself in Garry's mind as "life."

This strange disease of life escaped from the experimenter's laboratory and began to spread over all that planet. Everywhere it spread, it infected other matter. The experimenter tried to extirpate it but the infection was too widely spread. At last he and his fellows abandoned that diseased world.

But the disease got loose from that world to other worlds. Spores of it, driven by the push of light beams to other suns and planets, spread out in every direction. The life disease was adaptable, took different forms on different worlds, but always it grew and propagated, infected more and more matter.

The force creatures assembled their forces to wipe out this loathsome infection but could not. While they stamped it out on one world, it spread on two others. Always, too, some hidden spore escaped them. Soon nearly all the worlds of the central portion of the supergalaxy were leprous with the life plague.

Garry saw the force creatures make a last great attempt to stamp out this pathology infecting their universe. The attempt failed; the plague continued its resistless spread. The force creatures then saw that it would spread until it had infected all the worlds in the supergalaxy.

They determined to prevent this at all costs. They resolved to break up the supergalaxy, to detach the uninfected outer parts of it from the diseased central portion. It would be a stupendous task but the force creatures were not daunted by it.

Their plan entailed giving to the supergalaxy a rotatory movement of great speed. This they accomplished by generating tremendous waves of continuous force through the ether, waves so directed that gradually they started the supergalaxy rotating on its center.

Faster and faster the giant star swarm turned as time went on. The life disease was still spreading at its center but now the force creatures had hope. They continued their work until the supergalaxy was turning so fast that it could no longer hold together against its own centrifugal force. It broke up like a bursting flywheel.

Garry saw that break-up, as though from high above. He saw the colossal, spinning star cloud disintegrating, swarm after swarm of stars breaking from it and flying away through space. Countless numbers of these smaller new galaxies broke from the parent supergalaxy until at last only the inmost core of the supergalaxy was left.

It was still rotating, and still had the spiral form caused by its rotation. On it now the life plague had spread to nearly every world. The last swarm of clean, uninfected stars had broken away from it and was flying away like the others.

But as this last swarm departed, there took place a ceremony and a punishment. The force creatures had passed judgment upon that one of their number whose experiments had loosed the life plague upon them and had made necessary this great break-up.

They decreed that he should remain forever in this diseased galaxy that all the others were leaving. They imprisoned him in a shell of frozen force so constructed that never could he open it from within. They set that polyhedronal shell floating in the diseased galaxy they left behind.

Garry Adams saw that glowing polyhedron floating in aimless orbits in the galaxy, as the years passed in millions. The other galaxies sped farther and farther away from this infected one in which the life disease now covered every possible world. Only this one force creature remained here, prisoned eternally in the polyhedron.

Garry dimly saw the polyhedron, in its endless orbit through the suns, chance to strike upon a world. He saw——

He saw only mists, gray mists. The vision was passing and suddenly Garry was aware that he stood in hot sunlight. He stood by the glowing polyhedron, dazed, rapt.

And Dr. Peters, dazed and rapt, too, was working mechanically on something beside him, a triangular thing of copper and ebonite pointed at the polyhedron.

Garry understood instantly and cried out in horror as he leaped toward the astronomer. "Peters, *don't!*"

Peters, only partly awakened, looked dazedly down at the thing which his hands were busy finishing.

"Smash it!" Garry yelled. "The thing inside the polyhedron kept us occupied with that vision so it could keep you working unconsciously to set it free. Don't—oh, Lord!"

For as Garry yelled, the dazed scientist's hands had clicked together the last parts of the copper and ebonite triangle, and from its apex leaped a yellow beam that smote the glowing polyhedron.

The yellow flash spread instantly over the faceted, glowing bulk, and as Garry and the waking Peters stared petrifiedly, they saw the polyhedron dissolving in that saffron flare.

The faceted sides of frozen force melted and vanished in a moment. Up out of the dissolved prison cage burst and towered the Thing that had been in it.

A forty-foot pillar of blazing, blue light, crowned by a disk of light, it loomed supernally splendid in sudden darkness, for with its bursting forth the noonday sunlight had snapped out like turned-off electricity. It swirled and spun in awful, alien glory as Peters and Garry cried out and threw their hands before their blinded eyes.

From the brilliant pillar there beat into their minds a colossal wave of exultation, triumph beyond triumph, joy vaster than any human joy. It was the mighty paean of the Thing, that went out from it not in sound but in thought.

It had been prisoned, cut away from the wide universe, for age after slow-crawling age, and now at last it was free and rejoicing in its freedom. In unbearable madness of cosmic rapture it loomed in the noonday darkness.

Then it flashed up into the heavens like a giant lightning bolt of blue. And as it did so, Garry's darkening brain failed and he staggered into unconsciousness.

He opened his eyes to bright noonday sunlight, which was streaming through the window beside him. He was lying in the cabin and the day was again brilliant outside, and somewhere near by a metallic voice was speaking.

He recognized that the voice was coming from his own little battery radio. Garry lay unmoving, unremembering for the moment, as the excited voice hurried on.

"——far out as we can make out, the area affected extended from Montreal as far south as Scranton, and from Buffalo in the West to some miles in the Atlantic beyond Boston, in the East.

"It lasted less than two minutes, and in the whole area was a complete blotting out of the sun's light and heat in that time. Also, practically all electrical machinery ceased to function and the telegraph and telephone lines went completely dead.

"People living in certain Adirondack and Northwest Vermont sections have reported also some physical effects. They consisted of a sudden sensation of extreme joy, coincident with the darkness, and followed by brief unconsciousness.

"No one yet knows the cause of this amazing phenomenon though it may be due to a freak of solar forces. Scientists are now being consulted on the matter, and as soon as they——"

Garry Adams by this time was struggling weakly up to a sitting position in the bunk, clutching at its post.

"Peters!" he called over the metallic voice of the radio. "Peters——"

"I'm here," said the astronomer, coming across the cabin.

The scientist's face was pale and his movements a little unsteady, but he, too, was unhurt.

"I came back to consciousness a little sooner than you did and carried you up here," he said.

"That—that Thing caused all the darkness and other things I've just been hearing of?" Garry cried.

Dr. Peters nodded. "It was a creature of force, force so terrific that its bursting forth here damped the heat and light radiations of the sun, the electrical currents of machines, even the electro-nervous impulses of our brains."

"And it's gone; it's really gone?" the reporter cried.

"It's gone after its fellows, out into the void of intergalactic space after the galaxies that are receding from our own," said Dr. Peters solemnly. "We know now why all the galaxies in the cosmos are fleeing from our own, know that ours is held an accursed galaxy, leprous with the disease of life. But I don't think we'll ever tell the world."

Garry Adams shook his head weakly. "We won't tell; no. And I think we'll try to forget it ourselves. I think we'll try."

I am positive I knew of the expanding universe and of the receding galaxies before I read "The Accursed Galaxy." After all, I read the enormously popular books by Arthur S. Eddington and James Jeans on relativity and astronomy. Nevertheless, nothing made the receding galaxies so vivid to me as Hamilton did, and I have never read an explanation of that recession more dramatic or compelling than the one in this story. Every once in a while, I can feel myself almost believing it.

I never used Hamilton's view of life as a cosmic disease in my science fiction, but in a science article I once wrote named "Recipe for a Planet," in the July 1961 issue of The Magazine of Fantasy and Science Fiction, I ended with an imaginary recipe for a planet from "Mother Stellar's Planetary Cook-book."

Part of it went, "Cool slowly till the crust hardens and a thin film of adhering gas and moisture appears. (If it does not appear, you have overheated.) Place in an orbit at a comfortable distance from a star and set to spinning. Then wait. In several billion years, it will ferment at the surface. The fermented portion, which is called life, is considered the best part by connoisseurs."

This may not seem like much, but here there is no unconscious influence. When I spoke of the surface fermenting, I thought, very consciously, of Hamilton's "The Accursed Galaxy," which I had read twenty-six years before.

As the summer wore on, I became increasingly aware that I would have to go to the tuition-free College of the City of New York (which everyone called City College). I didn't want to, but there was no choice. My father might somehow have managed to find the money for tuition at Columbia College, but he did not have the heart to try for Seth Low Junior College and I didn't see my way clear to putting pressure on him to do so.

I didn't want to go to City College, because everyone told me that City graduates could not get into medical school, and I still saw no reasonable future for myself that didn't involve medical school. However, not-wanting-to wasn't going to help me. I had applied to City College just in case I couldn't get into Columbia, and they had accepted.

Came September, then, I went to City College and stayed there three days. I remember only two things about those three days. We had a physical examination and since I was still as skinny as a stick, I was put down as PD where everyone else had WD. I asked what PD meant and I was told "poorly developed." Everyone else, obviously, was "well developed."

The other thing I remember was that we were all given an intelligence test, and about a month later, when the tests were scored, I received a letter asking me to come in for further testing because I had astonished them. By that time I wasn't in City College any more, however, and I was glad they would have no opportunity to test me further. "Poorly developed" indeed!!

In any case, on the third day at City College a letter arrived from Seth Low Junior College. I was away at school, and my father, sensing something urgent, opened it and found they were inquiring as to why I had not showed up for registration. He called them up and explained we lacked the money for tuition. They at once offered a one-hundred-dollar scholarship.

This my father could not resist, and off I went to Seth Low Junior College, but not before I had objected very vehemently to my father's opening my mail. He kept saying, "But if I hadn't, you might have missed this opportunity," while I kept answering to the effect that I was almost sixteen and mustn't be treated like a baby.

I decided to major in zoology and took a general course in that subject in my freshman year. It is hard to believe it as I look back on it, but I actually dissected animals in that course. My most horrifying memory is the dissection of a cat in the second semester. I had to find a homeless alley cat and chloroform it. Unbelievable! In later years, when I was working at a medical school, I refused to do any animal experiments and invariably walked out of the lab when animals were brought in for the purpose. (I recognize the necessity of animal experimentation—but for other people.)

My sharpest memory is, as you might expect, of a trifle. Our zoology lectures were given in an old-fashioned room with a tile floor. At one point during one of those lectures, I needed a handkerchief and pulled one out of my pocket. In the same pocket was a glass "shooter" I had there for some reason (because it looked pretty, I think, and I enjoyed looking at the light through it). It came out with the handkerchief and went bouncety-bouncety-bounce over the tile floor.

The professor waited patiently while the class held its breath and I, red-faced, struggled to retrieve the shooter. When I had done so, and silence had fallen, the professor said, contemptuously, "Well, this is a *junior* college," and the dam broke and the laughter from the other students began and continued—and continued—

A small thing, and not worth remembering, except that it soured me on zoology. I ended the course with good marks, but the incident of the dropped shooter, even more than killing the cat, made it easy for me to consider switching majors, and that, in turn, deflected the current of my life.

Part Seven

1936

IN EARLY 1936, I recognized a great desire within myself that could no longer be repressed. I wanted a typewriter.

I had frequently seen typewriters, but always in business offices, where they were outside my world. They might as well have been in jewelry-store windows.

My closest approach to a typewriter had come in 1928, when my father had bought his second candy store. We moved in upstairs above the store, and there was an overlap of a few days before the previous proprietors moved out.

There was a typewriter in the apartment. I was eight years old at the time, had not yet discovered science fiction, and certainly did not dream of writing. Nevertheless, there was a strange attraction between it and myself—a kind of dim love-at-first-sight. I remember touching it and looking at it curiously and half depressing the keys and wondering how it worked and hoping that somehow it would remain there when the previous owners moved out.

It didn't. They took it away.

And, of course, there was no chance at all that we ourselves might get one. So I wrote *The Greenville Chums at College* in pencil, and over the course of the next five years graduated to nothing better than a fountain pen.

By 1936, though, I knew I had to have a typewriter. It was simply too onerous to write by hand, and I wanted to get down to serious labors in literary endeavor. My best talking point, of course, was that I was in college now and would have to write themes and term papers, so surely a typewriter was necessary. Armed with that talking point, I approached my father.*

* As I write that, it sounds awful. Why should I put pressure on my poor father? If I wanted a typewriter so badly, why didn't I go out, earn money somehow, and buy

My father said that he would see what he could do, and he did very well. One day he came back with a typewriter he had bought for ten dollars. It was secondhand, of course, and quite old, but it was a standard-size Underwood No. 5 in perfect working order.

It is queer that I cannot remember the day, or even the month, on which I got my very first typewriter. It was surely a gala day, and a significant one, such as I can rarely have experienced, yet my memory is a blank in that respect.

Need I say that I didn't know how to type?

I got to work experimentally, however, typing with one finger. My father, coming up one day for his afternoon nap, stopped to watch his college-boy son type, and frowned.

He said, "Why do you type with one finger, instead of with all your fingers like on a piano?"

I said, "I don't know how to do it with all my fingers, Papa."

My father had an easy solution for that. "Learn!" he thundered. "If I catch you typing with one finger again, I will take away the typewriter."

I sighed, for I knew he would. Fortunately, there lived, just across the street, a young lady who was one year older than myself and for whom, for three years now, I had felt a pure and puppyish passion—the only love affair, if it could possibly be dignified by that title, of my teen years. She was taking a commercial course in high school and knew how to type.

I asked her how to type and she showed me how to place my hands on the typewriter keys and which fingers controlled which keys. She watched me while, very slowly, I typed the word "the" with left-hand-first-finger, right-hand-first-finger, and left-hand-middle-finger. She then offered to give me periodic lessons.

An excuse to be alone with her every once in a while was just what I was looking for, but I had my pride. No one was ever allowed to teach me

---

one for myself? Right! The only trouble is that I was already working every day in the candy store, and, alas, it was unpaid labor. Nor did I ever get an allowance I could save up. My first allowance came at the age of nine, when I was told I could have ten cents a week. I asked if I could do whatever I wanted with that money. Told that I could, I went out and bought three Spanish stamps and started a stamp collection. The allowance was at once withdrawn on the grounds that I was spending it frivolously. I think my mother had a vague notion that I should have bought clothes with that dime. In my early teens I was given another allowance: a dollar a week this time. Precautions were taken, however, against my penchant for frivolity. I never saw the money. It was put aside toward payment of the premiums on an insurance policy that had been bought in my name. It was for a thousand dollars and when it finally came due and I was given the money, I didn't need it particularly. I would rather have had the dollar a week.

any more than I required to begin teaching myself. "That's all right," I said, "I'll practice."

And I did. I've been typing for thirty-seven years now, and I can do ninety words a minute for hours at a time.† I've practiced a great deal!

Naturally, when I began to type, I used both sides of the paper, single-spaced, and no margins. I had to save paper. Eventually, I learned to use one side and to double space, but to this very day I can't bring myself to leave respectable margins. I also tend to use typewriter ribbons and carbon paper until they are deader than they should be. It is not a matter of economy; I have no reason to economize in that direction.

It's just that I've never recovered from having to extract money for paper and typewriter ribbons from the candy store.

Yet even though I was now the owner of a typewriter, I still could not bring myself to write science fiction. I was beginning to edge toward it, though. I began, for the first time, to write fantasy.

During the 1930s, there were fantasy magazines of a kind on the market. One was *Weird Tales,* which was actually older by a couple of years than *Amazing Stories* itself. Its stories were reminiscent of Edgar Allen Poe and were fearfully overwritten. The author most typical of *Weird Tales* was H. P. Lovecraft, whose style revolted me.

There were also pulp magazines devoted to "terror stories," containing as much sex and sadism as the times allowed. I could read them by now, for my father had abandoned any attempt to tell a college boy what to read and what not to read, but I found them dreadful.

Consequently the fantasy I wrote was nothing like these, but rather something I made up entirely by myself. It involved (as I recall) a group of men wandering on some quest through a universe in which there were elves, dwarves, and wizards and in which magic worked. I had no idea that I was trying to anticipate Tolkien's *Lord of the Rings.*

Even though I was writing fantasy, I was still reading science fiction avidly. The coming of college did not dim my interest—perhaps because I entered so young. (I was still a teen-ager when I graduated from college.)

Not only did I continue to read *Astounding Stories* with furious attention, issue by issue, but I also read *Amazing Stories* and *Wonder Stories* at times, finding a few gems now and then.

There was, for instance, "He Who Shrank," by Henry Hasse, which appeared in the August 1936 issue of *Amazing Stories.*

† To be perfectly truthful, I've sacrificed accuracy for speed, and don't pretend that I don't make errors. I just x out, however. My editors don't mind, or, if they do, they maintain a discreet silence.

HE WHO SHRANK

by Henry Hasse

Years, centuries, aeons, have fled past me in endless parade, leaving me unscathed: for I am deathless, and in all the universe alone of my kind. Universe? Strange how that convenient word leaps instantly to my mind from force of old habit. Universe? The merest expression of a puny idea in the minds of those who cannot possibly conceive whereof they speak. The word is a mockery. Yet how glibly men utter it! How little do they realize the artificiality of the word!

That night when the Professor called me to him he was standing close to the curved transparent wall of the astrono-laboratory looking out into the blackness. He heard me enter, but did not look around as he spoke. I do not know whether he was addressing me or not.

"They call me the greatest scientist the world has had in all time."

I had been his only assistant for years, and was accustomed to his moods, so I did not speak. Neither did he for several moments and then he continued:

"Only a half year ago I discovered a principle that will be the means of utterly annihilating every kind of disease germ. And only recently I turned over to others the principles of a new toxin which stimulates the worn-out protoplasmic life-cells, causing almost complete rejuvenation. The combined results should nearly double the ordinary life span. Yet these two things are only incidental in the long list of discoveries I have made to the great benefit of the race."

He turned then and faced me, and I was surprised at a new peculiar glow that lurked deep in his eyes.

"And for these things they call me great! For these puny discoveries they heap honors on me and call me the benefactor of the race. They disgust me, the fools! Do they think I did it for them? Do they think I care about the race, what it does or what happens to it or how long it lives? They do not suspect that all the things I have given them were but accidental discoveries on my part—to which I gave hardly a thought. Oh, you seem amazed. Yet not even you, who have assisted me here for ten years, ever suspected that all my labors and experiments were pointed toward one end, and one end alone."

He went over to a locked compartment which in earlier years I had wondered about and then ceased to wonder about, as I became engrossed in my work. The professor opened it now, and I glimpsed but the usual array of bottles and test-tubes and vials. One of these vials he lifted gingerly from a rack.

"And at last I have attained the end," he almost whispered, holding the tube aloft. A pale liquid scintillated eerily against the artificial light in the ceiling. "Thirty years, long years, of ceaseless experimenting, and now, here in my hand—success!"

The Professor's manner, the glow deep in his dark eyes, the submerged enthusiasm that seemed at every instant about to leap out, all served to impress me deeply. It must indeed be an immense thing he had done, and I ventured to say as much.

"Immense!" he exclaimed. "Immense! Why—why it's so immense that—. But wait. Wait. You shall see for yourself."

At that time how little did I suspect the significance of his words. I was indeed to see for myself.

Carefully he replaced the vial, then walked over to the transparent wall again.

"Look!" he gestured toward the night sky. "The unknown! Does it not fascinate you? The other fools dream of some day traveling out there among the stars. They think they will go out there and learn the secret of the universe. But as yet they have been baffled by the problem of a sufficiently powerful fuel or force for their ships. And they are blind. Within a month I could solve the puny difficulty that confronts them; could, but I won't. Let them search, let them experiment, let them waste their lives away, what do I care about them?"

I wondered what he was driving at, but realized that he would come to the point in his own way. He went on:

"And suppose they do solve the problem, suppose they do leave the planet, go to other worlds in their hollow ships, what will it profit them? Suppose that they travel with the speed of light for their own life time, and then land on a star at that point, the farthest point away from here that is possible for them? They would no doubt say: 'We can now realize as never before the truly staggering expanse of the universe. It is indeed a great structure, the universe. We have traveled a far distance; we must be on the fringe of it.'

"Thus they would believe. Only I would know how wrong they were, for I can sit here and look through this telescope and see stars that are fifty and sixty times as distant as that upon which they landed. Comparatively, their star would be infinitely close to us. The poor deluded fools and their dreams of space travel!"

"But, Professor," I interposed, "just think—"

"Wait! Now listen. I, too, have long desired to fathom the universe, to determine what it is, the manner and the purpose and the secret of its creation. Have you ever stopped to wonder *what* the universe is? For thirty years I have worked for the answer to those questions. Unknowing, you helped me with your efficiency on the strange experiments I assigned to you at various times. Now I have the answer in that vial, and you shall be the only one to share the secret with me."

Incredulous, I again tried to interrupt.

"Wait!" he said. "Let me finish. There was the time when I also looked to the stars for the answer. I built my telescope, on a new principle of my own. I searched the depths of the void. I made vast calculations. And I proved conclusively to my own mind what had theretofore been only a theory. I know now without doubt that this our planet, and other planets revolving about the sun, are but electrons of an atom, of which the sun is the nucleus. And our sun is but one of millions of others, each with its allotted number of planets, each system being an atom just as our own is in reality.

"And all these millions of solar systems, or atoms, taken together in one group, form a galaxy. As you know, there are countless numbers of these galaxies throughout space, with tremendous stretches of space between them. And what are these galaxies? Molecules! They extend through space even beyond the farthest range of my telescope! But having penetrated that far, it is not difficult to make the final step.

"All of these far-flung galaxies, or molecules, taken together as a whole, form—what? Some indeterminable element or substance on a great, ultramacrocosmic world! Perhaps a minute drop of water, or a grain of sand, or wisp of smoke, or—good God!—an eyelash of some creature living on that world!"

I could not speak. I felt myself grow faint at the thought he had propounded. I tried to think it could not be—yet what did I or anyone know about the infinite stretches of space that must exist beyond the ranges of our most powerful telescope?

"It can't be!" I burst out. "It's incredible, it's—monstrous!"

"Monstrous? Carry it a step further. May not that ultra-world *also* be an electron whirling around the nucleus of an atom? And that atom only one of millions forming a molecule? And that molecule only one of millions forming—"

"For God's sake, stop!" I cried. "I refuse to believe that such a thing can be! Where would it all lead? Where would it end? It might go on—forever! And besides," I added lamely, "what has all this to do with—your discovery, the fluid you showed me?"

"Just this. I soon learned that it was useless to look to the infinitely large; so I turned to the infinitely small. For does it not follow that if such a state of creation exists in the stars above us, it must exist identically in the atoms below us?"

I saw his line of reasoning, but still did not understand. His next words fully enlightened me, but made me suspect that I was facing one who had gone insane from his theorizing. He went on eagerly, his voice the voice of a fanatic:

"If I could not pierce the stars above, that were so far, then I would pierce the atoms below, that were so near. They are everywhere. In every object I touch and in the very air I breathe. But they are minute, and to reach them I must find a way to make myself as minute as they are, and more so! This I have done. The solution I showed you will cause every individual atom in my body to *contract*, but each electron and proton will also decrease in size, or diameter, in direct proportion to my own shrinkage! Thus will I not only be able to become the size of an atom, but can go down, down into infinite smallness!"

II

When he had stopped speaking I said calmly: "You are mad."

He was imperturbed. "I expected you to say that," he answered. "It is only natural that that should be your reaction to all that I have said. But no, I am not mad, it is merely that you are unacquainted with the marvelous propensities of 'Shrinx.' But I promised that you should see for yourself, and that you shall. You shall be the first to go down into the atomic universe."

My original opinion in regard to his state of mind remained unshaken.

"I am sure you mean well, Professor," I said, "but I must decline your offer."

He went on as though I hadn't spoken:

"There are several reasons why I want to send you before I myself make the trip. In the first place, once you make the trip there can be no returning, and there are a number of points I want to be quite clear on. You will serve as my advance guard, so to speak."

"Professor, listen. I do not doubt that the stuff you call 'Shrinx' has very remarkable properties. I will even admit that it will do all you say it will do. But for the past month you have worked day and night, with scarcely enough time out for food and hardly any sleep at all. You should take a rest, get away from the laboratory for a while."

"I shall keep in contact with your consciousness," he said, "through a very ingenious device I have perfected. I will explain it to you later. The 'Shrinx' is introduced directly into the blood stream. Shortly thereafter your shrinkage should begin, and continue at moderate speed, never diminishing in the least degree so long as the blood continues to flow in your body. At least, I hope it never diminishes. Should it, I shall have to make the necessary alterations in the formula. All this is theoretical of course, but I am sure it will all work according to schedule, and quite without harm."

I had now lost all patience. "See here, Professor," I said crossly, "I refuse to be the object of any of your wild-sounding experiments. You should realize that what you propose to do is scientifically impossible. Go home and rest—or go away for a while—"

Without the slightest warning he leaped at me, snatching an object from the table. Before I could take a backward step I felt a needle plunge deep into my arm, and cried out with the pain of it. Things became hazy, distorted. A wave of vertigo swept over me. Then it passed, and my vision cleared. The Professor stood leering before me.

"Yes, I've worked hard and I'm tired. I've worked thirty years, but I'm not tired enough nor fool enough to quit this thing now, right on the verge of the climax!"

His leer of triumph gave way to an expression almost of sympathy.

"I am sorry it had to come about this way," he said, "but I saw that you would never submit otherwise. I really am ashamed of you. I didn't think you would doubt the truth of my statements to the extent of really believing me insane. But to be safe I prepared your allotment of the 'Shrinx' in advance, and had it ready; it is now coursing through your veins, and it should be but a short time before we observe the effects. What you saw in the vial is for myself when I am ready to make the trip. Forgive me for having to administer yours in such an undignified manner."

So angered was I at the utter disregard he had shown for my personal feelings, that I hardly heard his words. My arm throbbed fiercely where the needle had plunged in. I tried to take a step toward him, but not a muscle would move. I struggled hard to break the paralysis that was upon me, but could not move a fraction of an inch from where I stood.

The Professor seemed surprised too, and alarmed.

"What, paralysis? That is an unforeseen circumstance! You see, it is even as I said: the properties of 'Shrinx' are marvelous and many."

He came close and peered intently into my eyes, and seemed relieved.

"However, the effect is only temporary," he assured me. Then added: "But you will likely be a bit smaller when the use of your muscles returns, for your shrinkage should begin very shortly now. I must hurry to prepare for the final step."

He walked past me, and I heard him open his private cupboard again. I could not speak, much less move, and I was indeed in a most uncomfortable, not to mention undignified, position. All I could do was to glare at him when he came around in front of me again. He carried a curious kind of helmet with ear-pieces and goggles attached, and a number of wires running from it. This he placed upon the table and connected the wires to a small flat box there.

All the while I watched him closely. I hadn't the least idea what he was going to do with me, but never for a moment did I believe that I would shrink into an atomic universe; that was altogether too fantastic for my conception.

As though reading my thought the Professor turned and faced me. He looked me over casually for a moment and then said:

"I believe it has begun already. Yes, I am sure of it. Tell me, do you not feel it? Do not things appear a trifle larger to you, a trifle taller? Ah, I forgot that the paralyzing effect does not permit you to answer. But look at me—do I not seem taller?"

I looked at him. Was it my imagination, or some kind of hypnosis he was asserting on me, that made me think he was growing slightly, ever so slightly, upward even as I looked?

"Ah!" he said triumphantly. "You have noticed. I can tell it by your eyes. However, it is not I who am growing taller, but you who are shrinking."

He grasped me by the arms and turned me about to face the wall. "I can see that you doubt," he said, "so look! The border on the wall. If you remember, it used to be about even with your eyes. Now it is fully three inches higher."

It was true! And I could now feel a tingling in my veins, and a slight dizziness.

"Your shrinkage has not quite reached the maximum speed," he went on. "When it does, it will remain constant. I could not stop it now even if I wanted to, for I have nothing to counteract it. Listen closely now, for I have several things to tell you.

"When you have become small enough I am going to lift you up and place you on this block of Rehyllium-X here on the table. You will become smaller and smaller, and eventually should enter an alien universe consisting of billions and billions of star groups, or galaxies, which are only the molecules in this Rehyllium-X. When you burst through, your size in comparison with this new universe should be gigantic. However, you will constantly diminish, and will be enabled to alight on any one of the spheres of your own choosing. And—after alighting—you will continue—always down!"

At the concept I thought I would go mad. Already I had become fully a foot shorter, and still the paralysis gripped me. Could I have moved I would have torn the Professor limb from limb in my impotent rage—though if what he said was true, I was already doomed.

Again it seemed as though he read my mind.

"Do not think too harshly of me," he said. "You should be very grateful for this opportunity, for you are going on a marvelous venture, into a marvelous realm. Indeed, I am almost jealous that you should be the first. But with this," he indicated the helmet and box on the table, "I shall keep contact with you no matter how far you go. Ah, I see by your eyes that you wonder how such a thing could be possible. Well, the principle of this device is really very simple. Just as light is a form of energy, so is thought. And just as light travels through an 'ether' in the form of waves, so does thought. But the thought waves are much more intangible—in fact, invisible. Nevertheless the waves are there, and the coils in this box are so sensitized as to receive and amplify them a million times, much as sound waves might be amplified. Through this helmet I will receive but two of your six sensations: those of sound and sight. They are the two major ones, and will be sufficient for my purpose. Every sight and sound that you encounter, no matter how minute, reaches your brain and displaces tiny molecules there that go out in the form of thought waves and finally reach here and are amplified. Thus my brain receives every impression of sight and sound that your brain sends out."

I did not doubt now that his marvelous "Shrinx" would do everything he said it would do. Already I was but one-third of my original size. Still the paralysis showed no sign of releasing me, and I hoped that the Professor knew whereof he spoke when he said the effect would be but temporary. My anger had subsided somewhat, and I think I began to wonder what I would find in that other universe.

Then a terrifying thought assailed me—a thought that left me cold with apprehension. If, as the Professor had said, the atomic universe was but a tiny replica of the universe we knew, would I not find myself in the vast empty spaces between the galaxies *with no air to breathe*? In all the vast calculations the Professor had made, could he have overlooked such an obvious point?

Now I was very close to the floor, scarcely a foot high. Everything about me—the Professor, the tables, the walls—were gigantically out of proportion to myself.

The Professor reached down then, and swung me up on the table top amidst the litter of wires and apparatus. He began speaking again, and to my tiny ears his voice sounded a deeper note.

"Here is the block of Rehyllium-X containing the universe you soon will fathom," he said, placing on the table beside me the square piece of metal, which was nearly half as tall as I was. "As you know, Rehyllium-X is the densest of all known metals, so the universe awaiting you should be a comparatively dense one—though you will not think so, with the thousands of light-years of space between stars. Of course I know no more about this universe than you do, but I would advise you to avoid the very bright stars and approach only the dimmer ones. Well, this is good-by, then. We shall never see each other again. Even should I follow you—as I certainly shall as soon as I have learned through you what alterations I should make in the formula—it is impossible that I could exactly trace your course down through all the spheres that you will have traversed. One thing already I have learned: the rate of shrinkage is too rapid; you will be able to stay on a world for only a few hours. But perhaps that is best, after all. This is good-by for all time."

He picked me up and placed me upon the smooth surface of the Rehyllium-X. I judged that I must be about four inches tall then. It was with immeasurable relief that I finally felt the paralysis going away. The power of my voice returned first, and expanding my lungs I shouted with all my might.

"Professor!" I shouted. "Professor!"

He bent down over me. To him my voice must have sounded ridiculously high pitched.

"What about the empty regions of space I will find myself in?" I asked a bit tremulously, my mouth close to his ear. "I would last but a few minutes. My life will surely be snuffed out."

"No, that will not happen," he answered. His voice beat upon my eardrums like thunder, and I placed my hands over my ears.

He understood, and spoke more softly. "You will be quite safe in airless space," he went on. "In the thirty years I have worked on the problem, I would not be likely to overlook that point—though I will admit it gave me much trouble. But as I said, 'Shrinx' is all the more marvelous in the fact that its qualities are many. After many difficulties and failures, I managed to instill in it a certain potency by which it supplies sufficient oxygen for your need, distributed through the blood stream. It also irradiates a certain amount of heat; and, inasmuch as I consider the supposed sub-zero temperature of space as being somewhat exaggerated, I don't think you need worry about any discomfort in open space."

III

I was scarcely over an inch in height now. I could walk about, though my limbs tingled fiercely as the paralysis left. I beat my arms against my sides and swung them about to speed the circulation. The Professor must have thought I was waving good-by. His hand reached out and he lifted me up. Though he tried to handle me gently, the pressure of his fingers bruised. He held me in his open hand and raised me up to the level of his eyes. He looked at me for a long moment and then I saw his lips form the words "good-by." I was terribly afraid he would drop me to the floor a dizzy distance below, and I was relieved when he lowered me again and I slid off his hand to the block of Rehyllium-X.

The Professor now appeared as a giant towering hundreds of feet into the air, and beyond him, seemingly miles away, the walls of the room extended to unimaginable heights. The ceiling above seemed as far away and expansive as the dome of the sky I had formerly known. I ran to the edge of the block and peered down. It was as though I stood at the top of a high cliff. The face of it was black and smooth, absolutely perpendicular. I stepped back apace lest I lose my footing and fall to my death. Far below extended the vast smooth plain of the table top.

I walked back to the center of the block, for I was afraid of the edge; I might be easily shaken off if the Professor were to accidentally jar the table. I had no idea of my size now, for there was nothing with which I could compare it. For all I knew I might be entirely invisible to the Professor. He was now but an indistinguishable blur, like a far off mountain seen through a haze.

I now began to notice that the surface of the Rehyllium-X block was not as smooth as it had been. As far as I could see were shallow ravines, extending in every direction. I realized that these must be tiny surface scratches that had been invisible before.

I was standing on the edge of one of these ravines, and I clambered down the side and began to walk along it. It was as straight as though laid by a ruler. Occasionally I came to intersecting ravines, and turned to the left or right. Before long, due to my continued shrinkage, the walls of these ravines towered higher than my head, and it was as though I walked along a narrow path between two cliffs.

Then I received the shock of my life, and my adventure came near to ending right there. I approached one of the intersections. I turned the sharp corner to the right. I came face to face with the How-Shall-I-Describe-It.

It was a sickly bluish white in color. Its body was disc shaped, with a long double row of appendages—legs—on the under side. Hundreds of ugly looking spikes rimmed the disc body on the outer and upper edges. There was no head and apparently no organ of sight, but dozens of snake-like protuberances waved in my face as I nearly crashed into it. One of them touched me and the creature backed swiftly away, the spikes springing stiffly erect in formidable array.

This impression of the creature flashed upon my mind in the merest fraction of time, for you may be sure that I didn't linger there to take stock of its pedigree. No indeed. My heart choked me in my fright, I whirled and sped down the opposite ravine. The sound of the thing's pursuit lent wings to my feet, and I ran as I had never run before. Up one ravine and down another I sped, doubling to right and left in my effort to lose my pursuer. The irony of being pursued by a germ occurred to me, but the matter was too serious to be funny. I ran until I was out of breath, but no matter which way I turned and doubled the germ was always a hundred paces behind me. Its organ of sound must have been highly sensitive. At last I could run no more, and I darted around the next corner and stopped, gasping for breath.

The germ rushed a short distance past me and stopped, having lost the sound of my running. Its dozens of tentacular sound organs waved in all directions. Then it came unhesitatingly toward me, and again I ran. Apparently it had caught the sound of my heavy breathing. Again I dashed around the next corner, and as I heard the germ approach I held my breath until I thought my lungs would burst. It stopped again, waved its tentacles in the air and then ambled on down the ravine. Silently I sneaked a hasty retreat.

Now the walls of these ravines (invisible scratches on a piece of metal!) towered very high above me as I continued to shrink. Now too I noticed narrow chasms and pits all around me, in both the walls at the sides and the surface on which I walked. All of these seemed very deep, and some were so wide that I had to leap across them.

At first I was unable to account for these spaces that were opening all about me, and then I realized with a sort of shock that the Rehyllium-X was becoming *porous*, so small was I in size! Although it was the densest of all known metals, no substance whatsoever could be so dense as to be an absolute solid.

I began to find it increasingly difficult to progress; I had to get back and make running jumps across the spaces. Finally I sat down and laughed as I realized the futility and stupidity of this. Why was I risking my life by jumping across these spaces that were becoming wider as I became smaller, when I had no particular destination anyway—except down. So I may as well stay in one spot.

No sooner had I made this decision, however, than something changed my mind.

It was the germ again.

I saw it far down the ravine, heading straight for me. It might have been the same one I had encountered before, or its twin brother. But now I had become so small that it was fully fifteen times my own size, and the very sight of the huge beast ambling toward me inspired terror into my heart. Once more I ran, praying that it wouldn't hear the sound of my flight because of my small size.

Before I had gone a hundred yards I stopped in dismay. Before me yawned a space so wide that I couldn't have leaped half the distance. There was escape on neither side, for the chasm extended up both the walls. I looked back. The germ had stopped. Its mass of tentacles was waving close to the ground.

Then it came on, not at an amble now but at a much faster rate. Whether it had heard me or had sensed my presence in some other manner, I did not know. Only one thing was apparent: I had but a few split seconds in which to act. I threw myself down flat, slid backward into the chasm, and hung there by my hands.

And I was just in time. A huge shape rushed overhead as I looked up. So big was the germ that the chasm which had appeared so wide to me, was inconsequential to it; it ran over the space as though it weren't there. I saw the double row of the creature's limbs as they flashed overhead. Each one was twice the size of my body.

Then happened what I had feared. One of the huge claw-like limbs came down hard on my hand, and a sharp spur raked across it. I could feel the pain all through my arm. The anguish was insufferable. I tried to get a better grip but couldn't. My hold loosened. I dropped down—down—

IV

"This is the end."

Such was my thought in that last awful moment as I slipped away into space. Involuntarily I shut my eyes, and I expected at any moment to crash into oblivion.

But nothing happened.

There was not even the usual sickening sensation that accompanies acceleration. I opened my eyes to a Stygian darkness, and put out an exploring hand. It encountered a rough wall which was flashing upward past my face. I was falling, then; but at no such speed as would have been the case under ordinary circumstances. This was rather as if I were floating downward. Or was it downward? I had lost all sense of up or down or sideways. I doubled my limbs under me and kicked out hard against the wall, shoving myself far away from it.

How long I remained falling—or drifting—there in that darkness I have no way of knowing. But it must have been minutes, and every minute I was necessarily growing smaller.

For some time I had been aware of immense masses all around me. They pressed upon me from every side, and from them came a very faint radiance. They were of all sizes, some no larger than myself and some looming up large as mountains. I tried to steer clear of the large ones, for I had no desire to be crushed between two of them. But there was little chance of that. Although we all drifted slowly along through space together, I soon observed that none of these masses ever approached each other or deviated the least bit from their paths.

As I continued to shrink, these masses seemed to spread out, away from me; and as they spread, the light which they exuded became brighter. They ceased to be masses, and became swirling, expanding, individual stretches of mist, milky white.

They were nebulae! Millions of miles of space must stretch between each of them! The gigantic mass I had clung to, drawn there by its gravity, also underwent this nebulosity, and now I was floating in the midst of an individual nebula. It spread out as I became smaller, and as it thinned and expanded, what had seemed mist now appeared as trillions and trillions of tiny spheres in intricate patterns.

I was in the very midst of these spheres! They were all around my feet, my arms, my head! They extended farther than I could reach, farther than I could see. I could have reached out and gathered thousands of them in my hand. I could have stirred and kicked my feet and scattered them in chaotic confusion about me. But I did not indulge in such reckless and unnecessary destruction of worlds. Doubtless my presence here had already done damage enough, displacing millions of them.

I scarcely dared to move a muscle for fear of disrupting the orbits of some of the spheres or wreaking havoc among some solar systems or star groups. I seemed to be hanging motionless among them, or if I were moving in any direction, the motion was too slight to be noticeable. I didn't even know if I were horizontal or vertical, as those two terms had lost all meaning.

As I became smaller, of course the spheres became larger and the space between them expanded, so that the bewildering maze thinned somewhat and gave me more freedom of movement.

I took more cognizance now of the beauty around me. I remembered what the Professor had said about receiving my thought waves, and I hoped he was tuned in now, for I wouldn't have had him miss it for anything.

Every hue I had ever known was represented there among the suns and encircling planets: dazzling whites, reds, yellows, blues, greens, violets, and every intermediate shade. I glimpsed also the barren blackness of suns that had burnt out; but these were infrequent, as this seemed to be a very young universe.

There were single suns with the orbital planets varying in number from two to twenty. There were double suns that revolved slowly about each other as on an invisible axis. There were triple suns that revolved slowly about one another—strange as it may seem—in perfect trihedral symmetry. I saw one quadruple sun: a dazzling white, a blue, a green, and a deep orange. The white and the blue circled each other on the horizontal plane while the green and the orange circled on the vertical plane, thus forming a perfect interlocking system. Around these four suns, in circular orbits, sped sixteen planets of varying size, the smallest on the inner orbits and the largest on the outer. The effect was a spinning, concave disc with the white-blue-green-orange rotating hub in the center. The rays from these four suns, as they bathed the rolling planets and were reflected back into space in many-hued magnificence, presented a sight both beautiful and weird.

I determined to alight on one of the planets of this quadruple sun as soon as my size permitted, I did not find it hard to maneuver to a certain extent; and eventually, when I had become much smaller, I stretched alongside this solar system, my length being as great as the diameter of the orbit of the outermost planet! Still I dared not come too close, for fear the gravity of my bulk would cause some tension in the orbital field.

I caught glimpses of the surface of the outer, or sixteenth planet, as it swung past me. Through rifts in the great billowing clouds I saw vast expanses of water, but no land; and then the planet was moving away from me, on its long journey around to the other side of the suns. I did not doubt that by the time it returned to my side I would be very much smaller, so I decided to move in a little closer and try to get a look at the fifteenth planet which was then on the opposite side but swinging around in my direction.

I had discovered that if I doubled up my limbs and thrust out violently in a direction opposite that in which I wished to move, I could make fairly good progress, though the effort was somewhat strenuous. In this manner I moved inward toward the sun-cluster, and by the time I had reached the approximate orbit of the fifteenth planet I had become much smaller—was scarcely one-third as long as the diameter of its orbit! The distance between the orbits of the sixteenth and fifteenth planets must have been about 2,500,000,000 miles, according to the old standards I had known; but to me the distance had seemed but a few hundred yards.

I waited there, and finally the planet hove into view from out of the glorious aurora of the suns. Nearer and nearer it swung in its circle, and as it approached I saw that its atmosphere was very clear, a deep saffron-color. It passed me a scant few yards away, turning lazily on its axis opposite the direction of flight. Here, too, as on planet sixteen, I saw a vast world of water. There was only one fairly large island and many scattered small ones, but I judged that fully nine-tenths of the surface area was ocean.

I moved on in to planet fourteen, which I had noticed was a beautiful golden-green color.

By the time I had maneuvered to the approximate fourteenth orbit I had become so small that the light of the central suns pained my eyes. When the planet came in sight I could easily see several large continents on the lighted side; and as the dark side turned to the suns, several more continents became visible. As it swung past me I made comparisons and observed that I was now about five times as large as the planet. When it came around again I would try to effect a landing. To attempt a contact with it now would likely prove disastrous to both it and myself.

As I waited there and became smaller my thoughts turned to the Professor. If his amazing theory of an infinite number of sub-universes was true, then my adventure had hardly begun; wouldn't begin until I alighted on the planet. What would I find there? I did not doubt that the Professor, receiving my thought waves, was just as curious as I. Suppose there was life on this world—hostile life? I would face the dangers while the Professor sat in his laboratory far away. This was the first time that aspect of it occurred to me; it had probably never occurred to the Professor. Strange, too, how I thought of him as "far away." Why, he could merely have reached out his hand and moved me, universe and all, on his laboratory table!

Another curious thought struck me: here I was waiting for a planet to complete its circle around the suns. To any beings who might exist on it, the elapsed time would represent a year; but to me it would only be a number of minutes.

At that, it returned sooner than I expected it, curving around to meet me. Its orbit, of course, was much smaller than those of the two outer planets. More minutes passed as it came closer and larger. As nearly as I could judge I was about one-fifth its size now. It skimmed past me, so closely that I could have reached out and brushed its atmosphere. And as it moved away I could feel its steady tugging, much as if I were a piece of metal being attracted to a magnet. Its speed did not decelerate in the least, but now I was moving along close behind it. It had "captured" me, just as I had hoped it would. I shoved in closer, and the gravity became a steady and stronger pull. I was "falling" toward it. I swung around so that my feet were closest to it, and they entered the atmosphere, where the golden-green touched the blackness of space. They swung down in a long arc and touched something solid. My "fall" toward the planet ceased. I was standing on one of the continents of this world.

V

So tall was I that the greatest part of my body still extended out into the blackness of space. In spite of the fact that the four suns were the distance of thirteen orbits away, they were of such intense brilliance now that to look directly at them would surely have blinded me. I looked far down my tapering length at the continent on which I stood. Even the multi-colored light reflected from the surface was dazzling to the eye. Too late I remembered the Professor's warning to avoid the brighter suns. Close to the surface a few fleeting wisps of cloud drifted about my limbs.

As the planet turned slowly on its axis I of course moved with it, and shortly I found myself on the side away from the suns, in the planet's shadow. I was thankful for this relief—but it was only temporary. Soon I swung around into the blinding light again. Then into the shadow, and again into the light. How many times this happened I do not know, but at last I was entirely within the planet's atmosphere; here the rays of the sun were diffused, and the light less intense.

Miles below I could see but a vast expanse of yellow surface, stretching unbroken in every direction. As I looked far behind the curving horizon it seemed that I caught a momentary glimpse of tall, silvery towers of some far-off city; but I could not be sure, and when I looked again it had vanished.

I kept my eyes on that horizon, however, and soon two tiny red specks became visible against the yellow of the plain. Evidently they were moving toward me very rapidly, for even as I looked they became larger, and soon took shape as two blood-red spheres. Immediately I visioned them as some terrible weapons of warfare or destruction.

But as they came close to me and swerved up to where I towered high in the thin atmosphere, I could see that they were not solid at all, as I had supposed, but were gaseous, and translucent to a certain extent. Furthermore, they behaved in a manner that hinted strongly of intelligence. Without visible means of propulsion they swooped and circled about my head, to my utter discomfiture. When they came dangerously close to my eyes I raised my hand to sweep them away, but they darted quickly out of reach.

They did not approach me again, but remained there close together, pulsating in mid air. This queer pulsating of their tenuous substance gave me the impression that they were conferring together; and of course I was the object of their conference. Then they darted away in the direction whence they had come.

My curiosity was as great as theirs had seemed to be, and without hesitation I set out in the same direction. I must have covered nearly a mile at each step, but even so, these gaseous entities easily out-distanced me and were soon out of sight. I had no doubt that their destination was the city —if indeed it were a city I had glimpsed. The horizon was closer now and less curved, due to my decrease in height: I judged that I was barely five or six hundred feet tall now.

I had taken but a few hundred steps in the direction the two spheres had gone, when to my great surprise I saw them coming toward me again, this time accompanied by a score of—companions. I stopped in my tracks, and soon they came close and circled about my head. They were all about five feet in diameter, and of the same dark red color. For a minute they darted about as though studying me from every angle; then they systematically arranged themselves in a perfect circle around me. Thin streamers emanated from them, and merged, linking them together and closing the circle. Then other streamers reached slowly out toward me, wavering, cautious.

This, their manner of investigation, did not appeal to me in the least, and I swept my arms around furiously. Instantly all was wild confusion. The circle broke and scattered, the streamers snapped back and they were spheres again. They gathered in a group a short distance away and seemed to consider.

One, whose color had changed to a bright orange, darted apart from them and pulsated rapidly. As clearly as though words had been spoken, I comprehended. The bright orange color signified anger, and he was rebuking the others for their cowardice.

Led by the orange sphere they again moved closer to me; this time they had a surprise for me. A score of streamers flashed out quick as lightning, and cold blue flames spluttered where they touched me. Electric shocks ran through my arms, rendering them numb and helpless. Again they formed their circle around me, again the streamers emerged and completed the circle, and other streamers reached out caressingly. For a moment they flickered about my head, then merged, enveloping it in a cold red radiance. I felt no sensation at all at the touch, except that of cold.

The spheres began to pulsate again in the manner I had observed before, and immediately this pulsating began I felt tiny needlepoints of ice pierce my brain. A question became impinged upon my consciousness more clearly than would have been possible by spoken word:

"Where do you come from?"

I was familiar with thought transference, had even practiced it to a certain extent, very often with astonishing success. When I heard—or received—that question, I tried hard to bring every atom of my consciousness to bear upon the circumstances that were the cause of my being there. When I had finished my mental narration and my mind relaxed from the tension I had put upon it, I received the following impressions:

"We receive no answer; your mind remains blank. You are alien, we have never encountered another of your organism here. A most peculiar organism indeed is one that becomes steadily smaller without apparent reason. Why are you here, and where do you come from?" The icy fingers probed deeper and deeper into my brain, seeming to tear it tissue from tissue.

Again I tried, my mind focusing with the utmost clearness upon every detail, picturing my course from the very minute I entered the Professor's laboratory to the present time. When I finished I was exhausted from the effort.

Again I received the impression: "You cannot bring your mind sufficiently into focus; we receive only fleeting shadows."

One of the spheres again changed to a bright color, and broke from the circle. I could almost imagine an angry shrug. The streamers relaxed their hold on my brain and began to withdraw—but not before I caught the fleeting impression from the orange one, who was apparently addressing the others: "—very low mentality."

"You're not so much yourself!" I said aloud. But of course such a crude method as speech did not register upon them. I wondered at my inability to establish thought communication with these beings. Either my brain was of such a size as to prevent them from receiving the impression (remember I was still a four or five hundred foot giant on this world), or their state of mentality was indeed so much higher than mine, that I was, to them, lower than the lowest savage. Possibly both, more probably the latter.

But they were determined to solve the mystery of my presence before I passed from their world, as I would surely do in a few hours at my rate of shrinkage. Their next move was to place themselves on each side of me in vertical rows extending from far down near the ground up to my shoulders. Again the luminous ribbons reached out and touched me at the various points. Then as at a given signal they rose high into the air, lifting me lightly as a feather! In perfect unison they sped toward their city beyond the horizon, carrying me perpendicularly with them! I marveled at the manner in which such gaseous entities as these could lift and propel such a material giant as myself. Their speed must have exceeded by far that of sound—though on all this planet there was no sound except the sound of my body swishing through the air.

In a very few minutes I sighted the city, which must have covered an area of a hundred miles square near the edge of a rolling green ocean. I was placed lightly on my feet at the very edge of the city, and once more the circle of spheres formed around my head and once more the cold tendrils of light probed my brain.

"You may walk at will about the city," came the thought, "accompanied by a few of us. You are to touch nothing whatever, or the penalty will be extreme; your tremendous size makes your presence here among us somewhat hazardous. When you have become much smaller we shall again explore your mind, with somewhat different method, and learn your origin and purpose. We realize that the great size of your brain was somewhat of a handicap to us in our first attempt. We go now to prepare. We have awaited your coming for years."

Leaving only a few there as my escort—or guard—the rest of the spheres sped toward a great domed building that rose from a vast plaza in the center of the city.

I was very much puzzled as to their last statement. For a moment I stood there wondering what they could have meant—"we have awaited your coming for years." Then trusting that this and other things would be answered in the due course of their investigation, I entered the city.

It was not a strange city in so far as architecture was concerned, but it was a beautiful one. I marveled that it could have been conceived and constructed by these confluent globules of gas who at first glance seemed anything but intelligent, reasoning beings. Tall as I was, the buildings towered up to four and five times my height, invariably ending in domed roofs. There was no sign of a spire or angle as far as my eye could see; apparently they grated harshly on the senses of these beings. The entire plan of the city was of vast sweeping curves and circular patterns, and the effect was striking. There were no preconceived streets or highways, nor connecting spans between buildings, for there was no need of them. The air was the natural habitable element of this race, and I did not see a one of them ever touch the ground or any surface.

They even came to rest in mid air, with a slow spinning motion. Everywhere I passed among them they paused, spinning, to observe me in apparent curiosity, then went on about their business, whatever it was. None ever approached me except my guards.

For several hours I wandered about in this manner, and finally when I was much smaller I was bade to walk toward the central plaza.

In the circular domed building the others awaited my coming, gathered about a dais surmounted by a huge oval transparent screen of glass or some similar substance. This time only one of the spheres made contact with my brain, and I received the following thought: "Watch."

The screen became opaque, and a vast field of white came into view.

"The great nebula in which this planet is but an infinitesimal speck," came the thought.

The mass drifted almost imperceptibly across the screen, and the thought continued:

"As you see it now, so it appeared to us through our telescopes centuries ago. Of course the drifting motion of the nebula as a whole was not perceptible, and what you see is a chemically recorded reproduction of the view, which has been speeded up to make the motion visible on the screen. Watch closely now."

The great mass of the nebula had been quiescent, but as I watched, it began to stir and swirl in a huge spiral motion, and a vast dark shadow was thrown across the whole scene. The shadow seemed to recede—no, grew smaller—and I could see that it was not a shadow but a huge bulk. This bulk was entering the nebula, causing it to swirl and expand as millions of stars were displaced and shoved outward.

The thought came again: "The scene has been speeded up a million-fold. The things you see taking place actually transpired over a great number of years; our scientists watched the phenomenon in great wonder, and many were the theories as to the cause of it. You are viewing yourself as you entered our nebula."

I watched in a few minutes the scene before me, as these sphere creatures had watched it over a period of years; saw myself grow smaller, gradually approach the system of the four suns and finally the gold-green planet itself. Abruptly the screen cleared.

"So we watched and waited your coming for years, not knowing what you were or whence you came. We are still very much puzzled. You become steadily smaller, and that we cannot understand. We must hurry. Relax. Do not interfere with our process by trying to think back to the beginning, as you did before; it is all laid bare to us in the recesses of your brain. Simply relax, think of nothing at all, watch the screen."

I tried to do as he said, again I felt the cold probing tendrils in my brain, and a lethargy came over my mind. Shadows flashed across the screen, then suddenly a familiar scene leaped into view: the Professor's laboratory as I had last seen it, on the night of my departure. No sooner had this scene cleared than I entered the room, exactly as I had on that night. I saw myself approach the table close behind the Professor, saw him standing as he had stood, staring out at the night sky; saw his lips move.

The spheres about me crowded close to the screen, seemed to hang intent on every motion that passed upon it, and I sensed great excitement among them. I judged that the one who was exploring my mind, if not all of them, were somehow cognizant not only of the words the Professor and I spoke in those scenes, but of their meaning as well.

I could almost read the Professor's lips as he spoke. I saw the utter amazement, then incredulity, then disbelief, on my features as he propounded his theory of macrocosmic worlds and still greater macrocosmic worlds. I saw our parley of words, and finally his lunge toward me and felt again the plunge of the needle into my arm.

As this happened the spheres around me stirred excitedly.

I saw myself become smaller, smaller, to be finally lifted onto the block of Rehyllium-X where I became still smaller and disappeared. I saw my meeting with the germ, and my wild flight; my plunge into the abyss, and my flight down through the darkness, during which time the entire screen before me became black. The screen was slightly illuminated again as I traveled along with the great masses all around me, and then gradually across the screen spread the huge nebula, the same one these sphere creatures had seen through their telescopes centuries ago. Again the screen cleared abruptly, became transparent.

"The rest we know," came the thought of the one who had searched my brain. "The rest the screen has already shown. He—the one who invented the—what he called 'Shrinx'—he is a very great man. Yours has indeed been a marvelous experience, and one which has hardly begun. We envy you, lucky being; and at the same time we are sorry for you. Anyway, it is fortunate for us that you chose our planet on which to alight, but soon you will pass away even as you came, and that we cannot, and would not, prevent. In a very few minutes you will once more become of infinitesimal size and pass into a still smaller universe. We have microscopes powerful enough to permit us to barely glimpse this smaller atomic universe, and we shall watch your further progress into the unknown until you are gone from our sight forever."

I had been so interested in the familiar scenes on the screen that I had lost all conception of my steady shrinkage. I was now very much smaller than those spheres around me.

I was as interested in them as they were in me, and I tried to flash the following thought:

"You say that you envy me, and are sorry for me. Why should that be?"

The thought came back immediately: "We cannot answer that. But it is true; wonderful as are the things you will see in realms yet to come, nevertheless you are to be pitied. You cannot understand at present, but some day you will."

I flashed another thought: "Your organism, which is known to me as gaseous, seems as strange to me as mine, a solid, must seem to you. You have mentioned both telescopes and microscopes, and I cannot conceive how beings such as yourselves, without organs of sight, can number astronomy and microscopy among the sciences."

"Your own organs of sight," came back the answer, "which you call 'eyes,' are not only superfluous, but are very crude sources of perception. I think you will grant that loss of them would be a terrible and permanent handicap. Our own source of perception is not confined to any such conspicuous organs, but envelops the entire outer surface of our bodies. We have never had organs and appendages such as those with which you are endowed so profusely, for we are of different substance; we merely extend any part of our bodies in any direction at will. But from close study of your structure, we conclude that your various organs and appendages are very crude. I predict that by slow evolution of your own race, such frailties will disappear entirely."

"Tell me more about your own race," I went on eagerly.

"To tell everything there is to tell," came the answer, "would take much time; and there is little time left. We have a very high sociological system, but one which is not without its faults, of course. We have delved deep into the sciences and gone far along the lines of fine arts—but all of our accomplishments along these lines would no doubt appear very strange to you. You have seen our city. It is by no means the largest, nor the most important, on the planet. When you alighted comparatively near, reports were sent out and all of our important scientists hurried here. We were not afraid because of your presence, but rather, were cautious, for we did not know what manner of being you were. The two whom you first saw, were sent to observe you. They had both been guilty of a crime against the community, and were given the choice of the punishment they deserved, or of going out to investigate the huge creature that had dropped from the sky. They accepted the latter course, and for their bravery—for it was bravery—they have been exonerated."

VI

I would have liked greatly to ask more questions, for there were many phases that puzzled me; but I was becoming so very small that further communication was impossible. I was taken to a laboratory and placed upon the slide of a microscope of strange and intricate construction and my progress continued unabated down into a still smaller atomic universe.

The method was the same as before. The substance became open and porous, spread out into open space dotted with the huge masses which in turn became porous and resolved into far flung nebulae.

I entered one of the nebulae and once more star-systems swung all around me. This time I approached a single sun of bright yellow hue, around which swung eight planets. I maneuvered to the outermost one, and when my size permitted, made contact with it.

I was now standing on an electron, one of billions forming a microscopic slide that existed in a world which was in turn only an electron in a block of metal on a laboratory table!

Soon I reached the atmosphere, and miles below me I could see only wide patches of yellow and green. But as I came nearer to the surface more of the details became discernible. Almost at my feet a wide yellow river wound sluggishly over a vast plateau which fell suddenly away into a long line of steep precipices. At the foot of these precipices stretched a great green expanse of steaming jungle, and farther beyond a great ocean, smooth as green glass, curved to the horizon. A prehistoric world of jungles and great fern-like growths and sweltering swamps and cliffs. Not a breeze stirred and nowhere was there sight of any living thing.

I was standing in the jungle close to the towering cliffs, and for a half mile in every direction the trees and vegetation were trampled into the soil where my feet had swung down and contacted.

Now I could see a long row of caves just above a ledge half way up the side of the cliff. And I did not doubt that in each cave some being was peering furtively out at me. Even as I watched I saw a tiny figure emerge and walk out on the ledge. He was very cautious, ready to dash back into the cave at any sign of hostility on my part, and his eyes never left me. Seeing that nothing happened, others took heart and came out, and soon the ledge was lined with tiny figures who talked excitedly among themselves and gesticulated wildly in my direction. My coming must surely have aroused all their superstitious fears—a giant descending out of the skies to land at their very feet.

I must have been nearly a mile from the cliff, but even at that distance I could see that the figures were barbarians, squat and thick muscled, and covered with hair; they were four limbed and stood erect, and all carried crude weapons.

One of them raised a bow as tall as himself and let fly a shaft at me evidently as an expression of contempt or bravado, for he must have known that the shaft wouldn't reach half the distance. Immediately one who seemed a leader among them felled the miscreant with a single blow. This amused me. Evidently their creed was to leave well enough alone.

Experimentally I took a step toward them, and immediately a long line of bows sprang erect and scores of tiny shafts arched high in my direction to fall into the jungle far in front of me. A warning to keep my distance.

I could have strode forward and swept the lot of them from the ledge; but wishing to show them that my intentions were quite peaceful, I raised my hands and took several backward steps. Another futile volley of arrows. I was puzzled, and stood still; and as long as I did not move neither did they.

The one who had seemed the leader threw himself down flat and, shielding his eyes from the sun, scanned the expanse of jungle below. Then they seemed to talk among themselves again, and gestured not at me, but at the jungle. Then I comprehended. Evidently a hunting party was somewhere in that jungle which spread out around my feet—probably returning to the caves, for already it was nearing dusk, the sun casting weird conflicting streaks across the horizon. These people of the caves were in fear that I would move around too freely and perhaps trample the returning party under foot.

So thinking, I stood quietly in the great barren patch I had leveled, and sought to peer into the dank growth below me. This was nearly impossible, however, for clouds of steam hung low over the tops of the trees.

But presently my ears caught a faint sound, as of shouting, far below me, and then I glimpsed a long single file of the barbarian hunters running at full speed along a well beaten game path. They burst into the very clearing in which I stood, and stopped short in surprise, evidently aware for the first time of my gigantic presence on their world. They let fall the poles upon which were strung the carcasses of the day's hunt, cast but one fearful look up to where I towered, then as one man fell flat upon the ground in abject terror.

All except one. I doubt if the one, who burst from the tangle of trees last of all, even saw me, so intent was he in glancing back into the darkness from which he fled. At any rate he aroused his companions with a few angry, guttural syllables, and pointed back along the path.

At that moment there floated up to me a roar that lingered loud and shuddering in my ears. At quick instructions from their leader the hunters picked up their weapons and formed a wide semi-circle before the path where they had emerged. The limb of a large tree overhung the path at this point, and the leader clambered up some overhanging vines and was soon crouched upon it. One of the warriors fastened a vine to a large clumsy looking weapon, and the one in the tree drew it up to him. The weapon consisted merely of a large pointed stake some eight feet long, with two heavy stones fastened securely to it at the half way point. The one in the tree carefully balanced this weapon on the limb, directly over the path, point downward. The semicircle of hunters crouched behind stout lances set at an angle in the ground.

Another shuddering roar floated up to me, and then the beast appeared. As I caught sight of it I marveled all the more at the courage of these puny barbarians. From ground to shoulder the beast must have measured seven feet tall, and was fully twenty feet long. Each of its six legs ended in a wide, horny claw that could have ripped any of the hunters from top to bottom. Its long tapering tail was horny too, giving me the impression that the thing was at least partly reptilian; curved fangs fully two feet long, in a decidedly animal head, offset that impression, however.

For a long moment the monstrosity stood there, tail switching ceaselessly, glaring in puzzlement out upon the circle of puny beings who dared to confront it. Then, as its tail ceased switching and it tensed for the spring, the warrior on the limb above launched his weapon—launched it and came hurtling down with it, feet pressed hard against the heavy stone balance!

Whether the beast below heard some sound or whether a sixth sense warned it, I do not know; but just in time it leaped to one side with an agility belied by its great bulk, and the pointed stake drove deep into the ground, leaving the one who had ridden it lying there stunned.

The beast uttered a snarl of rage; its six legs sprawled outward, its great belly touched the ground. Then it sprang out upon the circle of crouching hunters. Lances snapped at the impact, and the circle broke and fled for the trees. But two of them never rose from the ground, and the lashing horned tail flattened another before he had taken four steps.

The scene took place in a matter of seconds as I towered there looking down upon it, fascinated. The beast whirled toward the fleeing ones and in another moment the destruction would have been terrible, for they could not possibly have reached safety.

Breaking the spell that was on me I swung my hand down in a huge arc even as the beast sprang for a second time. I slapped it in mid air, flattening it against the ground as I would have flattened a bothersome insect. It did not twitch a muscle, and a dark red stain seeped outward from where it lay.

The natives stopped in their flight, for the sound of my hand when I slapped the huge animal had been loud. They jabbered noisily among themselves, but fearfully kept their distance, when they saw me crouched there over the flattened enemy who had been about to wreak destruction among them.

Only one had seen the entire happening. He who had plunged downward from the tree was only momentarily stunned; he had risen dizzily to his feet as the animal charged out among his companions, and had been witness to the whole thing.

Glancing half contemptuously at the others, he now approached me. It must have taken a great deal of courage on his part, for, crouched down as I was, I still towered above the tallest trees. He looked for a moment at the dead beast, then gazed up at me in reverent awe. Falling prone, he beat his head upon the ground several times, and the others followed his example.

Then they all came forward to look at the huge animal.

From their talk and gestures, I gathered that they wanted to take it to the caves; but it would take ten of the strongest of them to even lift it, and there was still a mile stretch of jungle between them and the cliffs.

I decided that I would take it there for them if that was their want. Reaching out, I picked up the leader, the brave one, very gently. Placing him in the cupped hollow of my hand, I swung him far up to the level of my eyes. I pointed at the animal I had slain, then pointed toward the cliffs. But his eyes were closed tightly as if his last moment had come, and he trembled in every limb. He was a brave hunter, but this experience was too much. I lowered him to the ground unharmed, and the others crowded around him excitedly. He would soon recover from his fright, and no doubt some night around the camp fires he would relate this wonderful experience to a bunch of skeptical grandchildren.

Picking the animal up by its tapering tail I strode through the jungle with it, flattening trees at every step and leaving a wide path behind me. I neared the cliffs in a few steps, and those upon the ledge fled into the caves. I placed the huge carcass on the ledge, which was scarcely as high as my shoulders, then turned and strode away to the right, intending to explore the terrain beyond.

For an hour, I walked, passing other tribes of cliff dwellers who fled at my approach. Then the jungle ended in a point by the sea and the line of cliffs melted down into a rocky coast.

It had become quite dark now, there were no moons and the stars seemed dim and far away. Strange night cries came from the jungle, and to my left stretched wide, tangled marshes through which floated vague phosphorescent shapes. Behind me tiny fires sprang up on the face of the cliffs, a welcome sight, and I turned back toward them. I was now so much smaller that I felt extremely uneasy of being alone and unarmed at night on a strange planet abounding in monstrosities.

I had taken only a few steps when I felt, rather than heard, a rush of wings above and behind me. I threw myself flat upon the ground, and just in time, for the great shadowy shape of some huge night-creature swept down and sharp talons raked my back. I arose with apprehension after a few moments, and saw the creature winging its way back low over the marshes. Its wing spread must have been forty feet. I reached the shelter of the cliffs and stayed close to them thereafter.

I came to the first of the shelving ledges where the fires burned, but it was far above me now. I was a tiny being crouched at the base of the cliffs. I, an alien on this world, yet a million years ahead of these barbarians in evolution, peered furtively out into the darkness where glowing eyes and half-seen shapes moved on the edge of the encroaching jungle; and safe in their caves high above me were those so low in the state of evolution that had only the rudiments of a spoken language and were only beginning to learn the value of fire. In another million years perhaps a great civilization would cover this entire globe: a civilization rising by slow degrees from the mire and the mistakes and the myths of the dawn of time. And doubtlessly one of the myths would concern a great god-like figure that descended from the skies, leveled great trees in its stride, saved a famous tribe from destruction by slaying huge enemy beasts, and then disappeared forever during the night. And great men, great thinkers, of that future civilization would say: "Fie! Preposterous! A stupid myth."

But at the present time the god-like figure which slew enemy beasts by a slap of the hand was scarcely a foot high, and sought a place where he might be safe from a possible attack by those same beasts. At last I found a small crevice, which I squeezed into and felt much safer than I had out in the open.

And very soon I was so small that I would have been unnoticed by any of the huge animals that might venture my way.

VII

At last I stood on a single grain of sand, and other grains towered up like smooth mountains all around me. And in the next few minutes I experienced the change for the third time—the change from microscopic being on a gigantic world to a gigantic being floating amid an endless universe of galaxies. I became smaller, the distance between galaxies widened, solar systems approached and neared the orbit of the outermost planet. I received a very unexpected, but very pleasant, surprise. Instead of myself landing upon one of the planets—and while I was yet far too large to do so—the inhabitants of this system were coming out to land on me!

There was no doubt about it. From the direction of the inner planets a tapering silvery projectile moved toward me with the speed of light. This was indeed interesting, and I halted my inward progress to await developments.

In a few minutes the space rocket ship was very close. It circled about me once, then with a great rush of flame and gases from the prow to break the fall, it swooped in a long curve and landed gracefully on my chest! I felt no more jar than if a fly had alighted on me. As I watched it, a square section swung outward from the hull and a number of things emerged. I say "things" because they were in no manner human, although they were so tiny that I could barely distinguish them as minute dots of gold. A dozen of them gathered in a group a short distance away from the space ship.

After a few moments, to my surprise, they spread huge golden wings, and I gasped at the glistening beauty of them. They scattered in various directions, flying low over the surface of my body. From this I reasoned that I must be enveloped in a thin layer of atmosphere, as were the planets. These bird creatures were an exploring party sent out from one of the inner planets to investigate the new large world which had entered their system and was approaching dangerously close to their own planet.

But, on second thought, they must have been aware—or soon would be —that I was not a world at all, but a living, sentient being. My longitudinal shape should make that apparent, besides the movements of my limbs. At any rate they displayed unprecedented daring by coming out to land on me. I could have crushed their frail ship at the slightest touch or flung it far out into the void beyond their reach.

I wished I could see one of the winged creatures at closer range, but none landed on me again; having traversed and circled me in every direction they returned to the space ship and entered it. The section swung closed, gases roared from the stern tubes and the ship swooped out into space again and back toward the sun.

What tiding would they bear to their planet? Doubtless they would describe me as an inconceivably huge monstrosity of outer space. Their scientists would wonder whence I came; might even guess at the truth. They would observe me anxiously through their telescopes. Very likely they would be in fear that I would invade or wreck their world, and would make preparations to repulse me if I came too near.

In spite of these probabilities I continued my slow progress toward the inner planets, determined to see and if possible land upon the planet of the bird creatures. A civilization that had achieved space travel must be a marvelous civilization indeed.

As I made my way through space between the planets by means of my grotesque exertions, I reflected upon another phase. By the time I reached the inner planets I would be so much smaller that I could not determine which of the planets was the one I sought, unless I saw more of the space ships and could follow their direction. Another interesting thought was that the inner planets would have sped around the green sun innumerable times, and years would have passed before I reached there. They would have ample time to prepare for my coming, and might give me a fierce reception if they had many more of the space ships such as the one I had seen.

And they did indeed have many more of them, as I discovered after an interminable length of time during which I had moved ever closer to the sun. A red-tinged planet swung in a wide curve from behind the blazing green of the sun, and I awaited its approach. After a few minutes it was so close that I could see a moon encircling the planet, and as it came still nearer I saw the rocket ships.

This, then, was the planet I sought. But I was puzzled. They surely could not have failed to notice my approach, and I had expected to see a host of ships lined up in formidable array. I saw a host of them all right, hundreds of them, but they were not pointed in my direction at all; indeed, they seemed not to heed me in the least, although I must have loomed large as their planet came nearer. Perhaps they had decided, after all, that I was harmless.

But what seemed more likely to me was that they were confronted with an issue of vastly more importance than my close proximity. For as I viewed the space ships they were leaving the atmosphere of their planet, and were pointing toward the single satellite. Row upon row, mass upon endless mass they moved outward, hundreds, thousands of them. It seemed as though the entire population was moving *en masse* to the satellite!

My curiosity was immediately aroused. What circumstances or condition would cause a highly civilized race to abandon their planet and flee to the satellite? Perhaps, if I learned, I would not want to alight on that planet. . . .

Impatiently I awaited its return as it moved away from me on its circuit around the sun. The minutes seemed long, but at last it approached again from the opposite direction, and I marveled at the relativity of size and space and time. A year had passed on that planet and satellite, and many things might have transpired since I had last seen them.

The satellite swung between the planet and myself, and even from my point of disadvantage I could see that many things had indeed transpired. The bird people were building a protective shell around the satellite! Protection—from what? The shell seemed to be of dull gray metal, and already covered half the globe. On the uncovered side I saw land and rolling oceans. Surely, I thought, they must have the means of producing artificial light; but somehow it seemed blasphemous to forever bar the surface from the fresh pure light of the green sun. In a manner I felt sorry for them in their circumstances. But they had their space ships, and in time could move to the vast unexplored fields that the heavens offered.

More than ever I was consumed with curiosity, but was still too large to attempt a contact with the planet, and I let it pass me for a second time. I judged that when it came around again I would be sufficiently small for its gravity to "capture" me and sufficiently large that the "fall" to the surface would in no means be dangerous; and I was determined to alight.

Another wait of minutes, more minutes this time because I was smaller and time for me was correspondingly longer. When the two spheres hove into view again I saw that the smaller one was now entirely clad in its metal jacket, and the smooth unbroken surface shimmered boldly in the green glare of the sun. Beneath that barren metal shell were the bird people with their glorious golden wings, their space ships, their artificial light, and atmosphere, and civilization. I had but a glance for the satellite, however; my attention was for the planet rushing ever closer to me.

Everything passed smoothly and without mishap. I was becoming an experienced "planet hopper." Its gravity caught me in an unrelenting grip, and I let my limbs rush downward first in their long curve, to land with a slight jar on solid earth far below.

Bending low, I sought to peer into the murky atmosphere and see something of the nature of this world. For a minute my sight could not pierce the half gloom, but gradually the surface became visible. First, I followed my tapering limbs to where they had contacted. As nearly as I could ascertain from my height, I was standing in the midst of what seemed to be a huge mass of crushed and twisted metal!

Now, I thought to myself, I have done it. I have let myself in for it now. I have wrecked something, some great piece of machinery it seems, and the inhabitants will not take the matter lightly. Then I thought: the inhabitants? Who? Not the bird people, for they have fled, have barricaded themselves on the satellite.

Again I sought to pierce the gloom of the atmosphere, and by slow degrees more details became visible. At first my gaze only encompassed a few miles, then more, and more, until at last the view extended from horizon to horizon and included nearly an entire hemisphere.

Slowly the view cleared and slowly comprehension came; and as full realization dawned upon me, I became momentarily panic stricken. I thought insanely of leaping outward into space again, away from the planet, breaking the gravity that held me; but the opposite force of my spring could likely send the planet careening out of its orbit and it and all the other planets and myself might go plunging toward the sun. No, I had put my feet on this planet and I was here to stay.

But I did not feel like staying, for what a sight I had glimpsed! As far as I could see in every direction were huge, grotesque metal structures and strange mechanical contrivances. The thing that terrified me was that these machines were scurrying about the surface all in apparent confusion, seemed to cover the entire globe, seemed to have a complete civilization of their own, and nowhere was there the slightest evidence of any human occupancy, no controlling force, no intelligence, nothing save the machines. And I could not bring myself to believe that they were possessed of intelligence!

Yet as I descended ever closer to the surface I could see that there was no confusion at all as it had seemed at first glance, but rather was there a simple, efficient, systematic order of things. Even as I watched, two strange mechanisms strode toward me on great jointed tripods, and stopped at my very feet. Long, jointed metal arms, with claw-like fixtures at the ends, reached out with uncanny accuracy and precision and began to clear away the twisted debris around my feet. As I watched them I admired the efficiency of their construction. No needless intricacies, no superfluous parts, only the tripods for movement and the arms for clearing. When they had finished they went away, and other machines came on wheels, the debris was lifted by means of cranes and hauled away.

I watched in stupefaction the uncanny activities below and around me. There was no hurry, no rush, but every machine from the tiniest to the largest, from the simplest to the most complicated, had a certain task to perform, and performed it directly and completely, accurately and precisely. There were machines on wheels, on treads, on tracks, on huge multi-jointed tripods, winged machines that flew clumsily through the air, and machines of a thousand other kinds and variations.

Endless chains of machines delved deep into the earth, to emerge with loads of ore which they deposited, to descend again.

Huge hauling machines came and transported the ore to roaring mills.

Inside the mills machines melted the ore, rolled and cut and fashioned the steel.

Other machines builded and assembled and adjusted intricate parts, and when the long process was completed the result was—more machines! They rolled or ambled or flew or walked or rattled away under their own power, as the case might be.

Some went to assist in the building of huge bridges across rivers and ravines.

Diggers went to level down forests and obstructing hills, or went away to the mines.

Others built adjoining mills and factories.

Still others erected strange, complicated towers thousands of feet high, and the purpose of these skeleton skyscrapers I could not determine. Even as I watched, the supporting base of one of them weakened and buckled, and the entire huge edifice careened at a perilous angle. Immediately a host of tiny machines rushed to the scene. Sharp white flames cut through the metal in a few seconds, and the tower toppled with a thunderous crash to the ground. Again the white-flame machines went to work and cut the metal into removable sections, and hoisters and haulers came and removed them. Within fifteen minutes another building was being erected on the exact spot.

Occasionally something would go wrong—some worn-out part ceased to function and a machine would stop in the middle of its task. Then it would be hauled away to repair shops, where it would eventually emerge good as new.

I saw two of the winged machines collide in mid air, and metal rained from the sky. A half dozen of the tripod clearing machines came from a half dozen directions and the metal was raked into huge piles: then came the cranes and hauling machines.

A great vertical wheel with slanting blades on the rim spun swiftly on a shaft that was borne forward on treads. The blades cut through trees and soil and stone as it bore onward toward the near-by mountains. It slowed down, but did not stop, and at length a straight wide path connected the opposite valley. Behind the wheel came the tripods, clearing the way of all debris, and behind them came machines that laid down long strips of metal, completing the perfect road.

Everywhere small lubricating machines moved about, periodically supplying the others with the necessary oil that insured smooth movement.

Gradually the region surrounding me was being leveled and cleared, and a vast city was rising—a city of meaningless, towering, ugly metal— a city covering hundreds of miles between the mountains and sea—a city of machines—ungainly, lifeless—yet purposeful—for what? What?

In the bay, a line of towers rose from the water like fingers pointing at the sky. Beyond the bay and into the open sea they extended. Now the machines were connecting the towers with wide network and spans. A bridge! They were spanning the ocean, connecting the continents—a prodigious engineering feat. If there were not already machines on the other side, there soon would be. No, not soon. The task was gigantic, fraught with failures, almost impossible. *Almost?* A world of machines could know no almost. Perhaps other machines did occupy the other side, had started the bridge from there, and they would meet in the middle. And for what purpose?

A great wide river came out of the mountains and went winding toward the sea. For some reason a wall was being constructed diagonally across the river and beyond, to change its course. For some reason—or unreason.

Unreason! That was it! Why, why, why, I cried aloud in an anguish that was real; why all of this? What purpose, what meaning, what benefit? A city, a continent, a world, a civilization of machines! Somewhere on this world there must be the one who caused all this, the one intelligence, human or unhuman, who controls it. My time here is limited, but I have time to seek him out, and if I find him I shall drag him out and feed him to his own machines and put a stop to this diabolism for all time!

I strode along the edge of the sea for five hundred miles, and rounding a sharp point of land, stopped abruptly. There before me stretched a city, a towering city of smooth white stone and architectural beauty. Spacious parks were dotted with winged colonnades and statues, and the buildings were so designed that everything pointed upward, seemed poised for flight.

That was one half of the city.

The other half was a ruinous heap of shattered white stone, of buildings leveled to the ground by the machines, which were even then intent on reducing the entire city to a like state.

As I watched I saw scores of the flame-machines cutting deep into the stone and steel supporting base of one of the tallest buildings. Two of the ponderous air machines, trailing a wide mesh-metal network between them, rose clumsily from the ground on the outskirts of the city. Straight at the building they flew, and passed one on each side of it. The metal netting struck, jerked the machines backward, and the tangled mass of them plunged to the ground far below. But the building, already weakened at the base, swayed far forward, then back, hung poised for a long shuddering moment and then toppled to the ground with a thunderous crash amid a cloud of dust and debris and tangled framework.

The flame-machines moved on to another building, and on a slope near the outskirts two more of the air machines waited. . . .

Sickened at the purposeless vandalism of it all, I turned inland; and everywhere I strode were the machines, destroying and building, leveling to the ground the deserted cities of the bird people and building up their own meaningless civilization of metal.

At last I came to a long range of mountains which towered up past the level of my eyes as I stood before them. In two steps I stood on the top of these mountains and looked out upon a vast plain dotted everywhere with the grotesque machine-made cities. The machines had made good progress. About two hundred miles to the left a great metal dome rose from the level of the plain, and I made my way toward it, striding unconcerned and recklessly amidst the machines that moved everywhere around my feet.

As I neared the domed structure a row of formidable looking mechanisms, armed with long spikes, rose up to bar my path. I kicked out viciously at them and in a few minutes they were reduced to tangled scrap, though I received a number of minor scratches in the skirmish. Others of the spiked machines rose up to confront me with each step I took, but I strode through them, kicking them to one side, and at last I stood before an entrance-way in the side of the huge dome. Stooping, I entered, and once inside my head almost touched the roof.

I had hoped to find here what I sought, and I was not disappointed. There in the center of the single spacious room was The Machine of all Machines; the Cause of it All; the Central Force, the Ruler, the Controlling Power of all the diabolism running riot over the face of the planet. It was roughly circular, large and ponderous. It was bewilderingly complicated, a maze of gears, wheels, switchboards, lights, levers, buttons, tubing, and intricacies beyond my comprehension. There were circular tiers, and on each tier smaller separate units moved, performing various tasks, attending switchboards, pressing buttons, pulling levers. The result was a throbbing, rhythmic, purposeful unit. I could imagine invisible waves going out in every direction.

I wondered what part of this great machine was vulnerable. Silly thought. No part. Only it—itself. It was The Brain.

The Brain. The Intelligence. I had searched for it, and I had found it. There it was before me. Well, I was going to smash it. I looked around for some kind of weapon, but finding none, I strode forward bare-handed.

Immediately a square panel lighted up with a green glow, and I knew that The Brain was aware of my intent. I stopped. An odd sensation swept over me, a feeling of *hate*, of *menace*. It came from the machine, pervaded the air in invisible waves.

"Nonsense," I thought; "it is but a machine after all. A very complicated one, yes, perhaps even possessed of intelligence; but it only has control over other machines, it cannot harm me." Again I took a resolute step forward.

The feeling of menace became stronger, but I fought back my apprehension and advanced recklessly. I had almost reached the machine when a wall of crackling blue flame leaped from floor to roof. If I had taken one more step I would have been caught in it.

The menace, and hate, and imagined rage at my escape, rolled out from the machine in ponderous, almost tangible waves, engulfing me, and I retreated hastily.

I walked back toward the mountains. After all, this was not *my* world —not my universe. I would soon be so small that my presence amid the machines would be extremely dangerous, and the tops of the mountains was the only safe place. I would have liked to smash The Brain and put an end to it all, but anyway, I thought, the bird people were now safe on the satellite, so why not leave this lifeless world to the machines?

It was twilight when I reached the mountains, and from a high grassy slope—the only peaceful place on the entire planet, I imagined—I looked out upon the plain. Tiny lights appeared as the machines moved about, carrying on their work, never resting. The clattering and clanking of them floated faintly up to me and made me glad that I was a safe distance from it all.

As I stood out toward the dome that housed The Brain, I saw what I had failed to see before. A large globe rested there on a framework, and there seemed to be unusual activity around it.

A vague apprehension tightened around my brain as I saw machines enter this globe, and I was half prepared for what happened next. The globe rose lightly as a feather, sped upward with increasing speed, out of the atmosphere and into space, where, as a tiny speck, it darted and maneuvered with perfect ease. Soon it reappeared, floated gracefully down upon the framework again, and the machines that had mechanically directed its flight disembarked from it.

The machines had achieved space travel! My heart sickened with sudden realization of what that meant. They would build others—were already building them. They would go to other worlds, and the nearest one was the satellite . . . . encased in its protective metal shell . . . .

But then I thought of the white-flame machines that I had seen cut through stone and metal in a few seconds . . . .

The bird people would no doubt put up a valiant fight. But as I compared their rocket projectiles against the efficiency of the globe I had just seen, I had little doubt as to the outcome. They would eventually be driven out into space again to seek a new world, and the machines would take over the satellite, running riot as they had done here. They would remain there just as long as The Brain so desired, or until there was no more land for conquest. Already this planet was over-run, so they were preparing to leave.

The Brain. An intricate, intelligent mechanical brain, glorying in its power, drunk with conquest. Where had it originated? The bird people must have been the indirect cause, and no doubt they were beginning to realize the terrible menace they had loosed on the universe.

I tried to picture their civilization as it had been long ago before this thing had come about. I pictured a civilization in which machinery played a very important part. I pictured the development of this machinery until the time when it relieved them of many tasks. I imagined how they must have designed their machines with more and more intricacy, more and more finesse, until only a few persons were needed in control. And then the great day would come, the supreme day, when mechanical parts would take the place of those few.

That must have indeed been a day of triumph. Machines supplying their every necessity, attending to their every want, obeying their every whim at the touch of a button. That must have been Utopia achieved!

But it had proven to be a bitter Utopia. They had gone forward blindly and recklessly to achieve it, and unknowingly they had gone a step too far. Somewhere, amid the machines they supposed they had under their control, they were imbued with a spark of intelligence. One of the machines added unto itself—perhaps secretly; built and evolved itself into a terribly efficient unit of inspired intelligence. And guided by that intelligence, other machines were built and came under its control. The rest must have been a matter of course. Revolt and easy victory.

So I pictured the evolution of the mechanical brain that even now was directing activities from down there under its metal dome.

And the metal shell around the satellite—did not that mean that the bird people were expecting an invasion? Perhaps, after all, this was not the original planet of the bird people; perhaps space travel was not an innovation among the machines. Perhaps it was on one of the far inner planets near the sun that the bird people had achieved the Utopia that proved to be such a terrible nemesis; perhaps they had moved to the next planet, never dreaming that the machines could follow; but the machines had followed after a number of years, the bird people being always driven outward, the machines always following at leisure in search of new spheres of conquest. And finally the bird people had fled to this planet, and from it to the satellite; and realizing that in a few years the machines would come again in all their invincibility, they had then ensconced themselves beneath the shell of metal.

At any rate: they did not flee to a far-away safe spot in the universe as they could have very easily done. Instead, they stayed; always one sphere ahead of the marauding machines, they must always be planning a means of wiping out the spreading evil they had loosed.

It might be that the shell around the satellite was in some way a clever trap! But so thinking, I remembered again the white-flame machines and the deadly efficiency of the globe I had seen, and then my hopes faded away.

Perhaps some day they would eventually find a way to check the spreading menace. But on the other extreme, the machines might spread out to other solar systems, other galaxies, until some day, a billion years hence, they would occupy every sphere in this universe . . . .

Such were my thoughts as I lay prone there upon the grassy slope and looked down into the plain, down upon the ceaseless clatter and the ceaseless moving of lights in the dark. I was very small now; soon, very soon, I would leave this world.

My last impression was of a number of the space globes, barely discernible in the dusk below; and among them towering up high and round, was one much larger than the others, and I could guess which machine would occupy that globe.

And my last thought was a regret that I hadn't made a more determined effort to destroy that malicious mechanism, The Brain.

So I passed from this world of machines—the world that was an electron on a grain of sand that existed on a prehistoric world that was but an electron on a microscope-slide that existed on a world that was but an electron in a piece of Rehyllium-X on the Professor's laboratory table.

VIII

It is useless to go on. I have neither the time nor the desire to relate in detail all the adventures that have befallen me, the universes I have passed into, the things I have seen and experienced and learned on all the worlds since I left the planet of the machines.

Ever smaller cycles . . . . infinite universes . . . . never ending . . . . each presenting something new . . . . some queer variation of life or intelligence . . . . Life? Intelligence? Terms I once associated with things animate, things protoplasmic and understandable. I find it hard to apply them to all the divergencies of shape and form and construction I have encountered . . . .

Worlds young . . . . warm . . . . volcanic and steaming . . . . the single cell emerging from the slime of warm oceans to propagate on primordial continents . . . . other worlds, innumerable . . . . life divergent in all branches from the single cell . . . . amorphous globules . . . . amphibian . . . . crustacean . . . . reptilian . . . . plant . . . . insect . . . . bird . . . . mammal . . . . all possible variations of combinations . . . . biological monstrosities indescribable . . . .

Other forms beyond any attempt at classification . . . . beyond all reason or comprehension of my puny mind . . . . essences of pure flame . . . . others gaseous, incandescent and quiescent alike . . . . plant forms encompassing an entire globe . . . . crystalline beings sentient and reasoning . . . . great shimmering columnar forms, seemingly liquid, defying gravity by some strange power of cohesion . . . . a world of sound-vibrations, throbbing, expanding, reverberating in unbroken echoes that nearly drove me crazy . . . . globular brain-like masses utterly dissociated from any material substance . . . . intra-dimensional beings, all shapes and shapeless . . . . entities utterly incapable of registration upon any of my senses except the sixth, that of instinct . . . .

Suns dying . . . . planets cold and dark and airless . . . . last vestiges of once proud races struggling for a few more meager years of sustenance . . . . great cavities . . . . beds of evaporated seas . . . . small furry animals scurrying to cover at my approach . . . . desolation . . . . ruins crumbling surely into the sands of barren deserts, the last mute evidence of vanished civilizations . . . .

Other worlds . . . . a-flourished with life . . . . blessed with light and heat . . . . staggering cities . . . . vast populations . . . . ships plying the surface of oceans, and others in the air . . . . huge observatories . . . . tremendous strides in the sciences . . . .

Space flight . . . . battles for the supremacy of worlds . . . . blasting rays of super-destruction . . . . collision of planets . . . . disruption of solar systems . . . . cosmic annihilation . . . .

Light space . . . . a universe with a tenuous, filmy something around it, which I burst through . . . . all around me not the customary blackness of outer space I had known, but light . . . . filled with tiny dots that were globes of darkness . . . . that were burnt-out suns and lifeless planets . . . . nowhere a shimmering planet, nowhere a flaming sun . . . . only remote specks of black amid the high-satiated emptiness . . . .

How many of the infinitely smaller atomic cycles I have passed into, I do not know. I tried to keep count of them at first, but somewhere between twenty and thirty I gave it up; and that was long ago.

Each time I would think: "This cannot go on forever—it *cannot*; surely this next time I must reach the end."

But I have not reached the end.

Good God—how can there be an end? Worlds composed of atoms . . . . each atom similarly composed . . . . The end would have to be an indestructible solid, and that cannot be; all matter divisible into smaller matter . . . .

What keeps me from going insane? I want to go insane!

I am tired . . . . a strange tiredness neither of mind nor body. Death would be a welcome release from the endless fate that is mine.

But even death is denied me. I have sought it . . . . I have prayed for it and begged for it . . . . But it is not to be.

On all the countless worlds I have contacted, the inhabitants were of two distinctions: they were either so low in the state of intelligence that they fled and barricaded themselves against me in superstitious terror—or were so highly intellectual that they recognized me for what I was and welcomed me among them. On all but a few worlds the latter was the case, and it is on these types that I will dwell briefly.

These beings—or shapes or monstrosities or essences—were in every case mentally and scientifically far above me. In most cases they had observed me for years as a dark shadow looming beyond the farthest stars, blotting out certain star-fields and nebulae . . . . and always when I came to their world they welcomed me with scientific enthusiasm.

Always they were puzzled as to my steady shrinking, and always when they learned of my origin and the manner of my being there, they were surprised and excited.

In most cases gratification was apparent when they learned definitely that there were indeed great ultramacrocosmic universes. It seemed that all of them had long held the theory that such was the case.

On most of the worlds, too, the beings—or entities—or whatever the case might be—were surprised that the Professor, one of my fellow creatures, had invented such a marvelous vitalized element as "Shrinx."

"Almost unbelievable," was the general consensus of opinion; "scientifically he must be centuries ahead of the time on his own planet, if we are to judge the majority of the race by this creature here"—meaning me.

In spite of the fact that on nearly every world I was looked upon as mentally inferior, they conversed with me and I with them, by various of their methods, in most cases different variations of telepathy. They learned in minute detail and with much interest all of my past experiences in other universes. They answered all of my questions and explained many things besides, about their own universe and world and civilization and scientific achievements, most of which were completely beyond my comprehension, so alien were they in nature.

And of all the intra-universal beings I have had converse with, the strangest were those essences who dwelt in outer space as well as on various planets; identifiable to me only as vague blots of emptiness, total absences of light or color or substance; who impressed upon me the fact that they were Pure Intelligences, far above and superior to any material plane; but who professed an interest in me, bearing me with them to various planets, revealing many things and treating me very kindly. During my sojourn with them I learned from experience the total subservience of matter to influences of mind. On a giant mountainous world I stepped out upon a thin beam of light stretched between two crags, and willed with all my consciousness that I would not fall. And I did not.

I have learned many things. I know that my mind is much sharper, more penetrative, more grasping, than ever before. And vast fields of wonder and knowledge lie before me in other universes yet to come.

But in spite of this, I am ready for it all to end. This strange tiredness that is upon me—I cannot understand it. Perhaps some invisible radiation in empty space is satiating me with this tiredness.

Perhaps it is only that I am very lonely. How very far away I am from my own tiny sphere! Millions upon millions . . . . trillions upon trillions . . . . of light-years . . . . Light years! Light cannot measure the distance. And yet it is no distance: I am in a block of metal on the Professor's laboratory table . . . .

Yet how far away into space and time I have gone! Years have passed, years far beyond my normal span of life. I am eternal.

Yes, eternal life . . . . that men have dreamed of . . . . prayed for . . . . sought after . . . . is mine—and I dream and pray and seek for death!

Death. All the strange beings I have seen and conversed with, have denied it. I have implored many of them to release me painlessly and for all time—but to no avail. Many of them were possessed of the scientific means to stop my steady shrinkage—but they would not stop it. None of them would hinder me, none of them would tamper with the things that were. Why? Always I asked them why, and they would not answer.

But I need no answer. I think I understand. These beings of science realized that such an entity as myself should never be . . . . that I am a blasphemy upon all creation and beyond all reason . . . . they realized that eternal life is a terrible thing . . . . a thing not to be desired . . . . and as punishment for delving into secrets never meant to be revealed, none of them will release me from my fate . . . .

Perhaps they are right, but oh, it is cruel! Cruel! The fault is not mine, I am here against my own will.

And so I continue ever down, alone and lonely, yearning for others of my kind. Always hopeful—and always disappointed.

So it was that I departed from a certain world of highly intelligent gaseous beings; a world that was in itself composed of a highly rarefied substance bordering on nebulosity. So it was that I became even smaller, was lifted up in a whirling, expanding vortex of the dense atmosphere, and entered the universe which it composed.

Why I was attracted by that tiny, far-away speck of yellow, I do not know. It was near the center of the nebula I had entered. There were other suns far brighter, far more attractive, very much nearer. This minute yellow sun was dwarfed by other suns and sun-clusters around it—seemed insignificant and lost among them. And why I was drawn to *it*, so far away, I cannot explain.

But mere distance, even space distance, was nothing to me now. I had long since learned from the Pure Intelligence the secret of propulsion by mind influence, and by this means I propelled myself through space at any desired speed not exceeding that of light; as my mind was incapable of imagining speed faster than light, I of course could not cause my material body to exceed it.

So I neared the yellow sun in a few minutes, and observed that it had twelve planets. And as I was far too large to yet land on any sphere, I wandered far among other suns, observing the haphazard construction of this universe, but never losing sight of the small yellow sun that had so intrigued me. And at last, much smaller, I returned to it.

And of all the twelve planets, one was particularly attractive to me. It was a tiny blue one. It made not much difference where I landed, so why should I have picked it from among the others? Perhaps only a whim—but I think the true reason was because of its constant pale blue twinkling, as though it were beckoning to me, inviting me to come to it. It was an unexplainable phenomenon; none of the others did that. So I moved closer to the orbit of the blue planet, and landed upon it.

As usual I didn't move from where I stood for a time, until I could view the surrounding terrain; and then I observed that I had landed in a great lake—a chain of lakes. A short distance to my left was a city miles wide, a great part of which was inundated by the flood I had caused.

Very carefully, so as not to cause further tidal waves, I stepped from the lake to solid ground, and the waters receded somewhat.

Soon I saw a group of five machines flying toward me; each of them had two wings held stiffly at right angles to the body. Looking around me I saw others of these machines winging toward me from every direction, always in groups of five, in V formation. When they had come very close they began to dart and swoop in a most peculiar manner, from them came sharp staccato sounds, and I felt the impact of many tiny pellets upon my skin! These beings were very warlike, I thought, or else very excitable.

Their bombardment continued for some time, and I began to find it most irritating; these tiny pellets could not harm me seriously, could not even pierce my skin, but the impact of them stung. I could not account for their attack upon me, unless it be that they were angry at the flood I had caused by my landing. If that were the case they were very unreasonable, I thought; any damage I had done was purely unintentional, and they should realize that.

But I was soon to learn that these creatures were very foolish in many of their actions and manners; they were to prove puzzling to me in more ways than one.

I waved my arms around, and presently they ceased their futile bombardment, but continued to fly around me.

I wished I could see what manner of beings flew these machines. They were continually landing and rising again from a wide level field below.

For several hours they buzzed all around while I became steadily smaller. Below me I could now see long ribbons of white that I guessed were roads. Along these roads crawled tiny vehicles, which soon became so numerous that all movement came to a standstill, so congested were they. In the fields a large part of the populace had gathered, and was being constantly augmented by others.

At last I was sufficiently small so that I could make out closer details, and I looked more intently at the beings who inhabited this world. My heart gave a quick leap then, for they somewhat resembled myself in structure. They were four-limbed and stood erect, their method of locomotion consisting of short jerky hops, very different from the smooth gliding movement of my own race. Their general features were somewhat different too—seemed grotesque to me—but the only main difference between them and myself was that their bodies were somewhat more columnar, roughly oval in shape and very thin, I would say almost frail.

Among the thousands gathered there were perhaps a score who seemed in authority. They rode upon the backs of clumsy looking, four-footed animals, and seemed to have difficulty in keeping the excited crowd under control. I, of course, was the center of their excitement; my presence seemed to have caused more consternation here than upon any other world.

Eventually a way was made through the crowd and one of the ponderous four wheeled vehicles was brought along the road opposite to where I stood. I supposed they wanted me to enter the rough box-like affair, so I did so, and was hauled with many bumps and jolts over the rough road toward the city I had seen to the left. I could have rebelled at this barbarous treatment, but I reflected that I was still very large and this was probably the only way they had of transporting me to wherever I was going.

It had become quite dark, and the city was aglow with thousands of lights. I was taken into a certain building, and at once many important looking persons came to observe me.

I have stated that my mind had become much more penetrative than ever before, so I was not surprised to learn that I could read many of the thoughts of these persons without much difficulty. I learned that these were scientists who had come here from other immediate cities as quickly as possible—most of them in the winged machines, which they called "planes"—when they had learned of my landing here. For many months they had been certain that I would land. They had observed me through their telescopes, and their period of waiting had been a speculative one. And I could now see that they were greatly puzzled, filled with much wonderment, and no more enlightenment about me than they had been possessed of before.

Though still very large, I was becoming surely smaller, and it was this aspect that puzzled them most, just as it had on all the other worlds. Secondly in their speculations was the matter of *where* I had come from.

Many were the theories that passed among them. Certain they were that I had come a far distance. Uranus? Neptune? Pluto? I learned that these were the names of the outmost planets of this system. No, they decided; I must have come a much farther distance than that. Perhaps from another far-away galaxy of this universe! Their minds were staggered at that thought. Yet how very far away they were from the truth.

They addressed me in their own language, and seemed to realize that it was futile. Although I understood everything they said and everything that was in their minds, they could not know that I did, for I could not answer them. Their minds seemed utterly closed to all my attempts at thought communication, so I gave it up.

They conversed then among themselves, and I could read the hopelessness in their minds. I could see, too, as they discussed me, that they looked upon me as being abhorrent, a monstrosity. And as I searched the recesses of their minds, I found many things.

I found that it was the inherent instinct of this race to look upon all unnatural occurrences and phenomena with suspicion and disbelief and prejudiced mind.

I found that they had great pride for their accomplishments in the way of scientific and inventive progress. Their astronomers had delved a short distance into outer space, but considered it a very great distance; and having failed to find signs of intelligent life upon any immediate sphere, they leaped blindly and fondly to the conclusion that their own species of life was the dominant one in this solar system and perhaps—it was a reluctant perhaps—in the entire universe.

Their conception of a universe was a puny one. True, at the present time there was extant a theory of an expanding universe, and in that theory at least they were correct, I knew, remembering the former world I had left—the swirling, expanding wisp of gaseous atmosphere of which this tiny blue sphere was an electron. Yes, their "expanding universe" theory was indeed correct. But very few of their thinkers went beyond their own immediate universe—went deeply enough to even remotely glimpse the vast truth.

They had vast cities, yes. I had seen many of them from my height as I towered above their world. A great civilization, I had thought then. But now I know that great cities do not make great civilizations. I am disappointed at what I have found here, and cannot even understand why I should be disappointed, for this blue sphere is nothing to me and soon I will be gone on my eternal journey downward . . . .

Many things I read in these scientists' minds—things clear and concise, things dim and remote; but they would never know.

And then in the mind of one of the persons, I read an idea. He went away, and returned shortly with an apparatus consisting of wires, a headphone, and a flat revolving disc. He spoke into an instrument, a sort of amplifier. Then a few minutes later he touched a sharp pointed instrument to the rotating disc, and I heard the identical sounds reproduced which he had spoken. A very crude method, but effective in a certain way. They wanted to register my speech so that they would have at least something to work on when I had gone.

I tried to speak some of my old language into the instrument. I had thought I was beyond all surprises, but I was surprised at what happened. For nothing happened. I could not speak. Neither in the old familiar language I had known so long ago, nor in any kind of sound. I had communicated so entirely by thought transference on so many of the other worlds, that now my power of vocal utterance was gone.

They were disappointed. I was not sorry, for they could not have deciphered any language so utterly alien as mine was.

Then they resorted to the mathematics by which this universe and all universes are controlled; into which mathematical mold the eternal All was cast at the beginning and has moved errorlessly since. They produced a great chart which showed the conglomerated masses of this and other galaxies. Then upon a black panel set in the wall, was drawn a circle—understandable in any universe—and around it ten smaller circles. This was evidently their solar system, though I could not understand why they drew but ten circles when I had seen twelve planets from outer space. Then a tiny spot was designated on the chart, the position of this system in its particular galaxy. Then they handed the chart to me.

It was useless. Utterly impossible. How could I ever indicate my own universe, much less my galaxy and solar system, by such puny methods as these? How could I make them know that my own universe and planet were so infinitely large in the scheme of things that *theirs* were practically non-existent? How could I make them know that their universe was not *outside* my own, but *on my planet?*—superimposed in a block of metal on a laboratory table, in a grain of sand, in the atoms of glass in a microscopic slide, in a drop of water, in a blade of grass, in a bit of cold flame, in a thousand other variations of elements and substances all of which I had passed down into and beyond, and finally in a wisp of gas that was the cause of their "expanding universe." Even could I have conversed with them in their own language I could not have made them grasp the vastness of all those substances existing on worlds each of which was but an electron of an atom in one of trillions upon trillions of molecules of an infinitely larger world! Such a conception would have shattered their minds.

It was very evident that they would never be able to establish communication with me even remotely, nor I with them; and I was becoming very impatient. I wanted to be out of the stifling building, out under the night sky, free and unhampered in the vast space which was my abode.

Upon seeing that I made no move to indicate on the chart which part of their puny universe I came from, the scientists around me again conversed among themselves; and this time I was amazed at the trend of their thoughts.

For the conclusion which they had reached was that I was some freak of outer space which had somehow wandered here, and that my place in the scale of evolution was too far below their own for them to establish ideas with me either by spoken language (of which they concluded I had none) or by signs (which I was apparently too barbaric to understand)!! This—this was their unanimous conclusion! This, because I had not uttered any language for them to record, and because the chart of their universe was utterly insignificant to me! Never did it occur to them that the opposite might be true—that I might converse with them but for the fact that their minds were too weak to register my thoughts!

Disgust was my reaction to these short-sighted conclusions of their unimaginable minds—disgust which gave way to an old emotion, that of anger.

And as that one impulsive, rising burst of anger flooded my mind, a strange thing happened:

Every one of the scientists before me dropped to the floor in a state of unconsciousness.

My mind had, indeed, become much more penetrative than ever before. No doubt my surge of anger had sent out intangible waves which had struck upon their centers of consciousness with sufficient force to render them insensible.

I was glad to be done with them. I left the four walls of the building, emerged into the glorious expansive night under the stars and set out along the street in a direction that I believed would lead me away from the city. I wanted to get away from it, away from this world and the people who inhabited it.

As I advanced along the streets all who saw me recognized me at once and most of them fled unreasonably for safety. A group of persons in one of the vehicles tried to bar my progress, but I exercised my power of anger upon them; they drooped senselessly and their vehicle crashed into a building and was demolished.

In a few minutes the city was behind me and I was striding down one of the roads, destination unknown; nor did it matter, except that now I was free and alone as it should be. I had but a few more hours on this world.

And then it was that the *feeling* came upon me again, the strange feeling that I had experienced twice before: once when I had selected the tiny orange sun from among the millions of others, and again when I had chosen this tiny blue planet. Now I felt it for a third time, more strongly than ever, and now I knew that this feeling had some very definite purpose for being. It was as though something, some power beyond question, drew me irresistibly to it; I could not resist, nor did I want to. This time it was very strong and very near.

Peering into the darkness along the road, I saw a light some distance ahead and to the left, and I knew that I must go to that light.

When I had come nearer I could see that it emanated from a house set far back in a grove of trees, and I approached it without hesitation. The night was warm, and a pair of double windows opened upon a well-lighted room. In this room was a man.

I stepped inside and stood motionless, not yet knowing why I should have been drawn there.

The man's back was toward me. He was seated before a square dialed instrument, and seemed to be listening intently to some report coming from it. The sounds from the box were unintelligible to me, so I turned my attention to reading the man's mind as he listened, and was not surprised to learn that the reports concerned myself.

"—casualties somewhat exaggerated, though the property damage has reached millions of dollars," came the news from the box. "Cleveland was of course hardest hit, though not unexpectedly, astronomical computators having estimated with fair accuracy the radius of danger. The creature landed in Lake Erie only a few miles east of the city. At the contact the waters rose over the breakwater with a rush and inundated nearly one-third of the city before receding, and it was well that the greater part of the populace had heeded the advance warnings and fled . . . . all lake towns in the vicinity have reported heavy property damage, and cities as far east as Erie, and as far west as Toledo, have reported high flood waters . . . . all available Government combat planes were rushed to the scene in case the creature should show signs of hostility . . . . scientific men who have awaited the thing's landing for months immediately chartered planes for Cleveland . . . . despite the elaborate cordons of police and militiamen, the crowds broke through and entered the area, and within an hour after the landing roads in every direction were congested with traffic . . . . for several hours scientists circled and examined the creature in planes, while its unbelievable shrinkage continued . . . . the only report we have from them is that, aside from the contour of its great bell-shaped torso, the creature is quite amazingly correct anatomically . . . . an unofficial statement from Dr. Hilton U. Cogsworthy of the Alleghany Biological Society, is to the effect that such a creature *isn't*. That it cannot possibly exist. That the whole thing is the result of some kind of mass hypnotism on a gigantic scale. This, of course, in lieu of some reasonable explanation . . . . many persons would like to believe the 'mass hypnotism' theory, and many always will; but those who have seen it and taken photographs of it from every angle know that it does exist and that its steady shrinking goes on . . . . Professor James L. Harvey of Miami University has suffered a stroke of temporary insanity and is under the care of physicians. The habitual curiosity seekers who flocked to the scene are apparently more hardened . . . . the latest report is that the creature, still very large, has been transported under heavy guard to the Cleveland Institute of Scientific Research, where is gathered every scientist of note east of the Mississippi . . . . stand by for further news flashes . . . ."

The voice from the box ceased, and as I continued to read the mind of the man whose back was toward me, I saw that he was deeply absorbed in the news he had heard. And the mind of this person was something of a puzzle to me. He was above the average intelligence of those on this world, and was possessed of a certain amount of fundamental scientific knowledge; but I could see immediately that his was not a scientifically trained mind. By profession he was a writer—one who recorded fictitious "happenings" in the written language, so that others might absorb and enjoy them.

And as I probed into his mind I was amazed at the depth of imagination there, a trait almost wholly lacking in those others I had encountered, the scientists. And I knew that at last here was one with whose mind I might contact . . . . here was one who was different from the others . . . . who went deeper . . . . who seemed on the very edge of the truth. Here was one who thought: "—this strange creature, which has landed here . . . . alien to anything we have ever known . . . . might it not be alien even to our universe? . . . . the strange shrinking . . . . from that phenomenon alone we might conclude that it has come an inconceivable distance . . . . its shrinking may have begun hundreds, thousands of years ago . . . . and if we could but communicate with it, before it passes from Earth forever, what strange things might it not tell us!"

The voice came from the box again, interrupting these thoughts in his mind.

"Attention! Flash! The report comes that the alien space-creature, which was taken to the Scientific Research Institute for observation by scientists, has escaped, after projecting a kind of invisible mind force which rendered unconscious all those within reach. The creature was reported seen by a number of persons, after it left the building. A police squad car was wrecked as a direct result of the creature's "mind force," and three policemen were injured, none seriously. It was last seen leaving the city by the north-east, and all persons are ordered to be on the lookout and to report immediately if it is sighted."

Again the report from the box ceased, and again I probed into the man's mind, this time deeper, hoping to establish a contact with it which would allow for thought-communication.

I must have at least aroused some hidden mind-instinct, for he whirled to face me, overturning his chair. Surprise was on his face, and something in his eyes that must have been fear.

"Do not be alarmed," I flashed. "Be seated again."

I could see that his mind has not received my thought. But he must have known from my manner that I meant no harm, for he resumed his seat. I advanced further into the room, standing before him. The fear had gone out of his eyes and he only sat tensely staring at me, his hands gripping the arms of the chair.

"I know that you would like to learn things about myself," I telepathed; "things which those others—your scientists—would have liked to know."

Reading his mind I could see that he had not received the thought, so I probed even deeper and again flashed the same thought. This time he did receive it, and there was an answering light in his eyes.

He said "Yes," aloud.

"Those others, your scientists," I went on, "would never have believed nor even understood my story, even if their minds were of the type to receive my thoughts, which they are not."

He received and comprehended that thought, too, but I could see that this was a great strain on his mind and could not go on for long.

"Yours is the only mind I have encountered here with which I could establish thought," I continued, "but even now it is becoming weakened under the unaccustomed strain. I wish to leave my record and story with you, but it cannot be by this means. I can put your mind under a hypnotic influence and impress my thoughts upon your subconscious mind, if you have some means of recording them. But you must hurry; I have only a few more hours here at the most, and in your entire lifetime it would be impossible for you to record all that I could tell."

I could read doubt in his mind. But only for one instant did he hesitate. Then he rose and went to a table where there was a pile of smooth white paper and a sharp pointed instrument—pen—for recording my thoughts in words of his own language.

"I am ready," was the thought in his mind.

*　　*　　*　　*

So I have told my story. Why? I do not know, except that I wanted to. Of all the universes I have passed into, only on this blue sphere have I found creatures even remotely resembling myself. And they are a disappointment; and now I know that I shall never find others of my kind. Never, unless—

I have a theory. Where is the beginning or the end of the eternal All I have been traversing? Suppose there is none? Suppose that, after traversing a few more atomic cycles, I should enter a universe which seemed somehow familiar to me; and that I should enter a certain familiar galaxy, and approach a certain sun, a certain planet—and find that I was back where I started from so long ago: back on my own planet, where I should find the Professor in the laboratory still receiving my sound and sight impressions!! An insane theory; an impossible one. It shall never be.

Well, then, suppose that after leaving this sphere—after descending into another atomic universe—I should choose *not to alight on any planet?* Suppose I should remain in empty space, my size constantly diminishing? That would be one way of ending it all, I suppose. Or would it? Is not my body matter, and is not matter infinite, limitless, eternal? How then could I ever reach a "nothingness"? It is hopeless. I am eternal. My mind too must be eternal or it would surely have snapped long ago at such concepts.

I am so very small that my mind is losing contact with the mind of him who sits here before me writing these thoughts in words of his own language, though his mind is under the hypnotic spell of my own and he is oblivious to the words he writes. I have clambered upon the top of the table beside the pile of pages he has written, to bring my mind closer to his. But why should I want to continue the thought-contact for another instant? My story is finished, there is nothing more to tell.

I shall never find others of my kind . . . . I am alone . . . . I think that soon, in some manner, I shall try to put an end to it . . . .

I am very small now . . . . the hypnosis is passing from his mind . . . . I can no longer control it . . . . the thought-contact is slipping . . . .

EPILOGUE

National Press-Radio Service, Sept. 29, 1937 (through Cleveland *Daily Clarion*):—Exactly one year ago today was a day never to be forgotten in the history of this planet. On that day a strange visitor arrived—and departed.

On September 29, 1936, at 3:31 P.M., that thing from outer space known henceforth only as "The Alien" landed in Lake Erie near Cleveland, causing not so much destruction and terror as great bewilderment and awe, scientists being baffled in their attempts to determine whence it came and the secret of its strange steady shrinking.

Now, on the anniversary of that memorable day, we are presenting to the public a most unusual and interesting document purported to be a true account and history of that strange being, The Alien. This document was presented to us only a few days ago by Stanton Cobb Lentz, renowned author of "The Answer to the Ages" and other serious books, as well as of scores of short stories and books of the widely popular type of literature known as science-fiction.

You have read the above document. While our opinion as to its authenticity is frankly skeptical, we shall print Mr. Lentz's comment and let you, the reader, judge for yourself whether the story was related to Mr. Lentz by The Alien in the manner described, or whether it is only a product of Mr. Lentz's most fertile imagination.

"On the afternoon of September 29 a year ago," states Mr. Lentz, "I fled the city as did many others, heeding the warning of a possible tidal wave, should The Alien land in the lake. Thousands of persons had gathered five or six miles to the south, and from there we watched the huge shape overhead, so expansive that it blotted out the sunlight and plunged that section of the country into a partial eclipse. It seemed to draw nearer by slow degrees until, about 3:30 o'clock, it began its downward rush. The sound of contact as it struck the lake was audible for miles, but it was not until later that we learned the extent of the flood. After the landing all was confusion and excitement as combat planes arrived and very foolishly began to bombard the creature and crowds began to advance upon the scene. The entire countryside being in such crowded turmoil, it took me several difficult hours to return to my home. There I listened to the varied reports of the happenings of the past several hours.

"When I had that strange feeling that someone was behind me, and when I whirled to see The Alien standing there in the room, I do not presume to say that I was not scared. I was. I was very much scared. I had seen The Alien when it was five or six hundred feet tall—but that had been from afar. Now it was only ten or eleven feet tall, but was standing right before me. But my scaredness was only momentary, for something seemed to enter and calm my mind.

"Then, although there was no audible sound, I became aware of the thought: 'I know that you would like to learn things about myself, things which those others—your scientists—would have liked to know.'

"This was mental telepathy! I had often used the theory in my stories, but never had I dreamed that I would experience such a medium of thought in real fact. But here it was.

"'Those others, your scientists,' came the next thought, 'would never have believed nor even understood my story, even if their minds were of the type to receive my thoughts, which they are not.' And then I began to feel a strain upon my mind, and knew that I could not stand much more of it.

"Then came the thought that he would relate his story through my subconscious mind if I had some means of recording it in my own language. For an instant I hesitated; and then I realized that time was fleeing and never again would I have such an opportunity as this. I went to my desk, where only that morning I had been working on a manuscript. There was paper and ink in plenty.

"My last impression was of some force seeming to spread over my mind; then a terrific dizziness, and the ceiling seemed to crash upon me.

"No time at all had seemed to elapse, when my mind regained its normal faculties; but before me on the desk was a pile of manuscript paper closely written in my own longhand. And—what many persons will find it hard to believe—standing upon that pile of written paper upon my desk top, was The Alien—now scarcely two inches in height—and steadily and surely diminishing! In utter fascination I watched the transformation that was taking place before my eyes—watched until The Alien had become entirely invisible. Had descended down into the topmost sheet of paper there on my desk . . . .

"Now I realize that the foregoing document and my explanation of it will be received in many ways. I have waited a full year before making it public. Accept it now as fiction if you wish. There may be some few who will see the truth of it, or at least the possibility; but the vast majority will leap at once to the conclusion that the whole thing is a concoction of my own imagination; that, taking advantage of The Alien's landing on this planet, I wrote the story to fit the occasion, very appropriately using The Alien as the main theme. To many this will seem all the more to be true, in face of the fact that in most of my science-fiction stories I have poked ridicule and derision and satire at mankind and all its high vaunted science and civilization and achievements—always more or less with my tongue in my cheek however, as the expression has it. And then along comes this Alien, takes a look at us and concludes that he is very disappointed, not to mention disgusted.

"However, I wish to represent a few facts to help substantiate the authenticity of the script. Firstly: for some time after awakening from my hypnosis I was beset by a curious dizziness, though my mind was quite clear. Shortly after The Alien had disappeared I called my physician, Dr. C. M. Rollins. After an examination and a few mental tests he was greatly puzzled. He could not diagnose my case; my dizziness was the after effect of a hypnosis of a type he had never before encountered. I offered no explanation except to say that I had not been feeling well for the past several days.

"Secondly: the muscles of my right hand were so cramped from the long period of steady writing that I could not open my fingers. As an explanation I said that I had been writing for hours on the final chapters of my latest book, and Dr. Rollins said: 'Man, you must be crazy.' The process of relaxing the muscles was painful.

"Upon my request Dr. Rollins will vouch for the truth of the above statements.

"Thirdly: when I read the manuscript the writing was easily recognizable as my own free, swinging longhand up to the last few paragraphs, when the writing became shaky, the last few words terminating in an almost undecipherable scrawl as The Alien's contact with my mind slipped away.

"Fourthly: I presented the manuscript to Mr. Howard A. Byerson, fiction editor of the National Newspaper Syndicate Service, and at once he misunderstood the entire idea. 'I have read your story, Mr. Lentz,' he said a few days later, 'and it certainly comes at an appropriate time, right on the anniversary of The Alien's landing. A neat idea about the origin of The Alien, but a bit farfetched. Now, let's see, about the price; of course we shall syndicate your story through our National Newspaper chain, and—'

" 'You have the wrong idea,' I said. 'It is not a story, but a true history of The Alien as related to me by The Alien, and I wish that fact emphasized: if necessary I will write a letter of explanation to be published with the manuscript. And I am not selling you the publication rights, I am merely giving you the document as the quickest and surest way of presenting it to the public.'

" 'But surely you are not serious? An appropriate story by Stanton Cobb Lentz, on the eve of the anniversary of The Alien's landing, is a scoop; and you—'

" 'I do not ask and will not take a cent for the document,' I said; 'you have it now, it is yours, so do with it as you see fit.'

"A memory that will live with me always is the sight of The Alien as last seen by me—as last seen on this earth—as it disappeared into infinite smallness there upon my desk—waving two arms upward as if in farewell . . . .

"And whether the above true account and history of The Alien be received as such, or as fiction, there can be no doubt that on a not far off September, a thing from some infinite sphere above landed on this earth—and departed."

The beautiful elaborateness of "He Who Shrank" was one of the factors that kept me convinced that science fiction was beyond me, that only demigods could write such material.

And, of course, what fascinated me most about "He Who Shrank" was the notion of taking an idea to its ultimate and having it close the circle.

I never forgot. The time came when I had the chance to do it, and the result was my short story "The Last Question," my personal favorite of all the short stories I have ever written.

By the time I had a chance to read "He Who Shrank," I had completed my freshman year at college. And Seth Low Junior College had completed its tenth and last year. Columbia University had, for some reason, cut its throat. (No, I am not paranoid enough to think it was on account of me.)

That didn't leave me homeless, you understand. It merely meant that, rather than waiting till my junior year, I would go up to the Morningside Heights campus in my sophomore year. There I would take my course with the Columbia College elite.

There was still the matter of raising money for tuition. The one-hundred-dollar scholarship I had received the year before had been a one-shot, for the freshman year only. My father therefore managed to persuade one of his customers to arrange a summer job for me in 1936. I got it at the cost of lying a little about my age.

It was a thoroughly unskilled job. What I had to do was to help pull out lengths of rubberized fabric, cut measured lengths of it, pile one length on top of another, and fold them into rolls.

It was very dull, but it brought in the breath-taking sum of fifteen dollars per week. (A full fifteen dollars, for there were no deductions in those days.) I might have earned more, but I had to beg off overtime, since, job or no job, I had to put in as much time as possible in the candy store.

Also I applied for help from the NYA (National Youth Administration), and that paid me fifteen dollars a month for such things as library research for a professor who was writing a book, and preparing mathematical tables for a psychologist.

One way or another, my father and I always managed to scrape together enough money to keep me in school.

In September 1936, then, I began to take courses at Morningside Heights, and I was not to leave the campus (except for a four-year hiatus during World War II) for thirteen years, and three degrees.

The fact that I was at the Morningside campus, however, and went from course to course with the sophomores of Columbia College, did not make me one of them. I was not allowed to register at the college. Along with the other Seth Low rabble, I was put into the category of "University Undergraduate."

This meant that when I got my bachelor's degree at last, my diploma said nothing about Columbia College. I received my bachelor's degree from nothing less than Columbia University as a whole—the entire institution. What's more, I didn't get the fancy A.B. ("bachelor of arts"), which the Ivy League gentlemen of the college received. I got a B.S. ("bachelor of science"), educationally the equivalent, but socially the inferior.

At the time, I didn't care. The diploma said "Columbia," and it seemed a matter of little moment what word followed. As for "Bachelor of Science," that seemed appropriate to me, since, by graduation time, I intended to be a professional scientist.

It was not until a quarter century later that I discovered I had been snobbishly shortchanged. And after all that time lapse, I was still petty enough to grow suddenly angry. I stopped making financial contributions to Columbia.

In the fall of 1936, by the way, I changed my major. I had grown cold to zoology, as I described earlier, and when I took my first course in general chemistry in my sophomore year, I fell in love with it. I switched to chemistry as my major at once, and my desire to go to medical school (never very ardent) began to fade further. Dimly, I began to realize that I wanted to be a chemist. (In the end, I was a biochemist, teaching at a medical school, so I got what I wanted, while paying what service I could to my father's ambitions on my behalf.)

During 1936, those doddering ancients *Amazing Stories* and *Wonder Stories* continued to weave downhill. Both had shifted to bimonthly publication in 1935. *Wonder Stories* was so poorly distributed that my father's newsstand hardly ever got any issues and I hardly ever saw it. The March –April 1936 issue was its last. It was dead.

Amazing Stories continued, however, and I saw every issue. There were even times when I found stories in it that I liked every bit as much as those in *Astounding Stories*. There was, for instance, "The Human Pets of Mars," by Leslie F. Stone, in the October 1936 *Amazing Stories*.

THE HUMAN PETS OF MARS

by Leslie Frances Stone

CHAPTER I

Mists had hung above Washington all the morning, then with their clearing at noon the city grew aware of the strange machine hovering a few thousand feet in the air, above the Washington Monument. Never had there been seen a stranger ship. Golden in color, it looked like a huge round cheese-box, or a drum, only monstrous in size, a good thousand feet in diameter.

The President, from the verandah of the White House, saw it. People crowded to office windows, and into the streets. As far as Chevy Chase they saw it, and housewives came into the streets to stare in wonder and in fear. Then, as it was seen that the thing was about to land, was drifting to the municipal golf-links on Haines Point in Lower Potomac Park, wild excitement reigned. Some motorists thought to escape from the city, heading northward, or crossed the river to the Virginia shore; but most of them followed the drum-ship, pushing in upon the Point, driving the hurriedly augmented police-force half crazy.

Orders were dispatched from the White House. The Police Commissioner was directed to deploy his corps upon the golf-links; every fort near the city was warned to stand in readiness for action; planes were ordered out from Bolling Field and the Naval Hangars. No one had any idea from where the golden ship had come. Was it in peace or in war? Did it come from the other side of the world?

Now it was descending, dropping lightly upon the links. A circular opening in its side gave a glimpse of its shining interior, golden as its exterior. People shrieked and screamed, however, as the Things from within emerged into the sunlight. Those who had been crowding the police forward fought to retreat, restrained only by those behind, who also fought and screamed to get away . . . .

At first no one was certain of his impression, but already an intrepid radio announcer with his portable microphone was describing the horrors as they emerged from their ship. Six of them, forty feet tall. Octopods he called them at first, but a second glance showed them as having ten tentacles instead of eight, surmounted by a flabby sack-like body topped by a round soft head from which projected the tentacles, possessing a round rubbery toothless mouth and three lidless staring eyes. Five of the tentacles had large, padded foot-like extremities, while the remaining five, which were held furled around the hairless bodies, like rosettes, ended in small ten fingered hands, having two thumbs.

In color the creatures appeared a dull black over which lay a golden sheen that caught and reflected the light, and unlike true octopods the tentacles possessed no sucker cups, but were smooth. Decapods was a better name for them, and the announcer revised his first description by substituting that name.

After climbing from their ship, these awful visitants stood staring at the frightened mob, their lidless eyes flickering in this direction and that, but they made no hostile move toward the populace. From them could be heard high piping sounds, like the chirping of birds. Then, they discovered the Washington Channel that lay dimpling in the sun between the Point and the city-wharfs.

In one accord all six beasts moved toward the water, the people crowding out of their path. General Tasse, director of police, ordered a cordon of his men to block their way, but they proved no obstacle, as the monsters simply stepped over their ranks, carefully, so as not to tread upon them, and made their way to the water.

One of their number was seen to dip an unfurled "arm" into the water, then with a loud plop lowered itself into the Channel, the others following. There, like happy school-boys, they disported themselves, their gargantuan play causing high waves that went careening against either shore, rocking the yachts anchored there, swamping some of the smaller boats. Then, they were climbing ashore at the wharfs to make a peaceable tour of the city, doing no more damage than the pilfering of a few fruit carts along the Avenue, and scaring motorists out of their wits.

In a quandary Washington gave them the right of way, while scientists from the Smithsonian hurried to the city proper, hoping to communicate with them, to learn whence they had come, to study their science; but the monsters, who spoke among themselves in their high fluty tones, gave the scientists no time to catch up with them, simply stepping over each new obstacle put in their way. Capturing them, for the moment, seemed out of the question, and since they appeared completely unarmed, and apparently inoffensive as far as their intentions were an indication, nothing was done for the nonce, except that the police sought to untangle the traffic jams they caused everywhere.

General Tasse, abiding by orders, had tried to give them a motor-cycle escort, to clear the way ahead, but the beasts had disregarded this honor, as they seemed to disregard everything else of their startled hosts, deserting the escort whenever something in another street attracted their attention, leaving the police officers to catch up with them as best they could.

For several hours this continued, and in that time engineers from the Bureau of Standards attempted to make something of the unprotected ship, having hurried to the Point in auto-gyros. Only, as the decapods themselves defied the attention of the scientists, so had their ship's motors defied the engineers. Never had they seen such machines, no two alike, resembling nothing of Earth.

For instance, one machine was found to be six-sided, and each part simply a multiple of pentagons. Another had eight sides, a third was a series of three-sided figures, everything within coinciding with that shape. In color they were golden, like the ship itself, and transparent. On entering the drum-ship, the engineers had been startled to discover that whereas they could not see within the ship from without, from inside, they could see everything beyond perfectly clearly. Altogether, the ship was alluringly obscure.

The march of the decapods lasted for about three hours, although, actually, they did not get very far—merely wandering through the business district of the city and some of its monumental Government Buildings— owing to the fact that they went, for the most part, in circles. Now, they seemed restless, anxious to return to their ship, and in a body they headed for the Washington Monument, like a finger pointing to the sky. Reaching its foot, one of their number proceeded to climb the obelisk—on the OUTSIDE.

A few minutes later it descended once again, joining its fellows. It had taken bearings, found the drum-ship, and under its leadership, the five others started back for the municipal links, crossing the railroad embankment to do so.

Possibly, the capture of life specimens of this world came only as a second thought to the decapods when, suddenly, a child excitedly dashed in front of them to reach its mother beyond them. A prolonged shriek went up from the crowd of onlookers who had milled over the golf-links all these hours. For the child never reached its mother. Instead, it found itself lifted high in the air, in the hand of the foremost of the decapods!

With only a thought to save the child Officer McCarthy spurred his horse, Prince, forward. And the next instant, he, too, like the child was raised aloft with his horse. He may have saved himself, but his first reaction was to cling to his kicking horse, and when he had straightened in his saddle, he found himself too high in the air to dare to jump . . . .

CHAPTER II

The Bureau of Standards engineers were still delving into the unguessable secrets of the drum-ship when it was discovered that the monsters were returning. Pell-mell they ran out, piling helter-skelter into their autogyros. That is, all but Brett Rand and his chum George Worth. Never in his twenty-seven years had Brett come upon a machine whose essentials he could not grasp in an hour's time. It was said of him that he had teethed upon a Stilson wrench, and it was true that when other kids were taking toys apart he was putting small motors together, and making them "go." Where his fellows were ready to give up, he was only beginning to tinker.

Had there been a wire or cable, he might have traced it to its source, but there was nothing among those multisided machines of transparent golden metal that he could actually put his finger on as familiar. Somehow, he had removed the top of a peculiarly flat machine, and with an experienced screw-driver was feeling around the strange array of parts, although, to tell the truth, there were no screws to tempt his implement.

It was only by super-human effort that George managed to pull him away from the machine, to drive into his one-track mind that the decapods at that moment, were returning to the ship. Brett had not liked being disturbed, in fact, a sharp elbow caught George under the chin, sent him a-sprawl. But he came back and managed to draw Brett toward the doorway. Only it was too late.

The decapods were upon them; one already about to enter the ship. And not empty-handed either. In one arm was a wildly kicking horse, in whose tilted saddle a police-officer clung, in another a small girl of about six, who, in turn, clasped a mewing kitten to her breast. An ashen-faced negro was caught in a third coiled arm, while in the fourth, a belligerent, red-faced matron dressed in neat serge and wearing a stiff sailor hat, pummeled the monster with a tightly rolled umbrella. Other beasts following the first were also loaded down with captives, men, women, youths; white and black, without discrimination. There was even a wire-haired terrier among the captives.

At bay, the two young men scarcely knew what to do. Behind them lay the motor room, a large circular chamber in the center of the ship, reached by a corridor. And from that opened half a dozen wedge-shaped rooms, shaped so, to conform to the contour of the ship. Retreating before the oncoming monsters with their captives, they reached the central room first, then dashed into one of the smaller chambers, bare, but for a number of metallic straps hanging here and there from the ceiling, with a wide circular mat upon the floor.

Outside, they could hear the rat-tat of gun-fire; the police and soldiers attempting to rescue the prisoners, shooting low at the feet of the deca-pods, shots that simply *ricocheted from their flesh without the least dam-age*. Planes circled overhead, also firing upon the drum-ship, but with no apparent effect. The shells *simply bounced back!*

Through the wall of their retreat Brett and George saw the monsters deposit their prisoners in a second chamber, then close the door upon them, and turn to their machines. There were some tootings when the top was found off the machine Brett had tinkered with, and looking up one of the beasts discovered the culprits. The next instant it was coming to-ward them.

Brett still retained his screw-driver. Certainly he did not consider it much of a defensive weapon, his was more the natural reaction of a treed man as he let it fly toward the decapods. However, the missile never reached the eye for which Brett had unconsciously aimed, as a small hand caught it mid-air, the beast scarcely changing its stride as it came on.

"LOOK OUT," cried George, "it's going to gas us. Cover your face . . . ."

But there was no protection from the orange vapor that suddenly issued from the creature's small mouth. It filled the room, and the pair found themselves drifting away . . . .

What followed had been a page out of a nightmare. Brett, sinking into the artificial coma induced by the orange gas, was aware of a terrific det-onation, then a horrible sinking sensation that gripped his stomach—and oblivion.

He woke to a semi-consciousness aware of a splitting headache and an awful nausea. There was darkness around him, a deep black velvety dark-ness, in which great sparkling stars shone in the middle distances. He was aware of a groaning and moaning all around him, but was unable to orient himself, going into one intermittent doze after another. That he was fed during the hours that followed, he could remember, although the thought of food made his stomach turn over. However, unable to avoid the ministrations of a nurse bending over him with a large scooplike spoon, he had been forced to partake, the first mouthful, oddly enough, easing his sickness. The undefinable stuff had been both food and drink, quenching thirst and settling the stomach.

Then, after an indeterminable period, had come the cessation of the motor's throbbing present through his dreams, and with his fellow cap-tives he was borne from the ship, mind clear once more, into a strange towering building wherein monsters, the same as those who had captured him, examined him, probed and pinched. Long afterwards he could still hear the screams of the three who had died under the knife, their living flesh having been dissected by their inhuman captors.

From there they had been carried into an immense hall where took place an assembling of thousands of decapods. The chamber held a wide dais, ten feet high, and before it the captives were awaiting the next event.

Finding himself still whole, Brett raised himself upon his elbow to look around. The chamber was perhaps a thousand yards in diameter, oval in shape, with two great doorways at either end, through which the black decapods were pouring. He shuddered anew at the sight of them, then turned his eyes to his fellows, who were likewise beginning to take cognizance of their surroundings.

He recognized the severely dressed matron whom he had seen the day of their capture, still wearing her stiff hat, and holding her umbrella in one hand. Immediately he dubbed her the Militant Matron, the term fitted so well. Near her, feet sprawled out before him, squatted a middle-aged man in a neat business-suit, florid of face, who even in these circumstances could retain his pomposity. "The Senator" seemed the title best to fit him. A colored woman lay supine on the floor not far away, moaning and sighing as she mumbled something about the "Lawd's jedgement," and beside her sat a tooth-chattering blue-jeaned negro.

There were more, a pale faced man of indeterminate age, nondescript of coloring, who may have been a haberdasher's clerk,—a small young matronish-looking woman with a face filled with terror,—a tall, lean, dehydrated spinster,—a not too neatly dressed young man with inquisitive eyes that darted here and there, taking everything in. Then, there was the small girl with her kitten, still held tightly in her arms, who stared around with wide-open eyes, and a little boy a few years her senior lying on the floor, sobbing his heart out, while not far away crouched a seventeen-year-old girl, with ultra-high heels, a rumpled though modish silk dress, and a tiny crush hat, clasping an oversize purse against her chest.

There were others, but Brett's survey suddenly came to an end, for on turning around he found himself staring into the coolest pair of the bluest eyes he had ever seen. She would never have won a beauty contest, her features were too irregular, her mouth too generously wide, yet she possessed that inner something, which so often lifts the ordinary-appearing woman out of mediocrity. Fair-skinned, with a mop of chestnut hair framing an oval face, her main features were the bright intelligent blue eyes with their steady gaze.

"We—we seem to have arrived," she murmured. "Will you pinch me please, so I can find out if I'm dreaming or not?"

Brett gave another glance around. "No, I don't think we're dreaming, but those creatures certainly look like they've come out of a nightmare." He jerked his head toward the monsters slowly filling the vast hall in great circles, each squatting on the floor as it found its place among its fellows.

"And I thought it would be a great thing to do a paper on them, for biology class. I'm studying at the George Washington University that is— I was . . . ."

"And I—" Brett suddenly realized that, but for his intense interest in those damnable machines, George and he would not be here. Contrition filled his heart, and he looked around for George. George was coming toward him, carrying the little eight-year-old boy in his arms.

"Will someone please look after this kid? He's crying his eyes out for his mother . . . ."

The blue-eyed girl took the boy from George's arms. "I wanna go home, I want my muvver," he was muttering.

At that the little girl with the kitten looked up from her pet, and crawled to their side. "It's all right," she told the little boy. "This is just one of my bad dreams. I have lots of 'em, but I always wake up in my own little bed at home!"

And, as if that settled the question, she turned back to her mewing kitten. The boy looked at the speaker and grunted, then closed his eyes without a word. Brett and the girl exchanged glances.

But there was no more room for conversation, the hall had filled up; hundreds and hundreds of decapods squatted in close ranks. Suddenly, as if at a signal they all stood up, turning their bodies so that they faced one of the two doorways, through which was coming an immense monster, some ten feet taller than the tallest.

"Must be the high Mogul," muttered George, "look, he's got a retinue, too."

The massive creature was progressing down a lane opened for it, surrounded by ten smaller creatures, smaller even than the majority of the decapods. Reaching the dais, the Mogul as George had called him, took his place upon the platform, half reclining, while his ten followers stood at attention in a circle around him. Thereupon, a great sound went up from the throats of his subjects, and every beast unfurled its five arms, raising them on high. Not until the rites that followed were at end, did they drop them again.

Unaware of what was to take place the captives drew together, waiting nervously. The negro wench began to pray in a high hysterical voice, a woman sobbed in the gathering, and Brett heard the "Senator" declare: "I'll have them know that they can't do this to a citizen of the United States . . . ."

Now six decapods were coming forward until they stood just on the edge of the circle surrounding the dais, beyond the captives. One of their number commenced to speak in its high fluty tones, addressing the giant creature on the dais. For twenty minutes or so it orated, and no sooner had it ceased than a second of the six took its place.

"Looks like an endurance test," whispered Brett to George when half an hour later the third decapod commenced to speak.

"You know, I believe these are the six monsters that brought us here. They're reporting upon their expedition . . . ."

"Yes, but our captors possessed a golden sheen. These are all solid black . . . . Why—of course—they were wearing armour, George. That's the reason our bullets didn't hurt them."

"Right—some of that transparent gold of theirs . . . ."

"Have you any idea where we are?"

"Only that we're no longer on Earth. Notice how light you feel? As if you've had a few pounds lifted from your shoulders?"

Brett raised an arm. "Why yes, there is a difference here. Notice how much faster we're all breathing? Wherever this world is, George, it's smaller than Earth. And to think I got you into this, when . . . ."

"Aw don't start that stuff, kid. It may not be as bad as it seems. There, the last chappie is making his speech. Maybe we'll find out where we stand now . . . ."

Looking up Brett saw that the sixth decapod was now making its speech, but he was unprepared for what happened next, as a long tentacle shot into the midst of the captives, grabbing up the little six year old with her kitten! Hands caught him on either side as he started to the defense of the child. It was George and the blue-eyed girl.

"Wait—perhaps they won't hurt her. She's being shown off to the Mogul."

Brett cooled down as he saw the child had come to no harm, but now stood on the dais before the huge squatting monster. Unconcerned, she gave him look for look, but let out a wail when the same hand that had grabbed her up, pulled her pet out of her arms. But it was only to hold the tabby before the Mogul's eyes, then it was returned to its owner. Thereupon, the child was lifted to the floor once again, and this time it was the policeman, McCarthy, and his horse that were hoisted to the platform.

McCarthy had been standing beside the animal with hand on its muzzle, trying to calm it, for the creature was wild-eyed and all in a tremble. It gave a high squeal as the long arm came down upon it. Unceremoniously McCarthy was lifted to the saddle, regardless of the fact that he was placed there backwards; and it was only by gripping the saddle wildly that he managed to stick on, as he and the kicking horse went through the air.

He swung himself around in the saddle, just as the horse reared on its hind feet, thereby displaying a fine feat of horsemanship as he held his seat. But as soon as he had quieted the horse, the same hand that had put him there plucked him from the saddle. Then, no sooner was he on his feet than he was placed upon the saddle once again. This was repeated a number of times for the edification of the ruler who tittered in his high shrill voice over this phenomenon. Evidently, the decapod could not understand just why the horse and man came apart. A murmuring came from the close packed ranks of the assembly as well.

When the pair were returned to their places on the floor it came the turn of the Militant to be examined. Her face went beet-red and when she stood before the Mogul she told him in no uncertain terms what she thought of her treatment, explaining that whereas she was a D.A.R. and an F.F.V. it behooved the creatures to return her straightwith to her Virginia home.

She might as well have talked to the wind for all the attention the monsters paid her. One of the negroes was lifted to her side, and by the manner of the lecturer the others saw that the decapod was pointing out the difference of the coloring of the pair to the king.

Following that, each captive in turn was lifted to the platform to be oogled, and then returned to his place. Brett had looked forward with loathing to the touch of the decapod tentacle, but when it came his turn, he found that the arm felt like old well-worn leather, its temperature only slightly below that of his own.

The inspection ended, the Mogul next addressed the assembly and the six intrepid explorers. Then, he seemed to be giving instructions. Six long arms darted among the captives, and six of them were indiscriminately plucked up. Next, the ten creatures of the Mogul's retinue chose those among the group that they desired, lifting them high in their arms. Two more decapods were called forth from the innermost circle surrounding the dais, to pick up the two other captives, and the assembly was at an end.

Dropping off the platform, the Mogul hurried from the chamber followed by a creature bearing McCarthy and his horse aloft, then one by one the others followed with their burdens.

Outdoors Brett discovered they were in a great plaza covered with red sand, in the center of which was an artificial lake fed by a canal coming from a "thicket" of towers that surrounded the plaza on all sides. Overhead was a blood-red sun riding in a copperish sky.

The towers, for the most part, were uniform in size and height, some fifty feet in diameter, rising about four hundred feet into the air, and were of the same golden metal that the decapods appeared to use in all their projects. Across the plaza from the large building that had contained the assembly chamber, was a second tower of the same size. These two buildings broke the monotony of the uniformity of the decapod city.

Brett suddenly discovered that the Earth captives were not to be kept together, instead their captors were going off in all directions, some crossing the plaza, some going southward and others northward. To his wonder, he saw the ruler climbing the tower they had just quitted—*on the outside*.

A closer scrutiny showed that the monster was climbing by means of heavy bars affixed to the wall at intervals of ten feet, climbing hand over hand, until he looked like a pin-wheel. And following him came the creature bearing McCarthy and his horse, the pair held in one furled arm while the other four were used to pull the monster up the unique staircase.

In the side of the building he saw round openings spaced fifty feet apart, and it was into one of these doorways that the captives were borne. His own horse was already moving away from the tower in company with the pair carrying the Militant Matron, and the tall blue-jeaned negro whose name he was to learn as Jeff.

Looking around for George, Brett found he was being taken across the plaza. The blue-eyed girl had already disappeared as had some of the others.

At a tower not far from the Royal Palace wherein McCarthy had disappeared with the Mogul, Brett's captor came to a halt, and he realized they were about to mount it. The decapod took a firmer hold around his waist and grasping the nearest rung of the ladder started upward. With only those stationary bars between heaven and earth Brett trembled more than once, but the creature was sure-handed, and shortly they were entering the topmost chamber of the tower.

The room conformed to the shape of the building, fifty feet in diameter, circular; and its walls, like the sides of the drum-ship were transparent. But for a number of hanging straps and a heavy red mat in the center of the room, it was bare. He had been puzzled by those hanging straps in the drum-ship, but now he was to learn their purpose.

Dropping him on the smooth floor, the beast crossed the room to a strap dangling to within ten feet of the floor, and climbed upon it. It constituted the decapodian chair, and from that vantage spot the weird creature surveyed him—like a spider watching a fly, was the man's thought.

Giving it stare for stare he slowly got to his feet. A sidelong glance showed him that he was nearest to the door they had come through. Could he reach it before the monster? Then his shoulders sagged. He could never get down that inhuman ladder. He was truly a prisoner, three hundred and fifty feet above the ground. With resignation he awaited the beast's next move.

It came as the monster flashed out a long tentacle that grabbed him up—and tossed him the full length of the room!

Dazed, he slowly struggled to his feet, wondering what sardonic play this was to be, when he found himself unceremoniously dragged back across the floor toward the beast. Yet no sooner had it brought him to its feet than it tossed him again against the furthest wall! With rising choler he shook his fist at it, asking himself if first it intended to break his bones, before devouring him, railing at the thought that he was so defenseless.

His answer was repeated dragging over the floor, a third toss across the room, a third drag back. But the fourth toss found him lying where he had fallen, bruised and weak, mind in a whirl. Then into his consciousness came half-understanding. Suddenly he realized that with each drag across the floor had come a high piping tone from the monster. Even now it was piping at him.

Slowly he got to his feet, to try out his analysis. This time the engaging arm did not come out to meet him as he limped toward his master—answering its whistle.

He understood. He was being taught to "come here!"—even as he had taught his own dogs to answer his call—only less ferociously.

Reaching the spot just below where the beast was dangling from its overhead strap he paused, waiting. A tiny hand came down to pat his cheek, then to make certain he had really learned his lesson it shoved him away again—more gently this time. And with more alacrity the man obeyed the whistle. He had learned.

Slipping to the floor the beast next moved over to the matting where it squatted, drawing Brett toward it. He found himself laid upon the floor to the accompaniment of soft pattings and a chucking, like that used by a hen to call her chicks under her wing. Making no move, he awaited the creature's next action, and heard again the high whistle. Rising and coming to its side he received another pat on his cheek. He had learned to "lie down."

Several times this was repeated, then certain he had learned both simple lessons, the decapod appeared to lose interest in him, leaving him to his own devices for the time. But Brett did not want to be left alone. He decided it was high time to teach the monster that he, likewise, was a thinking creature.

Feeling around in his pockets he was disappointed to find he was without a pencil. In fact, his pockets yielded little else but a handkerchief, some coins and bills, a cigarette lighter without fuel. He remembered that on that memorable day when the decapods had invaded Washington, he had risen late, and failed to stock his pockets with his usual accessories. He didn't even have cigarettes.

However, that did not matter. He would try some other expedient. The decapod, he found, had its eyes turned away from him, was looking at the red sun that had sunk somewhat since they had entered the room, lying now just above the tower-tops. Going to its side, he tapped an arm lying in reach, to attract the creature's attention.

Slowly it turned its head to look at him, and even cocked its head when he addressed it, moving his lips slowly, forming words that he knew it could not understand. A little hand reached out toward his mouth, but beyond that the beast showed little interest in his demonstration. Thereupon, he pointed toward the lowering sun, and squatting on the floor used his finger to draw an imaginary sun there. But he could have saved the effort. Glancing up again, he found that the monster had turned away, was rising to go to the open doorway.

He watched in despair as it peered outside, looking down at the ground, realizing that the creature's mind told it that he was an inferior animal, and that was all there was to it. Having an intelligence of a vastly different order than that of Man, the decapods were unable to conceive the fact that an Earth-man was a thinking entity. Possibly to them Man was no more than a new type of animal; his buildings and industry having impressed them no more than the community life of an ant impresses the average man—aside from his wonder at the analogy of that life to his own.

Man to them was no more than the animals he himself domesticates. Possibly, too, they judged the buildings of Washington natural outcroppings of Nature, since they were unlike their own tower-buildings.

Thinking thus, Brett realized his own status, and that of his fellow-captives. They were pets—nothing else. To be regarded as no higher a development than the creatures indigenous to this land, that, later, he was to learn, the beasts tamed for their own pleasure.

It was a hard pill to swallow, and sorrowfully he considered the plight of his fellows, wondering how they were taking this intelligence. Would they submit or attempt to fight back? He thought of the blue-eyed girl and of George. Would they appreciate their new standing and act accordingly? Then, he smiled as he thought of the Militant Matron and the pompous Senator. He'd like to have seen them in the process of their "training."

CHAPTER III

Considering these things the man realized that the room was growing dark, that the sun was sinking, painting the sky garishly in deep reds, blues and greens. But before the chamber became wholly dark a newcomer entered.

Staying at its post beside the doorway, the first decapod suddenly began to chirp loudly in some excitement. Glancing through the transparent wall of the tower, Brett discovered that a second monster was mounting it. Immediately the room was filled with shrill tootings, and to his wonder the new arrival was giving the other a terrific whacking on its body and limbs.

He drew back, expecting a fight, but instead the pair settled themselves upon the matting in the center of the room quite amicably. He saw that the newcomer was somewhat larger than the first, ebon black in color, its tentacles more massive, its body thicker, whereas in contrast, the smaller beast was almost a chocolate brown. Could it be that they were male and female, and that this was an ordinary home-coming?

That it was, he learned in the days that followed. Each morning the black male left the city of towers in a small replica of the drum-ship that had brought Brett and his fellows here, returning at evening to the tower-room.

Following their greetings to each other, the smaller decapod, whom Brett dubbed Missis, for want of a better name—calling the other Mister in turn—dragged him forward to show him off to her lord and master. By her shrill whistlings Brett guessed she was explaining the happenings of the day, the Mogul's presentation of the pet to her. Mister did not appear overjoyed by the addition to his family circle, and it seemed to Brett that Missis was arguing with him about her new acquisition. But after a while they both settled upon the matting, leaving Brett to make himself comfortable on the cold floor.

Sleep was far from his mind. In the first place he was uncomfortably chilly, and with the setting of the sun, the room had become cold, bitterly so. Also he was hungry, not knowing when last he had eaten; but even those considerations did not count as high as the predicament in which he found himself.

That he was no longer on Earth he realized; knowing that nowhere upon the home planet could such monsters have managed to subsist, to develop their sciences to the high degree that was apparent. Earth's moon, Luna, as a possibility, he could discount, since it possessed no atmosphere, and Earth would have shown in its sky. Venus, too, was out of the question, for the sun's rays would surely be warmer there than upon Earth. That left Mars as a possibility, else one of the moons of Jupiter—that is, if they were still within the confines of the solar system.

But considering the distance of Sol from its nearest neighbor, some twenty-five trillions of miles, he doubted that the decapods could have brought them so far, unless their machines had a means of traversing space faster than light itself.

No, things pointed more directly at Mars, the red-planet. That red sun and copperish sky, the slightly lessened gravity-pressure, the thinness of the air, thin, as if he were breathing upon a mountain top, seemed to indicate Mars.

Sitting upon the floor, looking through the transparent ceiling of the tower-room, he was given positive proof that he was actually upon Mars. From the east he saw a moon rising, a small round globe, inordinately bright, silvering everything around him and blotting out some of the stars by its brilliancy. But that was not all. Even as he stared at the sky, a second moon was making its appearance, but unlike the first it came out *of the west*, out of the west, wherein the sun had newly dropped; whereas the first moon had appeared coming in the opposite direction!

This second satellite was even more brilliant than the first, but that wasn't its only unique feature. It acted as no self-respecting moon should, mounting the sky in rapid strides, blotting out star after star as it progressed swiftly to its zenith, which, according to Brett's wrist watch, would be reached in less than two hours!

Although not an astronomer he remembered enough of his university studies to realize that the two moons overhead were none less than the twin moons of Mars . . . . Phobos and Deimos; whose brilliancy was due to their proximity to the surface, Deimos being only 12,000 miles or so away, Phobos, a mere 2,170 miles. It came to him, too, that Phobos' queer antics were due to the fact that its period was only about 7 hours long, whereas Deimos' revolutionary period was 30 hours, and that Phobos, in consequence, made three revolutions to Mars' single rotation, its apparent motion and actual motion being the same, so that it rose in the west and passed across the sky to the east for its setting, taking but eleven hours to travel from meridian to meridian.

Considering these factors the man was momentarily happy over his discovery, but his joy was short-lived. Mars—49,000,000 miles from home—forty-nine millions of miles of empty Space . . . .

Shivering with cold in his thin summer suit, he crouched upon one end of the matting, awaiting morning through the long watches of a night that seemed never ending.

He must have dozed toward morning, but with the sun's rising he heard the stirrings of the monsters on their pallet. Here was no morning ablutions, no housekeeping facilities, but he found that the decapod went elsewhere for that. Plucking him from the floor the female led the way to the open doorway and started with him to descend the tower ladder, the larger and heavier beast following. Other beasts were leaving their domiciles on all sides, a general exodus of them.

Brett's searching eyes found a number of his fellow captives; the negro, Jeff, dwelt in a tower opposite his own, and as they reached the ground he descried the Militant Matron riding the arm of her chocolate brown mistress some distance ahead. Several other beasts, he now found, possessed pets besides the new arrivals. One bore a blue-skinned fish-like creature with a flat, seal-like head and long flippers. Another carried an animal with a distinctly fish head, oogling eyes and a long squid-like body.

It came to him then that life here had come out of the sea, that possibly even now they were living on the bottom of a sea long dead. He discovered that they were headed for the lake in the center of the wide plaza. As they reached the brink the decapods were plunging in, diving and splashing lubricously. Reaching the shore his own "mistress" dived in, taking Brett with her, regardless of the fact that he was fully clothed, and the water icy. Immediately his clothes sucked up water, dragging him low. Mistaking his trouble for an inability to swim Missis fortunately kept a hand upon him, preventing his sinking, but shortly he was blue and shivering.

As they climbed from the water at last the pair of decapods oogled his sodden condition. Hoping he could do something for himself, the decapod dropped him on the sand. Hurriedly he climbed out of his garments, wringing out the water as best he could. His action, evidently, astounded the monsters; his disrobing appearing to them as if he had peeled off his skin. As he cast aside each article they picked them up to study them, tooting shrilly at each other.

Speculatively he looked at the sun; but its wan rays told him it would be hours before they could dry the clothes for him. Dolefully he replaced his outer shirt, then his trousers, damp and clammy, and draped the underthings and coat over his arm while he stuffed his socks into his shoes to prevent the leather shrinking, slinging them around his neck by their strings.

Mister spoke impatiently to Missis and Brett was once more picked up. He found they were headed for the huge building across the plaza that was the replica of the Royal Palace. They entered at the first level wherein the decapods were already at breakfast, standing before a long twenty-foot-high counter that encircled the room, behind which a number of the creatures were serving them food in large bowls.

Placed upon the counter between his mistress and master, Brett looked at the food, a thick, mushy substance that gave off a faint fishy odor. With large scoops, many times bigger than a man-sized spoon, the pair of decapods prepared to devour the ten pounds or so of the stuff that their plates held, but made no offer of any to the man. He watched hungrily as they ate. Unappetizing though the stuff looked it seemed better than nothing, his stomach was clamouring for sustenance.

Then, when he was ready to give up, deciding he was not to be fed at all, he saw Missis lay down her scoop, and reaching out to Brett, shoved him toward the dish in which a fair amount of food remained. He understood. He was to have table scraps!

The man in him wanted to rebel, but in the face of hunger fastidiousness was gone. Picking up the scoop, he managed to get it to his mouth. He recognized the food as that which had been fed to him aboard the drum-ship; both his hunger and thirst were quenched by it.

Along the counter he saw others of his kind, likewise making the best of the meal, while a number of the animals native to this unknown world wolfed down their own breakfast. Across from him, sat the Militant Matron. A deep puddle of water had gathered around her, dripping from every part of her clothes; her sailor hat hung limply about her face, and yet, somehow, she managed to retain something of her dignity as she ate from her bowl, daintily, with a natural-sized spoon. She would, thought Brett, be just the one to carry such an implement upon her person.

Finishing breakfast, the next thing on the program was to see Mister off for the day. In a large open space, adjoining the plaza was a landing field in which a great number of drum-shaped ships were parked, replicas of the one that had brought them from Earth, but smaller, large enough only to hold two decapods comfortably. Missis stood with Brett upon her arm until the ship of her spouse had taken off. The ship had neither propeller nor wings, but mounted straight into the air without visible means of propulsion. Brett would have given what little he owned to learn the motive principle.

All the ships turned in one direction over the city, and then Missis was returning to the lake-side where dozens of strolling decapods joined her, and among which Brett was glad to see a number of his fellows.

After showing him off to a number of her "friends" the creature placed Brett on the sand, watching warily that he did not run away. For the present he was interested only in his fellow-captives, anxious to learn how they had fared. His heart lifted when George came hurrying toward him.

CHAPTER IV

They each had the same experiences to relate. "They're treating us just as if we were dogs," averred George disgustedly, "as if we hadn't a grain of intelligence. And that bath! Ugh, I'm still half frozen."

Not far from where they stood the Militant Matron was talking to the pompous looking little man, whom Brett had dubbed the Senator, the woman waxing indignant over her treatment at the hands of her captors. In precise tones she was telling what she thought of creatures unable to recognize her true value, and complaining of indigestion brought on by their unnatural food, as well as her deplorable condition following her enforced wetting. Several times the Senator cleared his throat, trying to get a word in edgewise.

Huddled on the sands a little distance away were the three negroes, Jeff, the woman Mattie and the third, who was a mulatto, in a once neat over-fashionable suit, now water-wrinkled. The woman was moaning about the "punishment ob de Lawd." Standing by the lake timidly surveying the others, was the spinster to whose arm clung the high-school girl in her absurdly high heels. She had made an attempt to keep herself presentable despite the condition of her bedraggled clothes. There was fresh rouge on her cheeks and lips that only made the whiteness of her face the more noticeable.

Three men, a portly elderly man who may have been a merchant, the nondescript clerk, and the fellow with the over-inquisitive eyes, stood in a group discussing their predicament in low tones, glancing now and then at the decapods standing or squatting beside the lake, keeping an eye upon their charges.

Not far away, sobbing on the sands sat a small pink-faced young matron Brett had noticed the previous day. Her hands covered her face, while racking sobs shook her body.

Certainly, nowhere had Brett seen a more despondent-looking gathering. Then he forgot them all, as he discovered the girl he was hopefully seeking. She was leading the six-year-old child who clasped a damp kitten to her breast. Feeling his eyes upon her, the girl came to Brett's side.

"Jill is worried about her kitten," she told him, "the poor little thing seems ailing."

The child held up her kitten for him to see, but he had to admit he could do nothing for it. Snuggling it close, the tot dropped to the ground, all her concern wrapped up in the little cat.

Again the girl's eyes met Brett's. She smiled warmly, "Please pardon the dishabille, but I left home too hurriedly to have my luggage sent ahead." Then she added, "I'm Dell Wayne by the way . . . ."

Her flippancy in the face of their predicament shocked him for a moment, then he grinned. He liked a girl who knew how to laugh. He realized that they may need a little laughter here. And she did look disheveled with a long slit in a water-stained silk skirt, a sagging wool sweater upon which a tie whose color was none too fast, had left a scarlet smear. Also, her hose and slippers had been removed. Carrying his own shoes and underthings and wearing only trousers and shirt he realized he himself was a none too prepossessing figure.

"I was just wondering when the next mail goes out so I can send for my wardrobe, particularly a bathing suit," he rejoined, adding, "Incidentally, my cable address is Brett Rand . . . ."

She did not answer because she was listening to the words of the "Senator" and the dehydrated spinster who came strolling along. They heard the woman saying: "Isn't this awful, Congressman Howell? Oh, you'll do something to get us out of here, won't you? Oh, I know you will. I said to Cleone—she's one of my pupils—why with Congressman Howell here, everything will be all right!"

He replied: "Ah, Miss Snowden, of course, of course—er—I shall do what I can. I shall—er—see that these—er—monsters learn who I am. The

United States is not going to permit them to get away with this—er—high-handed sort of thing. Now, Miss—er—Snowden, don't worry at all. I shall have us all—er—all back home before this—er—day is over. I'm—eh hem—on my way now to see some—er—thing in—er—er—authority." And he moved away.

Dell Wayne sighed for him. "Poor dear, I'm afraid he's going to be terribly disappointed."

Brett glanced at her covertly. "You seem to have taken this thing neatly on the chin, Miss Wayne . . . ."

Her chin lifted sharply. "What else are we to do? Oh, I realize that we're in an awful position, far from home, slaves of things that don't realize our capabilities. We won't be able to stand this sort of life they're forcing on us, the cold, the dousing in the lake, the food . . . . but I guess that old saying is right—'Where there's life there's hope', perhaps we can find a way out of this mess, somehow. Can't you think of something—?"

"There's one chance—to get a ship to take us back home, but I admit that, even if I had a ship, I'd not know what to do with it," and he recounted his experiences with the machines of the decapods previous to his capture.

They spoke of these things for some minutes, each making impossible suggestions, when George came up to them carrying the eight-year-old boy, followed by a gangling fifteen year old who hung back, eyeing the group as he anxiously waited for them to notice him, to draw him into their midst.

"Say, can't something be done for this kid?" George asked. "He's running a fever . . . ."

Dell took the boy and brought out a handkerchief. "He's burning up. Someone wet this for me, please."

The fifteen year old, whose name turned out to be Forrest Adam, ran to do her bidding, but beyond dampening the little boy's hot face, they could do nothing for him. All he could do was to cry for his mother.

The woman who had been crying on the sand came over. "Give him to me," she ordered. "He's just the age of my little Jacky at home. We can understand each other's needs." But even as she took the boy from Dell the beast, to whom he belonged, came to pluck him from her unwilling arms, taking him away.

Other decapods were reaching out for their charges, and Brett had only time to call good-bye to Dell and George, when he, too, was lifted up and carried "home."

CHAPTER V

Reaching the tower-room Missis proceeded to inspect the sodden clothes Brett had been carrying, and, without so much as a "by your leave," began to undress him completely. The man tried to fight her off, but the monster paid his struggles no attention. When her little double thumbed hands stumbled over buttons, he, perforce, assisted her, rather than have her pull them off.

When that was done she commenced to dress him again, with his assistance, putting on the garments he had discarded, now half dry. Some she tried to put on backwards, but he corrected her. Yet, no sooner was he reclothed than she started the whole business of undressing him again, like a child with a new toy.

Resignedly the man allowed himself to be dressed and undressed until she tired of the play; then when she lay on her pallet for a nap, he was glad to follow suit. But he could not sleep. His mind was too full. He realized with Dell that unless something were done shortly, all those who had fallen into the hands of the decapods with him, would be dead. It was his fault entirely that George was here, but though he had tried to broach that subject, to tell how he regretted having gotten his chum into this mess, George had shut him up immediately. If it was only for what he owed George, something had to be done—and there were those others. A plan was already forming itself in his mind, yet it was too intangible a thing upon which to put much faith.

Several days slipped by, the program being the same as on the first day, beginning with the forcible wetting in the lake, the same food, seeing Mister off in his flying ship, meeting fellow-captives on the lake shore for an hour or so before returning to the quiet of the tower-room to await Mister's nightly return.

McCarthy and his horse, as well as the wire-haired terrier had shown up the second day, and Brett had made the acquaintance of the rest of the Earthlings, the inquisitive man who turned out to be a news reporter, the merchant, Thomas Moore, Hal Kent who was a government clerk instead of a haberdasher, Cleone, the high-school girl who usually could be found clinging to Miss Snowden's thin arm.

McCarthy's concern was only for his horse, which was evidently dying on its feet, unable to digest the food of the decapods. The fifteen year old was perhaps the only happy person in the whole gathering. He had confessed to Brett that though he had read avidly all pseudo-scientific stories he could lay his hands upon, he'd never dreamed he would actually partake of such an experience. He was certain that rescue would come!

Jerry Ware, the reporter, was almost as cheerful, his mind centered only upon the scoop that should be his, when they got back "home."

And more and more Brett realized that that home-coming had to be soon. The conditions under which they were living were already telling upon the majority. Not only was the little boy, Tad, dying, but Jill was running a fever, and everyone could complain of indigestion, headaches, nausea and colds. None of them knew what it was to be comfortable, thinly clad as they were, with what clothing they possessed rewetted each day; the nights reaching almost freezing temperatures. The fact that the kitten and horse were first to sicken, with the younger children coming down with fever, proved that the food was altogether too rich for their constitutions, and it would be only a matter of days before the adults would become feverish as well.

Considering this, on the third day, Brett suggested to those who listened the necessity of vigorous exercise to offset the ill-effects of the food. The younger members of the party were willing enough, but under the leadership of the Militant Matron, who was really a Mrs. Joshua White-Smythe, the others had other plans. She explained. "We're going to follow the canal out of this place—and walk home, if necessary. The canal must lead to a river, and rivers always go to the sea . . . ."

Brett heard and objected. "Good heavens, can't you people realize yet that you're not on Earth any longer? That it's not a matter of 'walking home'?"

There was a tense moment, then Mrs. White-Smythe swung a pair of supercilious eyes upon him. "I suppose you think we're on the moon. Silly idea. As if anyone could live on the moon—or stars!"

"I'm afraid we're a lot further away than the moon, madam. Earth is far enough away to appear as a star to us now." Brett was certain he had picked Earth from among the celestial bodies the previous night.

Congressman Howell laughed at that. "Of course we're on Earth. *I* know we are. We're in the *Gobi* desert!"

"Why, of course. Haven't scientists been finding large bones here, and calling them dinosaur bones?" sniffed Miss Snowden.

"But these creatures haven't bones—ugh—they don't feel like they have them, anyway," spoke up Cleone.

"The next thing you'll be saying," said Howell severely, "is that we're on Mars . . . ."

"We are on Mars!"

"Mars!" It was a bombshell.

Dell who had been nursing Jill in her arms came to Brett's side. "You're sure of that?"

"Gee—I knew it," cried Forrest. "Those moons, they're Phobos and Deimos, aren't they, Mr. Rand?" (So much for his voracious study.)

Brett explained his reasons for his contention, pointing out the lessened gravity force, the red-dust atmosphere, the lessened warmth of the sun's rays, the presence of the twin moons, even now showing in the daytime sky.

George nodded. "Sounds logical, Brett. I've considered the same possibilities myself, but look here—scientists claim there isn't sufficient oxygen on Mars to sustain human life. This air is thin, but breathable . . . ."

Brett agreed. "I thought of that too, but it's my conviction that this city lies in a deep depression in the surface. From my tower, I can see a distant line of cliffs on the horizon—either a mountain chain, or the rim of this valley. If it's the latter, we're on some ancient sea-bottom. That would explain why astronomers have never detected oxygen in the atmosphere—because it lies below the surface!"

"Gosh, that sounds reasonable."

"Say, you know astronomers have plotted out some 'marshy areas' that show seasonal changes," put in Forrest, "they usually show up at the end of a canal. I guess we're in one of those areas, huh?"

"Possibly."

"Yes, but what of those seasonal changes, Brett? Observers have seen green spots, you know, following the dissolving of the icecaps."

"This, I imagine is the dry-season. I stumbled over some dried-up roots this morning. Wouldn't be surprised, if at certain seasons, some sort of vegetation grows here . . . ."

"Glory be. Let it come right away. Prince and I need it," McCarthy put in.

Suddenly there was a sobbing in the crowd. It came from Mrs. Burton, the young matron who was rocking Tad in her arms. "If what you say is true," she murmured through her tears, "then—I'll never see my John or little Jacky again . . . ."

Cleone added her tear-filled voice. "Oh, I'll never disobey Mama again. She warned me not to go to the Point to see that awful ship. Oh, I wish I was dead!"

"Hit's de punishment ob de Lawd."

No one noticed that, led by Howell and Mrs. White-Smythe, Miss Snowden, Moore, Kent, and the mulatto, Harris, were leaving the circle. Even their mistresses did not notice as they moved slowly along the lake shore toward the place where the canal joined the lake.

"You'll save us, won't you, Brett?" asked Dell. "You'll find a ship and get us home—before it's too late . . . . ?" She looked down at Jill lying in her arms, a tear spilling on the child's cheek. Brett noticed that her voice held a slight strain of hysteria.

He drew George aside to tell him of his plan. "I've not been idle. I've been making a play for that big brute of mine, been jumping all over him when he gets home nights, turning hand-springs—anything and every-thing to make him notice me . . . ."

"Good idea, and yet . . . ."

"Oh, I know there's plenty of objections. Still it's better than no plan at all . . . ."

"Sure, Brett, I'll do the same thing—perhaps one of us'll succeed."

CHAPTER VI

That night when Mister came home, true to his word, Brett literally flung himself on the monster, doing everything in his power to make the big fellow notice him. He had already discovered that the audibility of his voice-tones was below the sound range of the decapods; that partly ac-counted for the fact that the Earth people had failed in making the beasts realize their mental rating. He could roar at the top of his voice and the creatures paid no heed, no more than they heard his stirrings around in the night. Their voice-range, on the other hand, was often above his own sound-range, their lowest key was either a high "d" or "e". He could see their mouths move without hearing their voices, and the male's tones were even higher than those of the female.

Hence his only way of attracting attention was by his antics, and by taking a flying leap, with the aid of the lessened gravity, he would land high on Mister's body, clinging there until, perforce, the beast would put out a hand to steady him, or pluck him off. And the creature appeared to like these attentions. On the fourth morning he even deigned to give Brett a scoop of food from his plate.

That same night Brett found himself the recipient of a new piece of at-tire. It consisted of a heavy metal girdle fastened to a forty-foot long metal cable. He had seen one of the seal-things wearing a similar belt and leash, nor did he like its implication, not guessing that later it was to prove his salvation.

In the middle of the night he became horribly sick. He was cramped, and had a dizzy headache. And like most of his companions he was suffer-ing from a bad head-cold, that the bath of the following morning did not help.

And to make matters worse, on leaving the dining hall, Missis made use of the leash, snapping the belt around his middle and placing him on the ground. He was forced to run top-speed to keep up with her. Reaching the "air-port," he examined the girdle's buckle, but it was of an intricate mechanism that he could not unfasten. It angered him, because he had intended to run after Mister, make him understand that he wanted to spend the day with him. But the leash foiled him.

He was, of consequence, the most despondent of those gathered on the lake shore that day, eyeing his bedraggled, ailing fellows with jaundiced eye, realizing more fully how very bad they all looked, wan, listless. Then he gave a start. He almost chuckled. Nothing could be more ludicrous than the sight before him. The Militant Matron was sporting a black-eye!

Studying her further, he discovered that she had somehow in twenty-four hours been subjected to considerable mauling. Her face bore other bruises beside the shiner, and her clothes were almost in tatters. Also she was limping . . . .

She, however, was not the only one who appeared to have sustained maltreatment. The Congressman, although he did not have a black-eye, looked equally as bad as she, all semblance of neatness gone, his face scratched and bruised, while one trouser leg was ripped from knee to cuff.

Glancing quickly around Brett found others in the same pitiful condition. Miss Snowden, Moore, Kent and Harris were likewise in a ragged, bruised state. And all looked rather hang-dog about it.

Shortly, he learned what had taken place when the six had wandered away from their fellows the previous day, intent upon finding their way back to civilization. Hurrying along the canal, it seemed, they had made good progress. The canal had widened out, the towers growing more sparse, when they found themselves stalked on all sides by strange decapods. Then they had been surrounded.

At first the curious creatures had been content with poking at them, pinching them; but tiring of that, one had plucked Kent up. From one beast to another he had passed. The others struggled, but were each plucked from the ground. Then had come squabbling among the ever increasing number of monsters, those on the outskirts resenting the slowness with which their fellows examined the curiosities. Fights started here and there, until it was a wonder the Earthlings were not torn limb from limb. Only the timely intervention of a troop of decapods wielding club-like metal rods had saved them. Taken to a massive tower-building they had been turned over to creatures of some authority who examined them thoroughly. Later, they had been returned to their own mistresses, much the worse for the experience.

So ended the first break for liberty.

Howell kept away from the others the remainder of the morning, but when he could catch Brett's eye, he motioned him to come to his side. "Young man," said he, "I do not believe this—er—story of yours about our being upon Mars—but—er—a—you strike me as a man to be depended upon. I heard you making plans with your young friend. Now, listen to me. You—er—get me out of here, and I'll pay you well—er—ten thousand dollars. No—I'll pay fifteen—twenty, whatever you say. Only save me. I'm sick—I'll die unless I get medical attention—but for God's sake get me home . . . ."

Brett listened quietly enough, though with every word his gorge was rising, but he managed to keep his voice under control as he asked, "And what about the others, Congressman . . . . ?"

The man hemmed and hawed a moment, then: "What of them? Let them get out as best they can. After all, *I* am needed in Washington, I have my duty to perform. Two of us have a much better chance—whereas . . . ."

Had the man been younger Brett would have struck him down. He had much he would have liked to say, but he knew he could not trust himself if he let himself go, so he turned on his heel, after one scathing look. It was the last and only time Howell approached him, but he did, later, draw George aside. That young man, however, saw fit to give him a piece of his mind, telling Brett about it later.

"The dirty-so-in-so. Thank God, he's only one out of the rest of them. It's men like him that . . . ."

But Brett waved aside his denunciations. "Forget about him. Listen, we've got to do something. Understand? We're all sick, dying on our feet. We've got to have some setting-up exercises to offset the richness of our food, and general conditions here. Mosey around and see if you can't start something."

"Yeah, I know. The kid, Tad, didn't show up this morning. We're afraid he's dead, and the baby Jill is getting worse. It won't help that her kitten died last night, either . . . ."

Brett's proposal was received in various ways. Howell positively refused to join the group, the negroes grumbled and refused point-blank to do anything for themselves, the three of them forming a praying bee around Mattie whose high hysterical voice was beginning to color all their dreams. Surprisingly it was the Militant Matron that jumped at the idea, organizing the group, wading in after slackers, leading the calisthenics. It was the outlet that she had needed to adjust herself. Brett grinned secretly. He bet with himself that the mayor, as well as all the *worth-while* people of her home-town, usually toed the mark when she was about.

The next day Brett had his piece of luck. Jumping at the end of his long leash, trying to make Mister understand he wanted to accompany him to the *office* that day the catch on his belt suddenly gave way, freeing him. It took him but a moment to realize his advantage, and without a backward glance at Missis, he started on a run after the departing male, about to board his ship. Making a flying leap, he landed on one of the beast's five legs, clung there for dear life.

CHAPTER VII

Mister halted in his tracks, Missis came running up, but reaching down for the man. Brett clung to the male, refusing to be pried off. With much shrill tooting the pair conferred. The female appeared to object to leaving her pet to Mister's care, but his careful groundwork seemed about to bear fruit. The beast hesitated.

Then to his chagrin, at a word from Missis, the male held him out to her. Shrieking at the top of his voice and digging his fingers into the leathery tentacle, Brett again refused to be freed. Missis gave him a long glance. He took it for reproach, but didn't care. Then she said something to Mister that made that worthy chuckle. Thereupon, she turned away, leaving Brett in full possession!

With beating heart he rode his master's arm. They entered the waiting machine. It contained two compartments, the first holding the controls and two queer motors, the second bare, but for a mat and a few hanging straps. High on the wall of the control room was a huge plaque studded with dials, levers and buttons, and before it hung a series of straps in which Mister slung himself.

Carefully the man, squatting on an arm, watched the decapod manipulate the controls. One small hand depressed an octagonal-shaped lever, a second hand turning, in quick succession, three knobs, each of different form. At the touch of the lever the ship was filled with a terrific roar, and with the twisting of the dials came such pressure that Brett lost consciousness.

But the spasm was of short duration, for when he reopened his eyes, they were just leaving the sanded floor of the port. Unaffected by the contusion of the take-off, the beast was twisting a long red bar, which, after he took his hand away, began to oscillate jerkily, continuing to do so all through the trip that followed.

Since the ship was made of the golden transparent metal of the decapods Brett could look in every direction. He saw that they had risen above the tower city, a thousand feet or so, and were now moving away in a straight line. Looking through the floor he could see the plan of the city, a mass of towers, intersected by two canals, dotted with plazas, an occasional monster tower rising high above its fellows. The city had more length than breadth, and he discovered that, true to his supposition, it lay in a deep depression in the planet's surface. Far away, on either side, was the rim of the valley, great dark cliffs.

They were following one of the two canals, and when the city ended abruptly, strips of some growing stuff of bright unnatural green took its place. Here and there monster gardeners tended the plants, keeping a steady flow of water in the ditches from the canal.

Where the canal made a great bend they deserted it, rising over the valley rim into a land that was naught but sand, silent dunes that lay supine, or swirled under wind-eddies. Shortly, a second city came to view, standing beside a second canal. The towers here were twice the circumference of those left behind, but much lower, none rising more than seventy-five feet. Interposed among them were other strange shapes of structures, some tall and slender, others squat and flat, or many sided. Then, there were cone-shaped edifices with the cone's point toward the ground, the wide, flat plane at the top, upheld by interlaced girders. An evil-looking, green smoke rose from many of the buildings, showing why the decapods set their factories far from their residential cities.

Between this conglomeration were wide plazas in which flying machines were already parked, or just arriving. Other machines had preceded them or trailed them from the city of towers, while more approached from opposite directions. As soon as they landed, their pilots hurried into one or another of the various shaped piles.

Realizing they were about to land, Brett clung tightly to Mister's muscular arm, trying to keep his eyes open to watch how the landing was made. A touch halted the oscillating bar, the three knobs were twisted to their original position, and the ship was floating to a landing as lightly as a feather.

They entered a round building filled with activity, monsters moving among queer machines that covered most of the floor space. At one end of the long chamber stood a high counter, and it was to this desk that Mister hastened. Climbing to his hanging "chair," the decapod placed Brett on a clear space on the counter itself, pushing him down to indicate that he was to stay where he was put.

On a wide plaque in front of him was a series of bars, odd-shaped knobs and round flat keys, and without wasting time Mister set to work, depressing keys and twisting knobs. Sometimes all five hands were engaged; again only one. Brett had no idea what it was for, but as the decapod glanced occasionally at the various throbbing machines, he concluded that this control-board was, in some way, connected with them. If only he could have asked questions!

The monotony of watching those moving hands made the man drowsy. A touch, later, awoke him. Mister and he were surrounded by several machinists, the machines were stilled. Brett was placed on the floor and was commanded by Mister's tootings to "jump." This meant turning handsprings, somersaulting without number, making high leaps into the air, flip-flopping and what-not. Brett had always been proud of his muscular control, and Mars' gravity allowed him feats he could never have accomplished at home. Then, he was picked up, handed around as each monster examined him, texture of skin, hair and clothing.

Placed on the table again, he watched the machines restart, and for several hours Mister worked silently and efficiently at his task. Brett wondered at the activity, but there was nothing to tell him what was being done, since the room was otherwise bare except for the machines. At last, the machines were stopped once more, and there was a general exodus from the building. The work-day was at an end.

Outside, the man was the cynosure of all eyes, and had to show-off again for his master's fellows. This time, when they climbed into the flying machine, he was prepared for the take-off, managing to hold on to his senses as he watched everything the pilot did, memorizing each process.

He felt better for what little he had accomplished, having forged the first link in the chain that meant escape, but he foresaw that it was not to be as simple as he had hoped. There was the question of the ship's space-worthiness, of fuel. True, he could see no outlet but the single entrance, which, by its very solidity, pointed to the fact that, once closed, it hermetically sealed the ship. But there was also the question of how he and his companions were to manipulate those giant controls. He could, undoubtedly, reach them from the hanging straps, but were Earth muscles equal to turning them?

His fellows crowded around him the next morning. They had guessed his absence of the previous day had to do with the workings of his plot to escape. He narrated all he had seen, but told only George of his many fears. "We know nothing of the machinery, not even how the ship is fueled. And we'll be taking a chance on its space-worthiness."

"You saw nothing that looked like fuel tanks?"

"No. My guess would be that the power is derived either from stored energy in the machines themselves or from solar or cosmic rays . . . ."

"Hum—that is a problem. But say, I tell you what. To-night, let's sneak out and give these ships a once-over, top to bottom. We can't wait much longer. Jill died in Dell's arms yesterday. She's pretty much broken up over it. Mrs. White-Smythe keeled over, too, and we had a difficult time of it, bringing her around; and several others are mighty sick . . . ." Even as he spoke George was doubled up with a cramp that twisted his face and made him catch at Brett to keep his balance.

"Yes, I realize we're all in a bad way. Getting many of those spasms, George?"

"Oh, I'm all right, so so, anyway. Yes, we've got to get out of here . . . ."

"But what's puzzling me is how we're to get out of the towers? Drop from rung to rung? You and I might manage, but how 'bout the others—the women . . . . ?"

"I've got that figured out, Brett. Most of us have leashes now, you see. Here's what we'll do," and George explained his idea. They planned to meet an hour or so after sunset, with the rising of Deimos.

CHAPTER VIII

It seemed to Brett that Missis and Mister would never fall asleep, but at last their quiet breathing told him all was well. Tip-toeing more from habit than need, since he knew his nocturnal stirrings never disturbed them, he crept to the open doorway. Deimos was just showing over the rim of the valley leaving the ground still in shadow.

Picking up the long cable of his leash he studied the ladder below him. Luckily, one of the rungs was fastened just five feet beneath the doorway. It was broad and round, jutting out from the building's side some two feet, its end a broad knob.

Swinging over the door-sill, he felt around with his feet until he found the rung, then balancing himself carefully slid down until he straddled it. Next, he pulled the cable that he held in one hand after him, and draped it over the rung so that its ends hung clear, dangling several feet below the next rung beneath. Taking both sides of the cable in his hands, he went down until his feet met the step.

Chuckling over the simplicity of the thing, he repeated the same performance over and over again, until, at last, the ground was underfoot. For a few moments he stood listening, to discover if his descent had disturbed any of the neighbors, but the decapods were all sound sleepers, nothing stirred in the night. Coiling up the cable, he hastened to his rendezvous.

George was at the landing field before him, since his tower home was nearer. In the moonlight he was inspecting one of the flying machines.

"You're right," he told Brett, "these things have no storage tanks of any sort, but look here, what do you make of these?"

He pointed to a mesh-work of wires embedded in the very stuff of which the golden ship was made. In the daylight they would have appeared invisible, but the moon's rays glinted upon their surfaces, silvering them.

"Antenna! There's some way of drawing power out of the air. Whether it comes from artificial beams or from the cosmos itself, there's no telling. Possibly, we'll never know, but I'd take a chance it's either solar or cosmic rays—they couldn't broadcast a beam from here to Earth. Of course, we could tell better if only we could find that big ship that brought us here . . . ."

"How 'bout trying this one out? We might as well learn if we can handle it . . . ."

Brett thoughtfully paused to consider the question before giving an answer when they both grew aware of the fact that they were not the only ones abroad in the city. Across the plaza loomed the figure of a huge decapod. In one hand it carried a long metal bar. "A night watchman . . . ." breathed George.

Luckily, they were unseen as the beast was gazing in an opposite direction. Hastily they dodged under cover among the massed machines, watching breathlessly until the police guard turned back among the towers.

"Whee—that was close! Wonder what these things have to guard against? They haven't anything for anyone to steal!"

"No telling, no more than we cannot explain lots of things about them. I guess this ends our chance at trying out the ship. No use giving our hand away yet. We've got to make the break *en masse*, and take the consequences . . . ."

They went in one of the ships to study the controls, but there seemed no connecting links between them and the motors. They were as much in the dark as before.

A paling of the stars in the east warned them that morning was at hand. Separating, they hurried to their respective towers. On the way Brett all but ran into a second guard, moving between the buildings. Again luck was with him, and he slipped out of sight. Reaching his own tower, Brett was faced with the monumental task of reclimbing the glassy wall.

A running jump carried him high enough to grasp the first of the ladder rungs, but from there on it was a gruelling job of lassoing each succeeding rung, standing upright and hooking the cable over the rung above his head. The sun was showing above the valley rim as he swung his foot over the sill of his chamber. In a few moments the beasts had begun to awaken.

That same morning Brett apprised their fellows of the details of the plot that George and he had carefully worked out between them. Looking around he realized that there was no time to lose. They were all sallow, pathetically thin. Everyone had a cough, sneezing and wheezing. A few had to hold their chests when coughing spasms seized them. And they were all sick from the rich, unnatural food of their captors. Even Dell who had been the most uncomplaining showed a peaked, wan face in which the blue eyes seemed over large and bright. Only the little dog, Jock, did not seem to have suffered any. Each day he had friskily re-greeted the new friends he had made.

"I'm not going to conceal any facts from you," Brett explained. "We've possibly one chance in a thousand to get home. For one thing, these flying machines may not be hermetically sealed, and once we're out in Space, we'll suffocate—even so we don't know how long our air will suffice without renewal—not very long, anyway. Secondly, we're taking a chance on fuel. Then, again, we don't know, when once in Space, if we can find Mother Earth. None of us know a thing about spatial navigation, we're none of us astronomers, and we may miss Earth entirely—and fall into the Sun. In fact, I'm afraid that a thousand to one chance is a small margin . . . .

"But we do know one thing, and that is, if we remain here much longer, none of us'll live to tell the tale anyway. We're dying on our feet, so it's up to each of you to decide for yourself. You must come willingly . . . ."

He did not know whether it was the "hope that springs eternal" or whether it was a fatalistic courage that caused them to give a unanimous consent, but there was not a single nay in the little gathering. Even, Mattie who had insisted right along that this was "Gawd's jedgement" found it in herself to let loose a wild Hallelujah.

Each member of the party was told just what he or she was to do as Brett warned them that the first step toward escape depended largely upon themselves, illustrating how the descent from the towers was to be accomplished. A count showed that three or four of their masters had neglected to provide their "pets" with leashes, and therefore, it fell upon several of the stronger men to help those unfortunates. The hour set for the exodus was at Deimos' rising.

As Brett flung his leg over the sill of his doorway, he saw the dark shadow on the neighboring tower that he knew to be the big negro, Jeff. Almost at the same time both reached the ground and, as pre-scheduled, hurried to the building that had housed the Militant Matron. They saw her peering out the third story chamber, waiting for them. She had a leash, but the nearest ladder rung was ten feet below her.

The negro, to Brett's surprise, insisted upon going up after her, explaining that besides being a "champeen" riveter who knew his scaffolds, he had also served on a western ranch as a cow-puncher. And true to his word he lassoed the rung above Mrs. White-Smythe's head, carefully paying out the cable until its other end swung to the woman's waiting hand.

Bravely the heavy matron dared put her weight upon it, carrying the negro on the other end aloft, until she reached the rung from which he had been lifted, hanging on until he could join her on the single support. When, at last, they reached the ground she had something to say to the darky. "Boy," said she, "if you're ever out of a job you come see me. I never believed I'd get out of that place alive!"

Proceeding on their way the three picked up Jerry Ware the reporter who had with him the little school-girl, Cleone, and Mrs. Burton, impatient over any delay that might keep her longer from "John" and little "Jacky." The rest of the Earthlings were housed on opposite sides of the plaza, and were to meet them later.

Brett led the way to the great dining hall, now empty; keeping his eyes open the while for "police men," but not a single decapod showed up to halt their progress. The moonlight shone on the long high counter behind which stood the large vats of Martian food ready for the morning horde. Bad as the food was for them, part of the plan was to carry off a few casks to sustain them upon their homeward journey, for the Earthlings had no way of knowing how long that trip was to be.

However, since there was no opening in the counter, they had to devise a way of getting the casks over it. The decapods simply stepped over the barrier, but not so the Earthlings. Jeff, the tallest and huskiest of the men was made the under-stander, and Ware climbed to his shoulders. He was slenderer than Brett, and Brett knew that the reporter could never haul either himself or Jeff to the counter's top, so it became necessary for Brett to climb up first. Standing on Jerry's shoulders, that threatened collapse, he swung himself to the edge of the counter, and managed to draw himself upon it.

Uncoiling his leash that was slung around his shoulders he dropped its end into Jerry's hand and quickly hauled him to his side. Together they drew Jeff to the counter top. It was Jeff who held the cable for Jerry and Brett to slide down to the floor on the other side where stood the vats.

The vats were great open containers, but stored to one side were dozens of tubs, six feet high and four in diameter. Turning six of them on their sides the men rolled them in position below Jeff. The cable end was tied securely around the first, and Brett skinned up the leash to stand beside Jeff and help in drawing the heavy cask to the counter top. That done, they rolled it to the other side, and slung it to the floor where the women there untied the noose. One by one the other tubs were lifted over the counter.

As they toiled more of the party made their appearance as scheduled, then the heavy tubs were rolled out of the hall toward the machine the Earthlings had chosen for their escape. When the containers were inside Brett counted noses. Everyone was there—except McCarthy.

The boy, Forrest, remembered having seen McCarthy that night. "I called him," he said, "but he was going the other way. He just waved and called back that he'd be along directly . . . ."

"Hum—I guess he's gone to the grave of his horse to say good-bye. He took Prince's death hard," observed George.

"Here he comes now!"

McCarthy was coming on a run, something white clutched under his arm. It was Jock, the wire-haired terrier. "Glory be," said the man as he caught his breath. "I just couldn't leave this little feller behind, even if he is only a dog . . . ." He had climbed half way up a tower to get the animal.

"Well, come on. It'll be light soon. Inside everyone!"

The fifty-foot ship held them all, and the heavy door was swung closed. Then Brett and George climbed the straps until they were opposite the control plaque.

With his heart in his throat Brett tentatively touched the octagonal lever that he had watched Mister depress, after warning everyone to beware of the take-off. He was astonished at the ease with which the lever reacted under his hand. A light touch depressed it. But it was more difficult with the three knobs. It took both George and him with all their combined strength to turn them. Then, they waited for the roar of the take-off.

It DID NOT COME!

CHAPTER IX

Brett and George stared at each other. They could feel a slight pulsation throughout the ship, but that was all.

"Maybe we didn't twist the knobs far enough . . . ." whispered George. Brett nodded. Again they worked on them. They found they could turn them still farther; yet nothing happened!

Again the pair looked at each other, neither daring to voice his thoughts. Below them, their companions grew restive, wondering at the delay. It was Forrest who had a suggestion.

"Maybe—it's because the sun's not up—that it depends on the sun's rays . . . ."

Brett glanced thoughtfully at the boy. Perhaps he was right. One guess was as good as another. Lifting his eyes to the east, he saw that the sun would rise shortly.

A bright red was already tinting the sky. Then—gradually, so slowly it seemed it would never break the mist on the horizon, a slender sliver of blood red cut the gloom.

"THE SUN!"

Never had sun worshipers greeted that orb with more fervor, but their exultation was of short duration.

With a roar that was like a dozen claps of thunder, the ship sprang into action, mounting the sky so rapidly no one within witnessed the take-off. Thrown to the floor by the terrific pressure, they lost all consciousness and the machine was a wild thing climbing straight into the heavens.

Out of the blackness of oblivion Brett, at last, opened his eyes. He found himself on the floor below the strap to which he had been clinging. Beside him lay George, not yet stirring. Here and there someone moaned, tried to get up. And it was only by concentrating all his will that Brett was able to lift a hand, then his head, and lastly his body. It was as if a thousand-pound weight held him down.

He realized that the copper-sky was already losing some of its color, that Mars was dwindling rapidly beneath him.

Panting, he strove to reclimb the straps, to reach the controls. Fighting the pressure was like fighting a monster. He got to his knees, bringing one foot forward to jack up his body. A hanging strap came within reach of a hand, and that helped. His climb upward was a bitter thing to watch, so slow, so painful as one dragging hand followed the other, like something out of a nightmare, or a slow-motion camera.

Opposite the controls at last, he was uncertain of what to do. Should he twist the red lever as Mister had done to level off the flight? Or twist the dials to starting point? Sluggishly his mind milled over the question, then he decided first to start the oscillating bar.

Eyes blurred with the sweat of his gigantic effort, he felt rather than saw the bar. The lightest of taps started it oscillating and he almost screamed with joy when he found the pressure subsiding. Soon, he was feeling normal again.

The others were rising to their feet; George climbed the adjoining strap to his side. "We've done it! We've done it!" came the cries from all sides, as they forgot the ordeal they had just experienced, staring with fascinated eyes at the copper ball rolling off to the right, its form becoming more evidently diminishing. They had left Mars behind—were in free space!

For a while George eyed the oscillating bar. Then he spoke. "Now what?" he wanted to know. "How do we guide this thing?"

Brett pointed to the bar. "Mister swung that right or left—but your guess is as good as mine. Where is Earth?"

Together they looked into the great panorama of the firmament spread out before them like a great black velvet mantle dotted with multicolored jewels. The sun glowered at them like an evil enraged eye.

"There's the sun, directly ahead. Ugh what a furnace. Earth must show somewhere in its vicinity—with Mercury and Venus. We ought to know it because it will show its phases to Mars, like the moon does to Earth . . . ."

"Righto . . . . There—see that pale green star there—see, about a degree beyond the silver crescent—in half-moon. That's Earth, George, I know it is!"

George studied thoughtfully, turning now and then to eye other glittering objects round about. After a while he was ready to conclude that the greenish half-moon was Earth, the silvery body below it, Venus. "If only we could see the moon alongside, we could be certain."

On the floor beneath them was Forrest listening to their conversation. Suddenly he cried out. "There it is! See that faint glow of light along the dark side? It's the moon—LUNA!"

They, too, found the light-glow he spoke of, showing faintly along the planet's limb. It was sufficient to convince them that the pale green planet was Earth. But how to head their ship in that direction was their quandary. It seemed that the ship lay in a course diagonally across the heavens.

Tentatively Brett touched the oscillating red bar fearing to halt it altogether, but it did not stop as it moved in its socket. They waited breathlessly. "It's working . . . ." cried George, "only we're swinging more directly toward the sun . . . ."

Again Brett pushed the stick ever so slightly. Again they waited. The sky seemed to swing around them as the green half-moon moved slowly until it lay directly in their path. Those below who had listened quietly to the pair of engineers cheered, certain now that their pilots were to bring them home—safely.

"Guess there's nothing else to do here now, Brett. Might as well climb down and let the ship do the rest . . . ."

But Brett thought differently. "No, one of us must stay on duty at all times—to keep an eye on the 'stick.' We can know if the ship leaves her course by centering Earth just above the plaque. See that little finger-like piece sticking up? We'll go by that. Right now it cuts Earth in half."

"All right. I'll take the first trick."

Of those aboard, only McCarthy possessed a watch that ran, since it was encased in a water-proof jacket. Now he wound it up. George was to take a four-hour shift, then Brett would relieve him, trying to get some sleep in the meantime.

As he slid down the strap Brett found Dell awaiting him. "You've been wonderful," she averred. "If only we could have saved the children, everything would be top-hole."

Brett waved aside her congratulations. "We're not there yet," he pointed out. He was sorry as soon as he had said that, but he needed something to cover up his embarrassment. And Dell understood. She chuckled happily. "Do you know—when we *do* get home, I'm going to start a movement to release every pet in the land!"

"Now I know what it means to a dumb brute thrown in with creatures whose language is not its language, who make their will its will."

"I guess there's a lot in that—not being able to talk back. God knows it's been a horrible enough experience for all of us." He wanted to say more, but he seemed to be going to sleep on his feet. The girl noticed his discomfort, and suggested that he rest. He scarcely knew that he lay down, falling asleep almost as soon as he reached the bare floor. He hadn't had any sleep to mention in the last three or four days. But it seemed almost immediately that they were waking him again. Someone was shaking his shoulder, crying in his ear. "Brett, Brett—wake up. The DECAPODS HAVE CAPTURED US!"

CHAPTER X

Sleep was immediately banished. Rising to his feet he stared out of the ship's transparent wall, to behold an awesome sight. For there—scarcely a thousand yards away, loomed the great drum-ship of the Decapods.

"They're dragging us back to Mars!"

The men were grim-faced, the women in tears. Mattie was moaning and praying at the same time.

A glance told him it was true. Far more swiftly than they had come, the drum-ship was dragging them back, away from the sun, away from the Earth, back toward Mars . . . . There was no visible grapple, but such a bond existed now between the two ships nevertheless.

In terse words George told what had happened. How, suddenly, the huge ship had come upon them, invisible until it was quite close; then the sun glinting on its golden sides appraised them of its proximity. But they hadn't realized, at first, that it had them in its grip.

Brett climbed to the controls to see that nothing had been touched, only now the oscillating bar was swinging aimlessly back and forth. For a moment he studied the bank of controls, a row of buttons whose purpose he did not know. He pointed these out to George. "Shall we try them? No telling what they're intended for . . . ."

George agreed. "I thought of them, yet was afraid to try them out."

"It can't hurt to try. Death awaits us on Mars. I'm going to try this first green button here. Hold on . . . ." And as he spoke he pressed the first of a row of six green buttons that studded the bottom of the control bank.

Breathlessly they waited. Nothing happened!

"Wrong," muttered Brett, and he pressed the second.

"THEY'RE FALLING BEHIND!" went up the cry in the ship.

Looking around Brett saw this was true. It appeared that they were stationary, that the larger ship was rapidly dwindling in size. "Whatever you did," cried George jubilantly, "you've counteracted their power . . . ." Then—"Good Lord—here they come back!"

As he cried out the enemy grew larger, racing down upon them.

Brett gave his full attention to the controls, again twisting the three great knobs to the full extent of their thread, then he juggled the "stick," until Earth once more lay directly in their path. Difficult though it was to judge their rate of acceleration, it seemed that their own ship gained on the other, the growth of the pursuer being less rapid than before. Still it was evident that the drum-ship possessed a greater speed, eating up the short advantage they had gained almost immediately.

"Well," he said somberly. "I guess there's nothing else to do but try the rest of the buttons. Here goes."

As he spoke he depressed the third button! A cry of astonishment went up in the ship. They could no longer see outside; they were enveloped in a hazy aura that enclosed the entire machine. And the next instant the whole ship rocked, seemed to tilt—then righted itself.

They waited, and again there came a rocking that ceased after a few moments. When the third rocking came and passed, Brett cried out: "They're firing upon us from the big ship . . . ."

As if to prove his words their ship rocked again. After that, however, it did not come again, though five, ten minutes passed.

"Think they've given up?"

"Maybe, but I don't like this fog around us. Wonder what the next button will do?"

"Try it," ordered George.

This time the haze faded away; again they could see the Void wherein the drum-ship loomed like a great evil eye a thousand yards behind.

"LOOK OUT! THEY'RE GOING TO FIRE AGAIN!"

Brett had seen the pencil of light leave the ship's side even as George yelled, and at the same time he punched the third button again. Immediately they were reenveloped in the haze that was like a shining white fog. The rocking was heavier than before, tossing the machine around like a cork.

"I've got it! This haze is a power screen to protect us from their rays? Wonder if this ship's got one of those rays?"

"THE FIFTH BUTTON!" declared George.

Brett nodded. "Yeah—but how do we use it?"

"Their ray seems to come directly from the front of their ship—perhaps, if we turned around . . . . ?"

Brett lost no time in acting on the suggestion, shoving the oscillating stick about. They could feel no movement, but when he had the stick pointing at right-angles to its former position he depressed the button that dissolved the power screen, keeping a finger close to the accompanying button in case the drum-ship had the march on them.

It lay in the same position as before, its very presence a menace, but Brett found that their ship was somewhat off center. Again he moved the "stick," bringing the control panel in direct line with the big ship.

Then, his hand went to the fifth button on the panel before him. And at the same time the drum-ship struck.

A cry went up from the watchers. Some covered their faces with their hands, others stared, grim-faced, waiting . . . .

The two rays had met. Almost in dead center between the ships. There was a terrific flash of lurid, evil light, though no sound came to them in that soundless void. Brett did not wait as he flashed on their power screen once again.

He waited a reasonable time before lifting the screen. George was ready to depress the beam button, so that almost simultaneously, with the flashing out of the screen, the pencil ray cut the blackness.

A shout went up in the little ship as the long light-beam impinged itself upon the shell of the decapods' ship, but Brett did not wait to learn the result, hiding their ship immediately within their protective cloud. He let five minutes go before he dared look out.

The big ship was still there, its distance greater, however, although it was unscathed, wrapped now in a dense brilliant cloud that sparkled like diamond facets in the sun's rays that it had imprisoned.

Disappointment filled the hearts of the Earthlings as Brett again re-enveloped them in their own screen. "There's nothing to be done," he admitted, "but to go on. As long as we have the screen we're safe, and *vice-versa*. We'll turn about and try to head for home . . . ."

As he spoke he pressed the "stick" back to its original position, releasing the screen long enough to center the focus of the ship on the green half-moon that was "home." A glance backward showed that the enemy was still clothed in its fog.

He ordered George to get some rest, suggesting that it was time for the serving of some food. Jerry had pilfered half a dozen scoops, the only ones within reach when they raided the dining hall, and the Earthlings lined up for their rations. When they had all eaten sparingly, those who could bring themselves to compose their minds for sleep, did so, disposing themselves as best they could on the bare floor. The women gathered in the adjoining room for what little privacy it offered them with only a transparent wall between.

Brett slid down his strap to the floor. Forrest came to his side. "Gee, Mr. Rand, you were great. You know this is just like the stories I read, only I wish you could have 'gotten' that ole ship out there . . . ."

"I wish so too, but it looks like stale-mate for the present. No use risking ourselves. Later, perhaps, they'll grow careless."

He looked around for Dell, and saw her in the other room bending over one of the women. Walking to the small machines in the center of the ship he studied them speculatively. From them came the soft throb that filled the air, yet he could see no moving parts. Then, for the first time he noticed a feature he had not seen before.

In the floor was a circular disk, about four feet in diameter. In its center was a smaller disk set below the floor's level. Hesitantly he reached out a hand to touch it. And at his touch the whole piece of the larger disk moved aside, revealing a circular chamber about a foot deep. On its floor was a second knob like the one on the plate above.

"I wonder," he said aloud, and looked for something detachable upon his person. A button on his sleeve filled his want, and he tugged until it came free. Laying it on the lower disk, he closed the upper one and waited, but nothing happened. Through the transparent metal he could see the button lying as he had placed it.

"Must be some sort of control . . . ." he muttered. "Ah—here it is . . . ." He had discovered a tiny lever, scarcely an inch long imbedded in the knob, and he shoved it over with his thumb. Staring through the top disk he saw the floor beneath fall away, revealing the emptiness of Space. The button slid off the disk, and then the contraption closed automatically with a snap.

"An air-lock!" he mused. "Gosh, had I found that before, I'd have known for certain this ship was air-tight. A nice little arrangement to throw away trash . . . ."

Several hours later he climbed to the control panel. Releasing the fog screen a minute he verified their course, replacing the screen again. A single glance behind revealed the decapods' ship still wrapped in its protective shroud of glistening light. Then his eye fell upon the sixth button of the series that had proven so providential. What, he wondered, would that button do?

After a moment's hesitation he decided to risk it, and pressed the key. To his surprise a small circular portion of the panel slid to one side revealing a smooth polished surface on which dots of light shone. A startled glance showed him a greenish half-moon held in dead-center of the disk. He almost shouted with joy! No longer need he switch off their power screen to determine their position, for this was no less than a vision-screen. They no longer were flying blind!

CHAPTER XI

Hours slipped by. George awakened, and most of the others roused themselves. They dined again, and George took his place before the controls. Brett suggested now that they give the women more privacy than they had. He had noticed a number of hooks stuck in the partitioning wall, and decided that a screen could be provided if each man relinquished either his suit coat or outershirt. It was warm in the ship, and they would not need them. Mrs. White-Smythe contributed her suit coat, and Mrs. Burton had a silk jacket, so that a sizable curtain could be hung by means of one of the "dog-leashes" across the wall.

"Now, if we had some water, we could make ourselves half-way presentable," observed Dell looking at her unwashed hands.

"We've got water," declared Forrest. "One of those tubs is full. Shake it, and you can hear it gurgle . . . ."

A rush was made toward the cask he designated. The top was pried off (a small handle was provided on each tub for that purpose) and sure enough water was found within.

Brett considered. Their food precluded the need of drinking water, yet the very sight of it made him thirsty. He saw several people running a tongue over their lips. They would all enjoy a cooling drink. But he shook his head. He feared that once they started on the water, they would want more and more, and one barrel would not last long. Yet, they'd all feel better if they could lave their dry skins. He explained all this, but there was only one dissenter. It was Congressman Howell.

"Since when are you giving orders, Mr. Rand?" he wanted to know. "I don't recall any election of officers for this cruise . . . ."

Brett looked up in surprise. There had been no selection of officers, and actually there seemed no need. He had simply taken the lead up to this point, because it seemed the only natural thing to do, especially since no one else had demanded the job.

A deep silence followed Howell's words. Brett started to answer. "You're right, of course, I . . . ."

But he got no further. It was the Militant Matron who spoke up. "I think Mr. Rand's done an excellent job of it so far, Congressman, and if there's any point in electing him—I, for one, cast my vote for him. Without him, we'd still be back there—on Mars." (So she admitted the truth now.) "He's been the only man here with guts—yes, I said guts—to rescue us, and I think he should be our captain. How 'bout it, folks?"

She turned to the others, and her response was a cheer from all sides. Disgruntled Howell slipped away.

Taking turns with the five food scoops (the sixth was used as a ladle) each man and woman received their water ration. They could do no more than wet their faces and hands with it. However, one of the women had the brilliant idea of dumping all their water into the air-lock receptacle in their room (a second lock had since been found in that chamber) and using the combined water to wash out such clothing as they could manage.

Brett in the meantime ran his hand through his straggly beard as he waited his water ration, wishing for a razor to remove it. But he knew, or thought there wasn't one in the crowd; that is until Forrest sidled over to him.

"Want a razor, Mr. Rand?"

Brett looked up and grinned.

"I got one," admitted the boy in a whisper as he ran a hand over his virgin chin. "Some older fellows were kidding me 'bout not shaving yet—back home, you know. So the day the decapods came—I had bought a razor. I—I thought I'd shave and make the hair grow.

"I never said anything about it before, 'cause I thought I'd get laughed at, but if you told 'em I bought it for my dad . . . ."

The man could have hugged him. The razor, an ordinary safety affair was rusted, but he did not care. He almost shouted when Forrest brought out a tube of shaving cream that all this while had reposed in his pocket.

The others crowded around, begging for next go. Forrest insisted his hero have the first shave, the others, he said with a negligent wave of his hand, could draw straws for it—or something.

The backing of the power screen made a dim mirror of the ship's walls, and Brett used that for his shave. After some difficulty in hacking away the hirsute growth, and nicking himself more than once he managed a fairly clean shave. Then he relinquished the razor to the next in turn. Luckily, the boy had likewise purchased a package of blades. Each man kept his blade for further use.

Dell made her appearance with the other women. "I feel like a new woman," she laughed. "One could scarcely believe that a little water could work such wonders . . . ."

The effect of their ablutions was to give the Earthlings a new lease on life, an uplift in their morale. Their eyes had brightened, and their cheery voices filled the ship.

When it came his turn at the controls Brett again threw off the power screen to ascertain if the decapods were still on their trail. No sooner was the screen replaced than a rocking shook the ship. The decapods were most assuredly on their tail.

He conferred with George. Should they again attempt to rid themselves of the enemy? They decided to consult the others on the momentous question. The majority vote was for War!

Once more the ship was swung out of its course, turned about so it could face the enemy, and Brett worked until the big ship lay centered in the vision-screen. Then with one finger he depressed the button that released their own screen, while almost immediately, he switched it on again. There followed a rocking of the ship as a pencil beam from the decapods' machine flashed across the Void.

Twice he used the same tactics, and twice the other struck; but the third time the decapods resorted to the same strategy, dropping their own screen. Instantly Brett shot out his ray. It worked.

"A HIT! A Hit!" cried George, and they saw the big ship stagger, side-slip and try to right itself. Only it could not. It was careening wildly, from side to side. But the decapods were not done yet. A white beam cut the blackness, but the ray was wild, and did not come anywhere near their ship.

Twice the decapods attempted to restore their protective screen, and though it flashed on each time, it faded almost instantly. Again Brett used his ray upon it, but now the other was quickly dwindling in size and the range was too great.

For several minutes they followed it, but hurt though it was, the big ship could accelerate more quickly, and was swiftly moving away—back in the direction from which it had come—back to Mars . . . .

Breathing a sigh of relief the pilot turned about, heading for Earth once again. Earth was still far, far away, and there was no way of computing how long the voyage would be.

With no further interruptions the monotony of space began to tell upon the travelers, voices grew low, eyes lack-luster, bodies listless with nothing to occupy mind or body. They commenced to hate the sight of food, most of them suffering from cramps as well as from the colds they had brought from Mars.

Brett commenced to wonder if they *should* reach home alive. He realized he was feeling pretty rotten himself, only the excitement of the escape and the fight with the decapods had taken his mind from it, but now that he had time to allow himself to dwell upon his condition, he knew that he was actually sick.

Endless hours slipped by, and with them the sickness aboard grew apace. Clarice and Mrs. Burton were very sick, staying in the other room, not even coming out at meal time. Mattie who had taken to prayers again, calling upon God as witness to their sins, sometimes forgot to pray as she moaned instead. Miss Snowden sat slumped in a corner most of the time, and the Militant Matron, though she tried to help Dell cheer the others, was visibly sick. Several men were in the same condition, refusing food, and Forrest's eyes were over-bright.

Swung in the seat woven from the overhead straps facing the control panel or lying in his corner Brett found that there were long lapses of time in which his mind seemed away from his body. His body grew to be something unattached, his lucid moments becoming fewer and fewer. Sometimes he thought he was on Mars, sometimes at his desk in the Bureau of Standards back home. Sometimes he heard himself talking aloud, to no one in particular.

"It's the food," he heard Dell mutter to George one time. "It's rotting . . . ."

That woke him up. He hurried to the open tub they were using, three of the others were empty. He tasted it, and only with effort kept from retching. It was rotted.

He called George. "Let's open the last barrel." It too was rotting. "No more food," he said.

The next meal time, only water was doled out from the now half-empty barrel. No one seemed to notice the change, nor care. Brett crawled up to the control board to check the course. The green mantled Earth lay in dead-center of the screen, but it still seemed far away. He grew panicky. Perhaps they no longer moved!

CHAPTER XII

For a long time he stared at that far away globe. For a time he forgot what it actually was; it had revolved into a symbol, a symbol of attainment, but outside that he could not remember. It seemed that the Void had always been, all that he had ever known. Only he could not put out of his mind that deep longing he felt for that greenish half-globe with its diminutive moon alongside, for Luna had since detached itself slightly from the side of Earth and rode the darkness, shedding its light on the mother planet.

Once someone aroused him to tell him that Clarice was dead, and Mattie was fast sinking, but the words scarcely meant anything. He knew that Kent had already passed away, and that several others were in a deep coma from which they could not be aroused.

The next time his brain roused itself he became aware of a distinctly unpleasant odor around him. He puzzled over it a while before he realized that it came from their fouled food supply. Something snapped within him, and he was more fully alert than he had been for some time. He realized the need of ridding the ship of the stuff. Before this, he had puzzled about their air-supply, afraid that that might also give out on them, but he had come to know that one of the ship's two motors was designed to keep it clean and pure. Only with that putrefaction rising from the tubs, the air would soon grow stale. They had to be emptied.

Glancing about for help he saw George sleeping, making vague stirrings that bespoke a troubled body. Moore, the merchant, lay supine, snoring spasmodically, the little rolls of fat gone from his face, his skin an unhealthy yellow. Howell lay in a strange unnatural position. Leaning over him Brett realized he was dead. The mulatto, Harris, was doubled in a knot, sweat streaking from his face. Jeff the big negro and Jerry the reporter seemed the only two that looked normal. Forrest was breathing with difficulty, and McCarthy lay with an arm around the dog, mumbling in a delirium. Shaking Jeff and Jerry awake Brett told them what had to be done. None of them were strong enough for the task, but together they managed to push the pair of casks to the air-lock, tip them over so their contents spilled into the small receptacle. When it filled up, they closed and dumped it. This procedure had to be repeated many times, the three of them suffering time and time again over their ugly task as the evil smell of the mass affected them. They were forced to scoop out the bottoms, but at last it was finished, the casks tightly closed.

The dead presented another problem, but they did not like the thought of consigning them to space. Dragging the bodies to one side they covered them with a few coats taken from the screen shielding the women.

On, on drifted the ship of death, moving slowly toward its objective. From his place on the floor Brett raised his eyes from time to time to the body of George slumped within the straps above his head, eyes closed. But those facts scarcely registered upon his brain as he drifted again into the unreal realm of a deathlike sleep. Several times he sought to drag himself out of his lethargy, but each time the effort was too great. He did not know that like a sleep-walker he had gotten up a number of times to wander among the others, putting a hand to a forehead here and there. When next he awoke, he found his arms wrapped around a thin though warm body.

Focusing eyes with some difficulty he found that it was Dell Wayne who lay within his grasp. He was startled by her appearance, her sunken cheeks, the depths of her eye sockets. He grew frightened, fearing that she was dead, and laid his head upon her heart. It beat. The movement awakened her. Somehow she managed a smile. "Brett—good Brett," she murmured in a scarcely audible voice. "I—I guess this is the end—isn't it? It's been nice knowing you—Brett . . . ."

The import of her words fell upon him, and suddenly he knew he did not want to die. "NO—No . . . . we shan't die—we can't. We've come too far together for that—I can't let you die—you understand? Why, Dell—I love you—I love you. We can't die—yet . . . ."

She did not answer, smiling at him instead, an enigmatical smile. Then, they both were silent, drifting again into that half-way death of sleep.

The first shout did not rouse them, nor the second. It took a heavy shaking on the part of the boy, Forrest, to awaken them. "Earth—" he was shrieking . . . . "Earth—in our path. Can't you understand? We're almost —home—HOME!"

The last word did it. Brett woke, staring wildly into the wilder eyes of the boy. "Home?" he asked querulously, "HOME?"

Then he was struggling to his feet, dragging Dell with him. He glanced out the ship's side (the power screen had long since been down, after they had ascertained that the decapod ship was really gone). It was true. Before them, filling most of their sky, loomed the broad green globe of Earth. To one side shone a thin sliver of the moon. They were already within Luna's orbit.

Weak though he was Brett managed to climb up to the control panel, staring with yearning eyes at the great body before him, picking out the familiar features of the continents as the globe was turning slowly, half in darkness, half in light.

How long he hung there in the straps, he did not know. Below him he could hear the stirrings of his fellows, almost all aroused now by Forrest. He knew it must have taken hours, that slow approach to the globe, but it did not matter, nothing mattered as the lineaments of Earth grew before his eyes, sometimes blotted by that line of darkness. Gradually it lost its globular form, horizons straightened out, and with a suddenness that startled him, he found that the sky around them was no longer dead black—that it was taking on color—pale blue at first, then deeper and deeper. They were well within the atmosphere blanket!

Now it seemed they were falling, falling too swiftly as land and water rushed up to meet them. "Do something, do something," his brain commanded, "do something before we crash."

The knobs—three of them must be turned. With both hands he tugged and pulled; then someone was helping him, and he found it was George. The ship leveled off, and now the same speed that had seemed so incredibly slow out in space swung them rapidly through the air, five miles or so above the landscape. Again the acceleration was lessened and Brett jiggled the "stick." They had reached Earth at its most southern point, and he turned the ship northward.

Those who had the power to do so had risen to their feet, crowding to the walls to stare hungrily at the twilighted land beneath. Night came upon them, and still they moved on, on. Brett knew when they crossed the equator by the constellations; steered his course by the pole-star. Dawn was breaking when he realized they lay off the Virginian coast. There was that great arm of land that was the eastern shore of Chesapeake Bay. He headed the ship over the bay, followed it, trying to name the rivers emptying into it.

He found the river he sought, the lordly Potomac and followed its course. Soon they saw the beautiful pattern that was Washington, the tiny sliver of stone that was the Monument. A few minutes later the ship hovered above Haines Point, and Brett halted the oscillating stick.

Instantly the ship nosed down, dropping evenly to the ground, forward motion halted. As the land came up to meet them, George and he twisted the three dials to neutral. The journey was at end.

Like a feather the ship settled upon the grass of the municipal golf-links, not far from the spot, where, on that memorial day, five weeks since, the great drum-ship of the decapods had rested.

Again Washington had witnessed the early morning arrival, but there were only police, and soldiers to receive the travelers. Bolling Field and the Naval Airdrome had dispatched planes to the scene, machine-guns pointed downward menacingly. A shout of wonder greeted the first of the emaciated passengers to disembark. Willing hands helped them while those unable to walk were carried out tenderly.

A week later Brett Rand with an arm around his wife received the news-reporters in his brother's home. Still thin and wan from their experience the pair expressed their joy of being "home."

"I'm going to make a life work of freeing every animal pet in the land!" declared Mrs. Rand when asked if she was going to follow a "career."

"After our honeymoon," Brett said, "George and I are going to study the decapod ship. There are great things to be learned there, mechanisms entirely new to science . . . ."

"And that, boys, is one tall order!" It was George, speaking from the shadows.

———

This story, "The Human Pets of Mars," does not hold up on rereading as well as many of the other stories in this book did, and I am keenly embarrassed by the simple-minded portrayal of the Blacks in the tale. Yet I well remember thinking the story was absolutely great when I read it for the first time.*

I admit that even when I read the story I was dubious as to the possibility of Earthmen taking over completely alien vessels and learning to handle them so well as to be able to outrace, outmaneuver, and outfight those to the manner born.

Still, the story of indomitable men winning out over immense odds is always popular, and such situations appealed to me both in my reading and in my writing. A great many of my stories will pit one man against a world, though for sheer derring-do, my novel The Currents of Space springs first to mind.

It was sometime in late 1936, encouraged, I believe, by my pleasure in "The Human Pets of Mars," that I could finally resist no more. I had

* Stone was one of the few women writing science fiction in the 1930s. There are many of them now. They compete on equal terms with the men and win more than their share of the honors—but Stone was a pioneer.

grown tired of the endless pages of my fantasy, which was getting nowhere, and I decided to try, for the very first time, science fiction!

I don't remember the details of that first piece of science fiction I ever tried to write, but, of course, it was a novel. Once again, as though incapable of learning, I began a long, incoherent, invertebrate tale, like the fantasy that had just died, and (for that matter) like "The Greenville Chums at College" five years earlier. I made it up as I went along and I never knew on one page what the next page would hold.

That, in itself, is not so bad. Even today when I write a novel, I don't know the details to come and tend to make it up as I go along. Nowadays, though, I know the ending at all times; I know where I am heading. Up through the age of seventeen, I apparently had never realized that this was fundamental—that it was important to know the direction at least.

I was bound to get weary of such endless, meandering efforts, and, therefore, as soon as I found myself mired in literary quicksand, which sooner or later I always did, I quit. The science fiction novel died just as my previous attempts did.

What I now remember about my science fiction epic is that there was a great deal of talk about the fifth dimension at the start and that later on there was some catastrophe that destroyed photosynthesis (though not on Earth, I think). I remember one sentence word for word: "Whole forests stood sere and brown in midsummer." Why I remember that, I don't know.

The manuscript still existed sometime after I had actually begun to publish my stories. I remember looking at it once (perhaps as late as 1940) and noting that, on the whole, my vocabulary was more complex in that story than in the later stories I published. I was still naïve enough at that time to think that this spoke poorly for the stories I published—as though I had declined in literary ability because my style had grown more direct.

Indeed, it is rather embarrassing as I look back on it now to realize how little I learned about writing through careful study and intelligent consideration of what I read, and how much I advanced through mere intuition. Until I was a published writer, I remained completely ignorant of the fact that there were books on how to write and courses on the subject one could take.

Of course, I sometimes say, quite emphatically, that it is a good thing I never took courses or read books on how to write. I say that it would have spoiled my natural style, that it would have made me observe an artificial caution, that it would have hedged me about with rules that I could not have followed without wearing myself out.

That, of course, may be simple rationalization designed to resign me to what was.

Well, it *was*. Whatever the reason, that's the way it was. I spent all my school time concentrating my real attention on the sciences (chemistry in particular) and mathematics, and paying very little attention to my English courses, which bored me. When it came to writing, I just followed where my intuition led me.

Like the Clayton *Astounding, Wonder Stories* had an unexpected rebirth. It was sold to a chain of pulps that featured several magazines with the word "Thrilling" in the title. Therefore, after a three-month hiatus, *Thrilling Wonder Stories* reached the newsstand with the August 1936 issue. And it was only fifteen cents.

It was rather a comedown. *Wonder Stories* had, to the end, shown a faded gentility, and the Paul covers, which had been tightly associated with science fiction for ten years, had continued to lend it glamour. *Thrilling Wonder Stories*, however, was entirely pulp—in its name, its stories, and even its art work. Indeed, its early covers featured extraterrestrial creatures with protruding eyes to such an extent that fans began to speak of "bug-eyed monsters," a term quickly abbreviated to "bems," as a way of deriding unsophisticated science fiction.

And yet *Thrilling Wonder Stories* had occasional interesting stories in it, too. In its third issue, December 1936, there was "The Brain Stealers of Mars," by John W. Campbell, Jr.

THE BRAIN STEALERS OF MARS

by John W. Campbell, Jr.

CHAPTER I

Imitation of Life

Rod Blake looked up with a deep chuckle. The sky of Mars was almost black, despite the small, brilliant sun, and the brighter stars and planets that shone visibly, Earth most brilliant of all, scarcely sixty million miles away.

"They'll have a fine time chasing us, back there, Ted." He nodded toward the brilliant planet.

Ted Penton smiled beatifically.

"They're probably investigating all our known haunts. It's their own fault if they can't find us—outlawing research on atomic power."

"They had some provocation, you must admit. Koelenberg should have been more careful. When a man takes off some three hundred square miles of territory spang in the center of Europe in an atomic explosion, you can't blame the rest of the world for being a bit skittish about atomic power research."

"But they might have had the wit to see that anybody that did get the secret would not wait around for the Atomic Power Research Death Penalty, but would light out for parts and planets quite unknown and leave the mess in the hands of a lawyer till the fireworks quieted down. It was obvious that when we developed atomic power we'd be the first men to reach Mars, and nobody could follow to bring us back unless they accepted the hated atomic power and used it," argued Blake.

"Wonder how old Jamison Montgomery Palborough made out with our claims," mused Penton. "He said he'd have it right in three months, and this is the third month and the third planet. We'll let the government stew, and sail on, fair friend, sail on. I still say that was a ruined city we saw as we landed."

"I think it was, myself, but I remember the way you did that kangaroo leap on your neck the first time you stepped out on the moon. You certainly saw stars."

"We're professionals at walking under cockeyed gravities now. Moon —Venus—"

"Yes, but I'm still not risking my neck on the attitude of a strange planet *and* a strange race at the same time. We'll investigate the planet a bit first, and yonder mudhole is the first stop. Come on."

They reached the top of one of the long rolling sand dunes and the country was spread out below them. It looked exactly as it had been from the last dune that they had struggled up, just as utterly barren, utterly bleak, and unendingly red. Like an iron planet, badly neglected and rusted.

The mudhole was directly beneath them, an expanse of red and brown slime, dotted here and there with clumps of dark red foliage.

"The stuff looks like Japanese maple," said Blake.

"Evidently doesn't use chlorophyl to get the sun's energy. Let's collect a few samples. You have your violet-gun and I have mine. I guess it's safe to split. There's a large group of things down on the left that look a little different. I'll take them while you go straight ahead. Gather any flowers, fruits, berries or seeds you see. Few leaves—oh, you know. What we got on Venus. General junk. If you find a small plant, put on your gloves and yank it out. If you see a big one, steer clear. Venus had some peculiarly unpleasant specimens."

Blake groaned. "You telling me. I'm the bright boy that fell for that pretty fruit and climbed right up between the stems of a scissor tree. Uhuh. I shoot 'em down. Go ahead, and good luck."

Penton swung off to the left, while Blake slogged ahead to a group of weird-looking plants. They were dome-shaped things, three feet high, with a dozen long, drooping, sword-shaped leaves.

Cautiously Blake tossed a bit of stone into the center of one. It gave off a mournful, drumming boom, but the leaves didn't budge. He tried a rope on one leaf but the leaf neither stabbed, grabbed, nor jerked away, as he had half expected after his lesson with the ferocious plants of Venus. Blake pulled a leaf off, then a few more. The plant acted quite plant-like, which pleasantly surprised him.

The whole region seemed seeded with a number of the things, nearly all about the same size. A few, sprinkled here and there, were in various stages of development, from a few protruding sword-leaves, to little three-inch domes on up to the full-grown plant. Carefully avoiding the larger ones, Rod plucked two small ones and thrust them into his specimen bag. Then he stood off and looked at one of the domes that squatted so dejectedly in the thick, gummy mud.

"I suppose you have some reason for being like that, but a good solid tree would put you all in the shade, and collect all the sunlight going. Which is little enough." He looked at them for some seconds picturing a stout Japanese maple in this outlandish red-brown gum.

He shrugged, and wandered on, seeking some other plant. There were few others. Apparently this particular species throttled out other varieties very thoroughly. He wasn't very anxious anyway; he was much more interested in the ruined city they had seen from the ship. Ted Penton was cautious.

Eventually Blake followed his winding footsteps back toward the ship, and about where his footsteps showed he'd gathered his first samples, he stopped. There was a Japanese maple there. It stood some fifteen feet tall, and the bark was beautifully regular in appearance. The leaves were nearly a quarter of an inch thick, and arranged with a peculiar regularity, as were the branches. But it was very definitely a Japanese maple.

Rod Blake's jaw put a severe strain on the hinges thereof. It dropped some three inches, and Blake stared. He stared with steady, blank gaze at that perfectly impossible Japanese maple. He gawked dumbly. Then his jaw snapped shut abruptly, and he cursed softly. The leaves were stirring gently, and they were not a quarter of an inch thick. They were paper thin, and delicately veined. Further, the tree was visibly taller, and three new branches had started to sprout, irregularly now. They sprouted as he watched, growing not as twigs but as fully formed branches extending themselves gradually. As he stared harder at them they dwindled rapidly to longer twigs, and grew normally.

Rod let out a loud yip, and made tracks rapidly extending themselves toward the point where he'd last seen Ted Penton. Penton's tracks curved off, and Rod steamed down as fast as Mars' light gravity permitted, to pull up short as he rounded a corner of another sword-leaf dome clump. "Ted," he panted, "come over here. There's a—a—weird thing. A—it looks like a Japanese maple, but it doesn't. Because when you look at it, it changes."

Rod stopped, and started back, beckoning Ted.

Ted didn't move.

"I don't know what to say," he said quite clearly, rather panting, and sounding excited, though it was a quite unexciting remark, except for one thing. He said it in Rod Blake's voice!

Rod stiffened. Then he backed away hurriedly, stumbled over his feet and sat down heavily in the sand. "For the love of—Ted—Ted, wh-what did you s-s-say?"

"I don't know wh-what to s-s-say."

Rod groaned. It started out exactly like his own voice, changed rapidly while it spoke, and wound up a fair imitation of Ted's. "Oh, Lord," he groaned, "I'm going back to the ship. In a hurry."

He started away, then looked back over his shoulder. Ted Penton was moving now, swaying on his feet peculiarly. Delicately he picked up his left foot, shook it gently, like a man trying to separate himself from a piece of flypaper. Rod moved even more rapidly than he had before. Long, but rapidly shrinking roots dangled from the foot, gooey mud dropping from them as they shrank into the foot. Rod turned again with the violet-gun in his hand. It thrummed to blasting atomic energy, and a pencil beam of ravening ultra-violet fury shot out and a hazy ball of light surrounded it.

The figure of Ted Penton smoked suddenly, and a hole the size of a golf ball drove abruptly through the center of the head, to the accompaniment of a harsh whine of steam and spurts of oily smoke. The figure did not fall. It slumped. It melted rapidly, like a snow-man in a furnace, the fingers ran together, the remainder of the face dropped, contracted, and became horrible. It was suddenly the face of a man whose pouched and dulled eyes had witnessed and enjoyed every evil the worlds knew, weirdly glowing eyes that danced and flamed for a moment in screaming fury of deadly hate—and dissolved with the last dissolution of the writhing face.

And the arms grew long, very long and much wider. Rod stood frozen while the very wide and rapidly widening arms beat up and down. The thing took off and flapped awkwardly away, and for an instant the last trace of the hate-filled eyes glittered again in the sun.

Rod Blake sat down and laughed. He laughed, and laughed again at the very funny sight of the melting face on the bat-bodied thing that had flown away with a charred hole in the middle of its grape-fruit-sized head. He laughed even louder when another Ted-Penton-thing came around the corner of the vegetable clump, on the run. He aimed at the center of its head. "Fly away!" he yelled as he pressed the little button down.

This one was cleverer. It ducked. "Rod—for the love of—Rod, shut up," it spoke.

Rod stopped, and considered slowly. This one talked with Ted Penton's voice. As it got up again he aimed more carefully and flashed again. He wanted it to fly away too. It ducked again, in another direction this time, and ran in rapidly. Rod got up hastily and ran. He fell suddenly as some fibrous thing lashed out from behind and wrapped itself unbreakably about his arms and body, binding him helplessly.

Penton looked down at him, panting heavily.

"What's the trouble, Rod; and why in blazes were you shooting your gun at me?"

Rod heard himself laugh again, uncontrollably. The sight of Ted's worried face reminded him of the flying thing, with the melted face. Like an overheated wax figure. Penton reached out a deliberate hand and cracked him over the face, hard. In a moment Rod steadied, and Penton removed the noose from his arms and body. Blake sighed with relief.

"Thank God, it's you, Ted," he said. "Listen, I saw you—*you*—not thirty seconds ago. You stood over there, and I spoke to you. You answered in *my* voice. I started off, and your feet came up out of the ground with roots on them, like a plant's. I shot you through the forehead, and you melted down like a wax doll to a bat-thing that sprouted wings and flew away."

"Uhh—" said Penton soothingly. "Funny, at that. Why were you looking for me?"

"Because there's a Japanese maple where I was that grew while my back was turned, and changed its leaves while I looked at it."

"Oh, Lord," said Penton unhappily, looking at Rod. Then more soothingly, "I think we'd better look at it."

Rod led the way back on his tracks. When the maple should have been in sight, it wasn't at all. When they reached the spot where Rod's tracks showed it should have been, it wasn't there. There was only a somewhat wilted sword-bush. Rod stared blankly at it, then he went over and felt it cautiously. It remained placidly squatted, a slightly bedraggled lump of vegetation.

"That's where it was," said Blake dully. "But it isn't there any more. I know it was there."

"It must have been an—er—mirage," decided Penton. "Let's get back to the ship. We've had enough walking practice."

Rod followed him, wonderingly shaking his head. He was so wrapped up in his thoughts, that he nearly fell over Penton, when Ted stopped with a soft, unhappy, gurgling noise. Ted turned around and looked at Rod carefully. Then he looked ahead again.

"Which," he asked at length, "is you?"

Rod looked ahead of Penton, over his shoulder. Another Rod was also standing in front of Penton. "My God," said Rod, "it's me this time!"

"I am, of course," said the one in front. It said it in Rod Blake's voice. Ted looked at it, and finally shut his eyes.

"I don't believe it. Not at all. *Wo bist du gewesen, mein Freund?*"

"*Was sagst du?*" said the one in front. "But why the *Deutsch?*"

Ted Penton sat down slowly and thoughtfully. Rod Blake stared at Rod Blake blankly, slightly indignant.

"Let me think," said Penton unhappily. "There must be some way to tell. Rod went away from me, and then I come around the corner and find him laughing insanely. He takes a shot at me. But it looks, and talks like Rod. But he says crazy things. Then I go for a walk with him—or it—and meet another one that at least seems less insane than the first one. Well, well. I know German of course, and so does Rod. Evidently this thing can read minds. Must be like a chameleon, only more so."

"What do you mean?" asked Rod Blake. It doesn't particularly matter which one.

"A chameleon can assume any color it wants to at will. Lots of animals have learned to imitate other animals for safety, but it takes them generations to do it. This thing, apparently, can assume any shape or color at will. A minute ago it decided the best form for the locality was a sword-bush. Some of these things must be real plants then. Rod thought of a maple tree, thought of the advantages of a maple tree, so it decided to try that, having read his mind. That was why it was wilted-looking; this isn't the right kind of country for maple trees. It lost water too fast. So it went back to the sword-bush.

"Now this one has decided to try being Rod Blake, clothes and all. But I haven't the foggiest notion which one *is* Rod Blake. It won't do a bit of good to try him on languages we know, because he can read our minds. I know there must be some way. There must—there must—Oh yes. It's simple. Rod, just burn me a hole in that thing with your violet-gun."

Rod reached for his gun at once with a sigh of relief and triggered quickly. The phoney Rod melted hastily. About half of it got down into the boiling mud before Rod incinerated the rest with the intense ultra-violet flare of the pistol. Rod sighed. "Thank the Lord it was me. I wasn't sure for a while, myself."

Ted shook himself, put his head in his hands, and rocked slowly. "By the Nine Gods of the Nine Planets, what a world! Rod, for the love of heaven, stay with me hereafter. Permanently. And whatever you do, don't lose that pistol. They can't grow a real violet-gun, but if they pick one up, may God help us. Let's get back to the ship, and away from this damned place. I thought you were mad. My error. It's just the whole bloody planet that's mad."

"I was—for a while. Let's move."

They moved. They moved hastily back across the sand dunes to the ship.

CHAPTER II

The Secret of the Thushol

"They're centaurs," gasped Blake. "Will you look at that one over there —a nice little calico. There's a beautiful little strawberry roan. What people! Wonder why the city is so dilapidated, if the people are still here in some numbers. Set 'er down, will you, Ted. They haven't anything dangerous, or they'd have a better city."

"Uhmmm—I suppose that's right. But I'd hate to have one of those fellows nudge me. They must weigh something noticeable, even here—about twelve hundred pounds back on Earth. I'm setting down in that square. You keep your hand on that ten-inch ion-gun while I step out."

The ship settled with a soft *thumpf* in the deep sandy dust of the ruined city square. Half a hundred of the centaurs were trotting leisurely up, with a grizzled old Martian in the lead, his mane sparse and coarse. Ted Penton stepped out of the lock.

"Pholshth," the Martian said after a moment's inspection. He extended his hands out horizontally from his shoulders, palms upward and empty.

"Friends," said Ted, extending his arms in a similar gesture, "I am Penton."

"Fasthun Loshthu," explained the centaur, indicating himself. "Penshun."

"He sounds like an ex-soldier," came Blake's voice softly. "Pension. Is he O.K.?"

"I think so. You can leave that post anyway, and shut off the main atomics, start auxiliary B, and close the rooms. Lock the controls with the combination and come on out. Bring your ion-gun as well as your ultraviolet. Lock the lock doors."

"Blazes. I want to come out this afternoon. Oh well, O.K." Blake went to work hurriedly and efficiently. It was some thirty seconds before he was through in the power room. He stepped eagerly into the lock.

He stopped dead. Penton was on his back, moving feebly, the old centaur bent over him, with his long, powerful fingers fixed around the man's throat. Penton's head was shaking slowly back and forth on the end of his neck, in a loose, rather detached-looking way.

Blake roared and charged out of the lock, his two powerful pistols hastily restored to his holsters. He charged out—and sailed neatly over the centaur's back, underestimating Mars' feeble grip. In an instant he was on his feet again, and returning toward his friend when a skillful left forefoot caught his legs, and sent him tumbling as the heavy bulk of an agile young centaur landed on his back. Blake turned; a smaller, lighter body far more powerfully muscled. In a moment the Earthman broke the centaurs' grip and started through the six or seven others that surrounded him.

A grunted word of command dissolved the mêlée, and Blake stood up, leaping toward Penton.

Penton sat on the ground, rocking slowly back and forth, his head between his hands. "Oh, Lord, they all do it here."

"Ted—are you all right?"

"Do I sound it?" Penton asked unhappily. "That old bird just opened up my skull and poured a new set of brains in. Hypnotic teaching—a complete university education in thirty seconds—all done with hypnotism and no mirrors used. They have the finest education system. God preserve us from it."

"*Shthuntho ishthu thiu lomal?*" asked the old Martian pleasantly.

"*Ishthu psoth lonthul timul,*" groaned Penton. "The worst of it is, it works. I know his language as well as I know English." Suddenly he managed a slight grin. He pointed to Blake and said: "Blake *omo phusthu ptsoth.*"

The old centaur's lined, sparsely bearded face smiled like a pleased child's. Blake looked at him uneasily.

"I don't like that fellow's fa—" He stopped, hypnotized. He walked toward the old Martian with blank eyes and the grace of an animated tailor's dummy. He lay down in sections, and the old Martian's long, supple fingers circled his neck. Gently they massaged the back of his spine up to the base of his skull.

Penton smiled sourly from where he sat. "Oh, you don't like his face, eh? Wait and see how you like his system."

The centaur straightened. Slowly Blake sat up. His head continued to nod and weave in a detached sort of way, till he gingerly reached up, felt around for it and took it firmly in his hands. He rested his elbows on his knees.

"We didn't both have to know his blasted language," he managed bitterly at last. "Languages always did give me headaches anyway."

Penton watched him unsympathetically.

"I hate repeating things, and you'll find it useful, anyway."

"You are from the third planet," the Martian stated politely.

Penton looked at him in surprise, started up, then rose to his feet gingerly.

"Get up slowly, Blake, I advise you for your own good." Then to the Martian: "Why, yes. But you knew! How?"

"My great-great grandfather told me of this trip to the third planet before he died. He was one of those that returned."

"Returned? You Martians have been to Earth?" gasped Blake.

"I guessed that," said Penton softly. "They're evidently the centaurs of legend. And I think they didn't go alone from this p¹anet."

"Our people tried to establish a colony there, many, many years ago. It didn't succeed. They died of lung diseases faster than they could cross space. The main reason they went in the first place was to get away from the *thushol*. But the *thushol* simply imitated local Earth-animals and thrived. So the people came back. We built many ships, hoping that since we couldn't go, the *thushol* would. But they didn't like Earth." He shook his head sorrowfully.

"The *thushol*. So that's what you call 'em." Blake sighed. "They must be a pest."

"They were then. They aren't much any more."

"Oh, they don't bother you any more?" asked Penton.

"No," said the old centaur apathetically. "We're so used to them."

"How do you tell them from the thing they're imitating?" Penton asked grimly. "That's what I need to know."

"It used to bother us because we couldn't," Loshthu sighed. "But it doesn't any more."

"I know—but how do you tell them apart? Do you do it by mind-reading?"

"Oh, no. We don't try to tell them apart. That way they don't bother us any more."

Penton looked at Loshthu thoughtfully for some time. Blake rose gingerly, and joined Penton in his enwrapped contemplation of the grizzled Martian. "Uhmmmm," said Penton at last, "I suppose that is one way of looking at it. I should think it would make business rather difficult though. Also social relations, not knowing whether it was your wife or just a real good imitation."

"I know. We found it so for many years," Loshthu agreed. "That was why our people wanted to move to Earth. But later they found that three of the ship commanders were *thushol*, so the people came back to Mars where they could live at least as easily as the *thushol*."

Penton mentally digested this for some moments, while the half hundred centaurs about stood patiently, apathetically motionless.

"We have myths on Earth of centaurs, people like you, and of magic creatures who seemed one thing, but when captured became snakes or tigers or other unpleasant beasts, but if held long enough reverted to human shape and would then grant a wish. Yes, the *thushol* are intelligent; they could have granted a simple Earth barbarian's wish."

Loshthu shook his head slowly.

"They are not intelligent, I believe. Maybe they are. But they have perfect memories for detail. They would imitate one of our number, attend our schools, and so learn all we knew. They never invented anything for themselves."

"What brought about the tremendous decline in your civilization? The *thushol?*"

The centaur nodded.

"We forgot how to make space ships and great cities. We hoped that would discourage the *thushol* so they would leave us. But they forgot too, so it didn't help."

"Good Lord," Blake sighed, "how in the name of the Nine Planets do you live with a bunch like that?"

Loshthu looked at Blake slowly.

"Ten," he said. "Ten planets. You can't see the tenth with any practicable instrument till you get out beyond Jupiter. Our people discovered it from Pluto."

Blake stared at him owlishly. "But how can you live with this gang? With a civilization like that—I should think you'd have found some means of destroying them."

"We did. We destroyed all the *thushol*. Some of the *thushol* helped us, but we thought that they were our own people. It happened because a very wise, but very foolish philosopher calculated how many *thushol* could live parasitically on our people. Naturally the *thushol* took his calculations to heart. Thirty-one percent of us are *thushol*."

Blake looked around with a swiftly unhappy eye.

"You mean—some of these here are *thushol?*" he asked.

Loshthu nodded.

"Always. They reproduced very slowly at first, in the form of an animal that was normally something like us, and reproduced as did other animals. But then they learned to imitate the amœbæ when they studied in our laboratories. Now they simply split. One big one will split into several small ones, and each small one will eat one of the young of our people, and take its place. So we never know which is which. It used to worry us." Loshthu shook his head slowly.

Blake's hair rose slightly away from his head, and his jaw dropped away. "My God," he gasped. "Why didn't you do something?"

"If we killed one we suspected, we might be wrong, which would kill our own child. If we didn't, and just believe it our own child anyway, it at least gave us the comfort of believing it. And if the imitation is so perfect one can't tell the difference, what is the difference?"

Blake sat down again, quietly.

"Penton," he sighed, at length, "those three months are up, let's get back to Earth—fast."

Penton looked at him. "I wanted to a long time back. Only I thought of something else. Sooner or later, some other man is going to come here with atomic power, and if he brings some of those *thushol* back to Earth with him, accidentally, thinking it's his best friend—well, I'd rather kill my own child than live with one of those, but I'd rather not do either. They can reproduce as fast as they can eat, and if they eat like an amœba —God help us. If you maroon one on a desert island, it will turn into a fish, and swim home. If you put it in jail it will turn into a snake and go down the drain pipe. If you dump it in the desert it will turn into a cactus and get along real nice, thank you."

"Good God."

"And they won't believe us, of course. I'm sure as blazes not going to take one back to prove it. I'll just have to get some kind of proof from this Loshthu."

"I hadn't thought of that. What can we get?"

"All I can think of is to see what they can let us have, then take all we can, and make a return trip with reputable and widely believed zoologists and biologists to look into this thing. Evolution has produced some weird freaks, but this is a freakier weirdness than has ever been conceived."

"I still don't really believe it," Blake said. "The only thing I am firmly convinced of is my headache."

"It's real enough and logical enough. Logical as hell. And hell on Earth if they ever get there. Evolution is always trying to produce an animal that can survive anywhere, conquer all enemies, the fittest of the surviving fit. All life is based on one thing: protoplasm. Basically, it's the same in every creature, every living thing, plant and animal, amœba and man. It is just modified slightly, hooked together in slightly different ways. The *thushol* are built of protoplasm—but infinitely more adaptable protoplasm. They can do something about it, make it take the form of a bone cell and be part of a thigh bone, or be a nerve cell in a brain. From some of that ten-second-college-course Loshthu poured into me, I gather that at first the *thushol* were good imitations outside, but if you cut into one, you could see that the organs weren't there. Now they have everything. They went through Martian medical colleges, of course, and know all about what makes a centaur tick, and so they make themselves with the same kind of tickers. Oh, very nice."

"They don't know much about us. Maybe with the X-ray fluoroscope screen we could have told those imitations of us," suggested Blake.

"Oh, no, by no means. If we knew the right form, they'd read it in our minds, and have it. Adaptive protoplasm. Just think, you couldn't kill it in an African jungle, because when a lion came along, it would be a little, lady lion, and when an elephant showed up, it would be a helpless baby elephant. If a snake bit it, I suppose the damned thing would turn into something immune to snake bites—a tree, or something like that. I just wonder where it keeps the very excellent brain it evidently has."

"Well, let's find out what Loshthu can offer us by way of proofs."

CHAPTER III
Mind-Readers and Company

It developed that the Martians had once had museums. They still had them, because nobody was sufficiently interested to disturb their age-long quiet. Martians lived centuries, and their memories were long; but once or twice in a lifetime did a Martian enter the ancient museums.

Penton and Blake spent hours in them, intensive hours under Loshthu's guidance. Loshthu had nothing but time, and Penton and Blake didn't want to linger. They worked rapidly, collecting thin metal sheaves of documents, ancient mechanisms, a thousand things. They baled them with rope that they had brought from the ship when they moved it nearer the museum. Finally, after hours of labor, bleary-eyed from want of sleep, they started out again to the ship.

They stepped out of the gloomy dusk of the museum into the sun-lit entranceway. Immediately, from behind a dozen pillars, a leaping, flashing group of men descended upon them, tore the books, the instruments, the data sheaves from their hands. They were upset, slugged, trampled on and spun around. There were shouts and cries and curses.

Then there was silence. Twelve Pentons and thirteen Blakes sat, lay or stood about on the stone stairway. Their clothes were torn, their faces and bodies bruised, there was even one black eye, and another developing swiftly. But twelve Pentons looked exactly alike, each clasping a bit of data material. Thirteen Blakes were identical, each carrying a bit of factual mustiness under his arm or in his hand.

Loshthu looked at them, and his lined, old face broke into a pleased smile. "Ah," he said. "There are more of you. Perhaps some can stay with us to talk now."

Penton looked up at Loshthu, all the Pentons did. Penton was quite sure he was *the* Penton, but he couldn't think of any way to prove it. It was fairly evident that *thushol* had decided to try Earth again. He began to wonder just—"

"Loshthu, just why," asked one of the Pentons in Penton's voice, "did the *thushol* not stay on Earth if they could live there?"

Penton was quite sure he had been the one to think of that partic—

"Pardon me, but wasn't that the question I was going to ask?" said another Penton in well-controlled fury. Penton smiled gently. It seemed evident that—

"I can apparently be spared the trouble of doing my own talking. You all help so," said one of the numerous Pentons angrily.

"Say, how in hell are we going to tell who's who?" demanded one of the Blakes abruptly.

"That damned mind-thief stole my question before I had a chance—"

"Why you—you—you talking! I was just about—"

"I think," said one of the Pentons wearily, "you might as well stop getting peeved, Blake, because they'll all act peeved when you do. What do you know. I beat all my imitators to the draw on that remark. A noble achievement, you'll find, Rod. But you might just as well pipe down, and I'll pipe down, and we'll see what our good friend, Loshthu, has to say."

"Eh," sighed Loshthu. "You mean about the *thushol* leaving Earth? They did not like it. Earth is a poor planet, and the people were barbarians. Evidently they are not so now. But the *thushol* do not like work, and they found richer sustenance on Mars."

"I thought so," said Penton. (Does it matter which one?) "They've decided that Earth is richer than Mars now, and want a new host. Don't draw that pistol, Blake! Unfortunately, my friend, we had twenty-five ion-guns and twenty-five violet-guns made up. If we'd had more we would have more companions. We were exceedingly unfortunate in equipping ourselves so well in the matter of clothing, and being so thoughtful as to plan all of it right, so we carried a lot of each of the few kinds. Exceedingly. However, I think we can improve things a little bit. I happen to remember that one ion-gun is out of commission, and I had the coils out of two of the violet-guns to repair them. That makes three guns out of service. We will each stand up and fire, one at a time, at the sand in front there. The line forms on the right."

The line formed. "Now," continued that particular Penton, "we will each fire, beginning with myself, one at a time. First ion, then violet. When one of us evidences lack of a serviceable gun, the others will join in removing him rapidly but carefully. Are we ready? Yes?" That Penton held up his ion-gun, and pushed the button.

It didn't fire, and immediately the portico stank with his smoke.

"That's one," said the next Penton. He raised his ion-gun and fired. Then his violet-gun. Then he raised it and fired again, at a rapidly dissolving Blake. "That makes two. That one evidently found, when we fired at the first one, that his didn't work. We have one more to eliminate. Next?"

Presently another Blake vanished. "Well, well," said Penton pleasantly, "the Blake-Penton odds are even. Any suggestions?"

"Yes," said Blake tensely. "I've been thinking of a patch I put in one suit that I ripped on Venus." Another Blake vanished under the mutual fire.

"There's one more thing I want to know. Why in blazes are those phonies so blasted willing to kill each other, and though they know which is which, don't kill us? And how did they enter the ship?" Rod demanded. Or at least a Rod.

"They," said two Pentons at once. Another one looked at them. "Bad timing, boys. Rodney, my son, we used a combination lock. These gentlemen are professional mind-readers. Does that explain their possession of the guns? I've been thinking right along of one way to eliminate these excessive excrescences, consisting of you going into a huddle with your tribe, and eliminating all but the one you know to be yourself, and I doing the same. Unfortunately, while they're perfectly willing to kill each other so long as they don't die, they will prevent their own deaths by adequate, unfortunately adequate defense.

"Now since these little gun tests and others have been made I think it fairly evident that we are not going to leave this planet until the two right men are chosen and only two go into that ship with us. Fortunately they can't go without us, because while they can read minds, it takes more than knowledge to navigate a space ship, at least such knowledge as they can get from us. It takes understanding, which mere memory will not supply. They need us.

"We will, therefore, march dutifully to the ship, and each of us will replace his guns carefully in the prepared racks. I know that I'm the right Penton—but you don't. So no movement will be made without the unanimous agreement of all Pentons and Blakes."

Blake looked up, white-faced.

"If this wasn't so world-shakingly serious, it would be the damnedest comic opera that ever happened. I'm afraid to give up my gun."

"If we all give them up, I think it puts us even. We have some advantage in that they don't want to kill us, and if worst comes to worst, we could take them to Earth, making damned sure that they didn't get away. On Earth we could have protoplasmic tests made that would tell the story. By the way, that suggests something. Yes indeed, I think we can make tests here. Let us repair to this ship."

CHAPTER IV

Penton's Strategy

The Blakes sat down and stayed down. "Ted, what in blazes can we do?" His voice was almost tearful. "You can't tell one of these ghastly things from another. You can't tell one from me. We can't—"

"Oh, God," said another Blake, "that's not me. That's just another one of those damned mind stealers."

Another one groaned hopelessly.

"That wasn't either." They all looked helplessly at the line of Pentons. "I don't even know who's my friend."

Penton nodded. All the Pentons nodded, like a grotesquely solemn chorus preparing to recite some blessing. They smiled in superhuman unity. "That's all right," they said in perfect harmony. "Well, well. A new stunt. Now we all talk together. That makes things easier. I think there may be a way to tell the difference. But you must absolutely trust me, Blake. You must give up your guns, putting all faith in my ability to detect the right one, and if I'm wrong, realize that I will not know. We can try such simple tests as alcohol, whiskey, to see if it makes them drunk, and pepper to see if it burns their tongues—"

"It won't work," said Blake tensely. "Lord, Penton, I can't give up my guns—I won't—"

Penton, all the Pentons smiled gently. "I'm half again as fast as you are, Blake, and no Martian-born imitation of you is going to be faster. Maybe these Martian imitations of me are as fast as I am. But you know perfectly well that I could ray the whole gang of you, all ten of you, out of existence before any one of you could move a finger. You know that, don't you, Rod?"

"Lord, yes, but Ted, Ted, don't do that—don't make me give up my guns—I've got to keep them. Why should I give up mine, if you keep yours?"

"That probably was not you speaking, Rod, but it doesn't matter. If it wasn't what you thought, we could do something about it. Therefore, that is what you wanted to say, just as this is what I wanted to say, whether I said it or not. Oh, Lord preserve us. It talks with my voice! But anyway, the situation is this; one of us has to have unquestioned superiority over the other gang. Then, the one with the whip hand can develop proof of identity, and enforce his decisions. As it is, we can't."

"Let me be that one, then," snapped one Blake.

"I didn't mean that," sighed another. "That wasn't me."

"Yes it was," said the first. "I spoke without thinking. Go ahead. But how are you going to make the others give up their guns? I'm willing. You can't make them?"

"Oh, yes I can. I have my faithful friends, here," said Penton grimly, his eleven hands waving to his eleven counterparts. "They agree with me this far, being quite utterly selfish."

"But what's your system. Before I put my neck in the noose, I have to know that noose isn't going to tighten on it."

"If I had a sound system in mind—I'm carefully refraining from developing one—they'd read it, weigh it, and wouldn't agree at all. They still have hopes. You see that pepper and alcohol system won't work perfectly because they can read in my mind the proper reaction, and be drunk, or have an inflamed tongue at will, being perfect actors. I'm going to try just the same. Rod, if you ever trusted me, trust me now."

"All right, come on. We'll go to the ship, and any one of these things that doesn't part with its gun is *not* me. Ray it."

Blake rose jerkily, all ten of him, and went down to the ship.

The Pentons followed faithfully after. Abruptly Penton rayed one Blake. His shoulder blades had humped curiously and swiftly. Wings were developing. "That helps," said Penton, holstering his guns.

The Blakes went on, white-faced. They put the weapons in the racks in the lock stoically. The Martians had seen the, to them, inconceivably swift movements of Penton's gun hands, and Penton knew that he, himself, had done the raying that time. But he still didn't know a way to prove it without causing a general mêlée which would bring about their own deaths. That wasn't so important. The trouble was that given fifty years, the rest of the world would descend on this planet unwarned. Then all Earth would be destroyed. Not with flame and sword and horrible casualty lists, but silently and undetectably.

The Blakes came out, unarmed. They shuffled and moved about uneasily, tensely, under the watchful eyes of eleven Pentons armed with terrifically deadly weapons.

Several Pentons went into the ship, to come out bearing pepper, saccharine tablets, alcohol, the medicine chest. One of them gathered them together and looked them over. "We'll try pepper," he said, rather unhappily. "Line up!"

The Blakes lined up, hesitantly. "I'm putting my life in your hands, Ted," said two of them in identical, plaintive tones.

Four Pentons laughed shortly. "I know it. Line up. Come and get it."

"First," he sighed, after a moment, "stick out the tongue, patient."

With unsteady hands he put a bit of pepper from the shaker on the fellow's tongue. The tongue snapped in instantly, the Blake clapped his hands to his mouth, gurgling unpleasantly. "Waaaar!" he gasped. "Waar—achooo—damnt!"

With hands like flashing light, Penton pulled his own, and a neighbor's ion-gun. In a fiftieth of a second all but the single gagging, choking, coughing Blake were stinking, smoking, swiftly dissolving and flowing rubbish. The other Penton methodically helped destroy them.

Blake stopped gagging in surprise.

"My God, it might not have been the right one!" he gasped.

The ten Pentons sighed softly. "That finally proves it. Thank God. Definitely. That leaves me to find. And it won't work again, because while you can't read my mind to find the trick that told, these brothers of mine have. The very fact that you don't know how I knew, proves that I was right."

Blake stared at him dumbly. "I was the first one—" he managed between a cough and a sneeze.

"Exactly. Go on inside. Do something intelligent. Use your head. See what you can think of to locate me. You have to use your head in some such way that they don't mind-read it first, though. Go ahead."

Blake went, slow-footed. The first thing he did was to close the lock-door, so that he was safely alone in the ship. Blake went into the control room, donned an air-suit complete with helmet, and pushed a control handle over. Then a second. Presently he heard curious bumpings and thumpings, and strange floppings and whimperings. He went back rapidly, and rayed a supply chest and two crates of Venusian specimens that had sprouted legs and were rapidly growing arms to grasp ray pistols. The air in the ship began to look thick and greenish; it was colder.

Contentedly Blake watched, and opened all the room doors. Another slithering, thumping noise attracted him, and with careful violet-gun work he removed an unnoticed, extra pipe that was crawling from the cross-brace hangers. It broke up into lengths that rolled about unpleasantly. Rod rayed them till the smallest only, the size of golf balls with curious blue-veined legs, staggered about uncertainly. Finally even they stopped wriggling.

Half an hour Rod waited, while the air grew very green and thick. Finally, to make sure, he started some other apparatus, and watched the thermometer go down, down till moisture grew on the walls and became frost, and no more changes took place. Then he went around with an opened ion-gun with a needle beam and poked everything visible with it.

The suction fans cleared out the chlorine-fouled atmosphere in two minutes, and Blake sat down wearily. He flipped over the microphone switch and spoke into the little disc. "I've got my hand on the main ion-gun control. Penton, I love you like a brother, but I love Earth more. If you can induce your boy friends to drop their guns in a neat pile and retire—

O. K. If not, and I mean if not within thirty seconds, this ion-gun is going into action and there won't be any more Pentons. Now, drop!"

Grinning broadly, with evident satisfaction, ten Pentons deposited twenty heart-cores of ultra-essence of destruction, and moved off. "Way off," said Blake grimly. They moved.

Blake collected twenty guns. Then he went back into the ship. There was a fine laboratory at one end, and with grim satisfaction, he took down three cotton-stoppered tubes, being very careful to handle them with rubber gloves. "You never did man a good turn before, tetanus, but I hope you spread high, wide and handsome here—"

He dumped them into a beaker of water, and took beaker and glass down to the lock and out. The ten waited at a distance.

"All right, Penton. I happen to know you took a shot of tetanus anti-vaccine some while ago, and are immune. Let's see if those blasted brain stealers can steal the secret of something we know how to make, but don't know anything about. They can gain safety by turning into a chicken, which is immune, but not as human creatures. That's a concentrated dose of tetanus. Go drink it. We can wait ten days if we have to."

Ten Pentons marched boldly up to the beaker, resting beside the ship. One stepped forward to the glass—and nine kept right on stepping. They stepped into the lee of the ship where the ion-gun could not reach.

Blake helped Penton into the ship with a broad grin.

"Am I right?"

"You're right," sighed Penton, "but God knows why. You can't get tetanus by swallowing it, and lockjaw doesn't develop so quickly as ten days."

"I didn't know for sure," grinned Blake. "They were too busy trying to find out what I was doing to follow your mind. Ah—there they go. Will you ray them or shall I?" asked Blake politely, sighting the ion-gun at the nine flapping, rapidly vanishing things scuttling across the red, rusty planet. The ship dipped sharply in pursuit. "There's one thing—ahhh—" he straightened as the incredible glare died in thin air. "I want to know. How in blazes did you pick me out?"

"To do what you did requires some five hundred different sets of muscles in a beautifully coordinated neuromuscular hookup, which I didn't believe those things could imitate without a complete dissection. I took the chance it was you."

"Five hundred sets of muscles! What the heck did I do?"

"You sneezed."

Rod Blake blinked slowly, and slowly his jaw tested again its supports and their flexibility.

John Campbell is, of course, the most unusual personality in all the history of magazine science fiction. He sold a story to *Amazing Stories* when he was only seventeen, but the editor lost it and Campbell had no carbon copy. His first published story, "When the Atoms Failed," appeared in the January 1930 issue of that magazine. He was not quite twenty then.

At the time, Edward E. Smith was the outstanding science fiction writer, thanks to his *Skylark of Space*. Its sequel, *Skylark Three*, a three-part serial appearing in the August, September, and October 1930 *Amazing Stories*, made his position secure as the champion of the "super-science epic." (In later times, such stories were referred to as "space opera"* by the increasingly sophisticated science fiction readers.)

No sooner had *Skylark Three* concluded, when Campbell's story "Solarite" appeared in the November 1930 *Amazing Stories*. It was the second story in what was eventually called the "Arcot, Wade and Morey" series. In these, Campbell challenged Smith's position and managed to share the throne with him.

I was fascinated by the super-science epic, as most science fiction readers of the thirties were. I never wrote anything that could be considered one in the strict sense of the term, but the Foundation trilogy was my own version of the form, with the accent on politics and sociology rather than on physical science.

But though Smith remained with the super-science epic throughout his career, Campbell did not. In the November 1934 *Astounding Stories*, Campbell published a story called "Twilight." For it, he used the pen name Don A. Stuart (a form of his then wife's maiden name), in order, deliberately, to dissociate it from the super-science associations of his name. "Twilight" was the second story (a half year after Weinbaum's "A Martian Odyssey," which was the first) to point the way to another and better level of science fiction. The accent was on people, on emotion, and on good, understated writing.

I did not miss it as I missed "A Martian Odyssey." I read it when it first appeared—and I didn't like it. Indeed, I liked none of the dozen stories Campbell wrote under the Stuart pseudonym in the next three years.

The fault was mine. I have reread some of them since, and I am ashamed of myself for having remained stuck at the lower level. I had found them too quiet, too downbeat, too moving. I wanted action and adventure, and I was simply incapable of following Campbell up to the Stuart level. I eventually did, but it took a few years. I was not as good a man as Campbell was.*

---

* I did not, by the way, know that Stuart was really Campbell until after I met John for the first time, in 1938. See *The Early Asimov*.

But Campbell was not content to be Don A. Stuart alone. He had tackled Smith when Smith was king, in 1930. Now, in 1936, he tackled Weinbaum when Weinbaum was king. "The Brain Stealers of Mars" was the first of five "Penton and Blake stories." In each one, the two men were up against the dangerous life-forms of another planet.

It impressed me, and for quite a while I tried to write Penton and Blake stories. An early example, which was a complete failure, was "Ring Around the Sun." Then I wrote "Reason," which involved Gregory Powell and Michael Donovan. I wrote and published four of what I called in my own mind "Powell and Donovan stories" in conscious and deliberate imitation of Penton and Blake.

However, the Powell and Donovan stories involved my positronic robots and the three laws of robotics, and eventually Susan Calvin took over. As often happened in my case (and I suppose in the case of other writers, too), no matter how I tried to shape my stories, they ended up shaping me.

Toward the end of 1936, one more short story in *Amazing Stories* impressed me. It was "Devolution," again by Edmond Hamilton, in the December issue. It's the third story by him I couldn't forget from my teen-age years, and all three had to do, one way or another, with the origin or development of life, and all took a sardonic view of mankind.

(Oh, before I give you the story. The issue in which it appears contains the second part of a serial by John W. Campbell, Jr. It was "Uncertainty," and it's too long for inclusion in this book. But, at random, I flipped a page and read, "A rain of atomic bombs struck the protected metal . . ." Oh, we science fiction readers were escaping, all right. The rest of the world didn't worry about atomic bombs for nine more years.)

DEVOLUTION

by Edmond Hamilton

Ross had ordinarily the most even of tempers, but four days of canoe travel in the wilds of North Quebec had begun to rasp it. On this, their fourth stop on the bank of the river to camp for the night, he lost control and for a few moments stood and spoke to his two companions in blistering terms.

His black eyes snapped and his darkly unshaven handsome young face worked as he spoke. The two biologists listened to him without reply at first. Gray's blond young countenance was indignant but Woodin, the older biologist, just listened impassively with his gray eyes level on Ross' angry face.

When Ross stopped for breath, Woodin's calm voice struck in. "Are you finished?"

Ross gulped as though about to resume his tirade, then abruptly got hold of himself. "Yes, I'm finished," he said sullenly.

"Then listen to me," said Woodin, like a middle-aged father admonishing a sulky child.

"You're working yourself up over nothing. Neither Gray nor I have made one complaint yet. Neither of us have once said that we disbelieve what you told us."

"You haven't *said* you disbelieve, no!" Ross exclaimed with anger suddenly reflaring. "But don't you suppose I can tell what you're thinking?

"You think I told you a fairy story about the things I saw from my plane, don't you? You think I dragged you two up here on the wildest wild-goose chase, to look for incredible creatures that could never have existed. You believe that, don't you?"

"Oh, *damn* these mosquitoes!" said Gray, slapping viciously at his neck and staring with unfriendly eyes at the aviator.

Woodin took command. "We'll go over this after we've made camp. Jim, get out the duffle-bags. Ross, will you rustle firewood?"

They both glared at him and at each other but grudgingly they obeyed. The tension eased for the time.

By the time darkness fell on the little riverside clearing, the canoe was drawn up on the bank, their trim little balloon-silk tent had been erected, and a fire crackled in front of it. Gray fed the fire with fat knots of pine while Woodin cooked over it coffee, hot cakes and the inevitable bacon.

The firelight wavered feebly up toward the tall trunks of giant hemlocks that walled the little clearing on three sides. It lit up their three khaki-clad, stained figures and the irregular white block of the tent. It gleamed out there on the riffles of the McNorton, chuckling softly as it flowed on toward the Little Whale.

They ate silently, and as wordlessly cleaned the pans with bunches of grass. Woodin got his pipe going, the other two lit crumpled cigarettes, and then they sprawled for a time by the fire, listening to the chuckling, whispering river-sounds, the sighing sough of the higher hemlock branches, the lonesome cheeping of insects.

Woodin finally knocked his pipe out on his bootheel and sat up.

"All right," he said, "now we'll settle this argument we were having."

Ross looked a little shamefaced. "I guess I got too hot about it," he said subduedly. Then added, "But all the same, you fellows do more than half disbelieve me."

Woodin shook his head calmly. "No, we don't, Ross. When you told us that you'd seen creatures unlike anything ever heard of while flying over this wilderness, Gray and I both believed you."

"If we hadn't, do you think two busy biologists would have dropped their work to come up here with you into these unending woods and look for the things you saw?"

"I know, I know," said the aviator unsatisfiedly. "You think I saw something queer and you're taking a chance that it will be worth the trouble of coming up here after.

"But you don't believe what I've told you about the looks of the things. You think that sounds too queer to be true, don't you?"

For the first time Woodin hesitated in answering. "After all, Ross," he said indirectly, "one's eyes can play tricks when you're only glimpsing things for a moment from a plane a mile up."

"Glimpsing them?" echoed Ross. "I tell you, man, I saw them as clearly as I see you. A mile up, yes, but I had my big binoculars with me and was using them when I saw them.

"It was near here, too, just east of the forks of the McNorton and the Little Whale. I was streaking south in a hurry for I'd been three weeks up at that government mapping survey on Hudson's Bay. I wanted to place myself by the river forks so I brought my plane down a little and used my binoculars.

"Then, down there in a clearing by the river, I saw something glisten and saw—the things. I tell you, they were incredible, but just the same I saw them clear! I forgot all about the river forks in the moment or two I stared down at them.

"They were big, glistening things like heaps of shining jelly, so translucent that I could see the ground through them. There were at least a dozen of them and when I saw them they were gliding across that little clearing, a floating, flowing movement.

"Then they disappeared under the trees. If there'd been a clearing big enough to land in within a hundred miles I'd have landed and looked for them, but there wasn't and I had to go on. But I wanted like the devil to find out what they were and when I took the story to you two, you agreed to come up here by canoe to search for them. But I don't think now you've ever fully believed me."

Woodin looked thoughtfully into the fire. "I think you saw something queer, all right, some queer form of life. That's why I was willing to come up on this search.

"But things such as you describe, jelly-like, translucent, gliding over the ground like that—there's been nothing like that since the first protoplasmic creatures, the beginning of life on earth, glided over our young world ages ago."

"If there were such things then, why couldn't they have left descendants like them?" Ross argued.

Woodin shook his head. "Because they all vanished ages ago, changed into different and higher forms of life, starting the great upward climb of life that has reached its height in man.

"Those long-dead, single-celled protoplasmic creatures were the start, the crude, humble beginnings of our life. They passed away and their descendants were unlike them. We men are their descendants."

Ross looked at him, frowning. "But where did they come from in the first place, those first living things?"

Again Woodin shook his head. "That is one thing we biologists do not know and can hardly speculate upon, the origin of those first protoplasmic forms of life.

"It's been suggested that they rose spontaneously from the chemicals of earth, yet this is disproved by the fact that no such things rise spontaneously *now* from inert matter. Their origin is still a complete mystery. But, however they came into existence on earth, they were the first of life, our distant ancestors."

Woodin's eyes were dreaming, the other two forgotten, as he stared into the fire, seeing visions.

"What a glorious saga it is, that wonderful climb up from crude protoplasm creatures to man! A marvelous series of changes that has brought us from that first low form to our present splendor.

"And it might not have occurred on any other world but earth! For science is now almost sure that the cause of evolutionary mutations is the radiations of the radioactive deposits inside the earth, acting upon the genes of all living matter."

He caught a glimpse of Ross' uncomprehending face, and despite his raptness smiled a little.

"I can see that means nothing to you. I'll try to explain. The germ-cell of every living thing on earth contains in it a certain number of small, rod-like things which are called chromosomes.

"These chromosomes are made up of strings of tiny particles which we call genes. And each of these genes has a potent and different controlling effect upon the development of the creature that grows from that germ-cell.

"Some of these genes control the creature's color, some control his size, some the shape of his limbs, and so on. Every characteristic of the creature is predetermined by the genes in its original germ-cell.

"But now and then the genes in a germ-cell will be greatly different from the genes normal to that species, and when that is so, the creature that grows from that germ-cell will be greatly different from the fellow-creatures of its species. He will be, in fact, of an entirely new species. That is the way in which new species come into existence on earth, the method of evolutionary change.

"Biologists have known this for some time and they have been searching for the cause of these sudden great changes, these mutations, as they are called. They have tried to find out what it is that affects the genes so radically.

"They have found experimentally that X-Rays and chemical rays of various kinds, when turned upon the genes of a germ-cell, will change them greatly. And the creature that grows from that germ-cell will thus be a greatly changed creature, a mutant.

"Because of this, many biologists now believe that the radiation from the radioactive deposits inside earth, acting upon all the genes of every living thing on earth, are what cause the constant change of species, the procession of mutations, that has brought life up the evolutionary road to its present height.

"That is why I say that on any other world but earth, evolutionary progress might never have happened. For it may be that no other world has similar radioactive deposits within it to cause by gene-effect the mutations. On any other world, the first protoplasmic things that began life might have remained forever the same, down through endless generations.

"How thankful we ought to be that it was not so on earth! That mutation after mutation has followed, life ever changing and progressing into new and higher species, until the first crude protoplasm things have advanced through countless changing forms into the supreme achievement of man!"

Woodin's enthusiasm had carried him away as he talked but now he stopped, laughing a little as he relit his pipe.

"Sorry that I lectured you like a college freshman, Ross. But that's my chief subject of thought, my *idée fixe*, that wonderful upward climb of life through the ages."

Ross was staring thoughtfully into the fire. "It does seem wonderful the way you tell it. One species changing into another, going higher all the time—"

Gray stood up by the fire and stretched. "Well, you two can wonder over it but this crass materialist is going to emulate his remote invertebrate ancestors and return to a prostrate position. In other words, I'm going to bed."

He looked at Ross, a doubtful grin on his blond young face, and said, "No hard feelings now, feller?"

"Forget it," the aviator grinned back. "The paddling *was* hard today and you fellows *did* look mighty skeptical.

"But you'll see! To-morrow we'll be at the forks of the Little Whale and then I'll bet we won't scout an hour before we run across those jelly-creatures."

"I hope so," said Woodin yawningly. "Then we'll see just how good your eyesight is from a mile up, and whether you've yanked two respectable scientists up here for nothing."

Later as he lay in his blankets in the little tent, listening to Gray and Ross snore and looking sleepily out at the glowing fire embers, Woodin wondered again about that.

What had Ross actually seen in that fleeting glimpse from his speeding plane? Something queer, Woodin was sure of that, so sure that he'd come on this hard trip to find it. But what exactly?

Not protoplasmic things such as he described. That couldn't be, of course. Or could it? If things like that had existed once, why couldn't they —couldn't they—

Woodin didn't know he'd been sleeping until he was wakened by Gray's cry. It wasn't a nice cry, it was the hoarse yell of someone suddenly assaulted by bone-freezing terror.

He opened his eyes at that cry to see the Incredible looming against the stars in the open door of the tent. A dark, amorphous mass humped there in the opening, glistening all over in the starlight, and gliding into the tent. Behind it were others like it.

Things happened very quickly then. They seemed to Woodin to happen not consecutively but in a succession of swift, clicking scenes like the successive pictures of a motion picture film.

Gray's pistol roared red flame at the first viscous monster entering the tent, and the momentary flash showed the looming, glistening bulk of the thing, and Gray's panic-frozen face, and Ross clawing in his blankets for his pistol.

Then that scene was over and instantly there was another one, Gray and Ross both stiffening suddenly as though petrified, both falling heavily over. Woodin knew they were both dead now, but didn't know how he knew it. The glistening monsters were coming on into the tent.

He ripped up the wall of the tent and plunged out into the cold starlight of the clearing. He ran three steps, he didn't know in what direction, and then he stopped. He didn't know why he stopped dead but he did.

He stood there, his brain desperately urging his limbs to fly, but his limbs would not obey. He couldn't even turn, could not move a muscle of his body. He stood, his face toward the starlit gleam of the river, stricken by a strange and utter paralysis.

Woodin heard rustling, gliding movements in the tent behind him. Now from behind, there came into the line of his vision several of the glistening things. They were gathering around him, a dozen of them it seemed, and he now could see them quite clearly.

They weren't nightmares, no. They were real as real, poised here around him, humped, amorphous masses of viscous, translucent jelly. Each was about four feet tall and three in diameter, though their shapes kept constantly changing slightly, making dimensions hard to guess.

At the center of each translucent mass was a dark, disk-like blob or nucleus. There was nothing else to the creatures, no limbs or sense-organs. He saw that they could protrude pseudopods, though, for two, who held the bodies of Gray and Ross in such tentacles, were now bringing them out and laying them down beside Woodin.

Woodin, still quite unable to move a muscle, could see the frozen, twisted faces of the two men, and could see the pistols still gripped in their dead hands. And then as he looked on Ross' face he remembered.

The things the aviator had seen from his plane, the jelly-creatures they three had come north to search for, they were the monsters around him! But how had they killed Ross and Gray, how were they holding him petrified like this, who were they?

"We will permit you to move but you must not try to escape."

Woodin's dazed brain numbed further with wonder. Who had said those words to him? He had heard nothing, yet he had *thought* he heard.

"We will let you move but you must not attempt to escape or harm us."

He *did* hear those words in his mind, even though his ears heard no sound. And now his brain heard more.

"We are speaking to you by transference of thought impulses. Have you sufficient mentality to understand us?"

Minds? Minds in these things? Woodin was shaken by the thought as he stared at the glistening monsters.

His thought apparently had reached them. "Of course we have minds," came the thought answer into his brain. "We are going to let you move, now, but do not try to flee."

"I—I won't try," Woodin told himself mentally.

At once the paralysis that held him abruptly lifted. He stood there in the circle of the glistening monsters, his hands and body trembling violently.

There were ten of them, he saw now. Ten monstrous, humped masses of shining, translucent jelly, gathered around him like cowled and faceless genii come from some haunt of the unknown. One stood closer to him than the others, apparently spokesman and leader.

Woodin looked slowly around their circle, then down at his two dead companions. In the midst of the unfamiliar terrors that froze his soul, he felt a sudden aching pity as he looked down at them.

Came another strong thought into Woodin's mind from the creature closest him. "We did not wish to kill them, we came here simply to capture and communicate with the three of you.

"But when we sensed that they were trying to kill us, we slew quickly. You, who did not try to kill us but fled, we harmed not."

"What—what do you want with us, with me?" Woodin asked. He whispered it through dry lips, as well as thinking it.

There was no mental answer this time. The things stood unmoving, a silent ring of brooding, unearthly figures.

Woodin felt his mind snapping under the strain of silence and he asked the question again, screamed it.

This time the mental answer came. "I did not answer, because I was probing your mentality to ascertain whether you are of sufficient intelligence to comprehend our ideas.

"While your mind seems of an exceptionally low order, it seems possible that it can appreciate enough of what we wish to convey to understand us.

"Before beginning, however, I warn you again that it is quite impossible for you to escape or to harm any of us and that attempts to do so will result disastrously for you. It is apparent you know nothing of mental energy, so I will inform you that your two fellow-creatures were killed by the sheer power of our wills, and that your muscles were held unresponsive to your brain's commands by the same power. By our mental energy we could completely annihilate your body, if we chose."

There was a pause, and in that little space of silence Woodin's dazed brain clutched desperately for sanity, for steadiness.

Then came again that mental voice that seemed so like a real voice speaking in his brain.

"We are children of a galaxy whose name, as nearly as it can be approximated in your tongue, is Arctar. The galaxy of Arctar lies so many million light-years from this galaxy that it is far around the curve of the sphere of the three-dimensional cosmos.

"We came to dominance in that galaxy long ages ago. For we were creatures who could utilize our mental energy for transport, for physical power, for producing almost any effect we required. Because of this we rapidly conquered and colonized that galaxy, travelling from sun to sun without need of any vehicle.

"Having brought all the matter of the galaxy Arctar under our control, we looked out upon the realms beyond. There are approximately a thousand million galaxies in the three-dimensional cosmos, and it seemed fitting to us that we should colonize them all so that all the matter in the cosmos should in time be brought under our control.

"Our first step was to proliferate our numbers so as to multiply our number to that required for the great task of colonization of the cosmos. This was not difficult since of course, reproduction with us is a matter of mere fission. When the requisite number of us were ready, they were divided into four forces.

"Then the whole sphere of the three-dimensional cosmos was quartered out among those four forces. Each was to colonize its division of the cosmos and so in their tremendous hosts they set out from Arctar, in four different directions.

"A part of one of these forces came to this galaxy of yours eons ago and spread out deliberately to colonize all its habitable worlds. All this took great lengths of time, of course, but our lives are of length vastly exceeding yours, and we comprehend that racial achievement is everything and individual achievement is nothing. In the colonization of this galaxy, a force of several million Arctarians came to this particular sun and, finding but this one planet of its nine nearer worlds habitable, settled here.

"Now it has been the rule that the colonists of all these worlds throughout the cosmos have kept in communication with the original home of our race, the galaxy Arctar. In that way, our people, who now hold the whole cosmos, are able to concentrate at one point all their knowledge and power, and from that point go forth commands that shape great projects for the cosmos.

"But from this world no communications have ever been received since shortly after the force of colonizing Arctarians came here. When this was first noted the matter was deferred, it being thought that within a few more million years report would surely be made from this world too. But still no word came, until after more than a thousand million years of this silence the directing council at Arctar ordered an expedition sent to this world to ascertain the reason for such silence on the part of its colonists.

"We ten form that expedition and we started from one of the worlds of the sun you call Sirius, a short distance from your own sun, where we too are colonists. We were ordered to come with full speed to this world and ascertain why its colonists had made no report. So, wafting ourselves by mental energy through the void, we crossed the span from sun to sun and a few days ago arrived on your world.

"Imagine our perplexity when we floated down here on your world! Instead of a world peopled in every square mile by Arctarians like ourselves, descended from the original colonists, a world completely under their mental control, we find a planet that is largely a wilderness of weird forms of life!

"We remained at this spot where we had landed and for some time sent our vision forth and scanned this whole globe mentally. And our perplexity increased for never had we seen such grotesque and degraded forms of life as presented themselves to us. And not one Arctarian was to be seen on this whole planet.

"This has sorely perplexed us, for what could have done away with the Arctarians who colonized this world? Our mighty colonists and their descendants surely could never have been overcome and destroyed by the pitifully weak mentalities that now inhabit this globe. Yet where, when, are they?

"That is why we sought to seize you and your companions. Low as we knew your mentalities must be, it seemed that surely even such as you would know what had become of our colonists who once inhabited this world."

The thought-stream paused a moment, then raced into Woodin's mind with a clear question.

"Have you not some knowledge of what became of our colonists? Some clue as to their strange disappearance?"

The numbed biologist found himself shaking his head slowly. "I never —I never heard before of such creatures as you, such minds. They never existed on earth that we know of, and we now know almost all of the history of earth."

"Impossible!" exclaimed the thought of the Arctarian leader. "Surely you must have some knowledge of our mighty people if you know all the history of this planet."

From another Arctarian's mind came a thought, directed at the leader but impinging indirectly on Woodin's brain.

"Why not examine the past of the planet through this creature's brain and see what we can for ourselves?"

"An excellent idea!" exclaimed the leader. "His mentality will be easy enough to probe."

"What are you going to do?" cried Woodin shrilly, panic edging his voice.

The answering thoughts were calming, reassuring. "Nothing that will harm you in the least. We are simply going to probe into your racial past by unlocking the inherited memories of your brain.

"In the unused cells of your brain lie impressed inherited racial memories that go back to your remotest ancestors. By our mental power of command we shall make those buried memories temporarily dominant and vivid in your mind.

"You will experience the same sensations, see the same scenes, that your remote ancestors of millions of years ago saw. And we, here around you, can read your mind as we now do, and so see what you are seeing, looking into the past of this planet.

"There is no danger. Physically you will remain standing here but mentally you will leap back across the ages. We shall first push your mind back to a time approximating that when our colonists came to this world, to see what happened to them."

No sooner had this thought impinged on Woodin's mind than the starlit scene around him, the humped masses of the Arctarians, suddenly vanished and his consciousness seemed whirling through gray mist.

He knew that physically he was not moving yet mentally he had a sense of terrific velocity of motion. It was as though his mind was whirling across unthinkable gulfs, his brain expanding.

Then abruptly the gray mists cleared. A strange new scene took hazy form inside Woodin's mind.

It was a scene that he sensed, not saw. By other senses than sight did it present itself to his mind, yet it was none the less real and vivid.

He looked with those strange senses upon a strange earth, a world of gray seas and harsh continents of rock without any speck of life upon them. The skies were heavily clouded and rain fell continually.

Down upon that world Woodin felt himself dropping, with a host of weird companions. They were each an amorphous, glistening, single-celled mass, with a dark nucleus at its center. They were Arctarians and Woodin knew that *he* was an Arctarian, and that he had come with the others a long way through space toward this world.

They landed in hosts upon the harsh and lifeless planet. They exerted their mentalities and by sheer telekinetic force of mental energy they altered the material world to suit them. They reared great structures and cities, cities that were not of matter but of *thought*. Weird cities built of crystallized mental energy.

Woodin could not comprehend a millionth of the activities he sensed going on in those alien Arctarian cities of thought. He realized a vast ordered mass of inquiry, investigation, experiment and communication, but all beyond his present human mind in motives and achievement. Abruptly all dissolved in gray mists again.

The mists cleared almost at once and now Woodin looked on another scene. It was later in time, this one. And now Woodin saw that time had worked strange changes upon the hosts of Arctarians, of which he still was one.

They had changed from unicellular to multicellular beings. And they were no longer all the same. Some were sessile, fixed in one spot, others mobile. Some betrayed a tendency toward the water, others toward the land. Something had changed the bodily form of the Arctarians as generations passed, branching them out in different lines.

This strange degeneration of their bodies had been accompanied by a kindred degeneration of their minds. Woodin sensed that. In the thought-cities the ordered process of search for knowledge and power had become confused, chaotic. And the thought-cities themselves were vanishing, the Arctarians having no longer sufficient mental energy to maintain them.

The Arctarians were trying to ascertain what was causing this strange bodily and mental degeneration in them. They thought it was something that was affecting the genes of their bodies, but what it was they could not guess. On no other world had they ever degenerated so!

That scene passed rapidly into another much later. Woodin now *saw* the scene, for by then the ancestor, whose mind he looked through, had developed eyes. And he saw that the degeneration had now gone far, the Arctarians' multicellular bodies more and more stricken by the diseases of complexity and diversification.

The last of the thought-cities now were gone. The once mighty Arctarians had become hideous, complex organisms degenerating ever further, some of them creeping and swimming in the waters, others fixed upon the land.

They still had left some of the great original mentality of their ancestors. These monstrously-degenerated creatures of land and sea, living in what Woodin's mind recognized as the late Paleozoic age, still made frantic and futile attempts to halt the terrible progress of their degradation.

Woodin's mind flashed into a scene later still, in the Mesozoic. Now the spreading degeneration had made of the descendants of the colonists a still more horrible group of races. Great webbed and scaled and taloned creatures they were now, reptiles living in land and water.

Even these incredibly-changed creatures possessed a faint remnant of their ancestors' mental power. They made vain attempts to communicate with Arctarians far on other worlds of distant suns, to apprise them of their plight. But their minds were now too weak.

There followed a scene in the Cenozoic. The reptiles had become mammals, the downward progress of the Arctarians had gone farther. Now only the merest shreds of the original mentality remained in these degraded descendants.

And now this pitiful posterity had produced a species even more foolish and lacking in mental power than any before, ground-apes that roamed the cold plains in chattering, quarrelling packs. The last shreds of Arctarian inheritance, the ancient instincts toward dignity and cleanliness and forbearance, had faded out of these creatures.

And then a last picture filled Woodin's brain. It was the world of the present day, the world he had seen through his own eyes. But now he saw and understood it as he never had before, a world in which degeneration had gone to the utmost limit.

The apes had become even weaker bipedal creatures, who had lost almost every atom of inheritance of the old Arctarian mind. These creatures had lost, too, many of the senses which had been retained even by the apes before them.

And these creatures, these humans, were now degenerating with increasing rapidity. Where at first they had killed like their animal forebears only for food, they had learned to kill wantonly. And had learned to kill each other in groups, in tribes, in nations and hemispheres. In the madness of their degeneracy they slaughtered each other until earth ran with their blood.

They were more cruel even than the apes who had preceded them, cruel with the utter cruelty of the mad. And in their progressive insanity they came to starve in the midst of plenty, to slay each other in their own cities, to cower beneath the lash of superstitious fears as no creatures had before them.

They were the last terrible descendants, the last degenerated product, of the ancient Arctarian colonists who once had been kings of intellect. Now the other animals were almost gone. These, the last hideous freaks, would soon wind up the terrible story entirely by annihilating each other in their madness.

Woodin came suddenly to consciousness. He was standing in the starlight in the center of the riverside clearing. And around him still were poised the ten amorphous Arctarians, a silent ring.

Dazed, reeling from that tremendous and awful vision that had passed through his mind with incredible vividness, he turned slowly from one to the other of the Arctarians. Their thoughts impinged on his brain, strong, somber, shaken by terrible horror and loathing.

The sick thought of the Arctarian leader beat into Woodin's mind.

"So *that* is what became of our Arctarian colonists who came to this world! They degenerated, changed into lower and lower forms of life, until these pitiful insane things, who now swarm on this world, are their last descendants.

"This world is a world of deadly horror! A world that somehow damages the genes of our race's bodies and changes them bodily and mentally, making them degenerate further each generation. Before us we see the awful result."

The shaken thought of another Arctarian asked, "But what can we do now?"

"There is nothing we can do," uttered their leader solemnly. "This degeneration, this awful change, has gone too far for us ever to reverse it now.

"Our intelligent brothers became on this poisoned world things of horror and we cannot now turn back the clock and restore them from the degraded things their descendants are."

Woodin found his voice and cried out thinly, shrilly.

"It isn't true!" he cried. "It's all a lie, what I saw! We humans aren't the product of downward devolution, we're the product of ages of upward evolution! We must be, I tell you! Why, we wouldn't want to live, I wouldn't want to live, if that other tale was true. It can't be true!"

The thought of the Arctarian leader, directed at the other amorphous shapes, reached his raving mind.

It was tinged with pity, yet strong with a superhuman loathing.

"Come, my brothers," the Arctarian was saying to his fellows. "There is nothing we can do here on this soul-sickening world.

"Let us go, before we too are poisoned and changed. And we will send warning to Arctar that this world is a poisoned world, a world of degeneration, so that never again may any of our race come here and go down the awful road that those others went down.

"Come! We return to our own sun."

The Arctarian leader's humped shape flattened, assumed a disk-like form, then rose smoothly upward into the air.

The others too changed and followed, in a group, and a stupefied Woodin stared up at them, glistening dots lifting rapidly into the starlight.

He staggered forward a few steps, shaking his fist insanely up at the shining, receding dots.

"Come back, damn you!" he screamed. "Come back and tell me it's a lie!

"It must be a lie—it must—"

There was no sign of the vanished Arctarians now in the starlit sky. The darkness was brooding and intense around Woodin.

He screamed up again into the night but only a whispering echo answered. Wild-eyed, staggering, soul-smitten, his gaze fell on the pistol in Ross' hand. He seized it with a hoarse cry.

The stillness of the forest was broken suddenly by a sharp crack, that reverberated a moment and then died rapidly away. Then all was silent again save for the chuckling whisper of the river hurrying on.

On the whole, I am an optimistic writer, and my heroes generally win out in the end and the world is saved. Yet, for years I had noticed that stories with sad endings, or ironical ones, or paradoxical ones struck me harder than those with conventionally happy ones, and stayed with me longer.

And, every once in a while, it seemed to me that the downbeat was better and was even necessary in my own usually upbeat stories. It was remembering stories like "Devolution" that gave me the courage to try such endings.

For instance, there is my story "The Ugly Little Boy" (published in the magazines as "The Lastborn"), which ended in such utter tragedy that many readers have written to tell me that they were crying at the end. (So was I when I wrote it.) Yet it seemed not a tragic ending at all when I thought about it later. It ended with the triumph of love, and there is no greater triumph than that.

But, you know, I cannot resist the insertion at this point of a short-short story of my own (only one thousand words long, so forgive me), which was written in the spirit of disenchantment you find in "Devolution."

My story, entitled "Big Game," was written on November 18, 1941, just about five years after I read "Devolution." I mentioned "Big Game" in *The Early Asimov* (see page 366) as the last of the eleven science fiction stories I had written but had been unable to publish. In that book I said, "I wish I could remember what 'Big Game' was about. . . . The title, however, recalls nothing to my mind, and the story now no longer exists."

But apparently it did indeed exist. I have been handing material to Boston University, as I mentioned earlier in this book, and among some old manuscripts I hadn't looked through was one of the never-published "Big Game."

After *The Early Asimov* appeared, some fan of mine, poking through some of the material in Boston University's library (with permission), came across the manuscript, had it Xeroxed, and sent a copy to me.

So here it is, the only story of mine that exists (as far as I know—perhaps I had better not be too sure of myself any more) but has never, till now, been published.

BIG GAME

by Isaac Asimov

"I see by the papers," I said, over my beer, "where the new time machine at Stanford has been sent forward in time two days with a white mouse inside. No ill effects."

Jack Trent nodded gravely and said, "What they ought to do with one of those things is to go back a few million years and find out what happened to the dinosaurs."

I had been watching Hornby at the next table for the last few minutes in a casual fashion, and the fellow looked up and caught my eye at that point. He was alone, and had a bottle—quarter empty—to himself. Maybe that's why he spoke then.

Anyway, he grinned and said to Jack, "Too late, old fellow. I did that myself ten years ago and found out. The bigwigs say it was climatic changes. It wasn't." He raised his glass to us in a silent toast and tossed it off.

We looked at each other. Neither of us knew Hornby, except by sight, but Jack's right eyelid flickered and his head motioned slightly. I grinned, and we moved over to that next table and ordered two more beers.

Jack looked at Hornby solemnly. "You invented a time machine, did you?"

"Long ago." Hornby smiled amiably and filled his glass again. "Better than the ones those amateurs at Stanford rigged up. I've destroyed it, though. Lost interest."

"Tell us about it. You say it wasn't climate that knocked off the big lizards?"

"Why should it be?" He glanced quickly out of eye corners. "Climate didn't annoy them for millions of years. Why should a sudden dry spell wipe them out so completely and finally, while other creatures lived on comfortably?" He tried to snap his fingers derisively, but didn't succeed, and ended by muttering, "Not logical!"

"What did?" I asked.

Hornby hesitated doubtfully, and teetered his bottle. Then he said, "Same thing that knocked off the bison. Intelligent life!"

"Men from Mars?" I suggested. "It was a little too early for the inhabitants of Atlantis."

Hornby grew truculent quite suddenly. He was more than half gone, I imagine. "I saw them, I tell you," he said violently. "They were reptiles, and not large, either. They were four feet tall and bipeds. Why not? Those dinosaurs had millions of years to evolve. They crawled and climbed and flew and swam. They were all shapes, sizes, and varieties. Why shouldn't one develop a brain—and kill off all the rest?"

I said, "No reason, except that no fossil saurian has ever been discovered with a brain-case capable of holding the gray matter of anything more than a kitten." Jack nudged me—he wanted Hornby to rattle on—but I hate bull.

Hornby merely gave me a look of contempt. "You don't find many fossils of intelligent animals. They don't fall into mudholes, you know, as a general rule. Besides, it so happens they *were* pinheads, and what of it? How much of *your* brain do you use? Not a fifth, if that, and the rest is waste, or God knows what. Those reptiles had kitten brains, but they used it *all*." Then he fired up, "And don't ask why we don't find traces of their cities or machines. I don't think they built any. Their intelligence was of an entirely different order from ours. They tried to tell me what their life was like, but I couldn't understand—except that their great amusement was the hunting of big game."

"How did they try to tell you?" asked Jack. "Telepathy?"

"I think so. They had brains, I tell you. I just looked at them, and they looked at me, and then I *knew*. I knew lots of things. I didn't hear or feel anything; I just *knew*. I can't explain, really. Try it someday." His eyes were brooding, fixed on his glass. "I wish I could have stayed longer. Might have learned more." He shrugged.

"Why didn't you?" I asked.

"It wasn't safe," he said. "I could tell that. I was a freak to them, remember, and they were curious about me. Not about my body, of course; that didn't bother them. It was my brain." He smiled crookedly at us. "It was so big, you know. They wondered what I could use it all for. They were going to dissect me to find out, so I didn't stay."

"How did you get away?"

"I wouldn't have, if they hadn't sighted a triceratops at that moment. They dropped everything and ran off with their little metal rods in their hands. Those were their weapons, you see. There's your answer. Those brainy little reptiles killed saurians with all the enthusiasm of a big-game hunter bagging lions. They would rather knock off a tyrannosaurus than eat. Why not? Those huge beasts must have been magnificent prizes. All the rest, too, from the pterodactyl to the ichthyosaurus" (he couldn't pronounce them very well, but we got his meaning), "none of them could stand up against the midget beasts that killed them for fun or glory. And they went fast, too. *We* killed off hundreds of millions of bison in thirty years, didn't we?"

He tried to snap his fingers again. Then, with bitterness, "Climatic changes, hell! But who'd believe the truth?"

He fell silent, and Jack nudged him. "But say, old fellow, what killed off those little lizards? Why aren't they still around, running things?"

Hornby looked up, and gazed at Jack fixedly, "I never went back to find out, but I know what happened. The only fun they got out of life was this big-game hunting. I told you I found that out when I looked in their eyes. So when they ran out of brontosauri and diplodoci, they turned to the very biggest: themselves! And they did just as good a job at that." Truculently he added, "Why not? Aren't men doing the same thing?"

And yet, perhaps it's not important that a few of my stories have never been published. I suspect that I waste nothing. For instance, once I reread "Big Game," I realized that I had made use of the plot and expanded it into "Day of the Hunters," which appeared in the November 1950 *Future Fiction*. That story, however, never appeared anywhere else, not even in *The Early Asimov*, which traced my career only through 1949, so I doubt that its existence disturbs the novelty (if any) of "Big Game."

*   *   *   *

As 1936 ended, my father sold his third candy store and, after some complications, bought his fourth, at 174 Windsor Place, in the Park Slope section of Brooklyn. (I always described it as being "on the other side of Prospect Park," for whenever I said I lived near the Park, the other person always said, "On Flatbush Avenue?" and I always said, "No, on the other side.")

Times were improving now, and the candy store we bought proved the best of the lot. This time my father stayed put till it came time to retire.

Part Eight

1937

THE YEAR 1937 was a quiet one. I completed my sophomore year at Columbia and began my junior year without any particular crises.

Astounding Stories continued to dominate the science fiction field more and more. *Thrilling Wonder Stories* seemed of little account to me, and *Amazing Stories* continued to stumble wearily toward its end. And yet there was one story in that magazine during 1937 that hit me hard. That was *By Jove!* a three-part serial by Walter Rose, in the February, April, and June 1937 issues.

I remember very little about the plot except for sympathetic giant insects on Jupiter. (Rose never wrote anything but this and one short story, at least in science fiction.) Yet, even as the serial was running, and it is too long, of course, to include here, my views on Jupiter changed utterly, thanks to something John W. Campbell, Jr., was doing.

It seems that everything Campbell did influenced me even when he was not doing science fiction.

You see, every once in a while a science fiction magazine would run a non-fiction piece that dealt with some subject the editor conceived to be of interest to science fiction readers. Generally, such articles tended to be a little mystic in content, and I was never satisfied with that. *Astounding Stories,* for instance, published *Lo!* a book by Charles Fort, in eight installments beginning with the April 1934 issue. It irritated the devil out of me, since to me it seemed to be an incoherent mass of quotations from newspapers out of which ridiculous conclusions were drawn.

But then, beginning in the June 1936 issue of *Astounding Stories,* came an eighteen-part series called *A Study of the Solar System,* by Campbell. It was real science.

For the first time, I read a modern account of the Solar System. (Until then, I had gotten my astronomy out of more or less out-of-date books in the public library.) For the first time, astronomy was made truly dramatic to me in Campbell's somewhat overcharged prose. And of all the parts of that long series, the one that affected me most was the ninth part, "Other Eyes Watching," which dealt with Jupiter and appeared in the February 1937 *Astounding Stories*.

OTHER EYES WATCHING

by John W. Campbell, Jr.

All space flamed with an intolerable incandescence; for two thousand million miles, titanic streamers of flame shot out, wove and twined, streamers that flared dull-red and cooling where they stretched to breaking, then great clots that swirled in blue-white heat of new creation. Dimming slowly in the distance, the Wrecker was vanishing, the vagrant star that had lashed worlds out of the Sun as it swept by.

Two worlds, each blazing with the blue-white heat of the violent racking their already incandescent masses were receiving, had neared, swung, passed on. Two suns, each a million miles in diameter—not quaking, since they were not solid, but flaming gas—had swept by at frightful, hurtling speeds, engendering gravitational stresses, as they passed within not millions of miles, but hundreds of miles of each other, that must have made the infinite fabric of space creak to the awful strains. Each a million-mile ball of incredibly hot matter—nearing, nearing—flames leaping out that were to make worlds, whole solar systems—shrieking at each other with a roaring thunder whose mere vibrations of sound would have pulverized this planet—and passing.

But this is the thing that paralyzes my thoughts: I cannot conceive that this thing, this blasting of flames that made worlds, the explosions that scattered giant planets over three billion miles of space—all that flaming catastrophe—took place, was, and was done in not more than three *hours!* So inconsequential a thing as reading through this magazine will take longer than that. But in that almost instantaneous, Gargantuan catastrophe—worlds were made, set spinning, established—and the star that caused it passed on forever.

The flaming drift of flame that it left shrieking through two thousand million miles of space cooled slowly, flaming filaments of wispy heat being drawn by mighty gravities of forming planets, till nearly all that scattered matter was collected in nine major clumps.

But it could not stay, for the frightful heats that had been buried under cooler layers of the stars had been torn out into open space, and it could not even radiate till it began to collect properly. (Hot atoms can radiate only when they collide with others.)* Our Earth condensed; others swiftly lost the hydrogen, the other light gases. But out farther from the Sun, the mightiest of all the groupings dragged at those atoms of flying hydrogen with a savage grip that slowed them as they struggled up one—five—ten —twenty million miles from the heart of the mass that was to be Jupiter.

The Sun was far off, and the mighty drag it exerted to aid the gases in escaping the inner planets was weakened here. The gases, their speed exhausted in a running fight that lasted twenty million miles, fell back, captured. Half a million miles, and they could get free from Mars. But Jupiter? Not a chance! Already there were flaming aggregations that had half succeeded in escaping, only to be trapped as satellites rotating tens of millions of miles out, but captured, definitely.

Jupiter dragged them back. Heavy metals were there, and condensing now, under the pressure of inconceivable tons of that captured stuff, to a liquid, terrifically compressed core. On to them piled the greater tons of these returning, captured atoms. More, more, more turned liquid, as the cold of space drank in their heat slowly. Ages passed, and the heat went rapidly. The core grew cold, as the core of all other planets had cooled.

And now Jupiter, last to cool, felt the chill of its far position. The Sun gave no great heat at this distance. That vast atmosphere which had condensed out first the metals, then the oxides, the compounds, finally water, till all the compounds had churned in the slowly cooling furnace and had reached a new stability, wound up, at last, with a condition something like this: Every last trace of oxygen had found something to grip, and hold. Down it had gone, as silicon dioxide or iron oxide or calcium oxide, some as trillions of tons of water. Fluorine, most active of non-metals, had beaten even the oxygen to a mate. Chlorine was coming out, the bromine and iodine; sulphur and phosphorus had gone down with the oxygen.

Everything was happily united—save for the inert gases that didn't want to be: helium and xenon and radon and argon. And two others: hydrogen and nitrogen. Nitrogen, because it isn't ordinarily very anxious to do anything about it. It's not a confirmed-bachelor element; but it usually takes the stimulus of high temperatures to make nitrogen active. Then, of course, nitrogen becomes so virulently active it will drive even oxygen out of combination!

* One estimate places the temperature of that matter freshly torn from a star at more than 600,000° centigrade.

Hydrogen didn't unite simply because there was too much of it. Most plentiful of all elements in those vast flames the three-hour catastrophe had thrown out to make planets, it had gone down, by the trillions of tons, with oxygen to make water. By the millions, it had gone contentedly to rest with chlorine. It had combined with everything that it could combine with—and there simply wasn't enough. So, there was hydrogen and nitrogen in the atmosphere, no half-hearted twenty per cent of hydrogen; most of that atmosphere was hydrogen.

Unfortunately, hydrogen and nitrogen, while they unite to form ammonia, do not do so very willingly, as Earth chemists know. During the War, Germany spent millions developing very complex and expensive apparatus to force the unwilling elements together. Haber, the inventor, should have been killed, by all rights, in one of the almost innumerable explosions they had trying to force these two into combination.

The principal point of the process is pressure—pressure in large doses—and they tried to use enormous steel retorts, made of metal of the finest quality and nine inches thick. But hydrogen has a nasty habit of forming a compound with iron—iron hydride—under these conditions, and that compound is twice as brittle as glass and not a tenth as strong. The retorts, fifty feet long and three feet in diameter, for all those nine-inch walls, blew up. Hydrogen and nitrogen do not unite readily, except under great pressure——

Pressure! Of all things Jupiter has, pressure is outstanding. Pressure that would make the bottoms of our seas seem near vacuum conditions. The hydrogen and nitrogen inevitably combined. Ammonia takes less room than the two gases; the elements were literally crushed together—not to ammonia water, but to liquid ammonia, for Jupiter was cold, bitterly cold. Water was the stuff that made those great chalky mountains along the torrid equator, where the vast, intensely blue seas washed at them, and steamed slowly. Seas, of little, low, choppy waves, crushed under the gravity of that 86,000-mile world—seas of liquid ammonia.

The cold snows of the north—65,000 miles away around the titanic globe—were solid ammonia. And that atmosphere was hydrogen and ammonia vapor—and methane, carbon tetrahydride. That is the principal constituent of natural gas here on Earth, an excellent fuel. Not on Jupiter. On Jupiter it is the waste product, the incombustible residue. Gasoline would be a safe cleaning fluid there, utterly incombustible. There, they would say that hydrogen would not burn, but oxygen was an excellent fuel.

But that is not all that is strange in the chemistry of the giant planet. Jupiter is possessed of a climate ideal for life! The temperature is mild, about 120 degrees below zero centigrade, 185 below Fahrenheit. Yes that's a mild temperature! It's mild for life on an entirely different basis, an ammonia basis. Remember that in the discussion of the possible life media, I said that ammonia, though unstable, was a possible medium? That hydrogen could function as the active gas at low temperatures under great pressure? These conditions are fulfilled, for ammonia is stable, and the enormous pressure makes hydrogen active.

So a life is possible there, a life that breathes in a pure, invigorating atmosphere of hydrogen, with gentle breezes of ammonia! Its foods are, perhaps oxidizing agents instead of reducing agents. There are many organic compounds that we know which are capable of this action, compounds called peroxides which are violently explosive at the temperature of Earth, but stable at temperatures so low that Jupiter would find them normal.

Chemistry of life would be strangely different. Perhaps if there are intelligent, but not-too-intelligent inhabitants, they attempt to forget their woes on Saturday nights with the aid of a bottle of ethylamine, C_2H_5NH, instead of that ancient Earthly staple, ethyl alcohol, C_2H_5OH. To them, perhaps that compound H_2O is a solid, white salt; at any rate, it is an immensely important part of their diet.

And what sort of a world do they live in? It must be a savage world of small animals. No great 100-foot monsters ever lived on the land of Jupiter, for they would have been crushed under their own weight. The animals would be small so that they could be active. Elephants never jump. Perhaps beings corresponding to men would be no more than two feet tall, but muscled so powerfully as to make any hand-to-hand encounters with such people (impossible due to the differences in atmosphere and pressure) a dangerous business indeed. Swift-moving beyond belief, in order to keep up with an environment lashed by a gravity two and a half times as swift as ours.

Things fall more swiftly. The spring of an attacking animal there would be a blur of motion to our eyes, for if it were not, he would not be able to spring any distance before that snapping gravity jerked him back to the ground.

They would have hard ground of low, almost flat country, where even the strength of mountains cannot lift themselves high against an overwhelming, eternal gravity. Though Jupiter is 300 times as massive as Earth, its gravity is not, fortunately, 300 times as great at the surface, because the surface is so far from the center of the planet. At one hundred thousand miles from the center of Earth, the gravity is one three hundredth that an equal distance from the center of Jupiter, but the latter planet is larger—and the surface is farther from the center.

But the hills are low, for the gravity is still intense. The trees are low, scrubby things, perhaps with many stalks supporting a widespreading network of branches. There's reason for that, too—two good ones. The gravity—always that—and the winds. Not the gentle zephyrs of a minor planet like Earth, but howling, roaring, shrieking tornadoes that seem leftover memories of that wild day when planets were created in three brief hours. Winds that shriek past at two hundred miles an hour. Those are the steady, day-in-and-day-out trade winds of Jupiter—gentle things that they expect every day of the long, long year. At least, we know they exist in the upper atmosphere, and surely something more than a hint of them goes raving around the surface.

Speaking of surface—Jupiter has lots of that! How much of it is flooded, we have no way of guessing, but the planet is about 265,000 miles in circumference, and it spins around that circumference at a mad pace: once each ten hours, 26,500 miles an hour. But if ever a Jovian Magellan set out to circle his world, he would be tackling a task that even light would require a very distinctly measurable time to accomplish. Jupiter is a full-size planet, no accidental scrapings dropped behind that world!

And that fearfully heavy atmosphere is going to introduce difficulties when they start to make airplanes. The planes are easy enough—almost anything with a flat surface will fly in an atmosphere as thick as that frightfully compressed stuff is. But speed is something quite different. It takes more than streamlining to wriggle a path through that ultracondensed soup.

Under the circumstances, probably an automobile would have the better of it, for, could we see a Jovian driver, we would undoubtedly praise the gods of the universe that we couldn't ride with him. They would have a habit of taking right-angle turns at forty to fifty miles an hour, braking the car to a dead stop from seventy miles an hour in about fifteen feet, and jittering through traffic with the general effect of one of those trick movies of a wild ride through New York.

Why? Because brakes there would have a far greater effect; the mass of the car, its inertia, would be unchanged, while its weight, and consequent pressure against the surface would be two and a half times as great. The jarring decelerations, approaching the severity of a full-fledged collision, would not bother the concentrated balls of muscular strength a Jovian would have to be, anyway. Swinging a corner at forty would be no trick at all, when the car was held to the road by Jupiter's savage clutch.

But top speeds? That forty or fifty would be like doing approximately the same speed through water. If the brakes stop a car quickly, so does the air. What they'd burn for gasoline, I don't know—perhaps pure hydrogen peroxide—but they would burn it at a frightening rate, to make any speed.

And what would they build these automobiles of? Not iron—remember what happened to Haber's steel retorts. Iron is a hopelessly brittle metal under those conditions.* Not aluminum—for in the strongly alkaline rains of that world, aluminum would melt away in no time. Silver would run away in liquid streams of ammonia-silver complex salts. So would copper. None of the noble metals—they're all too heavy, by far, even if they are not as rare as on Earth, though they probably are. They would develop an utterly alien metallurgy, and a completely alien chemistry.

What do they burn in their gas stoves? Oxygen? Would they be able to develop radio where radio vacuum tubes would be crushed instantly by the brutal hand of that atmospheric pressure? Even if the tube is built sufficiently strong to stand the pressure, hydrogen atoms would seep through, as they diffuse through almost any material we know of. Perhaps, though, they would develop Alexanderson alternators for sending, which are nothing but specially designed dynamos; and receive by crystal detectors. Still—even our best sets would never receive messages around that world—a quarter of a million miles.

But are there any people there to worry about such things? We can't know, of course, but we can say this: There is an active liquid, not water, but one we have reason to believe is an excellent substitute. They have an atmosphere containing an active gas. They certainly have reason to develop life—a nice mild climate, lots of land and "water" area in all probability. The Sunlight may be a bit diluent, but it's there.

Yes, those people may be based on a weird chemistry that makes liquid ammonia their "Adam's ale," and hydrogen their air; but the chemistry is possible. They might fry an egg—of a Jovian chicken—on the freezer tray of a Terrestrial refrigerator, but based on an ammonia scale, they have the proper temperature. They have day and night—shorter than those of any other planet of the system—to distribute the Sun's heat evenly.

If some strange and utterly alien creature from other solar systems were to come to make a guess as to which of Sol's children bore life, which do you suppose he would choose? Tiny planets—the Terrestrial type—with an almost perfect vacuum for atmosphere—or mighty worlds like Jupiter? I think I would choose Jupiter, were it not that I just happen to have special, one might say "inside," dope. My personal economy is based on water.

I'm glad of that. That and the atmosphere I breathe. For I wonder if there are on Jupiter, peoples more intelligent than we, gazing out through

* You may be interested in one solution of the problem of getting hydrogen under great pressure safely. They use two retorts, one inside the other, like an arm in a sleeve. The "arm" is the hydrogen retort, with hydrogen at a pressure, let us say, of 2000 pounds to the square inch. The sleeve is a heavy steel retort about it. Between the two, in the hollow, is nitrogen at 2010 pounds. The hydrogen leaks and weakens the inner retort, but that's under no real strain. The nitrogen keeps it from reaching the outer sleeve, taking all the strain safely because it is not "weakened" by seeping hydrogen.

mighty telescopes, wondering and longing, imagining life on tiny, more Sunward worlds—and vainly wishing. Wishing, and knowing that they cannot leave. For just as surely as no near-evacuated vessel made of matter could resist for a day, that awful, crushing atmosphere of Jupiter, so surely could no vessel made of matter resist the frightful, bursting pressure should it venture into space charged with that ultra-compressed air. Burdened by an enormously heavy air, seeking to escape an enormously massive planet—and the filtering, seeping hydrogen escaping steadily through the very atoms of the metal. I wonder if they look—and wish——

———

Campbell was, of course, no more accurate about Jupiter than astronomers generally were in 1937—who could reasonably expect him to be—but he presented the 1937 viewpoint effectively, and I never forgot it. Jupiter, after that, could not be a world of giant insects. It was a world of a giant atmosphere containing methane and ammonia.

Stories of mine such as "The Callistan Menace," "Not Final," and, particularly, "Victory Unintentional," were written with Campbell's "Other Eyes Watching" firmly in mind.

Campbell's articles taught me more. They taught me that non-fiction could be as interesting as fiction. Well enough done, I found, it could compete with the fiction in a science fiction magazine and grab the attention. I always turned to Campbell's article first in those issues in which the series appeared.

The time was to come, over a dozen years later, when *Astounding* would print non-fiction articles by me, and, still later, *The Magazine of Fantasy and Science Fiction* would begin a regular series of non-fiction articles by me that would run far longer than any other such series in the history of the field. (As I write this, I am working on my 181st monthly article in that series.)

And all the articles I write for science fiction magazines, indeed all the non-fiction I write, I trace back to my pleasure at reading Campbell's articles on astronomy.

There was no question that I was beginning to value science for its own sake and was beginning to enjoy science fiction not only for the quality of its writing and the excitement of its action, but for the accuracy of its science. Consequently, when I came across John D. Clark's "Minus Planet," in the April 1937 *Astounding Stories,* I found an entirely new dimension of pleasure in it.

MINUS PLANET

by John D. Clark

Now that it's all over, and we have escaped the more serious of the possible consequences, we wonder why we were so slow to see what was happening. For it might have been foreseen. We knew that the position of man in the universe was precarious enough, and that the very existence of matter itself wasn't much more stable. That is—we knew it, but we didn't realize it. There *is* a difference, and that difference was almost enough to eliminate not only man but the Earth itself from celestial history.

The warnings were plain enough. They lasted for years. Biologists had noticed that the evolution of animal and plant life in the northern hemisphere was steadily accelerating, due, probably, to the gradual and completely inexplicable increase in the intensity of the cosmic rays from the direction of Polaris.

These rays increased the number of mutations in the germ plasm of all living matter exposed to them. New varieties of plants, freak animals, queer monsters born to normal men and women, were coming into the world at a steadily increasing rate. There were advantages, of course. Many of the new varieties of plants and animals were extremely useful, and there were geniuses as well as monsters born to commonplace human beings. But, on the whole, the inhabitants of the planet didn't like the situation. The scientists liked it even less than did anybody else. You see, they couldn't explain it—and when a scientist can't explain something, he is likely to be annoyed. It makes him look so foolish.

It was on January 15, 2156, that the astrophysicist, Dr. James Carter, had the first glimmer of light—literally. He was working on the new five-hundred-inch reflector of the Mt. McKinley observatory at the time, and noticed a darkening of his photographic plate from the spectrometer focused on Polaris in the northern sky. He repeated his observation, and got the same result; a uniform darkening over the whole spectral range.

"As though," he said to his assistant, "the whole damned spectrum were light struck! And I never knew any source of light that would give a continuous spectrum from infra-red to cosmic rays, with the cosmics the strongest. There doesn't seem to be any line structure at all—just as though there were a hot body out there heated to a few billion degrees centigrade!"

The assistant, Dr. Michael Poggenpohl, usually known as Doc Mike, wrinkled his diminutive nose, and scratched his flaming head. "That," he remarked, "doesn't make sense! A body that hot on the outside wouldn't stay that way. And where did it come from, anyway, Jimmy?"

Jimmy uncoiled his six foot three of giraffelike build from his usual thinking position (in which he rested comfortably on the back of his neck), lighted a cigarette, and grunted. The noise was not gracious, but neither was his mood nor the expression on his somewhat battered face.

"Right now, I want some information on where this alleged source of light is. Will you make arrangements for the observatories on Mars and Venus to take simultaneous observations with us on the northern sky? No, I don't want a spectrum. I *have* a spectrum, and it has me baffled. I merely want a simple photographic observation. Everything this object, whatever it is, is sending out, seems to affect the plate. And I want to know *where* it is. The question of *what* it is, can wait. Move on now, little one, and pretend that you're earning the money the commissariat of science is paying you!"

Mike held his nose insultingly, and moved to obey. "And how about the jack," he asked sweetly, "that they're foolish enough to waste on you?"

"It's not waste, old fruit. Geniuses have to be supported. I'm the genius!"

"I've been wondering what it was. I thought you must be somebody's uncle. O. K., I'll get the messages off right away. The light-beam operator ought to be able to get in touch with Mars directly, but Venus is on the other side of the Sun right now, and he'll have to relay to him."

"Don't bother me with trifles! Go away and let me think in peace!"

"You mean loaf," said Mike, and departed.

But Jimmy didn't loaf when the other man had gone. He reached for a dozen reference books, a slide rule, and a wad of paper, and immediately became oblivious to all about him. He remained in that state for some hours, and only returned to the world when Mike reappeared with the televised plates from the other observatories. They all showed the same thing: a small, brilliant point against the background of the northern constellations.

It had evidently been overlooked previously, since it was almost invisible to the eye, even through the largest telescope, and appeared only on the photographic plate, which was sensitive to the invisible ultra-violet, gamma, and cosmic radiation which accounted for the major part of its energy. The plates were sent via pneumatic tube to the calculating room, with a request that the distance of the unknown body be determined, if possible, from the observations of the three planets. The two scientists sat down to think it over.

"Mike, what do you know about matter, anyway? What's it composed of?"

"What's the matter? I thought *you* were the genius. And why ask a kindergarten question at this time of day, anyway?"

"Go on, go on. I'm asking the questions. What's matter made of?"

"Well, if you must know, it seems to be made of assorted particles of electricity. An atom consists of a heavy, positive nucleus, with a lot of light, negative electrons floating around it. To be precise, the nucleus consists of, say, 'z' protons and 'n' neutrons. They weigh almost the same, and the protons have unit positive charges, while the neutrons are neutral. The whole nucleus has a positive charge, then, of plus 'z'. (Ordinary hydrogen hasn't any neutrons—just a single lone proton for a nucleus.) Then, of course, there are 'z' negative electrons floating around outside to neutralize the whole affair. You ought to know, though! You developed the method of splitting the nucleus on a commercial scale to get the energy out of it!"

"Yes, yes, I know. But what is a proton made of?"

"That? Oh, it seems to be a neutron closely tied up with a positron— a *positive* electron that doesn't weigh much of anything."

"Then, candidate, what are the fundamental units of matter?"

"What is this, anyhow? Another damned Ph.D. exam? The *fundamental* particles would be the neutron, with most of the mass and no charge, and the positron and electron, with positive and negative charge respectively, and no mass to speak of. And so what?"

"Very good, Rollo. And now, what is light?"

"T'hell with light! I can think of lots better things to discuss." He flicked the communicator switch, and the round face of the commissary clerk looked out at him from the view plate. "Send up two—no—four liters of beer! And make sure it's cold!"

Carter grinned like a ghoul, and slid farther down in his neck. "Make that six liters, will you? But this is serious. What happens when a positron meets an electron?"

"All right," Doc Mike said wearily. "You get a photon of light coming out of where the two met. Can be most any frequency—usually very high, cosmic or gamma. I wish he'd hurry with that beer! And what's this all about, anyway?"

"Wait and see—and get ready for a trip. I need the information on those plates, though, and several sets of observations some days apart. Here's the beer!"

II.

Two weeks later two frightened scientists looked at each other over the final results from the calculating room. The figures were before them. The unknown, which continued to radiate faintly but continuously in its peculiar fashion, was some ten thousand million miles from the Earth, and was coming closer. And unless the gods of mathematics had completely forsaken them, within two years it would hit the Earth, or come so close to it that the latter would be as thoroughly wrecked as though it had sustained a direct hit.

The body was not large—no larger than the Moon—but its manner of radiation was unique. High-frequency light comes from a hot body. And a body that small *couldn't* be that hot; it would have cooled off long ago. And if it *were* that hot, the intensity of the radiation received by the Earth would have been much greater—greater, in fact, than that received from the Sun, in spite of the small size of the unknown and its great distance from the Earth. It just didn't make sense. And it didn't make sense to the other astronomers of the solar system. Nothing had appeared in the popular press, nor was it likely to. An iron-clad censorship had been clamped down. The danger was serious enough, and panic would make it worse.

Carter spoke. "We're going out to take a look, Mike. Or I am, anyway. Would you like to come along?"

"Uh-huh. You need somebody to take care of you. When do we leave?"

"In half an hour. My ship is ready to go. It has a lot of new gadgets on it, too. This should be a good chance to try them out. Let's go."

Just half an hour later the rocket blasted free from the snow-covered space port near the observatory. It was an improved experimental model of those used at the time, all of which depended upon the principle discovered and developed by Carter himself, which had made space travel something more than an insane gamble.

Hydrogen gas was fed into the converter, where terrific static and magnetic fields converted it into helium. Immense energy, developed from the loss of mass, appeared in the process, which energy imparted a tremendous velocity to the flaming helium gas which escaped through the rocket jets at the stern of the ship. An acceleration up to ten times that of gravity could be maintained, but five gravities was the usual limit for any length of time. More than that, and the passengers lost consciousness. Five was uncomfortable enough, but men in good training could stand it, if they didn't attempt to move from their padded and pivoted chairs.

The trip was uneventful. A week later the rocket was circling cautiously around the unknown body. It was about the size of the Moon, but little could be seen of its surface, which appeared to be under a continuous bombardment with some immensely high explosive. The flashes from the explosions, consisting mainly of cosmic, gammas, and UV's, were evidently the source of the light which had puzzled the observers. Carter and Poggenpohl crouched behind their lead-glass screens and watched.

"Looks like a fluorescent screen being bombarded by electrons, Jimmy. Somewhat larger scale, though. More bombardment on the forward side, too."

"Yes, there is. It looks as though it were sweeping a path through space as it approaches the Earth. Man that gun, will you, please, and fire a solid shot at it when we go around the rear of it again?"

"O. K. Don't see what you're driving at, though. Do you expect a bell to ring, like in a shooting gallery? I'll signal when I fire, and aim directly at the center when we're exactly behind it."

The minute went by, then, "Ready—fired! Watch for it!"

There was no need to watch. Twenty minutes later, when the hundred-pound piece of steel hit the surface of the wandering planet, there was a tremendous flash, dwarfing those which had been observed.

Carter appeared to be pleased, or at least satisfied, and called to the other. "All right, Mike. I'm going to cut the rockets and let the ship take up an orbit around this peculiar object. You take the measurements of distance to the surface and time the orbit, and I'll measure its diameter. Considering the fate of that piece of steel you sent out of the gun, I don't think we'll land this time. It might be unhealthy."

There followed a period of several hours, during which the only sound was the click of the calculating machine, and Mike's gasp as he saw the final result. "Good Lord, Jimmy! This cockeyed animal isn't any bigger than the Moon, and she weighs as much as Jupiter! Are we nuts—or is it?"

Jimmy laughed as he cut in the rockets and swung the ship around for home. "The latter, Mike! *It's* demented—completely. We're no crazier than usual. Gather around and I'll explain."

"It's about time! Now, *what* have you got up your sleeve, anyway?"

"You remember, when we first saw this thing, I put you through a quiz on matter? I had a hunch then, and I've proved it. You described the sort of matter with which we are familiar. Look here. You said that matter was made up of neutrons and positrons, in the last analysis, in the nuclei, and of electrons on the outside. Well, there is another sort of matter possible. What is to prevent an *electron* from combining closely with a neutron, and forming a *negative* proton? The possibility was mentioned way back in 1934, and I think the old boy even gave his hypothetical particle a name—an 'antron,' I think he called it. Now take some of these antrons, and some extra neutrons, and make a nucleus out of them, and then release enough positrons on the outside to balance the antrons. And one has an atom with a *negative* atomic number, since the atomic number of an atom, of course, is the number of positive charges on the nucleus.

"And now one makes a whole universe with these minus elements. And one makes oneself out of them, too, and lives in the place, and can't tell the difference between it and a regular universe. All the physical laws will be the same—but just wait until part of your new universe hits part of a regular universe! Then there'll be the devil to pay and no pitch hot! Figure it out. What do you think will happen?"

"Uh—let's see. First the outer electrons in our matter will neutralize the outer positrons in the reverse matter—and there'll be a hell of a lot of light or other radiation—UV, gamma, cosmic and what not. Then the nuclei will get together. Nothing will happen to either set of neutrons. But the positrons on the protons will neutralize the electrons on the antrons, and there'll be another burst of radiation and a lot of neutrons left over. So the net result will be a mob of neutrons and a flock of radiation. What do you think? Is that thing out there"—he gestured toward the anomalous planet they were leaving behind—"out of a reverse universe?"

"I think so. It has all the symptoms. Long, long ago, how long ago, Heaven only knows, it escaped from some nebula in outer space—some nebula that's built in reverse—and headed this way. And here it is. The glowing and flashing surface is the result of its contact with cosmic dust— the little particles of matter that drift around through all space. And every time it picks some up there's a flash; all the charged particles are neutralized and head away from it as light. And it has added a few more neutrons to its collection. They probably sift down to the center of gravity of the thing. That's why it's so infernally heavy."

"Then, teacher"—Mike was having an idea—"it was probably a rather ordinary planet when it started out on its travels. Barring being built backward, that is! I'd make a guess that it was about half the mass of Jupiter when it started, and, I suppose, had about half the volume. But every time it picked up some normal matter it both shrunk and got heavier. The mass of the positrons and electrons lost would be too small to lose sleep over, and, on the average, it would pick up one neutron for every one of its own freed from a nucleus.

"So it's 'most used up now—an awful flock of neutrons left, and just a little bit of normal reverse matter. The neutrons will have most of the mass, and the reverse matter will take up almost all of the space. Neutrons don't take up any volume to speak of."

"Right. So now it has twice the mass it started with, approximately, and a minute fraction of its original volume. When the rest of the reverse matter is finally neutralized it will be a little heavier, and so small that it'll be completely invisible. Maybe there'll be a few cubic centimeters of neutrons, or some absurd amount like that, with all that mass. But we'd better hurry! It won't be very amusing if that neutralizing is done with some of the Earth's surface! Hold tight—here comes some acceleration!"

III.

Ten days later Carter and Poggenpohl presented their report to the commissariat of science of the United States of America, and two days later they attended an emergency meeting of the heads of the departments of science of the governments of the world. Carter was speaking.

"So you see, gentlemen, what the situation is. You all understand the theory of the phenomenon, and you know that the observatories of the world and of the other two inhabited planets have checked our own telescopic observations. In addition, there is the phenomenon we observed when the six-inch projectile hit this—this——"

"Call it 'Gus,'" whispered Mike disrespectfully.

Jimmy glared at him, and continued, "—this—minus planet. I am aware of no alternative theory to explain the behavior of this anomalous body, and most of you appear to be inclined to adhere to the one Dr. Poggenpohl and I have presented." He looked around the table and saw nothing but a succession of reluctant nods.

"Then, the question is, what to do about it? If it were normal matter it would be bad enough. But then, it might be possible to install huge rocket tubes on the intruder and drive it out of its course sufficiently to miss the Earth by a safe margin. But what can we do with this thing, when, if we touch it, we shall be annihilated? And if we don't touch it, we shall be annihilated anyhow. At least the Earth, and those who can't escape to the other planets will be annihilated, and that means ninety-nine per cent of the population. For you know that our combined rocket fleets aren't enough to move one per cent of the Earth's population in the time we have available. And even if we could move them—the other planets are only barely inhabitable by man, and certainly could not support all of us."

"There's one thing we must do," remarked the science commissary of the Russians, "and that is to keep this situation a secret, for the present at least. For if we don't, there will be such a rush for the few rockets we have that half the world's population will be killed in a few days in the panic. And the rockets themselves will be smashed. We won't be able to do anything at all with them."

"There's no doubt at all on that point," said the delegate from the Federated States of Europe. "I take it that the meeting is unanimous on that point?" There was another chorus of nods, but this time more enthusiastic. "But has anybody any idea of how to move this—minus planet—out of the course it's following?"

There was a sodden silence, and then Mike rose slowly to his feet, his red hair bristling with what looked like an idea. "Gentlemen, there's one other way to move our little country cousin out of his course. Hit him with something heavy that's moving fast enough to do the job."

"But what will happen to that thing, whatever it is? Won't it be annihilated?"

"Not so you could notice it, when it comes to the effect. All the electrons and positrons will be gone, and it won't be normal matter any more, but the neutrons will be left, and they will have the momentum they started with."

"Very well, Herr Poggenpohl, but what can we hit it with that will be big enough to make any difference? All the space ships in the solar system, firing all their biggest guns for a year, wouldn't be enough to do anything to its course! After all, it weighs as much as Jupiter!"

"There's one projectile available that would be big enough to make quite a perceptible dent in its path: the Moon! We can spare it. All it does is produce the tides. Mount rocket tubes on the Moon, pry it up out of the solar system, and sock the intruder so that its course will be changed and it will fall into the Sun! We can do that if we hit it while it's still far enough away from the system."

The council gasped at the suggestion, and there was a chorus of excited protests, which slowly died, as the sheer magnitude of the plan gripped the imaginations of the assembled scientists. Nobody thought of putting the question to a formal vote, and in twenty minutes the meeting had been changed, automatically, into an executive council, which was in an excited argument about ways and means, in which calculating machines, reference books, celestial mechanics, the quantum theory, and polylingual profanity played a prominent part.

Carter pounded on the table and shouted until he managed to attract the attention of the disputants. "Gentlemen," he said, "I suggest that we present our plans to the various governments, in order to obtain their coöperation in the execution of our project. And I also suggest that publicity can do no harm now, since we have an apparently practicable remedy for the difficulty. The amateur astronomers will let the cat out of the bag very soon, anyway, if we don't make some statement. And finally, may

I suggest that we request the President of the United States to make a television broadcast, explaining the situation to the public, asking their coöperation, and assuring them that the said situation is, as it were, well in hand?"

The assembled scientists stared blankly at him, nodded absent-mindedly, and returned to their discussion, more violently than before. Carter grinned at Mike, lighted a cigarette, and wandered out of the room, in search of a communicator in some place that was quiet enough so that he could make his message to the President heard above the din.

The President revealed the danger to the world in one of his famous fireside broadcasts, concluding with a request that every one remain quietly at his normal duties, unless called upon to coöperate in some way with the scientists who were working at what appeared to be a practicable method of saving the planet.

The heads of the other governments of the world made similar broadcasts.

As might be expected, most of the population of the Earth paid no attention at all to the broadcasts, being quite unable to realize the situation. The Earth had never been destroyed, therefore it could not be destroyed, and the scientists were crazy as usual. That attitude was typical of the major part of the inhabitants of the globe—the great, average masses.

But there were two other attitudes apparent. On the one side there were those intelligent enough to understand the danger and the measures that were being taken against it. They were the scientists, engineers, and technicians of the world, and the well-educated part of the other classes of the population.

On the other side were the unbalanced, the fanatics, and the extremely ignorant, who were the tools of the first two. They rioted, for no apparent reason, but merely because they were frightened, they tried to make up in two years for the dullness of their lives, not realizing that the dullness of those lives was largely due to the dullness of their intellects. Some of them—and they were less trouble than the others—merely got drunk and remained that way. A few of them actively obstructed the work that had to be done.

One of them, one Obidiah Miller, who had been, it was rumored, a circuit rider in the Tennessee Mountains, was the most virulent. He was an ignorant man, but he possessed a native shrewdness which, combined with his surprising oratorical powers and his religious fanaticism, had a tremendous effect on the more ignorant and weak-minded portions of the population.

Fanatics are always followed by fools, of which there is an inexhaustible supply. When the danger appeared, the intelligent parts of the populace decided that the reasonable thing to do was to coöperate with the scientists who were trying to cope with it. The fanatics proclaimed, and the fools believed, that the approaching calamity was the judgment of God on an impious world. Especially did they protest that the Moon should not be moved. First, because it couldn't be moved; second, because the Lord hadn't intended it to move; and third, because, since God had evidently intended that the minus planet should destroy the Earth for its wickedness, it would be an act of impiety even to attempt to avert the collision.

"Would ye seek, brethren, to attempt to stave off the Day of Judgment, as foretold in the Holy Scriptures? Would ye seek"—his hill-billy accent rolled out over the sheep-faced crowd—"to avert the day when the righteous shall be raised to the right hand of God, and the wicked shall be cast down to Hell? Will ye let the wicked meddlers into matters that are best left alone attempt to stave off the almighty hand of God? Wreck the space ports! Smash the rockets! Kill the idolaters!"

There was an answering rumble from the crowd, as Mike and Jimmy slipped away from its outskirts. "The 'idolaters,' " Mike remarked, as they sidled into a building, "sounds like us. I would recommend, with all due respect to the gentleman's religious convictions, that steps be taken. With an ax, for choice, before he starts gumming the works."

"There appears to be something in what you say. Personally, I have no desire to become a martyr to science before it's absolutely necessary. Let's get the chief of the Federal police on the wire, and have him gather our friend in and send his congregations home. And some guards with machine guns and things around the space ports might not be amiss. We haven't any time to be bothered by fools!"

In the next few days there was an epidemic of raids on the pseudo-religious protest meetings, and there was a great gathering-in of the more rabid of the fanatics, including Obidiah Miller, who was planted, gently but firmly, in a lunatic asylum. Guards were placed around the space ports, and assigned to the more important of the scientists who were employed on the gigantic task. There were a few attempts at sabotage and assassination, but all of them failed.

The work was pressed. The astronomical observatory on the Moon was dismantled and carried to the Earth piecemeal, as were many of the valuable fittings of the space port there. Since the development of atomic power, this port was not as necessary as it had been in the old days of combustion rockets. Then, the huge atomic drills, operated by men in space suits, started the excavation of the deep shafts that were to act as rocket tubes. Some fifty of them were drilled, most of them parallel, but a few at divergent angles, to act as the steering mechanism of the huge space ship into which Luna was being converted. At the bases of these shafts the reaction chambers were excavated, and lined with refractory material. The automatic fuel-supply system was installed, whereby millions of tons of the very material of the satellite itself were carried to the reaction chambers.

There, the lighter elements, oxygen, silicon, aluminum, etc., were to be converted into iron vapor, which was to be driven out of the rocket tubes by the atomic energy released in the process. Iron itself, though common on the Moon, was not suitable as a fuel, since, in respect to *atomic* changes, it is the most stable of all the elements. The whole fuel system was automatically controlled, with all controls in duplicate.

The controlling mechanism, which consisted, in effect, of fifty throttles—one for each rocket tube—was arranged to be controlled by remote radio control from a space ship, which would convoy the huge projectile to its destination. All the rocket tubes, of course, were on one hemisphere of the Moon, since there would be no need of stopping it in its course, once it had been started.

Thousands of men were needed for the construction work—of all types from manual laborers to astrophysicists. And all of them were working at high pressure. Work never stopped for months at a time. Accidents were many—an atomic drill is not the safest instrument in the universe, and working in a space suit is always dangerous.

As a result, the work took a steady toll of lives, and there was a steady inflow of new labor onto the job. But the work went on in spite of accidents. It had to. When a man was killed, if there was anything at all left of him, the body was tossed to one side and another man took his place. The record of the construction would be an epic in itself—one which there is no space to record here.

The plan of operation was simple—in theory. The Moon was to be gradually dragged away from the Earth—gradually, to avoid inducing huge tides and devastating Earthquakes, then driven north "above" the solar system, out of the plane of the ecliptic. It was to be driven into the minus planet at such an angle and at such a velocity that the latter would be deflected away from the Earth, and the residual mass of neutrons would fall directly into the Sun, where they would do no harm. It was calculated that the normal matter of the Moon would a little more than neutralize the negative matter of the minus planet, so that the residue that finally reached the Sun would consist of a small planetoid of normal matter surrounding an extremely massive core of neutrons.

IV.

It was July 6, 2157. Carter and Poggenpohl were rechecking the calculations of the course the Moon would have to take on its last voyage.

Finally, they finished with the last decimal and leaned back. "And that, my boy, is how it shall be done!" Jimmy threw his pencil at the calculating machine and inserted his face into a liter of beer.

"All you have to do is push the button and save the world. We'll have to do some reckoning, though, on the initial escape from the Earth. Otherwise, if we're a little brusque about it, the tides will put New York under fifty feet of water, and the mayor might possibly be annoyed with us. How far behind schedule are those Primates of engineers, who are supposed to be building the rocket tubes on that soon-to-be excompanion of our more romantic moments?"

"They ain't. Bill Douglas was here last night, and he said that they would be ready to go in two weeks. And we have three to spare. He's a week ahead of schedule. There's just a little more wiring to do. And we don't have to do any calculating on tidal effects, either. I did it myself a month ago. It won't be as tough as it looks—a gradual acceleration of the Moon's velocity in its orbit, and a gradual, simultaneous acceleration away from the Earth. I planned those rocket tubes, too, so that they won't shower the Earth with vaporized iron. They won't point this way until they're a long way from here. You stick to my firing chart, and you'll get away with it. And I figured what the tides would be, too, so you don't have to worry about that. I done it with my little calculator!"

"I say—I thought *I* was the genius around here! I'll have to have the brass hats increase your salary fifteen, or possibly twenty, cents a week!"

"You don't have to worry about that, either!" Mike grinned like a gargoyle. "I've already attended to it. I caught the commissary of science in a good mood the other day and hit him for five hundred dollars more per week. Got it, too. In fact, it's already spent. You're invited to come and help drink some of it to-night."

"Accepted without qualification. How about those tides, though? How bad will they be?"

"Not so bad. About three meters maximum above mean high water along the coast. They've almost finished building concrete sea walls around the cities and the important communications along the coast, and they're evacuating the other coastal lowlands. But *you* wouldn't know about that. You've been too busy with that trick integraph of yours to know whether you're alive or——"

A buzz of the communicator interrupted Mike. He flicked the switch, and the agitated face of the chief of the Federal police appeared on the screen. "Dr. Poggenpohl! That nut, Obidiah Miller, escaped from the loony bin last night! We haven't been able to track him down. Probably get him in a couple of days, but watch yourself in the meantime, and warn Dr. Carter. I'll send over a couple more guards. No sense in taking any chances now."

"Thanks, chief. I'll warn Dr. Carter. But there isn't much our little friend can do right now. The job's almost done. Thanks for the warning, though." He flicked off the switch. "Oh, hell, nothing we can do about it! I only hope he stays away from here. I *don't* like nuts. They get in my hair. And by the way, there's another guy who is cursing us up one side and down the other. The power commissary is quite wrathy.

"We're taking the Moon away from him, and he can't produce any tidal power any more. He'll have to rip up all his plants and convert them into atomic-power outfits. He doesn't love us. He wants to write off the original investment on the old plants, so that his department can make a good showing. And they didn't have any upkeep to speak of, and the power was free and required no brains whatever to produce. So, as I remarked, he does not love us. In fact, I think that he'd like to boil us in oil or do something else equally lingering and humorous to us."

"Oh, well. Invite him to the party. Perhaps, if we get him tight enough he won't mind it so much."

V.

It was August 1, 2157. The last of the construction crews had been removed from the Moon; all the movable equipment had been returned to the Earth, and everything was ready for the start. The control space ship was waiting for Carter and Poggenpohl, who were to guide the Moon on its last journey. In twenty hours, at exactly 16:27, GMT, August 2, 2157, the first rocket was to be fired.

Mike had strolled out to the ship, where he was intent on inspecting his quarters, when there was a frantic ringing of alarm bells, and a white-faced field attendant raced across the field. "Dr. Poggenpohl! Stop! There's trouble on the Moon! Just got word. A——" He stopped suddenly as Jimmy ran up alongside of him.

"There's going to be hell, Mike! That damned nut Miller's gummed things. When he got loose he got himself included in one of the last construction crews on the Moon, and when they left for Earth he hid and stayed there. And he's wrecked the remote-control apparatus completely!"

"How do you know?"

"He had to brag about it. He called me up on the communicator three minutes ago and told me what he'd done. Just wanted to rub it in. He's a martyr, of course. Perfectly willing to die with the Earth if he can keep everybody else from living. And there isn't any time to fix the control;

we have to start in twenty hours, come hell or high water. And *they'll* both come if we don't. Wait until I catch that messiah! I'll roast his liver over a slow fire!"

"What are you going to do about it, Jimmy? That damned minus planet will rip us out by the roots if we don't do something fast!"

"I'm going to the Moon and run the thing by hand. Tell them to get the experimental rocket ready."

"The hell you say! You'll get yourself annihilated! And how are you going to do it, anyway?"

"Oh, there's an auxiliary control for the tubes on the Moon itself, off to one side of the rocket area. Rather on the edge, between the rocket hemisphere and the forward or blank hemisphere. I can control it from there—if I can get there before our friend Obidiah thinks of smashing it, too."

"Maybe so, but you'll get yourself killed just the same. How are you going to get out from under when the two hit?"

"I'll have the rocket parked alongside," said Jimmy, "and dive into it when I have Luna lined up for a direct hit. I've a pretty good chance— maybe one in ten, or so. I'll go alone, of course. There's no sense in anybody else's taking the chance."

"That's what you think!" Mike's red hair bristled even more belligerently than usual, and he glared up at the other's face. "I'm going along. You can't handle that brute alone for a week—you're just nuts! And if you can draw to an inside straight, so can I!

"Hey!" he shouted across the field. "Provision the experimental rocket for two men for four weeks! And make it fast! I'll tear your liver out if I have to wait twenty minutes! Jimmy, get your gun! We'll have to settle with Obidiah."

Nobody's liver was torn out. Fifteen minutes later the little rocket roared clear of the field with the two men inside. Ten hours later they were in their space suits, bounding in long, ungainly leaps across the Lunar landing field toward the control room. In the helmet radio, Jimmy could hear Mike cursing fluently in three languages. "Lord," he thought, "if that ape has smashed things already—then we *shall* be in a jam!"

They reached the control cubicle, and peered in the ports. The control board was invisible from there. They crept into the air lock. As the inner door swung silently open they saw a gaunt figure in a space suit raising a huge spanner over the main controls.

Jimmy's gun roared. The figure pitched forward between the levers, and the spanner clanged to the floor. "This is no time for chivalry, Mike. Throw that thing out the air lock, will you, while I see if the controls are all right? The fool must have just remembered the direct controls. It's lucky that we arrived when we did!"

It was August 2, 2157, 16:24 GMT. The rocket had been moored by huge steel cables, with a quick-release arrangement, against the door of the control room. Three minutes to go.

Both men were in the padded and pivoted chairs before the control board. "We, who are about to die," Jimmy said casually, "salute you. Is everything ready?" He swung the safety-release lever over, activating the control buttons. "Will you tell them that I died in the odor of sanctity?"

"No," said Mike, "I will not. Your odor is not of sanctity. It reminds me more of beer. You may fire when you are ready, Gridley!"

Jimmy glued his eyes to the firing chart, and his fingers to the first bank of buttons. Twenty seconds to go. Mike shivered a little, and tried to disguise the shiver with a yawn. He started counting seconds.

"Ten—nine—eight—seven—six—five—four—three—two—one—fire!"

There was a shattering, ground-transmitted roar. The Moon under their feet trembled, and through the ports, silhouetted against a hellish glare, they saw the construction scaffolding fall to the ground. The roaring increased. It was like a continuous explosion. Mike tore his handkerchief into bits, stuffed pieces into his ears, and did the same for Jimmy, who was too busy with the controls to do anything for himself.

The roar increased and the flares waxed to an absolutely unendurable brightness, and there was a feeling of acceleration, as though the floor beneath their feet were tilting. Mike covered the ports against the glare, and sat down again. He lighted two cigarettes, one of which he placed in Jimmy's mouth.

The wall against which the rocket was moored had become the floor. The Moon was traveling faster than it had for millions of years, and was gradually drawing away from the Earth. They had no instruments with which to observe the latter, but Mike could imagine the growing tides, the tremblers, and the spectacle in the sky. "I hope they make movies from the Earth," he remarked to nobody in particular. "I'd like to see them if we ever get out of this."

He broke open some food and water, ate, and took the controls while Carter ate, and then, plugging his ears more thoroughly, lay down on an air mattress and went placidly to sleep, after setting an alarm to wake him, with an electric shock, after six hours. Any alarm depending on sound for its effect would be completely useless.

When he awoke and took the controls, the Earth was far behind, and the minus planet was a brilliant spot on the view plate, a little left of dead center. It was coming closer all the time. The roaring of the jets continued unabated. The whole hemisphere of the Moon "below" them, when he ventured to look, was one white glare, with the incandescent iron vapor shooting hundreds of miles into space.

August 12th, 3:28: The last watch was in progress. Jimmy was at the controls. Both of them were in their space suits, and the doors of the control-room air lock, which now appeared, because of the acceleration, to be below them, were wide open directly over the open, outer door of the air lock of the rocket, into which a rope dangled from a stanchion beside the control board.

The minus planet was visible through the port in the opposite wall— now the roof—filling most of the sky, and rapidly growing larger. The acceleration was still at maximum, as the greatest possible velocity at the time of the collision was not only desirable but necessary. The seconds sped, and yet dragged, as the minus planet grew.

3:30: Jimmy held up two fingers. Two minutes more! He waved Mike toward the air lock. The latter looked around the room to see if he had forgotten anything, and then slid "down" into the rocket's air lock and grabbed the control that would free the moorings.

3:31: The minus planet was bigger—much bigger. It filled most of the sky. Mike gazed anxiously up at Jimmy.

3:32: Jimmy leaped from the controls and slid down into the air lock. He tossed out the rope as Mike released the moorings and slammed the outer door of the lock. There was the sudden baffling sensation of weightlessness, as all acceleration left the ship, which was now falling freely after the Moon, toward the intruder. There was a *whoosh* as they opened the inner door, not waiting for the pressure to equalize, and pulled themselves by the guide rails toward the control cabin. The gyroscopes were already turning over at full speed, and the rocket tubes had been warmed up.

3:34: Mike slammed himself into the control seat, swung the stick which controlled the motors turning the ship around the stabilizing gyroscopes, and, heading her out to one side of the impending collision, jammed on the maximum safe acceleration of five gravities. Jimmy had managed to reach a chair, and was attempting to pull off his space suit, but the acceleration forced his arms down by his sides, and almost pulled him through the seat of the chair. Mike shoved the acceleration up another notch, and switched on all the view plates.

4:45: The acceleration was still on at six gravities, but neither of the men were interested in it. Their eyes were glued to the view plate, which bore on the impending collision. It was a matter of seconds. Already the Moon was breaking up, and most of the rocket tubes had gone out. Then——

There was a blinding flash on the view plate, and it went black, burned out by the tremendous impact of the radiation. Mike cut the acceleration to zero, and fainted. But Jimmy didn't know it. He was unconscious.

About an hour later they came to—bruised, battered, and burned by the radiation which had filtered through the supposedly ray-proof walls of the ship. They switched on an acceleration of half a gravity, so that they could navigate comfortably in the rocket, and swung her ninety degrees around the gyros, so that they could see the remains of the intruder through the side ports. The view plates were useless. There was a small, incandescent planetoid falling toward the Sun. Mike turned a spectrometer on it, gazed a minute, and then grinned all over his blistered face. "It looks like we've done it! There isn't a damned bit of minus matter left on the thing. It glows like a normal hot body—like a young Sun about the size of Ceres."

Jimmy tried to grin back, and couldn't. His face hurt too much. "Right-oh! The Moon neutralized the last of it, with some left over. There's nothing there now except neutrons and some white hot iron, silicon, and whatever else the Moon was made of. It's terrifically heavy, and it's hotter than the seven hinges of hell, but it's nothing to fear. It will fall into the Sun in a month or so. But *you* look like the way I feel, and that's like the latter end of a misspent life. You'd better strip. I'll get the antiburn goo from the medicine chest, and we can butter ourselves up. Then, we can let the ship coast a while while we get some sleep. And finally, if there's enough of her left to navigate, we can wend our way homeward. But sleep is what I want most right now——"

Two weeks later, two tanned and filthy astrophysicists stepped out of the air lock of a burned and blistered rocket onto the tarmac of the space port at Washington, stopped short, and gazed with horror at the galaxy of gold braid and blazing stuffed shirts that approached them. They glanced from side to side with the expression of hunted animals, and then, with the mien of early Christian martyrs, stepped forward to undergo the horrors of an official reception by the combined governments of the solar system.

———

By 1937, I had learned of anti-matter, and Clark's story, which was the first ever to deal with it in science fiction, excited me tremendously. I felt he was talking my language as a burgeoning chemist and that other, more ordinary readers would not understand it as I did. (This was a good feeling.)

John Clark was, of course, a professional chemist himself* and a Ph.D. was appended to his name under the story. (E. E. Smith was also a Ph.D.)

Looking back on "Minus Planet" now, some thirty-six years after it was written, I find that it is a little dated. A proton is looked at in the story as a neutron plus a positron, but it's actually more likely to be made up of mesons or quarks.

It's also interesting that the interloping body of anti-matter was discovered by optical telescope and that science fiction writers uniformly imagined an astronomical future in which telescopes would be just like the 100-incher of the 1930s, only larger. Nobody, including Clark in this story, foresaw the possibility of radio telescopes, though the basic discovery had been made in 1931.

Stories such as "Minus Planet" were convincing demonstrations that it wasn't enough for writers to make use of hoary catchwords like "radium" and "fourth dimension." They had to keep abreast of the latest developments in science.

And by 1937, I was beginning to realize that my knowledge of science was progressing to the point where I clearly knew more about it than most science fiction writers. That meant that my awe was vanishing and that, more and more, I became convinced that I knew enough to write science fiction.

As I look back on it now, I think that my appreciation of "Minus Planet" and my eagerness to be another John Clark contributed strongly to my decision (at last!) to write a science fiction story not merely for my own amusement but for possible publication.

My long-winded science fiction novel had suffocated to death some months before, and on May 29, 1937, about two months after I read "Minus Planet," I began, for the first time, a science fiction short story. I called it "Cosmic Corkscrew," and I worked at it, in fits and starts, for about a month.

However, it was another false start. As soon as I began to imagine myself writing with the intent of publishing, I froze. I managed to get the story half finished, and then I put it away in a drawer and forgot about it for nearly a year.

My enjoyment of science fiction had risen steadily through the years, ever since I first began reading it, in 1929, and in 1937 it reached its peak. I remember exactly when that peak came.

* He worked on rocket fuels during the war and recently wrote an excellent book on the subject, *Ignition!* to which I wrote the introduction. We met in 1942 and have been good friends ever since. He wrote only one other story, "Space Blister," which appeared in the August 1937 issue. Despite my periodic urgings, he has written no more fiction.

It came in the month of August 1937, when I was spending the summer waiting for my junior year at Columbia to begin. In that month, the September 1937 issue of *Astounding Stories* arrived, and I remember the precise feelings that swept over me as I sat in the living room of our apartment and read the first installment of Edward E. Smith's new four-part serial, *Galactic Patrol*.

Never, I think, did I enjoy any piece of writing more, any piece of any kind. Never did I savor every word so. Never did I feel so keen a sense of loss when I came to the end of the first installment and knew that I would have to wait a full month for the second.

Never anything like it before. Never anything like it after.

And in the September 1937 issue was another story, a novelette by Nat Schachner, "Past, Present, and Future," and at the time I enjoyed it nearly as much as I did *Galactic Patrol*.

Schachner was one of my favorite writers for the Tremaine *Astounding*. Among the stories I wish I could have included in this anthology (well, I couldn't include them all—even after I had cut the number to the bone, the fine gentlemen at Doubleday turned pale at the length of the book) were "Ancestral Voices," in the December 1933 issue (the first of the thought-variants, I think), "The Ultimate Metal," in the February 1935 issue, and "The Isotope Men," in the January 1936 issue.

However, "Past, Present, and Future" was far and away my favorite among his stories.

PAST, PRESENT, AND FUTURE

by Nat Schachner

Kleon stood on the edge of the jungle, stared out at the bright-blue bay. The great trireme, with its steeply pitched banks of oars, burned furiously. Fire and smoke crackled up to the tropic sun, licked like running tongues around the poop, swirled with final fury over the god Poseidon, whose wooden beard and pointing trident adorned the high-beaked prow.

As the god tottered and fell, charred beyond recognition, into the briny waters, Kleon bowed his head, uttered the classic prayer of Homer. It was an omen, a sign to him that never again would he see his native vines and twisted olive trees, that never again would he discourse with the philosophers or hear the godlike Alexander shout the Macedonian charge against the Persian hosts.

Slowly the embers died, slowly the sound of the crackling timbers ceased. Behind him, framed against a tangle of festooned trees and outlandish blooms, cowered his crew. They were not of his race; they were swart Egyptian sailors from Thebes, impressed by the mighty Alexander for his fleet against Arabia and the Indian potentates.

They held their spears uneasily, bracing themselves against the terrible wrath of their young commander, knowing that they had been guilty of foulest treachery, yet not sorry withal for what they had done. Their eyes feasted hungrily on the women by their sides—whom they had found inhabiting this incredible land where strange stars glowed overhead and the earth teemed with food and shelter and sustenance for the taking. These women were tall and light and straight, with copper-colored skins and laughing eyes that were a delight to sailors who had seen not even a mermaid for many moons.

Why should they leave these newfound delights, this gentle race of friendly people who called themselves Mayas in their own liquid tongue, to embark once more on restless Oceanus and steer back toward the setting sun? That was tempting the gods too much. This time, they were sure, their bones would molder in the sunless caverns of the fathomless seas, or their ship sweep over the rim of the world into the maw of old Chaos.

No, they had had enough of tempting the spirits of the waters. Only Isis and Osiris had saved them thus far, since the great wind had sprung up in the Indian Ocean and separated them from the fleet of Nearchus, admiral of Alexander, as it skirted the hostile coasts. They would stay here, with the people who thought them and their blond young commander, forsooth, gods from across the sea. Had they not kneeled and worshiped Kleon when the trireme had sailed into the fantastic bay? Had they not cried on him and called him by some outlandish name, as though he had been long expected? Quetzal—that was it.

Yet Kleon, in his Greek obstinacy, had ordered them, after a month of soft surrender to the balmy airs, after replenishment of food and water casks, to the oars again, to brave once more the perils they had so miraculously escaped. His mouth had set in a grim, hard way to all their protestations.

So they had burned the ship! It would be impossible for Kleon, for all his Greek learning, for all the magic arts he had learned among the wizards of the Persians, the Hindus, and the one-eyed Anthropophagi who lurked in caves on the Roof of the World, to force them to breast the waves again.

Yet, because he was their commander and they were but Egyptian slaves, because he wore bright armor and knew how to wield with slashing strokes the Macedonian short sword at his side, they cowered and were uneasy—though they outnumbered him an even hundred to one.

And still the Greek, terrible in his armor like the young sun god, made no move. The trireme was a dead-black hulk on the silent waters. The Mayas, black-haired, tall, stared at the stranger they had hailed as Quetzal, with fixed adoration. Even the raucous birds of many hues, who seemed to mock them from the trees with human cries, were still.

Hotep, the steersman, approached him timidly. "You are not angry with us, noble Kleon," he pleaded. "We have done only that which seemed best. Here, among these people, we are as gods. Why breast the floods to suffer hunger and thirst and hideous monsters, and perchance, the outraged edges of the world, to return once more to—slavery and back-bending toil and the hewing of fierce weapons?"

Kleon turned slowly. "You have done best for yourselves, no doubt," he said evenly. "You are slaves, Egyptians. You will mingle with these dwellers beyond the flood and find no demeanment in it. You will teach them what you know of the arts and be content. But I am a Greek and these are barbarians. I will not waste my life among such as these—and you. Life is a precious depository for the *noumena*, the metaphysical thought, or it is nothing. On the farther side of the world mighty Alexander marches to new triumphs, and the Grecian culture marches with him. Here is stagnation, minds that know not science or noble philosophy. What have I, a Greek, to do with these—or with you, for that matter, O Hotep?"

The Egyptian bowed humbly. He was not offended. In the elder days his race had been mighty, but the world had gone topsy-turvy, and the old gods had yielded to new. That was why he and his comrades were content to remain in this new land the balance of their days.

"What do you wish from us, great Kleon?" he asked.

The Greek stared at him speculatively, turned his gaze from the ocean, from the charred husk of the trireme, slid past the trembling crew, past the copper-colored natives, flung inland over the impenetrable jungle to the blue rise of ground that marked the backbone of the interior. Smoke curled lazily from a cone-shaped top. His blue eyes glinted; a strange luster crept into their being. When he spoke he seemed to commune with himself rather than hold conversation with Hotep.

"When Alexander left Persepolis and marched for dreadful months through strange Asian lands and stranger peoples to the Indus, we passed over the very top of the world. There we came upon a race of learned holy men, so old, so wasted with time's attritions, that verily they seemed in sooth what they maintained—survivors from an elder day, when earth was clad in ice and Zeus himself had not been born.

"I spent some time with them, O Hotep, and they opened their minds to me, a curious seeker after knowledge. They told me of the days before the ice came, when the world was young and the bleak hills were covered with strange verdure and mighty cities; they spoke with the air of participants in great civilizations long since buried. In full sooth their knowledge was beyond that of Aristotle himself. They averred that when the frozen waters pressed inexorably southward from the northern pole their civilization died, but such was the secret science of their priests that some few were able to immure themselves in caverns, there to repose for long centuries in immortal inanition, to awake at a predetermined time when their science taught them the ice would have ebbed back again to the frozen Boreal regions.

"I was skeptical, as the Sophists had taught me to be, but they took me to sealed caverns, into which I was able to peer through a strange instrument that made transparent the solid rock, and behold, I saw some of their sleepers still. These, they averred, had set their awakening for a later era than the rest, desiring to taste the farther future. A thousand more years must elapse before these would stir and breathe again."

"It is incredible," murmured Hotep politely.

The face of Kleon was a contemplative mask. "They taught me the secret," he mused. "The sight of yon mountain, where the Titans rumble underground and the Cyclopes forge their thunderbolts, reminded me of the tale."

He squared his shoulders suddenly. His voice lashed out as it was wont to do when he had led a phalanx into battle. "Hotep, slaves, listen to me!"

They jumped at his clarion tones, forgetful that he was but one and they were an even hundred. "Yes, gracious lord," they chorused.

"You have done a foul deed. You are cattle, and this idle land and idler folk will satisfy your limited desires. But I am a Greek, and must blaze always with a bright, clean flame, or life is valueless. I do not intend to rust away my remaining days among barbarians. Therefore, if you seek my forgiveness, you must follow my will in the exactest degree."

Hotep moved stealthily back to the mass of his comrades, firmed his grip on his spear. Did the Greek, perchance, have some mad notion of building a new trireme from the heavy forest trees, and blunder toward the west? Rather would he——

Kleon did not seem to see the hostile gestures of his men. "I too, shall brave the future," he declared. "The present is an empty amphora for my spirit; I wish to fill myself with the bright wine of days that are yet unborn. I shall immure myself in a cavern, even as those priests who inhabited the Roof of the World, and do thus and so as they had taught me. I shall set a time for my awakening—let me see—yea, ten thousand years. Who knows what strange and marvelous visions will greet my eye in that tremendous span of years!"

Spears dropped with dull thuds from nerveless fingers; black beards gaped in ludicrous astonishment, confused voices called on Horus and Ammon-Ra. The copper folk, all unwitting, knowing not the meaning of the god, Quetzal, nevertheless, prostrated themselves in fear before his flashing eye, the sound of his speech that surged like the many billowed sea.

Hotep burst out in gasping words. "Lord, have you in sooth gone mad? These tales of magic have addled your brain! They but mocked you. It is impossible——"

"It is enough," Kleon broke in sharply, "that I command it." He fingered his sword significantly.

A wave of hasty assent rose like incense from the crew. Why should they not do the mad Greek's bidding? Even so, would they be freed from ever-present dread of their treachery and meditated vengeance. They would live their lives among these gentle folk, take their women for wives, and loll in ease and security after much buffetings. Let the Greek be immured, if he wished, in the bowels of the earth, let him wait for that fantastic future he described.

It took almost a year to perform the task. But Kleon drove his crew and these pliable folk, who called themselves Mayas, relentlessly. Now that the die was cast, now that he had pondered on it nights and days, he was eager for that future which the gymnosophists of the Roof of the World had promised him; indeed, he was very eager.

He required a volcano; for the gases generated in the smithies of the Cyclopes were necessary for his entombment. He found the blue cone from which the smoke eternally wisped some fifty stadia inland. He caused its base to be cleared, and there the Egyptians built for him a small pyramid, patterned according to the one of Cheops, on which the copper-colored Mayas toiled willingly like submissive beasts of burden. Underneath the tapering stone they inclosed a chamber, rough-hewn, built against the millenniums, air-sealed against all outer contamination. From the chamber they led vents of stone to the bowels of the fire-breathing mountain, so that, by ingenious tappets, the swirling gases of brimstone and sulphurous pungency might be inducted in due proportions.

Then they withdrew and Kleon busied himself in secret. From his leather jerkin underneath the armor he drew a leaden globule. This had been given him by the gymnosophists with appropriate instructions. Within its hollow shell was a lustrous, ever-burning substance—a substance that burned, yet consumed itself only after thousands and thousands of years.

Kleon handled the pellet gingerly, prepared its mechanism so that, at a pressure, tiny openings would appear, so regulated as to emit the radiations of the interior element in specified amounts, and cease completely after ten thousand years. He, a Greek, of course, did not know that he held in his hand an ounce of pure, elemental radium, the secret of whose isolation from its salts had been known to that preglacial civilization, and had been since lost to the new-born world.

Then, as he had been taught, he arranged a comfortable niche in which to spread himself, saw to it that certain hinged stones devised by Hotep fell swiftly and smoothly into place on swinging pivots to cut off all entrance and exit, placed over a secret spring that controlled the pivots a tiny disk of laminated, fluorescent substance, likewise furnished by the ancients from the Roof of the World. On this was trained the perforations from the pellet of radium.

The potent radiations from the sacred element, they told him, would disintegrate each lamination of the disk in exactly one thousand years. Therefore, Kleon peeled off the excess layers and left but ten to withstand the steady buffets of the radium. As the bombardment finally pierced the last fluorescent layer, the unobstructed rays would then impinge on the naked spring that actuated the mechanism of the pivoting stones. They would turn smoothly in their sockets; air would rush in from outer vents, whiff away the preservative gases, and he, Kleon, would then awake as though from a short, dreamless nap, ten thousand years into the future.

They had tried to explain to him the exact interaction of pure, elemental radium with the special mixture of sulphurous oxides, hydrochloric acid, sulphocyanides and hydrocarbons of which volcanic gases are compounded, but chemistry was not a science of which the Greeks had any knowledge. It was sufficient for Kleon that the products of the interaction had certain effects on body tissues and organs. They acted as an arrester of vital processes, a bath in which all life remained suspended indefinitely with blood uncongealed and flesh both fresh and firm.

At last the day arrived. Kleon felt his heart beat unduly fast. Suppose the gymnosophists had been but playing on his Greek credulity, suppose they were magicians whose feats were illusions; suppose, instead, he would die within this tomb and never emerge. He laughed, and the sound of his laughter was hollow in his ears. He did not fear death, yet——

They were within the pyramid, within the sacred chamber—only Hotep and he. Outside, guarding the entrance, was his crew, spears uplifted in reverence in accordance with his strict instructions. Beyond, covering the cleared space around the pyramid, flat on their faces in adoration, lay the Mayas. Quetzal, the blond white god, it had been announced to them, intended to sleep. He was weary of the wickedness of the world. But some day, refreshed, mighty, he would arise and bring to his children, the Mayas, eternal life, peace and unexampled prosperity.

"I think," Kleon told Hotep with a grim smile, "that will be sufficient to protect me from harm." He looked shrewdly at the Egyptian. "I think also," he continued, "that you will find it profitable to perpetuate the legend."

Hotep grinned slyly in his beard. "You have an all-penetrating eye, noble Kleon. I shall make myself high priest of Quetzal, and my children after me."

"I didn't doubt it," Kleon commented dryly. Then his face became an expressionless mask. He tested the vents, the ensealing stone. "It is time, O Hotep. Do you retire and swing the stone into place behind you. Then, as you value your life and the honor of your approaching priesthood, seek no more entrance to my abode."

The Egyptian struggled for utterance in his black beard, bowed suddenly, and retired. The huge, rough-hewn stone clicked softly into place. The chamber was sealed.

Kleon, as one already dead, went about his preparations. A smoky torch was all his illumination. The laminated disk swung into position over the spring. The lead pellet fitted snugly into its niche. A touch of the mechanism and infinitesimal holes in the lead trained on the disk. A curious stream of radiance leaped out into the chamber. The fluorescent material of the ten-laminated disk glowed with a fiery bombardment. Kleon felt a strange tingling of his skin, as though innumerable atoms were popping into oblivion. He had been warned against the deadly effects of the unobstructed radium.

Half aghast at what he was about to do, he completed his preparations. Very carefully he laid himself down on his prepared pallet, hewn out of the solid wall, stretched himself out. By his side he laid his sword, and a keen-edged javelin. He was a fighting man, a leader of a phalanx. Who knew what manner of men he might meet in that remote, unimaginable future. In a corner of the chamber were sealed potteries, filled with dried food and water against his hunger and thirst on awakening.

He grimaced. Would he indeed awaken? His sinewy fingers held on the tiny metal lever at his side. A downward pressure and the smooth-shaped stones that sealed the vents from the volcano would open. After that——

The torch flickered smokily. Soon it would go out. The air in the inclosure was being fast used up. Breathing was becoming laborious. The stream of fiery radiance across the gloom seemed timeless; the disk pricked out in pin points of flame. The dry tingling of his skin increased. He gritted his teeth, swung down on the lever.

Three great stones moved noiselessly on their sockets; three smooth holes appeared suddenly in the wall. There was a faint rumble, a sucking sound. Gas billowed in, thick, yellow.

It swarmed through the underground chamber with clammy, twining tentacles. It beat around his head with acrid, suffocating vapors. The torch flickered, plunged into darkness. His body twitched; his lungs labored for air. The gas sucked in, stung and smarted.

But already a faint luminescence glimmered through the yellow, clogging surge. It spread. Fireflies glittered and danced. There was a crackling sound, new pungent odors. Chemical transformations beyond his knowledge were taking place.

Kleon felt a sudden release from the burning sensations. He tried to breathe, couldn't. He tried to move his limbs. They refused all action. The pounding of his heart slowed, died. A vast drowsiness assailed him. He was slipping. Time slipped with him.

This, then, was death. The chamber revolved slowly around him. His thoughts drifted through soft obstructions. Never again would he see his native vines, his gnarled olives—Athens—Alexander—comrades——

The chamber underneath the pyramid was very still. The vents to the volcano had closed automatically. The transformed gases laved the motionless body in their bath of inanition. The radium poured forth its ceaseless glow. The laminated disk glittered under the impact. All was silence. Time had ceased——

II.

Sam Ward wiped the sweat from the palms of his hands along the rough khaki of his trousers, and stared. He was tired, perspiring, bitten by stinging insects, broiled by the hot Guatemalan sun, and more than a bit disappointed. He had been led to expect more.

"There eet ees," the half-breed Indian pointed his grimy finger with half-triumphant, half-fearful gesture. "Juan nevaire lies. Now señor will pay heem the fifty dollars Mex he promise. Juan do not weesh to stay. There ees dangaire."

Sam did not answer. He took in the scene with practiced eyes. It was a find, all right, but there were innumerable higher and more elaborate ruins within the Yucatan Peninsula. There would be nothing here of start'ing importance.

Sam had done many things in the few years since he had left college. China and the war lords, diggings in the Mesopotamia coupled with certain unheralded brushes with the Bedouins, an unregulated, unauthorized stay with the Harvard excavations at Chichen-Itza in Yucatan. Then, finally, this comparatively tame, but well-paid assignment to investigate the inner jungles of Guatemala for possibilities of banana plantations on behalf of a New York syndicate.

At San Felipe, off the Pacific Coast, he had met Juan. A dirtier, frowsier, more drink-sodden half-breed did not exist. But Sam found him almost his sole source of information.

The whites were courteous, but vague. They shrugged expressive shoulders. The steamy jungles that rolled interminably inland up to the gaunt ramparts of the Sierra Madre were places most assuredly not to be visited. They were impenetrable, malarial, full of ticks and yellow fever, quaking with bottomless bogs, inhabited only by poisonous snakes and fierce animals, and, said his informants expressively, the Indians would not like it.

Sam Ward grinned at this latter bit of news. He felt perfectly competent to take care of himself. He was tall, broad-shouldered, with lean, hard muscles that rippled smoothly as he walked. He had been in jungles before, and he had faced men wilder than any beast or snake. A holster flapped carelessly at his side, and it housed a six-chambered revolver. It was fully loaded and Sam had used it with effect and deadly accuracy on certain necessary occasions. There were more bullets in his cartridge belt. No, Sam Ward did not much worry about the dislike of the Indians. He had a job to do for which his employers had paid liberally, and it would be done.

"But why," he asked carefully, "would the Indians not like it?"

His informant shrugged again. He was the mayor of San Felipe, short, stout, and a trifle asthmatic. "They do not tell, señor," he acknowledged. "They are Mayas, descendants of a stiff-necked race. Those jungles are sacred to them. There have been men gone in there, señor, but they never come out. So——"

Sam tried the Indians. They were tall and straight and handsome in a copper-colored way. No, señor! They would not guide him into the jungle, not even for twenty dollars Mex. Why? The god Quetzal would not like it; he was asleep, biding his time.

It was then he found Juan, outcast from white and red alike, vainly trying to cadge another drink of the fiery *tequila* from a flinty-hearted tavern keeper. Sam set him up, promised more, *mucho* more, for guidance into the forbidden territory. Juan babbled confusedly in terror, but yielded after a few more drinks skillfully applied.

Then came hours of hacking through thorny jungles, hours of slogging through bogs and fighting ticks and mosquitoes. It was a hell hole. Yet there were certain areas where the trees might be planted, if only the natives could be cajoled into work. A gamble any way you looked at it, Sam thought. He was ready to turn back.

Juan saw his gesture of disappointment. He thought fast. He knew how these fool Americans paid generously to be shown bits of stone in the jungle. His drink-colored brain had lost all fear.

"Maybe I show the gracious señor where Quetzal he sleep? Maybe eet ees worth fifty dollars Mex, huh, señor?" he said hopefully.

Sam pricked up his ears. "Quetzal? Nonsense! Every guttersnipe in Central America will show you where that fabulous god sleeps, for a consideration. I've seen enough unnecessary stones in Yucatan to last me a lifetime. Besides, the old Mayas built no cities on the Pacific side."

"Thees ees different," Juan persisted. He had noted joyfully that there had been no objection to the fifty dollars, and in his greed he lost all sense of superstitious fear. "Thees—what you call it—real theeng. I listen once to priests making talk in time of full moon."

Sam considered. The Sierra Madre loomed jagged and high a bare half dozen miles farther east. A smooth, symmetrical cone plumed lazy smoke into the air, tiredly, as though it had been doing so for incredible ages.

"Done!" Sam decided suddenly. Bananas had not worked out very well. Perhaps archæology might. Another Chichen-Itza? "But remember—no Quetzal, no money."

And now he stood, disappointed, staring at the smooth flanks of the volcano, and at the half overgrown, very low, plain pyramid that was almost lost in its shade. Mayan ruins, no doubt, and in a virgin territory.

But he had seen hundreds of similar ruins which had yielded nothing of particular importance.

"Quetzal in there," Juan insisted. "Please, señor, geeve me the fifty dollars Mex and let Juan go queekly. Quetzal maybe get angry."

Sam shook his head. "No sale," he grunted. "Show me Quetzal and I'll double it."

But he was talking to thin air. For the half-breed had swung suddenly on his bare heel, let out a startled yell, and dived headlong into the tangled jungles that inclosed them.

"Here, what the devil!" Sam cried and jerked at his gun.

Then he stopped, and his mouth set in a grim gash. He had seen certain gliding forms slip noiselessly through the thorn bushes and vanish. Mayas! They had been on his trail for hours, dogging his crashing progress through the jungle. Juan, he decided, would never get back to San Felipe. The odds were against Sam Ward's return, either, he thought quietly.

Slowly, he backed up to the overgrown pyramid, gun trained for the slightest movement in the encompassing jungle. There was none. If he could climb the ruin's crumbling, vegetation-covered slopes, he might be able to orient himself, find a way through the trackless forests.

His foot caught in a depression; he stumbled. He jerked around, nerves tense. There, at the base of the slope, practically screened from view by a mat of creepers, was a black hole. His foot had crashed through the tough lianas, burst them asunder.

Still wary, expecting every moment to hear the whistle of a blowpipe dart through the air, he bent to examine it. Luckily, he had a flashlight. He sprayed it down. The questing light illumined a passage, steeply slanting, straight, stretching fathomlessly.

Feverishly, Sam clawed away the remaining creepers. He forgot even the lurking Mayas, waiting to slay this invader of their ancient secrets. Maybe the drunken half-breed had been right, after all. For this passage was squared by human hands, and in a fashion different from those of the Yucatan pyramids. Vague familiarity tugged at his brain, exploded into sudden knowledge. He had seen passages just like this in Egypt, at the Great Pyramid of Cheops.

He knelt, sniffed at the air. It was cold and dank with the must of the underground, but it was breathable. He took a swift glance backward. There was not a rustle in the jungle, not even a bird cry. He smiled grimly. The Mayas were waiting patiently. Time was of no particular value to them. Well, let them wait. He also had plenty of time to die.

Meanwhile, the pyramid tugged at him, flooded him with eagerness. Its very shape, overgrown as it was, showed Egyptian influences. If he could prove that thesis, then the whole problem of the Mayas might be solved.

If! He laughed harshly. He had no illusions. The chances of his breaking through to San Felipe were mighty slim. Then he shrugged, even as the mayor had shrugged, even as a certain Kleon had shrugged over two millenniums before. His life was in the lap of the gods. In the meantime——

He ducked quietly into the passageway. Rocks and loose dirt slithered in after him. The echoes were like muffled thunder. Carefully, he picked his way along, always down, spraying the flash before him. The walls were rough-hewn, but neatly jointed, bare of all carving. It was cold and the air somewhat foul. Which meant that there was no other exit to the tunnel to create a ventilating draft.

Down, down he went, cautiously, watchful. Behind him were the Mayas, resentful of his desecration of their secrets; before him was—what?

He found out fast enough. He was staring blankly at a solid, barring wall. The tunnel had ended abruptly. He flashed his light carefully over its surface, and his heart leaped. Very faintly, almost smudged by obliterating time, he noted thin, straight cracks. A final capping stone had been heaved into position, incredible ages before. That meant there was a chamber within, sealed by long-forgotten men.

Juan had talked of Quetzal. So had the frowning Mayas. That, of course, was ridiculous. Quetzal was a myth, like—like—Zeus and Poseidon and all the Greek Pantheon.

Nevertheless, he must get in, even if he never lived to disclose to the world what he had found. But how? The great stone must weigh over a ton, and there was no way even to get a fingerhold in that thin line of division. It would require patient drilling with high-powered drills. He laughed at that. He might as well as ask for the moon.

Then his eyes narrowed. There had been tales, in Egypt, of cunning artifices, of secret springs that moved stones smoothly. He had never seen one, nor had any one else with whom he had talked. Always it was some vague other, third or fourth removed from the narrator, who had vouched for such finds.

Nevertheless, his sensitive fingers strayed and tapped and probed. With a lilt of exultation he edged a forefinger into a tiny, shallow concavity, discernible only to pressure, not to sight. He jabbed.

The wall seemed to disappear smoothly in front of him. He had not even seen the great stone turn on its pivoting axis. Light glowed beyond.

He jerked through the opening, swung his flash eagerly around. A short exclamation throttled his throat, died queerly on his lips. He was in a rough-hewn chamber, walled with blocks of solid stone. A strange radiance streamed from a tiny niche in the opposite wall, danced past him in a direct beam toward the way he had entered. This was in itself exciting enough. But in the farther corner, dimly illuminated by the queer, crackling luminance, ensconced in a recess carved out of the solid rock, a figure stretched motionless.

Dead, of course, but queerly lifelike, queerly fresh and untouched by the countless years of immurement. He seemed as if he were merely asleep, awaiting some last trump.

Sam pressed forward. His limbs were strangely sluggish, his breathing heavy. There was a curious yellow smoke within the chamber, glowing with an inner light, that stirred clammily about him. Sam paid no attention, attributing his thudding heart to the excitement of his find.

For the man on that bed of rock was blond of hair and white of skin. His features, composed in the embalmment of death, were regular, classical, as if chiseled on a medallion. Armor incased his limbs, still untarnished, still bright.

Unbidden, wild theories flashed through Sam. This was no swarthy Maya chieftain. This was—Quetzal? The legend of that bright, blond god who had come out of the Pacific, blue-eyed, bringing civilization to the Mayas. Could it possibly be——

Then, and then only, did Sam Ward feel the choking sensation in his throat, the nightmare clogging of his limbs, the electric prickling of his skin. The gas! An embalming gas, whose secret had been lost in the mists of time, whose preservative influence was doubtless responsible for the incredible condition of the blond-haired mummy. He must get out quickly —give it a chance to dissipate——

The cry that welled from his lips was strangely thin. The pivoted stone through which he had come had disappeared. In its place was a solid, blank-seeming wall. He had not heard it close behind him. Yet he could have sworn there had been a guttural chuckle, the stealthy pad of naked feet. The Mayas had crawled soundlessly after him, had immured him for all eternity!

He stared at the fluorescent disk that glowed uncannily on the stone. His thought processes were becoming curiously fogged. He tried to laugh. The sound was dull, far-off. Irony! He had made the greatest find of modern times, and he could not shout it from the housetops. Quetzal had taken his revenge. Perhaps, in some future time, remote archæologists would break into this chamber, find an incredible sight. A fair-haired god in bright armor—and another mummy, dressed in rough khaki, obviously of the twentieth century. He could envisage their bewilderment, their learned explanations.

The flash dropped from his paralyzed fingers; his limbs swayed pendulously. He tried to breathe, couldn't. His heart no longer pounded. He was floating on a huge, yellow sea. His brain fought on a moment, failed. He fell, sprawled out on his back.

The flash sent its aimless beam along the stone floor, died out eventually. But the glow from the leaden pellet persisted, as it had for more than two thousand years before. Time ticked on wearily in the outside world. Civilizations rose and fell; wars decimated the earth; incredible events took place.

But within the chamber silence reigned and the radium clock burned on with ceaseless energy. Two figures lay, side by side, motionless, untouched. Outside, storm and sun and air-carried seeds built up over the low pyramid layer on layer of soil. The Mayas were forgotten. The last priest, descendant of one Hotep, prayed for the last time with bleared, hopeless eyes. Juan rotted into mother earth, a tiny poisoned dart between his shoulder blades. Sam Ward, too, was forgotten. For a few weeks there had been a flurry in San Felipe. But the search was halfhearted, and there was no way to determine where he had been lost in the jungle.

Kleon—a Greek—and Sam Ward—an American—heirs of different ages, united eternally in subterranean death, while the world wagged on to a fantastic future!

III.

Tomson was curiously near to the vulgar emotion of anger as he stepped into the conveyor tube that would drop him to the lowest subterranean level of Hispan. He did not like to leave his cubicle on the middle level. There was home, his laboratory, his equipment, his calculation chamber. The atmospheric pressure was carefully attuned to his delicate body; the temperature did not vary by a hundredth of a degree from the warmth that was best adapted to the efficient working of his mind. In all the fifty years of his life he had not stirred more than half a dozen times from his level, and never this far down to the lowermost diggings of the Worker caste.

Why should he? He held his ordered niche in the system of Hispan. It had been fixed from birth, was comfortable, unalterable. Any other mode of existence was inconceivable. There had always been Olgarchs, there would always be the need for his class, the Technicians; and as for the Workers—well, no one paid much attention to them. They worked out their lives in the bowels of the earth, tended the mighty machines that made Hispan possible, dug and bred and died in humble anonymity.

Tomson dropped steadily down the conveyor tube that ran the vertical length of Hispan. A field of force hummed always in the tube. Travelers regulated the speed of ascent or descent by resistor packs attached to their belts. A slight shift to the right or left of the rheostat lever and positive or negative resistance to the field of force built up quickly in the required degree, and determined the speed and direction of flight.

Tomson passed the secondary levels of the lesser Technicians and his bald, bulging forehead wrinkled. It had been Harri who had respectfully but insistently begged his presence in the subterranean diggings. Damn the fellow, with his twitching face and excitable gesticulations of hands and legs. Why couldn't he have handled this alleged new situation himself and not have disturbed Tomson's intellectual concentrations? Didn't he know how highly organized and easily disrupted the delicate body and brain case of a chief Technician was? Down here in the Worker levels were crude pressures, fit only for hulking creatures, and temperatures that fluctuated by as much as a whole degree either way.

He shivered as he dropped, was tempted to return to his quarters and let Harri struggle with the problem himself. But Harri was obviously floundering, frightened even; and if anything went wrong the Olgarchs would hold him, Tomson, responsible. He sighed, and sped up the tempo of his fall.

The levels flashed by with clicking signals, tier on tier of them. Each one held its ordered niche in the society of Hispan. He had passed the ten sections of the lesser Technicians, dropped through the storage levels, the incubator tiers, the subsidiary power units; then he fled past the myriad swarming cells of the Workers, down through the factories where the food pellets were synthesized, past the levels of the intricate machines, and the eternal flames of the atom crushers.

There were others rising and descending in the force field of the conveyor tube. All greeted him as he flashed by, some with the decent nods of equals, others with respectful salutations in nice gradations of humbleness according to the level of abode. He returned them with the proper bend of head and twist of hand—and suddenly bent his slight form almost double.

A young man had just stepped out on the platform of the Workers' eating level, twisted his resistor pack, was rising in the conveyor tube. He was tall and well-formed, not spindly and bulging of forehead as Tomson, nor clumsily heavy as the Workers. He moved with a quick, calm grace, and his tawny hair was almost radiant. His features were aristocratic, high-bred, and were saved from superciliousness only by a frank, careless smile which he flashed on Workers, Technicians and equals alike, much to the scandal of his fellow Olgarchs.

He returned Tomson's respectful genuflection with the same grin, and was gone, a tawny portent, flashing upward to the highest Olgarchic tier. Tomson straightened out, so startled that he forgot the proper meticulous nod to the next Worker who humbly saluted him.

What was Beltan, an Olgarch, doing in the Worker levels? It was not, of course, the province of a Technician, even a chief, to question the goings and comings of the Olgarchs; but very rarely, and only for serious reasons, did any of the ruling caste deign to leave their parks and palaces. Tomson realized that Beltan was different from his fellows. With the others, like Gano, the dark, saturnine head, he knew his place and was at ease. Not so with Beltan.

The yellow-haired young Olgarch was forever poking his nose into nooks and corners of all the levels, had sought certain technical and scientific information from Tomson about which his fellows had never bothered, had actually, on occasion, spoken to a Worker. This in itself was an unheard-of thing, and Tomson disapproved of it strongly. Let each man order his actions in conformity with custom and station—even an Olgarch.

The bottom of the great shaft shot up to meet the Technician. In his bemusement he had barely time to switch the lever and come to a floating halt. He had reached the end of this three-thousand-foot drop.

He shivered, drew his scanty garment close around his thin shoulders. He coughed slightly. His sensitive skin detected the unforgivable variation of temperature in these depths. Why, it was surely a degree and a half below blood heat, the equable bath in which his body was wholly at ease.

Harri was waiting for him at the bottom of the conveyor tube. His sharp-nosed features betrayed his mingled anxiety and relief at the sight of the chief Technician. Now all responsibility was lifted from his own shoulders. Harri, like all lesser Technicians, was able to sustain only a minimum of such an onerous commodity as independent thought and action. He was of the caste who contacted the Workers directly, engineered their operations, directed their activities. They were the administrative branch, whereas the chief Technicians performed executive duties only; planned, experimented, made scientific discoveries.

"What is the meaning of this?" Tomson asked sharply. "Must a chief be disturbed from his important meditations simply because you are too lazy to think your problem out?"

Harri suffered from a nervous tic. A good many Technicians of both classes were thus afflicted. The neural system was overdeveloped compared to the muscular and vascular supports. His nearsighted eyes blinked rapidly; his arms and legs jerked uncontrollably. "I am sorry, Tomson," he declared humbly, "for breaking in upon your meditations. But a situation has arisen. You see, you gave instructions for a crew of Workers to blast new areas from the underlying rock. I was placed in charge."

"I know—I know!" Tomson grumbled impatiently. "We need more fuel for the atom crushers. Get on with your story."

"It is simply this, Tomson," Harri hurried. "In accordance with proper procedure, I turned on the penetro ray before I gave the order to blast. It sometimes happens there are materials embedded in the rock stratum we could otherwise use. I declare, my heart almost ceased its necessary functions at what the ray disclosed. I stopped all work, hastened to contact you at once. This represents a problem not in my sphere of action."

"What," demanded Tomson, "did you see that scared you into the loss of all faculties?"

"You shall determine for yourself. Look!"

They were standing below the lowermost level. During the course of thousands of years, as Hispan required more and more power for its purpose, the solid rock that underlay the city had gradually been penetrated to greater and greater depths. The rock was blasted with shattering electro-dissonances, the resulting powder fed into the atom crushers, and there, in shielded furnaces, the electrons burst from the atom shells, flashed into annihilation, and furnished energy for all the mighty machines that powered the city.

Within the still unfinished cavern, blasted from glistening quartzite, stood twoscore Workers. They were powerful, husky men, towering over the intellectualized Technicians, and their bodies were knotted and twisted with muscles. They stood by the boring machines and blasters, immobile, waiting patiently for the end of the conference of their chiefs. If they waited for hours it did not matter. Nothing mattered. It was all routine. They worked their shift, and they returned to the eating level, ate their pellets in silence in long community barracks, shifted to the mating quarters, performed their necessary acts, ascended next to the recreation level, where, for a few precious hours, they talked, quarreled, jested, saw selected audio visions of innocuous comedy at which they roared unthinkingly, and, by signal, shifted to the final sleeping unit, there to be awakened by further signal to continue the endless round.

Harri's finger jittered toward the control mechanism of the penetro ray, switched it on. The machine hummed with blue light. The solid rock seemed to dissolve in front of it, to become transparent as the clearest glass. Tomson stared, started violently in spite of himself. It was not proper for a chief Technician to show vulgar surprise in front of inferiors.

The vague outlines of a mathematical pyramid glimmered beneath, surrounded by encrusting pressure strata. Within its tapering body a passage showed, clogged with sediment and crumbled stone. At the farther end it opened into a shadowy chamber. He stepped quickly forward, adjusted the depth of the ray to bring its contents into bold relief.

Two bodies lay sprawled—one outstretched within a niche, clad in shining metal, the other twisted on the stony floor as if he had fallen unawares. Neither was a man of Hispan, in lineaments or dress. They seemed strangers from another world—preserved in every detail as if they had just fallen asleep, yet obviously dead. A yellowish gas, slightly iridescent, filled the chamber.

Tomson wrinkled his vestigial nose. The delicate instrument next to the ray apparatus was fluctuating violently. Powerful radiations were filtering through the layers of rock. He permitted himself a most unseemly exclamation of astonishment. Within a corner of the immuring chamber he saw the shadow of a pellet, through whose eyelets thin shafts of radiance were streaming. Metallic radium, its atoms breaking down through countless centuries, emitting ceaseless packets of alpha, beta and gamma rays!

"What shall we do?" Harri asked worriedly.

For the moment Tomson's shoulders sagged. He would have wished not to have the responsibility of a decision. Should he call on Gano, head of the Olgarchs, for his orders in this emergency? Then he straightened his frail body. No! This was his province; he must handle it himself.

He tried to keep his voice from quavering as he issued what he thought were crisp commands. "Blast away the outside layers of rock, Harri, then the inner wall of the chamber. But be careful not to harm anything within. We must examine the bodies of these strange beings who have been buried, for who knows how long, under the very foundations of Hispan."

Harri gave orders. The Workers obediently moved into action. The borers hummed and bit through the hard stone like so much melted butter; the blasters whiffed the surrounding layers into impalpable dust, which was instantly sucked into vacuum conveyors and whirled aloft to the atom crushers for conversion into power.

"That's enough." Harri gestured.

The borers stopped, the blasters died, and the last thin layer was gone. The chamber lay exposed to their view.

The thin yellow gas swirled out, dispersed into scattering particles. The air rushed in, laved the silent figures. At a word, a Worker lumbered over to the radium pellet, thrust it into a leaden receptacle, sealed the top. It did not matter if his hand were burned by the deadly radiations in the process.

Harri gulped. His eyes almost bulged out of his head; the skin twitched over his face with rapid jerks. "Look, Tomson," he gasped feebly. "They're alive!"

Tomson felt the perspiration start out on his bald brow, in spite of the fact that the temperature was more than a degree below his accustomed normal. The Workers looked uneasy. Alarm gaped on their lowering faces. The chief Technician had sufficient presence of mind to order them sharply to their quarters, though their shift had still some time to go. It was unprecedented, but so was the situation in which he found himself.

The Workers went hastily, shuffled into the conveyor tube, lifted swiftly to empty eating quarters, chattering at what they had seen.

Tomson and Harri were left alone to face those risen from the dead.

IV.

Sam Ward was the first to return to the interrupted processes of life. He had been under the retardant influences a lesser period than Kleon. As the preservative gases fled, and fresh, clean air took their place, he opened his eyes. He yawned; he stretched unwittingly. He did not know what had happened. It seemed, for the first few seconds, that he had merely aroused from a particularly deep and healthful sleep.

Then he blinked. Was he dreaming? What the devil was this place? Who were those curious creatures who stared at him as if he were a new species of insect? His eye fell on the outstretched figure of the man in armor. The figure was moving, was sitting up!

With an exclamation, awareness flooded Sam. San Felipe, Juan, the jungle, the pyramid, the Mayas, the stumbling into this cave, the entrapment, then—blankness——

He jerked to his feet swiftly. The gun whipped out of its holster, leveled. "All right," he said harshly. "What is this masquerade about?" His question was directed to the two outlandish figures before him. This jungle was spewing forth more and more strange things. They were not Mayas, but neither were they members of any human race he had ever come across. And those intricate machines that filled the background of the cavern. He was sufficient of a physicist and engineer to realize that they were far in advance of the year 1937.

Tomson shook his head sagely. This was indeed a matter for Gano. His brain clicked keenly. After all, he was a chief Technician. He knew something of the history of the world in the dim days before it died, and Hispan was isolated in a protective film. These were primitives of those earlier eras, somehow immured in this underground chamber, overlaid with the rocky accretions of centuries. The radium pellet, the gas that had dissipated, had kept life intact, though static.

It did not surprise him either that the stranger spoke an archaic variant of the tongue of Hispan. There had been a universal language on earth before it died. As for the curiously fashioned bit of metal in his hand, that was obviously a weapon. Doubtless solid pellets issued from its orifice. He was not afraid. Fear had been bred out of the Technician class. Besides, one touch of the blaster inset at his side, and stranger, weapon and all, would go to feed the energy units of the atom crushers.

"Masquerade?" he repeated slowly. "That is a word I do not know. But you require much explanation—you, your comrade, and this place in which you have laid as one dead. The questioning I shall leave to Gano."

Sam Ward lowered his gun. Surprise at the clipped, curious syllables of this little man with the high, bald forehead and single belted garment of lustrous material gaped his jaw. It was English, in a sense, and understandable, but——

At this instant Kleon rose lithely to his feet, caught up his short Macedonian sword. He seemed like a god among mortals—his fair blond hair, his calm blue eyes that took them all in with one sweeping glance. This, then, was the future, ten thousand years ahead. The gymnosophists from the Roof of the World had not lied. He was disappointed, a bit contemptuous. Were these the beings of the future? Could a Greek of Alexander's day, steeped in Aristotle and Aeschylos, find meet companionship with these spindly, feeble creatures who stood before him?

Then his eyes met those of Sam Ward. Ah, this was a different manner of man. He took in, approvingly, the tall, well-shouldered body, the evidence of power and muscular development, the steady gray of eyes, the level brow. Here was a man who could fight as at a frolic—and judge wisely—a healthy mind in a healthy body.

Sam was bewildered. Quetzal had come to life. These others—— It was getting damned confusing, nightmarish even. He whirled on Kleon. "And who the devil are you—Quetzal, Maya, or what?"

Kleon stared quietly. This was a language strange to him, a bit barbarous, if the truth must be told, with its harsh consonants and lack of mellifluous vowels. Yet there were two words—Quetzal, Maya. He understood them. Those copper-colored Cimmerians on whose far shore his trireme had been driven had called themselves Mayas, and they had termed him Quetzal, and bowed down in worship.

"Your tongue is unknown to me, my friend of a future that is now," he said calmly. "But I recognize the words Quetzal and Maya. The barbarians called me Quetzal; why, I do not know. But I am Kleon of Athens, who had journeyed far with mighty Alexander, and whose ship had been driven to a strange coast. There was no return; Hotep and the Egyptian slaves burned the ship. It was not meet for a Greek to rust out his life with barbarians. I therefore availed myself of certain magic taught me by the gymnosophists and slept into the future, hoping then to meet beings fitter to converse with an Athenian. Ten thousand years should have elapsed. I confess I am taken with your presence, stranger, but these two others are beneath my notice. Are they perchance your slaves?"

Sam Ward did not even know he had slid his gun back into its holster.

This was becoming entirely too incredible. First two weakling creatures who spoke a distorted English, yet were obviously of an advanced civilization. Now the god in shining armor, risen from the dead, speaking in ancient Greek, avowing matters beyond all possibility. For Sam had studied Greek at college and recognized the long surges, the mighty flow of that noblest of all languages.

He shook his head violently to clear his addled brain. Ten thousand years ahead! That meant eight thousand years for him. Good Lord! Had he slept that long? Were these others representatives of that far-distant future? He opened his mouth to speak, fumbling for the dimly remembered Greek.

But Tomson had decided that enough time had been wasted. He had understood the tongue of the man in the coarse-fibered clothes, but not this other in shining metal.

"Enough," he interrupted peremptorily. "These are matters for Gano, the head of the Olgarchs, to settle. You will come with me."

Sam was slowly regaining his poise. His pulses even leaped at the incredible adventure that was opening its doors to him. "O. K.," he said. "Lead on to this Gano."

But Kleon did not move. He had not followed Tomson's words, but the gesture was unmistakable. He took no orders from a slave.

Sam read his mind and grinned. "It's all right, friend Kleon, alias Quetzal," he translated haltingly into Greek. "These men are from that future you told me about. They are not my slaves. I am from another time myself, some two thousand years after you. Sam Ward is my name, and my country America. It did not exist in your day. I stumbled into your pyramid, and slept along with you. I don't think they mean us any harm."

Kleon's face lighted with gladness and a certain astonishment. "You speak Greek, Sam Ward, yet you speak it as a barbarian would. The accents are false and the quantities wrong." Sam grimaced wryly at that. His professors at college had been most careful in inculcating those accents and quantities. They represented the true Attic Greek in all its purity, they had averred.

"As for fear of harm"—Kleon straightened himself proudly, gestured significantly with sword and javelin—"these, my good weapons, are sufficient protection against such puny things as these men of the future."

Sam knew better. He had a hunch that even his own six-chambered revolver, with its fleet spew of death, might not be able to cope with the unimaginable weapons available to the year 10,000 A. D. Brawn, cold steel, meant little in such a case. But, of course, Kleon knew of nothing beyond the sword, the spear and bow.

Nevertheless, they followed the pair. Tomson and Harri, in spite of appearance, radiated a certain power, a certain feeling that it would be wise not to resist. They came to the great conveyor tube. Sam looked up its circular orifice, stretching almost five thousand feet aloft, and wondered. Were they expected to climb those smooth, coldly glowing walls?

Tomson jerked resistor packs from an emergency kit, strapped them on the two strangers. "Do as I do," he said, "and do not fear."

Sam moved the lever over obediently. Kleon understood and followed suit. Sam Ward could not repress a startled cry; Kleon called upon Hermes, the god of swiftness. They were catapulting upward at breath-taking speed.

Sam caught glimpses of a mighty civilization as he fled smoothly up: platforms which led into levels crowded with swarming humanity; huge machines that glowed and blasted and spun and gyrated; endless quarters; glittering miles of strange sights; laboratories; enormous sectors of fiery tumult, tier on tier, until he grew dizzy.

Then, new levels—a different world. Underneath lay teeming life, sprawling vastness, machinery, technique. Here were soft green patches shimmering under dewy artificial luminance; flowers of strange blooms and stranger fragrance; a soft, lapping interior lake, blue as cobalt, warmed and perfumed; multicolored buildings, spaciously set, gracious with curves and melting outlines; noble figures who gazed through transparent sections at their upward rush with incurious eyes and returned to their dalliance.

Then, suddenly, the mighty shaft ended. Tomson gestured and switched the lever to neutral. Sam and Kleon did likewise. Harri had quit them at the level of the lesser Technicians. Only the chief Technicians could converse with the Olgarchs.

They glided to a halt, whipped over to a landing platform. For an awful moment Sam thought he was slipping, would plummet downward the five thousand feet he had journeyed. The solid stance felt grateful to his muscles.

Tomson beckoned them on. A frescoed panel opened. They went in.

A simultaneous exclamation burst from ancient Greek and middle-period American alike. Sam blinked. At first it seemed as if they had come out upon a sky of lambent hue. Above them stretched a vault like that of heaven itself, with glowing stars, a silver moon that swung in slow orbit from side to side. Then he realized what it was. A very cunning and magnificent representation, on a vaulted dome, of an ancient sky, projected by invisible mechanisms, even like the planetariums of the twentieth century. Which meant that this building, or city, or world, whichever it might be, was wholly inclosed from the rest of earth—a cosmos self-contained, unitary.

He had not long to speculate. Tomson beckoned them into a tear-drop conveyance of white metal. They got in. A pressure on an inset and they darted off, rising low in the air, skimming over the level at a speed that Sam estimated at five hundred miles per hour. Yet there was no motor, no gears, no whirling propeller. Nor did the wind whip through them as it should. Sam could only figure that somehow the strange vehicle carried its own shell of air along with it.

Kleon pressed close to him, gripped his sword fiercely. This was magic beyond his knowledge. Sam grinned encouragingly at the Greek. "Something like this was in my time also," he told him. "It is better than horses or chariots."

An understanding had arisen between the two. They felt closer akin to each other than to Tomson, who represented the future. And Sam, however lamely, could speak the Grecian tongue.

Sam leaned over the side, breathless. It was paradise over which they were skimming. Everywhere, up to the dim slope of the domed horizon, were white-glowing dwellings, noble parks, artificial lakes, limpid, pellucid; skimming cars like their own, carrying commanding figures, tall as themselves, nobly proportioned, quite unlike the Technician who guided them. Nowhere was there any sign of machinery, of activating power, of the teeming swarms of the lower levels.

"Something tells me," Sam gritted between his teeth, "I'm not going to like this."

But there was no time for further observations. The conveyor car dipped, glided to the ground in front of a building gleaming in blue and gold. They were in a great park. Fountains splashed; music played softly; trees festooned with bright orange blossoms waved in an invisible breeze.

They got out quietly. Tomson stepped upon an oblong section of red metal; bowed toward the blank walls of the building with low genuflection. Sam watched him with narrowed eyes.

Kleon nodded with a pleased smile. "I knew he was but a slave," he said to the strange companion with whom he had been thrust into this future. "Only a slave would bend so humbly. Soon we shall meet his lord. I, a free Greek, am the equal of any one."

A voice issued from the building. "Enter, Tomson. You have done well." The wall seemed to roll back on itself. They went in. The wall retracted behind them.

V.

Tomson said nervously, "Forgive this unusual intrusion, head of the Olgarchs. But this is a problem which only you can solve."

Sam and Kleon stood a little apart, both straight and proudly erect. Of an equal height, the Greek was blond and blue-eyed, chiseled of feature; the American darker-hued, weather-tanned, keen of eye, firm-chinned. Two thousand years of civilization separated them; yet they were both men, in the sense that Tomson, for all his trained knowledge and intellectuality, was not.

Blue eyes and gray gazed steadily at Gano, head of the Olgarchs, apex of the city of Hispan. Gano did not resemble much the other Olgarchs of whom they had caught fleeting glimpses. He was thickset, sturdy of body and limb, with a massive head and craggy features. His hair was midnight black and his nose boldly jutting. But his eyes were decisive, penetrating, yet impenetrable themselves. He sat on a low divan, his long, thin fingers idling over a desk panel before him on which colored squares glowed and darkened in irregular succession. A signal board, Sam rightly decided.

Gano nodded. "I know, Tomson," he said brusquely, as one too busy to waste precious moments. "I have received visor-signals of your find and of your coming." He turned, surveyed the two men of an older day keenly from under shaggy brows, said, "One speaks the language of Hispan, in a fashion. The other does not. We must remedy that." He raised his voice slightly. "Beltan, take these creatures whom the foundations of our city have yielded and teach them the proper speech, so that we may converse at ease."

From a corner of the long, simply furnished room a figure arose. Sam had not noticed him before. He came toward them casually. He smiled and his whole face lighted with the brightness of his smile. Sam warmed to him at once. "This chap is more like it," he told himself.

Beltan was an Olgarch, one of the ruling class, but he did not seem to take his position seriously. He even grinned at Tomson. It made the Technician uneasy. It was not proper. He knew his place in the scheme of things, and Beltan should likewise. But Kleon relaxed his grip on his sword. He, too, recognized a man in this Olgarch of the future, a man after his own heart.

"Strange," thought Sam, watching the pair, "how alike they are! Proud poise of head, bright, tawny hair, clean-cut, classical features, a certain arrogance of those who never knew superiors. They'll hit it off pretty well —even if ten thousand years separate them. As for me"—he shrugged his shoulders—"this Beltan looks all right. But Gano, the others, the whole set-up, I'm afraid that——"

Beltan said with a certain light mockery, "Come with me, you two who have survived from some remote past. Let me teach you the nice intricacies of our proper tongue. Then you may judge if it were wise for you to leave your own time for the noble hierarchy that is Hispan."

"At times," Gano cut in sharply, "your nonsense bores me, Beltan."

The young Olgarch bowed. There was a twinkle in his eye. "At times it bores me, too, noble Gano. That is one of the penalties of having been born an Olgarch."

Gano frowned, turned abruptly to the Technician. "Return to your duties, Tomson."

The chief Technician muttered submissive words, fled from the room. There was a shocked expression on his face. Sam grinned. Tomson, he felt, had a good bit of a Mid-Victorian Philistine in his make-up.

Kleon muttered aside to the American. "What do they say?"

"They say," Sam told him, "they will teach us their tongue. I know something of it already. But for you it may be hard."

Beltan took them out of the council chamber, into a side room on whose walls abstract figures were stamped in gold.

"How," inquired Sam, "do you expect to make much headway with my very recent friend, Kleon? He is a Greek before my time, and knows nothing of English."

"English?" repeated Beltan with raised eyebrows. "Ah, you mean Hispana. He will learn as fast as you who have a smattering. Perhaps you are not familiar with the Inducto-learner." He waved toward a metal helmet suspended at the end of a long, transparent tube, whose other end entered the ceiling and disappeared.

Sam shook his head. "Never heard of it," he confessed. "In my day we spent half our life learning things and the other half in forgetting them."

Beltan laughed. "We Olgarchs waste no time in achieving knowledge. It comes to us ready-made. The Technicians toil and we garner the fruits. It is simple enough. An Olgarch on birth, or you, for that matter, place your head within the reception chamber. Short waves, oscillating at high speeds, and automatically attuned to the wave length of your particular brain, pulse through the tube. The latter leads to the cubicles of the chief Technicians. At the signal, the proper Technician adjusts his own sending unit. He concentrates on the subject of which knowledge is desired. His thoughts, converted into current, are transmitted inside your skull, make the necessary impress on your neurone paths. Behold, you have learned, well and painlessly."

Sam was impressed. "And the Technicians, do they learn the same way?"

Beltan looked surprised. "Of course not. This is for the Olgarchs only. But do you enter, Sam Ward."

Sam hesitated, grinned and placed his head boldly within the helmet. Beltan made the necessary adjustment. Then he pressed buttons on an instrument board.

At first Sam felt only a gentle tingling, a slight massage of his skull. Then words began to flow into his consciousness, thoughts which he had not originated. His mind was no longer his own; alien speech beat upon him—words that were the same as those to which he had been accustomed, yet strange.y distorted, clipped, shorn of unnecessary syllables. Subtly, the feeling grew that this was right and proper, the older speech an anachronism, not fit for present use.

When Beltan gestured for the removal of the helmet Sam was speaking Hispana, the English of the ninety-eighth century. "There, you see," remarked the Olgarch approvingly. "It is all very simple. And now, Kleon, who have been called the Greek, do you likewise."

Kleon was a very brave man, otherwise he would not have thrust his head without hesitation into the inclosure. This was powerful magic, he was certain, more powerful even than the incantations of the gymnosophists. Aristotle, Zeno, would never have approved of these barbarous practices. But he went——

VI.

Back in the council chamber the four men sat again—Gano, Beltan, Sam Ward and Kleon. They understood each other now, spoke the same tongue. But their thought processes were wholly different. Nor could this be helped. Heredity, environment, custom, the training of a lifetime, slow evolutionary molding could not be changed in a moment, not even by the marvelous science of Hispan.

Gano was courteous, if condescending. He listened patiently, first to the story of the Greek, then to the supplemental tale of the American. To him they were primitive savages of an elder day, interesting because of that, but wholly inferior to the Olgarchs and Technicians of Hispan. But Beltan listened with quiet eagerness to their respective pictures of earlier civilizations, of the glory of Greece and the march of Alexander into Asia, of the literature and drama of that ancient conglomerate of city states. It is true that he smiled at the naïve scientific conceptions that Kleon brought forth, but the concepts of the Grecian philosophers struck him forcibly.

To Sam's story of the world of the twentieth century he listened more skeptically and with a certain fastidious distaste. The particular glory of that era—the march of science—he dismissed as mere halting steps toward the future. But the story of war and greed and human conflict, of waste and incredible futility, of shorn forests and mineral resources, of the World War and the League of Nations, of concentration camps and the Spanish madness, brought grimaces to his lips.

"No wonder," he said slowly, "the whole world died not long after your time. Your twentieth century represented a retrogression, a relapse into futile barbarism from the rather noble era of Kleon."

Sam bristled at that. No man likes to hear his own century impugned, and another cried up in its place, especially by the member of a third epoch. "Perhaps," he said heatedly, "I have been a bit more honest in my descriptions than Kleon. For example, he told you nothing of the slavery that existed in his day, the very fundamental upon which his civilization was based."

"I see nothing wrong in that," Kleon declared with dignity. "It is only right that those whose brains are dull and whose backs are strong should support in leisure those who can bring forth large thoughts and meditations. Has not this Hispan likewise its slaves—its Technicians and Workers —to bring the flower of Olgarchs like Gano and Beltan into being?"

Gano relaxed not a muscle of his face, but Beltan threw back his head and laughed. "By the hundred levels of Hispan, even in that early age the Greeks had learned the art of flattery. You are not quite right, friend Kleon. These are no slaves; these are but fixed castes of society, each with its duties firmly ordered. Hispan could not long exist without such strict, efficient subdivisions. Neither Workers nor Technicians are other than content with their lot." He smiled bitterly. "That is left only as the last privilege of the Olgarchs."

"Rather," Gano interposed calmly, "it is your peculiar privilege, Beltan. No one else of our class feels the necessity for such a primitive emotion. Sometimes I think you are a sport, a mutant, not a true Olgarch."

Sam turned to the head of the Olgarchs. "What," he asked with a certain irony, "is the true function of the Olgarchs in this society of Hispan? The Technicians, I understand, supervise and create the scientific mechanism by which the city lives; the Workers lend their brawn and muscle to its functioning; but the Olgarchs?"

Gano frowned. "We live," he answered sharply. "We are the reason for the creations of the Technicians, the labors of the Workers. We are the flower to which they are the roots and stems and leaves. They work, so that we may enjoy."

Kleon nodded approvingly. "Hispan is not far apart from Athens," he said. "There is much good in your system."

Sam set his teeth. "That," he declared, "has always been the rationalized justification for slavery, even to this future time. Has it ever occurred to you that the slaves—call them Technicians, Workers, Helots, what you will—would also like to live?"

"They are content, happy," Gano answered softly. "Ask Tomson, if you will, whether this is not the best of all possible worlds."

Beltan leaned forward. "Have you already forgotten, Sam Ward," he mocked, "what you have told us of conditions in your own world? What were the Workers then if not slaves? Slaves who worked at the beck of others, who toiled far longer hours than the Workers of Hispan, who starved in times of depression and starved only more slowly while employed, who went to war to fight and kill for the benefit of others. Did you not have also your Technician class who toiled in laboratories and created new inventions for the benefit of your wealthy, your Olgarchs?"

"Yes, I suppose so," Sam admitted unwillingly. "But at least they were free to work or not to work."

"To starve, you mean." Then, suddenly, the irony was gone from Beltan's voice, and a certain fierce sincerity took its place. "It isn't the plight of the Workers and Technicians that matters. They are well taken care of in Hispan; they do their work and are happy and content. No, it is the plight of the Olgarchs, the lords of Hispan, that matters most profoundly.

"Gano, here, at least has the illusion that he is performing a necessary function. The chief Technicians listen respectfully to his orders, obey them. But the city would flourish just the same if Gano never gave an order. As for the rest of us, we haven't even that poor illusion. We sit and dawdle and wrap ourselves in fine garments, listen to fine music, eat delicate fare, strut and stroll and discuss in noble-sounding, empty phrases. We are parasites, aimless, unnecessary. We are excrescences on the body politic. The city could see us vanish and continue its course without a single jar."

Gano was on his feet, his black brow clouded. "Beltan," he said sharply, "even an Olgarch may go too far."

Beltan's nostrils quivered. There was defiance in his gaze. Then he subsided with a quizzical smile. "You are right, Gano," he murmured. "Even an Olgarch may go too far."

Kleon was puzzled. He was mightily taken with Beltan, but he did not understand his dissatisfaction. "If the uses of philosophy fail," he interposed, "as they sometimes do, there is always the heady pursuit of war against the barbarian, the stranger."

The young Olgarch said sadly: "There are no barbarians or strangers, unless it be you two. The city of Hispan is all that remains of the world."

Sam gasped. "Do you mean that New York, London, Paris, the great countries, have been wiped out? How? Why?"

Beltan did not seem to see Gano's frown, or seeing, paid no heed.

"The story," he replied, "is not often told, and then only to Olgarchs. But since you already know about the once external world, there is no harm in telling it to you. Not long after your time, Sam Ward, in about the twenty-seventh century, the nations then existing had withdrawn more and more into their own boundaries. It was the logical, if mad development of tendencies in your own era. Nationalism, self-sufficiency, I believe, were the watchwords.

"The process accelerated, so our records report," Beltan continued. "Soon even the national borders grew too large. The nationalistic tendencies, the patriotisms, grew fiercer, more local. Each nation, cut off from intercourse with other nations, bounded by impregnably fortified frontiers, dependent only on itself for its economy, found quarrels arising within its own confines. The fires of localism, of hatred for aliens, of patriotic fervor, finding nothing outside to feed upon, gnawed at their own vitals. Men of one community, a subdivision, a State, a city, decried the men of other communities, boasted of their superiority. They began to fight in internecine warfare.

"New nationalisms sprang up—nationalisms and hates based on smaller units. The countrysides became deserted, as the undefended farms and villages were devastated by the armies of opposing cities. The people collected in the towns, where there was a measure of protection. Soon the cry arose: New York for New Yorkers; London for the men of London; Paris for the Parisians!"

It was now Kleon's turn to nod. Evolution, he reflected, was but an eternal recurrence. For what was this Olgarch of the future describing but Greece in the time of Pericles and the Peloponnesian War?

"Soon," Beltan went on, "earth was broken up into a vast number of self-contained, heavily fortified cities. The old national boundaries were gone; newer and smaller ones took their place. Science advanced. Food was synthesized from inorganic elements; the secret of atomic power was discovered. The units grew smaller and smaller, drew away from each other. They fought, but the defenses were impregnable. The unfortified countryside became wholly deserted, unnecessary. It grew in the course of years into a tangle of wild forests, of desert stretches. All intercourse ceased. The cities rose vertically instead of horizontally along the earth, inclosed themselves in impassable barriers.

"Generation on generation added to these barriers, improved them with new methods of science. Such a one incloses Hispan, once a colony of your United States, now the sole survivor of all the teeming cities that once populated earth. A shield of neutron metal, impassable by any means known even to our science, was built up, layer on layer, around our city. No one knows how unimaginably thick it may be. No one has ever tried to penetrate its width."

Sam was appalled. He tried to grasp the story entire. It was logical, he admitted, up to a certain point. The forces involved were already at work

Beltan's tone was sharp, quick. "Have you any proof of that?"

"None whatever," Sam admitted. "Call it intuition if you like, or merely the memory of somewhat similar propaganda methods in my own twentieth century."

The flame that lifted in Beltan's eyes died. "In any event," he said dully, "there is no way of ever finding out. The neutron walls cannot be pierced."

Kleon had been singularly silent. His fair brow was furrowed; he seemed plunged in profound thought. Now he raised his head suddenly. "Is there," he demanded, "a mountain, within the confines of Hispan where the Titans are wont to groan uneasily?"

Beltan stared. "I do not understand."

"He means," explained Sam, "a volcano."

"No; there is not."

"Then," shouted Kleon, "by the one-eyed Cyclopes, there is a way of escape."

"What the devil——" Sam cried.

"Listen to me," the Greek said fiercely. "The pyramid Hotep built for me to sleep into this stupid future lay close to the flanks of such a volcano."

"That's true," Sam averred. "I remember it. But what of it?"

"This! According to the formula of the gymnosophists I required the gases from the smoking mountain for my chambered sleep. I drew them in by cunning vents which pierced the central fires. These opened to the day at the top of the mountain. Stones, nicely pivoted, sealed the vents after the gases poured into the chamber. Only I know the secret of their presence, of the springs by which they may pivot once more. The pyramid is within the city; the burning mountain is without. We shall escape by means of those passages which lead far underground from one to the other."

Sam pounded the Greek's shoulder. "Kleon, you are a genius." Then a thought struck him, clouded his joy. "Out of the frying pan into the fire." He grimaced. "Your passages lead to the central fires, you say. That means to the inner crater. We'd suffocate or frizzle to death."

"The mountain may have ceased its complaining long since," Kleon answered calmly. "And brave men die but once."

"Right!" Sam chuckled. "We start at once. We still have the gadgets that Tomson gave us. They'll drop us down the shaft." He stuck out his hand to Beltan. "Good-by," he said. "Thanks! You were the one bright spot in Hispan."

The Olgarch's eyes were inscrutable. "Warnings of your descent down

in his own time. But to think that all the world had died, except for this enshrouded city of Hispan! "What happened to the others?" he insisted.

He saw the quick, warning glance that Gano flashed. He noted Beltan's hesitation. "On that," the latter admitted reluctantly, "the records are somewhat garbled. It seems there was a cataclysm some time in the forty-first century. A celestial body from outer space, traveling at high speed, smashed into the earth, destroyed a goodly part, laid waste all the cities but Hispan."

"Why Hispan alone?"

"Because our city was the only one inclosed with neutron walls. Not even the impact of millions of tons could penetrate its solidity."

"And no attempt was ever made to explore outside, to investigate conditions?"

Gano rose suddenly. "There is no way out," he said smoothly, "and there have been questions enough. We have been patient with your rather primitive ignorance, but it is time to call a halt. And remember," he finished meaningly, "these tales which Beltan, who should have known better, has told you must go no further. Only the Olgarchs know of these, and Tomson, the chief Technician, the Workers, the other Technicians even, have no faintest idea that there is a world, a universe beyond this city of Hispan. To them there never was a sun or moon or stars, or earth of other cities and peoples. This is the round entire, the circumscription of their destinies. See to it that they hear no other."

"I see," Sam answered grimly. He was beginning to understand. It was only by a tremendous effort that he held back the rising wrath within him. But Kleon, child of an earlier, franker era, held no inhibitions. "I am a Greek," he declared proudly, "and bow to no man. My speech is my own, and subject to no restrictions."

Sam nudged him sharply. The brave fool was making trouble for them both.

Gano surveyed them thoughtfully, then nodded to Beltan as though he had not heard. "We shall decide on our course later," he said evenly, "when the council meets. In the meantime let these two be held in your quarters. *You* will take care of them."

Kleon's hand strayed to his sword. Sam's mouth set in a straight line. Very casually, his fingers touched the butt of his revolver. He knew what Gano meant. They were prisoners. The Greek, by his defiance, had brought this upon them. Yet he liked the headstrong warrior all the more for his folly. He was a man!

Beltan said with peculiar intonation, "Please come without delay."

Sam relaxed. He sensed the warning against resistance in the Olgarch's voice. Gano's delicately veined forefinger rested on a green square on the signal board. Intuitively, Sam felt that the slightest pressure would release blasting death against them.

"O. K.," he said laconically, in the elder speech. "Let's go, Kleon."

VII.

In silence the three entered a waiting car; in silence they sped over the noble park lands to a small, blank-walled building near the center of the level. In silence Beltan escorted them inside, the slide panel clicking smoothly behind them.

Sam cast a swift glance around. The walls were bare and smooth, the furnishings simple. There were no windows or doors other than the way they had entered. "We are prisoners, are we not?" he demanded.

Beltan looked at them with a certain pity. "I am afraid worse than that," he admitted. "Your presence in Hispan will give rise to talk, to questionings. You must eventually come in contact with the other castes. You know things of which they have no knowledge. Discontent may arise, dissatisfaction. The ordered peace and security of Hispan may be broken. You especially, Sam Ward, have subversive ideas. You do not like our distribution of functions?"

"I do not," Sam answered emphatically.

Beltan sighed. "I thought as much. As for you, Kleon, you are more sympathetic. But you spoiled it with your defiance of Gano. Still," he meditated, "if you would but admit your hastiness of speech, perhaps an exception might be made in your favor."

Kleon gazed at him with candid blue eyes. "Would that mean I must desert Sam Ward?"

"I'm afraid so."

The Greek stood poised like a young god. "Then I remain with him."

"Even if it means death?"

"Even so."

Beltan turned swiftly to the American. "And you," he inquired, "would you be willing to give an oath that your tongue would always remain submissive to the Olgarchs? Remember," he added hastily, "an answer to the contrary will mean a quiet dissolution. I am but one against many. In any event I shall plead your cause in the council, but my fellow Olgarchs will feel as Gano does."

Sam swallowed hard, but there was no tremor in his voice. "Kleon was right," he answered steadily. "We are not slaves. We can give no such promises."

Beltan sighed again. There was regretful admiration in that sigh. "You

are both brave men," he said. "It seems that elder, more primitive day bred sturdier frames than now. Yet you must die. I see no way out."

Sam fingered his gun. He glanced significantly at Kleon. "At least," he remarked evenly, "we'll go out fighting."

Kleon rattled his sword. "By Zeus and Ares," he swore, "you speak sooth, friend Sam. We'll take a goodly number of these Olgarchs to the lower realms along with us."

"You won't have the chance," Beltan assured them. "Gano controls your fates literally at his finger tips. A pressure on the proper square before him and lethal rays sweep through this structure."

Somehow Sam's gun was in his hand, its cold muzzle pressed against the Olgarch's ribs. "I'm sorry to have to do this," he said crisply, "but we don't give up very easily. You, Beltan, will show us a means of escape, or you die along with us."

The Olgarch looked at the two desperate men. Kleon's sword was out, its keen point pressed against his other side. He shook his head slowly. "I am not afraid to die," he answered with simple dignity. "I am weary of this aimless dalliance to which I am bound. Slay, if you will."

Sam stepped back, sheathed his gun. Kleon raised his sword in salut[e] "You, too, are a man," the American approved. "We three, I think, giv[e] the chance, could conquer the universe."

A slow, unaccustomed red spread over the Olgarch's aristocratic [fea]tures. "Believe me," he spoke earnestly, "I am your friend." Then he m[ade] a despairing gesture. "But there is no escape. I cannot help you. No [nook] or cranny of Hispan is remote from the search screens of the Ol[garch] council."

"I wouldn't stay here if I could," Sam declared harshly. "Your [own] Hispan is a stench in my nostrils, with its brutal caste system, its [year] round. Me—I prefer freedom and space and a bit of anarchy even, [where] men are human beings and not mere soulless cogs in a hierarchic [pattern] no matter how efficient. There must be a way to get out."

"There isn't," Beltan replied somberly. "The neutron walls are [impregn]able. And outside, besides wild desolation in which no man may li[ve] are lethal gases: Cyanogen, carbon monoxide, phosgene, produc[ed by] collision. The atmosphere has been destroyed. We do not even kn[ow] if anything, remains of earth, of the sun itself."

"That," Sam retorted with a grin, "is mere propaganda. Your [own] ancestors must have been singularly adept at that sort of thing. [Gano] tells me they foisted that tale even on themselves, in order t[o keep] position intact. If ever Workers or Technicians or even mut[ants] like yourself came in contact with other forms of civilizatio[n with] methods, there might be comparisons not at all favorable to [Hispan] the conveyor tube will be signaled back to Gano from every level," he said. "You'll never reach your buried pyramid."

"We'll chance it," Sam retorted.

"I won't permit such chances."

Sam looked at him incredulously. "You mean you're backing down? I thought you were our friend."

"I mean," Beltan replied quietly, "I am going with you. The levels will respect my presence."

"You're a good egg," Sam said with feeling. "But it's no go. You'd only get into a mess of trouble when you come back."

"I'm not coming back," the Olgarch retorted patiently.

"Huh! What's that?"

"I mean I'm going out into the strange new world with you." He smiled quizzically. "Didn't you say a little while before that we three, given the chance, could conquer the universe?"

"But—but——" Sam spluttered. "Why, damn it, you can't do this. The chances of our getting through, or of survival even if we do, are a thousand to one. Why should you give up everything——"

"Because I am tired of this life; because in rawness and chaos I may find again that soul you spoke of; because—I am your friend."

The three men, products of three different ages, stared at one another with level brows. Sam felt an unaccustomed lump in his throat, spoke gruffly. "Then we'd better get started—before Gano gets on our trail."

VIII.

It was easier than they had anticipated.

Under Beltan's guidance they darted in his conveyor car for the tube, bailed into the great shaft with swiftness and dispatch. Down five thousand feet they catapulted, meeting Technicians and Workers on their way, getting humble salutes because of the Olgarchic presence, curious glances as they whirled ever downward.

Then the final excavation, the still-yawning chamber which the blasters had laid bare. Harri, back on the job, looked up in alarm at this unprecedented invasion of an Olgarch. But Beltan took the trouble to explain. The sleepers, he said, were going to disclose to him the method by which they had slept intact these many ages. In the meantime, it was unnecessary for Harri and his corps of Workers to remain. And they were, he added with authority, to hold their tongues.

In seconds the final level was clear.

"Now"—Sam grinned—"strut your stuff, O Kleon." He had noted Beltan's anxious glances at the visor screen implanted in the upper shaft.

It was an even more anxious moment before the Greek found what he was looking for. A tiny, almost imperceptible depression in the ancient wall. A simultaneous exhalation of withheld breath burst from three pair of lips as the section of the wall turned on itself, disclosed a dark hole within. Sam, remembering his former experience, would have held back to determine if hot, volcanic gases would belch forth. But the Olgarch had cried out sharply. "Quick, run! We're discovered!"

They dived headlong into the baleful opening. Kleon flung around, thrust his shoulder against the massive stone. It swung smoothly and soundlessly back into position. They crouched, panting, in utter darkness.

Just in time, too! For at that moment there was a low, humming sound that rose swiftly to an unbearable scream. "Gano has turned on the blasters," said Beltan with a groan. "They'll shear through this thickness of rock in two or three seconds."

But the scream of rushing power gave way to a mightier roar. There was a huge crash, a tumbling, grinding noise. The solid rock swayed crazily underfoot. Then there was silence.

"The pyramid has fallen," Kleon told them shakenly. "There must be a hundred feet of earth and rock and stone behind. All return is blocked."

"Then the answer is *forward*," Sam responded with a cheerfulness he did not quite feel. If the volcano was still active, if, in the course of long centuries, the crater had become clogged with lava——

It was a long, steep, arduous climb in total darkness—silent, except for grunts and low curses as they bumped blindly into jagged edges. Up, always up, in fetid, clammy atmosphere——

Then the path widened suddenly and they were at the bottom of a huge bowl. Sam looked up fearfully, then let out a great shout that brought the echoes tumbling about them. "The stars! I see the stars!"

High overhead, framed in limited blue, were tiny pin points of light, peering down incuriously upon them. There followed a mad scramble, a clawing and backward slithering in crumbling, weathered lava flows of an ancient epoch. The volcano was extinct. The air was foul but breathable.

Then they were out, staring with avid eyes upon the enveloping scene. It was night and the fresh breeze stirred their hair, ruffled their clothes. Three men, of different civilizations, clad in different habits, united only in a common bond of escape, emerged into an incredible world!

To one side, framed by the heights of the Sierra Madre, reared a vast, light-quenching surface. Five thousand feet it sprang, massive, somber, swinging over the plain to either side as far as the eye could reach. The neutron-walled city of Hispan!

To the other side, past the mountains, a great wilderness stretched interminably without end, without beginning. There was no sign of life, of human habitation, of anything but tangled, savage-crowding trees. There wasn't a light, an airplane, not even a boat on the tideless darkness of the ocean beyond. Even the stars were strange, the old configurations gone.

Sam shivered. It was cold, but it was not that which made his flesh crawl. Suppose the tale of Hispan had been true? Suppose there were no other cities, no other human beings in that shoreless jungle? Suppose——

He turned to the others, grinned. "At least one thing is certain," he said lightly, "the air is good. If deadly gases once existed, they have long since been dissipated or made chemically harmless." He raised his voice, "Forward, comrades, to whatever destiny awaits us!"

"Forward!" cried Kleon, the Greek.

"Forward!" spoke Beltan, the Olgarch.

The three men turned their faces resolutely toward the East, toward the home of the rising sun. Slowly, they descended the mountain.

Of the two stories in the September 1937 *Astounding Stories,* the serial, *Galactic Patrol,* did not stand up. Years later, I got a copy of the hard-back version and sat down to relive past glories—but they weren't there. I found the book unreadable.

Yet, when I just reread "Past, Present, and Future" in the process of organizing this anthology, I found it just as much fun now as it had been then.

Schachner was alive to the gathering dangers of the 1930s and the mounting threat of Nazi Germany. His stories were filled with social problems therefore, with himself always on the side of the democratic angels.

I absorbed it all and I am glad of it now as I look back on it. Had the John Clark type of story been the only kind that had impressed me, I would have been sharply limited. (It is perhaps not for nothing that Clark wrote only two stories.) As it was when I came to write *The Foundation Trilogy,* there were times when the voice of Schachner sounded in my ear.

Part Nine

1938

FROM THE START, the year 1938 brought changes both for me and for the science fiction world. I had written another letter to *Astounding Stories,* and it was printed. (Thereafter, for about half a year, I wrote one every month and it was printed every month.)

A fellow alumnus of Boys High saw the letter, recognized my name, noticed my address, and wrote to me, inviting me to attend a meeting of the Queens Science Fiction League. (Or perhaps it was the Greater New York chapter.)

In any case, I actually got time off from the candy store (it was Sunday afternoon, when business was slow anyway) and attended. For the first time, I was associated with other science fiction readers. I met a number of young men who were to stay my friends for decades and who were to become notable in the science fiction world. As examples, there were Fred Pohl, Richard Wilson, Donald Wollheim, Sam Moskowitz, and Scott Meredith.

After nine years of isolation, I was never to be alone in science fiction again.

A sadder note was struck by the fact that the Teck *Amazing* finally gave up. The April 1938 issue was the eighty-ninth under the editorship of T. O'Conor Sloane, and the last.

Amazing Stories itself did not die, or even skip an issue; at least, its name didn't. It was bought by Ziff-Davis Publications, and the June 1938 issue came out in a new incarnation. The design of the name was changed, and the cover (horrors!) was a photograph rather than a painting.

The Ziff-Davis *Amazing* deliberately struck a lower level in writing and plotting, aiming for the younger reader. It proceeded to do well financially. With the October 1938 issue it went monthly, and there were to be periods when it had the highest monthly circulation ever achieved by a science fiction magazine.

Nevertheless, I considered it trash and disliked it intensely. It was the first science fiction magazine I did not read even when it was available. (It is rather embarrassing for me to have to admit, therefore, that my first two sales and my first two published appearances and my first two checks were to, in, and from the Ziff-Davis *Amazing*. I didn't really feel that I had arrived till I appeared in the pages of *Astounding*, with my third published story.)

But the overwhelming fact of 1938 was John W. Campbell, Jr. With the October 1937 issue, he had taken over the editorship of *Astounding Stories*. He remained, however, under the direction of Tremaine, who moved up to the post of Editorial Director. For seven issues, Campbell had to move slowly.

Nevertheless, he did manage to introduce changes. The March 1938 issue, for instance, was no longer *Astounding Stories*. It was *Astounding Science Fiction*, and the design of the name was changed to something altogether tasteful and attractive. I don't ordinarily welcome change in anything I have grown accustomed to, but that one I greeted gladly.

With the April 1938 issue, Tremaine left Street & Smith, and the fifty-fifth issue of the Tremaine *Astounding* was the last. It had been great while it lasted, but something far greater still was at hand. The May 1938 issue was the first of the Campbell *Astounding*. With that issue, Campbell was in complete charge and was to remain absolute ruler of the magazine for thirty-three years, up to the very day of his death.

Almost as soon as Campbell took over, the whole magazine breathed a new life. Campbell was looking for new authors and for a new kind of science fiction.

My fate had come to meet me. The June 1938 issue changed date of publication and was late. In mortal fear that the magazine had died, I actually traveled to Street & Smith Publications, Inc., to investigate (see *The Early Asimov*). That trip, the stimulation of my contacts with other fans, the new excitement of the Campbell era in birth, drove me back to writing.

Late in May 1938, I dug out the nearly forgotten manuscript of "Cosmic Corkscrew" and got back to work again. Even as I finished it, the July 1938 issue of *Astounding Science Fiction* came out, and in it was "The Men and the Mirror," by Ross Rocklynne. It was one of a series (and the best) that dealt with a detective who was pursuing a criminal only to find himself, and the criminal too, caught in a dilemma involving the laws of physics.

THE MEN AND THE MIRROR

by Ross Rocklynne

The men were plunging down the gently curving surface of the mirror.

Above them were the stars of the universe, whose light was caught by the mirror, radiated and reradiated by its concave surface, and, unimpaired, was flung back into space as a conglomerate glow.

There were two of these men. One was Edward Deverel, a worldly wise, carefree giant of a man whose profession—up until the recent past—had been that of pirating canal boats on the planet Mars. The other, a hard, powerful man, was Lieutenant John Colbie, whose assignment it was to apprehend this corsair of the canals.

Theirs was a real predicament, for they were unable to produce, at present, any means of escape from the prison this smooth, shining, deep bowl of a mirror presented.

As to how it all came about——

When Colbie, after his twelve-hour trek along the ammonia river which ran from the lake into which the Fountain poured its noxious ammonia liquids, finally reached Jupiter City, he was in a state of fatigue under which his muscles, every one of them, seemed to scream out a protest. He pressed the buzzer that let those within the air-lock understand that he was demanding admittance, and was decidedly relieved to see the huge valve swing open, throwing a glow of luminescence on the wildly swirling gases that raced across the surface of that mighty, poisonous planet Jupiter. Two men came forward. They covered him with hand weapons, and urged him inside the lock. The keeper of the lock desired to know Colbie's business, and Colbie demanded that he be taken before the commander of the garrison—who was also mayor of the city—as things had, of necessity, to be run on a military basis.

Riding through the streets of the city, he was both thrilled and awed, after that tortuous ordeal in the wilds of Jupiter, by the consciousness of the great genius of the human race—that it was able, in the face of so many killing difficulties, to erect this domed city, so well equipped with the luxuries of Earthly life. For outside the city there was a pressure of fifteen thousand pounds to the square inch. There was a gravitation two and a half times that of Earth. There was not a breathable drop of oxygen in the atmosphere, and not a ray of light ever penetrated the vast cloud layer to the planet's surface. But man had built the city, and it would remain forever, so solidly and efficiently was it constructed.

When Colbie came before the dome commander, that individual listened to his story, eyeing him keenly in the meanwhile.

"So you're Lieutenant John Colbie, of the Interplanetary Police Force," he mused. "Yet, not less than thirty-six hours ago another man stood before me and presented proof that he was John Colbie. One of you is wrong, I'd say, and no mistake about it."

"I've told you my story—that other man was a criminal, Edward Deverel by name, and I was put on his trail. I caught up with him on Vulcan, near the Sun, and we found it was hollow by the simple expedient of falling through a cavity on its surface. I had Deverel prisoner then, but he proved a bit too smart for me. We were trapped there, well enough, at the center of gravity. But he figured that the gases filling the planet's interior would expand as the planet came to perihelion, thus forming currents which Deverel used to his advantage in escaping the trap and eluding me at the same time. I found him again, but we were wrecked above Jupiter, fell into a pit with a liquid ammonia lake at the bottom. And Deverel, using, I'll have to admit, remarkably astute powers of deduction, figured that the lake drained by means of a siphon of some height. He eluded me that way, and I was left in the pit. I finally caught on—from some deliberate hints he had let drop—and followed him through the siphon. But he was waiting for me at the other end, demanded my credentials, and extracted from me a promise that I'd stay where I was for twenty-four hours." Colbie grinned in slight mirth. "So after twenty-four hours I came on. And now he's gone."

" 'Fraid he is," admitted the other. "I had no reason to suspect he was an imposter, so I gave him a ship. Come to think of it, he seemed in a mighty hurry. Hm-m-m. How can I identify you as Lieutenant John Colbie?"

"Easy," snapped Colbie. "I'm not unknown. There must be a few IPF men in the city. Let some of them identify me."

"Good idea." The man grimaced. "Something I should have done with the other man. However, that's past. No use replotting an orbit you've swung. I'll hunt up an IPF man or two."

And this he did. Within the space of a few hours, the commander had no doubt that the man who stood before him was one Lieutenant John Colbie, a native of Earth, and in the service of the Interplanetary Police Force.

"Well, we'll outfit you again, Lieutenant," he assured Colbie. "What's your course of action after that?"

Colbie, lolling in a deep chair, bathed, resplendent in borrowed clothing and refreshingly combed hair, cigarette drooping from a corner of his square lips, said, "My assignment was to apprehend a certain criminal; those are my orders. I just have to keep on trying."

"Not if things go as they have," said the other, smiling in such a manner that his sarcasm should have been without edge; but he saw immediately that he had said the wrong thing, for Colbie's eyes narrowed half angrily. "Sorry," he added quickly. And then apologetically, "Don't blame you a bit. Must be a sore point. How come you aren't in any especial hurry?" He deftly changed the subject.

"I should say I'm not in a hurry!" Colbie exclaimed feelingly. "I've been space-tied for a few months now, and I have to stuff a few of the civilized benefits into my life now and then. There's no need for haste, anyway. Only way I can find Deverel is by deducing his destination, then going there."

"Where do you think he went?" queried the other man interestedly.

"The new planet. I notice there's quite a lot about it in the papers. It's been making its way into the solar system for the past five or six months, I understand. It's a real wanderer—probably been zipping through interstellar space for ages. There's a good chance that's where Deverel's gone. He's curious, insanely curious about all things bizarre, and he won't be able to resist it—I hope," he added.

"Good lead, anyway. It'll be a worthwhile experience, too. No exploring parties have set foot on it. You two—if Deverel is there—will be the first to set foot on it. Hope you have good luck, this time," he added sincerely.

Colbie drew smoke into lungs that had not known cigarette smoke for a full half-year. "If there's any doubt in your mind, commander, let me assure you that Deverel's already up for trial, as far as my capturing him is concerned. Yes, I feel it in my bones. He's going back with me, this time."

The two men then looked up statistics on the new planet. It was a large sphere of celestial flotsam, somewhere near five thousand miles in diameter, of extremely low density for its bulk. It was traveling at the good clip of eighty-two miles per second toward the Sun, but it was estimated that the speed would be cut in half by a near passage by Jupiter. Finally it would take up an orbit that would be located somewhere between those of Jupiter and Neptune.

Shooting through space at furious velocity in his new cruiser, Colbie's lips were set and grim. His nerves were on edge. There was a flame in his brain. Truth to tell, he was so furious at Deverel's repeated escapes that the more he thought about it, the less he found himself able to think straight.

He could see the new planet as a small, gray dot against the ubiquitous veil of stars. It was not yet named, but was destined to be called Cyclops, for a reason to be seen. And with the passing hours it grew in apparent size, until, seven days after Colbie had shot upward into space, fighting Jupiter's gravitational fingers, it was a vast bulk in the heavens less than ten thousand miles distant. Colbie dived for it. He still had enormous speed, and was checking it with the greatest deceleration he could stand. When he came near enough to the planet, he used its gravitation as a further check. He started to circle it—and forthwith saw the "eye" of Cyclops staring up at him.

It was a mirror—a concave reflector, rather. But it looked like the eye of the planet, an eye that reflected starlight. Starlight, yes, because it was a reflector that caught the rays of the stars and threw them back to space. Indeed, Colbie, gazing on it awestruck, could see no slightest difference between the brilliance of the stars and the brilliance of that colossal mirror.

"Lord!" he whispered to himself, feeling half-reverent. He suddenly had a sensation of smallness, and realized in that second what an infinitesimal part of the universe he was. He lived for only the fraction of a second and surely was no larger than a sub-electron. For that mirror was artificial, had been fabricated by the powerful tools and intelligence of a race which had certainly lived at least thousands, perhaps millions of years ago. Who could tell how far Cyclops had traveled, plunging at steady pace across the void that separates our solar system from the nearest star? Who could tell the manner of people who had constructed it? One could only say that they had been engineers on a scale which human beings could not at present comprehend.

The mirror was perfect. Colbie took various readings on it, after the first mighty upsurge of awe had ebbed away. He found the diameter, about two miles less than a thousand; the depth, an approximate three hundred; and the shape, perfectly circular, perfectly curved. The albedo was so close to 1 that his instruments could not measure the infinitesimal fraction that it lacked!

And thereat, Colbie sat down and whistled loud and long. Man knew of no perfect reflector; it was deemed impossible, in fact. All materials will reflect light in some small degree, but more often the greater amount is absorbed. But the material of this colossus among reflectors reflected all light save an absolutely negligible amount of that which impinged on its surface. For Colbie knew that *some* of it was certainly absorbed—he did not believe in impossibilities. It was impossible that that mirror didn't absorb some light. His instruments had been unable to measure it, but of course there were instruments on Earth that would measure that absorption when the time came for it. But they would have to be delicate indeed. Even at that, however, the albedo of this mirror was a thing almost beyond belief, and certainly beyond comprehension.

The mirror disappeared around the curve of the planet as Colbie's ship plunged on, decreasing its velocity slowly but surely. Colbie forced his thoughts once more to the issue paramount in his mind—that of locating Deverel. But his exciting discovery of the mirror stayed in the back of his mind, and he was determined to know more about it. And he did; more thoroughly, in fact, than he liked at the time.

He now had his velocity under control. Hoping that Deverel had not detected his presence above the new planet, he gave himself up to the one problem that was perplexing him—where would Deverel have landed? Near the mirror; that was a certainty. Somewhere near the rim of the giant reflector—but that was anywhere on a circle three and a half thousand miles in circumference.

He finally resolved to scour the area in which Deverel would have landed. Training his single telescope downward so that it would sweep the entire area, he applied his photo-amplifiers to the light received, and then, keeping at a distance of about fifty miles from the surface of the planet so that Deverel could not possibly sight him with the naked eye, he darted around that circle at low speed, eye glued to the eyepiece of the telescope. He hoped thus to see the outlaw's ship.

And he did. It lay at the base of one of those mountains of Cyclops that flaunted a sharp peak thousands of feet up into the sky. That mountain swept down to foothills that terminated abruptly in a level plain scarcely more than seven or eight miles from the rim of the great mirror.

Colbie sighed in lusty relief, entirely glad that his assumption of Deverel's destination had now been proven absolutely correct.

Shooting the ship upward, and then, keeping that single landmark—the mountain—in view, he came up behind it, and, by dint of much use of forward, stern, and under jets, jockeyed the cruiser to rest far enough around the curve of the mountain so that the outlaw should not note his advent.

He put out a vial to draw in a sample of the planet's atmosphere, but as he had with good reason suspected, that atmosphere was nonexistent. The undistorted brightness of the stars had almost made him sure of it. He struggled into a spacesuit, buckled on his weapons, attached oxygen tank, screwed down his helmet, opened the air-lock and jumped down to the planet's surface. It was hard. Examining it, he found that it consisted of ores in a frozen, earthy state. Whether this was true of the entire planet he did not know.

He started around the curved base of the mountain, and, after the first mile, discovered that traveling across the surface of Cyclops was a terrific task. The planet was seamed and cracked in dozens of places; great gaping cracks which presented definite handicaps to a safe journey of any length. He found that he had to take precautions indeed, and often searched extensively for crevices narrow enough to leap with safety. He worried along, taking his time, but he was beginning to realize that he might not have as much of that at his disposal as he had indicated to the dome commander back on Jupiter.

So that, after a good many hours, he rounded the breast of the mountain and caught the black shine of Deverel's falsely acquired ship.

But he saw nothing of Deverel.

He threw himself to the ground. Suddenly he was painfully conscious that his heart was thumping. The thought of physical danger in no way caused this condition—he was simply afraid that Deverel might elude capture again by putting his tricky mentality to work. The competition between these two—law and disorder personified—had become a personal contest. Truth to tell, the IP man respected and rather admired Deverel's uncanny ability to escape him, not the fact that he had escaped. Colbie had to bring him back, but respected Deverel's unusual genius at escaping tight spots. But—he had to bring the man in, or admit the outlaw a better man than he.

In this uneasy state of mind, he lay there, projector out. It could shoot explosive missiles at thousands of feet per second, and was, in this, the twenty-third century, the ultimate in destructive hand weapons.

Now, as he lay there, his eyes constantly on the ship and the area about, he turned his thoughts in a new direction. In the name of all that was holy, why had Deverel come here? Hadn't he realized it was the first place Colbie would look? Certainly he must have known it. Then why had he come?

Colbie thought he saw the answer. Deverel had planned on leaving this planet long before the space policeman had arrived. He had had a full thirty-six hours' start on Colbie, and he decided that would give him enough time for the opportunity he so craved—to visit this new planet, and determine to his own satisfaction whether or not there was anything about it which would satisfy that love he had for the bizarre.

He had had sufficient time. Sufficient time to satisfy himself as to the nature of the mirror; sufficient time to leave again, and break up his trail in the trackless wastes of space.

But he hadn't left.

Why?

And then Colbie began to feel acute mental discomfort. And the longer he lay there, the worse it became. He became conscience stricken. And why? Because Deverel might be lying in there sick, and Colbie could not risk coming out into the open until he knew absolutely Deverel's whereabouts. And perhaps Deverel lay in there dying. Space sickness is a recognized malady, and it is not infrequent. It is ascribed to any number of causes, among which are noted positive and negative deceleration, a missing vital element in synthetic air, and the lack of gravitation. Its only cure is absolute rest under a decent gravitation. And—such a cure was impossible for a man who was dependent on no one but himself.

Colbie squirmed uncomfortably. "The fool might be dying!" he snapped angrily to himself. "While I'm lying here. But I can't give myself away."

But his nerves grew more and more tense. He dreaded the thought of Deverel sick in there while he was able to give him help. And in the end he sprang to his feet, determined he wouldn't let the uncertainty of the situation wear on him any longer.

And then his radio receiver woke to life, and screeched calmly though waveringly, "You're out there, Colbie. You *would* be there. Listen—" the voice dwindled away, and then came back in renewed strength. "I'm sick, Colbie, rottenly sick. I think I'm going to do the death act. It's the stomach that really hurts, though there's the ears too. They hurt, too, and they send the blind staggers right through the brain. I'm sweating—" The voice ebbed, rushed back. "If you want to—come in and give me a hand—will you? Then you can take me back—" The voice groaned off, and sliding sounds came through the receiver.

But already Colbie was tearing out into the open, racing across the space separating him from the ship, a wave of pity for the helpless man breaking over him.

The outer valve was open. Colbie climbed in, drew it shut, manipulated the controls of the inner valve, and debouched into the ship proper.

He was now amidships, standing opposite the lazaret. Forward was the control cabin and vital machinery, abaft, in the stern compartment, were sleeping and living quarters.

Colbie bounded aft, swung through a door, and saw a pitiable sight indeed. The room was incredibly littered with such items as soiled clothing, and dishes with the scum of meals dried onto them. In the middle of the room was a table, and on that table an electric fan was whirling full blast, flinging a steady current of air upon a man who lay stark naked on a bunk which seemed the ultimate in human filth.

Deverel lay there, twisting, squirming, panting, moaning, his eyes rolling, and rivulets of sweat bubbling up from his queerly yellow skin, and flowing down to encounter a plain, stained mattress.

The first thing Colbie did was to snap off that venomous, killing fan. In fact, to sweep it from the table with one blow of his open palm. The next was to take Deverel's pulse. It was quick, dangerously high, but certainly not predicting the close approach of death. In another day it might have ceased altogether, but at present there was plenty of chance.

Deverel's eyes lolled over to Colbie's, and his lips drew back painfully over handsome white teeth.

"Glad you came," he whispered, and then his head dropped back and his eyes closed. He was not asleep; the knowledge that he was now in the hands of a competent person sent him into a dead faint.

Colbie knew what to do in cases like this. He went forward to the control room, manipulated oxygen tank valves, and increased the quantity of oxygen in the air. He got all the clean linen he could find, and bathed Deverel from head to foot in lukewarm water. He turned the mattress over, put on clean sheets, and then lifted Deverel lightly as a baby back on to it. Then he stuck a thermometer into the outlaw's mouth.

He cleaned the room, occupying a full hour in washing dishes with a minimum of valuable water. Then he took meats and vegetables from the refrigerator, where they had doubtless reposed for months perfectly frozen, and started a pot of soup.

And that was all he could do for a while.

He sat down and waited, taking many readings on the thermometer.

And Deverel's temperature went down. His breathing became even, and then he slept. Thirteen hours later he awoke.

"Hi, Lieutenant," he said.

"Hi, yourself!" Colbie put down the magazine with which he had been really enjoying himself for the first time in months. "How's the temperature?" he inquired.

"Gone. Thanks a lot," he added carelessly, but he was serious. "You know I mean it, too."

"Sure." Colbie waved it aside. "A pleasure—I was glad to do it, y'know." He fingered the pages of the magazine abstractedly. He jerked a thumb. "How'd you know I was out there?"

"Didn't *know* it." Deverel laughed. "It's a cinch if you weren't out there you wouldn't have heard me say I knew you were."

"That's right." Colbie laughed, too, and blue eyes and gray eyes met each other in mutual amusement. "Like some soup?"

Deverel said enthusiastically that he did. So that these two men, mutually respecting enemies of each other, sat down and ate for all the world as if each was an affectionate friend of the other.

For many days life was easy. No grueling flights through harsh space. No anxieties. No dread of death to come. No fear of insanely impersonal meteors. Here on Cyclops, the planet of the great mirror, living was a pleasure.

Deverel regained his health. He was finally able to get out of bed and walk around. With that done, it was not long before Deverel was considered a well man once more. Of course, the old life then had to be recognized. There had been a tacit understanding between the two men—for a little while their personal relationships did not stand. That was fair.

But that understanding had to be sundered eventually, and Deverel did not put the time off. The moment he felt his strength had returned in full measure, he said: "Well, it's been fun while it lasted. But it's time for us to sort of assume our natural antagonisms. So you put me in irons—right away. Or I'll give you a swift, underhanded poke to the jaw."

Colbie regarded him judicially. "Fair enough," he conceded. "You wouldn't mind getting me about the heaviest pair of leg and arm irons from the lazaret, would you?" he inquired quizzically.

"Not at all," murmured Deverel politely.

"Wait a minute," Colbie said uneasily. He leaned forward. "Now look. Did you notice the mirror?"

"Certainly. And damned curious about it, too."

"And I. Now suppose we let this unwritten pact of mutual noninterference drag on for a while, just enough to allow us to explore? Y'know, I haven't got a time limit on me—"

"Oh"—Deverel waved a scornful hand—"neither have I. Let's let it drag on, shall we?" he said in the unconscious manner of a youngster excited over the prospect of a pleasing new toy. "You've got my promise, Colbie—I won't try to get away."

They saluted each other with a grin, and forthwith made ready for their adventure in exploration.

Sleep was the first preparation. After a good many hours, they set off across the gouged, forbidding plain. The stars looked down at them unwinkingly through the vacuum separating them from Cyclops' harsh terrain. Behind the men loomed the sharp, high peaks of the mountain in whose proximity Deverel had put down his stolen cruiser.

They were decked out as completely as they deemed advisable. They had oxygen, water, and food for at least a day. Colbie had decided not to carry his projector. It was a clumsy weapon, and he saw no possible use for it. Thus, attached by a two-hundred-foot hank of rope, which was suited in composition to the demands the cold and vacuum of space might make upon it, they wended their starlit way across Cyclops. When they were not using the rope fording dangerous chasms, they wound it up about them. They progressed steadily toward the rim of the reflector which probably had been constructed long before man had made the first full stride toward harmonized society.

Twice, Colbie slipped at the termination of a leap which taxed all his physical powers, and twice would have plunged into the apparently bottomless gorges below; and twice Deverel braced himself against the rims of the pits, and pulled the Interplanetary man back to safety. In both cases they made extended searches for narrower crevices.

Slowly but surely they worked their way to the rim, and finally struck level country. The last mile was a true plain, so unmarred that they suspected it must have been smoothed over artificially at some long-gone period. It struck Colbie that this would have been a much better place for Deverel to have put his ship down. Deverel explained that at the moment the first spasm of sickness had hit him, he was not in a frame of mind to care where he landed.

They came, then, to the rim.

They regarded with awe the black wall. It was composed of some dully hued metal. It stretched away from them in a slow curve that lost itself to their eyes many miles to either side of them. It was perfectly formed and unmarred in the slightest particular, about twice as tall as a man.

Deverel struck a pose, and said vibrantly, "The mirror!" But certainly he was not unshaken by the anciently constructed reflector.

Colbie put in wonderingly, "Some things a man can't believe. I wonder how old this thing is—wonder who made it—how they made it! Lord, what engineers they must have been! What a job!"

"What a contract for the firm that landed the bid!" Deverel put in, smiling. "What do you say we top it? I've got an itch to see it firsthand—touch it."

Colbie nodded, and Deverel braced himself against the wall, forming a cup with his heavily gloved hands. "Up you go! But once you get up," he warned, "careful you don't topple. That'd mean trouble in large doses."

"Don't worry about that," Colbie said grimly. "If any one falls, it's going to be you, not me."

He put one foot in the outlaw's hands. Deverel heaved. Colbie shot up and caught both hands around the rim, which sloped inward. That done, he drew himself upward so that he was sitting carefully on the rim, facing Deverel.

With much effort and care, he drew Deverel beside him, and then, as if with mutual consent, they twisted their heads and sent their eyes out over the great mirror.

At once, all sense of perspective and balance left them. Light from all directions smote them, blinded them, sent a haze into their minds. Downward and to all sides and above, there was light. In fact, the light of the stars and the light of the mirror were indistinguishable in the split second when that bewildering sensation of instability struck them. Colbie thought fleetingly and in panic that he was poised upside down on the most insecure foothold in the universe. He could not decide, in that split second, which was the true sky.

So—he clutched at the wrong sky, and toppled over the rim.

Deverel, feeling precisely the same sensations, would have recovered in time had not the rope attaching him to Colbie forcefully jerked at him a second before he had fully decided which way was up. So they both fell down the angle of the mirror, and were, in a second, shooting haphazardly, horridly, through an interminable pressing mist of light and nothing but light.

They were plunging downward so swiftly, and yet so lightly, that they might have been wafted along on an intangible beam of force. For they felt nothing. Not the slightest sensation of *sliding*—only a sense of acceleration *downward*.

After that first moment of heart-stopping horror, after the first panic, the first moment of unutterable vertigo had passed, Colbie's nerves started quivering violently. Deliberately he quieted them by closing his eyes and clenching his fists. Then he opened fists and eyes both, and looked around for Deverel. Deverel was about five feet behind him.

Deverel was looking at him from eyes that were extremely concerned.

"And I said to be careful," he snapped angrily. Colbie started to open his lips with hot words, but Deverel waved a hand disgustedly. "I know, I know. My fault, too." He drew a long breath and occupied himself putting his head where his feet were.

Colbie did the same, and then very gingerly tried to stay his fall, by pressing his hands and feet on the surface of the mirror. This had not the slightest effect on his position or his velocity. He found that it was extremely difficult to twist his body except by flinging his arms around, but he accomplished this not by any aid the mirror gave him. His hands in no slightest degree rubbed against the mirror's surface. In fact, he felt no sensation which told him that his hands might have touched a surface. It was as if he had run a finger over a vat of some viscous slime, as if the slime had imparted no heat, no cold, had not adhered to his finger, had not impeded its motion in any way, had merely guided it along a path determined by its own surface!

He closed his eyes painfully. The trend of his thoughts hinted of insanity. He tried to analyze his sensations. He was falling. Falling straight down, at the acceleration the gravity of this planet gave his body. But he knew he was merely gliding along at a downward angle. He was simply being guided by a substance which in no degree impeded the action of gravity. That must mean—

No friction!

The words exploded in his brain—and exploded crazily from his mouth. "*No friction!*"

Deverel stared at him, and then frantically made tests. He tried to rub that surface. He felt nothing, nothing that held his hand back—as if it had slid along infinitely smooth ice.

"You're right," he said, staring stupidly. "That's what it must be. Hell —it's frictionless!" And then he cried, "But that can't be!" and his lips twitched. "There can't be anything that's frictionless. You know that. It can't be done!"

Colbie shook his head as one speaking to a child. "No, Deverel," he found himself saying in a kindly voice, an insistent but pitying voice, "it has no rub. You put your hand on it and push. And does it hold your hand back? No." He shook his head sadly. "They made this stuff frictionless."

And as they shot downward into the sea of light, they held each other with their dumbfounded eyes.

The outlaw sharply shook his head. "We're making fools of ourselves. Let's face it. There isn't any friction. Now—now we're up against something."

"I know it."

Colbie almost drunkenly squirmed around, and finally maneuvered until he was sitting, his feet crossed under him, his eyes trained hypnotically into the downward distance. Or was there any distance? There was no horizon. The stars, and the conglomerate glow of the mirror that was the absolute reflection of the stars, merged with each other.

"We've got to pull ourselves together," he said stubbornly. "Let's think this out. We've got to get used to it."

"Right." And Deverel did the first sensible thing by twisting and looking behind him. They had toppled over the rim of the mirror almost exactly two minutes ago, and though their velocity had steadily been mounting, there was a horizon back there which could be seen. It was mainly indicated by that lofty, slowly rising mountain which loomed up against the rim of the mirror. He felt that it was a good landmark—somehow, that was the place they had to get back to.

"Now look," he said seriously to Colbie, "let's talk this over." His voice was slightly metallic as it came through Colbie's earphones. "Before I landed on this planet I took some readings on that mirror same as you, and I guess I came to the same conclusions.

"Long ago, maybe a million years, there was a race of men—or beings— who lived on a planet that circled a sun just like ours, perhaps. They had a satellite, this planet we're on. They were engineers on a monster scale. I have no doubt they could have remade their planet, and even their solar system, exactly to suit themselves—and maybe they did. But they made this satellite over to suit themselves, that's certain. They gouged out—how I wouldn't know—a section of this planet that corresponded to the bottom part of a sphere. The radius of that sphere—I figured it—is about 1600 miles out in space. Then, so help me—I wouldn't know this, either—they coated that gouged-out surface with some substance which, when it hardened, formed an absolutely smooth surface. You came to the same conclusions I did, didn't you? That it was such a perfect reflector you couldn't measure the amount it didn't reflect?"

Colbie, listening with interest, nodded. "And we should have seen that such a good reflector would be frictionless, too. Couldn't be any other way. And say!" he exclaimed. "This stuff can't be frictionless. We knew it couldn't reflect *all* light. It simply reflects all but a negligible amount of light, and it's got a negligible amount of friction, too!"

"That's right!" Deverel was genuinely relieved. "That idea of no friction at all had me going cuckoo. 'Course not—there can't be any surface that's got no friction at all. The molecular state of matter forbids it. No matter how close you crowd the molecules, they still make an infinitesimally bumpy surface.

"Now why did they make the mirror? Only reason I can see—power. They must have had a heat engine. It generated power in huge amounts, undoubtedly, and perhaps the power they took in that way was broadcast back to their planet. Or perhaps it was a weapon—another mirror, plane this time, which could rotate and train a searing beam of heat on an enemy ship. Would that ship blister! And they might have been able to rotate this satellite at will, too—

"Then something happened. Those people lost their satellite. Maybe their own planet exploded. Maybe their sun exploded, and this planet went shooting away, and finally our Sun grabbed it.

"And that's a fair explanation—the only one, as far as I see. Unless, of course, it was meant to be something that was in the experimental stage and was never completed."

"The magical mirror," Colbie interspersed softly. But neither of them then knew exactly what magical characteristics it did possess.

For a moment they were silent. "Well"—Deverel had a shrug in his voice —"we can't do anything now—can we? Shall we eat?"

"Why not?"

They ate in the strange manner necessitated by spacesuits. By buttons in a niche outside their suits they manipulated levers which reached into a complicated mechanism, pulling out food pills—tasteless things—and water, which they sucked through a tube.

"Now," said Deverel, smacking his lips as if he had just eaten a square meal, "this is just another situation, and not a fairy tale. Proved it by eating, which is so mortal it's disgusting. Where we bound?"

"For the bottom—"

"Ho—not at all! We're almost at bottom now—notice how the angle's been straightening out? It's almost 180° now. Let's see. Phew!" He had looked at his chronometer. "We've fallen three hundred miles in something like eight or nine minutes." Colbie started to protest, but the outlaw said, "Sure, to all intents and purposes we've simply fallen three hundred miles —the depth of the mirror. Remember, there isn't any friction that'd hold us back, and the inclined surface we came down on just guided us. And that means we're going to bounce right back to the other rim—see?"

"Ye gods, yes!" yelled Colbie, then grimaced. "But we won't quite reach the rim. Just that damnably small amount of friction will hold us back fifty or some feet. If there weren't any friction things would be simple— we'd reach the other rim exactly."

"Sure. And climb over. Gravity gave us the momentum going down, but she'll occupy herself taking it away at the same rate going up."

While they had been talking, they had passed bottom—quite definitely. They were going up, for the angle was slowly but surely increasing.

"We won't make it," Colbie said disconsolately. "There's the rub."

In the thoughtfully melancholy voice of the Danish prince, Deverel muttered, "Aye, there's the rub; for in that sleep of death, what dreams may come, when we have shuffled off this mortal coil, must give us pause."

"And that's appropriate, isn't it!" Colbie sneered.

"I played Hamlet once. Long time ago, of course, but I was pretty good. You know that second act scene where he—"

"Skip it! Forget it—I don't want to hear it. Let's get on. There is the friction—infinitesimal. It doesn't help at all when you try to change or retard your motion; but in the long run, it'll build up a total resistance great enough to keep us from the rim."

"Check, check, and check," agreed the outlaw, touching the fingers of his left hand with the index finger of his right.

"That's our situation. Looks hopeless."

"Maybe," Deverel declared. "Let me add some further facts. We're dropping down at an acceleration of twelve feet a second per second. At bottom, three hundred miles down, we had a terrific final velocity. Don't know exactly what it is, but there's a formula for it. Going up, gravity will be right on our tails, lopping off twelve feet of speed for every second. Notice I say up and down. I mean it. Our angular speed is something else again, and is certainly much greater."

Then, as he saw Colbie's impatient look, "I don't know how we get out. Normally, when you get in some place, you go out the same way—but they closed the door on us. And, of course, I don't see how we can change direction."

The IP man crossed his legs under him the other way for a change. He squinted upward. "Getting near top again. Damn that light. After a while, I'll go blind."

"Shut your eyes," Deverel told him callously, then, "Lord," he remarked whimsically, his cynical, yet friendly, eyes crinkling. "I'm glad we're what we are, Colbie. You have to chase me and I always feel obliged to run. Then we run into the most interesting experiences. I've had plenty of good times looting canal boats on Mars—did I ever tell you how hard it was squeezing the rings off the Empress' fingers? I used plenty of soap and water—and she was horrified at the way I wasted the water—but somehow I'm glad they got after me. And you are, too," he added as if in self-defense.

"Sure," Colbie remarked. "But in a way I'm not. You're a likeable fellow. I admit it. But you haven't got the instinct to help make an organized unit of society—you're a gear out of mesh. 'Course, there's others like you—but it's you I have to take in. I suppose I'll do it, too."

"Forgetting the mix-up we're in?"

"No. Just trying to match your own superb confidence in crises like this one."

"*Touché.*" The outlaw grinned. "Any ideas to match your confidence?"

"Not a shard."

"Me either—yet. By the way"—and here Deverel regarded Colbie thoughtfully—"I'm keeping anything I learn to myself—anything that might get us out, I mean."

"Meaning?" Colbie's eyes hardened.

"I'll sell what I know for a price."

"Ho! Freedom, I guess!" Colbie said sardonically.

"Well—not that, exactly. I'll tell you what it is, if I ever get anything to sell."

Colbie studied him, shrugged his shoulders carelessly. He looked over his shoulder, but he didn't see the approaching rim.

"Our angle's much steeper." Deverel followed his thought. "The rim isn't far away. Couple minutes yet."

"We won't make it though," Colbie said regretfully, "unless there's something else we don't know anything about."

In a few minutes, they saw the rim outlined against the black sides of an uneven mountain range which might have been set back from the rim anywhere from ten to twenty miles. They regarded its stubborn approach with anxiety.

So slowly it came toward them—and so rapidly their velocity was being decreased to the zero point! Nerves tensed, fists clenched, eyes strained. But intuitively, rather than from any deliberate mental calculation, they felt that they would not reach it. Their velocity was simply not enough.

And it wasn't. Slowly—compared to their earlier enormous velocities— they rose toward the rim which was so painfully near, yet so infinitely difficult to reach. One moment, then, they were rising; the next, falling. There had been no pause, or if there had been it was nestled close to that infinitesimal space of time which man will never measure. They began to fall.

In a voice that held words of chagrin—true to human nature, he had not given up hope—Colbie said, "Missed it—by about ten vertical feet, as a close guess. Next time we swing across this damned mirror we'll miss it by twenty feet."

"Something like that," Deverel agreed abstractedly. At the moment they had fallen, he had noted the time down to the exact fraction of a second. And he kept it in mind. Not that he had any idea of its ultimate benefit then, but he felt it might be a good thing to know. "Let's see," he was muttering to himself, and using Colbie's phrase, went on, "the time for one swing across—"

And he didn't finish the sentence. For an idea, a conception so alluring, so utterly startling, leaped into his mind, that he drew his breath inward through his suddenly meeting teeth. "Lord!" he whispered, and almost as if he were stunned, he dropped back, lying full length, his head cupped in the palms of his joined hands. And he saw the stars.

The two men were zooming along at a good fast clip that was building on itself. They were guided by the frictionless stuff of the mirror, and pulled by the force of gravity.

And above were the stars. So cold, so remote, so harshly, quietly beautiful. Deverel was looking at them, hard. They were exciting stars. They never changed their position as a whole. They looked the same as when they—the men—had gone plunging down the curve of the mirror.

While Deverel lay there on his back, his brow wrinkled in thought, Colbie watched him, watched him for a good many minutes, while they plummeted into the depths of the shining bowl. In an incredibly short time, they reached bottom—and Colbie grew tired of trying to read the outlaw's thoughts. He tried to rise to his feet. He went through a number of gyrations, which left him lying face down, looking at his own reflections.

Deverel had come out of his brown study, and was watching amusedly. "If there were a large enough area on the soles of your feet, m'lad, you could stand easily enough. But when you sit down, the center of gravity of your body is considerably lowered, and it's easy. So you'll never stand up unless by some miracle of balance."

This bit of wisdom was apparent. Colbie sat down, drew the water tube into his mouth, and sucked with abandon. Then he regarded Deverel knowingly. "Been thinking, eh? What about?"

"The mirror," Deverel replied solemnly. "I have to keep it to myself, though—sorry!"

"Likely!" There was a tigerish snarl implied in Colbie's voice overtones.

Deverel's worldly wise eyes grew sardonic. "Sure—I've been doing a lot of figuring, and I've found out a lot of stuff. Interesting, unusual. But there's something missing, Colbie—something I can't put my finger on. If I had it—and I will get it—I could get us out of here. Any suggestions?" he concluded, regarding Colbie sidewise out of a laughing eye.

"If I had them," pointedly, "I'd keep 'em. By the way, are you being fair? Withholding information? I'm referring to your promise—that you wouldn't try to get away."

"I did make a promise, just as you said—that I wouldn't try to get away.

And I haven't. And I won't until you tell me it's all right if I try. Get it?"
He fixed Colbie with a rigidly extended index finger, and went on in tight
tones of significance. "Let's be ourselves from now on, Colbie—outlaw and
cop! Right now, we're just partners in adventure. But you, just by saying
so, can make us what we really are—and I'd be your prisoner. D'you see?
Do that, Colbie, and I'll get us out of here!"

Colbie felt a slow flush rising to his face. Suddenly he felt utterly humiliated; felt as if his intelligence had been insulted and mocked at.
Colbie's voice exploded, an eruption of searing wrath. "No! Listen," he
went on in a low, deadly, flat voice, "the answer is no. No from now on.
I don't give a damn. I don't give a damn if we slide back and forth here
for eternity—that's what we'll do if you wait for me to give in to you and
your damned insulting demand. You've got the brass—" Colbie choked
apoplectically, and stopped. He waved his arms helplessly, glaring at the
other man. After a while he went on, his voice now even, "You suggest I
haven't got the mentality or the resource to find my—our—way out of
here. Maybe I haven't. Maybe I'm a damned dummy. But I'll tell you something that's going to make you squirm; you're going to see *me* outbluff
you! And *you're* going to give in to *me!* Remember it."

He sank back, glaring.

Deverel's eyes were popping. "Well!" he exclaimed in astonishment.
"Phew! Glad you got that off your chest—you sure take the fits!"

A lot of thought went on under Deverel's helmet, and in a way they
amused him. But they were all directed toward one end—escape. This was
a new Colbie, an undreamed-of Colbie, he saw here, and he was going to
be a tough nut to crack! So Deverel finally said, "You're going to outbluff
me, you said."

"Sure. Now, ever, and always. Something else, my dear mental marvel
—it's you that's going to do the thinking." His voice was contemptuous.
"Now, go ahead and use that so superior gray matter you're claiming."

Deverel's lips twitched. He said, shrugging, "If that's the way you want
it. But you're crazy."

Colbie refused to answer.

"Well." The outlaw laughed lightly. "Now we've got our own personal
feud mapped out. We won't be on speaking terms for maybe two or three
hours. Incidentally, we'll be bored to death. We won't even enjoy ourselves
the least bit. That's the way people do when they're mad at each other. If I
were a kid, or if we were medium-close relatives, I'd say all right—but we're
two grown men."

"I get it." Colbie put a grin on his face.

"Good!" Deverel exclaimed. "Now where are we, Colbie? Near the top
again. There's the rim, too!"

It was true. The rim was there—but it was not the same section of the
rim from which they had dropped. Deverel realized it. That mountain,

that landmark, did not show up against the rim. They had gone across the mirror twice. By common sense, they should have returned to their starting point. But had they returned, Deverel would have been startled indeed.

They came to the apex of the second trip across—and dropped back, once more missing it by an additional ten vertical feet. Once more they plunged downward into the depths of the shining bowl.

On the way down, Colbie was silent. Unable to help himself, his thoughts began to revolve. How could they get out? But his thoughts revolved futilely. He was unable to look at the matter objectively. Had he been solving a puzzle on paper, the answer would have come soon enough. He was well enough equipped on the laws of motion to have solved it. But, being a part of the brain-teaser himself, he was helpless.

But undoubtedly he should have noticed that the position of the stars in the heavens never changed.

They passed bottom, went sloping upward again, in a monotony of evenly decreasing speed that was maddening, at least to Colbie.

Deverel was not silent. He occupied himself in a frivolous manner, talking, laughing, cracking jokes. He enjoyed himself thoroughly. He could make himself at home anywhere, and in the strangest circumstances. It was one of his admirable qualities.

Finally he called, "How about it, Lieutenant? Making any headway?"

Colbie came out of it. "Know less than I did before," he admitted sadly. The light of the stars, and the light which the mirror so faithfully threw back into space, were beginning to irritate him, too.

"Damn shame." Deverel sounded regretful. "I've got a lot of dope on this strange vale o' paradise," he added sadly, "but I can't find the missing link that'd put it to some advantage. And to be frank, the time to put it to the best advantage will be in less than an hour. A crucial moment, I mean." He was staring intently at Colbie.

"Damn the crucial moment," Colbie said coldly.

"Well, there'll be several crucial moments," Deverel said, laughing softly. "The best possible times for us to get out—but I don't know yet how we'll get out. You say I have to do the thinking? But it won't hurt if we talk things over a little, will it?"

Colbie said it was all right with him. After all, the whole thing was up to Deverel from now on. No number of solutions would help if Deverel didn't give in.

They discussed the color of the strange substance. Did it have one? No, certainly not; it absorbed no light, hence was the color of any light it reflected. Could they, as a single system of two bodies, change their direction of motion? No. They were a closed system, and as such had a single center of gravity which would continue on its present course forever, unless some outside force intervened. They could jerk, they could squirm, but for every action in one direction, there would be equal reaction in the other. Was this substance either hot or cold as determined by human senses? No. For it could absorb no heat, nor could it, therefore, transmit heat. The first would convey the impression of coldness, the second that of warmth—

It was an amusing subject, and exhaustless. But Deverel plucked no fruit from its many branches. They were still hopelessly marooned within the bowl of the incredible mirror.

They hit the apex of the third swing across the great mirror—and fell downward again. They bounced back up from the bottom, zoomed upward through the sea of luminescence, fell downward again the fifth time.

And Deverel said, "It's coming. It's here. The first Crucial Moment. But we have to pass it up."

The sixth apex dwindled away, found Deverel looking longingly at the sharply rising mountain which he had placed in his head as a landmark, "the place they had to get back to."

"I know when we have to get out," he told Colbie anxiously, "but the how of it knocks me! Every trip across we take, we fall nearer the bottom by ten feet. Right now we're about sixty feet below the plane of the rim of the mirror. How are we going to rise that sixty feet?"

"You have me there," said Colbie nonchalantly.

Deverel regarded him seriously. Colbie was an uncaring idiot—didn't seem to give a damn whether they got out or not. But Deverel was beginning to feel whole new quantities of respect for the IP man. There was certainly more to him than he had hitherto suspected. He smiled. "Still holding out?"

Colbie said he was.

"Well, you know I won't give in." Deverel said harshly, "I'm supposed to be damned fool enough to think my way back to Earth with you, back to jail. I've outbluffed better men than you, Colbie, and I'll stick this one out, too. Are we going to be damned fools? You know, if this was off my mind, I could devote myself a lot better to the one problem that fuddles me up."

But Colbie said that he was sorry he couldn't help the outlaw get the suspense off his mind. And Deverel's teeth closed with a snap. Colbie, looking at the hard sardonic features, wondered vaguely, perhaps with a slight inward shudder, what would be the outcome of it all.

Then ensued utter weariness. For interminable minute after interminable minute, they swept dizzyingly down and up through the pressing, aching mist of light. Their eyes became tortured, their brains became inflamed, their muscles stiffened, their nerves jangled. They became irritable and touchy. The monotony was man-killing, especially in view of the fact that the manner of their salvation was yet a thing of the future—or perhaps a thing of no solution.

Deverel was up against a blank wall, and his every word had a snarl in it. "There's some way it can be done," he insisted, as they were dropping down after the tenth plunge across the great mirror. "And I have to find it soon. We're a hundred feet below the rim now. You could help me, Colbie —you've the brains for it, I know you have. But you're lazy, damn it. You insist on sitting back there and letting me do all the thinking. Suggest something, won't you?"

Colbie answered seriously, "Deverel, I have been thinking. But it's no good. What is it you know? What strange characteristics has the mirror got that both you and I don't already know?" He paused, shaking his head. "I can't see the trees for the forest—I'll admit it." He was genuinely sorry he couldn't help, and was more than a little touched by the outlaw's desperate search for the final link in the chain he had evidently fabricated. "Why not tell me what it's all about?" he suggested. "Maybe I can go on from what you've found out."

"No sale!" Deverel snorted angrily. "What I know is my trump card— you'd know as much as I do. Wouldn't do me any good."

"Won't do you any good, anyway—unless you give in." Colbie grinned easily.

"And you can bet everything you've got I won't!" Deverel snapped. And then looked queerly at Colbie. "You really have made up your mind, haven't you?" he demanded. He shrugged his shoulders sulkily. "But maybe you'll change it. That's what I'm banking on, anyway. You're not the type that can hold out forever."

Colbie shrugged his own shoulders in indifference, and then crossed his legs a different way. Thinking better of it, he lay flat on his back, and by virtue of swinging his arms one way and his legs the other, started to whirl about. Elsewhere, the action might have seemed childish, but here it was one of a strictly limited number of amusements.

While this aimless gyration, which, once started, continued unabated, may have amused Colbie at first, it very soon had a much different effect. Abruptly he sat up—still spinning lazily—and stared at Deverel. A slow grin appeared on his lips, went into temporary eclipse as he turned around, and appeared again as the rope holding them together wound up about him. "Your difficulty," he asked judiciously, "lies in being unable to make up for that hundred feet or so we've lost to friction, I take it?"

Deverel looked at him keenly and nodded.

Colbie's face split in a slow, broad grin. "I haven't got it all figured out. I said I'd let you do that. But I know how to make up for that difference. It takes cooperation, and maybe if you know how to do it, you'll give me the rest of that information sooner. Because I won't cooperate till you do. You think what I was doing, and you'll get it."

Deverel looked at him blankly. Then—"I've got it!" he gurgled. "I knew it could be done—and it's easy!"

He was talking rapidly, excitedly. "I've got the whole thing worked out, now. Everything I need! It's only a question of waiting. Two or three more times across the mirror— Now listen," he went on rapidly. "You have to tell me it's all right. This'll get us out, both of us. You will, won't you?" he demanded anxiously.

Then he saw Colbie's mask of a face and shouted furiously, "Don't be a damned fool, Colbie! You don't want to die, do you? You know you won't be able to stand death from lack of water and food—you know it! Now's the time to make up your mind." He was feverish.

"I made up my mind quite a while ago," Colbie pointed out. "If I hadn't, I wouldn't have contributed your clinching link just now."

Deverel laughed harshly. "You're going to stick with it," he jeered. "You're going to let a principle kill you! Well, I'm going to let it kill me, too—and I'm not as scared of death as you are. In fact, it'd be better if I did die; I've got too much hell in store for me, one way and another. So I don't really care. How do you like that?" he ripped out savagely.

"It's all right with me—I always knew you didn't give much of a damn about anything, Deverel." He smiled disarmingly.

Deverel regarded him in blank amazement, an amazement that swiftly turned into sheer, obvious admiration. Until that moment, Deverel had doubted that Colbie was sure of his intentions; now he knew it, and the knowledge gave him a new picture of Colbie.

Colbie yawned; and then Deverel's rage apparently broke all bounds. He called Colbie every foul name under the Sun, reviled him with the unprintable verbal scum of innumerable space ports—and then stopped short.

"Hell, I didn't mean that," he muttered. He waved a hand. "Sorry—I mean it. It's just that"—he summoned a grin—"there went the second Crucial Moment. Rather, the minute we drop down from the eleventh apex—there it goes. It's about a minute away. We're now, to all intents and purposes, a mean one hundred ten feet below the rim. Phew!"

"What are these crucial moments?" Colbie inquired in genuine bewilderment.

Deverel laughed in amused disgust. "There are several of them—I think. And the more of them we pass up, the more crucial the next one is. Get it? At last we come to the Final Crucial Moment! And after we pass that up—" Deverel shook his head. "After that, there's no more hope. No more Crucial Moments." After a while, he said listlessly, "I'll tell you when they come around."

They swept down and they swept up. Angles decreased and angles increased. The rim loomed up through the gloom of light, and dropped away. Constant acceleration, followed by just as constant deceleration. And light and still more light and nothing else but light.

Two men against the magical mirror!

Seventeen times the rim dropped away, and each time they approached it was farther away—ten feet higher than before. And then Deverel remarked wearily, "The third Crucial Moment—one hundred seventy feet below the rim." He cocked an eye—a bleary eye—at Colbie, who was so exhausted and blinded by the incessant play of light from the mirror that he was apathetic. "What are you thinking about?"

"Just waiting," Colbie returned tiredly, "for you to give the word!"

Deverel laughed harshly. "And I'll never give it. Listen. In less than an hour comes the—"

"The fourth Crucial Moment," put in Colbie acidly.

"Wrong. The final." He waited for this to take effect, but it had none at all. Then he snarled, "You're going to hold out—good Lord!" For a moment he was speechless, glaring at the other man. Then unaccountably, he laughed. "We're two of a kind—two stubborn fools. I didn't know you had it in you," he remarked frankly. "I really believe you're going to—" and he broke off.

"That I'm going to hold out past the time that really means something to us?" Colbie asked him quizzically. He nodded slowly.

Deverel sank back in disgust.

They topped the eighteenth, the nineteenth, the twentieth apex. Deverel was jumpy, irritated. "About half an hour," he said nervously. "That's all we've got. I mean it. When that time goes, then we kiss life good-bye. I wish you'd see reason, Colbie. Either we both die—or I go free, and you live, too, and we're just as if we never came to this planet. Just think of that—life again!"

Deverel watched Colbie intently, but the IP man was absolutely unaffected. The outlaw had been hoping against hope that Colbie would, in the last vital moments, give in. He had determined to wait that long, just on the chance. Now that chance was definitely out, and Deverel had to play a card he had long ago decided to use if worse came to worse. It might win—and it might lose.

So in the next few moments—with the verve and ability of a natural actor (he *had* played Hamlet when he was a younger man)—he increased his nervousness, the desperation of his manner, the snarl in his voice.

"Twenty-five minutes, Colbie. Give us plenty of time." Colbie was obdurate. They were on the twenty-second trip across. Deverel's rasping voice went on later, "Twenty minutes. And here comes the rim."

The rim came toward them, slowly. More and more slowly, and then gently started dropping away. The twenty-third trip.

"Fifteen minutes, Colbie." Deverel's voice had the rasp of a buzz saw in it. He was actually nervous now. The amount of time was pretty small. So that suddenly he said in a tone of voice that was deprived of every trace of moisture, "Colbie."

Colbie met his eyes, and what he saw there made his own open wider.

"You guessed it, Colbie." The outlaw's tone was dull. He spread his hands. "I'm done. I've cracked. Good Lord!" he burst out. "You don't give a damn! That's what gets me—I can't understand it. Listen—you may think I'm scared to die, that I'm not the kind of fellow I've painted myself to be—but I am. I'm careless with my life. I won't care at all when my number's due. What I can't stand is the fact that it isn't due! There's a way out. And it's only your stubborn refusal that's blocking the way. But I guess when you come down to it, it's me—"

"It's I—" Colbie corrected mildly.

"It's I that's blocking the way. So I give up. You win. You're the world-beater of this crowd. You're the champion holder-outer, the prince of don't-give-a-damners! Colbie, you've got me in tears. Honest, I feel like blubbering like a kid. I can't understand you—sitting there—" he groped.

The IP man regarded Deverel steadily. "You're funny," he muttered. "I knew you'd give in, just because of that. You have dash—impulsiveness—a quick love of life. I'm just a stolid space-cop."

And Deverel suddenly thrust out his jaw angrily. "I gave in, didn't I? And don't think I haven't got half a notion to take it back. I'm capable of it." His eyes challenged the other's.

Colbie said slowly, "No. Don't do it—forget it. We were fools—you decided not to be one. That's all there is to it." Once more he met the eyes of the other man, this time thoughtfully, then he nodded his head in slow determination. His head came up, and a sparkle entered his eyes.

"What do we do?" he demanded. "Spill it—let's get out of this forsaken place. I don't like the lighting arrangements! Come on!"

Deverel went into action.

"Wind yourself up on this rope," his voice cracked out, full of the energy of real desperation now. "Closer—come on! All right." He braced his feet against Colbie, and pushed. Colbie went whirling dizzily away, the rope uncoiling. He came to the end of the rope. Deverel then pulled in such a manner that he utilized to the fullest extent Colbie's rotatory motion. Colbie came spinning back, winding up. Deverel lashed out with his feet. Colbie unwound again, this time in a new direction. Time after time he came back, whirled away again. Deverel manipulated Colbie in the same way a small boy does a certain toy called the jo-jo.

Swiftly, each was swinging around the other in an ellipse with a shifting axis.

"Get it?" panted Deverel. "We've got a circular motion started. It isn't affecting our course in the slightest, though. We're a closed system. For every action a reaction. I'm swinging around you, too. Now, you stop spinning—it isn't necessary now." Colbie flailed about with his arms and, in the course of two revolutions, swung around Deverel in a true circle. And all the while they were hurtling up the slope of the mirror, at a rate dictated by no other force than the retarding power of gravity.

Deverel was gasping. "Now—draw up on the rope. Pulls us nearer the center of the circle we're making and we go faster—our angular velocity increases. Now we're going."

And they were. By dint of prodigious exertions, they worked their angular velocity up to such a point that the centrifugal force was putting a terrific strain on their laboring lungs.

And finally the outlaw gasped, "Enough! We're going plenty fast. If we go any faster, we'll split wide open. We'd keep on whirling like this until the slight bit of friction wore it down—that is, if we didn't use it to escape this trap. And we're going to use it, too! The rim should be along in —two minutes, seventeen seconds flat. Oh, yes, I figured that out to the hair's breadth."

Suddenly he was shouting out loud, "And there it is—the rim! Now, look, honest to God, I don't know which of us is going over." His eyes feverishly watched the approach of the rim, whenever it swung into his line of vision. It was etched against the mountains. Throbbing seconds beat away into the past. Colbie's pulses were hammering. How often afterward he thought of the snapping suspense the looming mirror engendered in him then! It was like a monster—mysterious and brutal. Deverel's voice came again, "I think it's going to be you. It *has* to be you! Yes!

"We're a closed system, remember. Now say we have an explosion. You fly that way, I fly the other. But we each retain the kinetic energy given us by centrifugal force."

Cocking a wild, red-rimmed, bleary eye on the approaching rim, he coiled himself up two feet nearer Colbie. They gyrated more swiftly. Colbie shouted in protest.

Deverel snarled, "Can't help it. The rope has to be parallel to the rim the minute we hit the apex." He blinked his eyes to get the sweat out, looked at the chronometer above his eyes. Seven seconds to go. Deverel was shuddering—he had so damned many things to do at once. He had to regulate their angular velocity—his timing sense—the sense which tells us how many whole steps we can make to reach a curb exactly—was telling him how many gyrations they would make in order to hang poised, for an infinitesimal second, parallel to the rim. With one hand, he had to extract a razor-sharp knife from an outside space kit. And he had to keep an eye on his chronometer, for he had to know exactly when they reached the apex of this, the twenty-third trip across the great mirror.

And perhaps the greatest miracle of that whole insane adventure was that everything worked itself out just as Deverel was planning. The rope, its human weights swinging dizzily at its ends, came parallel to the mirror's rim on the exact, nonexisting moment they reached the climb's apex. And in that exact moment, Deverel slashed at the rope close to where it was fastened about him.

Colbie experienced no change of pace—simply a sudden release of pressure. The operation had been smoothly performed. At the exact moment when they, as a single system, had no upward and no downward motion, Deverel had severed the rope. Colbie simply shot straight toward the rim at the velocity he had been rotating at that particular moment.

He plummeted up the slope of the mirror, gravity now definitely fighting him. He lost twelve feet in upward velocity every second. Would the kinetic energy his body now contained be sufficient to stave off that deadly deceleration? Would gravity whittle it down to zero, somewhere below the rim?

"Colbie," he gritted, speaking softly to himself, "if you've never prayed before, try it now!"

And perhaps the prayers did the trick, or it might have been the computations Deverel's keen brain worked out. Using the factors of their individual weights on this planet, and the two-hundred-foot length of rope, and the time for one revolution, he had known the approximate kinetic energy each man would develop, had known that Colbie would go over the rim with a liberal margin to spare.

Up past the rim Colbie shot. Over the rim—and up into space. And there, fifty feet above the planet, he stopped rising. The moment of falling was heart-stopping. His spacesuit was tough—but would it stand the strain? He didn't have much time to theorize about it. He hit, and he hit hard. He felt as if every bone in his body was crushed in the moment before his consciousness faded away.

When he came back to consciousness, he knew a sharp, agonizing pain below the knee of his right leg. "Broken," he thought dismally, and grimaced as he almost involuntarily tried to move the injured member. He couldn't move it at all.

Then the thought of Deverel came back. Good Lord, he was still on the mirror!

"Deverel!" he shouted.

A cheery voice came back. "All here and right as rain." Then the voice became anxious. "What's wrong? I was trying to get in touch with you."

"Broken leg, I guess."

"Hurt?"

"Damnably!" Colbie gritted his teeth.

"I was afraid something like that would happen," the outlaw answered with sympathy. "I'm sorry it had to be you—I would have taken the rap if we'd have swung around right. But we didn't. That was my gamble for escape."

"How are you getting out?" Colbie demanded. Then in sudden panic, "And what if *you* break a leg?"

"Ho! I'll get out, and I won't break a leg either. I have to travel across the mirror, you know, and I'll lose ten vertical feet. How far did you fall?" he asked anxiously. Colbie told him. "Fine! Not bad at all for a rough calc."

"You did a fine job all around," Colbie told him feelingly. "That's right, you'll go over the rim, too. You've got gravitational *and* centrifugal force acting on you."

"Now listen, Colbie, you're on the wrong part of the rim, d'you know that?"

No, Colbie hadn't known it. So their ships were on the other side?

"No, not on the other side. About a sixth of the circle of the rim around from where you are."

"Well, then, where are you bound?"

"For the ships."

Colbie gasped. "You're crazy! You're headed directly opposite from where I am."

"Oh, no, I'm not," Deverel sang sweetly. "I'm headed right for a point on the mirror a sixth of its rim removed from you in the direction the planet rotates. Now quit gasping like a fish, and listen to the most gorgeous and unbelievable part of this whole adventure. Do you think we went straight across the mirror?"

"Certainly!"

"We didn't! Now here's the bombshell—" He paused, and then said, *"We were the bob of a pendulum!"*

"What?" Colbie shouted it in dismay. "Lord, Deverel, you're crazy, crazy as a loon! A pendulum! We weren't hanging from anything, from a string, or cable or—Lord!"

"Getting it?" The voice was sympathetic. "Don't you see? We *were* a pendulum. And the beautiful part was that we didn't need to hang from anything so we could vibrate. A string, or something like that, would have ruined the effect entirely. As it is, we were a perfect, simple pendulum, the which that has, so far, existed only in theory! See, there wasn't any friction, and there was a perfect vacuum. There was just gravity. It pulled us down and up and down and up and down and up. And there was a force which wouldn't let us travel in any path except a perfect curve, the path a pendulum takes!

"And what is so characteristic of the pendulum? Why, the periods of vibration are the same! Do you think that knowledge didn't come in handy when I wanted to know *to the dot,* exactly when we'd reach the apex? You bet it did! And then there's something else about a pendulum —I'm surprised you didn't notice. At the Earth's pole the plane of vibration of a pendulum turns around once every twenty-four hours, in a direction opposite to that at which the Earth rotates. Rather, it appears that way. Actually, it is the Earth that turns around under the pendulum! And that's what happened to us. Didn't you notice that the stars as a whole never changed positions all during the time we were on the mirror? They didn't. We were a pendulum. The plane of our vibration was fixed in relation to space. This crazy planet revolved around under us because there wasn't any friction to say 'no'! So I figured it out diagrammatically—right! In my head! And if you think that wasn't a brain-twister—!

"I timed the first two or three vibrations after this pendulum stuff came up and hit me. I found each trip across took seventeen minutes, forty-five and four-tenths seconds. And I knew the period of rotation of this planet—fifty-two minutes, twenty-five and a fraction seconds. Notice anything about those figures, any general relation?"

"I get it," Colbie replied. He was sweating. His leg felt numb from the hip down. "One vibration took about one-third as long as the planet takes to make a revolution."

"Exactly! I'll keep talking, Colbie, help you forget the leg. And not only that, but the bottom of the mirror is a pole of the planet! So we were a true pendulum, vibrating at a planet's pole. And the length of our 'string,' the radius of the sphere, of which the mirror is a part, was out in space about sixteen hundred miles!

"Now in our vibrations, we always went through the center of the mirror, but we never went across to the other side. That is, one swing always began and ended in one-half the mirror. In relation to space, our plane of vibration was always the same; in relation to the mirror, it was a curve which crept round the mirror, touching the rim six times.

"I had the devil of a time!" Deverel exclaimed. "I had to formulate a law which would tell me absolutely where each vibration would end, on the mirror, and thus how many times we'd have to swing across before we got back to our starting point—our original starting point. And finally I got this: One swing from rim to rim ends at that point on the rim which is opposite its starting point at end of swing. Get it? Well, if you don't, draw a diagram of a circle divided into six sixty-degree wedges—and follow the law out." And Colbie actually did draw such a diagram later. "In other words, it took us six swings from rim to rim to bring us back to our starting point. Those were the Crucial Moments. If we'd have got out at the wrong places, Colbie, we'd have starved before we traveled the distance back to the ships—if we knew where they were. Then, too, there was a chance one of us would end up pretty badly hurt! And one of us did—you had to drop back further than I'll have to.

"And that's all there is to it. I let you out at the end of the twenty-third trip from rim to rim. I'm getting out at the end of the twenty-fourth—what I really believe would have been the Final Crucial Moment. We couldn't have developed enough centrifugal force to send us over the rim if we'd gone around the mirror six more times, and fallen, as a consequence, sixty additional feet farther away from it. How's your leg?" he inquired.

"Rotten!" Colbie muffled a groan.

"Keep your chin up!" Deverel snapped. "Seven minutes and I'll be over the rim, and I'll hotfoot it back to the ships. It may take several hours before I get back here," he added in anxiety.

"I'll be all right," Colbie mumbled.

In the next few hours they kept in constant touch. Deverel made the rim, landed unharmed. He set off across the gouged plateau with both speed and care. He made the ships unharmed; and less than fifteen minutes later, the most beautiful sight in the world for Colbie was the sight of that slim, black IPF cruiser as it came zooming above Cyclops straight toward him.

It landed. Deverel stepped out. He picked Colbie up in his strong arms, carried him inside the ship, took off his spacesuit, and bared his broken leg. It was a simple fracture, and was still in a healthy condition. Deverel went to work on it, put it in splints after having given it a wrench which accomplished the dual purpose of sending Colbie into a faint and setting the broken bone. Deverel put it in splints, and then bundled the IP man into bed.

Six weeks later, when Colbie was able to hobble around on a makeshift crutch, Deverel was still there.

"You make a nice nurse," Colbie told him over a meal one day. "Thanks —a lot."

"Skip it!" The outlaw grinned. "You weren't such a bad nurse yourself. I'd have been gone before now if you hadn't stepped in." He gulped a cup of coffee. "You're well enough, I figure," he said uneasily. "'Bout time to go?"

Thoughtfully, uneasily, Colbie said, "Sure—I guess it is."

So that the next day Deverel sat down at the controls and touched them lightly. The ship shot upward into the eternal night of Cyclops, zoomed feather-light out over the strangest, most magical mirror ever to exist. And Colbie, looking at it, knew that he would always think of it with more affection than fear. He would always think of it as a child's colossal toy. It had so many amusing characteristics that he halfway felt it'd be a pleasure to go zooming down its infinitely smooth surface once again.

A dream world, he thought, if there ever was one.

Once landed near Colbie's ship, the outlaw said sardonically, "I guess we transfer from this ship to yours?"

Colbie met his eyes seriously for a moment, then got up from where he was sitting, and limped back and forth in the close confines of the cabin.

His teeth were set, his eyes frowning, his fists opening and closing. He sat down again and got up. The look on his face was almost savage.

Suddenly he waved a hand violently, and a snarl contorted his features. He swung around, looking at the outlaw with hot, gray eyes. "I can't do it!" he snapped. He shoved out his jaw. "Not after what we've been through. Damn it, Deverel," he panted, "I don't like this job. I feel too friendly for you. I like you too damn much. You're a real guy. Hell, you could have run out any time you wanted to in the past six weeks.

"No. No, I can't do it. It'd be like"—he groped—"like taking unfair advantage, somehow. So," he said bitterly, "you're free." He forced a smile onto his face. "I'll write it in my report like this—'Captured outlaw, but he put one over on me and escaped.'"

"Right," Deverel agreed steadily.

"So I'll be going. I'll be here for, oh, about twenty-four hours. You going any place in particular?" he inquired politely.

"No-o-o," Deverel replied thoughtfully. "Don't know as I have any particular destination. Drop you a postcard? I will, if you think you need me for anything."

"Don't bother. I never have much trouble finding you," Colbie said airily. Then he put on a spacesuit. Deverel worked the valves, and a moment later Colbie stood in the air-lock. For a moment, the two men stood there, saluting each other with grave eyes. Then the inner door closed and the outer opened.

Deverel watched Colbie enter his ship.

Then he sat down and, incandescent gases flaring from her stern jets, the slim cruiser accelerated until it was swallowed up in the trackless, illimitable wastes of space.

I loved the story. It is a problem story, using authentic science (though the solution is inadequate, as a reader pointed out in the magazine's letter column at considerable length a few months later).

The time was to come when I was to try to write problem stories, but doing one as pure as "The Men and the Mirror" isn't easy. The closest approach in my case was perhaps "Paté de Foie Gras."

But "The Men and the Mirror" has a melancholy distinction for me. It was the last story I could thoroughly enjoy untrammeled by anything beyond science fiction *readership*. It was the last time I could experience the unalloyed delight of the uninvolved.

You see, I had become more than a fan. As soon as I finished "Cosmic Corkscrew," I took it to the offices of *Astounding Science Fiction*. There I met John Campbell for the first time. To be sure, "Cosmic Corkscrew" was rejected, but I was already working on another story (which was eventually sold and published as "The Callistan Menace").

It meant that I was evicted from Paradise. There was no longer, *ever*, any chance to read science fiction with complete enjoyment. I had become a writer, a competitor. If a published story was clearly worse than I could write, I was filled with contempt and annoyance. If it was clearly better, I was filled with envy and anxiety. I could no longer relax.

But never mind . . .

I was evicted from one Paradise only to enter another.

In the August 1938 issue of *Astounding Science Fiction* there appeared "Who Goes There?" by Campbell himself, under his Don A. Stuart pseudonym. (By then, I knew who Stuart was.) This was, beyond any doubt, one of the very best science fiction stories ever written—perhaps the very best of any length below that of a novel.

It was a rewrite of his "The Brain Stealers of Mars," which is included in this anthology, but "Who Goes There?" is at a much higher level. It was as though Campbell was, by example, showing the science fiction world exactly what he wanted. "The Brain Stealers of Mars" was the story as it might be before, but "Who Goes There?" was as it was now and as *he* wanted it to be.*

Therefore, with the August 1938 issue of *Astounding Science Fiction* and with the story "Who Goes There?" The Golden Age of Science Fiction (with capitals) begins, and any book entitled *Before the Golden Age* must end.

And I was *part* of the Golden Age. In October 1938, three months after I read "Who Goes There?" (with delight mingled with despair), I made my first sale—to the Ziff-Davis *Amazing*. And three months after that, I finally sold a story to Campbell.

I was there. Like science fiction itself, I had moved up to a higher level. On that higher level, joys were not unalloyed, for the despair of a story that would not work out was there and the chilling dread of the deadly rejection slip. But the unprecedented pleasures of the occasional sale also existed.

For what followed then, for the story of my next eleven years with its struggles and vicissitudes (and stories) I refer you to *The Early Asimov*, which must now be viewed as the second volume of my peculiarly designed autobiography.

—Unless, of course, you have already read it.

* "Who Goes There?" was eventually made into the financially successful but science fictionally contemptible motion picture *The Thing*, for which John was paid a mere few hundred dollars in total. When I expressed indignation at this, Campbell characteristically shrugged it off. He said, "It helps spread science fiction among the outsiders. That's all that counts."

S